PORT MORTUARY

PORT MORTUARY

PATRICIA CORNWELL

THORNDIKE
WINDSOR
PARAGON

This Large Print edition is published by Thorndike Press, Waterville, Maine USA and by AudioGo Ltd, Bath, England.
Copyright © 2010 by CEI Enterprises, Inc.
A Kay Scarpetta Novel.
Thorndike Press, a part of Gale, Cengage Learning.

Thorndike Press® Large Print Basic.
The text of this Large Print edition is unabridged.
Other aspects of the book may vary from the original edition.
Set in 16 pt. Plantin.

LIBRARY OF CONGRESS CATALOGING-IN-PUBLICATION DATA

Cornwell, Patricia Daniels.
 Port mortuary / by Patricia Cornwell.
  p. cm. — (Thorndike Press large print basic)
 "A Kay Scarpetta novel."
 ISBN-13: 978-1-4104-3158-5
 ISBN-10: 1-4104-3158-4
 1. Scarpetta, Kay (Fictitious character)—Fiction. 2. Medical examiners (Law)—Fiction. 3. Forensic pathologists—Fiction. 4. Women physicians—Fiction. 5. Terrorism—Prevention—Fiction. 6. United States. Dept. of Defense—Fiction. 7. Cambridge (Mass.)—Fiction. 8. Large type books.
 I. Title.
 PS3553.O692P575 2010
 813'.54—dc22   2010042422

Published in the U.S. in 2010 by arrangement with G. P. Putnam's Sons, a member of Penguin Group (USA) Inc.
Published in the U.K. in 2011 by arrangemen with Little, Brown Book Group.
U.K. Hardcover: 978 1 445 85443 4 (Windsor Large Print)
U.K. Softcover: 978 1 445 85444 1 (Paragon Large Print)

Printed in the United States of America
1 2 3 4 5 6 7 15 14 13 12 11

A NOTE TO MY READERS

While this is a work of fiction, it is not science fiction. The medical and forensic procedures, and technologies and weapons, you are about to see exist now, even as you read this work. Some of what you are about to encounter is extremely disturbing. All of it is possible.

Also real and fully operational at this writing are various entities, including the following:

Port Mortuary at Dover Air Force Base
Armed Forces Medical Examiner (AFME)
Armed Forces DNA Identification Laboratory (AFDIL)
Armed Forces Institute of Pathology (AFIP)
Department of Defense (DoD)
Defense Advanced Research Projects Agency (DARPA)
Royal United Services Institute (RUSI)

12/10

Special Weapons Observation Remote Direct-Action System (SWORDS)

Although completely within the realm of possibility, the Cambridge Forensic Center (CFC), the Georgia Prison for Women, Otwahl Technologies, and the Mortuary Operational Removal Transport (MORT) are creations of the author's imagination, as are all of the characters in this story and the plot itself.

My thanks —
To all the fine men and women of the Armed Forces Medical Examiner System and the Armed Forces Institute of Pathology, who have been kind enough during my career to share their insights and highly advanced knowledge, and to impress me with their discipline, their integrity, and their friendship.

As always, I'm deeply indebted to Dr. Staci Gruber, director of the Cognitive and Clinical Neuroimaging Core, McLean Hospital, and assistant professor, Harvard Medical School, Department of Psychiatry.

And, of course, my gratitude to Dr. Marcella Fierro, former chief medical examiner of Virginia, and Dr. Jamie Downs, medical examiner, Savannah, Georgia, for their expertise in all things pathological.

To Staci
You have to live with me
while I live it —

1

Inside the changing room for female staff, I toss soiled scrubs into a biohazard hamper and strip off the rest of my clothes and medical clogs. I wonder if *Col. Scarpetta* stenciled in black on my locker will be removed the minute I return to New England in the morning. The thought hadn't entered my mind before now, and it bothers me. A part of me doesn't want to leave this place.

Life at Dover Air Force Base has its comforts, despite six months of hard training and the bleakness of handling death daily on behalf of the U.S. government. My stay here has been surprisingly uncomplicated. I can even say it's been pleasant. I'm going to miss getting up before dawn in my modest room, dressing in cargo pants, a polo shirt, and boots, and walking in the cold dark across the parking lot to the golf course clubhouse for coffee and something to eat before driving to Port Mortuary, where I'm not in charge. When I'm on duty for the Armed Forces Medical Examiner, the AFME, I'm no longer a chief. In fact, I'm outranked by quite a number of people, and critical decisions aren't mine to make, assuming I'm even asked. Not so when I return to Massachusetts, where I'm depended on by everyone.

It's Monday, February 8. The wall clock above the shiny white sinks reads 16:33 hours, lit up red like a warning. In less than ninety minutes I'm supposed to appear on CNN and explain what a forensic radiologic pathologist, or RadPath, is and why I've become one, and what Dover and the Department of Defense and the White House have to do with it. In other words, I'm not just a medical examiner anymore, I suppose I'll say, and not just a habeas reservist with the AFME, either. Since 9/11, since the United States invaded Iraq, and now the surge of troops in Afghanistan — I rehearse points I should make — the line between the military and civilian worlds has forever faded. An example I might give: This past November during a forty-eight-hour period, thirteen fallen warriors were flown here from the Middle East, and just as many casualties arrived from Fort Hood, Texas.

Mass casualty isn't restricted to the battle-field, although I'm no longer sure what constitutes a battlefield. Maybe every place is one, I will say on TV. Our homes, our schools, our churches, commercial aircraft, and where we work, shop, and go on vacation.

I sort through toiletries as I sort through comments I need to make about 3-D imaging radiology, the use of computerized tomography, or CT, scans in the morgue, and I remind myself to emphasize that although my new headquarters in Cambridge, Massachusetts, is the first civilian facility in the United States to do virtual autopsies, Baltimore will be next, and eventually the trend will spread. The traditional postmortem examination of dissect as you go and take photographs after the fact and hope you don't miss something or introduce an artifact can be dramatically improved by technology and made more precise, and it should be.

I'm sorry I'm not doing *World News* tonight, because now that I think of it, I'd rather have this dialogue with Diane Sawyer. The problem with my being a regular on CNN is that familiarity often breeds contempt, and I should have thought about this before now. The interview could get personal, it occurs to me, and I should have mentioned the possibility to General Briggs. I should have told him what happened this morning when the irate mother of a dead soldier ripped into me over the phone, accusing me of hate crimes and threatening to take her complaints to the media.

Metal bangs like a gunshot as I shut my locker door. I pad over tan tile that always feels cool and smooth beneath my bare feet, carrying my plastic basket of olive oil shampoo and conditioner, an exfoliant scrub made of fossilized marine algae, a safety razor, a can of shaving gel for sensitive skin, liquid detergent, a washcloth, mouthwash, a toothbrush, a nail brush, and fragrant Neutrogena oil I'll use when I'm done. Inside an open stall, I neatly arrange my personal effects on the tile ledge and turn on the water as hot as I can stand it, hard spray blasting as I move around to get all of me, then lifting my face up, then looking down at the floor, at my own pale feet. I let water pound the back of my neck and head in hopes that stiff muscles will relax a little as I mentally enter the closet inside my base lodging and explore what to wear.

General Briggs — John, as I refer to him when we're alone — wants me in an airman battle uniform, or better yet, air force blues, and I disagree. I should wear civilian clothes, what people see me in most of the time when I do television interviews, probably a simple dark suit and ivory blouse with a collar, and the understated Breguet watch on a leather strap that my niece, Lucy, gave me. Not the Blancpain with its oversized black face and ceramic bezel, which also is from her, because she's obsessed with timepieces, with anything technically complicated and expensive. Not pants but a skirt and heels, so I come across as nonthreatening and accessible, a trick I learned long ago in court. For some reason, jurors like to see my legs while I describe in graphic anatomical detail fatal wounds and the agonal last moments of a victim's life. Briggs will be displeased with my choice in attire, but I reminded him during the Super Bowl last night when we were having drinks that a man shouldn't tell a woman what to wear unless he's Ralph Lauren.

The steam in my shower stall shifts, disturbed by a draft, and I think I hear someone. Instantly, I'm annoyed. It could be anyone, any military personnel, doctor or otherwise, whoever is authorized to be inside this highly classified facility and in need of a toilet or a disinfecting or a change of clothes. I think about colleagues I was

15

just with in the main autopsy room and have a feeling it's Captain Avallone again. She was an unavoidable presence much of the morning during the CT scan, as if I don't know how to do one after all this, and she drifted like ground fog around my work station the rest of the day. It's probably she who's just come in. Then I'm sure, because it's always her, and I feel a clenching of resentment. *Go away.*

"Dr. Scarpetta?" her familiar voice calls out, a voice that is bland and lacking in passion and seems to follow me everywhere. "You have a phone call."

"I just got in," I shout over the loud spatter of water.

It's my way of telling her to leave me be. *A little privacy, please.* I don't want to see Captain Avallone or anyone right now, and it has nothing to do with being naked.

"Sorry, ma'am. But Pete Marino needs to talk to you." Her unemphatic voice moves closer.

"He'll have to wait," I yell.

"He says it's important."

"Can you ask him what he wants?"

"He just says it's important, ma'am."

I promise to get back to him shortly, and I probably sound rude, but despite my best intentions I can't always be charming. Pete

16

Marino is an investigator I've worked with half my life. I hope nothing terrible has happened back home. No, he would make sure I knew if there was a real emergency, if something was wrong with my husband, Benton; with Lucy; or if there was a major problem at the Cambridge Forensic Center, which I've been appointed to head. Marino would do more than simply ask someone to let me know he's on the phone and it's important. This is nothing more than his usual poor impulse control, I decide. When he thinks a thought, he feels he must share it with me instantly.

I open my mouth wide, rinsing out the taste of decomposing charred human flesh that is trapped in the back of my throat. The stench of what I worked on today rises on swells of steam deep into my sinuses, the molecules of putrid biology in the shower with me. I scrub under my nails with anti-bacterial soap I squirt from a bottle, the same stuff I use on dishes or to decon my boots at a scene, and brush my teeth, gums, and tongue with Listerine. I wash inside my nostrils as far up as I can reach, scouring every inch of my flesh, then I wash my hair, not once but twice, and the stench is still there. I can't seem to get clean.

The name of the dead soldier I just took

care of is Peter Gabriel, like the legendary rock star, only this Peter Gabriel was a private first class in the army and had been in the Badghis Province of Afghanistan not even a month when a roadside bomb improvised from plastic sewer pipe packed with PE-4 and capped with a copper plate punched through the armor of his Humvee, creating a molten firestorm inside it. PFC Gabriel took up most of my last day here at this huge high-tech place where the armed forces pathologists and scientists routinely get involved in cases most members of the public don't associate with us: the assassination of JFK; the recent DNA identifications of the Romanov family and the crew members of the *H.L. Hunley* submarine that sank during the Civil War. We're a noble but little-known organization with roots reaching back to 1862, to the Army Medical Museum, whose surgeons attended to the mortally wounded Abraham Lincoln and performed his autopsy, and I should say all this on CNN. Focus on the positive. Forget what Mrs. Gabriel said. I'm not a monster or a bigot. *You can't blame the poor woman for being upset,* I tell myself. She just lost her only child. The Gabriels are black. *How would you feel, for God's sake? Of course you're not a racist.*

I sense a presence again. Someone has entered the changing room, which I've managed to fog up like a steam shower. My heart is beating hard because of the heat.

"Dr. Scarpetta?" Captain Avallone sounds less tentative, as if she has news.

I turn off the water and step out of my stall, grabbing a towel to wrap up in. Captain Avallone is an indistinct presence hovering in haze near the sinks and motion-sensitive hand dryers. All I can make out is her dark hair and her khaki cargo pants and black polo shirt with its embroidered AFME gold-and-blue shield.

"Pete Marino . . ." she starts to say.

"I'll call him in a minute." I snatch another towel off a shelf.

"He's here, ma'am."

"What do you mean *'here'?*" I almost expect him to materialize in the changing room like some prehistoric creature emerging from the mist.

"He's waiting for you out back by the bays, ma'am," she informs me. "He'll take you to the Eagle's Rest so you can get your things." She says it as if I'm being picked up by the FBI, as if I've been arrested or fired. "My instructions are to take you to him and assist in any way needed."

Captain Avallone's first name is Sophia.

19

She's army, just out of her radiology residency, and is always so damn military-correct and obsequiously polite as she lingers and loiters. Right now is not the time. I carry my toiletry basket, padding over tile, and she's right behind me.

"I'm not supposed to leave until tomorrow, and going anywhere with Marino wasn't part of my travel plans," I tell her.

"I can take care of your vehicle, ma'am. I understand you're not driving. . . ."

"Did you ask him what the hell this is about?" I grab my hairbrush and my deodorant out of my locker.

"I tried, ma'am," she says. "But he wasn't helpful."

A C-5 Galaxy roars overhead, on final for 19. The wind as usual is out of the south.

One of many aeronautical principles I've learned from Lucy, who is a helicopter pilot among other things, is that runway numbers correspond to directions on a compass. Nineteen, for example, is 190 degrees, meaning the opposite end will be 01, oriented that way because of the Bernoulli effect and Newton's laws of motion. It's all about the speed air needs to flow over a wing, about taking off and landing into the wind, which in this part of Delaware blows

20

in from the sea, from high pressure to low, from south to north. Day in and day out, transport planes bring the dead and take them away along a blacktop strip that runs like the River Styx behind Port Mortuary.

The shark-gray Galaxy is the length of a football field, so huge and heavy it seems scarcely to move in a pale sky of feathery clouds that pilots call mare's tails. I would know what type of airlifter it is without looking, can recognize the high pitch of its scream and whistle. By now I know the sound of turbine engines producing a hundred and sixty thousand pounds of thrust, can identify a C-5 or a C-17 when it's miles out, and I know helicopters and tilt rotors, too, can tell a Chinook from a Black Hawk or an Osprey. During nice weather when I have a few moments to spare, I sit on a bench outside my lodgings and watch the flying machines of Dover as if they're exotic creatures, such as manatees or elephants or prehistoric birds. I never tire of their lumbering drama and thundering noise, and the shadows they cast as they pass over.

Wheels touch down in puffs of smoke so close by I feel the rumble in my hollow organs as I walk across the receiving area with its four enormous bays, high privacy wall, and backup generators. I approach a blue van I've never seen before, and Pete Marino makes no move to greet me or open my door, and this bodes nothing one way or another. He doesn't waste his energy on manners, not that being gracious or particularly nice has ever been a priority of his for as long as I can remember. It's been more than twenty years since the time when we first met in Richmond, Virginia, at the morgue. Or maybe it was a homicide scene where I first was confronted with him. I really can't recall.

I climb in and shut the door, stuffing a duffel bag between my boots, my hair still damp from the shower. He thinks I look like hell and is silently judging. I can always tell by his sidelong glances that survey me from head to toe, lingering in certain places that are none of his business. He doesn't like it when I wear my AFME investigative garb, my khaki cargo pants, black polo shirt, and tactical jacket, and the few times he's seen me in uniform I think I scared him.

"Where'd you steal the van?" I ask as he backs up.

"A loaner from Civil Air." His answer at least tells me nothing has happened to Lucy.

The private terminal on the north end of the runway is used by nonmilitary personnel who are authorized to land on the air force base. My niece has flown Marino here, and it crosses my mind they've come as a surprise. They showed up unannounced to spare me from flying commercial in the morning, to escort me home at last. Wishful thinking. That can't be it, and I look for answers in Marino's rough-featured face, taking in his overall appearance rather much the way I do a patient at first glance. Running shoes, jeans, a fleece-lined Harley-Davidson leather coat he's had forever, a Yankees baseball cap he wears at his own peril, considering he now lives in the Republic of the Red Sox, and his unfashionable wire-rim glasses.

I can't tell if his head is shaved smooth of what little gray hair he has left, but he is clean and relatively neat, and he doesn't have a whisky flush or a bloated beer gut. His eyes aren't bloodshot. His hands are steady. I don't smell cigarettes. He's still on the wagon, more than one. Marino has many wagons he is wise to stay on, a train of them working their way through the unsettled territories of his aboriginal inclinations. Sex, booze, drugs, tobacco, food, profanity, bigotry, slothfulness. I probably should add mendacity. When it suits him, he's evasive or outright lies.

"I assume Lucy's with the helicopter . . . ?"

I start to say.

"You know how it is around this joint when you're doing a case, worse than the damn CIA," he talks over me as we turn onto Purple Heart Drive. "Your house could be on fire and nobody says shit, and I must have called five times. So I made an executive decision, and Lucy and me headed out."

"It would be helpful if you'd tell me why you're here."

"Nobody would interrupt you while you were doing the soldier from Worcester," he says to my amazement.

PFC Gabriel was from Worcester, Massachusetts, and I can't fathom why Marino would know what case I had here at Dover. No one should have told him. Everything we do at Port Mortuary is extremely discreet, if not strictly classified. I wonder if the slain soldier's mother did what she threatened and called the media. I wonder if she told the press that her son's white female military medical examiner is a racist.

Before I can ask, Marino adds, "Apparently, he's the first war casualty from Worcester, and the local media's all over it. We've gotten some calls, I guess people getting confused and thinking any dead body with a Massachusetts connection ends up with us."

"Reporters assumed we'd done the autopsy in Cambridge?"

"Well, the CFC's a port mortuary, too. Maybe that's why."

"One would think the media certainly knows by now that all casualties in theater come straight here to Dover," I reply. "You're certain about the reason for the media's interest?"

"Why?" He looks at me. "You know some other reason I don't?"

"I'm just asking."

"All I know is there were a few calls and we referred them to Dover. So you were in the middle of taking care of the kid from Worcester and nobody would get you on the phone, and finally I called General Briggs when we were about twenty minutes out, refueling in Wilmington. He made Captain Do-Bee go find you in the shower. She single, or does she sing in Lucy's choir? Because she's not bad-looking."

"How would you know what she looks like?" I reply, baffled.

"You weren't around when she stopped by the CFC on her way to visit her mother in Maine."

I try to remember if I was ever told this, and at the same time I'm reminded I have no idea what has gone on in the office I'm

25

supposed to run.

"Fielding gave her the royal tour, the host with the most." Marino doesn't like my deputy chief, Jack Fielding. "Point being, I did try to get hold of you. I didn't mean to just show up like this."

Marino is being evasive, and what he's described is a ploy. It's made up. For some reason he felt it necessary to simply appear here without warning. Probably because he wanted to make sure I would go with him without delay. I sense real trouble.

"The Gabriel case can't be why you just showed up, as you put it," I say.

"Afraid not."

"What's happened?"

"We've got a situation." He stares straight ahead. "And I told Fielding and everybody else that no way in hell the body was being examined until you get there."

Jack Fielding is an experienced forensic pathologist who doesn't take orders from Marino. If my deputy chief opted to be hands-off and defer to me, it likely means we've got a case that could have political implications or get us sued. It bothers me considerably that Fielding hasn't tried to call or e-mail me. I check my iPhone again. Nothing from him.

"About three-thirty yesterday afternoon in

Cambridge," Marino is saying, and we're on Atlantic Street now, driving slowly through the middle of the base in the near dark. "Norton's Woods on Irving, not even a block from your house. Too damn bad you weren't home. You could have gone to the scene, could have walked there, and maybe things would have turned out different."

"What things?"

"A light-skinned male, possibly in his twenties. Appears he was out walking his dog and dropped dead from a heart attack, right? Wrong," he continues as we pass rows of concrete and metal maintenance facilities, hangars, and other buildings that have numbers instead of names. "It's broad daylight on a Sunday afternoon, plenty of people around because there was an event at whatever that building is, the one with the big green metal roof."

Norton's Woods is the home of the American Academy of Arts and Sciences, a wooded estate with a stunning building of timber and glass that is rented out for special functions. It is several houses down from the one Benton and I moved into last spring so I could be near the CFC and he could enjoy the close proximity of Harvard, where he is on the faculty of the medical school's Department of Psychiatry.

"In other words, eyes and ears," Marino goes on. "A hell of a time and a place to whack somebody."

"I thought you said he was a heart attack. Except if he's that young, you probably mean a cardiac arrhythmia."

"Yeah, that was the assumption. A couple of witnesses saw him suddenly grab his chest and collapse. He was DOA at the scene — supposedly. Was transported directly to our office and spent the night in the cooler."

"What do you mean *'supposedly'*?"

"Early this morning Fielding went into the fridge and noticed blood drips on the floor and a lot of blood in the tray, so he goes and gets Anne and Ollie. The dead guy's got blood coming out of his nose and mouth that wasn't there the afternoon before, when he was pronounced. No blood at the scene, not one drop, and now he's bleeding, and it's not purge fluid, obviously, because he sure as hell isn't decomposing. The sheet he's covered with is bloody, and there's about a liter of blood in the body pouch, and that's fucked up. I've never seen a dead person start bleeding like that. So I said we got a fucking problem and everybody keep your mouth shut."

"What did Jack say? What did he do?"

28

"You're kidding, right? Some deputy you got. Don't get me started."

"Do we have an identification, and why Norton's Woods? Does he live nearby? Is he a student at Harvard, maybe at the Divinity School?" It's right around the corner from Norton's Woods. "I doubt he was attending whatever this event was. Not if he had his dog with him." I sound much calmer than I feel as we have this conversation in the parking lot of the Eagle's Rest inn.

"We don't have many details yet, but it appears it was a wedding," Marino says.

"On Super Bowl Sunday? Who plans a wedding on the same day as the Super Bowl?"

"Maybe if you don't want anybody to show up. Maybe if you're not American or are un-American. Hell if I know, but I don't think the dead guy was a wedding guest, and not just because of the dog. He had a Glock nine-mil under his jacket. No ID and was listening to a portable satellite radio, so you probably can guess where I'm going with this."

"I probably can't."

"Lucy will tell you more about the satellite-radio part of it, but it appears he was doing surveillance, spying, and maybe whoever he was fucking with decided to

29

return the favor. Bottom line, I'm thinking somebody did something to him, causing an injury that was somehow missed by the EMTs, and the removal service didn't notice anything, either. So he's zipped up in the pouch and starts bleeding during transport. Well, that wouldn't happen unless he had a blood pressure, meaning he was still alive when he was delivered to the morgue and shut inside our damn cooler. Forty-something degrees in there and he would have died from exposure by this morning. Assuming he didn't bleed to death first."

"If he has an injury that would cause him to bleed externally," I reply, "why didn't he bleed at the scene?"

"You tell me."

"How long did they work on him?"

"Fifteen, twenty minutes."

"Possible during resuscitation efforts a blood vessel was somehow punctured?" I ask. "Antemortem and postmortem injuries, if severe enough, can cause significant bleeding. For example, maybe during CPR a rib was fractured and caused a puncture wound or severed an artery? Any reason a chest tube might have been placed presumptively and that caused an injury and the bleeding you've described?"

But I know the answers even as I ask the

questions. Marino is a veteran homicide detective and death investigator. He wouldn't have commandeered my niece and her helicopter and come to Dover unannounced if there was a logical explanation or even a plausible one, and certainly Jack Fielding would know a legitimate injury from an accidental artifact. *Why haven't I heard from him?*

"The Cambridge Fire Department's HQ is maybe a mile from Norton's Woods, and the squad got to him within minutes," Marino says.

We are sitting in the van with the engine off. It is almost completely dark, the horizon and the sky melting into each other with only the faintest hint of light to the west. *When has Fielding ever handled a disaster without me? Never.* He absents himself. Leaves his messes for others to clean up. That's why he's not tried to get hold of me. Maybe he's walked off the job again. How many times does he need to do that before I stop hiring him back?

"According to them, he died instantly," Marino adds.

"Unless an IED blows someone into hundreds of pieces, there's really no such thing as dying instantly," I reply, and I hate it when Marino makes glib statements. Dy-

31

ing instantly. Dropping dead. Dead before he hit the ground. Twenty years of these generalities, no matter how many times I've told him that cardiac and respiratory arrests aren't causes of death but symptoms of dying, and clinical death takes minutes at least. It isn't instant. It isn't a simple process. I remind him again of this medical fact because I can't think of anything else to say.

"Well, I'm just reporting what I've been told, and according to them, he couldn't be resuscitated," Marino answers, as if the EMTs know more about death than I do. "Was unresponsive. That's what's on their run sheet."

"You interviewed them?"

"One of them. On the phone this morning. No pulse, no nothing. The guy was dead. Or that's what the paramedic said. But what do you think he's going to say — that they weren't sure but sent him to the morgue anyway?"

"Then you told him why you were asking."

"Hell, no, I'm not retarded. You don't need this on the front page of the *Globe*. This hits the news, I may as well go back to NYPD or maybe get a job with Wackenhut, except no one's hiring."

"What procedure did you follow?"

"I didn't follow shit. It was Fielding. Of course, he says he did everything by the book, says Cambridge PD told him there was nothing suspicious about the scene, an apparent natural death that was witnessed. Fielding gave permission for the body to be transferred to the CFC as long as the cops took custody of the gun and got it to the labs right away so we could find out who it's registered to. A routine case, and not our fault if the EMTs fucked up, or so Fielding says, and you know what I say? It won't matter. We'll get blamed. The media will go after us like nothing you've ever seen and will say everything should move back to Boston. Imagine that?"

Before the CFC began doing its first cases this past summer, the state medical examiner's office was located in Boston and was besieged by political and economic problems and scandals that were constantly in the news. Bodies were lost or sent to the wrong funeral homes or cremated without a thorough examination, and in at least one suspected child-abuse death the wrong eyeballs were tested. New chiefs came and went, and district offices had to be shut down due to a lack of funding. But nothing negative ever said about that office could

33

compare to what Marino is suggesting about us.

"I'd rather not imagine anything." I open my door. "I'd rather focus on the facts."

"That's a problem, since we don't seem to have any that make much sense."

"And you told Briggs what you just told me?"

"I told him what he needed to know," Marino says.

"The same thing you just told me?" I repeat my question.

"Pretty much."

"You shouldn't have. It was for me to tell. It was for me to decide what he needs to know." I'm sitting with the passenger's door open wide and the wind blowing in. I'm damp from the shower and chilled. "You don't raise things up the chain just because I'm busy."

"Well, you were busy as hell, and I told him."

I climb out of the van and reassure myself that what Marino has just described can't be accurate. Cambridge EMTs would never make such a disastrous mistake, and I try to conjure up an explanation for why a fatal wound didn't bleed at the scene and then bled profusely, and I contemplate computing time of death or even the cause of it for someone who died inside a morgue refrigerator. I'm confounded. I haven't a clue, and most of all I worry about him, this young man delivered to my door, presumed dead. I envision him wrapped in a sheet and zipped inside a pouch, and it's the stuff of old horrors. Someone coming to inside a casket. Someone buried alive. I've never had such a ghastly thing happen, not even close, not once in my career. I've never known anyone who has.

"At least there's no sign he tried to get out of the body bag." Marino tries to make both of us feel better. "Nothing to indicate he might have been awake at some point and started panicking. You know, like clawing at the zipper or kicking or something. I guess if he struggled he would have been in a weird position on the tray when we found him this morning, or maybe rolled off it. Except I wonder if you would suffocate in one of those bags, now that I think of it. I guess so, since they're supposed to be watertight. Even though they leak. You show me a body bag that doesn't leak. And that's the other thing. Blood drips on the floor leading from the bay to the fridge."

"Why don't we continue this later." It's check-in time. There are plenty of people in the parking lot as we walk toward the inn's modern but plain stucco entrance, and Marino has a big voice that projects as if he's perpetually talking inside an amphitheater.

"I doubt Fielding has bothered to watch the recording," Marino adds anyway. "I doubt he's done a damn thing. I haven't seen or heard from the son of a bitch since first thing this morning. MIA once again, just like he's done before." He opens the glass front door. "I sure as hell hope he doesn't shut us down. Wouldn't that be something? You do him a fucking favor and give him a job after he walked off the last one, and he destroys the CFC before it's even off the ground."

Inside the lobby with its showcases of awards and air force memorabilia, its comfortable chairs and big-screen TV, a sign welcomes guests to the home of the C-5 Galaxy and C-17 Globemaster III. At the front desk I silently wait behind a man in the muted pixilated tiger stripes of the army combat uniform, or ACU, as he buys shaving cream, water, and several mini bottles of Johnnie Walker Scotch. I tell the clerk that I'm checking out earlier than planned, and yes, I'll remember to turn in my keys, and of course I understand I'll be charged the usual government rate of thirty-eight dollars for the day even though I'm not staying the night.

"What is it they say?" Marino goes on. "No good deed goes unpunished."

"Let's try not to be quite so negative."

"You and me both gave up good positions in New York, and we shut down the office in Watertown, and this is what we're left with."

I don't say anything.

"I hope like hell we didn't ruin our careers," he says.

I don't answer him because I've heard enough. Past the business center and vending machines, we take the stairs to the second floor, and it is now that he informs me that Lucy isn't waiting with the helicopter at the Civil Air Terminal. She's in my room. She's packing my belongings, touching them, making decisions about them, emptying my closet, my drawers, disconnecting my laptop, printer, and wireless router. He's waited to tell me because he knows damn well that under ordinary circumstances, this would annoy me beyond measure — doesn't matter if it's my computer-genius, former-federal-law-enforcement niece, whom I've raised like a daughter.

Circumstances are anything but ordinary, and I'm relieved that Marino is here and

Lucy is in my room, that they have come for me. I need to get home and fix everything. We follow the long hallway carpeted in deep red, past the balcony arranged with colonial reproductions and an electronic massage chair thoughtfully placed there for weary pilots. I insert my magnetic key card into the lock of my room, and I wonder who let Lucy in, and then I think of Briggs again and I think of CNN. I can't imagine appearing on TV. What if the media has gotten word of what's happened in Cambridge? I would know that by now. Marino would know it. My administrator, Bryce, would know it, and he would tell me right away. Everything is going to be fine.

Lucy is sitting on my neatly made bed, zipping up my cosmetic case, and I detect the clean citrus scent of her shampoo as I hug her and feel how much I've missed her. A black flight suit accentuates her bold green eyes and short rose-gold hair, her sharp features and leanness, and I'm reminded of how stunning she is in an unusual way, boyish but feminine, athletically chiseled but with breasts, and so intense she looks fierce. Doesn't matter if she's being playful or polite, my niece tends to intimidate and has few friends, maybe none except Marino, and her lovers never last.

Not even Jaime, although I haven't voiced my suspicions. I haven't asked. But I don't buy Lucy's story that she moved from New York to Boston for financial reasons. Even if her forensic computer investigative company was in a decline, and I don't believe that, either, she was making more in Manhattan than she's now paid by the CFC, which is nothing. My niece works for me pro bono. She doesn't need money.

"What's this about the satellite radio?" I watch her carefully, trying to interpret her signals, which are always subtle and perplexing.

Caplets rattle as she checks how many Advil are in a bottle, deciding not enough to bother with, and she clunks it in the trash. "We've got weather, so I'd like to get out of here." She takes the cap off a bottle of Zantac, tossing that next. "We'll talk as we fly, and I'll need your help copiloting, because it's going to be tricky dodging snow showers and freezing rain en route. We're supposed to get up to a foot at home, starting around ten."

My first thought is Norton's Woods. I need to pay a retrospective visit, but by the time I get there, it will be covered in snow. "That's unfortunate," I comment. "We may have a crime scene that was never worked as one."

"I told Cambridge PD to go back over there this morning." Marino's eyes probe and wander as if it is my quarters that need to be searched. "They didn't find anything."

"Did they ask you why you wanted them to look?" That concern again.

"I said we had questions. I blamed it on the Glock. The serial number's been ground off. Guess I didn't tell you that," he adds as he looks around, looking at everything but me.

"Firearms can try acid on it, see if we can restore the serial number that way. If all else fails, we'll try the large-chamber SEM," I decide. "If there's anything left, we'll find it. And I'll ask Jack to go to Norton's Woods and do a retrospective."

"Right. I'm sure he'll get right on it," Marino says sarcastically.

"He can take photographs before the snow starts," I add. "Or someone can. Whoever's on call —"

"Waste of time," Marino says, cutting me off. "None of us was there yesterday. We don't know the exact damn spot — only that it was near a tree and a green bench. Well, that's a lot of help when you're talking about six acres of trees and green benches."

"What about photographs?" I ask as Lucy continues going through my small pharmacy of ointments, analgesics, antacids, vitamins, eyedrops, and hand sanitizers spread over the bed. "The police must have taken pictures of the body in situ."

"I'm still waiting for the detective to get those to me. The guy who responded to the scene, he brought in the pistol this morning. Lester Law, goes by Les Law, but on the street he's known as Lawless, just like his father and grandfather before him. Cambridge cops going back to the fucking *Mayflower.* I've never met him."

"I think that about does it." Lucy gets up from the bed. "You might want to make sure I didn't miss anything," she says to me.

Wastebaskets are overflowing, and my bags are packed and lined up by a wall, the closet door open wide, nothing inside but empty hangers. Computer equipment, printed files, journal articles, and books are gone from my desk, and there is nothing in the dirty-clothes hamper or bathroom or in the dresser drawers I check. I open the small refrigerator, and it is empty and has been wiped clean. While she and Marino begin carrying my belongings out, I enter Briggs's number into my iPhone. I look out at the three-story stucco building on the other side of the parking lot, at the large plate-glass window in the middle of the third floor. Last night I was in that suite with him and other colleagues, watching the game, and life was good. We cheered for the New Orleans Saints and ourselves, and we toasted the Pentagon and its Defense Advanced Research Projects Agency, DARPA, which had made CT-assisted virtual autopsies possible at Dover and now at the CFC. We celebrated mission accomplished, a job well done — and now this, as if last night wasn't real, as if I dreamed it.

I take a deep breath and press send on my iPhone, going hollow inside. Briggs can't be happy with me. Images flash on the wall-mounted flat-screen TV in his living room, and then he walks past the glass, dressed in the combat uniform of the army, green and sandy brown with a mandarin collar, what he typically wears when he's not in the morgue or at a scene. I watch him answer his phone and return to his big window, where he stands, looking directly at me. From a distance we are face-to-face, an expanse of tarmac and parked cars between the armed forces chief medical examiner and me, as if we're about to have a standoff.

"Colonel." His voice greets me somberly.

"I just heard. And I assure you I'm taking

care of this, will be on the helicopter within the hour."

"You know what I always say," his deep, authoritative voice sounds in my earpiece, and I try to detect the degree of his bad mood and what he's going to do. "There's an answer to everything. The problem is finding it and figuring out the best way to do that. The proper and appropriate way to do that." He's cool. He's cautious. He's very serious. "We'll do this another time," he adds.

He means the final briefing we were scheduled to have. I'm sure he also means CNN, and I wonder what Marino told him. What exactly did he say?

"I agree, John. Everything should be canceled."

"It has been."

"Which is smart." I'm matter-of-fact. I won't let him sense my insecurities, and I know he sniffs for them. I know damn well he does. "My first priority is to determine if the information reported to me is correct. Because I don't see how it can be."

"Not a good time for you to go on the air. I don't need Rockman to tell us that."

Rockman is the press secretary. Briggs doesn't need to talk to him because he already has. I'm sure of it.

"I understand," I reply.

"Remarkable timing. If I was paranoid, I might just think someone has orchestrated some sort of bizarre sabotage."

"Based on what I've been told, I don't see how that would be possible."

"I said if I was paranoid," Briggs replies, and from where I stand, I can make out his formidable sturdy shape but can't see the expression on his face. I don't need to see it. He's not smiling. His gray eyes are galvanized steel.

"The timing is either a coincidence or it's not," I say. "The basic tenet in criminal investigations, John. It's always one or the other."

"Let's not trivialize this."

"I'm doing anything but."

"If a living person was put in your damn cooler, I can't think of much worse," he says flatly.

"We don't know —"

"It's just a damn shame after all this." As if everything we've built over the past few years is on the precipice of ruin.

"We don't know that what's been reported is accurate —" I start to say.

"I think it would be best if we bring the body here," he interrupts again. "AFDIL can work on the identification. Rockman will make sure the situation is well contained. We've got everything we need right here."

I'm stunned. Briggs wants to send a plane to Hanscom Field, the air force base affiliated with the CFC. He wants the Armed Forces DNA Identification Lab and probably other military labs and someone other than me to handle whatever has happened, because he doesn't think I'm competent. He doesn't trust me.

"We don't know if we're talking about federal jurisdiction," I remind him. "Unless you know something I don't."

"Look. I'm trying to do what's best for all involved." Briggs has his hands behind his back, his legs slightly spread, staring across the parking lot at me. "I'm suggesting we can dispatch a C-Seventeen to Hanscom. We can have the body here by midnight. The CFC is a port mortuary, too, and that's what port mortuaries do."

"That's not what port mortuaries do. The point isn't for bodies to be received, then transferred elsewhere for autopsies and lab analysis. The CFC was never intended to be a first screening for Dover, a preliminary check before the experts step in. That was never my mandate, and it wasn't the agreement when thirty million dollars was spent

45

on the facility in Cambridge."

"You should just stay at Dover, Kay, and we'll bring the body here."

"I'm requesting you refrain from intervening, John. Right now this case is the jurisdiction of the chief medical examiner of Massachusetts. Please don't challenge me or my authority."

A long pause, then he states rather than asks, "You really want that responsibility."

"It's mine whether I want it or not."

"I'm trying to protect you. I've been trying."

"Don't." That's not what he's trying. He doesn't have confidence in me.

"I can deploy Captain Avallone to help. It's not a bad idea."

I can't believe he would suggest that, either. "That won't be necessary," I reply firmly. "The CFC is perfectly capable of handling this."

"I'm on the record as having offered."

On the record with whom? It occurs to me uncannily that someone else is on the line or within earshot. Briggs is still standing in front of his window. I can't tell if anyone else might be in the suite with him.

"Whatever you decide," he then says. "I'm not going to step on you. Call me as soon as you know something. Wake me up if you

46

have to." He doesn't say good-bye or good luck or it was nice having me here for half a year.

2

Lucy and Marino have left my room. My
suitcases, rucksacks, and Bankers Boxes are
gone, and there is nothing left. It is as if I
was never here, and I feel alone in a way I
haven't for years, maybe decades.

I look around one last time, making sure
nothing has been forgotten, my attention
wandering past the microwave, the small
refrigerator-freezer and coffeemaker, the
windows with their view of the parking lot
and Briggs's lighted suite, and, beyond, the
black sky over the void of the empty golf
course. Thick clouds pass over the oblong
moon, and it glows on and off like a signal
lantern, as if telling me what is coming
down the tracks and if I should stop or go,
and I can't see the stars at all. I worry that
the bad weather is moving fast, carried on
the same strong south wind that brings in
the big planes and their sad cargo. I should
hurry, but I'm distracted by the bathroom

mirror, by the person in it, and I pause to look at myself in the glare of fluorescent lights. *Who are you now? Who really?*

My blue eyes and short blond hair, the strong shape of my face and figure, aren't so different, I decide, are remarkably the same, considering my age. I have held up well in my windowless places of concrete and stainless steel, and much of it is genetic, an inherited will to thrive in a family as tragic as a Verdi opera. The Scarpettas are from hearty Northern Italian stock, with prominent features, fair skin and hair, and well-defined muscle and bone that stubbornly weather hardship and the abuses of self-indulgence most people wouldn't associate with me. But the inclinations are there, a passion for food, for drink, for all things desired by the flesh, no matter how destructive. I crave beauty and feel deeply, but I'm an aberration, too. I can be unflinching and impervious. I can be immutable and unrelenting, and these behaviors are learned. I believe they are necessary. They aren't natural to me, not to anyone in my volatile, dramatic family, and that much I know is true about what I come from. The rest I'm not so sure about.

My ancestors were farmers and worked for the railroads, but in recent years my mother has added artists, philosophers, martyrs, and God knows what to the mix as she has set about to research our genealogy. According to her, I'm descended from artisans who built the high altar and choir stalls and made the mosaics at Saint Mark's Basilica and created the fresco ceiling of the Chiesa dell'Angelo San Raffaele. Somehow I have a number of friars and monks in my past, and most recently — based on what, I don't know — I share blood with the painter Caravaggio, who was a murderer, and have some tenuous link to the mathematician and astronomer Giordano Bruno, who was burned at the stake for heresy during the Roman Inquisition.

My mother still lives in her small house in Miami and is prepossessed with her efforts to explain me. I'm the only physician in the family tree that she knows of, and she doesn't understand why I've chosen patients who are dead. Neither my mother nor my only sibling, Dorothy, could possibly fathom that I might be partly defined by the terrors of a childhood consumed by tending to my terminally ill father before I became the head of the household at the age of twelve. By intuition and training, I'm an expert in violence and death. I'm at war with suffering and pain. Somehow I always end up in charge or to blame. It never fails.

I shut the door on what has been my home not just for six months but more than that, really. Briggs has managed to remind me where I'm from and headed. It's a course that was set long before this past July, as long ago as 1987, when I knew my destiny was public service and didn't know how I could repay my medical school debt. I allowed something as mundane as money, something as shameful as ambition, to change everything irrevocably and not in a good way — indeed, in the worst way. But I was young and idealistic. I was proud and wanted more, not understanding then that more is always less if you can't be sated.

Having gotten full rides through parochial school and Cornell and Georgetown Law, I could have begun my professional life unburdened by the obligations of debt. But I'd turned down Bowman Gray Medical School because I wanted Johns Hopkins badly. I wanted it as badly as I'd ever wanted anything, and I went there without benefit of financial aid, and what I ended up owing was impossible. My only recourse was to accept a military scholarship as some of my peers had done, including Briggs, whom I was acquainted with in the earliest stage of my profession, when I was assigned to the Armed Forces Institute of Pathology, the AFIP, the parent organization of the AFME. A quiet stint of reviewing military autopsy reports at Walter Reed Army Medical Center in Washington, D.C., Briggs led me to believe, and once my debt was paid, I'd move on to a solid position in civilian legal medicine.

What I didn't plan on was South Africa in December of '87, what was summertime on that distant continent. Noonie Pieste and Joanne Rule were filming a documentary and about my same age when they were tied up in chairs, beaten, and hacked, broken bottle glass shoved up their vaginas, their windpipes torn out. Racially motivated crimes against two young Americans. "You're going to Cape Town," Briggs said to me. "To investigate and bring them home." Apartheid propaganda. Lies and more lies. *Why them and why me?*

As I take the stairs down to the lobby, I tell myself not to think about this right now. *Why am I thinking about it at all?* But I know why. I was yelled at over the phone this morning. I was called names, and what happened more than two decades ago is now before me again. I remember autopsy reports that vanished and my luggage gone through. I remember being certain I would turn up dead, a convenient accident or suicide, or staged murder, like those two women I still see in my head. I see them as clearly as I did then, pale and stiff on steel tables, their blood washing through drains in the floor of a morgue so primitive we used handsaws to open their skulls, and there was no x-ray machine, and I had to bring my own camera.

I drop off my key at the front desk and replay the conversation I just had with Briggs, and I have clarity. I don't know why I didn't see the truth instantly, and I think of his remote tone, his chilly deliberateness, as I watched him through glass. I've heard him talk this way before, but usually it is directed at others when there is a problem of a magnitude that places it out of his hands. This is about more than his personal opinion of me. This is about something beyond his typical calculations and our conflicted past.

Someone has gotten to him, and it wasn't the press secretary, not anyone at Dover but higher up than that. I feel certain Briggs conferred with Washington after Marino divulged information, running his mouth and spinning his wild speculations before I'd had the chance to say a word. Marino shouldn't have discussed the Cambridge case or me. He's set something into motion he doesn't understand, because there's a lot he doesn't understand. He's never been military. He's never worked for the federal government and is clueless about international affairs. His idea of bureaucracy and intrigue is local police department policies, what he rubber-stamps as bullshit. He has no concept of power, the kind of power that can tilt a presidential election or start a war.

Briggs would not have suggested sending a military plane to Massachusetts for the transfer of a body to Dover unless he's gotten clearance from the Department of Defense, the DoD — in other words, the Pentagon. A decision has been made and I'm not part of it. Outside, in the parking lot, I climb into the van and won't look at Marino, I'm so angry.

"Tell me more about the satellite radio," I say to Lucy, because I intend to get to the bottom of this. I intend to find out what Briggs knows or has been led to believe.

"A Sirius Stiletto," Lucy says from the dark backseat as I turn up the heat because Marino is always hot while the rest of us freeze. "It's basically nothing more than storage for files, plus a power source. Of course, it also works as a portable XM radio, just as it's designed to, but it's the headphones that are creative. Not ingenious but technically clever."

"They've got a pinhole camera and a microphone built in," Marino offers as he drives. "Which is why I think the dead guy was the one doing the spying. How could he not know he had an audiovisual recording system built into his headphones?"

"He might not have known. It's possible someone was spying on him and he had no idea," Lucy says to me, and I sense she and Marino have been arguing about it. "The pinhole is on top of the headband but in the edge of it and hard to see. Even if you noticed, it wouldn't necessarily cross your mind that built inside is a wireless camera smaller than a grain of rice, an audio transmitter that's no bigger, and a motion sensor that goes to sleep after ninety seconds if nothing's moving. This guy was walking around with a micro-webcam that was recording onto the radio's hard drive and an additional eight-gig SD card. It's too soon for me to tell you if he knew it — in other words, if he rigged this up himself. I know that's what Marino thinks, but I'm not at all sure."

"Does the SD card come with the radio, or was it added aftermarket?" I inquire.

"Added. A lot of storage space, in other

words. What I'm curious about is if the files were periodically downloaded elsewhere, like onto his home computers. If we can get hold of them, we might know what this is about."

Lucy is saying that the video files she has looked at so far don't tell us much. She has reason to suspect the dead man has a home computer, possibly more than one of them, but she hasn't found anything that might tell us where he lived or who he is.

"What's stored on the hard drive and SD card go back only as far as February fifth, this past Friday," she continues. "I don't know if that means the surveillance just started or, more likely, these video files are large and take up a lot of space on the hard drive. They probably get downloaded somewhere, and what's on the hard drive and SD card gets recorded over. So what's here may be just the most recent recordings, but that doesn't mean there aren't others."

"Then these video clips were probably downloaded remotely."

"That's what I would do if it were me doing the spying," Lucy says. "I'd log in to the webcam remotely and download what I wanted."

"What about watching in real time?" I then ask.

"Of course. If he was being spied on, whoever's doing it could log on to the webcam and watch him as it's happening."

"To stalk him, to follow him?"

"That would be a logical reason. Or to gather intelligence, to spy. Like some people do when they suspect their person is cheating on them. Whatever you can imagine, it's possible."

"Then it's possible he inadvertently recorded his own death." I feel a glint of hope and at the same time am deeply disturbed by the thought. "I say 'inadvertently' because we don't know what we're dealing with. For example, we don't know if he intentionally recorded his own death, if he's therefore a suicide, and I'm not ready to rule out anything."

"No way he's a suicide," Marino says.

"At this point, we shouldn't rule out anything," I repeat.

"Like a suicide bomber," Lucy says. "Like Columbine and Fort Hood. Maybe he was going to take out as many people as he could in Norton's Woods and then kill himself, but something happened and he never got the chance."

"We don't know what we're dealing with," I say again.

"The Glock had seventeen rounds in the

magazine and one in the chamber," Lucy tells me. "A lot of firepower. You could certainly ruin someone's wedding. We need to know who got married and who attended."

"Most of these people have extra magazines," I reply, and I know all about the shootings at Fort Hood, at Virginia Tech, at far too many places, where assailants open fire without necessarily caring who they kill. "Usually these people have an abundance of ammunition and extra guns if they're planning on mass murder. But I agree with you. The American Academy of Arts and Sciences is a high-profile place, and we should find out who got married there yesterday and who the guests were."

"I figure you're a member," Marino says to me. "Maybe you got a contact for getting a list of members and a schedule of events."

"I'm not a member."

"You're kidding."

I don't offer that I haven't won a Nobel Prize or a Pulitzer and don't have a Ph.D., just an M.D. and a J.D., and they don't count. I could remind him that the Academy may not be relevant anyway, because nonmembers can rent the building. All it takes is connections and money. But I don't feel like giving Marino detailed explanations.

He shouldn't have called Briggs.

"Good news and not so good about the recordings." Lucy reaches over the back of the seat and hands me her iPad. "Good news, as I've pointed out, is it doesn't appear anything's been deleted, at least not recently. Which could be an argument in favor of him being the one doing the spying. You might speculate that if someone had him under surveillance and had something to do with his death, that person likely would have logged on to the Web address and scrubbed the hard drive and SD before people like us could look."

"Or how about remove the damn radio and headphones from the damn scene?" Marino says. "If he was being stalked, hunted down, and whoever's doing it whacked him? Well, if it was me, I'd grab the headset and radio and keep walking. So I'm betting he was the one doing the recording. I don't believe for a minute someone else was. And I'm betting this guy was involved in something, and whatever the reason for the spy equipment, he was the only one who knew about it. What sucks is there's no recording of the perp, of whoever whacked him, which is significant. If he was confronted by someone while he was walking his dog, why didn't the headphones record it?"

"The headphones didn't record it because he didn't see the person," Lucy replies. "He wasn't looking at whoever it was."

"Assuming there was a person who somehow caused his death," I remind both of them.

"Right," she says. "The headphones pretty much pick up whatever the wearer is looking at, the camera on the crown of his head, pointing straight out like a third eye."

"Then whoever whacked him came up from behind," Marino states conclusively. "And it happened so fast the victim never even turned around. Either that or it was some kind of sniper attack. Maybe he was shot with something from a distance. Like a dart with poison. Aren't there some poisons that cause hemorrhaging? May sound far-fetched, but shit like this happens. Remember the KGB spy poked with an umbrella that had ricin in the tip? He was waiting at a bus stop, and no one saw a thing."

"It was a Bulgarian dissident who worked for the BBC, and it's not a certainty it was an umbrella, and you're getting deeper into the woods without a map," I tell him.

"Ricin wouldn't drop you in your tracks, anyway," Lucy says. "Most poisons won't. Not even cyanide gas. I don't think he was poisoned."

"This isn't helpful," I answer.

"My map is my experience as a cop," Marino says to me. "I'm using my deductive skills. They don't call me Sherlock for nothing." He taps his baseball cap with a thick index finger.

"They don't call you Sherlock at all." Lucy's voice from the back.

"It's not helpful," I repeat, looking at his big shape as he drives, at his huge hands on the wheel, which rubs against his gut even when he's in what he considers his fighting shape.

"Aren't you the one always telling me to think outside the box?" Defensiveness hardens his tone.

"Guessing isn't helpful. Connecting dots that might be the wrong dots is reckless, and you know it," I say to him.

Marino has always been inclined to jump to conclusions, but it's gotten worse since he took the job in Cambridge, since he went to work for me again. I blame it on a military presence in our lives that is as constant as the massive airlifters flying low over Dover. More directly, I blame it on Briggs. Marino is ridiculously enamored of this powerful male forensic pathologist who is also a general in the army. My connection to the military has never mattered to him or even been acknowledged, not when it was part of my past, not when I was recalled to a special status after 9/11. Marino has always ignored my government affiliations as if they don't exist.

He stares straight ahead, and headlights of an approaching car illuminate his face, touched by disgruntledness and a certain lack of comprehension that is part of who he is. I might feel sorry for him because of the affection I can't deny, but not now. Not under the circumstances. I won't let on that I'm upset.

"What else did you share with Briggs — in addition to your opinions?" I ask Marino.

When he doesn't answer, Lucy does. "Briggs saw the same thing you're about to see," she says. "It wasn't my idea, and I didn't e-mail them, just so we're clear."

"Didn't e-mail what exactly?" But I know what exactly, and my incredulity grows. Marino sent evidence to Briggs. It's my case, and Briggs has been given information first.

"He wanted to know," Marino says, as if that's a good enough reason. "What was I supposed to tell him?"

"You shouldn't have told him anything. You went over my head. It's not his case," I reply.

"Yeah, well, it is," Marino says. "He was appointed by the surgeon general, meaning he basically was hired by the president, so I'd say that means he outranks everyone in this van."

"General Briggs isn't the chief medical examiner of Massachusetts, and you don't work for him. You work for me." I'm careful how I say it. I try to sound reasonable and calm, the way I do when a hostile attorney is trying to dismantle me on the witness stand, the way I do when Marino is about to erupt into an unseemly display of loud profanities and slammed doors. "The CFC has a mixed jurisdiction and can take federal cases in certain situations, and I realize it's confusing. Ours is a joint initiative between the state and federal governments and MIT, Harvard. And I realize that's an unprecedented concept and tricky, which is why you should have let me handle it instead of bypassing me." I try to sound easygoing and matter-of-fact. "The problem about involving General Briggs prematurely, about involving him precipitously, is things can take on a life of their own. But what's done is done."

"What do you mean? 'What's *done*'?" Marino sounds less sure of himself. I detect an anxious note, and I'm not going to help him out. He needs to think about what has been done, because he's the one who did it.

"What's the not-so-good news?" I turn around and ask Lucy.

"Take a look," she says. "It's the last three recordings made, including a minute here and there when the headset was jostled by the EMTs, the cops, and this morning by me when I started looking at it in my lab."

The iPad's display glows brightly, colorfully, in the dark, and I tap on the icon for the first video file she has selected, and it begins to play. I see what the dead man was seeing yesterday at three-oh-four p.m., a black-and-white greyhound curled up on a blue couch in a living room that has a heart-of-pine floor and a blue-and-red rug.

The camera moves as the man moves because he has the headphones on and they are recording: a coffee table covered with books and papers neatly stacked, and what looks like architectural or engineering drafting vellum with a pencil on top; a window with wooden blinds that are closed; a desk with two large flat-screen monitors and two silver MacBooks, a phone plugged into a charger, possibly an iPhone, and an amber glass smoking pipe in an ashtray; a floor lamp with a green shade; a fleece dog bed

and scattered toys. I get a glimpse of a door that has a dead bolt and a sliding lock, and on a wall are framed photographs and posters that go by too abruptly for me to see the details. I will wait to study them later.

So far I observe nothing that tells me who the man is or where he lives, but I get the impression of the small apartment or maybe the house of someone who likes animals, is financially comfortable, and is mindful of security and privacy. The man, assuming this is his place and his dog, is highly evolved intellectually and technically, is creative and organized, possibly smokes marijuana, and has chosen a pet that is a needy companion, not a trophy but a creature that has suffered cruelty in a former life and can't possibly fend for itself. I feel upset for the dog and worry about what has happened to it.

Certainly the EMTs, the police, didn't leave a helpless greyhound in Norton's Woods yesterday, lost and alone in the New England weather. Benton told me it was eleven degrees this morning in Cambridge, and before the night is out, it will snow. Maybe the dog is at the fire department's headquarters, well fed and attended to around the clock. Maybe Investigator Law took it home or some other police person

did. It's also possible no one realized the dog belonged to the man who died. Dear God, that would be awful.

"What happened to the greyhound?" I have to ask.

"Got no idea," Marino says, to my dismay. "Nobody knew until this morning when Lucy and me saw what you're looking at. The EMTs don't remember seeing a greyhound running loose, not that they were looking, but the gate leading into Norton's Woods was open when they got there. As you probably know, the gate's never locked and is wide open a lot of the time."

"He can't survive in freezing conditions. How could people not notice the poor thing unleashed and running loose? Because I can't imagine he wasn't running around in the park for at least a few minutes before he ran out of the open gate. Common sense would tell you that when his master collapsed, the dog didn't suddenly flee from the woods and onto the street."

"A lot of people take their dogs off the leashes and let them run loose in the parks like Norton's Woods," Lucy says. "I know I do with Jet Ranger."

Jet Ranger is her ancient bulldog, and he doesn't exactly run.

"So maybe nobody noticed because it

didn't look out of the ordinary," she adds.

"Plus, I think everybody was a little pre-occupied with some guy dropping dead," Marino states the obvious.

I look out at military housing on a poorly lit road, at aircraft that are bright and big like planets in the overcast dark. I can't make sense of what I'm being told. I'm surprised the greyhound didn't stay close to his master. Maybe the dog panicked or there's some other reason no one noticed him.

"The dog's bound to show up," Marino goes on. "No way people in an area like that are going to ignore a greyhound wandering around by itself. My guess is one of the neighbors or a student has it. Unless it's possible the guy was whacked and the killer took the dog."

"Why?" I puzzle.

"Like you've been saying, we need to keep an open mind," he answers. "How do we know that whoever did it wasn't watching nearby? And then at an opportune moment, took off with the dog, acting like it belonged to him?"

"But why?"

"It could be evidence that would lead to the killer for some reason," he suggests. "Maybe lead to an identification. A game. A thrill. A souvenir. Who the hell knows? But you'll notice from the video clips at one point the leash was taken off him, and guess what? It hasn't showed up. It didn't come in with the headphones or the body."

The dog's name is Sock. On the iPad's display, the man is walking and clucking his tongue, telling Sock it's time to go. *"Let's go, Sock,"* he coaxes in a pleasant baritone voice. *"Come on, you lazy doggie, it's time for a walk and a shit."* I detect a slight accent, possibly British or Australian. It could be South African, which would be weird, a weird coincidence, and I need to get South Africa off my mind. *Focus on what's before you,* I tell myself as Sock jumps off the couch, and I notice he has no collar. Sock — a male, I assume, based on the name — is thin, and his ribs show slightly, which is typical for greyhounds, and he is mature, possibly old, and one of his ears is ragged as if once torn. A rescue retired from the racetrack, I feel sure, and I wonder if he has a microchip. If so and if we can find him, we can trace where he's from and possibly who adopted him.

A pair of hands enters the frame as the man bends over to loop a red slip lead around Sock's long, tapered neck, and I notice a silver metal watch with a tachymeter on the bezel and catch the flash of yellow gold, a signet ring, possibly a college ring. If the ring came in with the body, it might be helpful, because it might be engraved. The hands are delicate, with tapered fingers and light-brown skin, and I get a glimpse of a dark-green jacket and baggy black cargo pants and the toe of a scuffed brown hiking boot.

The camera fixes on the wall over the couch, on wormy chestnut paneling and the bottom of a metal picture frame, and then a poster or a print rises into view as the man stands up, and I get a close look at a reproduction of a drawing that is familiar. I recognize da Vinci's sixteenth-century sketch of a winged flapping device, a flying machine, and I think back a number of years — when was it exactly? The summer before 9/11. I took Lucy to an exhibition at London's Courtauld Gallery, "Leonardo the Inventor," and we spent many entranced hours listening to lectures by some of the most eminent scientists in the world while studying da Vinci's conceptual drawings of water, land, and war machines: his aerial screw, scuba gear, and parachute, his giant crossbow, self-propelled cart, and robotic knight.

The great Renaissance genius believed

that art is science and science is art, and the solutions to all problems can be found in nature if one is meticulous and observant, if one faithfully seeks truth. I have tried to teach my niece these lessons most of her life. I have repeatedly told her we are instructed by what is around us if we are humble and quiet and have courage. The man I am watching on the small device I hold in my hands has the answers I need. *Talk to me. Tell me. Who are you, and what happened?*

He is walking toward the door that is dead-bolted with the slide lock pulled across, and the perspective abruptly shifts, the camera angle changes, and I wonder if he has adjusted the position of the head-phones. Maybe he didn't have them completely over his ears and now he's about to turn on music as he heads out. He walks past something mechanical and crude-looking, like a grotesque sculpture made of metal scrap. I pause on the image but can't get a good look at whatever it is, and I decide that when I have the luxury of time I'll replay the clips as often as I want and study every detail carefully, or if need be, get Lucy to forensically enhance the images. But right now I must accompany the man and his dog to the wooded estate not even a block from Benton's and my house. I must witness what happened. In several minutes he will die. *Show me and I'll figure it out. I'll learn the truth. Let me take care of you.*

The man and the dog go down four flights of stairs in a poorly lit stairwell, footsteps sounding light and quick against uncarpeted wood, and the two of them emerge on a loud, busy street. The sun is low, and patches of snow are crusty on top with black dirt, reminding me of crushed Oreo cookies, and whenever the man glances down, I see wet pavers and asphalt, and the sand and salt from snow removal. Cars and people move jerkily and lurch as he turns his head, scanning as he walks, and music plays in the background, Annie Lennox on satellite radio, and I hear only what is audible outside the headphones, what is being picked up by the mike inside the top of the headband. The man must have the volume turned up high, and that's not good, because he might not hear someone come up behind him. If he's worried about his security, so worried that he double-locks his apartment door and carries a gun, why isn't he worried about not hearing what is going on around him?

But people are foolish these days. Even reasonably cautious people multitask ridiculously. They text-message and check e-mail while driving or operating other dangerous machinery or while crossing a busy street. They talk on their cell phones while riding bicycles and while Rollerblading, and even while flying. How often do I tell Lucy not to answer the helicopter phone; doesn't matter that it's Bluetooth-enabled and hands-free. I see what the man sees and recognize where he's walking, on Concord Avenue, moving at a good clip with Sock, past redbrick apartment buildings and the Harvard Police Department and the dark-red awning of the Sheraton Commander Hotel across the street from the Cambridge Common. He lives very near the Common, in an older apartment building that has at least four floors.

I wonder why he doesn't take Sock into the Common. It's a popular park for dogs, but he and his greyhound continue past statues and cannons, lampposts, bare oak trees, benches, and cars parked at meters lining the street. A yellow Lab chases a fat squirrel, and Annie Lennox sings, *"No more 'I love you's' . . . I used to have demons in my room at night . . ."* I am the man's eyes and ears at the time the headphones are recording, and I have no reason to suspect he knows about the hidden camera and mike or that any such thing is on his mind at all.

I don't get the sense he has a dark plan or is spying as he walks his dog. Except that he has a Glock semiautomatic pistol and eighteen rounds of nine-millimeter ammunition under his green jacket. Why? Is he on his way to shoot someone, or is the gun for self-protection, and if so, what did he fear? Maybe it was a habit of his, a normal routine to walk around armed. There are people like that, too. People who don't think twice about it. Why did he grind the serial number off the Glock, or did someone else do it? It enters my mind that the hidden recording devices built into his headphones might be an experiment of his or a research project. Certainly Cambridge and its surrounds are the mecca of technical innovations, which is one of the reasons the DoD, the Commonwealth of Massachusetts, Harvard, and MIT agreed to establish the CFC on the north bank of the Charles River in a biotech building on Memorial Drive. Maybe the man was a graduate student. Maybe he was a computer scientist or an engineer. I watch what is on the iPad's display, abrupt, shaky images of Mather Court apartments, a playground, Garden Street, and the tilted, worn headstones of the Old Burying Ground.

In Harvard Square, his attention fixes on the Crimson Corner newsstand, and he seems to think of walking in that direction, perhaps to buy a paper from the overstocked selection that Benton and I love. This is our neighborhood, where we prowl for coffee and ethnic food, and papers and books, ending up with takeout and armloads of wonderful things to read that we pile on the bed on weekends and holidays when I'm home. The *New York Times* and the *Los Angeles Times,* the *Chicago Tribune,* and the *Wall Street Journal,* and if one doesn't mind news a day or two old, there are fat papers from London, Berlin, and Paris. Sometimes we find *La Nazione* and *L'espresso,* and I read to us about Florence and Rome, and we look at ads for villas to rent and fantasize about living like the locals, about exploring ruins and museums, the Italian countryside and the Amalfi Coast.

The man pauses on the crowded sidewalk and seems to change his mind about something. He and Sock trot across the street, on Massachusetts Avenue now, and I know where they are headed, or I think I do. A left on Quincy Street, and they are walking more briskly, and the man has a plastic bag in his hand, as if Sock isn't going to hold out much longer. Past the modern Lamont

Library and the Georgian Revival brick Harvard Faculty Club and Fogg Museum, and the Gothic stone Church of the New Jerusalem, and they turn right on Kirkland Avenue. It is the three of us. I am with them, cutting over to Irving, turning left on it, minutes from Norton's Woods, minutes from Benton's and my house, listening to Five for Fighting on the satellite radio . . . *"even heroes have the right to bleed . . ."*

I feel a growing sense of urgency with each step as we move closer to the man dying and the dog being lost in the bitter cold, and I desperately don't want it. I'm walking with them as if leading them into it because I know what's ahead and they don't, and I want to stop them and turn them back. Then the house is on our left, three-story, white with black shutters and a slate roof, Federal-style, built in 1824 by a transcendentalist who knew Emerson, Thoreau, and the Norton of *Norton's Anthology* and Norton's Woods. Inside the house, Benton's and my house, are original woodwork and molding, and plaster ceilings with exposed beams, and over the landings of the main staircase are magnificent French stained-glass windows with wildlife scenes that light up like jewels in the sun. A Porsche 911 is in the narrow brick driveway, exhaust fog-

75

ging out of the chrome tailpipes.

Benton is backing up his sports car, the taillights glowing like fiery eyes as he brakes for a man and his dog walking past, and the man has his headphones turned toward Benton, maybe admiring the Porsche, a black all-wheel-drive Turbo Cabriolet that he keeps as shiny as patent leather. I wonder if he will remember the young man in the bulky green coat and his black-and-white greyhound or if they really registered at the time, but I know Benton. He'll become obsessed, maybe as obsessed with the man and his dog as I am, and I search my memory for what Benton did yesterday. Late afternoon he dropped by his office at McLean because he'd forgotten to bring home the case file of the patient he was to evaluate today. A few degrees of separation, a young man and his old dog, who are about to be parted forever, and my husband alone in his car heading to the hospital to pick up something he forgot. I'm watching it all unfold as if I'm God, and if this is what it's like to be God, how awful that must be. I know what's going to happen and can't do a thing to stop it.

3

I realize the van has stopped and Marino and Lucy are getting out. We are parked in front of the John B. Wallace Civil Air Terminal, and I stay put. I continue to watch what is playing on the iPad as Lucy and Marino begin unloading my belongings.

Cold air rushes in through the open tailgate while I puzzle over the man's decision to walk Sock in Norton's Woods, in what's called Mid-Cambridge, almost in Somerville. Why here? Why not closer to where he lived? Was he meeting someone? A black iron gate fills the display, and it is partially opened and his hand opens it wide, and I realize he has put on thick black gloves, what look like motorcycle gloves. Are his hands cold, or is there another reason? Maybe he does have a sinister plan. Maybe he intends to use the gun. I imagine pulling back the slide of a nine-millimeter pistol and pressing the trigger while wearing bulky gloves, and it seems illogical.

I hear him shake open the plastic bag, and then I see it as he looks down and I catch a glimpse of something else, what looks like a tiny wooden box. *A stash box,* I think. Some of them are made of cedar and even have a tiny hygrometer in them like a humidor, and I recall the amber glass smoking pipe on the desk inside the apartment. Maybe he likes to walk his dog in Norton's Woods because it is remote and usually quite private, and of little interest to the police unless there is a VIP or high-level event that requires security. Maybe he enjoys coming here and smoking weed. He whistles at Sock, bends over, and slips the lead off him, and I can hear him say, *"Hey, boy, do you remember our spot? Show me our spot."* Then he says something that's muffled. I can't quite make it out. *"And for you,"* it sounds like he says, followed by, *"Do you want to send one . . . ?"* Or *"Do you send one . . . ?"* After playing it twice I still can't understand what he is saying, and it may be that he is bent over and talking into his coat collar.

Who is he talking to? I don't see anyone nearby, just the dog and the gloved hands, and then the camera angle shifts up as the man straightens up and I see the park again, a vista of trees and benches, and off to one side a stone walkway near the building with the green metal roof. I catch glimpses of people and conclude by the way they are bundled up for the cold that they aren't wedding guests but most likely are walking in the park just like the man is. Sock trots toward shrubs to leave his deposit, and his master moves deeper into the gracious wooded estate of ancient elms and green benches.

He whistles and says, *"Hey, boy, follow me."*

In shaded areas around thick clumps of rhododendrons the snow is deep and churned up with dead leaves and stones and broken sticks that make me think morbidly of clandestine graves, of sloughed-off skin and weathered bones that have been gnawed on and scattered. He is scanning, looking around, and the hidden camera pauses on the three-tier green metal roof of the glass-and-timber building I can see from the sun-porch at Benton's and my house. As the man turns his head, I see a door on the first floor that leads outside, and the camera pauses again on a woman with gray hair standing outside the door. She is dressed in a suit and a long brown leather coat and is talking on her phone.

The man whistles and makes a gritty

sound as he walks on the slate gravel path toward Sock, to pick up what the dog has left . . . *"and this emptiness fills my heart . . ."* Peter Gabriel sings. I think of the young soldier with the same name who burned up in his Humvee, and I smell him as though his foul odors are still trapped deep inside my nose. I think of his mother and her grief and anger on the phone when she called me this morning. Forensic pathologists aren't always thanked, and there are times when those left behind act as if I am the reason their loved one is dead, and I try to remember that. *Don't take it personally.*

The gloved hands shake out the rumpled plastic bag again, the type one gets at the market, and then something happens. The man's gloved hand flies up at his head, and I hear the jostle of his hand hitting the headphones as if he's swatting at something, and he exclaims, *"What the . . . ? Hey . . . !"* in a breathy, startled way. Or maybe it is a cry of pain. But I don't see anything or anyone, just the woods and distant figures in it. I don't see his dog, and I don't see him. I back up the recording and play it again. His black gloved hand suddenly enters the frame, and he blurts out, *"What the . . . ?"* then, *"Hey . . . !"* I decide he sounds stunned and upset, as if something has knocked the wind out of him.

I play it again, listening for anything else, and what I detect in his tone is protest and maybe fear, and, yes, pain, as if someone has elbowed him or bumped him hard on a busy sidewalk. Then the tops of bare trees rush up and around. Chipped bits of slate zoom in and get large as he thuds down on the path, and either he is on his back or the headphones have come off. The screen is fixed on an image of bare branches and gray sky, and then the hem of a long black coat swishes past, flapping as someone walks swiftly, and another loud jostling noise and the picture changes again. Bare branches and a gray sky but different branches showing through the slats of a green bench. It happens so fast, so unbelievably fast, and then the voices and the sounds of people get loud.

"Someone call nine-one-one!"

"I don't think he's breathing."

"I don't have my phone. Call nine-one-one!"

"Hello? There's . . . uh, yeah, in Cambridge. Yes, Massachusetts. *Je-sus!* Hurry, hurry; they fucking have me on hold. Je-sus, hurry! I can't believe this. Yes, yes, a man, he's collapsed and doesn't seem to be breathing . . . Norton's Woods at the corner of Irving and Bryant . . . Yes, someone is trying CPR. I'll stay on . . . I'm staying on. Yes, I mean, I don't . . . She wants to know if he's still not breathing. No, no, he's not breathing! He's not moving. He's not breathing! . . . I didn't really see it, just looked over and noticed he was on the ground, suddenly he was on the ground . . ."

I press pause and get out of the van, and it is cold and very windy as I walk quickly into the terminal. It is small, with restrooms and a sitting area, and an old television is turned on. For a moment I watch Fox News and fast-forward the video on the iPad while Lucy leans against the front desk and pays the landing fee with a credit card. I continue to stare at images of bare branches showing between the slats of green-painted wood, certain now that the headphones ended up under a bench, the camera fixed straight up as the XM radio plays. . . . *"Dark lady laughed and danced . . ."* The music is louder because the headphones aren't pressed against the man's head, and it seems absurdly incongruous to be listening to Cher.

Voices off-camera are urgent and excited, and I hear the sounds of feet and the distant wail of a siren as my niece chats with an older man, a retired fighter pilot now working at Dover part-time as a fixed base operator, he is happy to tell her.

". . . In 'Nam. So that would have been, what, an F-Four?" Lucy chats with him.

"Oh, yeah, and the Tomcat. That was the last one I flew. But Phantoms were still around, you know, as late as the eighties. You build them right and they last like you wouldn't believe. Look how long the C-Five's been around. And still some Phantoms in Israel, I think. Maybe Iran. Nowadays those left in the U.S., we use them for unmanned targets, as drones. One hell of an aircraft. You ever seen one?"

"In Belle Chasse, Louisiana, at the Naval Air Station. Took my helicopter down there to help with Katrina."

"They've been experimenting with hurricane-busting, using Phantoms to fly into the eye." He nods.

The screen on the iPad goes black. The headphones weren't recording anymore, and I'm convinced that when the man fell to the ground they must have ended up some distance away under a bench. The motion sensor wasn't detecting enough activity to prevent it from dozing, and that's curious to me. How exactly did his headphones get knocked off and end up where they did? Maybe someone kicked them out of the way. It could have been accidental if that's what happened, perhaps by a person trying to help him, or it could have been deliberate by a person who was covertly recording him, stalking him. I think of the hem of the black coat flapping by, and I fast-forward intermittently, looking for the next images, listening for sounds, but nothing until four-thirty-seven p.m., when the woods and the darkening sky swing wildly, and bare hands loom large and paper crackles as the headphones are placed inside a brown bag, and I hear a voice say, ". . . Colts all the way." And another voice says, "Saints are gonna take it. They got . . ." Then murky darkness and muffled voices, and nothing.

Finding the TV remote on the arm of a couch inside the terminal, I switch the channel to CNN and listen to the news and watch the crawl, but not a word about the man on the video clips. I need to ask about Sock again. Where is the dog? It's not acceptable that no one seems to know. I fix on Marino as he enters the sitting area, pretending not to see me because he is sulking, or maybe he regrets what he's done and is embarrassed. I refuse to ask him anything, and it feels as if the missing dog is somehow his fault, as if everything is Marino's fault. I don't want to forgive him for e-mailing the video clips to Briggs, for talking to him first.

If I don't forgive Marino for once, maybe he'll learn a lesson for once, but the problem is I'm never quite able to convince myself of any case I make against him, against anyone I care about. Catholic guilt. I don't know what it is, but already I am softening toward him, my resolve getting weaker. I feel it happening as I search channels on the television, looking for news that might damage the CFC, and he walks over to Lucy, keeping his back to me. I don't want to fight with him. I don't want to hurt his feelings.

I walk away from the TV, convinced at least for the moment that the media doesn't know about the body waiting for me in my Cambridge morgue. Something as sensational as that would be a headline, I reason. Messages would be landing nonstop on my iPhone. Briggs would have heard about it and said something. Even Fielding would have alerted me. Except I've heard nothing from Fielding about anything at all, and I try to call him again. He doesn't answer his cell phone, and he's not in his office. Of course not. He never works this late, for God's sake. I try him at his home in Concord and get voicemail again.

"Jack? It's Kay," I leave another message. "We're about to take off from Dover. Maybe you can text or e-mail me an update. Investigator Law hasn't called back, I assume? We're still waiting for photographs, and have you heard anything about a missing dog, a greyhound? The victim's dog, named Sock, last seen in Norton's Woods." My voice has an edge. Fielding is ducking me, and it's not the first time. He's a master at disappearing acts, and he should be. He's staged enough of them. "Well, I'll try you again when we land. I assume you'll meet us at the office, probably sometime between nine-thirty and ten. I've sent messages to Anne and Ollie, and maybe you can make sure they are there. We need to take care of this tonight. Maybe you could check with Cambridge PD about the dog? He might have a microchip. . . ."

It sounds silly to belabor my point about Sock. What the hell would Fielding know about it? He couldn't be bothered to go to the scene, and Marino's right. Someone should have gone.

Lucy's Bell 407 is black with dark tinted glass in back, and she unlocks the doors and baggage compartment as wind buffets the ramp.

A wind sock is stiffly pointed north like a horizontal traffic cone, and that's good and bad. The wind will still be on our tail but so will the storm front, heavy rains mixed with sleet and snow. Marino begins to load my luggage while Lucy walks around the helicopter, checking antennas, static ports, rotor blades, the emergency pop-out floats and the bottles of nitrogen that inflate them, then the aluminum alloy tail boom and its gear box, the hydraulic pump and reservoir.

"If someone was spying on him, covertly recording him, and realized he was dead, then the person had something to do with it," I say to her, apropos of nothing. "So wouldn't you expect that person to have remotely deleted the video files recorded by the headphones, at least gotten rid of them on the hard drive and SD card? Wouldn't such a person want to make sure we didn't find any recordings or have a clue?"

"Depends." She grabs hold of a handle on the fuselage and inserts the toe of her boot into a built-in step, climbing up.

"If it were you doing it," I ask.

"If it were me?" She opens fasteners and props open a panel of the lightweight aluminum skin. "If I didn't think anything significant or incriminating had been recorded, I wouldn't have deleted them." Using a small but powerful SureFire flashlight, she inspects the engine and its mounts.

"Why not?"

Before she can answer, Marino walks over to me and says to no one in particular, "I got to make a visit. Anybody else needs to, now's the time." As if he's the chief steward and reminding us that there is no restroom on the helicopter. He's trying to make up to me.

"Thanks, I'm fine," I tell him, and he walks off across the dark ramp, back to the terminal.

"If it were me, this is what I'd do after he's dead," Lucy continues as the strong light moves over hoses and tubing, as she makes sure nothing is loose or damaged. "I'd download the video files immediately by logging on to the webcam, and if I didn't see anything that worried me, I'd leave them be."

She climbs up higher to check the main rotor, its mast, its swashplate, and I wait until she is back on the tarmac before I ask, "Why would you leave them be?"

"Think about it."

I follow her around the helicopter so she can climb up and check the other side. She almost seems amused by my questions, as if what I'm asking should be obvious.

"If they're deleted after he's dead, then someone else did it, right?" she says, checking under cowling, the light probing care-fully.

Then she drops back down to the ramp.

"Of course he couldn't do it after he was dead." I wait to answer her, because she could get hurt climbing all over her helicopter, especially when she's up around the rotor mast. I don't want her distracted. "So that's why you would leave them if you were the one spying on him and knew he was dead or were the one responsible for his death."

"If I were spying on him, if I followed him so I could kill him, hell, yes, I'd leave the last video recordings made, and I wouldn't grab the headphones from the scene, either." She shines the brilliant light along the fuselage again. "Because if people saw him wearing them out there in the park or on his way to the park, why are they now missing? The headphones are rather beefy and noticeable."

We walk around to the nose of the helicopter.

"And if I take the headphones, I'd have to take his satellite radio, too, dig in his coat pocket and get that out, have to take time to go to all this trouble after he's on the ground, and hope nobody saw me. And what about earlier files downloaded somewhere, assuming the spying has gone on for a while? How is that explained if there's no recording device that shows up and we find recordings on a home computer or server somewhere? You know what they say." She opens an access panel above the pitot tube and shines the light in there. "For every crime, there are two — the act itself and then what you do to cover it up. Be smarter to leave the headphones, the video files, alone, to let cops or someone like you or me assume he was recording himself, which is what Marino believes, but I doubt it."

She reconnects the battery. Her rationale for disconnecting it whenever she leaves the helicopter for any period of time is that if someone manages to get inside the cockpit and is lucky while fiddling with the throttle and switches, they could accidentally start the engine. But not if the battery is disconnected. Doesn't matter her hurry, Lucy always does a thorough preflight, especially if she's left her aircraft unattended, even if it's on a military base. But it doesn't escape my attention that she is checking everything more thoroughly than usual, as if she suspects something or is uneasy.

"Everything A-okay?" I ask her. "Everything in good shape?"

"Making sure of it," she says, and I feel

her distance more strongly. I sense her secrets.

She trusts no one. She shouldn't. I never should have trusted some people, either, going back to day one. People who manipulate and lie and claim it is for a cause. The right cause, a godly or just cause. Noonie Pieste and Joanne Rule were smothered to death in bed, probably with a pillow. That's why there was no tissue response to their injuries. The sexual assaults, the hacks with machetes and slashes with broken glass, and even the ligatures binding them when they were tied up in the chairs, all of it postmortem. A godly cause, a just cause, in the minds of those responsible. An unthinkable outrage, and they got away with it. To this day they did. *Don't think about it. Focus on what is before you, not on the past.*

I open the left-front door and climb up on a skid, the wind gusting hard. Maneuvering myself around the collective and cyclic and into the left seat, I fasten my four-point harness as I hear Marino opening the door behind me. He is loud and big, and I feel the helicopter settle from his weight as he climbs into the back, where he always sits. Even when Lucy flies with only him as a passenger, he isn't allowed up front where there are dual controls that he can nudge or bump or use as an armrest because he doesn't think. He just doesn't think.

Lucy gets in and begins another preflight, and I help her by holding the checklist, and together we go through it. I've never had a desire to fly the various aircraft my niece has owned over the years, or to ride her motorcycles or drive her fast Italian cars, but I'm fine to copilot, am handy with maps and avionics. I know how to switch the radios to the necessary frequencies or enter squawks and other information into the transponder or Chelton Flight System. If there was an emergency, I probably could get the helicopter safely to the ground, but it wouldn't be pretty.

". . . Overhead switches in the off position," I continue going down the list.

"Yes."

"Circuit breakers in."

"They are." Lucy's agile fingers touch everything she checks as we go down the plastic-laminated list.

Momentarily, she flips on the boost pumps and rolls the throttle to flight idle.

"Clear to the right." As she looks out her side window.

"Clear to the left." As I look out at the dark ramp, at the small building with its lighted windows and a Piper Cub tied down a safe distance away in the shadows, its tarp shaking in the wind.

Lucy pushes the start switch, and the main rotor blade begins to turn slowly, heavily, thudding faster like a heartbeat, and I think of the man. I think of his fear, of what I detected in those three words he exclaimed.

"What the . . . ? Hey . . . !"

What did he feel? What did he see? The lower part of a black coat, the loose skirt of a black coat swishing past. Whose coat? A wool dress coat or a trench coat? It wasn't fur. Who was wearing the long, black coat? Someone who didn't stop to help him.

"What the . . . ? Hey . . . !" A startled cry of pain.

I replay it in my mind again and again. The camera angle dropping suddenly, then fixing straight up at bare branches and gray sky, then the hem of the long, black coat moving past in the frame for an instant, maybe a second. Who would step around someone in distress as if he was an inanimate object, such as a rock or a log? What kind of human being would ignore someone who grabbed his chest and collapsed? The person who caused it, perhaps. Or someone who didn't want to be involved for some reason. Like witnessing an accident or assault and speeding off so you don't become part of the investigation. A man or a woman? Did I see shoes? No, just the hem or skirt of the coat flapping, and then another jostling sound and the picture was replaced by different bare trees showing through the underside of a green-painted bench. Did the person in the long black coat kick the headphones under the bench there so they didn't record something else that was done?

I need to look at the video clips more closely, but I can't do it now. The iPad is in back, and there isn't time. The blades rapidly beat the air, and the generator is on-line. Lucy and I put our headsets on. She flips more overhead switches, the avionics master, the flight and navigation instruments. I turn the intercom switch to "crew only" so Marino can't hear us and we can't hear him while Lucy talks to the air traffic controller. The strobes, the pulse and night scanner landing lights, blaze on the tarmac, painting it white as we wait for the tower to clear us for takeoff. Entering destinations in the touch-screen GPS and in the moving map display and the Chelton, I correct the altimeters. I make sure the digital fuel indicator matches the fuel gauge, doing most things at least twice, because Lucy believes in redundancy.

The tower releases us, and we hover-taxi to the runway and climb on course to the northeast, crossing the Delaware River at eleven hundred feet. The water is dark and ruffled by the wind, like molten metal flowing thickly. The lights of land flicker through trees like small fires.

4

We change our heading, veering toward Philadelphia, because the visibility deteriorates closer to the coast. I flip the intercom switch so we can check on Marino.

"You all right back there?" I'm calmer now, too preoccupied with the long black coat and the man's startled exclamation to be angry with Marino.

"Be quicker to cut through New Jersey," his voice sounds, and he knows where we are, because there is an in-flight map on a video screen inside the rear passenger compartment.

"Fog and freezing rain, IFR conditions in Atlantic City. And it isn't quicker," Lucy replies. "We'll be on 'crew only' most of the time so I can deal with flight following."

Marino is cut out of our conversation again as we are handed off from one tower to the next. The Washington sectional map is open in my lap, and I enter a new GPS destination of Oxford, Connecticut, for an eventual fuel stop, and we monitor weather on the radar, watching blocks of solid green and yellow encroach upon us from the Atlantic. We can outrun, duck, and dodge the storms, Lucy says, as long as we stay inland and the wind continues to favor us, increasing our ground speed to what at this moment is an impressive one hundred and fifty-two knots.

"How are you doing?" I keep up my scan for cell towers and other aircraft.

"Better when we get where we're going. I'm sure we'll be fine and can outrun this mess." She points at what's on the weather radar display. "But if there's a shadow of a doubt, we'll set down."

She wouldn't have come to pick me up if she thought we might have to spend the night in a field somewhere. I'm not worried. Maybe I don't have enough left in me to worry about yet one more thing.

"How about in general? How are you doing?" I say into the mike, touching my lip. "You've been on my mind a lot these past few weeks." I try to draw her out.

"I know how hard it is to keep up with people under the circumstances," she says. "Every time we think you're coming back, something changes, so we've all quit think-ing it."

Three times now the completion of my fellowship was delayed by one urgent mat-ter or another. Two helicopters shot down in one day in Iraq with twenty-three killed. The mass murder at Fort Hood, and most recently, the earthquake in Haiti. Armed forces MEs got deployed or none could be spared, and Briggs wouldn't release me from my training program. A few hours ago, he attempted to delay my departure again, suggesting I stay in Dover. As if he doesn't want me to go home.

"I figured we'd get to Dover and find out you had another week, two weeks, a month," Lucy adds. "But you're done."

"Apparently, they're sick of me."

"Let's hope you don't get home only to turn around and go back."

"I passed my boards. I'm done. I've got an office to run."

"Someone needs to run it. That's for sure."

I don't want to hear more damning com-ments about Jack Fielding.

"And things are fine elsewhere?" I ask.

"They've almost finished the garage, big enough for three cars even with the washing bay. Assuming you tandem park." She starts on a construction update, reminding me how disengaged I've been from what's going on at my own home. "The rubberized flooring is in, but the alarm system isn't ready. They weren't going to bother with glass breakers, and I said they had to. Unfortunately, one of the old wavy-glass windows original to the building didn't survive the upgrade. So you've got a bit of a breeze in the garage at the moment. Did you know all this?"

"Benton's been in charge."

"Well, he's been busy. You got the freq for Millville? I think one-two-three-point-six-five."

I check the sectional and affirm the frequency and enter it into Comm 1. "How are you?" I try again.

I want to know what I'm coming home to in addition to a dead man awaiting me in the morgue cooler. Lucy won't tell me how she is, and now she's accusing Benton of being busy. When she says something like that, she doesn't mean it literally. She's very tense. She's obsessively watching the instruments, the radar screens, and what's outside the cockpit, as if she's expecting to get into a dogfight or to be struck by lightning or to have a mechanical failure. I'm sensing something is off about her, or maybe I'm the one in a mood.

"He has a big case," I add. "An especially bad one."

We both know which one I mean. It's been all over the news about Johnny Donahue, the patient at McLean, a Harvard student who last week confessed to murdering a six-year-old boy with a nail gun. Benton believes the confession is false, and the cops, the DA, are unhappy with him. People want the confession to be genuine, because they don't want to think someone like that might still be loose. I wonder how the evaluation went today, as I envision Benton's black Porsche backing out of our driveway on the video clips I just watched. He was on his way to McLean to pick up Johnny Donahue's case file when a young man and a greyhound walked past our house. Several degrees of separation. The human web connecting all of us, connecting everyone on earth.

"Let's keep one-two-seven-point-three-five on Comm Two so we can monitor Philly," Lucy is saying, "but I'm going to try to stay out of their Class B. I think we can, unless this stuff pushes in any tighter from the coast."

She indicates the green and yellow shapes on the satellite weather radar display that show precipitation moving closer, as if trying to bully us northwest into the bright skyline of downtown Philadelphia, fly us into the high-rises.

"I'm fine," she then says. "Sorry about him, because I can tell you're pissed." She points her thumb toward the back, meaning Marino. "What'd he do besides be his usual self?"

"Were you listening when he talked to Briggs?"

"That was in Wilmington. I was busy paying for fuel."

"He shouldn't have called him."

"Like telling Jet Ranger not to drool when I get out the bag of treats. It's Pavlovian for Marino to shoot off his mouth to Briggs, to show off. Why are you more surprised than usual?" Lucy asks as if she already knows the answer, as if she's probing, looking for something.

"Maybe because it's caused a worse problem than usual." I tell her about Briggs wanting the body transported to Dover.

I tell her that the chief of the Armed Forces Medical Examiners has information he's not sharing, or at least I suspect that he is withholding something important from me. Probably because of Marino, I say. Because of what he's managed to stir up by going over my head.

"I don't think that's all of it by a long shot," Lucy says as her tail number is called out over the air.

She presses the radio switch on her cyclic and answers, and as she talks to flight following, I enter the next frequency. We hopscotch from airspace to airspace, the shapes on the weather radar mostly yellow now and bird-dogging us from the southeast, indicating heavy rains that at this altitude will create hazardous conditions as supercooled water particles hit the leading edges of the rotor blades and freeze. I watch for moisture on the Plexiglas windscreen and don't see anything, not one drop, while I wonder what Lucy is referring to. What's not it by a long shot?

"Did you notice what was in his apartment?" Lucy's voice in my headset, and I assume she means the dead man and what I watched on the video clips recorded by his headphones.

"You said that's not all of it." I go back to that first. "Tell me what you're referring to."

"I'm about to and didn't want to bring it up in front of Marino. He didn't notice, wouldn't know what it was, anyway, and I didn't point it out because I wanted to talk to you and I'm not sure he should know about it, period."

"Didn't point out what?"

"My guess is Briggs didn't need it pointed out," Lucy goes on. "He had a lot more time to look at the video clips than you did, and he or whoever else he's showed them to would have recognized the metal contraption near the door, sort of looks like a six-legged creepy crawler welded together with wires and composite pieces and parts, about the size of a stackable washer and dryer. Picked up by the camera for a second when the man and Sock were on their way out to Norton's Woods. I'm sure it wasn't lost on you, of all people."

"I caught a glimpse of what I thought was a crude metal sculpture." Obviously, I missed a connection she's made. A big one.

"A robot, and not just any robot," Lucy informs me. "A prototype developed for the military, what was supposed to be a tactical packbot for the troops in Iraq, and then another creative purpose was suggested that went over like the proverbial lead balloon."

A glint of recognition, and an ominous feeling begins working its way up from my gut, tightening my chest, creating awareness, then a memory.

"This particular model didn't last long," she continues, and I think I know what she's talking about.

MORT. Mortuary Operational Removal Transport. *Good God.*

"Never made it into service and is obsolete if not silly now, replaced by biologically inspired legged robots that can carry heavy loads over rough or slippery terrain," she says. "Like the quadruped called Big Dog that's all over YouTube. Damn thing can carry hundreds of pounds all day long in the worst conditions imaginable, jumps like a deer and regains its balance if it trips or slips or you kick it."

"MORT," I go ahead and say it. "Why would he have a packbot like MORT in his apartment? I think I'm misunderstanding something."

"You ever see it in person back then, when you got into a debate about it on Capitol Hill? And you're not misunderstanding anything. I'm talking about MORT."

"I never saw MORT in person." I saw it on videotaped demonstrations only, and I got into more than one debate, especially with Briggs. "Why would he have something like that?" I ask again about what Lucy claims is in the dead man's apartment.

"Creepy as hell. Like a giant mechanical ant, gas-powered," she says. "Sounds like a chain saw when it's ambulating slowly on its short, clunky legs with two sets of grippers in front like Edward Scissorhands. If you saw it coming at you, you'd run like hell or maybe lob a grenade at it."

"But in his apartment? Why?" I remember demonstrations that I found horrifying, and heated discussions that became nasty skirmishes with colleagues including Briggs at the AFME, at Walter Reed, and in the Russell Senate Office Building.

MORT. The epitome of wrongheaded automation that became the source of a controversy in military and medical intelligence. It wasn't the technology that was such a terrible idea, it was the suggestion of how it should be used. I remember a hot summer morning in Washington, the heat rising off a sidewalk crowded with Boy Scouts touring the capital as Briggs and I argued. We were hot in our uniforms, frustrated and stressed, and I remember walking past the White House, people everywhere, and wondering what would be next. What other inhumanities would be offered by technology? And that was almost a decade ago, almost the Stone Age compared to now.

"I'm pretty sure — in fact, more than pretty sure — that's what's parked inside the guy's apartment," Lucy is saying. "And you don't buy something like that on eBay."

"Maybe it's a model," I suggest. "A facsimile."

"No way. When I zoomed in on it, I could see the composite parts in detail, some wear and tear on it from usage, probably from R-and-D on hard terrain and it got scraped up a little. I could even see the fiber-optic connectors. MORT wasn't wireless, which was just one of a number of things wrong with it. Not like what they're doing today with autonomous robots that have onboard computers and receive information through sensors controlled by man-wearable units instead of lugging around a cumbersome Pelican case–based one. Like the military guys are doing so their field-embedded operators are hands-free when they're out with their robotic squads. This whole new thing with lightweight ruggedized processors that you can wear in your vest, say you're operating an unmanned ground vehicle or the armed robots, the SWORDS unit, the Special Weapons Observation Remote Direct-Action System. A robotic infantry armed with M-two-forty-nine light machine guns. Not something I'm comfortable with, and I know how you feel about that."

"I'm not sure that there are words for how

I feel about it," I reply.

"Three SWORDS units so far in Iraq, but they haven't fired their weapons yet. Nobody's sure how to get a robot to have that kind of judgment. Artificial EQ. A rather daunting prospect but I'm sure not impossible."

"Robots should be used for peacekeeping, surveillance, as pack mules."

"That's you but not everyone."

"They should not make decisions about life and death," I go on. "It would be like autopilot deciding whether we should fly through these clouds rolling toward us."

"Autopilot could if my helicopter had moisture and temperature sensors. Throw in force transducers and it will land all by itself as light as a feather. Enough sensors and you don't need me anymore. Climb in and push a button like the Jetsons. Sounds crazy, but the crazier, the better. Just ask DARPA. You got any idea how much money DARPA invests in the Cambridge area?"

Lucy lowers the collective, losing altitude and bleeding off speed as another ghostly patch of clouds rolls toward us in the dark.

"Besides what it's invested in the CFC?" she then says.

Her demeanor is different, even her face is different, and she's no longer trying to hide what has come over her. I know this mood. I know it all too well. It is an old mood I haven't seen in a while, but I know it like I know the symptoms of a disease that has been in remission.

"Computers, robotics, synthetic biology, nanotechnology, the more off the wall, the better," she continues. "Because there's no such thing as mad scientists anymore. I'm not sure there's any such thing as science fiction. Come up with the most extreme invention you can imagine, and it's probably being implemented somewhere. It's probably old news."

"You're suggesting this man who died in Norton's Woods is connected to DARPA."

"Somehow he is, in some capacity. Don't know how directly or indirectly," Lucy answers. "MORT isn't being used anymore, not by the military, not for any purpose, but was *Star Wars* stuff about eight or nine years ago when DARPA stepped up funding for military and intelligence-gathering applications of robotics, bio and computer engineering. And forensics and other applications germane to our war dead, to what happens in combat, in theater."

It was DARPA that funded the research and development of the RadPath technology we use in virtual autopsies at Dover and now at the CFC. DARPA funded my four-month fellowship that turned into six.

"A substantial percentage of research grants are going to Cambridge area labs, to Harvard and MIT," Lucy says. "Remember when everything became about the war?"

It's getting harder to remember a time when that wasn't true. War has become our national industry, like automotives and steel and the railroads once were. That's the dangerous world we live in. I don't believe it can change.

"The brilliant idea that robots like MORT could be utilized in theater to recover casualties so troops didn't risk their lives for a fallen comrade?" Lucy reminds me.

Not a brilliant idea but an unfortunate one. A supremely stupid one, I thought at the time and still do. Briggs and I weren't on the same side about it. He'll never give me credit for saving him from a PR misstep that could have injured him badly.

"The idea was aggressively researched for a while and then got tabled," Lucy adds.

It got tabled because using robots for such a purpose supposes they can decide a fallen soldier, a human being, is fatally injured or dead.

"DoD got a lot of shit for it, at least internally, because it seemed cold-blooded and inhumane," she says.

Deservedly. No one should die in the grippers of something mechanical dragging them off the battlefield or out of a crashed vehicle or from the rubble of a building that has collapsed.

"What I'm getting at is the early generations of this technology have been buried by DoD, relegated to a classified scrap yard or salvaged for pieces and parts," Lucy says. "Yet your guy in the cooler has one in his apartment. Where'd he get it? He's got a connection. He has drafting paper on the coffee table. He's an inventor, an engineer, something like that, and somehow involved in classified projects that require a high level of security clearance, but he's a civilian."

"How can you be so sure he's a civilian?"

"Believe me, I'm sure. He's not experienced or trained, and he sure as hell isn't military intel or a government agent or he wouldn't walk around listening to music turned up loud and armed with an expensive pistol that has the serial number ground off — in other words, he probably bought it on the street. He'd have something that would never be traced to him or anyone, something you use once and toss. . . ."

"We don't know who the gun is traced to?" I want to make sure.

"Not that I know of, not yet, which is ridiculous. This guy isn't undercover. Hell, no. I think what he is is scared," Lucy says as if she knows it for a fact. "Was," she adds. "He *was*. And someone had him under surveillance — my belief, anyway — and now he's dead. In my opinion, it's not a co-incidence. I suggest you exercise extreme caution when talking to Marino."

"Sometimes he has terrible judgment, but he's not trying to do me in."

"He's also not medical intel like you are, and his understanding only goes so far as not discussing cases with his buddies at the bowling alley and not talking to reporters. He thinks it's perfectly fine to confide in people like Briggs, because he's got no sense when it comes to military brass." Lucy's demeanor is as uneasy and somber as I've seen her since I can't remember when. "In a case like this one, you talk to me, you talk to Benton."

"Have you told Benton what you just told me?"

"I'll let you explain about MORT, because he's not likely to understand what it is. He wasn't around when you went through all that with the Pentagon. You tell him, and then all of us can talk. You, him, me, and that's it, at least for now, because you don't know who is what, and you damn well better have your facts straight and know who's us and who's them."

"If I can't trust Marino with a case like this, or any case, for that matter, why do I have him?" Defensiveness sharpens my tone, because Marino was her idea, too.

She encouraged me to hire him as CFC's chief of operational investigations, and she talked him into it, too, although it wasn't exactly a hard sell. He'd never admit it, but he doesn't want to be anywhere I'm not, and when he realized I was going to be in Cambridge, he suddenly got disenchanted with the NYPD. He lost interest in Assistant DA Jaime Berger, whose office he was assigned to. He got into a feud with his landlord in the Bronx. He started complaining about New York taxes, even though he'd been paying them for several years. He said it was intolerable having no place to ride a motorcycle and no place to park a truck, even though he owned neither at the time. He said he had to move.

"It's not about trust. It's about acknowledging limitations." It's an uncharacteristically charitable thing for Lucy to say. Usually, people are simply bad or useless and deserve whatever punishment she decides.

She eases up on the collective and makes

subtle adjustments with the cyclic, increasing our speed and making sure we don't climb into the clouds. The night around us is impenetrably dark, and there are stretches where I can't see lights on the ground, suggesting we are flying over trees. I enter the frequency for McGuire so we can monitor its airspace while keeping an eye on the Traffic Collision Avoidance System, the TCAS. It is showing no other aircraft anywhere. We might be the only ones flying tonight.

"I don't have the luxury to allow for limitations," I tell my niece. "Meaning I probably made a mistake hiring Marino. I probably made a bigger one hiring Fielding."

"Not probably, and not the first time. Jack walked out on you in Watertown and went to Chicago, and you should have left him there."

"In all fairness, we lost our funding in Watertown. He knew the office was probably going to close, and it did."

"That's not why he left."

I don't respond, because she's right. It isn't why. Fielding wanted to move to Chicago because his wife had been offered a job there. Two years later, he asked if he could come back. He said he missed working for me. He said he missed his family. Lucy, Marino, Benton, and me. One big, happy family.

"It isn't just them. You have a problem with everybody there," Lucy then says.

"So nobody should have been hired. Including you, I suppose."

"Probably not me, either. I'm not exactly a team player." She was fired by the FBI, by ATF. I don't think Lucy can be supervised by anybody, including me.

"Well, this is a nice thing to come home to," I reply.

"That's the danger with a prototype installation that no matter what anyone says is in fact both civilian and military, has both local and federal jurisdiction and also academic ties," Lucy says. "You're neither-nor. Staff members don't exactly know how to act or aren't capable of staying within boundaries, assuming anyone even understands the boundaries. I warned you about that a long time ago."

"I don't remember you warning me. I just remember you pointing it out."

"Let's enter the freq for Lakehurst and squawk VFR, because I'm ditching flight following," she decides. "We get pushed any farther west and we're going to have a crosswind that will slow us down more than twenty knots and we'll be grounded for the night in Harrisburg or Allentown."

Snowflakes are crazed like moths in landing lights and the wind of our blades as we set down on the wooden dolly. The skids tentatively touch, then spread heavily as the weight settles, and four sets of headlights begin to move toward us from the security gate near the FBO.

The headlights move slowly across the ramp, illuminating snow that is falling fast, and I recognize the silhouette of Benton's green Porsche SUV. I recognize the Suburban and the Range Rover, both of them black. I don't know the fourth car, a sleek, dark sedan with a chrome mesh grille. Lucy and Marino must have driven here separately today and left their SUVs with the line crew, which makes sense. My niece always arrives at the airport well in advance of everyone else so she can get the helicopter ready, so she can check it from the pitot tube on its nose to the stinger on its tail boom. I haven't seen her like this in a while, and as we wait the two minutes in flight idle before she finishes the shutdown, I try to remember the last time, pinpoint it exactly, in hopes of figuring out what's happening. Because she isn't telling me.

She won't unless it fits into her overall plan, and there is no getting information out of her when she's not ready to offer it, which can be never in extreme situations. Lucy thrives on covert behavior, is far more comfortable being who she's not than who she is, and that's always been the case, going back to her earliest years. She feeds on the power of secrecy and is energized by the drama of risk, of real danger. The more threatening, the better. All she's revealed to me so far is that an obsolete robot in the dead man's apartment is a DARPA-funded packbot called MORT that at one time was intended for mortuary operations in theater, in other words, body removal in war, a mechanical Grim Reaper. MORT was insensitive and inappropriate, and I fought it aggressively years ago, but the peculiarity of the dead man having such a thing in his apartment doesn't explain Lucy's behavior.

When was it that she scared me so badly, not that it's been only once, but the time I thought she might end up in prison? Seven or eight years ago, I decide, when she came back from Poland, where she was involved in a mission that had to do with Interpol, with special ops that to this day I'm unclear about. I'll never know just how much she would tell me if I pushed hard enough, but I won't. I've chosen to remain foggy about what she did over there. What I know is enough. It's more than enough. I would never say that about Lucy's feelings, health, or general well-being, because I care intensely about every molecule of her, but I can say it about some complex and clandestine aspects of the way she has lived. For her own good and mine, there are details I will not ask about. There are stories I don't want to be told.

During the last hour of our flight here to Hanscom Field, she got increasingly preoccupied, impatient, and impossibly vigilant, and it is her vigilance that has a special caliber. That's what I recognize. Vigilance is the weapon she draws when she feels threatened and goes into a certain mode I used to dread. In Oxford, Connecticut, where we stopped for fuel, she wouldn't leave the helicopter unattended, not for a second. She supervised the fuel truck and made me stand guard in the cold while she trotted inside the FBO to pay because she didn't trust Marino with guard duty, as she put it. She told me that when they had refueled in Wilmington, Delaware, earlier today en route to Dover, he was too busy on the phone to care about security or notice what was going on around them.

She said she watched him through the window as he paced on the tarmac, talking and gesturing, no doubt swept up in telling Briggs about the man who allegedly was still alive when he was locked inside my cooler. Not once did Marino look at the helicopter, Lucy reported to me. He was oblivious when another pilot strolled over to check it out, squatting so he could inspect the FLIR, the Nightsun, and peering through Plexiglas into the cabin. It didn't enter Marino's mind that the doors were unlocked, as was the fuel cap, and of course there is no such thing as securing the cowling. One can get to the transmission, the engine, the gear boxes, the vital organs of a helicopter, by the simple release of latches.

All it takes is water in the fuel tank for a flameout in flight, and the engine quits. Or sprinkle a small amount of contaminant into the hydraulic fluid, maybe dirt, oil, or water into the reservoir, and the controls will fail like power steering in a car, but a little more serious when you're two thousand feet in the air. If you really want to create havoc, contaminate both the fuel and the hydraulic fluid so you have a flameout and a hydraulic failure simultaneously, Lucy described in gory detail as we flew with the intercom on "crew only" so Marino couldn't hear. That would be especially unfortunate after dark, she said, when emergency landings, which are difficult enough, are far worse, because you can't see what's under you and had better hope it isn't trees, power lines, or some other obstruction.

Of course, the sabotage she fears most is an explosive device, and she's obsessed in general with explosives and what they're really used for and who is using them against us, including the U.S. government using them against us if it suits certain agendas. So I had to listen to that for a while before she went on to depress me further by explaining how simple it would be to plant such a thing, preferably under luggage or a floor mat in back so that when it detonates it takes out the main fuel tank beneath the rear seats. Then the helicopter turns into a crematorium, she told me, and this made me think of the soldier in the Humvee again and his devastated mother lashing out at me over the phone. I was making unfortunate associations most of the time we were flying, because for better or worse, any disaster described evokes vivid examples from my own cases. I know how people die. I know exactly what will happen to me if I do.

Lucy cuts the throttle and pulls the rotor brake down, and the instant the blades stop turning, the driver's door of Benton's SUV opens. The interior light doesn't go on. It won't in any one of the three SUVs on the ramp, because cops and federal agents, including former ones, have their quirks. They don't sit with their backs to the door. They hate to fasten their seat belts, and they don't like interior lights in their vehicles. They are imprinted to avoid ambushes and restraints that might impede their escape. They resist turning themselves into il-luminated targets. They are vigilant but not as vigilant as Lucy has been these past few hours.

Benton walks toward the helicopter and waits near the dolly with his hands in the pockets of an old black shearling coat I gave him many Christmases ago, his silver hair mussed by the wind. He is tall and lean against the snowy night, and his features are keen in the uneven shadow and light. Whenever I see him after a long separation, it is with the eyes of a stranger, and I'm drawn to him all over again, just like the first time long ago in Virginia when I was the new chief, the first woman in America to run such a large medical examiner system, and he was a legend in the FBI, the star profiler and head of what was then the Behavioral Science Unit at Quantico. He walked into my conference room, and I was suddenly unnerved and unsure of myself, and it had nothing to do with the serial murders we were there to discuss.

"You know this guy?" he says into my ear as we hug. He kisses me lightly on the lips, and I smell the woodsy fragrance of his aftershave and feel the soft leather of his coat against my cheek.

I look past him to a man climbing out of the sedan, what I now can see is a dark-blue or black Bentley that has the throaty purr of a V12 engine. He is big and overweight, with a jowly face and a fringe of thinning hair that flails in the wind. Dressed in a long overcoat, the collar up around his ears, and with gloves on, he stands a polite distance away with the detached demeanor of a limo driver. But I sense his awareness of us. He seems most interested in Benton.

"He must be waiting for someone else," I decide as the man looks at the helicopter, then looks at Benton again. "Or he's mixed up."

"Can I help you?" Benton steps closer to him.

"I'm looking for Dr. Scarpetta?"

"And why might you be looking for Dr. Scarpetta?" Benton is friendly but firm, and he gives nothing away.

"I was sent here with a delivery, and the instructions I got is the party would be on Dr. Scarpetta's helicopter or meeting it. What branch of service you with, or maybe you're Homeland Security? I see it's got a FLIR, a searchlight, a lot of special equipment. Pretty high-tech; how fast does it go?"

"What can I do for you?"

"I'm supposed to give something directly to Dr. Scarpetta. Is that you? I was told to ask for identification." The driver watches Lucy and Marino carry my belongings out of the passenger and baggage compartments. The driver isn't interested in me, not so much as a glance. I'm the wife of the tall, handsome man with silver hair. The driver thinks Benton is Dr. Scarpetta and that the helicopter is his.

"Let's get you out of here before this turns into a blizzard," Benton says, walking toward the Bentley in a way that gives the driver no choice but to follow. "I hear we're getting six to eight inches, but I think we're in for more, like we need it, right? What a winter. Where are you from? Not here. The south somewhere. I'm guessing Tennessee."

"You can tell after twenty-seven years? Guess I need to work on talking Yankee. Nashville. Was stationed here with the Sixty-sixth Air Base Wing and never got around to leaving. I'm not a pilot, but I drive pretty good." He opens the passenger door and leans inside. "You fly that thing yourself? I've never been in one. I knew right away your chopper wasn't air force. I guess if you're CIA, you're not going to tell me. . . ."

Their voices drift back to me as I wait on the ramp where Benton left me. I know better than to follow him to the Bentley but am unwilling to sit inside our car when I have no idea who the man is or what delivery he's talking about or how he knew someone named Scarpetta would be at Hanscom, either on a helicopter or meeting it, and what time it would land. The first person who comes to mind is Jack Fielding. It's likely he knows my itinerary, and I check my iPhone. Anne and Ollie have answered my text messages and are already at the CFC, waiting for us. But nothing from Fielding. *What is going on with him?* Something is, something serious. This can't be nothing more than his usual irresponsibility or indifference or erratic behavior. I hope he's all right, that he's not sick or injured or fighting with his wife, and I watch Benton tuck something into a coat pocket. He heads straight to the SUV, and that's his message to me. Get in and don't ask questions on the ramp. Something just transpired that he doesn't like, despite his relaxed, friendly act with the driver.

"What is it?" I ask him as we shut our doors at the same time Marino opens the back and starts shoving in my boxes and bags.

Benton turns up the heat and doesn't answer as more of my belongings are loaded, and then Marino comes around to my door. He raps a knuckle on the glass.

"Who the hell was that?" He stares off in the direction of the Bentley, and snow is falling thick and hard, frosting the bill of his baseball cap and melting on his glasses.

"Did many people know you and Lucy were heading out to Dover today?" Benton leans his shoulder against me as he talks to him.

"The general. And Captain What's-her-name, Avallone, when I called trying to get a message to the Doc. And certain people at our office knew. Why?"

"Nobody else? Maybe a mention in passing to the EMTs, to Cambridge police?"

Marino pauses, thinking, and a look passes over his face. He's not sure whom he told. He's trying to remember, and he's calculating. If he did something foolish, he won't want to admit it, has heard quite enough about how indiscreet he is. He doesn't intend to be chastised yet again, although, to be fair, he wouldn't have had a reason to behave as if it was classified information that he and Lucy were flying to Delaware to pick me up. It's not a state secret where I've been, only why I've been there, and I was supposed to come home tomorrow, anyway.

"No big deal if you did." Benton seems to be thinking the same thing I am. "I'm just trying to figure out how a messenger knew to meet the helicopter here, that's all."

"What kind of messenger drives a Bentley?" Marino says to him.

"Apparently, the kind who's been told your itinerary, including the helicopter's tail number," Benton replies.

"Goddamn Fielding. What the hell's he doing? He's fucking lost it, that's what." Marino takes off his glasses and then has nothing to wipe them with, and his face looks naked and strange without his old wire-rims. "I mentioned to a few people that you were probably coming back today instead of tomorrow. I mean, obviously certain people knew because of the problem we have with the dead guy bleeding and everything else." He directs this at me. "But Fielding's the one who knew exactly what you were doing, and he sure as hell knows Lucy's helicopter, since he's been in it before. Shit, you don't know the half of it," he adds darkly.

"We'll talk at the office." Benton wants him to shut up.

"What the hell do we really know about him? What the fuck's he up to? It's damn time to quit protecting him. He's sure as hell not protecting you," he says to me.

"Let's talk about this later," Benton replies with a warning in his tone.

"Setting you up somehow," Marino says to me.

"Now's not the time to get into it." Benton's voice flattens out.

"He wants your job. Or maybe he just doesn't want you to have it." Marino looks at me as he digs his hands into the pockets of his leather jacket and steps away from my window. "Welcome home, Doc." Flakes of snow blowing into the car are cold and wet on my face and neck. "Good to be

reminded who you can really trust, right?"
He stares at me as I roll up the glass.

Anticollision beacons flash red and white
on the wingtips of parked jets as we drive
slowly across the ramp toward the security
gate, which has just swung open.

The Bentley drives through, and we are
right behind it, and I notice its Massachusetts plate doesn't have *livery* stamped on it,
suggesting the car isn't owned by a limousine company. I'm not surprised. Bentleys
are unusual, especially around here, where
people are understated and conservation-
minded, even those who fly private. I seldom
see Bentleys or Rolls-Royces, mostly Toyo-
tas or Saabs. We pass the FBO for Signature,
one of several flight services on the civilian
side of the airfield, and I place my hand on
the soft suede of Benton's coat pocket
without touching the creamy white envelope
barely protruding from it.

"Would you like to tell me what just happened?" It appears he was given a letter.

"Nobody should know you just flew here
or that you might be here, shouldn't know
anything about you personally or your
whereabouts, period," Benton says, and his
face and voice are hard. "Obviously, she
called the CFC and Jack told her. She's

certainly called there before, and who else but Jack?"

He says it as if it's really not a question, and I have no idea what he is referring to.

"I can't understand why he or anyone would talk to her, for Christ's sake," Benton goes on, but I don't believe he doesn't understand whatever it is he's talking about. His tone says something else entirely. I don't sense that he's even surprised.

"Who?" Because I have no idea. "Who's called the CFC?"

"Johnny Donahue's mother. Apparently, that's her driver." Indicating the car up ahead.

The windshield wipers make a loud rubbery sound as they drag across the glass, pushing away snow that is turning to slush as it hits. I look at the taillights of the Bentley in front of us and try to make sense of what Benton is telling me.

"We should look at whatever it is." I mean the envelope in his pocket.

"It's evidence. It should be looked at in the labs," he says.

"I should know what it is."

"I finished evaluating Johnny this morning," Benton then reminds me. "I know his mother has called the CFC several times."

"How do you know?"

"Johnny told me."

"A psychiatric patient told you. And that's reliable information."

"I've spent a total of almost seven hours with him since he was admitted. I don't believe he killed anyone. There are a lot of things I don't believe. But I do believe his mother would call the CFC, based on what I know," Benton says.

"She can't really think we would discuss the Mark Bishop case with her."

"These days people think everything is public information, that they're entitled," he says, and it's not like him to make assumptions and to indulge in generalities. His statement strikes me as glib and evasive. "And Mrs. Donahue has a problem with Jack," Benton adds, and that comment strikes me as genuine.

"Johnny's told you his mother has a problem with Jack. And why would she have an opinion about him?"

"Some of this I can't get into." He stares straight ahead as he drives on the snowy road, and the snow is falling faster and slashes through the headlights and clicks against glass.

I know when Benton is keeping things from me. Usually, I'm fine with it. Right now I'm not. I'm tempted to slide the envelope out of his pocket and look at what someone, presumably Mrs. Donahue, wants me to see.

"Have you met her, talked to her?" I ask him.

"I've managed to avoid that so far, although she's called the hospital, trying to track me down, called several times since he was admitted. But it's not appropriate for me to talk to her. It's not appropriate for me to talk about a lot of things, and I know you understand."

"If Jack or anyone has divulged details about Mark Bishop to her, that's about as serious as it gets," I reply. "And I do understand your reticence, or I think I do, but I have a right to know if he's done that."

"I don't know what you know. If Jack's said anything to you," he says.

"About what specifically?"

I don't want to admit to Benton and most of all to myself that I can't remember precisely when I talked to Fielding last. Our conversations, when we've had them, have been perfunctory and brief, and I didn't see him at all when I was home for several days over the holidays. He had gone somewhere, presumably taken his family somewhere, but I'm not sure. Long months ago, Fielding quit sharing the details of his personal life with me.

"Specifically, this case, the Mark Bishop case," Benton says. "When it happened, for example, did Jack discuss it with you?"

Saturday, January 30, six-year-old Mark Bishop was playing in his backyard, about an hour from here in Salem, when someone hammered nails into his head.

"No," I answer. "Jack hasn't talked about it with me."

I was in Dover when the boy was murdered, and Fielding took the case, which was extraordinarily out of character, and I thought so then. He's never been able to deal with children but for some reason decided to deal with this one, and it shocked me. In the past, if the body of a child was en route to the morgue, Fielding absented himself. It made no sense at all that Fielding would take the Mark Bishop case, and I'm sorry I didn't return home, because that was my first impulse. I should have acted on it, but I didn't want to do to my second in command what Briggs just did to me. I didn't want to show a lack of faith.

"I've reviewed it thoroughly, but Jack and I haven't discussed it, although I certainly indicated I would make myself available if there was a need." I feel myself getting defensive and hate it when I get that way.

"Technically, it's his case. Technically, I wasn't here." I can't stop myself, and I know it sounds weak, like I'm making excuses, and I feel annoyed with myself.

"In other words, Jack hasn't tried to share the details. I should say he's not shared his details," Benton says.

"Consider where I've been and what I've been doing," I remind him.

"I'm not saying it's your fault, Kay."

"What's my fault? And what do you mean, 'his' details?"

"I'm asking if you've asked Jack about it. If maybe he's avoided discussing it with you."

"You know how he is when it's kids. At the time, I left him a message that one of the other medical examiners could handle it, but Jack took care of it. I was surprised he did, but that's how it went. As I've said, I've reviewed all of the records. His, the police, the lab reports, et cetera."

"So you really don't know what's going on with it."

"It seems you're saying I don't."

Benton is silent.

"Know what's going on in addition to the latest? The confession made by the Donahue boy?" I try again. "Certainly I know what's been in the news, and a Harvard student confessing to such a thing has been all over it. Obviously, what you're getting at is there are details I've not been told."

Again Benton doesn't answer. I imagine Fielding talking to Johnny Donahue's mother. It's possible Fielding gave her details about where I would be tonight, and she sent her driver to deliver an envelope to me, although the driver didn't seem to know Dr. Scarpetta was a woman. I look at Benton's black shearling coat. In the dark, I can make out the vague white edge of the envelope in his pocket.

"Why would anyone from your office talk to the mother of the person who's confessed to the crime?" Benton's question sounds more like a statement. It sounds rhetorical. "We absolutely sure nothing was leaked to the media about your leaving Dover today, maybe because of this case?" He means the man who collapsed in Norton's Woods. "Maybe there's a logical explanation for how she knew. A logical explanation other than Jack. I'm trying to be open-minded."

It doesn't sound like he's trying to be open-minded at all. It sounds like he believes Fielding told Mrs. Donahue for a reason, one I can't begin to fathom. Unless it's what Marino said minutes ago, that Fielding wants me to lose my job.

"You and I both know the answer." I hear the conviction in my tone and realize how certain I am of what Jack Fielding could be capable of. "Nothing's been in the news that I'm aware of. And even if Mrs. Donahue found out that way, it doesn't explain her knowing the tail number of Lucy's helicopter. It doesn't explain how she knew I was arriving by helicopter or would land at Hanscom or at what time."

Benton drives toward Cambridge, and the snow is a blizzard of flakes that are getting smaller. The wind is beating the SUV, gusting and shoving, the night volatile and treacherous.

"Except the driver thought you were me," I add. "I could tell by the way he was dealing with you. He thinks you're Dr. Scarpetta, and Johnny Donahue's mother certainly must know I'm not a man."

"Hard to say what she knows," Benton answers. "Fielding's the medical examiner in this case, not you. As you said, technically you have nothing to do with it. Technically, you're not responsible."

"I'm the chief and ultimately responsible. At the end of the day, all ME cases in Massachusetts are mine. I do have something to do with it."

"It's not what I meant, but I'm glad to

hear you say it."

Of course it's not what he meant. I don't want to think about what he meant. I've been gone. Somehow I was supposed to be at Dover and at the same time get the CFC up and running without me. Maybe it was too much to ask. Maybe I've been deliberately set up for failure.

"I'm saying that since the CFC opened, you've been invisible," Benton says. "Lost in a news blackout."

"By design," I reply. "The AFME doesn't court publicity."

"Of course it's by design. I'm not blaming you."

"Briggs's design." I give voice to what I suspect Benton is getting at.

He doesn't trust Briggs. He never has. I've always chalked it up to jealousy. Briggs is a very powerful and threatening man, and Benton hasn't felt powerful or threatening since he left the FBI, and then there is a past Briggs and I share. He is one of very few people still in my life who predates Benton. It feels as if I was barely grown up when I first met John Briggs.

"The AFME didn't want you giving interviews about the CFC or publicly talking about anything relating to Dover until the CFC was set up and you were finished with your training," Benton goes on. "That's kept you out of the limelight for quite a while. I'm trying to remember the last time you were on CNN. At least a year ago."

"And coincidentally, I was supposed to step back into the limelight tonight. And coincidentally, CNN was canceled. The third time it's been canceled, as my return here was delayed and delayed."

"Yes. Coincidentally. A lot of co-incidences," Benton says.

Maybe Briggs has compromised me and done so intentionally. How brilliant it would be to groom me for a bigger job, the biggest job so far, while systematically making me less visible. To silence me. Ultimately, to get rid of me. The idea of it is shocking. I don't believe it.

"Whose coincidences, that's what you would need to know," Benton then says. "And I'm not stating as fact that Briggs did anything Machiavellian. He's not the entire Pentagon. He's just one gear in a very big machine."

"I know how much you dislike him."

"It's the machine I don't like. It's always going to be there. Just make sure you understand it so you don't get chewed up by it."

Snow clicks and bounces against glass as

we pass stretches of open fields and dense woods, and a creek runs hard against the guardrail to our right as we pass over a bridge. The air must be colder here, the snow small and icy as we drive in and out of pockets of changing weather that I find unsettling.

"Mrs. Donahue knows that the chief medical examiner and director of the CFC, someone named Dr. Scarpetta, is Jack's boss," Benton then says. "She had to know that if she went to the trouble to have something delivered to you. But maybe that's all she knows," he summarizes, offering an explanation for what just happened at the airport.

"Let's look at whatever it is." I want the envelope.

"It should go to the labs."

"She knows I'm Jack's boss but doesn't know I'm a woman." It seems preposterous, but it's possible. "Even though all she had to do was Google me."

"Not everybody Googles."

I'm reminded of how easy it is for me to forget that there are still technically unsophisticated people in the world, including someone who might have a chauffeur and a Bentley. Its taillights are far ahead of us now on the narrow two-lane road, getting smaller and more distant as the car drives too fast for the conditions.

"Did you show the driver your identification?" I ask.

"What do you think?"

Of course Benton wouldn't. "So he didn't realize you're not me."

"Not from anything I did or said."

"I guess Mrs. Donahue will continue to think Jack works for a man. Strange that Jack would tell her how to find me and not indicate how her driver might recognize me, at least indicate I'm not a man. Not even use pronouns that might indicate it. Strange. I don't know." I'm not convinced of what we're conjecturing. It doesn't feel right.

"I wasn't aware you were having so many doubts about Jack. Not that they aren't warranted." Benton is trying to draw me out. The FBI agent in him. I've not seen it in a while.

"Just don't say I'm twice bitten or thrice bitten or whatever. Please," I say with feeling. "I've heard it enough today."

"I'm saying I wasn't aware."

"And all I've been aware of is my usual misgivings and denials about him," I reply. "I've not had sufficient information to be more concerned than usual." My way of asking Benton to give me sufficient information if he has it, to not act like a cop or a mental-health practitioner. *Don't hold back,* I'm telling him.

But he does hold back. He doesn't say a word. His attention is fixed straight ahead, his profile sharp in the low illumination of the dashboard lights. This is the way it's always been with us. We step around confidential and privileged information. We dance around secrets. At times we lie. In the beginning, we cheated, because Benton was married to someone else. Both of us know how to deceive. It isn't something I'm proud of, and I wish it didn't continue to be necessary professionally. Especially right this minute. Benton is dancing around secrets, and I want the truth. I need it.

"Look, we both know what he's like, and yes, I've been invisible since the CFC opened," I continue. "I've been in a vacuum, doing the best I can to handle things long distance while working eighteen-hour days, not even time to talk to my staff by phone. Everything's been electronic, mostly e-mails and PDFs. I've hardly seen anyone. I should never have placed Jack in charge under the circumstances. When I hired him yet again and rode out of town, I set everyone up for exactly what's happened. And you did tell me so, and you aren't the only one."

"You've never wanted to believe you've got a serious problem with him," Benton says in a way that unsteadies me further. "Even if you've had plenty of them. Sometimes there's simply no sufficient evidence that will make us accept a truth we can't bear to believe. You can't be objective when it comes to him, Kay. I'm not sure I've ever understood the reason."

"You're right, and I hate it." I clear my throat and calm my voice. "And I'm sorry."

"I just don't know if I'll ever figure it out." He glances over at me, both hands on the wheel, and we're alone on a snow-blown road that is poorly lit, driving through a snowy darkness. The Bentley is no longer visible up ahead. "I'm not judging you."

"He wrecks his life and needs me again."

"It's not your fault he wrecks his life unless you haven't told me something. Actually, no matter what, it wouldn't be your fault. People wreck their own lives. They don't need others to do it."

"That's not entirely true. He didn't choose what happened to him as a child."

"And that's not your fault, either," Benton says, as if he knows more about Fielding's past than I've ever told him, what few details I have. I've always been careful not to probe my staff, especially not to probe

141

Fielding. I know enough about his early tragedies to be mindful of what he might not want to talk about.

"Of course it sounds stupid," I add.

"Not stupid. Just a drama that will always end the same way. I've never completely understood why you feel the need to act it out with him. I feel like something happened. Something you've not told me."

"I tell you everything."

"We both know that's not true about either of us."

"Maybe I should just stick with dead people." I hear the bitterness in my tone, the resentment seeping through barriers I've carefully constructed most of my life. Maybe I don't know how to live without them anymore. "I know how to handle dead people just fine."

"Don't talk like that," Benton says quietly.

It's because I'm tired, I tell myself. It's because of what happened this morning when the black mother of a dead black soldier disparaged me over the phone and called me names, referred to my following not the Golden Rule but the *White Rule.* Then Briggs tried to override my authority. It's possible I've been set up by him. It's possible he wants me to fail.

"It's such a goddamn stereotype," Benton

then says.

"Funny thing about stereotypes. They're usually based on something."

"Don't say things like that."

"There won't be any more problems with Jack. The drama will end, I promise. Assuming he hasn't already ended it, hasn't walked off the job. He's certainly done that before. He has to be fired."

"He's not you, never was or could be, and he's not your damn child." Benton thinks it is as simple as that, but it isn't.

"He has to be let go," I answer.

"He's a forty-six-year-old forensic pathologist who's never earned the trust you show him or anything the hell you do for him."

"I'm done with him."

"You are done with him. I'm afraid that's true and you're going to have to let him go," Benton says, as if a decision was made already, as if it isn't up to me. "What is it you feel so guilty about?" There's something in his tone, something about his demeanor. I can't put my finger on what it is. "Way back in your Richmond days when you were just getting started with him. Why the guilt?"

"I'm sorry I've caused so many problems." I evade his question. "I feel I'm the one who's let everybody down. I'm sorry I've not been here. I can't begin to express how sorry I am. I take responsibility for Jack, but I won't allow it anymore."

"Some things you can't take responsibility for. Some things aren't your fault, and I'm going to keep reminding you of that, and you'll probably keep believing it's your fault, anyway," my husband the psychologist says.

I'm not going to discuss what is my fault and what isn't, because I can't talk about why I've always been irrationally loyal to Jack Fielding. I came back from South Africa, and my penance was Fielding. He was my public service, what I sentenced myself to as punishment. I was desperate to do right by him because I was convinced I'd wronged everyone else.

"I'm taking a look." I mean at what is in Benton's coat pocket. "I know how to look at a letter without compromising it, and I need to see what Mrs. Donahue wrote to me."

I slide the envelope out, holding it lightly by its edges, and discover the flap is sealed with gray duct tape that partially covers an address engraved in an old-style serif type-face. I recognize the street as one in Boston's Beacon Hill, near the Public Garden, very close to where Benton used to own a brownstone that was in his family for generations. On the front of the envelope is *Dr. Kay Scarpetta: Confidential* written elaborately with a fountain pen, and I'm careful about touching anything else with bare hands, especially the tape. It is a good source for fingerprints, for DNA and microscopic materials. Latent prints can be developed on porous surfaces such as paper by using a reagent such as ninhydrin, I calculate.

"Maybe you've got a knife handy." I place the envelope in my lap. "And I need to borrow your gloves."

Benton reaches across me and opens the glove box, and inside is a Leatherman multitool knife, a flashlight, a stack of napkins. He pulls a pair of deerskin gloves out of his coat pockets, and my hands are lost in them, but I don't want to leave my fingerprints or eradicate those of someone else. I don't turn on the map-reading light, because the visibility is bad and getting worse. Illuminating what I'm doing with the flashlight, I slip a small blade into a corner of the envelope.

I slit it along the top and slide out two folded sheets of creamy stationery that are of heavy stock with a watermark I can't make out clearly, what looks like some type of emblazonment or family crest. The letterhead is the same Beacon Hill address,

145

and the two pages are typed with a typewriter that has a cursive typeface, which is something I haven't seen in many years, maybe a decade at least. I read out loud:

Dear Dr. Scarpetta,

I hope you will excuse what I'm sure must seem an inappropriate and presumptuous gesture on my part. But I am a mother as desperate as a mother could possibly be.

My son Johnny has confessed to a crime I know he did not commit and could not have committed. Certainly he's had difficulties of late that resulted in our seeking treatment for him, but even so, he's never demonstrated any serious behavior problems, not even when he began Harvard as a withdrawn and bullied fifteen-year-old. If he was going to have a breakdown, I should think it would have been then, having left home for the first time and not possessing the normal skills for interacting with others and making friends. He did remarkably well until this past fall semester of his senior year, when his personality became alarmingly altered. <u>But he did not kill anyone!</u>

Dr. Benton Wesley, a consultant for the

FBI and a member of the McLean Hospital staff, knows quite a lot about my son's background and developmental obstacles, and perhaps he is at liberty to discuss these details with you, since he hasn't seemed inclined to discuss them with your assistant, Dr. Fielding. Johnny's is a long, complex story, and I need you to hear it. Suffice it to say that when he was admitted at McLean last Monday, it was because he was deemed to be a danger to himself. He had not harmed anybody else or so much as intimated that he might. Then suddenly out of the blue he confessed to such a vicious and horrible crime, and in short order was transferred to a locked ward for the criminally insane. I ask you, how is it possible the authorities have been so quick to believe his ludicrous and deluded tales?

I must talk to you, Dr. Scarpetta. I know your office performed the autopsy on the little boy who died in Salem, and I believe it is reasonable to request a second opinion. Of course you know Dr. Fielding's conclusion — that the murder was premeditated, carefully planned, a cold-blooded execution that was an initiation for a satanic cult. Something as monstrous as that is absolutely inconsistent with anything my son could do to anyone, and he has never had anything to do with cults of any description. It is outrageous to assume that his fondness for books and films with a horror or supernatural or violent theme might have influenced him to "act out."

Johnny suffers from Asperger's syndrome. He is spectacularly gifted in some areas and completely incompetent in others. He has very rigid habits and routines that he is obsessive about, and on January 30, he was eating brunch at The Biscuit with the person he is closest to, a supremely gifted graduate student named Dawn Kincaid, just as they do every Saturday morning from ten a.m. until one p.m. He could not, therefore, have been in Salem when the little boy was killed mid-afternoon.

Johnny has the remarkable ability to remember and parrot the most obscure details, and it is clear to me that what he has said to the authorities has come straight from what he's been told about the case and what's been in the news. He truly does seem to believe he is guilty (for reasons I can't begin to comprehend), and even claims that a "puncture wound" to his left hand was from the nail gun misfiring when he used it on the boy, which is fabricated. The wound is self-inflicted, a stab wound from a steak knife, and one of the many reasons we took him to McLean to begin with. My son seems determined to be severely punished for a crime he didn't commit, and the way things are going, he will get his wish.

Below are numbers to contact me. I hope you will have compassion and that I hear from you soon.

Sincerely,
Erica
Erica Donahue

I return the sheets of heavy, stiff stationery
to their envelope, then wrap the letter in
napkins from the glove box to protect it as
much as possible inside the zip-up compartment of my shoulder bag. If I have learned
nothing else, it is that you can't go back.
Once potential evidence has been cut
through, contaminated, or lost, it's like an
archaeologist's trowel shattering an ancient
treasure.

"She doesn't seem to know you and I are
married," I comment as trees thrash in the
wind along the roadside, snow swirling
whitely.

"She might not," Benton replies.

"Does her son know?"

"I don't discuss you or my personal life
with patients."

"Then she may not know much about
me."

I try to work out how it might be possible

that Erica Donahue wouldn't tell her driver that the person he was to deliver the letter to is a small blonde woman, not a tall man with silver hair.

"She uses a typewriter, assuming she typed this herself," I continue to deduce. "And anyone who would go to so much trouble taping up the envelope to ensure confidentiality probably isn't going to let someone else type the letter. If she still uses a typewriter, it's unlikely she goes on the Internet and Googles. The watermarked engraved stationery, the fountain pen, the cursive typeface, possibly a purist, someone very precise, who has a very certain and set way of doing things."

"She's an artist," Benton says. "A classical pianist who doesn't share the same high-tech interests as the rest of her family. Husband's a nuclear physicist. Older son's an engineer at Langley. And Johnny, as she pointed out, is incredibly gifted. In math, science. Writing that letter won't help him. I wish she hadn't."

"You seem very invested in him."

"I hate it when people who are vulnerable are an easy out. Because someone is different and doesn't act like the rest of us, he must be guilty of something."

"I'm sure the Essex County prosecutor

wouldn't be happy to hear you say that." I've assumed that's who hired Benton to evaluate Johnny Donahue, but Benton isn't acting like a consultant, certainly not like one for the DA's office. He's acting like something else.

"Misleading statements, lack of eye contact, false confessions. A kid with Asperger's and his never-ending isolation and search for friends," Benton says. "It's not uncommon for such a person to be overly influenced."

"Why would someone want to influence Johnny to take the blame for a violent crime?"

"All it takes is the suggestion of something suspicious, such as what a weird coincidence that you were talking crazy about going to Salem, and then that little boy was murdered there. Are you sure you hurt your hand when you stuck it in a drawer and got stabbed by a steak knife, or did it happen some other way and you don't remember? People see guilt, and then Johnny sees it. He's led to say what he thinks people want to hear and to believe what he thinks people want to believe. He has no understanding of the consequences of his behavior. People with Asperger's syndrome, especially teenagers, are statistically overrepresented among innocent people who are arrested and convicted of crimes."

Snowflakes are suddenly large and blowing wildly like white dogwood petals in a violent wind. Benton downshifts the Tiptronic transmission and lightly touches the brakes.

"Maybe we should pull over." I can't see the road as the headlights bounce off whiteness swarming all around us.

"Some freakish storm cell, like a microburst." He leans close to the steering wheel, peering straight ahead, as angry gusts of wind buffet us. "I think the best thing is to drive out of it."

"Maybe we should stop."

"We're on pavement. I can see which lane we're in. Nothing's coming." He looks in the mirrors. "Nothing's behind us."

"I hope you're right." I'm not just talking about the snow. Everything seems ominous, as if sinister forces surround us, as if we're being warned.

"It wasn't a smart thing for her to do. An emotional thing, maybe even a well-intended thing, but not smart." Benton drives very slowly through chaotic whiteness. "It's hearsay, but it won't be helpful. It's best you don't call her."

"I'll need to show the letter to the police,"

153

I reply. "Or at least tell them about it, so they can decide what they want to do."

"She's just made things worse." He says it as if he's the one deciding things. "Don't get mixed up in this by calling her."

"Other than her trying to influence the medical examiner's office, how has she made things worse?" I ask.

"Several key points she incorrectly makes. Johnny doesn't read horror or supernatural or violent fiction or go to movies like that, at least not that I'm aware of, and that detail won't help him. Also, Mark Bishop wasn't murdered mid-afternoon. It was closer to four. Mrs. Donahue may not realize what she just implied about her son," Benton says as the white squall ends as suddenly as it began.

Flakes are small and icy again, swirling like sand over pavement and accumulating in shallow drifts on the roadsides.

"Johnny was at The Biscuit with his friend, that's true," Benton continues, "but according to him, he was there until two, not one. Apparently, he and his friend had been there numerous times, but I'm not aware of him having some rigid regimen of being there every Saturday with her from ten to one."

The Biscuit is on Washington Street,

barely a fifteen-minute walk from our house in Cambridge, and I think of Saturdays when I've been home, when Benton and I have wandered into the small café with its chalkboard menu and wooden benches. I wonder if Johnny and his friend were ever in there when we were.

"What does his friend say about what time they left the café?" I ask.

"She claims she got up from the table around one p.m. and left him sitting there because he was acting strange and refused to leave with her. According to her statement to the police, Johnny was talking about going to Salem to get his fortune read, was talking wildly about that, and was still at the table when she walked out the door."

I find it interesting that Benton would have looked at a police statement or know the details of what a witness said. His role isn't to determine guilt or innocence or even to care but to evaluate if the patient is telling the truth or malingering and is competent to stand trial.

"Someone with Asperger's would have a hard time with the concept of a fortune being read or cards being read or anything of that nature," Benton is saying, and the more he tells me, the more perplexed I am.

He's talking to me as if he's a detective

and we're working the case together, yet he's cryptic when it comes to Jack Fielding. There's nothing accidental about it. My husband rarely lets information slip, even if he gives the appearance otherwise. When he thinks I should know information he can't tell me, he finds a way for me to figure it out. If he decides it's best I don't know, he won't help me. It's the frustrating way we live, and at least I can say I'm never bored with him.

"Johnny can't think abstractly, can't comprehend metaphors. He's very concrete," Benton is saying.

"What about other people inside the café?" I ask. "Could anybody in the café verify what the friend said or what Johnny claims?"

"Nothing more definitive than he and Dawn Kincaid were in there that Saturday morning," Benton says, and I don't remember when I've seen him so disturbed by someone he has evaluated. "Don't know about it being a weekly routine, and by the time Johnny confessed, several days had passed. Amazing what shitty memories people have, and then they start guessing."

"Then all you have is what Johnny says and now what his mother says in this letter," I reiterate what I'm hearing. "He says he left The Biscuit at two, which might not have given him enough time to get to Salem and commit the murder at around four. And his mother is saying he left at one, which could have given him enough time to do it."

"As I said, it's not helpful. What's in his mother's letter is quite bad for him. So far the only real alibi anyone can offer that might show his confession is bullshit is a problematic timeline. But an hour makes all the difference, or it could."

I imagine Johnny getting up from his table at The Biscuit at around one p.m. and heading to Salem. Depending on traffic and when he was actually out of Cambridge or Somerville and heading north on I-95, he could have been at the Bishops' house in the historic district by two or two-thirty.

"Does he have a car?" I ask.

"He doesn't drive."

"A taxi, the train? Not a ferry this time of year. They don't start running again until spring, and he would have had to board it in Boston. But you're right. Without a car, it would have taken him longer to get there. An hour would make a difference for someone who had to find transportation."

"I just don't understand where she got that detail," Benton says. "Well, maybe from him. Maybe he's changed his story yet again. Johnny said he left The Biscuit at two, not one, but maybe he's changed that rather critical detail because he thinks it's what someone wants to hear. However, it would be unusual, very unusual."

"You were just with him this morning."

"I'm not the one who would influence him to change a detail."

Benton is saying that the detail is new and he doesn't believe that Johnny has changed his story about what time he left the café. It would seem Mrs. Donahue simply made a mistake, but when I try to imagine that, something feels wrong.

"How would he have gotten to Salem at all?" I ask.

"He could have taken a taxi or a train, but there's no evidence he did either. No sightings of him, no receipts found, nothing to prove he was ever in Salem or had any connection with the Bishop family. Nothing except his confession," Benton says as his eyes cut to the rearview mirror. "And what's important about that is his story is exactly what's been in the news, and he changes the details as news accounts and theories change. That part of his mother's letter is accurate. He parrots details word for word. Including if somebody suggests a scenario or information — leads him, in other words.

Suggestibility, vulnerable to manipulation, acting in a way that generates suspicion, hallmark signs in Asperger's." He glances in the mirror again. "And attention to detail, to minutiae that can seem bizarre to others. Like what time it is. He's always maintained he left The Biscuit at two p.m. Three minutes past two, to be exact. You ask Johnny what time it is or what time he did something, and he'll tell you practically to the second."

"So why would he change that detail?"

"In my opinion, he wouldn't."

"Seems like he'd be better off saying he left earlier if he really wants people to believe he murdered Mark Bishop."

"It's not that he wants people to believe it. It's that he believes it. Not because of what he remembers but because of what he doesn't remember and because of what's been suggested to him."

"By whom? Sounds like he confessed before he was ever a suspect and interrogated. So he wasn't enticed into a false confession by the police, for example."

"He doesn't remember. He's convinced he suffered a dissociative episode after he left The Biscuit at two p.m., somehow got to Salem and killed a boy with a nail gun —"

"He didn't," I interrupt. "That much I can tell you with certainty. He didn't kill Mark Bishop with a nail gun. Nobody did."

Benton doesn't say anything as he speeds up, the snowflakes small again and sounding like grit hitting the car.

"Mrs. Donahue's also clearly misunderstood Jack's medical opinion." I talk with conviction as another part of me won't stop worrying about how I should handle her. I consider doing what Benton said and not calling her. I'll have my administrative assistant, Bryce, contact her instead, first thing in the morning, and say I'm sorry but I'm not able to discuss the Mark Bishop case or any case. It's important Bryce not give the impression that I'm too busy, that I'm unmoved by Mrs. Donahue's distress, and that makes me think of PFC Gabriel's mother again, of the painful things she said to me this morning at Dover. "I assume you've reviewed the autopsy report," I say to Benton.

"Yes."

"Then you know there is nothing in Jack's report that mentions a nail gun, only that injuries caused by nails penetrating the brain were the cause of death." I decide I can't possibly let Bryce make such a call on my behalf. I'll do it myself and ask Mrs.

Donahue not to contact me again. I'll emphasize it's for her own protection. Then I'm filled with doubt, going back and forth on what to do with her, no longer so sure of myself. I've always had confidence in my ability to handle devastated people, bereft and enraged people, but I don't understand what happened this morning. Mrs. Gabriel called me a bigot. No one has ever called me a bigot before.

"A nail gun hasn't been ruled out by the people who count," Benton informs me. "Including Jack."

"I find that almost impossible to believe."

"He's been saying it."

"First I've heard of it."

"He's been saying it to whoever will listen. I don't care what's in his written report, the paperwork you've seen," Benton repeats as he looks in the rearview mirror.

"Why would he say something contrary to lab reports?"

"I'm simply relaying to you what I know for a fact that he's been saying about a nail gun being the weapon."

"Saying a nail gun was used is absolutely contrary to scientific and medical fact." In my sideview mirror I see headlights far behind us. "A nail gun leaves tool marks consistent with a single mechanized blow, similar to a firing-pin impression on a cartridge case. Instead, what we have in this instance are tool marks on nails that are consistent with a handheld hammer, and there were hammer marks on the boy's scalp and skull and underlying pattern contusions. Nail guns often leave a primer residue similar to gunshot residue, but Mark Bishop's wounds were negative for lead, for barium. A nail gun wasn't used, and I'm frankly amazed if what you're implying is that the police, the prosecutor, believe otherwise."

"Not hard to understand a number of things people choose to believe in this case," Benton says, and he's sped up, driving the speed limit.

I look in my sideview mirror again, and the headlights are much closer. Bright bluish-white lights blaze in the mirror. A large SUV with xenon headlights and fog lamps. *Marino,* I think. And behind him, I hope, is Lucy.

"Wanting to believe that Johnny's confession is true, as I've said," Benton continues. "Wanting to think that it had to be a blitz attack, that Mark Bishop couldn't have seen it coming or he would have struggled like hell. No one wants to think a child was held down and knew what was about to happen to him as someone drove nails into his skull with a hammer, for Christ's sake."

"He had no defense injuries, no evidence of a struggle, no evidence of being held down. It's in Jack's report. I'm sure you've seen it, and I'm sure he explained all this to the prosecutor, to the police."

"I wish you'd done the damn autopsy." Benton cuts his eyes to his mirrors.

"What exactly has Jack been saying beyond what I've read in his paperwork? Besides the possibility of a nail gun."

Benton doesn't answer me.

"Maybe you don't know," I then say, but I believe he does.

"He said he couldn't rule out a nail gun," Benton replies. "He said it isn't possible to tell definitively. He said this after he was asked because of what Johnny claimed in his confession. Jack was specifically and directly asked if a nail gun could have been used."

"The answer's definitively no."

"He would debate that with you. He said it isn't possible to tell definitively in this case. He said it's possible it was a nail gun."

"I'm telling you it's not possible, and it is possible to tell definitively," I reply. "And this is the first I've heard about a nail gun except for what's been on the Internet, which I have dismissed, since I dismiss most things in the news unless I am certain of the sources."

"He suggested if you pressed a nail gun against someone's head, you'd get what's similar to the muzzle mark made by a contact gunshot wound. And it's possible that's what we're seeing on the scalp and underlying tissue. And that's why there's no evidence of a struggle or that the boy knew what was happening."

"You wouldn't get a muzzle mark similar to a contact gunshot wound, and it's not possible," I reply. "The injuries I saw in photographs are hammer marks, and just because there was no evidence of a struggle doesn't mean the boy wasn't somehow coerced or coaxed or manipulated into cooperating. It sounds to me as if certain parties are choosing to ignore the facts of the case because of what they want to believe. That's extremely dangerous."

"I think Fielding is the one who might be ignoring the facts of the case. Maybe intentionally."

"Good God, Benton. He might be a lot of things . . ."

"Or it's negligence. It's one or the other," Benton says, and he has something in mind, I believe he does. "Listen. You did the best you could these past six months."

"What's that supposed to mean?" I know what it means. It means exactly what I've feared every single day that I've been gone.

"Remember when he was your fellow in the dark ages, in Richmond?" Benton is getting close to an area that is off-limits, even though he couldn't possibly know it. "From day one, he couldn't stand doing kids, that's absolutely true, as you've pointed out. If a kid was coming in, he'd run like hell, sometimes disappearing days at a time. And you'd drive around, trying to find him, going to his house, his favorite bar, the damn gym or tae kwon do, drinking himself into a stupor or kicking the shit out of someone. Not that any of us like dealing with dead children, for Christ's sake, but he's got a real problem."

I should have encouraged Fielding to go into surgical pathology, to work in a hospital lab, looking at biopsies. Instead, I mentored and encouraged him.

"But he took the Mark Bishop case," Benton says. "He could have passed him off to one of your other docs. I just hope he didn't lie; I sure as hell hope he didn't do that on top of everything else." But Benton thinks Fielding is lying. I can tell.

"On top of what else?" I ask as I look into

my sideview mirror, wondering why Marino is on our bumper.

"I hope someone didn't encourage him to suggest the possibility of a nail gun even if he knows better." Benton has a way of looking in his mirrors without moving his head. All his years of undercover work, of watching his back because he really had to. Some habits never die.

"Who?" I ask.

"I don't know."

"You sound like you do know. You're not going to tell me." It is useless to push him. If he's not telling me, it's because he can't. Twenty years of the dance and it never gets easier.

"The cops want this case solved, that's for damn sure," Benton says. "They want a nail gun to be the weapon, because it's what Johnny has confessed to and because the thought is easier to deal with than a hammer. It concerns me that someone has influenced Jack."

"Someone has? Or you're just guessing that someone has."

"It concerns me that it might be Jack who is influencing people," Benton says next, and that's what he really thinks.

"I wish Marino would get off our bumper. He's blinding me with his damn lights.

What's he doing?"

"It's not Marino," Benton says. "His Suburban doesn't have lights like that, and he has a front plate. This one doesn't. It's from out of state, a state that doesn't require a front plate, or it's been removed or is covered with something."

I turn around to look and the lights hurt my eyes. The SUV is only a few car lengths behind us.

"Maybe someone trying to pass us," I wonder aloud.

"Well, let's see, but I don't think so." Benton slows down, and so does the SUV. "I'll make you pass us, how about that," and he's talking to the driver behind us. "Grab the number from the rear plate as he goes by," Benton says to me.

We are almost stopped in the road, and the SUV stops, too. It backs up quickly and makes a U-turn, going the other way, fishtailing as it speeds off in the snowy night on the snowy road. I can't make out the plate on its rear bumper or any detail about the SUV except that it is dark and large.

"Why would someone be following us?" I say to Benton as if he might know.

"I have no idea what that was," Benton says.

"Someone was following us. That's what

that was. Staying too close because of the weather, because visibility is so bad you would have to stay close or you could easily lose the person if they turned off."

"Some jerk," Benton says. "Nobody sophisticated. Unless he deliberately wanted us to know he was back there or thought we wouldn't notice."

"How's it even possible? We just drove through a blizzard. Where the hell did it come from? Out of nowhere?"

Benton picks up his phone and enters a number.

"Where are you?" he says to whoever answers, and after a pause he adds, "A large SUV with fog lights, xenons, no front plate, on our ass. That's right. Made a U-turn and sped off the other way. Yes, on Route Two. Anything like that just pass you? Well, that's weird. Must have turned off. Well, if . . . Yes. Thanks."

Benton places his phone back on the console and explains, "Marino's a few minutes behind us, and Lucy's right behind him. The SUV's vanished. If someone's stupid enough to follow us, he'll try again and we'll figure it out. If the point was to intimidate, then whoever it is doesn't know his target."

"Now we're a target."

"Anyone who knows wouldn't try it."

"Because of you."

Benton doesn't answer. But what I said is true. Anyone who knows anything about Benton would be aware of how foolhardy it is to think he can be intimidated. I feel his hard edge, his steely aura. I know what he can do if threatened. He and Lucy are similar if confronted. They welcome it. Benton's simply cooler, more calculating and restrained than my niece will ever be.

"Erica Donahue." That's the first thought to come to mind. "She's already sent one person to intercept us, and I doubt she realizes how dangerous her son's charming, handsome Harvard psychologist is."

Benton doesn't smile. "Wouldn't make sense."

"How many people know our whereabouts?" There is no point in trying to lighten the mood, which is unrelentingly intense. Benton has his own caliber of vigilance. It is different from Lucy's, and he is far better at concealing it. "Or my whereabouts. How many people know?" I go on. "Not just the mother or the driver. What did Jack do?"

Benton speeds up again and doesn't answer me.

"You're not thinking Jack has some reason

to intimidate us. Or try," I then say.

Benton doesn't reply, and we drive in silence and there is no sign of the SUV with the fog lamps and xenon headlights.

"Lucy suspects he's drinking a lot." Benton finally starts talking again. "But you should get that from her. And from Marino." His tone is flat, and I hear the unforgiveness in it. He has nothing but disdain for Fielding, even if he is silent about it most of the time.

"Why would Jack lie? Why would he try to influence anyone?" I'm back to that.

"Apparently, he's been coming in late and disappearing, and he's having his skin problems again." Benton doesn't answer my question. "I hope to hell he's not doing steroids on top of everything else, especially at his age."

I resist the usual defense that when Fielding is acutely stressed, he has problems with eczema, with alopecia, and that he can't help it. He's always been obsessed with his body, is a classic case of megarexia or muscle dysmorphia, and most likely this can be attributed to the sexual abuse he suffered as a young boy. It would sound absurd to go down the list, and I'm not going to do it this time. For once, I won't. I continue checking my sideview mirror. But the xenon headlights and fog lamps are gone.

"Why would he lie about this case?" I ask again. "Why would he want to influence anybody about it?"

"I can't imagine how you could make a kid stay still for that," Benton says, and he's thinking about Mark Bishop's death. "The family was inside the house and claim they didn't hear screams, didn't hear anything. They claim that Mark was playing one minute and the next he was facedown in the yard. I'm trying to envision what happened and can't."

"All right. We'll talk about that, since you're not going to answer my question."

"I've tried to picture it, to reconstruct it, and draw a blank. The family was home. It's not a big yard. How is it possible no one saw someone or heard anything?"

His face is somber as we drive past Lanes & Games, where Marino bowls in a league. What is the name of his team? *Spare None.* His new buddies, law enforcement and military people.

"I thought I'd seen it all, but I just can't picture how it happened," Benton again says, because he can't or won't tell me what is really on his mind about Fielding.

"A person who knew exactly what he was doing." I can envision it. I can imagine in painful detail what the killer did. "Someone who was able to put the boy at ease, perhaps lure him into doing what he was told. Maybe Mark thought it was part of a game, a fantasy."

"A stranger showed up in his yard and got him to play a game that involved having nails hammered into his head — or pretending to, which is more likely," Benton considers. "Maybe. But a stranger? I don't know about that. I've missed talking to you."

"It wasn't a stranger, or at least didn't seem like one to Mark. I suspect it was someone he had no reason to distrust — no matter what he was asked to do." I base this on what I know about his injuries or lack of them. "The body showed no signs that he was terrified and panicky, someone trying to fight or escape. I think it's likely he was familiar with the killer or felt inclined to co-operate for some reason. I've missed talking to you, but I'm here now and you're not talking to me."

"I am talking to you."

"One of these days I'm going to slip Sodium Pentothal into your drink. And find out everything you've never told me."

"If only it worked, I would reciprocate. But then we'd both be in serious trouble. You don't want to know everything. Or you shouldn't. And I probably shouldn't, either."

"Four p.m. on January thirtieth." I'm thinking about how dark it would have been when Mark was murdered. "What time did the sun set that day? What was the weather?"

"Completely dark at four-thirty, cold, overcast," says Benton, who would have found out those details first thing if he was the one investigating the case.

"I'm trying to remember if there was snow on the ground."

"Not in Salem. A lot of rain because of the harbor. The water warms up the air."

"So no footprints were recovered in the Bishops' yard."

"No. And at four it was getting dark and the backyard was in shadows because of shrubbery and trees," Benton says, as if he's the detective on the case. "According to the family, Mrs. Bishop, the mother, went out at four-twenty to make Mark come into the house, and she found him facedown in the leaves."

"Why are we assuming he had just been killed when she found him? Certainly his physical findings would never allow us to pinpoint his time of death to exactly four p.m."

"The fact that the parents recall looking out the window at approximately a quarter of four and seeing Mark playing," Benton says.

" 'Playing'? What does that mean exactly? What kind of playing?"

"Don't know exactly." Benton and his evasiveness again. "I'd like to talk to the family." I suspect he's already talked to them. "There are a lot of missing details. But he was playing by himself in the yard, and when his mother looked out the window at around four-fifteen, she didn't see him. So she went out to make him come into the house and found him, tried to rouse him, and picked him up and rushed him inside. She called nine-one-one at exactly four-twenty-three p.m., was hysterical, said that her son wasn't moving or breathing, that she was worried he had choked on something."

"Why would she think he might have choked?"

"Apparently, before he went out to play, he'd put some leftover Christmas candy into his pocket. Hard candies, and the last thing she said to him as he was going out the door was not to suck on candy while he was running or jumping."

I can't help but think that this is the sort of detail Benton would have gotten from the Bishops in person. I feel he has talked to them.

"And we don't know what kind of playing he was doing? He's by himself, running and jumping?" I ask.

"I just got involved in this case after Johnny confessed to it." Benton is evasive again. For some reason, he doesn't want to talk about what Mark was doing in his backyard. "Mrs. Bishop later told police she didn't see anybody in the area, that there was no sign of anybody having been on their property, and she didn't know until Mark got to the emergency room that he'd been murdered. The nails had been hammered in all the way, and his hair hid them, and there was no blood. And his shoes were missing. He was wearing a pair of Adidas while play-ing in the yard, and they were gone and haven't shown up."

"A boy playing in his yard in the near dark. Again, hard to imagine he would co-operate with a stranger. Unless it was someone who represented something he instinctively trusted." I continue making that point.

"A fireman. A cop. The guy who drives the ice-cream truck. That sort of thing," Benton considers easily, as if this is safe to talk about. "Or worse. A member of his own family."

"A member of his family would kill him in such a sadistic, hideous fashion and then take his shoes? Taking the shoes sounds like a souvenir."

"Or supposed to look like one," Benton says.

"I'm no forensic psychologist," I then say. "I'm playing your role, and I shouldn't. I'd like to see where it happened. Jack never went to the scene, and he should have made a retrospective visit." My mood settles lower as I say that. He didn't go to Mark Bishop's scene, and he didn't go to Norton's Woods.

"Or another kid. Kids playing a game that turned deadly," Benton says.

"If it was another kid," I reply, "he was remarkably well informed anatomically."

I envision the autopsy photographs, the boy's head with his scalp reflected back. I envision the CT scans, three-dimensional images of four two-inch iron nails penetrating the brain.

"Whoever did it couldn't have picked more lethal locations to drive the nails," I explain. "Three went through the temporal bone above the left ear and penetrated the pons. One was nailed into the back of the skull, directed upward, so it damaged the cervicomedullary junction, or upper cervical spinal cord."

"How fast would that have killed him?"

"Almost instantaneously. The nail to the back of the head alone could have killed him in minutes, as little time as it takes to die after you can no longer breathe. Injury at the C-one and C-two levels of the spinal cord interferes with breathing. The police, the prosecutor, a jury, for that matter, would have a hard time believing another child could have done that. It seems that causing death, almost immediate death, was the intention, and it was premeditated, unless the hammer and nails were at the scene, in the yard or house, and by all accounts they weren't. Correct?"

"A hammer, yes. But what house doesn't have a hammer? And the tool marks don't match. But you know that from lab reports. No nails like the ones that killed him. Those weren't found at the family's home, and no nail gun," Benton says.

"These were L-head nails, typically used in flooring."

"According to the police, no nails like that were found at the residence," he repeats.

"Iron, not stainless steel." I continue with details from photographs, from lab reports, and all the while I hear myself, I'm aware that I'm going over the case with Benton as if it's mine. As if it's his. As if we are working it the way we used to work cases in our early days together. "With traces of rust despite their protective zinc coating, which suggests they weren't just purchased," I go on. "That maybe they'd been lying around somewhere and exposed to moisture, possibly saltwater."

"Nothing like that at the scene. No L-head flooring nails, no iron nails at all," Benton says. "The father's been spreading the rumor about a nail gun, at least publicly."

"Publicly. Meaning he told the media," I assume.

"Yes."

"But when? He told the media when? That's the important question. Where did the rumor come from and when? Do we know for a fact it started with the father, because if it did, that's significant. It could mean he's offering an alibi, suggesting a weapon he doesn't have, that's he trying to lead the police in the wrong direction."

"We're thinking the same thing," Benton says. "Mr. Bishop might have suggested it to the media, but the question is, did someone suggest it to him first?"

I detect more subtleties. It occurs to me that Benton knows how the rumor about a nail gun started. He knows who started it, and it's not difficult to guess what he's implying. Jack Fielding is trying to influence what people think about this case. Maybe Fielding is the one behind the rumor that is now all over the news.

"We should do a retrospective. I'm trying to remember the name of the Salem detective." There's so much to do, so much I've missed. I hardly know where to start.

"Saint Hilaire. First name James."

"Don't know him." I'm a stranger to my own life.

"He's convinced of Johnny Donahue's guilt, and I'm really concerned it's just a matter of time before he's charged with first-degree murder. We have to move fast. When Saint Hilaire reads what Mrs. Donahue just wrote to you, it will be worse. He'll be more convinced. We have to do something quickly," Benton says. "I'm not supposed to give a damn, but I do because Johnny didn't do it and no jury is going to like him. He's inappropriate. He misreads people, and they misread him. They think he's callous and arrogant. He laughs and giggles when something isn't funny. He's rude and blunt and has no idea. The whole thing is absurd. A travesty. Probably one of the most classic examples of false confessions I've ever seen."

"Then why is he still on a locked unit at

McLean?"

"He needs psychiatric treatment, but no, he shouldn't be locked up on a unit with psychotic patients. That's my opinion, but no one's listening. Maybe you can talk to Renaud and Saint Hilaire and they'll listen to you. We'll go to Salem and review the case with them. While we're there, we'll look around."

"And Johnny's breakdown?" I ask. "If his mother is to be believed, he was fine his first three years at Harvard and suddenly has to be hospitalized? He's how old?"

"Eighteen. He returned to Harvard last fall to begin his senior year and was noticeably altered," Benton said. "Aggressive verbally and sexually, and increasingly agitated and paranoid. Disordered thinking and distorted perceptions. Symptoms similar to schizophrenia."

"Drugs?"

"No evidence whatsoever. Submitted to testing when he confessed to the murder and was negative; even his hair was negative for drugs, for alcohol. His grad-school friend Dawn Kincaid is at MIT, and she and Johnny were working together on a project. She became so concerned about him she finally called his family. This was in December. Then a week ago, Johnny was admitted to McLean with a stab wound to his hand and told his psychiatrist that he'd murdered Mark Bishop, claiming he took the train to Salem and had a nail gun in a backpack, said he needed a human sacrifice to rid him of an evil entity that had taken over his life."

"Why nails? Why not some other weapon?"

"Something to do with the magical powers of iron. And most of this has been in the news."

I recall seeing something on the Internet about devil's bone, and I mention that.

"Exactly. What iron was called in ancient Egypt," Benton replies. "They sell devil's bone in some of the shops in Salem."

"Lashed together in an X that you carry in a red satin pouch. I've seen them in some of the witcheries. But not the same type of nails. The ones in the witcheries are more like spikes, are supposed to look antique. And I doubt they're treated with zinc, that they're galvanized."

"Supposedly, iron protects against malevolent spirits, and thus the explanation for Johnny using iron nails. That's his explanation. And his story's completely unoriginal; as you just pointed out, it was one of the theories all over the news the days before he confessed to the murder." Benton pauses, then adds, "Your own office has suggested black magic as a motive, presumably because of the Salem connection."

"It's not our job to offer theories. Our job is to be impartial and objective, so I don't know what you mean when you say we suggested such a thing."

"I'm just telling you it's been discussed."

"With whom?" But I know.

"Jack's always been a loose cannon. But he seems to have lost what little impulse control he had," Benton says.

"I think we've established that Jack is a problem I can no longer attempt to solve. What project?" I go back to what Benton mentioned about Johnny Donahue's female MIT friend. "And what's Johnny's major?"

"Computer science. Since early last summer, he was interning at Otwahl Technologies in Cambridge. As his mother pointed out, he's unusually gifted in some areas. . . ."

"Doing what? What was he doing there?" I envision the solid façade of precast rising up like the Hoover Dam not far from where we just drove past, the part of Cambridge where the SUV with xenon lights was following us before it vanished.

"Software engineering for UGVs and related technologies," Benton says, as if it is no great matter because he doesn't know what I do about UGVs.

Unmanned ground vehicles. Military robots like the prototype MORT in the dead man's apartment.

"What's going on here, Benton?" I say with feeling. "What in God's name is going on?"

The storm has settled in, the wind much calmer now, and the snow is already several inches deep. Traffic is steady on Memorial Drive, the weather of little consequence to people used to New England winters.

The rooftops of MIT fraternity houses and playing fields are solid white on the left side of the road, and on the other side the snow drifts like smoke over the bike path and the boathouse and vanishes into the icy blackness of the Charles. Farther east, where the river empties into the harbor, the Boston skyline is ghostly rectangular shapes and smudges of light in the milky night, and there is no air traffic over Logan, not a single plane in sight.

"We should meet with Renaud as soon as possible — the sooner, the better." Benton thinks Essex County District Attorney Paul Renaud should know that there may be something more to Johnny Donahue's confession, that somehow the Harvard senior and a dead man in my cooler could be connected. "But if this involves DARPA?" Benton adds.

"Otwahl gets DARPA funding. But it isn't DARPA, isn't DoD. It's civilian, an international private industry," I reply. "But certainly it's closely tied to government through substantial grants, tens of millions, maybe a lot more than that, since their rather clumsy invention of MORT."

"The question is what else they're focused on. What are they focused on now that could have significance in all this?"

"I honestly can't say, not for a fact. But you know the obvious just by looking at the place." Were we to drive back toward Hanscom, we would pass within a mile of Otwahl Technologies and its adjoining superconducting test facility, a massive self-contained complex with its own private police force. "Neutron science, most likely, because of materials science and how it applies to new technologies."

"Robotics," Benton says.

"Robots, nanotechnology, software engineering, synthetic biology. Lucy knows something about it."

"Probably more than something."

"Knowing her, yes. A lot more than something."

"They're probably making damn humanoids so we never run out of soldiers."

"They might be." I'm not joking.

"And Briggs would know about the robot in this guy's apartment." Benton means the dead man's apartment. "Because of video clips? What else about that? I wonder if he said something to Jack about it, called and alerted him by asking questions."

I explain it further, giving a more detailed account of the man and the recordings Lucy discovered — recordings that Marino inappropriately e-mailed to Briggs before I had a chance to review them first, and when I did get a chance to see them, it was only superficially, en route to the Civil Air Terminal in Dover. I tell Benton all about the ill-fated six-legged robot, the Mortuary Operational Removal Transport, known as MORT, that is parked inside the apartment near the door, and I remind him of the controversies, of the disagreements I had with certain politicians and especially with Briggs over using a machine to recover casualties in theater or anywhere.

I describe the heartlessness, the horror, of a gas-powered metal construction that sounded like a chain saw lurching across the earth to recover wounded or dead human beings by grasping them in grippers that looked like the mandibles of a bull ant. "Think of the message it sends if you're dying on the battlefield and this is what your comrades send for you," I say to Benton. "What kind of message does it send to the victim's loved ones if they see it on the news?"

"You used inflammatory language like that when you testified before a defense appropriations Senate subcommittee," Benton assumes.

"I don't remember what I said verbatim."

"I'm sure you didn't make any friends at Otwahl. You probably made enemies you have no idea about."

"It wasn't about Otwahl or any other technology company. All Otwahl did was create an unmanned robotic vehicle. It was people at the Pentagon that came up with its so-called useful purpose. I think originally MORT was supposed to be a packbot, nothing more. I didn't even remember Otwahl was the company until tonight. They were never a preoccupation of mine. My disagreement was with the Pentagon, and I was going to stand my ground." I almost say *this time.* But I catch myself. Benton doesn't know about the time I didn't stand my ground.

"Enemies who haven't forgotten. Those kinds of enemies never forget. I'm sorry I wasn't privy to all this when it was going on," Benton says, because he wasn't around when I was making enemies on Capitol Hill. He was in a protective witness program and not exactly in a position to give me advice or counsel or even assure me that he wasn't dead. "You must have files on it, records from back then."

"Why?"

"I'd like to take a look, get up to speed. It might explain a few things."

"What things?"

"I'd like to look at what you have from back then," Benton says.

Transcripts from my testimony, video recordings of the segments aired on C-SPAN: What I have would be in my safe in our Cambridge basement — along with certain items I don't want him to see. A thick gray accordion file and photographs I took with my own camera. Bloodstained squares of white cardboard improvised before the days of FTA DNA collection kits, because if blood is air-dried it can last forever, and I knew where technology was headed. Plain white envelopes with finger-nail cuttings and pubic combings and head hair. Oral, anal, and vaginal swabs, and cut and torn bloody underpants. An empty Chablis bottle, a beer can. Materials I smuggled from a dark continent half a world away more than two decades ago, evidence I shouldn't have had, items I shouldn't have had privately tested, but I did. I seriously consider that if Benton was aware of the Cape Town cases, he might not feel the same about me.

"You know the old saying, revenge is best served cold," he goes on. "You fucked a huge multimillion-dollar project, a joint venture between DoD and Otwahl Technologies, and stepped on toes, and although a number of years have passed, I suspect there are people out there who haven't forgotten, even if you have. And now here you are, working with DoD in Otwahl's backyard. A perfect opportunity to calculate revenge, to pay you back."

"Pay me back? A man dropping dead in Norton's Woods is payback?"

"I just think we should know the cast of characters."

Then we stop talking about it, because we have reached the girder bridge that connects Cambridge to Boston, the Mass Ave Bridge, or what the locals refer to as the Harvard Bridge or MIT Bridge, depending on their loyalties. Just ahead, my headquarters rises like a lighthouse, silo-shaped with a glass dome on top, seven stories sided in titanium and reinforced with steel. The first time Marino saw the CFC he decided it looked like a dum-dum bullet, and in the snowy dark, I suppose it does.

Turning off Memorial Drive, away from the river, we take the first left into the parking area, illuminated by solar security lights and surrounded by a black PVC-coated fence that can't be climbed or cut. I dig a remote control out of my bag and push a button to open the tall gate, and we drive over tire tracks that are almost completely covered in fresh white powder. Anne and Ollie's cars are here, parked near the CFC's all-wheel-drive cargo vans and SUVs, and I notice one is missing, one of the SUVs. There should be four, but one of them is gone and has been since before it began to snow, probably the on-call medicolegal investigator.

I wonder who is on duty tonight and why that person is out in one of our vehicles. At a scene, or is the person at home, and I look around as if I've never been here before. Above the fence on two sides are lab buildings that belong to MIT, glass and brick, with antennas and radar dishes on the roofs, the windows dark except for a random few glowing dimly, as if someone left a desk light or a lamp on. Snow streaks the night and is loud like a brittle rain as Benton pulls close to my building, into the space designated for the director, next to Fielding's spot, which is empty and smooth with snow.

"We could put it in the bay," Benton says hopefully.

"That would be a little spoiled, since no one else can," I reply. "And it's unauthorized, anyway. For pickups and deliveries only."

"Dover's worn off on you. Am I going to have to salute?"

"Only at home."

We climb out, and the snow is up to the ankles of my boots and doesn't pack under them because it is too cold, the flakes tiny and icy. I enter a code in a keypad next to a shut bay door that begins to retract loudly as Marino and Lucy drive into the lot. The receiving bay looks like a small hangar sealed with white epoxy paint, and mounted in the ceiling is a monorail crane, a motorized lifter for moving bodies too large for manual handling. There is a ramp inside leading to a metal door, and parked off to the side is our white van-body truck, what at Dover we refer to as a bread truck, designed to transport up to six bodies on stretchers or in transfer cases and to serve as a mobile crime scene lab when needed.

As I wait for Marino and Lucy, I'm reminded I'm not dressed for New England. My tactical jacket was perfectly adequate in Delaware, but now I'm thoroughly chilled. I try not to think about how good it would be to sit in front of the fire with a single-malt Scotch or small-batch bourbon, to catch up with Benton about things other than tragedy and betrayal and enemies with long memories, to get away from everyone. I want to drink and talk honestly with my husband, to put aside games and subterfuge and not wonder what he knows. I crave a normal time with him, but we don't know what that is. Even when we make love we have our secrets and nothing is normal.

"No updates except Lawless." Marino answers a question no one asked as the bay door clanks down behind us. "He e-mailed scene photographs — finally. But says no luck with the dog. No one's called to report a lost greyhound."

"What greyhound?" Benton asks.

I was too busy describing MORT and didn't mention much else I saw on the video clips. I feel foolish. "Norton's Woods," I reply. "A black-and-white greyhound named

192

Sock that apparently ran off while the EMTs were busy with our case."

"How do you know his name is Sock?"

I explain it to him as I hold my thumb over the glass sensor of the biometric lock so it can scan my print. Opening the door that leads into the lower level of the building, I mention that the dog might have a microchip that could supply useful information about the owner's identification. Some rescue groups automatically microchip former racing greyhounds before putting them up for adoption, I add.

"That's interesting," Benton says. "I think I saw them."

"He stared right at you as you were pulling out of the driveway in your sports car about three-fifteen yesterday afternoon," Lucy tells him as we enter the processing area, an open space with a security office, a digital floor scale, and a wall of massive stainless-steel doors that open into cooler rooms and a walk-in freezer.

"What are you talking about?" Benton asks my niece.

"All that time in the car driving through a blizzard and you didn't catch him up on things?" Lucy says to me, and she's not easy to be around when she gets like this.

I feel a prick of annoyance even though

she's right. *She knows you, too,* enters my mind. *She knows you just as well as you know her.* She knows damn well when something is bothering me that I stubbornly keep to myself, and I've been bothered and feeling stubborn since I left Dover. It was stupid of me not to go into the sort of detail that Benton can do something with. I don't know of anyone more psychologically astute, and he would have plenty to say about the minutiae picked up by the recorders concealed inside the dead man's headphones.

Instead, I obsessed about DARPA because I was really obsessing about Briggs. I can't get past what happened earlier today, about what happened decades ago, about how what he caused never seems to end. He knows about that dark place in my past, a place I take no one, and a part of me will never forgive him for creating that place. It was his idea for me to go to Cape Town. It was his goddamn brilliant plan.

"He and the greyhound walked right past your driveway just minutes before he died," Lucy is telling Benton, but her gaze is steady on me. "If you hadn't left, you would have heard the sirens. You probably would have headed over there to see what was going on and maybe would have some useful information for us."

She looks at me as if she is looking at the dark place. It's not possible she could know about it, I reassure myself. I've never told her, never told Benton or Marino or anyone. The documents were destroyed except for what I have. Briggs promised that decades ago when I left the AFIP and moved to Virginia, and I already knew reports were missing without being told. Lucy doesn't have the combination to my safe, I remind myself. Benton doesn't. No one does.

"If you drop by my lab," Lucy is saying to Benton, "I'll show the video clips to you."

"You haven't seen them," I say to Benton, because I'm not sure. He's acting as if he hasn't seen them, but I don't know if it's just more of the same, more secrets.

"I haven't," he answers, and it sounds like the truth. "But I want to, and I will."

"Weird you're in them," Lucy says to him. "Your house is in them. Really weird. Sort of freaked me out when I saw it."

The night security guard sits behind his glass window, and he nods at us but doesn't get up from his desk. His name is Ron, a big, muscular dark-skinned man with closely shorn hair and unfriendly eyes. He seems afraid of me or skeptical, and it's obvious he's been instructed to maintain his post, not to be sociable, no matter who it is. I can only imagine the stories he's heard, and Fielding enters my thoughts again. What has happened to him? What trouble has he caused? How much has he hurt this place?

I walk over to the security guard's window and check the sign-in log. Since three p.m., three bodies have come in: a motor-vehicle fatality, a gunshot homicide, and an asphyxiation by plastic bag that is undetermined.

"Is Dr. Fielding here?" I ask Ron.

Retired marine corps military police, he is always neat and proud in his midnight-blue uniform with American flag and AFME patches on the shoulders and a brass CFC security shield pinned to his shirt. His face is wary and not the least bit warm behind his glass partition as he answers that he hasn't seen Fielding. He tells me that Anne and Ollie are here but no one else. Not even the on-call death investigator is in. Randy, he informs me in a monotone, and every other word is *ma'am,* and I'm reminded of how cold and condescending *ma'am* this and *ma'am* that can sound and how tired I got of hearing it at Dover. Randy is working from home because of the weather, Ron reports. Apparently, Fielding told him that was okay, even though it's not. That is against the rules I established. On-call investigators don't work from home.

"We'll be in the x-ray room," I inform Ron. "If anybody else shows up, you can find us in there. But unless it's Dr. Fielding, I need to know who it is and give clearance. Actually, I probably should know if Dr. Fielding shows up, too. You know what, no matter who it is, I need to know."

"If Dr. Fielding comes in you want me to call, ma'am. To alert you," Ron repeats, as if he's not sure that's what I meant, or maybe he's arguing.

"Affirmative," I make myself clear. "No one should just walk in, doesn't matter if they work here. Until I tell you otherwise. I want everything airtight right now."

"I understand, ma'am."

"Any calls from the media? Any sign of them?"

"I keep looking, ma'am." Mounted on three walls are monitors, each split into quadrants that are constantly rotating images picked up by security cameras outside the building and in strategic areas such as the bays, corridors, elevators, lobby, and all doors leading into the building. "I know there's some concern about the man found in the park." Ron looks past me at Marino, as if the two of them have an understanding.

"Well, you know where we'll be for now."

I open another door. "Thank you."

A long white hallway with a gray tile floor leads to a series of rooms located in a logical order that facilitates the flow of our work. The first stop is ID, where bodies are photographed and fingerprinted and personal effects not taken by the police are removed and secured in lockers. Next is large-scale x-ray, which includes the CT scanner, and beyond that are the autopsy room, the soiled room, the anteroom, the changing rooms, the locker rooms, the anthropology lab, the Bio4 containment lab reserved for suspected infectious or contaminated cases. The corridor wraps around in a circle that ends where it began, at the receiving bay.

"What does security know about our patient from Norton's Woods?" I ask Marino. "Why does Ron think there's a concern?"

"I didn't tell him anything."

"I'm asking what he knows."

"He wasn't on duty when we left earlier. I haven't seen him today."

"I'm wondering what he's been told," I repeat patiently, because I don't want to squabble with Marino in front of the others. "Obviously, this is a very sensitive situation."

"I gave an order before I left that everyone needed to be on the lookout for the media," Marino says, taking off his leather jacket as we reach the x-ray room, where the red light above the door indicates that the scanner is in use. Anne and Ollie won't have started without me, but it's their habit to deter people from walking into an area where there are levels of radiation much higher than are safe for living patients. "Wasn't my idea for Randy or the others to work from home, either," Marino adds.

I don't ask how long that's been going on or who the "others" are. Who else has been working from home? This is a state government facility, a paramilitary installation, not a cottage industry, I feel like saying.

"Damn Fielding," Marino then mutters. "He's fucking up everything."

I don't answer. Now is not the time to discuss how fucked up everything is.

"You know where I'll be." Lucy walks off toward the elevator, and with an elbow pushes a hands-free oversized button. She disappears behind sliding steel doors as I pass my thumb over another biometric sensor and the lock clicks free.

Inside the control room, forensic radiologist Dr. Oliver Hess is seated at a work station behind lead-lined glass, his gray hair unruly, his face sleepy, as if I got him out of bed. Past him, through an open door, I can see the eggshell-white Siemens Somatom Sensation and hear the fan of its water-cooled system. The scanner is a modified version of the one used at Dover, equipped with a custom head holder and safety straps, its wiring subsurface, its parameter sealed, its table covered by a heavy vinyl slicker to protect the multimillion-dollar system from contaminants such as body fluids. Slightly angled down toward the door to facilitate sliding bodies on and off, the scanner is in the ready status, and technologist Anne Mahoney is placing radio-opaque CT skin markers on the dead man from Norton's Woods. I get a strange feeling as I walk in. He is familiar, although I've never seen him before, only parts of him on recordings I watched on an iPad.

I recognize the tint of his light-brown skin and his tapered hands, which are by his sides on top of a disposable blue sheet, his long, slender fingers slightly curled and stiff with rigor.

In the video clips I heard his voice and saw glimpses of his hands, his boots, his clothing, but I did not see his face. I'm not sure what I imagined but am vaguely disturbed by his delicate features and long, curly brown hair, by the spray of light freckles across his smooth cheeks. I pull the sheet back, and he is very thin, about five-foot-eight and at most one hundred and thirty pounds, I deduce, with very little body hair. He could easily pass for sixteen, and I'm reminded of Johnny Donahue, who isn't much older. Kids. Could that be a common denominator? Or is it Otwahl Technologies?

"Anything?" I ask Anne, a plain-looking woman in her thirties with shaggy brown hair and sensitive hazel eyes. She's probably the best person on my staff, can do anything, whether it is different types of radiographic imaging or helping in the morgue or at crime scenes. She is always willing.

"This. Which I noticed when I undressed him." Her latex-sheathed hands grip the body at the waist and hip, pulling it over so I can see a tiny defect on the left side of the back at the level of the kidneys. "Obviously missed at the scene because it didn't bleed out, at least not much. You know about his bleeding, which I witnessed with my own two eyes when I was going to scan him early this morning? That he bled profusely from his nose and mouth after he was bagged and transported?"

"That's why I'm here." I open a drawer to

retrieve a hand lens, and then Benton is by my side in a surgical mask and gown and gloves. "He's got some sort of injury," I say to him as I lean close to the body and magnify an irregular wound that looks like a small buttonhole. "Definitely not a gunshot entrance. A stab wound made by a very narrow blade, like a boning knife but with two edges. Something like a stiletto."

"A stiletto in his back would drop him in his tracks?" Benton's eyes are skeptical above his mask.

"No. Not unless he was stabbed at the base of his skull and it severed his spinal cord." I think of Mark Bishop and the nails that killed him.

"Like I said at Dover, maybe something was injected," Marino offers as he walks in covered from head to foot with personal protective clothing, including a face shield and hair cover, as if he's worried about airborne pathogens or deadly spores, such as anthrax. "Maybe some kind of anesthesia. A lethal injection, in other words. That could sure as hell drop you in your tracks."

"In the first place, an anesthesia like sodium thiopental is injected into a vein, as are pancuronium bromide or potassium chloride." I pull on a pair of examination gloves. "They aren't injected into the person's back. Same thing with mivacurium, with succinylcholine. You want to kill somebody decisively and quickly with a neuromuscular blocker, you'd better inject it intravenously."

"But if they were injected into a muscle, it would still kill you, right?" Marino opens a cabinet and gets out a camera. He rummages in a drawer and finds a plastic six-inch ruler for size reference. "During executions, sometimes the injection misses the vein and goes into the muscle, and the inmate still dies."

"A slow and very painful death," I reply. "By all accounts, this man's death wasn't slow, and this injury wasn't made by a needle."

"I won't say the prison techs do it on purpose, but it happens. Well, it's probably on purpose. Just like some of them chill the cocktail, making sure the dirtbag feels it hit, the ice-cold hand of death," Marino says for Anne's benefit, because she is passionately anti–capital punishment. His way of flirting is to offend her whenever he can.

"That's disgusting," she says.

"Hey. It's not like they cared about the people they whacked, right? Like they cared if they suffered, right? What goes around comes around. Who hid the damn label maker?"

"I did. I lie awake at night figuring out ways to get you back."

"Oh, yeah? For what?"

"For just being you."

Marino digs in another drawer, finds the label maker. "He looks a hell of a lot younger than what the EMTs said. Anybody notice that besides me? Don't you think he looks younger than his twenties?" Marino asks Anne. "Looks like a damn kid."

"Barely pubescent," she agrees. "But then, all college kids are starting to look like that to me. They look like babies."

"We don't know if he was a college student," I remind everyone.

Marino peels the backing off a label printed with the date and case number, and sticks it on the plastic ruler. "I'll canvas the area over there by the common, see if any supers in apartment buildings recognize him, just do it my damn self to keep the rumor mill quiet. If he lives around there, and it sure seems like it, based on what's on the videos, someone's got to remember him and his greyhound. Sock. What kind of name is that for a dog?"

"Probably not his full name," Anne says. "Race dogs have these rather elaborate registered kennel names, like Sock It to Me or Darned Sock or Sock Hop."

"I keep telling her she should go on *Jeopardy,*" Marino says.

"It's possible his name might be in a registry," I comment. "Something with Sock in it, assuming we have no luck with a microchip."

"Assuming you find the damn dog," Marino says.

"We're running his prints, his DNA. Right away, I hope?" Benton stares intently at the body, as if he's talking to it.

"I printed him this morning and no luck, nothing in IAFIS. Nothing in the National Missing and Unidentified Persons System. We'll have his DNA tomorrow and run it through CODIS." Marino's big gloved hands place the ruler under the man's chin. "It's kind of strange about the dog, though. Someone's got to have him. I'm thinking we should put out info for the media about a lost greyhound and a number people can call."

"Nothing from us," I reply. "Right now we're staying away from the media."

"Exactly," Benton says. "We don't want the bad guys knowing we're even aware of the dog, much less looking for it."

" 'Bad guys'?" Anne says.

"What else?" I walk around the table, doing what Lucy calls a "high recon," looking carefully at the body from head to toe.

Marino is taking photographs, and he says, "Before we put him back in the fridge this morning, I checked his hands for trace, collected anything preliminarily, including personal effects."

"You didn't tell me about personal effects. Just that he didn't seem to have any," I reply.

"A ring with a crest on it, a steel Casio watch. A couple keys on a keychain. Let's see, what else? A twenty-dollar bill. A little wooden stash box, empty, but I swabbed it for drugs. The stash box on the video clip. For a second you could see him holding it right after he got to Norton's Woods."

"Where was it recovered?" I ask.

"In his pocket. That's where I found it."

"So he took it out of his pocket at the park and then put it back in his pocket before his terminal event." I remember what I watched on the iPad, the small box held in the black glove.

"I'd say we should be looking for the snorting or smoking variety," Marino says. "I'm betting weed. Don't know if you noticed," he says to me, "but he had a glass pipe in an ashtray on his desk."

"We'll see what shows up on tox," I reply. "We'll do a STAT alcohol and expedite a

206

drug screen. How backed up are they up there?"

"I'll tell Joe to move it to the head of the line," Anne refers to the chief toxicologist, whom I brought with me from New York, rather shamelessly stole him from the NYPD crime labs. "You're the boss. All you've got to do is ask." She meets my eyes. "Welcome back."

"What kind of crest, and what does the keychain look like?" Benton asks Marino.

"A coat of arms, an open book with three crowns," he says, and I can tell he enjoys having Benton at a disadvantage. The CFC is Marino's turf. "No writing on it, no phrase in Latin, nothing like that. I don't know what the crests for MIT and Harvard are."

"Not what you described," Benton answers. "Okay if I use this?" He indicates a computer on the counter.

"The keychain is one of those steel rings attached to a leather loop, like you'd snap around your belt," Marino goes on. "And as we all know, no wallet, not even a cell phone, and I think that's unusual. Who walks around with no cell phone?"

"He was taking his dog out and listening to music. Maybe he wasn't planning to be out very long and didn't want to talk on the phone," Benton says as he types in search words.

I pull the body over on its right side and look at Marino. "You want to help me with this?"

"Three crowns and an open book," Benton says. "City University of San Francisco." He types some more. "An online university specializing in health sciences. Would an online university have class rings?"

"And his personal effects are in which locker?" I ask Marino.

"*Numero uno.* I got the key if you want it."

"I would. Anything the labs need to check?"

"Can't see why."

"Then we'll keep his personal effects until they go to a funeral home or to his family, when we figure out who he is," I reply.

"And then there's Oxford," Benton says next, still searching the Internet. "But if the ring he had on was Oxford, it would have *Oxford University* on it, and you said it didn't have any writing or motto."

"It didn't," Marino replies. "But it looks like someone had it made, you know, plain gold and engraved with the crest, so maybe it wouldn't be as official as what you order from a school and wouldn't have a motto or

208

writing."

"Maybe," Benton says. "But if the ring was made, I have a hard time imagining it's for Oxford University, would be more inclined to think if someone went to an online college he might have a ring made because maybe there's no other way to get one, assuming you want to tell the world you're an alum of an online college. This is the City University of San Francisco coat of arms." Benton moves to one side so Marino can see what's on the computer screen, an elaborate crest with blue-and-gold mantling, and a gold owl on top with three gold fleur-de-lis, then below three gold crowns, and in the middle an open book.

Marino is holding the body on its side, and he squints at the computer screen from where he's standing and shrugs. "Maybe. If it was engraved, you know, if the person had it made for him, maybe it wouldn't be that detailed. That could be it."

"I'll look at the ring," I promise as I examine the body externally and make notes on a clipboard.

"No reason to think he was in a struggle, and we might get a perp's DNA or something off the watch or whatever. But you know me." Marino resumes what he was saying to me about processing the dead man's personal effects. "I swabbed every-thing anyway. Nothing struck me as unusual except that his watch had quit, one of those self-winding kind that Lucy likes, a chrono-graph."

"What time did it stop?"

"I got it written down. Sometime after four a.m. About twelve hours after he died. So he's got a nine-mil with eighteen rounds but no phone," he then says. "Okay. I guess so, unless he didn't leave it at home and in fact somebody took it. Maybe took the dog, too. That's what I keep wondering."

"There was a phone on a desk in the video clips I saw," I remind him. "Plugged into a charger near one of the laptops, I believe. Near the glass smoking pipe you men-tioned."

"We couldn't see everything he did in there before he left. I figured he might have grabbed his phone on his way out," Marino supposes. "Or he might have more than one. Who the hell knows?"

"We'll know when we find his apartment," Benton says as he prints what he's found on the Internet. "I'd like to see the scene pho-tos."

"You mean when I find the apartment." Marino puts the camera down on a coun-tertop. "Because it's going to be me poking around. Cops gossip worse than old women. I find where the guy lives, then I'll ask for help."

On a body diagram, I note that at eleven-fifteen p.m. the dead man is fully rigorous and refrigerated cold. He has a pattern of dark-red discoloration and positional blanching that indicates he was flat on his back with his arms straight by his sides, palms down, fully clothed, and wearing a watch on his left wrist and a ring on his left little finger for at least twelve hours after he died.

Postmortem hypostasis, better known as lividity or livor mortis, is one of my pet tattletales, although it is often misinterpreted even by those who should know better. It can look like bruising due to trauma when in fact it is caused by the mundane physiological phenomenon of noncirculating blood pooling into small vessels due to gravity. Lividity is a dusky red or can be purplish with lighter areas of blanching where areas of the body rested against a firm surface, and no matter what I'm told about the circumstances of a death, the body itself doesn't lie.

"No secondary livor pattern that might indicate the body moved while livor was still forming," I observe. "Everything I'm seeing is consistent with him being zipped up inside a pouch and placed on a body tray and not moving." I attach a body diagram to a clipboard and sketch impressions made by a waistband, a belt, jewelry, shoes and socks, pale areas on the skin that show the shape of elastic or a buckle or fabric or a weave pattern.

"Certainly suggests he didn't even move his arms, didn't thrash around, so that's good," Anne decides.

"Exactly. If he'd come to, he would have at least moved his arms. So that's real good," Marino agrees, keys clicking as an image fills the screen of the computer terminal on a countertop.

I make a note that the man has no body piercings or tattoos, and is clean, with neatly trimmed nails and the smooth skin of one who doesn't do manual labor or engage in any physical activity that might cause calluses on his hands or feet. I palpate his head, feeling for defects, such as fractures or other injuries, and find nothing.

"Question is whether he was facedown when he fell." Marino is looking at what Investigator Lester Law e-mailed to him. "Or is he on his back in these pictures because the EMTs turned him over?"

"To do CPR they would have had to turn him faceup." I move closer to look.

Marino clicks through several photos, all of them the same but from different perspectives: the man on his back, his dark-green jacket and denim shirt open, his head turned to one side, eyes partly closed; a close-up of his face, debris clinging to his lips, what looks like particles of dead leaves and grass and grit.

"Zoom in on that," I tell Marino, and with a click of the mouse, the image is larger, the man's boyish face filling the screen.

I return to the body behind me and check for injuries of his face and head, noting an abrasion on the underside of the chin. I pull down the lower lip and find a small laceration, likely made by his lower teeth when he fell and hit his face on the gravel path.

"Couldn't possibly account for all the blood I saw," Anne says.

"No, it couldn't," I agree. "But it suggests he hit the ground face-first, which also suggests he dropped like a shot, didn't even stumble or try to break his fall. Where's the pouch he came in?"

"I spread it out on a table in the autopsy room, figured you'd want to have a look," Anne tells me. "And his clothes are air-drying in there. When I undressed him, I put everything in the cabinet by your station. Station one."

"Good. Thank you."

"Maybe somebody punched him," Marino offers. "Maybe distracted him by punching or elbowing him in the face, then stabbed him in the back. Except that probably would have been recorded, would be on the video clips."

"He would have more than just this laceration if someone punched him in the mouth. If you look at the debris on his face and the location of the headphones" — I'm back at the computer, clicking on images to show them — "it appears he fell facedown. The headphones are way over here, what looks like at least six feet away under a bench, indicating to me that he fell with sufficient force to knock them a fair distance and disconnect them from the satellite radio, which I believe was in a pocket."

"Unless someone moved the phones, perhaps kicked them out of the way," Benton says.

"That was my other thought," I reply.

"You mean like somebody who tried to help him," Marino says. "People crowding around him and the headphones ended up under a bench."

"Or someone did it deliberately."

There is something else I notice. Clicking through the slideshow, I stop on a photograph of his left wrist. I zoom in on the steel tachymeter watch, move in close on its carbon-fiber face. The time stamp on the photograph is five-seventeen p.m., which is when the police officer took it, yet the time on the watch is ten-fourteen, five hours later than that.

"When you collected the watch this morning" — I direct this to Marino — "you said it appeared to have stopped. You sure it wasn't simply that the time was different than our local time?"

"Nope, it was stopped," he says. "Like I said, one of those self-winding watches, and it quit at some point early in the morning, like around four a.m."

"Seems it might have been set five hours later than Eastern Standard Time." I point out what I'm seeing in the photograph.

"Okay. Then it must have stopped around eleven p.m. our time," Marino says. "So it was set wrong to begin with and then it quit."

"Maybe he was on another time zone because he'd just flown in from overseas," Benton suggests.

"Soon as we finish up here, I got to find his apartment," Marino says.

I check the quality-control numbers in the quality-control log, making sure standard deviation is zero and the noise level of the system or variation is within normal limits.

"We ready?" I say to everyone.

I'm eager to do the scan. I want to see what is inside this man.

"We'll do a topogram, then collect the data set before going to three-D recon with at least fifty percent overlapping," I tell Anne as she presses a button to slide the table into the scanner. "But we'll change the protocol and start with the thorax, not the head, except, of course, for using the glabella as our reference."

I refer to the space between the eyebrows above the nose that we use for spatial orientation.

"A cross-sectional of the chest exactly correlating with the region of interest you've marked." I go down the list as we return to the control room. "An in situ localization of the wound; we'll isolate that area and any associated injury, any clues in the wound track."

I seat myself between Ollie and Anne, and then Marino and Benton pull up chairs behind us. Through the glass window I can see the man's bare feet in the opening of the scanner's bore.

"Auto and smart MT, noise index eighteen. Point-five segment rotation, point-six-two-five detector configuration," I instruct. "Very thin slice ultra-high resolution. Ten-millimeter collimation."

I can hear the electronic pulsing sounds as detectors begin rotating inside the x-ray tube. The first scan lasts sixty seconds. I watch in real time on a computer screen, not sure what I'm seeing, but it shouldn't be this. It occurs to me the scanner is malfunctioning or that some other patient's scan is displayed, the wrong file accessed. *What am I looking at?*

"Jesus," Ollie says under his breath, frowning at images in a grid, strange images that must be a mistake.

"Orient in time and space, and let's line up the wound back to front, left to right, and upward," I direct. "Connect points to get the penetration of the wound track, well, such as it is. There is a wound track and then it disappears? I don't know what this is."

"What the hell am I looking at?" Marino

asks, baffled.

"Nothing I've ever seen before, certainly not in a stabbing," I reply.

"Well, for one thing, air," Ollie announces. "We're seeing a hell of a lot of air."

"These dark areas here and here and here." I show Marino and Benton. "On CT, air looks dark. As opposed to the brighter white areas, which show higher density. Bone and calcification are bright. You can get a pretty good idea of what something is by the density of the pixels."

I reach for the mouse and move the cursor over a rib so they can see what I mean.

"CT number is one thousand one hundred and fifty one. Whereas this not-so-bright area here" — I move the cursor over an area of lung — "is forty. That's going to be blood. These dullish dark areas you're seeing are hemorrhage."

I'm reminded of high-velocity gunshots that cause tremendous crushing and tearing of tissue, similar to injury caused by the blast wave from an explosion. But this isn't a gunshot case. This isn't from a detonated explosive device. I don't see how either could be true.

"Some kind of wound that travels through the left kidney, superiorly through the diaphragm and into the heart, causing

219

profound devastation along the way. And all this." I point to murky areas around internal organs that are displaced and sheared. "More subcutaneous air. Air in the paraspinal musculature. Retroperitoneal air. How did all this air get inside of him? And here and here. Injury to bone. Rib fracture. Fracture of a transverse process. Hemopneumothorax, lung contusion, hemopericardium. And more air. Here and here and here." I touch the screen. "Air surrounding the heart and in the cardiac chambers, as well as in the pulmonary arteries and veins."

"And you've never seen anything like this?" Benton asks me.

"Yes and no. Similar devastation caused by military rifles, antitank cannons, some semiautomatics using extreme shock-fragmenting high-velocity ammunition, for example. The higher the velocity, the greater the kinetic energy dissipates at impact and the greater the damage, especially to hollow organs, such as bowel and lungs, and non-elastic tissue, such as the liver, the kidneys. But in a case like that, you expect a clear wound track and a missile or fragments of one. Which we aren't seeing."

"What about air?" Benton asks. "Do you see these pockets of air in cases like that?"

"Not exactly," I reply. "A blast wave can

create air emboli by forcing air across the air-blood barrier, such as out of the lungs. In other words, air ends up where it doesn't belong, but this is a lot of air."

"A hell of a lot," Ollie concurs. "And how do you get a blast wave from a stabbing?"

"Do a slice right through those coordinates," I say to him, indicating the region of interest marked by a bright white bead — the radio-opaque CT skin marker that was placed next to the wound on the left side of the man's back. "Start here and keep moving down five millimeters above and below the region of interest specified by the markers. That cut. Yes, that's the one. And let's reformat into virtual three-D volume rendering from inside out. Thin, thin cuts, one millimeter, and the increment between them? What do you think?"

"Point-seventy-five by point-five will do it."

"Okay, fine. Let's see what it looks like if we virtually follow the track, what track there is."

Bones are as vivid as if they are laid bare before us, and organs and other internal structures are well defined in shades of gray as the dead man's upper body, his thorax, begins to rotate slowly in three-dimension on the video display. Using modified software originally developed for virtual colonoscopies, we enter the body through the tiny buttonhole wound, traveling with a virtual camera as if we are in a microscopic spaceship slowly flying through murky grayish clouds of tissue, past a left kidney blown apart like an asteroid.

A ragged opening yawns before us, and we pass through a large hole in the diaphragm. Beyond is shattering, shearing, and contusion. *What happened to you? What did this?* I don't have a clue. It's a helpless feeling to find physical damage that seems to defy physics, an effect without a cause. There's no projectile. There's no frag, nothing metal I can see. There's no exit wound, only the buttonhole entrance on the left side of his back. I'm thinking out loud, repeating important points, making sure everyone understands what is incomprehensible.

"I keep forgetting nothing works down here," Benton comments distractedly as he looks at his iPhone.

"Nothing exited, and nothing is lighting up." I calculate what must be done next. "No sign of anything ferrous, but we need to be sure."

"Absolutely no idea what could have done this," Benton states rather than asks as he gets up from his chair, making rustling sounds as he unties his disposable gown. "You know the old saying, nothing new under the sun. I guess like a lot of old sayings, it's not true."

"This is new. At least to me," I reply.

He bends over and pulls off his shoe covers. "No question he's a homicide."

"Unless he ate some really bad Mexican food," Marino says.

It vaguely drifts through my thoughts that Benton is acting suspiciously.

"Like a high-velocity projectile, but there's no projectile, and if it exited the body, where's the exit wound?" I keep saying the same thing. "Where the hell's the metal? What the hell could he have been shot with? An ice bullet?"

"I saw a thing about that on *MythBusters*. They proved it's impossible because of heat," Marino says, as if I'm serious. "I don't know, though. Wonder what would happen if you loaded the gun and kept it in the freezer until you were ready to fire it."

"Maybe if you're a sniper in the interior of Antarctica," Ollie says. "Where'd that idea come from, anyway? *Dick Tracy?* I'm asking for real."

"I thought it was James Bond. I forget which movie."

"Maybe the exit wound isn't obvious,"

223

Anne says to me. "Remember that time the guy was shot in the jaw and it exited through his nostril?"

"Then where's the wound track?" I reply. "We need better contrast between tissues, need to be damn sure there's nothing we're missing before I open him up."

"If you need my help with that, I can call the hospital," Benton says as he opens the door. I can tell he's in a hurry, but I'm not sure why.

It's not his case.

"Otherwise, I'll check on what Lucy's found," Benton says. "Take a look at the video clips. Check on a couple other things. You don't mind if I use a phone up there."

"I'll make the call," Anne says to him as he leaves. "I'll get it arranged with McLean and take care of the scan."

It's been a theoretical possibility this day would come, and we are cleared with the Board of Health, and with Harvard and its affiliate McLean Hospital, which has four magnets ranging in strength from 1.5 to 9 Tesla. Long ago I made sure the protocols were in place to do MRIs on dead bodies in McLean's neuroimaging lab, where Anne works as a part-time MR tech for psychiatric research studies. That's how I got her. Benton knew her first and recommended her. He picks well, is a fine judge of character. I should let him hire my damn staff. I wonder whom he is going to call. I'm not sure why he is here at all.

"If that's what you want, we can do it right now," Anne is saying to me. "There shouldn't be a problem, won't be anyone around. We'll just go right up to the front door and get him in and out."

At this hour, psychiatric patients at McLean won't be wandering around the campus. There's little risk of them happening upon a dead body being carried in or out of a lab.

"What if someone shot him with a water cannon?" Marino stares as if transfixed at the rotating torso on the video screen, the ribs curving and gleaming whitely in 3-D. "Seriously. I've always heard that's the perfect crime. You fill a shotgun shell with water, and it's like a bullet when it goes through the body. But it doesn't leave a trace."

"I've not had a case like that," I reply.

"But it could happen," Marino says.

"Theoretically. However, the entrance wound wouldn't be like this one," I reply. "Let's get going. I want him posted and safely out of sight before everyone starts arriving for work." It's almost midnight.

225

Anne clicks on the icon for *Tools* to take measurements and informs me the width of the wound track before it blows through the diaphragm is .77 to 1.59 millimeters at a depth of 4.2 millimeters.

"So what that tells me . . ." I start to say.

"How about inches," Marino complains.

"Some type of double-edged object or blade that doesn't get much wider than half an inch," I explain. "And once it penetrated the body up to an approximate depth of two inches, something else happened that caused profound internal damage."

"What I'm wondering is how much of this abnormality we're seeing is iatrogenic," Ollie says. "Caused by the EMTs working on him for twenty minutes. That's probably the first question we'll get asked. We have to keep an open mind."

"No way. Not unless King Kong did CPR," I reply. "It appears this man was stabbed with something that caused tremendous pressure in his chest and a large air embolus. He would have had severe pain and been dead within minutes, which is consistent with what's been described by witnesses, that he clutched his chest and collapsed."

"Then why all the blood after the fact?" Marino says. "Why wouldn't he have been hemorrhaging instantly? How the hell's it possible he didn't start bleeding until after he was pronounced and on his way here?"

"I don't know the answer, but he didn't die in our cooler." I am at least sure of that. "He was dead before he got here, would have been dead at the scene."

"But we got to prove he started bleeding after he was dead. And dead people don't start bleeding like a damn stuck pig. So how do we prove he was dead before he got here?" Marino persists.

"Who do we need to prove it to?" I look at him.

"I don't know who Fielding's told since we don't even know where the hell he is. What if he's told somebody?"

Like you did, I think, but I don't say it. "That's why one should be careful about divulging details when we don't have all the information." I couldn't sound more reasonable.

"We got no choice about it." Marino won't let it go. "We have to prove why a dead person started bleeding."

I collect my jacket and tell Anne, "A head and full-body CT scan first. And on MR, full-body coil, every inch of him, and upload what you find. I'll want to see it right away."

"I'm driving," Marino says to her.

"Well, pull it into the bay to warm it up. One of the vans."

"We don't want him warming up. Matter of fact, think I'll put the AC on full-blast."

"Then you can ride just the two of you. I'll meet you there."

"Seriously. He warms up, he might start bleeding again."

"You've been watching too much *Saturday Night Live*."

"Dan Aykroyd doing Julia Child? Remember that? *'You'll need a knife, a very, very sharp knife.'* And blood spurting everywhere."

The three of them bantering.

"That was so funny."

"The old ones were better."

"No kidding. Roseanne Roseannadanna."

"Oh, God, I love her."

"I've got them all on DVD."

I hear them laughing as I walk away.

Scanning my thumb, I let myself into the area that is the first stop after Receiving, where we do identifications, a white room with gray countertops that we simply call ID.

Built into a wall are gray metal evidence lockers, each of them numbered, and I use the key Marino gave me to open the top one on the left, where the dead man's personal effects have been safely stored until we receipt them to a funeral home or to a family when we finally know who he is and who should claim him. Inside are paper bags and envelopes neatly labeled, and attached to each are forms Marino has filled out and initialed to maintain chain of custody. I find the small manila envelope containing the signet ring, and initial the form and put down the time I removed it from the locker. At a computer station I pull up a log and enter the same information, and then I think about the dead man's clothes.

I should look at them while I'm down here, not wait until I do the autopsy, which will be hours from now. I want to see the hole made by the blade that penetrated the man's lower back and created such havoc inside him. I want to see how much he might have bled from that wound, and I leave ID and walk along the gray tile corridor, backtracking. I pass the x-ray room, and through its open door I catch a glimpse of Marino, Anne, and Ollie, still in there, getting the body ready for transport to McLean, joking and laughing. I quickly go past without them noticing, and I open the double steel doors leading into the autopsy room.

It is a vast open space of white epoxy paint and white tile and exposed shiny steel tracks with cool filtered lighting running horizontally along the length of the white ceiling. Eleven steel tables are parked by wall-mounted steel sinks, each with a foot-operated faucet control, a high-pressure spray hose, a commercial disposal, a specimen rinse basket, and a sharps container. The stations I carefully researched and had installed are mini-modular operating theaters with down-draft ventilation systems that exchange air every five minutes, and there are computers, fume hoods, carts of surgical instruments, halogen lights on flexible arms, dissecting surfaces with cutting boards, containers of formalin with spigots, and test-tube racks and plastic jars for histology and toxicology.

My station, the chief's station, is the first one, and it occurs to me that someone has been using it, and then I feel ridiculous for thinking it. Of course people would have been using it while I've been gone. Of course Fielding probably did. *It doesn't matter, and why should I care?* I tell myself as I notice that the surgical instruments on the cart aren't neatly lined up the way I would leave them. They are haphazardly placed on a large white polyethylene dissecting board as if someone rinsed them and didn't do it thoroughly. I grab a pair of latex gloves out of a box and pull them on because I don't want to touch anything with my bare hands.

Normally, I don't worry about it, not as much as I should, I suppose, because I come from an old school of forensic pathologists who were stoical and battle-scarred and took perverse pride in not being afraid of or repulsed by anything. Not maggots or purge fluid or putrefying flesh that is bloated and turning green and slipping, not even AIDS, at least not the worries we have now when we live with phobias and federal regulations about absolutely everything. I remember when I walked around without protective clothing on, smoking, drinking coffee, and touching dead patients as any doctor would, my bare skin against theirs as I examined a wound or looked at a contusion or took a measurement. But I was never sloppy with my work station or my surgical instruments. I was never careless.

I would never return so much as a teasing needle to a surgical cart without first washing it with hot, soapy water, and the drumming of hot water into deep metal sinks was a pervasive sound in the morgues of my

past. As far back as my Richmond days —
even earlier, when I was just starting at Walter Reed — I knew about DNA and that it
was about to be admissible in court and
become the forensic gold standard, and
from that point forward, everything we did
at crime scenes and in the autopsy suite and
in the labs would be questioned on the witness stand. Contamination was about to
become the ultimate nemesis, and although
we don't make a routine of autoclaving our
surgical instruments at the CFC, we certainly don't give them a cursory splash
under the faucet and then toss them onto a
cutting board that isn't clean, either.

I pick up an eighteen-inch dissecting knife
and notice a trace of dried blood in the
scored stainless-steel handle and that the
steel blade is scratched and pitted along
the edge and spotted instead of razor-sharp
and as bright as polished silver. I notice
blood in the serrated blade of a bone saw
and dried bloodstains on a spool of waxed
five-cord thread and on a double-curved
needle. I pick up forceps, scissors, rib
shears, a chisel, a flexible probe, and am
dismayed by the poor condition everything
is in.

I will send Anne a message to hose down
my station and wash all of its instruments

before we autopsy the man from Norton's Woods. I will have this entire goddamn autopsy room cleaned from the ceiling to the floor. I will have all of its systems inspected before my first week home has passed, I decide, as I pull on a fresh pair of gloves and walk to a countertop where a large roll of white paper — what we call butcher paper — is attached to a wall-mounted dispenser. Paper makes a loud ripping sound as I tear off a section and cover an autopsy table midway down the room, a table that looks cleaner than mine.

I cover my AFME field clothes with a disposable gown, not bothering with the long ties in back, then return to my messy station. Against the wall is a large white polypropylene drying cabinet on hard rubber casters with a double clear acrylic door, which I unlock by entering a code in a digital keypad. Hanging inside are a sage-green nylon jacket with a black fleece collar, a blue denim shirt, black cargo pants, and a pair of boxer briefs, each on its own stainless-steel hanger, and on the tray at the bottom are a pair of scuffed brown leather boots, and next to them, a pair of gray wool socks. I recognize some of the clothing from the video clips I saw, and it gives me an unsettled feeling to look at it now. The cabinet's centrifugal fan and HEPA exhaust filters make their low whirring sound as I look at the boots and the socks by picking them up one by one, finding nothing remarkable. The boxer briefs are white cotton with a crossover fly and elastic waistband, and I note nothing unusual, no stains or defects.

Spreading the coat open on the butcher paper–covered table, I slip my hands into the pockets, making sure nothing has been left in them, and I collect a clothing diagram and a clipboard and begin to make notes. The collar is a deep-pile synthetic fur and covered with dirt and sand and pieces of dry brown leaves that adhered to it when the man collapsed to the ground, and the heavy knit cuffs are dirty, too. The sage nylon shell is a very tough material, which appears to be tear-resistant and waterproof with a black fiberfill insulation, none of it easily penetrable unless the blade was strong and very sharp. I find no evidence of blood inside the liner of the coat, not even around the small slit in the back of it, but the areas of the outer shell, the shoulders, the sleeves, the back, are blackened and stiff with blood that collected in the bottom of the body pouch after the man was zipped inside it and then was transported to the CFC.

I don't know how long he might have bled out while he was inside the bag and then the cooler, but he didn't bleed from his wound. When I spread open the denim shirt, long-sleeved, a men's size small, which still smells faintly of a cologne or an after-shave, I find only a spot of dark blood that has dried stiffly around the slit made by the blade. What Marino and Anne have reported seems to be accurate, that the man began bleeding from his nose and mouth while he was fully clothed inside the body bag, his head turned to the side, probably the same side it was turned to when I examined him in the x-ray room a little while ago. Blood must have dripped steadily from his face into the bag, pooling in it and leaking from it, and I can see that easily when I look at it next, an adult-size cadaver pouch, typical of ones used by removal services, black with a nylon zipper. On the sides are webbing handles attached with rivets, and that's often where the problem with leakage oc-curs, assuming the bag is intact with no tears or flaws in the heat-sealed seams. Blood seeps through rivets, especially if the pouch is really cheap, and this one is about twenty-five dollars' worth of heavy-duty PVC, likely purchased by the case.

As I imagine what I just saw on the CT

scan and realize how quickly the damage occurred in what clearly was a blitz attack, the bleeding makes no sense at all. It makes even less sense than it did when Marino first told me about it in Dover. The massive destruction to the man's internal organs would have resulted in pulmonary hemorrhage that would have caused blood to drain out of the nose and mouth. But it should have happened almost instantly. I don't understand why he didn't bleed at the scene. When the paramedics were working to resuscitate him, he should have been bleeding from his face, and this would have been a clear indication that he hadn't dropped dead from an arrhythmia.

As I leave the autopsy room to go upstairs, I envision the video clips again and remember my wondering about his black gloves and why he put them on when he entered the park. Where are they? I haven't seen a pair of gloves. They weren't in the evidence locker or in the drying cabinet, and I checked the pockets of the coat and didn't find them. Based on what I saw in the recordings covertly made by the man's headphones, he had the gloves on when he died, and I envision what I saw on Lucy's iPad when I was riding in the van to the Civil Air Terminal. A black-gloved hand entered the frame as if the man was swatting at something and there was a jostling sound as his hand hit the headphones while his voice blurted out, *"What the . . . ? Hey . . . !"* Then bare trees rushing up and around, then chipped bits of slate looming large on the ground and the thud of him hitting, and then the hem of a long black coat flapping past. Then silence, then the voices of people surrounding him and exclaiming that he wasn't breathing.

The x-ray room door is closed when I get to it, and I check inside, but everyone is gone, the control room empty and quiet, the CT scanner glowing white in the low lights on the other side of the lead-lined glass. I pause to try the phone in there, hoping Anne might answer her cell, but if she's already at McLean and in the neuroimaging lab, it will be impossible to reach her through the thick concrete walls of that place. I am surprised when she answers.

"Where are you?" I ask, and I can hear music in the background.

"Pulling up now," she says, and she must be inside the van with Marino driving and the radio on.

"When you removed his clothing," I say, "did you see a pair of black gloves? He may have been wearing a pair of thick black gloves."

A pause, and I hear her say something to Marino and then I hear his voice, but I can't make out what they're saying to each other. Then she tells me, "No. And Marino says when he had the body in ID first thing, there were no gloves. He doesn't remember gloves."

"Tell me exactly what happened yesterday morning."

"Just sit right here for a minute," I hear her say to Marino. "No, not there yet or they'll come out. The security guys will. Just wait here," she says to him. "Okay," she says to me. "A little bit after seven yesterday morning, Dr. Fielding came to x-ray. As you know, Ollie and I are always in early, by seven, and anyway, he was concerned because of the blood. He'd noticed blood drips on the floor outside the cooler and also inside it, and that the body was bleeding or had bled. A lot of blood in the pouch."

"The body was still fully clothed."

"Yes. The coat was unzipped and the shirt was cut open, the EMTs did that, but he was clothed when he came in and nothing was done until Dr. Fielding went in there to get him ready for us."

"What do you mean, 'to get him ready'?"

I've never known Fielding to get a body ready for autopsy, to actually go to the trouble to move it out of the refrigerator and into x-ray or the autopsy room, at least not since the old days when he was in training. He leaves what he considers mundane tasks to those whom he still calls *dieners* and whom I call autopsy technicians.

"I only know he found the blood and then hurried to get us because he took the call from Cambridge PD, and as you know, it was assumed the guy was a sudden death that was natural, like an arrhythmia or a berry aneurysm or something."

"Then what?"

"Then Ollie and I looked at the body, and we called Marino and he came and looked, and it was decided not to scan him or do the post yet."

"He was left in the cooler?"

"No. Marino wanted to process him in ID first, to get his prints, swabs, so we could get started with IAFIS and DNA, with anything that might help us figure out who he is. The important point is there were no gloves at that time, because Marino would have had to take them off the body so he could print him."

"Then where are they?"

"He doesn't know, and I don't, either."

"Can you put him on, please?"

I hear her hand him the phone, and he says, "Yeah. I unzipped the pouch but didn't take him out of it, and there was a lot of blood in it, like you know."

"And you did what, exactly?"

"I printed him while he was in the pouch, and if there had been gloves, I sure as hell would have seen them."

"Possible the squad removed the gloves at the scene and put them inside the pouch and you didn't notice? And then they got misplaced somehow?"

"Nope. I looked for any personal effects, like I told you. The watch, ring, keychain, the stash box, the twenty-dollar bill. Took everything out of his pockets, and I always look inside the pouch for the very reason you just said. In case the squad or the removal service tucks something in there, like a hat or sunglasses or whatever. The headphones, too. And the satellite radio. They were in a paper bag and came in with the body."

"What about Cambridge PD? I know Investigator Lawless brought in the Glock."

"He receipted it to the firearms lab around ten a.m. That was all he brought in."

"And when Anne put his clothing inside

the drying cabinet, well, obviously she didn't have the gloves if you say they weren't there in the first place."

I hear him say something, and then Anne is back on the phone, saying, "No. I didn't see gloves when I put everything else in the cabinet. That was around nine p.m., almost four hours ago, when I undressed the body to get it ready for the scan, not long before you got to the CFC. I cleaned the cabinet to make sure it was sterile before I put his other clothing in there."

"I'm glad something's sterile. We need to clean my station."

"Okay, okay," she says, but not to me. "Wait. Jesus, Pete. Hold on."

And then Marino's voice in my ear: "There were other cases."

"I beg your pardon?"

"We had other cases yesterday morning. So maybe someone removed the gloves, but I got no friggin' idea why. Unless they maybe got picked up by mistake."

"Who did the cases?"

"Dr. Lambotte, Dr. Booker."

"What about Jack?"

"Two cases in addition to the guy from Norton's Woods," Marino says. "A woman who got hit by a train and an old guy who wasn't under the care of a physician. Jack didn't do shit, was gone with the wind," Marino says. "He doesn't bother with the scene, and so we get a body that starts bleeding in the fridge and now we got to prove the guy was dead."

9

The directorate of what officially is called the Cambridge Forensic Center and Port Mortuary is on the top floor, and I have discovered that it is difficult to tell people how to find me when a building is round.

The best I've been able to do on the infrequent occasions I've been here is to instruct visitors to get off the elevator on the seventh floor, take a left, and look for number 111. It's only one door down from 101, and to comprehend that 101 is the lowest room number on this floor and 111 is the highest requires some imagination. My office suite, therefore, would occupy a corner at the end of a long hallway if there were corners and long hallways, but there aren't. Up here there is just one big circle with six offices, a large conference room, the reading room for voice-recognition dictation, the library, the break room, and in the center a windowless bunker where

Lucy chose to put the computer and questioned documents lab.

Walking past Marino's office, I stop outside 111, what he calls CENTCOM, for Central Command. I'm sure Marino came up with the pretentious appellation all on his own, not because he thinks of me as his commander but rather he's come to think of himself as answering to a higher patriotic order that is close to a religious calling. His worship of all things military is new. It's just one more thing that is paradoxical about him, as if Peter Rocco Marino needs yet another paradox to define his inconsistent and conflicted self.

I need to calm down about him, I say to myself as I unlock my heavy door with its titanium veneer. He isn't so bad and didn't do anything so terrible. He's predictable, and I shouldn't be surprised in the least. After all, who understands him better than I do? The Rosetta stone to Marino isn't Bayonne, New Jersey, where he grew up a street fighter who became a boxer and then a cop. The key to him isn't even his worthless alcoholic father. Marino can be explained by his mother first and foremost, and then his childhood sweetheart Doris, now his ex-wife, both women seemingly docile and subservient and sweet but not harmless. Not hardly.

I push buttons to turn on the flush-mount lighting built into the struts of the geodesic glass dome that is energy-efficient and reminds me of Buckminster Fuller every time I look up. Were the famed architect-inventor still among the living, he would approve of my building and possibly of me but not of our morbid raison d'être, I suspect, although at this stage of things I would have a few quibbles with him, too. For example, I don't agree with his belief that technology can save us. Certainly, it isn't making us more civilized, and I actually think the opposite is true.

I pause on gunmetal-gray carpet just inside my doorway as if waiting for permission to enter, or maybe I'm hesitant because to appropriate this space is to embrace a life I've rather much put off for the better part of two years. If I'm honest about it I should say I've put it off for decades, since my earliest days at Walter Reed, where I was minding my own business in a cramped, windowless room of AFIP headquarters when Briggs walked in without knocking and dropped an eight-by-eleven gray envelope on my desk with *CLASSIFIED* stamped on it.

December 4, 1987. I remember it so

vividly I can describe what I was wearing and the weather and what I ate. I know I smoked a lot that day and had several straight Scotches at the end of it because I was excited and horrified. The case of all cases, and the DoD wanted me, picked me over all others. Or more accurately, Briggs did. By spring of the following year, I was discharged from the air force early, not on good behavior but because the Reagan administration wanted me gone, and I left under certain conditions that are shameful and cause pain even now. It is karmic that I find myself in a building of circles. Nothing has ended or begun in my life. What was far away is right next to me. Somehow it's all the same.

The most blatant sign of my six-month absence from a position I've yet to really fill is that Bryce's adjoining administrative office is comfortably cluttered while mine is empty and stark. It feels forlorn and lonely in here, my small conference table of brushed steel bare, not even a potted plant on it, and when I inhabit a space there are always plants. Orchids, gardenias, succulents, and indoor trees, such as areca and sago palms, because I want life and fragrances. But what I had in here when I moved in is gone and has been gone, overwatered and too much fertilizer. I gave Bryce detailed instructions and three months to kill everything. It took him less than two.

There is virtually nothing on my desk, a bow-shaped modular work station constructed of twenty-two-gauge steel with a black laminate surface and a matching hutch of file drawers and open shelves between expansive windows overlooking the Charles and the Boston skyline. A black granite countertop behind my Aeron chair runs the length of the wall and is home to my Leica Laser Microdissection System and its video displays and accoutrements, and nearby is my faithful backup Leica for daily use, a more basic laboratory research microscope that I can operate with one hand and without software or a training seminar. There isn't much else, no case files in sight, no death certificates or other paperwork for me to review and initial, no mail, and very few personal effects. I decide it's not a good thing to have such a perfectly arranged, immaculate office. I'd rather have a landfill. It's peculiar that being faced with an empty work space should make me feel so overwhelmed, and as I seal Erica Donahue's letter in a plastic bag I finally realize why I'm not a fan of a world that is fast becoming paperless. I like to see the enemy, stacks of what I must conquer, and I take comfort in reams of friends.

I'm locking the letter in a cabinet when Lucy silently appears like an apparition in a voluminous white lab coat she wears for its warmth and what she can conceal beneath it, and she's also fond of big pockets. The oversized coat makes her seem deceptively nonthreatening and much younger than her years, in her low thirties is the way she puts it, but she'll forever be a little girl to me. I wonder if mothers always feel that way about their daughters, even when the daughters are mothers themselves, or in Lucy's case, armed and dangerous.

She probably has a pistol tucked into the back waistband of her cargo pants, and I realize how selfishly happy I am that she's home. She's back in my life, not in Florida or with people I have to force myself to like. Manhattan prosecutor Jaime Berger is included in this mix. As I look at my niece, my surrogate only child, walking into my office, I can't avoid a truth I won't tell her. I'm glad if she and Jaime have called it quits. That's really why I haven't asked about it.

"Is Benton still with you?" I inquire.

"He's on the phone." She shuts the door

behind her.

"Who's he talking to at this hour?"

Lucy takes a chair, pulling her legs up on the seat, crossing them at the ankles. "Some of his people," she says, as if to imply he's talking to colleagues at McLean, but that's not it. Anne is handling the hospital, and she and Marino are there and getting started on the scan. Why would Benton be talking to them or anyone else at McLean?

"It's just the three of us, then," I comment pointedly. "Except for Ron, I assume. But if you want the door shut, I suppose that's fine." It's my way of letting her know that her hypervigilant and secretive behavior isn't lost on me and I wish she would explain it. I wish she would explain why she feels it necessary to be evasive if not blatantly untruthful to me, her aunt, her almost-mother, and now her boss.

"I know." She slides a small evidence pillbox out of her lab coat pocket.

"You know? What do you know?"

"That Anne and Marino went to McLean because you want an MRI. Benton filled me in. Why didn't you go?"

"I'm not needed and wouldn't be particularly helpful, since MR scans aren't my specialty." There is no MRI scanner at Dover's port mortuary, where most bodies

249

are war casualties and are going to have metal in them. "I thought I'd take care of a few things, and when I'm satisfied I know what I'm looking for, I'll get started on the autopsy."

"Kind of a backward way to look at things, when you stop to think about it," Lucy muses, her eyes green and intensely fixed on me. "It used to be you did the autopsy so you knew what you were looking for. Now it's just a confirmation of what you already know and a means of collecting evidence."

"Not exactly. I still get surprises. What's in the box?"

"Speaking of." She slides the small white box across the unobstructed surface of my ridiculously clean desk. "You can take it out and don't need gloves. But be careful with it."

Inside the box on a bed of cotton is what looks like the wing of an insect, possibly a fly.

"Go ahead, touch it," Lucy encourages, leaning forward in her chair, her face bright with excitement, as if she's watching me open a gift.

I feel the stiffness of wire struts and a thin transparent membrane, something like plastic. "Artificial. Interesting. What is this exactly, and where did you get it?"

"You familiar with the holy grail of fly-bots?"

"I confess I'm drawing a blank."

"Years and years of research. Millions and millions of research dollars spent on building the perfect flybot."

"Not intimately aware of it. Actually, I don't think I know what you're talking about."

"Equipped with micro-cameras and transmitters for covert surveillance, literally for bugging people. Or for detecting chemicals or explosives or possibly even biological hazards. The work's been going on at Harvard, MIT, Berkeley, a number of places here and overseas, even before cyborgs, those insects with embedded microelectromechanical systems, machine-insect interfaces. Which then spread to doing shit like that to other living creatures, like turtles, dolphins. Not DARPA's finest moments, you ask me."

I place the wing back on the square of cotton. "Let's back up. Start with where you got this."

"I'm worried."

"You and me both."

"When Marino had him in ID this morning" — Lucy means the dead man from

Norton's Woods — "I wanted to tell him about the recording system I discovered in the headphones, so I go downstairs. He's fingerprinting the body, and I notice what at a glance looks like a fly wing stuck to the guy's coat collar along with some other debris, like dirt and pieces of dead leaves from his being on the ground."

"It didn't get dislodged by the EMTs," I comment. "When they opened his coat."

"Obviously, it didn't. Was snagged on the fur, the fake-fur collar," Lucy says. "Something struck me about it, you know, I got a funny feeling and I took a closer look."

I get a hand lens out of my desk drawer and turn on an examination light, and in the bright illumination the magnified wing doesn't look natural anymore. What one would assume is the base of the wing, where it attaches to the body, is actually some sort of flexure joint, and the veins running through the wing tissue are shiny like wires.

"Probably a carbon composite, and there are fifteen joints in each wing drive, which is pretty amazing." Lucy describes what I'm seeing. "The wing itself is an electroactive polymer frame, which responds to electrical signals, causing the fanfold wings to flap as fast as the real deal, your everyday housefly. Historically, a flybot takes off vertically like a helicopter and flies like an angel, which has been one of its major design obstacles. That and coming up with something micromechanical that's autonomous but not bulky — in other words, biologically inspired so it has the necessary power to move around freely in whatever environment you put it in."

"Biologically inspired, like da Vinci's conceptualized inventions." I wonder if she is reminded of the exhibition I took her to in London and if she noticed the poster in the living room of the dead man's apartment. Of course she noticed. Lucy notices everything.

"The poster over the couch," she says.

"Yes, I saw it."

"In one of the video clips, when he was putting the leash on his dog. How creepy is that?" Lucy says.

"I'm not sure I know why it's creepy."

"Well, I had the luxury of looking at the recordings more carefully than you did." Lucy's demeanor again, the nuances I've come to recognize as surely as I detect the subtle changes in tissue under the microscope. "It's for the same exhibition you took me to at the Courtauld, has the date on it for that same summer," she says calmly and with a certain goal in mind. "We might have been there when he was, assuming he went."

That's the goal. This is what Lucy thinks. A connection between the dead man and us.

"Having the poster doesn't mean he did," she goes on. "I realize that. It doesn't mean it in a way that would hold up in court," she adds with a hint of irony, as if she's making a dig at Jaime Berger, the prosecutor I'm increasingly suspicious she's no longer with.

"Lucy, do you have some idea of who this man is?" I go ahead and ask.

"I just think it's bizarre to consider he might have been at that gallery when we were. But I'm certainly not saying he was. Not at all."

It's not what she really thinks. I can see it in her eyes and hear it in her voice. She suspects he might have been there when we were. How could she begin to conclude such a thing about a dead man whose name we don't know?

"You're not hacking again," I say bluntly, as if I'm asking about smoking or drinking or some other habit that could be bad for her health.

I've thought more than once that Lucy might have found a way to trace the covertly recorded video files to a personal computer or server somewhere. To her, a firewall and other security measures to protect proprietary data are nothing more than a speed bump on the road to getting what she wants.

"I'm not a hacker," she says simply.

That's not an answer, I think but don't say.

"I just find it an unusual coincidence that he might have been at the Courtauld when we were," she goes on. "And I think it's likely he has that poster because he has some connection to that exhibit. You can't buy them now. I checked. Who would have one unless they went or someone close to them did?"

"Unless he's much older than he looks, he would have been a child then," I point out. "That was in the summer of 2001."

I'm reminded that the time on his watch was five hours ahead of what it should have been for this part of the world. It was set for the United Kingdom's time zone, and the exhibition was in London. That proves nothing. *A consistency but not evidence,* I tell myself.

"That exhibit was exactly the kind of thing a precocious little inventor in the making would love," Lucy says.

"The same way you did," I reply. "I think you walked through it four times. And you bought the lecture series on CD, you were so enthralled."

"It's quite a thought. A little boy in the gallery at the exact moment we were."

"You say that as if it's a fact." I continue to push the same point.

"And almost a decade later I'm here, you're here, and his dead body is here. Talk about six degrees of separation."

It jolts me to hear her refer to something else I was thinking about earlier. First the London exhibit, now the great web that is all of us, the way lives around the planet somehow interconnect.

"I never really get used to it," she is saying. "Seeing someone and then later they're murdered. Not that I can envision him as a boy at a gallery in London, not that I see some little kid's face in my mind. But I might have been standing next to him or even talked to him. In retrospect it's always hard to comprehend that if you had known what was ahead, maybe you could have changed someone's destiny. Or your own."

"Did Benton tell you the man from Norton's Woods was murdered, or did you get that from someone else?"

"We were catching up."

"And you told him about the flybot while you were just now catching up inside your lab." It's not a question.

I feel sure she's told Benton about the robotic fly wing and whatever else she thinks he should know. She's the one who was emphatic in the helicopter a little while ago that he is the only person she really trusts right now, except for me. Although I don't exactly feel trusted. I sense she is sifting through information and selective about what she offers when I wish she wouldn't hold back. I wish she wouldn't be evasive or lie. But one thing I've learned about Lucy is that wishing makes nothing true. I can wish my life away with her and it won't change her behavior. It won't change what she thinks or does.

I turn off the lamp and return the small white box to her. "What do you mean, 'flies like an angel'?"

"Those artistic renderings of angels hovering. I know you've seen them." Lucy reaches for a pad of call sheets and a pen neatly placed next to the phone. "Their bodies are vertical, like someone with a jet pack on, as opposed to insects and birds, whose bodies are horizontal in flight. These little flybots fly vertically, like angels, and that's been one of their flaws, that and their size. Finding the solution is what I mean by 'holy grail.' It's eluded the best and the brightest."

She sketches something to show me, a stick figure that looks like a cross flying through the air.

"If you want an insect like a common housefly to literally be a fly on the wall conducting covert surveillance," she continues, "it should look like a fly, not like a tiny body that's upright with wings attached. If I were having a meeting in Iran with Ahmadinejad and something flew by vertically and landed vertically on a windowsill like a micro–Tinker Bell, I believe I'd notice it and be slightly suspicious."

"If you were meeting with Ahmadinejad in Iran, I'd be slightly suspicious for a lot of reasons. Forgetting why my patient had the wing of one of these things on his coat, assuming this wing is part of an intact flybot —" I start to say.

"Not exactly a flybot," she interrupts. "Not necessarily a spybot, either. That's what I'm getting to. I think this is the holy grail."

"Then whatever it is, what might it have been used for?"

"Let your imagination be the limit," she answers. "I could make quite a list but can't know definitively, not from one wing, although I can tell a few things that are significant. Unfortunately, I couldn't find the rest of it."

"You mean on the body, on his coat? Find it where?"

"At the scene."

"You went to Norton's Woods."

"Sure," she says. "As soon as I realized what the wing was from. Of course I headed straight there."

"We were together for hours." I remind her that she could have told me before now. "Just you and me in the cockpit all the way here from Dover."

"Funny thing about the intercom. Even when I'm sure it's off in back, I'm still not sure. Not if it's something I can't afford having anyone overhear. Marino shouldn't know about this." She indicates the small white box with the wing in it.

"Why exactly?"

"Believe me, you don't want him to know a damn thing about it. It's a very small piece of something a lot bigger, in more ways than one."

She goes on to assure me that Marino knows nothing about her going to Norton's Woods. He is unaware of the tiny mechanical wing or that it was a motivating factor in her encouraging him to bring me home from Dover early, to safely escort me in her helicopter. She didn't mention any of this to me until now, she continues to explain, because she doesn't trust anyone at the moment. Except Benton, she adds. And me, she adds. And she's very careful where she has certain conversations, and all of us should be careful.

"Unless the area has been cleared," she says, and what she means is swept, and the implication is that my office is safe or we wouldn't be having this conversation inside it.

"You checked my office for surveillance devices?" I'm not shocked. Lucy knows how to sweep an area for hidden recorders because she knows how to spy. The best burglar is a locksmith. "Because you think who might be interested in bugging my office?"

"Not sure who's interested in what or why."

"Not Marino," I then say.

"Well, that would be as obvious as a Radio-Shack nanny cam if he did it. Of course not. I'm not worried about him doing something like that. I just worry that he can't keep his mouth shut," Lucy replies. "At least not when it comes to certain people."

"You talked about MORT in the helicopter. You weren't worried about the intercom, about Marino, when it came to MORT."

"Not the same thing. Not even close," she says. "Doesn't matter if Marino runs his mouth to certain people about a robot in the guy's apartment. Other people already know about it, you can rest assured of that. I can't have Marino talk about my little friend." She looks at the small white box. "And he wouldn't mean anything bad. But he doesn't understand certain realities about certain people. Especially General Briggs and Captain Avallone."

"I didn't realize you knew anything about her." I've never mentioned Sophia Avallone to Lucy.

"When she was here. Jack showed her around. Marino bought her lunch, was kissing her uniformed ass. He doesn't get it about people like that, about the fucking Pentagon, for that matter, or someone he stupidly assumes is one of us, you know, is safe."

I'm relieved she realizes it, but I don't want to encourage her to distrust Marino, not even slightly. She's been through enough with him and finally they are friends again, close like they were when she was a child and he taught her to drive his truck and to shoot and she aggravated the hell out of him and it was mutual. She gets science from my genetics, but she gets her affinity

261

for cop stuff, as she refers to it, from him. He was the big, tough detective in her life when she was a know-it-all difficult wunderkind, and he has loved and hated her as many different times as she has loved and hated him. But friends and colleagues now. Whatever it takes to keep it that way. *Be careful what you say,* I tell myself. *Let there be peace.*

"From which I conclude Briggs doesn't know about this." I indicate the small white box on my desk. "And Captain Avallone doesn't."

"I don't see how."

"Is my office bugged right now?"

"Our conversation is completely safe," she replies, and it isn't an answer.

"What about Jack? Possible he knows about the flybot? Well, you didn't tell him."

"No damn way."

"So unless someone's called him looking for it. Or maybe its wing."

"You mean if the killer called here looking for a missing flybot," Lucy says. "And I'm just going to call it that for purposes of simplicity, although it's not just a garden-variety flybot. That would be pretty stupid. That would imply the caller had something to do with the guy's homicide."

"We can't rule out anything. Sometimes

killers are stupid," I reply. "If they're desperate enough."

Lucy gets up and goes into my private bathroom, where there is a single-cup coffeemaker on a counter. I hear her filling the tank with tap water and checking the small refrigerator. It is almost one a.m. and the snow hasn't eased up, is falling hard and fast, and when the small flakes blow against the windows, the sound is like sand blasting the glass.

"Skim milk or cream?" Lucy calls out from what is supposed to be my private changing area, which includes a shower. "Bryce is such a good wife. He stocked your refrigerator."

"I still drink it black." I start opening my desk drawers, not sure what I'm looking for.

I think about my sloppy work station in the autopsy room. I think of people helping themselves to what they shouldn't.

"Yeah, well, then why is there milk and cream?" Lucy's loud voice. "Green Mountain or Black Tiger? There's also hazelnut. Since when do you drink hazelnut?" The questions are rhetorical. She knows the answers.

"Since never," I mutter, seeing pencils, pens, Post-its, paper clips, and in a bottom drawer, a pack of spearmint gum.

It is half-full, and I don't chew gum. Who likes spearmint gum and would have reason to go into my desk? Not Bryce. He's much too vain to chew gum, and if I caught him doing it, I would disapprove, because I consider it rude to chew gum in front of other people. Besides, Bryce wouldn't root around inside my desk, not without permission. He wouldn't dare.

"Jack likes hazelnut, French vanilla, shit like that, and he drinks it with skim milk unless he's on one of his high-protein, high-fat diets," Lucy continues from inside my bathroom. "Then he uses real cream, heavy cream, like what's in here. I suppose if you had guests, were expecting visitors, you might have cream."

"Nothing flavored, and please make it strong."

"He's a superuser just like you are," Lucy's voice then says. "His fingerprints are stored in every lock in this place just like yours are."

I hear the spewing of hot water shooting through the K-Cup and use it as a welcome interruption. I refuse to engage in the poisonous speculation that Jack Fielding has been in my office during my absence, that maybe he's been helping himself while he drinks coffee, chews gum, or who the hell knows what he's been up to. But as I look around, it doesn't seem possible. My office feels unlived-in. It certainly doesn't appear as if anyone has been working in here, so what would he be doing?

"I went over to Norton's Woods before Cambridge PD did, you know. Marino asked them to go back because of the serial number being eradicated from the Glock. But I got there first." Lucy talks on loudly from inside the bathroom. "But I had the disadvantage of not knowing exactly where the guy went down, where he was stabbed, we now know. Without the scene photographs, it's impossible to get an exact location, just an approximate one, so I combed every footpath in the park."

She walks out with steaming coffee in black mugs that have the AFME's unusual crest, a five-card poker draw of aces and eights, known as the dead man's hand, what Wild Bill Hickok supposedly was holding when he was shot to death.

"Talk about a needle in a haystack," she continues. "The flybot's probably half the size of a small paper clip, about the size of, well, a housefly. No joy."

"Just because you found a wing doesn't mean the rest of it was ever out there," I remind her as she sets a coffee in front of me.

"If it's out there, it's maimed." Lucy returns to her chair. "Under snow as we speak and missing a wing. But very possibly still alive, especially when it gets exposed to light, assuming it's not further damaged."

" 'Alive'?"

"Not literally. Likely powered by micro–solar panels as opposed to a battery that would already be dead. Light hits it and abracadabra. That's the way everything is headed. And our little friend, wherever he is, is futuristic, a masterpiece of teeny-tiny technology."

"How can you be so sure if you can't find most of it? Just a wing."

"Not just any wing. The angle and flexure joints are ingenious and suggest to me a different flight formation. Not the flight of an angel anymore. But horizontal like a real insect flies. Whatever this thing is and whatever its function, we're talking about something extremely advanced, something

I've never seen before. Nothing's been published about it, because I get pretty much every technical journal there is online, plus I've been running searches with no success. By all indications, it's a project that's classified, top secret. I sure hope the rest of it is out there on the ground somewhere, safely covered with snow."

"What was it doing in Norton's Woods in the first place?" I envision the black-gloved hand entering the frame of the hidden video camera, as if the man was swatting at something.

"Right. Did he have it, or did someone else?" She blows on her coffee, holding the mug in both hands.

"And is someone looking for it? Does someone think it's here or think we know where it is?" I ask that again. "Has anyone mentioned to you that his gloves are gone? Did you happen to notice when you were downstairs while Marino was printing the body? It appears the victim put on a pair of black gloves as he arrived at the park, which I thought was curious when I watched the video clips. I assume he died with the gloves on, and so where are they?"

"That's interesting," Lucy says, and I can't tell if she already knew the gloves are missing.

I can't tell what she knows and if she's lying.

"They weren't in the woods when I was walking around yesterday morning," she informs me. "I would have seen a pair of black gloves, saying they were accidentally left by the squad, the removal service, the cops. Of course, they could have been and were picked up by anybody who happened along."

"In the video clips, someone wearing a long black coat walks past right after the man falls to the ground. Is it possible whoever killed him paused just long enough to take his gloves?"

"You mean if they're some type of data gloves or smart gloves, what they're using in combat, gloves with sensors embedded in them for wearable computer systems, wearable robotics," Lucy says, as if it is a normal thing to consider about a pair of missing gloves.

"I'm just wondering why his gloves might be important enough for someone to take them, if that's what's happened," I reply.

"If they have sensors in them and that's how he was controlling the flybot, assuming the flybot is his, then the gloves would be extremely important," Lucy says.

"And you didn't ask about the gloves

when you were downstairs with Marino? You didn't think to check gloves, clothing, for sensors that might be embedded?"

"If I had the gloves, I would have had a much better chance of finding the flybot when I went back to Norton's Woods," Lucy says. "But I don't have them or know where they are, if that's what you're asking."

"I am asking that because it would be tampering with evidence."

"I didn't. I promise. I don't know for a fact that the gloves are data gloves, but if they are, it would make sense in light of other things. Like what he's saying on the video clip right before he dies," she adds thoughtfully, working it out, or maybe she's already worked it out but is leading me to believe what she's saying is a new thought. "The man keeps saying, 'Hey, boy.' "

"I assumed he was talking to his dog."

"Maybe. Maybe not."

"And he said other things I couldn't figure out," I recall. " 'And for you' or 'Do you send one' or something like that. Could a robotic fly understand voice commands?"

"Absolutely possible. That part was muffled. I heard it, too, and thought it was confusing," Lucy says. "But maybe not if he was controlling the flybot. 'For you' could be *four-two*, maybe, as in the number four?

'And' could be *N,* as in north? I'll listen again and do more enhancement."

"More?"

"I've done some. Nothing helpful. Could be he was telling the flybot GPS coordinates, which would be a common command to give a device that responds to voice — if you're telling it where to go, for example."

"If you could figure out GPS coordinates, maybe you could find the location, find where it is."

"Sincerely doubt it. If the flybot was controlled by the gloves, at least partially controlled by sensors in them, then when the victim waved his hand, probably at the moment he was stabbed?"

"Right. Then what?"

"I don't know, but I don't have the flybot, and I don't have the gloves," Lucy says to me while looking at me intently, her eyes directly on mine. "I didn't find them, but I sure wish I had."

"Did Marino mention that someone may have been following Benton and me after we left Hanscom?" I ask.

"We looked for the big SUV with xenon lights and fog lamps. I'm not saying it means anything, but Jack's got a dark-blue Navigator. Pre-owned, bought it back in October. You weren't here, so I guess you haven't seen it."

"Why would Jack follow us? And no. I don't know anything about him buying a Navigator. I thought he had a Jeep Cherokee."

"Traded up, I guess." She drinks her coffee. "I didn't say he would follow you or did. Or that he would be stupid enough to ride your bumper. Except in a blizzard or fog, when visibility's really bad, a rather inexperienced tail might follow too close if the person doesn't know where the target is going. I don't see why Jack would bother. Wouldn't he assume you were on your way here?"

"Do you have an idea why anyone would bother?"

"If someone knows the flybot is missing," she says, "he or she sure as hell's looking for it, and possibly would spare nothing to find it before it gets into the wrong hands. Or the right hands. Depending on who or what we're dealing with. I can say that much based on a wing. If that's why you were followed, it would make me less likely to suspect that whoever killed this guy found the flybot. In other words, it could very well still be missing or lost. I probably don't need to tell you that a top-secret proprietary technical invention like this could be worth a fortune, especially if someone could steal the idea and take credit for it. If such a person is looking for it and has reason to fear it may have come in with the body, maybe this person wanted to see where you were going, what you were up to. He or she might think the flybot is here at the CFC or might think you have it off-site somewhere. Including at your house."

"Why would I have it at my house? I haven't been home."

"Logic has nothing to do with it when someone is in overdrive," Lucy answers. "If I were the person looking, I might assume you instructed your former FBI husband to hide the flybot at your house. I might assume all kinds of things. And if the flybot is still at large, I'm still going to be looking."

I remember what the man exclaimed, can hear his voice in my head. *"What the . . . ? Hey . . . !"* Maybe his startled reaction wasn't due solely to the sudden sharp pain in his lower back and tremendous pressure in his chest. Maybe something flew at his face. Maybe he had on data gloves, and his startled reaction is what caused the flybot to get broken. I imagine a tiny device mid-flight, and then struck by the man's black gloved hand and crushed against his coat collar.

"If someone has the data gloves and looked for the flybot before the snow started, is it really possible the person wouldn't have found it?" I ask my niece.

"Sure, it's possible. Depends on a number of things. How badly damaged it is, for example. There was a lot of activity around the man after he went down. If the flybot was there on the ground, it could have been crushed or damaged further and rendered completely unresponsive. Or it could be under something or in a tree or a bush or anywhere out there."

"I assume a robotic insect could be used as a weapon," I suggest. "Since I don't have a clue what caused this man's internal injuries, I need to think about every possibility imaginable."

"That's the thing," Lucy says. "These days, almost anything you can imagine is possible."

"Did Benton tell you what we saw on CT?"

"I don't see how a micromechanical insect could cause internal damage like that," Lucy answers. "Unless the victim was somehow injected with a micro-explosive device."

My niece and her phobias. Her obsession with explosives. Her acute distrust of government.

"And I sure as hell hope not," she says. "Actually, we'd be talking about nanoexplosives if a flybot was involved."

My niece and her theories about superthermite, and I remember Jaime Berger's comment the last time I saw her at Thanksgiving when all of us were in New York, having dinner in her penthouse apartment. "Love doesn't conquer all," Berger said. "It can't possibly," she said as she drank too much wine and spent a lot of time in the kitchen, arguing with Lucy about 9/11, about explosives used in demolitions, nanomaterials painted on infrastructures that would cause a horrendous destruction if impacted by large planes filled with fuel.

I have given up reasoning with my phobic, cynical niece, who is too smart for her own good and won't listen. It doesn't matter to her that there simply aren't enough facts to support what has her convinced, only allegations about residues found in the dust right after the towers collapsed. Then, weeks later, more dust was collected and it showed the same residues of iron oxide and aluminum, a highly energetic nanocomposite that is used in making pyrotechnics and explosives. I admit there have been credible scientific journal articles written about it, but not enough of them, and they don't begin to prove that our own government helped mastermind 9/11 as an excuse to start a war in the Middle East.

"I know how you feel about conspiracy theories," Lucy says to me. "That's a big difference between us. I've seen what the so-called good guys can do."

She doesn't know about South Africa. If she did, she would realize there isn't a difference between the two of us. I know all too well what so-called good guys can do. But not 9/11. I won't go that far, and I think of Jaime Berger and imagine how difficult it would be for the powerful and established Manhattan prosecutor to have Lucy as a partner. Love doesn't conquer all. It really is true. Maybe Lucy's paranoia about 9/11 and the country we live in have driven her back into a personal isolation that historically is never broken for long. I really thought Jaime was the one, that it would last. I now feel certain it hasn't. I want to tell Lucy I'm sorry for that and I'm always here for her and will talk about anything she wants, even if it goes against my beliefs. Now is not the time.

"I think we need to consider that we might be dealing with some renegade scientist or maybe more than one of them up to no good," Lucy then tells me. "That's the big point I'm trying to make. And I mean serious no good, extreme no good, Aunt Kay."

It relieves me to hear her call me Aunt Kay. I feel all is right with us when she calls me Aunt Kay, and she rarely does it anymore. I don't remember the last time she did. When I'm her Aunt Kay I can almost ignore what Lucy Farinelli is, which is a genius who is marginally sociopathic, a diagnosis that Benton scoffs at, nicely but firmly. Being marginally sociopathic is like being marginally pregnant or marginally dead, he says. I love my niece more than my own life, but I've come to accept that when she is well behaved, it is an act of will or simply because it suits her. Morals have very little to do with it. It's all about the end justifying the means.

I study her carefully, even though I won't see what's there. Her face never gives away information that could really hurt her.

I say to her, "I need to go ahead and ask you one thing."

"You can ask more than one." She smiles and doesn't look capable of hurting anything or anyone unless you recognize the strength and agility in her calm hands and the rapid changes in her eyes as thoughts flash behind them like lightning.

"You aren't involved in whatever this is." I mean the small white box and the flybot wing inside it. I mean the dead man who is getting an MRI at McLean — someone we may have crossed paths with at a da Vinci exhibition in London months before 9/11, which Lucy incredibly believes was orchestrated from within our own government.

"Nope." She says it simply and doesn't flinch or look the slightest bit uncomfortable.

"Because you're here now." I remind her she works for the CFC, meaning she works for me, and I answer to the governor of Massachusetts, the Department of Defense, the White House. I answer to a lot of people, I tell her. "I can't have —"

"Of course you can't. I'm not going to get you into trouble."

"It isn't just you anymore —"

"No need to have this conversation," she interrupts again, and her eyes blaze. They are so green they don't look real. "Anyway, he doesn't have thermal injury, right? No burns?"

"None that I can see so far. That's correct," I reply.

"Okay. So if someone poked him with a modified shark bang stick? You know, one of those speargun shafts with something like a shotgun cartridge attached to the tip? Only in this case, a tiny, tiny charge containing nanoexplosives?"

I push the power button to start my desktop computer. "It wouldn't look like what I just saw. It would look like a contact gunshot wound minus the patterned abrasion made by the muzzle of a gun. Even if we're talking about using nanoexplosives as opposed to some type of firearm ammunition on the tip of a shaft or something shaft-like, you're right, you'd see thermal injury. There should be burns at the entrance and also to underlying tissue. I assume you're implying something like a flybot could be used to deliver nanoexplosives. Is that what you fear this so-called renegade scientist or more than one of them might be doing?"

"Deliver. Detonate. Nanoexplosives, drugs, poisons. Like I said, let your imagination be the limit what a device like this might be capable of."

"I need to take a look at the security footage that shows the body bag leaking." As I look for files in my computer. "I'm not going to have to go see Ron for that, am I?"

Lucy comes around to my side of the desk and starts typing on my keyboard, entering her system administrator's password that grants complete access to my kingdom.

279

"Easy as pie." She taps a key to open a file.

"Nobody could get into my files without your knowing."

"Not in cyberspace. But I can't know if someone's been in your physical space, especially since I'm not up here all the time, in fact, not even most of the time, because I work remotely when I can," she says, but I'm not sure I believe she wouldn't know.

In fact, I don't believe it.

"But no way anyone has gotten into your password-protected files," she says, and that I do believe. Lucy wouldn't permit it. "You can monitor the security cameras from anywhere, by the way. Even from your iPhone if you want. All you need is access to the Internet. I found this earlier and saved it as a file. Five-forty-two p.m. That's what time it was yesterday when this was captured by a closed-caption security camera in the receiving area."

She clicks on play and turns up the volume, and I watch two attendants in winter coats pushing a stretcher bearing a black body bag along the lower level's gray tile hallway.

Wheels click as they park the stretcher in front of the cooler, and now I can see Janelle, stocky with short brunette hair, tough-looking with a surprising number of tattoos, as best I recall. Someone Fielding found and hired.

Janelle opens the massive stainless-steel door, and I hear the rush of blowing air.

"Put it . . ." She points, and I notice she is wearing her coat, a dark jacket with *FORENSICS* in large, bright yellow letters on the back. She's in scene clothes, including a CFC baseball cap, as if she's going out in the cold or just came in.

"That tray there?" an attendant asks as he and his partner lift the body bag off the stretcher. The bag bends freely as they carry it, the body inside it as flexible as in life. "Shit, he's dripping. Dammit. He'd better not have AIDS or something. On my pants, my damn shoes."

"The lower one." Janelle directs them to a tray inside the cooler, stepping out of the way and not interested that blood is dripping from the body bag and spotting the gray floor. She doesn't seem to notice.

"Janelle the magnificent," Lucy comments as the video recording ends abruptly.

"Do you have the MLI log?" I want to see what time the medicolegal investigator — in other words, Janelle — came and went yesterday. "Obviously, she was on call during the evening?"

281

"She worked a double shift on Sunday, worker bee that she is," Lucy says. "Filled in for Randy, who was scheduled for evenings over the weekend but called in sick. Meaning he stayed home to watch the Super Bowl."

"I hope not."

"And Dandy Randy's not here now because of the weather. Supposedly on call at home. Must be nice to have a take-home SUV and get paid for staying home," Lucy says, and I hear the contempt in her flinty tone and see it in the hardness of her face. "I guess you can tell you got your work cut out for you. Assuming you ever quit making excuses for people."

"I don't make them for you."

"That's because there aren't any."

I look at the log Janelle kept yesterday, a template on my video display that has very few fields filled in.

"I don't mean to state what's as plain as the nose on my face, but there's not much you really know about what goes on," Lucy says. "You don't know the finer points of the day-to-day in this place. How could you?" She returns to her side of the desk and picks up her coffee, but she doesn't sit back down. "You haven't been here. You've sort of never been here since we opened for business."

"This is it? This is the entire log for Sunday?"

"Yup. Janelle came in at four. If what she entered into the log is to be believed." Lucy stands there, drinking her coffee, eyeing me. "And she runs with quite a pack, by the way. Forensic fuck buddies. Most of them cops, a few of them data-entry and clerical. Whoever she can be a hero to. You know she's on a dodgeball team? What kind of person plays dodgeball? Someone with finesse."

"If she came in at four, why is she dressed in scene clothes, including her jacket? As if she just came in from the cold?"

"Like I said, if what she entered in the log is to be believed."

"And David was on before that and didn't respond to anything, either?" I ask. "Jack could have sent him to Norton's Woods. David was sitting right here, so why didn't Jack tell him to go to the scene? It's maybe fifteen minutes from here."

"And you don't know that, either." Lucy walks into the bathroom and rinses her mug. "You don't know if David was sitting right here," she says as she walks back out and hovers near my closed office door. "I don't want to be the one to tell you . . ."

"It would seem you are the only one to tell me. No one else is telling me a damn thing," I reply. "What the hell is happening around here? People just show up when they feel like it?"

"Pretty much. The other MEs, the MLIs, in and out, marching to their own drummer. It trickles down from the top."

"It trickles down from Jack."

"At least on your side of things. The labs are another story, because he's not interested in them. Except firearms." She leans against the closed door, slipping her hands into the pockets of her lab coat.

"He's supposed to be in charge in my absence. Jack's the codirector of the entire CFC Port Mortuary." I can't keep the protest out of my tone, the note of outrage.

"Not interested in the labs, and scientists don't pay any attention to him, anyway. Except firearms, like I said. You know Fielding and guns, knives, crossbows, hunting bows. Never met a weapon he didn't love. So he messes with the firearms and tool-mark lab and has managed to fuck them up, too. Piss off Morrow until he's on the verge of quitting. I do know he's actively looking for another job, and there's no good reason his lab didn't finish with the Glock the dead guy had on him. The eradicated serial number. Shit. He bolted out of here this morning and didn't bother."

"He bolted out of here?"

"He was driving off when I was returning from Norton's Woods. This was about ten-thirty."

"Did you talk to him?"

"No. Maybe he wasn't feeling well. I don't know, but I don't understand why he didn't make sure someone took care of the Glock. Using acid on a drilled-off serial number? How long does that take to at least try? He must have known it was important."

"He might not have," I answer. "If the Cambridge detective is the only one who talked to him, why would he think the Glock was important? At that time, no one had a clue the man from Norton's Woods was a homicide."

"Well, I guess that's a relevant point. Morrow probably doesn't even know we went to get you, that you're back from Dover. Fielding vanished, too, when he knew damn well there was a major problem that most people with a brain in their head would decide was his fault. He's the one who took the call about the guy in Norton's Woods. He's the one who didn't go to the scene or make sure somebody did. The reason Janelle is dressed for the great outdoors, in my opinion? She didn't get here at four, the time she entered into the log. She got here just in time to let in the attendants and sign in the body and then turned right around and left. I can find out. There will be an entry for when she disabled the alarm to enter the building. Depends on whether you want to make a federal case out of it."

"I'm surprised Marino hasn't made sure I know the extent of the problems." It's all I can think to say. The inside of my head has gone dark.

"Like the boy crying wolf," Lucy says, and it's true.

Marino complains so much about so many people, I scarcely hear him. Now we're back to my failures. I haven't paid attention. I haven't listened. Maybe I wouldn't have listened no matter who told me.

"I've got a few things to take care of. You know how to find me," Lucy says, and she opens my door and leaves it open after she walks out.

I pick up the phone and try Fielding's numbers again. I don't leave any messages this time, and it crosses my mind that his wife isn't answering their home phone, either. She would see my office name and number on caller ID. Maybe that's why she doesn't pick up, because she knows it's me. Or maybe his family has gone somewhere, is out of town. On a Monday night in the middle of a snowstorm, when he knows damn well I've rushed home from Dover to take care of an emergency case?

I walk out and scan my thumb to unlock the door to the right of mine. I stand inside my deputy chief's office and slowly scan it as if it is a crime scene.

11

I picked his office, insisting on one as nice as mine, generously large, with a private shower. He has a river and city view, although his shades are down, which I find unnerving. He must have closed them when it was still light out, and I don't know why he would do that. Not for a good reason, I think. Whatever Jack Fielding has done, it all bodes badly.

I walk around and open each shade, and through expansive glass that is a reflective gray tint, I can make out the blurred lights of downtown Boston and billowing waves of freezing moisture, an icy snow that clicks and bites like teeth. The tops of high-rises, the Prudential and Hancock towers are obscured, and gusting wind moans in low tones around the dome over my head. Below, Memorial Drive is churned up by traffic, even at this hour, and the Charles is formless and black. I wonder how deep the snow is by now and how deep it will get before it moves off to the south. I wonder if Fielding will ever return to this room I designed and furnished for him, and somehow it feels that he won't, even though there is no evidence he's gone for good.

The biggest difference between our work spaces is his is crowded with reminders of the occupant, his various degrees, certificates, and commendations, his collectibles on shelves, autographed baseballs and bats, tae kwon do trophies and plaques, and models of fighter planes and a piece from a real one that crashed. I go over to his desk and survey Civil War relics: a belt buckle, a mess kit, a powder horn, a few minié balls that I remember him collecting during our early days in Virginia. But there are no photographs, and that makes me sad. In some places I can see what's gone in blank spaces of wall where he's not bothered to fill in the tiny holes left from hanging hooks he removed.

It stings that he no longer displays familiar pictures taken when he was my forensic pathology fellow, candid shots of us in the morgue or the two of us out at death scenes with Marino, the lead homicide detective for Richmond PD in the late eighties, the early nineties, when both Fielding and I were just getting started, although in completely different ways. He was the good-looking doctor beginning his career, while I was shifting mine into the private sector, transitioning into civilian life and the role of chief, doing my best not to look back. Maybe Fielding isn't looking back, although I don't know why. His old days were good days compared to mine. He didn't help cover up a crime. He's never had anything on par with that to hide from. Not that I know of, but I have to wonder. What do I know anymore?

Not much, except I sense he's gotten rid of me, maybe gotten rid of all of us. I sense he's gotten rid of more than he ever has before. It is something I'm convinced of without knowing exactly why. Certainly his personal property is still here, his Gore-Tex rain suit on a hanger, and his neoprene hip waders, his dive bag of scuba gear and scene case stowed in a closet, and his collection of police patches and police and military challenge coins. I remember helping him move into this office. I even helped him arrange his furniture, both of us complaining and laughing and then griping some more as we moved the desk, then his conference table, then moved them again and again.

"What is this, Laurel and Hardy?" he said.

"You going to push a mule up the stairs next?"

"You don't have stairs."

"I'm thinking of getting a horse," he said as we moved the same chairs we'd just moved earlier. "There's a horse farm about a mile from the house. I could board the horse there, maybe ride it to work, to crime scenes."

"I'll add that to the employee handbook. No horses."

We joked and teased each other, and he looked good that day — vital and optimistic, his muscles straining against the short sleeves of his scrubs. He was just incredibly built and healthy-looking then, his face still boyishly handsome, his dark blond hair messy, and he hadn't shaved for several days. He was sexy and funny, and I remember the whispers and giggles of some of the female staff as they walked past his open door, finding excuses to stare at him. Fielding seemed so happy to be here and with me, and I remember both of us placing photographs and reminiscing about our early days together — photographs that now are gone.

In their place are ones I don't recall. The pictures are prominently arranged on his shelves and walls, formal poses of him with politicians and military brass, one with General Briggs and even Captain Avallone, perhaps from the tour Fielding gave her. He looks wooden and bored. In a photograph of him in tae kwon do white, mid-flight and kicking an imagined enemy, he looks angry. He looks red-faced and hateful. As I study recent family portraits, I decide he doesn't look content in them, either, not even when he is holding his two little girls or has his arm around his wife, Laura, a delicate blonde whose prettiness is eroding, as if a trying existence is mapping its course on her physically, etching lines and furrows into a topography that once was graceful and smooth.

She is number three for him, and I can trace his decline as I scan his captured moments in chronological order. When he married her, he looked energetic, with no sign of a rash, and he didn't have any unseemly bald patches. I pause to admire how amazing he was, shirtless and as hard-bodied as stone in running shorts, washing his Mustang, a '67, cherry red with Le Mans stripes down the center of the hood. Then as recently as this past fall, the thickening around his middle; the splotchy, flushed skin; the strands of hair combed back and held in place with gel to hide his alopecia.

At a martial arts competition not even a month ago, he doesn't look as fit or as spiritually balanced in his grandmaster's uniform and black belt. He doesn't look like someone who finds joy in beautiful form or technique. He doesn't look like someone who honors other people or has self-control or respect for anything. He looks dissipated. He looks slightly deranged. He looks perfectly miserable.

Why? I silently ask that earlier photograph of him with his prized car, when he was stunning to behold and seemed carefree and vital, the sort of man it would be easy to fall in love with or to place in charge or to trust with your life. *What changed? What made you so unhappy? What was it this time?* He hates working for me. He hated it the last time, in Watertown, where he didn't stay long, and now the CFC, and he hates that more, it's obvious. This past late summer, when he started looking so bad, is when we finally opened our doors to criminal justice, taking cases. But I wasn't even in Massachusetts then, just one weekend over Labor Day. It can't be my fault. It's always been my fault. I've always blamed myself for Fielding's downfalls, and he's had more of them than I care to count.

I pick him up and he falls again, only

harder each time. It gets uglier. It gets bloodier. Again and again. Like a child who can't walk, and I won't accept it until he's injured beyond fixing. The drama that will always end predictably is the way Benton has described it. Fielding shouldn't be a forensic pathologist, and it's because of me that he is. He would have been better off if he'd never met me in the spring of 1988 when he wasn't sure what he wanted in life and I said I know what you should do. Let me show you. Let me teach you. If he'd never come to Richmond, if he'd never run into me, he might have picked a way to spend his days that would have suited him. His career, his life, would have been about him and not about me.

That really is the bottom line, that he does the best he can in an environment totally destructive to him and finally can't take it any longer and decompensates, disintegrates, and remembers why he is what he is and who shaped him, and then I loom as huge in his wretched life as a billboard. His answer to these crises is always the same. He vanishes. One day he simply drops off the radar, and what I find in his wake is awful. Cases he mishandled or neglected. Memos that show his lack of control and dangerous judgment. Hurtful voicemails he didn't bother to delete because he wanted me to hear them. Damaging e-mails and other communications he hoped I'd find. I sit in his chair and start opening drawers. I don't have to rummage long.

The file folder isn't labeled and contains four pages printed at eight-oh-three yesterday morning, February 8, a speech that based on other information in the header and news section is from the Royal United Services Institute's website. A century-old British think tank with satellite offices strategically located around the world, RUSI is dedicated to advanced innovations in national and international security, and I can't imagine Fielding's interest. I can't fathom him caring about a keynote address given by Russell Brown, the shadow secretary of state for defense, on his views about the "defense debate." I skim the conservative member of Parliament's not-so-startling comments that it isn't a given the UK will always act as part of an alliance and the economic impact of the war is catastrophic. He makes repeated allusions to misinformation methodically propagated, which is as close as the respectable MP is going to come to outright accusing the United States of orchestrating the invasion of Iraq and dragging the UK along for the ride.

Unsurprisingly, the speech is political, as is almost everything right now in Britain, which holds its general election in three months. Six hundred and fifty seats are being contested, and a major campaign issue is the more than ten thousand British troops fighting the Taliban in Afghanistan. Fielding isn't military, has never paid much attention to foreign affairs or elections, and I don't know why he would have the slightest interest in what is happening in the UK. I don't recall that he's ever even been to the UK. He's not the sort to be interested in a general election over there or RUSI or any think tank, and knowing him as well as I do, I suspect he intended for me to find this file. He wanted me to see it after he pulled another one of his vanishing stunts. What is it he wants me to know?

Why is he interested in RUSI? And did he come across the speech himself on the Internet, or did someone send it to him? If it was sent to him, by whom? I consider asking Lucy to go into Fielding's e-mail, but I'm not ready to be that heavy-handed, and I don't want to be caught. I can lock the door, but my superuser deputy chief could still walk in, because I don't have confidence that Ron or anyone else will keep Fielding in the security area if he shows up. I have no faith that Ron, who was unfriendly to me and seems to have little regard for me, will detain Fielding or try to get hold of me to ask for clearance. I don't trust that my staff is loyal to me or feels safe with me or follows my orders, and Fielding could reappear at any moment.

That would be like him. To vanish without warning, then show up just as unexpectedly and catch me red-handed, sitting at his desk, going through his electronic files. It's just one more thing he'll use against me, and he's used plenty against me over the years. What has he been doing behind my back? Let's see what else I find, and then I'll know what to do. I look at the time stamp again and imagine Fielding sitting in this very chair at eight-oh-three yesterday morning printing the speech, while Lucy, Marino, Anne, and Ollie, while everybody, was in an uproar because of what was in the cooler downstairs.

How odd that Fielding would be up here in his office while that was going on, and I wonder if he even cared that a man might have been locked inside our refrigerator while still alive. Of course, Fielding would have to care. How could he not? If the worst had turned out to be true, he would be blamed. Ultimately, I would be the one all over the news and likely out of a job, but he would go down with me. Yet he was up here on the seventh floor, in his office and out of the fray, as if he already had his mind made up, and it occurs to me that his disappearance may be related to something else. I lean back in his chair and look around, my attention landing on the pad of call sheets and a ballpoint pen near his phone. I notice faint indentations on the top sheet of paper.

Turning on a lamp, I pick up the pad and hold it at various angles, trying to make out indented writing left like a footprint when someone wrote a note on a top sheet of paper that is no longer there. One thing about Fielding, he doesn't have a light touch, not when he's wielding a scalpel or typing on a keyboard or writing something by hand. For a devotee of martial arts, he is surprisingly rough, is easily frustrated and quick to flare up. He has a childish way of holding a pencil or pen with two fingers on top instead of one, as if he's using chopsticks, and it's not uncommon for him to break lead or nibs, and he's hell on Magic Markers.

I don't need ESDA or a Docustat or vacuum box or some other indented writing-recovery unit to detect what I can see the old-fashioned way in oblique lighting with my own eyes. Fielding's barely legible scribble. What appears to be two separate notes. One is a phone number with a 508 area code and "MVF8/18/UK Min of Def Diary2/8." Then a second one: "U of Sheffield today @ Whitehall. Over and out." I look again, making sure I read the last three words correctly. *Over and out.* The end of a radio transmission, like *Roger Wilco over and out* but also a song performed by a heavy-metal band that Fielding used to play in his car all the time when he first came to Richmond. *"Over and out / every dog has its day."* What he'd sing to me when he'd threaten to quit, when he'd had enough, or when he was teasing, flirting, pretending to be fed up. Did he write *over and out* on a call sheet with me in mind or for some other reason?

I find a legal pad in a drawer and write what I've discovered indented on the pad of call sheets and begin doing the best I can to figure out what Fielding was up to and thinking about, what it is he wants me to know. If I came in here to snoop, I was going to find the printout and the indented writing. He knows me. He would think that way, because he knows damn well how my mind works. The University of Sheffield is one of the top research institutions in the world, and Whitehall is where RUSI is headquartered, literally in the former White-hall Palace, the original location of Scotland Yard.

Logging on to Intelliquest, a search engine Lucy created for the CFC, I type in RUSI and the date February 8 and Whitehall. What comes up is the title of a keynote address, *Civilian-Military Collaboration,* the lecture Fielding must be referring to that was delivered at RUSI at ten a.m. UK time, what is now yesterday morning for me. The speaker was Dr. Liam Saltz, the controversial Nobel laureate whose doomsday opinions about military technology make him a natural enemy of DARPA. I wasn't aware he was on the faculty at the University of Sheffield. I thought he was at Berkeley. He used to be at Berkeley, and now he's at Sheffield, I read on the Internet as I think, rather dazed, of the exhibit at the Courtauld in the summer before 9/11, where Lucy and I heard Dr. Saltz lecture. Not long after that, Dr. Saltz, like me, was a vocal critic of MORT.

I ponder the title of the lecture Dr. Saltz delivered not even twenty-four hours ago. *Civilian-Military Collaboration.* That certainly sounds tame for the rabble-rousing Dr. Saltz, who is as jolting as an air-raid siren in his warnings that America's two-hundred-plus-billion-dollar allocation to future combat systems — specifically, unmanned vehicles — has put us on the road to ultimate annihilation. Robots might seem to make sense when you consider sending them into the battlefield, he rails, but what happens when they come home like used Jeeps and other military surplus? Eventually they will find their way into the civilian world, and what we'll have is more policing and surveillance, more insensate machines doing the jobs of humans, only these machines will be armed and equipped with cameras and recording devices.

I've heard Dr. Saltz on the news, painting terrifying scenarios of "copbots" responding to crime scenes and unmanned "robocruisers" pursuing vehicles to write up occupants for traffic violations or hauling people in for outstanding warrants or, God forbid, getting a message from sensors to use force. Robots Tasering us. Robots shooting us to death. Robots that look like huge insects dragging our wounded and dead off a battlefield. Dr. Saltz testifying before the same Senate subcommittee I did but not at the same time. Both of us wreaking havoc for a technology company named Otwahl that I'd completely forgotten about until just hours ago.

I've met him only once, when both of us happened to be on CNN and he pointed at me and quipped, "Autbotsies."

"I beg your pardon," I answered, unclipping my mike as he walked onto the set.

"Robotic autopsies. Someday they'll take your place, my good doctor, maybe sooner than you think. We should have a drink after the show."

He was a bright-eyed man who looked like a lost hippie with his long, graying ponytail and wasted face, and he had the electricity of an exposed live wire. That was two years ago, and I should have taken him up on his invitation and waited around CNN. I should have had a drink with him. I should have gotten better versed in what he believes, because it isn't all crazy. I haven't seen him since then, although I can't escape his presence in the media, and I try to recall if I've ever mentioned him to Fielding for any reason at all. I don't think so. I can't figure out why I would. Connections. What are they? I search some more.

The University of Sheffield in South Yorkshire has an excellent medical school, that much I already know. *Rerum Cognoscere Causas,* its motto, *To discover the causes of things,* how apropos, how ironic. I need causes. *Research,* and I click on that. Global warming, global soil degradation, rethinking engineering with pioneering computer software, new findings in human embryonic stem cells' DNA changes. I go back to the indented notes on the call sheet.

MVF8/18/UK Min of Def Diary2/8.

MVF is our abbreviation for motor-vehicle fatality, and I instigate another search, this time mining the CFC database. I enter MVF and the date 8/18, August 18 last summer, and a record is returned, the case of a twenty-year-old British man named Damien Patten who was killed in a taxicab accident in Boston. Fielding didn't do the autopsy, one of my other MEs did, and in the narrative I notice that Damien Patten was a lance corporal in the 14th Signal Regiment and was on leave and had come to Boston to get married when he was killed in the taxicab accident. I get a funny feeling. Something registers.

I execute another search using the keywords February 8 and UK Ministry of Defense Diary. I end up on its official news blog, and an entry in the diary lists British soldiers killed in Afghanistan yesterday. I run down the list of casualties, looking for anything that might mean something to me. A lance corporal from 1st Battalion Coldstream Guards. A lance sergeant from 1st Battalion Grenadier Guards. A kingsman from 2nd Battalion Duke of Lancaster's Regiment. Then there is a sapper, or combat engineer, with the Counter-Improvised Explosive Device Task Force, who was killed in the mountainous terrain of northwestern Afghanistan. In the Badghis Province. Where my patient PFC Gabriel was killed on Sunday, February 7.

I execute another search, although one detail I already know without having to look it up is how many NATO troops died in Afghanistan on February 7. At Dover, we always know. It's as routine as preparing for ugly storms, a depressingly morbid report that controls our lives. Nine casualties, and four of them were Americans killed by the same roadside improvised explosive device that turned PFC Gabriel's Humvee into a blast furnace. But again, that was on the seventh, not the eighth. It occurs to me that the British soldier who died on the eighth might have been injured the day before.

I check and I'm right. The IED sapper, Geoffrey Miller, was twenty-three, recently married, and was wounded in a roadside bombing in the Badghis Province early Sunday but died the next day in a military medical center in Germany. Possibly the same roadside bombing that killed the Americans we took care of at Dover yesterday morning — in fact, it's likely. I wonder if Sapper Miller and PFC Gabriel knew each other, and how the British man killed in a taxicab, Damien Patten, might be connected. Was Patten acquainted with Miller and Gabriel in Afghanistan, and what does Fielding have to do with any of this? How are Dr. Saltz or MORT or the dead man from Norton's Woods connected, or are they?

Miller's body will be repatriated this Thursday, returned to his family in Oxford, England. I read on, but I can't find anything else about him, although I certainly am capable of getting more information about a slain British soldier if I need it. I can call the press secretary, Rockman. I can call Briggs, and I should, anyway, I remember. Briggs asked me to — in fact, ordered me — demanding that I keep him informed about the Norton's Woods case, to wake him up if need be the minute I have information. But I won't. No way. Not now. I'm not sure whom I can trust, and as that thought lingers, I realize the trouble I'm in.

What does it say when you can't ask for help from the very people you work with? It says everything, and it's as if the ground is opening up beneath my feet and I'm falling into the unknown, a cold, lightless, empty space where I've been before. Briggs wanted to do an end run, to usurp my authority and transfer the Norton's Woods case to Dover. Fielding has been sneaking around in my absence, meddling in affairs that are none of his business and even using my office, and now he's ducking me, or at least I hope that's all it is. My staff is committing mutiny, and any number of people, strangers to me, seem to know the details of my return home.

It is almost two a.m., and I'm tempted to try the indented telephone number Fielding scribbled on a call sheet and surprise whoever answers, wake the person up and perhaps get a clue as to what is going on. Instead, I do a polite computer search to see who or what the number with the 508 area code might belong to. The report summary shocks me, and for a moment I sit very still and try to calm myself. I try to push back the walls of dismay and confusion crowding in.

Julia Gabriel, mother of PFC Gabriel.

On the screen in front of me are her home and business addresses, her marital status, the salary she earns as a pharmacist in

Worcester, Massachusetts, and the name of her only child and his age, which was nineteen when he died in Afghanistan on Sunday. I was on the phone with Mrs. Gabriel for the better part of an hour before I autopsied her son, trying to explain as gently as I could the impossibility of collecting his sperm while she raised her voice at me and cried and accused me of personal choices that aren't mine to make and ones I didn't make and would never make.

Saving sperm from the dead and using it to impregnate the living isn't something that causes me a moral dilemma. I really have no personal opinion about what truly is a medical and legal question, not a religious or ethical one, and the choice should be up to those involved, certainly not up to the practitioner. What matters to me is that the procedure, which has become increasingly popular because of the war, is done properly and legally, and my supposed views on posthumous reproduction rights were moot in PFC Gabriel's case, anyway. His body was burned and decomposing, his pelvis so charred that his scrotum was gone and the vas deferens containing semen along with it, and I wasn't about to tell Mrs. Gabriel that. I was as compassionate and gentle as I could be and didn't take it personally as she vented her grief and rage on the last doctor her son would ever see on this earth.

Peter had a girlfriend who was willing to have his children just like his friend was doing, it was a pact they'd made, Mrs. Gabriel went on, and I had no idea whose friend or what she was talking about. Peter's friend told him of another friend who got killed in Boston on his wedding day this past summer, only Mrs. Gabriel never mentioned Damien Patten by name, the British man killed in a taxicab this past August 18. *"All three of them dead now, three young, beautiful boys dead,"* Mrs. Gabriel said to me over the phone, and I had no idea who she was talking about. I think I do now. I think she meant Patten for sure, the friend of the friend whom PFC Gabriel had some sort of pact with. I wonder if the friend of Patten's was this other casualty that Fielding seems to have led me to, Geoffrey Miller, an IED sapper.

All three of them dead now.

Did Fielding discuss the Patten case with Mrs. Gabriel, and who did she talk to first, Fielding or me? She called me at Dover at around quarter of eight. I always fill out a call sheet, and I remember writing down the time as I sat in my small office at Dover's Port Mortuary, looking at the CT scans and their coordinates that would help me locate with GPS precision the frag and other objects that had penetrated the badly burned body of her son. Based on what she said to me as I now try to reconstruct that conversation, she likely talked to Fielding first. That might explain her repeated references to "other cases."

Someone had planted an idea in her head about what we do for other cases. She was under the distinct impression that we routinely extract semen from casualties and in fact encourage it, and I recall being puzzled, because the procedure has to be approved and is fraught with legal complications. I couldn't imagine what had given her such an idea, and I might have asked her about it, had she not been so busy castigating me and calling me names. What kind of monster would prevent a woman from having her dead boyfriend's children or stop the mother of a dead son from being a grandmother? We do it for our other cases, why not her son? she wept. *"I have no one left,"* she cried. *"This is bullshit bureaucracy, go on and admit it,"* she yelled at me. *"Bureaucratic bullshit to cover up yet another hate crime."*

"Anyone home?" Benton is in the doorway.

Mrs. Gabriel called me a military bigot.

"You do unto others as long as they're white," she said. *"That's not the Golden Rule but the White Rule,"* she said. *"You took care of that other boy who got killed in Boston, and he wasn't even a U.S. soldier, but not my son, who died for his country. I suppose my son was the wrong color,"* she went on, and I had no idea what she meant or what she was basing such an accusation on. I didn't try to figure it out because it seemed like hysteria, nothing more, and I forgave her for it on the spot. Even though it obviously hurt me badly and I've not been able to put it out of my mind since.

"Hello?" Benton is walking in.

"Another hate crime, only it will be found out and people like you won't get rewarded this time," and she wouldn't explain what she was thinking when she said something so terrible as that. But I didn't ask her to elaborate, and I didn't give her venomous comments much credence at the time, because being yelled at, cursed, threatened, and even attacked by people who are otherwise civilized and sane isn't a new experience. I don't have shatterproof glass installed in the lobbies and viewing rooms of offices where I've worked because I'm afraid of the dead throwing a fit or assaulting me.

"Kay?"

My eyes focus on Benton holding two coffees and trying not to spill them. Why would Julia Gabriel have called here before calling me at Dover? Or did Fielding call her, and in either event, why would he have talked to her? Then I remember Marino telling me about PFC Gabriel being the first casualty from Worcester and the media calling the CFC as if the body was here instead of at Dover, about a number of phone calls here because of the Massachusetts connection. Maybe that's how Fielding found out, but why would he get on the phone with the slain soldier's mother, even if she called here by mistake and needed to be reminded her son was at Dover? Of course she knew that. How could Mrs. Gabriel not know her son was flown into Dover? I can't see any legitimate reason for Fielding to have talked to her or what he possibly could have said that was helpful, and how dare him.

He's not military or even a consultant for the AFME. He's a civilian and has no right to probe into details relating to war casualties or national security or to engage in conversations about such matters, which are plainly defined as classified. Military and medical intelligence are none of his business. RUSI is none of his business. The election in the UK isn't, either. The only thing that should be Fielding's damn business is what he has so resoundingly neglected, which is his enormous responsibility here at the CFC and what should be his damn loyalty to me.

"That's nice of you," I say to Benton in a detached way. "I could use a coffee."

"Where were you just now? Besides in the middle of an imagined fight. You look like you might kill someone."

He comes close to the desk, watching me the way he does when he's trying to read what I'm thinking because he's not about to trust what I say. Or maybe he knows what I have to say is only the beginning of things and that I'm clueless about the rest of it.

"You okay?" He sets the coffees on the desk and moves a chair close.

"No, I'm not okay."

"What's wrong?"

"I think I just discovered what it means when something reaches critical mass."

"What's the matter?" he asks.

"Everything."

12

"Please shut the door." It occurs to me I'm starting to act like Lucy. "I don't know where to begin, so many things are the matter."

Benton closes the door, and I notice the simple platinum band on his left ring finger. Sometimes I'm still caught by surprise that we're married, so much of our lives consumed by each other whether we've been together or apart, and we always agreed we didn't have to do it, to be official and formal, because we're not like other people, and then we did it anyway. The ceremony was a small, simple one, not a celebration as much as a swearing in, because we really meant it when we said until death do us part. After all we'd been through, for us to say it was more than words, more like an oath of office or an ordination or perhaps a summary of what we'd already lived. And I wonder if he ever regrets it. For example, right now does he wish he could go back to how it was? I wouldn't blame him if he thinks about what he's given up and what he misses, and there are so many complications because of me.

He sold his family brownstone, an elegant nineteenth-century mansion on the Boston Common, and he can't have loved some places we've lived or stayed in because of my unusual profession and preoccupations, what is a chaotic and costly existence despite my best intentions. While his forensic psychology practice has remained stable, my career has been in flux these past three years, with the shutting down of a private practice in Charleston, South Carolina, then my office in Watertown closing because of the economy, and I was in New York and then Washington and Dover, and now this, the CFC.

"What the hell is going on in this place?" I ask him as if he knows and I don't understand why he would. But I feel he does, or maybe I'm just wishing it because I'm beginning to experience desperation, that panicky sensation of falling and flailing for something to grab hold of.

"Black and extra-bold." He sits back down and slides the mug of coffee closer. "And not hazelnut. Even though you have quite a stash of it, I hear."

"Jack's still not shown up, and no one has heard from him, I assume."

"He's definitely not here. I think you're as safe in his office as he's been in yours." Benton says it as if he means more than one thing, and I notice how he's dressed.

Earlier he had on his winter coat and in the x-ray room was covered in a disposable gown before heading upstairs to Lucy's lab. I didn't really notice what he was wearing underneath his layers. Black tactical boots, black tactical pants, a dark red flannel shirt, a rubber waterproof watch with a luminescent dial. As if he's anticipating being out in the weather or someplace that might be hard on his clothes.

"So Lucy told you it appears he's been using my office," I say. "For what purpose I don't know. But maybe you do."

"Nobody's needed to tell me there's a looting mentality at — what is it Marino calls this place? CENTCOM? Or does that just refer to the inner sanctum, or what's supposed to be the inner sanctum, your office. No captain of the ship, and you know what happens. The Jolly Roger flag goes up, the inmates run the asylum, the drunks manage the bar, if you'll excuse me for mixing metaphors."

"Why didn't you say something?"

"I don't work at the CFC. Or for it. Just an invited guest on occasion," he says.

"That's not an answer, and you know it. Why wouldn't you protect me?"

"You mean in the manner you think I should," he says, because it's silly to suggest he wouldn't protect me.

"What has been going on around here? Maybe if you tell me, I can figure out what needs to be done," I then say. "I know Lucy's been catching you up. It would be nice if someone would catch me up. In detail, and with openness and full disclosure."

"I'm sorry you're angry. I'm sorry you've come home to a situation that is upsetting. Your homecoming should have been joyful."

"Joyful. What the hell is joyful?"

"A word, a theoretical concept. Like full disclosure. I can tell you what I've witnessed firsthand, what happened when I met here several times. Case discussions. There have been two that involved me." He stares off. "The first was the BC football player from last fall, not long after the CFC took over the Commonwealth's forensic cases."

Wally Jamison, age twenty, Boston College's star quarterback. Found floating in

Boston Harbor on November 1 at dawn. Cause of death exsanguination due to blunt-force trauma and multiple cutting injuries. Tom Booker's case, one of my other MEs.

"Jack didn't do that one," I remind him.

"Well, if you ask him, you might get a different impression," Benton informs me. "Jack reviewed the Wally Jamison case as if it was his. Dr. Booker wasn't present. This was last week."

"Why last week? I don't know anything about it."

"New information, and we wanted to talk to Jack, and he seemed eager to cooperate, to offer a wealth of information."

" 'We'?"

Benton lifts his coffee, then changes his mind and sets it back down on Fielding's sloppy desk with all its collectibles that are all about him. "I think Jack's attitude is he may not have done the autopsy, but that's just a technicality. An NFL draft was right up the alley of your ironman freak of a deputy chief."

" 'Ironman freak'?"

"But I suppose it was his bad luck to be out of town when Wally Jamison got beaten and hacked to death. Wally's luck was a little worse."

Believed to have been abducted and murdered on Halloween. Crime scene unknown. No suspect. No motive or credible theory. Just the speculation of a satanic cult initiation. Target a star athlete. Hold him hostage in some clandestine place and kill him savagely. Chatter on the Internet and on the news. Gossip that's become gospel.

"I don't give a shit what Jack's feeling is or what's right up his goddamn alley," says a hard part of me that's old and scarred over, a part of me that is completely fed up with Jack Fielding.

I realize I'm enraged by him. I'm suddenly aware that at the core of my unhealthy relationship with him is molten fury.

"And Mark Bishop, also last week. Wednesday was the football player. Thursday was the boy," Benton says.

"A boy whose murder might be related to some initiation. A gang, a cult," I interject. "A similar speculation about Wally Jamison."

"*Speculation* being the operative word. Whose speculation?"

"Not mine." I think angrily of Fielding. "I don't speculate unless it's behind closed doors with someone I trust. I know better than to put something out there, and then the police run with it, then the media runs with it. Next thing I know, a jury believes it, too."

"Patterns and parallels."

"You're connecting Mark Bishop and Wally Jamison." It seems incredible. "I fail to see what they might have in common besides speculation."

"I was here last week for both case consults." Benton's eyes are steady on me. "Where was Jack last Halloween? Do you know for a fact?"

"I know where I was, that's about the only fact I know. While I've been at Dover, that's all I've known and all I was supposed to know. I didn't hire him so I could goddamn babysit him. I don't know where the hell he was on Halloween. I guess you're going to tell me he wasn't out somewhere taking his kids trick-or-treating."

"He was in Salem. But not with his kids."

"I wouldn't know that and don't know why you do or why it's important."

"It wasn't important until very recently," Benton says.

I stare at his boots again, then at his dark pants with their flannel lining and cargo and rear slash pockets for gun magazines and flashlights, the type of pants he wears when he's working in the field, when he goes to crime scenes or is out on the firing or explosive-ordnance-disposal ranges with cops, with the FBI.

"Where were you before you picked me up at Hanscom?" I ask him. "What were you doing?"

"We have a lot to deal with, Kay. I'm afraid more than I thought."

"Were you dressed in field clothes when you picked me up at the airport?" It occurs to me that he might not have been. He's changed his clothes. Maybe he hasn't done anything yet but is about to.

"I keep a bag in my car. As you know," Benton says. "Since I never know when I might get called."

"To go where? You've been called to go somewhere?"

He looks at me, then out the window at the chalky skyline of Boston in the snowy dark.

"Lucy says you've been on the phone." I continue to prod him for information I can tell I'm not going to get right now.

"I'm afraid nonstop. I'm afraid there's more than I thought," and then he doesn't continue. That's all he's going to say about it. He's headed out somewhere, has someplace to go. It's not a good place. He's been talking to people and not about anything good and he's not going to inform me right now. Full disclosure and joy. When there is such a thing, it is only a taste, a hint of what we don't have the rest of the time.

"You met on Wednesday and then on Thursday. Discussing the Wally Jamison and Mark Bishop cases here at the CFC." I go back to that. "And I assume Jack was in on the Mark Bishop discussion as well. He was involved in both discussions. And you didn't mention this a little while ago when we were talking in the car."

"Not such a little while ago. More than five hours ago. And a lot has happened. There have been developments since we were in the car, as you know. Not the least of which is what we now realize is another murder. Number three."

"You're linking the man from Norton's Woods to Mark Bishop and Wally Jamison."

"Very possibly. In fact, I'd say yes."

"What about the meetings last week? With Jack? He was there," I push.

"Yes. Last Wednesday and Thursday. In your office."

"What do you mean my office? This building? This floor?"

"Your personal office." Benton indicates my office next door.

"In my office. Jack conducted meetings in my office. I see."

"He conducted both meetings in your office. At your conference-room table in there."

"He has his own conference table." I look at the black lacquered oval table with six ergonomic chairs that I got at a government auction.

Benton doesn't respond. He knows as well as I do that Fielding's inappropriate decision to use my personal office has nothing to do with the furniture. I think of what Lucy mentioned about sweeping my office for covert surveillance devices, although she never directly said who might be doing the spying or if anyone was. The most likely candidate for the sort of individual who might bug my office and get away with it is my niece. Maybe motivated by the knowledge that Fielding was helping himself to what isn't rightfully his. I wonder if what's been going on in my private space during my absence has been secretly recorded.

"And you never mentioned this to me at that time," I continue. "You could have told me when it happened. You could have fully disclosed to me that he was using my damn office as if he's the damn chief and director of this goddamn place."

"The first I knew of it was last week when I met with him. I'm not saying I hadn't heard things about the CFC and about him."

"It would have been helpful if I'd known these things you were hearing."

"Rumors. Gossip. I didn't know certain things for a fact."

"Then you should have told me a week ago when you knew it for a fact. On the Wednesday you had your first meeting and discovered it was in my office, in an office Jack didn't have permission to use. What else haven't you told me? What new developments?"

"I'm telling you as much as I can and when I can. I know you understand."

"I don't understand. You should have been telling me things all along. Lucy should have. Marino should have."

"It's not that simple."

"Betrayal is very simple."

"No one is betraying you. Marino and Lucy aren't. I'm certainly not."

"Implying that somebody is. Just not the three of you."

He is quiet.

"You and I talk every day, Benton. You should have told me," I then say.

"Let's see when I might have overwhelmed you with all this, overwhelmed you with a lot of things while you've been at Dover.

When you'd call at five a.m. before you'd head over to Port Mortuary to take care of our fallen heroes? Or at midnight when you'd finally log out of your computer or quit studying for your boards?"

He doesn't say it defensively or unkindly, but I get his not-so-subtle point, and it's justified. I'm being unfair. I'm being hypocritical. Whose idea was it that when we have virtually no time for each other we shouldn't dwell on work or domestic minutiae or they will be all that's left? Like cancer, I'm quick to offer my clever medical analogies and brilliant insights when he's the psychologist, he's the one who used to head the FBI's profiling unit at Quantico, he's the one on the faculty of Harvard's Department of Psychiatry. But it's me with all the wisdom, all the profound examples, comparing work and niggling domestic details and emotional injuries to cancers, to scarring, to necrosis, and my prognostications that if we're not careful, one day there's no healthy tissue left and death will follow. I feel embarrassed. I feel shallow.

"No, I didn't approach certain subjects until we were driving here, and now I'm telling you more, telling you what I can," Benton says to me with stoical calm, as if we are in a session of his and any moment

324

he will simply announce we have to stop.

I won't stop until I know what I must. Some things he must tell me. It's not just fairness, it's about survival, and I realize I'm feeling unsure of Benton as if I don't quite know him anymore. He's my husband, and I'm touched by a perception that something has been altered, a new ingredient has been added to the house special.

What is it?

I study what I'm intuiting as if I can taste what has changed.

"I mentioned my concern that Jack's interpretation of Mark Bishop's injuries is problematic," Benton goes on, and he's guarded. He's calculating every word he says as if someone else is listening or he will be reporting our conversation to others. "Well, based on what you've described about the hammer marks on the little boy's head, Jack's interpretation is just damn wrong, couldn't be more wrong, and I suspected it at the time when he was going over the case with us. I suspected he was lying."

" 'Us'?"

"I told you I've heard things, but I honestly haven't been around Jack."

"Why do you say 'honestly'? As opposed to *dishonestly,* Benton?"

"I'm always honest with you, Kay."

"Of course you aren't, but now is not the time to go into it."

"Now isn't. I know you understand." And he holds my stare for a long moment. He's telling me to please let it go.

"All right. I'm sorry." I will let it go, but I don't want to.

"I hadn't seen him for months, and what I saw for myself was . . . Well, it was pretty obvious during those discussions last week that something's off with him, severely off," Benton resumes. "He looked bad. His thoughts were racing all over the map. He was hyperfluent, grandiose, hypomanic, aggressive, and red-faced, as if he might explode. I certainly felt he wasn't being truthful, that he was deliberately misleading us."

"What do you mean 'us'?" And it begins to occur to me what I'm picking up.

"Has he ever been in a psychiatric hospital, been in treatment, maybe been diagnosed with a mood disorder? He ever mentioned anything like that to you?" Benton questions me in a way that I find unexpected and unnerving, and I'm reminded of what I sensed in the car when we were driving here. Only now it's more pronounced, more recognizable.

He is acting the way he used to when he was still an agent, when he was empowered by the federal government to enforce the law. I detect an authority and confidence he hasn't manifested in years, a sure-footedness he lacked after his reemergence from protective deep cover. He came back feeling lost, weak, like nothing more than an academician, he often complained. *Emasculated,* he would say. *The FBI eats its young, and they've eaten me,* he would say. *That's my reward for going after an organized-crime cartel. I finally get my life back and don't want what's left of it,* he would say. *It's a husk. I'm a husk. I love you, but please understand I'm not what I was.*

"He ever been delusional or violent?" Benton is asking me, and it isn't just a clinician talking.

I'm feeling interrogated.

"He had to expect you would tell me he's been using my office as if it's his. Or that I'd find out." I think of Lucy again, of spying and covert recordings.

"I know he has a temper," Benton says, "but I'm talking about physical violence possibly accompanied by dissociative fugue, disappearing for hours, days, weeks, with little or no recall. What we're seeing with some of these men and women who return from war, disappearances and amnesia triggered by severe trauma and often confused with malingering. The same thing Johnny Donahue is supposedly suffering from, only I'm not sure how much of it has been suggested to that poor damn kid. I wonder where the idea came from, if someone's suggested it to him."

He says it as if he really doesn't wonder it.

"Jack's certainly famous for coming across as a malingerer, of avoiding his responsibilities going back to the beginning of time," Benton then says.

I created Fielding.

"What haven't you told me about him?" Benton goes on.

I made Fielding what he is. He is my monster.

"A psychiatric history?" Benton says. "Off-limits even to me, even to the FBI. I could find out, but I won't violate that boundary."

Benton and the FBI. One and the same again. Not a street agent again. I can't imagine that. A criminal investigative analyst, a criminal intelligence analyst, a threat analyst. The Department of Justice has so many analysts, agents who are a combination academic and tactical. If you're going to go to prison or get shot, may as well be at the hand of a cop who's got a Ph.D.

"What might you know about Jack, your protégé, that I don't?" Benton asks me. "Besides that he's a sick fuck. Because he is. Somewhere some part of you knows it, Kay."

I'm Briggs's monster, and Fielding is mine. Going back to the beginning of time.

"I'm well aware of sexual abuse," Benton says blandly, as if he doesn't care what happened to Fielding when he was a child, as if Benton really doesn't give a damn.

Not a psychologist but something else speaking, and I'm sure. Cops, federal agents, prosecutors, those who protect and punish, are hardened to excuses. They judge "subjects" and "persons of interest" by what they do, not by what was done to them. People like Benton don't give a damn about why or if it couldn't be helped, doesn't matter the definitions, distillations, and predictions he so astutely, so skillfully, renders. In his heart Benton has no sympathy for hateful, harmful people, and his years of being a clinician and consultant have been cruel to him, have been unfulfilling and have felt fake, he's confessed to me more than once.

"That much is a matter of public record since the case went to trial." Benton feels the need to tell me something I've never asked Fielding about.

I don't remember when and how I first heard of the special school Fielding attended as a boy near Atlanta. Somehow I know, and all that comes to mind is references he's made to a certain "episode" in his past, that what he experienced with a certain "counselor" makes it excruciatingly difficult for him to handle any tragedy involving children, especially if they were abused. I'm certain I never pushed him to volunteer the details. Back in those days especially, I wouldn't have asked.

"Nineteen seventy-eight," Benton says, "when Jack was fifteen, although he was twelve when it started, went on for several years until they were caught having sex in the back of her station wagon parked at the edge of the soccer field as if she wanted to be caught. She was pregnant. Anther pathetic story about boarding schools, this one, thank God, not Catholic but for troubled teens, one of these private treatment center–slash–academies that has *Ranch* in its name. What the therapist did to get convicted of ten counts of sexual battery on a minor isn't what you haven't told me about Jack."

"I don't know the details," I finally answer him. "Not all of them or even most of them.

I don't remember her name, if I ever knew it; didn't know she was pregnant. His child? Did she have it?"

"I've reviewed the case transcripts. Yes. She had it."

"I wouldn't have had a reason to look at the case transcripts." I don't ask why Benton has a reason. He's not going to reveal that to me right now, and maybe he never will. "What a shame there's one more child in the world Jack's raised poorly. Or not at all," I add. "How sad."

"Kathleen Lawler hasn't had such a good life, either," Benton starts to say.

"How sad," I repeat.

"The woman convicted of molesting Jack," he says. "I don't know about the child, a girl, born in prison, given up for adoption. Considering the mutant genetic loading, probably in prison, too, or dead. Kathleen Lawler was in one mess after another, currently in a correctional facility for female offenders in Savannah, Georgia, serving twenty years for DUI manslaughter. Jack communicates with her, is a prison pen pal, although he uses a pen name, and that's not what you haven't told me, because I doubt you know about it. Actually, I can't imagine you do."

"Who else was at the meetings last week?"

I'm so cold my fingernails are blue, and I wish I'd brought my jacket in here. I notice a lab coat on the back of Fielding's door.

"It crossed my mind while we were sitting in your office," says Benton, the former FBI agent, the former protected witness and master of secrets, who isn't acting like a former anything anymore.

He's acting like he's investigating a case, not just a consultant on one. I'm convinced that what I suspect is true. He's back with the Feds. Things end where they begin and begin where they end.

"An affective disorder. I've thought hard about it, tried to remember him from the old days. Done a lot of reflecting on the old days." Benton talks matter-of-factly, as if he has no feelings about what he's divulging and accusing me of. "He's never been normal. That's my point. Jack has significant underlying pathology. That's why he was sent off to boarding school. To learn to manage his anger. When he was six years old he stabbed another little kid in the chest with a ballpoint pen. When he was eleven he hit his mother in the head with a rake. Then he was sent to the ranch near Atlanta, where he only got angrier."

"I have no idea what he did when he was growing up," I reply. "It's not a common practice to conduct extensive background checks on doctors one might hire, in fact, was unheard of when I was getting started, when he was getting started. I'm not an FBI agent," I add pointedly. "I don't dig up everything I can about people and go around questioning neighbors they grew up around. I don't question their teachers. I don't track down their pen pals."

I get up from Fielding's desk.

"Although I probably should have. I probably will from now on. But I've never covered up for him," I go on. "Never protected him that way. I admit I've been too forgiving. I admit I've fixed his disasters or tried to. But never covered up something I shouldn't, if that's what you're saying I've done. I would never do anything unethical for him or anyone." *Not anymore,* I add silently. I did it once but never again, and I never did it for Jack Fielding. Not even for myself but for the highest law of the land.

I walk across the office, cold and exhausted and ashamed of myself. I remove Fielding's lab coat from the hook at the top of the closed door.

"I don't know what it is you think I've not told you, Benton. I have no idea what he's involved with or whom. Or his delusions or dissociative states and blackouts. Not in my presence, and he's never shared information like that, if it's true."

I put on the lab coat, and it is huge, and I detect the faint sharp odor of eucalyptus, like Vicks, like Bengay.

"Maybe a mood disorder with a touch of narcissism and intermittent explosive anger," Benton goes on as if I just said nothing. "Or it could be the drugs, maybe his damn performance-enhancement drugs as usual, the sorry bastard. He doesn't represent the CFC well, I'm sorry as hell to make the understatement of the century, and it wasn't lost on Douglas and David, and that got the CFC off on the wrong foot, as long ago as early November, when they got involved in the Wally Jamison kidnapping and murder. You can imagine what's gotten back to Briggs and others. Jack is one inch from ruining everything, and that opens up a place to opportunists. Like I said, it creates a looting mentality."

I pause before a window and look down on the dark, snowy street as if I might find something there that will remind me of who I am. Something to give me strength, something to find comfort in.

"He's done a lot of damage." Benton's voice behind me. "I don't know that it's been intentional. But I suspect some of it

has been because of his complicated relationship with you."

Snow is blowing at a sharp angle, hitting
the window almost horizontally and making
rapid clicks that remind me of fingernails
tapping, of something restless and disturbed. When I look at the snow as it hits
the glass, it makes me dizzy. It gives me
vertigo to look at it and then to look down.

"Is that what this is about, Benton? My
complicated relationship with him?"

"I need to know about it. It's better it's
me instead of someone else asking you."

"You're saying everything is damaged and
ruined because of it. That it's the root of
everything wrong." I don't turn around but
stare out and down until I can't look at the
flying flakes of ice and the road below and
the dark river or the volatile winter night
any longer. "That's what you believe." I
want him to verify what he just said. I want
to know if what's been damaged and ruined
while I've been gone includes Benton and
me.

"I just need to know anything you haven't
told me," he answers instead.

"I'm sure you and others need to know." I
don't say it nicely as my pulse picks up.

"I understand things from the past don't

335

get resolved easily. I understand complications."

I turn around and meet his stare, and what I see in it isn't just cases and dead people or my mutinous office or my deranged deputy chief. I see Benton's distrust of me and my past. I see him doubting my character and who I am to him.

"I never slept with Jack," I tell him. "If that's what you're trying to find out so someone else is spared the discomfort of asking me. Or is it my discomfort you're so worried about? I never did. It won't come out because it isn't there. If that's what you're trying to ask me, that's your answer. You can pass it along to Briggs, to the FBI, to the attorney general, to whoever you goddamn want."

"I would understand when Jack was your fellow, when both of you were just getting started in Richmond."

"I try not to make it a practice to have sex with people I mentor," I say with a surprising flare of irritability. "I'd like to think I bear no similarity to what's-her-name Lawler, the former therapist locked up in Georgia."

"Jack wasn't twelve when you met him."

"It never happened. I don't do that with people I mentor."

"And when people mentor you?" Benton's eyes are steady on me as I stand by the window.

"That's not why John Briggs and I have a problem," I answer angrily.

13

I return to Fielding's desk and sit back down in his chair as I finger something slick and filmy inside one of his lab coat pockets. I pull out a square of transparent plastic that is paper-thin.

"The CFC didn't need to make a bad first impression with the Feds, but I'm confident you'll change it." Benton says it as if he regrets what he's just asked me, as if he's sorry about what he just confronted me with in the line of duty.

I sniff what Fielding must have peeled off a eucalyptus-laced pain-relieving patch, and resentfully think, *Yes, indeed, the Feds. I'm so glad I can change what the goddamn Feds must think of me.*

"I don't want you to feel negative about everything here, everything you've come home to," Benton continues. "It wouldn't be helpful if you are. There is a lot to take care of, but we'll get there. I know we will.

I'm sorry our conversation had to move in certain directions. I'm really sorry we had to get into all this."

"Let's talk about Douglas and David." I remind him of names he referred to moments earlier. "Who are they?"

"I have no doubt you'll prevail and make this place work, make it what it was meant to be, which is stellar and unlike anything anywhere. Better than what they have in Australia, in Switzerland, even better than any place where they were doing it first, including Dover, right? I have complete confidence in you, Kay. I don't want you to ever forget that."

The more Benton assures me of his confidence, the less I believe it.

"Law enforcement respects you, the military does," he adds, and I don't believe that, either.

If it were true, he wouldn't have to say it. *So what?* I then think, with hostility that seems to come from nowhere. I don't need people to like or respect me. It isn't a popularity contest. Isn't that what Briggs always says? *It's not a popularity contest, Colonel,* or if he's being more personable, *It's not a popularity contest, Kay,* and he smiles wryly, a steely glint of mischief in his eyes. He doesn't give a shit if anybody likes him, and in fact thrives on people not liking him, and I'm going to start thriving on it, too. The hell with everyone. I know what I need to do, which is something. I will do something, oh, yes, I will. Thinking I'm going to come home to this and just take it, do nothing about it, let whoever it is have his way? No. Hell, no. Not going to happen. Whoever would entertain an idea like that sure as hell doesn't know me.

"Who are Douglas and David?" I again ask, and I sound snappish.

"Douglas Burke and David McMaster," Benton says.

"I don't know them, and who are they to you?" Now I'm the one doing the interrogating.

"FBI's Boston Field Office, Metro Boston Homeland Security. You haven't gotten to know the locals, not key ones, but you will. Including the coast guard. I'm going to help you get to know everyone around here if you'll permit me to. For once I might be useful. I've missed being useful to you. I know you're upset."

"I'm not upset."

"Your face is flushed. You look upset. I don't mean to upset you. I'm sorry I have. But it's something I've needed to know for several reasons."

"And are you satisfied?"

"It's critical to know where you are in all this and who you are in it," he says as I hold the flimsy plastic backing, a square about the size of a cigarette pack.

I lift it up to the light and see Fielding's large fingerprints on the transparent film and smaller ones that must be mine. Fielding is chronically straining muscles, always achy and sore, especially when he's abusing anabolic steroids. When he's back to his old, bad tricks he smells like a damn menthol cough drop.

"What do Homeland Security, the coast guard, have to do with anything we're talking about?" I'm opening desk drawers, looking for Nuprin, Motrin, or Bengay patches, for Tiger Balm, for anything that might confirm what I suspect.

"Wally Jamison's body was floating in the harbor at the coast guard's ISC, their Integrated Support Command. Right there under their nose. Which I believe was the point," Benton replies as he watches me.

"Or the point was the wharf right there that's deserted after dark. One of the few wharves in the area that you can drive a car on. I sure as hell know that area. So do you. We know it, and some of the people who work there probably would recognize us, we've walked around there so many times, right next door to where we stay once in a blue moon when we can get away and be alone and be civil to each other." I sound sarcastic and mean.

"Authorized personnel only. Might I ask what you're looking for? I'm sure it's something that will be in plain view."

"It's my office. This entire place is my office. I'll look at whatever the hell I want. Plain view or not." My pulse is flying, and I feel agitated.

"The wharf isn't open to the public. Not just anybody can drive a car on it," Benton replies as he watches me carefully, worried. "I didn't mean to upset you this much."

"We walk over there all the time and no one asks for our IDs. They're not standing around with submachine guns. It's a tourist area." I'm argumentative and combative, and I don't want to be.

"The coast guard ISC isn't a tourist area. There's a guard gate you have to go through to get out on the pier," Benton says very calmly, very reasonably, and he continues looking at his iPhone. He looks at it and then at me, back and forth, reading both of us.

"I miss it. Let's spend a few days there soon." I try to sound nice because I'm acting awful. "Just the two of us."

"Yes. We will. Soon," he says. "We'll talk and get everything straight."

I imagine it with startling clarity, our favorite suite that reaches out into the water like a fingertip at the Fairmont hotel on Battery Wharf, directly next door to the coast guard ISC. I see the ruffled dark-green water of the harbor and hear it washing against pilings as if I'm there. I hear the creaking of docks, the clanking of rigging lines against masts, and the bass tones of the horns the big ships sound as if all of it is audible inside Fielding's office.

"And we won't answer our phones, and we'll go for walks and get room service and watch the tall ships, the tugboats, the tankers from our window. I would love that. Wouldn't you love it?" But I don't sound nice as I say it. I sound pushy and angry.

"We'll do it this weekend if you want. If we can," he says as he reads something on his iPhone, scrolling down with his thumb.

I move my coffee away and the corner of the desk looks rounded, not squared. Too much caffeine and my heart is beating hard. I feel light-headed and edgy.

"I hate it when you look at your phone all the time," I say before I can stop myself. "You know how much I hate it when we're

343

talking."

"It can't be avoided right now," he says as he looks at it.

"Exit off Ninety-three, get on Commercial Street, and you're right there," I resume arguing. "A convenient way to get rid of a body. Drive it there and dump it in the harbor. Nude, so whatever trace evidence there might have been from the car trunk, for example, was probably washed away." I shut a bottom drawer and sound peculiar to myself as I mutter distractedly, "Pain-relieving patches. None. And I didn't see any in my desk drawers, either. Only chewing gum. I've never been a gum chewer. Well, when I was a little kid. Dubble Bubble at Halloween, with the colorful waxy yellow wrapper that's twisted on the ends."

I see it. I smell it. My mouth waters.

"Here's a secret I've never told anyone. I'd recycle. Chew it and wrap it up again. For days until there was no flavor left."

My mouth is watering, and I swallow several times.

"I stopped chewing gum when I stopped trick-or-treating. See, you've reminded me of trick-or-treating, something I haven't thought of in so many years I can't believe it's just popped into my head. Sometimes I forget I was ever a child. Ever young and stupid and trusting."

My hands are shaking.

"Better not to like something you can't afford, so I didn't make a habit of gum."

I'm trembling.

"Better not to look like you grew up low-class, especially if you did grow up low-class. When have you ever seen me chew gum? I won't. It's low-class."

"Nothing about you is low-class." Benton watches me carefully, guardedly, and I see what is in his eyes. I'm scaring him.

But I can't stop myself. "I've worked damn hard in life not to look low-class. You didn't know me when I was getting started and had no idea what people are really like, people who have complete power over you, people you worship really, and what they're capable of luring you into so that you never feel the same about yourself. And then you bury it like that beating heart under the floorboards in Edgar Allan Poe, but you always know it's there. And you can't tell anyone. Even when it keeps you awake at night. You can't even tell the person you're closest to that there's this cold, dead heart under the floorboards and it's your fault it's under there."

"Christ, Kay."

"It's odd that everything we love seems to

be in close proximity to something hateful and dead," enters my mind next. "Well, not everything."

"Are you all right?"

"I'm fine. Just stressed out, and who the hell wouldn't be? Our house is a stone's throw from Norton's Woods, where someone was murdered yesterday, and he may have been at the Courtauld Gallery at the same time Lucy and I were the summer before Nine-Eleven, which she thinks was caused by us, by the way. Liam Saltz was there, too, at the Courtauld, one of the lecturers. I didn't meet him then, but Lucy has him on CD. I can't remember what he talked about."

"I'm curious why you would bring him up."

"A link on a website that Jack was looking at for some reason."

Benton doesn't say anything, and he doesn't take his eyes off me.

"You and I go in The Biscuit when I'm home on weekends, maybe we've been in there at the same time Johnny Donahue and his MIT friend were," I go on and can't keep up with my thoughts. "We love Salem and the oils and candles in the shops there, the same shops that sell iron spikes, devil's bone. Our favorite getaway in Boston is next to where Wally Jamison's body was found the morning after Halloween. Is someone watching us? Does someone know everything we do? What was Jack doing in Salem on Halloween?"

"Wally's body got where it was by boat, not the wharf," Benton replies, and I don't know where he got the information.

"All these things in common. You'd think we live in a small town."

"You don't look good."

"You're sure it was a boat. I feel like I'm having a hot flash." I touch my cheek, press my hand against it. "Lord. That will be next. So much to look forward to."

"More relevant is the fact that someone deliberately dumped his body where the hundred-foot cutters are homeported with guardsmen on board." Benton watches my every move. "And starting around daybreak, support staff and other personnel show up for work and the wharf is a parking lot. All these people getting out of their cars and seeing a mutilated body floating in the water. That's brazen. Killing a little kid in his own backyard while his parents are inside the house is brazen. Killing someone on Super Bowl Sunday in Norton's Woods while a VIP wedding is going on is brazen. Doing all this in our own neighborhoods is brazen. Yes."

"First you know it's a boat. Next you know it was a VIP wedding, not just a wedding but a VIP wedding." I don't ask but state. He wouldn't say it if he didn't know it. "Why was Jack in Salem? Doing what there? You can't even get a hotel room in Salem on Halloween. You can't even drive, there are so many people."

"Are you sure you're all right?"

"Do you think it's personal?" I ask as I obsess about what a small world it is. "I come home and this is my welcome. To have all this ugliness and death and deceit and betrayal practically in my lap."

"To some extent, yes," Benton says.

"Well, thank you for that."

"I said, 'to some extent.' Not everything."

"You said you think it's personal. I want to know exactly how it is personal."

"Try to calm down. Breathe slowly." He reaches for my hand, and I won't let him touch me. "Slowly, slowly, Kay."

I pull away from him, and he returns his hand to his lap, to the iPhone in it that flashes red every other second as messages land. I don't want him to touch me. It's as if I have no skin.

"Is there anything to eat in this place? I can send out for something," Benton says.

"Maybe it's low blood sugar. When did you eat last?"

"No. I couldn't right now. I'll be fine. Why do you say 'VIP'?" I hear myself ask.

He looks at his phone again, the tiny red light flashing its alert. "Anne," he says to me as he reads what just landed. "She's on her way, should be here in a few minutes."

"What else? I can download the scan in here, take a look."

"She didn't send it. She tried to call you. Obviously, you're not at your desk. There were undercover agents at the wedding. Protecting a VIP, but obviously he wasn't the one who needed it," Benton says. "Nobody was looking for the one who needed protecting. We didn't know he was going to be there."

I take another deep breath, and I try to diagnose a heart attack, if I might be having one.

"Did the agents see what happened?" Mount Auburn would be the closest hospital. I don't want to go to the hospital.

"Ones stationed by the outside doors weren't looking at him and didn't see it. They saw people rushing around him when he collapsed. There was no reason he was of interest, and the agents maintained their posts. They had to. In case it was some diversionary maneuver. You always maintain your post when you're on a protective detail; with rare exception, you don't divert."

I focus on the discomfort in the center of my chest and my shortness of breath. I'm sweating and light-headed, but there's no pain in my arms. No pain in my back. No pain in my jaw. No radiating pain, and heart attacks don't cause altered thinking. I look at my hands. I hold them in front of me as if I can see what's on them.

"When you saw Jack last week, did he smell like menthol?" I ask, and then I say, "Where is he? What exactly has he done?"

"What about menthol?"

"Extra-strength Nuprin patches, Bengay patches, something like that." I get up from Fielding's desk. "If he's wearing them all the time and reeks of eucalyptus, of menthol, it's usually an indication he's abusing himself physically, tearing the hell out of himself physically in the gym, in his tae kwon do tournaments, has chronic and acute muscle and joint pain. Steroids. When Jack's on steroids, well . . . That's always been the prelude to other things."

"Based on what I saw last week, he's on something."

I'm already taking off Fielding's lab coat.

I fold it into a neat square and place it on top of his desk.

"Is there a place you can lie down?" Benton says. "I think you should lie down. The on-call room downstairs. There's a bed. I can't take you home. You can't be there right now. I don't want you going out of this building, not without me."

"I don't need to lie down. Lying down won't help. It will make it worse." I walk into Fielding's bathroom and snatch a trash basket liner from a box under the sink.

Benton is on his feet, watching what I'm doing, keeping an eye on me as I tuck the folded lab coat inside the liner and return to the bathroom. I scrub my hands and face with soap and hot water. I wash any area of skin that might have come into contact with the plastic film I found in Fielding's lab coat pocket.

"Drugs," I announce when I sit back down.

Benton returns to his chair, tensely, as if he might spring up again.

"Something transdermal that certainly isn't Nuprin or Motrin. Don't know what, but I will find out," I let him know.

"The piece of plastic you were touching."

"Unless you poisoned my coffee."

"Maybe a nicotine patch."

"You wouldn't poison me, would you? If you don't want to be married anymore, there are simpler solutions."

"I don't see why he'd be on nicotine unless as a stimulant? I guess so. Something like that."

"It's not something like that. I used to live off nicotine patches and never felt like this, not even when I would light up while I still had a twenty-one-milligram patch on. A true addict. That's me. But not drugs, not whatever this is. What has he done?"

Benton stares at his coffee mug, tracing the AFME crest on the black glazed ceramic. His silence confirms what I suspect. Whatever Fielding is involved in, it's connected to everything else: to me, to Benton, to Briggs, to a dead football player, to a dead little boy, to the man from Norton's Woods, to dead soldiers from Great Britain and Worcester. Like planes lit up at night, connected to a tower, connected in a pattern, at times seeming at a standstill in the dark air but having been somewhere and going somewhere, individual forces that are part of something bigger, something incomprehensibly huge.

"You need to trust me," Benton says quietly.

"Has Briggs been in contact with you?"

"Some things have been going on for a while. Are you all right? I don't want to go before I know you are."

"This is what I've trained for, made so many sacrifices for." I decide to accept it. Acceptance makes it easier for me to know what to do. "Six months of being away from you, of being away from everyone, of giving up everything so I could come home to something that's been going on for a while. An agenda."

I almost add *just like in the beginning,* when I was barely a forensic pathologist and was too naïve to have a clue about what was happening. When I was quick to salute authority, and worse, to trust it, and much worse, to respect it, and even worse than that, to admire it, and worst of all, to admire John Briggs so much I would do anything he wanted, absolutely anything. Somehow I've managed to land in the same spot. The same thing again. An agenda. Lies and more lies, and innocent people who are disposable. Crimes as coldly carried out as any I've ever seen. Joanne Rule and Noonie Pieste are graphically in my mind, as real as they've ever been.

I see them on dented gurneys with rust in their welded seams and wheels that stick, and I remember my feet sticking as I walked across an old white stone floor that would not stay clean. It was always bloody in the Cape Town morgue, with bodies parked everywhere, and the week I was there I saw cases as extreme in their grotesqueness as that continent is extreme in its magnificent beauty. People hit by trains and run over on the highway, and domestic and drug deaths in the shantytowns, and a shark attack in False Bay, and a tourist who died from a fall on Table Mountain.

I have the irrational thought that if I go downstairs and walk into my cooler, the bodies of those two slain women will be waiting for me just as they were on that December morning after I'd flown nineteen hours in a small coach seat to get to them. Only they had already been looked at by the time I showed up, and that would have been true if I'd flown Mach II on the Concorde or been a block away from them when they were murdered. It wasn't possible for me to get to them fast enough. Their bodies may as well have been on a movie set, they were so staged. Innocent young women murdered for the sake of a news story, for the sake of power and influence and votes, and I couldn't put a stop to it.

I not only couldn't stop it, I helped make it happen, because I made it possible for it to happen, and I replay what PFC Gabriel's mother said about hate crimes and being rewarded for them. My office at Dover is right next to Briggs's command suite. I remember someone walking past my closed door several times while I was talking to her. Whoever it was paused at least twice. It crossed my mind at the time that someone might be waiting to come in but could hear through the door that I was on the phone and was unwilling to interrupt. The more likely answer is that someone was listening. Briggs has started something, or someone allied with him has, and Benton's right, it's been going on for a while.

"Then these last six months have been nothing more than a political ploy. How sad. How tawdry. How disappointing." My voice is steady, and I sound completely calm, the way I get before I do something.

"Are you okay? Because we should go downstairs if you're okay. Anne is here. We should talk to her, and then I need to go." Benton has gotten up and is near the door, waiting for me with his phone in hand.

"Let me guess. Briggs made sure I got this position so he could keep it open for whom-ever he really has in mind." I go on and my heart has slowed and my nerves feel steadier, as if they're firing normally again.

"Wanted me to keep the seat warm. Or was I the excuse to get this place built, to get MIT, get Harvard, get everybody on board, to justify some thirty million in grants?"

Benton reads something else as messages drop out of the thin air, one after another.

"He could have saved himself a lot of trouble," I say as I get up from the desk.

"You're not going to quit," Benton says, reading what someone has just sent to him. "Don't give them that satisfaction."

" 'Them.' Then it's more than one."

He doesn't answer as he types with his thumbs.

"Well, it's always been more than one. Take your pick," I say as we walk out together.

"If you quit, you give them exactly what they want." As he reads and scrolls down on his phone.

"People like that don't know what they want." I shut Fielding's door behind us, making sure it's locked. "They just think they do."

We begin our descent in my bullet-shaped building that on dark nights and gloomy days is the color of lead.

I'm explaining to Benton the indented writing on a pad of call sheets as we glide down in an elevator I researched and selected because it reduces energy consumption by fifty percent. It can't be a coincidence that Fielding was interested in a keynote address Dr. Liam Saltz just gave at Whitehall, I say, while numbers change on a digital display, while we gently sink from floor to floor in the soft glow of LEDs in my environmentally friendly hoisting machine that no one who works here appreciates in the least, from what I've heard. Mostly there are complaints because it is slow.

"He's one extreme, and DARPA's certainly the other, neither of them always right, that's for sure." I describe Dr. Saltz as a computer scientist, an engineer, a philosopher, a theologian, whose sport, whose art, most assuredly isn't war. He hates wars and those who make them.

"I know all about him and his art." Benton doesn't say it in a positive way as we stop gently and the steel door slides open with scarcely a sound. "I certainly remember from that time at CNN when you and I got into a spat because of him."

"I don't remember getting into a spat." We are back in the receiving area, where Ron is sternly alert behind his glass partition, exactly as we left him long hours ago.

In split screens of video displays I see cars parked in the lot behind the building, SUVs that aren't covered with snow and have their headlights on. Agents or undercover police, and I remember windows glowing in MIT buildings rising above the CFC fence, I remember noticing it at the time Benton drove us here, and now I know why. The CFC has been under surveillance, and the FBI, the police, aren't making any effort to disguise their presence now. I feel as if the CFC is on lockdown.

Ever since I walked out of Port Mortuary at Dover, I have been accompanied or locked inside a secured building, and the reason isn't what was presented, at least not the only reason. No one was trying to get me home as quickly as possible because of a body bleeding inside the cooler. That was a priority but certainly not the only one and maybe not even the top one. Certain people used that as an excuse to escort me, certain people, such as my niece, who was armed and playing bodyguard, and I can't believe Benton wasn't involved in that decision, no matter what he did or didn't know at the time.

"Maybe you remember him hitting on you," Benton is saying as we follow the gray corridor.

"You seem to think I'm having sex with everyone."

"Not with everyone," he says.

I smile. I almost laugh.

"You're feeling better," he says, touching my arm tenderly as he walks with me.

Whatever got into me has passed, and I wish it wasn't such a godforsaken hour of the morning. I wish someone was in the trace evidence lab so we could take a look at the plastic film I was exposed to, probably try the scanning electron microscope first, then Fourier transform infrared or whatever detectors it takes to figure out what is on Fielding's pain-relieving patches. I've never taken anabolic steroids and don't know firsthand how that would feel, but I can't imagine it's what I felt upstairs. Not that quickly.

Cocaine, crystal methamphetamine, LSD, whatever could get into my system instantly and transdermally, hopefully nothing like that, either, but what would I know about how that would feel? Not an opioid like fentanyl, which is the most common narcotic delivered by a patch. A strong pain reliever like fentanyl wouldn't have caused me to react the way I did, but again, I'm not sure. I've never been on fentanyl. Everybody reacts differently to medications, and uncontrolled substances can be contaminated with impurities and have variable doses.

"Really. You seem like yourself." Benton touches me again. "How are you feeling? You okay for sure?"

"Worn off, whatever it was. I wouldn't do the case if it wasn't, if I felt even remotely impaired," I tell him. "I guess you're coming to the autopsy room." Since we're headed there.

"A drink. Right." He is back to Liam Saltz. "He bumps into you at CNN and asks you to have a drink with him at midnight. That's not exactly normal."

"I'm not sure how to take that. But I don't feel flattered."

"His reputation with women is on a par with certain politicians who will remain unnamed. What's the buzzword these days? A sexual addiction."

"Well, if you're going to have one."

We walk past the x-ray room, and the door is shut, the red light off because the scanner isn't in use. The lower level is empty and silent, and I wonder where Marino is. Maybe he's with Anne.

"He had any contact with you since then? That was what? About two years ago?" Benton asks. "Or maybe with some of your compatriots at Walter Reed or Dover?"

"Not with me. I wouldn't know about others, except no one involved with the armed forces is a fan of Dr. Saltz's. He's not considered patriotic, which really isn't fair if you analyze what he's actually saying."

"Problem is nobody seems to understand what anybody is saying anymore. People don't listen. Saltz isn't a communist. He's not a terrorist. He hasn't committed treason. He just doesn't know how to curb his enthusiasm and muzzle his big mouth. But he's not of interest to the government. Well, he wasn't."

"Suddenly, he is." I assume that's what Benton will tell me next.

"He wasn't at Whitehall yesterday. Wasn't even in London." Benton waits until now to inform me of this as we pause before the locked double steel doors of the autopsy room. "I don't guess you found that part on the Internet when you were trying to make heads or tails of Jack's indented writing," Benton adds in a tone that is shaded with other meanings. A hint of hostility, not directed at me but at Fielding.

"How do you know where Liam Saltz was or wasn't?" I ask at the same time I think about what Benton mentioned upstairs. He referred to the event at Norton's Woods as a VIP wedding and mentioned a security presence. Undercover agents, Benton told me, although it was during an interval when I wasn't thinking as clearly as I should have been.

"Did his keynote address by satellite on a big video screen. Well attended by the audience at Whitehall," Benton says as if he was there. "He had a complication, a family matter, and had to leave the country."

I think of the man beyond these closed steel doors. A man whose wristwatch when he died may have been set to UK time. A man with an old robot called MORT inside his apartment, the same robot that Liam Saltz and I testified against, persuading people in power to disallow its use.

"Is that why Jack was looking him up, looking up RUSI or whatever he was looking at early yesterday morning?" I ask as I scan open the lock to the autopsy room.

"I'm wondering how that happened, if he got a call and then looked him up or maybe knew he was in Cambridge for some reason," Benton replies. "I'm wondering a lot of things that hopefully will get answered soon. What I do know is Dr. Saltz was here for the wedding. The daughter of his current wife, whose biological father was supposed to give her away, then got the swine flu."

"I text-messaged you," Anne tells me, and she's shrouded in blue as she works on a computer that is contained in a waterproof stainless-steel enclosure, the sealed keyboard mounted at a height suitable for typing while standing. Behind her on the autopsy table of station one, which is now shiny and clean, is the man from Norton's Woods.

"I'm sorry," I say to her abstractedly as I think of Liam Saltz and worry what his connection might be to this dead man, beyond robots, particularly MORT. "My phone's in my office, and I've not been in there," I say to Anne, and then I ask Benton, "Does he have other children?"

"He's at the Charles Hotel," Benton replies. "Someone's on the way to talk to him. But to answer your question, yes, he does. He has a number of children and stepchildren from multiple marriages."

"I wanted to let you know I didn't feel comfortable uploading his scans and e-mailing them," Anne then says to me. "Don't know what we're dealing with and thought it was better to play it extra-safe. If you're going to hang around, you need to cover up." She directs this to Benton. "Got no clue what this one's been exposed to, but he didn't set off any alarms. At least he's not radioactive. Whatever he's got in him isn't, thank God."

"I assume all was quiet at the hospital. No incidents," Benton says to her. "I'm not staying."

"Security escorted us in and out, and we didn't see anyone else — no patients or staff, at any rate."

"You found something in him?" I ask her.

"Trace amounts of metal." Anne's gloved hands move on the computer's keyboard and click the mouse, both freshly overlaid with industrial silicone. Fielding's sloppy presence is noticeably gone from the autopsy room, and I see water in the sink of station one — my station — and a big sponge, the surgical instruments bright and shiny and neatly arranged on the dissecting board. I spot a mop that wasn't here earlier, and a whetstone on a countertop.

"I'm amazed," I say to her as I look around.

"Ollie," she says, clicking the mouse. "I called him, and he drove back and spruced up the place."

"You're kidding."

"It's not that we haven't tried while you were gone. Jack's been using this work space, and we've learned to stay away."

"How can there be metal that didn't show

up on CT?" Benton watches her scroll through files she created at the neuroimaging lab, looking for the images she wants from the MRI.

"If it's really small," I explain to him how it's possible. "A threshold size of less than point-five millimeter and I wouldn't expect it to be detected on CT. That's why we wanted to rule out the possibility by using MR, and apparently it's a good thing."

"Although maybe not if he was alive," Anne says, clicking on a file. "You don't want something ferromagnetic in a living person, because it's going to torque. It's going to move. Like metal shavings in the eyes of people involved in professions that expose them to something like that. They may not even know it until they get an MRI. Then they know it; boy, do they ever. Or if they have body piercings they don't tell us about, and we've seen that enough times," she says to Benton. "Or, God forbid, a pacemaker. Metal moves, and it heats up."

"Theories?" I ask her, because I can't imagine an event or a weapon that could create what has just filled the video display.

"Your guess is as good as mine," she answers as we study high-resolution images of the dead man's internal damage, a dark distorted area of signal voids that starts just inside the buttonhole wound and becomes increasingly less pronounced the deeper the penetration inside the organs and soft tissue structures of the chest.

"Because of the magnetic field, even with what must be particles incredibly minute, you're going to get artifact. Right here," I point out to Benton. "These very dark and distorted areas where there's no signal penetration. You get this blooming artifact along the wound track, what's left of the wound track, because the signal's been blown out by metal. He's got some sort of ferromagnetic foreign bodies inside him, all right."

"What could do that?" Benton asks.

"I'm going to have to recover some of it, analyze it." I think of what Lucy said about thermite. It would be ferromagnetic just as bullets are, both metal composites having iron oxide in common.

"Point-five? The size of dust?" Benton's eyes are distracted by other thoughts.

"A little bigger," Anne replies.

"About the size of gunshot residue, grains of unburned powder," I add.

"A projectile like a bullet could be reduced to frag no bigger than grains of gunshot powder," Benton considers, and I can tell he is connecting what I'm saying with something else, and I think of my niece and wonder exactly what she said to him while they were together in her lab earlier. I think of shark bang sticks and nanoexplosives, but there are no thermal injuries, no burns. It wouldn't make sense.

"No projectile I've ever seen," Anne says, and I agree. "Do we know anything more about who he might be?" She means the body on the table. "I wasn't trying to eavesdrop."

"Hopefully soon," Benton replies.

"It sounds like you might have an idea," Anne says to him.

"Our first clue was he showed up at Norton's Woods at the same time Dr. Saltz was inside the building, and that was something to check because of certain interests these two individuals would have in common." He means robots, I suspect.

"I don't think I know who that is," Anne says to him.

"A scientist who won a Nobel Prize and is an expatriate," Benton says, and as I observe him with Anne I'm reminded they are colleagues and friends, that he treats her with an easy familiarity, with trust that he doesn't exhibit around most people. "And if he" — Benton indicates the dead man — "knew Dr. Saltz was coming to Cambridge, the question was how."

"Do we know if he knew that?" I ask.

"Right now we don't for a fact."

"So Dr. Saltz was at the wedding. But this one wasn't dressed for a wedding." Anne indicates the nude dead body on the table. "He had his dog with him. And a gun."

"What I know so far is the bride is a daughter from a different marriage," Benton says as if this detail has been carefully checked. "The daughter's father, who was supposed to give her away, got sick. So she asked her stepfather, Dr. Saltz, at the last minute, and he couldn't physically be in two places at once. He flew into Boston on Saturday and made his appearance at White-hall via satellite. A sacrifice on his part. The last thing he felt like doing, I'm sure, was to reenter the U.S. and show up at Cambridge."

"The undercover agents?" I ask. "For him? If so, why? I know he has enemies, but why would the FBI be offering protection to a civilian scientist from the UK?"

"That's the irony," Benton says. "The security at the event wasn't about him, was about those attending the wedding, most of them from the UK because of the groom's family. The groom is Russell Brown's son, David. Both Liam Saltz's stepdaughter Ruth and David attend Harvard Law, which is one reason the wedding was here."

Russell Brown. The shadow secretary of state for defense, whose speech I just read on the RUSI website.

"He shows up at an event like that and is armed," I say as I move closer to the steel table. "A gun with the serial number eradicated?"

"Right. Why?" Benton asks. "To protect himself, or was he a potential assailant? Or to protect himself for a reason that's unrelated to the wedding and the people I've just mentioned?"

"Possibly top-secret technology he was involved in," I offer. "Technology worth quite a lot of money," I add. "Technology people might kill for."

"And maybe did kill for," Anne says as she looks at the dead young man.

"Hopefully, we'll know soon," Benton says.

I look at the dead man rigid on his back, his curled fingers and the position of his arms, his legs, his hands, his head, exactly as they were earlier, no matter how much he has been disturbed during transport and scans. Rigor mortis is complete, but he won't resist me strenuously as I examine him, because he's thin. He doesn't have much muscle fiber for calcium ions to have gotten trapped in after his neurotransmitters quit. I can break him easily. I can bend him to my will.

"I've got to go," Benton says to me. "I know you want to get this taken care of. I'll need your help with something by the time you're ready to get away from here, and you're not to get away on your own. Make sure she calls me," he says to Anne as she labels test tubes and specimen containers. "Call me or call Marino," he adds. "Give us an hour's advance notice."

"Marino will be with you . . . ?" I start to ask.

"We're working on something. He's already there."

I no longer question what Benton is referring to when he says "we," and he looks one more time at me, his eyes meeting mine with the intimacy of a lingering touch, and he leaves the autopsy room. I hear the receding sound of his brisk footsteps along the hard tile corridor, then his voice and another voice as he talks to someone, perhaps Ron. I can't make out a word they are saying, but they sound serious and intense before silence returns abruptly. I imagine Benton has left the receiving area, and on a video display I'm startled by him.

Picked up by security cameras, he walks through the bay as he zips up the shearling coat I gave him so long ago I don't remember the year, only that it was in Aspen, where he used to have a place.

I watch him on closed-circuit TV opening the side door that is next to the massive bay door, and then another camera picks him up outside my building as he walks past his green SUV parked in my spot. He gets into a different SUV, dark and big with bright headlights that the snow slashes through, the wipers sweeping side to side, and I can't see who is driving. I watch the SUV in my snow-covered lot, backing up, moving forward, and pausing as the big gate opens, and finally out of sight in the bitter weather at the empty hour of four a.m., with my husband in the passenger's seat, driven by someone, maybe his FBI friend Douglas, both of them headed to a destination that for some reason I've not been told about.

14

Inside the anteroom I prepare for battle the way I always do, suiting up in armor made of plastic and paper.

I never feel like a doctor, not even a surgeon, as I get ready to conduct a post-mortem examination, and I suspect only people who deal with the dead for a living can understand what I mean by that. During my medical school residencies I was no different from other doctors, tending to the sick and injured on wards and in emergency rooms, and I assisted in surgical procedures in the OR. So I know what it is to incise warm bodies that have a blood pressure and something vital to lose. What I'm about to do couldn't be more different from that, and the first time I inserted a scalpel blade into cold, unfeeling flesh, made my first Y-incision on my first dead patient, I gave up something I've never gotten back.

I abandoned any notion that I might be

godlike or heroic or gifted beyond other mortals. I rejected the fantasy that I could heal any creature, including myself. No doctor has the power to cause blood to clot or tissue or bone to regenerate or tumors to shrink. We don't create, only prompt biological functions to work or not work properly on their own, and in that regard, doctors are more limited than a mechanic or an engineer who actually builds something out of nothing. My choice of a medical specialty, which my mother and sister still consider morbid and abnormal, probably has made me more honest than most physicians. I know that when I administer my healing touch to the dead they are unmoved by me or my bedside manner. They stay just as dead as they were before. They don't say thank you or send holiday greetings or name their children after me. Of course I was cognizant of all this when I decided on pathology, but that's like saying you know what combat is when you enlist in the marines and get deployed to the mountains of Afghanistan. People don't really know what anything is really like until it really happens to them.

I can never smell the acrid, oily, pungent odor of unbuffered formaldehyde without being reminded of how naïve I was to assume that the dissection of a cadaver donated to science for teaching purposes is anything like the autopsy of an unembalmed person whose cause of death is questioned. My first one took place in the Hopkins hospital morgue, which was a crude place compared to what is beyond this room where I am this minute folding my AFME field clothes and placing them on a bench, not bothering with the locker room or modesty at this hour. The woman whose name I still recall was only thirty-three and left behind two small children and a husband when she died of postoperative complications from an appendectomy.

To this day I'm sorry she was my science project. I'm sorry she was ever put in a position to be any pathology resident's project, and I remember thinking how absurd it was that such a healthy young human being had succumbed to an infection caused by the removal of a rather useless wormlike pouch from the large intestine. I wanted to make her better. As I worked on her, practiced on her, I wanted her to come to and climb off that scratched-up steel pedestal table in the center of the dingy floor inside that dreary subterranean room that smelled like death. I wanted her alive and well and to feel I'd had something to do with it. I'm not a surgeon. What I do is excavate so I can make my case when I go to war with killers or, less dramatically but more typically, with lawyers.

Anne was thoughtful enough to find a pair of freshly laundered scrubs, size medium and the institutional green I'm accustomed to, and I put them on, then over them a disposable gown, which I tie snugly in back before I pull shoe covers out of a dispenser and cover a pair of rubber medical clogs Anne dug up somewhere. Next are protective sleeves, a hair cover, a mask, and a face shield, and finally I double-glove.

"Maybe you could scribe for me," I say to her as I return to the autopsy room, a big, empty vista of gleaming white and bright steel. Only the three of us are here, if I include my patient on the first table. "In the event I don't get to dictate my findings directly afterward, as it appears I may have to leave."

"Not by yourself," she reminds me.

"Benton took the car key," I remind her.

"Wouldn't stop you, since we have vehicles, so don't try to fool me. When it's time, I'm calling him, and there won't be an argument." Anne can say almost anything and not sound disrespectful or rude.

She takes photographs while I swab the

entrance wound on the lower back. Then I swab orifices in the off chance this homicide might involve a sexual assault, although I don't see how, based on what has been described.

"Because we're looking for a unicorn." I seal anal and oral swabs in paper envelopes and label and initial them. "Not your everyday pony, and I'm not going to believe anything, anyway, since I didn't go to the scene."

"Well, nobody did," Anne says. "Which is a shame."

"Even if somebody had, I'd still be looking for a unicorn."

"I don't blame you. I wouldn't trust what anybody says if I were you."

"If you were me." I lock a new blade into a scalpel as she fills a labeled plastic jar with formalin.

"Unless it's me who's talking," she replies without looking at me. "I wouldn't lie or cheat or help myself to things that aren't mine. I would never treat this place as if it belongs to me. Never mind. I shouldn't get into it."

I won't let her get into it. It isn't necessary to put her in a position like that, betraying the people who have betrayed me. I know what it feels like to be put in a position like that. It's one of the worst feelings there is and promotes lying, overtly or by omission, and I know that feeling, too. An untruth that lodges intact in the core of your being like undigested corn found in Egyptian mummies. There's no getting rid of such a thing, of undoing it, without going in to get it, and I'm not sure I have the courage for that, as I think of the worn wooden steps leading down into the basement of the house in Cambridge. I think of the rough stone walls belowground and the fifteen-hundred-pound safe with its two-inch-thick composite triple-lock door.

"I don't suppose you've heard any rumors about where everybody is," I then say. "When you were with Marino at McLean." I begin the Y incision, cutting from clavicle to clavicle, then long and deep straight down with a slight detour around the navel and terminating at the pubic bone in the lower abdomen. "Did you get any idea of who is in our parking lot and what's going on? Since I seem to be under house arrest for reasons no one has been inclined to make completely clear."

"The FBI." Anne doesn't tell me something I don't know as she walks to the wall where clipboards hang from hooks next to rows of plastic racks for blank forms and diagrams. "At least two agents in the parking lot, and one followed us. Someone did." She collects the paperwork she needs and selects a clipboard after making sure the ballpoint pen attached to it by a cord has ink. "A detective, an agent. I don't know who followed us to the hospital, but someone who clearly had alerted security before we got there." She returns to the table. "When we rolled up at the neuroimaging lab, there were three McLean security guys, most excitement they've had in years. And then this person in an SUV, a dark-blue Ford, an Explorer or an Expedition."

Maybe what Benton just drove away in, and I ask Anne, "Did he or she get out of the SUV? I assume you didn't talk to whoever it was?" I reflect back soft tissue. The man is so lean he has just the thinnest layer of yellow fat before the tissue turns beefy red.

"It was hard to see, and I wasn't going to walk right up and stare. The agent was still sitting in the SUV when we left and followed us back here."

She picks up rib cutters from the surgical cart and helps me remove the breastplate, exposing the organs and significant hemorrhage, and I smell the beginning of cells breaking down, the faintest hint of what promises to be putrid and foul. The odors emitted by the human body as it decomposes are uniquely unpleasant. It isn't like a bird or an opossum or the largest mammal one can think of. In death we are as different from other creatures as we are in life, and I would recognize the stench of decaying human flesh anywhere.

"How do you want to do this? En bloc? And deal with the metal after we have the organs on the cutting board?" Anne asks.

"I think we need to synchronize what we're doing inch by inch, step by step. Line things up with the scans as best we can, because I'm not sure I'm going to be able to see whatever these ferromagnetic foreign bodies are unless I'm looking right at them with a lens." I wipe my bloody gloved hands on a towel and step closer to the video display, which Anne has divided into quadrants to give me a choice of images from the MRI.

"Distributed a lot like gunshot powder," she suggests. "Although we can't see the actual metal particles because they canceled the signal."

"True. More blooming artifact, more voids at the beginning than the end. Greatest amount at the entrance." I point my bloody gloved finger at the screen.

"But no residue of anything on the surface," she says. "And that's different from a gunshot wound, a contact wound."

"Everything about this is different from a gunshot wound," I answer.

"You can see that whatever this stuff is, it starts here." She indicates the entrance wound on the lower back. "But not at the surface. Just beneath it, maybe half an inch beneath it, which is really weird. I'm trying to imagine it and can't. If you pressed something against his back and fired, you'd get gunshot residue on the clothes and in the entrance wound, not just an inch inside and then deeper."

"I looked at his clothes earlier."

"No burns or soot, no evidence of GSR," she says.

"Not grossly," I correct her, because not being able to see gunshot residue doesn't mean it isn't there.

"Exactly. Nothing visually."

"What about Morrow? I don't suppose he came downstairs yesterday while Marino had the body in ID, printing him, collecting personal effects. I don't suppose someone thought to ask Morrow to do a presumptive test for nitrites on the clothing, since we didn't know at that time there could be GSR or that there was even an entrance

wound that correlates with cuts in the clothing."

"Not that I know of. And he left early."

"I heard. Well, we still can test presumptively, but I'd be really surprised if that's
what we're seeing on MR. When Morrow or
maybe Phil gets in, let's get them to do a
Griess test just to satisfy my curiosity before
we move on to something else. I'm betting
it will be negative, but it's not destructive,
so nothing lost."

It's a simple, quick procedure involving
desensitized photographic paper that is
treated with a solution of sulfanilic acid,
distilled water, and alpha-naphthol in
methanol. When the paper is pressed against
the area of clothing in question and then
exposed to steam, any nitrite residues will
turn orange.

"Of course, we're going to do SEM-
EDX," I add. "But these days it's a good
idea to do more than one thing, since slowly
but surely lead is going to disappear from
ammunition, and most of these tests are
looking for lead, which is toxic to the
environment. So we need to start checking
for zinc and aluminum alloys, plus various
stabilizers and plasticizers, which are added
to the gunpowder during manufacturing.
Here in the U.S., at any rate. Not so much

in combat, where poisoning the environment with heavy metals is considered a fine idea, since the goal is to create dirty bombs, the dirtier the better."

"Not our goal, I hope."

"No, not ours. We don't do that."

"I never know what to believe."

"I do know what to believe, at least about some things. I know what comes back to us when our service people are returned to Dover," I reply. "I know what's in them. I know what isn't. I know what's manufactured by us and what's manufactured by others, the Iraqi insurgency, the Taliban, the Iranians. That's one of the things we do, materials analysis to figure out who is making what, who is supplying it."

"So when I hear these things about weapons or bombs made in Iran . . ."

"That's where it comes from. It's how the U.S. knows. Intelligence from our dead, from what they teach us."

We leave it at that, our talk of the war, because of this other war that has killed a man who is too young to be finished. A man who took an old greyhound for a walk in the civilized world of Cambridge and ended up in my care.

"They've developed some really interesting technology in Texas that I want us to look into." I return to gunshot residue because it is safer to talk about that. "Combining solid phase micro-extraction with gas chromatography coupled with a nitrogen phosphorus detector."

"As Texas should, since it's a state law that everybody carry a gun. Or is it that firearms are tax-deductible, like farming and raising livestock is around here?"

"Well, not quite," I reply. "But we'll want to look into doing something similar at the CFC, since of all places I would expect a growing prevalence of *green* ammunition."

"Of course. Don't pollute the environment while you're doing a drive-by shooting."

"What scientists have come up with at Sam Houston can detect as little as one gunpowder particle, which isn't relevant in this case, since we know this man has metal in him, almost at a microscopic level but plenty of it. Preliminarily, at any rate, Marino should have used a GSR kit on the hands at least. Since this man was armed."

"I do know that he did that much before he printed him," Anne says. "Because of the gun, although no sign it had been fired. But I saw him using a stub on the hands when I walked into ID at one point."

"But not the wound, because you discovered it later. It wasn't swabbed."

"I haven't done anything. I wouldn't have. Not my department."

"Good. I'll take care of it when I get to it, when we turn him over," I decide. "Let's take out the bloc so I can blot the raw surfaces of the injured track. I'm going to use the MRI as my map and blot as much of the metal material as I can, in hopes that even if we can't see it, we're getting some of it. We know it's metal. The question is, what kind of metal and what is it from?"

In wall-mounted steel cabinets with glass doors I find a box of blotting paper while Anne lifts the bloc of organs out of the body and places it on the dissecting board.

"I can't tell you what a problem it is these days, people with metal in them," she comments as she collects organ fragments from the chest cavity, which is opened and empty like a china cup, the ribs gleaming opaquely through glistening red tissue. "Including old bullets of the non-green variety. We get these research subjects in after the hospital's advertised for volunteers, and of course I mean the *normals,* right? All these people who come in and they're just as normal as the day is long, right? And have nothing to report. Uh, right. Like it's real normal to have an old bullet in you."

She returns fragments of the left kidney, the left lung, and the heart to their correct anatomical positions on the bloc of organs as if she's piecing together a puzzle.

"Happens more often than you think," she says. "Well, not more often than someone like you would think, since we see things like that in the morgue all the time. And then you get the old routine that bullets are lead, and lead isn't magnetic, so it's fine to scan the person. Usually, one of the psychiatrists who doesn't know any better and can't seem to remember from one time to the next that, no, wrong again. Lead, iron, nickel, cobalt. All bullets, pellets, are ferromagnetic, I don't care if they're so-called green, they're going to torque because of the magnetic field. That could be a problem if someone's got a fragment in him that's in close proximity to a blood vessel, an organ. God forbid something was left in the brain if some poor person was shot in the head eons ago. Paxil, Neurontin, or the like aren't going to help the poor person's mood disorder if an old bullet relocates to the wrong place."

She rinses a fragment of kidney and places it on the dissecting board.

"We're going to need to measure how much blood is in the peritoneum." I'm looking at the hole in the diaphragm that I saw hours earlier when I followed the wound track during the CT scan. "I'm going to guess at least three hundred MLs, originating through the lacerated diaphragm, and at least fifty MLs in his pericardium, which normally might suggest some time interval before death because of how much he bled. But the severity of these injuries, which are similar to blast injuries? He had no survival time. Only as long as it took for his heart and respiration to quit. If I were willing to use the term *instant death,* this would qualify as one."

"This is unusual." Anne hands me a tiny fragment of kidney that is hard and brown with tan discoloration and retracted edges. "I mean, what is that? It almost looks fixed or cooked or something."

There is more. As I pull a light closer and look at the bloc of organs, I notice hard, dry fragments of the left lung's lower lobe and of the heart's left ventricle. Using a steel beaker, I scoop pooled blood and hematoma out of the mediastinum, or the middle section of the chest cavity, and find more fragments and tiny, hard, irregular blood clots. Looking closely at the disrupted left kidney, I note perirenal hemorrhage and interstitial emphysema, and more evidence of the same abnormal tissue changes in areas closest to the wound track, areas most susceptible to damage from a blast. But what blast?

"Reminds me of tissue that's been frozen, almost freeze-dried," I say as I label sheets of blotting paper with an abbreviation for the location the sample came from. LLL for left lower lobe and LK for left kidney and LV for left ventricle of the heart.

In the strong light of a surgical lamp and the magnification of a hand lens I can barely make out dark silvery specks of whatever was blasted through this man when he was stabbed in the back. I see fibers and other debris that won't be discernible until they are looked at under a microscope, but I feel hopeful. Something was deposited that likely was unintended by the perpetrator, trace evidence that might give me information about the weapon and the person who used it. I turn the fume hood on the lowest setting so there is nothing more than an exchange of air, and I begin gently blotting.

I touch the sterile paper to the surfaces of fragmented tissue and the edges of wounds, and one by one lay the sheets inside the hood, where the gently circulating air will facilitate evaporation, the drying of blood without disturbing anything adhering to it. I collect samples of the freeze-dried-looking tissue and save them in plasticized cartons and also in small jars of formalin, and I tell Anne we're going to want a lot of photographs and that I'll ask colleagues of mine to look at images of internal damage and of the tannish tough tissue. I'll ask if they've ever seen anything like it before, and as I'm saying all this, I'm wondering who I mean. Not Briggs. I wouldn't dare send anything to him. Certainly not Fielding. No one who works here. No one at all comes to mind except Benton and Lucy, whose opinions won't help or matter. It's up to me whether I like it or not.

"Let's turn him over," I say, and empty of organs, he is light in the torso and head-heavy.

I measure the entrance wound and describe what it looks like and exactly where it is, and I examine the wound track through the bloc of organs, finding every area that was punctured by what I'm now certain was a narrow double- and single-edged blade.

"If you look at the wound, you can clearly see the two sharp ends of it, the corners of the buttonhole made by two sharp edges," I explain to Anne.

"I see." Her eyes are dubious behind her plastic glasses.

"But look here, where the wound track

terminates in the heart. Can you see how both ends of the wound are identical, both very sharp?" I move the light closer and hand her a magnifying lens.

"Slightly different from the wound on his back," she says.

"Yes. Because when the blade terminated in the heart muscle, it didn't penetrate as deeply; just the tip went in. As opposed to when these other wounds were made." I show her. "The tip penetrated and was followed by the length of the blade running through, and as you can see, the one end of the wound is just a little blunted and slightly stretched. You especially can see it here, where it penetrated the left kidney and kept going."

"I think I see what you're saying."

"Not what you would expect with a butterfly knife, a boning knife, a dagger, all of which are double-edged, both sides of the blade sharp from tip to handle. This brings to mind something spear-tipped — sharp on both sides at the tip but single-edged after that, like I've seen in some fighting knives or, in particular, something like a bowie knife or bayonet, where the top of the blade has been sharpened on both edges to make penetration easier in stabbings. So what we've got is an entrance that is three-eighths of an inch linear; both ends of the wound are sharp, with one that is slightly more blunted than the other. And the width expands to five-eighths of an inch." I measure, and Anne writes it down on a body diagram.

"So the blade is three-eighths of an inch at the tip, and at its widest it's five-eighths. That's pretty narrow. Almost like a stiletto," she says.

"But a stiletto is double-edged, the entire blade is."

"Homemade? A blade that injects something that explodes?"

"Without causing thermal injury, without causing burns. In fact, what we're seeing is more consistent with frostbite, where the tissue feels hard and is discolored," I remind her as I measure the distance from the wound on the man's back to the top of his head. "Twenty-six inches, and two inches to the left of the mid-spine. Direction is up and anterior, with extensive subcutaneous and tissue emphysema along the track, perforating the transverse process on the left twelfth rib paraspinally. Perforating paraspinal muscle, perirenal fat, left adrenal, left kidney, diaphragm, left lung, and pericardium, terminating in the heart."

"How long a blade for something to

perforate all that?"

"At least five inches."

She plugs in the autopsy saw, and we turn the body on its back again. I place a headrest under the neck and incise the scalp from ear to ear, following the hairline so the sutures won't be visible afterward. The top of the skull is white like an egg as I reflect the scalp back and pull the face down like a sock, like something sad, the features collapsing as if he is crying.

15

I don't realize the sun is up and the arctic front has marched off to the south until I open my office door and am greeted by a clear blue sky beyond tall windows.

I look down seven floors, and there are a few cars moving slowly on the white-frosted furrowed road below, and going the other way, a snowplow truck with its yellow blade held up like a crab claw as it scuttles along, looking for the right spot, then lowering the blade with a clank I can't hear from up here and scraping pavement that's not going to be completely cleared because of ice.

The riverbank is white, and the Charles is the color of old blue bottle glass and wrinkled by the current, and beyond in the distance the skyline of Boston catches the early light, the John Hancock Tower soaring far above any other high-rise, overbearing and sturdy, like a solitary column left standing in the ruins of an ancient temple. I think about coffee, and it is a fleeting urge as I wander into my bathroom and look at the coffeemaker on the counter by the sink and the boxes of K-Cups that include hazelnut.

I'm beyond being helped by stimulants, not sure I'd feel caffeine except in my gut, which is empty and raw. Intermittently, I'm stabbed by nausea, then I'm hungry, then nothing at all, just the gauziness of sleeplessness and the persistent hint of a headache that seems more remembered than real. My eyes burn, and thoughts move thickly but push with force like a heavy surf pounding against the same unyielding questions and tasks to be done. I won't wait for anyone, given a choice. I can't wait. There is no choice. I will overstep boundaries if need be, and why shouldn't I? Boundaries I've set have been stepped on right and left by others. I will do things myself, those things I know how to do. I am alone, more alone than I was because I've changed. Dover has changed me. I will do what is necessary, and it might not be what people want.

It is half past seven, and I've been downstairs all this time because Anne and I took care of other cases after we finished with the Norton's Woods man, whose name we are no closer to discovering, or if it is known, I've not been informed. I know intimate details about him that should be none of my business, but not the most important facts: who he is, what he was and hoped to become, his dreams, and what he loved and hated. I sit down at my desk and check the notes Anne made for me downstairs and add a few of my own, making sure I will remember later he had eaten something with poppy seeds and yellow cheese shortly before he died and the total amount of blood and clot in the left hemithorax was one thousand three hundred milliliters and the heart was disrupted into five irregular fragments that were still attached at the level of the valves.

I will want to emphasize this to the prosecution, it occurs to me, because I'm thinking about court. For me it all ends there, at least on the civilian side of my life. I imagine the prosecutor using inflammatory language I can't use, telling the jury that the man ate cheese and a poppy-seed bagel and took his rescued old dog for a walk, that his heart was blown to pieces, causing him to hemorrhage almost three units of blood or more than a third of all the blood in his body in a matter of minutes. The autopsy didn't reveal the purpose of the man's death, although provisionally, at least the cause of it is simple, and I absently write it down as I continue to ponder and meditate and make plans.

Atypical stab/puncture to the left back.

A pathological diagnosis that seems trite after what I just saw, and one that would give me pause, were I to come across it somewhere. I'd find it cryptic, almost tongue-in-cheek and coy, like a bad joke if one knows the rest of it, the massive blast-like disruption of the organs and that the death is a vicious and calculated homicide. I envision the hem of the long black coat quickly flapping past and what must have happened just seconds before when the person wearing it plunged a blade into the victim's lower back. For an instant he felt the physical response, the shock and pain as he exclaimed, *"Hey . . . !"* and clutched his chest, collapsing on his face on the slate path.

I imagine the person in the black coat quickly bending over to snatch off the man's black gloves and briskly walking away, perhaps tucking the blade up a sleeve or into a folded newspaper or I don't know. But as I imagine it, I believe the person in the long black coat is the killer and was covertly recorded by the dead man's head-phones, and it causes me to wonder again who was doing the spying. Did the killer plant micro–recording devices in the victim's headphones so he could be followed? And I imagine a figure in a long black coat walking swiftly through the shaded woods, coming up behind the victim, who couldn't hear anything but the music in his headphones as he's stabbed in the back, and he falls too fast to turn around. I wonder if he died not knowing who did this to him. And afterward? Is it what Lucy proposed? Did the person in the long black coat view the video files and decide it wasn't necessary to delete them from a webcam site somewhere, that in fact it was clever to leave them?

There are reasons for all things, I tell myself what has always been true but never feels that way while I'm in the middle of the problem. There are answers, and I will find them, and while the physics of how the fatal injury was executed may seem difficult to divine, I assure myself there are tracks the killer left behind. I have captured footprints on blotting paper. I will follow them to who did this. *You won't get away with it,* I think, as if I'm talking to the person in the long black coat. *I hope whoever you are, you have nothing to do with me, that you aren't someone I taught to be meticulous and clever.* I have decided that Jack Fielding is on the run or in custody. It even enters my mind that he might be dead. But I'm exhausted. I'm sleep-deprived. My thoughts aren't as disciplined as they should be. He can't be dead. Why would he be dead? I have seen the dead downstairs, and he wasn't among them.

My other patients of the morning were simple enough and asked little of me as I tended to them: a motor-vehicle fatality, and I could smell the booze and his bladder was full, as if he'd been drinking until the moment he left the bar and climbed behind the wheel in a snowstorm that careened him into a tree; a shooting in a run-down motel, and the needle tracks and prison tattoos of yet one more among us who died the way he lived; an asphyxia by a plastic dry-cleaning bag tied around an old widow's neck with an old red satin ribbon, maybe left over from a holiday during better times, her stomach full of dissolved white tablets, and next to the bed an empty bottle of a benzodiazepine prescribed for sleeplessness and anxiety.

I have no messages on my office and cell phones, no e-mails that matter to me at the moment and under the circumstances. When I checked Lucy's lab, she wasn't there, and when I checked with security, I discovered that even Ron has left, replaced by a guard I've never met, gangly and jug-eared like Ichabod Crane, someone named Phil who says Lucy's car isn't in the lot and the instructions are that the security guards aren't to let anyone into the building, not through the lower level or the lobby, without clearing it with me. Not possible, I let Phil know. Employees should be showing up already, or they will be at any minute, and I can't be the gatekeeper. Let anybody in who has a right to be here, I told him before I came upstairs. Except Dr. Fielding, and when I added that, I could tell it wasn't necessary. The guard named Phil clearly was aware that Fielding can't just show up or won't or maybe isn't able to, and besides, the FBI dominates my parking lot. I can see their SUVs clear as the bright, cold day on the video display on my desk.

I swivel my chair around to the polished black-granite countertop behind me, to my arsenal of microscopes and what accompanies them. Pulling on a pair of examination gloves, I slit open one of the white envelopes I sealed with white paper tape right before I came upstairs, and I pull out a sheet of blotting paper that is stained with a generous smear of dried blood that came from the area of the left kidney where I saw a dense collection of metallic foreign bodies in the

MRI. Turning on the lamp of my materials microscope, a Leica I have depended on for years, I carefully move the paper to the stage. I tilt the eyetubes to a viewing angle that won't strain my neck and shoulders and realize right away that the settings have been changed for someone much taller than me who is right-handed, someone who drinks coffee with cream and chews spearmint gum, I suspect. The ocular focus and interocular distance have been changed, too.

Switching to left-hand operation and adjusting the height so it is better suited for me, I start with a magnification of 50X, manipulating the focus knob with one hand as I use the other to move the sheet of blotting paper on the stage, lining up the bloody smear until I find what I'm looking for, bright whitish-silver chips and flakes in a constellation of other particles so minute that when I bump the magnification up to 100X, I can't make out their characteristics, only the rough edges and scratches and striations on the largest particles, what looks like unburned metal chips and filings that have been milled by a machine or a tool. Nothing I see reminds me of gunshot residue, doesn't even remotely resemble the flakes, disks, or balls I associate with gunpowder or the ragged fragments or particulate of a projectile or its jacket.

More curious is other debris mixed with blood and its obvious elements, the colorful confetti of detritus that constitutes everyday dust tangled with red cells piled up like coins, and granular leukocytes reminiscent of amoeba that are caught as if frozen in time, swimming and cavorting with a louse and a flea that at a magnified size remind me why seventeenth-century London went into a panic when Robert Hooke published *Micrographia* and revealed the piercing mouthparts and claws of what infested cats and mattresses. I recognize fungi and spores that look like sponges and fruit, spiny pieces of insect legs and insect egg cases that look like the delicate shells of nuts or spherical boxes carved of porous wood. As I move the paper on the stage, I find more hairy appendages of long-dead monsters, such as midges and mites and the wide compound eyes of a decapitated ant, the feathery antenna of what may have been a mosquito, the overlapping scales of animal hair, maybe from a horse or a dog or a rat, and reddish-orange flecks that could be rust.

I reach for the phone and call Benton. When he answers, I hear voices in the background and am subjected to a bad connection.

"A knife sharpened or shaped on something like a lathe, possibly a rusty one in a workshop or basement, possibly an old root cellar where there are mold, bugs, decaying vegetables, probably damp carpet," I say right off as I begin an Internet search on my computer, typing the keywords *knife* and *exploding gases.*

"What was sharpened?" Benton asks, and then he says something to someone else, something like *need the keys* or *need to keep.* "I'm moving, not in a good place," he gets back to me.

"The weapon used to stab him. A lathe, a grinder, possibly old or not taken care of, with traces of rust, based on the metal shavings and very fine particulate I'm seeing. I think the blade was honed, perhaps to make it thinner and to sharpen the tip on both edges, to turn the tip into a spear, so whatever might have been used for sharpening and polishing, a rasp, a file."

"You're talking about power tools that are old and rusty. A lot of rust?"

"Metalworking tools of some type, not necessarily power tools; I'm not in a position to be that detailed. I'm not an expert in metalworking and I don't know how much rust. Just that I found what looks like flakes of it." *Exploding intestines. How to clean your spark plugs. Common gases associated with metalworking and hand-forged knives,* I silently read what is on my computer screen as I then say to Benton, "Not that I pretend to be a trace-evidence examiner, but microscopically it's nothing I've not seen before, just never seen it blown into a body. But then I've never really looked. I've never had a reason to look for something like this, am unaccustomed to using blotting paper internally when someone has been stabbed. I suppose there could be all sorts of invisible fibers, debris, particulate, injected inside people who've been shot, stabbed, impaled, or God knows what."

I type *injection knife* into the search field because as I listen to myself, I'm reminded of remote delivery darts, of weapons powered by CO_2 to fire what's basically a long-range immobilization or tranquilizing missile with a small explosive charge and a hypodermic needle. Why couldn't you do the same thing with a knife, as long as it had a way to be powered and a narrow channel bored through the blade with an outlet hole near the tip?

"I'm walking outside to the car now," Benton says. "Will be there in forty-five minutes to an hour if the traffic's not too bad. The roads aren't bad. One-twenty-eight isn't too bad."

"Well, this wasn't hard." I'm disappointed. Nothing with so much potential for lethal damage should be this easy to find.

"What isn't hard?" Benton says as I look in amazement at an image of a steel combat knife with a gas outlet hole near the tip and a neoprene handle in a foam-lined plastic case.

"A CO_2 cartridge screws into the handle. . . ." I skim out loud. "Thrust the five-inch stainless-steel blade into the target as you use your thumb to push the release button, which it appears is part of the guard hub. . . ."

"Kay? Who's with you right now?"

"Injects a freezing ball of gas the size of a basketball or more than forty cubic inches at eight hundred pounds of pressure per square inch," I go on, looking at images on an elaborate website as I wonder how many people have such a weapon in their homes, their cars, their camping gear, or are walking around with it strapped to their sides. I have to admit it is ingenious, possibly one of the scariest things I've ever seen. "Can drop a large mammal in a single stab . . ."

"Kay, are you by yourself?"

"Freezes wound tissue instantly, thus

delaying bleeding and attracting other predators, so if you have to defend yourself against a great white shark, for example, it won't begin bleeding into the water and attracting other sharks until you are well out of the way." I skim and summarize and feel sickened. "It's called a WASP. You can add it to your shopping cart for less than four hundred dollars."

"Let's talk about it when I see you," Benton says over the phone.

"I've never heard of it." I read more about a compressed gas injection knife I can order right now as long as I'm over eighteen years of age. "Advertised for Special Ops, SWAT, pilots who are stranded in open water, scuba divers. Apparently developed to kill large marine predators — as I said, sharks, mammals, maybe whales and those in wet suits. . . ."

"Kay?"

"Or grizzly bears, for example, while you're minding your own business on a friendly hike through the mountains." I make no effort to keep the sarcasm out of my tone, to hide the anger I feel. "And, of course, military, but nothing I've seen in military casualties —"

"I'm on a cell phone," Benton interrupts me. "I'd rather you don't mention this to anyone else. No one in your office, or have you already?"

"I haven't already."

"You're by yourself?" he asks me again.

Why wouldn't I be? But I say, "Yes."

"And maybe you could delete it from your history, empty your cache, in case anybody decides to view your recent searches."

"I can't stop Lucy from doing that."

"I don't care if Lucy does it."

"She's not here. I don't know where she went."

"I know," he says.

"All right, then." He's not going to tell me where she is or where anybody is, it seems. "I'll make evidence rounds, take care of as much as I can and meet you downstairs in back when you get here." I hang up and try to reason through what just happened. I try not to feel hurt by him as I logically sort it out.

Benton didn't sound surprised or especially concerned. He didn't seem alarmed by what I've discovered but by my discovering it and the possibility that I might have told someone else, and that probably means the same thing I've been sensing since I returned home from Dover. Maybe I'm not the one finding things out. Maybe I'm simply the last one to know and nobody wants me to find out anything. What an unexpected predicament to be in, if not an unprecedented one, I think, as I do what Benton asked and empty the cache and clear the history, making it problematic for anyone to see what I've been searching on the Internet. As I do this I wonder who really asked: my husband, or was it the FBI asking? Who was just talking to me and telling me what to do as if I don't know better?

It's almost nine, and most of my staff is already here, those who aren't using the snow as an excuse to stay home or to go somewhere else they'd rather be, such as skiing in Vermont. On the security monitor I've watched cars pull into the lot and seen some people coming through the back door but far more arriving by way of the civilized entrance on the ground floor, through the stone lobby with its formidable carvings and flags, avoiding the dreary domain of the dead on the lower level. The scientists rarely need to meet the patients whose body fluids and belongings and other evidence they test, and then I hear the sounds of my administrator, Bryce, unlocking the door in the hallway that opens onto his adjoining office.

I reseal the blotting paper in a clean envelope and unlock a drawer to gather other items I've been keeping safe as I try not to sink into a dark space, thinking dark thoughts about what I just looked at on a website and what it implies about human beings and their capacity to create imaginative ways to do harm to other creatures. In the name of survival, it crosses my mind, but then rarely is it really about staying alive; instead, it's about making sure something else doesn't, and the power people feel when they can overpower, maim, kill. How terrible, how awful, and I have no doubt about what happened to the man from Norton's Woods, that someone came up behind him and stabbed him with an injection knife, blasting a ball of compressed gas into his vital organs, and if it was CO_2, there is no test that will tell us. Carbon dioxide is ubiquitous, literally as present as the air we exhale, and I envision what I saw on CT, the dark pockets of air that had been blown into the chest and what that must have felt like, and how I will answer the same question I'm always asked.

Did he suffer?

The truthful answer would be no one knows such a thing except the person who is dead, but I would say no, he didn't suffer. I would say he felt it. He felt something catastrophic happening to him. He wasn't conscious long enough to suffer during the agonal last moments of his life, but he would have felt a punch to his lower back accompanied by tremendous pressure in his chest as his organs ruptured, all of it happening at once. That would have been the last thing he felt except possibly a glimmer, a flash, of a panicked thought that he was about to die, and then I stop thinking about it because to obsess and imagine further would become useless and self-indulgent theorizing that is paralyzing and nonproductive. I can't help him if I'm upset.

I'm worthless to anyone if I feel what I feel, just as it was when I took care of my father and became an expert at pushing down emotions that climbed up inside me like some desperate creature trying to get out. "I worry what you have learned, my little Katie," my father said to me when I was twelve and he was a skeleton in the back bedroom, where the air was always too warm and smelled like sickness and light seeped wanly through the slatted shades I kept closed most of the way his last months. "You have learned things you shouldn't ever have to learn but especially at your age, my little Katie," he said to me as I made the bed with him still in it, having learned to wash him religiously so he wasn't overcome by pressure sores, to change his soiled sheets by moving his body, a body that seemed hollowed out and dead except for the heat of his fever.

I would gently rock my father to his side, holding him up on one side, then the other, leaning him against me because he could not get up in the end, couldn't even sit up. He was too weak to help me move him during what his doctor called the blast phase of chronic myeloid leukemia, and at times he enters my mind and I feel the weight of him against me when I'm swathed in protective clothing, peering through protective glasses, at work at my hard steel table.

I fill out lab analysis requests that will need to be signed by each scientist I receipt various items to so I can keep the chain of evidence intact. Then I get up from my desk.

16

Knocking once, I open the door that leads into Bryce's office.

Our shared entrance is directly across from the door to my private bath, which I've learned to keep open a crack. When both gray metal doors are shut I have had a tendency to get mixed up and walk in on Bryce when I'm interested in coffee or washing up or I find myself about to hand paperwork to a toilet and a sink. He is at his desk with his chair rolled back and has taken off his coat, which is draped over the back, but he still has on his big designer sunglasses that look ridiculously heavy, as if drawn on with a dark-brown crayon. He struggles with a pair of L.L.Bean snow boots that don't go with his typically deliberate ensemble, which today is a navy cashmere blazer, tight black jeans, a black turtleneck, and a tooled leather belt with a big silver buckle shaped like a dragon.

"I'll be on the phone and can't be disturbed," I tell him as if I've been here every day for these past six months, as if I've never been gone. "Then I have to leave."

"Is someone going to tell me what's going on around here? And welcome home, boss." He looks up at me, his eyes masked by the big, dark glasses. "I don't suppose the unmarked cars in the parking lot are a surprise party, because I know I'm not throwing one. Not that I wouldn't and wasn't intending to eventually, but whoever they are, they aren't here because of me, and when I asked one of them to be so kind as to give me an explanation and please move his ass so I could park in my spot, he was shall we say *testy?*"

"The case from yesterday morning," I start to say.

"Oh, is that why? Well, no wonder." His face brightens as if what I just said is somehow good news. "I knew it was going to be important, I somehow knew it. But he didn't really die here, please tell me it's not true, that you didn't find anything to suggest anything so outrageous or I guess I'll just start looking for another job right this minute and tell Ethan we're not about to buy that bungalow we've been looking at. I'm sure you've figured out what happened

411

by now, knowing you. You probably figured it out in five minutes."

He pulls off the other boot, moving both of them to the side, and I notice he's spiked his hair and has shaved off the mustache and beard he had when I saw him last. Compactly built, Bryce is slight but strong with a blond choirboy prettiness, to use a cliché, because it happens to be true. He doesn't look like himself with facial hair, which is probably the point, to look like someone else, to be transformed into a formidable and virile character like James Brolin, or to be taken seriously like Wolf Blitzer, heroes of his. My top administrator and trusted right hand has many, a host of famous imagined friends he speaks of easily as if the act of tuning into them on one of his big-screen TVs or saving them with TiVo makes them as real as next-door neighbors.

Seriously good at what he does for me, with degrees in criminal justice and public administration, Bryce Clark at a glance seems misplaced, as if he wandered off the set of *E!,* and I have used this to my advantage over the few years he's worked for me. Outsiders and even people who work here don't always realize that my recovering Mormon compulsive-talking clotheshorse of a chief of staff is not to be trifled with. If nothing else, he's voyeuristic and adores "filling me in," as he puts it. He likes nothing better than to gather information like a magpie and carry it back to his nest. He is dangerous if he detests you. It's unlikely you'll know it. His banter and deliberate affect are a bunker that his more dangerous self hides behind, and in that way he reminds me of my former secretary, Rose. Those who made the mistake of treating her like a silly old woman one day found themselves missing a limb.

"The FBI? Homeland Security? No one I've seen before." Bryce is bent over in his chair as he unzips a nylon gym bag, his stocking feet planted on the floor.

"Probably the FBI —" But he isn't going to let me finish.

"Well, the one who was so rude totally looked the part, all buff in a gray suit and camel-hair coat. I think the FBI fires people if they get fat. Well, good luck hiring in America. Drop-dead good-looking, I'll give him that. Did you see him back there? Do we know his name and what field office he's with? Not anyone I've met from Boston. Maybe he's new."

"Who?" My thoughts run into a wall.

"Lord, you are tired. The agent in that big, bad black Ford Expedition, the spitting image of the football player on *Glee* — oh, you probably don't watch that, either, it's only the best show on TV and I can't imagine you don't love Jane Lynch, unless you don't know who she is, since you probably didn't catch *The L Word,* but maybe *Best in Show* or *Talladega Nights?* My God, what a hoot. The Bureau boy in the black Ford looks exactly like Finn —"

"Bryce . . ."

"Anyway, I saw all the blood, how much the body from Norton's Woods bled inside his pouch, and it was god-awful, and I thought to myself, *This is it. The end of this place.* Meanwhile, Marino's huffing and puffing and about to blow the house down, pitching a fit as only Marino can about someone delivered alive and dying in the fridge. So I told Ethan we might have to tuck away our pennies because I might be unemployed. And the job market right now? Ten percent unemployment or some nightmare like that, and I seriously doubt *Doctor G* is going to hire me because every morgue worker on the planet wants to be on her show, but I would ask you to pick up the phone and recommend me to her, please, if this place goes down the toilet. Why can't we do a reality show? I mean, really. You had your own show on CNN some years ago; why can't we do something here?"

"I need to talk to you about —" But there's no point when he gets like this.

"I'm glad you're here, but sorry you had to come home for something so god-awful. I stayed awake all night wondering what I was going to tell reporters. When I saw those SUVs behind the building, I thought it was the media, was fully expecting television trucks —"

"Bryce, you need to calm down and maybe take your sunglasses off —"

"But nothing in the news that I know of, and not one reporter has called me or left a message here or anything —"

"I need to go over a few things, and you really need to shut up, please," I interrupt him.

"I know." He takes off his sunglasses as he works his foot into a black high-top sneaker. "I'm just a little overwrought, Dr. Scarpetta. And you know how I get when I'm over-wrought."

"Have you heard from Jack?"

"Where's the Mouth of Truth when you need it?" As he ties his sneakers. "Don't ask me to pretend, and I would respectfully request that you inform him I don't answer directly to him anymore. Now that you're home, thank God."

"Why do you say that?"

"Because all he does is order me around as if I work in the drive-through window at Wendy's. He barks and snaps as his hair falls out, and then I wonder if he's going to kick someone, maybe me, or strangle me with his umpteenth-degree black belt or whatever the fuck he has, excuse my French. And it's gotten worse, and we weren't supposed to bother you at Dover. I told everybody to leave you alone. Everybody's told everybody to leave you alone or they'll answer to me. I'm just realizing you've been up all night. You look awful." His blue eyes look me up and down, studying the way I'm dressed, which is in the same khaki cargo pants and black polo shirt with the AFME crest that I put on at Dover.

"I came straight here and don't have anything to change into." I finally get a word in edgewise. "I don't know why you bothered replacing your L.L.Beans with an old pair of Converse left over from basketball camp."

"I know you have a better eye than that, and I know you know I never went to basketball camp, because I always went to music camp every summer. Hugo Boss, half price at Endless-dot-com, plus free shipping," he adds, getting up from his chair.

416

"I'm making coffee, and you want some. And no, I've not heard from Jack, and you don't need to tell me there's a problem and it might have to do with those agents in our parking lot, who obviously have a personality disorder. I don't know why they can't make an effort to be friendly. If I wore a big gun and could arrest people, I'd be Little Miss Sunshine to everyone, smile and be so nice. Why not?" Bryce brushes past me, walking into my office, disappearing into the bathroom. "I can run by your house and pick up a few things if you want. Just tell me. A business suit or something casual?"

"If I get stuck here . . ." I start to say I might take him up on it.

"We really do need to arrange some sort of closet for you, a little haute couture at HQ. Ohhhh, wardrobe?" his voice sings out as he makes coffee. "Now if we had our own show, we'd have wardrobe, hair, makeup, and you'd never find yourself in the same dirty clothes and odiferous of death, not that I'm saying you're . . . Well, anyway. Best of all would be if you went home and straight to bed." As hot water shoots loudly through a K-Cup. "Or I could run out and get you something to eat. I find when I'm tired and sleep-deprived . . ." He emerges from my bathroom with two coffees and says, "Fat. There's a time and a place for everything. Dunkin' Donuts, their croissant with sausage and egg, how 'bout it? You might need two. You actually look a little thin. Life in the military really doesn't suit you, dear boss."

"Are you aware of a woman named Erica Donahue calling here?" I ask him as I return to my desk with a coffee I'm not sure I should drink. Opening a drawer, I search for Advil in hopes there really might be a bottle hiding somewhere.

"She did. Several times." Bryce carefully sips the hot coffee, leaning against the frame of the open doorway that connects us.

When he offers nothing else, I ask, "When did she call?"

"Starting after it was in the news about her son. That was a week ago, I think, when he confessed to killing Mark Bishop."

"You talked to her?"

"Most recently, all I really did was direct her call to Jack again when she was looking for you."

" 'Again'?"

"You should get his part from him. I don't know his details," Bryce says, and it's not like him to be careful with me. He's cautious suddenly.

"But he talked to her."

"This was, let me see. . . ." He has a habit of gazing up at the dome as if the answers to all things are there. It's also a favorite delaying tactic of his. "Last Thursday."

"And you talked to her. Before you transferred her call to Jack."

"Mostly I listened."

"What was her demeanor, and what did she say?"

"Very polite, sounded like the upper-class intelligent woman she is, based on what I hear. I mean, there's a ton of stuff about the Donahue family and Johnny Hinckley Junior. He's almost that notorious. . . . *And when he saw what he had done, he holstered his trusty nail gun.* . . . But you probably don't read all this shit on these gore-sites like Morbidia Trivia, Wicked-whatever-pedia, Cryptnotes, or whatever, and I do have to follow them as part of my job, part of my being informed about what's being said out there in sensational sin-loving cyberland."

He's comfortable again. He's uncomfortable only when I probe him about Fielding.

"Mom was an almost famous concert pianist in a former life, played in a symphony orchestra. I think in San Francisco," Bryce goes on. "I happened to notice some Twittering about her being taught by Yundi

Li, but I seriously doubt Li gives lessons, and he's only twenty-eight, so I don't believe it for a second. Of course she's in an uproar, can you imagine? They say her son is a savant, has these bizarre abilities, like knowing tire treads. The detective from Salem, Saint Hilaire, who is anything but, and you don't know him yet, was talking about it. Apparently, Johnny Donahue can look at a tread pattern in a dirt parking lot and go, 'That's a Bridgestone Battle Wing front motorcycle tire.' I just came up with that because Ethan has those on his BMW, which I wish he didn't love so much, because to me they're all donorcycles. Supposedly, Johnny can do math problems in his head, and I'm not talking if a banana costs eighty-nine cents how much is a bunch of six? More Einsteinian, like what is nine times a hundred and three to the square root of seven or something? But then you probably know all this. I'm sure you've been keeping up with the case."

"What exactly did she want to discuss with me? Did she tell you?" I know Bryce. He wouldn't hand off someone like Erica Donahue without letting her talk until she ran out of words or patience. He's too much of a snoop, his mind a chatterbox gossip mill.

"Well, obviously he didn't do it, and if someone would really look into the facts without having their mind made up, they'd see all the inconsistencies. The conflicts," Bryce replies, blowing on his coffee, not looking at me.

"What conflicts, exactly?"

"She says she talked to him the day of the murder at around nine in the morning, before he headed off to that café in Cambridge that's now become so famous right around the corner from you?" Bryce continues. "The Biscuit? Lines out the door because of all the publicity. Nothing like a murder. Anyway, he wasn't feeling well that day, according to Mom. Has terrible allergies or something and was complaining his pills or shots or whatever weren't working anymore, and he was dosing up big-time and felt *punk* is the word she used. So I guess if someone has itchy eyes and a runny nose, he's not going to kill anyone. I didn't want to tell her that a jury wouldn't put much stock in a sneezy defense —"

"I need to make a call and then make my rounds," I cut him off before he digresses the rest of the day. "Can you check with Trace Evidence and see if Evelyn is in, and if so, please tell her I have a few things that are rather urgent. What I've got needs to

421

start with her and then fingerprints, then DNA, then toxicology, then one item in particular will come back up here to Lucy's lab. There was no one over there a while ago. What about Shane, are we expecting him, because I'm going to need an opinion about a document?"

"It's not like we're a rugby team stranded in a blizzard in the Andes and are going to resort to cannibalism, for God's sake."

"It was quite a storm all night."

"You've been down south too long. There's what? Eight inches? A bit icy but nothing for around here," Bryce says.

"Actually, if you could ask Evelyn to come upstairs immediately and let her into Jack's office." I decide I'm not going to wait as I remember the lab coat folded up inside the trash-can liner.

I explain to Bryce what's in the pocket and that I want it checked right away on SEM and I also want a nondestructive chemical analysis.

"Be very, very careful not to open the bag and touch anything," I say to Bryce. "And tell Evelyn there are fingerprints on the plastic film. Meaning there will also be DNA."

With my administrator silently out of range

on the other side of our shared shut door, I decide to hold off calling Erica Donahue until I have a chance to think about what I'm going to do. I need to think about everything.

I want to reread her letter and make sure of my intentions, and as I ponder and remember what's happened since I left Dover, as I look out at the bright blue sky of a new day, I know I'm still hungover from the last mother I dealt with. I feel poisoned by the memory of Julia Gabriel on the phone as someone loitered outside my closed door at Port Mortuary. The names she called me and what she accused me of were bitter and vile, but I didn't really let it get to me in a way that gave power to her words until I found what I did in Fielding's office. Since then a shadow that is chilled and dark like a sunless part of the moon is at the back of my thoughts and moods. I don't know what is being said or decided about me or what has been resurrected like some cold-blooded thing that never died and now is stirring.

What records have been found, and what has been gone through that I have secretly feared all these years and at the same time forgotten? Although the truth was always there, like something unseemly out of sight in a closet, something that I never look for but, if reminded, I know it's not gone, because it was never thrown out or returned to its rightful owner, which should never have been me. But the ugly matter was handed over as if it was mine. And it was left hanging. As long as what was done in South Africa stayed hidden in my closet instead of where it belonged, I'd be fine, was the message I got when I returned to Walter Reed after working those two deaths and was thanked for my service to the AFIP, to the air force, and was free to leave early. Debt paid in full. They had just the position for me in Virginia, where I would prosper as long as I remembered loyalty and took my dirty laundry with me.

Has it happened again? Has Briggs done the same thing to me again and soon will send me packing? Where this time? Early retirement crosses my mind. It's all coming out with more ugliness piled on, and that's not survivable, I decide, because I don't know what else to think. Briggs has told someone, and someone told Julia Gabriel, who has accused me of hatred, prejudice, callousness, dishonesty, and I must remember that this noxious miasma permeates any decisions I might make right now, that and fatigue. *Be exceedingly careful. Use your head. Don't give yourself up to emotions, and easy as pie* drifts through my mind. What Lucy said about security recordings, and I pick up my phone and buzz Bryce.

"Yes, boss," he says brightly, as if we haven't chatted in days.

"Our security recordings from the closed-circuit cameras everywhere," I say. "When was Captain Avallone here from Dover? I understand Jack gave her a tour."

"Oh, Lord, that was a while ago. I believe November. . . ."

"I recall she went home to Maine the week of Thanksgiving," I tell him. "I know she was gone from Dover that week because I had to stay. We were shorthanded."

"That sounds about right. I think she was here that Friday."

"Were you with them on the grand tour?"

"I was not. I wasn't invited. And Jack spent a lot of time with her in your office, just so you know. In there with the door shut. They ate lunch in there at your table."

"This is what I need you to do," I tell him. "Get hold of Lucy, text-message her or whatever you need to do, and let her know I want a review of every security recording that has Jack and Sophia on it, including anything in my office."

"In your office?"

"How long has he been using it?"

"Well . . ."

"Bryce? How long?"

"Pretty much the entire time. He helps himself when he wants to impress people. I mean, he doesn't use it for his casework very often, mostly when he's being ceremonial. . . ."

"Tell Lucy I want recordings of my office. She'll know exactly what I mean. I want to see what Jack and the captain were talking about."

"How delicious. I'll get right on it."

"I'm about to make an important call, so please don't disturb me," I then say. As I hang up, I realize Benton will be here soon.

But I resist the temptation to rush. Wise to slow down, to allow thoughts and perceptions to sort themselves out, to strive for clarity. *You're tired. Exercise caution, and play it smart when you're this tired.* There's one way to do this right, and every other way is wrong. You won't know the right way until it happens, and you won't recognize it if you're wound up and muddled. I reach for my coffee but change my mind about that, too. It won't help at this point, will only make me jittery and upset my stomach more. Pulling another pair of examination gloves out of a box on the granite counter

426

behind my desk, I remove the document from the plastic bag I sealed it in.

I slide the two folded sheets of heavy paper out of the envelope I slit open in Benton's SUV as we drove through a blizzard what now seems like a lifetime ago but has only been twelve hours. In the light of morning and after so much has happened, it seems more unusual than it did that this classical pianist whom Bryce described as intelligent and reasonable would have used duct tape on her fine engraved stationery. Why not regular tape that is transparent instead of this ugly wide strip of lead-gray across the back? Why not do what I do when I enclose a private memo in an envelope and simply sign your name or initials over the seal of the flap? What was Erica Donahue afraid would happen? That her driver might want to read what she wrote to someone named Scarpetta whom he apparently had never heard of?

I smooth open the pages with my cotton-gloved hand and try to intuit what the mother of a college boy who has confessed to murder transferred to the keys of her typewriter, as if what she felt and believed as she composed her plea to me is a chemical I can absorb that will get me into her mind. It occurs to me I've come up with such an analogy because of the plastic film I found in the pocket of Fielding's lab coat. Hours beyond that unnerving druggy experience, I can see just how bad it really was and that I could not have been myself with Benton, and how uncomfortable it must have been for him. Maybe that's why he's being so secretive and is lecturing me about divulging information to whoever happens to be nearby, as if I, of all people, don't know better. Maybe he doesn't trust my judgment or self-control and fears that the horrors of war changed me. Maybe he's not so sure that the woman who came home to him from Dover is the one he knows.

I'm not who you used to know floats through my head. *I'm not sure you ever knew me* is a whisper in my thoughts, and as I read the neat rows of single-spaced type, I find it remarkable that in two pages there isn't one mistake. I see no evidence of white-out or correction tape, no misspellings or bad grammar. When I think back to the last typewriter I used, a dusky pink IBM Selectric I had in Richmond the first few years I was there, I remember my chronic aggravation with ribbons that broke or having to swap out the golf ball–like element when I wanted to change fonts, and dealing with a dirty platen that left smudges on paper, not to mention my own hurried fingers hitting the wrong keys, and while my spelling and grammar are good, I'm certainly not infallible.

As my secretary Rose used to say when she'd walk in with my latest effort typed on that damn machine, *"And on what page is this in Strunk and White, or maybe it's in the MLA style guide and I just can't find it? I'll redo it, but every time you type something yourself?"* And she'd flap her hand in that characteristic gesture of hers that said to me *Why bother?,* and then I stop those thoughts because it makes me sad when I think about her. I've missed Rose every day since she died, and if she were here right now, somehow things would be different. Things would feel different, if nothing else. For me she was my clarity. For her I was her life. No one like Rose should be gone from this earth, and I still can't believe it, and now is not a good time to think about the blond young man in black high-top sneakers sitting next door instead of her. I need to focus. Focus on Erica Donahue. What will I do with this woman? I am going to do something, but I must be shrewd.

She must have typed her letter to me more than once, as many times as it took to make it impeccable, and I'm reminded that when her driver rolled up in the Bentley he didn't seem to know that the intended recipient of the envelope sealed with duct tape is a woman, and indeed seemed to think a silver-haired man was me. I remind myself that the mother of Johnny Donahue also doesn't seem aware that the forensic psychologist evaluating him, this same silver-haired man, is my husband, and also contrary to what's in her letter, there is no unit for the "criminally insane" at McLean, nor has anyone deemed that Johnny is criminally insane, which is a legal term and not a diagnosis. According to Benton, she also has other facts wrong.

She has confused details that may very well hurt her son, possibly damaging an alibi that potentially is his strongest. Claiming he left The Biscuit in Cambridge at one p.m. instead of at two, as Johnny maintains, she has made it far more believable that he could have found transportation and gotten to Salem in time to kill Mark Bishop around four that afternoon. Then there is her reference to her son reading horror novels and enjoying horror films and violent entertainment, and finally what she said about Jack Fielding and a nail gun and a satanic cult, none of that correct or proven.

Where did she get those dangerous details

— where, really? I suppose Fielding could have put such ideas in her head when he talked to her on the phone, if it's true he's the one now spreading these rumors, that he's lying, which is what Benton seems to think. Regardless of what Fielding did or didn't do or his truths or untruths or his reasons for anything that is happening, my questions come back to the mother of Johnny Donahue. I make myself bring all of it back to her, because what I fail to see is motivation that is logical. Her delivering this letter to me really doesn't sit well at all. It feels off. It feels wrong.

For one so meticulous about typos and sentence construction, not to mention the attention she must pay to her music, it strikes me that she doesn't seem to care nearly as much as she should about the facts of her son's confession to one of the most heinous acts of violence in recent memory. Every detail counts in a case like this, and how could an intelligent, sophisticated woman with expensive lawyers not know that? Why would she take the chance of divulging anything to someone like me, a complete stranger, especially in writing, when her son faces being locked up for the rest of his life in a forensic psychiatric facility like Bridgewater or, worse, in a prison, where a convicted child-killer with Asperger's, a so-called savant who can work the most difficult math problems in his head but is impaired when it comes to everyday social cues, isn't likely to survive very long?

I refresh myself on all these facts and relevant points at the same time I realize I'm feeling and behaving as if they matter to me. And they shouldn't. I'm supposed to be objective. *You don't take sides, and it's not your job to care,* I tell myself. *You don't care about Johnny Donahue or his mother one way or the other, and you're not a detective or the FBI,* I think sternly. *You're not Johnny's defense attorney or his therapist, and there's nothing for you to get involved in,* I then say to myself severely, because I don't feel convinced. I'm struggling with impulses that have become impossibly strong, and I'm not sure how to turn them off or if I can or should. I do know I don't want to.

Some of what I've grown accustomed to not only at Dover but on non-combat-related matters that are the jurisdiction of the AFME or what basically is the federal medical examiner is far too compatible with my true nature, and I don't want to go back to the staid old way of doing things. I'm military and I'm not. I'm civilian and I'm not. I've been in and out of Washington and lived on an air force base and routinely been sent on recovery missions of air crashes and accidents during training exercises and deaths on military installations or fatalities involving special forces, the Secret Service, a federal judge, even an astronaut in recent months, handling a multitude of sensitive situations I can't talk about. What I'm feeling is the *not* part of the equation. I'm not any one thing, and I'm not feeling at all inclined to surrender to limitations, to sit on my hands because something isn't my department.

As an officer involved in medical intelligence, I'm expected to investigate certain aspects of life and death that go far beyond the usual clinical determinations. Materials I remove from bodies, the types of injuries and wound ballistics, the strengths and failures of armor, and infections, diseases, lesions, whether from parasites or sand fleas, and extreme heat, dehydration, and boredom, depression, and drugs are all matters of national defense and security. The data I gather aren't just for the sake of families and usually aren't destined for criminal court but can have a bearing on the strategies of war and what keeps us safe domestically. I'm expected to ask questions. I'm expected to follow leads. I'm expected to pass along information to the surgeon general, the Department of Defense, to be intensely industrious and proactive.

You're home now. You don't want to come across as a colonel or a commander, certainly not as a prima donna. You don't want to get a case null prossed or thrown out of court. You don't want to cause trouble. Isn't there enough already? Why would you encourage more? Briggs doesn't want you here. Be careful you don't justify his position. Your own staff doesn't seem to want you here or know you're here. Don't make it easy for you not to be. Your only legitimate purpose in contacting Erica Donahue is to ask her kindly not to contact you or your office again, for her own good, for her own protection.

I decide to use those exact words, and I almost believe my motivation as I call the home phone number typed at the end of her letter.

17

The person who answers doesn't seem to understand what I'm saying, and I have to repeat myself twice, explaining that I'm Dr. Kay Scarpetta and I'm responding to a letter I just received from Erica Donahue, and is she available, please?

"I beg your pardon," the well-modulated voice says. "Who is this?" A woman's voice, I'm fairly sure, although it is low, almost in the tenor range, and could belong to a young man. In the background a piano plays, unaccompanied, a solo.

"Is this Mrs. Donahue?" I'm already getting an uncomfortable feeling.

"Who is this, and why are you calling?" The voice hardens and enunciates crisply.

I repeat what I said as I recognize a Chopin étude, and I remember a concert at Carnegie Hall. Mikhail Pletnev, who was stunning in his technical mastering of a composition that is very hard to play. The music of someone detailed and meticulous who likes everything just so. Someone who isn't careless and doesn't make mistakes. Someone who wouldn't mar a fine engraved envelope by slapping on duct tape. Someone who isn't impulsive but very studied.

"Well, I don't know who this really is," says the voice, what I now believe is Mrs. Donahue's voice, stony and edged with distrust and pain. "And I don't know how you got this number, since it's unlisted and unpublished. If this is some sort of crank call, it's absolutely outrageous, and whoever you are, you should be ashamed of yourself —"

"I assure you this is not a crank call," I interrupt before she can hang up on me as I think about her listening to Chopin, Beethoven, Schumann, worrying her life away, agonizing over a son who probably has caused her anguish since she gave birth to him. "I'm the director of the Cambridge Forensic Center, the chief medical examiner of Massachusetts," I explain authoritatively but calmly, the same voice I use with families who are on the verge of losing control, as if she is Julia Gabriel and about to shriek at me. "I've been out of town, and when I arrived at the airport last night, your driver was there with your letter, which I've carefully read."

"That's absolutely impossible. I don't have a driver, and I didn't write you a letter. I've written no one at your office and have no idea what on earth you're talking about. Who is this? Who really, and what do you want?"

"I have the letter in front of me, Mrs. Donahue."

I look at it on top of my desk and smooth it open again, being careful and deliberate as it nags at me to ask her about Fielding and why she called him and what he said to her. It nags at me that I don't want her to hate me or think I'm unfeeling or anything other than honest. It's possible Fielding disparaged me to her the same way I suspect he did with Julia Gabriel. I'm close to asking, but I stop myself. What has been said, and what has Erica Donahue been led to believe? But not now. *Self-control,* I tell myself.

Mrs. Donahue asks indignantly, "What does it say that's supposedly from me?"

"A creamy rag paper with a watermark." I hold the top sheet of paper up to my desk lamp, adjusting the shade so the bulb shines directly through the paper, showing the watermark clearly, like the inner workings of a soft-shell crab showing through pearly skin. "An open book with three crowns," I say, and I'm shocked.

I don't let her hear it in my voice. I make sure she can't begin to sense what is racing through my mind as I describe to her what I'm seeing, like a hologram, in the sheet of paper I hold up to the light: an open book between two crowns, with a third crown below, and above that three cinquefoil flowers. And it is the flowers Marino neglected to mention that so glaringly aren't Oxford's coat of arms, that so glaringly aren't the coat of arms for the online City University of San Francisco. What I'm looking at isn't what Benton found on the Internet early this morning while all of us were in the x-ray room, but it's what I saw on the gold signet ring I took out of the evidence locker before I came upstairs after looking at the dead man's clothes.

I open the small manila envelope and shake the ring out into the palm of my gloved hand. The gold catches the lamplight and is bright against white cotton as I turn it different ways to look at it, noting it is badly scratched and the bottom of the band is worn thin. The ring looks old, like an antique, to me.

"Well, that sounds like my crest and my paper. I admit it does," Mrs. Donahue is

438

saying over the phone, and then I read to her the Beacon Hill address engraved on the envelope and letterhead, and she confirms it also is hers. "My personal stationery? How is that possible?" She sounds angry, the way people get when they're scared.

"What can you tell me about your crest? Would you mind explaining it to me?" I ask.

I look at the identical crest engraved in the yellow-gold signet ring that I now hold under a hand lens. The three crowns and the open book are large in the magnifying glass, and the engraving is almost gone in spots, the five-petal flowers, the cinquefoils especially, just a ghost of what was once deeply etched because of the age of the ring, which has been subjected to wear and tear by someone, or perhaps by a number of people, including the man from Norton's Woods, who was wearing it on the little finger of his left hand when he was murdered. There can be no mistake he had it on, that the ring came in with his body. There was no mix-up by police, a hospital, a funeral home. The ring was there when Marino removed the man's personal effects yesterday morning and locked them up and kept the key until he turned it over to me.

"My family name is Fraser," Mrs.

439

Donahue explains. "It's my family coat of arms, that particular emblazon for Jackson Fraser, a great-grandfather who apparently changed the design to incorporate elements such as Azure in base, a border Or, and a third crown Gules, which you can't see unless you're looking at a replica of the coat of arms that displays the tinctures, such as what is framed in my music room. Are you saying someone wrote a letter on my stationery and had a driver hand-deliver it to you? I don't understand or see how it's possible, and I don't know what it means or why someone would do something like that. What kind of car was it? We certainly don't have a driver. I have an old Mercedes, and my husband drives a Saab and isn't in the country right now, anyway, and we've never had a driver. We only use drivers when we travel."

"I'm wondering if your family coat of arms is on anything else. Embroidered, engraved, besides being framed on the wall in your music room, anywhere else it might appear. If it's known or published, if someone could have gotten hold of it." No matter how I phrase it, it sounds like a peculiar thing to quiz her about.

"Get hold of it to do what ultimately? What goal?"

"Your stationery, for example. Let's think about that and what the ultimate goal might be."

"Is what you have engraved or printed?" she then asks. "Can you tell the difference between engraved and printed by looking at what you have?"

You don't know who he is, I'm thinking. *You don't know that the man who died wearing that ring isn't a member of her family, a relative,* and I remember Benton saying Johnny Donahue has an older brother who works at Langley. What if he happened to be in Cambridge yesterday, staying at an apartment near Harvard, maybe a friend's apartment that has an obsolete packbot in it, a friend with a greyhound, a friend who perhaps works in a robotics lab? What if the older brother or some other man significant to Mrs. Donahue had just been overseas, in the UK, and had flown back here unexpected and is dead and she doesn't know, the Donahue family doesn't know? What does Johnny's brother look like?

Don't ask her.

"The stationery is engraved," I answer Mrs. Donahue's question.

What if her family is somehow connected with Liam Saltz or with someone who might have attended his daughter's wedding on

441

Sunday? Might the Donahues have a connection to a member of Parliament named Brown?

Stay away from it.

"Well, you can't pull engraved stationery out of a hat, have it made in a minute," Mrs. Donahue is saying.

Now I'm looking at the envelope, at the duct tape on the back that I didn't cut through, that I thought to preserve.

"Especially if you don't have the copperplates," she adds.

We use sticky-sided tape all the time in forensics, to collect trace evidence from carpet, from upholstery, to lift fibers, paint chips, glass fragments, gunshot residue, minerals, even DNA and fingerprints, from all types of surfaces, including human bodies. Anybody could know that. Just watch television. Just Google "crime scene investigative techniques and equipment."

"If someone got hold of my copperplates? But who? Who could have them?" she protests. "Without those, it would take weeks. And if you do press proofs, which of course I do, add several more weeks. This makes no sense."

She wouldn't put duct tape on the back of her elegant envelope that took many weeks to engrave. Not this precise, proud woman who listens to Chopin études. If someone else did, then I might have an idea why. Especially if it was someone who knows me or knows the way I think.

"And yes, the crest is on a number of things. It's been in my family for centuries," she adds, because she wants to talk. There is much pent up inside her, and she wants to let it out.

Allow it.

"Scottish, but you probably guessed that based on the name," she then says. "Framed on the wall in the music room, as I mentioned, and engraved on some of my family silverware, and we did have some silver stolen years ago by a housekeeper who was fired but never charged with anything because we really couldn't prove it to the satisfaction of the Boston police. I suppose my family silver could have ended up in a pawnshop around here. But I don't see what that could have to do with my stationery. It sounds as if you're implying someone might have made engraved stationery identical to mine with the goal of impersonating me. Or someone stole it. Are you suggesting identity theft?"

What to say? How far do I go?

"What about anything else that might have been stolen, anything else with your family crest on it?" I don't want to directly ask her about the ring.

"Why do you ask? Is there something else?"

"I have a letter that is supposedly from you," I reiterate instead of answering her questions. "It's typed on a typewriter."

"I still use a typewriter," she verifies, and sounds bewildered. "But usually I write letters by hand."

"Might I ask with what?"

"Why, a pen, of course. A fountain pen."

"And the type style on your typewriter, which is what kind? But you might not know the typeface. Not everybody would."

"It's just an Olivetti portable I've had forever. The typeface is cursive, like handwriting."

"A manual one that must be fairly old." As I look at the letter, at the distressed cursive typeface made with metal typebars striking an inked ribbon.

"It was my mother's."

"Mrs. Donahue, do you know where your typewriter is?"

"I'm going to walk over there, to the cabinet in the library where it's kept while I'm not using it."

I hear her moving into another area of the house, and it sounds as if she sets what must be a portable phone down on a hard surface. Then a series of doors shut, perhaps cabinet doors, and a moment later she is back on with me and almost breathless as she says, "Well, it's gone. It's not here."

"Do you remember when you saw it last?"

"I don't know. Weeks ago. Probably around Christmas. I don't know."

"And it wouldn't be someplace else. Perhaps you moved it or someone borrowed it?"

"No. This is terrible. Someone took it and probably took my stationery, too. The same one who wrote to you as if it was me. And I didn't. I most assuredly didn't."

The first person to come to mind is her own son Johnny. But he is at McLean. He couldn't possibly have borrowed her typewriter, her pen, her stationery, and then hired a man and a Bentley to deliver a letter to me. Assuming he could have known when I was flying in last night on Lucy's helicopter, and I'm not going to ask his mother about that, either. The more I ask her, the more information I give.

"What's in the letter?" she persists. "What did someone write as if it's from me? Who could have taken my typewriter? Should we call the police? What am I saying? You are the police."

445

"I'm a medical examiner," I correct her matter-of-factly as Chopin's tempo quickens, a different étude. "I'm not the police."

"But you are, really. Doctors like you investigate like the police and act like the police and have powers they can abuse like the police. I talked to your assistant, Dr. Fielding, about what's being blamed on my son, as I know you're very well aware. You must know I've called your office about it and why. You must know why and how wrong it is. You sound like a fair-minded woman. I know you haven't been here, but I must say I don't understand what's been condoned, even from a distance."

I swivel around in my chair, facing the curved wall behind me that is nothing but glass, my office shaped exactly like the building if you laid it on its side, cylindrical and rounded at one end. The morning sky is bright blue, what Lucy calls severe clear, and I notice something moving in the security display, a black SUV parking in back.

"I was told you called to speak to him," I reply, because I can't say what is about to boil out of me. What isn't fair? What have I condoned? How did she know I haven't been here? "I can understand your concern, but —"

"I'm not ignorant," Mrs. Donahue cuts me off. "I'm not ignorant about these things, even if I've never been involved in anything so awful ever before, but there was no reason for him to be so rude to me. I was within my rights to ask what I did. I fail to understand how you can condone it, and maybe you really haven't. Maybe you aren't aware of the entire sordid mess, but how could you not be? You're in charge, and now that I have you on the phone, perhaps you can explain how it's fair or appropriate or even legal for someone in his position to be involved in this and have so much power."

The word *careful* flashes in my mind, as if there is a warning light in my head flashing neon-red.

"I'm sorry if you feel he was rude or unhelpful." I abide by my own warning and am careful. "You understand we can't discuss cases with . . ."

"Dr. Scarpetta." Sharp piano notes sound as if responding to her or the other way around. "I would never and I most assuredly did not," she says emotionally. "Will you excuse me while I turn this down? You probably don't know Valentina Lisitsa. If only I could just listen and not have all these other dreadful things banging in my head, like pots and pans banging in my head! My stationery, my typewriter. My son! Oh, God, oh, God." As the music stops. "I didn't ask Dr. Fielding prying questions about someone who was murdered, much less a child. If that's what he's told you I called about, it's absolutely untrue. Well, I'll just say it. A lie. A damn lie. I'm not surprised."

"You called wanting to speak to me," I say, because that's all I really know other than her claims to Bryce about Johnny and his innocence and allergies. She obviously has no idea I've not talked to Fielding, that no one has, it seems. And the more I downplay what she's saying or outright ignore it, the louder she'll get and the more she'll volunteer.

"Late last week," she says with energy. "Because you're in charge and I've gotten nowhere with Dr. Fielding, and of course you understand my concern, and this really is unacceptable if not criminal. So I wanted to complain, and I'm sorry about your coming home to that. When I realized who you are, that it wasn't some crank call, my first thought was it's about my filing a complaint with your office, not anything as official as I'm making it sound, at least not yet, although our lawyer certainly knows and the CFC's legal counsel certainly knows. And now maybe I won't need to file anything. It depends on what you and I agree upon."

Agree upon about what? I think but I don't ask. She knew I was coming home, and that doesn't fit with what she supposedly wrote to me, either. But it fits with a driver meeting me at Hanscom Field.

"What is in the letter? Can you read it to me? Why can't you?" she says again.

"Is it possible someone else in your family might have written to me on your stationery and borrowed your typewriter?" I suggest.

"And signed my name?"

I don't answer.

"I'm assuming I supposedly signed whatever you got or you'd have no reason to think it's from me other than an engraved address, which could be my husband, who unavoidably is in Japan on business, has been since Friday, although it is the most inopportune time to be away. He wouldn't write such a thing, anyway. Of course he wouldn't."

"The letter purports to be from you," I reply, and I don't tell her it is signed "Erica" above her name typed in cursive and that the envelope is addressed in an ornate script in the black ink of a fountain pen.

"This is very upsetting. I don't know why you won't read it to me. I have a right to know what someone said as if they're me. I suppose our attorney will have to deal with you after all, the attorney representing Johnny, and I assume it's about him, this letter that's a lie, a fraud. Probably the dirty trick of the same ones who are behind all this. He was perfectly fine until he went there, and then he became Mr. Hyde, which is a harsh thing to say about your own child. But that's the only way I can think to say it so you understand how dramatically he was altered. Drugs. It must be, although the tests are negative, according to our lawyer, and Johnny would never take them. He knows better. He knows what thin ice he already skates on because of his unusualness. I don't know what else it could be except drugs, that somebody introduced him to something that changed him, that had a terrible effect, to deliberately destroy his life, to set him up. . . ."

She continues to talk without pause, getting increasingly upset, as a knock sounds on my outer door and someone tries the knob, then at the same time Bryce opens our adjoining door and I shake my head no at him. *Not now.* Then he whispers that Benton is at my door, and can he let him in? And I nod, and he shuts one door and another opens.

I put Mrs. Donahue's call on speaker-phone.

Benton closes the door behind him as I hold up the letter to indicate whom it is I'm talking to. He moves a chair close to me while Mrs. Donahue continues to speak, and I jot a note on a call sheet.

Says didn't write it — not her driver or Bentley.

". . . at that place," Mrs. Donahue's voice sounds inside my office as if she is in it.

Benton sits and has no reaction, and his face is pale, drained, and exhausted. He doesn't look well and smells of wood smoke.

"I've never been there because they don't allow visitors unless they have some special event for staff. . . ." her voice continues.

Benton picks up a pen and writes on the same call sheet *Otwahl?* But it seems perfunctory when he does it. He doesn't seem particularly curious.

"And then you have to go through security on a par with the White House, or maybe more extreme than that," Mrs. Donahue says, "not that I know it for a fact, but according to my son, who was frightened and a wreck the last few months he was there. Certainly since summer."

"What place are you talking about?" I ask her as I write another note to Benton.

Typewriter missing from her house.

He looks at the note and nods as if he already knew that Erica Donahue's old Olivetti manual typewriter is gone, possibly stolen, assuming what she's just told me is true. Or maybe he somehow knows she's told me this, and then it intrudes upon my thoughts that my office probably is bugged. Lucy's saying she has swept my office for covert surveillance devices likely means she planted them, and my attention wanders around the room, as if I might find tiny cameras or microphones hidden in books or pens or paperweights or the phone I'm talking on. It's ridiculous. If Lucy has bugged my office, I'm not going to know. More to the point, Fielding wouldn't know. I hope I catch him saying things to Captain Avallone, not realizing the two of them were being recorded secretly. I hope I catch both of them in the act of conspiring to ruin me, to run me out of the CFC.

". . . where he had his internship. That technology company that makes robots and things nobody is supposed to know about . . ." Mrs. Donahue is saying.

I watch Benton fold his hands in his lap, lacing his fingers as if he is placid when he's anything but low-key and relaxed. I know the language of how he sits or moves his eyes and can read his restiveness in what seems the utter stillness of his body and mood. He is stressed-out and worn-out, but there is something else. Something has happened.

". . . Johnny had to sign contracts and all these legal agreements promising he wouldn't talk about Otwahl, not even what its name means. Can you imagine that? Not even something like that, what *Otwahl* means. But no wonder! What these damn people are up to. Huge secret contracts with the government, and greed. Enormous greed. So are you surprised things might be missing or people are being impersonated, their identities stolen?"

I have no idea what *Otwahl* means. I assumed it was the name of a person, the one who founded the company. Somebody Otwahl. I look at Benton. He is staring vacantly across the room, listening to Mrs. Donahue.

". . . Not about anything, certainly not what goes on, and anything he did there belongs to them and stays there." She is talking fast, and her voice no longer sounds as though it is coming from her diaphragm but from high up in her throat. "I'm terrified. Who are these people, and what have they done to my son?"

"What makes you think they've done

something to Johnny?" I ask her as Benton quietly, calmly writes a note on the call sheet, his mouth set in a firm, thin line, the way he looks when he gets like this.

"Because it can't be coincidental," she replies, and her voice reminds me of the cursive typeface of her old Olivetti. Something elegant that is deteriorating, fading, less distinct and slightly bleary. "He was fine and then he wasn't, and now he's locked up at a psychiatric hospital and confessing to a crime he didn't commit. And now this," she says hoarsely, clearing her throat. "A letter on my stationery or what looks like my stationery, and of course it's not from me and I have no idea who delivered it to you. And my typewriter is gone. . . ."

Benton slides the call sheet to me, and I read what he wrote in his legible hand.

We know about it.

I look at him and frown. I don't understand.

". . . Why would they want him accused of something he didn't do, and how have they managed to brainwash him into thinking he murdered that child?" Mrs. Donahue then says yet again, "Drugs. I can only assume drugs. Maybe one of them killed that little boy and they need someone as a scapegoat. And there was my poor Johnny, who is gullible, who doesn't read situations the way others do. What better person to pick on than a teenager with Asperger's. . . ."

I am staring at Benton's note. *We know about it.* As though if I read it more than once I'll comprehend what it is he knows about or what it is that he and his invisible others, these entities he refers to as "we," know about. But as I sit here, concentrating on Mrs. Donahue and trying to decipher what she is truly conveying while I cautiously extract information from her, I have the feeling Benton isn't really listening. He seems barely interested, isn't his typically keen self. What I detect is he wants me to end the call and leave with him, as if something is over with and it's just a matter of finishing what has already ended, just a matter of tying up loose ends, of cleaning up. It is the way he used to act when a case had wrung him out for months or years and finally was solved or dropped or the jury reached a verdict, and suddenly everything stopped and he was left harried but spent and depressed.

"You started noticing the difference in your son when?" I'm not going to quit now, no matter what Benton knows or how spent he is.

"July, August. Then by September for sure. He started his internship with Otwahl last May."

"Mark Bishop was killed January thirtieth." It is as close as I dare come to pointing out the obvious, that what she continues to claim about her son being framed doesn't make sense, the timing doesn't.

If his personality began changing last summer when he was working at Otwahl and yet Mark Bishop wasn't murdered until January 30, what she's suggesting would mean someone programmed Johnny to take the blame for a murder that hadn't happened yet and wouldn't happen for many months. The Mark Bishop case doesn't fit with something meticulously planned but as a senseless and sadistic violent attack on a little boy who was at home, playing in his yard, on a weekend late afternoon as it was getting dark and no one was looking. It strikes me as a crime of opportunity, a thrill kill, the evil game of a predator, possibly one with pedophilic proclivities. It wasn't an assassination. It wasn't the black-ops takeout of a terrorist. I don't believe his death was premeditated and executed with a very certain goal in mind, such as national security or political power or money.

". . . People who don't understand Asperger's assume those who have it are violent, are almost nonhuman, don't feel the same things the rest of us do or don't feel anything. People assume all sorts of things because of what I call *unusualness,* not sickness or derangement but unusual. That's the disadvantage I mean." Mrs. Donahue is talking rapidly and with no ordered sequence to her thoughts. "You point out behavior changes that are alarming and other people think it's just him. Just Johnny because of his unusualness, which is a sad disadvantage, as if he needed yet one more disadvantage. Well, that's not what this is, not about his unusualness. Something horrific got started when he did at that place, at Otwahl last May. . . ."

It also enters my mind what Benton mentioned hours earlier, that Mark Bishop's death might be connected to others: the football player from BC, who was found in the Boston Harbor last November, and possibly the man who was murdered in Norton's Woods. If Benton is right, then Johnny Donahue would have to be framed for all three of these homicides, and how could he be? He was an inpatient at McLean when the killing occurred in Norton's Woods, for example. I know he couldn't have committed that homicide, and I fail to see how he could be set up to take the blame for it unless he wasn't on the hospital ward, unless he was on the loose and armed with an injection knife.

Benton writes another note. *We need to go.* And he underlines it.

"Mrs. Donahue, is your son on any medications?" I ask.

"Not really."

"Prescription or perhaps over-the-counter medications?" I inquire without being pushy, and it requires effort on my part, because my patience is frayed. "Maybe you can tell me anything at all he might have been taking before he was hospitalized or any other medical problems he might have."

I almost say "might have had," as if he is dead.

"Well, a nasal spray. Especially of late."

Benton raises his hands palms up as if to say *This isn't news.* He knows about Johnny's medication. His patience is frayed, too, and signs of it are breaking through his imperviousness. He wants me to get off the phone and to go with him right now.

"Why of late? Was he having respiratory problems? Allergies? Asthma?" I ask as I pull a pair of gloves out of the dispenser and hand them to Benton. Then I give him the manila envelope containing the ring.

"Animal dander, pollens, dust, gluten, you name it, he's allergic, has been treated by allergists most of his life. He was doing fine until late summer, and then nothing seemed to work very well anymore. It was a very bad season for pollens, and stress makes things worse, and he was increasingly stressed," she says. "He did start using a spray again that has a type of cortisone in it. The name just fled from me. . . ."

"Corticosteroid?"

"Yes. That's it. And I've wondered about it in terms of it affecting his moods, his behavior. Things such as insomnia, ups and downs, and irritability, which, as you know, became extreme, culminating in him having blackouts and delusions, and ultimately our hospitalizing him."

"He started using it again? So he's used the corticosteroid spray before?"

"Certainly, over the years. But not since he started a new treatment, which meant he didn't need shots anymore. For about a year it was like a magical cure; then he got bad again and resumed the nasal spray."

"Tell me about the new treatment."

"I'm sure you're familiar with drops under the tongue."

I'm aware that sublingual immunotherapy has yet to be approved by the FDA, and I ask, "Is your son part of a clinical trial?" I scribble another note to Benton.

Spray and drops to the labs stat. And I underlined *stat,* which means *statim,* or immediately.

"That's right, through his allergist."

I look at Benton to see if he knows about this, and he glances at my note as he puts on the gloves, and next he glances at his watch. He's going to look at the ring only because I asked him to. It's as if he's already seen it or already knows it isn't important or has his mind made up. Something has ended. Something has happened.

". . . What's called an off-label use that his doctor supervises, but no more trips to his office for shots every week," Mrs. Donahue says, and she seems momentarily soothed as she talks about her son's allergies instead of everything else, her pain in remission, but it won't last.

If someone has tampered with Johnny's medications, it might explain why his allergies got bad again. What he was placing under his tongue or spraying up his nose might have been sufficiently altered chemically to render the medications ineffective, not to mention extremely harmful. I look at Benton as he examines the signet ring. He has no expression on his face. I hold up a sheet of stationery so he can see the water-mark. He has no visible reaction, and I notice a cobweb in his hair. I reach over and remove it, and he returns the ring to the envelope. He meets my eyes and widens them the way he does at parties and dinners when he's telegraphing *Let's go now.*

". . . Johnny takes several drops under his tongue daily, and for a while had excellent results. Then it stopped working as well, and he's been miserable at times. This past August he resumed the spray but only seemed to get worse, and along with it were these very disturbing changes in his personality. They were noted by others, and he did get in trouble for acting out, was kicked out of that class, as you know, but he wouldn't have harmed that child. I don't think Johnny was even aware of him, much less would do something. . . ."

Benton takes off the gloves and drops them in the trash. I point at the envelope, and he shakes his head. *Don't ask Mrs. Donahue about the ring.* He doesn't want me to mention it, or maybe it isn't necessary for me to bring it up to her because of what Benton knows that I don't, and then I notice his black tactical boots. They are covered with gray dust that wasn't there earlier when we were talking in Fielding's

461

office. The legs of his black tactical pants also are quite dusty, and the sleeves of his shearling coat are dirty, as if he brushed up against something.

". . . It was the main thing I wanted to ask, more of a personal matter directed at him as a man who teaches martial arts and is supposed to abide by a code of honor," Mrs. Donahue says, grabbing my attention back, and I wonder if I've misunderstood her. I can't possibly have heard what I just did. "It was that more than the other, not at all what you assumed or what he told you. Lying, I'm sure, because as I've said, if he claims I called him to ask for details about what was done to that poor child, then he was lying. I promise I didn't ask about Mark Bishop, who wasn't known to us personally, by the way. We only saw him there sometimes. I didn't ask for information about him. . . ."

"Mrs. Donahue, I'm sorry. You're cutting in and out." It's not really true, but I need her to repeat what she said and to clarify.

"These portable phones. Is this better? I'm sorry. I'm pacing as I talk, pacing all over the house."

"Thank you. Could you please repeat the last few things you said? What about martial arts?"

462

I listen with another jolt of disbelief as she reminds me of what she assumes I know, that her son Johnny is acquainted with Jack Fielding through tae kwon do. When she called this office several times to talk to Fielding and eventually to complain to me, it is because of this relationship. Fielding was Johnny's instructor at the Cambridge Tae Kwon Do Club. Fielding was Mark Bishop's instructor, taught a class of Tiny Tigers, but Johnny didn't know Mark, and certainly they weren't in the same class, weren't taught together, Mrs. Donahue is adamant about that, and I ask her when Johnny started taking lessons. I tell her I'm not sure about the details and must have an accurate account if I'm to deal appropriately and fairly with her complaint about my deputy chief.

"He's been taking lessons since last May," Mrs. Donahue says while my thoughts scatter and bounce like caroms. "You can understand why my son, who's never really had friends, would be easily influenced by someone he adores and respects. . . ."

"Adores and respects? Do you mean Dr. Fielding?"

"No, not hardly," she says acidly, as if she truly hates the man. "His friend was involved in it first, has been for quite some time. Apparently, a number of women are quite serious about tae kwon do, and when she began working with Johnny and they became friends, she encouraged him, and I wish he hadn't listened. That and, of course, Otwahl, that place and whatever goes on there, and look what's happened. But you can certainly imagine why Johnny would want to be powerful and able to protect himself, to feel less picked on and alone when the irony, of course, is that those days for him really were gone. He wasn't bullied at Harvard. . . ."

She goes on, rambling and less crisp and commanding now, and her despair is palpable. I can feel it in the air inside my office as I get up from my desk.

". . . How dare him. That certainly constitutes a violation of his medical oath if anything does. How dare him continue to be in charge of the Mark Bishop case in light of what we all know the truth is," she says.

"Can you be specific about what truth you're referring to?" I look out my windows at the blindingly bright morning. The sun and the glare are so intense, my eyes water.

"His bias." Her voice sounds behind me, on speakerphone. "He's never been fond of Johnny or particularly nice to him, would make tactless comments to him in front of the others. Things such as 'You need to look at me when I'm talking to you instead of at the goddamn light switch.' Well, as I'm sure you're aware, because of Johnny's unusualness, his attention gets caught up on things that don't make sense to others. He has poor eye contact and can be offensive because people don't understand it's just the way his brain works. Do you know much about Asperger's, or has your husband . . ."

"I don't know much." I don't intend to get into what Benton has or hasn't told me.

"Well, Johnny gets fixated on a detail of no significance to anyone else and will stare at it while you're talking to him. I'll be telling him something important and he's looking at a brooch or a bracelet I'm wearing, or he makes a comment or laughs when he shouldn't. And Dr. Fielding berated him about laughing inappropriately. He belittled him in front of everyone, and that's when Johnny tried to kick him. Here this man has however many degrees of a black belt someone can have, and my son, who weighs all of a hundred and forty pounds, tried to kick him, and that was when he was forced to leave the class for good. Dr. Fielding forbade him from ever coming back and threatened to blackball him if he tried to take lessons anywhere else."

"When was this?" I hear myself as if I'm someone else speaking.

"The second week of December. I have the exact date. I have everything written down."

Six weeks before Mark Bishop was murdered, I think, dazed, as if I'm the one who has been kicked. "And you suggested to Dr. Fielding —" I start to say to the phone on my desk as if I'm looking at Mrs. Donahue and she can see me.

"I certainly did!" she says excitedly, defiantly. "When Johnny started babbling his nonsense about having killed that boy during a blackout and that their tae kwon do instructor did the autopsy! Can you imagine my reaction?"

Their tae kwon do instructor. Who else is she referring to? Johnny's MIT friend, or are there others? Who else might Fielding have been teaching, and what could have caused Johnny Donahue to confess to a murder Benton believes he didn't commit? Why would Johnny think he did something so horrific during a so-called blackout? Who influenced him to the extent he would admit to it and offer details such as the weapon being a nail gun when I know for a fact that isn't true? But I'm not going to ask Mrs.

Donahue anything else. I've gone too far; everything has gone too far. I've asked her more than I should, and Benton already knows the answers to anything I might think of. I can tell by the way he's sitting in his chair, staring down at the floor, his face as hard and dark as my building's metal skin.

18

I hang up the phone and stand before my curved wall of glass, looking out at a patchwork of slate tiles and snow punctuated by church steeples stretching out before me in the kingdom of CFC.

I wait for my heart to slow and my emotions to settle, swallowing hard to push the pain and anger back down my throat, distracting myself with the view of MIT, and beyond it, Harvard and beyond. As I stand inside my empire of many windows and look out at what I'm supposed to manage if the worst happens to people, I understand. I understand why Benton is acting the way he is. I understand what has ended. Jack Fielding has.

I vaguely remember him mentioning not long after he moved here from Chicago that he had volunteered at some tae kwon do club and couldn't always be available to do cases on weekends or after hours because of his dedication to teaching what he referred to as his art, his passion. On occasion he would be gone to tournaments, he told me, and he assumed he would be granted "flexibility." As acting chief during my long absences, he expected flexibility, he reiterated, almost lecturing me. The same flexibility I would have if I were here, he stated, as if it was a known fact that I have flexibility when I'm home.

I remember being put off by his demands, since he's the one who called me asking for a job at the CFC, and the position I foolishly agreed to give him far surpasses any he's ever had. In Chicago he wasn't afforded much status, was one of six medical examiners and not in line for a promotion of any kind, his chief confided in me when we spoke of my hiring Fielding away from there. It would be a tremendous professional opportunity and good for him personally to be around family, the chief said, and I was deeply moved that Fielding thought of me as family. I was pleased that he had missed me and wanted to come back to Massachusetts, to work for me like in the old days.

And the irony that should have infuriated me, and one I certainly should have pointed out to Fielding instead of indulging him as usual, was this notion of flexibility, as if I come and go as I please, as if I take vacations and run off to tournaments and disappear several weekends each month because of some art or passion I have beyond what I do in my profession, beyond what I do every damn day. My passion is what I live every damn day, and the deaths I take care of every damn day and the people the deaths leave behind and how they pick up and go on, and how I help them somehow do that. I hear myself and realize I've been saying these things out loud, and I feel Benton's hands on my shoulders as he stands behind me while I wipe tears from my eyes. He rests his chin on top of my head and wraps his arms around me.

"What have I done?" I say to him.

"You've put up with a lot from him, with way too much, but it's not you who's done anything. Whatever he was on, was taking and probably dealing . . . Well. You had a brush with it earlier, so you can imagine." He means whatever drugs Fielding might have used to saturate his pain-relieving patches, and whatever drugs he might have been selling.

"Have you found him?" I ask.

"Yes."

"He's in custody? He's been arrested? Or

you're just questioning him?"

"We have him, Kay."

"I suppose it's best." I don't know what else to ask except how Fielding is doing, which Benton doesn't answer.

I wonder if Fielding had to be placed in a four-point restraint or maybe in a padded room, and I can't imagine him in captivity. I can't imagine him in prison. He won't last. He will bat himself to death against bars like a panicked moth if someone doesn't kill him first. It also crosses my mind that he is dead. Then it feels he is. The feeling settles numbly, heavily, as if I've been given a nerve block.

"We need to head out. I'll explain as best I can, as best we know. It's complicated; it's a lot," I hear Benton say.

He moves away, no longer touching me, and it is as if there is nothing holding me here and I will float out the window, and at the same time, there is the heaviness. I feel I've turned into metal or stone, into something no longer alive or human.

"I couldn't let you know earlier as it became clear, not that all of it is clear yet," Benton says. "I'm sorry when I have to keep things from you, Kay."

"Why would he, why would anyone . . . ?" I start to ask questions that can never be answered satisfactorily, the same questions I've always asked. Why are people cruel? Why do they kill? Why do they take pleasure in ruining others?

"Because he could." Benton says what he always does.

"But why would he?" Fielding isn't like that. He's never been diabolical. Immature and selfish and dysfunctional, yes. But not evil. He wouldn't kill a six-year-old boy for fun and then enjoy pinning the crime on a teenager with Asperger's. Fielding's not equipped to orchestrate a cold-blooded game like that.

"Money. Control. His addictions. Righting wrongs that go back to the beginning of his time. And decompensating. Ultimately destroying himself because that's who he was really destroying when he destroyed others." Benton has it all figured out. Everybody has it figured out except me.

"I don't know," I mutter, and I tell myself to be strong. I have to take care of this. I can't help Fielding, I can't help anyone, if I'm not strong.

"He didn't hide things well," Benton then says as I move away from the window. "Once we figured out where to look, it's become increasingly obvious."

Someone setting people up, setting up

everything. That's why it's not hidden well. That's why it's obvious. It's supposed to be obvious, to make us think certain things are true when maybe they aren't. I won't accept that the person behind all this is Fielding until I see it for myself. *Be strong. You must take care of it. Don't cry over him or anyone. You can't.*

"What do I need to bring?" I collect my coat off a chair, the tactical jacket from Dover that isn't nearly warm enough.

"We have everything there," he says. "Just your credentials in case someone asks."

Of course they have everything there. Everything and everyone is there except me. I collect my shoulder bag from the back of my door.

"When did you figure it out?" I ask. "Figure it out enough to get warrants to find him? Or however it's happened?"

"When you discovered the man from Norton's Woods was a homicide, that changed things, to say the least. Now Fielding was connected to another murder."

"I don't see how," I reply as we walk out together, and I don't tell Bryce I'm leaving. At the moment I don't want to face anyone. I'm in no mood to chat or to be cordial or even civilized.

"Because the Glock had disappeared from

the firearms lab. I know you haven't been told about that, and very few people are aware of it," Benton says.

I remember Lucy's comments about seeing Morrow in the back parking lot at around ten-thirty yesterday morning, about a half hour after the pistol was receipted to him in his lab, and he couldn't be bothered with it, according to Lucy. If she knew about the missing Glock, she withheld that crucial information, and I ask Benton if she deliberately lied by omission to me, the chief, her boss.

"Because she works here," I say as we wait for the elevator to climb to our floor. It is stuck on the lower level, as if someone is holding open the door down there, what staff members sometimes do when they are loading a lot of things on or off. "She works for me and can't just keep information from me. She can't lie to me."

"She wasn't aware of it then. Marino and I knew, and we didn't tell her."

"And you knew about Jack and Johnny and Mark. About tae kwon do." I'm sure Benton did. Probably Marino, too.

"We've been watching Jack, been looking into it. Yes. Since Mark was murdered last week and I found out Jack taught him and Johnny."

I think of the photographs missing from Fielding's office, the tiny holes in the wall from the hanging hooks being removed.

"It began to make sense that Jack took control of certain cases. The Mark Bishop case, for example, even though he hates to do kids," Benton goes on, looking around, making sure no one is nearby to overhear us. "What a perfect opportunity to cover up your own crimes."

Or some other person's crimes, I think. Fielding would be the sort to cover for someone else. He desperately needs to be powerful, to be the hero, and then I remind myself to stop defending him. *Don't unless you have proof.* Whatever turns out to be true, I'll accept it, and it occurs to me that the photographs missing from Fielding's office might have been group poses. That seems familiar. I can almost envision them. Perhaps of tae kwon do classes. Pictures with Johnny and Mark in them.

I wonder but don't ask if Benton removed those photographs or if Marino did, as Benton continues to explain that Fielding went to great lengths to manipulate everyone into believing that Johnny Donahue killed Mark Bishop. Fielding used a compromised, vulnerable teenager as a scapegoat, and then Fielding had to escalate his manipulations further after he took out the man from Norton's Woods. That's the phrase Benton uses. *Took out.* Fielding took him out and then heard about the Glock found on the body and realized he'd made a serious tactical error. Everything was falling apart. He was losing it, decompensating like Ted Bundy did right before he was caught, Benton says.

"Jack's fatal mistake was to stop by the firearms lab yesterday morning and ask Morrow about the Glock," Benton continues. "A little later it was gone and so was Jack, and that was impulsive and reckless and just damn stupid on his part. It would have been better to let the gun be traced to him and claim it was lost or stolen. Anything would have been better than what he did. It shows how out of control he was to take the damn gun from the lab."

"You're saying the Glock the man from Norton's Woods had is Jack's."

"Yes."

"It's definitely Jack's," I repeat, and the elevator is moving now, making a lot of stops on its way up, and I realize it is lunchtime. Employees heading to the break room or heading out of the building.

"Yes. The dead man has a gun that could be traced to Fielding once acid was used on the drilled-off serial number," Benton says, and it's clear to me that he knows who the dead man is.

"That was done. Not here." I don't want to think of yet something else done inside my building that I didn't know.

"Hours ago. At the scene. We took care of the identification right there."

"The FBI did."

"It was important to know immediately who the gun was traced to. To confirm our suspicions. Then it came here to the CFC and is safely locked up in the firearms lab. For further examination," Benton says.

"If Jack is the one who murdered him, he should have realized the problem with the Glock when he first was called about the case on Sunday afternoon," I reply. "Yet he waited until Monday morning to be concerned about a gun he knew could be traced to him?"

"To avoid suspicion. If he'd started asking the Cambridge police a lot of questions about the Glock prior to the body being transported to the CFC, or demanded that the gun be brought in immediately when the labs were closed, it would have come across as peculiar. Antennas would have gone up. Fielding slept on it and by Monday morning was probably beside himself and planning what he was going to do once the gun was brought in. He would take it and flee. Remember, he hasn't been exactly rational. It's important to keep in mind he's been cognitively impaired by his substance abuse."

I think about the chronology. I reconstruct Fielding's steps yesterday morning, based on information from his desk drawer and the indented writing on his call-sheet pad. Shortly after seven a.m. it seems he talked to Julia Gabriel before she called me at Dover, and about a half hour later he entered the cooler, and minutes after that he told Anne and Ollie the body from Norton's Woods was inexplicably bloody. It seems more logical to consider it was at this point that Fielding recognized the dead man and realized the Glock he'd heard about from the police would be traced to him. If he didn't recognize the dead man until Monday morning, then Fielding didn't kill him, I say to Benton, who replies that Fielding had a motive I couldn't possibly know about.

The dead man's stepfather is Liam Saltz, Benton informs me. It was confirmed a little while ago when an FBI agent went to the Charles Hotel and talked to Dr. Saltz and showed him an ID photograph Marino took of the man from Norton's Woods. He was Eli Goldman, age twenty-two, a graduate student at MIT and an employee at Otwahl Technologies, working on special micromechanical projects. The video clips from Eli's headphones were traced to a webcam site on Otwahl's server, Benton tells me, but he won't elaborate on who did the tracing, if Lucy might have.

"He rigged up the headphones himself?" I ask as the elevator finally gets to us and the doors slide open.

"It appears likely. He loved to tinker."

"And MORT? How did he get that? And what for? More tinkering?" I know I sound cynical.

I know when people have their damn minds made up, and I'm not ready for my mind to be made up. Not one damn thing should be decided this fast.

"A facsimile, a model he made as a boy," Benton explains. "Based on photographs his stepfather had taken of the real thing when he was lobbying against it some eight or nine years ago when you and Dr. Saltz testified before the Senate subcommittee. Apparently, Eli was making models of robots and inventing things since he was practically in diapers."

We slowly sink from floor to floor while I

ask why Otwahl would hire the stepson of a detractor like Liam Saltz, and I want to know what Otwahl means, because Mrs. Donahue said the name meant something. "O. T. Wahl," Benton replies. "A play on words, because the last name of the company's founder is Wahl. *On the Wall,* as in a fly on the wall, and Eli's last name isn't Saltz," Benton adds, as if I didn't hear him when he told me it's Goldman. Eli Goldman. But Otwahl would have done a background check on him, I point out. Certainly they would have known who his stepfather is, even if their last names aren't the same.

"MORT was a long time ago," Benton says as the elevator doors open on the lower floor. "And I don't know that Otwahl had a clue Eli and his stepdad were philosophically simpatico."

"How long had Eli worked there?"

"Three years."

"Maybe three years ago Otwahl wasn't doing anything that Eli or his stepfather would have been concerned about," I suggest as we walk along gray tile while Phil the security guard watches us from behind his glass partition. I don't wave at him. I'm not friendly.

"Well, Eli was worried and had been for months," Benton says. "He was about to give his stepfather a demonstration of technology that he wasn't going to approve of at all, a fly that could be a fly on the wall and spy and detect explosives and deliver them or drugs or poisons or who knows what."

Nanoexplosives or dangerous drugs delivered by something as small as a fly, I think, as we walk past staff I've not seen in months. I don't stop to chat. I don't wave or say hello or even have eye contact.

"He's about to give his stepfather important information like that and conveniently dies," I reply.

"Exactly. The motive I mentioned," Benton says. "Drugs," he says again, and then he tells me more, gives me details the FBI learned from Liam Saltz just a few hours earlier.

I feel sad and upset again as I envision what Benton is saying about a young man so enamored of his famous stepfather that whenever they were to see each other, Eli always set his watch to it, mirroring Dr. Saltz's time zone in anticipation of their reunion, a quirk that has its roots in Eli's poignant past of broken homes and parental figures missing in action and adored from afar. I remember what I watched on the video clips, Eli and Sock walking to

Norton's Woods, and then I imagine Dr. Saltz emerging from the building in the near dark after a wedding Eli wasn't invited to. I imagine the Nobel laureate looking around and wondering where his stepson was, having no idea of the terrible truth. Dead. Zipped up inside a pouch and unidentified. A young man, barely more than a boy. Someone Lucy and I may have crossed paths with at an exhibit in London the summer of 2001.

"Who killed him, and what for?" I say as we pass through the empty bay, the CFC van-body truck gone. "I don't see how what you've just said explains Eli being murdered by Jack."

"It all points in the same direction. I'm sorry. But it does."

"I just don't see why and for what." I open the door leading outside, and it is too beautiful and sunny to be so cold.

"I know this is hard," Benton says.

"A pair of data gloves?" I say as we begin to pick our way over snow that is glazed and slick. "A micromechanical fly? Who would stab him with an injection knife, and why?"

"Drugs." Benton goes back to that again. "Somehow Eli had the misfortune of getting involved with Jack or the other way around. Strength-enhancing, very dangerous drugs. Probably was using and selling, and Eli was the supplier, or someone at Otwahl was. We don't know. But Eli being killed while he was out there with a flybot and about to meet his stepfather wasn't a coincidence. It's the motive, I mean."

"Why would Jack be interested in a flybot or a meeting?" I ask as we move very slowly, one step at a time, my feet about to go out from under me. "A damn ice-skating rink," I complain, because the parking lot wasn't plowed and it needs to be sanded. Nobody has been running this place the way it ought to be run.

"I'm sorry, we're way over here." We head slowly toward the back fence. "But that's all there was. The drug connection," Benton then says. "Not street drugs. This is about Otwahl. About a huge amount of money. About the war, about potential violence on an international and massive scale."

"Then if what you're saying is right, it would seem to imply Jack was spying on Eli. Rigged up the headphones with hidden recording devices and followed him to Norton's Woods. That would make sense if the murder was to stop Eli from showing his stepfather the flybot or turning it over to him. How else would Jack know what Eli was about to do? He must have been spying on him, or someone was."

"I doubt Jack had anything to do with the headphones."

"My point exactly. Jack wouldn't be interested in technology like that or capable of it, and he wouldn't be interested in a place like Otwahl. You're not talking about the Jack I know. He's much too limbically driven, too impatient, too simple, to do what you've just described." I almost say *too primitive,* because that has always been part of his charm. His physicality, his hedonism, his linear way of coping with things. "And the headphones don't make sense," I insist. "The headphones make me think someone else might be involved."

"I understand how you feel. I can understand why you'd want to think that."

"And did Dr. Saltz know his adoring stepson was into drugs and had an illegal gun?" I ask. "Did he happen to mention the headphones or other people Eli might have been involved with?"

"He knew nothing about the headphones and not much about Eli's personal life. Only that Eli was worried about his safety. As I said, he'd been worried for months. I know this is painful, Kay."

"Worried about what, specifically?" I ask as we walk very slowly, and someone is going to get hurt out here. Someone is going to slip and break bones and sue the CFC. That will be next.

"Eli was involved in dangerous projects and surrounded by bad people. That's how Dr. Saltz described it," Benton says. "It's a lot to explain and not what you might imagine."

"He knew his stepson had a gun, an illegal one," I repeat my question.

"He didn't know that. I assume Eli wouldn't have mentioned it."

"Everyone seems to be doing a lot of assuming." I stop and look at Benton, our breath smoking out in the brightness and the cold, and we are at the back of the parking lot now, near the fence, in what I call the hinterlands.

"Eli would know how Dr. Saltz feels about guns," Benton says. "Jack probably sold the Glock to him or gave it to him."

"Or someone did," I reiterate. "Just as someone must have given him the signet ring with the Donahue crest on it. I don't suppose Eli was also involved in tae kwon do." I look around at SUVs that don't belong to the CFC, but I don't look at the agents inside them. I don't look at anyone as I shield my eyes from the sun.

"No," Benton answers. "The football

player wasn't, either, Wally Jamison, but he used the gym where they're held, used Jack's same gym. Maybe Eli had been to that gym, too."

"Eli doesn't look like someone who uses a gym. Hardly a muscle in his body," I comment as Benton points a key fob at a black Ford Explorer that isn't his and the doors unlock with a chirp. "And if Jack killed him, why?" I again ask, because it makes no sense to me, but maybe it's my fatigue. No sleep and too much trauma, and I'm too tired to comprehend the simplest thing.

"Or maybe the connection has to do with Otwahl and Johnny Donahue and other illegal activities Jack was involved in that you're about to find out. What he was doing at the CFC, how he was earning his money while you were gone." Benton's voice is hard as he says all that while opening my door for me. "Don't know everything but enough, and you were right to ask what Mark Bishop was doing in his backyard when he was killed. What kind of playing he was doing. I almost couldn't believe it when you asked me that, and I couldn't tell you when you asked. Mark was in one of Jack's classes, as Mrs. Donahue implied, for three- to six-year-olds, had just started in December and was practicing tae kwon do in his yard when someone, and I think we know who, appeared, and again, you're probably right about how it happened."

As he goes around to the driver's side to get in, and I dig in my bag for my sunglasses, impatient and frustrated as a lipstick, pens, and a tube of hand cream spill on the plastic floor mat. I must have left my sunglasses somewhere. Maybe in my office at Dover, where I can scarcely remember being anymore. It seems like forever ago, and right now I am sickened beyond what I could possibly describe to anyone, and it doesn't please me to hear I was right about anything. I don't give a damn who is right, just that someone is, and I don't think anybody is. I just don't believe it.

"A person Mark had no reason to distrust, such as his instructor, who lured him into a fantasy, a game, and murdered him," Benton goes on as he starts the SUV. "And then trumped up a way to blame it on Johnny."

"I didn't say that part." I stuff items back into my bag as I grab my shoulder harness and fasten up, then I decide to take my jacket off, and I undo the seat belt.

"What part?" Benton enters an address in the GPS.

"I never said Jack trumped up a way to make Johnny believe he drove nails into

Mark Bishop's head," I reply, and the SUV is warm from when Benton drove it here, and the sun is hot as it blazes through glass.

I take off my jacket and toss it in back, where there is a large, thick box with a FedEx label. I can't tell whom it is for and I'm not interested, probably some agent Benton knows, probably whoever Douglas is, and I suppose I'll find out soon enough. I fasten my shoulder harness again, working so hard I'm practically out of breath, and my heart is pounding.

"I didn't mean that part was from you. There are a lot of questions. We need you to help us answer everything we possibly can," Benton says.

We begin backing up, pulling out of my parking lot, waiting for the gate to open, and I feel handled. I feel humored. I'm not sure I remember ever feeling so nonessential in an investigation, as if I'm an obstruction and a nuisance people have to be politically correct with because of my position, but not taken seriously and unwanted.

"I thought I'd seen it all. I'm warning you, it's bad, Kay." Benton's voice has no energy as he says that. It sounds hollow, like something gutted.

The gray frame house with the old stone foundation and a cold cellar in back were built by a sea captain in centuries past. The property is scrubbed and eroded by harsh weather, directly exposed to what blows in from the sea, and sits alone at the end of a narrow, icy street coarsely sanded by city emergency crews. Where branches have snapped, ice is shattered on the frozen earth and sparkles like broken glass in a high sun that offers no warmth, only a blinding glare.

Sand makes a gritty sound against the underside of the SUV while Benton drives very slowly, looking for a place to park, and I look out at the brightness of the sandy road and the heaving deep blue of the sea and the paler blue of the cloudless sky. I no longer feel the need for sleep or that I could if I tried. Having last gotten up at quarter of five yesterday morning in Delaware, I have been awake some thirty hours since, which isn't unheard of for me, isn't really remarkable if I pause to calculate how often it happens in a profession where people don't have the common courtesy to kill or to die during business hours. But this is a different type of sleeplessness, foreign and unfamiliar, with the added excitement bordering on hysteria from being told, or having it implied at least, that I've lived much of my life with something deadly and I'm the reason it turned deadly.

No one is stating such a thing in exactly those words, but I know it to be true. Benton is diplomatic, but I know. He's not said it's my fault people are brutally dead and countless others have been disrespected and defiled, not to mention those harmed by drugs, people whose names we may never know, guinea pigs or "lab rats," as Benton put it, for a malevolent science project involving a potent form of anabolic steroid or testosterone laced with a hallucinogenic to build strength and muscle mass and enhance aggression and fearlessness. To create killing machines, to turn human beings into monstrosities with no frontal cortex, no concept of consequences, human robots that savagely kill and feel no remorse, feel virtually nothing at all, including pain. Benton has been describing what

Liam Saltz told the FBI this morning, the poor man bereft and terrified.

Dr. Saltz suspects Eli got involved with a treacherous and unauthorized technology at Otwahl, found himself in the midst of DARPA research gone bad, gone frighteningly wrong, and was about to warn his humanitarian Nobel laureate stepfather and to offer proof and to beg him to put a stop to it. Fielding put a stop to Eli because Fielding was using these dangerous drugs, perhaps helping to distribute them, but mostly my deputy chief with his lifelong lust for strength and physical beauty and his chronic aches and pains was addicted. That's the theory behind Fielding's vile crimes, and I don't believe it is that simple or even true. But I do believe other comments Benton has continued to make. I was too good to Fielding. I've always been too good to him. I've never seen him for what he is or accepted his potential to do real harm, and therefore I enabled him.

Snow turned to freezing rain where the ocean warms the air, and the power is still out from downed lines in this area of Salem Neck called Winter Island, where Jack Fielding owns a historic investment property I had no idea about. To get to it you have to pass the Plummer Home for Boys, a lovely mossy green mansion set on a gracious spread of lawn overlooking the sea, with a distant view of the wealthy resort community of Marblehead. I can't help but think about the way things begin and end, the way people have a tendency to run in place, to tread water, to really not get beyond where and how it all started for them.

Fielding stopped his life where it took off for him so precipitously, in a picturesque setting for troubled youths who can no longer live with their families. I wonder if it was deliberate to pick a spot no more than a stone's throw from a boys' home, if that factored into his subconscious when he decided on a property I'm told he intended to retire to or perhaps sell for a profit in the future when the real-estate market turns around and after he'd finished much-needed improvements. He'd been doing the work on the house and its outbuilding himself and doing it poorly, and I'm about to see the manifestation of his disorganized, chaotic mind, the handiwork of someone profoundly out of control, Benton has let me know. I'm about to see the way my enabled protégé lived and ended.

"Are you still with us? I know you're tired," Benton says as he touches my arm.

"I'm fine." I realize he's been talking and I tuned him out.

"You don't look fine. You're still crying."

"I'm not crying. It's the sun. I can't believe I left my sunglasses somewhere."

"I've said you can have mine." His dark glasses turn toward me as he creeps along the sandy, gritty-sounding road in the glaring sun.

"No, thank you."

"Why don't you tell me what's going on with you, because we're not going to have a chance to talk for a while," he says. "You're angry with me."

"You're just doing your job, whatever it is."

"You're angry with me because you're angry at Jack, and you're afraid to be angry at him."

"I'm not afraid of what I feel about him. I'm more afraid of everyone else," I reply.

"Meaning what, exactly?"

"It's something I sense, and you don't agree with me, so we should leave it at that," I say to him as I look out the window at the cold, blue ocean and the distant horizon, where I can make out houses on the shore.

"Maybe you could be a little more specific. What do you sense? Is this a new thought?"

"It isn't. And it's nothing anybody wants

to hear," I answer him as I stare out at the bright afternoon while we continue to troll for a place to park.

I'm not really helping him look for a spot. Mostly I'm sitting and staring out the window while my mind goes where it wants to, like a small animal darting about, looking for a safe place. Benton probably thinks I'm pretty useless. He's aided and abetted my uselessness by waiting this long to come get me for something that's been going on for hours. I'm showing up in medias res, as if this is a musical or an opera and it's no big deal for me to wander in during the middle or toward the end, depending on which act we're in.

"Christ, this is ridiculous. You would think someone would have left us something. I should have had Marino put cones out, save us something." Benton vents his anger at parked cars and the narrow street, then says to me, "I want to hear whatever it is. New thought or not. Now, while we have a minute alone."

There is no point in saying the rest of it, of telling him again what I sense, which is a calculating, cruel logic behind what was done to Wally Jamison, Mark Bishop, and Eli Goldman, behind what happened to Fielding, behind everything, a precisely formulated agenda, even if it didn't turn out as planned. Not that I know the plan in its entirety, maybe not even most of it, but what I sense is palpable and undeniable, and I won't be talked out of it. *Trust your instincts. Don't trust anything else. This is about power. The power to control people, to make them feel good or frightened or to suffer unbearably. Power over life and death.* I'm not going to repeat what I'm sure sounds irrational. I'm not going to tell Benton yet again that I sense an insatiable desire for power, that I feel the presence of a murderous entity watching us from a dark place, lying in wait. Some things are over, but not everything is, and I don't say any of this to him.

"I'm just going to have to tuck it in here, and the hell with it." He isn't really talking to me but to himself, easing as close to a rock wall as he can so we don't stick halfway out into the slick, sandy street. "We'll hope some yahoo doesn't hit me. If so, he'll be in for an unpleasant surprise."

I suppose he means it wouldn't be fun to realize the door you just dinged or the bumper you just scraped or the side you just swiped is the property of the FBI. The SUV is a typical government vehicle, black with tinted glass and cloth seats, and emergency strobes hidden behind the grill, and on the floor in back are two coffee cups neatly held in place inside their cardboard to-go box along with a balled-up food bag. The war wagon of a busy agent who is tidy but not always in a convenient spot to toss out trash. I didn't know that Douglas was a woman until Benton referred to the special agent who's assigned this car as "she" a little while ago while he was telling me about *her* running the license plate of the Bentley that met us at Hanscom last night, a 2003 four-door black Flying Spur personally owned by the CEO of a Boston-based niche service company that supplies "discreet concierge-minded chauffeurs" who will drive any vehicle requested, explaining why the Bentley didn't have a livery license plate.

The reservation was made online by someone using an e-mail address that belongs to Johnny Donahue, an inpatient at McLean with no Internet access when the e-mail was sent yesterday from an IP address that is an Internet café near Salem State College, which is very close to here. The credit card used belongs to Erica Donahue, and as far as anybody knows, she doesn't do anything online and won't touch a computer. Needless to say, the FBI and the police don't believe she or her son booked the Bentley or the driver.

The FBI and the police believe Fielding did, that he likely got access to Mrs. Donahue's credit card information from payments she made to the tae kwon do club for lessons her son took until he was told not to come back after he tried to kick his instructor, my deputy chief, a grandmaster with a seventh-degree black belt. It isn't clear how Fielding might have gained access to Johnny's e-mail account unless he somehow manipulated the vulnerable and gullible teenager into giving him the password at some point or learned it by some other means.

The chauffeur, who isn't suspected of anything except not bothering to research Dr. Scarpetta before he delivered something to her, received the assignment from dispatch, and according to dispatch, no one who works at the elite transportation company ever met the alleged Mrs. Donahue or talked to her over the phone. In the notes section of the online reservation, an "exotic luxury car" was requested for an "errand," with the explanation that further instructions and a letter to be delivered would be dropped off at the private driving company's headquarters. At approximately six p.m., a manila envelope was slipped through the mail slot in the front door, and some three hours later, the chauffeur showed up at Hanscom Field with it and decided that Benton was me.

We get out into the cold, clean air, and ice is everywhere, lit up by the sun as if we are inside an illuminated crystal chandelier. Shielding my eyes with my hand, I watch the dark-blue sea as it rolls and contracts like muscle, pushing itself inland to smash and boil against a rock-strewn shore where no one lives. Right here a sea captain once looked out at a view that I doubt has changed much in hundreds of years, acres of rugged coastline and beach with copses of hardwood trees, untouched and uninhabitable because it is part of a marine recreational park, which happens to have a boat launch.

A little farther down, past the campground, where the Neck wraps around toward the Salem Harbor, is a yacht yard where Fielding's twenty-foot Mako was shrink-wrapped and on a jack stand when police found it this morning. I'm vaguely aware he has a dive boat because I've heard him mention it, but I didn't know where he keeps it. I never would have imagined twenty-four hours ago that it might become the focus of a homicide investigation, or that his dark-blue Navigator SUV with its missing front license plate would, or that his Glock pistol with its drilled-off serial number would, or that everything Fielding owns and has done throughout his entire existence would.

Overhead, an orange Dauphin helicopter, an HH-65A, also known as a Dolphin, beats low across the cold blue sky, its enclosed Fenestron ten-bladed tail rotor making a distinctive modulated sound that is described as low noise but to me has a quiet high pitch, is ominously whiny, reminding me a bit of a C-17. Homeland Security is conducting air surveillance, and I've been told that, too. I don't know why federal law enforcement has taken to the air or the land or the sea unless there is a concern about the overall security of the Salem Harbor, a significant port with a huge power plant. I have heard the word *terrorism* mentioned, just in passing by Benton and also by Marino when I had him on the phone a few minutes ago, but these days I hear that word a lot. In fact, I hear it all the time. Bioterrorism. Chemical terrorism. Domestic terrorism. Industrial terrorism. Nanoterrorism. Technoterrorism. Everything is terrorism if I stop to think about it. Just as every violent crime is hateful and a hate crime, really.

I continue going back to Otwahl, every-thing leading me back to Otwahl, my thoughts carried on the wing of a flybot or, as Lucy puts it, not a flybot but the holy grail of flybots. Then I think about my old nemesis MORT, a life-size model of it perched like a giant mechanical insect inside a Cambridge apartment rented by Eli Gold-man, and next I worry about the controver-sial scientist Dr. Liam Saltz, who must be heartbroken beyond remedy. Maybe he simply got caught in one of those ghastly coincidences that happens in life, his tragic misfortune to be the stepfather of a brilliant young man who slipped into bad science, bad drugs, and illegal firearms.

A kid too smart for his own good, as Benton puts it, murdered while wearing an antique signet ring missing from Erica Donahue's house, just as her stationery is missing, and her typewriter and a fountain pen, items that Fielding must have gotten hold of somehow. He must have gotten his hands on all sorts of things from the rich Harvard student he bullied, Johnny Donahue, and it doesn't matter if it all feels wrong to me. I can't prove that Fielding didn't exchange the gold ring for drugs. I can't prove he didn't exchange the Glock for drugs. I can't say that's not why Eli had the ring and the gun, that there's some other reason far more nefarious and dangerous than what Benton and others are proposing.

I can say and have said that Eli Goldman was an obstruction to the mercenary progress of a company like Otwahl, and Otwahl is the common denominator in everything, more so than tae kwon do or Fielding. As far as I'm concerned, if Fielding is as directly and solely responsible as everyone is claiming, then we should be taking a very hard and different look at Otwahl and wonder what he had to do with the place beyond being a user or a research subject or even someone who helped distribute experimental drugs until they brought about his complete annihilation.

"Otwahl and Jack Fielding," I said to Benton a little while ago. If Fielding is guilty of murder and case-tampering and obstruction of justice and all sorts of lies and conspiracies, then he's intimately connected with Otwahl, right down to its parking lot, where his Navigator likely got tucked out of sight last night during a blizzard. "You have to make that connection in a meaningful way," I repeatedly told Benton on our drive to this desolate spot that is achingly beautiful and yet ruined, as if Fielding's property is an ugly stain on the canvas of an exquisite seascape.

"Otwahl Technologies and an eighteenth-century sea captain's house on Salem Neck," I said to my husband, and I asked his opinion, his honest and objective opinion. After all, he should have a very well-informed and completely objective opinion because of his alliance with the well-informed and completely objective *we*'s, as I stated it, these anonymous comrades of his, the shadowy rank and file of an FBI he doesn't belong to anymore, he claims, and of course I don't believe him. He is FBI, all right, as secretive and driven as I remember him from times long past, and maybe I could put up with that if I didn't feel so utterly alone.

He's not even listening to me anymore, pretty much checked out when I made the comment a few minutes ago that Fielding must have some link to Otwahl beyond his teaching martial arts to a few brainy students who had internships with the technology behemoth. The connection must be more than just drugs, I said. Drug-impregnated pain-relieving patches can't be the entire explanation for what I'm about to find inside a tiny stone outbuilding that

Fielding was turning into a guest quarters before he supposedly found another use for it that has earned it several new names.

The Kill Cottage, I think darkly, bitterly. *The Semen's House,* I think cynically.

Destined to be Salem's latest attraction during Halloween, which lasts all of October, with a million people making a pilgrimage here from all over the land. Another example of a place made famous by atrocities that don't seem real anymore, tall tales, almost cartoonish, like the witch on her broom depicted on the Salem logo that is on police patches and even painted on the police cruiser doors. Be careful what you hate and murder, because one day it will own you. The Witch City, as people have dubbed the place where those men and women were herded up to what is now called Gallows Hill Park, a spot similar to where Fielding bought a sea captain's house. Places that don't change much. Places that are now parks. Only Gallows Hill is ugly, and it should be. An open field ravaged by the wind, and barren. Mostly rocks, weeds, and patchy, coarse grass. Nothing grows there.

Thoughts like these are solar flares, and peak and spike with a timing I can't seem to control, as Benton touches my elbow, then grips it firmly, while we cross the sandy dead-end street that has turned into a parking lot of law-enforcement vehicles, marked and unmarked, some with the Salem logo, silhouettes of witches straddling their brooms. Pulled up close to the sea captain's house, almost right up against the back of it, is the CFC's white van-body truck that Marino drove here hours earlier while I was in the autopsy room and then upstairs, having no idea what was happening some thirty miles northeast. The back of the truck is open, and Marino is inside, wearing green rubber boots and a bright yellow hard hat and a bright yellow level-A suit, what we use for demanding jobs that require protection from biological and chemical hazards.

Cables snake over the diamond-steel floor and out the open metal doors, over the unpaved icy drive, and disappear through the front of the stone cottage, what must have been a charming, cozy outbuilding before Fielding turned it into a construction site of exposed foundation blocks, the ground frozen with ice that is gray. The area behind the sea captain's house is an eyesore of spilled cement and toppled piles of lumber and bricks, and rusting tools, shingles, weather stripping, and nails everywhere. A wheelbarrow is covered loosely with a black tarp that flaps, the entire perimeter strung with yellow crime scene tape that shakes and jumps in the wind.

"We got enough juice in this thing for lights and that's it, got about a hundred and twenty minutes of run time left," Marino says to me as he digs inside a built-in storage bin.

What he's referring to is the auxiliary power unit, the APU, which can keep the truck's electrical system running while the engine is off and supplies a limited amount of emergency power externally.

"Assuming the power doesn't come back on, and maybe we'll get lucky. I've heard it could anytime, the main problem being those poles knocked over by snapped-off trees you probably drove past on Derby Street on your way here. But even if we get the electricity back, it won't help much in there." He means in the stone outbuilding. "No heat in there. It's cold as shit, and after a while it gets to you, I'm just telling you," he says from inside the truck while Benton and I stand outside in the wind and I flip up the collar of my jacket. "Cold as our damn fridge at the morgue, if you can imagine working in there for hours."

As if I've never worked a scene in frigid

weather and am unfamiliar with a morgue cooler.

"Course, there are some advantages to that if the power goes out, which it's going to do in these parts when you get storms, and he didn't have a backup generator," Marino continues.

He means that Fielding didn't.

"And that's a lot of money to lose if the freezer quits. Which is why plugging in a space heater and turning it on high was for the obvious reason of ruining the DNA so we'd never know who he'd taken the shit from. Do you think that's possible?" he asks me.

"I'm not sure which part of it —" I start to say.

"That we won't ID them. Possible we won't?" Marino continues talking nonstop, as if he's been drinking coffee since I saw him last. His eyes are bloodshot and glassy.

"No," I reply. "I don't think it's possible. I think we'll find out."

"So you don't think it's as worthless as tapioca."

"Christ," Benton says. "I could have done without that. Christ, I wish you'd stop with the fucking food analogies."

"Low copy number." I remind Marino we can get a DNA profile from as little as three human cells. Unless virtually every cell is degraded, we'll be okay, I assure him.

"Well, it's only fair we really try." Marino talks to me as if Benton's not here, directing his every comment to me as if he's in charge and doesn't want to be reminded of my FBI or former FBI husband. "I mean, what if it was your son?"

"I agree we have to ID them and let their next of kin know," I reply.

"And get sued, now that I think of it," Marino reconsiders. "Well, maybe we shouldn't tell anyone. Seems to me we just need to know who it came from. Why tell the families and open a can of worms?"

"Full disclosure," Benton says ironically, as if he really knows what that is. He is looking at his iPhone, reading something on it, and he adds, "Because a lot of them probably already know. We're assuming Fielding arranged with them up front to pay for the service he was offering. It's not possible to hide anything."

"We're not going to," I answer. "We don't hide things, period."

"Well, I'll tell you. I'm thinking we really should install cameras inside our cooler, not just outside in the hall and the bay and certain rooms but actually in there," Marino says to me, as if it has always been his belief that we should have cameras inside the coolers, probably inside the freezer, too. In fact, he's never mentioned the idea before now. "I wonder if cameras would work in a cooler. . . ." he is saying.

"They work outdoors. It gets colder in the winter around here than it is in the cooler," Benton comments dully, barely listening to Marino, who is full of himself, enjoying his role in the drama that has unfolded, and he's never liked Fielding. I can't think of a bigger *I told you so.*

"Well, we got to do it," Marino says to me. "Cameras and no more of this shit, of people doing shit they think they can get away with."

I look behind us at boots and shoes lined up outside the opening that leads into the cottage. The Kill Cottage, the Semen's Cottage. Some cops are calling it the Little Shop of Horrors.

"Cameras," I hear Marino as I stare at the stone cottage. "If we had them in the cooler, we'd have it all on tape. Well, hell, maybe it's a good thing. Shit, imagine if something like that got leaked and ended up on YouTube. Fielding doing that to all these dead bodies. Jesus. I bet you have cameras like that at Dover, though."

He hands us folded bright yellow suits like his.

"Dover must have cameras in the coolers, right?" he goes on. "I'm sure DoD would spring for it, and nothing like the present to ask, right? In light of the circumstances, I don't think anything's off the table when it comes to beefing up security at our place. . . ."

I realize Marino is still talking to me, but I don't answer because I'm worrying about what's in the cab of the truck. I'm suddenly overwhelmed by pity as I stand outside in the cold and wind and glare, my level-A suit folded up and tucked under my arm while Benton is putting his on.

And Marino goes on quite cheerfully, as if this is quite the carnival. ". . . Like I said, a good thing it's cold. I can't imagine working this on one of those ninety-degree days like we used to get in Richmond, where you can wring water out of the air and nothing's stirring. I mean, what a fucking pig. Don't even look at the toilet in there; probably the last time it was flushed was when they were still burning witches around here. . . ."

"They were hanged," I hear myself say.

Marino looks at me with a blank expression on his big face, and his nose and ears are red, the hard hat perched on top of his

bald head like the bonnet of a yellow fire-
plug.

"How's he doing?" I indicate the cab of
the truck and what's inside it.

"Anne's a regular Dr. Dolittle. Did you
know she wanted to be a vet before she
decided to be Madame Curie?" He still says
curry, like curry powder, no matter how
many times I've told him it's *Cure-ee,* like
the element curium that's named after
Madame *Cure-ee.*

"I tell you what, though," he then says to
me. "It's a good thing the heat hadn't been
off in the house more than five, six hours
before anybody got here. Dogs like that
don't have much more hair than I do. He'd
dug himself under the covers in Fielding's
rat's nest of a bed and was still shivering
like he was having a seizure. Of course, he
was scared shitless. All these cops, the FBI
storming in with all their tactical gear, the
whole nine yards. Not to mention I've heard
that greyhounds don't like to be left alone,
have, what do you call it, separation anxiety."

He opens another storage bin and hands
me a pair of boots, knowing my size without
asking.

"How do you know it's Jack's bed?" I ask.

"It's his shit everywhere. Who else's would it be?"

"We need to be sure of everything." I'm going to keep saying it. "He was out here in the middle of nowhere. No neighbors, no eyes or ears, the park deserted this time of year. How do you know for a fact he was alone out here? How can you be absolutely certain he didn't have help?"

"Who? Who the hell would help him do something like this?" Marino looks at me, and I can see it on his big face, what he thinks. I can't be rational about Fielding. That's exactly what Marino thinks, probably what everybody thinks.

"We need to keep an open mind," I reply, then I indicate the cab of the truck again and ask again about the dog.

"He's fine," Marino says. "Anne got him something to eat, chicken and rice from that Greek diner in Belmont, made him a nice comfy bed, and the heat's blasting, feels like an oven, probably sucking up more to keep his skinny ass warm than we're using in the cellar. You want to meet him?"

He hands us heavy black rubber gloves and disposable nitrile ones, and Benton blows on his hands to warm them as he continues text-messaging and reading whatever is landing on his phone. He doesn't

511

seem interested in anything Marino and I are saying.

"Let me take care of things first," I tell Marino, because I don't have it in me at the moment to see an abandoned dog that was left alone in a pitch-dark house with no heat after his master was murdered by the person who stole him. Or so the theory goes.

"Here's the routine," Marino then says, grabbing two bright yellow hard hats and handing them to us. "Over there, where you'll see plastic tubs for decon." He points at an area of dirt near a sheet of plywood that serves as the cottage's front door. "You don't want to track anything beyond the perimeter. Suits and boots go on and off right over there."

Lined up next to three plastic tubs filled with water is a bottle of Dawn dishwashing detergent and rows of footwear, the boots and shoes of the people inside, including what I recognize as a pair of tan combat boots, men's size. Based on what I'm seeing, there are at least eight investigators working the scene, including someone who might be army, someone who might be Briggs. Marino bends over to check the status display on the diamond-steel-encased APU in the back of the truck, then thuds down the diamond-steel steps out into the glare and sparkle of ice that coats bare trees as if they have been dipped in glass. Hanging everywhere are long, sharp icicles that remind me of nails and spears.

"So what you can do is put your gear on now," Marino says for my benefit as Benton wanders off, busy with his phone, communicating with someone and not listening to us.

Marino and I begin walking to the cottage, careful not to slip on ice that is frozen unevenly over rutted dirt and mud and debris that Fielding never cleaned up.

"Leave your shoes here," Marino tells me, "and if you need to use the facilities or go out for fresh air, just make sure you swish your boots off before you go back in. There's a lot of shit in there you don't want to be tracking everywhere. We don't even know exactly what shit, could be shit we don't know about, my point is. But what we do know isn't something you want to be tracking all over, and I know they say the AIDS virus can't live very long postmortem or whatever, but don't ask me to find out."

"What's been done?" I unfold my suit, and the wind almost blows it out of my hands.

"Things you're not going to want to do and shouldn't be your problem." Marino works his huge hands into a pair of purple gloves.

"I'll do anything that needs to be done," I remind him.

"You're going to need your heavy rubber gloves if you start touching a lot of stuff in there." Marino puts those on next.

I feel like snapping at him that I'm not here to sightsee. Of course I'll be touching things. But I don't intend to stoop to saying I've shown up to work a crime scene as if I'm one of the troops reporting to Marino and will be saluting him next. It's not that I don't understand what Marino is doing, what Benton is doing, what everyone is doing. Nobody wants me guilty of the very thing Mrs. Donahue accused Fielding of, ironically. Not that I want to have a conflict, either, and I understand I shouldn't be the one examining someone who worked for me and who, as rumor has it, I had sex with at some point in my life.

What I don't understand is why I'm not bothered more than I am. The only sadness I'm aware of right now is what I feel about a dog named Sock who is sleeping on towels in the cab of the CFC truck. If I see the dog I'm afraid I'll break down, and every other thought is an anxious one about him. Where will he go? Not to an animal shelter.

I won't allow that. It would make sense if Liam Saltz took him, but he lives in England, and how would he get the dog back to the UK unless it is in the cargo area of a jet, and I won't permit that, either. The pitiful creature has been through enough in this life.

"Just be careful." Marino continues his briefing as if I don't know a damn thing about what is going on around here. "And just so you know, we got the van making runs back and forth like clockwork."

Yes, I know. I'm the one who set it up. I watch Benton wander back toward the truck, talking to someone on his phone, and I feel forgotten. I feel extraneous. I feel I'm not helpful or of interest to anything or anyone.

"Pretty much nonstop, already thirty or forty DNA samples in the works, a lot of it not completely thawed, so maybe you're right and we'll be lucky. The van makes an evidence run and then turns around and comes right back, is on its way back here now even as we speak," Marino says.

I bend over and untie one of my boots.

"Anne drives like a damn demon. I didn't know that. I always figured she'd drive like an old lady, but she's been sliding in and out of here like the damn thing's on skis.

It's something," Marino says, as if he likes her. "Anyway, everybody's working like Santa's helpers. The general says he can bring in backup scientists from Dover. You sure?"

At the moment I don't know what I want, except a chance to evaluate the situation for myself, and I've made that clear.

"It's not your decision," I answer Marino, untying my other boot. "I'll handle it."

"Seems like it would be helpful to have AFDIL." Marino says it in a way that makes me suspicious, and I eye the tan combat boots by the decon tubs.

It's awkward enough that Briggs is here, and it enters my mind that he might not be the only one who's shown up from Dover.

"Who else?" I ask Marino as I lean against cinder blocks for balance. "Rockman or Pruitt?"

"Well, Colonel Pruitt."

Another army man, Pruitt is the director of the Armed Forces DNA Identification Laboratory, AFDIL.

"He and the general flew in together," Marino adds.

I didn't ask either of them to come, but they didn't need me to ask, and besides, Marino asked, at least he admitted to inviting Briggs. Marino told me about it during the drive here, over the phone. He said by the way he hoped I didn't mind that he took the liberty, especially since Briggs supposedly had been calling and I supposedly hadn't been answering, so Briggs hunted down Marino. Briggs wanted to know about Eli, the man from Norton's Woods, and Marino told him what was known about the case and then told him "everything else," Marino informed me, and he hoped I didn't mind.

I replied that I did mind, but what's done is done. I seem to be saying that a lot, and I said as much to Marino while I was on the phone with him during the car ride here. I said certain things were done because Marino had done them, and I can't run an office like that, although what was implicit but not stated was that Briggs is here for that very reason. He's here because I can't run an office. Not like that. Not at all. If I could run the CFC as the government and MIT and Harvard and everyone expected, nobody would be working this crime scene, because it wouldn't exist.

My yellow suit is stiff and digs into my chin as I pull my green rubber boots on, and Marino moves the makeshift plyboard door out of the way. Behind it is a wide sheet of heavy translucent plastic nailed to the top of the door frame, hanging like a curtain.

"Just so we're clear, I'm maintaining the chain of custody," I tell him the same thing I said earlier. "We're doing this the way we always do it."

"If you say so."

"I do say so."

I have a right to say so. Briggs isn't above the law. He has to honor jurisdiction, and for better or for worse, this case is the jurisdiction of Massachusetts and the principalities where the crimes have occurred.

"I just think any help we can get . . ." Marino says.

"I know what you think."

"Look, it's not like there's going to be a trial," he then says. "Fielding saved the Commonwealth a lot of fucking money."

20

The air is heavy with the smell of wood smoke, and I notice that the fireplace in the far wall is crammed with partially burned pieces of lumber topped by billowy clouds of whitish-gray ash, delicate, as if spun by a spider, but in layers. Something clean-burning, like cotton cloth, I think, or an expensive grade of paper that doesn't have a high wood-pulp content.

Whoever built the fire did so with the flue closed, and the assumption is that Fielding did, but no one seems quite sure why, unless he was out of his mind or hoping that eventually his Little Shop of Horrors would burn to the ground. But if that was his intention, he certainly didn't go about it in the right way, and I make a mental note of a gas can in a corner and cans of paint thinner and rags and piles of lumber. Everywhere I look I see an opportunity for starting a conflagration easily, so the fireplace makes no sense unless he was too deranged in the end to think clearly or wasn't trying to burn down the building but to get rid of something, perhaps to destroy evidence. Or someone was.

I look around in the uneven, harsh illumination of temporary low-voltage extension lights hanging from hooks and mounted on poles, their bulbs enclosed in cages. Strewn over an old scarred, paint-spattered workbench are hand tools, clamps, drill bits, paintbrushes, plastic buckets of L-shaped flooring nails and screws, and power tools, such as a drill with screwdriver attachments, a circular saw, a finishing sander, and a lathe on a metal stand. Metal shavings, some of them shiny, and sawdust are on the bench and the concrete floor, everything filthy and rusting, with nothing protecting Fielding's investment in home improvement from the sea air and the weather but heavy plastic and more ply-board stapled and nailed over windows. Across the room is another doorway that is wide open, and I can hear voices and other sounds drifting up from stairs leading down into the cellar.

"What have you collected in here?" I ask Marino as I look around and imagine what I saw under the microscope. If I could magnify samples from Fielding's work space, I suspect I would see a rubbish dump of rust, fibers, molds, dirt, and insect parts.

"Well, it's obvious when you look at the metal shavings some of them are recent because they haven't started rusting and are really shiny," Marino replies. "So we got samples, and they've gone to the labs to find out if under the scope they look anything like what you found in Eli Saltz's body."

"His last name isn't Saltz," I remind him for the umpteenth time.

"You know, to compare tool marks," Marino says. "Not that there's much of a reason to doubt what Fielding did. We found the box."

The box the WASP came in.

"A couple spent CO_2-two cartridges, a couple extra handles, even the instruction book," Marino goes on. "The whole nine yards. According to the company, Jack ordered it two years ago. Maybe because of his scuba diving." He shrugs his big shoulders in his big yellow suit. "Don't know, except he didn't order it two years ago to kill Eli. That's for damn sure. And two years ago Jack was in Chicago, and I guess you might ask what he needed a WASP for." Marino walks around in his big green boots and keeps looking at the opening to the stairs leading down, as if he's curious about what's being said and done down there. "The only thing that will kill you in the Great Lakes that I know of is all the mercury in the fish."

"It's with us. We have the box and the CO-two cartridges. We have all of it." I want to know which labs. I want to make sure Briggs isn't sending my evidence to the AFME labs in Dover.

"Yeah, all that stuff. Except the knife that was in the box, the WASP itself. It still hasn't shown up. My guess is he ditched it after stabbing the guy, maybe threw it off a bridge or something. No wonder he didn't want anyone going to the Norton's Woods scene, right?" Marino's bloodshot eyes look at me, then distractedly look around, the way people act when nothing they are looking at is new. He'd been here many hours before I showed up.

"What about in here?" I squat in front of the fireplace, which is open and built of old firebrick that is probably original to the building. "What's been done here?" My hard hat keeps slipping over my eyes, and I take it off and set it on the floor.

"What about it?" Marino watches me from where he's standing.

I move my gloved finger toward the whitish ashes, and they are weightless, lifting and stirring as the air moves, as if my thoughts are moving them. I contemplate the best way to preserve what I'm seeing, the ashes much too fragile to move in toto, and I'm pretty sure I recognize what has happened in the fireplace, or at least some of what occurred. I've seen this before but not recently, maybe not in at least ten years. When documents are burned these days, usually they were printed, not typed, and were generated on inexpensive copying paper with a high wood-pulp content that combusts incompletely, creating a lot of black sooty ash. Paper with a high cotton-rag content has a completely different appearance when it is burned, and what comes to mind immediately is Erica Donahue's letter that she claims she never wrote.

"What I recommend," I say to Marino, "is we cover the fireplace so the ashes aren't disturbed. We need to photograph them in situ before disturbing them in any way. So let's do that before we collect them in paint cans for the documents lab."

His big booted feet move closer, and he says, "What for?"

What he's really asking is why I am acting like a crime scene investigator. My answer, should I give one, which I won't, is because somebody has to.

"Let's finish this the way it should be done, the way we know how and have always done things." I meet his glassy stare, and what I'm really saying is nothing is over. I don't care what everyone assumes. It's not over until it is.

"Let's see what you've got." He squats next to me, our yellow suits making a plastic sound as we move around, and their faint odor reminds me of a new shower curtain.

"Typed characters on the ash." I point, and the ashes stir again.

"Now you're a psychic and ought to get a job in one of the magic shops around here if you can read something that's been burned."

"You can read some of it because the expensive paper burns clean, turns white, and the inked characters made by a typewriter can be seen. We've looked at things like this before, Marino. Just not in a long time. Do you see what I'm looking at?" I point, and the air moves and the ashes stir some more. "You can actually see the inked engraving of her letterhead, or part of it. Boston and part of the zip code. The same zip code on the letter I got from Mrs. Donahue, although she says she didn't write it and her typewriter is missing."

"Well, there's one in the house. A green one, an old portable on the dining-room table." He gets up and bends his legs as if his knees ache.

"There's a green typewriter next door?"

"I figured Benton told you."

"I guess he couldn't tell me everything in an hour."

"Don't get pissed. He probably couldn't. You won't believe all the shit next door. Appears when Fielding moved here he never really moved his shit in. Boxes everywhere. A fucking landfill over there."

"I doubt he had a portable typewriter. I doubt that's his."

"Unless he was in cahoots with the Donahue kid. That's the theory of where a lot of shit has come from."

"Not according to his mother. Johnny disliked Jack. So how does it make sense that Jack would have Mrs. Donahue's typewriter?"

"If it's hers. We don't know it is. And then there's the drugs," Marino says. "Obviously, Johnny's been on them since about the time he started taking tae kwon do lessons from Fielding. One plus one equals two, right?"

"We're going to find out what adds up and what doesn't. What about stationery or paper?"

"Didn't see any."

"Except what seems to be in here." I remind him it appears some of Erica Donahue's stationery might have been burned, or maybe all of it was, whatever was left over from the letter someone wrote to me, pretending to be her.

"Listen . . ." Marino doesn't finish what he's about to say.

He doesn't need to. I know what he's going to say. He's going to remind me I can't be reasonable about Fielding, and Marino thinks he should know, all right. Because of our own history. Marino was around in the early days, too. He remembers when Fielding was my forensic pathology fellow in Richmond, my protégé, and in the minds of a lot of people, it seems, a lot more than that.

"This was here just like this?" I then ask, indicating a roll of lead-gray duct tape on the workbench.

"Okay. Sure," he says as he squats by an open crime scene case on the floor and gets out an evidence bag, because the roll of tape can be fracture-matched to the last strip torn off it. "So tell me how the hell he might have gotten hold of it, and what for?"

He means Fielding. How did Jack Fielding get hold of Erica Donahue's typewriter, and what was his purpose in writing a letter allegedly from her and having it hand-delivered to me by a driver-for-hire who usually works events like bar mitzvahs and weddings? Did Johnny Donahue give Fielding the typewriter and stationery? If so, why? Maybe Fielding simply manipulated Johnny. Lured him into a trap.

"Maybe a last-ditch effort to frame the kid," Marino then says, answering his own question and voicing what I'm pondering and about to dismiss as a possibility. "A good question for Benton."

But Benton is off somewhere, talking on his phone or maybe conferring with his FBI compatriots, maybe with the female agent named Douglas. It bothers me when I think about her, and I hope I'm just paranoid and raw and have no reason to be concerned about the nature of his relationship with Special Agent Douglas. I hope the extra coffee cup in the back of her SUV wasn't Benton's, that he hasn't been riding around with her, spending a lot of time with her while I was at Dover and then before that, in and out of Washington. Not just an enabler and a bad mentor, now I'm a bad wife, it occurs to me. Everything feels wrecked. It feels over with. It feels as if I'm working my own death scene, as if the life I knew somehow didn't survive while I was away, and I'm investigating, trying to reconstruct what did me in.

"This is what we need to do right now," I tell Marino. "I assume no one has touched the typewriter, and is it an Olivetti, or do you know?"

"We've been pretty tied up over here." What he's saying is that the police have more important matters to tend to than an old manual typewriter. "We found the dog in there, like I told you. And a bedroom it appears Fielding was using, and you can tell he was in and out living here, but this is where it happened." He indicates the outbuilding we're in. "The typewriter's in a case on the dining-room table. I opened it to see what was inside, but that's it."

"Swab the keys for DNA before you pack it up and transport it to the labs, and I want those swabs going out on the next evidence run the van makes. I want those swabs analyzed first, because they might tell us who wrote that letter to me," I tell him.

"I think we know who."

"Then the typewriter goes to Documents so we can compare the typeface to what's on the letter I got, a cursive typeface, and we'll analyze the duct tape that's on the envelope and see if it came from the roll we just found and what trace is on it or DNA or fingerprints or who knows what. Don't be surprised if it points to the Donahues. If trace is from their house or fingerprints or DNA is from that source."

"Why?"

"Framing their son."

"I didn't know Jack was that damn smart," Marino says.

"I didn't say he framed anyone. I've not tried and convicted him or anyone," I reply flatly. "We have his DNA profile and finger-prints for exclusionary purposes, just as we have all of ours. So he should be easy to include or exclude, and any other profiles, and if there are? If we find DNA from more than one source, which we certainly should expect? We run the profiles through CODIS immediately."

"Sure. If that's what you want."

"We run them right away, Marino. Because we know where Jack is. But if anyone else is involved, including the Donahues? We can't waste time."

"Sure, Doc. Whatever you want," Marino says, and I can read his thoughts.

This is Jack Fielding's house, it's his Kill Cottage, his Little Shop of Horrors. Why go to all this trouble? But Marino's not going to say it to me. He's assuming I'm in denial.

I'm holding out the remote and irrational hope that Fielding didn't kill anyone, that someone else magically was using his property and his belongings and is responsible for all of this, someone other than Fielding, who is the victim and not the monster everyone now believes he is.

"We don't know if his family's been here," I remind Marino patiently and quietly, but in a sobering tone. "His wife, his two little girls. We don't know who's been in the house and touched things."

"Not unless they've been coming here from Chicago to stay in this dump."

"When exactly did they move out of Concord?" That's where his family was living with him, in a house Fielding had rented that I helped him find.

"Last fall. And it fits with everything," Marino makes yet one more assumption. "The football player and what happened after Fielding's family moved back to Chicago and he came here, fixing up this place while he was living in it like a hobo. He could have sent you a goddamn e-mail and let you know it wasn't working out for him personally around here. That his wife and kids bolted not long after the CFC started taking cases."

"He didn't tell me. I'm sorry he didn't."

"Yeah, well, don't say I should have." Marino seals the roll of duct tape in a plastic evidence bag. "It wasn't my business. I wasn't going to start out my new career here by ratting on the staff and telling you that Fielding was the usual fuck-up right out of the box and you sure as hell should have expected it when you thought it was such a brilliant idea to take him back."

"I should have expected this?" I hold Marino's bloodshot, resentful stare.

"Put on your hard hat before you go down. There's a lot of shit hanging from the ceilings, like all these damn lights strung up like it's Christmas. I got to go back out to the truck, and I know you need a minute."

I adjust the ratchet of my hard hat, making it tighter, and the reason Marino isn't going into the cellar with me isn't because I need a minute. It isn't because he's sensitive enough to offer me a chance to deal with what's down there without him by my side, breathing down my neck. That might be what he's talked himself into, but as I listen to him swishing his boots in the tubs just outside the door, stepping in and out of the water, I can only imagine how distasteful a scene like this must be to him. It has little to do with the unpleasantness of body fluids thawing and breaking down or even

531

his squeamishness about hepatitis or HIV or some other virus and everything to do with how the body fluids got here. Marino's ablution in the plastic tubs filled with water and dishwashing fluid are his attempt to cleanse himself of the guilt I know he feels.

He never saw Fielding doing any of it, and that's the problem Marino faces. The way he would think about it is he should have noticed, and as I've explained to Benton while we were driving here and then explained to Marino over the phone, the extraction of sperm isn't much different from a vasectomy, except when such a procedure is performed on a dead body, it's even quicker and simpler, for obvious reasons. No local anesthesia is needed, and the doctor doesn't have to be concerned with how the patient is feeling or if he might have second thoughts or any other emotional response.

All Fielding had to do was make a small puncture on one side of the scrotum and inject a needle into the vas deferens to extract sperm. He could have done this in minutes. He probably didn't do it during the autopsy but before it by going into the cooler when nobody was around, making certain he got to the body as quickly after death as possible, which in retrospect might explain why he noticed the man from Norton's Woods was bleeding before anybody else did. Fielding went into the cooler first thing when he got to the building early Monday morning to acquire his latest involuntary sperm donation, and that's when he noticed blood in the tray under the body bag. So he walked rapidly down the corridor and notified Anne and Ollie.

If anybody would have noticed something like this going on during the six months I was at Dover it was Anne, I told Marino. She never saw what Fielding was doing or had a clue, and we know he extracted sperm from at least a hundred patients based on what has been found in a freezer in the cellar and what's broken all over the floor, potentially a hundred thousand dollars, maybe much more, depending on what he charged and if he did it on a sliding scale, taking into account what the family or other interested party could afford. Liquid gold, as cops are calling what Fielding was selling on a black market of his own creation, and I can't stop thinking about his choice of Eli as an involuntary donor, assuming this was Fielding's intention, and we'll never really know.

But at the time Fielding went into the cooler yesterday morning, there was only one young male body fresh enough to be a suitable candidate for a sperm extraction, and that was Eli Goldman. The other male case was elderly, and it's highly unlikely he had loved ones who might be interested in buying his semen, and a third case was a female. If Fielding murdered Eli with the injection knife, would he then be so brazen and reckless as to take the young man's sperm, and who was he planning to sell it to without incriminating himself? If he'd tried something like that, he may as well have confessed to the homicide.

It continues to tug at my thoughts that Fielding didn't know who the unidentified dead young male was when he was notified about the case on Sunday afternoon. Fielding didn't bother going to the scene, wasn't interested, and had no reason at that time to be interested. I continue to suspect he didn't have a clue until he walked into the cooler, and then he recognized Eli Goldman because they had a connection somehow. Maybe it was drugs, and that's why Eli had one of Fielding's guns. Maybe Fielding had given or sold the Glock to Eli. For sure someone did. Drugs, the gun, maybe something else. If only I could have been in Fielding's mind when he walked into the cooler at shortly after seven yesterday morning. Then I would know. I would know everything.

I move a hanging light out of my way so it doesn't knock my hard hat as I go down stone steps in my bulky yellow suit and big rubber boots.

A cold sweat is rolling down my sides, and I am worrying about Briggs and what it will be like when I'm confronted with him, and I'm worrying about a greyhound named Sock. I am worrying about everything I can possibly worry about because I can't bear what I'm about to see, but it is better this way, and as much as I complain about Marino, he really did do the right thing. I wouldn't have wanted Fielding's body transported to the CFC. I wouldn't want to see it for the first time in a pouch on a steel gurney or tray. Marino knows me well enough to decide that given the choice, I would demand to see Fielding the way he died, to satisfy myself that it was exactly as it appears, and that what Briggs determined when he examined the body hours earlier is the same thing I observe and that Briggs and I share the same opinion about Fielding's cause and manner of death.

The cellar is whitewashed stone with a vaulted stone ceiling and no windows, and it is too small a space for so many people, all of them dressed the way I am, in bright yellow with thick black gloves and green rubber boots and bright yellow hard hats. Some people have on face shields, others surgical masks, and I recognize my own scientists, three from the DNA lab, who are swabbing an area of the stone floor that is littered with shattered glass test tubes and their black plastic stoppers. Nearby is the space heater Marino mentioned, and an upright stainless-steel laboratory cryogenic freezer, the same make and model that we use in labs where we have to store biological samples at ultra-low temperatures.

The freezer door is open wide, the adjustable shelves inside empty because someone, presumably Fielding, removed all the specimens and smashed them to the stone floor, then turned on the space heater. I notice partial labels adhering to glass fragments on a floor that is otherwise clean, the cellar appearing whitewashed with something non-glossy, like primer, like a winemaker's cave that has been turned into a laboratory with a steel sink and steel countertop, racks for test tubes, and large steel tanks of liquid nitrogen, and central to the main room I'm in, a long metal table that Fielding probably was using for shipping and several chairs, one of them pulled out a little, as if someone might have been sitting in it. I look at the chair first, and I look for blood, but I don't see any.

The table is covered with white butcher paper, and arranged on it are pairs of elbow-length bright-blue cryogloves, ampoules, rollerbases, smudge-proof pens, and long corks and measuring sticks for storage canisters, and stacked underneath are white cardboard boxes called CryoCubes, which are inexpensive vapor shippers we typically use for sending biological materials that are placed inside an aluminum canister, where they can remain frozen at minus 150 degrees centigrade for up to five days. These special packing containers can also be used to ship frozen semen, and in fact are often referred to as "semen tanks" and are favored by animal breeders.

I can only assume that Fielding's equipment and materials for his illegal and outrageous cottage industry were purloined from the CFC, that in the dark of night or after hours, he somehow managed to sneak what he wanted out of the labs without security batting an eye. Or it is possible he simply ordered what he needed and charged it to us but had it shipped directly here, to the sea captain's house. Even as I'm piecing together what he might have done, he is so close to me I could touch him, under a disposable blue sheet on his clean white primer–painted floor that is stained with blood at one edge of the plasticized paper, a spot of blood that is part of a large pool under his head, based on what I know. From where I'm standing, I can see the blood has begun to separate and coagulate, is in the early stages of decomposition, a process that would have been dramatically slowed because of the ambient temperature in the cellar. It is cold enough to see your breath, as cold as a morgue refrigerator.

The flashgun of a camera goes off, and then goes off again as a broad-shouldered figure in blaze yellow photographs the one area of whitewashed wall down here that is blackened and foul, where a total station on a bright yellow tripod has been set up, and I'm guessing the electro-optical distance-measuring system has already mapped the scene, recording the coordinate data of every feature, including what Colonel Pruitt is photographing. He catches me looking at him and lowers the camera to his side as I walk over to a wall where I smell death, the faintest musty, pungent stench of blood that has broken down and dried over months in a sunless, cold environment. I smell mildew.

I smell dust, and I notice piles of torn dirty carpet and plywood nearby against a different wall, and I can tell by dust and dirt on the white floor that the carpet and wood was recently dragged to where it is.

Bolted into stone at the height of my head are a series of steel screw-pin anchor shackles that I associate with sling assemblies used in hoisting. Based on coils of rope, grease guns, clamps, a cargo trolley, and grab hooks and swivel rings in the ceiling, I surmise that Fielding devised a creative rig for changing out the heavy tanks of liquid nitrogen, and at some point the system was perverted into one I suspect he never intended when he began extracting semen and selling it.

"From what I'm able to figure out so far, the main thing used was the splitting maul, which would account for both the blunt-force and cutting injuries," Pruitt begins without so much as a hello, as if our meeting here is normal, nothing more than a continuum of our time together at Dover. "Basically, a long-handled sledgehammer on one side, the other side sharp like an ax. It was under carpet and wood, along with a Boston College letter jacket, a pair of sneakers, other items of clothing that we think were Wally Jamison's. This entire area was under that stuff over there." He indicates the carpet and wood that was moved, what I surmise was used to cover the crime scene. "All of it, including the splitting maul, of course, has been packaged and sent to your place already. Did you see the weapon yet?" Pruitt says, shaking his head.

"No."

"Can't imagine someone coming after me with something like that. Jesus. Shades of Lizzie Borden. And pieces of bloody rope from being strung up." He points to the shackles and rings bolted into stone that is crusty and black with old blood, and I almost imagine I can smell fear down here, the unimaginable terror of the football player tortured and murdered on Halloween.

"Why didn't he clean this up?" I ask the first question that comes to mind as I look at a scene that doesn't appear to have been touched after Wally Jamison was brutally and sadistically murdered down here.

"I guess he took the path of least resistance and just covered everything up with plyboard and old carpet," Pruitt replies. "That's why there's a lot of dirt and fibers everywhere. Appears after the homicide, he didn't bother washing things down at all. Just heaped old carpet on top and leaned all these boards against the wall." He points again to the pile of old torn carpet of different colors, and near it, the large sheets of plyboard stacked on the white floor near a closed access door that leads outside the cellar.

"I don't know why he wouldn't have washed it down," I repeat. "That was three months ago. He just left a crime scene, practically left it like a time capsule? Just threw carpet and plyboard over it?"

"One theory is he got off on it. Like people who photograph or film what they do so they can continue getting off on it after the fact. Every time he came down here, he knew what was behind the boards and carpet, what was hidden under them, and got off on it."

Or someone got off on it, I think. Jack Fielding has never gotten off on gore. For a forensic pathologist, he was actually rather squeamish. Benton will say it was the influence of drugs. Everyone is probably saying that, and maybe it's true. Fielding was altered, that much I don't doubt.

"Some of us can help you with this, you know," Pruitt then says, looking at me through a plastic face shield that clouds up intermittently as he breathes the cold cellar air. His hazel eyes are alert and friendly as they look at me, but he is troubled. How could anybody not be, and I wonder if he senses what I do. I wonder if he has a feeling in his gut that something is wrong with all this. I wonder if he's asking the question I am right now as I look at the blackened whitewashed wall with the rusting shackles bolted into the stone.

Why would Jack Fielding do something like this?

Extracting semen to sell to bereft families is almost understandable. One can easily blame greed or even a lust for the gratification, the power he must have felt when he was able to give back life where it had been taken. But as I envision the photographs, video recordings, and CT scans I've seen of Wally Jamison's mutilated body, I'm reminded of what went through my thoughts at the time. His murder seemed sexually and emotionally driven, as if the person who swung the weapon at him had feelings for him, certainly had a rage that didn't quit until Wally was lacerated, sliced, cut, and contused beyond recognition and bled to death. Afterward, his nude body was transported, probably by boat, probably by Fielding's boat, and dumped in the harbor at the coast guard station, an act that Benton describes as brazen, as a taunt to law enforcement. And that doesn't sound like Fielding, either. For such a fierce, muscle-bound grandmaster, he was rather much a coward.

"Thank you. Let's see what's needed," I say to Pruitt.

"Well, you know the DNA that's needed. Hundreds of samples already, not just the semen that needs to be reconnected with its donor but everything else being swabbed."

"I know. It's a huge job and will go on for quite a while because we don't know what's happened in here. Just part of it. What was in the freezer and then whatever else was done in addition to what I'm supposing must have been the homicide of the BC student, Wally Jamison." As I say his name I envision him, square-jawed with curly black hair and bright blue eyes, and powerfully built. Then what he looked like later. "What time did you get here?"

"John and I flew in early, got here about seven hours ago."

I don't ask him where Briggs is now.

"He did the external exam and will go over those details with you when you're ready," Pruitt adds.

"And nobody had touched him prior to that?" Fielding's body was discovered shortly after three a.m. Or that's what I've been told.

"When John and I got here, the body was covered just like he is now. The Glock isn't here. After the FBI restored the eradicated serial number, the gun was bagged and is now at your labs," Pruitt tells me what Benton did.

"I didn't know about it until a little while ago. When I was being driven here."

"Look. If I'd been here at three a.m. and it was up to me?" He starts to say he would have told me everything that was going on. "But the FBI wanted to keep things contained, since no one's been sure if he was a lone wolf." He means if Fielding was. "Because of all the other factors, like Dr. Saltz and the MP and so on. The fear of terrorism."

"Yes. Only not the brand of terrorism the Bureau usually has to worry about. This is a different brand of terrorism," I comment. "It feels personal. Doesn't it feel personal? What are you thinking about all this?"

"Nobody had touched the body when the police, the FBI found it." Pruitt doesn't want to tell me what he thinks about it. "I do know he was the same temperature as the room by then, had been down here for a while, but you should talk to John about it."

"You're saying his body was the same temperature as the ambient air at three a.m."

"It's forty degrees, or around that. Maybe a few degrees warmer because of all the people down here. But you need to get the details from John."

Pruitt stares off at the human-shaped mound draped with a blue sheet on the other side of the cellar, near the freezer, near thawing fluids on the stone floor, where investigators have knee pads on and are collecting one shard of glass at a time and swabbing, and packaging each item separately in paper envelopes that they label with permanent markers. I won't do the calculations until I check the body, but already what I'm hearing adds to what I suspect. Something is wrong.

21

The stain on the whitewashed wall is an ugly darkness some six feet above the stone floor, probably where Wally Jamison's head and neck were when he was shackled and beaten and cut to death.

Spraying out from the largest stain are a constellation of pinpoint spatters, tiny black marks that at close inspection are elongated, are angled, the cast-off blood from the weapon as it was repeatedly swung, as it was repeatedly bloodied from impacting with human flesh, and I envision the wood-splitting maul Pruitt mentioned, and I agree with him. What a terrible way to die. Then I think of the injection knife. Another horrendous way to die. Sadism.

"He should have had a system of keeping track of the samples," I say to Pruitt as I watch the investigators in bright yellow, on their hands and knees, some of them people I don't know. Maybe Saint Hilaire from

Salem. Maybe Lester "Lawless" Law from Cambridge. I'm not sure who is here, really, just that the FBI is working in conjunction with a special task force comprising investigators from various departments who are members of the North Eastern Massachusetts Law Enforcement Council, NEMLEC. "If he really was selling extracted semen," I continue my train of thought, "I would assume he had a way of logging the specimens." I direct his attention to bits of gummy labels still adhering to broken glass on the floor. "Finding information like that will help us with identification, maybe preliminarily supply it, and then we can verify through DNA. If all of the specimens came from CFC cases, we should have DNA on blood-spot cards in each case file."

"I know Marino is looking into that, has somebody pulling every case of young males who would have been viable candidates. Especially if Fielding did the autopsies."

"With all due respect, that was my direction, not Marino's." I hear the defensiveness I can't keep out of my tone, but I've had enough of my new self-appointed acting chief Pete Marino. I've had enough references that imply he runs my office.

"We've not found a log yet," Pruitt adds. "But Farinelli's over there with his laptop, which was as dead as he was when we got here. Maybe the log will be on that."

It always seems strange when investigators refer to my niece by her last name. Lucy must be next door in the house, where there are no lights or heat, unless the power has come back on. I realize that down here I might not know, since we are using auxiliary lights brought in and set up. I walk over to an open Pelican case near the bottom of the stairs and find a flashlight, then return to the wall to shine the light over bloodstains to see what else they have to tell me before I look at the person who supposedly caused them, my deputy chief, working alone in his Kill Cottage. *My deputy chief, the lone wolf who had no help in all this,* I think skeptically and with growing anger at the police, the FBI, at everyone who started working the scene without me.

Below the darkest area on the white-washed wall is a corresponding dark area on the whitewashed floor, a myriad of drips that combine into a solid stain, what I can tell was a pool of blood that is almost black and flaking, much of it having soaked into the porous whitewashed stone. Some of the drops at the edge of the large stained area are perfectly round, with only a small amount of distortion or scalloping around the edges from the roughness of the stone, passive spatters from the victim bleeding. Other stains are smeared from someone, possibly the assailant, stepping on them or dragging something over them while they were still wet. Maybe dragging carpet and plyboards over them, I think. The only bloodstains that show a direction of travel are those on the wall and the ceiling, black and elongated or with a teardrop shape, and I believe most of these were projected by the repeated swings and impacts of the weapon.

The victim was upright when he bled, shackled to the wall, it would seem, and what I can't tell is the timing of at least one blow that I know was fatal. Did it happen early on or later? *The earlier, the better,* I can't help but think as I imagine what was done, as I reconstruct the pain and suffering and most of all his terror. I hope he hadn't been subjected to the abuse for long when an artery was breached, most likely the carotid on the left side of his neck. The distinctive wave pattern on the wall is from arterial blood spurting out under high pressure in rhythm to the beats of his heart, and I remember photographs I saw, the deep gashes to his neck.

Wally Jamison would have lived only

minutes after receiving such an injury, and I wonder how long the cutting and beating went on after it was too late to hurt him anymore. I wonder about the rage and what the connection might have been between Wally Jamison and Jack Fielding. It had to be more than that they simply went to the same gym. Wally wasn't involved in martial arts, and as far as anyone knows, he wasn't acquainted with Johnny Donahue or Eli Goldman or Mark Bishop. He didn't work or intern at Otwahl, either, and apparently had nothing to do with robotics or other technologies. What I know about Wally Jamison is that he was from Florida, a senior at BC, where he was majoring in history and somewhat of a celebrity because of football, and a partier, a ladies' man. I can't come up with a single reason why Fielding might have known him, unless it was some chance encounter they had, perhaps because of the gym and then perhaps drugs, the hormonal cocktail Benton mentioned.

Wally Jamison's toxicology was negative for illegal or therapeutic drugs or alcohol, but we don't routinely test for steroids unless we have reason to suspect a death may be related to them. Wally's cause of death wasn't a question. There certainly was no reason to think steroids killed him, at least not directly, and now it may be too late to go back. We're not going to get another sample of his urine, although we can try testing his hair, where the molecules of drugs, including steroids, might have accumulated inside the hair shaft. A test like that would be a long shot for detecting steroids, and it isn't going to tell us if Wally got them from Fielding or knew Fielding or was murdered by him. But I'm willing to try anything, because as I look around this cellar and see the shape of Fielding's body under a sheet on the floor, I want to know why. I have to know and won't accept that he was crazy, that he'd lost his mind. That's just not good enough.

Returning to the Pelican case near the stairs, I find a pair of knee pads and put them on before kneeling by the rounded blue sheet, and when I pull it back from Jack Fielding's face, I'm not prepared for how present he looks. That's the word that comes to mind, *present,* as if he's still here, as if he's asleep but not well. There is nothing vital or vibrant about him, and my brain races through the details I'm seeing, the stiff strands of hair from the gel he used to hide his baldness, the red splotches on his face, which is puffy and pale, and I pull the sheet off, and it rustles as I move it out of my way. I sit back on the heels of my rubber boots and look him over, taking in his gelled sandy-brown hair that was thinning on top and gone in spots, and the dried blood around his ear and pooled under his head.

I imagine Fielding pointing the barrel of the Glock inside his left ear and pulling the trigger. I try to get into his mind, try to conjure up his last thoughts. Why would he do that? Why his ear? The side of the head is common in gunshot suicides, but not the ear, and why his left side and not his right? Fielding was right-handed. I used to tease him about having what I called "extreme handedness" because he couldn't do anything useful with his left hand, nothing that required any degree of dexterity or skill. He certainly didn't shoot himself in his left ear while holding the pistol in his right hand, not unless he'd become a contortionist in my absence, and maybe that will be one more speculation everyone will come up with. But I need to check the angle. I point my right finger into my left ear canal as best I can, pretending my index finger is the barrel of the Glock.

"Things really aren't that bad," a deep voice says. "It hasn't come to that, has it?" General John Briggs says.

I look up at him standing over me, his legs

552

spread, his hands behind his back, big and bulky in bright yellow, but he's not wearing a face shield or gloves or a hard hat, his face ruggedly compelling, hawklike, it's been described as, and shadowed with stubble. He's a dark man, and no matter how often he shaves, he always looks as if he needs to, his eyes the same dark gray as the titanium veneer on my building, his black hair thick with very little gray for his age, which is exactly sixty.

"Colonel," he then says, and he squats next to me and picks up the flashlight I was using earlier and had left upright on the stone floor. "I imagine you're wondering the same thing I am." He turns on the light.

"I seriously doubt it," I reply as he shines the light inside Fielding's left ear.

"I'm wondering where he was," Briggs says. "Looking for high-velocity spatter, something to indicate if he was right here? Because why? Was he standing by his cryogenic freezer and just stuck a gun in his ear?"

I take the light from him so I can direct it where I want as I look inside Fielding's ear, and mostly what I see is dark dried blood that is crusty, but as I lean closer I can make out the small black entrance wound, a contact wound, and that is elongated. It is angled. A large amount of blood is under his head, a dried pool of it that is thick and looks sticky because the cellar is moist, and I smell blood that is beginning to break down, the sweetish foul odor that is faint, and I detect alcohol. It wouldn't surprise me if Fielding was drinking in the end. Whether he shot himself or someone else did, he probably was compromised, and I remember the big SUV with the xenon lights that tailed Benton and me some sixteen hours ago while we were driving through a blizzard to the CFC. The current assumption is that Fielding was in that SUV, that it was his Navigator and he'd removed the front plate so we couldn't tell who was behind us.

Nobody has satisfactorily offered why he might have decided to tail Benton and me or how he managed to disappear instantly, seemingly into thin air, after Benton stopped in the middle of the snowy road in hopes whoever was on our bumper would pass us. I seem to be the only one consumed by the fact that Otwahl Technologies is very close to the area where the big SUV with xenon lights and fog lamps vanished, and if someone had a gate opener or code to that place or was familiar to the private police, that person could have tucked the Navigator in there, rather much like vanishing in the Bat Cave, is how I described it to Benton, who didn't seem impressed. *"Why would Jack Fielding have that kind of access to Otwahl?"* I asked Benton as we were driving here. *"Even if he was involved with some of the people who work there, would he have access to its parking lot? Could he have pulled in so quickly and been confident the private police who patrol the grounds would have been fine with it?"*

"With all the white-painted surfaces in here," Briggs is saying to me, "you'd think we could find something that might indicate where the shooting occurred."

I look at Fielding's hands. They are as cold as the stone in the cellar, and he is completely rigorous. As muscle-bound as he is, it is like moving the arms of a marble statue as I shine the flashlight on his thick, strong hands, examining them, noting his clean, trimmed nails and surprised by them. I expected them to be dirty, as crazy and out of control as everyone believes he was. I notice his calluses, which he's always had from using free weights in the gym or working on his cars or doing home repairs. It appears he died holding the pistol in his left hand, or it is supposed to look like he did, his fingers curled tightly and the impression in his palm made by the Glock's nonslip stippled grip. But I don't notice a fine mist of blood that might have blown back on his skin when he pulled the trigger. Back spatter is an artifact that can't be staged or faked.

"We'll do GSR on his hands," I comment, and I notice that Fielding isn't wearing his wedding band. The last time I saw him, he had it on, but that was in August, and he was still living with his family, from what I understand.

"The muzzle of the gun had blood," Briggs tells me. "Internal muzzle staining from blood being sucked in."

The phenomenon is caused by explosive gases when the barrel of a gun is pressed against the skin and fired.

"The ejected cartridge case?" I inquire.

"Over there." He indicates an area of the whitewashed floor about five feet from Fielding's right knee.

"And the gun? In what position?" I slide my hands under Fielding's head and feel the hard lump of jagged metal under the scalp above his right ear, where the bullet exited his skull and is trapped under his skin.

"Still gripped in his left hand. I'm sure you noticed the way his fingers are curled and the impression of the grip in his palm. We had to pry the gun out of his hand."

"I see. So he shot himself with his left hand even though he's right-handed. Not impossible but unusual, and he either was already lying right here on the floor when he did it or fell with the gun still gripped in his hand. A cadaveric spasm and he clenched it hard. And fell neatly on his back just like this. Well, that's quite a thing to imagine. You know me and cadaveric spasms, John."

"They do happen."

"Like winning the lottery," I answer. "That happens, too. Just never to me."

I feel fractured bone shift beneath my fingers as I gently palpate Fielding's head and envision a wound path that is upward and slightly back-to-front, the bullet lodging approximately three inches from the lower angle of his right jaw.

"He shot himself like this?" I turn my left hand into a gun again, and point my purple nitrile–gloved index finger at an awkward angle, as if I'm going to shoot myself in the left ear. "Even if he held the pistol in his left hand when he wasn't left-handed, it's slightly awkward and unusual, the way my elbow has to be down and behind me, don't you think? And I might expect a fine mist of back spatter on his hand. Of course, these things aren't set in stone," I say inside Fielding's white-painted stone cellar.

"Odd thing about shooting yourself in the ear," I comment, "is people generally are squeamish because of the anticipated noise, not rational, because you're about to die anyway, but it's human nature. Like shooting yourself in the eye. Almost nobody does."

"You and I need to talk, Kay," Briggs says.

"And most of all, the timing of when the cryogenic freezer was gone into," I then say. "And the space heater turned on and what was burned upstairs, possibly Erica Donahue's stationery. If Jack did all that before he killed himself, then why is there no semen or broken glass on the floor under him?" I am manipulating Fielding's big body, and he is deadweight, completely stiff and unwilling as I move him a little, looking under him at a floor that is white and clean. "If he came down here and broke all these test tubes and then shot himself in the ear, there should be glass and semen under his body. It's all around him but none under him. There's a shard of glass in his hair." I pick it out and look at it. "Someone broke all this after he was dead, after he was already lying here on the floor."

"He could have gotten glass in his hair when he broke test tubes, violently smashed everything," Briggs says, and he sounds patient and kind, for him. He almost seems to feel sorry for me. My insecurities again.

"Do you have your mind made up, John? You and everyone else?" I look up into his compelling face.

"You know damn better than that," he says. "We have a lot to talk about, and I'd rather not do it here in front of the others. When you're ready, I'll be next door."

The power came back on in Salem Neck at about half past two, about the time I was finishing with Jack Fielding, kneeling next to him on that cold stone floor until my feet started tingling and my knees were aching and burning, despite the pads I had on.

The flush-mounted lights in his old outdated kitchen are illuminated, the house quite chilly but with the promise of warmth in the forced air I feel coming out of floor vents as I walk around in my tactical boots and field clothes and jacket, having taken off my protective gear except for disposable gloves. The white porcelain sink is filled with dishes, and the water is scummy with soap, a coagulated slick of yellowish grease floating on it, and the sheer yellow curtain cover-

559

ing the window over the sink is stained and dingy.

Wherever I look I find remnants of food and garbage and hard drinking and am reminded of the squalor of countless scenes I've worked, of their rot and spoilage, their musty, mildewy smells, of how often it is that the life preceding the death was the real crime. Fielding's last months on earth were far more tortured than he deserved, and I can't accept that he wanted anything he made for himself. This is not what he scripted for his ultimate destiny, it's not what he was born to, and I continue thinking of that favorite phrase of his when he would remind me he wasn't *born to* this or *born to* that, especially if I asked him to do something he found distasteful or boring.

I pause by a wooden table with two wooden chairs beneath a window that faces the icy street and the choppy dark-blue water beyond it, and the table is deep in old newspapers and magazines that I spread around with my gloved hand. The *Wall Street Journal,* the *Boston Globe,* the *Salem News,* as recent as Saturday, I note, and I recall seeing several papers covered with ice on the sidewalk in front, as if they were tossed there and no one brought them inside the house before the big storm. There

560

are about half a dozen *Men's Health* magazines, and I notice the mailing labels are for Fielding's Concord address. The January and February issues were forwarded here, as was a lot of other mail in the pile I sift through. I recall that Fielding's rental of the house in Concord began almost a year ago, and based on the clutter and furniture I recognize as his and what I've been told about his domestic problems, it would make sense that he didn't renew the lease. He relocated to a drafty antique house that is completely lacking in charm because of the run-down condition it's in, and while I can imagine what he envisioned when he fell in love with the place, something changed for him.

What happened to you? I look around at the squalor he's left in his wake. *Who were you in the end?* I envision his dead hands and remember their coldness and their rigor and how heavy they felt as I held them. They were clean, his nails well kempt, and that very small detail doesn't seem to fit with everything else I'm seeing. *Did you make this appalling mess? Or did someone else? Has some other person who is slovenly and crazed been inside your house?* But I also know that consistency really is the hobgoblin of little minds, that what Ralph

561

Waldo Emerson wrote is true. People aren't easily explained or defined, and what they do isn't always consistent. Fielding may very well have been falling apart along with everything around him but was still vain enough to have good hygiene. It could be true.

But I'm not going to know. His CT scan, his autopsy won't tell me. There's so much I won't know, including why he never told me about his place in Salem. Benton says that Fielding purchased the house right after he moved to Massachusetts, which was a year ago this past January, but he never mentioned it to me. I'm not sure he was hiding anything criminal he was up to or intended to be up to, but rather I have a feeling he wanted something that was just his, something that didn't concern me and that I had no opinion about and wasn't going to improve or change or help him with. He didn't want my mentoring him as he set about to turn an eighteenth-century sea captain's safe harbor into his own or into an investment or whatever he originally dreamed of having all to himself.

If that's the truth, then how sad, I think as I look out at water sparkling like sapphires, rolling and crashing against the gray, rocky shore across the icy, sandy street. I walk through a wide opening that once had pocket doors, into a dining room of exposed dark oak beams in a white plaster ceiling that is water-stained, noting that the tarnished brass hanging onion lantern belongs in an entryway, not over the walnut table, which is dusty and surrounded by chairs that don't match and need new upholstery. I don't blame Fielding for not wanting me here. I'm too critical, too sure of my goddamn good taste and informed opinions, and it's no wonder I drove him to distraction. Not just an enabler but also a bad mother when I had no right to even be a good one. It wasn't my place to be anything to him except a responsible boss, and if he were here I would tell him I'm sorry. I would ask him to forgive me for knowing him and caring, because what help was it? What damn good did I do?

I focus on a disturbed area of dust at one end of the table, where someone was eating or working, perhaps where the Olivetti typewriter was, and the chair in front of it is in better shape than the others. Its faded, threadbare red-velvet cushion is intact and probably safe to sit on, and I think about Fielding in here typing. I try to place him at this table with its old casement windows, the view in here a dreary one of the gravel drive, and it's impossible for me to envision him hunched over in a small chair beneath a hanging lantern, typing a two-page letter over and over on engraved watermarked paper until he had a final version that was flawless.

Fielding and his big, impatient fingers, and he was never much of a typist, was self-taught, what he called "hunt and pick" instead of hunt and peck, and the point of that document supposedly from Erica Donahue is illogical if it came from him. Considering the condition Fielding was in, based on what Benton saw when he met with him last week in my office, it doesn't seem plausible to me that my deputy chief would have gone to such lengths to set up and frame a Harvard student for Mark Bishop's homicide. Why would Fielding have killed that six-year-old boy? I don't buy what Benton says, that Fielding was killing himself as a child when he drove nails into Mark Bishop's head. Fielding was putting an end to his own childhood of abuse, Benton told me, and I'm not persuaded.

But I have to remind myself that there are many things in life that make sense to the people who are doing them while the rest of us never figure it out. Even when we're told why, the explanation often doesn't fit with any template that has rhyme or reason. I pause before a casement window, not quite ready to leave this room and enter the next one, where I can hear Briggs walking around in his desert boots. He is talking to someone on his phone, and I pull out mine to check my text messages and see that there is one from Bryce.

Can U call Evelyn!?

I try her in the trace evidence lab and another microscopist answers, a young scientist named Matthew.

"You anywhere near a computer?" Matthew's voice, confident and tense with excitement. "Evelyn's just down the hall in the ladies' room, but we want to send you something totally weird, and I keep thinking it's a mistake or like the weirdest contamination ever. You know a hair is about eighty thousand nanometers, right? So imagine something four nanometers, in other words, a hair would be twenty thousand times the diameter of what we found. And it's not organic, even though the elemental fingerprint is mostly pure carbon, but we've also detected trace residues of what appears to be phencyclidine. . . ."

"You found PCP?" I interrupt his breathless talk.

"PCP, angel dust, a really trace amount,

just a minuscule amount. Using FTIR. At a magnification of one hundred, just plain ol' light microscopy, and you can see the granules and a lot of other microscopic debris, especially cotton fibers, on the backing of the pain-relieving patch, okay? Probably some of these granular structures are PCP, maybe Nuprin, Motrin, too, whatever the patch originally was, possibly other chemicals there."

"Matthew, slow down."

"Well, at one hundred and fifty thousand X with SEM you'll see what I'm talking about as big as a bread box, Dr. Scarpetta, what we want to send you."

"Go ahead, and if nothing else, I'll go out to the truck and log in. Send PDFs, though, and I'll try on my iPhone. What are you talking about, exactly?"

"Sort of like buckyballs, like a dumbbell made out of buckyballs but with legs. It's definitely man-made, about the size of a strand of DNA, like I said, four nanometers and pure carbon, except for whatever it was meant to deliver. And also traces of polyethylene glycol that we're conjecturing was the outer coating for what was meant to be delivered."

"Explain the *meant-to-deliver* part. Something built on nanoscale to deliver a trace amount of PCP or what?"

"This isn't my area, obviously, and we don't have an AFM, an atomic force microscope, here, hint, hint. Because I'd say we've just entered a new day where we have to start looking for things like this, things you might need to magnify millions of times. And in my opinion, something like an AFM would have to have been used to assemble this, do the nanoassembly, to manipulate the nanotubes, the nanoparticles, while you're trying to get them to stick together, using a nanoprobe or whatever. Well, we could probably handle a lot of this with SEM, but an AFM would be a good idea if this is what's headed down the pike and about to slam into us head-on, Dr. Scarpetta."

"You don't know what you've found, but it's a nanobot of some type, possibly, in your opinion, for the delivery of a drug or drugs? You found one on the film backing that was in the lab coat pocket?" I don't say whose lab coat.

"Just one admixed with the particulate and fibers and other debris because we didn't analyze the entire piece of film, just the specimen we mounted on a stub. The rest of the plastic film's at fingerprints right now, and then it's going to DNA, then to

GC-Mass-Spec," Matthew says. "And it's broken or degraded."

"What is?"

"The nanobot. Or it looks broken, or maybe it's deteriorating, like it was supposed to have eight legs but I'm seeing four on one side and two on the other. I'm e-mailing this to you now, a couple photographs we took so you can see it for yourself."

I'm able to pull up the images on my iPhone, and it is an inexplicable feeling to note the eerie symmetry, to have it enter my mind that the nanobot looks like a molecular version of a micromechanical fly. I can't know if Lucy's holy grail of flybots looks like this nanobot magnified thousands of times, but the artificial structure in the photographs is insectlike with its grayish, buckyball elongated body. The delicate nanowire arms or legs that are still intact are bent at right angles with gripperlike appendages on the tips, possibly for grabbing onto the walls of cells or burrowing into blood vessels or organs, to find the target, in other words, and adhere to it while delivering medicine or perhaps illegal drugs destined for certain brain receptors.

No wonder Johnny Donahue's drug screen was negative, it occurs to me. If nanobots were added to his sublingual allergy extracts or, better yet, to his corticosteroid nasal spray, the drugs might have been below the level of detection. More astonishingly, the drugs may not have penetrated the blood-brain barrier at all, but would have been programmed to bind to receptors in the frontal cortex. If the drugs never entered the bloodstream, they wouldn't have been excreted in urine. They wouldn't have ended up in hair, and that's the point of nanotechnology's use in medicine, to treat diseases and disorders with drugs that aren't systemic and therefore are less harmful. As is true with everything else, whatever can be used for good most assuredly will be used for evil.

Fielding's living room is bare floors and walls, and stacked almost to the ceiling are dusty brown boxes, all the same size, with the moving company Gentle Giant's logo on the sides, scores of cartons in cubed piles as if they've never been touched since they were carried in here.

In the midst of this cardboard bunker Briggs sits, reminding me of a Matthew Brady photograph of a Civil War general, in his muted sandy-green fatigues and boots, a Mac notebook in his lap, his broad-shouldered back straight against the straight-back chair. I decide it would be like him to sit and make me stand, to choreograph our conversation so I feel small and subservient to him, but he gets up, and I tell him no, thank you, I'll stand. So both of us do, moving to a window, where he places his laptop on a sill.

"I find it interesting he has a wireless network in here," Briggs says right off, looking out at the view of the ocean and the rocks across the icy street that is covered with tan sand. "With all you've seen in here, would you expect him to have wireless?"

"Maybe he wasn't the only person in here."

"Maybe."

"At least you'll entertain the possibility. That's more than anybody else seems to be doing." I place my iPhone on the windowsill so he can see what is in the small display, and he looks at it, and then he looks away.

"Imagine two types of nanobots," he says, as if he's talking to someone on the other side of the wavy old window, as if his attention is out there on the sunlight and sparkling water and not on the woman standing next to him, a woman who always feels young and insecure with him, no matter her age or who she grew up to become.

"A nanobot that is biodegradable," he says, "that vanishes at some point after delivering a minute dose of a psychoactive drug, and then a second type of nanobot that self-replicates."

I always feel like someone else with Briggs, someone other than myself, and as I stand next to him, our sleeves touching and feeling his heat, I think of the wonderful and the terrible ways he has shaped me.

"The self-replicating one is what worries us most. Imagine if you got something like that inside you," he says, and what's inside me is the irresistible force that is General John Briggs, and I understand what Fielding felt and how much he must have revered and resented me.

I understand how awful and wonderful it is to be overwhelmed by someone. Like a drug, it occurs to me. An addiction you desperately want to get over and desperately want to keep. Briggs will always have the same effect on me, I think. I won't get over it in this life.

"And the self-replicating nanobot enables the sustained release of something like testosterone," Briggs says, and I feel his energy, the intensity of him, and I'm aware of how close we are standing to each other, drawn to each other, just as we've always been and should never have been. "A drug like PCP couldn't replicate, of course, so that would be a dead-end hit, would be repeated only as the subject repeats his or her nasal spray or injections or applies a new transdermal patch impregnated with biodegradable nanobots. But something your body naturally produces could be programmed to replicate, so the nanobot is replicating, flowing freely through the body, through your arteries, latching onto target areas, like the frontal cortex of your brain, without the need of a battery. Self-propelled and replicating."

Briggs looks at me, and his eyes are hard but there is something in them that he's always held for me, an attachment that is as constant as it is conflicted. I'm vividly reminded of who we were at Walter Reed, when our futures held mystery and limitless possibility, when he was older and profoundly formidable to me and I was a prodigy. He called me Major Prodigy, and then I returned from South Africa and went to Richmond and he didn't call me at all, not for years. What we had with each other was complex and unfathomable, and I'm reminded all over again when I'm with him.

"We wouldn't need wars anymore," he says. "Not the sort of wars you and I know,

Kay. We're on the threshold of a new world where our old wars will seem easy and humane."

"Jack Fielding wasn't that kind of scientist," I reply. "He didn't manufacture those patches and probably would have been extremely resistant and unnerved had someone attempted to entice him into using drugs delivered by nanobots. I would be stunned if he even knew what a nanobot is or would have a clue this was what he was letting loose in his system. He probably thought he was taking some new form of steroid, a designer steroid, something that would help him in his bodybuilding, help alleviate his chronic pain from decades of overuse, help him fight aging. He hated getting older. Getting old wasn't an option to him."

"Well, he won't have to worry about it."

No, he won't, that's for sure. What I say is, "I don't accept that he killed himself because he didn't want to get old. I haven't accepted he killed himself, and have extreme doubts about it."

"I understand you got an exposure to one of his patches," Briggs then says, "and I'm sorry about that, but if you hadn't, you wouldn't know the rest of it. Kay Scarpetta high. Now, that's quite a thought. I'm sorry

I wasn't there to see that."

Benton must have told him.

"This is what we're up against, Kay," Briggs says. "Our brave new world, what I call neuroterrorism, what the Pentagon is calling it, the big fear. Make us crazy and you win. Make us crazy enough and we'll kill ourselves, saving the bad guys the trouble. In Afghanistan, give our troops opium, give them benzodiazepines, give them hallucinogenics, something to take the edge off their boredom, and then see what happens when they climb into their choppers and fighter jets and tanks and Humvees. See what happens when they come home addicts, come home deranged."

"Otwahl," I comment. "We're developing weapons like this?"

"*We* aren't. That's not what DARPA's paying all these millions for, dammit. But someone at Otwahl is, and we don't think it's just one. A cell of superbrains engaging in experiments not authorized or approved, and in fact as dangerous as it gets."

"I assume you know who."

"Damn kids," he says, gazing out at the bright afternoon. "Seventeen, eighteen, with IQs off the charts and full of passion but nothing home up here." He taps his forehead. "I don't need to tell you about boys especially, their frontal lobes not done, like a half-baked cookie until they're in their early to mid-twenties, and yet there they are, fucking around in nanotech labs or with superconductors and robotics and synthetic biology, you name it. Difficult enough we give them guns and throw them into stealth bombers, but we have rules," he says in a hard tone. "We have structures, regimens, leadership, the strictest of supervision, but what the hell do you think goes on at a place like Otwahl where the objective isn't national security and discipline but money and ambition? Those damn whiz kids like Johnny Donahue and his gang over there don't know shit about Afghanistan or Pakistan or Iraq, for Christ's sake. They've never set foot on a military base."

"I don't see Jack's connection to it beyond his teaching martial arts to a few of them." The sky is a spotless deep turquoise, and below it, the blue ocean heaves.

"He got tangled up with them, and my guess is unwittingly became a science project. You know all too well what goes on with research projects and clinical trials, only the type we're familiar with are supervised and strictly monitored by human-study review boards. So where do you get volunteers if you're an eighteen-year-old

Harvard or MIT technical engineer at Otwahl? We can only guess that Jack made his contacts likely through the gym, through tae kwon do. All of us are painfully aware of his lifelong problems with substance abuse, mainly steroids, so now someone is going to deliver the elixir of life, the fountain of youth, through pain-relieving patches. But he sure as hell didn't get what he bargained for. Neither did Wally Jamison, Mark Bishop, or Eli Goldman."

"Wally Jamison didn't work at Otwahl."

"For a while he dated someone who does. Dawn Kincaid, another one of the neuro-terrorists over there."

"Johnny Donahue's best friend," I say. "And where is she right now?" I ask. "It seems everyone you've mentioned is dead. Except her." I feel an alarm going off inside me.

"Missing in action," Briggs says. "Didn't show up at Otwahl yesterday or today, supposedly is on vacation."

"I'm sure."

"Exactly. We'll find her and get the rest of the story, because no question she's going to be the one to tell it, since her expertise is nanoengineering, nanoscale chemical synthesis. Based on what we've learned, she's likely the one developing these nasty little

nanobots that found their way to Jack Fielding and turned him into a Mr. Hyde, to put
it mildly."

"Mr. Hyde," I repeat. "The same thing
Erica Donahue says happened to her son,"
I point out. "Only I doubt Johnny killed
anyone."

"He didn't kill that boy."

"You're convinced Jack did."

"Out of control, sloppy," Briggs says.

"And then he killed Eli." My comment
hangs in the air, and I wonder if it sounds
as hollow to Briggs as it does to me. I
wonder if he can hear how strongly I don't
believe it.

"You realize this is because of the damn
swine flu." He continues staring out at the
day blazing beyond dusty old glass. "If the
stepdaughter's biological father hadn't gotten sick, Liam Saltz wouldn't have had the
pleasure of giving her away at her wedding,
and he wouldn't have come to the U.S., to
Cambridge, to Norton's Woods, at the last
minute. And Jack wouldn't have had to
stab Eli in the back with a damn injection
knife."

"To stop him from telling Dr. Saltz what
you're telling me."

"We can't ask Jack, unfortunately."

"Maybe I could understand it if Eli was

577

going to tell Dr. Saltz or someone that Jack was selling semen he was stealing from dead bodies. Maybe that would be a motive."

"We don't know what Eli knew. But he likely was aware of Jack and his drugs, obviously was well enough acquainted with him to have one of his guns. That must have been a bad feeling when Jack found out from the Cambridge police that the dead man had a Glock on him with an eradicated serial number."

"Sounds like Marino's filled you in. Told you all this as if it's an irrefutable case history. And it's not. It's a theory. We don't have tangible evidence that Jack killed anyone."

"He knew he was in trouble. That much I think is safe to say," Briggs replies.

"As much as anything is safe to say. I agree he wouldn't have removed the Glock from the lab had he not feared he had a problem. My question is whether he was covering for himself or for someone else."

"He knew damn well we'd restore the serial number, that we'd trace the pistol to him."

" 'We,' " I reply. "I've been hearing that word a lot of late."

"I know how you feel about it." Briggs plants his hands on the windowsill and leans forward, as if his lower back aches. "You think I'm trying to take something away from you. You believe it." He smiles grimly. "Captain Avallone came here last fall."

"Someone that junior? So it wouldn't raise suspicions?"

"Exactly, to appear casual, an informal drop-in while she was on her way somewhere else. When the fact is we were hearing things we didn't like about how your second in command was running the CFC. And I don't need to tell you we have a vested interest. The AFME does, DoD does, a lot of people do. It isn't yours to ruin."

"It isn't mine at all," I answer. "Obviously, I did a terrible job before I even started —"

"You haven't done a terrible job," he cuts me off. "I'm just as much to blame. You picked Jack or, better put, gave in to his wish to come back, and I didn't get in your way, and I sure as hell should have. I didn't want to step on you, and I should have stepped all over you about that decision you made. I figured in four months you'd be home, and I honestly didn't imagine the havoc that man could cause in such a short period of time, but he was mixed up with the Otwahl Technologies Rat Pack, doing drugs and losing it."

"Is that why you delayed my leaving

Dover? So you could find time to replace the leadership at the CFC? Find time to replace me?" I say it as bravely as I can.

"The opposite. To keep you out of it. I didn't want you tarred by it. I delayed you as many times as I could without an out-and-out abduction, and then the father of the bride in London gets the damn swine flu, and a dead body starts bleeding. And your niece shows up in her chopper at Dover, and I tried to get you to stay by offering to transport the body to Dover, but you wouldn't, and that was the end of it. And here we are again."

"Yes, again."

"We've been in our messes before. And we probably will again."

"You didn't send Lucy to pick me up."

"I did not. And I don't think she's likely to take orders from me. Thank God she never thought about enlisting. Would end up in Leavenworth."

"You didn't ask her to bug my office."

"A suggestion made in passing so we could know exactly what Jack was doing."

"Your making a suggestion in passing is like a cannibal offhandedly inviting someone to dinner," I reply.

"Quite an analogy."

"People pay attention to your suggestions,

and you know it."

"Lucy pays attention if it suits her."

"What about Captain Avallone? Did she conspire with Jack, conspire against me?"

"Never. I told you why she showed up last November for her tour. She's quite loyal to you."

"So loyal that she told Jack about Cape Town." I surprise myself by saying it out loud.

"That never happened. Sophia knows nothing about Cape Town."

"Then how did Julia Gabriel know?"

"When she was yelling at you? I see," he says, as if I've just answered a question I didn't know he'd asked. "I stopped outside your door to have a word with you and could hear you talking on the phone, could hear you were somewhat intensely involved. She talked to me, too. Talked to a number of people after getting word on the grapevine that we routinely extract semen at Dover, that every medical examiner's office does this routinely, which is utter bullshit. We would never do such a thing unless it was absolutely proper and approved. She got this impression because Jack was covertly doing that at the CFC and had done so in the case of the man who got killed in a Boston taxicab on his wedding day. Someone connected to Mrs. Gabriel's son. And I think you can understand how she got the idea that her son Peter should get the same special treatment."

"She knows nothing about me personally. She didn't mean it personally. You're sure."

"Why would you believe these negative things about you personally?" he says.

"I think you know why, John."

"No damn way she was referring to anything specific. She's an angry, militant woman and was just venting when she called you the same names she called me, called several other people at Dover. Bigots. Racists. Nazis. Fascists. A lot of staff got christened a lot of ugly names that morning."

Briggs steps back away from the window and collects his laptop off the sill, his way of saying he has to go. He can't have a conversation that lasts more than twenty minutes, and in fact the one we just had is lengthy for him and has tried his patience and gotten too close to too many things.

"One favor you could do for me that would be greatly appreciated," he says. "Please stop telling people I thought MORT was the best thing since sliced bread."

Benton, I think. I guess the two of them have gotten quite cozy.

"Not so, but I understand your remembering it that way, and I'm sorry we butted heads about it," Briggs goes on. "However, given a choice of a robot dragging a dead body off the battlefield and a living person risking his life and limb to do it? That's what I call a Sophie's choice. No good choice, only two bad ones. You weren't right, and I wasn't, either."

"Then we'll leave it at that," I answer. "Both of us made bad decisions."

"It's not like we hadn't made them before," he mutters.

He walks with me out of the sea captain's house, passing through rooms I've already been in. Every space seems empty and depressing, as if there never was anybody home. It doesn't feel that Fielding ever lived here, just parked himself as he worked demonically on his renovations and labored secretly in his cellar, and I just don't know what drove him. Maybe it was money. He'd always wanted money and was never going to get it in our trade, and that bothered him about me, too. I do better than most. I plan well, and Benton has his inheritance, and then there is Lucy, who is obscenely rich from computer technologies she's been selling since she was no older than the neuro-terrorists Briggs just talked about. Thank

God Lucy's inventions are legal, as best I know.

She's inside the CFC truck with Marino and Benton, and the yellow suits and hard hats are off, and everyone looks tired. Anne has driven off in the van again, making another delivery to the labs while more evidence waits for her here, white boxes filled with white paper evidence bags.

"There's a package for you in your car," Briggs says to me in front of the others. "The latest, greatest level four-A armor, specifically designed for females in theater, which would be fine if you ladies would bother with the plates."

"If the vest isn't comfortable," I start to say.

"I think it is, but I'm built a little different from you. Problem's going to be if it won't completely close on the sides. We've seen that too many times, and the projectile finds that one damn opening."

"I'll try it out for you," Lucy offers.

"Good," Marino says to her. "You put it on, and I'll start shooting, see if it works."

"Or trauma from blunt force, which is what most people seem to forget about," I tell Briggs. "The round doesn't penetrate the body armor, but if the blunt force from the impact goes as deep as forty-four millimeters, it's not survivable."

"I haven't been to the range in a while," Lucy chats with Marino. "Maybe we can borrow Watertown's. You been to their new one?"

"I bowl with their range master."

"Oh, yeah, your team of cretins. What's it called? Gutter Balls."

"Spare None. You should bowl with us sometime," Marino says to Briggs.

"Would it be acceptable to you, Colonel, if AFDIL sends in backup scientists to help out at the CFC, for God's sake?" Briggs is saying to me. "Since it seems we have an avalanche of evidence that just keeps coming."

"Any help would be greatly appreciated," I reply. "I'll work on the vest right away."

"Get some sleep first." Briggs says it like an order. "You look like hell."

22

Massachusetts Veterinary Referral Hospital has twenty-four-hour emergency care, and although Sock doesn't seem to be in any distress as he snores curled up like a teacup dog, a Chihuahua or poodle that can fit in a purse, I need to find out what I can about him. It is almost dark, and Sock is in my lap, both of us in the backseat of the borrowed SUV, driving north on I-95.

Having identified the man who was murdered while walking Sock, I intend to bestow the same kindness toward the rescued race dog, because no one seems to know where he came from. Liam Saltz doesn't know and wasn't aware his stepson Eli had a greyhound, or any pet. The superintendent of the apartment building near Harvard Square told Marino that pets aren't allowed. By all accounts, when Eli rented his unit there last spring, he didn't have a dog.

"This doesn't really need to be done tonight," Benton says as we drive and I pet the greyhound's silky head and feel great pity for him. I'm careful about his ragged ears because he doesn't like them touched, and he has old scars on his pointed snout. He is quiet, like something mute. *If only you could talk,* I think.

"Dr. Kessel doesn't mind. We should just do it while we're out," I reply.

"I wasn't thinking about whether some vet minded or not."

"I know you weren't." As I stroke Sock and feel that I might want to keep him. "I'm trying to remember the name of the woman who is Jet Ranger's nanny."

"Let's not go there."

"Lucy's never home, either, and it works out just fine. I think it's Annette, or maybe Lanette. I'll ask Lucy if Annette or Lanette could stop by during the day, maybe first thing each morning. Pick up Sock and take him to Lucy's place so he and Jet Ranger can keep each other company. Then Annette or whatever her name is could bring Sock back to Cambridge at night. What would be so hard about that?"

"We'll find Sock a home when the time is right." Benton takes the Woburn exit, the sign illuminating an iridescent green as our headlights flash over it and he slows down on the ramp.

"You're going to have a lovely home," I tell Sock. "Secret Agent Wesley just said so. You heard him."

"The reason you can't have a dog is the same reason it's always been a bad idea," Benton's voice says from the dark front seat. "Your IQ drops about fifty points."

"It would be a negative number, then. Minus ten or something."

"Please don't start baby talk or gibberish or whatever it is you speak to animals."

"I'm trying to figure out where to stop for food for him."

"Why don't I drop you off and I'll run to a convenience store or market and pick up something," Benton then says.

"Nothing canned. I need to do some research first about brands, probably a small-batch food for seniors because he's not a spring chicken. Speaking of, let's do chicken breasts, white rice, whitefish like cod, maybe a healthy grain like quinoa. So I'm afraid you'll need a real grocery store. I think there's a Whole Foods somewhere around here."

Inside Mass Vet Referral, I'm shown along a long, bright corridor lined with examination rooms, and the technician who accompanies us is very kind to Sock, who is rather sluggish, I notice. He is light on his small feet, slowly ambling along the corridor as if he's never run a race in his life and couldn't possibly.

"I think he's scared," I say to the tech.

"They're lazy."

"Who would think that of a dog that can run forty miles an hour?" I comment.

"When they have to, but they don't want to. They'd rather sleep on the couch."

"Well, I don't want to tug him. And his tail's between his legs."

"Poor baby." The tech stops every other second to pet him.

I suspect Dr. Kessel alerted the staff of the greyhound's sad circumstances, and we've been shown nothing but consideration and compassion and quite a lot of attention, as if Sock is famous, and I sincerely hope he won't be. It wouldn't be helpful if news of him became public, becoming chatter on the Internet and voyeurism or the usual tasteless jokes that seem to crop up around me. Do I take Sock to the morgue? Is Sock being trained as a cadaver dog? What does Sock do when I come home smelling like dead bodies?

He doesn't have a fever, and his gums and teeth are healthy, his pulse and respiration are normal, and no sign of a heart murmur or dehydration, but I won't allow Dr. Kessel to draw blood or urine. We'll reserve a thorough checkup for another time, I suggest, because the dog doesn't need more trauma. "Let him get to know me before he associates me with pain and suffering," I suggest to Dr. Kessel, a thin man in scrubs who looks much too young to have finished veterinary school. Using a small scanner he calls a wand, he looks for a microchip that might have been implanted under the skin of Sock's bony back as the dog sits on the examination table and I pet him.

"Well, he's got one, a nice little RFID chip right where it ought to be over his shoulders," Dr. Kessel says as he looks at what appears in the wand's display. "So what we have is an ID number, and let me give the National Pet Registry a quick call and we'll find out who this guy belongs to."

Dr. Kessel makes the call and takes notes. Momentarily, he hands me a piece of paper with a phone number and the name Lost Sock.

"That's quite a name for a race dog, huh, boy?" the vet says to him. "Maybe he lived up to it and that's why he got put out to pasture. A seven-seven-zero area code. Any idea?"

"I don't know."

He goes to a computer on a countertop and types the area code into a search field and says, "Douglasville, Georgia. Probably a vet's office there. You want to call from here and see if it's open? You're a long way from home," he says to Lost Sock, and I already know I won't call him that.

"You won't be lost ever again," I tell him as we return to the car, because I don't want to make the phone call in front of an audience.

The woman who answers simply says hello, as if I've reached a home number, and I tell her I'm calling about a dog that has this phone number on a microchip.

"Then he's one of our rescues," she says, and she has a Southern drawl. "Probably from Birmingham. We get a lot of them retired from the racetrack there. What's his name?"

I tell her.

"Black and white, five years old."

"Yes. That's correct," I reply.

"Is he all right? Not hurt or anything? He hasn't been mistreated."

"Curled up in my lap. He's fine."

"A sweetheart, but they all are. The nice thing about him is he's cat- and small dog–tolerant and does fine with children as long as they don't yank or tug on his ears. If you hold on a minute, I'll pull him up on my computer and see what I can find out about where he's supposed to be and with whom. I remember a student took him but can't think of her name. Up north. He was wandering loose or what? And where are you calling from? I know he's been trained and socialized, went through the program with flying colors, so you have a really nice dog, and I'm sure his owner must be just beside herself looking for him."

" 'Trained and socialized'?" I ask as I think about Sock being owned by a female student. "What program? Is your rescue group involved in a special program of some sort that takes greyhounds to retirement communities or hospitals, something like that?"

"Prisons," she says. "He was released from the racetrack last July and went through our nine-week program where inmates do the actual training. In his case, he went to the Georgia Prison for Women in Savannah."

I remember Benton telling me about the woman incarcerated in a prison located in Savannah, the therapist convicted of molesting Jack Fielding when he was a troubled boy and sent to live on a ranch near Atlanta.

"We got involved with them because they

were already training bomb-sniffing dogs, and we thought why not see if they want to do something a little more warm and fuzzy," the woman says, and I put her on speakerphone and turn up the volume, "like taking one of these sweet babies. The inmate learns patience and responsibility, and what it feels like to be loved unconditionally, and the greyhound learns commands. Anyway, Lost Sock was trained by a female inmate at the Georgia Prison for Women who said she wanted him when she finally gets out, but I'm afraid that won't be for a while. He was then adopted by someone she recommended, the young woman in Massachusetts. Do you have something to write with?"

She gives me the name Dawn Kincaid and several phone numbers. The address is the one where we just were in Salem, Jack Fielding's house. I seriously doubt Dawn Kincaid lived there all of the time, but she may have been there often. I doubt she was living with Eli Goldman all of the time, either, but it could be that he babysat her dog. Obviously, he knew her, both of them at Otwahl, and I remember that Briggs said Dawn Kincaid's area of expertise was chemical synthesis and nanoengineering. Anyone who is an expert in nanoengineering likely would consider it child's play to rig a pair of headphones with hidden micro audio and video recorders. She likely would have had easy access to Eli's headphones and portable satellite radio. She worked with him. Her dog was in his apartment, meaning she may have been a frequent visitor there. She may have stayed there. She might have a key.

Bryce is still at the CFC when I reach him, and I tell him I made a photocopy of Erica Donahue's letter before it was submitted to the labs, and to please find the file and read the phone numbers. I jot them down and ask what's going on with the DNA lab.

"Working around the clock," Bryce says. "I hope you're not coming back here tonight. Get some rest."

"Did Colonel Pruitt return to Dover, or is he at the labs?"

"I saw him a little while ago. He's here with General Briggs, and some of their people are coming from Dover. Well, they're your people, too, I guess. . . ."

"Get hold of Colonel Pruitt and ask him if per my directive the profiles from the typewriter are going into CODIS immediately, before everything else. Maybe they already have? He'll know what I mean. But what's really important is I want a familial search done, checking any profiles against Jack Fielding's exclusionary DNA, and a familial search done in CODIS that includes a comparison with the profile of an inmate at the Georgia Prison for Women in Savannah. Her name is Kathleen Lawler." I spell the name for him. "A repeat offender . . ."

"Where?"

"The women's prison near Savannah, Georgia. Her DNA should be in the CODIS database. . . ."

"What's that got to . . . ?"

"She and Jack had a child together, a girl. I want a familial search to see if we get a match with anything recovered. . . ."

"He what? He what with who?"

"And the latent prints on the plastic film . . ." I start to say.

"Okay. Now you're scrambling my brains. . . ."

"Bryce. Get unscrambled and be quiet, and you'd better be writing this down."

"I am, boss."

"I want the prints from the film compared to Fielding and to me, and I want DNA done ASAP on that, too. See who else might have touched the film. Maybe whoever made or altered the patch the film came from. And my guess is Otwahl might print its employees, have their prints on file over there. A place that security-minded. It's really important we know exactly who supplied those tampered-with patches. Colonel Pruitt and General Briggs will understand all this."

Next I get Erica Donahue on the phone as Benton drives through Cambridge, taking the same roads Eli did the last time he walked here with Sock on Sunday, on his way to meet his stepfather, to blow the whistle on Otwahl Technologies to a man who could do something about it.

"A welcome guest meaning how often?" I ask Mrs. Donahue after she tells me over speakerphone that Dawn Kincaid has been to the Donahues' home on Beacon Hill many times and is always a welcome guest. The Donahues adore her.

"For dinner or just dropping by, especially on the weekends. You know she came up the hard way, had to work for everything and has had so much misfortune, her mother killed in a car crash, and then her father dying tragically, I forget from what. Such a lovely girl, and she's always been so sweet to Johnny. They met when he started at Otwahl last spring, although she's older, in a Ph.D. program at MIT, transferred from Berkeley, I believe, and just incredibly bright and so attractive. How do

596

you know her?"

"I'm afraid I don't. We've not met."

"Johnny's only friend, really. Certainly the closest one he's ever had. But not romantic, although I've hoped for it, but I don't think that will ever be. I believe she's seeing someone else at Otwahl, a scientist she's working with there."

"Do you know his name?"

"I'm sorry, I don't recall it if I ever knew. I think he's originally from Berkeley as well, and then ended up here because of MIT and Otwahl. A South African. I've heard Johnny rather rudely refer to the Afrikaans nerd Dawn dates, and some other names I won't repeat. And before that it was a dumb jock, according to my son, who's a bit jealous. . . ."

"A dumb jock?" I ask.

"A terribly rude thing to say about someone who died so tragically. But Johnny lacks tact. That's part of his unusualness."

"Do you know the name of the man who died?"

"I don't remember. That football player they found in the harbor."

"Did Johnny talk about that case with you?"

"You're not going to imply that my son had something to do with —"

I calmly reassure her I'm not implying anything of the sort, and I end the call as the SUV crunches through the frozen snow blanketing our Cambridge driveway. At the end of it, under the bare branches of a huge oak tree, is the carriage house, our remodeled garage, its double wooden doors illuminated in our headlights.

"You heard that for yourself," I say to Benton.

"It doesn't mean Jack didn't do it. It doesn't mean he didn't kill Wally Jamison or Mark Bishop or Eli Goldman," he says. "We need to be careful."

"Of course we need to be careful. We're always careful. None of this you already knew?"

"I can't tell you what a patient told me. But let's put it this way, what Mrs. Donahue just said is interesting, and I didn't say I'm convinced about Fielding. I'm saying we just need to be careful because we don't know certain things for a fact right now. But we will. I can promise you that. Everyone's looking for Dawn Kincaid. I'll pass this latest information along," Benton says, and what he's really saying is there's nothing we can do about it or nothing we should do about it, and he's right. We can't go out like a two-party posse and track down Dawn

Kincaid, who probably is a thousand miles from here by now.

Benton stops the SUV and points a remote at the garage. A wooden door rolls up, and a light goes on inside, illuminating his black Porsche convertible and three other empty spaces.

He tucks the SUV next to his sports car, and I slip the lead over Sock's long, slender neck and help him out of my lap, then out of the backseat and into the garage, which is very cold because of the missing window in back. I walk Sock across the rubberized flooring and look through the gaping black square and at our snowy backyard beyond it. It is very dark, but I can make out disturbed snow, a lot of footprints, the neighborhood children again using our property as a shortcut, and that's going to stop. We have a dog, and I will get the backyard walled or fenced in. I will be the mean, crabby neighbor who doesn't allow trespassing.

"What a joke," I comment to Benton as we walk out of the detached garage and onto the slick, snowy driveway, the night sharply cold and white and very still. "You decide to get an alarm system for the garage. So we have one that doesn't work and anybody could climb right in. When are we getting a new window?"

We head to the back door, walking carefully over crusty snow, which Sock clearly doesn't like, snatching his paws up as if he's walking over hot coals and shivering. Dark trees rock in the wind, the night sky scattered with stars, the moon small and bone-white high above the roofs and treetops of Cambridge.

"It sucks," he says, shifting the bag of groceries to his other arm as he finds the door key. "I'll make sure to get them out here tomorrow. It's just I haven't been around and someone has to be home."

"How big a deal to get fencing in back for Sock? So we can let him out and not be afraid he'll run off."

"You told me he doesn't like to run." Benton unlocks the door of the glassed-in porch.

Beyond it are the dark shapes of trees in Norton's Woods. The timber building with its three-tiered metal roof hulks darkly against the night, no lights on inside. I feel sad as I look at the American Academy of Arts and Sciences headquarters and think of Liam Saltz and his slain stepson. I wonder if the maimed flybot is still out there somewhere, buried and frozen, no longer alive, as Lucy put it, because the sun can't find it. I have a funny feeling someone has it. Maybe the FBI, I decide. Maybe people from DARPA, from the Pentagon. Maybe Dawn Kincaid.

"I think we need boots for him," I say. "They make little booties for dogs, and he needs something like that so he doesn't cut his paws on the ice and frozen snow."

"Well, he won't go very far in this cold." Benton opens the door and the alarm begins to beep. "Trust me. You'll have a hard time making him go out in this weather. I hope he's housebroken."

"He needs a couple of coats. I'm surprised Eli or Dawn or whoever didn't have coats for him. Greyhounds need them up here. This really isn't the right part of the world for greyhounds, but it is what it is, Sock. You're going to be warm and well fed and fine."

Benton enters the code on the keypad and resets the alarm the instant he's shut the door behind us, and Sock leans against my legs.

"You build a fire, and I'm making drinks," I tell Benton. "Then I'll cook chicken and rice or maybe switch to cod and quinoa but not right now. He's been eating chicken and rice all day, and I don't want him sick. What

601

would you like? Or maybe I should ask what's in the house."

"Some of your pizza's still in the freezer."

I turn on lights, and the stained-glass windows in the stairwell are dark but will be gorgeous from the outside, backlit by lights inside the house. I imagine the French wildlife scenes brilliantly lit up when I take Sock out at night and how cheerful that will be. I imagine playing with him in the backyard in the spring and summer, when it's warm, and seeing the vibrant windows lit up at night and of how peaceful and civilized that will be. Living on the edge of Harvard and coming home from the office to my old dog, and I'll plant a rose garden in back, and I think how good that sounds.

"Nothing to eat for me right now," Benton says, taking off his coat. "First things first. A very strong drink, please."

He goes into the living room, and Sock's nails click against hardwood, then are silent on rugs as we pass from room to room and into the kitchen, where I feel him leaning against my legs as I open dark cherry cabinets above stainless-steel appliances. Wherever I move, he moves and presses against me, pushing against the back of my legs as I get out tumblers, then ice from the freezer, and then a bottle of our very best

Scotch, a Glenmorangie single-malt aged twenty-five years that was a Christmas gift from Jaime Berger. My heart aches as I pour drinks and think of Lucy and Jaime breaking up and of people who are dead, and of what Fielding did to his life, and now he's dead. He'd been killing himself all along, and then someone finished it for him, stuck a Glock in his left ear and pulled the trigger, most likely when he was standing near the cryogenic freezer, where he stored ill-gotten semen before shipping it to wives, mothers, and lovers of men who died young.

Who would Fielding trust so much as to allow the person into his cellar, to share his illegal venture capitalism with, to let borrow his sea captain's house and probably everything he owned? I remember what his former boss told me, the chief in Chicago. He commented he was glad Jack was moving to Massachusetts to be near family, only he wasn't referring to Lucy, Marino, and me, not to any of us, not even to his current wife and their two kids. I have a feeling the chief meant someone I never knew existed before now, and if I weren't so selfish and egotistical, maybe the thought would have occurred to me sooner.

How typical of me to assume such importance in Fielding's life, and he wasn't thinking of me at all when he told his former chief what he did about family. Fielding probably meant the daughter from his first love, probably the first woman he ever had sex with, the therapist at the ranch near Atlanta who bore his daughter, and then gave her up just as Fielding was given up. A girl with genetic loading, as Benton put it, that would land her in prison if she didn't end up dead. And she moved here last year from Berkeley, and then Fielding moved back here from Chicago.

"Nineteen seventy-eight," I say as I walk into the dark, cozy living room of built-in bookcases and exposed old beams. The lights are out, and a fire crackles and glows on the brick hearth, and sparks swarm as Benton moves a log with the poker. "She would be about Lucy's age, about thirty-one." I hand him a tumbler of Scotch, a generous pour with only a few cubes of ice. The whisky looks coppery in the firelight. "Do you think it's her? That Dawn Kincaid is his biological daughter? Because I do. I hope you didn't already know about her."

"I promise I didn't. If it's true."

"You really weren't focused on Dawn Kincaid or a child Fielding had with the woman in prison."

"I really wasn't. You need to remember

how recent this all has been, Kay." We settle next to each other on the sofa, and then Sock settles in my lap. "Fielding wasn't on anybody's radar until last week, at least not for anything criminal, nothing violent. But I should have gone to the trouble to find out about the baby adopted," Benton says, and he sounds slightly angry with himself. "I know I would have eventually, and I hadn't yet because it didn't seem important."

"In the grand scheme of things and at the time, it wasn't. I'm not trying to put you on the defensive."

"I knew from the records I reviewed that the baby, a girl, was given up for adoption while the mother was in prison the first time. An adoption agency in Atlanta," he says. "Maybe like some adopted children, she set about to find out who her biological parents were."

"As smart as she is, that probably wasn't hard."

"Christ." Benton takes a swallow of Scotch. "It's always the one thing you think doesn't matter, the one thing you think can wait."

"I know. That's almost always how it works out. The detail you don't want to bother with."

We sit on the sofa, looking at the fire, and

Sock is curled up on top of me. He is attached to me. He won't let me out of his sight. He has to be touching me, as if he's certain I'll disappear and he'll be abandoned in a run-down house again where horrible things happen.

"I think there is a very good probability that's what the DNA is going to tell us about Dawn Kincaid," Benton continues in a flat tone. "I wish we could have known it before, but there wasn't a reason to look."

"You don't have to keep saying that. Why would you have looked? What would a baby he fathered when he was a teenager have to do with what's gone on?"

"Obviously, it might have."

"Twenty-twenty hindsight."

"I knew he was writing Kathleen Lawler, e-mailing her, but there's nothing criminal about that, nothing even suspicious, and no mention of anyone by the name of Dawn, just an *interest* they had in common. I recall that phrase, the interest they shared. I thought he fucking meant crime, maybe their old crime and how it changed who they were forever, that was the *interest* they had in common," he says ruefully, trying to figure it out as he talks. "Now I have to wonder if the interest they shared might be their child, might even be Dawn Kincaid.

Just unfortunate that Jack never got past that part of his life, that he was still connected to Kathleen Lawler, and probably she to him. And then a daughter who got his intelligence, his good parts and his bad parts. And the mother's good and really bad parts. And who the hell knows all the places that daughter's been bounced around to but never lived with her father, who I suspect she never knew while she was growing up. Of course, this is complete speculation on our part."

"Not really. It's like an autopsy. Most of the time it tells me what I already know."

"I'm afraid we might know. I'm afraid we really might, and it's a horror story, really. Talk about bad seed and the sins of the father."

"Some would say it was the sins of the mother in this case."

"I should make some phone calls," Benton says as he drinks and sits in front of the fire, staring into it.

He is angry with himself. He can't tolerate missing that one thing, as he calls it. In his mind, he should have made it a burning priority to track down a baby born to a woman in prison more than thirty years ago, and that really is unreasonable. Why would he think it mattered?

"Jack never mentioned Dawn Kincaid to me or a daughter who was given up for adoption, absolutely nothing like that. I had no idea." The whisky has heated me up, and I pet Sock, feeling the bumps of his ribs, like a washboard, and feeling the sadness that has settled inside me and won't go away. "I seriously doubt she ever lived with him until maybe very recently, don't see how. Not in Richmond, absolutely not. And it's unlikely his wives would have allowed a daughter from that early criminal liaison to be part of their lives, assuming they knew. He probably didn't tell them, except to allude to his difficulty with cases involving dead children. If he even said that much to the women in his life."

"He said it to you."

"I wasn't just a woman in his life. I was his boss."

"That's not all."

"Please not again, Benton. Really. It's getting to be ridiculous. I know you're in a mood and both of us are tired."

"It's the thought of you not being honest with me. I don't care what you did back then. I don't have a right to care about what you did before we were together."

"Well, you do care, and you have a right to care about anything you want. But how many times do I have to tell you?"

"I remember the first time we socialized."

"How dated that sounds, no pun intended. Like two people on a Sunday night in the fifties." I reach for his hand.

"Nineteen eighty-eight, that Italian place in the Fan. Remember Joe's?"

"Every time I was out with the cops, that's where we'd end up. Nothing like a big plate of baked spaghetti after a homicide scene."

"You hadn't been the chief long." Benton talks to the fire, and he strokes my hand gently, both of our hands resting on top of Sock. "I asked you about Jack because you were so industrious about him, so vigilant, so focused, and I thought it was unusual. The more I probed, the more evasive you got. I've never forgotten it."

"It wasn't because of him," I answer. "It was because of the way I felt about me."

"Because of Briggs. Not an easy man to be under. And I don't mean that the way it just came out. Not that you would necessarily be the one under him or anyone. Probably on top."

"Please don't be snide."

"I'm teasing you, and both of us are too tired and frayed around the edges for teasing. I apologize."

"What happened is my fault, anyway. I

won't blame him or anyone," I continue. "But he was God back then. To someone like me. I was really very sheltered. I think all I'd ever done was go to school, study, consumed by residencies, Lord, how many years of them, like a long dream of working hard and rarely sleeping, and of course doing what I was told by people in authority. In the early days hardly questioning it. Because I felt I didn't deserve to be a doctor. I should have run my father's small grocery store, been a wife and mother, lived simply, like everyone else in my family."

"John Briggs was the most powerful person you'd ever come across. I can see why," Benton says, and I sense he might know Briggs better than I've imagined. I wonder how much they've talked these past six months, not only about Fielding but about everything.

"Please don't be threatened by him," I'm saying as I wonder what Benton knows about Briggs and, most of all, what Benton knows about me. "My past with him doesn't matter anymore. And it was about my perception, anyway. I needed him to be powerful. I needed that back then."

"Because your father was anything but powerful. All those years he was ill, with you taking care of him, taking care of everyone. You wanted someone who would take care of you for once."

"And when you get what you want, guess what happens. John took terrible care of me. Or it would be more accurate if I said that I took terrible care of myself. I knew — better yet, was persuaded — to go against my conscience and to be led into something that wasn't right."

"Politics," Benton says as if he knows.

"What would you know about what happened back then?" I look at him, and shadows move on his keenly handsome face in the firelight.

"I think it's something like two years' service for every year of medical or law school paid for by the military. So unless my math is really bad, you owed the U.S. government eight years of service with the air force, more specifically, the AFIP, AFME."

"Six. I finished Hopkins in three years."

"Okay, that's right. But you served what, a year? And every time I've asked about it, you give me the same song and dance about the AFIP wanting to set up a fellowship program in Virginia and they decided to plant you there as chief."

"We did start an AFIP fellowship program. In those days there weren't that many offices if you were AFIP and wanted to specialize in forensics. So we added Richmond. And now, of course, us. The CFC. We'll be gearing up for that soon. Any minute I've got to get that going."

"Politics," Benton says again as he takes a drink of Scotch. "You've always felt guilty about something, and for the longest time I thought it was Jack. Because you'd had an affair with him, repeating his original injury. A powerful woman in charge of him has sex with him, victimizing him again, returning him to the scene of the original crime. For you? That would have been unpardonable."

"Except I didn't."

"You promise."

"I promise."

"Well, you did something." He's not going to stop until we have it before us.

"Yes, I did, but it was before Jack," I answer.

"You did what you were ordered to do, Kay. And you've got to let it go," he says, because he knows. It's obvious he does.

"I never told their families," I reply, and Benton doesn't say anything. "The two women murdered in Cape Town. I couldn't call their families and tell them what really happened. They think it was racism, gang members during Apartheid. A high crime rate of blacks killing whites suited certain political leaders back then. They wanted it to be true. The more, the better."

"Those leaders are gone now, Kay."

"You should make your phone calls, Benton. Call Douglas or whoever and tell them about Dawn Kincaid and who she probably is and the tests I've ordered."

"The Reagan administration is long gone, Kay." Benton's going to make me talk about it, and I'm convinced it's been talked about before. Briggs probably said something to him because Briggs knows damn well how haunted I am.

"What I did isn't long gone," I reply.

"You didn't do a damn thing that was wrong. You had nothing to do with their deaths. I don't have to know all the details to say that much," Benton says as he laces his fingers in mine, our joined hands gently rising and sinking in rhythm to Sock's breathing.

"I feel as if I had everything to do with it," I answer.

"You didn't," he says. "Other people did, and you were forced to be silent. Do you know how often it is I can't tell what I know? My whole life has been like that. The alternative is to make things worse. That's the test. Does telling make it worse and cause others to be persecuted and killed. *Primum non nocere.* First, do no harm. That's what I weigh everything against, and I sure as hell know you do the same."

I don't want a lecture right now.

"Do you think she did it?" I ask as Sock breathes slowly, contentedly, as if he's lived here always and is home. "Killed all of them?"

"Now I'm wondering." He looks at his drink, and it turns the color of honey in the firelight.

"To put Jack out of his misery?"

"She probably hated him," Benton says. "That's why she would have been drawn to him, wanted to get to know him as an adult, if that's what she did."

"Well, I don't think he shackled Wally Jamison in his cellar and hacked him to death. If Wally came to the house in Salem willingly, probably it was upon Dawn's invitation, to see her. Maybe play out some fantasy, a game, a macabre sex game on Halloween. Maybe she did a similar thing to Mark Bishop, and when she has them under control, under her spell, exactly where she wants them, she strikes. A rush, a thrill, for someone diabolical like that."

"Liam Saltz's second wife, Eli's mother, is South African," Benton says. "As is her husband from that earlier marriage, Eli's biological father, and Eli was wearing a ring that likely was taken from the Donahue house, likely taken by Dawn along with the typewriter, the stationery. Maybe used the duct tape to collect fibers, trace evidence, DNA from the Donahue house, while she was at it. Make it look like the letter really did come from the mother, making sure that Johnny's alibi was weakened further by it."

"Now you're thinking irrationally like me," I reply wryly. "That's what I believe happened, or close to it."

"The game," Benton muses in that tone he has when he hates what someone has done. "Games and more games, elaborate, intricate dramas. I can't wait to meet the fucking bitch. I really can't wait."

"Maybe you've had enough Scotch."

"Not half enough. Who better to manipulate Johnny Donahue than someone like that, some attractive brain trust of a woman who's older? To plant the idea in that poor kid's head that he murdered a six-year-old while he was delusional and having memory lapses because of drugs she was spiking his meds with? Spiking Fielding's meds with. Who knows who else? A poisonous person who destroys the people she's supposed to love, pays them back for every crime committed against her, and you pile on her genetic predisposition and maybe the same cocktail Fielding was on?"

"That would be the perfect storm, as they say."

"Let's see what kind of killing machine I can be and get away with it," he says in that tone of his, and if I could look into his eyes, I know what would be in them. Complete contempt. "And after it's ended, no one is left standing but her. Fucking bulletproof."

"You could be right." And I remember the box I left in the car. "Why don't you make your phone calls."

"Borderline, sadistic, manipulative, narcissistic."

"I guess some people are everything." I set down my glass on the coffee table and ease Sock off my lap and onto the rug.

"Some people just about are."

"I forgot the box Briggs left for me," I say as I get up from the sofa. "And I'll take Sock out back. You ready to go potty?" I ask the dog. "Then I'll warm up pizza. I don't suppose we have anything for salad. What the hell have you eaten the entire time I've been gone? Let me guess. You run over to Chang An for Chinese food and live on that for the next three days."

"That would be really good right now."

"You've probably been doing it every week."

"I'd rather have your pizza anytime."

"Don't try to be nice," I reply.

I walk into the kitchen for Sock's lead and slip it around his neck and find a flashlight in a drawer, an old Maglite that Marino gave me aeons ago, long and black aluminum, powered by fat D batteries, reminding me of the old days, when police used to carry flashlights the size of nightsticks instead of everything being so small, like the SureFire lights Lucy likes and what Benton keeps in his glove box. I disarm the alarm system and worry about Sock, about how cold it is, realizing as we go down the back steps in the dark that I didn't bother with a coat for me, and I notice that the motion-sensor light attached to the garage is out. I try to remember if it was out an hour or so ago when we got home, but I'm not sure. There is so much to fix, so much to change, so much to do. Where will I start when tomorrow comes?

Benton didn't lock the door to the detached garage, because what would be the point with an open window the size of a big-screen TV? Inside the remodeled carriage house it is dark and bitterly cold, and air blows in through the open black square that I can barely make out, and I turn on the Maglite and it doesn't work. The batteries must be dead, and how stupid of me not to check before I left the house. I point the key at the SUV, and the lock chirps but the interior light doesn't go on because it's a damn Bureau car, and Special Agent Burke isn't about to have an interior light that comes on. I feel around on the backseat for the box, which is quite large, and I realize it won't be easy to carry it and deal with Sock. In fact, I can't.

"I'm sorry, Sock," I say to the dog as I feel him shivering against my legs. "I know it's cold in here. Just give me a minute. I'm so sorry. But as you're discovering, I'm a very stupid person."

I use the car key to slit the tape on top of the box and pull out a vest that is familiar even if I've not examined this particular brand, but I recognize the feel of tough nylon and the stiffness of ceramic-Kevlar plates that Briggs or someone has already inserted into the internal pockets. I tear open the Velcro straps on the sides to open up the vest so I can sling it over my shoulder. I feel the weight of the vest draped over me as I shove the car door shut, and Sock jumps away from me like a rabbit. He yanks the lead out of my hand.

"It's just the car door, Sock. It's all right, come here, Sock. . . ." I start to call out at the same time something else moves inside the garage near the open window, and I turn around to see what it is, but it is too dark to see anything.

"Sock? Is that you over there?"

The dark, frigid air moves around me, and the blow to my back feels like a hammer hitting me between my shoulder blades, as if a loud hissing dragon is attacking me, and I lose my balance.

A piercing scream and hissing, and a warm, wet mist spatters my face as I fall hard against the SUV and swing with all my might at whatever it is. The Maglite cracks like a bat against something hard that gives beneath the weight of the blow and then moves, and I swing again and hit something again, something that feels different. I smell the iron smell of blood and taste it on my lips and in my mouth as I swing again and again at air, and then the lights are on and the glare is blinding and I'm covered with a fine film of blood as if I've been spray-painted with it. Benton is inside the garage, pointing a pistol at the woman in a huge black coat facedown on the rubberized floor. I notice blood pooling under her bloody right hand, and near it, a severed fingertip with a glittery white French nail, and near that, a knife with a thin steel blade and a thick black handle with a release button on the shiny metal guard.

"Kay? Kay? Are you all right? Kay! Are you all right?"

I realize Benton is shouting at me as I crouch by the woman and touch the side of her neck and find her pulse. I make sure she is breathing and turn her over to check her pupils. Neither of them is fixed. Her face is bloody from the Maglite smashing into it, and I am startled by the resemblance, the dark blond hair cut very short, the strong features, and the full lower lip that look like Jack Fielding's. Even the small ears close to the sides of her head look like his, and I feel the strength in her upper body, her shoulders, although she isn't a large person, maybe five-foot-six or -seven and slender but with large bones like her dead father. All this is flooding my senses as I tell Benton to rush into the house and call 911, and to bring a container of ice.

A warm front moved in during the night and brought more snow, this time a gentle snow that falls silently, muting all sound, covering everything that is ugly, softly rounding whatever is sharp and hard.

I sit up in bed inside the master bedroom on the second floor of the house in Cambridge, and snow is coming down, piling in the bare branches of an oak tree on the other side of the big window nearest me. A moment ago a fat gray squirrel was there, perfectly balanced on the smallest twig, and we were eye to eye, his cheeks moving as he stared through the window at me while I sifted through the paperwork and photographs in my lap. I smell old paper and dust and the medicine smell of the wipes I used on Sock, who I suspect hadn't had his ears cleaned in recent memory, maybe not ever, not the way I cleaned them. He didn't like it at first, but I talked him into it with a soft voice and a sweet-potato treat that Lucy brought by when she gave me a container of the same wipes she uses on her bulldog. The miconazole-chlorhexidine is good for pachydermatis, I made the mistake of mentioning to my niece very early this morning when she stopped by to check on me.

Jet Ranger wouldn't appreciate being called a pachyderm, Lucy retorted. He's not an elephant or a hippopotamus, and there's only so much one can do about his weight. She has him on a new diet for seniors, but he can't exercise because of his bad hips, and the snow gives him a rash on his paws for some reason, and his legs are too short for snow this deep, so he can't go on even the briefest walk this time of year, she went on and on, and I'd truly offended her. But that's the way Lucy can get when she's worried and scared, and most of all she's upset she wasn't here last night. She's angry she wasn't here to deal with Dawn Kincaid, but I'm not sorry in the least. I can't say I'm proud of myself for giving someone a linear skull fracture and a concussion, but if Lucy had been in the garage instead of me, there would be one more person dead. My niece would have killed Dawn Kincaid for sure, probably shot her, and there are enough people dead.

It's also possible that Lucy wouldn't have survived the encounter, I don't care what she says. It depends on two details that made the difference in my still being here and Dawn Kincaid being locked up on the forensic ward of an area hospital. I don't think she was expecting me to walk into the garage. I think she was lurking on the other side of the gaping window, waiting for me to take Sock into the dark backyard. But I surprised her by entering the garage first to get what I'd left in the car, and by the time she slipped through the big space where the window was supposed to be, I'd already opened the box and slung the level IV-A tactical vest over my shoulder. When she stabbed at my back with the injection knife, it hit a nylon-covered ceramic-Kevlar plate, and the terrific jolt caused by that absolute stopping action caused her fingers to slide along the blade. She cut three fingers to the bone and severed the tip of her pinkie at the same time she was releasing the CO_2, and a mist of her blood sprayed all over me.

My point to Lucy was that unless she'd caused Dawn to lose the surprise element for the attack and unless Lucy also just happened to have on body armor or at least have it draped over her torso, she might not have been as fortunate as I was. So my niece should stop saying it's a damn shame she wasn't here last night, claiming that she sure as hell would have taken care of things, as if I didn't, because I did, even though it was luck. I think I took care of things just fine and only hope I can take care of a far more important matter that hasn't killed me yet but at times has certainly felt like it might.

"She'd told me there had been catcalls and ugly comments," Mrs. Pieste is telling me over the phone as I go over her daughter's case with her. "Calling her a Boer. Telling the Boers to go home, and as you know, that's Afrikaans for farmer but it's really meant to disparage all white South Africans. And I kept telling the man from the Pentagon that I didn't care about the reason, whether it was Noonie and Joanne being white or American or assumed to be South African. And, of course, they weren't South African. I didn't care why. I just didn't want to believe the suffering he described."

"Do you remember who that man from the Pentagon was?" I ask.

"A lawyer."

"It wasn't a colonel in the army," I hope out loud.

"It was some young lawyer at the Pentagon who worked for the secretary of defense. I don't remember his name."

Then it wasn't Briggs.

"A fast-talking one," Mrs. Pieste adds disdainfully. "I remember I didn't like him. But I wouldn't have liked anybody who told me the things he did."

"The only comfort I can offer out of all of this," I repeat, "is Noonie and Joanne didn't suffer the way you've been led to believe. I can't say with absolute certainty that they weren't aware of being smothered, but it is extremely likely they weren't aware because they were drugged."

"But that would have been tested for," Mrs. Pieste's voice says, and she has a Massachusetts accent, can't pronounce R's, and I didn't realize she's originally from Andover. After Noonie's murder, the Piestes moved to New Hampshire, I just found out.

"Mrs. Pieste, I think you understand nothing was tested as it was supposed to be," I reply.

"Why didn't you?"

"The medical examiner in Cape Town —"

"But you signed the death certificate, Dr. Scarpetta. And the autopsy report. I have copies that lawyer from the Pentagon sent me."

"I didn't sign them." I refused to sign documents that I knew were a lie, but knowing they were a lie made me guilty of it anyway. "I don't have copies, as hard as that probably is for you to believe," I then say. "They weren't supplied to me. What I have are my own notes, my own records, which I mailed back to the U.S. before I left South Africa because I worried my luggage would be gone through, and it was."

"But you signed what I have."

"I promise I didn't," I reply calmly but firmly. "My guess is certain people made certain my signature was forged on those falsified documents in the event I decided to do what I'm doing now."

"If you decided to tell the truth."

It's so hard to hear it stated so bluntly. The truth. Implying what I've told or not told over the years makes me a liar.

"I'm sorry," I tell her again. "You had a right to know the truth back then, at the time of your daughter's death. And the death of her friend."

"I can see why you didn't say anything back then, though," Mrs. Pieste says, and she sounds only slightly upset. Mostly she sounds interested and relieved to be talking about something that has dominated her life for most of it. "When people do things like this, no telling where they'll stop. Well, there's no limit. Other people would have gotten hurt. Including you."

"I wouldn't have wanted anybody else to get hurt," I reply, and I feel worse if what she's saying is that I was silent out of fear for my own safety. I was afraid of a lot of things and a host of people I couldn't see. I was afraid of other people dying, of people being wrongly accused.

"I hope you understand that when I read the death certificate and autopsy report, not that I understand most of the medical terms, well, one would think the findings are yours," Mrs. Pieste says.

"They absolutely weren't, and they are false. There was no tissue response to the injuries. All of it was postmortem. In fact, hours after the deaths, Mrs. Pieste. What was done to Noonie and Joanne occurred many hours after they had died."

"If there wasn't a test for drugs, then how can you be sure they were given something?" her voice goes on, and I hear the sound of another phone being picked up.

"This is Edward Pieste," a man's voice says. "I'm on, too. I'm Noonie's father."

"I'm so sorry for your loss." It sounds weak, perfectly insipid. "I wish I had exactly the right words to say to both of you. I'm sorry you were lied to and that I permitted it, and although I won't make excuses . . ."

"We understand why you couldn't say what happened," the father replies. "The feelings back then, and our government secretly in collusion with those who wanted to keep Apartheid alive. That's why Noonie was making that documentary. They wouldn't let the film crew into South Africa. Each of them had to go in as if they were tourists. A big dirty secret, what our government was doing to support the atrocities over there."

"It wasn't that big of a secret, Eddie." Mrs. Pieste's voice.

"Well, the White House put on the good face."

"I'm sure they told you about the documentary Noonie was making? She had such a future," Mrs. Pieste says to me as I look at a picture of her daughter that I wouldn't want the Piestes to ever see.

"About the children of Apartheid," I reply. "I did see it when it aired here."

"The evils of white supremacy," she says. "Of any supremacy, period."

"I missed the first part of what the two of you have been talking about," Mr. Pieste says. "Was out shoveling the driveway."

"He doesn't listen," his wife says. "A man his age shoveling snow, but he's the hard head." She says it with sad affection. "Dr.

Scarpetta was telling me Noonie and Joanne were drugged."

"Really. Well, that's something." He says it with no energy in his tone.

"I got to the apartment several days after their deaths and did a retrospective. It was staged, of course; their crime scene was staged," I explain. "But there were beer cans, plastic cups, and a wine bottle in the kitchen trash, a bottle of white wine from Stellenbosch, and I managed to get the cans, the bottle, and cups along with other items, and have them sent back to the States, where I had them tested. We found high levels of GHB in the wine bottle and two of the cups. Gamma hydroxybutyric acid, commonly known as a date-rape drug."

"They did say there was rape," Mr. Pieste says with the same empty affect.

"I don't know for a fact that they were raped. There was no physical sign of it, no injuries except staged ones inflicted postmortem, and swabs I had tested privately here in the U.S. were negative for sperm," I reply, looking through photographs of the nude bodies bound to chairs I know the women weren't sitting in when they were murdered. I look at close-ups showing a livor mortis pattern that told me the women were lying in bed on rumpled sheets for at least twelve hours after death.

I go through photographs I took with my own camera of hacking and cutting injuries that barely bled, and ligatures that scarcely left a mark on the skin because the brutes behind all this were too ignorant to know what the hell they were doing, someone hired or assigned by government or military operatives to spike a bottle of local wine and have drinks with the women, possibly a friend or they thought the person was friendly or safe, when, of course, he was anything but, and I tell them that serology tests I had done after I got home indicated the presence of a male. Later, when I had DNA testing done, I got the profile of a European or white male who remains unknown. I can't say for a fact it is the profile of the killer, but it was someone drinking beer inside the apartment, I add.

As much as one can reconstruct anything, I tell the Piestes what I think happened, that after Noonie and Joanne were drugged and groggy or unconscious, their assailant helped them to bed and smothered them with a pillow, and I based this on pinpoint hemorrhages and other injuries, I explain. Then for some reason this person must have left. Maybe he wanted to come back later with others involved in the conspiracy, or it could be that he waited inside the apartment for his compatriots to arrive, I don't know. But by the time the women were bound and cut and mutilated so savagely, they had been dead for a while, and it couldn't have been more obvious to me when I finally saw them.

"Up here we got about four inches already," Mr. Pieste says after a while, after he's heard enough. "That on top of ice. Did you get the ice down there in Cambridge?"

"I guess we should complain about this to someone," Mrs. Pieste says. "Does it matter how long it's been?"

"It never matters how long it's been when you're talking about the truth," I reply. "And there's no statute of limitation on homicide."

"I just hope they didn't lock up someone who shouldn't have been," Mrs. Pieste then says.

"The cases have remained unsolved. Attributed to black gang members but no arrests," I tell them.

"But it was probably someone white," she says.

"Someone white was drinking beer inside the apartment, that much I can say with reasonable certainty."

"Do you know who did it?" she asks.

"Because we would want them punished," her husband says.

"I only know the type of people who likely did it. Cowardly people all about power and politics. And you should do what you feel, what's in your heart."

"Eddie, what do you think?"

"I'll write a letter to Senator Chappel."

"You know how much good that will do."

"Then to Obama, Hillary Clinton, Joe Biden. I'll write everyone," he says.

"What will anybody do about it now?" Mrs. Pieste says to her husband. "I don't know that I can live through it again, Eddie."

"Well, I need to go clear the walk again," he says. "Got to stay on top of the snow, and it's really coming down. Thank you for your time and trouble, ma'am," he says to me. "And for going ahead and telling us. I know that wasn't an easy decision, and I'm sure my daughter would appreciate it if she was here to tell you herself."

After I hang up, I sit on the bed for a while, the paperwork and photographs back in the gray accordion file they've been in for more than two decades. I'll return the file to the safe in the basement, I decide. But not now. I don't feel like going down into the basement and into that safe right now, and I think someone has just pulled into our driveway. I hear snow crunching, and I'm not in a good state of mind to see whoever it is. I'll stay up here for a little while longer. Maybe make a grocery list or contemplate errands or just pet Sock for a minute or two.

"I can't take you for a walk," I tell him.

He is curled up next to me, his head on my thigh, unperturbed by the sad conversation he just overheard and having no idea what it says about the world he lives in. But then he knows cruelty, maybe knows it better than the rest of us.

"No walks without a coat," I go on, petting him, and he yawns and licks my hand, and I hear the beeping of the alarm being disarmed, then the front door shuts. "I think we're going to try boots," I tell Sock as Marino's and Benton's voices drift up from the entryway. "You probably aren't going to like these little shoes they make for dogs and are likely to get quite annoyed with me, but I promise it's a good thing. Well, we have company." I recognize Marino's heavy footsteps on the stairs. "You remember him from yesterday, in the big truck. The big man in yellow who gets on my nerves most of the time. But for future reference, you have no reason to be afraid of him. He's not a bad person, and as you may be aware, people who have known each other for a very long time tend to be ruder to each other than they are to people they don't like half as much."

"Anybody home?" Marino's big voice precedes him into the bedroom as the doorknob turns, and then he knocks as he opens the door. "Benton said you was decent. Who were you talking to? You on the phone?"

"He's clairvoyant, then," I reply from the bed, where I'm under the covers, nothing but pajamas on. "And I'm not on the phone and wasn't talking to anyone."

"How's Sock? How ya doing, boy?" he then says before I can answer. "How come he smells funny? What did you put on him, flea medicine? This time of year? You look okay. How are you feeling?"

"I cleaned his ears."

"So, how are you doing, Doc?"

Marino looms over me, and his presence seems larger than usual because he's in a heavy parka and a baseball cap and hiking boots while I'm in nothing but flannel, modestly tucked under a blanket and a duvet. He has a small black case in his hands that I recognize as Lucy's iPad, unless he's managed to get one of his own, which I doubt.

"I didn't get hurt. There's nothing wrong with me. I've just been staying in this morning, taking care of a few things," I say to him. "I'm assuming Dawn Kincaid is fine. Last I heard, she was stable."

"Stable? You're joking, right?"

"I'm talking about her physical condition. The reattachment of her finger and the damage to the rest of them, the other three that were cut so severely. It's probably a good thing for her it was so cold in the garage. And, of course, we thought to pack her hand and her severed finger in ice. I'm hoping that helped. Do you know? I haven't heard a word. What's her status? I've not heard any reports since she was admitted last night."

"You're kidding, right?" Marino's eyes look at me, and they're just as bloodshot as they were yesterday in Salem.

"I'm not kidding. Nobody's told me a word. Benton said earlier he would check, but I don't think he has."

"He's been on the phone with us all morning."

"Maybe you'd be so kind as to call the hospital and check."

"Like I give a flying fuck if she loses a

635

finger or all of her damn fingers," Marino says. "Why would you give a fuck? You afraid she'll sue you? That must be it, and wouldn't that figure? She probably will. Will sue you for maybe losing the use of her hand so she can't build nanobots or whatever anymore, a psycho like that. I guess psychopaths are stable in the mental illness sense of the word. Can you be crazy and a psychopath? And still be put together well enough to work at a place like Otwahl? Her case is going to be one big damn problem. If she gets out, well, can you imagine?"

"Why would she get out?"

"I'm just telling you the case is going to be a problem. You won't be safe if she's on the loose again. None of us will be."

He helps himself to the foot of the bed, and the bed sinks and it feels like I'm suddenly sitting uphill as he makes himself comfortable, petting Sock and informing me that the police and the FBI found the "rat hole" Dawn Kincaid had rented, a one-bedroom apartment in Revere, just outside of Boston, where she stayed when she wasn't with Eli Goldman or with her biological father, Jack Fielding, or whoever else she had entangled in her web at any point in time. Marino slips the iPad out of its case and turns it on as he lets me know that he and Lucy and quite a number of other investigators have been searching the rat-hole apartment for hours, going through Dawn's computer and everything she has, including everything she's stolen.

"What about her mother?" I ask. "Has anybody talked to her?"

"Dawn's been in contact with her for a number of years, visiting her in prison down there in Georgia now and then. Reconnected with her and with Fielding on and off over the years. Latches on when she wants something, a first-class manipulator and user."

"But does the mother know what's happened up here?"

"Why do you care what a fucking child molester thinks?"

"Her relationship with Jack wasn't that simple. It's not as easily explained as you so eloquently just put it. I'd hate for her to hear about him on the news."

"Who gives a shit."

"I never want anybody to find out that way," I reply. "I don't care who it is. Her relationship with him wasn't simple," I repeat. "Relationships like that never are."

"Plain and simple to me. Black and white."

"If she hears it on the news," I reply, and

637

I realize I'm perseverating. "I always hate for that to happen. Such an inhumane way for people to find out terrible things like this. That's my concern."

"A klepto," Marino then says, because his only interest is the case and what the investigators have been discovering at Dawn Kincaid's apartment.

Apparently, she is a bona fide klepto, to quote Marino. Someone who seemed to have taken souvenirs from all sorts of people, he goes on, including items stolen from people we have no idea about. But some of what investigators have found so far has been identified as jewelry and rare coins from the Donahue house, and also several rare autographed musical manuscripts that Mrs. Donahue had no idea were missing from the family library.

Recovered from a locked chest in a closet in Dawn's apartment were guns believed to have been removed from Fielding's collection, and his wedding band. Also in this same trunk, a martial-arts carry bag, I'm told, and inside it, a black satin sash, a white uniform, sparring gear, a lunch bag filled with rusty L-shaped flooring nails, and a hammer, and a pair of boy's Adidas tae kwon do shoes believed to be the ones Mark Bishop was wearing while practicing kicks in his backyard the late afternoon he was killed. Although no one is quite certain how Dawn lured the boy into lying facedown and allowing her to play some gruesome game with him that included "pretending" to hammer nails into his head, or more specifically, the first nail.

"The one that went in right here," Marino continues speculating, pointing to the space between the back of his neck and the base of his skull. "That would have killed him instantly, right?"

"If we must use that phrase," I reply.

"I mean, she probably helped him in some of Fielding's Tiny Tiger classes, maybe?" he continues to spin the story. "So the kid's familiar with her, looks up to her, and she's hot, I mean really good-looking. If it was me, I'd tell the kid I'm going to show him a new move or something and to lie down in the yard. And of course the kid's going to do what an expert says, what someone teaching him says, and he lies down and it's almost dark out and then boom! It's over."

"Someone like that can never get out," I reply. "She'll do more and do it worse next time, if that's even possible."

"Denying everything. She's not talking, except to say Fielding did it all and she's innocent."

"He didn't."

"I'm with you."

"She's going to have a hard time explaining what's in her apartment," I point out, as I continue going through photographs. Marino must have taken hundreds.

"She's good-looking and charming and smart as hell. And Fielding's dead."

"Incriminating." I've said this several times as I look through the photographs on the iPad. "Should be very helpful to the prosecution. I'm not sure why you think the case will be a problem."

"It's going to be. The defense will pin it all on Fielding. The psycho bitch will get a dream team of big-shot lawyers, and they'll make the jury believe Fielding did all of it." Marino leans closer to me, and the slope of the bed changes again, and Sock is snoring quietly, not interested in his former owner or her rat hole, which has a dog bed in it, Marino shows me.

He leans close to me, clicking through several photographs of the dog's plaid bed and several toys, and I indicate I'd rather look at the photographs myself. He and Sock are on top of me, and I'm feeling smothered.

"I just thought I'd show you, since I'm the one who took them," Marino says.

"Thank you. I'll manage. You did a very good job with the photographs."

"Point is, it's obvious the dog stayed here." Marino means Sock stayed in Dawn Kincaid's rat hole. "And also with Eli and with Fielding," he adds. "To give her credit, I guess she liked her dog."

"She left him in Jack's house with no heat and all alone." I click through photographs that are overwhelmingly incriminating.

"She doesn't give a shit unless it suits her. When it doesn't, she gets rid of it one way or another. So she cared about him when it suited her."

"That's the more likely story," I agree.

I look at photographs of an unmade double bed, then other pictures of a tiny bedroom shockingly filled with junk, as if Dawn Kincaid is a hoarder.

"Plus, she had another reason to leave him," Marino goes on. "If she leaves the dog at Fielding's house, then maybe we think he's the one who killed everyone, then killed himself. The dog is there. His red leash is there. The boat that was probably used to dump Wally Jamison's body is there, and Wally's clothes and the murder weapon are in Fielding's basement. The Navigator with the missing front plate is there. You're supposed to think Fielding was following you and Benton when you left Hanscom. Fielding's deranged. He's watching you. He's following you, trying to intimidate you, or spying, or maybe he was going to kill you, too."

"He was dead by the time we were followed. Although I can't be exact about time of death, I'm calculating he'd been dead since Monday afternoon, probably was murdered not long after he got home to Salem after leaving the CFC with the Glock he'd removed from the lab. It was Dawn in the Navigator tailing us Monday night. She's the one deranged. She rode our bumper to make sure we knew we were being followed, then disappeared, probably ducked out of sight in Otwahl's parking lot. So eventually we'd think it was Jack, who in fact already had been murdered by her with a pistol she probably gave to her boyfriend, Eli, before she murdered him, too. But you're right. It's likely she tried to set things up so all of it got blamed on Jack, who isn't around to defend himself. She set up Jack and made it look like he was setting up Johnny Donahue. It's terrifying."

"You got to make the jury buy it."

"That's always the challenge, no matter the case."

"It's bad the dog was at Fielding's house,"

Marino repeats. "It connects him to Eli's murder. Hell, it's on video clips that Eli was walking the dog when he was whacked."

"The microchip," I remind him. "It traces back to Dawn, not to Jack."

"Doesn't mean anything. He kills Eli and then takes the dog, and the dog would know Fielding, right?" Marino says, as if Sock isn't inches away from him, sleeping with his head on my leg. "The dog would be familiar with Fielding because Dawn was staying over there in Salem, had the dog at Fielding's house some of the time or whatever. So Fielding kills Eli, then takes the dog as he walks off, or this is what Dawn wants us to think."

"It's not what happened. Jack didn't kill anyone," as I conclude that Dawn's apartment has the same brand of squalor that I observed at Fielding's house in Salem.

Clutter and boxes everywhere. Clothes piled in mounds and strewn in odd places. Dishes piled in the sink. Trash overflowing. Mounds of newspapers, computer printouts, magazines, and on a dining-room table, a large number of items tagged and placed there by police, including a GPS-enabled sports watch that is the same model as one I gave Fielding for his birthday several years ago, and a Civil War military dissection set in a rosewood case that is identical to one I gave him when he worked for me in Richmond.

There is a close-up of a pair of black gloves, one of them with a small black box on the wrist, what Marino describes as lightweight flexible wireless data gloves with built-in accelerometers, thirty-six sensors, and an ultra-low-profile integrated transmitter-receiver, only I have to infer all this, sift it out of his mispronunciations and mangled descriptions. The gloves, which were closely examined by both Briggs and Lucy at the scene, are clearly intended for gesture-based robotic control — specifically, to control the flybot that Eli had with him when he was murdered by the woman who had given him the stolen signet ring he was wearing when his body came to the CFC.

"Then the flybot was in her apartment," I presume. "And did Benton offer you any coffee?"

"I'm coffeed out. Some of us haven't been to bed yet."

"I'm in bed working. Doesn't mean I've slept."

"Must be nice. I'd like to stay home and work in bed." He takes the iPad from me and searches through files.

"Maybe we could adjust your job description. You can stay home and work in bed a certain number of days each year, depending on your age and decrepitude, which we'll have to evaluate. I suppose I'll be the one to evaluate it."

"Oh, yeah? Who's gonna evaluate yours?" He finds a photograph he wants me to see.

"Mine doesn't need evaluating. It's obvious to one and all."

He shows me a close-up of the flybot, only at a glance it's hard to know what it is, just a shiny, wiry object on a square of white paper on Dawn Kincaid's dining-room table. The micromechanical device could be an earring, it occurs to me. A silver earring that was stepped on, which is exactly what is suspected, Marino tells me. Lucy thinks the flybot was stepped on while the EMTs were working on Eli, then later Dawn found it when she returned to Norton's Woods, possibly wearing the same long black wool coat that she had on in my garage, a coat that I believe was Fielding's. A witness claims to have observed a young man or woman, the person wasn't sure which, in a big black coat walking around Norton's Woods with a flashlight, several hours after Eli Goldman died there. The individual in the big coat was out there alone, and the person who saw him or her thought it was strange because he or she did not have a dog and seemed to be looking for something while making odd hand gestures.

"It must have been huge on her and practically dragged on the ground," Marino says, getting up from the bed. "I'm not saying she was trying to look like a man, but with her short hair and the big coat, and a hat and glasses on or whatever? As long as you don't see her rack. She's got quite a rack. Has that in common with her dad, right?"

"I've never known Jack to have large breasts."

"I mean both of them built."

"So she returned when she assumed it was safe to do so, and even though the flybot was badly damaged, it responded to radio frequency signals sent by the data gloves?" I turn off the iPad and hand it to him.

"I think she just saw it on the ground, think it was shiny in the flashlight and she found it that way. Lucy says the bug is DOA. Squashed."

"Do we know exactly what it does or was supposed to do?"

Marino shrugs, towering over me again, still in his parka, which he hasn't bothered to unbutton, as if he didn't intend to stay long. "This isn't my area of expertise, you know. I didn't understand half of what they were talking about, Lucy and the general. I just know the potential for whatever this thing is supposed to do is something to be concerned about, and DoD intends to do some sort of inspection of Otwahl to see what the hell is really going on over there. But I'm not sure we don't already know exactly what the hell is going on over there."

"Meaning what?"

He returns the iPad to its case and says, "Meaning I worry there's R-and-D going on that the government damn well knows about but just doesn't want anyone else to know, and then you get kids out of control and the shit hits the fan. I think you get my drift. When are you coming back to work?"

"Probably not today," I tell him.

"Well, we got a shitload of things to do and undo," he says.

"Thanks for the warning."

"Buzz me if you need something. I'll call the hospital and let you know how the psycho's doing."

"Thanks for stopping by."

I wait until the sound of his heavy footsteps stops at the front door, and then the door shuts again, and then a pause, and Benton resets the alarm. I hear his footsteps, which are much lighter than Marino's, as he walks past the stairs, toward the back of the house where he has his office.

"Come on, let's get up," I say to Sock, and he opens his eyes and looks at me and yawns. "Do you know what bye-bye means? I guess not. They didn't teach you that at the prison. You just want to sleep, don't you? Well, I've got things to do, so come on. You're really quite lazy, you know. Are you sure you ever won a race or even ran in one? I don't think I believe it."

I move his head and put my feet on the floor, deciding there must be a pet shop around here that has everything a skinny, lazy old greyhound might need for this kind of weather.

"Let's go for a ride." I talk to Sock as I find my slippers and a robe. "Let's see what Secret Agent Wesley is doing. He's probably in his office on the phone again, what do you bet? I know, he's always on the phone, and I agree, it's quite annoying.

"Maybe he'll take us shopping, and then I'm going to make a very nice pasta, home-made pappardelle with a hearty Bolognese sauce, ground veal, red wine, and lots of mushrooms and garlic.

"I need to explain up front that you only get canine cuisine; that's the rule of the house. I'm thinking quinoa and cod for you today." I continue talking as we go down the stairs. "That will be a nice change after all that chicken and rice from the Greek diner."

ABOUT THE AUTHOR

Patricia Cornwell is author of seventeen previous novels featuring Dr. Kay Scarpetta. Her most recent bestsellers include *The Scarpetta Factor, Scarpetta, The Front, Book of the Dead, At Risk,* and *Portrait of a Killer: Jack the Ripper—Case Closed.* Her earlier works include *Postmortem*—the only novel to win the Edgar, Creasey, Anthony, and Macavity awards and the French Prix du Roman d'Aventure in a single year—and *Cruel and Unusual,* which won Britain's prestigious Gold Dagger Award for the best crime novel in 1993. *Book of the Dead* won the 2008 Galaxy British Book Awards' Books Direct Crime Thriller of the Year award, making Cornwell the first American to win this prestigious U.K. award. Dr. Kay Scarpetta herself won the 1999 Sherlock Award for the best detective created by an American author.

RANDOM
HOUSE
LARGE
PRINT

A Traitor
to
Memory

Elizabeth George

RANDOM HOUSE
LARGE PRINT

Library of Congress
Cataloging-in-Publication Data
George, Elizabeth.
A traitor to memory / by Elizabeth George.
p. cm.
ISBN 0-375-43113-6
1. Violinists—Fiction.   2. England—Fiction.
3. Large type books.   I. Title.

PS3557.E478 T72 2001
813'.54—dc21
00-054695

1   3   5   7   9   10   8   6   4   2

FIRST LARGE PRINT EDITION

This Large Print Edition published in
accord with the standards of the N.A.V.H.

For the other Jones girl,
wherever she might be

"O my son Absalom,
My son, my son, Absalom!
Would God I had died for thee."

II Samuel
Chapter 19
Verse 4

A Traitor
to
Memory

*F*AT GIRLS *can do. Fat girls can do. Fat girls can do and do and do.*

As she trod the pavement towards her car, Katie Waddington used her regular mantra in rhythm with her lumbering pace. She said the words mentally instead of aloud, not so much because she was alone and afraid of seeming batty but rather because to say them aloud would put further demands on her labouring lungs. And they had trouble enough to keep going. As did her heart which, according to her always sententious GP, was not intended to pump blood through arteries that were being fast encroached upon by fat.

When he looked at her, he saw rolls of flesh, he saw mammae hanging like two heavy flour sacks from her shoulders, he saw a stomach that drooped to cover her pubis and skin that was cratered with cellulite. She was carrying so much weight on her frame that she could live for a year on her own tissues without eating, and if the doctor was to be believed, the fat was moving in on her vital organs. If she didn't do something to curb herself at table, he declared each time she saw him, she was going to be a goner.

"Heart failure or stroke, Kathleen," he told her with a shake of his head. "Choose your poison. Your condition calls for immediate action, and that action is *not* intended to include ingesting anything that can turn into adipose tissue. Do you understand?"

How could she not? It was *her* body they were talking about and one couldn't be the size of a hippo in a business suit without noticing that fact when the opportunity arose to have a glimpse at one's reflection.

But the truth of the matter was that her GP was the only person in Katie's life who had difficulty accepting her as the terminally fat girl she'd been from childhood. And since the people who counted took her as she was, she had no motivation to shed the thirteen stone that her doctor was recommending.

If Katie had ever harboured a doubt about being embraced by a world of people who were increasingly buffed, toned, and sculpted, she'd had her worth reaffirmed this night as it was every Monday, Wednesday, and Friday when her Eros in Action groups met from seven till ten o'clock. There, the sexually dysfunctional populace of Greater London came together for solace and solution. Directed by Katie Waddington—who'd made the study of human sexuality her lifelong passion—libidos were examined; erotomania and -phobia were dissected; frigidity, nymphomania, satyrism, transvestitism, and fetishisms were admitted to; erotic fantasies were encouraged; and erotic imagination was stimulated.

"You saved our marriage," her clients gushed. Or their lives, or their sanity, or frequently their careers.

Sex is commerce was Katie's motto, and she had nearly twenty years of approximately six thousand grateful clients and a waiting list of two hundred more to prove this true.

So she walked to her car in a state that was somewhere between self-satisfaction and absolute rapture. She might be anorgasmic herself, but who was to know as long as she had success in consistently promoting happy orgasm in others? And that's what the public wanted, after all: guilt-free sexual release upon demand.

Who guided them to it? A fat girl did.

Who absolved them of the shame of their desires? A fat girl did.

Who taught them everything from stimulating erogenous zones to simulating passion till passion returned? A terminally hugely preposterously fat girl from Canterbury did and did and did.

That was more important than counting calories. If Katie Waddington was meant to die fat, then that was the way she'd die.

It was a cool night, just the way she liked it. Autumn had finally come to the city after a beastly summer, and as she trundled along in the darkness Katie relived, as she always did, the high points of her evening's group session.

Tears. Yes, there were always tears as well as hand wringing, blushing, stammering, and sweating aplenty. But there was generally a special moment as well, a breakthrough moment that made listening to hours of repetitious personal details finally worth-while.

Tonight that moment had come in the persons of Felix and Dolores (last names withheld) who'd joined EiA with the express purpose of "recapturing the magic" of their marriage after each of them had spent two years—and twenty thousand pounds—in explor-ing their individual sexual issues. Felix had long since admitted seeking satisfaction outside the realm of his wedding vows, and Dolores had herself owned up to enjoying her vibrator and a picture of Laurence Olivier as Heathcliff far more than the marital em-brace of her spouse. But on this night, Felix's rumina-tions on why the sight of Dolores's bare bum brought on thoughts of his mother in her declining years was too much for three of the middle-aged women in the group who attacked him verbally and so viciously that Dolores herself sprang passionately to his defence, ap-parently flooding away her husband's aversion to her backside with the sacred water of her tears. Husband and wife subsequently fell into each other's arms, lip-locked, and cried out in unison, "You've saved our marriage!" at the meeting's conclusion.

She'd done nothing more than give them a forum, Katie admitted to herself. But that's all some people really wanted, anyway: an opportunity to humiliate themselves or their beloved in public, creating a situ-ation from which the beloved could ultimately rescue or be provided rescue.

There was a genuine gold mine in dealing with the

sexual dilemmas of the British population. Katie considered herself more than astute to have realised that fact.

She yawned widely and felt her stomach growl. A good day's work and a good evening's work meant a good meal as a reward to herself followed by a good wallow with a video. She favoured old films for their nuances of romance. Fading to black at the crucial moment got her juices flowing far more efficiently than close-ups of body parts and a sound track filled with heavy breathing. *It Happened One Night* would be her choice: Clark and Claudette and all that delicious tension between them.

That's what's missing in most relationships, Katie thought for the thousandth time that month. Sexual tension. There's nothing left to the imagination between men and women any longer. It's a know-all, tell-all, photograph-all world, with nothing to anticipate and even less left secret.

But she couldn't complain. The state of the world was making her rich, and fat though she was, no one gave her aggro when they saw the house she lived in, the clothes she wore, the jewellery she bought, or the car she drove.

She approached that car now, where she'd left it that morning, in a private car park across the street and round the corner from the clinic in which she spent her days. She found that she was breathing more heavily than usual as she paused on the kerb before crossing. She put one hand on a lamppost for support and felt her heart struggling to keep to its job.

Perhaps she *ought* to consider the weight loss programme her doctor had suggested, she thought. But
a second later, she rejected the idea. What was life *for*
if not to be enjoyed?

A breeze came up and blew her hair from her
cheeks. She felt it cooling the back of her neck. A
minute of rest was all she needed. She'd be fit as ever
when she caught her breath.

She stood and listened to the silent neighbourhood. It was partly commercial and partly residential,
with businesses that were closed at this hour and
houses long ago converted to flats with windows
whose curtains were drawn against the night.

Odd, she thought. She'd never really noticed the
quiet or the emptiness of these streets after dark. She
looked round and realised that anything could happen in this sort of place—anything good, anything
bad—and it would be solely left to chance if there
was a witness to what occurred.

A chill coursed through her. Better to move on.

She stepped off the kerb. She began to cross.

She didn't see the car at the end of the street till its
lights switched on and blinded her. It barreled towards her with a sound like a bull.

She tried to hurry forward, but the car was fast
upon her. She was far too fat to get out of its way.

GIDEON

16 AUGUST

I WANT to begin by saying that I believe this exercise to be a waste of my time, which, as I attempted to tell you yesterday, is exactly what I do not have to spare just now. If you wanted me to have faith in the efficacy of this activity, you might have given me the paradigm upon which you are apparently basing what goes for "treatment" in your book. Why does it matter what paper I use? What notebook? What pen or what pencil? And what difference does it make where I actually do this nonsensical writing that you're requiring of me? Isn't the simple fact that I've *agreed* to this experiment enough for you?

Never mind. Don't reply. I already know what your answer would be: Where is all this anger coming from, Gideon? What's beneath it? What do you recall?

Nothing. Don't you see? I recall absolutely nothing. That's why I've come.

Nothing? you say. Nothing at all? Are you sure

that's true? You do know your name, after all. And
apparently you know your father as well. And where
you live. And what you do for a living. And your
closest associates. So when you say nothing, you must
actually be telling me that you remember—

Nothing *important* to me. All right. I'll say it. I remember nothing that I count as important. Is that
what you want to hear? And shall you and I dwell on
what nasty little detail about my character I reveal
with that declaration?

Instead of answering those two questions, however, you tell me that we'll begin by writing what
we do remember—whether it's important or not.
But when you say *we,* you really mean *I'll* begin by
writing and what I'll write is what *I* remember. Because as you so succinctly put it in your objective,
untouchable psychiatrist's voice, "What we remember can often be the key to what we've chosen to
forget."

Chosen. I expect that was a deliberate selection of
words. You wanted to get a reaction from me. I'll
show her, I'm supposed to think. I'll just show the little termagant how much I can remember.

How old are you, anyway, Dr. Rose? You say
thirty, but I don't believe that. You're not even my
age, I suspect, and what's worse you look like a
twelve-year-old. How am I supposed to have confidence in you? Do you honestly think you're going to
be an adequate substitute for your father? It was he I
agreed to see, by the way. Did I mention that when
we first met? I doubt it. I felt too sorry for you. The

only reason I decided to stay, by the way, when I walked into the office and saw you instead of him is that you looked so pathetic sitting there, dressed all in black as if that could make you look like someone competent to handle people's mental crises.

Mental? you ask me, leaping onto the word as if it were a runaway train. So you've decided to accept the conclusion of the neurologist? Are you satisfied with that? You don't need any further tests in order to be convinced? That's very good, Gideon. That's a fine step forward. It will make our work together easier if you've been persuaded that there's no physiological explanation for what you're experiencing.

How well spoken you are, Dr. Rose. A voice like velvet. What I should have done was turn straight round and come back home as soon as you opened your mouth. But I didn't because you manoeuvred me into staying, didn't you, with that "I wear black because my husband died" nonsense. You wanted to evoke my sympathy, didn't you? Forge a bond with the patient, you've been told. Win his trust. Make him *suggestible*.

Where's Dr. Rose? I ask you as I enter the office.

You say, I'm Dr. Rose. Dr. Alison Rose. Perhaps you were expecting my father? He had a stroke eight months ago. He's recovering now, but it's going to take some time, so he's not able to see patients just now. I've taken over his practise.

And away you go, chatting about how it came about that you returned to London, about how you miss Boston, but that's all right because the memories were too painful there. Because of him, because of your husband, you tell me. You even go so far as to give me his name: Tim Freeman. And his disease: colon cancer. And how old he was when he died: thirty-seven. And how you'd put off having children because you'd been in medical school when you first got married and when it finally came time to think of reproducing, he was fighting for his life and you were fighting for his life as well and there was no room for a child in that battle.

And I, Dr. Rose, felt sorry for you. So I stayed. And as a result of that staying, I'm now sitting at the first-floor window overlooking Chalcot Square. I'm writing this rubbish with a biro so that I can't erase anything, per your instructions. I'm using a loose-leaf notebook so that I can add where necessary if something miraculously comes to me later. And what I'm not doing is what I ought to be doing and what the whole world expects me to be doing: standing side by side with Raphael Robson, making that infernal ubiquitous nothing between the notes disappear.

Raphael Robson? I can hear you query. Tell me about Raphael Robson, you say.

I had milk in my coffee this morning, and I'm paying for it now, Dr. Rose. My stomach's on fire. The flames are licking downwards through my gut. Fire moves up, but not inside me. It happens the opposite, and it always feels the same. Common distension of the stomach and the bowels, my GP tells me. Flatus, he intones, as if he's offering me a medical benediction. Charlatan, quack, and fourth-rate saw-bones.

I've got something malignant devouring my intestines and he calls it wind.

Tell me about Raphael Robson, you repeat.

Why? I ask. Why Raphael?

Because he's a place to start. Your mind is giving you the place to start, Gideon. That's how this process is going to work.

But Raphael isn't the beginning, I inform you. The beginning is twenty-five years ago, in a Peabody House, in Kensington Square.

17 AUGUST

That's where I lived. Not in one of the Peabody Houses, but in my grandparents' house on the south side of the square. The Peabody Houses are long gone now, replaced by two restaurants and a boutique the last time I checked. Still, I remember those houses well and how my father employed them to fabricate the Gideon Legend.

That's how he is, my father, ever prepared to use what comes to hand if it has the potential to get him where he wants to go. He was restless in those days, always full of ideas. I see now that most of his ideas were attempts to allay my grandfather's fears about him, since in Granddad's eyes, Dad's failure to establish himself in the Army presaged his failure at everything else as well. And Dad knew that's what Granddad believed about him, I suppose. After all, Granddad wasn't a man who ever kept his opinions to himself.

He hadn't been well since the war, my grandfather. I supposed that's why we lived with him and Gran. He'd spent two years in Burma as a prisoner of the Japanese, and he'd never recovered from that completely. I suspect that being a prisoner had triggered something inside him that would have remained dormant otherwise. But in any event, all I was ever told about the situation was that Granddad had "episodes" which called for his being carted off for a "nice countryside holiday" every now and again. I can't remember any specific details about these episodes, as my grandfather died when I was ten. But I do remember that they always began with some fierce and frightening banging about, followed by my grandmother weeping, and my grandfather shouting "You're no son of mine" at my father as they took him away.

They? you ask me. Who are they?

The goblin people is what I called them. They looked like anyone else on the street, but their bodies were inhabited by snatchers of the soul. Dad always let them into the house. Gran always met them on the stairs, crying. And they always passed her without a word because all the words they had to say had already been said more than once. They'd been coming for Granddad for years, you see. Long before I was born. Long before I watched from between the stairway balusters, crouched there like a little toad and frightened.

Yes. Before you ask, I do remember that fear. And

something else as well. I remember someone drawing me away from the balusters, someone who peeled off my fingers one by one to loosen my grip and lead me away.

Raphael Robson? you're asking me, aren't you? Is this where Raphael Robson appears?

But no. This is years before Raphael Robson. Raphael came after the Peabody House.

So we're back to the Peabody House, you say.

Yes. The House and the Gideon Legend.

19 AUGUST

Do I remember the Peabody House? Or have I manufactured the details to fill in an outline that my father gave me? If I couldn't remember what it smelled like inside, I would say that I was merely playing a game by my father's rules to be able to conjure the Peabody House out of my brain at a time like this. But because the scent of bleach can still transport me back to the Peabody House in an instant, I know the foundation of the tale is true, no matter how much of it has been embroidered upon over the years by my father, my publicist, and the journalists who've spoken to them both. Frankly, I myself no longer answer questions about the Peabody House. I say, "That's old ground. Let's till some fresh soil this time round."

But journalists always want a hook for their story and, limited by my father's firm injunction that only my career is open for discussion when I'm interviewed, what better hook could there be than the one my father created out of a simple stroll in the garden of Kensington Square:

I am three years old and in the company of my grandfather. I have with me a tricycle on which I am trundling round the perimeter of the garden while Granddad sits in that Greek-temple affair that serves as a shelter near the wrought iron fence. Granddad has brought a newspaper to read, but he isn't reading. Instead, he's listening to some music coming from one of the buildings behind him.

He says to me in a hushed voice, "It's called a concerto, Gideon. This is Paganini's D major concerto. Listen." He beckons me to his side. He sits at the very end of the bench and I stand next to him with his arm round my shoulders, and I listen.

And I know in an instant that this is what I want to do. I somehow know as a three-year-old what has never left me since: that to listen is to be but to play is to live.

I insist that we leave the garden at once. Granddad's hands are arthritic and they struggle with the gate. I demand that he hurry "before it's too late."

"Too late for what?" he asks me fondly.

I grab his hand and show him.

I lead him to the Peabody House, which is where the music is coming from. And then we're inside, where a lino floor has recently been washed and the air stings our eyes with the smell of bleach.

Up on the first floor, we find the source of the Paganini concerto. One of the bed-sitting rooms is

the dwelling place of Miss Rosemary Orr, long retired from the London Philharmonic. She is standing
in front of a large wall mirror, and she's got a violin
under her chin and a bow in her hand. She isn't playing the Paganini, though. Instead, she's listening to a
recording of it with her eyes closed and her bow
hand lowered and tears coursing down her cheeks
and onto the wood of her instrument.

"She's going to wreck it, Granddad," I inform my
grandfather. And this rouses Miss Orr, who starts and
no doubt wonders how an arthritic old gentleman
and a runny-nosed boy come to be standing at the
door to her room.

But there is no time for her to voice any conster-
nation, for I go to her and take the instrument from
her hands. And I begin to play.

Not well, of course, for who would believe that an
untrained three-year-old no matter his natural talent
could possibly pick up a violin and play Paganini's
Concerto in D Major the first time he's heard it? But
the raw materials are there within me—the ear, the
inherent balance, the passion—and Miss Orr sees this
and insists that she be allowed to instruct the precocious child.

So she becomes my first instructor in the violin.
And I remain with her until I am four and a half years
old, at which time it is decided that a less conventional manner of instruction is required for my talent.

So that is the Gideon Legend, Dr. Rose. Do you
know the violin well enough to see where it lapses
into fantasy?

We've managed to promulgate the legend by actually calling it a legend, by laughing it off even as it is told. We say, Stuff and nonsense, all of it. But we say that with a suggestive smile. Miss Orr's long dead, so she can't refute the story. And after Miss Orr there was Raphael Robson, who has limited investments to make in the truth.

But here's the truth for you, Dr. Rose, because despite what you may think concerning my reaction to this exercise in which I've agreed to engage, I am interested in telling you the truth.

I am in the garden of Kensington Square that day with a summer play group sponsored by a nearby convent, populated by the infant inhabitants of the square, and directed by three of the college students who live in a hostel behind the convent. We are collected daily from our individual houses by one or another of our three keepers and we are led hand-in-hand into the central garden where, it is hoped and for a nominal fee, we will learn the social skills that are engendered through cooperative play. This will stand us in good stead when we take our places at primary school. Or so the plan is.

The college students occupy us with games, with crafts, and with exercise. And once we are set busily to whatever task they've chosen that day, they—unbeknownst to our parents—repair to that same Greek-temple affair where they chat amongst themselves and smoke cigarettes.

This particular day is earmarked for biking although what passes for biking is actually tricycle riding round the perimeter of the garden. And while I trundle round and round on my tricycle at the tail end of the small pack, a boy like myself—although I don't remember his name—takes out his willie and urinates openly upon the lawn. A crisis ensues, during which the malefactor is marched directly home amid a thorough telling-off.

This is when the music begins, and the two college students who remain after the child has been removed haven't the slightest idea what it is that we're listening to. But I want to go to that sound and I insist with a force so unusual in me that one of the students—it's an Italian girl, I think, because her English isn't good although her heart is big—says that she will help me track it down. And so we do, to the Peabody House where we meet Miss Orr.

She is neither playing, pretending to play, nor weeping when the college girl and I find her in her sitting room. Rather, she is giving a music lesson. She ends every lesson—I learn—by playing a piece of music on her stereo for her student. Today she is playing the Brahms concerto.

Do I like music? she wants to know.

I have no answer. I don't know if I like it, if what I feel is liking or something else. I only know that I want to be able to make those sounds. But I'm shy and say nothing of this, and I hide behind the Italian girl's legs until she clutches my hand and apologises in her broken English and shoos me back to the garden.

And that's the reality.

You want to know, naturally, how this inauspicious

beginning to my life in music metamorphosed into the Gideon Legend. How, in other words, did the discarded weapon left—shall we say?—to collect one hundred years of lime deposits in a cave become Excalibur, the Sword in the Stone? I can only speculate, as the Legend is my father's invention and not my own.

The children from the play group were taken to their homes by their student keepers at the end of the day, and reports were given on each child's development and comportment. What else were the parents spending their money on if not to receive hopeful daily indications that a suitable level of social maturity was being achieved?

God knows what the display in public of what should have been a private bodily function earned the willie waver that afternoon. In my case, the Italian student reported on my meeting with Rosemary Orr.

This would have occurred in the sitting room, I dare say, where Gran would have been presiding over the afternoon tea she never failed to make for Granddad, enveloping him in an aura of normalcy as a hedge against the intrusion of an episode. Perhaps my father was there as well, perhaps we were joined by James the Lodger, who helped us make ends meet by renting one of the vacant bedrooms on the fourth floor of the house.

The Italian student—although let me say now that she might as easily have been Greek or Spanish or

Portuguese—would have been invited to join the family for refreshment, which would then have given her the opportunity to tell the tale of our meeting with Rosemary Orr.

She says, "The little one, he wants to find this music we are listening, so we trail it up—"

"She means 'hearing' and 'track it down,' I think," the lodger interposes. His name is James, as I've said, and I've heard Granddad complain that his English is "too bloody perfect to be real" so he must be a spy. But I like to listen to him anyway. Words come from James the Lodger's mouth like oranges, plump and juicy and round. He himself is none of that, except for his cheeks, which are red and get redder still when he realises everyone is attending to him. He says, "Do go on," to the Italian-Spanish-Greek-Portuguese student. "Don't take the slightest notice of me."

And she smiles because she likes the lodger. She'd like him to help her with her English, I expect. She'd like to be friends with him.

I myself have no friends—despite the play group—but I don't notice their absence because I have my family, and I bask in their love. Unlike most children of three, I do not lead an existence separate from the adults in my limited world: taking my meals alone, entertained and exposed to life by a nanny or some other child minder, making periodic appearances in the bosom of the family, spinning my wheels until such a time as I can be packed off to school. Instead,

I am *of* the world of the adults with whom I live. So I see and hear much of what happens in my home and if I don't remember events, I remember the impressions of events.

So I recall this: the story of the violin music being told and Granddad plunging into the midst of the tale with an expatiation on Paganini. Gran's used music for years to soothe him when he's teetering on the edge of an episode and while there's still a hope of heading it off, and he talks about trills and bowing, about vibrato and glissandi with what sounds like authority but is likely, I know now, delusion. He's big and booming in his grandiloquence, an orchestra in and of himself. And no one interrupts or disagrees when he says to everyone but in reference to me, "This boy shall play," like God declaring Himself for light.

Dad hears this, attaches to it a significance that he shares with no one, and swiftly makes all the necessary arrangements.

So it is that I come to receive my first lessons in the violin from Miss Rosemary Orr. And from these lessons and from that report from the play group, my father develops the Gideon Legend which I've dragged through life like a ball and chain.

But why did he make it a story about your grandfather? you want to know, don't you? Why not just keep the central characters but fudge on the details here and there? Wasn't he worried that someone would step forward, refute the story, and tell the real tale?

I give you the only answer I can, Dr. Rose: You'll have to ask my father.

21 AUGUST

I remember those first lessons with Rosemary Orr: my impatience locking horns with her devotion to minutiae. "Find your body, Gideon dear, find your body," she says. And with a one-sixteenth tucked between my chin and my shoulder—for this was in the days when that was the smallest instrument one could obtain—I endure Miss Orr's perpetual adjustments to my position. She arches my fingers over the fingerboard; she stiffens my left wrist; she grips my shoulder to prevent its intrusion into the bowing; she straightens my back and uses a long pointer to tap the insides of my legs to alter my stance. All along while I play— when she at last *allows* me to play—her voice rings out above the scales and arpeggios that are my initial assignments: "Body up, shoulder down, Gideon dear." "Thumb under *this* part of the bow, not on the silver part, please, and not on the side." "The whole *arm* up-bows." "Strokes are big and detached." "No, no! You use the *fleshy* part of the fingers, dear." Continually, she has me play one note and set up for the next. Over and over we engage in this exercise until she is satisfied that all body parts which exist as extensions of the right hand—that is to say the wrist, the elbow, the arm, and the shoulder blade—function along with the bow like an axis and wheel, with the body parts keeping the bow on course.

I learn that my fingers must work independently of each other. I learn to find that balancing point on the fingerboard which will later allow my fingers to shift as if through air alone from one position to the next on the strings. I learn to listen for and to find the ringing tone of my instrument. I learn up bow and down bow, the golden mean, *staccato* and *legato, sul tasto* and *sul ponticello.*

In short, I learn method, theory, and principle, but what I do not learn is what I hunger to learn: how to rupture the spirit to bring forth the sound.

I persevere with Miss Rosemary Orr for eighteen months, but soon I tire of the soulless exercises that dominate my time. Soulless exercises were not what I heard issuing forth from her window that day in the square, and I rail against having to be part of them. I hear Miss Orr excuse this to my father, "He is, after all, a very small child. It's to be expected that, at such a young age, his interest wouldn't be held for long." But my father—who is already doing two jobs to keep the family at Kensington Square—has not attended my thrice-weekly lessons and thus he can't perceive the manner in which they're bleeding life from the music I love.

My grandfather, however, has been there all along because during the eighteen months that I have been with Miss Orr, he has not experienced anything resembling an episode. So he's taken me to my lessons and he's listened from a corner of the room, and with his sharp eyes absorbing the form and the content of my lessons and his parched soul thirsty for Paganini, he has drawn the conclusion that his grandson's prodigious talent is being held back, not nurtured, by well-meaning Rosemary Orr.

"He wants to make *music,* damn it," Granddad roars at my father when they discuss the situation. "The boy's a bloody *artist,* Dick, and if you can't see that much when it's painted in front of you, you've got no brains and you're no son of mine. Would you feed a thoroughbred from the pig trough? I don't bloody think so, Richard."

Perhaps it is fear that garners my father's cooperation, fear that another episode will be forthcoming if he does not acquiesce in Granddad's plan. And it is a plan that my grandfather makes immediately apparent: We live in Kensington, no great distance from the Royal College of Music, and it is there that a suitable instructor of the violin shall be found for his grandson Gideon.

So it is that my grandfather becomes my saviour and the trustee of my unspoken dreams. So it is that Raphael Robson enters my life.

22 AUGUST

I am four years and six months old, and although I know now that Raphael would only have been in his early thirties at the time, to me he is a distant, awesome figure who commands my complete obedience from the first moment we meet.

He isn't a pleasing figure to behold. He sweats copiously. I can see his skull through his baby-fine hair.

His skin is the white of river-fish flesh and it is patched with scales from too much time in the sun. But when Raphael picks up his violin and plays for me—for that is our introduction to each other— whatever he looks like fades to insignificance, and I am clay for him to mould. He chooses the Mendelssohn E minor, and he gives his entire body to the music.

He doesn't play notes; he exists within sounds. The allegro fireworks he produces on his instrument mesmerise me. In a moment he has been transformed. He is no sweating, patchy-skinned cough drop, but Merlin, and I want his magic for myself.

Raphael doesn't teach method, I discover, saying in his interview with my grandfather that "It's the work of the violinist to develop his own method." Instead, he improvises exercises for me. He leads and I follow. "Rise to the *opportunity*," he instructs me over his own playing and watching mine. "*Enrich* that vibrato. Don't be afraid of *portamenti*, Gideon. Slide. Make them flow. *Slide.*"

And this is how I begin my real life as a violinist, Dr. Rose, because all that has gone before with Miss Orr was a prelude. I take three lessons a week at first, then four, and then five. Each lesson lasts three hours. I go at first to Raphael's office at the Royal College of Music, Granddad and I on the bus from Kensington High Street. But the extended hours of waiting for me to finish my lessons are a trouble to Granddad, and everyone in the house is terrified that they will provoke an episode sooner or later without my grandmother there to contend with it. So eventually an arrangement must be made for Raphael Robson to come to me.

The cost is, of course, enormous. One does not ask a violinist of Raphael's calibre to commit vast stretches of his teaching time to one small student without recompensing him for his travel, for the hours lost from instructing other students, and from the increased time he will be spending on me. Man does not, after all, live on the love of music alone. And while Raphael has no family to support, he does have his own mouth to feed and his own rent to pay and the money must be raised somehow to see to it that he wants for nothing that would make it necessary for him to reduce his hours with me.

My father is already working at two jobs. Granddad gets a small pension from a Government grateful for the wartime sacrifice of his sanity, and it has been in the course of preserving that sanity that my grandparents have never moved to less expensive but more trying surroundings in the post-war years. They've cut back to the bone, they've let out rooms to lodgers, and they've shared the expense and the work of running a large house with my father. But they have not allowed for having a child prodigy in the family—and that is what my grandfather insists upon calling me—nor have they budgeted for what the costs will be in nurturing that prodigy to fulfill his potential.

And I don't make it easy on them. When Raphael suggests another lesson here or there, another hour or two or three with our instruments, I am passionate about my need for this time. And they see how I thrive under Raphael's tutelage: He steps into the house and I am ready for him, my instrument in one hand and my bow in the other.

So an accommodation must be made for my lessons, and my mother is the one who makes it.

ONE

IT WAS the knowledge of a touch—reserved for him but given to another—that drove Ted Wiley out into the night. He'd seen it from his window, not intending to spy but spying all the same. The time: just past one in the morning. The place: Friday Street, Henley-on-Thames, a mere sixty yards from the river, and in front of her house from which they'd departed only moments before, both of them having to duck their heads to avoid a lintel put into a building in centuries past when men and women were shorter and when their lives were more clearly defined.

Ted Wiley liked that: the definition of roles. She did not. And if he hadn't understood before now that Eugenie would not be easily identified as his woman and placed into a convenient category in his life, Ted had certainly reached that conclusion when he saw the two of them—Eugenie and that broomstick stranger—out on the pavement and in each other's arms.

Flagrant, he'd thought. She *wants* me to see this.

She wants me to see the way she's embracing him, then curving her palm to describe the shape of his cheek as he steps away. God damn the woman. She *wants* me to see this.

That, of course, was sophistry, and had the embrace and the touch occurred at a more reasonable hour, Ted would have talked himself out of the ominous direction his mind began taking. He would have thought, It can't mean *anything* if she's out in the street in daylight in public in a shaft of light from her sitting room window in the autumn sunshine in front of God and everyone and most of all *me*. . . . It can't mean anything that she's touching a stranger because she knows how easily I can see. . . . But instead of these thoughts, what was *implied* by a man's departure from a woman's home at one in the morning filled Ted's head like a noxious gas whose volume continued to increase over the next seven days as he—anxious and interpreting every gesture and nuance—waited for her to say, "Ted, have I mentioned that my brother"—or my cousin or my father or my uncle or the homosexual architect who intends to build another room onto the house— "stopped for a chat just the other night? It went on into the early hours of the morning and I thought he'd never leave. By the way, you might have seen us just outside my front door if you were lurking behind your window shades as you've taken to doing recently." Except, of course, there was no brother or cousin or uncle or father that Ted Wiley knew of, and if there was a homosexual architect, he'd yet to hear Eugenie mention him.

What he *had* heard her say, his bowels on the rumble, was that she had something important to tell him. And when he'd asked her what it was and thought he'd like her to give it to him straightaway if it was going to be the blow that killed him, she'd said, Soon. I'm not quite ready to confess my sins yet. And she'd curved her palm to touch his cheek. Yes. *Yes.* That touch. Just *exactly* like.

So at nine o'clock on a rainy evening deep in November, Ted Wiley put his ageing golden retriever on her lead and decided that a stroll was in order. Their route, he told the dog—whose arthritis and aversion to the rain did not make her the most cooperative of walkers—would take them to the top of Friday Street and a few yards beyond it to Albert Road, where if by coincidence they should run into Eugenie just leaving the Sixty Plus Club, where the New Year's Eve Gala Committee were still attempting to reach a compromise on the menu for the coming festivities, why, that's what it would be: a mere coincidence and a fortuitous chance for a chat. For all dogs needed a walk before they kipped down for the night. No one could argue, accuse, or even suspect over that.

The dog—ludicrously albeit lovingly christened Precious Baby by Ted's late wife and resolutely called P.B. by Ted himself—hesitated at the doorway and blinked out at the street, where the autumn rain was falling in the sort of steady waves that presaged a lengthy and bone-chilling storm. She began to lower herself determinedly to her haunches and would have successfully attained that position had Ted not tugged her out onto the pavement with the desperation of a man whose intentions will not be thwarted.

"Come, P.B.," he ordered her, and he jerked the lead so that the choke chain tightened round her neck. The retriever recognised both the tone and the gesture. With a bronchial sigh that released a gust of dog breath into wet night air, she trudged disconsolately into the rain.

The weather was a misery, but that couldn't be helped. Besides, the old dog *needed* to walk. She'd become far too lazy in the five years that had passed since her mistress's death, and Ted himself had not done much to keep her exercised. Well, that would change now. He'd promised Connie he'd look after the dog, and so he would, with a new regime that began this very night. No more sniffing round the back garden before bedtime, my friend, he silently informed P.B. It's walkies and nothing else from now on.

He double-checked to make sure the bookshop's door was secure, and he adjusted the collar of his old waxed jacket against the wet and the chill. He should have brought an umbrella, he realised as he stepped out of the doorway and the first splash of rainwater hit his neck. A peaked cap was insufficient protection, no matter how well it suited him. But why the hell was he even *thinking* about what suited him? he pondered. Fire and ice, if anyone wormed a way in-

side his head these days, it would be to find cobwebs
and rot floating there.

Ted harrumphed, spat in the street, and began to
give himself a pep talk as he and the dog plodded past
the Royal Marine Reserve, where a broken gutter
along the roof erupted rainwater in a silver plume.
He was a catch, he told himself. Major Ted Wiley, retired from the Army and widowed after forty-two
years of *blissful* marriage, was a very fine catch for any
woman. Weren't available men scarce as uncut
diamonds in Henley-on-Thames? Yes. They were.
Weren't available men without unsightly nose hairs,
overgrown eyebrows, and copious ear hairs scarcer
still? Yes and yes. And weren't men who were clean,
in possession of their faculties, in excellent health,
dexterous in the kitchen, and of an uxorious disposi-
tion so rare in town as to find themselves victims of
something akin to a feeding frenzy the very moment
they chose to show themselves at a social gathering?
Damn right, they were. And he was one of them.
Everyone knew it.

Including Eugenie, he reminded himself.

Hadn't she said to him on more than one occasion,
You're a fine man, Ted Wiley? Yes. She had.

Hadn't she spent the last three years willingly accepting his company with what he *knew* was pleasure?
Yes. She had.

Hadn't she smiled and flushed and looked away
when they'd visited his mother at the Quiet Pines
Nursing Home and heard her announce in that irritating and imperious way of hers, I'd like a wedding

before I die, you two. Yes, yes, and yes. She had, she
had.

So what did a touch on a stranger's face mean in
light of all that? And why could he not expunge it
from his mind, as if it had become a brand and not
what it was: an unpleasant memory that he wouldn't
even have *had* had he not taken to watching, to wondering, to lurking, to having to *know,* to insisting
upon battening down the hatches in his life as if it
weren't a life at all but a sailing vessel that might lose
its cargo if he wasn't vigilant?

Eugenie herself was the answer to that: Eugenie,
whose spectral-thin body asked for nurture; whose
neat hair—thickly silvered though it was with grey—
asked to be freed from the hair slides that held it;
whose cloudy eyes were blue then green then grey
then blue but always guarded; whose modest but
nonetheless provocative femininity awakened in Ted
a stirring in the groin that called him to an action he
hadn't been capable of taking since Connie's death.
Eugenie *was* the answer.

And he was the man for Eugenie, the man to protect her, to bring her back to life. For what had gone
unspoken between the two of them these past three
years was the extent to which Eugenie had been
denying herself the very *communion* of her fellow men
for God only knew how long. Yet that denial had declared itself openly when he'd first invited her to join
him for a simple evening glass of sherry at the
Catherine Wheel.

Why, she's not been out with a man in *years,* Ted

Wiley had thought at her flustered reaction to his invitation. And he'd wondered why.

Now, perhaps, he knew. She had secrets from him, had Eugenie. *I have something important I want to tell you, Ted.* Sins to confess, she'd said. Sins.

Well, there was no time like the present to hear what she had to say.

At the top of Friday Street, Ted waited for the traffic lights to change, P.B. shivering close at his side. Duke Street was also the main thoroughfare to either Reading or Marlow, and as such it carried all manner of vehicles rumbling through town. A wet night like this did little to decrease the volume of traffic in a society that was becoming depressingly more reliant upon cars and even more depressingly desirous of a commuter lifestyle defined by work in the city and life in the country. So even at nine o'clock at night, cars and lorries splashed along the soaked street, their headlamps creating ochroid fans that reflected against windows and in pools of standing water.

Too many people going too many places, Ted thought morosely. Too many people without the slightest idea of why they're rushing headlong through their lives.

The traffic lights changed and Ted crossed over, making the little jog into Grey's Road with P.B. bumping along next to him. Despite the fact that they'd not walked even a quarter of a mile, the old dog was wheezing, and Ted stepped into the shallow doorway of Mirabelle's Antiques to give the poor retriever a breather. Their destination was almost in sight, he reassured her. Surely she could make it just a few more yards up to Albert Road.

There, a car park served as courtyard for the Sixty Plus Club, an organisation attending to the social needs of Henley's ever-growing community of pensioners. There, too, Eugenie worked as Director. And there Ted had met her, upon relocating to the town on the Thames when he could no longer bear in Maidstone the memories of his wife's lengthy death.

"Major Wiley, how lovely. You're on Friday Street," Eugenie had said to him, reviewing his membership form. "You and I are neighbours. I'm at number sixty-five. The pink house? Doll Cottage? I've been there for years. And you're at . . ."

"The bookshop," he'd said. "Just across the street. The flat's above it. Yes. But I'd no idea . . . I mean, I've not seen you."

"I'm always out early and back late. I know your shop, though. I've been in many times. At least when your mother was running it. Before the stroke, that is. And she's still well, which is lovely. Improving, isn't she."

He'd thought Eugenie was asking, but when he realised she wasn't—indeed, she was merely *affirming* information that she already had—then he also realised where he'd seen her before: at Quiet Pines Nursing Home, where three times each week Ted visited his mother. She volunteered there in the mornings, did Eugenie, and the patients referred to her as "our angel." Or so Ted's mother had informed him once as together they watched Eugenie entering a cubicle with an adult-sized nappie folded over her wrist. "She hasn't any relatives here, and the Home don't pay her a penny, Ted."

Then *why*, Ted had wanted to know at the time. Why?

Secrets, he thought now. Still waters and secrets.

He looked down at the dog, who'd sagged against him, out of the rain and determined to snooze while she had the chance. He said, "Come along, P.B. Not much farther now," and he looked across the street to see through the bare trees that there was not much more time either.

For from where he and the dog stood sheltered, he noticed that the Sixty Plus Club was disgorging its New Year's Eve Gala Committee. Raising their umbrellas and stepping through puddles like neophyte high-wire artists, the committee members called out their goodnights to one another with enough good cheer to suggest that a compromise on comestibles had been finally achieved. Eugenie would be pleased at this. Pleased, she'd no doubt be feeling expansive and ready to talk to him.

Ted crossed the street, eager to intercept her, his reluctant golden retriever in tow. He reached the low wall between the pavement and the car park just as the last of the committee members drove away. The lights in the Sixty Plus Club went out and the entry porch became bathed in shadow. A moment later, Eugenie herself stepped into the misty penumbra between the building and the car park, working upon the tie of a black umbrella. Ted opened his mouth to call her name, sing out a hearty hello, and make the offer of a personal escort back to her cottage. No time of night for a lovely lady to be alone on the streets, my dearest girl. Care for the arm of an ardent admirer? With dog, I'm afraid. P.B. and I were out for a final recce of the town.

He could have said all this, and he was indeed drawing breath to do so when he suddenly heard it. A man's voice called out Eugenie's name. She swung to her left, and Ted looked beyond her where a figure was getting out of a dark saloon car. Backlit by one of the streetlamps that dotted the car park, he was mostly shadow. But the shape of his head and that gull's-beak nose were enough to tell Ted that Eugenie's visitor of one in the morning had returned to town.

The stranger approached her. She remained where she was. In the change of light, Ted could see that he was an older man—of an age with Ted himself, perhaps—with a full head of white hair scraped back from his forehead and falling to touch the turned-up collar of a Burberry.

They began to talk. He took the umbrella from her, held it over them, and spoke to her urgently. He was taller than Eugenie by a good eight inches, so he bent to her. She lifted her face to hear him. Ted strained to hear him as well but managed to catch only "You've *got* to" and "My knees, Eugenie?" and finally, loudly, "Why won't you *see*—" which Eugenie interrupted with a rush of soft conversation and the placement of her hand on his arm. "*You* can say that to *me*?" were the final words Ted heard from the man before he jerked himself away from Eugenie's grasp, thrust the umbrella upon her, and stalked to his car. At this, Ted breathed a cirrus of relief into the cold night air.

It was a brief deliverance. Eugenie followed the stranger and intercepted him as he yanked open the door to his car. With the door between them, she continued to speak. Her listener, however, averted his face, and cried out, "No. *No,*" at which point she reached up to him and tried to curve her palm against his cheek. She seemed to want to draw him to her despite the car door that continued to act like a shield between them.

It was effective as a shield, that door, because the stranger escaped whatever caress Eugenie wanted to bestow upon him. He dived into the driver's seat, wrenched the door closed, and started the engine with a roar that resounded against the buildings on three sides of the car park.

Eugenie stepped away. The car reversed. Its gears ground like animals being dismembered. Its tyres spun wickedly against wet pavement. Rubber met tarmac with a sound like despair.

Another roar and the car was speeding towards the exit. Not six yards from where Ted watched in the shelter of a young liquidambar tree, the Audi—for now it was close enough for Ted to see the distinguishing quadruple circles on its bonnet—swerved into the street without so much as a moment's pause for its driver to determine if any other vehicles were in his way. There was just enough time for Ted to catch a glimpse of a profile that was twisted with emotion before the Audi veered left in the direction of Duke Street and there turned right for the Reading Road. Ted squinted after it, trying to make out the number plate, trying to decide if he'd ill-chosen his moment to happen upon Eugenie.

He didn't have much time to select between scarpering for home and pretending he'd just arrived, however. Eugenie would be upon him in thirty seconds or less.

He looked down at the dog, who'd taken the opportunity of this respite from their walk to deposit herself at the base of the liquidambar, where she now lay curled, with the apparent and martyred determination to sleep in the rain. How reasonable was it, Ted wondered, to suppose he could coax P.B. into a fast trot that would take them out of the immediate area before Eugenie reached the edge of the car park? Not very. So he would offer Eugenie the pretence that he and the dog had just arrived.

He squared his shoulders and gave a tug on the lead. But as he was doing so, he saw that Eugenie wasn't heading his way at all. Instead, she was walking in the opposite direction, where a path between buildings offered pedestrians access to Market Place. Where the blazes was she going?

Ted hastened after her, at a brisk pace that P.B. didn't much care for but couldn't avoid without serious risk of strangulation. Eugenie was a dark figure ahead of them, her black raincoat, black boots, and black umbrella making her an unsuitable ambler on a rainy night.

She turned right into Market Place, and Ted wondered for the second time where she was going. Shops were closed at this hour, and it wasn't in Eugenie's character to frequent pubs alone.

Ted endured a moment of agony while P.B. relieved herself next to the kerb. The dog's capacious bladder was legend, and Ted was certain that, in the lengthy wait for P.B. to empty a pool of steaming urine onto the pavement, he'd lose Eugenie to Market Place Mews or Market Lane when she crossed halfway down the street. But after a quick glance right and left, she continued on her way, towards the river. Passing by Duke Street, she crossed into Hart Street, at which point Ted began thinking that she was merely taking a circuitous route home, despite the weather. But then she veered to the doors of St. Mary the Virgin, whose handsome crenellated tower was part of the river vista for which Henley was famous.

Eugenie hadn't come to admire that vista, however, for she swiftly ducked inside the church.

"Damn," Ted muttered. What to do now? He could hardly follow her into the church, canine in tow. And hanging about outside in the rain wasn't an appealing idea. And while he could tie the dog to a lamppost and join her at her prayers—if praying was what she was doing in there—he couldn't exactly maintain the pretence of a chance encounter inside St. Mary the Virgin after nine in the evening, when

there was no service going on. And even if there *had*
been a service, Eugenie knew he wasn't a church-
goer. So what the hell else could he do now except
turn tail for home like a lovesick idiot? And all the
time seeing seeing still seeing that moment in the car
park when she touched him again, again that
touch . . .

Ted shook his head vigorously. He couldn't go *on*
like this. He had to know the worst. He had to know
tonight.

To the left of the church, the graveyard made a
rough triangle of sodden vegetation bisected by a
path that led to a row of old brick almshouses whose
windows winked brightly against the darkness. Ted
led P.B. in this direction, taking the time that Eugenie was inside the church to marshal his opening
statement to her.

Look at this dog, fat as a sow, he would say. We're
on a new campaign to slim her down. Vet says she
can't go on like this without her heart giving out, so
here we are and here we'll be nightly from now on,
making a circumvention of the town. May we toddle
along with you, Eugenie? Heading home, are you?
Ready to talk, are you? Can we make this the *soon*
you spoke to me about? Because I don't know how
much longer I can hold on, wondering what it is that
you want me to know.

The problem was that he'd decided upon her, and
he'd reached the decision without knowing if she'd
reached it as well. In the last five years since Connie's
death, he'd never had to *pursue* a woman, since

women had done the pursuing of him. And even if that had demonstrated for him how little he liked to *be* pursued—damnation itself, when had women become so flaming aggressive? he wondered—and even if what evolved from those pursuits tended to be a pressure to perform under which he had consistently wilted, yet there had been an intense gratification in knowing that the old boy still had It and It was highly in demand.

Except Eugenie wasn't demanding. Which made Ted ask himself whether he was man enough for everyone else—at least superficially—but for some reason not man enough for her.

Blast it all, *why* was he feeling like this? Like an adolescent who'd never been laid. It was those failures with the others, he decided, failures he'd never once had with Connie.

"You should see a doctor about this little problem of yours," that piranha Georgia Ramsbottom had said, twisting her bony back from his bed and donning his flannel dressing gown. "It's not normal, Ted. For a man your age? What are you, sixty? It's just not normal."

Sixty-eight, he thought. With a piece of meat between his legs that remained inert despite the most ardent of ministrations.

But that was because of their *pursuit* of him. If they'd only let him do what nature intended every man to do—be the hunter and not the hunted—then everything else would take care of itself. Wouldn't it? *Wouldn't* it? He needed to know.

A sudden movement within one of the squares of light from an almshouse window attracted his attention. Ted glanced that way to see that a figure had come into the room that the window defined. The figure was a woman, and as Ted looked curiously in her direction, he was surprised to see her raise the red jumper that she was wearing, lifting it over her head and dropping it to the floor.

He looked left and right. He felt his cheeks take on heat, despite the rain that was pelting him. Peculiar that some people didn't know how a lit window worked at night. They couldn't see out, so they believed no one could see in. Children were like that. Ted's own three girls had to be taught to draw the curtains before they undressed. But if no one ever taught a child to do that . . . peculiar that some people never learned.

He stole a glance in her direction again. The woman had removed her brassiere. Ted swallowed. On the lead, P.B. was beginning to snuffle in the grass that edged the graveyard path, and she headed towards the almshouses innocently.

Take her off the lead, she won't go far. But instead Ted followed, the lead looped in his hand.

In the window the woman began brushing her hair. With each stroke her breasts lifted and fell. Their nipples were taut, with deep brown aureoles encircling them. Seeing all this, his eyes fixed to her breasts as if they were what he'd been waiting for all evening and all the evenings that had preceded this evening, Ted felt the incipient stirring within him, and then that gratifying rush of blood and that throb of life.

He sighed. There was nothing wrong with him. Nothing at all. Being *pursued* had been the problem. Pursuing—and afterwards claiming and having—was the sure solution.

He tugged P.B.'s lead so the dog walked no farther. He settled in to watch the woman in the window and to wait for his Eugenie.

IN THE LADY Chapel of St. Mary the Virgin, Eugenie didn't so much pray as wait. She hadn't darkened the doorway of a house of worship in years, and the only reason she'd done so tonight was to avoid the conversation she'd promised herself that she'd have with Ted.

She knew he was following her. It wasn't the first time she'd come out of the Sixty Plus Club to see his silhouette under the trees on the street, but it *was* the first time she wouldn't allow herself to talk to him. So she hadn't turned in his direction when she could have done, at the natural moment to offer an explanation to what he'd witnessed in the car park. Instead, she'd headed for Market Place with no clear idea of where she was going.

When her gaze had fallen upon the church, she'd made the decision to slip inside and adopt an attitude of supplication. For the first five minutes in the Lady Chapel, she even knelt on one of the dusty hassocks, gazed upon the statue of the Virgin, and waited for the old familiar words of devotion to spring into her mind. But they would not. Her head was too filled with impediments to prayer: old arguments and accusations, older loyalties and the sins committed in the name of them, current importunacies and their implications, future consequences if she made an ignorant misstep now.

She'd made enough missteps in the past to devastate thirteen dozen lives. And she'd long ago learned that an action taken was the same as a pebble dropped into still water: The concentric rings that the pebble effects may lessen in substance, but they do exist.

When no prayer came to her, Eugenie rose from her knees. She sat with her feet flat on the floor and studied the face of the statue. You didn't make the choice to lose Him, did you? she asked the Virgin silently. So how can I ask you to understand? And even if you did understand, what intercession can I ask you to give me? You can't turn back time. You can't unhappen what happened, can you? You can't bring back to life what's dead and gone, because if you could, you would have done it to save yourself the torture of His murder.

Except they never say it was murder, do they? Instead, it's a sacrifice for a greater cause. It's a giving of life for something far more important than life. As if anything really is . . .

Eugenie put her elbows on her thighs and rested her forehead in the palms of her hands. If she was to believe what her erstwhile religion taught her to believe, then the Virgin Mary had known from the start exactly what would be required of her. She'd understood clearly that the Child she nurtured would be ripped from her life in the flowering of His manhood. Reviled, beaten, abused, and *sacrificed,* He would die ingloriously and she would be there to watch it all. And the only assurance she would ever have that His death had a greater meaning than what was implied by being spat upon and nailed up between two common criminals was simple faith. Because although religious tradition had it that an angel had appeared to put her in the picture of future events, who could really stretch their brains to fit around that?

So she'd gone on blind faith that a greater good existed somewhere. Not in her lifetime and not in the lifetime of the grandchildren she would never have. But there. Somewhere. Quite real. There.

Of course, it hadn't happened yet. Fast-forward two thousand brutal years and mankind was still waiting for the good to come. And what did she think, the Virgin Mother, watching and waiting from her throne in the clouds? How did she begin to assess the benefit against the cost?

For years newspapers had served to tell Eugenie that the benefits—the good—tipped the scales against the price she herself had paid. But now she was no longer sure. The Greater Good she'd thought she was serving threatened to disintegrate before her, like a woven rug whose persistent unraveling makes a mockery of the labour that went into its creation. And only she could stop that unraveling, if she made the choice to do so.

The problem was Ted. She hadn't intended to draw close to him. For so very long she hadn't allowed herself near enough to anyone to encourage confidence of any kind. And to feel herself even *capable* now—not to mention deserving—of establishing a connection to another human being seemed like a form of hubris that was certain to destroy her. Yet she wanted to draw close to him anyway, as if he were the anodyne for a sickness that she lacked the courage to name.

So she sat in the church. In part because she did not want to face Ted Wiley just yet, before the way was paved. In part because she did not yet possess the words to do the paving.

Tell me what to do, God, she prayed. Tell me what to say.

But God was as silent as He'd been for ages. Eugenie dropped an offering in the collection box and left the church.

Outside, it was still raining relentlessly. She raised her umbrella and headed towards the river. The wind was rising as she reached the corner, and she paused for a moment to wrestle against it as it struck her umbrella with more force than she expected and turned it inside out.

"Here. Let me help you with that, Eugenie."

She swung round and Ted was standing there, his old dog droopily at his side and rainwater dripping from his nose and jaw. His waxed jacket glistened brightly with damp, and his peaked cap clung to his skull.

"Ted!" She offered him the gift of her spurious surprise. "You look positively drowned. And poor P.B.! What are you doing out here with that sweet dog?"

He righted her umbrella and held it over both of them. She took his arm.

"We've begun a new exercise programme," he told her. "Up to Market Place, down to the church yard, and back home four times a day. What're *you* doing here? You haven't just come out of the church, have you?"

You know I have, she wanted to say. You just don't know why. But what she said was, lightly, "Decompressing after the committee meeting. You remember: the New Year's Eve committee? I'd given them a deadline to decide on the food. So much to be ordered, you know, and they can't expect the caterer to wait forever for them to make up their minds, can they?"

"On your way home now?"

"I am."

"And may I . . . ?"

"You know that you may."

How ridiculous it was, the two of them in such an idle conversation, with volumes of what needed saying deliberately going unsaid between them.

You don't trust me, Ted, do you? Why don't you trust me? And how can we foster love between us if we have no foundation of trust? I know you're worried because I'm not telling you what it was I said I wanted to tell you, but why can't you let the wanting to tell you be enough for now?

But she couldn't risk anything that would lead to

revelation at the moment. She owed it to ties far older than the tie she felt to Ted to put her house in order before burning it down.

So they engaged in insignificant chat as they walked along the river: his day, her day, who'd come into the bookshop and how his mother was getting on at Quiet Pines. He was hearty and cheerful; she was pleasant albeit subdued.

"Tired?" he asked her when they reached the door of her cottage.

"A bit," she admitted. "It's been a long day."

He handed her the umbrella, saying, "Then I won't keep you up," but he looked at her with such open expectation in his ruddy face that she knew her next line was supposed to be to ask him in for a brandy before bed.

It was her fondness for him that prompted the truth. She said, "I've got to go into London, Ted."

"Ah. Early morning, then?"

"No. I've got to go tonight. I've an appointment."

"Appointment? But with the rain, it'll take you more than an hour. . . . Did you say an *appointment?*"

"Yes. I did."

"What sort . . . ? Eugenie . . ." He blew out a breath. She heard him curse quietly. So, apparently, did P.B., because the old retriever raised her head and blinked at Ted as if with surprise. She was soaking, poor dog. At least, thank God, her fur was thick as a mammoth's. "Let me drive you in, then," Ted said at last.

"That wouldn't be wise."

"But—"

She put her hand on his arm to stop him. She raised it to touch his cheek, but he flinched and she stepped away. "Are you free for dinner tomorrow night?" she asked him.

"You know that I am."

"Then have a meal with me. Here. We'll talk then, if you'd like."

He gazed at her, trying—she knew—and failing to read her. Don't make the attempt, she wanted to tell him. I've had too much rehearsal for a rôle in a drama you don't yet understand.

She watched him steadily, waiting for his reply. The light from her sitting room came through the window and jaundiced a face already drawn with age and with worries he wouldn't name. She was grateful for that: that he wouldn't speak his deepest fears to her. The fact that what frightened him went unspoken was what gave her courage to contend with everything that frightened her.

He removed his cap then, a humble gesture that she wouldn't for all her life have had him make. It exposed his thick grey hair to the rain and removed the meagre shadow that had hidden the rubicund flesh of his nose. It made him look like what he was: an old man. It made her feel like what she was: a woman who didn't deserve such a fine man's love.

"Eugenie," he said, "if you're thinking you can't tell me that you . . . that you and I . . . that we aren't . . ." He looked towards the bookshop across the street.

"I'm not thinking anything," she said. "Just about London and the drive. And there's the rain as well. But I'll be careful. You've no need to worry."

He appeared momentarily gratified and perhaps a trifle relieved at the reassurance she meant to imply. "You're the world to me," he said simply. "Eugenie, do you know? You're the world. And I'm a bloody idiot most of the time, but I do—"

"I know," she said. "I know that you do. And we'll talk tomorrow."

"Right, then." He kissed her awkwardly, hitting his head on the edge of the umbrella and knocking it askew in her hand.

Rain dashed against her face. A car raced up Friday Street. She felt spray from its tyres hit her shoes.

Ted swung round. "Hey!" he shouted at the vehicle. "Watch your bloody driving!"

"No. It's all right," she said. "It's nothing, Ted."

He turned back to her, saying, "Damn it. Wasn't that—" But he stopped himself.

"What?" she asked. "Who?"

"No one. Nothing." He roused his retriever to her feet for the last few yards to their front door. "We'll talk, then?" he asked. "Tomorrow? After dinner?"

"We'll talk," she said. "There's so much to say."

SHE HAD VERY few preparations to make. She washed her face and cleaned her teeth. She combed her hair and tied a navy blue scarf round her head. She protected her lips with a colourless balm, and she put the winter lining into her raincoat to give herself more protection from the chill. Parking was always bad in London, and she didn't know how far she would have to walk in the cold and windy storm-stricken air when she finally arrived at her destination.

Raincoat on and a handbag hooked over her arm, she descended the narrow staircase. She took from the kitchen table a photograph in a plain wooden frame. It was one of a baker's dozen that she usually had arranged round the cottage. Before choosing from among them, she'd lined them up like soldiers on the table and there the rest of them remained.

She clasped this frame just beneath her bosom. She went out into the night.

Her car was parked inside a gated courtyard, in a space she rented by the month, just down the street. The courtyard was hidden by electric gates cleverly fashioned to look like part of the half-timbered buildings on either side. There was safety in this, and Eugenie liked safety. She liked the illusion of security afforded by gates and locks.

In her car—a secondhand Polo whose fan sounded like the wheezing of a terminal asthmatic—she carefully set the framed photo on the passenger seat and started the engine. She'd prepared in advance for this journey up to London, checking the Polo's oil and its tyres and topping up its petrol as soon as she'd learned the date and the place. The time had come later, and she'd balked at it at first, once she realised ten forty-five meant at night and not in the morning. But she had no leg to stand on in protesting, and she knew it, so she acquiesced. Her night vision wasn't what it once had been. But she would cope.

She hadn't counted on the rain, however. And as she left the outskirts of Henley and wound her way northwest to Marlow, she found herself clutching the steering wheel and crouching over it, half-blinded by the headlamps of oncoming cars, assailed by how the blowing rain diffracted the light in spearheads that riddled the windscreen with visual lacerations.

Things weren't much better on the M40, where cars and lorries put up sheets of spray with which the Polo's windscreen wipers could barely keep pace. The lane markings had mostly vanished beneath the standing water, and those that could be seen seemed to alternate between writhing snakelike in Eugenie's vision and side-stepping to border an entirely different traffic lane.

It wasn't until she reached the vicinity of Wormwood Scrubs that she felt she could relax the death hold she had on the steering wheel. Even then she didn't breathe with ease until she'd veered away from the motorway's sleek and sodden river of concrete and headed north in the vicinity of Maida Hill.

As soon as she could manage it, she pulled to the kerb at a darkened Sketchley's. There, she let out a lungful of air that felt as if it had been held back since she'd made the first turn into Duke Street in Henley.

She rooted in her handbag for the directions she'd written out for herself from the *A to Z*. Although she'd escaped the motorway unscathed, another quarter of the journey still had to be negotiated through London's labyrinthine streets.

The city at the best of times was a maze. At night it became a maze ill lit and in possession of a nearly laughable paucity of signposts. But at night in the rain it was Hades. Three false starts took Eugenie no farther than Paddington Recreation Ground before she got lost. Wisely, each time she returned the way she'd come, like a taxi driver determined to understand just where he'd made his first mistake.

So it was nearly twenty past eleven when she found the street she was looking for in northwest London. And she spent another maddening seven minutes circling round till she found a space to park.

She clasped the framed photo to her bosom again, took up her umbrella from the back seat of the car, and clambered out. The rain had finally abated, but the wind was still blowing. What few autumn leaves had remained on the trees were being wafted through the air to plaster themselves on the pavement, in the street, and against the parked cars.

Number Thirty-two was the house she wanted, and Eugenie saw that it would be far up the street, on the other side. She walked up the pavement for twenty-five yards. At that hour the houses she passed were mostly unlit, and if she hadn't been nervous enough about the coming interview, her state of anxiety was heightened by the darkness and by what her active imagination was telling her could be hidden there. So she decided to be careful, as a woman alone in a city on a rainy night in late autumn ought to be careful. She ventured off the pavement and proceeded on her way in the middle of the road, where she would have advance warning should anyone want to attack her.

She thought it unlikely. It was a decent neighbourhood. Still, she knew the value of caution, so she was grateful when the lights swept over her, telling her that a vehicle had turned into the street behind her. It was coming along slowly, the way she herself had come and doing what she herself had been doing, looking for that most precious of London commodities: a place to park. She turned, stepped back against the nearest vehicle, and waited for the car to pass her. But as she did so, it pulled to one side and blinked its lights, telling her that the way was hers.

Ah, she'd been mistaken, she thought, resettling her umbrella against her shoulder and going on her way. The car wasn't waiting for a parking space at all, but rather for someone to come out of the house in front of which it sat. She gave a quick glance over her shoulder when she reached this conclusion, and as if the unknown driver was reading her thoughts, the car's horn beeped once abruptly, like a parent who'd come calling for an unresponsive child.

Eugenie continued walking. She counted the house numbers as she passed. She saw Number Ten and Number Twelve. She'd gone barely six houses from her own car when the steady light behind her shifted, then went out altogether.

Odd, she thought. You can't just park in the street like that. And thinking this, she began to turn. Which was, as it happened, not the worst of her mistakes.

Bright lights blazed on. She was instantly blinded. Blinded, she froze as the hunted often do.

An engine roared and tyres wailed against the roadway.

When she was hit, her body flew up, her arms flung wide, and her picture frame shot up like a rocket into the cold night air.

TWO

J. W. PITCHLEY, aka TongueMan, had experienced an excellent evening. He'd broken Rule One—*never* suggest meeting *anyone* with whom one has engaged in cybersex—but it had all worked out, proving to him yet again that his instincts for picking fruit past its prime but all the juicier for having hung disregarded on the tree so long were as finely honed as a surgical tool.

Humility and honesty forced him to admit that it hadn't been that much of a risk, however. Any woman who called herself CreamPants was as good as advertising what she wanted, and if he'd had any doubts about that, five meetings on-line that had had him coming into his Calvin Klein jockeys without the slightest handshake of the organ on his part should have set his mind at rest. Unlike his four other current cyberlovers—whose spelling skill was, alas, often as limited as their imaginations—CreamPants had a capacity for fantasy that cooked his brain and a natural ability to express that fantasy that stiffened his cock like a divining rod the moment she logged on the net.

Creamy here, she would write. *R U rdy 4 it, Tongue?*
Oh my. Oh yes. He always was.

So he'd taken the metaphorical plunge himself this
time instead of waiting for his cyberspondent to do
so. This was wildly out of character for him. Usually,
he played along cooperatively, always there at the
other end of on-line encounters when one of his
lovers wanted action but never venturing into the
arena of embodiment unless or until his partner suggested it. Following this pattern, he'd successfully
transformed exactly twenty-seven Super Highway
encounters into twenty-seven intensely satisfying
trysts at the Comfort Inn on Cromwell Road—a
wise and cautious distance from his own neighbourhood and night-clerked by an Asian gentleman whose
memory for faces took a far back seat to his abiding
passion for videos of old BBC costume dramas. Thus,
only once had he found himself the victim of a
practical cyberjoke, agreeing to meet a lover called
DoMeHard and discovering two spotty-faced
twelve-year-olds dressed like the Kray brothers waiting for him instead. No matter, though. He'd sorted
them out quick enough and he was fairly certain
they'd not be trying *that* little caper on-line again.

But CreamPants had got to him. *R U rdy 4 it?* She
had him wondering almost from the first if she could
do in person what she could do with words.

That was always the question, wasn't it? And anticipating, fantasising, and securing the answer were
part of the fun.

He'd worked very hard to bring CreamPants

round to suggesting that they meet. He climbed to new and dizzying heights of descriptive licentiousness with the woman. To develop more ideas in the carnal vein, he'd spent six hours over a fortnight browsing through the paraphernalia of pleasure in those windowless shops in Brewer Street. And when he finally found himself spending his daily commute into the City wrapped up in lustful visions of their sated bodies inextricably twined on the hideously hued counterpane of a Comfort Inn bed—this, instead of reading the *Financial Times,* that daily staple of his career—he knew that he had to take action.

So *Want it 4 real?* he'd finally written to her. *R U rdy 4 a rsk?*

She'd been ready.

He made the suggestion that he always made when his cyberlovers requested a meeting: drinks at the Valley of Kings, easy enough to find, just a few steps away from Sainsbury's on Cromwell Road. She could come by car, by taxi, by bus, or by tube. And if upon first sight they found they didn't actually appeal to each other . . . just a quick martini in the bar and no regrets, okay?

The Valley of Kings possessed the same priceless quality as the Comfort Inn. Like the vast majority of service-oriented businesses in London, its waiters spoke virtually no English and to them every English person looked alike. He'd taken all twenty-seven of his cyberencounters to the Valley of Kings without the *maître d',* the waiters, or the bartender so much as blinking an eyelash in recognition of him, so he was confident that he could take CreamPants there as well without any of its employees betraying him.

He'd known who she was the moment she walked into the restaurant's saffron-scented bar. And he was gratified to see that yet again he'd somehow instinctively known who and what she would be. Fifty-five years old if she was a day, well-scrubbed, and wearing just the right amount of scent, she wasn't some slag out on the pull. She wasn't a Mile End shag bag trying to better herself or a Scouse-come-south in the hope of finding a bloke who'd raise her standard of living. She was instead exactly what he'd assumed that she'd be: a lonely divorcée whose kids were grown up and who was facing the prospect of being called *Gran* about ten years sooner than she wanted. She was eager to prove to herself that she still had a modicum of sex appeal despite the lines on her face and her incipient jowls. And never mind that he had his own reasons for choosing her despite the dozen years of difference between their ages. He was happy enough to supply her with the validation that she required.

Such validation took place in Room 109, first floor, perhaps ten yards away from the roar of traffic. Being on the street—a request he always made *sotto voce* prior to securing the room key—obviated the necessity of staying the night. It would be impossible for anyone in possession of normal hearing actually to *sleep* in any of the rooms that faced Cromwell Road. And since spending the night with a cyberlover was the last activity on his mind, being able to say "God, what a din" at one point or another usually sufficed as prelude to a gentlemanly exit.

So everything had gone according to plan: drinks had segued into a confession of physical attraction which had led to a stroll to the Comfort Inn, where vigorous coupling had resulted in mutual satisfaction. In person CreamPants—whose real name she coyly refused to reveal—was only slightly less imaginative than she was on the keyboard. Once all the sexual permutations, positions, and possibilities had been thoroughly explored between them, they fell away from each other, slick with sweat and other bodily fluids, and listened to the roar of lorries grinding up and down the A4.

"God, what a din," he groaned. "I should have thought of a better spot than this. We'll never sleep."

"Oh." She took her cue. "Not to worry. I can't stay anyway."

"You can't?" Pained.

A smile. "I hadn't actually planned on it. After all, there was always the chance that you and I wouldn't have made the same sort of connection in person as we did on the net. You know."

How he did. The only question now as he drove home was, What next? They'd gone at it like beavers for two solid hours, and they'd both enjoyed themselves immensely. They'd parted with promises made on both sides of "staying in touch" but there had been ever so slight an undercurrent in CreamPants' farewell embrace that belied her casual words and suggested to him that the course of wisdom called for steering clear of her for a time.

Which was ultimately, after a long, aimless drive in the rain for sexual decompression, what he decided to do.

He yawned as he turned into his street. He'd have an excellent night's doss after his exertions of the evening. There was nothing like spirited sex with a relative stranger of advancing years to set one up for slumber.

He squinted through the windscreen as the wipers lulled him with their steady rhythm. He cruised up the incline and flicked on the indicator for his driveway—more out of habit than necessity—and was thinking about how much longer it would be before LadyFire and EatMe each suggested a meeting, when he saw the heap of sodden garments lying next to a late-model Calibra.

He sighed. Wasn't society crumbling round his ears? Beneath a thin protection of their epidermis, people were becoming little more than pigs. After all, why on earth should *anyone* drop his jumble at Oxfam when he could *just* as easily toss it into the street? It was pathetic.

He was about to drive past, when a flash of white within the mass of soaked material caught his eye. He glanced over. A rain-drenched sock, a tattered scarf, a limp collection of women's knickers? What?

But then he saw. His foot plunged wildly on the brake.

The white, he realised, belonged to a hand, a wrist, and a short length of arm which itself protruded from the black of a coat. Part of a mannequin, he thought resolutely to still the hammering of his heart. Someone's pea-brained idea of a joke. It's too short to be a person, anyway. And there're no legs or head. Just that arm.

But he lowered his window in spite of these reassuring conclusions. His face spattered with the rain, he peered at the shapeless form on the ground. And then he saw the rest.

There *were* legs. There was a head as well. It merely hadn't seemed so upon an initial glance through the rain-streaked window because the head was bowed deeply into the coat as if in prayer and the legs were tucked completely under the Calibra.

Heart attack, he thought in spite of what his eyes told him otherwise. Aneurysm. Stroke.

Only what were the legs *doing* under that car? Under it, when the only possible explanation for *that* was . . .

He snatched up his mobile and punched in triple nine.

DCI ERIC LEACH'S body was screaming flu. He ached everywhere it was possible to ache. He was sweaty on the head, the face, and the chest; he had the chills. He should have phoned in ill when he first started feeling like crap in a basket. He should have gone to bed. There, he would have gleaned a double benefit. He would have caught up on the sleep he'd been missing since trying to reorganise his life post-divorce; he would have had an excuse when the phone call came through at midnight. Instead, here he was dragging his sorry shivering bum from an inadequately furnished flat into the cold, the wind, and the rain, where he was no doubt risking double pneumonia.

Live and learn, DCI Leach thought wearily. Next time he got married, he'd damn well stay married.

He saw the blue flashing lights of police vehicles as he made his final left turn. The hour was drawing on towards twenty past twelve, but the rising road in front of him was as bright as midday. Someone had hooked up floodlights, and these were complemented by the lightning-bolt hiccups of the forensic photographer.

The activity outside their houses had gathered a hefty collection of gawkers, but they were being held back by the crime scene tape that had been strung along the length of the street on both sides. Additional tape as well as barriers blocked the road at either end. Behind these, press photographers had already gathered, those vampires of the radio waves who continuously tuned in to the Met's frequency in the hope of learning that fresh blood was available somewhere.

DCI Leach thumbed a Strepsil out of its packet. He left his car behind an ambulance whose waterproof-shrouded attendants were lounging against its front bumper, drinking coffee from Thermos lids in an unhurried fashion that indicated which one of their services was going to be required. Leach nodded at them as he hunched his shoulders against the rain. He showed his warrant card to the gangling young PC who was in charge of keeping the press at bay, and he stepped past the barrier and approached the collection of professionals who were gathered round a saloon car halfway up the street.

He heard snatches of neighbourhood conversation as he wearily trudged up the slight incline. Most of it was murmured in the reverential tones employed by those who understood how impartial the reaper was when he sauntered by to do his grim business. But there was also the occasional ill-considered complaint about the confusion that ensued when a sudden death in the open demanded police examination. And when one of those complaints was spoken in just the sort of pinched-nose I-smell-something-decidedly-unpleasant-and-it's-you tone that Leach detested, he turned on his heel. He stalked in the direction of the protest, which was concluding with the phrase ". . . one's sleep being disturbed for no *apparent* reason other than to satisfy the baser inclinations of the tabloid photographers" and found its source, a helmet-haired ghoul with her entire life savings invested in a plastic surgery job that needed redoing. She was saying, "If one's council taxes can*not* protect one from this sort of thing—" when Leach cut her off by speaking to the nearest constable guarding the scene.

"Shut that bitch up," he barked. "Kill her if you have to." And he went on his way.

At the moment, the crime scene action was being dominated by the forensic pathologist, who beneath a makeshift shelter of polythene sheets was wearing a bizarre combination of tweeds, wellingtons, and up-market Patagonia rain wear. He was just completing his preliminary examination of the body, and Leach got enough of a look to see they were dealing with either a cross-dresser or a female of indeterminate age, badly mangled. Facial bones were crushed; blood seeped from the hole where an ear had once been; raw skin on the head marked the areas where hair had been ripped from the scalp; the head hung at a natural angle but with a highly unnatural twist. It was just the thing to have to look upon when one was already light-headed with fever.

The pathologist—Dr. Olav Grotsin—slapped his hands on his thighs and pushed himself to his feet. He snapped off his latex gloves, tossed them to an assistant, and saw Leach where the DCI stood, attempting to ignore his own ill health and assessing what could be assessed from his position of less than four feet from the corpse.

"You look like hell," Grotsin said to Leach.

"What've we got?"

"Female. One hour dead when I got here. Two at the most."

"You're sure?"

"About what? The time or the sex?"

"The sex."

"She's got breasts on her. Old but there. As for the

rest, I don't like cutting off their knickers in the street. You can wait till the morning on that, I presume."

"What happened?"

"Hit-and-run. Internal injuries. I'd venture to guess she's ruptured everything that could be ruptured."

Leach said, "Shit," and stepped past Grotsin to squat by the body. It lay a scant few inches from the driver's door of the Calibra, on its side with its back to the street. One arm was twisted behind it, and the legs were tucked beneath the Vauxhall's chassis. The Vauxhall itself was unblemished, Leach noted, which hardly surprised him. He couldn't see a driver hotly seeking a parking space and running over someone lying in the street in order to get it. He looked for tyre marks on the body and on the dark raincoat she wore.

"Her arm's dislocated," Grotsin was saying behind him. "Both legs are broken. And we've got a bit of candy floss as well. Turn her head and you'll see it."

"The rain didn't wash it off?"

"Head was protected under the car."

Protected was an odd choice of word, Leach thought. The poor sow was dead, whoever she was. Pink froth from her lungs may well have indicated that she didn't die instantly, but that was not much help to them and no help at all to the hapless victim. Unless, of course, someone had come upon her while she still lived and managed to catch a few critical words as she lay dying in the street.

Leach got to his feet and said, "Who phoned it in?"

"Right over there, sir." It was Grotsin's assistant

who replied, and she nodded across the street where
for the first time Leach saw that a Porsche Boxter was
double-parked with its hazard lights blinking. Two
police constables were guarding this vehicle at either
end, and just beyond them a middle-aged man in a
trench coat stood beneath a striped umbrella and anxiously alternated his gaze from the Porsche to the
broken body that lay some yards behind it.

Leach went over to examine the sports car. It
would be a short night's work if the driver, the vehicle, and the victim were forming a neat little triad
here on the street, but even as he approached the car,
Leach knew that this would not be likely. Grotsin
would hardly have used the words *hit-and-run* if only
the first term applied.

Still, Leach walked round the Boxter carefully. He
squatted in front of it and examined its front end and
its body. He went from there to the tyres and
checked each of these. He lowered himself to the
rain-washed pavement and scrutinised the Porsche's
undercarriage. And when he was done, he ordered
the car impounded for the crime team's analysis.

"Oh, I say. That can't be necessary" was the complaint made by Mr. Trench Coat. "I stopped, didn't
I? As soon as I saw . . . And I reported it. Surely you
can see that—"

"It's routine." Leach joined the man as a PC was
offering him a cup of coffee. "You'll have the car
back quick enough. What's your name?"

"Pitchley," the man said. "J. W. Pitchley. But see
here, this is an expensive car, and I see no reason . . .

Good God, if I'd hit her, the car would show the signs."

"So you know it's a woman?"

Pitchley looked flustered. "I suppose I thought . . . I did go over to it . . . to her. After I rang triple nine. I got out of the car and went to see if there was anything I could do. She might have been alive."

"But she wasn't?"

"I couldn't actually tell. She wasn't . . . I mean, I could see she was unconscious. She wasn't making a sound. She might have been breathing. But I knew not to touch. . . ." He gulped his coffee. Steam rose from the cup.

"She's a fair enough mess. Our pathologist concluded she's a woman by checking for breasts. What did you do?"

Pitchley looked aghast at the implication. He glanced over his shoulder to the pavement, as if worried that the collection of onlookers standing there could hear his exchange with the detective and would draw erroneous conclusions from it. "Nothing," he said in an undertone. "My God. I didn't do anything. Obviously, I could see that she was wearing a skirt beneath her coat. And her hair's longer than a man's—"

"Where it's not been ripped from her skull."

Pitchley grimaced but went on. "So when I saw the skirt, I just assumed. That's it."

"And that's where she was lying, is it? Right there by the Vauxhall?"

"Yes. Right there. I didn't touch her, didn't move her."

"See anyone on the street? On the pavement? On a porch? At a window? Anywhere?"

"No. No one. I was just driving along. There was no one anywhere except her, and I wouldn't have noticed her at all except her hand—or her arm or something . . . white, this was—caught my eye. That's it."

"Were you alone in your own car?"

"Yes. Yes, of course I was alone. I live alone. Over there. Just up the street."

Leach wondered at the volunteered information. He said, "Where were you coming from this evening, Mr. Pitchley?"

"South Kensington. I was . . . I was dining with a friend."

"The friend's name?"

"I say, am I being accused of something?" Pitchley sounded flustered rather than concerned. "Because if phoning the emergency services when one finds a body is grounds for suspicion, I'd like a solicitor with me when I— Hello, there. *Do* keep your distance from my car, would you please?" This last was directed towards a swarthy constable who was part of a fingertip search ongoing in the street.

More constables combed the area surrounding Pitchley and Leach, and it was from this group that a female PC presently emerged, a woman's handbag in her latex-gloved grip. She trotted towards Leach, and he donned his own gloves, stepping away from Pitchley with instructions to the man to give his address and phone number to one of the policemen guarding his car. He met the female constable in the middle of the street and took the handbag from her.

"Where was it?"

"Ten yards back. Beneath a Montego. Keys and wallet are in it. There's an ID as well. Driving licence."

"Is she local?"

"Henley-on-Thames," the constable replied.

Leach unfastened the handbag's clasp, fished out the keys, and handed them over to the constable. "See if they fit any of the cars in the area," he told her and as she set off to do so, he took out the wallet and opened it to locate the ID.

He first read the name without making a connection. Later he would wonder how he'd failed to twig her identity instantly. But he was feeling so much like trampled horse turds that it wasn't until he'd read not only her organ donor card but also the name imprinted on her cheques that he realised who the woman actually was.

Then he looked from the handbag he was holding to the crumpled form of its owner lying like so much discarded rubbish in the street. And as his body shuddered, what he said was, "God. Eugenie. Jesus Christ. *Eugenie.*"

FAR ACROSS TOWN, Detective Constable Barbara Havers sang along with the rest of the partygoers and wondered how many more choruses of jolly-good-fellowing she was going to have to live through before she could make her escape. It wasn't the hour of the night that bothered her. True, one in the morning meant that she was already cutting critically into her beauty rest, but since even doing a Sleeping-Beauty wouldn't make an inroad into her general appearance, she knew that she could live with the knowledge that if she managed to get four hours' kip at the end of the night, she was going to be one lucky bird. Rather, she was bothered by the reason for the party, exactly *why*, along with her colleagues from New Scotland Yard, she'd been crammed into an overheated house in Stamford Brook for the last five hours.

She knew that twenty-five years of marriage was something worth celebrating. She could count on the digits of her right hand the couples she knew who'd attained that hallmark of connubial longevity, and she wouldn't even have to use her thumb. But there was something about this particular couple that didn't strike her as right, and try as she had done from the moment she'd first stepped into the sitting room where yellow crepe paper and green balloons made a brave attempt to camouflage a shabbiness that had more to do with indifference than with poverty, she'd not been able to shake the feeling that the guests of honour and the company assembled were all taking part in a domestic drama for which she—Barbara Havers—had not been given a script.

At first she told herself that her disconnected

feeling came from partying with her superior officers, one of whom had saved her neck from the professional noose nearly three months earlier and one of whom had attempted to knot the rope himself. Then she decided her discomfort came from arriving at the party in her usual state—dateless—while everyone else had a companion in tow, including her fellow and favourite detective constable, Winston Nkata, who'd brought along his mother, an imposing woman six feet tall and dressed in the Caribbean colours of her birth. Finally, she settled on the simple fact of celebrating *anyone's* marriage as the source of her uneasiness. Jealous cow, I am, Barbara finally told herself with some disgust.

But even that explanation couldn't withstand much serious scrutiny, because under normal circumstances Barbara wasn't given to wasting energy on envy. True, there were reasons aplenty all round for her to feel that barren emotion. She was standing in a crowd of chattering couples—husbands and wives, parents and children, lovers and companions—and she herself was spouseless, partnerless, and childless without a single prospect on her horizon for changing those conditions. But having engaged in her usual reaction to this state of affairs by browsing the buffet table for edible distraction, she'd quickly won herself over to considering all the freedoms afforded her unattached status, and she'd dismissed any disquieting emotions that threatened to undermine her peace of mind.

Still, she didn't feel as bonhomous as she knew she

ought to be feeling at an anniversary party, and as the guests of honour took an overlarge knife in their clasped hands and began to assail a cake whose icing was decorated with roses, ivy, twined hearts, and the words *Happy Twenty-fifth, Malcolm & Frances,* Barbara surreptitiously stole glances round the crowd to see if anyone besides herself was giving more attention to his wristwatch than to the waning moments of the celebration. No one was. Each and every person was focused on Detective Superintendent Malcolm Webberly and his uxorial companion of a quarter of a century, the redoubtable Frances.

This evening represented Barbara's first encounter with Superintendent Webberly's wife, and as she watched the woman feeding her husband a forkful of cake and laughingly accepting her own forkful in turn, Barbara realised that she'd been avoiding any prolonged consideration of Frances Webberly for the entire evening. They'd been introduced by the Webberlys' daughter Miranda in her rôle of hostess and they'd made the sort of polite conversation one always made with the spouse of a colleague. *How many years have you known Malcolm?* and *Do you find it difficult working in a world with so many men to contend with?* and *What drew you to homicide investigations in the first place?* Still, throughout this conversation, Barbara had found herself itching for an escape from Frances, despite the fact that the other woman's words were kindly spoken, her periwinkle eyes fixed pleasantly on Barbara's face.

But perhaps that was it, Barbara decided. Perhaps the source of her uneasiness lay in Frances Webberly's eyes and what was hidden behind them: an emotion, a concern, a sense of something not quite as it should be.

Yet exactly what that something was Barbara couldn't have said. So she gave herself to what she earnestly hoped were the final moments of the shindig, and she applauded along with the rest of the company as the concluding "and so say all of us" was sung.

"Tell us how you've done it," someone from the crowd called out as Miranda Webberly stepped in to relieve her parents at the cake.

"By having no expectations," Frances Webberly said promptly and clasped both hands round her husband's arm. "I had to learn that early, didn't I, darling? Which is just as well since the only thing I actually *gained* from this marriage—aside from my Malcolm—is the two stone I've never been able to lose from carrying Randie."

The company joined her lighthearted laughter. Miranda merely ducked her head and continued cutting the cake.

"That sounds a fair bargain." This was said by Helen, the wife of DI Thomas Lynley. She'd just accepted a plate of cake from Miranda, and she touched the girl fondly on the shoulder.

"Spot on," Superintendent Webberly agreed. "We've got the best daughter on earth."

"Oh, you're right, naturally," Frances said, shooting Helen a smile. "I would be nowhere without Randie. But just you wait, Countess, till the time arrives when that slender body of yours starts to bloat and your ankles swell. Then you'll know what I'm talking about. Lady Hillier, may I offer you cake?"

There it was, Barbara thought, that something not right. *Countess*. And *Lady*. She was several beats off, was Frances Webberly, giving those titles a public airing. Helen Lynley never used her title—her husband was an earl as well as a detective inspector, but he'd go to the rack before mentioning that fact and his wife was just as reticent—and while Lady Hillier might indeed be the wife of Assistant Commissioner Sir David Hillier—who himself would go to the rack before *failing* to make his knighthood known to anyone within hearing distance—she was also Frances Webberly's own sister, and using her title, which Frances had done all night, seemed to be an effort to underscore for everyone differences between them that might otherwise have gone unremarked.

It was all very strange, Barbara thought. Very curious. Very . . . off.

She gravitated towards Helen Lynley. It seemed to Barbara that the simple word *countess* had driven a subtle wedge between Helen and the rest of the party, and as a result the other woman was tucking into her cake alone. Her husband appeared oblivious of this— typical man—since he was engaged in conversation with two of his fellow DIs, Angus MacPherson, who was working on his weight problem by ingesting a piece of cake the size of a shoebox, and John

Stewart, who was compulsively arranging the remaining crumbs from his own piece of cake in a pattern that resembled a Union Jack. So Barbara went to Helen's rescue.

"Is her countess-ship thoroughly chuffed by the evening's festivities?" she asked quietly when she reached Helen's side. "Or haven't enough forelocks been tugged in her direction?"

"Behave yourself, Barbara," Helen remonstrated, but she smiled as she said it.

"Can't do that. I've got a reputation to maintain." Barbara accepted a plate of cake and tucked into it happily. "You know, your slenderness," she went on, "you could at least *try* to look dumpy like the rest of us. Have you thought about wearing horizontal stripes?"

"There *is* that wallpaper I got for the spare room," Helen said thoughtfully. "It's vertical, but I could wear it on its side."

"You owe it to your fellow females. One woman maintaining her appropriate body weight makes the rest of us look like elephants."

"I'm afraid I won't be maintaining it for long," Helen said.

"Oh, I wouldn't go to Ladbrokes to put five quid—" Barbara suddenly realised what Helen was saying. She glanced at her in surprise and saw that Helen's face bore an uncharacteristically bashful half smile.

"Holy *hell*," Barbara intoned. "Helen, are you

really . . . ? You and the inspector? Hell. That's bloody *brilliant,* that is." She looked across the room at Lynley, his blond head cocked to listen to something that Angus MacPherson was saying to him. "The inspector hasn't said a word."

"We've only just found out this week. No one actually knows yet. That seemed best."

"Oh. Right. Yeah," Barbara agreed, but she didn't know what to think about the fact that Helen Lynley had just confided in her. She felt a sudden warmth swell over her and a quick pulsing in the back of her throat. "Gosh. Hell. Well, never fear, Helen. Mum'll be the absolute word at this end till you tell me otherwise." And as she realised her inadvertent pun, Helen did also, and they laughed together.

It was at this moment that Barbara caught sight of the caterer tiptoeing along the side of the dining room from the direction of the kitchen, a cordless phone in her hand.

"A call for the superintendent," she announced, but she managed to sound apologetic about the fact, and she added, "Sorry," as if there had actually been a chance in hell that she could have done something about it.

"Here comes trouble," DI Angus MacPherson rumbled as "At *this* hour?" Frances Webberly asked. She said anxiously, "Malcolm, good heavens . . . You can't . . ."

A sympathetic murmur rose from the guests. They all knew either first- or secondhand what a phone call at one in the morning meant. So did Webberly. He said, "Can't be helped, Fran," and he put a hand on her shoulder as he went to take the call.

DETECTIVE INSPECTOR THOMAS Lynley wasn't surprised when the superintendent excused himself from the party and climbed the stairs with the cordless receiver pressed to his ear. He *was* surprised, however, at the length of time that his superior officer was gone. At least twenty minutes passed during which the superintendent's guests finished their cake and coffee and made noises about heading for their respective homes. Frances Webberly protested at this, casting more than one vexed glance at the stairs. They couldn't leave just yet, she told them, not before Malcolm had the chance to thank them for being part of their anniversary party. Wouldn't they wait for Malcolm?

She didn't add what she would never say. If their guests left before her husband had completed his phone call, common courtesy suggested that Frances step into the front garden to bid farewell to the people who'd come to honour her marriage. And what had long gone unmentioned between Malcolm Webberly and most of his colleagues was the fact that Frances had not put a toe outside her house in more than ten years.

"Phobias," Webberly had explained to Lynley on the single occasion when he'd spoken about his wife. "It began with simple things that I didn't notice. By the time they had a tight enough hold on her to get

my attention, she was spending all day in the bedroom. Wrapped in a blanket, would you believe it?
God forgive me."

The secrets men live with, Lynley thought as he
watched Frances fluttering among her guests. There
was an edge to her gaiety that no one could miss, a
hint of the determined and the anxious to her pleasure. Randie had wished to surprise her parents with
an anniversary party at a local restaurant where there
would be more room, even a dance floor for the
guests. But that hadn't been possible considering
Frances's condition, so the venue was restricted to the
family's disintegrating old house in Stamford Brook.

Webberly finally descended the stairs as the company were making their farewells, ushered to the
door by his daughter, who wrapped her arm round
her mother's waist. It was a fond gesture on Randie's
part. It served the double purpose of reassuring
Frances even as it prevented her from tearing away
from the door.

"Not leaving?" Webberly boomed from the stairs,
where he'd lit a cigar that was sending a blue cloud in
the direction of the ceiling. "The night is young."

"The night is morning," Laura Hillier informed
him, fondly pressing her cheek to her niece's and saying her farewells. "Lovely party, Randie. You did
your parents proud." Her hand clasped in her husband's, she went out into the night, where the rain
that had been falling heavily all evening had finally
stopped.

Assistant Commissioner Hillier's departure gave

the rest of the company permission to go, and people began to do so, Lynley among them. He was waiting for his wife's coat to be unearthed from somewhere upstairs, when Webberly joined him at the door to the sitting room and said in a low voice, "Stay a moment, Tommy. If you will."

There was a drawn quality to the superintendent's face that prompted Lynley to murmur, "Of course." Next to him, his wife said spontaneously, "Frances, have you your wedding pictures anywhere at hand? I won't let Tommy take me home till I've seen you on your day of glory."

Lynley shot Helen a grateful look. Within another ten minutes, the remaining guests had departed and while Helen occupied Frances Webberly and Miranda helped the caterer clear away dishes and serving platters, Lynley and Webberly repaired to the study, a cramped room barely large enough for a desk, an armchair, and the bookshelves that furnished it.

Perhaps in deference to Lynley's abstemious habits, Webberly went to the window and wrestled with it to give some respite from his cigar smoke. Cold autumn air, heavy with damp, floated into the room.

"Sit down, Tommy." Webberly himself remained standing, next to the window, where the dim ceiling light cast him mostly in shadow.

Lynley waited for Webberly to speak. The superintendent, however, was chewing the inside of his lower lip, as if the words he wanted to say were there and he needed to taste them for their fluency.

Outside the house, a car's gears ground discordantly, while inside the doors to kitchen cupboards banged shut. These noises seemed to act like a spur upon Webberly. He looked up from his musing and said, "That was a bloke called Leach on the phone. We used to be partners. I haven't talked to him in years. It's rotten to lose touch that way. I don't know why it happens, but it just does."

Lynley knew that Webberly had hardly asked him to remain behind in order to hear the superintendent wax melancholy on the state of a friendship. One forty-five in the morning was hardly the hour to be discussing one's former mates. Still, to give the older man an opportunity to confide, Lynley said, "Is Leach still in the force, sir? I don't think I know him."

"Northwest London police," Webberly said. "He and I worked together twenty years ago."

"Ah." Lynley thought about this. Webberly would have been thirty-five at the time, which meant he was speaking of his Kensington years. "CID?" he asked.

"He was my sergeant. He's in Hampstead now, heading up the murder squad. DCI Eric Leach. Good man. Very good man."

Lynley studied Webberly thoughtfully: faded, thin straw-coloured hair hastily brushed across his forehead, natural ruddiness of complexion muted, neck holding the head at an angle that suggested too much weight on his shoulders. Everything about him spoke of a single explanation—bad news—and a single source—the phone call.

Webberly roused himself but didn't move from the

shadows as he spoke. "He's working a hit-and-run up in West Hampstead, Tommy. That's why he called. It happened round ten, eleven tonight. The victim's a woman." Webberly paused, seemed to be waiting for Lynley to make a response of some kind. When Lynley didn't do anything other than nod—unfortunately, hit-and-runs happened with a distressing frequency in an urban environment in which foreigners often forgot which side of the street they were supposed to be driving on and in which direction they ought to be looking if they were pedestrians—Webberly studied the tip of his cigar and cleared his throat. "From the state of things, Leach's crime scene people are guessing that someone knocked her down, then deliberately ran over her. And then got out, dragged her body to one side, and drove on his way."

"Christ," Lynley murmured reverently.

"Her handbag was found nearby. Car keys and ID were in it. The car itself wasn't far, right there on the street. Inside, on the passenger seat, was a London *A to Z*, along with specific directions to the street where she was killed. And an address was there as well: Number Thirty-two Crediton Hill."

"Who lives there?"

"The bloke who found the body, Tommy. The very same bloke who happened to drive up the street within an hour of her being hit."

"Was he expecting the victim at his home? Had they an appointment?"

"Not that we know of, but we don't know much.

Leach said the bastard looked like he'd swallowed an onion when they told him the woman had his address in her car. All he said was 'No. That's impossible,' and phoned his solicitor directly."

Which was, of course, his right. But there was certainly something suspicious about that being someone's first reaction to learning a murder victim was carrying his address.

Still, neither the hit-and-run nor the oddity of its discovery could explain to Lynley why DCI Leach had phoned Webberly at one in the morning or why Webberly was reporting that phone call to him now.

He said, "Sir, is DCI Leach in over his head for some reason? Is something wrong with the murder squad in Hampstead?"

"Why did he phone, you mean? And more importantly, why am I telling you?" Webberly didn't wait for a reply before he sank into his desk chair and said, "Because of the victim, Tommy. She's Eugenie Davies, and I want you involved. I want to move heaven and earth and hell if I have to, to get to the bottom of what happened to her. Leach knew that the moment he saw who she was."

Lynley frowned. "Eugenie Davies? Who was she?"

"How old are you, Tommy?"

"Thirty-seven, sir."

Webberly blew out a breath. "Then I suppose you're too young to remember."

GIDEON

23 AUGUST

I DIDN'T like the way you asked me the question, Dr. Rose. I was offended by your tone and the implication. Don't try to tell me there *was* no implication, because I'm not that much of a fool. And don't make allusions to the "real meaning" behind a patient's drawing inferences from your words in the first place. I know what I heard, I know what happened, and I can summarise both for you in a sentence: You read what I've written, saw an omission in the story, and pounced on it like a criminal barrister with a mind so closed as to be virtually useless.

Let me repeat what I said in our session: I made no mention of my mother until that final sentence because I was attempting to fulfil your assignment to me, which was to write what I remember, and I was writing *what* I was writing as it came into my mind. She did not come into my mind before then: before Raphael Robson became, virtually, my full-time instructor and companion.

But the Italian-Greek-Portuguese-Spanish girl *did* come into your mind? you ask me in that insufferably quiet calm placid manner of yours.

Yes, she did. What's that supposed to mean? That I have a heretofore unmentioned affinity for Portuguese-Spanish-Italian-Greek girls, arising from my unacknowledged indebtedness to an unnamed young woman who unknowingly started me on my path to success? Is that it, Dr. Rose?

Ah. I see. You give me no answer. You keep a safe distance in your father's chair and you fix your soulful eyes on me and I'm meant to take this distance between us as the Bosporus waiting for me to swim. Plunge into the waters of veracity, it suggests. As if I'm not telling the truth.

She was there. Of course she was there, my mother. And if I mentioned the Italian girl instead of my mother, it was for the simple reason that the Italian girl—and why can't I remember her blasted *name,* for God's sake?—figured in the Gideon Legend while my mother did not. And I *thought* you instructed me to write what I remembered, going back to the earliest memory I could recall. If that's not what you instructed me to do, if instead you wished me to manufacture the salient details of a childhood that is largely fiction but safely and antiseptically regurgitated in such a way that you can identify and label where and what you choose—

Oh yes, I am angry, before you point that out to me. Because I do not see what my mother, an analysis of my mother, or even a superficial conversation about my mother has to do with what happened at Wigmore Hall. And that's why I've come to see you, Dr. Rose. Let's not forget that. I've agreed to this process because there on the stage in Wigmore Hall, in front of an audience paying mightily to benefit the East London Conservatory—which is my own *charity,* mind you—I mounted the platform, I rested my violin on my shoulder, I picked up my bow, I flexed my left hand's fingers as usual, I nodded to the pianist and the cellist . . . and I could not play. God in heaven, do you know what that *means?*

This wasn't stage fright, Dr. Rose. This wasn't a temporary block against a single piece of music, which, by the way, I'd spent the last two weeks rehearsing. This was a total, utter, complete, and humiliating loss of ability. Not only had the music itself been ripped from my brain, but how to play the music—not to mention how to *live*—was gone as well. I may as well not ever have held a violin, let alone have spent the last twenty-one years of my life performing in public.

Sherrill began the Allegro, and I heard it without the slightest degree of recognition. And where I was supposed to join the piano and the cello: nothing. I knew neither what to do nor when to do it. I was Lot's son incarnate had he and not the man's wife been the one to turn and observe the destruction.

Sherrill covered for me. He feinted. He *improvised,* God help him, with Beethoven. He worked his way round to my entrance again. And again there was nothing. Just silence like a vacuum, and the silence roared like a hurricane in my head.

So I left the platform. Blindly, body shivering, vision tunneling, I walked. Dad met me in the Green Room, crying, "What? Gideon. For God's sake. *What?*" with Raphael only a step behind him.

I thrust my instrument into Raphael's hands and collapsed. Babble all round me and my father saying, "It's that bloody girl, isn't it? This is down to her. God damn it. Get a *grip,* Gideon. You have obligations."

And Sherrill, who'd left the platform in my wake, asking, "Gid? What happened? Lose your nerve? Shit. It happens sometimes."

While Raphael set my violin on the table saying, "Oh dear. I was afraid this would happen eventually." Because like most people he was thinking of himself, of his own countless failures to perform in a public venue like his father and his father before him. Every member of his family has a high-powered career in performance music save poor sweating Raphael, and I expect he's secretly been biding his time, waiting for disaster to befall me, making us official brothers in misery. He was the one who cautioned against climbing aboard the swift acceleration that occurred in my career after my first public concert when I was seven. Evidently, now he thinks the chickens of catastrophe, born of that acceleration, have come home to roost on my shoulders.

But it wasn't nerves that I felt in the Green Room,

Dr. Rose. And it wasn't nerves that I felt before, in front of that audience out in the Hall. It was instead some sort of shutdown, which feels irrevocable and complete. And what was odd about it was that despite the fact that I could hear all their voices—my father's, Raphael's, and Sherrill's—quite clearly, all I could see in front of me was white light shining on a blue, blue door.

Am I having an episode, Dr. Rose? Just like Granddad, am I having an episode that a nice calm countryside visit can cure? Please tell me, because music is not what I do, music is who I am and if I don't have it—the sound and the sheer *chivalry* of sound—I am nothing but an empty husk.

So what does it matter that in recounting my introduction to music, I made no mention of my mother? It was an omission of sound and fury, and you'd be wise to account its significance accordingly.

But to omit her now would be deliberate, you tell me. You say, Tell me about your mother, Gideon.

25 AUGUST

She went to work. She'd been a constant presence for my first four years, but once it became clear that she had a child of exceptional talent that needed fostering, which was going to be not only time-consuming but hideously expensive, she took a job to help out with the costs. I was given into the care of my grandmother—when I was not practising my instrument, having lessons with Raphael, listening to the recordings he brought for me, or attending concerts in his company—but my life had altered so appreciably from what it had been before that day I first heard the music in Kensington Square, I hardly noticed her absence. Prior to that, however, I do remember accompanying her—it seemed like every day—to early morning Mass.

She'd struck up a friendship with a nun at the convent in the square, and between them they'd arranged that my mother could attend the daily Mass that was said for the sisters. She was a convert to Catholicism, my mother. But as her own father was an Anglican minister, I wonder now how much her conversion had to do with devotion to a different dogma and how much it had to do with slapping her father in the face. He wasn't, as I was given to understand it, a very nice fellow. Other than that, I don't recall him.

This is not the case for my mother, but she's a shadowy figure for me because she left us. When I was nine or ten—I can't remember which—I arrived home from a concert tour of Austria to find that my mother had quit Kensington Square, leaving not a trace of herself behind. She took every article of clothing she possessed, each one of her books, and a number of family photographs. And off she went, like a figurative thief in the night. Except it was the day, I've been told. And she called a taxi. She left no note and no forwarding address, and I never heard from her again.

My father had been with me in Austria—Dad always traveled with me, and Raphael often accompanied us as well—so he was as much in the dark about where Mother had gone and why she had gone as I myself was. All I know is that we came home to find Granddad having an episode, Gran weeping on the stairs, and Calvin the Lodger trying to find the appropriate phone number with no one to help him.

Calvin the Lodger? you ask me. The earlier lodger—James, is that right?—he was gone?

Yes. He must have left the year before. Or the year before that. I don't remember. We had a number of lodgers over time. We had to, in order to make ends meet, as I've already noted.

Do you remember them all? you want to know.

I don't. Just those who figure large, I suppose. Calvin because he was there that night when I first learned my mother had gone. James because he was present when everything began.

Everything? you ask.

Yes. The violin. The lessons. Miss Orr. Everything.

26 AUGUST

I associate everyone with music. When I think of Rosemary Orr, I think of Brahms, the concerto that was playing the first time I met her. When I think of Raphael, it's the Mendelssohn. Dad is Bach, the solo violin sonata in G minor. And Granddad will always be Paganini. The twenty-fourth caprice was his favourite. "All those notes," he would marvel. "All those perfect notes."

And your mother? you ask me. What about her? Which piece of music do you associate with your mother?

Interestingly, I can't attach an actual piece of music to Mother the way I can with the others. I'm not sure why. A form of denial, perhaps? Repression of emotion? I don't know. You're the psychiatrist. Explain it to me.

I still do this with music, by the way. I still associate a person with a piece. Sherrill, for example, is Bartók's Rhapsody, which is what he and I initially played together in public, years ago, at St. Martin's in the Fields. We've never played it since and we were teenagers then—the American and the English *wunderkind* together made excellent press, believe me—but he'll always be Bartók when I think of him. That's just how it works in my mind.

And it's the same for people who aren't musical in the least. Take Libby, for instance. Have I told you about Libby? She's Libby the Lodger. Yes, like James and Calvin and all the others except she's of the present, not of the past, and she lives in the lower ground floor flat of my house in Chalcot Square.

I hadn't thought of letting it till she turned up at my door one day, ferrying a recording contract that my agent had decided had to be signed at once. She works for a courier service, and I didn't know she was a girl till she handed me the paperwork, took off her helmet, and said with a nod at the contracts, "Don't be bugged by this, okay? I just gotta ask. You a rock musician or something?" in that excessively casual and friendly fashion that seems to plague the native Californian.

I replied, "No. I'm a concert violinist."

She said, "No way!"

I said, "Way."

To which she produced such a blank expression that I thought I was dealing with a congenital idiot.

I won't ever sign contracts without having read them—no matter what my agent claims this reveals about my lack of trust in his wisdom—and rather than have the poor urchin—for so she seemed to me—wait on the front step while I read through the document, I asked her in and we climbed to the first floor, which is where the music room overlooks the square.

She said, "Oh wow. Sorry. You *are* somebody, aren't you?" as we climbed because she noticed the art work for the CD covers hanging along the staircase. "I feel like a real dope."

I said, "No need," and walked into the music room with her on my heels and my own head buried in clauses about accompanists, royalties, and time lines.

"Oh, this is awesome," she intoned while I went to the window seat where even now I'm writing in this notebook for you, Dr. Rose. "Who's this guy you're with in the picture? This guy with the crutches? Jeez. Look at you. You look seven years old!"

God. He's possibly the greatest violinist on earth and the girl's as ignorant as a tube of toothpaste. "Itzhak Perlman," I told her. "And I was six at the time, not seven."

"Wow. You actually *played* with him when you were only *six*?"

"Hardly. But he was kind enough to listen to me one afternoon when he was in London."

"Very cool."

And as I read she continued to wander, murmuring from her rather limited vocabulary of exclamations. She took particular pleasure—so it seemed—in an examination of my earliest instrument, that one-sixteenth that I keep in the music room on a little stand. I also keep the Guarneri there, the violin that I use today. It was in its case, and the case was open because when Libby arrived with the paperwork for me, I'd been in the midst of my morning practise. Obviously unaware of the trespass she was committing, she casually reached down and plucked the E-string.

She might as well have shot a pistol in the room. I leapt up and bellowed, "Don't *touch* that violin!" and so startled her that she reacted like a child who's been struck. She said, "Oh my gosh," and she backed away from the instrument with her hands behind her and her eyes filling. And then she turned away in embarrassment.

I set my paperwork aside and said, "Look. Sorry. Didn't mean to be a swine, but that instrument's two hundred and fifty years old. I'm rather careful with it, and I usually don't allow—"

Her back turned to me, she waved me off. She took several deep breaths before she shook her head vigorously, which made her hair puff out—have I mentioned that her hair is curly? Toast coloured, it is, and very curly—and she rubbed her eyes. Then she turned round and said, "Sorry about that. It's okay. I shouldn't have touched it and I totally wasn't thinking. You were right to tell me off, you really were. It's just that, like, for a second you were so totally rock, and I freaked."

Language from another planet. I said, "Totally rock?"

She said, "Rock Peters. Formerly Rocco Petrocelli and currently my estranged husband. I mean, as estranged as he'll let us be since he holds the purse strings and he's not exactly into loosening them to help me get established on my own."

I thought she looked far too young to be married to anyone, but it turned out that, despite her looks and what appeared to be a rather charming prepubescent plumpness, she was twenty-three years old and two years married to the irascible Rock. At the moment, however, I said, "Ah."

She said, "He's got, like, this hair-trigger temper among other things, such as not knowing monogamy is usually part of the marriage deal. I never knew when he was going to blow a fuse. After two years cowering round the apartment, I called it quits."

"Oh. Sorry." I admit that I felt uneasy with her unburdening of personal details. It's not that I'm unused to such displays. This tendency to confession and contrition seems peculiar to all the Americans I've ever known, as if they've somehow become acculturated to disbosoming themselves along with learning to salute their flag. But being used to something isn't exactly akin to welcoming it into your life. What, after all, is one to *do* with someone else's personal data?

She gave me more of it. She wanted a divorce; he did not. They continued to live together because she could not come up with the cash to break away from him. Whenever she came close to the amount she needed, he simply withheld her wages until she'd spent whatever nest egg she'd managed to accumulate. "And why he even *wants* me there is, like, the major mystery of my life, you know? I mean the man is *totally* governed by the herd instinct, so what's the point?"

He was, she explained, a womaniser without peer, an adherent to the philosophy that groups of females—"the herd, get it?"—should be dominated and serviced by a single male. "But the problem is that the entire female sex is the herd in Rock's mind. And he's got to hump them all just to keep them happy." Then she clapped her hand over her mouth and said, "Oops. Sorry." And then she grinned. And then she said, "Anyway. Gosh. Look at me. I'm, like, totally running *off* at the mouth. Got those papers signed?"

Which I hadn't. Who'd had an opportunity to read them? I said I'd sign them if she wouldn't mind waiting. She took herself to a corner and sat.

I read. I made one phone call to clarify a clause. I signed the contracts and returned them to her. She shoved them into her pouch, said thanks, and then cocked her head at me and asked, "Favour?"

"What?"

She shifted her weight and looked embarrassed. But she plunged ahead and I admired her for it. She said, "Would you . . . I mean, it's like, I've never actually heard a violin in person before. Would you please play a song?"

A song. She was indeed a philistine. But even a philistine is educable, and she'd asked politely. What would it hurt? I'd been practising anyway, working on Bartók's solo sonata, so I gave her part of the *Melodia,* playing it as I always play: putting the music before myself, before her, before everything. By the time I'd reached the end of the movement, I'd forgotten she was there. So I went on to the *Presto,* hearing as usual Raphael's injunction: "Make it an invitation to *dance,* Gideon. Feel its quickness. Make it flash, like light."

And when I was finished, I was brought back to an abrupt awareness of her presence. She said, "Oh wow. Oh wow. Oh *wow.* I mean, you are so totally excellent, aren't you?"

I looked her way to see that sometime during the playing she'd begun to cry, because her cheeks were wet and she was digging round in her leathers, looking—I presume—for something on which to wipe her dribbling nose. I was pleased to have touched her with the Bartók, and even more pleased to see that my assessment of her educability had been on target. And I suppose it was because of that assessment that I asked her to join me in my regular cup of midmorning coffee. The day was fine, so we took it in the garden, where, under the arbour, I'd been creating one of my kites on the previous afternoon.

I haven't mentioned my kites before this, have I, Dr. Rose? Well, there's nothing to them, actually. They're just something I do when I feel the need to take a break from the music. I fly them from Primrose Hill.

Ah yes. I can see that you're searching for meaning there, aren't you? What does creating and flying kites *symbolise* in the patient's history and in his present life? The unconscious mind speaks in all our actions. The conscious mind merely has to grasp the meaning behind those actions and wrestle it into comprehensible form.

Kites. Air. Freedom. But freedom from what? What need do I have to be free when my life is full and rich and complete?

Let me complicate the skein you've been commissioned to unravel by telling you that I fly gliders as well. No, not the gliders you sail into the air from a hilltop, watching as the currents take them. But gliders that you *pilot* up in the air, towed by a plane and released to find those same currents yourself.

My father finds this a particularly horrifying hobby. Indeed, it's become a subject so sore that we no longer discuss it. When he finally realised that I'd moved beyond his ability to influence me with regard to what few leisure hours I actually have, he shouted, "I wash my hands of you, Gideon!" and the topic became taboo between us.

It seems dangerous, you tell me.

No more than life, I reply.

And then you ask, What is it you like about glid-ing? The silence? The technical mastery of something so different to your chosen profession? Or is it the es-cape that you're seeking, Gideon? Or perhaps the inherent risks?

And I say that there is danger in digging too deeply for meaning when something can be so simply ex-plained: As a child and once my talent became appar-ent, I was not allowed a single activity that might injure my hands. Designing and creating kites, flying gliders . . . My hands are quite safe from harm.

But you do see the relevance of activities associated with the sky, don't you, Gideon? you ask me.

I see only that the sky is blue. Blue like the door. That blue blue door.

GIDEON

28 AUGUST

I DID what you suggested, Dr. Rose, and I've nothing to report apart from the fact that I felt a real fool. Perhaps the experiment would have turned out differently had I cooperated and done it in your office as you asked, but I couldn't get my mind round what you were talking about, and it seemed absurd. More absurd, even, than spending hours at this notebook when I could be practising my instrument as I used to. As I *want* to.

But I still haven't touched it.

Why?

Don't ask the obvious, Dr. Rose. It's gone. Can't you see that and what it means? The music is gone.

Dad was here this morning. He's only just left. He came round to see if I'd improved at all—for that you can read Have I tried to play again?—although he was good enough not to ask the question directly. But then, he didn't actually *need* to ask it since the Guarneri was in the position he'd left it when he brought me home from Wigmore Hall. I haven't even had the nerve to touch the case.

Why? you ask.

You know the answer. Because at the moment I lack the courage: If I can't play, if the gift, the ear, the talent, the genius, or whatever else you wish to call it is moribund or gone from me entirely, how do I exist? Not how do I go on, Dr. Rose, but how do I exist? How do I exist when the sum and substance of who I am and who I have been for the last twenty-five years is contained in and defined by my music?

Then let's look at the music itself, you say. If each person in your life is indeed associated in some way with your music, perhaps we need to examine your music much more carefully for the key to unlock what's troubling you.

I laugh and say, Did you intend that pun?

And you gaze at me with those penetrating eyes. You refuse to engage in levity. You say, So that final Bartók you were writing about, the solo sonata . . . Is that what you associate with Libby?

Yes, I associate the sonata with Libby. But Libby's nothing to do with my present problem. I assure you of that.

My father found this notebook, by the way. When he came round to check on me, he found it on the window seat. And before you ask, he wasn't nosy-parkering. My dad might be an insufferably single-minded bastard, but he isn't a spy. He's merely given the last twenty-five years of his life to supporting his only child's career, and he'd like to see that career stay afloat and not go swimming down the toilet.

His only child not for long, though. I'd forgotten all about that in these last few weeks. There's Jill to consider. I can't imagine having a new brother or sister at my age, let alone a stepmother less than ten years my senior. But these are the days of elastic families, and the course of wisdom suggests that one stretch with the changing definitions of spouse, not to mention of father, mother, and sibling.

But yes, I think it a little *odd,* this bit about my father and his production of a new family. It's not that I expected him to remain a divorced single man forever. It's just that after nearly twenty years in which he never to my knowledge even had a date with a woman—let alone a relationship whose depth might suggest the sort of physical intimacy that produces children—it's all come as something of a shock to me.

I'd met Jill at the BBC when I was previewing a rough cut of that documentary they filmed at the East London Conservatory. This was several years ago, just before she produced that outstanding adaptation of *Desperate Remedies*—Did you see it, by the way? She's quite a Thomas Hardy buff—and she was working in their documentary division then, if that's what it's called. Dad must have met her as well at that time, but I don't recall ever seeing them together and I can't say at what point they became each other's partner. I do recall being invited round to Dad's flat for a meal and finding her there in the kitchen, stirring away at something on the cooker, and while I was surprised to see her, I simply assumed she was there because she'd brought along a final copy of the documentary for us to preview. I suppose that might have been the start of their relationship. Dad became slightly less available to me after that evening, now I come to think about it. So perhaps everything began that night. But as Jill and Dad have never lived together—although Dad says that's being arranged for shortly after the baby's birth—I really had no reason to conclude there was anything at all between them.

And now that you know? you ask me. How do you feel? And when did you learn about them and the baby? And where?

I see the direction you're taking. But I have to tell you it's something of a non-starter.

I learned about my father's situation with Jill some months ago, not on the day of the concert at Wigmore Hall, not even during the week or the month of the concert, in fact. And there was no blue door anywhere in sight when I was given the news about my future half sibling. You see, I knew where you were heading, didn't I?

But how did you feel? you persist in asking. A second family for your father after all these years—

Not a second family, I hasten to tell you. A third.

His third family? You look at the notes you've been taking during our sessions and you see no reference to an earlier family, before my own birth. But there was one and there was a child from that family, a girl who died in infancy.

She was called Virginia, and I don't know exactly how she died or where or how long after her death my father ended his marriage to her mother or even who her mother was. In fact, the only reason I know about her existence at all—or about my father's earlier marriage—is that Granddad began shouting about it during one of his episodes. It was in the same vein as his "you're no son of mine" curses as he was being taken from the house. Except this time it was along the lines of Dad's not being any son of Granddad's because all he could ever produce was freaks. And I suppose I was given a hasty explanation by someone—Was it Mother who told me or was she gone by then?—since I must have assumed that, in shouting about freaks, Granddad meant me. So Virginia must have died because there was something wrong with her, a congenital condition perhaps. But I don't actually know what it was, because whoever it was who told me about her in the first place didn't know or wouldn't say and because the subject never came up again.

Never came up? you query.

But you know the dance, Doctor. Children don't mention topics that they associate with chaos, tumult, and contention. They learn quite early the consequences of stirring a pot best left alone. And I assume you can make the leap from there yourself: Since the violin was my sole concentration, once I was assured of my grandfather's esteem, I thought no more of the subject.

The subject of the blue door, however, is something else entirely. As I said when I began, I did exactly as you asked me to do and as we tried to do in your office. In my mind I recreated that door: Prussian blue with a silverish ring in its centre serving as a knob; two locks, I think, done in silver like the ring; and perhaps a house number or a flat number above the knob.

I darkened my bedroom and stretched out on my bed and closed my eyes and visualised that door; I visualised my approach to it; I visualised my hand grasping the ring that served as its knob and my fingers turning keys in the locks, the lower lock first with one of those old-fashioned keys with large and easily duplicated teeth, the upper lock next, which is modern, burglar proof, and safe. With the locks disengaged, I put my shoulder against the door, gave a slight push, and . . . Nothing. Absolutely nothing.

There is *nothing* there, Dr. Rose. My mind is a blank. You want to make interpretive leaps based on what I find behind that door, or what colour it is, or the fact that it has two locks, not one, and a ring for a knob—Could he be fleeing from commitment? you ask yourself—while I'm inspired by this exercise to tell you bloody sod all. Nothing has been revealed to me. Nothing lurks ghoul-like behind that door. It leads to no room that I can conjure up, it merely sits at the top of a staircase like—

Staircase, you leap. So there's a staircase as well?

Yes. A staircase. Which, we both know, means climbing, rising, elevating, clawing out of this pit . . . What *of* it?

You see the agitation in my scrawl, don't you? You say, Stay with the fear. It won't kill you, Gideon. Feelings won't kill you. You are not alone.

I never thought that I was, I say. Don't put words in my mouth, Dr. Rose.

2 SEPTEMBER

Libby was here. She knows something's not right since she hadn't heard the violin in days and she generally hears it for hours on end when I'm practising. That's largely why I hadn't let the lower ground floor flat once the original tenants left. I thought about it when I first bought and moved into this house in Chalcot Square, but I didn't want the distraction of a tenant coming and going—even by a separate entrance—and I didn't want to have to limit my hours of practise out of concern for someone else. I told Libby all this when she was leaving that day, when she'd zipped herself into her leathers, returned her helmet to her head just outside my front door, and caught sight of the empty flat below through the wrought iron railings. She said, "Wow. Is that for rent or anything?"

And I explained that I left it empty. There was a young couple living there when I first bought the building, I told her. But as they weren't able to develop a passion for the violin at odd hours of the night, they soon decamped.

She cocked her head. She said, "Hey. How old are you anyway? And do you always talk like a bottle's in your butt? When you were showing me the kites, you sounded totally normal. So what's up? Is this about being English or something? Step out of the house and all of a sudden you're Henry James?"

"He wasn't English," I informed her.

"Well. Sorry." She began to fasten her helmet's strap, but she seemed agitated because she had trouble with it. "I got through high school on Cliffs Notes, bud, so I wouldn't know Henry James from Sid Vicious. I don't even know why he popped into my head. Or why Sid Vicious did, for that matter."

"Who's Sid Vicious?" I asked her solemnly.

She peered at me. "Come on. You're joking."

"Yes," I said.

And then she laughed. Well, not laughed actually. It was more like a hoot. And she grabbed my arm and said, "You, *you,*" with such an inordinate degree of familiarity that I was both astounded and charmed. So I offered to show her the lower ground floor flat.

Why? you ask.

Because she'd asked about it and I wanted to show her and I suppose I wanted her company for a while. She was so absolutely un-English.

You say, I didn't mean why did you show her the flat, Gideon. I meant why are you telling me about Libby.

Because she was here, just now.
She's significant, isn't she?
I don't know.

3 SEPTEMBER

"It's Liberty, she tells me. "God, isn't that, like, totally the *worst?* My parents were hippies before they were yuppies, which was way before my dad made, like, a billion dollars in Silicon Valley. You *do* know about Silicon Valley, don't you?"

We are walking to the top of Primrose Hill. I have one of my kites. Libby's talked me into flying it this late afternoon, sometime last year. I ought to be rehearsing, since I'm due to record Paganini—the second violin concerto, this is—with the Philharmonic in less than three weeks and the *Allegro maestoso* has been giving me some trouble. But Libby's returned from a confrontation with the acidulous Rock about wages he's withheld from her again, and she's reported his response to her request for her money: "The jerk said, 'Fly a kite, bitch,' so I thought I'd take him up on it. Come on, Gideon, you're working too hard anyway."

I've been at it for six hours, two increments of three with an hour's break to walk over to Regent's Park at noon, so I agree to the plan. I allow her to choose the kite, and she selects a multi-level affair that spins and requires just the right wind velocity to show its best stuff.

We head off. We follow the curve of Chalcot

Crescent—more gentrification sourly remarked upon by Libby, who appears to prefer London decaying to London renewed—and dash across Regent's Park Road and thence into the park, where we set off up the side of the hill.

"Too much wind," I tell her, and I have to raise my voice because the wind gusts fiercely against the kite and the nylon slaps against me. "You've got to have perfect conditions for this one. I don't expect we'll even get it in the air."

That proves to be the case, much to her disappointment because it seems that she "just totally wanted to *put* it to Rock. The creep. He's threatening to tell whoever it is that gets told"—this with a wave of her hand in the vague direction of Westminster, by which I assume she must be talking about the Government—"that we were never really married in the first place. I mean *physically* married like in doing the deed with each other. Which is, like, just such a crock of shit that you wouldn't *believe.*"

"And what would happen if he told the Government that you weren't really married?"

"Except that we *were.* We are. Jeez, he makes me nuts."

As it turns out, she's afraid that her status in the country will change if her estranged husband has his way. And because she's moved from his doubtless—to my imagination—insalubrious home in Bermondsey to the lower ground floor flat in Chalcot Square, he's afraid that he's losing her for good, which he apparently doesn't wish to do despite his continued womanising. So they've had yet another row, the end of which was his directive to her about kite flying.

Sorry not to be able to accommodate her, I invite her for a coffee instead. It's over coffee that she tells me the name for which Libby is merely a diminutive: Liberty.

"Hippies," she says again of her parents. "They wanted their kids to have totally *far out* names"—this with a mock inhalation of an imaginary cannabis cigarette. "My sister's is even worse: Equality, if you can believe it. Ali for short. And if there'd been a third kid in the family . . ."

"Fraternity?" I say.

"You got it," she rejoins. "But I should be excessively glad they went for abstract nouns. I mean, God, it could be totally worse. My name could be Tree."

I chuckle. "Or perhaps just a type of tree: pine, oak, willow."

"Willow Neale. I could get behind that." She fingers through the packets of sugar on the table to find the dieters' sweetener. She is, I have discovered, a chronic dieter whose pursuit of bodily perfection has been "the rip tide in the otherwise peaceful ocean of my existence," she's said. She dumps the sweetener into her non-fat caffèlatte and says, "What about you, Gid?"

"Me?"

"Your parents. What are they like? Not former flower children, I bet."

She hadn't yet met my father, you see, although he had seen her from the music room late one afternoon when she returned home from work on her Suzuki and parked it in her accustomed place on the pavement, right next to the steps that lead down to the lower ground floor flat. She roared up and gunned the engine two or three times, as is her habit, creating a ruckus that caught Dad's attention. He went to the window, saw her, and said, "I'll be damned. There's an infernal cyclist actually chaining his motorbike to your front rails, Gideon. See here . . ." and he began to open the window.

I said, "That's Libby Neale. It's fine, Dad. She lives here."

He turned slowly from the glass. "What? That's a *woman* out there? She *lives* here?"

"Below. In the flat. I decided to let it out. Did I forget to tell you?"

I hadn't done. But my failure to mention Libby and the flat hadn't been so much a deliberate omission as a subject that hadn't come up. Dad and I talk every day, but our conversations are always about our professional concerns, like an upcoming concert, a tour he might be organising, a recording session that hadn't gone well, a request for an interview, or a personal appearance. Witness the fact that I didn't know a thing about his relationship with Jill until *not* mentioning it became more awkward than mentioning it: The sudden appearance of an obviously pregnant woman in one's life will demand some sort of explanation, after all. But otherwise, we've never had a chummy father-and-son relationship. We've both been absorbed with my music since my childhood, and this concentration on both our parts has precluded the possibility—or perhaps obviated the necessity—of the sort of soul baring that appears to be the hallmark of closeness between people these days.

Mind you, I don't regret for an instant that Dad and I have the sort of connection with each other that we have. It's firm and true, and if it's not the sort of bond that makes us want to hike the Himalayas together or paddle up the Nile, it's still a relationship that strengthens and supports me. Truth be told, if it were not for my father, Dr. Rose, I would not be where I am today.

4 SEPTEMBER

No. You will not catch me with that.

Where are you today, Gideon? you ask me blandly.

But I refuse to participate. My father plays no part in this, in whatever *this* is. If I cannot bring myself to even pick up the Guarneri, it is not my father's fault. I refuse to become one of those gormless pulers who lay the blame for their every difficulty at the feet of their parents. Dad's life was rough. He did his best.

Rough in what way? you want to know.

Well, can you imagine having Granddad for a father? Being sent off to school when you were six? Growing up with a steady diet of someone's psychotic episodes to feed you when you *were* at home? And always knowing that there was never a hope in hell that you could fully measure up no matter *what* you did because you were adopted in the first place and your father never let you forget it? No. Dad's done the best he could as a father. And he's done better than most as a son.

Better than yourself as a son? you ask me.

You'll have to get that information from Dad.

But what do you think about yourself as a son, Gideon? What comes first to your mind?

Disappointment, I say.

That you've disappointed your father?

No. That I mustn't. But that I might.

Has he let you know how important it is not to disappoint him?

Never once. Not at all. But . . .

But?

He doesn't like Libby. I somehow knew that he wouldn't like her or at least wouldn't like her being there. He would consider her a potential distraction or, worse, an impediment to my work.

You ask, Is that why he said, "It's that girl, isn't it?" when you had your blackout in Wigmore Hall? He leapt right to her, didn't he?

Yes.

Why?

It's not that he doesn't want me to be with some-one. Why wouldn't he? Family is everything to my father. But family is going to be stopped short if I don't marry someday and have children of my own.

Except there's another child on the way now, isn't there? The family will continue anyway, no matter what you do.

Yes, it will.

So now he can disapprove of every woman in your life without fearing the consequences of your taking that disapproval to heart and never marrying, can't he, Gideon?

No! I will not play this game. This is *not* about my father. If he doesn't like Libby, it's because he's concerned about the impact she could have on my music. And he's well within his rights to be concerned. Libby doesn't know a bow from a kitchen knife.

Does she interrupt your work?

No, she doesn't.

Does she display an indifference to your music?

No.

Does she intrude? Ignore requests for solitude? Make demands upon you that violate the time you've set aside for your music?

Never.

You said she was a philistine. Have you discovered that she clings to her ignorance like a badge of accomplishment?

No. I haven't.

But still your father doesn't like her.

Look, it's for my own good. He's never made a move that wasn't for my good. I'm here with you because of him, Dr. Rose. When he understood what had happened to me in Wigmore Hall, he didn't say "Buck up! Get a grip! You've a God damn audience who've paid to see you!" No. What he said was "He's ill" to Raphael. "Make our excuses," and he spirited me out of there. He took me home and he put me to bed and he sat next to me all night and he said, "We'll handle this, Gideon. Just sleep for now."

He instructed Raphael to find help. Raphael knew about your own father's work with blocked artists, Dr. Rose. And I came to you. Because my father wants me to have my music, I came to you.

5 SEPTEMBER

No one else knows. Just the three of us: Dad, Raphael, and I. Even my publicist isn't clear what's going on. Under a doctor's care, she's given out, telling the world that it's merely exhaustion.

I assume the interpretation given to that story is one variation or another of The Artist Piqued, and that's fine with me. Better the assumption that I stalked off the platform because I did not like the Hall's lighting than the truth reach public consumption.

Which truth is that? you ask.

Is there more than one? I want to know.

Certainly, you say. There's the truth of what's happened to you and the truth of why. What's happened is called psychogenic amnesia, Gideon. Why it's happened is the reason for our meetings.

Are you saying that until we know *why* I have this . . . this . . . what did you call it?

Psychogenic amnesia. It's like hysterical paralysis or blindness: Part of you that's always worked—in this case your musical memory, if you'd like to call it that—simply stops working. Until we know why you're experiencing this trouble, we won't be able to change it.

I'm wondering if you know how I recoil from that information, Dr. Rose. You impart it with perfect sympathy, but still I feel like a freak. And yes, *yes,* I know how that word resonates in my past, so you needn't point that out to me. I still hear Granddad howling it at my father as they drag him away, and I still apply that word to myself every day now. Freak, freak, freak, I call myself. Finish the freak off. Put an end to the freak.

Is that what you are? you ask me.

What else could I be? I never rode a bicycle, played rugby or cricket, hit a tennis ball, or even went to school. I had a grandfather given to fits of psychosis, a mother who would have been happier as a cloistered nun and probably ended up in a convent for all I know, a father who slaved at two jobs till I was established professionally, and a violin instructor who shepherded me from concert tours to recording engagements and otherwise never let me out of his sight. I was coddled, catered to, and worshipped, Dr. Rose. Who would emerge from conditions like that as anything other than a bona fide freak?

Is it any wonder that I'm riddled with ulcers? That I puke my guts out before a performance? That my brain sometimes pounds like a hammer in my skull? That I haven't been able to *be* with a woman in more than six years? That even when I *was* able to take a woman to bed, there was neither closeness, joy, nor passion in the act but merely a need to have done, have it over, have my paltry release, and then have her gone?

And what is the sum of all that, Dr. Rose, if not a sure-fire genuine freak?

7 SEPTEMBER

Libby asked this morning if something was wrong. She came upstairs in her usual leisure attire—denim dungarees, a T-shirt, and hiking boots—and she seemed about to head out for a stroll because she was wearing the Walkman she usually takes with her when she's engaging in one of her diet hikes. I was in the window seat, doing my duty with this journal, when she turned and saw me watching her. Up she came.

She's trying a new diet, she told me. The No-White Diet, as she calls it. "I've tried the Mayo diet, the cabbage-soup diet, the Zone diet, the Scarsdale diet, the you-name-it diet. Nothing's worked, so I'm on to this." *This,* she tells me, consists of eating whatever she wants as long as it isn't white. White foods unnaturally altered with food colouring count as white as well.

She is, I have learned, obsessed with her weight, and this is a mystery to me. She isn't fat, as far as I can tell, which admittedly isn't very far since she's always garbed either in her leathers for the courier service or in her dungarees. She doesn't appear to have any other clothes. But even if she *does* look slightly podgy to some people—and mind you, I'm not saying that she looks slightly podgy to me—it's probably owing to the fact that her face is round. Don't round faces make one look plump? I tell her this, but it's no consolation. "We live in skeletal times," she says. "You're lucky to be naturally skinny."

I've never told her the cost of this emaciation that she seems to admire. Instead, I've said, "Women are too obsessed with their weight. You look perfectly fine."

On one occasion when I say this, she responds with "So if I look so perfectly fine, take me on a date, why don't you?"

And this is how we begin to see each other. What an odd expression that is, "to see each other," as if we're incapable of seeing another person until we're socially involved. I don't much like it—"seeing each other"—because it smacks of a euphemism where one isn't needed. Dating, on the other hand, sounds so adolescent. And even if that weren't the case, I wouldn't call what we're doing dating.

So what are you doing with Liberty Neale? you want to know.

And you mean, Are you sleeping with her, Gideon? Is she the woman who's managed to melt the ice that's been in your veins these last years?

I suppose that depends on what you mean by sleeping with her, Dr. Rose. And there's another euphemism for you. Why do we use a term like *sleeping* when sleeping is the last thing we intend to do when we climb into bed with the opposite sex?

But yes, we are sleeping together. Now and again.

But by sleeping, I mean sleeping, not shagging. We're neither of us ready for anything else.

How did this come about? you want to know.

It was a natural progression. One night she made a meal for me at the end of a particularly exhausting day of rehearsals for a concert at the Barbican. I fell asleep on her bed where we'd been sitting, listening to a recording. She covered me with a blanket and joined me under it, and there we remained till morning. Now and again we sleep together still. I suppose we both find it comforting in some way.

Nurturing, you say.

In that it feels good to have her there, yes. Then it's nurturing as well.

Something that was missing during your childhood, Gideon, you point out. If everyone's concentration was on your growth and performance as an artist, it wouldn't be unusual for other more essential needs to have gone both unrecognised and unfulfilled.

Dr. Rose, I insist upon your accepting what I say: I had good parents. As I've said, my father worked endlessly just to make ends meet. Once it became clear that I had the potential, the talent, and the desire to be . . . let's call it who I am today, my mother went out and found a job as well to help cover all the expenses incurred. And if I didn't see my parents as often as I might have done because of this, I had Raphael with me for hours each day and when he wasn't there, I had Sarah-Jane.

Who was she? you ask.

She was Sarah-Jane Beckett. I don't quite know what to call her, actually. *Governess* is too anachronistic a term and Sarah-Jane would have sorted you out in fairly short order had you ever called her a governess. So I suppose we'd have to call her my teacher. As I noted earlier, I never attended school once it became apparent that the violin would be my life because regular school hours conflicted with my schedule of lessons. So Sarah-Jane was employed as my teacher. When I wasn't working with Raphael, I was working with her. And because we fitted in lessons where and as we could, she lived with us. In fact, she lived with us for years. She must have arrived when I was five or six—once my parents saw how impossible it was going to be for me to be educated in a traditional fashion—and she stayed until I was sixteen, at which time my education was complete and my schedule of concerts, recordings, rehearsals, and practise periods precluded any further courses of study. But until that point, I had daily lessons with Sarah-Jane.

Was she a surrogate mother? you want to know.

Always, *always* it comes back to my mother. Are you looking for Oedipal connections, Doctor? How about an unresolved Oedipal complex? Mother trots off to work when son is five, leaving him incapable of laying to rest his unconscious desire to jump her? Then Mother disappears when son is eight or nine or ten or however old he was because I do *not* remember nor do I care to, and she is never heard from again.

I remember, though, her silence. Odd. It's just come to me now. My mother's silence. And I remember waking up one night while she was still with us and finding her lying in bed with me. She's holding me and it's very difficult to breathe *because* of the way she's holding me. It's difficult because her arms are round me and she's got my head somehow. . . . Never mind. I don't remember.

How is she holding you, Gideon?

I don't remember. Just that I can't breathe very well but I can feel her breathing and it's very hot.

Her breath is hot?

No. Just the feeling. Where I am. I want to escape.

From her?

No. Just escape. Run, actually. Of course, this could all be a dream. It was so long ago.

Did it happen more than once? you want to know.

I see where you're heading, and I won't go there with you because I refuse to pretend that I remember what you seem to want me to remember. The facts are these: My mother is beside me in my bed, I am held by her, it is hot, I smell her perfume. And there's a weight on my cheek as well. I do feel that weight. It's heavy but inert and it smells of perfume. Odd, that I would recall that smell. I couldn't tell you what it was—her perfume, Dr. Rose—but I expect that if I ever smelled it again, I would know it at once and it would remind me of Mother.

I expect she was holding you between her breasts, you tell me. That's why you would both feel the weight and smell the perfume. Is it dark in your bedroom or is there a light?

I don't recall. Just the heat, that weight, the scent. And silence.

Have you lain that way with anyone else? With Libby perhaps? Or whoever preceded Libby?

God, no! And this is not about my mother! All right. Yes. Of *course* I know that her desertion of me—of us—looms large. I'm not an idiot, Dr. Rose. I come home from Austria, my mother is gone, I never see the woman again, never hear her voice, never read so much as a sentence in her handwriting addressed to me. . . . Yes, yes, I know the song: This is a Very Big Incident. And since I never heard from her again, I also see the logical connection that I would make as a child: It was my fault. Perhaps I make that connection when I am eight or nine or however old I was when she left, but it is not a connection that I recall making and it's not a connection that I make now. She left. End of story.

What do you mean, end of story? you ask.

Just that. We never spoke of her. Or at least I never spoke of her. And if my grandparents and father did, and if Raphael or Sarah-Jane or James the Lodger—

He was still there when she left?

He was there . . . Or was he? No. He couldn't have been. It was Calvin, wasn't it? Didn't I say earlier it was Calvin? Calvin the Lodger trying to phone for help in the midst of Granddad's episode after Mother left us . . . So James had long ago decamped as well.

Decamped, you say. There's a secrecy implied in *decamped,* you tell me. Was there secrecy behind James the Lodger's leaving?

There is secrecy everywhere. Silence and secrecy. That's how it seems. I walk into a room and a hush falls on it and I know they've been talking about my mother. And I am not allowed to speak of her.

What happens if you do?

I don't know because I never test the rule.

Why not?

The music is central. I have my music. I still have my music. My father, my grandparents, Sarah-Jane, and Raphael. Even Calvin the Lodger. We all have my music.

Is this rule stated? The rule about not asking after your mother? Or is it implied?

It must be . . . I don't know. She's not there to greet us when we return from Austria. She's gone but no one acknowledges that fact. The house has been wiped so clean of her that it's as if she never lived there in the first place. And no one says a word. They don't pretend she's taken a trip somewhere. They don't pretend she's suddenly died. They don't pretend she ran off with another man. They act as if she never existed. And life goes on.

You never asked about her?

I must have known that she was one of the subjects that we just didn't talk about.

One? There were others?

Perhaps I didn't miss her. I don't actually recall missing her. I don't even remember much about what

she looked like. Except that her hair was blonde and
she covered it with head scarves, the sort you always
see the Queen wearing. But this would have been in
church. And yes, I do remember being with her in
church. I remember her crying. Crying in church at
morning Mass with the nuns lined up in the first few
pews of that chapel of theirs in Kensington Square.
They're on the other side of this rood screen affair,
the nuns, except it's not really a rood screen but more
like a fence to keep a separation between them and
the rest of the public except there's no one else there
to *be* the rest of the public at early morning Mass.
There's just Mother and I. And the nuns are in front
in those special pews giving responses, and one of
them is dressed in that old way, in a habit, but all the
rest are done up normally but very plain and with
crosses on their chests. And during Mass, my mother
kneels, always kneels, with her head resting on her
hands. She weeps the whole time. And I don't know
what to do.

Why is she weeping? you want to know, of course.

She is always weeping, it seems. And this one
nun—the one dressed in the old way—comes up to
Mother after Communion but before the end of Mass
and she takes us both to a sitting room of some kind
in the convent next door and there she and Mother
talk. They sit in one corner of the room. I am in the
other corner, the far corner, where I've been given a
book to read and told to sit. I'm impatient to be back
home, though, because Raphael's assigned me a set of
exercises to master and if I master them to his liking,

we're to go to the Festival Hall as a reward. A concert. Ilya Kaler will be performing. He is not yet twenty years old but already he has won the Grand Prize at the Genoa Paganini Competition and I want to hear him because I intend to be far greater than Ilya Kaler.

How old are you? you want to know.

I must be six. Seven at the oldest. And I am impatient to go home. So I leave my corner and I approach my mother and I pull on her sleeve and say, "Mum. I'm bored," because that's what I always say, that's how I communicate. Not: I've got to practise for my lesson with Raphael, Mum. But: I'm bored and it's your duty as my mother to deal with my boredom. But Sister Cecilia—and yes, that's her name, I've remembered her name—disengages my hand from my mother's sleeve and leads me back to the corner and says, "You'll be stopping right here till you're called for, Gideon, and no nonsense about it," and I'm surprised because no one ever talks to me that way. I'm the prodigy, after all. I am—if there can be degrees of it—more unique than anyone within my universe.

The surprise of being disciplined in such a way and by such a woman in such a costume is perhaps what keeps me in my corner for another few minutes as Sister Cecilia and my mother huddle together at their end of the room. But then I begin kicking at a bookshelf to entertain myself and I kick too hard and books topple to the floor and a statue of the Virgin falls and breaks on the lino. We leave soon afterwards, my mother and I.

I excel at my lesson that morning. Raphael takes me to the concert as he's promised. He's arranged for me to meet Ilya Kaler and I've brought my violin and we play together. Kaler is brilliant, but I know I'll exceed what he has accomplished. Even then, I know this.

What happens to your mother? you ask.

She spends much of her time upstairs.

In her bedroom?

No. No. In the nursery.

In the nursery? Why?

And I know the answer. I *know* the answer. Where has it been for all these years? Why have I suddenly remembered now?

My mother's with Sonia.

8 SEPTEMBER

There are gaps, Dr. Rose. They exist in my brain like a series of canvases painted by an artist but incomplete and coloured only black.

Sonia is part of one of those canvases. I remember the *fact* of her now: that there was a Sonia, and that she was my younger sister. She died at a very early age. I remember this as well.

So that would be why my mother was weeping all those mornings at early Mass. And Sonia's death must have been one of the subjects we did not speak about. To speak about her death would be to bring on a new torrent of Mother's terrible grieving and we wished to spare her that.

I've been trying to conjure up a picture of Sonia, but nothing is there. Just the black canvas. And when I try to summon her up to take part in a specific memory—Christmas, for instance, or Guy Fawkes Night, or the annual taxi ride with Gran to Fortnum and Mason for a birthday lunch in the Fountain . . . anything . . . anything at all . . . nothing is there. I don't even remember the day that she died. Nor do I recall her funeral. I know just the *fact* that she died because suddenly she wasn't there any longer.

Just like your mother, Gideon? you ask me.

No. This is different. This *must* be different because this feels different. And all I know for certain is that she was my sister, that she died young. Then Mother was gone. Whether she left us soon after Sonia died or whether it was months or years later, I couldn't say. But why? Why can't I remember my sister? What happened to her? What do children die of: cancer, leukaemia, cystic fibrosis, scarlet fever, influenza, pneumonia . . . what else?

This is the second child to die, you point out to me.

What? What do you mean? The second child?

The second child of your father's to die, Gideon. You've told me about Virginia . . . ?

Children die, Dr. Rose. That's what happens sometimes. Every day of the week. Children fall ill. Children die.

THREE

"I DON'T really see how the caterer managed to cope in here, do you?" Frances Webberly asked. "Of course, it's quite good enough for us, this kitchen. I can't see that we'd actually use a dishwasher or a microwave even if we had one. But caterers . . . They're used to all the mod cons, aren't they? What a surprise it must have been for the poor woman to arrive and find us living practically in the Middle Ages."

At the table, Malcolm Webberly made no reply. He'd heard his wife's deliberately cheerful words, but his mind was elsewhere. To deflect a potential conversation that he didn't want to have with anyone, he'd set about polishing his shoes in the kitchen. He assumed that Frances, having known him for more than thirty years and thus being well aware of his aversion to doing two things at once, would see him at this modest industry and leave him to himself.

He very much wanted to *be* left to himself. He'd wanted that from the instant he'd heard Eric Leach say, "Malc, sorry it's so late, but I've got some news," and go on to tell him of Eugenie Davies' death. He needed the time alone to sort through his feelings, and while a sleepless night with his wife snoring lightly beside him had given him a number of hours to consider how the words *hit-and-run* actually affected him, he'd found that all he'd been able to do was to picture Eugenie Davies as he'd last seen her: with the river wind tossing her bright blonde hair. She'd covered that hair with a scarf the moment she'd stepped from her cottage, but during their walk the scarf had loosened and it was while she removed it, refolded it, and replaced it on her head that the wind flicked locks of hair round her shoulders.

Quickly, he'd said to her, "Why not leave it off? The light in your hair makes you look . . ." What? Beautiful? he'd wondered. But she'd never been a great beauty in all the years that he'd known her. Young? They were both a decade past their prime. He'd supposed the word he wanted was actually *peaceful*. The sunlight in her hair made an aureole round her head, which reminded him of seraphim, which spoke of peace. But as those thoughts came to him, he'd become conscious of the fact that he'd never seen Eugenie Davies truly at peace and that at the moment—despite that trick of the halo created by light and wind—she was not at peace still.

These thoughts in his mind once again, Webberly smeared polish industriously on his shoe. As he did so, he became aware that his wife was still talking to him. ". . . a lovely job, though. But thank heavens it was dark when the poor woman arrived because

Lord knows how she would have functioned had she got a good look at our garden." Frances laughed ruefully. " 'I'm still holding out for my pond and my lilies,' I told our Lady Hillier last night. She and Sir David are actually thinking of putting a hot tub in their conservatory. Did you know? I told her a conservatory hot tub is perfectly well and good if you like that sort of thing, but as for me, a little pond is all I've ever wanted. 'And we'll have it someday,' I told her. 'Malcolm says we'll have it, so we will.' Naturally, we'll have to find someone to scythe through the weeds and cart off that old lawn mower out there, but I didn't mention that to our Lady Hillier—"

Your sister Laura, Webberly thought.

"—as she'd hardly understand what I was talking about. She's had that gardener of hers since . . . I don't know how long. But when the time's right and the money's there, you and I will have our little pond, won't we?"

"I expect so," Webberly said.

Frances eased behind the table in the cramped little kitchen and gazed from the window into the garden. She'd stood there so often in the past ten years that she'd worn a shoe-sized place in the lino, and there were finger grooves in the window sill where she'd spent hours clutching onto the wood. What did she think as she stood there hour after hour every day? her husband wondered. What did she try—and fail—to do? A moment later he had his answer:

"The day looks quite fine," she told him. "Radio One claimed there's going to be more rain by this afternoon, but I think they've got it wrong. You know, I believe I'll go out and do some work in the garden this morning."

Webberly looked up. Frances, apparently feeling his eyes on her, swung round from the window, one hand still on the sill and the other tight on the lapel of her dressing gown. "I think I can do it today," she said. "Malcolm, I think I can do it."

How many times had she said that before? Webberly wondered. One hundred? One thousand? And always with that same mixture of hope and delusion. She was going to work in the garden, Malcolm, she was going to walk to the shops this afternoon, she would definitely sit on a bench in Prebend Gardens or take Alfie for a romp or try the new beautician that was so well-spoken-of . . . so many good and honest intentions coming to naught at the final moment when the front door stood implacably in front of Frances and, try as she might and God knows she tried, she couldn't force her right hand up far enough to grasp onto the knob.

Webberly said, "Frannie—"

She cut in anxiously. "It's the party that's made all the difference. Having our friends in . . . being surrounded like that. I feel as right as . . . well, as right as can be."

Miranda's appearance at the kitchen door saved Webberly from having to make a reply. With an "Ah. Here you are," she dropped her trumpet case onto the floor along with a weighty rucksack, and she went to the cooker, where Alfie—the family's Alsatian mix—was having a lengthy post-party lie-in on his blanket. She gave the dog a brisk rub between his ears, which he responded to by rolling over and offering his stomach for her ministrations. She cooperated, pausing to plant a kiss on his head and to accept a wet dog kiss in return.

"Darling, that's terribly unhygienic," Frances said.

"That's doggy love," Miranda replied. "Which, as we know, is the purest kind. Isn't it, Alf?"

Alfie yawned.

Miranda said, over her shoulder to her parents, "I'm off, then. I've two papers to hand in next week."

"So soon?" Webberly set his shoes to one side. "We've had you barely forty-eight hours. Cambridge can wait another day, can't it?"

"Duty calls, Dad. Not to mention the odd exam or two. You still want me to try for a first, I take it?"

"Hang on, then. Let me finish with these shoes and I'll drive you up to King's Cross Station."

"No need. I'll go by tube."

"Then I'll run you up to the Underground."

"Dad." Her voice was a model of patience. They'd walked this path often in her twenty-two years, so she was well-used to its twists and turns. "I need the exercise. Explain it to him, Mum."

Webberly protested. "But if it begins to rain on your way—"

"Heavens, Malcolm, she's not going to melt."

But they do, Webberly countered, in his mind. They melt, they break, they disappear in an instant.

And always when melting, breaking, or disappearing is the very last possibility in your head. Still, he knew the wisdom of compromise in a situation in which two females were beginning to join forces against him. So he said, "I'll walk a bit with you, then." And he added, "Alf needs his morning toddle, Randie," when Miranda rolled her eyes and was about to remonstrate against the idea of a father chaperoning his adult daughter down the street in broad daylight as if she were incapable of using a zebra crossing on her own.

"Mum?" Miranda looked to her mother for support. Frances said with a regretful shrug, "You've not taken Alfie yet yourself, have you, darling?"

Miranda surrendered with good-natured exasperation. "Oh, come along then, you twit. But I'm not waiting for the shoe polish routine to be done."

"I'll see to the shoes," Frances said.

Webberly fetched the dog's lead and followed his daughter out of the house. Outside, Alfie rooted an old tennis ball from the shrubbery. He knew the routine when Webberly was on the other end of the lead: It would be a stroll to Prebend Gardens, where his master would unhook the lead from his collar and throw the tennis ball across the grass, whereupon Alfie would dash after it, refuse to return it, and run wildly around for at least a quarter of an hour.

"I don't know who has less imagination," Miranda said as she watched the dog snuffle through the hydrangeas, "you or the dog. Just look at him, Dad. He *knows* what's up. There's not the least bit of surprise in store for him."

"Dogs like routine," Webberly told her as Alfie emerged triumphant, a hairy old ball in his jaws.

"Dogs, yes. But what about you? Do you *always* take him to the gardens, for God's sake?"

"It's my walking meditation twice a day," he told her. "Morning and night. Doesn't that satisfy?"

"Walking meditation," she scoffed. "Dad, you're such a fibber. Really." They set off to the right once beyond the front gate, following the dog to the end of Palgrave Street, where he made the expected left turn that would take them up to Stamford Brook Road and Prebend Gardens that lay just on the other side of it.

"It was a good party," Miranda said, linking her arm through her father's. "Mum seemed to like it. And no one mentioned . . . or wondered . . . at least not to me . . ."

"It was fine," Webberly said, squeezing his arm to his side to hold her closer. "Your mother enjoyed herself so much she was talking about working in the garden today." He felt his daughter looking at him but he kept his own eyes resolutely forward.

Miranda said, "She won't. You know she won't. Dad, why don't you insist she go back to that doctor? There's help for people like Mum."

"I can't force her to do more."

"No. But you could . . ." Miranda sighed. "I don't know. Something. *Some*thing. I don't understand why you won't take a stand, why you've never taken a stand with Mum."

"What d'you have in mind?"

"If she thought you meant to . . . well, if you said, 'This is it, Frances. I'm at my limit. I want you to go back to that psychiatrist or else.' "

"Or else? What?"

He could feel her deflate. "Yes. That's just it, isn't it? I know you'd never leave her. Well, of course, how could you and live with yourself? But there's got to be something you—we—haven't thought of yet." And then apparently to spare him from having to answer, she noted that Alfie was eyeing a cat up ahead of them with too much interest. She took the lead from her father and said, "Don't even *think* of it, Alfred," with a little jerk.

At the corner, they crossed and there they parted fondly, Miranda heading to the left, which would ultimately take her in the direction of Stamford Brook Underground station and Webberly striding onward along the green iron railings that formed the east boundary of Prebend Gardens.

Inside the wrought iron gate, Webberly took the dog off his lead and wrested the tennis ball from his jaws. He flung it as far as he could down the length of the green and watched as Alfie raced after it. Once the ball was in the dog's possession, Alfie did his usual: He loped to the far end of the lawn and began to race round the perimeter of the green. Webberly watched his progress from bench to bush to tree to path, but he himself remained where they'd entered, moving only to the paint-chipped black bench a short distance from the notice board on which announcements of coming events in the community were posted.

These he read without actually assimilating them: Christmas fêtes, antiques fairs, car boot sales. He noted with approval that the phone number of the local police station was prominently displayed and that a committee hoping to organise a Neighbourhood Watch programme was going to assemble in the basement of one of the churches. He saw all this but he couldn't have testified to any of it later. Because although he perceived those six or seven pieces of paper pinned behind the glass of the notice board, and although he went through the motions of reading each one of them, what he actually observed was Frances standing at the kitchen window while his daughter said kindly and with absolute faith in him, *Of course you'd never leave her . . . how could you?* That last especially seemed to reverberate round his skull like an echo with a killing sense of irony.

Leaving Frances had been the last thing on his mind that night he'd got the call to go to Kensington Square. The call had come via the Earl's Court Road station, where he was a recently promoted detective inspector with a newly assigned sergeant—Eric Leach—as his partner. Leach did the driving down Kensington High Street, which in those days was moderately less jammed than it tended to be now. Leach was new to the borough, so they overshot the mark and ended up winding through Thackery

Street, with its small-village feel so at odds with a huge city, and coming into the square from its south-east end. This put them directly in front of the house they were seeking: a red brick Victorian affair with a white medallion at the gable's peak giving the date of construction: 1879, relatively new in an area where the oldest building had been raised nearly two hundred years earlier.

A panda car, a tandem arrival at the scene along with the paramedics when the emergency call had first come through, still sat at the kerb although its lights were no longer flashing. The paramedics themselves were long since gone, as were the neighbours, who had doubtless assembled as neighbours will do when sirens scream into a residential area.

Webberly shoved open his door and walked to the house, where a low brick wall surmounted by black wrought iron fenced in a flagstone area with a central planter. An ornamental cherry tree grew there, and at that time of year it created a roseate blossom pool on the ground.

The front door was closed, but someone inside must have been waiting for them, because no sooner had Webberly put his foot on the bottom step than the door swung open and the uniformed constable who'd placed the call to the station admitted them into the house. He looked shaken. This was his first call to a child's death, he told them. He'd arrived in the wake of the ambulance.

"Two years old," he informed them in a hollow voice. "Dad'd been giving her kiss of life and the 'medics tried everything they could." He shook his head, looking stricken. "No chance. She was gone. Sorry, sir. I've a baby at home. Makes you think . . ."

"Right," Webberly said. "It's okay, son. I've a little one myself." He needed no reminding how fleeting life was, how vigilant a parent needed to be against anything that might snuff that life out. His own Miranda had just turned two.

"Where'd it happen?" Webberly asked.

"In the bath. Upstairs. But don't you want to talk to . . . ? The family're in the drawing room."

Webberly didn't need a young PC to tell him his business, but the boy was rattled, so there was no point sorting him out right then. He looked at Leach instead. "Tell them we'll be with them shortly. Then . . ." He jerked his head towards the stairs. He said to the constable, "Show me," and he followed him up a staircase that curved round an ornate oak plant stand from which an enormous fern drooped fronds towards the floor.

The nursery bathroom was on the second floor of the house along with the nursery, a loo, and another bedroom that was occupied by the other child in the family. The parents and grandparents had rooms just below on the first floor. The top floor was occupied by the nanny, a lodger, and a woman who . . . well, the constable supposed she'd be called a governess although the family didn't call her that.

"She teaches the children," the constable said. "Well, perhaps just the older one, I expect."

Webberly raised his eyebrows at the oddity of a

governess in this day and age, and he went into the bathroom where the tragedy had occurred. Leach joined him there, his duty done in the drawing room below. The constable returned to his post by the front door.

The two detectives surveyed the bathroom somberly. It was a mundane location for sudden death to make its mark. And yet it happened so often that Webberly wondered when people would finally learn not to leave a child unattended for even a second when it came to so much as an inch of water anywhere.

There was more than an inch of water in the tub, however. At least ten inches remained inside, cool now and with a plastic boat and five yellow ducklings floating motionless on its surface. A bar of soap rested on the bottom near the drain, and a stainless steel bath tray with worn rubber ends bridged the width of the tub and held a limp flannel, a comb, and a sponge. All of it looked perfectly normal. But there was also an indication that both panic and tragedy had been recent visitors to the room.

To one side, a towel rack lay overturned on the floor. A soaked bath mat was crumpled beneath a wash basin. A rattan wastepaper basket had been caved in. And across the white tiles were the footprints of the paramedics whose last concern would have been to keep the room neat and tidy as they attempted to revive a child.

Webberly could picture the scene as if he'd been there because he *had* been there before while on uniformed patrol: no panic among the 'medics but rather intense and what seemed like inhumanly impersonal calm; checks for pulse and respiration, for reaction from the pupils; the immediate initiation of CPR. They would know she was dead within moments but they would not say those words to anyone because their job was life, life at any cost, life at every cost, and they would work upon the child and whisk her from the house and continue to work upon her all the way to the hospital because there was always the chance that life could be wrung from the limp tatter that remained when the spirit left the body.

Webberly squatted by the wastepaper basket and used a pen to right it, having a look inside. Six crumpled tissues, perhaps half a yard of dental floss, a flattened tube of toothpaste. He said to Leach, "Check the medicine cabinet, Eric," while he himself went back to the tub and looked long and hard round its sides, round its taps and its spigot, along the grout that edged it, and into its water. Nothing.

Leach said, "Baby aspirin in here, cough syrup, some prescriptions. Five of them, sir."

"For who?"

"Made out for Sonia Davies."

"Note them all, then. Seal off the room. I'll speak to the family."

But it was more than the family he met in the drawing room because more than the family lived in the house, and more than only the house's inhabitants had been present when the tragedy supervened in their evening rituals. Indeed, the drawing room seemed to be bursting with people although there were but nine individuals present: eight adults and a small boy with an appealing fall of white-blond hair across his forehead. Chalky-faced, he stood in the protective circle of the arm of an old man who was, presumably, his grandfather and whose necktie—a souvenir of some college or club by the look of it— the boy grasped and twisted in his fingers.

No one spoke. They looked in shock, and they seemed to be grouped to offer each other what support they could. Most of this was being directed at the mother, who was sitting in one corner of the room, a woman in her thirties like Webberly himself, but whey of complexion with large eyes that were haunted and seeing again and again what no mother ever ought to see: her child's limp body in the hands of strangers who fought to save her.

When Webberly introduced himself, one of the two men who were hovering near the mother rose and said he was Richard Davies, the father of the child who'd been taken to hospital. The use of the euphemism was clear when he gave a glance in the direction of the little boy, his son. Wisely, he didn't wish to speak of the other child's death in front of her brother. He said, "We were at the hospital. My wife and I. They told us—"

At this a young woman—seated on a sofa accompanied by a man of her own age with his arm round her shoulders—began to cry. It was a horrible, guttural weeping that grew to the sort of sobs that lead to hysteria. "I do not *leave* her," she keened, and even through her lamentation Webberly could hear her heavy German accent. "I swear to God almighty that I do not leave her for even a minute."

Which begged the question of how she had died, of course.

They all needed to be interviewed, but not simultaneously. Webberly said to the German girl, "You were responsible for the child?"

At which the mother said, "I brought this down upon us."

"Eugenie!" Richard Davies cried, and the other man who'd been hovering over her, his face shining with a patina of sweat, said, "Don't *talk* like that, Eugenie."

The grandfather said, "We all know who's at fault."

The German girl wailed, "No! No! No! I do not leave her!" while her companion held her and said, "It's *okay,*" which it patently was not.

Two people said nothing: an elderly woman who kept her eyes glued onto Granddad and a tomato-haired woman in a neat pleated skirt who watched the German girl with undisguised dislike.

Too many people, too much emotion, growing confusion. Webberly told them all to disperse, save the parents. Remain in the house, he directed them. And someone stay with the little boy.

"I'll do that," Tomato-hair said, obviously the "governess" about whom the young PC had spoken. "Come along, Gideon. Let's have a look at your maths."

"But I'm to practise," the boy said, looking

earnestly from one adult to another. "Raphael did tell me—"

"Gideon, it's all right. Go with Sarah-Jane." The sweat-faced man left the mother's side, going to squat before the little boy. "You're not to worry about your music just now. Go with Sarah-Jane, all right?"

"Come along, lad." Grandfather stood, the little boy in his arms. The rest of the group followed him from the room till only the parents of the dead child remained.

Even now in the garden in Stamford Brook, with Alfie barking at the birds and chasing the squirrels and waiting for his master to call him back to the lead, even now in this park Webberly could see Eugenie Davies as she had been on that long-ago evening.

Dressed simply in grey trousers and a pale blue blouse, she didn't move an inch. She didn't look at him or at her husband. She only said, "Oh my God. What's to become of us?" And even then she spoke to herself, not to the men.

Her husband said, but rather to Webberly and not in answer to her, "We went to the hospital. There was nothing they could do. They didn't tell us that here. At the house. They didn't tell us."

"No," Webberly said. "That's not their job. They leave that to the doctors."

"But they knew. While they were here. They knew then, didn't they?"

"I expect so. I'm sorry."

Neither of them wept. They would, later, when

they realised that the nightmare they were currently experiencing was no nightmare at all but rather an extended reality that would colour what remained of their lives. But at the moment, they were dull with trauma: the initial panic, the crisis of frantic intervention, the invasion of strangers into their home, the agonising wait in a casualty ward, the approach of a doctor whose expression undoubtedly had said it all.

"They talked about releasing her later. The . . . her body," Richard Davies said. "He said we couldn't take her, couldn't make any arrangements. . . . Why?"

Eugenie's head lowered. A tear dropped onto her folded hands.

Webberly drew a chair over so that he was on the same level as Eugenie and he nodded to Richard Davies to sit as well, which he did, next to his wife, whose hand he took. Webberly explained to them as best he could: When an unexpected death occurred, when someone died who was not under the care of a physician who could sign a death certificate, when someone died in an accident—like a drowning—then a post-mortem examination was required by law.

Eugenie looked up. "Are you saying they'll cut her up? Cut her open?"

Webberly skirted the question by saying, "They'll determine the exact cause of her death."

"But we know the cause," Richard Davies said. "She . . . my God, she was in the bath. And then there was shouting, the women screaming. I ran upstairs and James came tearing down from—"

"James?"

"He lodges with us. He was in his room. He came running."

"Where was everyone else?"

Richard looked to his wife for some sort of answer. She shook her head, saying only, "Mother Davies and I were in the kitchen, starting dinner. It was Sonia's bath time and . . ." She hesitated, as if saying her daughter's name made more real what she could not bear to think about.

"And you don't know where everyone else was?"

Richard Davies spoke. "Dad and I were in his sitting room. We were watching that . . . God, that infernal, stupid football game. We were actually watching *football* while Sosy was drowning upstairs."

It seemed the diminutive form of their daughter's name was what broke Eugenie. She finally began to weep in earnest.

Richard Davies, caught up in his own grief and despair, didn't take his wife into his arms as Webberly would have had him do. He merely said her name, telling her uselessly that it was all right, that the baby was with God, who loved her as much as they did. And Eugenie herself above all people knew that, didn't she, she whose faith in God and God's goodness was absolute?

Cold comfort, that, Webberly thought. He said, "I'll want to talk to everyone else, Mr. and Mrs. Davies." And then to Richard Davies alone, "She might need a doctor," in reference to his wife. "Better phone him."

The drawing room door opened as he spoke and DS Leach entered. He nodded to indicate he'd completed his list and sealed the bathroom off, and Webberly told him to set up the drawing room to conduct interviews with the residents of the house.

"Thank you for helping us, Inspector," Eugenie said.

Thank you for helping us. Webberly thought about those words now as he lumbered to his feet. How curious it was that five simple words spoken in such a wretched voice had actually managed to transform his life: from detective to knight errant in the space of a single second.

It was because of the kind of mother she was, he told himself now as he called to Alfie. The kind of mother that Frances—God forgive her—could never have hoped to be. How could anyone help admiring that? How could any man help wanting to be of service to such a mother?

"Alfie, come!" he shouted as the Alsatian loped after a terrier with a Frisbee in his mouth. "Home. Come. We won't use the lead."

As if the dog actually understood this last promise, he dashed back to Webberly. He'd had an excellent run this morning, if his heaving sides and his dangling tongue were any indication. Webberly nodded towards the gate and the dog walked to it and sat obediently, eyes on Webberly's pockets for a treat to reward him for such a display of good manners.

"You'll have to wait till we get home," Webberly told him, and afterwards considered his own words.

Indeed, that's the way life played out, didn't it? At the end of the day and for too many years, everything that mattered in Webberly's sorry little world had found itself put off till he got home.

LYNLEY NOTED THAT Helen hadn't taken more than a mouthful of tea. She'd changed her position in bed, however, and she was observing him make a mess of his tie while he was watching her in the mirror.

"So she's someone Malcolm Webberly knew?" Helen asked. "How dreadful for him, Tommy. And on his anniversary night."

"I wouldn't go so far as to say he knew her," Lynley replied. "She was one of the principals in the first case he ran as a DI over in Kensington."

"That would have been years ago, then. It must have made an enormous impression on him."

"I dare say it did." Lynley didn't want to tell her why. Indeed, he didn't want to tell her anything else about that long-ago death that Webberly had investigated. The drowning of a child was horrific enough to contemplate under any circumstances, but under these newly changed circumstances in their lives, it seemed to Lynley that a certain amount of discretion and delicacy was going to be in order now that his wife was carrying a child of her own.

A child of *our* own, he corrected his thinking, a child to whom no harm would ever come. So elaborating on the harm that had befallen another child seemed like tempting fate. At least that was what

Lynley told himself as he went about the rituals of dressing.

In bed, Helen turned on her side, away from him, her knees drawn up and an extra pillow bunched into her stomach. "Oh Lord," she moaned.

Lynley went to her, sat on the edge of the bed, and smoothed her chestnut hair. "You've not touched much of your tea," he said. "Would you like something different this morning?"

"I'd like to stop feeling so wretched."

"What does the doctor say?"

"She's a font of wisdom on that front: 'I spent the first four months of every pregnancy embracing the bowl of the loo. It'll pass, Mrs. Lynley. It always does.' "

"Till then?"

"Think positive thoughts, I suppose. Just don't make them of food."

Lynley studied her fondly: the curve of her cheek and the way her ear lay like a perfect shell against her head. There was a greenish cast to her skin, though, and the way she was clutching onto the pillow suggested another round of sickness was fast on its way. He said, "I wish I could do this for you, Helen."

She laughed weakly. "That's just the sort of thing men say out of guilt when they know very well that the last thing on earth they would *ever* choose to do is to have a baby for anyone." She reached for his hand. "I do appreciate the thought, though. Are you off, then? You will have breakfast, won't you, Tommy?"

He assured her that he would have a meal. Indeed, he knew there was no escape from it. If Helen wasn't insisting upon his eating, then Charlie Denton—manservant, housekeeper, cook, valet, aspiring thespian, unrepentant Don Juan, or whatever else he was choosing to call himself on a given day—would bar the door until Lynley had downed a plate of something.

"What about you?" he asked his wife. "What d'you have on? Are you working today?"

"Frankly, I wish not, because I'd like to remain immobile for the next thirty-two weeks."

"Shall I phone Simon, then?"

"No. He's got that acrylamide business to sort out. They need it in two days."

"Yes, I see. But does he need you?" Simon Allcourt-St. James was a forensic scientist, an expert witness whose specialities took him into the witness box regularly to confirm the Crown Prosecution's evidence or to bolster the position of the defence. In this particular instance, he was working on a civil case in which the litigation involved determining how much acrylamide—absorbed through the skin—constituted a toxic dose.

"I like to think so," she replied. "And anyway . . ." She gazed at him, a smile curving her mouth. "I'd like to tell him our news. I told Barbara last night, by the way."

"Ah."

"*Ah?* Tommy, what's that supposed to mean?"

Lynley rose from the bed. He went to the

wardrobe, where the mirrored door illustrated the disaster he'd created with his tie. He unknotted it and began again. "You did tell Barbara that no one else knows, didn't you, Helen?"

Across from him, she struggled to sit up. The movement cost her, however, and she quickly sank back. "I told her that, yes. But now that she knows, I think we may as well tell—"

"I'd rather not just yet." The tie looked worse than the first time round. Lynley gave up on the effort, blamed it on the material, and fetched another. He was aware that Helen was watching him, and he knew she expected some very sound reasoning behind his decision. He said, "Superstition, darling. If we keep it to ourselves, there's less chance something might go wrong. It's silly, I know. But there you have it. I hadn't thought to tell anyone till . . . well, I guess till it took."

"Till it took." She repeated the phrase thoughtfully. "Are you worried, then?"

"Yes. Worried. Terrified. Nervous. Apprehensive. Preoccupied. And frequently incoherent. That's about it."

She smiled gently. "I love you, darling."

And that smile asked for a further admission. He owed her that much. "There's also Deborah to consider," Lynley said. "Simon'll be able to cope with the news, but it's going to hurt Deborah like the devil when you tell her you're pregnant."

Deborah was Simon's wife, a young woman with so many miscarriages to her name that it seemed like a deliberate act of cruelty to mention a successful pregnancy in her hearing. Not that she wouldn't feign joy for the couple. Not that she wouldn't *feel* that joy at some level. But at a deeper level where her own hopes lay, she would feel the hot brand of failure scorch the skin of dreams, and that skin had been scorched enough times already.

"Tommy," Helen said kindly, "Deborah's going to find out eventually. How much more hurtful is it going to be if she suddenly realises I've switched to maternity clothes without mentioning the fact that we're having a baby? She'll know *why* we haven't told her at that point. Don't you think that will hurt her even more?"

"I'm not suggesting we let it go that long," Lynley said. "Just for a while, Helen. For luck, actually, more than for Deborah. Will you do this for me?"

Helen studied him as he'd studied her. He felt himself chafing under her scrutiny, but he didn't turn from it, waiting for her answer. She said, "Are you happy about this baby, darling? Are you truly happy?"

"Helen, I'm delighted."

But even as he spoke, Lynley wondered why he did not feel that way. He wondered why what he actually felt was a duty he'd long left undone.

FOUR

JILL FOSTER was grunting through the final series of pelvic tilts with her antenatal trainer counting them when Richard came into the flat. He looked more haggard than she'd expected, and she didn't like the way this made her feel. He'd been divorced from Eugenie for sixteen years. As far as she could see, the identification of his former wife's body should merely be an inconvenient exercise undertaken as a helpful member of society doing his duty to assist the police.

Gladys, the antenatal trainer whom Jill had come to think of as a cross between an Olympic athlete and a fitness Nazi, said, "Ten more, Jill. Come along, now. You'll thank me when you're in labour, luv."

Jill grunted, "Can't."

"Nonsense. Take your mind off exhaustion. Think of that dress instead. You'll thank me at the end of the day. Do ten more."

The dress in question was a wedding gown, a Knightsbridge creation that had cost a small fortune and that hung from the sitting room door, where Jill had placed it to give her inspiration when the hun-gries came upon her and when the fitness Nazi was taking her through her sweating, miserable, and embarrassing paces. "I'm sending you Gladys Smiley, darling," Jill's mother had announced upon being told of the grandchild to come. "She's the best antenatal specialist in the south and that's including London, mind you. She's generally booked up, but she'll fit you in for me. Exercise is crucial. Exercise and diet, of course."

Jill had cooperated with her mother, not because Dora Foster *was* her mother but because she'd delivered five hundred babies at five hundred successful home births. So she knew what she was talking about.

Gladys counted down from ten. Jill was sweating like a race horse and feeling like a sow, but she managed a glowing smile for Richard. He'd argued against what he'd called "the unique absurdity" of Gladys Smiley from the first, and he was still standing firm against the idea of Dora Foster delivering her first granddaughter at the family home in Wiltshire. But since Jill had compromised on the wedding— agreeing to the more modern approach of postnatal connubiality rather than what she would have preferred: engagement, marriage, and childbirth in that order—she knew that Richard was ultimately going to have to give in to her desires. *She* was the one giving birth, after all. And if she wanted her mother to deliver her—her mother with thirty years of experience doing just that—then that's the way it was going to be. "You're not my husband yet, darling," Jill informed him pleasantly each time he protested. "I haven't yet said a word in front of anyone about loving, honouring, and obeying you."

She had him there, and she knew it. So did he. Which was why she was going to have her way in the end.

"Four . . . three . . . two . . . one . . . yes!" Gladys cried. "Excellent work. You keep this up and that little one'll slide right out of you. See if she doesn't." She handed Jill a towel and nodded at Richard, where he stood in the doorway, looking grey round his mouth. "Settled on a name, then, have you?"

"Catherine Ann," Jill said firmly as Richard said just as firmly, "Cara Ann."

Gladys looked from one to the other, saying, "Yes. Well. Keep up the good work, Jilly. I'll see you day after tomorrow, yes? Same time?"

"Hmm." Jill remained on the floor as Richard saw Gladys out of the flat. She was still there—feeling like a beached whale—when he came back into the sitting room. She said, "Darling, there is no way on earth that I'm naming a child Cara. I'd be the laughing stock of every one of my friends. Cara indeed. Honestly, Richard. She's a child, not a character in a romance novel."

In the normal course of events, he'd have argued. He'd have said, "Catherine is far too ordinary, so if it's not to be Cara, then it's not to be Catherine, and we'll have to compromise on something else."

Which was what they'd been doing since the day that they'd met when she'd found herself going head-to-head with the man during a documentary the BBC had been filming about his son. "You may speak to Gideon about his music," Richard Davies had informed her during the contract negotiations. "You may question him about the violin. But my son does not discuss his personal life or his history with the media, and I insist upon making that perfectly clear."

Because he doesn't *have* a personal life, Jill thought now. And what went for his history could have been summed up in four syllables: the violin. Gideon was music and music was Gideon. So it had been and always would be.

Richard, on the other hand, was electricity. She'd liked matching wits and battling wills with him. She'd found that appealing and sexy, despite the enormous gap in their ages. Arguing with a man was such an aphrodisiac. And so few men in Jill's life were actually *willing* to argue. Especially English men, who generally decomposed into passive-aggression at the first sign of a row.

Arguing, however, was not what Richard had in mind at the moment: arguing about the name of their daughter, the location of the freehold they had yet to purchase, the choice of wallpaper once that freehold was theirs, or the size and the date of their future wedding. All those had been subjects of past rows between them, but she could see he hadn't the heart for a heated discussion now.

His colourless face was an advertisement for what he'd undergone in the past few hours, and despite the fact that his clinging to the idea of Cara was rather more maddening than she'd anticipated it might be when he first suggested the name five months ago, Jill wanted to appear sympathetic to his recent experiences. No matter that she felt like saying, "What on *earth's* wrong? For God's sake, Richard, the beastly woman walked out on you nearly twenty years ago." She knew the wisdom of saying instead, "Was it bad, darling? Are you quite all right?" in the gentlest of tones.

Richard went to the sofa and sat, his scoliosis looking worse for the dejection that drooped his shoulders. He said, "I couldn't tell them."

She frowned. Couldn't tell them . . . ? "What, darling?"

"Eugenie. I couldn't tell them if the woman was actually Eugenie."

"Oh." In a small voice. Then, "She'd changed that much? Well, I suppose it's not that odd, is it, Richard? So long since you've seen her. And perhaps she's had a rough time . . ."

He shook his head. He dug two fingers into his eyebrows and rubbed. "It isn't that, although I couldn't have told them even if it was."

"Then what?"

"She was hit quite badly. They wouldn't say exactly what happened, even if they knew. But she looked as if a lorry had run over her. She was . . . She was mangled, Jill."

"My God." Jill struggled into a sitting position.

She put a supportive hand on his knee. This *was* something to go all grey in the face about. "Richard, I'm so terribly sorry. What an ordeal for you."

"They showed me a Polaroid first, which was good of them. But when I couldn't identify her from that, they showed me her body. They asked if there were distinguishing marks somewhere on her that might identify her. But I couldn't remember." His voice was dull, like an old copper coin. "All I could tell them was the name of her dentist twenty years ago and think of that, Jill. I could remember the name of her dentist but not if she had a birthmark somewhere that might tell the police that she is—that she was—Eugenie, my wife."

Former wife, Jill wanted to add. Deserting wife. Wife who selfishly left behind a child whom you raised to adulthood alone. *Alone*, Richard. Let's not forget that.

"But I could remember the name of her bloody dentist," he was saying. "And only because he's mine as well."

"What will they do?"

"Use the x-rays to make sure it's Eugenie."

"What do you think?"

He looked up. He seemed so tired. With an unaccustomed sense of guilt, Jill thought of how little sleep he was managing to get on her sofa and how kind and solicitous it was of him to stay the nights with her now when her time was drawing near. Since Richard had already had two children—although only one of them was actually still alive—Jill hadn't honestly expected him to be as lovingly concerned for her welfare as he'd been during most of the pregnancy. But from the moment her stomach had started to swell and her breasts had begun to grow heavier, he'd treated her with a tenderness she'd found rather poignant. It served to open her heart to him and to bind them more closely together. This unit they were forming was something she warmed to. It was what she'd longed for and dreamed of having and despaired of finding among men her own age.

"What I think," Richard said in answer to her question, "is that the likelihood of Eugenie's having had the same dentist since our marriage ended—"

Since she deserted you, Jill corrected him silently.

"—is fairly remote."

"I still don't understand how they connected you with her. And how they tracked you down."

Richard stirred on the sofa. In front of him on the large plump ottoman that served as a coffee table, he fingered the latest copy of *Radio Times*. Its cover featured a toothy American actress who'd agreed to simulate what would undoubtedly be a wildly imperfect English accent so she could play the part of Jane Eyre in yet another resurrection of that eponymous and utterly implausible Victorian melodrama. Jane Eyre indeed, Jill thought with a scoff, she who fostered within the soft brains of more than one hundred years of mentally pliable female readers the nonsensical belief that a man with a past as dark as licorice could be elevated by the love of a decent woman. What utter nonsense.

Richard wasn't answering. Jill said, "Richard, I don't understand. How did they connect you with Eugenie? I realise she must have kept your surname, but Davies isn't so uncommon that one would make the leap that you and she had once been married."

"One of the police on the scene," Richard said. "He knew who she was. Because of the case . . ." He aimlessly shifted the copy of *Radio Times* so that the one beneath it was on top. This one pictured Jill herself in modern garb among the costumed cast of her triumphant production of *Desperate Remedies,* filmed within weeks of Jill's final breakup with Jonathon Stewart, whose passionate vows to leave his wife "once our Steph has finished up at Oxford, darling" had proved to be just about as steadfast as his performance in bed had been reliable. Two weeks after "our Steph" had her diploma in her grubby little grasp, Jonathon was making another excuse which involved settling the wretched girl "in her new digs up in Lancaster, darling." Three days later Jill had pulled the plug on their relationship and buried herself in *Desperate Remedies,* whose title couldn't have been more appropriate to her emotional state at the time.

Jill said, "The case?" and a moment later realised what case he was speaking about. *The* case, of course, the only one that mattered. The case that had broken his heart, destroyed his marriage, and coloured the last two decades of his life. She said, "Yes, I suppose the police might remember."

"He was involved. One of the detectives. So when

he saw her name on her driving licence, he tracked me down."

"Yes. I see." She half-rolled into a kneeling position from which she was able to touch his curved shoulder. "Let me make you something. Tea, coffee."

"I could do with a brandy."

She lifted an eyebrow, although since he was looking at the magazine cover and not at her, he didn't see the action. She wanted to say, At this hour? Surely not, darling. But she heaved herself to her feet and went to the kitchen, where she took a bottle of Courvoisier from one of the sleek cupboards and poured him an exact two tablespoons, which seemed an adequate amount to restore him.

He joined her in the kitchen and took the glass without comment. He drank a sip and swirled the remaining liquid in the glass. He said, "I can't get the sight of her out of my mind."

This seemed too much to Jill. All right, the woman was dead. And yes, she'd died in a dreadful way, with much to be pitied. Indeed, it was a grim affair, having to look upon her broken body. But Richard hadn't had a single word from his former wife in nearly two decades, so why would he be so distraught at her death? Unless he was still carrying a torch for her . . . Unless, perhaps, he'd not been quite truthful about the death of their marriage and what he'd done with the corpse.

Jill said with care and placing a loving hand on his forearm, "I know this must be a terrible time for you.

But you've not actually . . . seen her in all these years, have you?"

A flicker in his eyes. Of their own accord, her fingers tightened. Don't make this into a Jonathon situation, she told him silently. Lie to me now, and I will end this, Richard. I will not live in a fantasy again.

He said, "No, I've not seen her. But I've spoken to her recently. A number of times in the last month or so." He seemed to feel the shield she put up to protect her heart from damage at this piece of news, because he went on hastily. "She phoned me because of Gideon. She'd read about what happened at Wigmore Hall. When he didn't recover from that . . . situation . . . quickly, she phoned to ask me about him. I haven't told you because . . . I don't actually know *why* I haven't told you. It didn't seem very important at the time. And beyond that, I didn't want anything to upset you in these final weeks . . . the baby. It hardly seemed fair to you."

"That's completely outrageous." Jill felt a swelling of righteous anger.

Richard said, "I'm sorry. We spoke for only five minutes . . . ten minutes at the most each time she phoned. I didn't consider—"

"I don't mean that," Jill interrupted. "I don't mean it's outrageous that you didn't tell me. But that she phoned you at all. That she had the audacity to phone you, Richard. That she could walk out of your life— out of *Gideon's* life, for God's sake—and then phone up when she reads about him because she's curious that he's had a bit of trouble at a performance. My *God,* what cheek."

Richard said nothing in reply to this. He merely swirled the brandy round in his glass and observed the thin patina it left on the sides. There was something more here, Jill concluded. She said, "Richard? What is it? There's something you're not telling me, isn't there?" And she felt once again a basic shutting down when confronted with the idea that a man with whom she was so intimately involved might not be as forthcoming as she required of him. Odd, she thought, how one humiliating and disastrous relationship had the potential to affect every involvement that followed it. "Richard? Tell me. Is there something more?"

"Gideon," Richard said. "I didn't tell him that she'd been phoning me about him. I didn't know *what* to tell him, Jill. It's not as if she was asking to see him, because she wasn't asking to see him at all. So what would have been the point, telling him? But now she's dead and he's got to be told about that and I'm terrified that hearing it is going to make him take a turn for the worse."

"Yes. I can see how it could."

" 'Is he well?' she wanted to know, Jill. 'Why isn't he playing, Richard?' she asked. 'How many concert engagements has he actually broken? And why? Why?' "

"What was she after?"

"She must have phoned me a dozen times in the

last two weeks alone," Richard said. "There she was, this voice from the past which I thought I'd *bloody* well recovered from and—" He stopped himself.

Jill felt the chill. It started from her ankles and swept up quickly to close round her heart. She said carefully, "Thought you'd recovered?" and tried to stop herself from thinking what she couldn't bear to think, but the words ricocheted round her head anyway: He still loves her. She walked out on him. She disappeared from his life. But he continued to love her. He climbed into my bed. He joined his body to mine. But all the time he was loving Eugenie.

No wonder he'd never remarried. The only question was: Why was he remarrying now?

The damn man read her mind. Or perhaps her face. Or maybe he felt the chill as well, since he said, "Because it took me that much time to find you, Jill. Because I love you. Because at my age, I never expected to love again. And every morning when I awake, even on that miserable sofa of yours, I thank God for the miracle that you love me. Eugenie is a distant part of my past. Let's not make her part of our future."

And the truth of it was, as Jill knew well, that they both had pasts. They were not adolescents, so neither of them could expect the other to come into their new life unburdened. The future was what was important, at the end of the day. Their future and the future of the baby. Catherine Ann.

HENLEY-ON-THAMES was easily accessible from London, especially when the morning commute along the M40 created tailbacks that extended in the opposite direction only. So DI Thomas Lynley and DC Barbara Havers were rolling south in the direction of Henley from Marlow just under an hour after having left Eric Leach's incident room in Hampstead.

DCI Leach, fighting off either a head cold or flu, had introduced them to a squad of detectives who, while slightly leery of the presence of New Scotland Yard among them, also seemed willing to accept their participation in a work load that currently included a series of rapes on Hampstead Heath and an arson in the Grade II-listed cottage of an ageing actress of both title and considerable reputation.

Leach detailed the preliminary findings from the post-mortem examination first, pending blood, tissue, and organ analysis, and they amounted to a multitude of injuries on a body that had ultimately been identified through dental records as belonging to one Eugenie Davies, aged sixty-two. First came the fractures she had sustained: the fourth and fifth cervical vertebrae, the left femur, ulna, and radius, the right clavicle, and the fifth and sixth ribs. Then came the internal ruptures: liver, spleen, and kidneys. The cause of death had been determined as massive internal haemorrhaging and shock, and the time had been set between ten o'clock and midnight. An evaluation of trace evidence on the body would be forthcoming.

"She was thrown about fifty feet," Leach told the detectives assembled in the incident room as they stood among the computers, the china boards, the filing cabinets, the copy machines, and the photographs.

"According to forensic she was then driven over at least twice, possibly three times, as indicated by contusions on the body and markings left on her mac."

A general murmur greeted this remark. Someone said, "Nice neighbourhood, that" with heavy irony.

Leach corrected the DC's misapprehension. "We're assuming a single car, not three, did the damage, McKnight. We'll hold that position till we hear otherwise from Lambeth. One hit from the vehicle put her flat out on the pavement. Then once over her, once in reverse, and back again."

Leach indicated several pictures on the china board before he went on. They depicted the street as it had been in the aftermath of the hit-and-run. He gestured to one in particular showing a section of tarmac photographed between two orange traffic cones with a line of cars along the pavement in the background. "The point of impact appeared to be here," he said. "And the body landed here, square in the centre of the road." Another set of traffic cones, plus a large rectangle of the street taped off. "The rain took care of some of the blood that would have been where the body landed. But it wasn't raining hard enough to carry away all the blood from the site or the tissue and bone fragments either. However, the body's not where the tissue and bone are. Instead, it's over here next to this Vauxhall at the kerb. And notice how she's tucked a bit under it? We reckon that our driver, having knocked her down and having done his bit of back and forthing over her body, then got out of his car, dragged the woman to one side, and drove off."

"She couldn't have been dragged beneath a set of wheels? Lorry, perhaps?" The question came from a DC who was noisily eating from a cup of instant noodles. "Why rule that out?"

"Nature of what few tyre marks we've got," Leach informed him, reaching for his coffee, which he'd left on a nearby desk heaped with files and computer printouts. He was more loosely strung than Lynley had expected upon their first introduction not forty minutes earlier in his office. Lynley took this as a good sign of what it was going to be like working with the DCI.

"But why not three cars, sir?" one of the other DCs asked. "The first knocks her down, drives off in a panic. She's wearing black so the next two don't even see her lying in the road and run over her before they know what's happened."

Leach took a gulp of coffee and shook his head. "You won't find anyone giving you good odds on our having three conscienceless citizens all in the same neighbourhood on the same night running over the same body and not one of them reporting it. And nothing in your scenario explains how the hell she ended up partway under that Vauxhall. Only one explanation does that, Potashnik, and it's why we're the ones looking at the situation."

There was a murmur of agreement at this.

"I'd put good money on the bloke who reported it being the driver we're looking for," someone from the back of the room called out.

"Pitchley pulled in a brief and put in the plug

straightaway," Leach acknowledged, "and that bears the stench of manure, you're right. But I don't think we've heard the last from him, and that car of his is going to be what unseals his lips, make no mistake."

"Pinch a bloke's Boxter and he'll sing 'God Save the Queen' on demand," a DC at the front pointed out.

"That's what I'm relying on," Leach agreed. "I'm not saying he's the driver who did her in in the first place, and I'm not saying he's not. But no matter which way the wind's blowing, he won't be getting that Porsche off us till we know why the dead woman was carrying his address. If it takes holding the Porsche to shake the information from him, then holding the Porsche and going over it six times with granny's hoover is exactly what's going to happen. Now . . ."

Leach went on to make the action assignments, most of which put his team into the street where the hit-and-run had occurred. It was lined with houses— some conversions and some individual homes—and the DCs were to get a statement from everyone in the area about what had been seen, heard, smelled, or dreamed about on the previous night. His directions allocated other DCs to dog the forensic lab: some of them monitoring the progress made on the examination of Eugenie Davies' car, others given the responsibility for pulling together all the information regarding trace evidence on the woman's body, still others matching the trace evidence from the body to the Boxter that the police had impounded. This same group would be evaluating any and all tyre prints left in the West Hampstead street and on Eugenie Davies' body and her clothes. A final group of constables— the largest—were assigned to search for a car with damage to its front end. "Body shops, car parks, car hire firms, streets, mews, and lay-bys on the motor- way," Leach informed them. "You don't run down a woman in the street and drive away with no damage."

"That does put the Boxter out of the running," a female DC noted.

"Possession of the Boxter's how we prise informa- tion from our man," Leach replied. "But there's no telling if—and where—this bloke Pitchley might have himself another car stowed away. And we'd be wise not to forget that."

The meeting concluded, Leach met with Lynley and Havers privately in his office. As their superior officer of record, he gave Lynley and Havers instruc- tions in a manner that suggested more than mere homicide—if that were not already enough—was in- volved in the case. But what that more was, he didn't mention. He merely handed over Eugenie Davies' address in Henley-on-Thames, telling them that the house was their starting point. He assumed, he told them pointedly, that they had enough experience be- tween them to know what to do with what they found there.

"What the hell was that supposed to mean?" Bar- bara asked now as they swung into Bell Street in Henley-on-Thames, where children were taking their morning exercise in a school yard. "And why've we been given the house while the rest of that lot are beating the pavement from West Hampstead to the river? I don't get it."

"Webberly wants us involved. Hillier's given his blessing."

"And *that's* reason enough to do some serious tip-toeing, 'f you ask me."

Lynley didn't disagree. Hillier had no love for either one of them. And Webberly's state of mind in his study on the previous evening had suggested a few things but declared nothing. He said, "I expect we'll sort things out soon enough, Havers. What's the address again?"

"Sixty-five Friday Street," she said, and with a glance at their street map, "Take a left here, sir."

Sixty-five turned out to be a dwelling seven buildings up from the River Thames on a pleasant street that mixed residences with a veterinarian's surgery, a bookshop, a dental clinic, and the Royal Marine Reserve. It was the smallest house that Lynley had ever seen—bar his own companion constable's tiny dwelling in London that often struck him as fit for Bilbo Baggins and no one else. It was painted pink and it consisted of two floors and a possible attic if the microscopic dormer window on the roof was any indication. Appropriately it bore an enamel plaque which named it Doll Cottage.

Lynley parked a short distance away from it, across the street from the bookshop. He fished the dead woman's set of keys from his pocket while Havers took the opportunity to light up and fortify her bloodstream with nicotine. "When are you going to drop that loathsome habit?" he asked her as he checked the front of the house for an alarm system and put the key in the lock.

Havers inhaled deeply and offered him her most maddening smile of tobacco-induced pleasure. "Listen to him," she said to the sky. "There may be something more obnoxious than a reformed smoker, but I don't know what it is. Child pornographer come to Jesus on the day of his arrest? Tory with a social conscience perhaps? Hmm. No. They don't quite match up."

Lynley chuckled. "Put it out in the street, Constable."

"I wouldn't even dwell on another option." She flicked the cigarette over her shoulder, after taking another three hits.

Lynley opened the door, which admitted them into a sitting room. This looked about as large as a shopping trolley, and it was furnished with near monastic simplicity and with a taste that veered towards Oxfam rejects.

"And I thought *I'd* achieved drab-with-a-vengeance," Havers remarked.

It wasn't an inappropriate description, Lynley thought. The furniture was of post-war vintage, crafted at a period of time when rebuilding a capital devastated by bombing had taken precedence over interior design. A threadbare grey sofa accompanied by a matching armchair of an equally disenchanting hue sat against one wall. They formed a little seating area round a blond-wood coffee table spread with magazines and two similar end tables, both of which someone had attempted to refinish unsuccessfully. Three lamps in the room all sported tasseled shades, two of them askew and the third bearing a large burn that could have been turned to the wall but wasn't. Nothing save a single print above the sofa, featuring an unattractive Victorian-era child with her arms round a rabbit, decorated the walls. On either side of a mouse-hole fireplace, fitted shelves held books, but they were spottily placed here and there, and it seemed as if something had stood among them but had been removed.

"Bloody poverty-stricken," Havers said in assessment. She was, Lynley saw, fingering through the magazines on the coffee table, her hands—latex gloved—fanning the publications out so even Lynley could see from his place by the bookshelves that they all bore pictorial covers that placed them years out of date.

Havers moved into the kitchen that lay just beyond the sitting room as Lynley turned to look at the bookshelves. She called out, "One mod con in here. She's got an answer machine, Inspector. Light's blinking."

"Play it," Lynley said.

The first disembodied voice floated from the kitchen as Lynley took his reading spectacles from his jacket pocket in order to examine more closely the few volumes on the fitted bookshelves.

A man's deep and sonorous voice said, *"Eugenie. Ian,"* as Lynley picked up a book called *The Little Flower* and opened it to see it was a biography of a Catholic saint called Therese: French, from a family of daughters, a cloistered nun, suffered an early death from whatever one would contract living in a cell with no heating in France in midwinter. *"I'm sorry about the row,"* the voice continued from the kitchen. *"Phone me, will you? Please? I've got the mobile with me,"* and he followed this declaration with a number that began with a recognisable prefix.

"Got it," Havers called out from the kitchen.

"It's a Cellnet number," Lynley said, and picked up the next book as the next voice—this one a woman's—left her message, saying, *"Eugenie, it's Lynn. Dearest, thank you so much for the call. I was out for a walk when you rang. It was so very kind of you. I hardly expected . . . Well. Yes. There it is. I'm just about coping. Thanks for asking. If you ring me back, I'll give you an update. But I expect you know what I'm going through."*

Lynley saw he was holding another biography, this one of a saint called Clare, an early follower of St. Francis of Assisi: gave away all she owned, founded an order of nuns, lived a life of chastity and died in poverty. He picked up a third book.

"Eugenie," another man's voice from the kitchen, but this one distraught and obviously familiar to the dead woman, since he spoke without attribution, saying, *"I need to speak with you. I had to ring again. I know you're there, so will you pick up the phone? . . . Eugenie, pick up the God damn phone."* A sigh. *"Look. Did you*

actually expect me to be happy about this turn of events? How could I be? . . . Pick up the phone, Eugenie." A silence was followed by another sigh. *"All right. Fine. If that's how you're going to play it. Flush history down the toilet and get on with things. I'll do the same."* The phone banged down.

"That sounds like a decent field to plough," Barbara called.

"Hit one-four-seven-one at the end of the messages and pray for good luck." The third book, Lynley saw, detailed the life of St. Teresa of Avila, and a quick examination of its jacket was enough to inform him that thematic unity was being achieved on the bookshelves: the convent, poverty, an unpleasant death. Lynley read this and frowned thoughtfully.

Another man's voice, again without attribution, came from the answer machine in the kitchen. He said, *"Hullo, darling. Still asleep or are you out already? I'm just ringing about tonight. The time? I've a bottle of claret that I'll bring along if that suits. Just let me know. I'm . . . I'm very keen to see you, Eugenie."*

"That's it," Havers said. "Fingers crossed, Inspector?"

"Metaphorically," he replied as in the kitchen Havers punched in 1471 to trace whoever had made the most recent call to Eugenie Davies' home. As she did so, Lynley saw that the rest of the books on the shelves were also biographies of Catholic saints, all of them female. None of them were recently published, most of them were at least thirty years old, and some of them had been printed prior to World War II. Eleven of them had the name *Eugenie Victoria Staines* inscribed on their fly leaves in a youthful hand; four of them were stamped *Convent of the Immaculate Conception,* and five others bore the inscription *To Eugenie, with fondest regards from Cecilia.* Out of one of this last group—the life of someone called Saint Rita—a small envelope fell. It bore no postmark or address, but the single sheet of paper had been dated nineteen years earlier in a beautifully schooled hand that had also written:

> *Dearest Eugenie,*
>   *You must try not to give in to despair. We can none of us understand God's ways. We can only live through the trials He chooses for us to endure, knowing that there is a purpose behind them which we may not be able to understand at the time. But we <u>will</u> understand eventually, dear friend. You must believe that.*
>   *We deeply miss you at morning Mass and all of us hope that you will return to us soon.*
>   *With Christ's love and my own, Eugenie,*
>   *Cecilia*

Lynley returned the paper to its envelope and snapped the book closed. He called out, "Convent of the Immaculate Conception, Havers."

"Are you recommending a lifestyle change for me, sir?"

"Only if it suits you. In the meantime, make a note

to track down the convent. We want someone called Cecilia if she's still alive, and I've a feeling that's where we might find her."

"Right."

Lynley joined her in the kitchen. The simplicity of the sitting room was repeated there. The kitchen hadn't been updated in several generations, from the look of it, and the only appliance that could be said to be remotely modern was the refrigerator, although even it appeared to be at least fifteen years old.

The answer machine was sitting on a narrow wooden work top. Next to it stood a papier-mâché holder containing several envelopes. Lynley picked these up as Havers went over to a small table and two chairs that abutted one of the walls. Lynley glanced over to see that the table was set not for a meal but for an exhibition: Three neat lines of four framed photographs apiece stood upon it as if for inspection. Envelopes in hand, Lynley went to Havers' side as she said, "Her kids, d'you think, Inspector?"

Every photograph indeed depicted the same subjects: two children who advanced in age in each picture. They began with a small boy—perhaps five or six years old—holding an infant who, in later pictures, turned out to be a little girl. From first to last, the boy looked desperately eager to please, wide-eyed and smiling so broadly and anxiously that every tooth in his mouth was on display. The little girl, on the other hand, seemed mostly unaware that a camera was focused on her at all. She looked right, she looked left, she looked up, she looked down. Only once—with her brother's hand on her cheek—had anyone managed to get her to look into the camera.

Havers said in her usual blunt fashion, "Sir, doesn't it look like there's something wrong with this kid? And she's the one that died, right? The one the superintendent told you about? This is her, right?"

"We'll need someone to confirm it," Lynley replied. "She could be someone else. A niece. A grandchild."

"But what d'you *think*?"

"I think yes," Lynley said. "I think she's the child who died." Drowned, he thought, drowned in what could have gone down as an accident but instead turned into something far more.

The photo must have been taken not long before she died. Webberly had told him that the girl had died at two, and Lynley saw that she couldn't have been much less than that at the time of this picture. But Webberly hadn't told him everything, he realised as he studied the photo.

He felt his guard go up and his suspicions heighten.

And he didn't much like either one of those sensations.

FIVE

MAJOR TED Wiley didn't think in terms of the police when the silver Bentley pulled to the kerb across the street from his bookshop. He was in the middle of ringing up a purchase at the till for a youthful housewife with a sleeping toddler in a push chair, and rather than concentrate on the presence of a luxury vehicle in Friday Street during non-Regatta season, he instead engaged the youthful housewife in conversation. She'd bought four books by Dahl, which clearly were not intended for herself, so it appeared she was one of the few modern young parents who understood the importance of introducing a child to reading. Along with the insidious dangers of cigarette smoking, this was one of Ted's favourite topics. He and his wife had read to all three of their girls—not that there had been a surfeit of other night-time activities for children to engage in in Rhodesia all those years ago—and he liked to think that the early start which he and Connie had given to them resulted in everything from respect for the written word to a determination to attend first-class universities.

So seeing a young mother in possession of a stack of children's books delighted Ted. Had she herself been read to as a child? he wanted to know. What were the little one's favourites? Wasn't it astonishing how quickly children attached themselves to a story they'd been read, demanding it over and over again?

Thus, Ted saw the silver Bentley only out of the corner of his eye. He gave it little thought other than, Fine motor, that. It was only when the car's occupants got out and approached Eugenie's house that he bade a friendly farewell to his customer and moved closer to the window to watch them.

They were an odd pair. The man was tall, athletically built, blond, and admirably dressed in the sort of well-made suit that ages over time like a fine wine. His companion wore red trainers, black trousers, and an overlarge navy pea jacket that hung to her knees. The woman lit up a fag before she had the car door closed, which made Ted's lip curl in distaste—the world's tobacco manufacturers were surely going to burn for eternity in a section of hell designed just for them—but the man walked straight to Eugenie's door.

Ted waited for him to knock, but he didn't. As his companion sucked at her cigarette like someone with a death wish, the man examined an object in his hand, which turned out to be a key to Eugenie's front door, because he inserted this key in the lock and after making a remark to his companion, they both went inside.

At this sight, Ted went numb from his feet to his

earlobes. First that unfamiliar man at one in the morning, then last night's encounter between Eugenie and that same individual in the car park, and now these two strangers in possession of a key to the cottage . . . Ted knew he had to get over there at once.

He glanced round the shop to see if any more customers were considering purchases. There were two others. Old Mr. Horsham—Ted liked to call him Old Mr. Horsham because it was such a relief to find someone out and about who was older than he himself—had taken a volume about Egypt off the shelf and appeared to be weighing it rather than inspecting it. And Mrs. Dilday was, as usual, reading another chapter from a book she had no intention of purchasing. Part of her daily ritual was to select a best seller, carry it casually to the back of the shop, where the armchairs were, read a chapter or two, mark her place with a grocery receipt, and hide the book among secondhand volumes of Salman Rushdie, where—considering the tastes of the average citizen in Henley—it would not be noticed.

For nearly twenty minutes Ted waited for these two customers to remove themselves from the premises so that he could invent a reason to go across the road. When Old Horsham finally bought Egypt for a gratifying sum, saying, "Saw action there in the war," as he handed over two twenty-pound notes, which he extricated from a wallet that looked old enough to have seen action with its owner, Ted then turned his hopes towards Mrs. Dilday. But this, he saw, was going to be fruitless. She was firmly ensconced in her favourite overstuffed armchair, and she'd brought a Thermos of tea with her as well. She was pouring, sipping, and reading quite happily, just as if she were in her own home.

Public libraries exist for a reason, Ted wanted to tell her. But instead he alternated between watching her, sending her mental messages about leaving at once, and peering out of the window for any kind of indication of who the people were in Eugenie's house.

In the midst of his mental imaging of Mrs. Dilday actually purchasing her novel and trotting off to read it, the telephone rang. His eyes still on Eugenie's house, Ted felt behind him for the receiver and picked it up on the fifth double ring.

He said, "Wiley's Books," and a woman asked, "Who's this speaking, please?"

He said, "Major Ted Wiley. Retired. Who's this?"

"Are you the only person who uses this line, sir?"

"What . . . ? Is this BT? Is there a problem?"

"Your phone number registers on one-four-seven-one as the last to have called this number that I'm speaking from, sir. It belongs to a woman called Eugenie Davies."

"Right. I phoned her this morning," Ted informed his caller, trying to keep his voice as steady as he could. "We've a dinner engagement." And then because he had to ask it although he already knew the answer, "Is something wrong? Has something happened? Who are you?"

The receiver at the other end was covered for a

moment as the woman spoke to someone else in the room. She said, "Metropolitan police, sir."

Metropolitan . . . that meant London. And suddenly Ted could see it again: Eugenie driving into London last night with the rain beating down against the roof of the Polo and the spray from the tyres arcing out into the road. "London police?" he asked nonetheless.

"That's right," the woman told him. "Where are you, exactly, sir?"

"Across from Eugenie's house. I've a bookshop . . ."

Another consultation. Then, "Would you mind stepping over here, sir? We've one or two questions we'd like to ask you."

"Has something . . ." Ted could barely force himself to say the words, but they had to be said. If nothing else, the police would expect to hear them. "Has something happened to Eugenie?"

"We can come to you if that's more convenient."

"No. No. I'll be there at once. I must close up first, but I'll—"

"Fine, Major Wiley. We'll be here for quite some time."

Ted walked to the back, where he told Mrs. Dilday that an emergency required him to shut up shop for a time. She said, "Dear me. I hope it's not your mum?" because that was indeed the most rational emergency: his mother's death, although at eighty-nine it was only the stroke that was preventing her from taking up kick-boxing in her declining years.

He said, "No, no. Just . . . There's something I need to take care of."

She peered at him intently but accepted the vague excuse. In a welter of nerves, Ted waited as she drank down the rest of her tea, donned her wool coat, thrust her hands into her gloves, and—without the least attempt to disguise her actions—put the novel she was reading behind a copy of *The Satanic Verses*.

Once she was gone, Ted hurried up the stairs to his flat. He found that his heart was alternately fluttering then pounding, and he was going rather light in the head. With the lightness came voices, so real that he swung round without thinking, anticipating a presence that was not there.

First the woman's voice again: "Metropolitan police. We've one or two questions we'd like to ask . . ."

Then Eugenie's: "We'll talk. There's so much to say."

And then, unaccountably, his own Connie's murmur coming to him from the grave itself, Connie, who'd known him as no one else had: "You're a match for any man alive, Ted Wiley."

Why now? he wondered. Why Connie now?

But there was no answer, only the question. And there was also what had to be faced and dealt with across the street.

AS LYNLEY BEGAN going through the letters he'd pulled from the papier-mâché holder, Barbara Havers went up the narrowest staircase she'd ever seen to the first floor of the tiny house. There, two very small

bedrooms and an antiquated bathroom opened off a
landing that wasn't much larger than a drawing pin's
head. Both bedrooms continued the theme of
monastic simplicity bordering on shabbiness that began in the sitting room below. The first room contained three pieces of furniture: a single bed covered
by a plain counterpane, a chest of drawers, and a bedside table on which stood yet another tasseled lamp.
The second bedroom had been turned into a sewing
room and contained, aside from the answer machine,
the only remotely modern appliance in the entire
building: an advanced sewing machine next to which
lay a considerable pile of tiny garments. Barbara fingered through these and saw that they were dolls'
clothes, elaborately designed and more elaborately
fashioned with everything from beadwork to faux
fur. There were no dolls anywhere in the sewing
room nor were there any in the bedroom next door.

There Barbara went first to a chest of drawers,
where she found a humble paucity of clothing, even
by her own indifferent standards of dress: threadbare
knickers, equally worn brassieres, a few jumpers, a
limp collection of tights. There was neither a fitted
clothes cupboard nor a wardrobe in the room, so the
few skirts, trousers, and dresses that the woman had
owned were folded carefully into the chest of drawers as well.

Among the trousers and the skirts, at the back of
the drawer, Barbara saw that a bundle of letters had
been tucked. She fished these out, removed the rubber band that held them together, laid them out

across the single bed, and saw that they had all been written in the same hand. She blinked at this hand. She took a moment to assimilate the fact that she recognised the black, decisive scrawl.

The envelopes bore postmarks as old as seventeen years. The most recent, she saw, had been sent just over one decade ago. She reached for this one and slid the contents out.

He called her "Eugenie my darling." He wrote that he didn't know where to begin. He said those things that men always say when they claim to have reached the decision that they no doubt intended to reach all along: She must never doubt that he loved her more than life itself; she must know, remember, and hold to her heart the fact that the hours they had spent to-gether had made him feel alive—truly and wonder-fully alive, my darling—for the first time in years; indeed, the feeling of her skin beneath his fingers had been like liquid silk shot through with lightning. . . .

Barbara rolled her eyes at the purple phrasing. She lowered the letter and gave herself a moment to re-act to it and, more important, to what it implied. Read more or not, Barb? she asked herself. Read more and she felt something akin to unclean. Not and she felt unprofessional.

She went back to the letter. He'd gone home, she read, intending to tell his wife everything. He'd screwed his courage to the sticking place—Barbara winced at the pilfering from Shakespeare—and held the image of Eugenie in his mind to give him the strength to deal a mortal blow to a perfectly good and decent woman. But he'd found her unwell, Eugenie darling, unwell in a manner that he couldn't explain in a mere letter, but that he <u>would</u> explain, would lay before her in all its desperate detail, when next they met. This <u>didn't</u> mean they would not be together at the end of the day, darling Eugenie. This didn't mean they had no future. Above all, this didn't mean everything that had passed between them counted for nothing, because that was not the case.

He'd concluded with, "Wait for me. I beg you. I'm coming to you, darling." And he'd signed it with the scrawl that Barbara had seen on notes, on Christmas cards, on departmental letters, and on memos for years.

At least she now knew what had seemed off at the Webberly party, she thought as she stuffed the letter back into its envelope. All that jolly-good-fellowing to celebrate twenty-five years of sham.

"Havers?" Lynley was in the doorway, spectacles sliding down his nose and a greeting card in his hand. "Here's something that fits in with one of the phone messages. What've you found?"

"Swap," she said, and handed over her envelope in exchange for what he was carrying.

This card was from someone called Lynn, with an envelope that bore a London postmark but no sender's address. Its message was simple:

Thank you so much for the floral tribute, dearest
Eugenie, and for your presence which meant so much to

*me. Life will go on. I know that. But, of course, it will
never be the same.*
Fondly,
Lynn

Barbara examined the date: a week ago. She agreed
with Lynley. Thematically, it sounded like the same
woman who'd left the message on the answer machine.

"Damn." This was Lynley's reaction to the letter
Barbara had handed to him. He gestured to the other
letters that lay across Eugenie Davies' bed. "What
about those?"

"All from him, Inspector, if the writing on the envelopes is anything to go by."

Barbara watched the play of reactions as they
crossed Lynley's face. She knew that her superior officer and she had to be thinking along the same lines:
Had Webberly known these letters—so embarrassing
and potentially damaging to him—would be in Eugenie Davies' possession? Had he merely suspected or
feared that they might be? And in either case, had he
arranged to have Lynley—and by extension Havers as
well—work the case in order to run interference no
matter which circumstance arose?

"D'you think Leach knows about them?" Barbara
asked.

"He phoned Webberly when he had a potential
i.d. on the body. At one in the morning, Havers.
What does that suggest to you?"

"And guess who he asked to go to Henley this morning." Barbara took the letter that Lynley handed back to her. "What's to do, then, sir?"

Lynley walked to the window. She watched as he gazed down at the street. She expected the regulation reply from him. Asking the question in the first place had been merely rote.

"We'll take them with us," he said.

She got to her feet. "Right. You've got evidence bags in the boot, haven't you? I'll fetch—"

"Not like that," Lynley said.

Barbara said, "What? But you just said take—"

"Yes. We'll take them with us." He turned back to her from the window.

Barbara stared at him. She didn't want to think what he was implying. *We'll take them with us.* Not, We'll bag them and log them as evidence, Havers. Not, Have a care with them, Barbara. Not, We'll have forensic check them for fingerprints, for the prints of someone other than the recipient who might have found them, might have read them, might have become consumed with jealousy because of them and despite their age, someone who might have looked for vengeance because of them. . . .

She said, "Hang on, Inspector. You can't mean—"

But she wasn't able to complete her protest.

Below them, someone knocked on the door.

LYNLEY ANSWERED IT to find an elderly gentleman in a waxed jacket and peaked cap standing on the pavement, his hands sunk into his pockets. His ruddy face was mapped with the markings of broken capillaries, and his nose was just that shade of rose that would deepen and grow purple over time. But it was his eyes that Lynley took note of most closely. They were blue, intense, and wary.

He introduced himself as Major Ted Wiley, Army, retired. "Someone from the police . . . You must be one of them. I had a call . . . ?"

Lynley asked the man to step inside. He introduced himself and then introduced Havers, who descended the stairs as Wiley moved tentatively into the room. The old gentleman looked round him, glanced at the stairs, then lifted his eyes to the ceiling as if he were trying to determine what Barbara Havers had been looking for or had found on the floor above.

"What's happened?" Wiley removed neither his hat nor his jacket.

"You're a friend of Mrs. Davies?" Lynley asked him.

The man didn't respond at once. It was as if he were trying to decide what the word *friend* actually meant in reference to his relationship with Eugenie Davies. He finally said, looking from Lynley to Havers and back again to Lynley, "Something's happened to her. You wouldn't be here otherwise."

"That was you on the phone, that last message on her machine? A man talking about plans for tonight?" Havers asked this. She remained by the stairs.

"We were . . ." Wiley seemed to hear the past tense and made the adjustment. "We're supposed to have dinner. Tonight. She said . . . You're from the Met and she went to London last night. So something's happened to her. Please tell me what."

"Sit down, Major Wiley," Lynley said. The old man didn't seem frail, but there was no telling the condition of his heart or his blood pressure from just one look at him, and Lynley didn't like to take risks with someone when he had bad news to pass on.

"It was raining hard last night," Wiley said, more to himself than to either Lynley or Havers. "I talked to her about driving in the rain. And the dark. Dark's bad enough but rain makes it worse."

Havers crossed the few feet to Wiley and took him by the arm. "Have a seat, Major," she said.

"It's bad," he responded.

"I'm afraid so," Lynley said.

"The motorway? She said she'd be careful. She said not to worry. She said we'd talk. Tonight. We'd talk. She wanted to talk." He was speaking not so much to them but to the coffee table in front of the sofa on which Havers had deposited him. She sat next to him, perched on the edge.

Lynley took the armchair. He said gently, "I'm afraid Eugenie Davies was killed last night."

Wiley turned his head to Lynley in what looked like slow motion. "The motorway," he said. "The rain. I didn't want her to go."

For the moment, Lynley didn't disabuse him of the notion that there had been a motorway car crash. The BBC early morning news had carried the story of the hit-and-run, but no mention had been made of Eugenie Davies' name at that time since her body had yet to be identified and her family had yet to be tracked down. Lynley said, "She left after dark, then? What time was this?"

Wiley said numbly, "Half past nine, I think? Ten? We were walking back from St. Mary the Virgin—"

"Evensong?" Havers had taken out her notebook and was jotting down the information.

"No, no," Wiley said. "There was no service. She'd gone in . . . to pray? I don't actually know be-cause . . ." He removed his cap then, as if he were in church himself. He held it with both hands. "I didn't go in with her. I had my dog. My golden. P.B.? That's her name. We waited in the church yard."

"This was in the rain?" Lynley asked.

Wiley twisted the cap. "Dogs don't mind rain. And it was time for her last walk of the evening. P.B.'s last walk."

Lynley said, "Can you tell us why she was going to London?"

Wiley gave the cap another twist. "She said she had an appointment there."

"With whom? Where?"

"I don't know. She said we'd talk tonight."

"About the appointment?"

"I don't know. God. I don't *know*." His voice frac-tured but Ted Wiley wasn't a retired Army man for nothing. He regained control within a second. Then he said, "How did it happen? Where? Did she skid? Hit a lorry?"

Lynley gave the facts to him, offering just enough details to tell Wiley where and how she had died. He

didn't use the word *murder* in his explanation. And
Wiley didn't interrupt to ask why the Metropolitan
police were trolling through the belongings of a
woman who, to all intents and purposes, was the victim of a simple hit-and-run.

But a moment after Lynley had finished his explanation, Wiley made the leap. He seemed to take
measure of the fact that Havers had descended the
stairs upon his arrival wearing latex gloves. He put
this together with the police punching one-four-
seven-one on Eugenie's phone. He added to this
what they had said about Eugenie's answer machine.
And he said, "This can't have been an accident. Because why would you . . . the two of you coming out
here from London . . ." His eyes focused on something else, perhaps someone else, a vision in the distance that seemed to prompt him to say, "That bloke
in the car park last night. This isn't an accident, is it?"
And he rose.

Havers rose as well and urged him back down. He
cooperated, but now he was changed, as if an unnamed purpose had begun to consume him. From
twisting his cap, he went to slapping it against his
palm. He said, quite as if he were giving an order to
a subordinate, "Tell me what happened to Eugenie."

There seemed little risk that he would have a heart
attack or stroke, so Lynley told him that he and
Havers were part of a murder squad, leaving him to
fill in the rest of the blanks. He went on to say, "Tell
us about the man in the car park," which Wiley did
without hesitation.

He'd walked up to the Sixty Plus Club, where Eugenie worked. He went with P.B. to accompany Eugenie home in the rain. When he got there, he observed her in an altercation with a man. Not a local man, Wiley said. This was someone from Brighton.

"She told you that?" Lynley asked.

Wiley shook his head. He'd got a glimpse of the number plate as the car sped off. He couldn't get it all, but he saw the letters: ADY. "I was worried about her. She'd been acting a little peculiar for several days, so I looked the letters up in the registration mark guide. I saw ADY is Brighton. The car was an Audi. Navy or black. I couldn't tell in the dark."

"You keep a copy handy?" Havers asked. "The registration mark guide? Is this a hobby or something?"

"It's in the bookshop. Travel section. I sell a copy now and then. People who want to give their kids something to do in the car. That sort of thing."

"Ah."

Lynley knew Havers' *ah*. She was watching Wiley curiously. He said, "You didn't intercede in the altercation between Mrs. Davies and this man, Major Wiley?"

"I came into the car park only at the end of it. I heard a few shouted words—on his part, this was. He got into the car. Took off before I was close enough to say anything. That was it."

"Who did Mrs. Davies say this man was?"

"I didn't ask her."

Lynley and Havers exchanged a look. Havers was the one to ask, "Why not?"

"As I said. She'd been acting peculiar, different from usual, for several days. I assumed there was something on her mind and . . ." Wiley shifted his eyes to his cap and seemed surprised to find it still in his hands. He stuffed it into his pocket. "See here. I'm not the sort who pries. I decided to wait for her to tell me whatever she wanted to tell me."

"Had you ever seen this man before?"

Wiley said no, no, he didn't know the man. He hadn't seen him before that moment, he didn't recognise the man at all, but he'd got a good look at him if the detectives wanted a description. When they said that they did, he provided it: the approximate age, the height, the iron-grey hair, the dominant hawk-like nose. "He called her Eugenie," Wiley concluded. "They knew each other." This, he said, he'd assumed from what he'd seen in the car park: Eugenie had touched the man's face, but he'd pulled away.

"But you still didn't ask her who he was?" Lynley said. "Why was that, Major Wiley?"

"It seemed . . . too personal, somehow. I thought she'd tell me when she was ready. If he was important."

"And she did say she had something she wanted to talk to you about," Havers noted.

Wiley nodded and let out a slow breath. "She did say that. She talked about confessing her sins."

"Sins," Havers said.

Lynley leaned forward, avoiding Havers' meaningful look in his direction. He said, "May we assume from all this that you and Mrs. Davies had a close relationship, Major Wiley? Were you friends? Lovers? Engaged?"

The question seemed to discomfort Wiley. He altered his position on the sofa. "It'd been three years. I wanted to be respectful with her, not like one of these randy modern blokes with nothing more on his mind. I was willing to wait. She finally said that she was ready, but she wanted to have a talk first."

"Which was what was supposed to happen tonight," Havers concluded. "That's why you phoned her."

It was.

Lynley asked the old gentleman to come into the kitchen with them, then. He said that there were other voices on Eugenie Davies' answer machine, and Major Ted Wiley—three years into a relationship with the dead woman, no matter what the relationship was—might be able to identify them.

In the kitchen, Wiley stood by the table and looked at the photographs of the two children. He reached for one of them, but he stopped himself when he finally seemed to take in the fact that Lynley and Havers were wearing gloves for a reason. As Havers readied the answer machine to play its messages again, Lynley said, "Are these Mrs. Davies' children, Major Wiley?"

"Her son and daughter," Wiley said. "Yes. They're her children. Sonia died a number of years ago. And

the boy . . . They were estranged, Eugenie and the
boy. Been estranged for I don't know how long. They
had some sort of falling-out ages back. She never
spoke of him to me except to say they no longer saw
each other."

"And Sonia? Did Mrs. Davies ever speak to you
about Sonia?"

"Just that she died young. But"—Wiley cleared his
throat and stepped away from the table as if wishing
to distance himself from what he was about to say—
"well, look at her. One can't be surprised that she
died young. They . . . they often do."

Lynley frowned, wondering that Wiley seemed
unaware of a case that certainly must have dominated
the newspapers at the time. He said, "Were you in
the country twenty years ago, Major Wiley?"

No, he'd been . . . Wiley seemed to do a backward
progression in his head, cataloguing the years he'd
spent on active duty in the Army. He said he'd been
in the Falklands then. But that was long ago and he
might have been in Rhodesia at the time . . . or what
was left of Rhodesia. Why?

"Mrs. Davies never told you that Sonia was murdered?"

Dumbly, Wiley returned his gaze to the photographs. He said, "She didn't tell me . . . She didn't
say . . . No, never once. Good God." He dug into his
back pocket and brought out a handkerchief, but he
didn't use it. Instead, he said only, "This lot don't belong here, on the table, you know. Did you move
them?" in apparent reference to the pictures.

"This is where we found them," Lynley told him.

"They should be scattered round the house. The sitting room. Upstairs. In here. That's how they always were." He pulled out one of the two chairs beneath the table and lowered himself into it heavily. He looked fairly spent at this point, but he nodded at Havers where she stood by the answer machine.

Lynley studied the major as he listened to the messages. He tried to read Wiley's reaction when he heard the voices of two other men on the machine. From their words and their tone, it was obvious that they were both involved with Eugenie Davies in some way. But if Wiley reached that conclusion himself and if that conclusion distressed him, he gave no indication other than colour in a face already so rubicund as to make measuring further redness impossible.

At the end of the messages, Lynley asked, "Do you recognise anyone?"

"Lynn," he said. "She did tell me that, Eugenie did. The child of a friend called Lynn passed away suddenly, and Eugenie went to the funeral. She told me that when she'd heard that the child had died, she knew how Lynn felt and she wanted to commiserate."

"Heard that she'd died?" Havers asked. "Heard from who?"

Wiley didn't know. He hadn't thought to ask. "I assumed the woman must have rung her up. This Lynn person," he said, "whoever she is."

"Do you know where the funeral was?"

He shook his head. "She went off for the day."

"When was this?"

"Last Tuesday. I asked her if she wanted me to go as well. Funerals being what they are, I thought she might welcome the company. But she said she and Lynn had some talking to do. 'I need to see her,' she said. That was all."

"Need to see her?" Lynley asked. "That's what she said?"

"Need. Yes. That's what she said."

Need, Lynley thought. Not want, but need. He considered the word and everything it implied. What follows need, he knew, is usually action.

But was that the case here in this kitchen in Henley, where it appeared several needs were colliding? There was Eugenie Davies' need to confess sin to Major Wiley. There was an unidentified man's need to talk to Eugenie, declared on her answer machine. And there was Ted Wiley's need . . . for what?

Lynley asked Havers to play the messages one more time, and he wondered if Wiley's slight change of posture—drawing his arms closer to his body— was an indication of steeling himself. He kept his gaze fixed on the major as once again the two men on the machine declared their need to speak to Eugenie.

I had to ring again, the one voice declared. *Eugenie, I need to speak with you.*

And there it was again: that word *need*. What would a man do with a desperate need?

HOW WD U do it 2 me if u cd?

TongueMan read the question from LadyFire without his usual surge of gratification. They'd been

dancing round this moment for weeks, despite an initial—and inaccurate—assessment of her on his part
which had suggested he'd have her ready for a go well
in advance of CreamPants. It just went to show that
you couldn't judge the outcome by someone's ability
to engage in suggestive cyberchat, didn't it? LadyFire
had come on strong at first in the descriptive arena,
but she'd faded quickly when the talk shifted from
fantasy fucks between celebrities (she'd been astonishing in her ability to convey a hot encounter between
a purple-haired rock star and their nation's monarch)
to fantasy fucks in which she herself was one of the
partners. Indeed, TongueMan had thought for a time
that he'd lost her altogether by pushing too soon and
revealing too much. He'd even considered moving
on to the next possibility—EatMe—and he was about
to do so when LadyFire reappeared on the cyber-
scene. She'd needed some time to think, evidently.
But now she knew what she wanted. So *How wd u do
it 2 me if u cd?*

TongueMan studied the question and took note of
the fact that his mind didn't kick into high gear at the
thought of another supercharged semi-anonymous
encounter with another cyberlover so soon after his
last. He was doing his best to forget his last anyway,
and especially to forget everything that had followed:
the flashing lights, the barriers blocking off both ends
of his street, the eyes of suspicion coming to rest on
him, the Boxter—damn them—being hauled off for
police inspection. But he'd handled it all well enough,
he decided. Yes. He'd handled it like a pro.

The Met certainly weren't prepared for someone who was wise to their ways, TongueMan thought. They expected one to lie down, belly up, the moment they started to ask their questions. They reckoned that Joseph Q. Average Citizen—eager to prove he had nothing to hide—would jump onto the cooperation trolley car and ride it to whatever destination the cops were hoping to take. So when the police said, "We have a few questions, if you wouldn't mind coming down to the station for a chat," most people sauntered right along without a second thought, assuming they had some sort of immunity from a legal system that anyone with a grain of sense knew could ride roughshod over the uninitiated in about five minutes.

TongueMan, however, was anything but a member of the uninitiated. He knew what could happen when one cooperated, blithely believing that doing one's civic duty was synonymous with demonstrating one's guilelessness. Bollocks, that. So when the cops said that his address had been in the possession of that woman in the street and could they ask him a few questions please, TongueMan knew which way the trolley ride was heading, and in short order he had his solicitor on the phone.

Not that Jake Azoff had liked being torn from his bed at midnight. Not that he didn't whine privately about "duty solicitors and what they are being paid by the Government to do." But there was no way on earth that TongueMan was going to place his future—not to mention his present—into the hands of a duty solicitor. True, the representation wouldn't have cost him a penny, but a duty solicitor had no vested interest in TongueMan's future, whereas Azoff—with whom he enjoyed a rather complicated relationship involving shares, bonds, mutual funds, and the like—actually did. Besides, what was he paying Azoff for, if not to be ready when legal advice of any sort was needed?

But TongueMan was worried. Obviously. He could lie to himself about it. He could attempt to distract himself by phoning in sick from work and logging onto the net for a few hours of pornographic fantasising with utter strangers. But his body couldn't prevaricate when it came to unacknowledged anxiety. And the fact that he was enjoying no physical reaction whatsoever to *How wd u do it 2 me if u cd?* said it all.

He typed *U wdnt 4get it soon.*

She typed *R u shy 2day? Cm on. Tell how.*

How? he wondered. Yes, that was it. How? He tried to be loose. Just let the mind roam. He was good at this. He was a master. And she was certainly what all the others had been: older and looking for a sign that she still had what it took.

He typed *Whr do u want my tong?* in an attempt to get her to do the work.

She typed *No fair. R U jst all tlk?*

He wasn't even talk today, TongueMan thought, which she'd discover soon enough if they carried on much longer in this vein. It was time to get huffy with LadyFire. A break was called for till he sorted himself out.

He typed *If thts wt u thnk, bby* and logged off. Let her stew in that juice for a day or two.

He checked how the market was doing before he pushed back from the keyboard. He swung his chair round and left the study, descending to the kitchen where the glass carafe on the coffee maker offered him a final cup. He poured and savoured the flavour of coffee the way he liked it: strong, black, and bitter. Rather like life itself, he decided.

He gave a brief laugh devoid of amusement. There was a real irony to the last twelve hours, and he was sure if he thought about it long enough, he'd discover what that irony was. But thinking about it was the last thing he wanted to do at the moment. With a Hampstead murder squad breathing down his neck, he knew he had to maintain his composure. That was the secret to life, composure: in the face of adversity, in the face of triumph, in the face of—

Something flicked against the kitchen window. Roused, Tongue-Man looked out to see two roughly dressed, unshaven men standing in the middle of his back garden. They'd come in from the park that ran the length of nearly all the Crediton Hill back gardens on the east side of the street. Since he had no fence between his property and the park, his visitors hadn't encountered much of an obstacle in gaining access. He was going to have to do something about that.

The two men saw him and nudged each other simultaneously. One of them called out, "Open up, Jay.

Long time, no see," and the other added, "We're giving you a break, coming in the back way" with a maddening smirk.

TongueMan cursed. First a body in the street, then the Boxter towed away, then himself under the eyes of the cops. And now this. Always guard against thinking a day couldn't possibly get worse, he told himself as he went to the dining room and opened the french windows.

"Robbie, Brent," he said to the men in greeting, every bit as if he'd seen them only last week. It was cold outside, and they were hunched against it, stamping their feet and blowing steam like two bulls waiting for the matador. "What're you doing here?"

"Ask us in?" Robbie said. "Not a very pleasant day for the garden, this."

TongueMan sighed. It seemed as if every time he took a step forward, something came along to drag him two steps back. He said, "What's this about, then?" But what he meant was, How did you find me this time?

Brent grinned, saying, "The usual, Jay," but at least he had the decency to look uncomfortable and to shift his feet.

Robbie, on the other hand, was the one to watch out for. Always had been and always would be. He'd throw Granny from the underground train if he thought he stood to gain by it, and TongueMan knew the last thing he could hope for was consideration, respect, or sympathy from the bloke.

"Street's blocked off." Robbie cocked his head in the general direction of the bottom of the road. "Something happen?"

"A woman was hit by a car last night."

"Ah." But the way Robbie said the word declared that he wasn't learning anything new. "And that's why you're not at work today?"

"I work from home sometimes. I've told you that."

"Might've, yeah. But it's been a while, ha'n't it?" He didn't go on to mention what hung between them unspoken: the time it had been since he'd last come calling and what he'd gone through to track down this address. Instead, he said, "But your office tol' me you had to cancel a meeting today and you phoned in with flu. Or was it a head cold? You remember, Brent?"

"You *talked* to my—" TongueMan stopped himself. This, after all, was the reaction Robbie sought. He said, "I thought we'd got that straight. I asked you not to speak to anyone but me when you phone me at work. You've got the private line. There's never any need to talk to my secretary."

"You ask for a lot," Robbie said. " 'N't that so, Brent?" This last was obviously meant to remind the other man—possessing the lesser intelligence—which side he was supposed to be on.

Brent said, "Right. You asking us in, or what, Jay? Cold out here."

Robbie added, as if superfluously, "There's three tabloid blokes down the end of the street. You know that, Jay? Wha's going on?"

TongueMan cursed in silence and stepped back from the door. The two men outside laughed, knocked hands in a clumsy high-five, crossed the flagstones, and came up the steps. "There's a boot scraper. Use it," TongueMan told them. Last night's rain had made a swamp of the ground beneath the trees that formed the boundary between the houses and the park. Robbie and Brent had tramped right through it like farmers raising pigs. "I've a decent Oriental carpet in here."

"Take the daisies off, Brent," Robbie said cooperatively. "How's that, Jay? We leave our mucked-up boots on the step. We know how to be proper guests, me and Brent."

"Proper guests wait for invitations."

"Wouldn't want to stand on that sort of ceremony."

Both men were inside, and they seemed to fill the room. They were enormous, and while they'd never used their size to intimidate him, he knew they wouldn't hesitate to use anything within their power to bend his will to theirs.

"Why's those tabloid blokes hanging about?" Robbie asked. "Far's I know, the only way tabloids get their stuff's if someone rings them up with something hot."

"Yeah," Brent said, bending to peer into the china cabinet, which he used as a mirror to inspect his hair. "Something hot, Jay." He jiggled the cabinet door.

"That's antique. Have a care, all right?"

"It looked dodgy, those blokes hanging round the barriers at the bottom of the road," Robbie said.

"So we had a word with them, me and Brent did, didn't we?"

"Yeah. A word." Brent opened the door and took out one of the china cups inside. "Nice, this. Old, is it, Jay?"

"Come on, Brent."

"He asked a question, Jay."

"Fine. It's old. It's early nineteenth century. If you're going to break it, just get it over with and spare me the suspense, all right?"

Robbie chuckled. Brent grinned and replaced the cup. He shut the cabinet with the care a neurosurgeon might give to repositioning a section of skull.

Robbie said, "One of the tabloid blokes said the cops're interested in someone on this street. Said a snout at the station tol' him the dead bird was carrying an address with her last night. Wouldn't give us the address, though, me and Brent, if he knew it. Thought we might be competition."

Small chance of that, TongueMan thought. But he anticipated the direction they were about to take, and he did what he could to brace himself for the inevitable course of the conversation.

"Tabloids," Robbie said. "Amazing what they c'n dig up 'less someone tries to head them off."

"Yeah. Amazing," Brent agreed. And then as if he'd merely been playing the other man's stooge instead of living the rôle, he said, "Rolling Suds, Jay. It needs some bolstering."

"I 'bolstered' it not six months ago."

"Right. But that was then, in spring. Season's slow

now. And there's this matter of . . . well, you know."
Brent glanced at Robbie.

Which was when the pieces clicked into place.
"You've borrowed against the business, haven't you?"
TongueMan said. "What is it this time? Horses?
Dogs? Cards? I'm not *about* to—"

"Hey, you listen." Robbie took a step forward as if
to demonstrate the considerable difference in their
sizes. "You owe us, mate. Who stood by you? Who
gave aggro to every Tom and Willie who even
thought 'bout whispering behind your back? Brent
got his *arm* broke because of you, and I—"

"I know the story, Rob."

"Good. So hear the ending, okay? We need some
oscar, we need it today, and if that's a problem, then
you best speak up."

TongueMan looked from one man to the other
and saw the future unrolling before him like an endless carpet with a repetitive design. He would sell up
again, move house again, establish himself, change his
job if necessary . . . and they would still find him.
And when they found him, they would trot out the
same manoeuvre they'd used with so much success
for so many years. This was the way it was going to
be. They believed he owed them. And they never
forgot.

"What do you need?" he asked them wearily.

Robbie named his price. Brent blinked and
grinned.

TongueMan fetched his chequebook and scrawled
the amount. Then he saw them out the way they had

come: through the dining room door and into the back garden. He watched till they ducked beneath the bare branches of the plane trees at the edge of the park. Then he went to the phone.

When he had Jake Azoff on the line, he took a breath that felt like a stab in the heart. "Rob and Brent found me," he informed his solicitor. "Tell the police I'll talk."

GIDEON

10 SEPTEMBER

I DON'T understand why you won't prescribe something for me. You're a medical doctor, aren't you? Or will the act of writing out a prescription for migraines reveal you as a charlatan? And please don't produce that tedious commentary about psychotropic medication again. We're not talking about antidepressants, Dr. Rose. About antipsychotics, tranquillisers, sedatives, or amphetamines. We are talking about a simple pain killer. Because what I have in my head is simple pain.

Libby's trying to help. She was here earlier and she found me where I'd been all morning: in my bedroom with the curtains drawn and a bottle of Harveys Bristol Cream tucked into the crook of my arm like a Paddington bear. She sat on the edge of the bed and loosened my grip on the bottle, saying, "If you're planning on getting blitzed on this, you'll be hurling chunks in an hour."

I groaned. Her style of language, so bizarre and so

graphic, was the last thing I needed to hear. I said, "My head."

She said, "The pits. But booze's going to make it worse. Let's see if I can help."

She put her hands on my head. The tips of her fingers, resting lightly on my temples, were cool and they traced small circles, small fresh circles that diminished the pounding in my veins. I felt my body relax beneath her touch, and it seemed to me that I could easily fall asleep with her sitting there so quietly.

She moved and lay next to me and placed her hand on my cheek. The same gentle touch of the same cool flesh. She said, "You're burning."

I murmured, "It's the headache."

She turned her hand so my cheek felt the backs of her fingers, then. Cool, they were so wonderfully cool.

I said, "Feels good. Thanks, Libby." I took her hand, kissed her fingers, and placed them back against my cheek.

She said, "Gideon . . . ?"

I said, "Hmm?"

"Oh, never mind." And then when I did just that, she sighed and went on. "D'you ever think about . . . us? I mean, like, where we're headed and all?"

I made no reply. It seems to me that it always comes down to this with women. That plural pronoun and the quest for validation: thinking about us confirms that there is an *us* in the first place.

She said, "D'you realise how much time we've spent together?"

"A great deal of time."

"Jeez, we've even, like, slept together."

Women, I have also noted, have a marvelous command of the obvious.

"So d'you think we should go on? D'you think we're ready for the next level in all this? I mean, I've got to say I feel totally ready. Really ready for what comes next. What about you?" And as she spoke, she lifted her leg to rest her thigh against mine, crossed my chest with her arm, and tilted her hips—just the ghost of a tilt, this was—to press her pubis against me.

And suddenly I am back with Beth, back at that point in a relationship when something more is supposed to happen between the man and the woman and when nothing does. At least, not for me. With Beth the next level was permanent commitment. We were lovers, after all, and had been lovers for eleven months.

She is the liaison between East London Conservatory and the schools from which the conservatory draws its students. A former music instructor, she is also a cellist. She is perfect for the conservatory in that she speaks the language of the instruments, the language of the music, and, most importantly, the language of the children themselves.

I am not aware of her at first. Not until we must deal with a parent whose child has run away from home, seeking a shelter that the conservatory cannot provide. The child, we learn, has been prevented from practising by the mother's boyfriend, who, we also learn, has other activities in mind for her. The girl has become little more than a servant in their squalid home. But that *little more* is defined by sexual favours she has been told to perform on both of them.

Beth is Nemesis to this pathetic excuse of a human couple. She is pure Fury. She waits for neither police nor Social Services to deal with the situation because she trusts neither police nor Social Services. She deals with it herself: with a private detective and with a meeting between herself and the couple during which she makes it clear what will happen to them both should this child come to any harm. And to make sure that they understand, she defines *harm* for them in the explicit street terms that they are accustomed to.

I am not there for any of this, but I hear of it from more than one of the other instructors. And the ferocity of her devotion to this student touches something within me. A longing, perhaps. Or perhaps a chord of recognition.

At any rate, I seek her out. We fall into *together* in the most natural fashion I can imagine. For a year all is well.

But then as it happens, she talks of having more. It's logical, I know. Pondering the next step is rational for a man and a woman, although perhaps more for a woman who has her basic biology to consider.

When the subject of *next* comes up between us, I know I should want what follows those professions of love we've made for each other. I realise that nothing stays the same forever and to expect that she and I will be forever content to be fellow musicians and ardent lovers is a form of delusion. But, still, when she broaches the idea of marriage and children, I feel myself grow cool. I avoid the topic at first and when it can no longer be shunted to one side with the excuse of rehearsals, practises, recording sessions, and personal appearances, I find that the coolness within me has increased in proportion and now has iced over the idea not only of a future with Beth but also a present with Beth as well. I can't be with her as I was before. I feel no passion, and I have no desire. I attempt to go through the motions at first but it's just not there for me any longer. Whatever *it* was: desire, fervour, attachment, devotion.

We grind against each other, then, which is probably the way it happens when a man and a woman are trying to preserve a connection that's already been severed. And in that grinding, we wear each other away until what we had is so distant a memory that we can no longer sift through the discord of our present to locate the harmony that defined our past. And it ends. We end. She goes on to find another man whom she marries twenty-seven months and one week later. I remain as I am.

So when Libby spoke of next levels, I felt my spirit shudder. And yet I knew it would always come down to this same conversation between me and a woman, as long as I allowed any woman into my life.

The *shouldn't*s began their bows in my mind. I

shouldn't have shown her the lower ground floor flat. I shouldn't have agreed to let it to her. I shouldn't have taken her out for coffee. I shouldn't have bought her a meal, played that first concerto on her stereo, flown kites from Primrose Hill with her, taken her soaring in the glider, eaten at her table, fallen asleep with her spooned into my body and her nightshirt accidentally hiked up so that I could feel her naked arse warm and soft resting against my flaccid penis.

That should have told her the tale: that flaccidity. That unchanging, indifferent, Laodicean flaccidity. But it did not. Or if it did, she did not wish to draw the conclusion implied by that lifeless piece of flesh.

I said, "It feels good, having you here like this."

She said, "It could feel better. We could have more." And she moved her hips three times in that way women have that unconsciously mimes the rotation against which a normal man wants to thrust.

But I, as we know, am not a normal man.

I knew that I was supposed to desire at least the act if not the woman herself. But I did not. Nothing stirred in me except, perhaps, the ice. And what came over me was stillness and shadow and that disembodied feeling of being outside myself, above myself, looking down on this pitiful excuse for a man and wondering what the hell it was going to *take*, for God's sake, to move the bastard.

Libby said, her cool hand on my hot cheek again, "What's wrong, Gideon?" And she became quite still on the bed next to me. She didn't move away, however, and the fear that a precipitate movement on my part might give her an idea I did not wish her to have prompted me to remain immobile as well.

I said, "I've been to the doctor. I've had all the tests. There's nothing to account for them, Libby. It happens."

"I'm not talking about the migraines, Gid."

"Then what?"

"Why aren't you playing? You always play. You're like a clock. Three hours every morning, three hours every afternoon. I've seen Rafe's car in the square every day, so I know he's been here, but I haven't heard either of you guys playing."

Rafe. She has that American tendency to give everyone a nickname. Raphael became Rafe the first time she met him. Nothing could suit him less, if you ask me, but he doesn't appear to mind the sobriquet.

And he has been here every day, as she pointed out. Sometimes for an hour, sometimes for two or three. He mostly paces while I sit in the window seat and write. He sweats, he mops his forehead and his neck with a handkerchief, he casts apprehensive looks in my direction, and he no doubt projects us into a future in which my anxiety state prematurely terminates an otherwise brilliant career and in which his reputation as my musical Rasputin is summarily ruined. He pictures himself as a footnote in history, one written in typescript so infinitesimal as to require a magnifying glass to be read.

I have been his hope for immortality-by-proxy. There he has been for fifty-whatever years, a man incapable of rising even to the level of concertmaster

despite his talent and his every best effort, condemned by a reservoir of stage fright that has un-
loosed its floodgates in a deluge of terror whenever
he's had a chance to audition. The man's a brilliant
musician in a family of equally brilliant musicians.
But unlike the rest of them—all playing in one orchestra or another, right down to his sister, who for
twenty-some years has played electric guitar in a hippie band called Plated Starfire—Raphael has excelled
only at passing his artistry on to others. Public performance has defeated him.

And I have been his claim to fame and the means
by which he's attracted, like a benevolent Pied Piper,
a following of hopeful prodigies and their parents for
more than two decades. But that's all set to be sacrificed if I don't get a grip on what's gone wrong in my
head. Never mind that Raphael has never once bothered to get a grip on what's wrong in *his* head—it
can't be normal for one man to sweat through three
shirts and one suit jacket every day of his life, can
it?—I am to devote all my waking hours to getting a
grip on what's wrong in mine.

Raphael, as I've said, is the person who tracked
you down initially, Dr. Rose. Or at least, he tracked
your father down once the neurologists decided that
there is nothing physically wrong with me. So he has
a vested interest in my recovery that's dual: Not only
has he been significant in bringing me into your care,
which might well put me into his debt in a very large
way should you and I overcome my problem, but
also my continued career as a violinist will mean *his*

continued career as my muse. So Raphael would very much like to see me get well.

You're thinking of this as cynicism, aren't you, Dr. Rose? A new wrinkle in the blanket of my character. But remember that I have experienced Raphael Robson for years, so I know how he thinks and what he intends, probably better than he knows himself.

For example, I know that he dislikes my father. And I know that Dad would have sacked him a dozen times throughout the years had Raphael's style of instruction—allowing the student to develop his own method rather than imposing a preformed method upon him—not been exactly what I needed to thrive.

Why does Raphael dislike your father? you ask me curiously, unsure if this animosity between them is what's at the root of my present difficulty.

I don't have an answer to that question, Dr. Rose, at least not an answer that's both lucid and complete. But I expect it has to do with my mother.

Raphael Robson and your mother? you clarify, and you look at me so intently that I wonder what nugget I've offered you.

So I dig into my mind. I try to see what is there. And I make a logical connection from examining everything I've been able to dredge out thus far because those words placed all in a row just now—Raphael Robson and my mother—have stirred something within me, Dr. Rose. I can feel an uneasiness creeping outward from my gut. I've chewed and swallowed something rotten, and I *feel* the consequences roiling round in me.

What have I inadvertently unearthed? Raphael Robson has disliked my father for twenty-plus years because of my mother. Yes. I feel something like truth in this. But why?

You suggest that I take myself back in time to a moment when they are together, perhaps. Raphael and my mother. But the canvas is there, that damned black canvas and if they are on it, the paint has long ago been obscured.

And yet you've placed their names together, Raphael's and your mother's, you point out to me. For their names to be linked, other links must exist, even if only within the subconscious mind. You're thinking of them together, you tell me. Do you see them together as well?

See them? Together? The idea is preposterous.

Which part? you ask. The seeing part or the together part, Gideon?

And I know where you're heading with both those alternatives. Don't think I don't. I'm to choose between Oedipal conflicts and the primal scene. That's where we're going, isn't it, Dr. Rose? Little Gideon can't abide the fact that his music instructor *a le béguin pour sa mère*. Or, what's worse, little Gideon walked in on *sa mère et l'amoureux de sa mère* in flagrante delicto, with *l'amoureux de sa mère* being Raphael Robson.

Why the coy switch to French? you ask me. What does using English do to the facts? How does using English feel, Gideon?

Absurd. Ridiculous. Outrageous. Raphael Robson and my mother as lovers? What a ludicrous notion.

How could she cope with his sweat? Even twenty years ago he sweats enough to water the garden.

12 SEPTEMBER

The garden. Flowers. God. I've remembered those flowers, Dr. Rose. Raphael Robson coming to the house with an enormous spray of flowers. They're for my mother, and she's there in the house, so it's either night time or she hasn't gone into work that day.

Is she ill? you ask me.

I don't know. But I see the flowers. Dozens of them. All different kinds, so many different kinds that I can't even name them. It's the largest bouquet I've ever seen and yes, yes, she must be ill because Raphael takes the flowers to the kitchen and arranges them himself in a number of vases that Gran digs out for him. But Gran can't stay to help him with the flowers because Granddad must be watched for some reason. For days and days we've had to keep an eye on Granddad, and I don't know why.

An episode? you ask me. Is he having a psychotic episode, Gideon?

I don't know. Just that *everyone* is out of sorts. Mother is ill. Granddad is being confined upstairs with music playing all the time to calm him. Sarah-Jane Beckett keeps huddling in corners with James the Lodger and if I get too close to them, she tightens her mouth and tells me to get back to my school prep when I haven't actually been given a lesson that's generated any prep in the first place. I've caught Gran

weeping on the stairs. I've heard Dad shouting somewhere: behind a closed door, I think. Sister Cecilia
has called in, and I've seen her talking to Raphael in
the upstairs corridor. And then there are all those
flowers. Raphael and flowers. Scores of flowers that I
can't even name.

He takes them to the kitchen and I'm required to
wait in the sitting room, where he has provided an
exercise for me to master. And I remember that exercise even today. It is scales. *Scales,* which I loathe
and which I feel are far beneath me. So I refuse to do
them. I kick over my music stand. I shout that I'm
bored, bored, *bored* with this *stupid* music and I won't
play it a minute more. I demand the telly. I demand
biscuits and milk. I *demand.*

And Sarah-Jane is there in a flash. She says—and I
do remember exactly what she says, Dr. Rose, because it is so foreign to my ears—"You're *not* the centre of the world any longer. Behave yourself."

Not the centre of the world *any longer?* you muse.
So this must be after Sonia was born.

It must be, Dr. Rose.

Can you make any connections, then?

What sort of connections?

Raphael Robson, the flowers, your grandmother
weeping, Sarah-Jane Beckett and the lodger gossiping—

I didn't say that they are gossiping. They're just
talking together, their heads together, sharing a secret
perhaps? I wonder. Are they lovers?

Yes, yes, Dr. Rose. I *see* how I return to the theme

of lovers. No need to point it out to me. And I know where you're heading, in an inexorable process that takes us towards my mother and Raphael. I see where that process is going to end if we examine the clues with rational calm. The clues are these: Raphael with those flowers, Gran crying and Dad shouting, Sister Cecilia in attendance, Sarah-Jane and the lodger tittering in a corner . . . I see where this takes us, Dr. Rose.

What stops you from saying it, then? you ask, with those sombre sad sincere eyes on mine.

Nothing stops me, except uncertainty.

If you say it, you'll be able to test how it feels, to see if it fits.

All right, then. All right. Raphael Robson has impregnated my mother and together they have produced this child, Sonia. My father realises he's been cuckolded—God, where did *that* word come from? I feel like I'm taking part in a Jacobean melodrama— and the shouting that ensues behind closed doors is his reaction. Granddad hears this, puts together the pieces, and is sent round the bend and on his way to another episode. Gran reacts to the chaos between Mother and Dad as well as to the potential of another episode. Sarah-Jane and the lodger are all agog with the excitement. Sister Cecilia is brought in to attempt to mediate the dispute, but Dad can't bear to live in the same house with a constant reminder of Mother's infidelity, and he demands that the baby be sent away somewhere, adopted or something. Mother can't bear the thought of this and she weeps in her room.

And Raphael? you ask.

He's the proud father, isn't he? Bearing flowers like every proud father before him.

How does that feel? you want to know.

It makes me want to have a shower. And not because of the thought of my mother "in the rank sweat of an unseamèd bed"—if you'll pardon the obvious allusion—but because of *him*. Because of Raphael. Yes, I do see that he may have loved my mother and hated my father for possessing what he himself wanted. But that my mother would have returned his love . . . would have thought of taking that sweaty and perpetually sun-incinerated body into her bed or wherever else they might have accomplished the act . . . this thought is too incredible to be embraced.

But children, you point out to me, always find the contemplation of their parents' sexuality abhorrent, Gideon. This is why the actual sight of intercourse—

I did not witness intercourse, Dr. Rose. Not between my mother and Raphael, not between Sarah-Jane Beckett and the lodger, not between my grandparents, not between my father and anyone. *Anyone.*

Your father and anyone? you are quickly upon it. Who is *anyone*? Where does *anyone* come from?

Oh God. I don't know. I don't *know.*

15 SEPTEMBER

I went to see him this afternoon, Dr. Rose. Ever since unearthing Sonia and then having the recollection of Raphael and those obscene flowers and the chaos in the house in Kensington Square, I've felt that I needed to talk to my father. So I went down to South Kensington and found him in the garden next to Braemar Mansions, which is where he's lived for the past few years. He was in the little green-house that he's commandeered from the rest of the residents of the building, and he was doing what he usually does with his free time. He was hovering over his infant hybrid camellias, examining their leaves with a magnifying glass, looking for either en-tomological intruders or incipient buds. I could not tell which. It's his dream to create a bloom worthy of the Chelsea Flower Show. Worthy of a prize at the show, I should say. Anything less would be a waste of his time.

From the street, I saw him inside the greenhouse, but as I don't have a key to the garden gate, I entered through the building. Dad has the first floor flat at the top of the stairs, and because I could see that the door was ajar up there, I headed up with the thought of se-curing it. But I found Jill inside at Dad's dining table, working on her laptop with her feet propped up on a hassock she'd brought in from the sitting room.

We exchanged pleasantries—what exactly does one say to one's father's young, pregnant mistress?—and she told me what I already knew, specifically that Dad was in the garden. She said, "He's nurturing the rest of his children," with one of those long-suffering rolls of the eyes that are intended to convey fond ex-asperation. But that phrase *the rest of his children* seemed heavily laden with meaning today, and I couldn't put it from my mind as I left her.

I realised that I'd failed to notice something before that was obvious to me as I made my way back through the flat. Walls, chest tops, table tops, and bookshelves announced a single bald fact that had never once touched upon my consciousness, and that fact was what I first dealt with when I entered the greenhouse, because it seemed to me that if I could wrest a truthful answer from my father, I would be one step closer to understanding.

Wrest? You seize upon that word, don't you, Dr. Rose? You seize upon it and everything it implies. Is your father less than truthful, then? you ask me.

I'd never thought him so. But now I wonder.

And what will you understand? you want to know. Wresting the truth from your father will take you one step closer to understanding what?

To understanding what has happened to me.

It's connected to your father?

I don't want to think so.

When I walked into the greenhouse, he didn't look up, and I thought about how his body has begun to suit him for this current employment, bending over small plants. His scoliosis seems to have worsened over the past few years, and although he's just sixty-two years old, he seems older to me because of his growing curvature. Looking at him, I wondered how Jill Foster—nearly thirty years his junior—had come to see him as a sexual object. What draws human beings together is a puzzle to me.

I said, "Why are there no pictures of Sonia in your flat, Dad?" An unexpected frontal assault seemed most likely to garner results. "You've got me from every angle at every age, with violin and without; but you haven't got Sonia. Why?"

He did look up then, but I think he was buying time, because he took a handkerchief from the back pocket of his jeans and he used it to polish the magnifying glass. He refolded the handkerchief, stowed the lens in a chamois sack, and took the sack to a shelf at the end of the greenhouse, where he keeps his gardening tools.

"Good afternoon to you as well," he said. "You had more of a greeting for Jill, I hope. Is she still on the computer?"

"In the kitchen."

"Ah. The screenplay proceeds apace. She's doing *The Beautiful and Damned*. Have I mentioned that? Ambitious to offer another Fitzgerald to the BBC, but she's determined to prove that an American novel about Americans in America can be made palatable for the British viewing public. We shall see. And how is your own American these days?"

That's what he's taken to calling Libby. She has no name other than "your American," although sometimes she becomes "your little American" or "your charming American." She's particularly my charming American when she commits a social solecism of some kind, as she does with what seems like religious fervour. Libby does not stand on ceremony, and Dad has not forgiven her for referring to him by his

Christian name when I first introduced them. Nor has he forgotten her immediate reaction to Jill's pregnancy: "Holy shit. You knocked up a *thirty*-year-old? Great going, Richard." Jill's older than thirty, of course, but that was a small matter next to the effrontery of Libby's mentioning the great gap in their ages.

"She's fine," I said.

"Still riding her motorcycle round London, then?"

"She's still working for the courier service, if that's what you mean."

"And how is she liking her Tartini these days? Shaken or stirred?" He removed his glasses, crossed his arms, and studied me in that way he always does, the way that says, "Steady on or I'll sort you out."

That look has managed to derail me on more than one occasion, and in combination with his comments about Libby, it probably should have derailed me then. But having a sister pop into my mind where there had been no sister before was enough to bolster me to face whatever attempt at obfuscation he might make. I said, "I'd forgotten Sonia. Not just how she died, but that she'd ever existed in the first place. I'd completely forgotten I ever *had* a sister. It's like someone took a rubber to my mind and erased her, Dad."

"Is that why you've come, then? To ask about pictures?"

"To ask about her. Why don't you have any pictures of her?"

"You're looking for something sinister in the omission."

"You have pictures of me. You have an entire exhibit of Granddad. You have Jill. You even have Raphael."

"Posing with Szeryng. Raphael was secondary."

"Yes. All right. But that begs the question. Why is there nothing of Sonia?"

He observed me for a good five seconds before he moved. And then he merely turned and began cleaning off the potting bench where he'd earlier been working. He picked up a brush and used it to sweep loose leaves and the remains of soil into a bucket, which he took from the floor. This done, he sealed the soil bag, capped a bottle of fertiliser, and returned his gardening tools to their respective cubby holes. He cleaned each tool as he put it away. Finally, he removed the heavy green apron he wore when working with his camellias, and he led the way out of the greenhouse and into the garden.

There's a bench at one side, and he made his way over to it. It sits beneath a chestnut tree, long the bane of my father's existence. "Too much God damn shade," he always grouses. "What the hell is supposed to grow in shadow?"

Today he seemed to welcome the shade, though. He sat and winced a little, as if he had a pain in his back, which he might well have had because of his spine. But I didn't want to ask about that. He'd avoided my question for long enough.

I said, "Dad, why is there—"

He said, "This comes of that doctor, doesn't it? That woman . . . what's her name?"

"You know it. Dr. Rose."

He muttered, "Shite," and pushed himself off the bench. I thought he was going to return to the house in a temper rather than talk about a subject that he clearly didn't want to address, but he eased himself to his knees and began pulling at weeds in the flower bed that lay before us. He said, "If I had my way, residents who don't take proper care of their plots would have their plots confiscated. Just look at this muck."

It was hardly that. True, too much water had produced mould and moss on the border stones, and weeds tangled with an enormous fuchsia that appeared to want trimming. But there was something appealing about the natural look of the plot, with its central birdbath overgrown with ivy and its stepping-stones sunk deeply into greenery. "I rather like it," I said.

Dad gave a derisive snort. He continued pulling weeds, tossing them over his shoulder and onto the gravel path. "Have you touched the Guarnerius yet?" he asked. He objectifies the violin that way, always has done. I prefer to call it by its maker's name, but Dad has melded the maker into the instrument, as if Guarneri himself had no other life.

"No. I haven't."

He leaned back on his heels. "That's brilliant, then. That's bloody brilliant. That's the great plan come to nothing, isn't it? Tell me, what's this gaining us? What exact advantage are you being blessed with as you and the good doctor take your shovels to the past? It's the present where our problem is, Gideon. I wouldn't think you'd need reminding of that."

"She's calling it psychogenic amnesia. She says that—"

"Bollocks. You had a case of *nerves.* You still have a case of nerves. It happens. Ask anyone. Good God. How many years did Rubinstein not play? Ten? Twelve? And d'you think he spent that time scribbling in a notebook? I expect not."

"He didn't lose the playing," I explained to my father. "He feared the playing."

"You don't know that you've lost it, do you? If you haven't picked up the Guarnerius yet, you don't know what you've lost and what you're just afraid that you've lost. Anyone with an ounce of common sense would tell you that what you're experiencing is cowardice: plain and simple. And the fact that this doctor hasn't brought herself round to mentioning the word . . ." He went back to his weeding. "Bollocks."

"You wanted me to see her," I reminded him. "When Raphael suggested it, you seconded the idea."

"I thought you'd be learning to cope with your fear. I thought that's what she'd be giving you. And if, by the way, I'd known it was going to be a flaming *she* in that doctor's chair, I would have thought twice about carting you round there to weep on her shoulder in the first place."

"I'm not—"

"This is what comes of that girl, that bloody blasted God damn *girl.*" And on the last word, he tugged a particularly entangled weed from the plot and up-rooted one of the dormant lilies in the process. He swore and began to pound the earth round the plant in an attempt to undo the damage. "This is how Americans think, Gideon, and I hope you see that," he informed me. "This is what comes of coddling an entire generation of layabouts who've had everything handed to them on a platter. They know nothing but leisure so they use that leisure to blame their anomie on their parents. She's encouraged this fault-finding in you, boy. Next, she'll be promoting chat shows as a venue for airing what ails you."

"That's not fair on Libby. She's nothing to do with this."

"You were bloody all right till she came along."

"Nothing's happened between us to cause this problem."

"Sleeping with her, are you?"

"Dad——"

"Shagging her properly?" He looked over his shoulder as he asked this last question, and he must have seen what I preferred to keep hidden. Seeing it, he said ironically, "Ah. Yes. But she is not the root of your problem. I see. So tell me, exactly what does Dr. Rose consider the appropriate moment for you to pick up the violin again?"

"We haven't talked about that."

He shoved himself to his feet. "That's bloody rich. You've seen her . . . what? . . . three times a week for how many weeks? Three? Four? But you haven't yet got round to talking about the problem? See anything singular in that state of affairs?"

"The violin—the playing—"

"You mean the not playing."

"All right. Yes. Not playing the violin. It's a symptom, Dad. It's not the disease."

"Tell that to Paris, Munich, and Rome."

"I'll make the concerts."

"Not the way you're going at it now."

"I thought you wanted me to see her. You asked Raphael—"

"I asked Raphael for help. Help to get you back on your feet. Help to put the violin in your hands. Help to get you back in the concert hall. Tell me—just tell me, swear to it, reassure me, anything—that that's what you're getting from this doctor. Because I'm on your side in this, son. I am on your side."

"I can't swear to it," I said, and I know that my voice reflected all the defeat I felt. "I don't know what I'm getting from her, Dad."

He wiped his hands on the sides of his jeans. I heard him curse in a low tone that seemed tinctured with anguish. He said, "Come with me."

I followed him. We went back into the building, up the stairs, and into his flat. Jill had made tea and she raised her cup to us, saying, "Some, Gideon? Darling?" as we passed the kitchen. I thanked her and demurred, but Dad made no response. Jill's face clouded in that way I've seen when Dad ignores her: not as if she's hurt but as if she's comparing his behaviour with some unmentioned catalogue of appropriate behaviours she's developed in her head.

Dad strode on, oblivious of this. He went to what I call the Granddad Room, where he keeps a bizarre but nonetheless revealing collection of memorabilia: everything from silver-encased childhood locks of Granddad's hair to letters from the "great man's" wartime commanding officer commending him upon his comportment while imprisoned in Burma. It sometimes seems to me that Dad has spent the better part of his life trying to pretend his father was either a normal or a supernormal man rather than what he actually was, a broken mind who spent more than forty years balancing on the brink of insanity for reasons no one would ever mention.

He shut the door behind us, and at first I thought he'd taken me into the room in order to recite some sort of panegyric to Granddad. I felt myself getting irritated at what I saw as yet another attempt on his part to deflect a proper conversation.

He's done this before? you want to know, don't you? It's the logical question.

And I would have to say Yes, he's done this before. I hadn't much considered that fact until recently. I hadn't actually *had* to consider it because my music was central to our relationship and that's always what we talked about. Practice sessions with Raphael, work at the East London Conservatory, recording sessions, personal appearances, concerts, tours . . . There was always my music to occupy us. And because I was so *engaged* with my music, any question I asked or subject I wanted to pursue could easily be avoided by directing my thoughts to the violin. *How's the Stravinski coming along? What about the Bach? Is* The Archduke *still giving you trouble?* God. *The Archduke.* It always gave me trouble. It's my Nemesis, that piece. It's my Waterloo. It is, in fact, what I was scheduled to play at Wigmore Hall. First time in public to master the bastard and I couldn't do it.

Ah. You see how easily I become distracted by the thought of my music, Dr. Rose. Even then I did it to myself, so you can imagine how skilfully Dad could manage to divert our conversations.

But this afternoon, I couldn't be distracted, and Dad must have realised this, because he didn't attempt either to regale me with a story of Granddad's feats of ostensible bravery during his imprisonment or to move me with a review of his gallant battle against a monstrous mental condition that had its tendrils buried deep in his brain. Instead, he shut the door behind us, and I realised he'd done so to gain us some privacy.

He said, "You're looking for something nasty, aren't you? Isn't that what psychiatrists are always after?"

"I'm trying to remember," I told him. "That's what this is about."

"How is remembering Sonia supposed to gain you ground with your instrument? Has your Dr. Rose explained that to you?"

You haven't, have you, Dr. Rose? All you've said is that we'll begin with what I can remember. I'll write about everything I have in my memory, but you don't explain how doing this exercise will manage to dislodge whatever it is that's blocking my ability to play.

And what has Sonia to do with my playing? She must have been a baby when she died. Because surely I would remember an older sibling, one who walked and talked, who played in the sitting room, who created mud puddles in the back garden with me. I would remember that.

I said, "Dr. Rose calls this psychogenic amnesia."

"Psycho . . . what?"

I explained it to him as you explained it to me. I ended with, "Because there's no physical cause for the memory loss—and you know the neurologists have cleared the screen on that—the cause has to come from somewhere else. From the psyche, Dad, and not from the brain."

"That's a load of rubbish," he said, but I could tell that the words were a form of bravado. He sat in an armchair and stared at nothing.

"All right." I sat as well, in front of the old roll top desk that belonged to Gran. I did what I'd never considered doing before because I'd never felt it necessary. I called his bluff. "All right, Dad. Accepted. It's rubbish. What should I do, then? Because if all I'm feeling is nerves and fear, I'd be able to play my music alone, wouldn't I? With no one there? With even Libby out of the house so that I could be certain I had no eavesdroppers anywhere? I could play then, couldn't I? And if I couldn't manage so much as a simple arpeggio, who'd be the wiser? Isn't that the case?"

He looked at me. "Have you tried, Gideon?"

"Don't you see? I haven't *had* to try. I don't need to try when I already know."

He moved his head, then, away from me. He seemed to go inward, and while he did so, I was aware of the silence in the flat and the silence outside, no breeze even blowing to susurrate the tree leaves. When he finally spoke, it was to say, "No one knows the pain of having a child before the child is born. It seems as if it'll be so simple, but it never is."

I made no reply. Was he speaking of me? Of Sonia? Or the other, that longer-ago child of a distant marriage, the one called Virginia, who had never been spoken of?

He went on. "You give them life and you know you'd do anything to protect them, Gideon. That's how it is."

I nodded, but he still wasn't looking at me so I said, "Yes." Affirmation of what, I couldn't tell you. But I had to say something, and that was what I said.

It seemed enough. Dad said, "Sometimes you fail. You don't intend to. You don't even contemplate failure. But it happens. It comes out of nowhere and it takes you by surprise and before you have a chance to stop—even to react in some useless way—it's on you. Failure." He met my eyes then, and the look he gave me was so filled with suffering that I wanted to retreat and to spare him whatever was causing him such pain. Hadn't it been bad enough that his childhood, adolescence, and adulthood had been filled with the sorrow of having a father whose infirmities tried his patience and depleted his reserves of devotion? Was he now supposed to be saddled with a son who appeared to be heading in the same direction? I wanted to retreat. I wanted to spare him. But I wanted my music more. I am a void without my music. So I said nothing. I let the silence lie like a gauntlet between us. And when my father could bear the unseen sight of that gauntlet no longer, he picked it up.

He stood and came towards me and for a moment I thought he intended to touch me. But instead he rolled back the top of my grandmother's desk. From his key ring, he inserted a small key in the central interior drawer. From the drawer, he took a neat stack of papers. These he carried back to his chair.

We'd arrived somewhere, and I was aware of the drama and significance of the moment, as if we'd crossed a boundary that neither of us had recognised as even existing before. I felt a churning in my gut as he fingered through the papers. I saw the sparkling crescent in the field of my vision that always heralds the pounding in my head.

He said, "I have no pictures of Sonia for the simplest of reasons. Had you thought it through—and had you been less distressed you probably would have—I'm certain you would have worked it out for yourself. Your mother took the pictures when she left us, Gideon. She took every one of them. Except for this."

He took a single snapshot from a soiled envelope.

He passed it to me. And for a moment, I found that I didn't want to take it from him, so fraught with meaning had Sonia suddenly become.

He read my hesitation. He said, "Take it, Gideon. It's all I have left of her."

So I took it, hardly daring to wonder what I might see, but somehow fearing what I would see all the same. I swallowed and steeled myself. I looked.

What was in the picture was this: a baby cradled in the arms of a woman I did not recognise. They were seated in the back garden of the Kensington Square house, on a striped deck chair in the sun. The woman's shadow fell across Sonia's face, but her own was fully exposed to the light. She was young and blonde. She was aquiline featured. She was very pretty.

"I don't . . . Who is this?" I asked my father.

"That's Katja," he said. "Gideon, that's Katja Wolff."

GIDEON

20 SEPTEMBER

THIS IS what I've been wondering ever since Dad showed me that photograph: If Mother took with her every picture of Sonia that was in the house, why did she leave that one picture behind? Was it because Sonia's face was so much in shadow that she might have been any baby and consequently not memorable to my mother, not something she could cling to in her grief . . . if grief was indeed what took her from us? Or was it because Katja Wolff was in it? Or was it because Mother didn't know about the photo in the first place? Because, you see, the one thing I cannot tell from the picture—which I have now with me and which I will show you when next we meet—is who took it of them?

And why did Dad have this particular picture, this picture in which the focal figure is not his daughter his very own daughter who died, but a young and smiling and golden woman who is not his wife was never his wife never became his wife and was certainly not the mother of that child.

I asked Dad about Katja Wolff because asking was the natural thing to do. He told me that she was Sonia's nanny. She was a German girl, he said, with very limited English. She'd made a dramatic and foolhardy escape from East to West Berlin in a hot air balloon that she and her boyfriend had manufactured in secret, and she'd gained some notoriety from that.

Do you already know this story, Dr. Rose? Perhaps not. You would have been less than ten years old at that time, I expect, and living . . . where? In America at that point?

Living here in England so much closer to where it all happened, I don't remember it myself. But it was, as Dad told me, quite a story then because Katja and her boyfriend didn't attempt their crossing from somewhere in the countryside, where it would have been at least marginally safer to go from east into west, but instead they sailed from East Berlin itself. The boy didn't make it all the way. The border guards got him. But Katja did make it. She earned her fifteen minutes that way and became a standard-bearer for freedom. Television news, front-page headlines, magazine stories, radio interviews. She ended up being invited to England.

I listened carefully as Dad told me all this, and I watched him closely. I looked for signs and for inner meanings, and I tried to make inferences, leaps, and deductions. Because even now in the situation in which I find myself—sitting here in the music room in Chalcot Square with the Guarneri fifteen feet away, taken from its *case* at least and surely that's progress God tell me that's progress, Dr. Rose, although I can't bring myself to lift the violin to the height of my shoulder—there are questions I'm afraid to ask my father.

What sorts of questions? you want to know.

Questions like these, questions that rise to my mind without effort: Who took that picture of Sonia and Katja? Why did my mother leave only that single picture behind? Did she even know about it? Did she actually *take* the other pictures or did he destroy them? And why, above all, did my father never speak of them before now: never speak to me of Sonia, of Katja, of my mother?

Obviously, he hadn't forgotten they existed. After all, once I brought Sonia up, he produced her picture and from its condition I'd swear before God that it was something he's held and contemplated hundreds of times. So why the silence?

People sometimes avoid, you tell me. They dodge subjects too painful for them to face.

Like Sonia herself? Her death? My mother? Her leaving? The pictures?

Katja Wolff perhaps?

But why would Katja Wolff be a painful subject to Dad? Except for the most obvious reason.

Which is?

You want me to say it, don't you, Dr. Rose? You want me to write it. You want me to stare at it sitting on this page, and thus to weigh its truth or its falsehood. But where the hell is that going to get me? She's holding my sister, she's cradling her just beneath her breast, her eyes look kind and her face is serene. One of her shoulders is bare because she's wearing a dress or a top with straps too loose and it's brightly coloured, bizarrely coloured, that dress or top, so much yellow and orange and green and blue. And that bare shoulder is smooth and round and yes all right it's an invitation and I'd have to be blind not to see it so if a man *is* taking that picture of Katja and if that man is my father—but it could be Raphael it could be James the Lodger it could be Granddad or the gardener or the postman or *any* man because she is splendid beautiful seductive and even I a cocked-up mess of a paltry excuse of a healthy laughable male can see who she is and what she is and how she's offering what she's offering—then that man has an alliance with her and I've a fairly good idea what sort it is.

So write about her, you instruct me. Write about Katja. Fill a page with her name alone if that's what it takes and see where filling that page takes you, Gideon. Ask your father if there are other pictures he can show you: family pictures, casual pictures, snapshots of holidays, fêtes, parties, gatherings, dinners, anything at all. Look at them closely. See who's in them. Read their expressions.

Look for Katja? I ask.
Look for what's there.

21 SEPTEMBER

Dad says I was nearly six when Sonia was born. I was just short of eight when she died. I phoned and asked him those two questions outright. Aren't you pleased, Dr. Rose? The horns were there and I actually grabbed them.

When I asked him how Sonia died, Dad said, "She drowned, son." The answer seemed to cost him much, and his voice seemed to come from a place that was distant. I felt a tightness inside me, having asked him anything at all, but that did not stop me going on. I asked him her age when she died: two years. And the strain in his voice told me that she had been quite old enough not only to have established a permanent place in his heart but also to have made an indelible mark on his spirit.

The sound of that strain and the comprehension that accompanied it explained so much to me about my father: his focus on me throughout my child-hood, his determination that I should have and see and be and experience the very best, his single-minded protection of me when I began my public ca-reer, his wariness of anyone who came too close and might do me harm. Having lost one child—no, my God, having lost *two* because Virginia his oldest had died young as well—he was not about to lose an-other.

So I finally understand why he's stayed so close, been so involved, finessed so much of my life and career. Early on I said aloud what I wanted—the violin, my music—and he did what it took to see to it that his remaining child was given just that, as if by providing me the means to my dream he would somehow assure my longevity. So he had two jobs; he sent Mother out to work as well; he employed Raphael; he arranged that I should be educated at home.

Except all this was *before* Sonia, wasn't it? It couldn't have been the result of Sonia's death. Because if, as he said, she was born when I was six years old, Raphael Robson and Sarah-Jane Beckett would already have been in place in the house. And James the Lodger would have been there as well. And into this already *established* group Katja Wolff would have come as Sonia's nanny. So that's what must have happened, isn't it: An established group was forced to accept an interloper in their midst. An intruder, if you will. A foreigner as well. And not just any, but a German foreigner. Briefly famous, yes. But German all the same: our wartime enemy and Granddad forever a prisoner of that war.

So Sarah-Jane Beckett and James the Lodger are whispering about *her* in that corner in the kitchen, not about my mother, not about Raphael, and not about those flowers. They are whispering about her because Sarah-Jane is like that, *was* like that from the first, a whisperer. Her whispering grows out of jealousy because Katja is lithe and pretty and seductive and Sarah-Jane Beckett—with her short red hair like a pudding bowl sprouting from her scalp and her body not much different to mine—sees how the men in the household look at Katja, especially James the Lodger, who helps Katja with her English and laughs when she says with a shiver, "*Mein Gott,* my corpse is not yet used to such rain in this country" instead of *my body,* which is what she means. She's asked if she would like a cup of tea, and she says, "Oh yes. Most voluntarily and with many gratitudes," and they laugh the men laugh but it's laughter that's charmed. My father, Raphael, James the Lodger, even Granddad.

And I remember that. Dr. Rose, I *remember.*

22 SEPTEMBER

So where has she been all these years, Katja Wolff? Buried with Sonia? Buried because of Sonia perhaps?

Because of Sonia? You pounce upon the word, don't you? Why *because,* Gideon?

Because of her death. If Katja was Sonia's nanny and Sonia died when she was two years old, Katja would have left us then, wouldn't she? I would have had no need for a nanny with Raphael and Sarah-Jane attending to me. So Katja would have left us after two years—perhaps even less—and that would be why I'd forgotten her. I was, after all, only eight at the time, and she wasn't my nanny but Sonia's, so I would have had little to do with her. I was consumed with my music, and when the violin wasn't devouring my time, my school lessons were. I'd already had my first public performances, and the fallout from them was an offer to study at Juilliard for a year. Imagine that. Juilliard. What age could I have been: seven? eight?

"A virtuoso in the making," I was called.

But I didn't want *making*. I wanted *made*.

23 SEPTEMBER

I don't go to Juilliard as things turn out, despite the honour and what it can mean to my development as an international musician. Because of the history of the place, scores of people three times my age would have done anything to have the same opportunity, to experience the endless possibilities that could come from having this extraordinary transcendent invaluable experience. . . . But there is no money, and even if there were, I am far too young to go that distance by myself, let alone to live there. And since my family cannot move there en masse, the opportunity passes me by.

En masse. Yes. I somehow know that en masse is the only way Juilliard will happen to me, money or not. So I say, Please *please* let me go, Dad, I must go, I want to go to New York because even then I know what it means in my present and can mean to my future. Dad says, Gideon, you know we can't go. You can't be there alone, and we can't go as a group. Naturally, I demand to know why. Why why why can't I have what I want when until this moment I have always had it. He says—and yes, I remember this well—Gideon, the world will come to you. I promise you that, I swear it, son.

But it's clear that we can't go to New York.

For some reason I *know* this even as I ask again and again and again, even as I bargain, beg, behave as badly as I've ever done, as I kick the music stand, fling myself into my grandmother's treasured demi-lune table and crack two of its legs . . . even then I *know* there will be no Juilliard no matter what I do. Alone, with my family, with one of my parents, accompanied only by Raphael, or with Sarah-Jane dogging my heels as my shadow or protector, I will not be going to that Mecca of music.

Know, you point out to me. Know before you ask, know as you ask, know despite everything you do to change . . . what, Gideon? What are you trying to change?

Reality, obviously. And yes, Dr. Rose, I know that's an answer that takes us nowhere. What's the reality that I already understand as a seven- or eight-year-old?

It appears to be this: We are not a rich family. Oh yes, we live in an area that not only indicates but also requires money, but the family's owned that house for generations and the only reason the family *still* owns it is due to the lodgers, to Dad's two jobs, to Mother's going to work, and to Granddad's pittance from the Government. But money is not something we ever discuss. Talk of money is like speaking of bodily functions at the dinner table. Yet I know I won't go to Juilliard and I feel a tightening inside me as I know this. It starts in my arms. It moves to my stomach. It rises upwards into my throat till I shout oh I shout and I remember what I shout, "It's because she's here!" And that's when I kick and pound and fling. That's when, Dr. Rose.

She's here?

She. Of course. It must be Katja.

26 SEPTEMBER

Dad was here again. He came for two hours and was replaced by Raphael. They wanted to make it look as if they weren't taking shifts at a death watch, so I had at least five minutes alone between the time Dad left and Raphael arrived. But what they don't know is that I saw them from the window. Raphael came walking into Chalcot Square from the direction of Chalcot Road, and Dad intercepted him in the middle of the garden. They stood on either side of one of the benches and they talked. At least, Dad talked. Raphael listened. He nodded and did what he always does: ran his fingers left to right on his scalp to arrange the fretwork that's left of his hair. Dad was passionate. I could tell that much from the way he gestured, one hand up at the level of his chest and closed into a fist like a punch withheld. The rest I didn't need to interpret because I knew what he was passionate about.

He'd come in peace. No mention of anything regarding my music. "Had to get away from her for a while," he sighed. "I've come to believe that women the world over in the last months of pregnancy are all the same."

"Jill's moved in, then?" I asked him.

"Why tempt fate?"

Which was his way of saying that they're sticking to their original plan: Have the baby first, combine their households second, and marry when the dust settles on the first two events. It's the fashion these days to go at relationships in that way, and Jill is an adherent to fashion. But I sometimes wonder how Dad feels about an arrangement so foreign to his other marriages. He's a traditionalist at heart, I believe, with nothing so important as his family and with only one way in mind to make a family. Once he learned Jill was pregnant, I can't see him doing anything but dropping hastily to one knee in order to claim her. Indeed, that's what he did with his first wife, although he doesn't know that I learned that from Granddad. He met her while he was on leave from the Army—his intended career, by the way—he got her pregnant, and he married her. That he's not gone the same route with Jill tells me it's Jill's agenda being followed.

"She sleeps when she can now," he told me. "It's always like that in the last six weeks or so. They're so blasted uncomfortable and if the baby's decided to be awake from midnight till five A.M. . . ." He brushed his hand through the air dismissively. "Then you've got what you've been waiting for for years: a nightly chance to read *War and Peace*."

"Are you staying with her now?"

"I'm doing time on the sofa."

"Not good for your back, Dad."

"Don't remind me."

"Have you settled on the name?"

"I still want Cara."

"She still wants—" and the import dawned upon me so suddenly that I scarcely said it but I forced myself to go on. "She's holding fast for Catherine?"

He and I locked eyes, and she was there between us, as if she were corporeal, immediate, and eternally that captivating girl in the picture. I said, even though my palms were damp and my gut was beginning to feel the first spark of a fire to come, "But that would remind you of Katja, wouldn't it? If you called the baby Catherine?"

His response was to get up and make coffee, and he took his time with the activity. He commented upon my choice of ready-ground beans and what they did to destroy freshness. He went from there to an expatiation of what the presence of yet another Starbucks—this one on Gloucester Road not far from Braemar Mansions—has done to the atmosphere of his neighbourhood.

As he did all this, the pain in my gut began to move slowly down where it planned, as always, to wreak havoc with my bowels. I listened to him make the leap from Starbucks to the Americanisation of global culture, and I pressed my arm hard against the lowest part of my intestines, willing the pain to stop and the urgency to ease, because if that did not happen, Dad would have won.

I let him exhaust the subject of America: international conglomerates dominating business, Hollywood megalomaniacs determining cinematic art forms, astronomical and singularly obscene salaries and share options becoming the measure of a capitalist's success. When he reached the peroration of his speech—evidenced by the fact that the great gulps he was taking from his coffee cup were becoming more frequent—I repeated my question, except this time I didn't ask it *as* a question. "Katja," I said. "Catherine would remind you."

He poured what remained of his coffee down the drain. He strode into the music room. As he moved, he said, "God damn it. *Show* me, Gideon." And then, "Ah. This is what's going for progress, is it?"

He'd seen the Guarneri back in its case and although the case was open, he somehow knew that I hadn't yet attempted to play it. He took it from the case and the absence of the reverence with which he'd touched that violin in the past told me just how angry—or agitated, irritated, infuriated, frightened, worried, I do not know which—he actually was. He held the instrument out to me, fingers round its neck with that brilliant scroll emerging from his fist like hope coiled round an unspoken promise. He said, "Here. Take it. Show me where we are. Show me exactly where weeks of excavating through the dreck of the past has taken you, Gideon. A note will do. A scale. An arpeggio. Or, miraculously because something tells me it would be miraculous at this point, a movement from the concerto of your choice. Any concerto. Too tough? Then what about a little encore piece?"

And the fire was in me but it was changed to a single coal. White hot, silver hot, incandescent, and it moved like acid down through my body.

And yes, yes, I see what my father has done, Dr. Rose. You don't need to point it out. I see what he's done. But in that moment I could only say, "I can't. Don't make me. I can't," like a nine-year-old who's been asked to play a piece that he cannot master.

Dad used that next, saying, "Perhaps that's beneath you. Too easy for you, Gideon. An insult to your talent. So let's start with *The Archduke*, shall we?"

Let's start with The Archduke. The acid ate through me, and what was left when the pain had knotted my viscera and rendered me useless was blame. I am at fault. I placed myself into this position. Beth set the programme for the Wigmore Hall benefit, and she said, "What about *The Archduke,* Gideon?" in absolute innocence. And because it was Beth who made the suggestion, Beth who'd already experienced my other more personal brand of failure, I couldn't bring myself to say, "Forget it. That piece is a jinx."

Artists believe in jinxes. The word *Macbeth* spoken inside a theatre has its counterpart in every field of art. So if I'd called *The Archduke* what I needed to call it—my personal jinx—Beth would have understood, despite the way she and I ended. And Sherrill wouldn't have cared as much as a sprat what we played. He would have said, in that Do-I-actually-give-a-shit American fashion of his that he uses to hide a monstrous talent, "Just point me to the keyboard, boys and girls," and that would have been that.

So it was all down to me and I let it happen. I am to blame.

Dad found me where I'd taken myself off to when I could not face the challenge he was issuing: in the shed in the garden, where I sketch the designs and make my kites. That's what I was doing then—sketching—and he joined me, the Guarneri replaced in its case and the case itself left inside the house.

He said, "You are the music, Gideon. That's what I want you for. That's all that I want."

I said, "That's what we're trying to get to."

He said, "It's bollocks, going at it this way, scratching in notebooks and having a nod-off on a screw doctor's sofa every three days."

"I don't lie on a sofa."

"You know what I mean." He placed his hand across the sketch I was working on, the better to force me to pay attention. He said, "We can hold people at bay only so long for you, Gideon. We're doing it—Joanne is doing a bloody brilliant job, in fact—but there's going to come a point when even a publicist like Joanne, loyal as she is, is going to start asking exactly what the term *exhaustion* means in a case in which that same exhaustion is showing no sign of improvement. When that happens, I'm either going to have to tell her the truth or I'm going to have to invent a fiction for her to offer people that might damn well make the situation worse."

"Dad," I said, "it's mad to think the tabloid-reading public gives a toss about—"

"I'm not talking about tabloids. Right. A rock star

disappears from view and the journalists are digging through his rubbish every morning, looking for something that will tell them why. That's not the case here and that's not what concerns me. What concerns me is the world that *we* live in with a schedule of concerts set up through the next twenty-five months, Gideon, as you well know, and with phone calls—almost daily, mind you—from musical directors enquiring about the state of your health. Which is, as you also know, a euphemism for your playing. 'Is he recovering from exhaustion?' means 'Do we tear up the contract or keep the programme in place?' " As he said all this, Dad slowly eased my drawing towards him, and although his fingers had begun to smear the lines that sketched out the two bottom spreaders, I didn't point this out to him and I didn't stop him. So he went on. "Now, what I'm asking you to do is simple: Walk inside that house, go up to the music room, and pick up that violin. Don't do it for me because this isn't about me and it never was. Do it for yourself."

"I can't."

"I'll be with you. I'll be next to you, holding you upright or whatever you want. But you've got to do it."

We stared at each other, Dr. Rose. I could feel him *willing* me out of that shed where I make my kites, out of the garden, and into the house.

He said, "You won't know if you've made progress with her, Gideon, unless you pick up the instrument and try."

By that he meant you, Dr. Rose. He meant these hours of writing I've been doing. He meant this sifting through the past we've engaged in which, it appeared, he was willing to assist me in . . . if I only gave him a demonstration that at the very *least* I could pick up the violin and scrape the bow across the strings.

So I said nothing, but I left the shed and went back to the house. In the music room, I walked not to the window seat, where I've done most of this notebook writing, but to the violin case instead. The Guarneri lay there, its top and its purfling gleaming, the repository of two hundred and fifty years of music-making shimmering from its F holes, its sides, and its pegs.

I can do this. Twenty-five years do not vanish in an instant. Everything I've learned, everything I know, every natural talent I ever possessed, may be obscured, may be buried under a landslide I cannot yet identify, but all of it is there.

Dad stood next to me at the violin case. He put his hand on my elbow as I reached for the Guarneri. He murmured, "I won't leave you, son. It's all right. I'm here."

And just at that moment, the phone began to ring.

Dad's fingers tightened on my elbow like a reflex. He said, "Leave it," in reference to the phone. And since that's what I've been doing for weeks, I had no trouble accommodating him.

But it was Jill's voice that spoke into the answer machine. When she said, "Gideon? Is Richard still there? I must speak to Richard. Has he left? Please pick up," Dad and I reacted identically. We both said, "The baby," and he strode to the phone.

He said, "I'm still here. Are you all right, darling?" And then he listened.

There was no simple yes or no in her reply. As she made it, Dad turned from me and said, "What sort of phone call?" He listened to another lengthy response and he finally said, "Jill . . . *Jill* . . . Enough. Why on earth did you answer it?"

She responded at length again. At the end of her reply, Dad said, "Wait. Hang on. Don't be silly. You're working yourself into a real state . . . I can hardly be responsible for an unsolicited and unidentified call when—" His face darkened suddenly as she apparently interrupted him. "God damn it, Jill. Listen to yourself. You're being completely irrational." And the tone in which he spoke those final words was one I'd heard him use before to dismiss a subject he didn't wish to pursue. Glacial, it was. Dismissive, superior, and in control.

But Jill was not one to release a topic so lightly. She went on again. He listened again. His back was to me, but I could see him stiffening. It was nearly a minute before he spoke.

"I'm coming home," he told her brusquely. "We're not having this discussion over the phone."

He rang off then, and it sounded to me as if she were in midsentence when he did so. He turned round and said with a glance at the Guarneri, "You've had a reprieve."

"Everything all right at home?" I asked him.

"Nothing's right anywhere," was his curt reply.

26 SEPTEMBER, 11:30 P.M.

The fact that I'd failed to play for him was undoubt-edly what Dad shared with Raphael in the square when he left me, because when Raphael joined me not three minutes after he and Dad parted, I could see the information incised on his face. His glance went to the Guarneri in its case.

"I can't," I said.

"He says you won't." Raphael touched the instrument gently. It was a caress that he might have given to a woman had any woman ever found him an object of sexual attraction. But no woman had done, as far as I knew. Indeed, it seemed to me as I watched him that I alone—and my violin—had prevented Raphael from leading a completely solitary life.

As if to confirm my thoughts, Raphael said, "This can't go on forever, Gideon."

"If it does?" I asked him.

"It won't. It can't."

"Do you take his side, then? Did he ask you out there"—here I nodded at the window—"to demand that I play for you?"

Raphael looked out at the square, at the trees whose leaves were beginning to change now, dressing themselves in the colours of early autumn. "No," he said. "He didn't ask that I force you to play. Not today. I dare say his mind was on other things."

I wasn't sure I believed him, considering the passion I'd witnessed in my father as he'd spoken to Raphael in the square. But I seized on the idea of "other things" and I used that to turn the conversation. "Why did my mother leave us?" I asked. "Was it because of Katja Wolff?"

Raphael said, "This isn't a subject for you and me."

"I've remembered Sonia," I told him.

He reached for the latch on the window, and I thought he meant to open it, either to let in the cool air or to climb outside onto the narrow balcony. But he did neither. He merely fumbled with the mechanism uselessly, and it came to me, watching him, how that simple gesture said so much about the lack in every interaction he and I had had that did not involve the violin.

I said, "I've *remembered* her, Raphael. I've remembered Sonia. And Katja Wolff as well. Why has no one ever spoken of them?"

He looked pained, and I thought he meant to avoid answering me. But just as I was ready to challenge his silence, he said, "Because of what happened to Sonia."

"What? What happened to Sonia?"

His voice contained wonder when he replied. "You really don't remember, do you? I always thought you never spoke of it because the rest of us didn't. But you don't remember."

I shook my head, and the shame of that admission swept through me. She was my *sister* and I could not remember a single thing about her, Dr. Rose. Until you and I began this process, I'd completely forgotten she'd ever existed. Can you begin to imagine how that feels?

Raphael went on, using great kindness to excuse the obsessive self-interest that had erased my younger sister from my mind. He said, "But you weren't even eight years old then, were you? And we never spoke of it once the trial was over. We barely spoke of it during the trial, and we agreed not to speak of it afterwards. Even your mother agreed, although she was broken by everything that happened. Yes. I can see how you might have wiped it all from your mind."

I said although my mouth was dry, "Dad told me that she drowned, that Sonia *drowned*. Why was there a trial? Who was tried? For what?"

"Your father didn't tell you more?"

"He didn't say anything other than Sonia drowned. He seemed so . . . He looked like he was paying a price just to tell me *how* she died. I didn't want to ask him for more. But now . . . a trial? That must mean . . . a *trial*?"

Raphael nodded, and all the possibilities implied by what I've recalled so far swarmed into my mind at once before he went on: Virginia died young, Granddad had episodes, Mother is weeping and weeping in her room, someone has taken a picture in the garden, Sister Cecilia is in the hall, Dad is shouting, and I'm in the sitting room, kicking at the legs of the sofa, upending my music stand, hotly and defiantly declaring that I *will* not play those infantile scales.

"Katja Wolff killed your sister, Gideon," Raphael told me. "She drowned her in her bath."

28 SEPTEMBER

He wouldn't say more. He simply shut off, shut down, or whatever it is that people do when they've reached the limit of what they can force themselves to speak of. When I said, "Drowned? *Deliberately? When? Why?*" and felt the apprehension that attended those words streak cold fingers down my spine, he said, "I can't say more. Ask your father."

My father. He sits on the edge of my bed and he watches me and I am afraid.

Of what? you ask me. How old are you, Gideon?

I must be young, because he seems so big, like a giant, when actually he's much the same size as I am now. He puts his hand on my forehead—

Are you comforted by the touch?

No. No, I shrink away.

Does he speak?

Not at first. He just sits with me. But after a moment he moves to place his hands on my shoulders as if he expects me to rise and wishes to hold me still where I lie so I might listen to him. So that's what I do. I lie there and we gaze at each other and then finally he starts to speak.

He says, "You're safe, Gideon. *You* are safe."

What's he talking about? you ask. Have you had a bad dream? Is that why he's there? Or is it something more? Katja Wolff, perhaps? Are you safe from her?

Or is this something from further back, Gideon, from the time before Katja lived at your house?

There've been people at the house. I remember that. I've been sent to my room in the company of Sarah-Jane Beckett, and she's talking talking talking to herself in a voice that I'm not meant to hear. She's pacing, talking, and pulling at her fingernails as if she wants to tear them off. She's saying, "I *knew* it. I could see this coming." She's saying, "Bloody little whore," and I know those are bad words, and I'm surprised and frightened because Sarah-Jane Beckett doesn't use bad words. "Thought we wouldn't know," she says. "Thought we wouldn't *notice*."

Notice what?

I don't know.

Outside my bedroom, there are footsteps and someone is crying, "Here! In here!" I recognise the voice as barely my father's because it is tinged with so much panic. Above his cries, I hear my mother, and she's saying, "Richard! Oh my God, Richard! Richard!" Granddad is raving, Gran is keening, and someone is calling for everyone to "clear the room, clear the room." This last is a voice I don't recognise, and when Sarah-Jane hears it, she stops pacing and murmuring and she waits with her head bent, standing next to the door.

And there are other voices—more strangers' voices—that I hear. One asks a series of sharp questions beginning with *how*.

And there are more footsteps, constant movement, metal toolboxes hitting the floor, orders being barked by a man, other tense male voices responding, and through it all, someone is crying out, "No! I do not leave her alone!"

That must be Katja, because she says *do* instead of *did,* which might be what someone unfamiliar with English would say in a moment of panic. And when she says this, weeping as she says it, Sarah-Jane Beckett puts her hand on the doorknob and says, "Little bitch."

I think she means to go into the corridor where all the noise is, but she doesn't do that. Instead, she looks towards the bed, where I'm watching her, and she says, "I won't be leaving now, I expect."

Leaving, Gideon? Had she been going somewhere? Was it time for her annual holiday?

No. I don't think that's what she's talking about. Somehow I think this leaving was to be permanent.

Perhaps she's been sacked as your home teacher?

That doesn't seem reasonable. If she's been sacked for incompetence, dishonesty, or some sort of malfeasance, what does Sonia's death have to do with keeping her on as my teacher? Which is what happens, Dr. Rose: Sarah-Jane Beckett remains my teacher until I'm sixteen, when she marries and moves to Cheltenham. So she was planning to leave for another reason, but that reason is cancelled with Sonia's death.

Does that make Sonia the reason that Sarah-Jane Beckett was leaving?

It seems so, doesn't it? But I can't think why.

SIX

Doll Cottage possessed an attic, which was
the last stop DC Barbara Havers and her superior officer made in Eugenie Davies' house. It was a
tiny garret tucked into the eaves. They gained access
to it through a hatch in the ceiling just outside the
bathroom. Once inside, they were reduced to crawling across an expanse of flooring whose dust-free
condition suggested that someone made regular visits,
either to clean or to look through the small room's
contents.

"So what d'you think?" Barbara asked as Lynley
pulled on a cord affixed to a light bulb in the ceiling.
A cone of yellow illumination shone down on him,
casting shadows from his forehead that hid his eyes.
"Wiley *says* she wanted to talk to him, but all he
would really have to do is play a little fast and loose
with the time line he's given us, and Bob would definitely be your et cetera."

"Is that your colourful way of indicating Major
Wiley has a motive?" Lynley asked her. "There are
no cobwebs in here, Havers."

"Already noted. No dust either."

Lynley ran his hand over a wooden sea chest that stood next to several large cardboard boxes. It had a hasp as a fastener, but there was no lock, so he lifted the top and peered inside as Barbara crawled to the first of the boxes. He said, "Three years of patient effort, establishing a relationship that he hoped would be more than what she had on offer. She informs him, reluctantly, that there can never be more between them than there is because—"

"Because of some bloke driving a navy—or black—Audi with whom she has a row in a car park?"

"Possibly. In frustration he follows her to London—Major Wiley, this is—and runs her down. Yes. I suppose it could have happened that way."

"But you don't think so?"

"I think it's early days yet. What've you got there?"

Barbara examined the contents of the box she'd opened. "Clothes."

"Hers?"

Barbara lifted the first garment out and held it up: a small child's pair of corduroy dungarees, pink, embroidered with yellow flowers. "The daughter's, I expect." She rustled downwards and scooped out an entire pile of clothing: dresses, jumpers, pyjamas, shorts, T-shirts, Babygros, shoes, and socks. All of it was thematically identical: The colours and the decorations indicated it had been used to dress the child who'd been murdered. Barbara packed it back into the box that had held it and turned to the next box as

Lynley lifted out the contents of the wooden sea chest.

The second box contained what appeared to be the linens and the other objects that had been used on a baby's cot. Peter Rabbit sheets lay folded neatly inside, and what accompanied them were a musical mobile, a well-worn Jemima Puddleduck, six other stuffed animals in a condition that suggested they'd been less favoured than Jemima, and the padding that was used round the sides of a cot to prevent a small child from banging her head.

The third box held bathing accoutrements: everything from rubber duckies to a miniature dressing gown. Barbara was about to comment on the macabre nature of having kept this particular set of items—considering the end that the child had met—when Lynley said: "This is interesting, Havers."

She looked up to see that he'd put on his glasses and was holding a stack of newspaper articles, the first of which he'd opened to peruse. Next to him on the floor he'd piled the rest of the sea chest's contents, which comprised a collection of magazines and newspapers and five leather albums suitable for photographs or scrapbooks. "What?" she asked him.

"She's kept a virtual library on Gideon."

"From newspapers? For what?"

"For playing his violin." Lynley lowered the magazine article he was looking at and said, "Gideon Davies, Havers."

Barbara rested back on her heels, a washing mitt

shaped like a cat in her hand. "Should I be swooning at this bit of news?"

"You don't know . . . ? Never mind," Lynley said. "I forget myself. Classical music isn't your forte. Were he the lead guitarist for Rotting Teeth—"

"Do I sense scorn for my musical preference?"

"—or some other group, no doubt you'd have leapt upon his name."

"Right," Barbara said. "So who is this bloke when he's at home in the shower?"

Lynley explained: a virtuoso violinist, a former child prodigy, the possessor of a worldwide reputation who'd made his professional debut before he was ten years old. "It appears that his mother kept everything associated with his career."

"In spite of her estrangement from him?" Havers said. "That suggests he was the one who wanted it. Or the dad, perhaps."

"Doesn't it, though," Lynley agreed, sifting through the material. "She's got a treasure trove here. Everything from his latest appearance especially, tabloids included."

"Well, if he's famous . . ." Barbara pulled out a smaller box from among the bathing items. She opened it to discover a collection of prescription medicines, all made out to the same person: Sonia Davies.

"No. This was something of a fiasco," Lynley told her. "A piece of music for a trio. At Wigmore Hall, this was. He refused to play. He left the platform at the start of the piece, and he hasn't played in public since."

"Got his knickers in a twist about something?"

"Perhaps."

"Stage fright?"

"Also possible." Lynley held up the newspapers: tabloids and broadsheets. "She appears to have collected every article that made mention of it, no matter how small."

"Well, she *was* his mum. What's in the albums?"

Lynley opened the first of these as Barbara moved to look over his shoulder. More newspaper articles had been preserved inside the leather volumes. These were accompanied by concert programmes, publicity pictures, and brochures for an organisation called East London Conservatory.

"I wonder exactly why they were estranged," Barbara asked, seeing all of this.

"That's certainly the question," Lynley replied.

They sorted through the rest of the contents of the boxes and the chest and found that everything inside was associated with either Gideon or Sonia Davies. It was as if, Barbara thought, Eugenie Davies had herself not existed before her children had. It was as if she had ceased to exist when she'd lost them. Except, of course, she'd actually lost only one of them.

"I expect we're going to have to track down Gideon," Barbara noted.

"He's on the list," Lynley agreed.

They replaced everything and lowered themselves back into the cottage proper. Lynley pulled the hatch's cover into position. He said, "Fetch those letters from the bedroom, Havers. Let's go over to the Sixty Plus Club. We might be able to fill in some gaps there."

Outside, they headed up Friday Street, away from the river, passing opposite Wiley's Books where, Barbara noted, Major Ted Wiley made no effort to hide the fact that he was watching them through the front window, standing just behind a display of picture books. He raised a handkerchief to his face as they moved along the pavement. Crying? Pretending to cry? Or just honking his nose? Barbara couldn't help wondering. Three years was a long time to wait for a commitment, only to be foiled at the end.

Friday Street was a mixed bag of businesses and residences. It gave way to Duke Street, where Henley Piano Galleries featured a display of violins and violas—along with a guitar, a mandolin, and a banjo—in the window. Lynley said, "Hang on a moment, Barbara," and sauntered over to study them. Barbara took the opportunity to light a fag, and she gazed at the instruments in collegial cooperation, wondering what she and Lynley were supposed to be seeing.

She finally said, "What? *What?*" to Lynley when he continued gazing, his fingers pulling meditatively at his chin.

He said, "He's like Menuhin. There are all sorts of similarities in their early careers. But one wonders if the family is similar. Menuhin had his parents' complete devotion from the first. If Gideon hadn't—"

"Menu-who?"

Lynley glanced her way. "Another prodigy, Havers." He folded his arms and shifted his weight, preparatory—it seemed—to settling in for a confab on the topic. "It's something to think about: what happens to the parents' lives when they discover they've produced a genius. A set of responsibilities falls upon them entirely different to those faced by the parents of average children. Now take that set of responsibilities and to them add the responsibilities faced by the parents of a different sort of child."

"A child like Sonia," Havers said.

"Those responsibilities are equally challenging, equally demanding, and equally difficult but in an entirely different way."

"But are they equally rewarding to the parents? And if they aren't, how do the parents cope? And what does the daily act of coping do to their marriage?"

Lynley nodded, looking to the violins again. Considering his words, Barbara wondered how far into his own future he was gazing as he studied the instruments. She hadn't yet mentioned to him the conversation she'd had with his wife on the previous evening. Now didn't seem like the time to do it. But on the other hand, he'd given her an entrée that was tough to ignore. And wouldn't it benefit him to have a friendly ear he could speak his potential concerns into during the months of Helen's pregnancy? He would hardly want to do so with his wife.

She said, "Bit worried, sir?" and dragged on her Player with marginal apprehension because, although she'd worked in partnership with Lynley for three years, they rarely ventured into the realm of their personal lives in conversation.

"Worried, Havers?"

She blew smoke from the side of her mouth, the better to avoid hitting him in the face with it when he turned back to her. She said, "Helen told me last night about . . . you know. I expect there're worries connected with that. Everyone now and again would have them. You know. I mean . . ." She rustled her hair and fastened the top button of her pea jacket, which she immediately then unfastened when it felt like a noose.

Lynley said, "Ah. The baby. Yes."

"Scary moments connected with that, I expect."

"Moments indeed," he replied evenly. Then he said, "Let's move on," and headed round the corner from the piano gallery, the conversation between them dismissed.

Odd answer, Barbara thought. Odd reaction. And she realised how stereotypical she'd expected to find his response to impending fatherhood. The man had a distinguished family tree. He had a title—no matter how anachronistic it was to have a title in the first place—and a family estate that he'd inherited in his early twenties. Wasn't he supposed to produce an heir to all that in fairly short order after marrying? And shouldn't he be delighted at the prospect of a duty fulfilled within a few months of having taken the marital plunge?

She frowned, then tossed the dog end of her fag

into the street, where it landed in a puddle at the
kerb. The volumes one didn't know about men, she
thought.

The Sixty Plus Club was a modest building that sat
on one side of a car park in Albert Road, and when
they entered, Barbara and Lynley were immediately
greeted by a large-toothed woman with red hair who
was dressed in a diaphanous flowery affair more suitable for a sunny garden party than for the grey November day outside. She displayed her fearsome oral
pearls at them and introduced herself as Georgia
Ramsbottom, club secretary, "by unanimous vote for
the fifth consecutive year." Could she assist them?
With a parent, perhaps, who might be reluctant to
enquire about the club's amenities? A mother recently widowed? A father trying to come to terms
with the passing of a beloved spouse? "Sometimes our
pensioners"—one of whom she obviously did not
consider herself to be, despite the shiny and taut facial
flesh that spoke of her efforts to retard the ageing
process—"drag their feet a bit when it comes to making life changes, don't they?"

"Not only pensioners," Lynley said pleasantly as he
produced his warrant card and introduced himself
and Barbara.

"Oh. Goodness me. Sorry. I naturally assumed . . ."
Georgia Ramsbottom lowered her voice. "Police?
I don't know that I can assist you. I'm only *elected*,
you see."

"Five consecutive years," Barbara noted helpfully.
"Cheers."

"Is there something . . . ? But then, you'll want to talk to our Director, won't you. She's not in yet today—I can't think why except to say Eugenie often has pressing business to attend to elsewhere—but I can ring her at home if you wouldn't mind waiting in the games room?"

She indicated the door through which she herself had come to greet them. Beyond it at small tables, foursomes sat playing cards, twosomes sat playing chess or draughts, and a onesome played Patience with very little of it, if his muttered "*Bugger* it" was anything to go by. She herself took a step towards a closed office on whose door the word *Director* was stenciled on a translucent window. She said, "I'll just pop in her office and phone her."

Lynley said, "You're speaking about Mrs. Davies, I take it?"

"Eugenie Davies. Yes, of course. She's generally here save for the periods she spends at one of her nursing homes. Very *good,* is our Eugenie. Very generous. A perfect example of . . ." She seemed at a loss to complete her metaphor, so she changed gears with, "But if you're looking for her, then you already know . . . ? I mean about her reputation for good works? Because otherwise . . ."

"I'm afraid she's dead," Lynley said.

"Dead," Georgia Ramsbottom repeated after a moment during which she stared at them in incomprehension. "Eugenie? Eugenie Davies? Dead?"

"Yes. Last night. In London."

"London? Was she . . . ? What on earth happened?

Oh my *God,* does Teddy know?" Georgia's eyes flicked to the doorway through which Lynley and Barbara had come. Her face said that she was inclined to dash out to bear the bad tidings to Major Wiley posthaste. "He and Eugenie," she said rapidly and in a low voice as if the cardplayers in the nearby room might attend to something other than their games. "They were . . . Well, of course, neither of them ever came out and *said* directly, but that was Eugenie all over, wasn't it? Very discreet. She wasn't one to divulge the intimate details of her life to just anyone. But one could see when they were together that Ted was besotted with her. And I, for one, was thrilled for them both because although Ted and I were an item ourselves when he first came to Henley, I'd concluded that he wasn't *quite* right for me, and when I passed him on to Eugenie, I couldn't have been happier that they just seemed to click. Chemistry. That certain something between them that he and I just never had. You know how it is." She showed her teeth again. "Poor darling Ted. Poor dear man. Such a pleasure, he is. Such a favourite here in the club."

"He knows about Mrs. Davies," Lynley said. "We've spoken to him."

"Poor man. First his wife. Now this. My God." She sighed. "Goodness. I shall have to let everyone know."

Barbara wondered fleetingly exactly how much the woman was going to enjoy the employment.

"If we may have access to her office . . ." Lynley indicated the room with a nod.

Georgia Ramsbottom said, "Oh, yes. Oh, of

course. It shouldn't be locked. It isn't usually. The phone's in there and if Eugenie's not here and it rings, someone must answer. Naturally. Because some of our members have spouses in nursing homes and a ringing phone could easily mean . . ." Her voice trailed off meaningfully. She turned the knob and swung the door open, waving Barbara and Lynley inside. She said, "If you wouldn't mind my asking . . ."

Lynley hesitated just inside the door. He turned to the woman as Barbara passed by, going to the single desk in the room and lowering herself into the chair. On the desk top was a daily diary, which she slid towards her as Lynley said, "Yes?"

"Was Ted . . . Is he . . ." She seemed to strive for a funereal tone. "Is Ted terribly distraught, Inspector? We're such *friends,* and one wonders if one should phone immediately? Or perhaps drop by to offer a word of comfort?"

Good grief, Barbara thought. The corpse wasn't cold yet. But, obviously, when a man came up for grabs, there was no time to waste. As Lynley made all the right well-bred noises about only a friend having the ability to judge the suitability of a phone call or a visit, and as Georgia Ramsbottom took herself off to the netherworld to chew this over, Barbara gave her attention to Eugenie Davies' diary, where she saw that the director of the social club kept herself busy with committee meetings that were associated with club events, visits to places called Quiet Pines, River View, and The Willows which seemed to be nursing homes, engagements with Major Wiley that were indicated by *Ted* written across a time, and a set of appointments designated by what seemed to be the names of pubs and hotels. These last appeared regularly throughout the year. They were inconsistent as to day and week, but they marked each month of the year at least once. Interestingly, the entries occurred not only in the previous months of the year, not only in the current month, but clear through to the end of the diary, which included the first six months of the coming year as well. Barbara pointed these out to Lynley as he ventured through a personal telephone directory that he'd pulled from the top right-hand drawer of the desk.

"Standing appointment," he said.

"As a pub crawler?" Barbara asked. "A hotel critic? I don't think so. Listen: Catherine Wheel, King's Head, Fox and Glove, Claridges . . . Now, that's something different. What does that suggest to you? It suggests an assignation to me."

"One hotel?"

"No, there are others. Here's the Astoria. And Lords of the Manor. Le Meridien as well. In town, out of town. She was seeing someone, Inspector, and I'll bet it wasn't Wiley."

"Phone the hotels. See if she booked a room."

"Grunt work."

"One of the job's chief glories."

As she placed the calls, Barbara went through the rest of Eugenie Davies' desk. The other drawers contained office supplies: business cards, envelopes and stationery, Sellotape and staples, rubber bands, scis-

sors, pencils, and pens. Filing folders held contracts
with suppliers of food products, furniture, computers, and copying equipment. By the time she'd
learned from the first of the hotels that there was no
record of a Eugenie Davies staying with them, Barbara had also concluded that there was nothing of a
personal nature inside her desk.

She turned her attention to the top of the desk as
Lynley bent over a computer that was set in sleep
mode. She delved into the dead woman's In tray.
Lynley sank into her cyberworld.

Like the hotels, the In tray, Barbara found, wasn't
exactly a fountain of riveting information. It held
three applications for membership to the Sixty Plus
Club—all from recent widows in their seventies—as
well as what appeared to be drafts of announcements
for upcoming activities. Barbara whistled softly when
she saw what the club had on offer for its members.
With the approaching holiday season, the pensioners
were scheduling themselves into an admirable round
of events: Everything from a coach trip to Bath for
dinner and the panto to a New Year's Eve Gala was
available. There were cocktail parties, dinners,
dances, Boxing Day outings, and midnight church
services advertised for the over-sixties crowd who
certainly weren't taking their golden years in anything resembling a supine position.

Behind her, Barbara heard the whir and beep of
Eugenie Davies' computer coming out of sleep. She
got up and went to the single filing cabinet as Lynley
took her place at the desk and swung the chair round

to face the computer behind it. The filing cabinet had a lock, but it wasn't fastened, so Barbara pulled open the first drawer and began leafing through the files. These appeared to be largely devoted to correspondence with other pensioners' organisations in the UK. However, there were also documents that dealt with the National Health, with a travel-and-study programme called Elder Hostel, with geriatric issues from Alzheimer's to osteoporosis, and with legal issues surrounding wills, trusts, and investments. A manila folder was devoted to correspondence from the children of adult members of the Sixty Plus Club. Most of these were letters of gratitude and appreciation for what the club was doing to bring Mum or Dad out of his or her shell. A few questioned the devotion Mum or Dad had apparently developed for an organisation unrelated to the immediate family. Barbara pulled this last group out and set them on the desk. No telling if a pensioner's relative had got a bit worried over Mum's or Dad's affection for the director of the club, not to mention where that affection might have led. She checked to make sure none of the letters were signed *Wiley*. None were, but that didn't mean that the major had no married daughter who'd written to Eugenie.

One of the files was particularly interesting, as it was filled with photographs of the club during a variety of events. As Barbara flipped through these, she noted that Major Wiley was a frequent subject of the pictures and that he was generally in the company of a woman who hung on his arm, draped herself over his shoulder, or sat in his lap. Georgia Ramsbottom. *Dear Teddy*. Ah yes, Barbara thought. She said, "Inspector," at the same moment as Lynley said, "Here's something, Havers."

Photographs in hand, she went to the computer. She saw that he had accessed the internet and that he'd brought Eugenie Davies' e-mail onto the screen. "She didn't have a password?" Barbara asked as she handed him the pictures.

"She had," Lynley said. "But it was easy enough to suss out, all things considered."

"One of the kids' names?" Barbara asked.

"*Sonia*," he said, and then a moment later, "Damn."

"What?"

"There's nothing here."

"No convenient message threatening her life? No arrangement for a trip to Hampstead? What about an invitation to Le Meridien?"

"Nothing at all." Lynley peered at the screen. "How do you trace someone's e-mail, Havers? Might she have old messages hidden somewhere?"

"You're asking me? I've only just got used to mobile phones."

"We need to find them. If they're here."

"We'll need to take it, then," Barbara said. "The computer, sir. There's going to be someone in London who'll be able to sort it out."

"There is indeed," Lynley replied. He sifted through the pictures she'd handed to him, but he didn't appear to give them much attention.

"Georgia Ramsbottom," Barbara prompted him. "She and dear Teddy appear to have been quite an item at one time."

"Sixty-year-old women running each other down in the road?" Lynley queried.

"It's a thought," Barbara said. "I wonder if her car's bashed up."

"Somehow I doubt it," Lynley replied.

"But we should have a look. I don't think we can—"

"Yes, yes. We'll have a look. It's bound to be in the car park." But he sounded dismissive, and Barbara didn't much like it when he set the photographs down summarily and returned to the computer, his mind made up. He logged off Eugenie Davies' e-mail, shut down the machine, and began to unplug it. "Let's trace where Mrs. Davies has been on the internet," he told her. "No one goes on-line without leaving a trail of breadcrumbs."

"CREAMPANTS." DCI ERIC Leach kept his face impassive. He'd been a cop for twenty-six years, and he'd long ago realised that in his line of work only a numbskull optimistically concluded he'd heard everything there was to hear from fellow members of the human race. But this one was clearly something for the books. "You did say Cream Pants, Mr. Pitchley?"

They were in an interview room at the police station: J. W. Pitchley, his solicitor—a diminutive man called Jacob Azoff with nostril hairs like feather dusters and a large coffee stain decorating his tie—a police constable called Stanwood, and Leach himself, who was doing the questioning as he tossed back Lemsip like cider and wondered sourly how long it was going to take his immune system to catch up with the single life he was back to leading. One night on a pub crawl and he became a breeding ground for every virus known to man.

Pitchley's solicitor had rung not two hours prior to this meeting. His client wanted to make a statement to the police, Azoff had informed Leach briefly. And he wanted to be assured that this statement would be confidential, just between us boys, treated with kid gloves, and blessed with holy water. In other words, Pitchley didn't want the press to get hold of his name, and if there was a ghost of a chance that the press were going to be *given* his name . . . et cetera, et cetera, et cetera. Yawn.

"He's walked that route before," Azoff had said in a tone that was portentous. "So if we can reach a preliminary agreement about the confidentiality of this conversation, Detective Chief Inspector Leach, I believe we have on our hands a man who deeply wishes to assist you with your enquiries."

So Pitchley and his brief had shown up, had been ushered through the back door of the station like covert operatives, had been given the refreshment they requested—fresh orange juice and sparkling mineral water with ice and lime not lemon, thank you—and had ensconced themselves at the interview table where Leach had pressed the tape recorder's play button, reciting the day, the time, and the names of all individuals present.

Pitchley's story had so far not altered from what he had told them on the previous night although he'd become more detailed as to arrangements and places and relatively more specific as to names. Unfortunately, aside from the sobriquets adopted by his partners in amorous encounters at the Comfort Inn, he was unable to come up with the *actual* name of anyone who could confirm his story.

Thus, Leach asked reasonably, "Mr. Pitchley, how is it that you expect us to track down this woman? If she wasn't willing to give her name to the bloke who was poking her—"

"We don't use that term," Pitchley said with some offence.

"—then how do you expect her to be forthcoming when the coppers want to track her down? Doesn't the withholding of her name suggest something to you?"

"We always—"

"Doesn't it suggest she might not *wish* to be tracked down in ways other than through the internet?"

"It's merely part of the game that we—"

"And if she doesn't wish to be tracked down, doesn't *that* suggest she's got someone hanging round—like a husband—who might not look kindly on a bloke—who's had a naked romp with his wife—showing up on the front steps with flowers and chocolates and the hope that she'll confirm his alibi?"

Pitchley's colour was growing high. But then, so was Leach's level of disbelief. With much hemming and hawing, the man had confessed to being an on-line Casanova who regularly seduced women of advancing years, none of whom gave him their names or ever knew his. Pitchley claimed that he couldn't remember the number of women he'd had assignations with since the birth of e-mail and chat rooms, and he certainly couldn't remember all their cyber-names, but he could swear on a stack of eighty-five religious books of DCI Leach's choice that he observed the same procedure with all of them once an agreement to meet had been reached: drinks and dinner in the Valley of Kings in South Kensington followed by several hours of athletically creative sexual intercourse at the Comfort Inn on Cromwell Road.

"So you'll be remembered at either the restaurant or the hotel?" Leach asked the man.

That might be, Pitchley was sad to admit, a bit of a problem. The waiters at the Valley of Kings were foreigners, weren't they? The night receptionist at the Comfort Inn was a foreigner as well. And foreigners often had a spot of difficulty remembering an English face, didn't they? Because foreigners—

"Two-thirds of bloody *London* are foreigners," Leach cut in. "If you can't come up with something more solid than what you've come up with so far, Mr. Pitchley, we're wasting our time."

"Might I remind you, DCI Leach, that Mr. Pitchley's visit to the station is voluntary," Jake Azoff pointed out at this juncture. His had been the orange juice, and Leach noticed that a particle of pulp clung to his moustache like a punk-dyed bird dropping. "Perhaps a more marked degree of civility would serve to encourage a deeper recollection on his part."

"I assume that Mr. Pitchley came to the station because he had something more to tell me than he told me last night," Leach retorted. "So far, we're getting a variation on a theme here, and all it's doing is producing more quicksand in which your boy is already up to his chest."

"I don't see how that conclusion is at all accurate," Azoff said, affronted by the implication.

"Don't you, now? Let me enlighten you. Unless I've been dreaming, Mr. Pitchley has just informed us that his hobby is to use the internet to root out women over fifty—to chat up and coax into bed. He's just informed us that he's enjoyed a rather marked degree of success in this arena. So much so that he can't even recall how many women have been on the receiving end of his erotic talents. Am I correct, Mr. Pitchley?"

Pitchley shifted position on his chair and took a sip of water. His skin was still flushed, and his hair—dust-coloured with a central parting that created wings which flopped into his face—swept downwards when he nodded. He kept his head lowered. From embarrassment or regret, as a means of obfuscation . . . Who the hell could tell?

"Fine. Let's continue. Now, we have an older woman who's run down by a vehicle on Mr. Pitchley's street, a few doors from his own home. This woman just happens to be in possession of Mr. Pitchley's address. What does that suggest to you?"

"I wouldn't draw any conclusion myself," Azoff said.

"Naturally. But it's my job to draw conclusions. And the conclusion I draw is that this lady was on her way to see Mr. Pitchley."

"We've made no admission that Mr. Pitchley was expecting or knew the woman in question."

"And if she *was* on her way to see him, we have from Mr. Pitchley's own lips one hell of an excellent reason why." Leach pressed his point by leaning forward, the better to see beneath Pitchley's protection of hair. "She was just round the age you like them, Pitchley. Sixty-two. Nice shape to her body—what was left of it, that is, after the car did its work with her. She was divorced. No remarriage. No children at home. I wonder if she'd got herself a computer? Something to use to while away the nights when she was feeling lonely out there in Henley?"

"That's just not possible," Pitchley said. "They never know where I live. They never know how to find me after we've . . . once we've . . . well, after we've left Cromwell Road."

"You just fuck 'em and flee," Leach said. "That's rich, that is. But what if one of them decided she didn't like that arrangement? What if one of them followed you home? Not last night, of course, but on another night. Followed you, saw where you live, and bided her time when you never contacted her again."

"She didn't. She *can't* have done."

"Why not?"

"Because I don't ever go directly home. I drive round for at least thirty minutes—sometimes an hour—once we leave the hotel to make certain . . ." He paused and managed to look relatively miserable about the admission he was making, "I drive round to make certain she's . . . well, not on my tail."

"Very wise," Leach said with irony.

"I know how it sounds. I know it makes me look a perfect shit. And if that's what I am, then that's what I am. But what I'm not is a man who'd run down a woman in the street and you damn well know it if you've examined my car and not used the opportunity to joyride it round London. So I'd like the Boxter returned, Inspector Leach."

"Would you, now?"

"I would. You wanted information, and I've given you information. I've told you where I was last night, I've told you why, and I've told you with whom."

"With CreamPants."

"All right. I'll go on-line again. I'll get her to come forward if that's what you want."

"You can do and will do," Leach agreed. "But by your own admission, I don't see how that's going to help much in the larger picture."

"Why? I can't have been in two places at once."

"True enough. But even if Miss CreamPants, or perhaps it's Mrs. CreamPants"—Leach couldn't hide his smirk and he didn't bother to try—"confirms your story, there's part of it she can't help you with, isn't there? She can't tell us where you drove for an hour or thirty minutes after you finished with her. And if you're about to argue that she may have followed you, then you're on thin ice again. Because if she followed you, there's a very good chance that Eugenie Davies, after a similar romp on the Cromwell Road, once did the same."

Abruptly, Pitchley pushed back from the table, and with so much force that his chair shrieked like a siren against the floor. "Who?" His voice was hoarse, as if it were sandpaper trying to speak. "Who did you say?"

"Eugenie Davies. The dead woman." Even as he spoke, DCI Leach read the new reality on the other man's face. "You know her. And by that name. You *know* her, Mr. Pitchley?"

"Oh God. Oh hell." Pitchley moaned.

Azoff said to his client in a flash, "Need five minutes?"

No answer was required of the suspect, because a quick tap sounded on the door of the interview room, and a female PC popped her head inside. She said to Leach, "DI Lynley on the phone, sir. Now or later?"

"Five minutes," Leach said curtly to Pitchley and Azoff. He picked up his paperwork and left them alone.

LIFE WASN'T A continuum of events, although it wore the guise of exactly that. Instead, it was actually a carousel. In infancy, one mounted a galloping pony and started out on a journey during which one assumed that circumstances would change as the expedition continued. But the truth of life was that it was an endless repetition of what one had already experienced . . . round and round and up and down on that pony. And unless one dealt with whatever challenges one was *meant* to deal with along the route, those challenges appeared again and again in one form or another till the end of one's days. If he hadn't subscribed to that notion before, J. W. Pitchley was a believer now.

He stood on the steps of the Hampstead police station with his solicitor and listened to the peroration of Jake Azoff's harangue. This consisted of a soliloquy on the topic of trust-and-veracity between a client and his lawyer. He was ending with, "Do you think I would have bloody well walked in there if I'd bloody well known what you were bloody well *hiding,* you twit? You made me look like a fool and what the *hell* do you think that does for my credibility with the cops?"

Pitchley wanted to say that the current situation wasn't *about* Azoff, but he didn't bother. He didn't say anything, which encouraged the solicitor to demand, "So what would you like me to call you, sir?" The *sir* was no indication of anything other than contempt, which coloured it appreciably. "Is it to be Pitchley or Pitchford for what remains of our legal relationship?"

"Pitchley's perfectly legal," J. W. Pitchley replied. "There's nothing dodgy in how I changed my name, Jake."

"In that, perhaps," Azoff retorted. "But I want the whys, the wherefores, and the hows in writing on my desk, by fax, messenger, e-mail, or carrier pigeon before six o'clock. And then we'll look at what happens next in our professional relationship."

J. W. Pitchley, AKA James Pitchford, AKA TongueMan to his cyberacquaintances, nodded co-operatively even though he knew Jake Azoff was blowing smoke in the air. Azoff's track record of managing his money was so appalling that he wouldn't be able to exist for a month without some-one at the helm of his investments, and Pitchley-Pitchford-TongueMan had been handling them for so many years and with such a degree of expertise in the financial legerdemain department that to give control over to a lesser fiscal guru would be to put Azoff within striking distance of the Inland Revenue, which the solicitor was understandably loath to have happen. But he needed to let off steam, did Azoff, and J. W. Pitchley—formerly James Pitchford and currently AKA TongueMan—couldn't really blame him. So he said, "Will do, Jake. Sorry about the sur-prise," and he watched as Azoff huffed, raised the col-lar of his overcoat against a chill wind, and set off down the street.

For his part, Pitchley, with no access to his car and no invitation from Azoff to drive him back to Cred-iton Hill, set off disconsolately for the railway station near Hampstead Heath and prepared to submit him-self to its insalubrious embrace. At least it wasn't the underground, he told himself. *And* there hadn't been a smash-up between competing railway lines vying for the Excellence in Ineptitude Award in at least a week.

He walked up Downshire Hill and veered right into Keats' Grove, where at the eponymous poet's house and library, a middle-aged woman was just leaving the waterlogged grounds, a large satchel in her right hand that was painfully sloping her shoulder with its weight. Pitchley-Pitchford slowed his footsteps when she turned right and headed in the same direction as the one he was taking. In another time, he would have hurried forward to assist her with her burden. It was, after all, the gentlemanly thing to do.

Her ankles, Pitchley-Pitchford saw, were a little too thick, but the rest of her was just as he liked a woman to be: a bit worn, a touch disheveled, and possessing a somewhat harried academic mien which suggested not only an agreeable level of intelligence but also the sort of lack of sexual confidence that he always found so stimulating. Chat-room women were invariably like this woman when he finally met them, which was why he was drawn to the internet, despite his own better judgement, not to mention the threat of sexually transmitted diseases. And, considering what he'd just been through at the Hampstead police station, even though the better part of his mind was lecturing him about the idiocy of future encounters with women whose names had thus far been inconsequential to him, the other part of his mind—his reptilian brain—would have no part of lessons learned or trepidation about the future. There *are* more important considerations than a bit of mess with the police, James, the lizard cerebellum declared. Dwell, for example, on the infinite pleasures to be given to and taken from the individual orifices of the female anatomy.

But that was pure madness, that kind of adolescent fantasising. What wasn't fantasy was the death of Eugenie Davies in Crediton Hill, Eugenie Davies, who had been carrying *his* address.

When he first knew Eugenie, he'd been James Pitchford, twenty-five years old, three years graduated from university and one year graduated from a bed-sit in Hammersmith the approximate size of a fingernail. A year in those lodgings had offered him access to the language school he needed where, for an exorbitant sum that took ages to recoup, he'd purchased individual instruction in his native language, suitable for business dealings, for academic purposes, for social gatherings, and for cowing doormen at fine hotels.

From there, he'd snagged his first job in the City from whose perspective a central London address had sounded so abso*lutely* right. And since he never invited office mates home for drinks, dinner, or anything else, there was no way for them to know that the letters, documents, and thick party invitations sent to a lofty address in Kensington were actually delivered to the fourth-floor bedroom he occupied, which was even smaller than the bed-sit he'd begun with in Hammersmith.

Cramped accommodation had been a small price to pay all those years ago, not only for the address but also for the companionship the address had afforded. In the time since those days in Kensington Square,

J. W. Pitchley had schooled himself not to think of that companionship. But James Pitchford, who had reveled in it and had deemed himself an unmitigated success in self-reinvention because of it, had scarcely lived a single moment without experiencing some passing thought about one member of the household or another. Especially Katja.

"You can help my talking English, please?" she had asked him. "I am here one year. I learn not as good as I wish. I will be so grateful." All those charming V's in place of W's when she spoke were her own variation of the abhorrent missing aitch he'd worked so hard upon.

He agreed to help her because she was so earnest in supplicating him. He agreed to help her because—although she couldn't know it and he would die before telling her—they were two of a kind. Her escape from East Germany, while far more dramatic and awe-inspiring, mirrored an earlier flight of his own. And although their motivations were different, the core of them was identical.

They already spoke the same language, he and Katja. If he could help her better herself through something as simple as grammar and pronunciation, he was glad to do so.

They met in her free time, when Sonia was asleep or with her family. They used his room or hers, where they each had a table that was just large enough for the books from which Katja did her grammar exercises and for the tape recorder into which she spoke. She was earnest in her efforts at dic-

tion, enunciation, and pronunciation. She was coura-
geous in her willingness to experiment in a language
that was as foreign to her as Yorkshire pudding. Indeed, it was for her courage that James Pitchford had
first learned to admire Katja Wolff. The sheer audacity that had carried her over the old Berlin Wall was
the stuff of a heroism he could only hope to emulate.

I will make myself worthy of you, he told her silently
as they sat together and worked on the mystery of irregular verbs. And while the table light shone on her
soft blonde hair, he visualised himself touching it,
running his fingers through it, feeling it caress his
naked chest as she lifted herself from their shared embrace.

On her chest of drawers across the room, the intercom broke into James Pitchford's reveries just
about as often as he allowed himself to dream them.
From two floors below, the child would whimper
and Katja's head would rise from her nightly lesson.

"It's nothing," he'd say because if it was something,
their shared time that was so precious to him and already too brief would be over for the evening. For if
Sonia Davies' whimper escalated to a cry, the possibilities were endless as to what the trouble might be.

"The little one. I must go," Katja said.

"Wait a moment." He used the opportunity to
cover her hand with his own.

"I cannot, James. If she weeps and Mrs. Davies
hears and finds me not with her . . . You know how
she is. And this is my job."

Job? he thought. It was more like indentured servitude. The hours were long, and the duties were end-less. Caring for a child so constantly ill required the efforts of more than one young woman with virtually no experience.

Even at twenty-five, James Pitchford could see this. Sonia Davies needed a professional nurse. Why she didn't have one was one of the mysteries of Ken-sington Square. He wasn't in a position to delve into this mystery, however. He needed to keep his head down and his profile obscure.

Still, when Katja hurried off to the child in the midst of an English lesson, when he heard her leap out of her bed in the middle of the night and rush down the stairs to come to the aid of the little girl, when he returned from work and found Katja feed-ing her, bathing her, occupying her with one stimu-lation or another, he thought protectively, The poor creature *has* a family, hasn't she? What are *they* doing to care for her?

And it seemed to him that the answer was nothing. Sonia Davies was left in Katja's charge while the rest of the crew hovered round Gideon.

Could he blame them? Pitchford wondered. And even if he could, had they any choice? The Davieses had embarked upon Gideon's fashioning long before Sonia's birth, hadn't they? They were already com-mitted to a course of action, as evidenced by the pres-ence of Raphael Robson and Sarah-Jane Beckett in their world.

Thinking of Robson and Beckett, Pitchley-Pitchford entered the railway station and dropped the required coins into a ticket machine. As he wandered out onto the platform, he reflected upon the astounding fact that he hadn't thought of either Robson or Beckett for years. Robson, of course, he might well have forgotten since the violin instructor had not lived among them. But it was strange that he hadn't given a passing consideration to Sarah-Jane Beckett in all this time. She had been, after all, so very much a presence.

"I find my position here more than suitable," she told him early in her employ, in that peculiar pre-Victorian manner of speaking she used when she was in full Governess Mode. "Whilst difficult at times, Gideon is a remarkable pupil, and I feel most privileged to have been chosen from nineteen candidates to be his instructor." She'd just joined the household, and her room would be up with his among the eaves on the house's top floor. They would have to share a bathroom the size of a pin head. No bath, just a shower in which an average-size man could barely turn around. She'd seen this on the day she moved in, looked at it disapprovingly, but finally sighed with martyred acceptance.

"I don't wash garments in the bathroom," she informed him, "and I prefer that you refrain from doing so as well. If we have consideration for each other in this small way, I dare say we shall manage quite well together. Where are you from, James? I can't quite place you. Normally, I'm very good at accents. Mrs. Davies, for instance, grew up in Hampshire. Can you tell? I quite like her. Mr. Davies as well. But the grandfather? He does seem a bit . . . Well. One doesn't like to speak ill, *but . . .*" She tapped a finger to her temple and lifted her eyes in the direction of the ceiling.

Barmy was the word James would have chosen at another time in his life. But instead he said, "Yes. He's a queer fish, isn't he? But if you give him a wide berth, you'll find he's harmless enough."

So for just over a year, they'd lived in harmony and with the spirit of cooperation. Daily, James left for his job in the City as Richard and Eugenie Davies took themselves to their own places of employment. The elder Davieses remained at home, where Granddad occupied himself in the garden and Gran kept house. Raphael Robson took Gideon through his sessions on the violin. Sarah-Jane Beckett gave the boy lessons in everything from literature to geology.

"It's astonishing working with a genius," she informed him. "The child is like a sponge, James. One would think he'd be hopeless at anything but music, but that isn't the case. When I compare him to what I had my first year in North London . . ." Again and as always, she used her eyes to express the rest: North London, that dwelling place of society's detritus. Fully half of her students there were black, she'd informed him. And the rest of them—with a pause for effect—were *Irish.* "One doesn't wish to cast aspersions on minorities, but there are limits to what one should expect oneself to endure in one's chosen career, don't you think?"

She spent time with him when she wasn't with

Gideon. She asked him out to the cinema or for a drink at the Greyhound, "just as friends." But often on those just-as-friends evenings, her leg pressed against his in the darkness as the celluloid flickered its images on the screen, or she took his arm as they entered the pub and she slid her hand from his biceps to his elbow to his wrist so that when their fingers touched it was only natural that they clasp and remain clasped once they were seated.

"Tell me about your family, James," she urged him. "Do tell me. I want every detail."

So he manufactured tales for her because telling tales had long ago become his stock in trade. He was flattered by the attention that she—an educated girl from the Home Counties—was willing to show him. He had held his own counsel and kept his head down for so many years that Sarah-Jane Beckett's interest in him stirred an appetite for companionship that he'd kept suppressed for most of his life.

She wasn't the companion he was seeking, however. And while he couldn't have said exactly who that companion would be in his evenings with Sarah-Jane, he felt no heaving of the earth when her leg touched his and no pleasurable longing for the pressure of something more than her palm against his own when she took his hand.

Then Katja Wolff arrived, and with Katja the situation was different. But then, Katja Wolff had been as different from Sarah-Jane Beckett as was humanly possible to be.

SEVEN

"SHE MIGHT have been meeting with the ex," DCI Leach said in reference to the man Ted Wiley had seen in the car park of the Sixty Plus Club. "Divorce doesn't mean goodbye forever, take it from me. He's called Richard Davies. Track him down."

"He could be the third male voice on her answer machine as well," Lynley acknowledged.

"What did that voice say again?"

Barbara Havers read the message from her notes. "Sounded angry," she added, and tapped her biro meditatively against the paper. "You know, I wonder if our Eugenie played men off against each other."

"You're thinking of this other bloke . . . Wiley?" Leach said.

"Could be something there," Havers noted. "We've got three separate men on her answer machine. We've got her—this is according to Wiley— arguing with a bloke in the car park. We've got her wanting to talk to Wiley, having something to tell him, something he apparently feels was important . . ." Havers hesitated and glanced at Lynley.

He knew what she was thinking and what she wanted to say: *We've also got love letters from a married man and a computer with access to the internet.* She was clearly waiting for him to give her the go-ahead to say this, but he held his tongue, so she finished lamely with, "We've got reason to look closely at every bloke who knew her, 'f you ask me."

Leach nodded. "Have at Richard Davies, then. Get what you can."

They were in the incident room, where detective constables were reporting in on the activities to which they'd been assigned. Following Lynley's phone call to the DCI on the way back into town, Leach had allocated further manpower to the PNC in order to trace all navy and black Audis with number plates ending in ADY. He'd put a constable on to BT for a list of the incoming and outgoing phone calls from Doll Cottage in Henley, and another constable was getting on to Cellnet to track down the mobile phone whose owner had left a message on Eugenie Davies' answer machine.

Of the activities reported as being completed so far that day, only the DC with the responsibility for gathering information from forensic had offered a useful detail: A number of minute paint particles had been found on the dead woman's clothing when it was examined. Further particles had also been found on her body, specifically upon her mangled legs.

"They're putting the paint under analysis," Leach said. "Broken down, it might well give us the make of the car that hit her. But that'll take time. You know the dance."

"Have you got a colour on the paint?" Lynley asked.

"Black."

"What colour is the Boxter you're holding?"

"As to that . . ." Leach told his team to get on with their work and he led the way back to his office, saying, "Car's silver. And it's clean. Not that I'd expect some bloke—no matter how much he's rolling in bunce—to run down a woman in a motor that cost more than my mum's house. We're still holding the car, though. It's proving useful."

He paused at a coffee machine and plugged in a few coins. A viscous liquid drizzled pathetically into a plastic cup. Leach said, "You?" and held the cup up in offer. Havers accepted, although she looked as if she regretted the decision once she tasted the brew; Lynley chose the course of wisdom and demurred. Leach purchased another cup for himself and took them into his office, where he used his elbow to shoot the door home. His phone was ringing, and he barked "Leach" into it as he set down his coffee and sank into his desk chair, nodding Lynley and Havers to chairs of their own. "Hello, love," he said to his caller, his face brightening. "Nope . . . Nope . . . She's what?" With a glance at the other detectives, "Esmé, I can't actually talk at the moment. But let me say this: *No one* has said anything at all about getting remarried, okay? . . . Yes. Right. We'll speak later, love." He dropped the receiver back into place, saying, "Kids. Divorce. It's a real nightmare."

Lynley and Havers made noises of sympathy. Leach slurped coffee and dismissed the phone call. He said, "Our bloke Pitchley came by for a little chat this morning, solicitor in tow" and he brought them up to date on what the man from Crediton Hill had revealed: that he not only had recognised the name of the hit-and-run victim, that he not only had once known the hit-and-run victim, but that he'd also lived in the very same house with the hit-and-run victim at the time of the murder of said victim's daughter. "He's changed his name from Pitchford to Pitchley for reasons he's not talking about," Leach concluded. "I like to think I would have twigged his identity eventually, but it's been twenty years since I last saw the bloke and a hell of a lot of fish have swum under the bridge in the meantime."

"Not surprising," Lynley said.

"Now that I know who he is, though, I've got to tell you he smells sweet to me for this business, Boxter or not. He's got something the size of a T-Rex marching through his conscience. I can feel it."

"Was he a suspect in the child's death?" Lynley asked. Havers, he noted, had flipped over a new page in her notebook and was jotting the information down on a sheet that looked stained with brown sauce.

"No one was a suspect at first. Until all the reports came in, it looked like a case of negligence.

You know what I mean: A flaming idiot goes to take a phone call while the toddler's in the bath. The kid tries to reach for a rubber ducky. She slips, knocks herself on the head, and the rest is academic. Unfortunate and tragic, but it happens." Leach slurped more coffee and picked up a document from his desk, which he used to gesture with. "But when the reports came in on the child's body, there were bruises and fractures no one could explain, so everyone became a suspect. It all came down to the nanny dead quick. And she was a real piece of work, she was. I might've forgotten Pitchford's face, but as to that German cow . . . There's not a chance in hell I'd ever forget her. Cold as a cod, that woman was. Gave us one interview—*one* interview, mind you, about a toddler that died in her care—and she never said another word. Not to CID, not to her solicitor, not to her barrister. Not to anyone. Took her right to silence straight to Holloway. Never shed a tear either. But then, what else could you expect from a Kraut? Family were mad to engage her in the first place."

From the corner of his eye, Lynley saw Havers tap her biro against the paper she was writing on. He glanced her way to see her eyes had narrowed at Leach. She wasn't a woman who put up with bigotry in any of its forms—from xenophobia to misogyny—and he could tell she was about to make a comment that wouldn't endear her to the detective chief inspector. He interceded, saying, "The German girl's origins worked against her, then."

"Her flaming Kraut personality worked against her."

" 'We will fight them on the beaches,' " Havers murmured.

Lynley shot her a look. She shot him one back.

Leach either didn't hear or chose to ignore Havers, for which Lynley was grateful. The last thing they needed was a division among them, with lines being drawn on the issue of political correctness.

The DCI leaned back in his chair and said, "The diary and phone messages are all you came up with?"

"So far," Lynley answered. "There was also a card from a woman called Lynn, but that doesn't appear to be germane at the moment. Her child died and Mrs. Davies went to the funeral, apparently."

"There was no other correspondence?" Leach asked. "Letters, bills, the like?"

Lynley said, "No. There was no other correspondence," and he didn't look Havers' way. "She had a sea chest filled with materials relating to her son, though. Newspapers, magazines, concert programmes. Major Wiley said that Gideon and Mrs. Davies were estranged, but from the look of her collection, I'd guess it wasn't Mrs. Davies who wanted the estrangement."

"The son?" Leach asked.

"Or the father."

"We're back to the argument in the car park, then."

"We could be. Yes."

Leach swallowed the rest of his drink and crushed

the plastic cup. He said, "But it's odd, don't you think, to have found so little information about her in the woman's own home?"

"It was a fairly monastic environment, sir."

Leach studied Lynley. Lynley studied Leach. Barbara Havers scribbled furiously into her notebook. A moment passed during which no one admitted to anything. Lynley waited for the DCI to give him the information he wanted. Leach didn't do it. He merely said, "Have at Davies, then. He shouldn't be tough to track down."

So the plans were set and the assignments made, and in short order Lynley and Havers were back in the street and heading for their respective cars. Havers lit a cigarette and said, "What're you going to do with those letters, Inspector?"

Lynley didn't pretend to need clarification. "I'm giving them back to Webberly," he said, "eventually."

"*Giving* them . . ." Havers drew in on her cigarette and blew the smoke out in a burst of frustration. "If word gets out that you've taken them from the scene and not turned them in . . . That *we've* taken them from the scene and not turned them in . . . Bloody hell, do you know where that puts us, Inspector? And on top of it, there's that computer. Why didn't you tell Leach about that computer?"

"I'll tell him, Havers," Lynley said. "Once I know exactly what's on it."

"Jesus in a basket!" Havers cried. "That's suppressing—"

"Listen, Barbara. There's only one way it would

come to light right now that we've got the computer and those letters, and we both know what that one way is." He looked at her evenly and waited for her to connect the dots.

Her expression altered. She said, "Hey. I don't grass, Inspector," and he could see the affront she'd taken.

He said, "That's why I work with you, Barbara," and he disarmed the Bentley's security system. He opened the door before he spoke to her again, over the car's roof. "If I've been brought in on this case to keep Webberly protected, I'd like to know that and I'd like it said to my face for once. Wouldn't you?"

"I'd like to keep my nose clean is what I'd like," Havers replied. "One of us got demoted two months ago, Inspector, and if memory serves me right, it wasn't you." She was white-faced, watching Lynley with an expression that was completely unlike the belligerent officer he'd worked with for the past several years. She'd taken a professional and psychological beating in the last five months, and Lynley realised that he owed her the opportunity to avoid another one. He said, "Havers, would you prefer to be out of this? That's not a problem. One phone call and—"

"I don't want to be out."

"But it could get dicey. It's *already* dicey. I more than understand how you might—"

"Don't talk rubbish. I'm in, Inspector. I'd just like us to have a little care with what we're doing."

"I'm taking care," Lynley assured her. "Those letters from Webberly are not an issue in this case."

"You'd better hope that's true," Havers replied. She pushed away from the Bentley. "Let's get on with it, then. What's next?"

Lynley accepted her words and dwelt for a moment on how best to approach the next phase of their job. "You've the look of a woman in need of spiritual guidance," he said. "Track down the Convent of the Immaculate Conception."

"What about you?"

"I'll follow our DCI's suggestion. Richard Davies. If he's seen or talked to his former wife recently, he might know what she wanted to confess to Wiley."

"He might *be* what she wanted to confess to Wiley," Havers pointed out.

"There's that as well," Lynley said.

JILL FOSTER HAD never run into a serious snag while she was ticking off accomplishments from the Master List that she'd first compiled as a fifteen-year-old schoolgirl. Reading all of Shakespeare (done by age twenty), hitchhiking the length of Ireland (done by twenty-one), taking a double first at Cambridge (by age twenty-two), traveling alone in India (by twenty-three), exploring the Amazon River (twenty-six), kayaking the Nile (twenty-seven), writing a definitive study of Proust (still in progress), adapting the novels of F. Scott Fitzgerald for television (also in the works) . . . From athleticism to intellectualism, Jill Foster hadn't experienced even a hiccup on her progress through life.

In the personal realm, however, she'd had more

difficulty. She'd placed the achievement of marriage and children before her thirty-fifth birthday, but she'd found it more challenging than she'd anticipated to attain a goal that involved the enthusiastic cooperation of another person. And it was marriage and children that she'd wanted: in that order. Yes, it was trendy to be "partners" with someone. Every third pop singer, film star, or professional athlete was living proof of that, congratulated in the tabloids on a daily basis for their mindless ability to reproduce, as if the act of reproduction itself took some sort of talent that only they possessed. But Jill was not a woman easily swayed by what bore the appearance of a trend, particularly when it came to her Master List of Accomplishments. One did not achieve one's goals by taking shortcuts that were nothing but passing vogues.

The aftermath of her affair with Jonathon had for a time seriously undermined her confidence in her ability to reach her marital and maternal objective. But then Richard had come into her life, and she'd quickly seen that an accomplishment that had so far eluded her was finally within her reach. In the world of her grandparents—even of her parents—to have become lovers with Richard before a formal commitment had been made between them would have been both foolhardy and ruinous. Indeed, even today there were probably a dozen agony aunts whose advice—considering Jill's ultimate objective—would have been to wait for the ring, the church bells, and the confetti before embarking on any kind of intimacy with one's intended bridegroom, or at least to have used what were euphemistically called "precautions" until such a time as the deal was signed, sealed, and registered in the customary way. But Richard's earnest pursuit of her in the aftermath of Jonathon's failure to leave his wife constituted a phase in Jill's life that was both flattering and essential. His desire *for* her had aroused an equal desire *in* her, and she was deeply gratified to feel it since, after Jonathon, she'd begun to wonder if she would ever feel that hot aching hunger—unlike any other hunger—for a man again.

And that hunger, Jill had found, was firmly tied to impregnation. It might have been due to a dawning knowledge of how few years she actually had left for childbirth, but every time she and Richard made love in those first months, her body had strained to take him into her more deeply, as if the sole act of surging towards him would ensure that their contact produced a child.

So she'd gone at marriage backwards, but what did it matter? They were happy with each other, and Richard was devotion itself.

Still, she had the occasional flicker of doubt, a memento left her by Jonathon's promises and Jonathon's lies. And while, when doubts surfaced, she reminded herself that the two men were absolutely nothing alike, there were times when a shadow cast on Richard's face or a silence in the midst of a discussion between them triggered a set of worries within her that she tried to tell herself were unnecessary and unreal.

Even if Richard and I don't marry, she would lecture herself in her worst moments, Catherine and I shall be perfectly all right. I've a career to fall back on, for heaven's sake. And the age of unmarried mothers being social pariahs has long since passed.

But that wasn't really the point, was it, her long-range-planning self would argue. The point was marriage and husband as well. And the larger point was family, which she chose to define as father-mother-child.

So now she said pleasantly to Richard with that ultimate goal in mind, "Darling, if you'd only see it, I know you'd agree." They were in Richard's car on the way to South Kensington from Shepherd's Bush in order to keep an engagement with an estate agent who was going to determine a selling price for Richard's flat. This was progress in the right direction to Jill's way of thinking, since they obviously couldn't live *en famille* in Braemar Mansions once the baby was born. There was far too little room.

She was privately grateful for this additional indication of Richard's positive marital intentions, but she hadn't yet been able to understand why they couldn't take the next step and have a look at a suitable detached house—completely renovated—that she'd managed to locate in Harrow. Looking at the house didn't mean they were going to have to *buy* it, for heaven's sake. And since she hadn't yet put her own flat up for sale—"let's not both be homeless at once," Richard had advised when she'd suggested doing so—there was little chance that having a simple

look at a building on offer would result in their own-
ing it on this very day. "It would give you a sense of
what I have in mind for us," she told him. "And if
you don't like what I have in mind once you see it,
at least we'll know straightaway and I can change
course." Not that she would, naturally. She would
merely expend more careful and subtle effort to bring
him round to her way of thinking.

"I don't need to see it to know what you have in
mind, darling," Richard replied as they trundled along
in moderately bearable traffic, considering the time of
day. "Modern conveniences, double glazing, fitted
carpet, and large gardens in both front and back." He
looked over at her and smiled affectionately. "Tell me
I've got it wrong and I'll buy you dinner."

"You'll buy me dinner either way," she told him.
"If I'm on my feet long enough to cook you a meal,
I'll swell up like a ham."

"But tell me I've got it wrong about the house."

"Oh, you know you haven't got it wrong," she
laughed. And she touched him fondly, smoothing her
fingers against his temple where his hair was grey.
"And don't begin a lecture, if you're thinking of one,
all right? I didn't go anywhere on my own to find it.
The estate agent drove me up to Harrow."

"Which is as it should be," Richard said. His hand
moved to her stomach, monstrously huge, the skin
stretched taut like a kettle drum. "Are you awake,
Cara Ann?" he enquired of their child.

Catherine Ann, Jill corrected him patiently. But
she didn't make the correction aloud. He'd somewhat

recovered from the distress in which he'd arrived in
Shepherd's Bush earlier that day. There was no point
to upsetting him all over again. While an argument
concerning the name of their child was hardly going
to cause an emotional upheaval, she did believe that
what Richard had been through deserved her sympathy.

He didn't still love the woman, she assured herself.
After all, they'd been divorced for years. It was
merely the shock of everything that had made him so
ill, having to gaze upon the bloodied corpse of someone who had once shared his life. That was something to make anyone ill, wasn't it? Asked to look
upon the broken body of Jonathon Stewart, wouldn't
she have reacted likewise?

With this in mind, she decided she could compromise on the house in Harrow. She was confident that
her willingness to do so would prompt an important
compromise on his part. She led into this compromise by saying, "All right, then. We won't go up to
Harrow today. But the modern bit, Richard. Are you
quite happy with that?"

"Decent plumbing and double glazing?" he asked.
"Fitted carpet, dishwasher, and all the rest? I dare say
I can live with it. As long as you're there. Both of
you, that is." He smiled at her, but still she sensed
something deeper in his eyes, looking like regret for
what might have been.

But he *doesn't* still love Eugenie, she thought insistently. He doesn't and he can't, because even if he
does, she's dead. She's dead.

"Richard," she said, "I've been thinking about the flats. Mine and yours. And which of them we *should* sell first, actually."

He braked for a light near Notting Hill station, where an unappealing crowd dressed in London black were clogging the pavements and distributing into the street their share of London rubbish. "I thought we'd decided all that."

"We had done, yes. But I've been thinking . . ."

"And?" He looked wary.

"Well, it seems to me that my flat would go faster, that's all. It's been done up. It's completely modernised. The building's smart. The neighbourhood's lovely. And it's freehold. I expect it would fetch quite enough for us to put money down on a house and not have to wait to sell both flats before we have a place for all of us."

"But we've already made the decision," Richard pointed out. "We've an estate agent coming—"

"We can put him off, surely. We can say we've changed our minds. Darling, let's face it. Your flat's hopelessly out of date. It's as ancient as Methuselah. And it's got less than fifty years left on the lease. It's in a good enough building—if the owners would ever get round to fixing it up—but it's going to be *months* before it sells. Whereas mine . . . You must see how different things could be."

The light changed and they continued through the traffic. Richard didn't speak till he made the turn into the antiques shop heaven that was Kensington

Church Street. He said, "Months. Yes. Right. It could take months to sell my flat. But is that really a problem? You can't want to move house for at least six months anyway."

"But—"

"It would be impossible in your condition, Jill. Worse, it would be nothing short of torture, and it might be dangerous." He swung them past the Carmelite Church and onwards down towards Palace Gate and South Kensington, weaving his way through buses and taxis. Another stretch of road, and he made the turn into Cornwall Gardens, going on to say, "Are you nervous, darling? You haven't said much about actually *having* the baby. And I've been preoccupied—first Gideon, now this . . . this other business—so I haven't done as right by you as I should have. Listen, I do know that."

"Richard, I quite understand how concerned you've been with Gideon unwell. I don't mean you to think—"

"I think nothing but that I adore you, you're having our child, and we've a life to establish together. And if you'd like me to be in Shepherd's Bush with you more frequently now that you're nearly due, I'm happy to do that."

"You're there every night already. I can hardly ask for more than that, can I?"

He reversed into a parking space some thirty yards distant from Braemar Mansions, after which he switched off the engine and turned to her. "You can

ask me for anything, Jill. And if it pleases you to offer your flat for sale before mine, then it pleases me.
But I won't have any part of your moving house
till you've had the baby and recovered from that,
and I seriously doubt your mother would disagree
with me."

Jill herself couldn't disagree. She knew her mother
would have a seizure at the thought of her packing up
her belongings and trekking *anywhere* other than from
kitchen to loo in less than three months after giving
birth. "Childbirth puts the female body through a
trauma, darling," Dora Foster would have said. "Coddle yourself. It may be your only chance to do so."

"Well?" Richard said, smiling at her fondly.
"What's your reply?"

"You are so wretchedly logical and reasonable.
How can I argue? What you've said makes such
sense."

He leaned towards her and kissed her. "You're ever
gracious in defeat. And if I'm not mistaken"—he
nodded towards the old Edwardian building as he
came round her side of the car and eased her up and
onto the pavement—"our estate agent is right on
time. Which bodes well, I think."

Jill hoped that was the case. A tall blond man was
mounting the front steps of Braemar Mansions, and as
Jill and Richard approached, he studied the line of
bells and pushed what appeared to be Richard's.

"You're looking for us, I believe," Richard called
out.

The man turned, saying, "Mr. Davies?"

"Yes."

"Thomas Lynley," he said. "New Scotland Yard."

LYNLEY ALWAYS MADE it a habit to gauge reactions when he introduced himself to people who weren't expecting him, and he did so now as the man and woman on the pavement paused before mounting the front steps to what was a considerably down-at-heel building at the west end of Cornwall Gardens.

The woman looked as if she'd normally be quite small, although at the moment she was swollen in every conceivable way from pregnancy. Her ankles in particular were the size of tennis balls, giving undue emphasis to her feet, which were themselves large and out of proportion to her height. She walked with the rolling gait of someone trying to keep her balance.

Davies himself walked with a stoop that promised to worsen as he grew older. He had hair that was faded from its original colour—ginger or blond, it was difficult to tell—and he wore it swept straight back from his forehead with no effort made to disguise its thinness.

Both Davies and the woman appeared surprised when Lynley introduced himself, the woman perhaps more so because she looked at Davies and said, "Richard? Scotland Yard?" as if she either needed his protection or wondered why the police were coming to call.

Davies said, "Is this about . . . ?" but changed course, perhaps with the realisation that a conversation on the front steps wasn't what he wanted to engage in with a police officer. He said, "Come in. We were expecting an estate agent. You've given us a surprise. This is my fiancée, by the way."

He went on to say that she was called Jill Foster. She looked to be somewhere in her thirties—plain but with very good skin and hair the colour of currants, cut simply just beneath her ears—and Lynley had assumed upon seeing her that she was another of Richard Davies' children or perhaps a niece. He nodded to her, taking note of the tightness with which she clutched Davies' arm.

Davies let them into the building, where he led the way up the stairs to his first-floor flat. It had a sitting room that overlooked the street, a dim rectangle broken by a window that was at the moment covered by shutters. Davies went to fold these back, saying to his fiancée, "Sit down, darling. Put your feet up," and to Lynley, "May I offer you something? Tea? Coffee? We're expecting an estate agent—as I said—and we haven't a great deal of time before he gets here."

Lynley assured them that the visit wouldn't take long, and he accepted a cup of tea to buy time to have a look round the sitting room at its clutter of belongings. These took the form of amateur photographs of outdoor scenes, countless pictures of Davies' virtuoso son, and a collection of hand-carved walking sticks that formed a circular decoration over the fireplace in the fashion of weaponry found in Scottish castles. There was also a surfeit of prewar furniture, stacks of newspapers and magazines, and a display of other memorabilia related to his son's career as a violinist.

"Richard's a bit of a pack rat," Jill Foster told Lynley as she lowered herself with some care into a chair whose need for re-stuffing and reupholstering was evidenced by the tufts of what looked like yellowish cotton wool pushing upwards like springtime's new growth. "You should see the other rooms."

Lynley picked up a photograph of the violinist in childhood. He was standing attentively, his instrument in his hand, gazing up at Lord Menuhin, who was in turn gazing down at him, instrument also in hand, smiling beneficently. "Gideon," Lynley said.

"The one, the only," Jill Foster replied.

Lynley glanced at her. She smiled, perhaps to take the sting from her words. "Richard's joy and the centre of his life," she said. "It's understandable but sometimes it does wear upon one."

"I expect it does. How long have you known Mr. Davies?"

With a grunt and a heave, she said, "Bother. This won't do," and moved from the armchair she'd chosen to lower herself to the sofa, where she raised her legs and put a cushion into position beneath her feet. She said, "God. Two more weeks. I begin to understand why they call it 'being delivered.'" She rested her back against a second cushion. Both were as threadbare as the furniture. "Three years now."

"He's looking forward to new fatherhood?"

"When most men his age are looking forward to

grandfatherhood," Jill replied. "But even at his age, yes. He's looking forward."

Lynley smiled. "My own wife's pregnant."

Jill's face altered brightly, the connection between them made. "Is she? Is this your first, Inspector?"

Lynley nodded. "I can take a leaf out of Mr. Davies' book. He seems devoted."

She smiled and rolled her eyes in good humour. "He's like a mother hen. Don't walk down the stairs too quickly, Jill. Don't take public transport. Don't drive in traffic. No. Don't drive at all, my dear. Don't go for a walk without a companion. Don't drink any-thing that contains caffeine. Carry your mobile everywhere you go. Avoid crowds, cigarette smoke, and preservatives. The list is endless."

"He's anxious for you."

"It's rather touching when it doesn't make me want to lock him in a cupboard."

"Did you have a chance to compare notes with his former wife? About her own pregnancies?"

"Eugenie? No. We never met. Previous wives and current wives. Or in my case wives-to-be. Some-times it's in the interest of wisdom to keep them apart, isn't it."

Richard Davies returned to them then, bearing a plastic tray on which sat a single cup and saucer ac-companied by a small jug of milk and a bowl of sugar cubes. He said to his fiancée, "Darling, you weren't wanting tea as well, were you?"

Jill said that she wasn't, and Richard settled in next to her, raising her painfully swollen feet to his lap after placing Lynley's tea on the side table next to the chair in which Jill had first been sitting.

"How can we help you, Inspector?" he asked.

Lynley took a notebook from his jacket pocket. He thought it an interesting question. Indeed, he thought all of Davies' behaviour interesting. He couldn't remember the last time he'd turned up on someone's doorstep unexpected, offered his identification, and been offered a cup of tea in welcome. The general responses to an unanticipated visit from the police were suspicion, alarm, and anxiety, no matter how hidden the recipient of the visit attempted to keep them.

Davies said, as if in expectation of just this reaction on Lynley's part, "I expect you've come about Eugenie. I wasn't much help to your Hampstead colleagues when I was asked to look . . . well, to look at her, actually. I hadn't seen Eugenie in years, and the injuries . . ." He raised his hands from his fiancée's feet, a hopeless gesture.

Lynley said, "I've come about Mrs. Davies. Yes."

At which point Richard Davies looked at his fiancée, saying, "Would you prefer to have a lie-down, Jill? I can let you know when the estate agent arrives."

"I'm fine," she said. "I share your life, Richard."

He squeezed her leg, saying to Lynley, "If you're here, then it must have been Eugenie. It would have been too much to hope for that someone other than Eugenie would have been carrying her identification."

"It was Mrs. Davies," Lynley said. "I'm sorry."

Davies nodded, but he didn't look mournful. He said, "It's been nearly twenty years since I last saw her. I feel sorry she had such an accident as she had, but my loss of her—our divorce—was long ago. I've had years to recover from her death, if you see what I mean."

Lynley could see. Permanent mourning on Davies' part would have suggested either a devotion to match Victoria's or an unhealthy obsession, which was fairly much the same. However, Davies had a misconception that wanted correcting. Lynley said, "I'm afraid it wasn't an accident. Your former wife was murdered, Mr. Davies."

Jill Foster raised herself from the cushion supporting her back. "But wasn't she . . . ? Richard, didn't you say . . . ?"

For his part, Richard Davies looked at Lynley steadily, his pupils growing larger. "I was told a hit-and-run," he said.

Lynley explained. Given information was always scant until they had the first of their reports from forensic. An initial inspection of the dead woman's body—not to mention where she'd been found—had certainly called for the conclusion that she'd been hit by someone who then fled the scene. But a closer examination had revealed that she'd been hit more than once, her body had been moved, and what tyre tracks they had found on her clothing and her corpse indicated the damage had been done by a single vehicle.

So their hit-and-run motorist was a murderer, and the death was no accident but a homicide.

"Good God." Jill held out a hand to Richard Davies, but he didn't take it. Instead, he seemed to go into himself, stunned, to a dark place from which she couldn't draw him.

Davies said, "But they gave me absolutely no indication . . ." He stared into nothing, murmuring, "God. How can things possibly get worse?" Then he looked at Lynley. "I shall have to tell Gideon. You will allow me to be the one to tell my son? He's been unwell for several months. He's been unable to play. This could push him . . . You *will* allow me to be the one? It won't be in the papers yet, will it? In the *Evening Standard*? Not before Gideon's been told?"

"That's in the hands of the press office," Lynley said. "But they'll hold back till the family's been notified. And you can help us with that. Aside from Gideon, are there other family members?"

"Her brothers, but God only knows where they are. Her parents were still alive twenty years ago, but they may well be dead by now. Frank and Lesley Staines. Frank was an Anglican priest, so you might start there—through the Church—to find him."

"And the brothers?"

"One younger, one older. Douglas and Ian. Again, I can't say if they're living or dead. When I first met Eugenie, she hadn't seen any of her family in years and she never saw them the entire time we were married."

"We'll try to find them." Lynley took up his cup in which a Typhoo tea bag drooped soggily against the side. He removed it and added a splash of milk before he said, "And you, Mr. Davies? When exactly did you last see your former wife?"

"When we were divorced. Perhaps . . . sixteen years ago? There were papers to sign in the course of the proceedings, and that was when I saw her."

"Since then?"

"Nothing. I'd spoken to her recently, though."

Lynley set his cup down. "When was this?"

"She'd been phoning regularly to ask about Gideon. She'd learned he wasn't well. This would have been . . ." He turned to his fiancée. "When was that awful concert, darling?"

Jill Foster met his gaze so steadily that the fact that he knew exactly when the concert had been was more than apparent. She said, "The thirtieth of July, wasn't it?"

"That sounds right, yes." And to Lynley, "Eugenie phoned shortly afterwards. I can't recall exactly when. Perhaps round the fifteenth of August. She'd kept in touch since then."

"The last time you spoke to her?"

"Sometime last week? I don't know exactly. I didn't think to make note of it. She phoned here and left a message. I phoned her back. There wasn't much to tell her, so the conversation was brief. Gideon— and I'd very much appreciate this bit staying confidential, Inspector—is suffering from acute stage fright. We've given out that it's exhaustion, but that's a bit of a euphemism. Eugenie wasn't taken in by it, and I doubt the public's going to accept it much longer."

"But she didn't visit your son? Did she contact him?"

"If she did, Gideon's said nothing to me about it. Which in itself would be a surprise. My son and I are quite close, Inspector."

Davies' fiancée lowered her eyes. Lynley made a mental tick next to the possibility of filial-paternal devotion's being a one-way street with only Richard Davies traveling down it. He said, "Your wife was on her way to see a man in Hampstead, evidently. She had his address with her. He's called J. W. Pitchley, but you may know him by his previous name, James Pitchford."

Davies' hands stopped caressing Jill Foster's feet. He became as still as a life-size Rodin.

"You remember him?" Lynley asked.

"Yes. I remember him. But . . ." Again, to his fiancée, "Darling, are you certain you don't want a lie-down?"

Her expression said volumes about her intentions: There was no way on earth that Jill Foster was going to toddle off to the bedroom now.

Davies said, "I'd be unlikely to forget anyone from that period of time, Inspector. Nor would you had you lived through it. James lodged with us for a number of years before Sonia, our daughter . . ." He left off the rest of the sentence, using that gesture with his fingers lifted briefly to express the rest.

"Have you any idea if your former wife kept in touch with this man? He's been interviewed and he himself says no. But in your phone conversations, did your wife ever mention him?"

Davies shook his head. "We never entertained any subject at all other than Gideon and Gideon's health."

"She made no mention of her family, then, of her life in Henley-on-Thames, of friends she may have made there? Of lovers?"

"Nothing at all like that, Inspector. Eugenie and I didn't part under the best circumstances. She walked out one day and that was the end of it. No explanation, no argument, no excuse. One day she was there; the next day she was gone, and four years later I heard from her solicitors. So the blood between us wasn't exactly flowing with the milk of human kindness. I'll admit that I wasn't particularly pleased to hear from her when I finally did."

"Could she have been involved with another man at the time she left you? This would be someone who may have recently re-entered her life."

"Pitches?"

"Pitchley," Lynley said. "Yes. Could she have been involved with Pitchley when he was James Pitchford?"

Davies considered this. "He was a good deal younger than Eugenie—fifteen years, perhaps? Ten? But Eugenie was an attractive woman, so I suppose it's possible there was something between them. Let me top up your tea, Inspector."

Lynley acquiesced to this idea. Davies eased himself from beneath Jill Foster's legs and took himself into the kitchen, where running water indicated a minute or two in which he'd be waiting for the kettle to boil. Lynley wondered about the time that this gained the man: why he wanted it, why he needed it. Surprise was piling upon shock, it was true, and Davies was of the generation for whom a display of emotion was tantamount to baring one's backside in Piccadilly Circus. And his fiancée was taking much careful notice of his every reaction, so he had good reason to want some moments to pull himself together. But still . . .

Richard Davies returned to them then, this time carrying a glass of orange juice as well, which he pressed upon his fiancée, saying, "You need the vitamins, Jill."

Lynley took his tea cup with thanks and said, "Your wife was involved with a man in Henley-on-Thames, a man called Wiley. Did she mention him to you in any of your conversations?"

"No," Davies said. "Really, Inspector, we confined ourselves to Gideon."

"Major Wiley tells us they were estranged, Gideon and his mother."

"Does he?" Richard asked. "I wouldn't choose that word myself. Eugenie left one day and never returned. If you want to call it estrangement, I suppose you can. I prefer abandonment."

"Her sin?" Lynley asked.

"What?"

"She told Major Wiley she had something she

wished to confess to him. Perhaps abandoning her child and her husband was it. She never was able to confess, by the way. Or so Major Wiley tells us."

"You think that Wiley . . . ?"

"We're just gathering information at this point, Mr. Davies. Is there anything you can add to what you've already told me? Is there anything your former wife might have said in passing that you didn't think of at the time as having significance, but that now—"

"Cresswell-White." Davies said it almost like a meditation, but when he repeated the name, he did so with more conviction. "Yes. There's Cresswell-White. I had a letter from him, so Eugenie must have done as well."

"And Cresswell-White is . . . ?"

"She *would* have had a letter from him, certainly, because when killers are released, the families are informed as a matter of course. At least, that's what my letter said."

"Killers?" Lynley said. "Have you had word about your daughter's killer?"

In answer, Richard Davies left the room and walked down a short corridor, where he entered another room. The sound of drawers and cupboards opening and shutting ensued. When he returned, he bore a legal-size envelope, which he handed over to Lynley. It contained a letter from one Bertram Cresswell-White, Esq., Queen's Counsel and all the window dressing, and it had been sent from Number Five Paper Buildings, Temple, London. It informed

Mr. Richard Davies that HM Prison Holloway would be releasing Miss Katja Wolff on parole on the date given below. Should Miss Katja Wolff harass, threaten, or even contact Mr. Davies in any way, Mr. Davies was to inform Mr. Cresswell-White, Q.C., immediately.

Lynley read the message and examined the date: twelve weeks to the day that Eugenie Davies had died. He said to Richard Davies, "Has she made contact with you?"

"No," Davies answered. "Had she done so, believe me, I swear to God I would have . . ." His bravado receded, the stuff of the younger man he no longer was. He said, "Might she have located Eugenie?"

"Mrs. Davies didn't mention her?"

"No."

"Would she have mentioned her had she seen her?"

Davies shook his head, not so much in denial as in confusion. "I don't know. At one time, yes. Of course she would have said something to me. But after all this time . . . I just don't know, Inspector."

"May I keep this letter?"

"Of course. Will you look for her, Inspector?"

"I'll have a man track her down." Lynley went through the rest of his questions, from which he learned only the identity of the Cecilia who'd written the note to Eugenie Davies: Sister Cecilia Mahoney, she was called, Eugenie Davies' close friend at the Convent of the Immaculate Conception. The convent itself was in Kensington Square, where the

Davies family had long ago lived. "Eugenie was a convert to Catholicism," Richard Davies said. "She hated her father—he was a raging maniac when he wasn't holier-than-thou from the pulpit—and it seemed the best way to get vengeance on him for a hellish childhood. At least that's what she told me."

"Were your children baptised Catholics, then?" Lynley asked.

"Only if she and Cecilia did it in secret. My own dad would have had a stroke otherwise." Davies smiled with fondness. "He was quite a tyrannical paterfamilias in his own way."

And have you taken a page from that book, Lynley wondered, despite your air of helpfulness now? But that was something he'd have to learn from Gideon.

GIDEON

1 OCTOBER

WHERE IS this taking us, Dr. Rose? You ask me to consider my dreams now as well as my memories, and I wonder if you know what you're doing. You ask me to write my random thoughts, to free myself from worrying about how they connect or where they might lead or how they might produce the key that will fit into the lock of my mind, and my patience with this process is wearing thin.

Dad informs me that your previous work in New York was primarily with eating disorders. He's been doing his prep where you're concerned—a few phone calls to the States was all it took—because as he sees no progress, he's begun to question how much more time I want to devote to dredging up the past instead of dealing with the present. "For God's sake, she doesn't work with musicians," he said when I spoke to him today. "She doesn't even work with other artists. So you can continue to fill her purse with money and get nothing in return—which is all that's been happening so far, Gideon—or you can try something else."

"What?" I asked him.

"If you're so insistent upon psychiatry as the answer, then at least try someone who'll address the problem. And the problem is the violin, Gideon. The problem is not what you do or do not remember about the past."

I said, "Raphael told me."

"What?"

"That Katja Wolff drowned Sonia."

There was silence at this, and as we were on the phone and not having the conversation in person, I could only guess at Dad's expression. His face would have hardened as the muscles tightened, and his eyes would have gone opaque. In telling me even as little as he told, Raphael had broken an agreement of twenty years' standing. Dad would not like that.

"What happened?" I asked.

"I won't discuss this."

"It's why Mother left us, isn't it?"

"I've told you—"

"Nothing. You've told me *nothing*. If you're so intent on helping me, why won't you help me with this?"

"Because *this* has sod all to do with your problem. But digging it all up, dissecting every nuance, and dwelling on them *ad infinitum* are brilliant ways to side-step the real issues, Gideon."

"I'm going at this the only way I can."

"Bollocks. You're following her dance steps like a nancy boy."

"That's bloody unfair."

"Unfair is being asked to stand to one side and watch your son throw his life away. Unfair is having lived solely for that son's benefit for a quarter of a century so that he can become the musician he wishes to be, only to have him fall to pieces the first time he has a setback. Unfair is crafting a relationship with that son unlike any I could ever have had with my own father and then being asked to step back while the love and trust that I've had with him for years gets transferred to some female psychiatrist with nothing more to recommend her than having managed to hike to Machu Picchu without having to be carried to the top."

"Jesus. How much nosing round have you done?"

"Enough to know how much time you're wasting. God damn it, Gideon"—but his voice wasn't hard when he said those words—"have you even tried?"

To play, naturally. That was what he needed to know. It was as if, to him, I'd ceased to be anything other than a music-making machine.

When I didn't reply, he said not unreasonably, "Don't you see, then, that this could be nothing more than a momentary blackout? A loose connection in your brain. But because you've never had the smallest blip in your career, you've panicked. Pick up the violin, for God's sake. Do it for yourself before it's too late."

"Too late for what?"

"To overcome the fear. Don't let it drag you down. Don't dwell on it."

At the end, his words didn't seem illogical. Instead, they seemed to indicate an action that was reasonable and sound. Perhaps I *was* making a mountain out of a dust speck, using a manufactured "illness of spirit" as a cover for a wound to my professional pride.

So I picked up the Guarneri, Dr. Rose. In the cause of optimism, I put the shoulder rest in place. I gave myself the break of sheet music—alleviating the pressure of having to produce a measure from memory by choosing the Mendelssohn that I'd played a thousand times before—and I found my body, as Miss Orr would have told me. I could even hear her: "Body up, shoulders down. Upbow with the *whole* arm. Only the tops of the fingers move."

I heard it all, but I could do none of it. The bow skittered across the strings, and my fingers flailed the gut with as much delicacy as a butcher dressing a pig.

Nerves, I thought. This is all about nerves.

So I tried a second time, and the sound was worse. And that's all it was that I produced: sound, Dr. Rose. I didn't come close to approaching music. As for actually playing the Mendelssohn . . . I might have been attempting a moon landing from the music room, so impossible was the task I'd undertaken.

How did it feel to make the attempt? you want to know.

How did it feel to close the coffin on Tim Freeman? I reply. Husband, companion, victim of cancer, and everything else that he was to you, Dr. Rose. How did it feel when your husband died? Because this is a death to me, and if there's going to be a resurrection, what I need to know is how it's going to be effected by sifting through the past and writing down my damn dreams. Tell me that, please. For God's sake, tell me.

2 OCTOBER

I didn't tell Dad.

Why? you ask.

I couldn't face it.

Face what?

His disappointment, I suppose. What it would do to him to know that I can't do what he wants me to do. He's fashioned his entire life round mine, and my entire life has been fashioned round my playing. Both of us are hurtling towards oblivion right now, and it seems an act of kindness if only one of us knows it.

When I set the Guarneri back into its case, I made my decision. I left the house.

On the front steps I met Libby, however. She was leaning next to the railing with a bag of marshmallows open on her lap. She didn't appear to be eating them, although she did look as if she were contemplating doing so.

I wondered how long she'd been sitting there, and when she spoke, I had my answer.

"I heard." She got to her feet, looked down at the bag, then stuffed it into the capacious front of her dungarees. "That's what's been wrong, isn't it, Gid? That's why you haven't been playing. Why didn't you *tell* me? I mean, I thought we were friends."

"We are."

"No way."

"Way," I said.

She didn't smile. "Friends help each other out."

"You can't help with this. I don't even know what's gone wrong with me, Libby."

She looked off bleakly into the square. She said, "Shit. What are we doing, Gid? Why're we flying your kites? Gliding your glider? Why the hell are we sleeping together? I mean, if you can't even talk to me—"

The conversation was a reenactment of a hundred discussions with Beth, with a slight change in subject. With her, it had been, "Gideon, if we can't even make love any longer . . ."

With Libby things hadn't gone far enough to make that a subject, for which I was grateful. I heard her out but had nothing to say. When she had finished talking and realised there would be no reply, she followed me to my car, saying, "Hey! Wait a minute. I'm talking to you. Wait a minute. *Wait.*" She grabbed my arm.

"I've got to go," I told her.

"Where?"

"Victoria."

"Why?"

"Libby . . ."

"Fine." And when I'd unlocked the car, she

climbed inside. "Then I'm coming with you," she said.

To rid myself of her, I would have had to remove her bodily from the car. And there was a set to her jaw and a steeliness in her eyes that told me she wouldn't be removed without putting up a monumental fight. I didn't have the energy or the heart for that, so I started the car and we drove to Victoria.

The Press Association has its offices just round the corner from Victoria Station on Vauxhall Bridge Road, and that's where I took us. On the way, Libby brought out the marshmallows, which she started to consume.

I said, "Aren't you on the No-White Diet?"

"These are coloured pink and green, in case you didn't notice."

"You once said white that's coloured artificially counts as white," I reminded her.

"I say lots of things." She slapped the plastic bag against her lap and appeared to reach a decision, because she said, "I want to know how long. And you'd better be totally straight with me."

"How long what?"

"How long not playing. Or playing like that. Just then. Like that. How long?" And then, in a switch that wasn't atypical of her, she said, "Never mind. I ought to have noticed before now. It's because of that bastard Rock."

"We can hardly blame your husband—"

"Ex. Please."

"Not yet."

"Close enough."

"Fine. But we can't blame him—"

"Loathsome as he is."

"—if I'm having a rough time just now."

"That's *so* not what I was talking about," she said, irritation in her voice. "There's more people on earth than you, Gideon. I was talking about myself. *I* would've noticed what's been happening with *you* if *I* hadn't been so strung out about Rock."

But I hardly heard what she said about her husband, because I was struck by her words: *more people on earth than you, Gideon,* and how they echoed almost exactly Sarah-Jane Beckett's sentiments all those years ago. *You're not the centre of the universe any longer.* And I couldn't see Libby in the car with me because all I could see was Sarah-Jane Beckett. I can see her still, I can see her eyes peering at me, her face bending over me. It's pinched, that face, with eyes that are narrowed to a band of stubby lashes.

What's she talking about when she says that? you ask me.

Yes. That's the question, all right.

I've been naughty while she was responsible for me. It's been left to her to determine my punishment, which has been a thorough wigging, Sarah-Jane style. There's a wooden box in Granddad's wardrobe and I've got into it. It's filled with old boot black, shoe polish, and rags, and I've used all this as paints. All along the first-floor corridor I've smeared brown polish and boot black on the walls. Bored, bored, *bored,* I've thought as I ruined the wallpaper and wiped my hands on the curtains. But I'm not bored, really, and Sarah-Jane knows. That's not why I've done it.

Do you know why you did it? you ask me.

I'm not sure now. But I think I'm angry, and I feel afraid. Quite distinctly and very much afraid.

I see the spark of interest in your face when I tell you this, Dr. Rose. Now we're getting somewhere. Angry and afraid. Emotion. Passion. Something, by God, that you can work with.

But I have little to add to that. Only this: When Libby said *more people on earth than you, Gideon*, what I felt distinctly was fear. It was a fear quite apart from the fear of never being able to play my instrument again, however. It was a fear that seemed entirely un-related to the conversation that she and I were hav-ing. Yet I felt it in such a sudden paroxysm that I heard myself cry "Don't!" at Libby, and all the while it wasn't Libby I was talking to at all.

And what is it you were afraid of? you inquire.

That, I would have thought, is obvious.

3 OCTOBER

We were directed up to the news library, a storage room where rack after rack of news cuttings are filed in manila folders and catalogued by subject along scores of rolling shelves. Do you know this place? News readers spend their days there, poring through every major paper, clipping and identifying stories which then become part of the library's collection.

Nearby, a single table and a photocopier serve members of the public who want to do research.

I told a poorly dressed, long-haired boy what I was looking for. He said, "You should've rung first. It'll take twenty minutes or so. That stuff's not kept up here."

I said that we'd wait, but I found that my nerves were tangled so excessively that I couldn't remain in the library once the young man had gone off on his search. I couldn't breathe, and in short order I found myself sweating as much as Raphael. I said to Libby that I needed some air. She followed me out onto Vauxhall Bridge Road. But I couldn't breathe there either.

"It's the traffic," I told Libby, "the fumes," and I found myself gasping like a winded runner. And then my viscera went into action: stomach clenching and bowels loosening, threatening a humiliating explosion right there on the pavement.

Libby said, "You look like hell, Gid."

I said, "No. No. I'm all right."

She said, "You're all right like I'm the Virgin Mary. C'mere. Get out of the middle of the sidewalk."

She led me round the corner to a coffee bar and sat me at a table. She said, "Don't move unless you're, like, going to faint, okay? In which case, put your head . . . somewhere. Where is it you're supposed to put your head? Between your knees?" Then she went to the counter and came back with some orange juice. "When was the last time you ate?" she asked.

And I—sinner and soft-spined poltroon—let her believe what she was believing. I said, "Can't remember exactly," and I downed the orange juice as if it were an elixir that could return to me everything that I have so far lost.

Lost? you repeat, ever vigilant for triggers.

Yes. What I've lost: my music, Beth, my mother, a childhood, memories that other people take for granted.

Sonia? you ask. Sonia as well? Would you have her back if you could, Gideon?

Yes, of course, is my reply. But a different Sonia.

And that answer stops me. Because contained within it is a reservoir of remorse for what I'd forgotten about my sister.

3 OCTOBER, 6:00 P.M.

When I was able to get my raging bowels under control and to breathe normally, Libby and I returned to the news library. There, five bulging manila envelopes awaited us, crammed with newspaper cuttings from over twenty years ago. They were roughly clipped from papers and dog-eared; they were musty smelling and discoloured with age.

While Libby searched out a second chair so that she could join me at the table, I reached for the first envelope and opened it.

KILLER NANNY CONVICTED leapt out at me, with the unspoken reassurance that little had changed with newspaper headlines in the last two decades. The

words were accompanied by a picture, and there she
was before me, my sister's killer. The photograph
looked as if it had been taken very early on in the legal process, since Katja Wolff had been caught by the
lens not at the Old Bailey or in prison somewhere but
in the Earl's Court Road as she came out of the Kensington police station in the company of a stubby man
in an ill-fitting suit. Just behind him, partially obscured by the doorway, was a figure I would not have
been able to make out had I not known the shape of
him and the size of him and the general look of him
from nearly twenty-five years of daily sessions on the
violin: Raphael Robson. I registered the presence of
these two men—assuming the former to be Katja
Wolff's solicitor—but what I focused on was Katja
herself.

Much had changed for her since the day of the
sunny picture that had been taken in the back garden.
Of course, that photograph had been posed while this
one had obviously been snapped in that frantic rush
that exists between the time a newsworthy figure
leaves a building and the time she enters a vehicle
which whisks her away. What was evident in the picture was that public notoriety—at least of this sort—
hadn't suited Katja Wolff. She looked thin and ill.
And whereas the back-garden shot had depicted her
smiling up at the camera openly and happily, this shot
had captured her trying to conceal her face. The photographer must have got in quite close, because the
picture wasn't grainy as one would expect from a

telephoto shot. Indeed, every detail of Katja Wolff's face seemed harshly highlighted.

Her mouth was pressed shut so her lips were thin. Dark skin formed half-moon bruises beneath her eyes. Her aquiline features had sharpened unappealingly from a loss in weight. Her arms were sticklike, and where her blouse formed a V, her collar bone looked like the edge of a plank.

I read the copy to find that Mr. Justice St. John Wilkes had passed the mandatory life sentence for murder upon Katja Wolff, with an unusual recommendation made to the Home Office that she serve no less than twenty years. According to the correspondent, who evidently had been present in the courtroom, the defendant had leapt to her feet upon hearing the sentence pronounced and demanded to speak. "Let me tell what happened," she was reported as saying. But her offer to speak now—after having maintained her right to silence not only through the trial but throughout the investigation as well— smacked of panic and deal-making, and it came too late.

"We know what happened," Bertram Cresswell-White, senior Treasury Counsel, declared later to the press. "We heard it from the police, we heard it from the family, we heard it from the forensic laboratory and from Miss Wolff's own friends. Placed in circumstances which she found increasingly difficult, seeking to vent her anger in a situation in which she felt she was being unfairly disciplined, and given the opportunity to rid the world of a child who was imperfect anyway, she willfully and with malice towards the Davies family shoved Sonia Davies beneath the water in her own bathtub and held her there—despite the child's pathetic struggles—until she drowned. At which point, Miss Wolff raised the alarm. This is what happened. This is what was proved. And it is for this that Mr. Justice Wilkes handed down the sentence required by law."

"She'll serve twenty years, Dad." Yes. Yes. That's what he says to Granddad when my father comes into the room where we are waiting for word: Granddad, Gran, and I. I remember. We are in the drawing room, lined up on the sofa, myself in the middle. And yes, my mother is there as well, and she's crying. As she always is, it seems to me, not just after Sonia's death but after Sonia's birth as well.

Birth is supposed to be a joyful time, but Sonia's birth could not have been. I finally realised that as I flipped the first news cutting over and looked at the second one—a continuation of the front-page story—that lay beneath it. For there I discovered a photograph of the victim, and to my shame I saw what I had forgotten or deliberately erased from my mind for more than two decades about my younger sister.

What I'd forgotten was the first thing that Libby noticed and mentioned when she rejoined me with a second chair, towing it along behind her as she came into the news library again. Of course, she didn't know it was my sister's picture since I hadn't told her why we'd come to the Press Association office in the first place. She'd heard me ask for cuttings on the Katja Wolff trial, but that was the extent of it.

Libby scooted herself to the table, half-turned towards me, and she reached for the picture, saying, "What've you got?" And then when she saw, she said, "Oh. She's Down's Syndrome, right? Who is she?"

"My sister."

"Really? But you've never said . . ." She looked from the picture to me. She went on carefully, either choosing her words or choosing how far she wished to go with their implications, "Were you, like . . . ashamed of her or something? I mean . . . Gosh. It's no big deal. Down's Syndrome, I mean."

"Or something," I said. "I was or something. Something contemptible. Something bad."

"What, then?"

"I couldn't remember her. Or any of this." I gestured to the files. "I couldn't remember any of this. I was eight years old, someone drowned my sister—"

"*Drowned* your—"

I clutched her arm to stop the rest. I had no need for the staff of the news library to know who I was. Believe me, my shame was great enough without having my identity attached to it openly.

"Look," I told Libby tersely. "Look for yourself. And I couldn't *remember* her, Libby. I couldn't remember the first bloody thing about her."

"Why?" she asked.

Because I didn't want to.

3 OCTOBER, 10:30 P.M.

I expect you to leap upon that admission with a warrior's triumph, Dr. Rose, but you say nothing. You merely watch me, and while you have schooled your features to betray nothing, you have little power over the light that comes to your eyes, dark though they might be. I see it there for just an instant—that spark again—and it tells me you wish me to hear what I myself have just said.

I couldn't remember my sister because I didn't *want* to remember her. That must be the case. We don't want to remember, so we choose to forget. Except isn't the truth that sometimes we simply don't need to remember. And other times we are *told* to forget.

Here's what I can't understand, though. My grandfather's episodes were the Great Unspoken in Kensington Square, and yet I remember them clearly. I have vivid memories of what led up to them, of the music that my grandmother used in an attempt to forestall them, of their occurrences and the chaos that accompanied them, and of the aftermath in which tears flowed as attendants fetched him for a spell in the country to rid him of them. Yet we never spoke of his episodes. So why do I remember them—and him—but not my sister?

Your grandfather figures larger in your life than your sister, you tell me, because of your music. He plays a leading part in the drama that is your musical history, even if a segment of his rôle takes place within the fiction that is the Gideon Davies Legend. To repress him as you've apparently repressed the memory of Sonia—

Repressed? Why *repressed*? Are you agreeing that I haven't *wanted* to have memories of my sister, Dr. Rose?

Repression isn't a conscious choice, you tell me, and your voice is quiet, compassionate, calm. It's associated with an emotional, psychological, or physical state too overwhelming for someone to handle, Gideon. For example, if as children we witness something terrifying or incomprehensible to us— sexual intercourse between our parents is a good illustration—we shove it out of our conscious awareness because at that age we have no tools to deal with what we've seen, to assimilate it in a fashion that makes sense to us. Even as adults, people who suffer horrific accidents generally have no memory of the catastrophe simply because it *is* horrific. We don't actively make the choice to shove an image from our mind, Gideon. We simply do it. Repression is how we protect ourselves. It's how our mind protects itself from something it isn't yet prepared to face.

Then what—*what*—can I not face about my sister, Dr. Rose? Although I did remember Sonia, didn't I? When I was writing about Mother, I remembered her. I'd blocked just one detail about her. Until I saw the picture, I didn't know she was Down's.

So the fact that she was *Down's* figures in all this,

doesn't it? It must, because it's the one detail that had to be revealed to me. I couldn't dredge it up. Nothing led me to it.

You weren't able to dredge up Katja Wolff either, you point out to me.

So Down's and Katja Wolff are connected, aren't they, Dr. Rose? They must be.

5 OCTOBER

I couldn't remain in the news library once I saw that picture of my sister and heard Libby voice what I myself could not say. I wanted to remain there. I had five envelopes of information in front of me, all detailing what had happened to my family twenty years ago. No doubt I would also have discovered within those envelopes every significant name of every person who had been involved in the investigation and the legal proceedings that followed it. But I found that I couldn't read any further once I saw that picture of Sonia. Because seeing that picture allowed me to visualise my sister under the water: with her so-round head turning side to side and her eyes—those eyes which even in a newspaper photograph show that she was born anomalous—looking looking always looking because they cannot keep themselves from looking upon her killer. This is someone she trusts, loves, depends upon, and needs, who is holding her down beneath the water, and she doesn't understand. She is only two years old, and even if she had been a normal child, she would not have understood what was happening. But she isn't normal. She wasn't born normal. And nothing in the two years that comprise her short life has ever been normal.

Abnormality. Abnormality leading to crisis. That's it, Dr. Rose. We have lurched from crisis to crisis with my sister. Mother weeps at Mass in the morning, and Sister Cecilia knows that she needs help. Not only does she need help to cope with the fact that she has given birth to a child who is different, imperfect, unusual, outstanding, or whatever else you want to call her, but she also needs practical help in the caring for her. Because despite the presence of one child a prodigy and the other child handicapped by a defect of birth, life must continue, which means Gran must still be in attendance on Granddad, Dad must have two jobs as before, and if I'm to continue with the violin, Mother must work as well.

The logical expense to cut is the violin and everything associated with it: release Raphael Robson from his duties, sack Sarah-Jane Beckett as my constant teacher, and send me to day school. With the enormous amount of money saved from these simple and expedient economies, Mother can stay at home with Sonia, see to her growing needs, and nurse her through the health traumas that come up continually.

But making this change is unthinkable to everyone, because at six and a half years old, I have already made my public debut, and to deny the world the gift of my music seems an act of egregious pettiness. Doing this, however, has certainly been mooted among my parents and grandparents. Yes. I remember now.

Mother and Dad are having a discussion in the drawing room and Granddad enters into it vociferously.
"Boy's a genius, a God damn *genius,*" he bellows at
them. And Gran is there, because I hear her anxious
"Jack, Jack," and I picture her scurrying to the stereo
and throwing on a Paganini for the savage breast re-
siding directly beneath Granddad's flannel shirt. "He's
already giving *concerts,* God damn it," Granddad rages.
"You'll cut him off from that over my dead body. So
for once in your life—just for flaming once, Dick—
will you please make the *right* decision?"

Neither Raphael nor Sarah-Jane is involved in this
debate. Their futures hang in the balance along with
my own, but they have as much say in what will happen as I do, which is none at all. The dispute goes on
for hours and days during my mother's convalescence
from her pregnancy, and both the dispute and the difficulties of my mother's recovery are exacerbated by
the health crises that Sonia experiences.

*The baby's been taken to the doctor . . . to hospital . . .
to Casualty.* There is all round us a pervasive sense of
tension, urgency, and fear that has never been in the
house before. People are stretched to the breaking
point with anxiety. Always the question hangs in the
air, What will happen next?

Crises. People are gone a great deal of the time.
There are gaps in which no one seems at home at all.
Just Raphael and I. Or Sarah-Jane and I. While
everyone else is with Sonia.

Why? you ask. What sort of crises did Sonia have?
I can only remember *He says he'll meet us at hospi-*

tal. Gideon, go to your room, and the sound of Sonia's weak crying, and I can hear that crying as it fades away when they carry her downstairs and out into the night.

I go to her room, which is next to mine. This is the nursery. A light has been left on, and there's some sort of machine next to her cot and straps that keep her hooked onto it while she sleeps. There is a chest of drawers with a carousel lamp on it, the same carousel lamp that I can remember watching turn round and round as I lay in my own cot, this very same cot. And I see the marks where I bit the railing, and I see the Noah's Ark transfers that I used to stare at. And I climb into the cot though I am six and a half years old and I curl up there and wait for what will happen.

What does happen?

In time, they return, as they always do, with medicine, with the name of a doctor they're to see in the morning, with a behavioural prescription or a cutting-edge diet that they're to adhere to. Sometimes they have Sonia with them. Sometimes she's being kept in hospital.

Which is why my mother weeps at Mass. And *yes,* this is what she and Sister Cecilia must be talking about when we go with her into the convent that day that I overturn the bookshelf and break the statue of the Virgin. She murmurs mostly, this nun, and I assume it's to comfort my mother, who must feel . . . what? Guilt because she's given birth to a child who's suffering one illness after the next, anxiety because the *what can happen next* is always loitering outside her front door, anger at the inequities of life, and sheer exhaustion from trying to cope.

Out of all this fertile turbulent soil must grow the idea of hiring a nanny. A nanny could be the solution for everyone. Dad could continue his two jobs, Mother could return to work, Raphael and Sarah-Jane could remain with me, and the nanny could help to care for Sonia. James the Lodger would be there to bring in extra funds, and perhaps another lodger could be accommodated. So Katja Wolff comes to us. As things turn out, she isn't a trained nanny, however. She hasn't been to a specialised course or a college to earn a certificate in child care. But she is educated and she is helpful, affectionate, grateful, and—it must be said—affordable. She loves children, and she needs the job. And the Davies family need help.

6 OCTOBER

I went to see Dad that same evening. If anyone holds the anamnestic key I'm trying to find, it's going to be my father.

I found him at Jill's flat, on the front steps of the building, in fact. The two of them were in the midst of one of those polite but tense arguments that loving couples have when they each have reasonable desires that have come into conflict. This one apparently involved whether Jill—as she approached her due date—was still going to drive herself round London.

Dad was saying, "That's dangerous and irresponsible. It's a wreck, that car. For God's sake, I'll send a taxi round for you. I'll drive you myself."

And Jill was saying, "Would you *stop* treating me like a piece of Lalique? I can't even breathe when you're like this."

She began to go inside the building, but he took her by the arm. He said, "Darling. Please," and I could tell how afraid for her he was.

I understood. My father hadn't been blessed with luck in his children. Virginia, dead. Sonia, dead. Two out of three were not the sort of odds to give a man peace of mind.

To her credit, Jill seemed to recognise this as well. She said, more quietly, "You're being silly," but I think there was a part of her that appreciated the degree to which Dad was solicitous for her well-being. And then she saw me standing on the pavement, hesitating between skulking off and striding forward with a hearty hello that attempted to demonstrate a level of bonhomie that I did not feel. She said, "Hullo. Here's Gideon, darling," and Dad swung round, releasing her arm, which freed her to unlock the front door and usher both of us up to her flat.

Jill's flat is everywhere modern in a period building that was gutted several years ago by a clever developer who completely updated it within. It's all fitted carpets, copper pans hanging from the kitchen ceiling, gleaming mod cons that actually work, and paintings that look as if they intend to slide off their canvases and do something questionable on the floor. It is, in short, perfectly Jill. I wonder how my father

is going to cope with her decorating preferences
when at last they begin to cohabit. Not that they're
not already as good as cohabiting. My father's hovering over Jill is becoming somewhat obsessive.

With his paranoia about the new baby rising daily,
I wondered if I should broach the subject of Sonia
with him. My body told me not: I found that my
head had begun a vague aching, and my stomach
burned, but it burned in a way that told me I could
not attribute it to anything other than nerves.

Jill said, "I've got some work to do, so I'll leave
you two to your own devices. I don't expect you've
come to visit me, have you?"

I suppose I *should* have considered dropping in to
see Jill now and again, especially as she is to be my
step-mother, odd though the proposition seems. But
I could tell by the way she asked her question that she
was merely sorting out information and not implying
anything the way so many women do.

I said, "There are one or two things . . ."

She said, "I expect there are. I'll be in the study,"
and she went in that direction.

When Dad and I were alone, we repaired to the
kitchen. Dad moved Jill's impressive coffee maker
into the centre of the work top and fetched some
espresso beans, which he poured inside. The coffee
maker—like the flat itself—is quintessentially Jill. It's
an amazing machine with a capability of producing
one fresh cup of anything in less than a minute: coffee, cappuccino, espresso, latte. It steams milk and
boils water and I expect it would do the washing up,

the laundry, and the hoovering if you programmed it thus. Dad used to scoff at the appliance, but I noticed that he was using it like a pro.

He took out two demitasse cups and their saucers. From a bowl near the sink, he found a lemon. He was searching for the proper knife with which to carve us each a curl of the peel when I spoke.

"Dad, I've seen a picture of Sonia. I mean a better picture than the one you showed me. A newspaper picture from the time of the trial."

He turned a dial on the coffee machine, replaced its single spout with a double one that he took from a drawer, and put the two small cups in position. He pushed a button. A gentle whirring ensued. He gave his attention to the lemon again, making a curving sliver that would have done credit to a chef at the Savoy. "I see," was all he said. He began a second slice.

"Why did no one tell me about it?" I asked.

"About what?"

"You know. The trial. How Sonia died. Everything. Why didn't we talk about it?"

He shook his head. He had finished the second lemon-peel curl—as perfectly carved as was the first—and when the espresso was done, he plopped a curl in each cup and handed me mine. He said, "Out here?" and cocked his head in the direction of the sitting room off which a terrace overlooked other similar period buildings nearby.

On a grey day such as this, the terrace didn't promise much comfort. But it did offer the benefit of privacy, which I wanted with Dad, so I followed him out.

As I suspected, we were completely alone there. The other terraces from the building were deserted. Jill's outdoor furniture was already covered, but Dad removed the plastic sheeting from two of the chairs and we sat. He set his espresso on his knee and zipped his parka. He said, "I didn't keep the newspapers. I didn't look at them. What I wanted more than anything was to forget. I realise that's probably anathema to the current thinking among mental health experts. Aren't we all supposed to wallow in recollection till we reek of the stench? But I don't come from an age when that was fashionable, Gideon. I lived through it—the days and weeks and months of it—and when it was over, I wanted nothing more than to forget it had ever happened."

"Is that how Mother felt as well?"

He lifted his cup. He drank, but he observed me as he did so. "I don't know how your mother felt. We couldn't talk about it. None of us could talk about it. To talk about it meant to relive it, and living through it once was horror enough."

"I need to talk about it now."

"More of your Dr. Rose's sterling recommendations? Sonia loved the violin, if that's of interest to you. She loved *you* and the violin, more precisely. She spoke very little—language comes late to a Down's child—but she could say your name."

That was like the precise administering of a

wound, a delicate but perfectly accurate incision into my heart. I said, "Dad—"

He cut in. "Never mind. That was low of me."

"Why did no one speak of her afterwards? After she . . . after the trial?" I asked the question but the answer was obvious: We never spoke of anything frightful. Granddad raged like a maniac periodically; he was carted, dragged, led, or carried out into the night or the morning or the heat of the afternoon and he did not return for weeks, and we did not mention the fact at any time. Mother vanished one day, taking with her not only every possession she owned but also every reminder that she had ever been part of the family, and we did not concern our-selves with a discussion of where she might have gone or why. And there I sat on my father's lover's terrace, wondering why we never spoke of Sonia's life or her death when we were and had always been a group of people who spoke of nothing: nothing painful, nothing heartbreaking, nothing horrifying, nothing grievous.

"We wanted to forget it had happened."

"Forget Mother had happened? Forget Sonia her-self had happened?"

He observed me and I saw that opaqueness in his eyes, that expression that had always succeeded so well in defining a territory whose landscape was ice, bitter wind, and endless smoke-coloured sky. "That's unworthy of you," he said. "I think you know what I'm talking about."

"But never to say her name. All those years. To me. Never to say even the words *your sister . . .*"

"There would have been profit in that, you think? You would have gained something had Sonia's murder become part of the daily fabric of our lives. Is that your conclusion?"

"I just don't understand—"

He drank down the rest of his espresso and put the cup on the terrace, next to the leg of his chair. His face was as grey as his hair, which swept back from his forehead as my own hair does, with that very same widow's peak in the centre, with those same indentations like fjords on either side. He said, "Your sister was drowned in her bath. She was drowned by a German girl we'd taken into our home."

"I know—"

"Nothing. That's what you know. You know what the papers might have told you but you don't know what it was to be there. You don't know that Sonia was murdered because she was growing progressively more difficult to care for and because the German girl—"

Katja Wolff, I thought. Why won't he say her name?

"—was pregnant."

Pregnant. The word was a snap of the fingers in front of my face. The word brought me back to my father's world and what he had lived through and what the present circumstances were asking him to live through again. I thought back to the picture of Katja Wolff smiling dreamily up at the camera in the

Kensington Square garden with Sonia in her arms. I thought of the picture of her leaving the police station, stick thin and ill-looking with features sharpened by excessive weight loss. Pregnant.

I murmured, "She didn't look pregnant in the picture," and I looked away from Dad to one of the other terraces where, I noticed, an Old English sheep dog was watching us curiously. As he saw me take note of him, he rose on his hind legs, front paws on the iron rail that surrounded the terrace. He began to bark. I shivered at the sound. He'd had his vocal cords removed and what remained was a hopeful but pathetic yelp that was air and muscle and mostly cruelty. It made me feel sick.

Dad said, "What picture?" And then he must have reckoned I was speaking of a photo I'd seen in the newspaper, because he said, "It wouldn't have shown. She was deadly ill at the start of her pregnancy, so she didn't put on weight, she lost it. We noticed first that she'd gone off food, that she didn't look well, and we thought it was a lover's spat of some kind. She and the lodger—"

"That would've been James."

"Yes. James. They were close. Obviously, a hell of a lot closer than we originally assumed. He liked to help her with her English when she had free time. We had no objection to that. Until she came up pregnant."

"Then what?"

"We told her she'd have to go. We weren't running a home for unmarried mothers, and we needed someone whose attention would be kept on Sonia, not on herself: her illness, her difficulty, her condition, whatever you want to call it. We didn't throw her out on the street or even tell her she had to leave at once. But as soon as she was able to find another . . . situation, job, she would have to go. That would have taken her away from James, though, and she snapped."

"Snapped?"

"Tears, anger, hysteria. She couldn't cope. Not with pregnancy, unremitting illness during pregnancy, looming homelessness, and your sister as well. Sonia was just out of hospital at the time. She needed constant care. The German girl snapped."

"I remember."

"What?" I could hear the reluctance behind the question, that conflict between Dad's desire to put an end to a reminiscence that was painful for him and his wish to liberate from a prison of mind the son he loved.

"Crises. Sonia being carried to the doctor, to hospital, to . . . I don't know where else."

He sank back in his chair and, like me, looked over at the dog who so wanted our attention. He said, "No place for a creature with complicated needs," and I couldn't tell if he was referring to the animal, to himself, to me, or to my sister. "At first it was her heart. An atrioseptal defect, it was called. It wasn't long—just after her birth—when we knew from her colour and her pulse that there was trouble. So they performed an operation on her and we thought,

Right. That's taken care of the problem. But then it was her stomach: duodenal stenosis. Very common among Down's children, we were told. As if her being Down's in the first place was as minor an issue as the poor creature having a wandering eye. More surgery then. After that, imperforate anus. Hmm, we were told, this particular little one appears to be at the farthest extreme of the syndrome. So *many* problems. Let's see if we can cut her open again. And again. And again. And then give her hearing aids. And bottles of medicine. And of course, we can only hope she'll be happy to have her body invaded and probed and rearranged on a regular basis till we get her sorted out."

"Dad . . ." I wanted to prevent the rest. He'd said enough. He'd gone through enough: not only to have lived through her suffering but also to have lived through her death. And before that death, to have borne his own grief, my mother's, and no doubt his parents' . . .

Before I could finish what I'd wanted to say to him, I heard my grandfather all at once again. I felt the breath leave me as if I'd taken a punch to the gut, but I had to ask. I said, "Dad, how did Granddad cope with all this?"

"Cope? He wouldn't attend the trial. He—"

"I don't mean the trial. I mean Sonia. How she . . . how she was."

And I can hear him, Dr. Rose. I can hear him howling as he always howled—Lear-like—although the storm that raged round him was not of the moors but of his own mind. Freaks! he's shouting. You're capable of giving me nothing but freaks! There's spittle at the corners of his mouth, and although my grandmother takes his arm and murmurs his name, he hears and is aware of nothing but the wind and the rain and the thunder in his head.

Dad said, "Your grandfather was a troubled man, Gideon. But a great and good man. His demons were fierce, but so was his battle against them."

"Did he love her?" I asked. "Did he hold her? Did he play with her? Did he think of her as his grandchild?"

"Sonia was ill for a great part of the time she was with us. She was very fragile."

"So he didn't, did he?" I asked my father. "He didn't . . . anything."

Dad made no reply. Instead, he rose and walked to the railing. The Old English sheep dog yelped in near soundlessness, pawing at his own rails with an eagerness that was as obvious as it was pathetic. "Why do they *do* that to animals?" Dad said. "For the love of God, it's so bloody unnatural. If people want a pet, they should accommodate the pet. If they don't, they should damn well get rid of it."

"You aren't going to tell me, are you?" I asked him. "About Granddad and Sonia. You aren't going to tell me."

"Your grandfather was who your grandfather was," my father replied. And that was the end of it.

EIGHT

LIBERTY NEALE knew that if she'd only had the luck to meet Rock Peters somewhere in Mexico and to marry him there, she wouldn't have been in her current position because she could have divorced the creep in a micro-flash and that would have been the end of it. But no, she hadn't met him in Mexico. She hadn't even *gone* to Mexico. She'd come to England because she'd been such a total zero in foreign language in high school that England was the closest place to California that resembled a foreign country, where people spoke a language that Libby understood. Canada hardly counted.

She would have preferred France—she had a major thing for croissants, although the less said about *that* the better—but a few days in London had provided her with a wider range of eating experiences than she'd anticipated, so she'd managed to settle in happily, out of the reach of her parents and, more importantly, thousands of miles away from that living example of human perfection, her older sister. Equality Neale was tall, thin, intelligent, articulate, and disgustingly successful at everything she did. *And* she'd been elected homecoming queen at Los Altos High School, which was enough to make anyone blow major chunks into the next time zone. So getting away from Ali had been priority numero uno, and London had made that possible.

But in London, Libby had met Rock Peters. In London, she had married the creep. And in London—where she hadn't yet got round to scoring anything closely resembling a work permit or a permanent resident's card despite her marriage—she was at Rock's mercy, whereas in Mexico, it would have been "kiss my ass, Jack," and money or not, she could have gotten away from him. She still wouldn't have had the bucks to do it, but that wouldn't have mattered because the thumb spoke a universal language and she wasn't afraid to put herself out on the road and use it. Which was something she couldn't do from England since hitching a ride across the Atlantic to get away from Rock wasn't exactly possible.

Rock had her . . . well, he had her by the balls, figuratively speaking. She wanted to stay in England because she didn't want to go home and admit defeat when *every* letter she got from California was filled to the brim with Ali's latest success. But to stay in England, she needed money. And to get money, she needed Rock. True, she could have made some bucks even more illegally than she was already making them, but getting caught would have meant getting deported, which would have meant back to Los Altos Hills, back to Mom and Dad, and back to

"Why don't you go to work for Ali for a time, Lib? In public relations, you could—" blah blah blah. No way in hell, Libby told herself, was she going to put herself anywhere *near* her sister.

So when Rock wanted something, she was basically his slave. Which was why she was back to screwing the shithead two or three times a week upon demand. She'd try to avoid it, usually by pointing out that there was a delivery needing to be made and since she was the most reliable of his couriers, shouldn't she make it? But that usually didn't work because when Rock wanted sex, Rock wanted sex, and it never took him much time to ride the train to the station anyway.

That was what had happened this day, back in the Bermondsey hovel above the grocery store where, if she concentrated on the traffic noises below, she'd always been able to avoid hearing Rock grunting in her ear like a constipated pig. As always, she'd been so pissed off after screwing him that she wanted to amputate his cock with a saw. That not being possible, she'd gone to her tap-dancing lesson instead.

She'd tapped herself into the sweat of the century, shuffling, chugging, flapping, and spanking till she was dripping wet. The instructor kept yelling, "Libby, what are you *doing* over there?" above the strains of "On the Sunny Side of the Street," but Libby had ignored her. It hadn't mattered whether she was in step, out of step, in line, out of line, or even in the same hemisphere as her fellow tappers. What mattered was doing something hard, something fast, something that was demanding and physical in order to put Rock Peters from her mind. If she didn't do that, she'd end up in front of the closest refrigerator, and approximately six billion calories later, she'd find herself recovered from Rock's brand of blackmail.

"Think of it this way, Lib," he'd say when it was over and she lay beneath him, defeated again, "It's tit for tat, pardon the pun," and he'd offer that grin she'd first thought so cool and later learned to recognise for the sign of contempt it actually was. "You scratch my itch and I scratch yours. 'Sides, you're not getting any from the fiddler, are you? I know when a bird's been rogered proper and you've the look of someone who hasn't had a decent shagging in more'n a year."

"That's right, I haven't, you total dickhead," she'd snap. "*Think* about it, Rock. And he's not a fiddler. He plays the violin."

"Ooooh. Pardon my French," he'd say. And it mattered exactly zero to the former Rocco Petrocelli that she'd put down his ability as a lover. To him, success in bed meant getting his rocks off. What happened to his partner was left to self-stimulation or coincidence.

Libby departed the dance studio in a better frame of mind, her leotard and tap shoes stuffed into her backpack and that outfit replaced by the leathers which she wore when she made her courier stops. Helmet under her arm, she strode to the Suzuki and she used the kick starter instead of the electric ignition, the better to think about tromping on Rock's face.

The streets were clogged—like, when *weren't* they clogged?—but she'd spent enough time on the bike to know not only which side streets to take but also how to squeeze between cars and delivery trucks when traffic had come to a standstill. She had a Walkman that she usually wore on deliveries, the recorder tucked into an inner pocket of her leathers and the helmet holding the earphones in place. She liked bubble-gum music, she liked it loud, and she generally sang along, because the combination of music blasting against her eardrums and her own voice singing at maximum volume pretty much took care of whatever was left in her head that she didn't want to think about.

But she didn't use the Walkman today. The tap dancing had wiped away the image of Rock's hairy body mashed on top of her and his salami-red cock shoving between her legs. And as for the rest of what was in her head: That was something she *wanted* to think about.

Rock was right: She still hadn't gotten Gideon Davies to bed—as in *really* to bed—and she couldn't figure out why. He seemed to like being with her, and he seemed normal in every way other than what wasn't happening between them in the sack. Yet in all the time she'd been living below him and hanging with him, they'd never progressed beyond the point where they'd been that first night when they fell asleep on her bed while listening to a CD. That was it with a capital *I* as far as the sex part went.

At first she'd thought the dude was gay and her radar had gone totally down for the count after being with Rock for so long. But he didn't *act* gay or do the gay scene in London or even have younger guys, older guys, or obviously *twisted* guys up to his place in private. All he had was his dad—who hated her guts and was all Mr. Major Attitude whenever she and he were actually breathing the same air for five seconds—and Rafe Robson, who hung around Gideon day and night like a case of the hives. All of this had long ago made Libby conclude that there was nothing strictly *wrong* with Gideon that a decent relationship couldn't straighten out . . . if she could just get him away from his keepers for a while.

Having left the South Bank, where her tap lesson was, having woven her way through the worst of the traffic through the City and upwards to Pentonville Road, she opted to shoot through the by-ways of Camden Town rather than take on the crush of cars, taxis, buses, and trucks that were always making a mess of every street within spitting distance of King's Cross Station. Her route to Chalcot Square wasn't a direct one as a result, but that was cool as far as Libby was concerned. She didn't mind having more time to plan an approach that might work as a breakthrough with Gideon. To her way of thinking, Gideon Davies had to be more than simply a man who'd been playing the violin since he was just out of diapers. Yeah, it was cool that he was a major big deal as a musician, but he was also a *person*. And that person was more than just the music he made. That person could exist whether he played the violin or not.

When Libby finally arrived in Chalcot Square, the first thing she saw was that Gideon wasn't alone. Raphael Robson's ancient Renault stood at the south edge of the square, parked with one wheel on the sidewalk like he'd been in a hurry. Through the lit window to Gideon's music room, Libby noted that the unmistakable shape of Rafe—handkerchief, as always, mopping up the sweat on his face—was moving about, and he was talking. Preaching, more likely. And Libby knew about what.

"Shit," she muttered as she gunned up to the house. She revved the engine a few times in the cause of letting off steam and she pulled the Suzuki onto its kick stand. Rafe Robson didn't usually turn up in Chalcot Square at this time of day, and to have him here now—no doubt droning on and on about what Gideon ought to be doing that he wasn't doing, which was naturally whatever Rafe *wanted* him to do—was a real bummer that, in combination with what she'd already been through, having to screw Rock Peters, really ticked her off.

She shoved through the gate in the wrought iron railing and didn't stop it from clanging against the concrete that defined the upper steps to the house. She flung herself downwards, banged her way into the basement flat, and without a second thought dived straight for the refrigerator.

She'd been trying to stay on the No-White Diet,

but now—tap dancing be damned—she was definitely craving something pale. Vanilla ice cream, popcorn, rice, potatoes, cheese. She thought she might
freak if she didn't have it.

Months ago, however, she'd prepared the refrigerator door for a moment just like this. Before she
could open the appliance, she was forced to look
upon a picture of herself at sixteen years of age, a
tubbo in a one-piece bathing suit standing next to her
size-five sister in a butt-floss bikini . . . *and* with a
perfect tan, of course. Libby had put a sticker over
Ali's face: a spider wearing a cowboy hat. But now
she peeled the sticker off, gazing long and hard upon
her sister, and just for good measure she read the message that she'd penned for herself across the refrigerator door. *IN THROUGH THE LIPS AND ONTO THE HIPS!!!*
She took her inspiration where she could.

She sighed and backed off, which was when she
heard it: the violin music floating down from above.
She thought for a moment, "Omigod! He's cracked
it," and she felt a surge of pleasure at the realisation
that Gideon's problems might be over, that his most
recent plan for solving his problem had actually done
the job.

This was very cool. This would make him happy.
And it had to be Gideon who was playing upstairs. It
wouldn't, after all, be Rafe Robson, who couldn't
possibly be so uncool as to torture Gid by playing the
violin in front of him while Gid was having such
trouble playing himself.

But just as she was celebrating the fact of Gideon

Davies' return to his music, the rest of the orchestra started grinding away. A CD, Libby thought despairingly. It was Rafe's little pep talk for Gideon's ears: See how you once played the music, Gideon? You did it then. You can do it now.

Why, Libby wondered, wouldn't they leave him the hell alone? Did they think he'd start playing if they bugged him enough? Because they sure as hell were beginning to bug her. "He's more than this stupid *music,*" she snarled at the ceiling above her.

She left the kitchen and marched to her own small CD player. There, she selected a disk that was guaranteed to drive Raphael Robson right up the wall. It was bubble gum squared, and she played it loud. Just for good measure, she opened her windows. Banging on the floor above ensued in short order. She turned the volume up to full blast. Time for a nice long bath, she thought. Bubble-gum music was, like, *so* perfect for soaking, soaping, and singing along.

Thirty minutes later, bathed and dressed and feeling that she'd made her point, Libby turned off the CD player and listened for any more sounds from above. Silence. She'd made her point.

She left the flat and popped her head above the level of the street to see if Rafe's car was still in the square. The Renault was gone, which meant Gideon might be ready for a visit from someone who cared more about him as a person than as a musician. She trotted up the stairs from her flat to his front door, where she gave a hearty knock.

No answer prompted her to turn back to the

square, taking a look for Gideon's Mitsubishi and seeing the GPS five cars along. Libby frowned, gave another knock, and called out, "Gideon? You still in
there? It's me."

This roused him. The dead bolt was released from
the other side of the door. The door swung open.

Libby said, "Hey, sorry about the music. I sort of
lost control and—" She cut her own words off. He
looked like hell. True, he hadn't looked good in
weeks, but now he was positively bird-doo on a
cracker. Libby's first thought was that Rafe Robson
had worked Gideon over by making him listen to his
own recordings. Bastard, she thought.

She said, "Where's good ol' Rafe? Gone to make
his report to your dad?"

Gideon merely stepped back from the door and let
her in. He went up the stairs, and she followed him.
His destination was where he'd obviously been when
she'd knocked on his door: the bedroom. The im-
print of his head on the pillow and his body on the
bed looked pretty recent.

A dim light was burning on the bedside table, and
the shadows not dispelled by its glow fell on Gideon's
face and made him look cadaverous. He'd been surrounded by an aura of anxiety and defeat since the
Wigmore debacle, but Libby saw that there was
something more edging that aura now, something
that looked . . . what? Excruciating, she realised. So
she said, "Gideon, what's wrong?"

He said simply, "My mother's been murdered."

She blinked. Her jaw dropped. She snapped it

closed. "Your *mom*? Your *mother*? Oh *no*. When? How? Holy *shit*. Sit down." She urged him over to his bed and he sat, his hands hanging limply between his knees. "What happened?"

Gideon told her what little there was to know. He concluded with, "Dad was asked to identify her body. The police've been to see him since. A detective, Dad said. He rang a while ago." Gideon clutched his arms around himself, bent forward, and rocked like a child. He said, "That's it, then."

"What?" Libby asked.

"There's no hope after this."

"Don't say that, Gideon."

"I might as well be dead, too."

"Jeez. Hey. Don't *say* that."

"It's the truth." He shivered as he said this and glanced round the room as if looking for something while he continued to rock.

Libby thought about what it meant that his mother was dead. She said, "Gideon, you're going to get through all this. You're going to get past it," and she tried to sound like she really meant those words, like whether he played his music or not was as important to her as it was to him.

She noticed that his shivering had turned to trembling. At the foot of his bed was a knitted blanket, and she grabbed this and dropped it around his thin shoulders. "You want to talk about it?" she asked him. "About your mom? About . . . I don't know . . . anything?" She sat beside him and put her arm around him. She used her other hand to close the blanket at his throat till he grasped it as well and clutched it.

He said, "She was on her way to see James the Lodger."

"Who?"

"James Pitchford. He lived with us when my sister was . . . when she died. And it's odd because I'd been thinking of him myself recently, although before that he hadn't crossed my mind in years." Gideon grimaced then, and Libby noticed that the hand not clutching the blanket was pressed into his stomach as if something inside were burning his guts. "Someone ran her down in James Pitchford's street," he said. "More than once, Libby. And because she was on her way to see James, Dad thinks the police are going to want to track down everyone who was involved . . . back then."

"Why?"

"Because of the kind of questions they asked him, I dare say."

"I don't mean why does he think the cops want to track down everyone. I mean why would they *want* to track down everyone. Is there a connection between then and now? I mean, obviously if your mom was going to see James Pitchford, there's some sort of connection. But if someone from twenty years ago killed her, why wait till now to do it?"

Gideon bent forward farther, his face contorted with pain. He said, "God. It feels like a coal's burning right through me."

"Here, then." Libby lowered him to bed. He curled on his side, his legs drawn up to his chest. She removed his shoes. His feet were sockless and as pale as milk, and he rubbed them together spasmodically, as if the friction could take his mind from the pain.

Libby lowered herself next to him, spooning her body into his beneath the blanket. She insinuated her hand beneath his arm and laid her palm on his stomach. She could feel his spine curved into her, every knob of it like a marble. He'd become so thin that she wondered how he kept his bones from poking through his papery skin.

She said, "I bet you've had a brain lock on this stuff, huh? Well, forget about it. Not for always. Just for now. Lay here with me and just forget."

"I can't," he said, and he gave a bitter laugh. "Remembering everything is my assignment." His feet rubbed. He curled into himself further still. Libby held him closer. He finally said, "She's out of gaol, Libby. Dad knew, but he didn't tell me. That's why the police want to look at twenty years ago. She's out of gaol."

"Who is? You mean . . . ?"

"Katja Wolff."

"Do they think she might have run down your mom?"

"I don't know."

"Why would she? It makes more sense that your mom would want to run down her."

"In the normal way of things," Gideon said. "Except nothing about my life has been normal, so there's no reason why my mother's death should be normal either."

"Your mom must have testified against her," Libby said. "And she could have spent her time locked up planning to get everyone who put her there. But if she did, how'd she find your mom, Gideon? I mean, you didn't even know where she was. How could this Wolff chick have tracked her down? And if she *did* track her down, and if she did kill her, why'd she kill her on this Pitchford guy's street?" Libby thought about her questions and then answered them herself. "To give Pitchford a message?"

"Or to give someone else one."

A PHONE CALL relayed to Barbara Havers what Lynley had learned from Richard Davies, including the name she needed to gain access to the Convent of the Immaculate Conception. There, he told her, she should find someone who could give her the where-abouts of a Sister Cecilia Mahoney.

The convent sat on a piece of land that was prob-ably worth a king's ransom, tucked among a host of listed properties dating from the 1690s. This would have been where the movers and shakers had built their rural retreats during the time that William and Mary had built their own little humble country cot-tage in Kensington Gardens. Now the movers and shakers in the square were the employees of several business establishments that had shoe-horned them-selves into the historic buildings, denizens of a second convent—where the bloody hell did *nuns* get the lolly to have digs round here? Barbara wondered—and inhabitants of a number of homes that had probably been handed down through families for more than three hundred years. Unlike some of the city squares that had suffered bomb damage or the ravages of greed from consecutive Tory governments with big business, vast profits, and the privatisation of everything in mind, Kensington Square stood largely untouched, with four sides of distinguished buildings overlooking a central garden where the fallen autumn leaves made an umber skirt on the lawn beneath each tree.

Parking was impossible, so Barbara pulled her Mini onto the pavement at the northwest edge of the square, where a strategically placed bollard prevented the traffic from the distant high street from creating a short cut and disturbing the quiet of the neighbourhood. She shoved her police identification onto what went for the Mini's dashboard. She clambered out and in short order found herself in the company of Sister Cecilia Mahoney, who was still a resident of the convent and who was, when Barbara called, at work in the chapel next door.

Barbara's first thought upon encountering the nun was that she didn't look much like one. Nuns were supposed to be women two or three decades past their prime who wore heavy black robes, clanking rosary beads, and veils and wimples from the Middle Ages.

Cecilia Mahoney didn't fit this picture. In fact,

when Barbara was directed to the chapel to find her, her first assumption when she saw the figure up on a small step ladder with a can of marble polish in her hand was that she was a tartan-skirted cleaning woman, since cleaning an altar that featured a statue of Jesus pointing to His own exposed, anatomically incorrect, and partially gilded heart was what she was doing. Barbara told this woman that, pardon me but she was looking for Sister Cecilia Mahoney, whereupon the woman turned and said with a smile, "Then it's me you're looking for," in a brogue that sounded as if she'd just landed from Killarney.

Barbara identified herself, and the nun took some care in climbing down from the steps. She said, "Police, is it? Why, you haven't the look of a policeman at all. Is there some sort of trouble, Constable?"

The chapel was dimly lit, but down from the steps Sister Cecilia put herself into a pool of rose light created by a single votive candle that burned on the altar she was polishing. It did much to flatter her, smoothing away the lines on her middle-aged face and casting highlights into hair that was short but whose curls—as black and as shiny as obsidian—couldn't be disciplined even by the slides she used to manage them. She had violet eyes, darkly lashed, and they looked upon Barbara kindly.

Barbara said, "Is there somewhere we can go to have a word?"

The nun said, "Sad to say, Constable, it's unlikely that we'll be disturbed in here if it's privacy you're wanting. Time was that would have been out of the question. But these days . . . even the students who live in our dormitory frequent the chapel only when they've got an exam and are hoping for God's intervention in the matter. Come. Let's go up here and you can tell me what it is that you're wanting to know." She smiled, revealing perfect white teeth, and went on to say, as if in explanation of her smile, "Or is it that you're wanting to join us in the convent, Constable Havers?"

"It might give me the fashion make-over I need," Barbara admitted.

Sister Cecilia laughed. "Come this way. It'll be a bit warmer by the main altar. I've an electric fire there for the Monsignor when he says Mass in the morning. He's become a bit arthritic, poor man."

Taking her cleaning supplies in hand, she led Barbara up the single centre aisle in the chapel, beneath a deep blue ceiling punctuated by gilded stars. Barbara saw that it was a church of women: Apart from the statue of Jesus and a stained glass window dedicated to St. Michael, all other windows and statues were female: St. Theresa of Lisieux, St. Clare, St. Catherine, St. Margaret. And atop the ornamental pillars on either side of each of the windows were carvings of even more women.

"Here we are." Sister Cecilia went to one side of the altar and switched on a large electric fire. As it began to heat, the nun explained that she'd continue her work right here in the sanctuary if the constable didn't mind. There was this altar to be seen to as well: the candlesticks and the marble to be polished, a reredos to be dusted, and altar cloths to be replaced. "But you might wish to sit by the fire, my dear. The cold seeps in."

As Sister Cecilia set to her cleaning, Barbara told her that she'd brought what might be bad news for the nun. Her name had been found inside several books on the lives of saints—

"Not a surprise, I hope, considering my calling," Sister Cecilia murmured as she removed the brass candlesticks from the altar and set them carefully on the floor next to Barbara. She went on to the altar cloths, folding and placing them over an ornate altar rail. She then fished in her bucket and brought out a jar and some rags, which she took with her to work upon the altar.

Barbara told her that the books in question had been among a collection kept by a woman who'd died on the previous evening. There had been a note penned to that woman as well, a note written by Sister Cecilia herself. "She was called Eugenie Davies," Barbara said.

Sister Cecilia hesitated. She'd just scooped up a palmful of marble polish and she held it motionless as she said, "Eugenie? Oh, I'm sorry to hear about that, I am. It's been years since I last saw the poor woman. Was it sudden, her passing?"

"She was murdered," Barbara said. "In West Hampstead. On her way to see a bloke called J. W. Pitchley, who was once James Pitchford."

Sister Cecilia moved to the altar slowly, like an underwater diver in a strong, cold current. She smoothed some polish onto the marble, using small round strokes, as her lips worked their way round a thought or a prayer.

"We've learned," Barbara said, "that the killer of the daughter—a woman called Katja Wolff—has recently got out of prison as well."

The nun turned from the altar at this, saying, "You can't be thinking poor Katja had anything to do with this."

Poor Katja. Barbara said, "Did you know the girl?"

"Of course I knew her. She lodged here at the convent before she went to work for the Davies family. They lived at that time just along the square."

Katja had been a refugee from the former East Germany, Sister Cecilia explained, and she went on to relate the facts of the girl's immigration to England.

Katja Wolff had dreamed as all girls dream, even girls from countries where freedom is so limited as to make the very *act* of dreaming imprudent. She had been born in Dresden of parents who believed in the system of economy and government under which they had lived. A teenager during the Second World War, her father had seen the worst that could happen when nations engage in conflict, and he embraced the lifestyle of equality for the masses, believing that only communism and socialism held out the promise that global destruction would not occur. As good Party workers with no members of the intelligentsia in their past for whose sins they would have had to pay, the family prospered under this system. From Dresden they moved to East Berlin.

"But Katja wasn't like the rest of them," Sister Cecilia said. "Indeed, Constable, God love the girl, but wasn't Katja Wolff living proof that children are born with their personalities intact."

Unlike her parents and her four siblings, Katja hated the atmosphere of socialism and the omnipresence of the State. She hated the fact that their lives were "described, prescribed, and circumscribed" from birth. And in East Berlin—so close to the West by the presence of that other half of the city just a few hundred yards across No Man's Land—she got her first taste of what could be if she only could escape the land of her birth. For from East Berlin for the first time she could see western television and from westerners who traveled to the East on business, she could learn what life was like in what the girl came to call The World of Bright Colours.

"She was expected to go to university, to study in one field of science or another, to marry, and to have babies who would be looked after by the State," Sister Cecilia explained. "This is what her sisters were doing and this is what her parents intended her to do as well. But she wanted to be a fashion designer." Sister Cecilia turned from the altar with a smile. "And can you not imagine, Constable Havers, how that idea was greeted by members of the Party?"

So she escaped, and in escaping *as* she'd escaped, she gained a degree of celebrity that had brought her to the attention of the convent, where there existed a programme for political refugees: one year at the convent to have shelter and food, to learn the language, and to assimilate into the culture if they could. "She came to us with not a word of English and only the clothes on her back, Constable. She was with us that full year before she went to the Davies family to help out with the new baby."

"Is that when you got to know them?"

Sister Cecilia shook her head. "It was years and years that I'd known Eugenie. She attended Mass here, so she was familiar to all of us, she was. We spoke now and again and I lent her a book or two— which is what you must have seen amongst her collection—but it was only after Sonia's birth that I came to know her better."

"I saw a picture of the little girl."

"Ah, yes." Sister Cecilia rubbed polish along the front of the altar, tucking her cloth into its ornate carving. "Eugenie was devastated when that baby was born. And I suppose any mother would feel the same. A period of adjustment is necessary—isn't it— when a child is born who isn't what we expect her to be. And indeed, it must have been worse for Eugenie and her husband than it might have been for other parents, because their first child was so gifted, you see."

"The violin player. Right. We know about him."

"Yes. Little Gideon. An astonishing lad." Sister Cecilia lowered herself to her knees and saw to the elaborate barley sugar column at the end of the altar. She said, "Eugenie didn't talk about little Sonia at first. All of us knew she was pregnant, of course, and we knew when she'd delivered the child. But the first we knew anything was wrong was when she returned to Mass one or two weeks later."

"She told you, then?"

"Ah no. Poor thing. She just wept. Wept her eyes out every morning for three or four days, there at the back of the chapel with that poor frightened little boy at her side, stroking her arm and watching her with those big eyes of his. As for us at the Immaculate Conception, we none had actually seen the infant, you understand. I'd gone to the house. But Eugenie was never 'available for visitors.'" Sister Cecilia clucked and went back to her bucket of cleaning items, from which she took another rag and set about buffing. "When I finally spoke to Eugenie and learned the truth from her, I understood her sorrow. But not the depth of it, Constable. That, I must tell you, I never understood. Now, perhaps it's because I'm not a mother and have no idea what it's like to give birth to a child who isn't perfect as the world deems perfection. But it seemed to me then—and it seems to me now—that God gives us what we're *meant* to have. We may not understand His reason for giving us *what* He gives us at the moment we're given it, but there is a plan for us which time allows us to comprehend." She rested on her heels and looked over her shoulder at Barbara, softening what she seemed to feel might be harsh words by adding, "But then, that's an easy thing for one such as myself to say, isn't it, Constable? Here I am"—she extended her arms—"surrounded by God's love manifesting itself in a thousand different ways every day. Who am I to judge another's ability—or lack of such—to accept the will of God, when I myself have been blessed with so much? Will you see to the candlesticks for me, dear? There's a tin of polish in the bucket there."

Barbara said, "Oh. Right. Sorry." She rooted through the bucket for the appropriate tin and a rag whose black spots suggested it was the correct one to use on the candlesticks. Housewifely chores were not exactly in her line, but she reckoned she could do a job on the brass without destroying it permanently. "When was the last time you talked to Mrs. Davies?"

"That would have been soon after Sonia's death. There was a service for the child." Sister Cecilia looked down at her polishing rag. "Eugenie wouldn't hear of a Catholic funeral because she'd stopped attending Mass herself. Her faith was gone: that God would have given her such an afflicted child in the first place, that God would have taken the child in such a way . . . Eugenie and I never spoke again. I tried to see her. I wrote to her as well. But she would have none of me, none of my faith, none of the Church. In the end I had to leave her to God, and I only pray the dear woman found peace at last."

Barbara frowned, candlestick in one hand and polish tin in the other. There was a vital part of the story that was missing, and it was named Katja Wolff. She said, "How exactly did the German girl end up working in the Davies household?"

"That was my doing." Sister Cecilia got to her feet with a little grunt. She genuflected in front of the tabernacle at the centre of the altar and then began to attack its marble sides. "Katja needed employment at the end of her year here at the convent. A position with the Davies family, which included her room and board, would have allowed her to save for design college. It seemed a solution created by God because Eugenie so needed someone to help her."

"And then the baby was killed."

Sister Cecilia looked over at her, one hand on the tabernacle. She said nothing but her face, muscles loosening so that expression was drained from it entirely, spoke the inference that she herself did not make.

Barbara said, "Have you stayed in contact with anyone else from that time, Sister Cecilia?"

"It's Katja you're asking about, is it, Constable?"

Barbara prised the lid from the brass polish and said, "If you like."

"I went once a month for two years to see her. First while she was on remand in Holloway, then when she was imprisoned. She spoke to me only once, in the beginning, when she was arrested. Then not again."

"What did she say?"

"That she did not kill Sonia."

"Did you believe her?"

"I did."

But then, she would have had to do so, Barbara thought, because believing that Katja Wolff had murdered a child would have been a monstrous burden to carry through the rest of life, especially for the woman—devoted or not to an omnipotent and sagacious God—who had facilitated the German girl's placement in that family. She said, "Have you heard from Katja Wolff since she got out of prison, Sister Cecilia?"

"Indeed, I have not."

"Would there be any reason, aside from a need to declare her innocence, that she might have contacted Eugenie Davies once she was released?"

"None at all," Sister Cecilia said firmly.

"You're certain of that?"

"I am. If Katja were to contact anyone at all from that terrible time, it would be no one from the Davies family. It would be myself. But I've not heard from her."

She sounded so positive, Barbara thought. She sounded so firm. Indeed, she sounded as if there were no wiggle room whatever in what she had to say in the matter. Barbara asked her why.

"Because of the baby," Sister Cecilia said.

"Sonia?"

"No. Katja's own child, the child she had in prison. When he was born, Katja asked me to place him with a family. So if she's out of prison and dwelling on her past, I think it's safe to say that what she wants is to know what happened to her son."

NINE

YASMIN EDWARDS locked up her shop for the evening the way she always did: with maximum care. Most of the businesses on Manor Place had been boarded up for ages, and they were suffering the way derelict buildings usually suffered south of the river: They had become the urban outdoor canvases for graffiti artists, and where they had front windows and not sheets of either steel or plywood, those windows were broken. Yasmin Edwards' shop was one of the few new or resurrected businesses in the Kennington neighbourhood, apart from two pubs which had long survived the urban rotting that had invaded the street. But then, when did pubs *not* survive, and when wouldn't they survive as long as there was drink to be served and blokes like Roger Edwards to guzzle it?

She tested the padlock that she'd put through the hasp, and she made certain that the grillwork was fixed properly in place. That done, she scooped up the four carrier bags which she'd filled inside the shop, and she walked in the direction of home.

Home was in the Doddington Grove Estate, a

short distance away. She lived in Arnold House—
had lived there for the last five years, since her release from Holloway and from the hoop-jumping
she'd had to do in open conditions—and she was
lucky to have a flat that overlooked the horticultural
centre across the street. It wasn't a park, a common,
or a garden square, true. But it was green and it was
a bit of nature and that's what she wanted for Daniel.
He was only eleven and he'd spent most of her
prison term in care—thanks to her younger brother,
who "couldn't cope with a kid, Yas, look, I'm sorry
but it's just a fac', i'n't it?"—and she was determined
to make it up to her son in every possible way that
she could.

He was waiting for her just outside the lift, across
the strip of tarmac that did for the Arnold House car
park. But he wasn't alone, and when Yasmin saw who
was chatting to her son, she doubled her pace. The
neighbourhood wasn't a bad one—could have been a
lot worse and wasn't *that* the truth?—but candymen
and chicken hawks could turn up anywhere, and if
one of them so much as suggested to her son that
there was a life to be had outside of school and study,
she would kill the flaming bastard.

This bloke looked just like a candyman with his
expensive togs and the glitter of a gold watch in the
lights from the car park. And he had the patter as
well. Because as Yasmin approached, calling, "Dan,
what you *do*ing out here this time of day?" she could
see that the man had her son in thrall to a conversation Dan was liking too well.

Both of them turned. Daniel called out, "Hi, Mum. Sorry. Forgot my key." The man said nothing.

Yasmin said, "Why'd you not come by the shop, then, tell me?" with all her suspicions on top alert.

Daniel dropped his head like he always did when he was embarrassed about something. He said, examining his trainer-shod feet—Nikes that had cost her a fortune—"Went over to the Army Centre, Mum. A bloke was inspecting them and they were all lined up outside and they let me watch and after they let me stay for tea."

Charity, Yasmin thought. Sodding *charity*. "They not think you had a home to go to?" she demanded.

"They know me, Mum. They know you. One said, 'Isn't your mummy the lady got the beads in her hair? Right pretty, she is.' "

Yasmin harrumphed. She'd been studiously ignoring her son's companion. She handed over two of the carrier bags to her son, said, "Mind how you go with these. You've some washing to do," and punched in the code to call the lift.

That was when the man spoke, saying in a voice that was south of the river like hers but more deeply influenced by West Indian roots, "Missus Edwards, that right?"

"I already had too much of what you're selling," she replied, but she spoke to the lift door and not to him. She said, "Daniel?" and he came to stand in front of her to wait for the lift. She put a protective hand on his shoulder. Daniel peered round at the man. She straightened him back to face the lift.

"Winston Nkata," the man then said. "New Scotland Yard."

That got her attention. He extended an identity card which she looked at before she looked at him. A copper, she thought. A brother *and* a copper. There was only one thing worse than a brother who was a raas, and that was a brother who joined the Bill.

She dismissed the identification with a toss of her head, and the beads at the ends of her multitude of plaits offered him the music of her contempt. He was looking at her the way men always looked at her, and she knew what he saw and what he was thinking. What he saw: the body, all six feet of her; the face coloured walnut, a face that could have been like a model's face with a model's bones and a model's skin except that her lip—her upper lip, this was—was split permanently and scarred like an exploding purple rose where that bastard Roger Edwards had broken a vase against it when she wouldn't give him her Sainsbury wages or go on the game to support his habit; the eyes, coloured coffee and angry, angry but wary as well; and if she took her coat off in the cold evening air, he'd see the rest of her but especially the summertime cropped top she wore because her stomach was flat and her skin there was smooth and if she wanted to show off a smooth, tight stomach to the world, then she was going to, no matter the weather. That's what he saw. And what he thought? What they all thought, what they always thought: Wouldn't mind doing her for a lark, long as she wears a bag on her head.

He said, "C'n I have a word, Missus Edwards?"

and he sounded the way they always sounded, like they'd lay in front of a bus for their mummies.

The lift arrived and the door slid open slowly, like there was melted cheese on its track. It slid like it was saying if you were so stupid as to get in and ride it to the third floor where you had your flat, you might not get out because the door might decide not to open again.

She tapped Daniel's shoulder to move him inside. The cop said, "Missus Edwards? C'n I have a word with you?"

She said, "Like I've a choice?" and punched the button marked three.

The cop said, "Cheers," and got inside.

He was big. That was what she noticed first in the harsh overhead light inside the lift. He was taller than she was by a good four inches. And he had a scar on his face as well. It ran like a chalk mark from the corner of his eye right down his cheek and she knew what it was—a razor slash—but not how he'd got it. So she said, "What's that, then?" with a nod at his face.

He glanced at Daniel, who was looking up at him the way he always looked at black men: with that face so shiny so open so wanting, that face that revealed what'd gone missing in his life since the night his mum had taken on Roger Edwards one last time. The cop said, "A r'minder, this is."

"Of what?"

"How stupid one bloke can be when he thinks he's cool."

The lift jerked to a stop. She made no comment.

The cop was closest to the door, so he got out first when it groaned open. But he made a point to hold the door back—like it was going to slide shut and smack either Yasmin or her son . . . fat lot he knew about the flaming lift. He stepped to one side, and she swept past him, saying, "Mind those bags, Dan. Don't drop the wigs. The terrace's dead grotty and you drop 'em, you'll never get the filth out."

She admitted them into the flat and switched on one of the lamps in what went for the sitting room. She said to her son, "Mind you fill the tub. Be easier with the shampoo this time round."

"Right, Mum," Daniel said. He shot a shy look at the cop—a look that so clearly said *This is our gaff, what you think of it, man?* that Yasmin ached for him, physically ached, and that ache made her angry because it told her once again just what she and Daniel had lost.

She said, "Get on with it, then," to her son and to the cop, "What you want, man? Who'd you say you were?"

Dan said, "Winston Nkata, Mum."

She said, "Told you what to do, d'n't I, Dan?"

He grinned, with those big white teeth—the teeth already of the man he'd become far sooner than she wanted for him—shining in a face that was lighter than her own, a mixture of the colours of her skin and Roger's. He disappeared into the bathroom, where he turned the bath taps on, setting the water to roaring in a way that announced he was doing his job smartly, just like Mum'd told him to do.

Winston Nkata stayed near to the door, and Yasmin found that this irritated her more than if he'd sauntered through the rooms of the flat—four rooms only so it wouldn't have taken him more than one minute even if he was studying what he saw in every one of those rooms—inspecting every piece of her property. She said, "What's this about, then?"

He said, "Mind 'f I look round?"

"Why? I'm not holding nothing. You got a warrant? And I checked in like I always check in with Sharon Todd last week. If she's told you different—if that bitch's told prison service *anything* different . . ." Yasmin could feel the scare creeping up her arms as she realised yet again the amount of power her parole officer had over what went for her freedom. She said, "She'd gone to see her GP. Least, that's what I was told, wasn't I? Had some sort of attack in the office, she did, and they told her to have it checked out straightaway. So when I got there . . ." She drew a breath to slow herself down. And she was angry— *angry*—at the fear that she felt and the fact that this man with his razor-scarred face had brought fear with him into her house. This copper held every card in the deck, and both of them knew it. She said with a shrug, "Look round, then. Whatever you want, you'll not find it here."

He engaged her eyes for a long clear time, and she refused to look away because to look away would tell him he'd squashed her beneath his thumb like a flea. So she stood where she was by the kitchen door while the water roared in the bathroom and Daniel saw to the wigs that wanted washing.

The cop said, "Cheers," with a nod that she was meant to believe was shy and polite. He went first to her bedroom and flipped on the light. She could see him move to the paint-chipped clothes cupboard, and he opened it, but he didn't empty the pockets of any of the garments inside, although he fingered several pairs of trousers. He didn't pull out the drawers in the chest, either. But he studied the top of it—particularly one hairbrush and the blond hairs caught up in its bristles, particularly the dish of beads that she used when she wanted a change on the ends of her plaits. He took the most time with the picture of Roger, twin to the picture that she had in the sitting room, triplet to the picture that stood in the other bedroom on the table next to Daniel's small bed, quadruplet to the picture that hung on the kitchen wall above the table. Roger Edwards, aged twenty-seven when the snap had been taken, one month arrived from New South Wales, and two days fresh from Yasmin's bed.

The cop came out of her bedroom, nodded at her politely, and went into Daniel's, where the music was the same: clothes cupboard, top of the chest, picture of Roger. He went from there to the bathroom, where Daniel started chatting to him straightaway, saying, "This is my reg'lar job, these wigs. Mum pr'vides them for ladies what have cancer, see? When they take their med'cine, their hair falls out mostly. Mum gives them hair. She does their faces as well."

"Gives them beards, does she?" the cop asked.

Daniel laughed. "Not with hair, man! She does them with make-up. Dead good she is at it, Mum is. I c'n show you a—"

"Dan!" Yasmin barked. "Mind you've a job to do." She saw her son duck back to the tub.

The cop came out of the bathroom, gave her another nod, and went into the kitchen. There a door led onto a tiny balcony where she dried their clothes, and he opened this door, peered outside, then closed it carefully and ran his hand—large like the rest of him—along the jamb like someone looking for splinters. He opened no cupboards or drawers. He did nothing else, in fact, except stand at the table and look at that same picture that he'd been looking at in every room.

He said, "Who's this bloke, then?"

"Dan's dad. My husband. He's dead."

"Sorry."

"No need to be sorry," she said. "I killed him. But I 'spect you know that already. I 'spect that's why you're here, right? Some Aussie with a habit for henry got found dead with a knife in his neck and you lot ran the specifics through your computers and Yasmin Edwards' name popped up like toast."

"I didn't know that," Winston Nkata said. "Sorry all the same."

He sounded . . . what? She couldn't put a name to it, just as she couldn't put the name she wanted to put to the expression in his eyes. And she felt the bubbling of rage grow in her, which was something that she couldn't think through and she could never explain. It was the rage she'd learned to feel young and always—*always*—at the hands of a man: blokes she met and thought well of for a day or a week or a month till who they were showed through what they pretended to be.

She snapped, "What you want, then? Why're you messing with me? Why're you outside chatting to my son like you were in'erested in something he got to tell you? 'F you think I done something, then you speak proper and you speak now or you get your bum *out* 'f here. Hear me? Because if you don't—"

He said, "Katja Wolff," and that stopped her. What the hell did he want with Katja? He said, "Probation service list this as her address. That right?"

"We got approval," Yasmin said. "I'm out five years. 'S no mark against me. We got approval."

"They got her working at a laundry up Kennington High Street," Winston Nkata said. "Stopped there first to have a word with her, but she'd not been in all day. Called in ill, they said. Flu. So I came here."

Alarms rang in Yasmin's head, but she made sure the sound of them didn't play on her face. She said, "So she's gone off to the doctor."

"All day?"

"NHS," she replied with a shrug.

He said as politely as he'd so far said everything else to her, "Fourth time she's phoned in like that, they tell me at the laundry, Missus Edwards. Fourth time in twelve weeks. Not happy, that lot in Kennington High Street. They spoke to her parole officer today."

Alarm bells were changing to full-blown sirens. The frights were charging up Yasmin's spine. But she knew how coppers lied to you when they wanted to rattle you into saying something they could twist like a rag, and harshly she reminded herself of that fact, saying inwardly, Bitch, don't you lose it now.

She said, "I don't know nothing about any of that. Katja lives here, right, but she goes her own way. I got 'nough on my mind with Daniel, don't I?"

He looked in the direction of her bedroom, where the full-size bed and the hairbrush on the chest and the clothes in the cupboard told a different story. And she wanted to scream, Yeah! And wha' *about* it, Charlie? You ever *been* inside? You ever known for five minutes what's it like to think that f'r a stretch of time that feels like forever you'll have exactly *no one* in your life? Not a friend, not a mate, not a lover, not a partner? You know what that's like?

But she said nothing. She merely met his eyes with defiance. And for five long seconds that felt like fifty, the only sound in the flat came from the bathroom, where Dan started singing some pop song as he scrubbed the wigs.

Then that sound was interrupted by another. A key scraped into the lock on the door. The door swung open.

And Katja was with them.

LYNLEY MADE CHELSEA his final stop of the day. After leaving Richard Davies with his card and with instructions to phone should he hear from Katja Wolff or have any further information to impart, he negotiated the congestion round South Kensington station and cruised down Sloane Street, where the streetlamps glowed on an upmarket neighbourhood of restaurants, shops, and houses and the autumn leaves patterned the pavements in bronze. As he drove, he thought about connections and coincidence and whether the presence of the former obviated the possibility of the latter. It seemed very likely. People were often in the wrong place at the wrong time, but rarely were they at the wrong place, at the wrong time, and with the intention of calling on someone who figured in a violent crime from their past.

He grabbed the first parking space he found in the relative vicinity of the St. James house, a tall umber brick building on the corner of Lordship Place and Cheyne Row. From the Bentley's boot, he took the computer he'd removed from Eugenie Davies' office.

When he rang the bell, he heard a dog's immediate barking. It came from the left—that would be from St. James's study, where Lynley could see through a window that a light was burning—and it approached the door with the enthusiasm of a canine doing the job properly. A woman's voice said, "Good grief, that's *enough*, Peach," to the dog who, in best dachshund fashion, completely ignored her. A bolt slid back, the outside light above the door flicked on, and the door itself swung open.

"Tommy! Hullo. What a treat!" It was Deborah St. James who'd answered the bell, and she stood with the long-haired dachshund in her arms, a squirming barking bunch of brandy-coloured fur who wanted nothing better than to sniff Lynley's leg, hands, or face to see if he met with her canine approval. "Peach!" Deborah remonstrated with the dog. "You know very well who this is. Stop it." She stepped back from the door, saying, "Come in, Tommy. Helen's already gone home, I'm afraid. She was tired, she said. Round four, this was. Simon accused her of keeping late nights to avoid compiling data on whatever it is they're doing—I can never keep it straight—but she swore it was because you'd had her up till dawn listening to all four parts of *The Ring*. Except I can't remember if there *are* four parts. Never mind. What have you brought us?"

Once the door was closed behind them, she put the dog on the floor. Peach gained a good whiff of Lynley's trousers, registered his scent, took a step backwards, and wagged her tail in greeting. "Thank you," he told the dachshund solemnly. She trotted into the study where a gas fire burned and a lamp was lit on St. James's desk. There, a number of printed pages were scattered, some of them bearing black-and-white photographs and some of them bearing only script.

Deborah led Lynley into the room, saying, "Do put that thing down somewhere, Tommy. It looks heavy."

Lynley chose a coffee table that stood in front of a sofa facing the fireplace. Peach came to investigate the computer before returning to a basket that exposed her to the best warmth of the fire. There, she curled herself into a ball, sighed happily, and watched the proceedings in a dignified head-on-paws position from which she blinked drowsily from time to time.

"You must be wanting Simon," Deborah said. "He's just upstairs. Let me fetch him for you."

"In a moment." Lynley said the words without thinking, and so quickly on the heels of her own that Deborah brought herself up short, smiled at him quizzically, and shoved a portion of her heavy hair behind one ear.

She said, "All right," and walked to an old drinks trolley by the window. She was a tallish woman, lightly freckled across the bridge of her nose, not thin like a model, not stout, but well-shaped and completely female. She wore black jeans and a sweater that was the colour of green olives and made an attractive contrast with her coppery hair.

He saw that the room was stacked along the walls and the bookshelves at floor level with dozens of mounted and framed photographs. Some of them were dressed in bubble wrap, which reminded him of Deborah's upcoming show in a gallery on Great Newport Street.

She said, "Sherry? Whisky? We've got a new bottle of Lagavulin that Simon's telling me is nothing short of potable heaven."

"Simon's not given to hyperbole."

"Like the fine man of science that he is."

"It must be good, then. I'll have the whisky. You're working on the show?"

"It's nearly ready. I'm at the catalogue stage." Handing over the whisky, she nodded to her husband's desk and said, "I've been going over the proofs. The pictures they've selected are fine, but they've edited out some of my timeless prose"—she grinned; her nose wrinkled as it always did, making her look much younger than her twenty-six years— "and I'm finding that I don't like that much. Look at me. My fifteen minutes arrive and straightaway I become the great *artiste*."

He smiled. "That's unlikely."

"Which part?"

"The part about fifteen minutes."

"You're very quick this evening."

"I speak only the truth."

She smiled at him fondly, then turned and poured herself a glass of sherry. She took it up, held it out, and said, "Here's to . . . Hmm . . . I don't know. What shall we drink to?"

Which was how Lynley knew that Helen had been as good as her word, not telling Deborah about the coming baby. He was relieved at this. At the same time, he was ill at ease. Deborah would have to know sometime, and he knew that he had to be the person to tell her. He wanted to do so now, but he couldn't think of a place to begin, apart from saying outright, Let's drink to Helen. Let's drink to the baby my wife and I have made. Which was, of course, completely impossible.

He said instead, "Let's drink to the sale of every one of your pictures next month. On opening night, to members of the royal family who will summarily demonstrate they've a taste for something beyond horses and blood sport."

"You never did get over your first fox hunt, did you?"

" 'The unspeakable in pursuit.' "

"Such a traitor to your class."

"I like to think it's what makes me interesting."

Deborah laughed, said, "Cheers, then," and took a sip of sherry.

For his part, Lynley took a deep gulp of the Lagavulin and considered everything that was going unsaid between them. What a thing it was to come face-to-face with one's cowardice and indecision, he thought.

He said, "What will you do after the show is mounted? Have you another project in mind?"

Deborah looked round at the photographs piled in their serried ranks and considered the question, head cocked and eyes thoughtful. "Bit frightening, that is," she admitted frankly. "I've been working on this since January. Eleven months now. And I suppose what I'd *like* to do if the gods allow it . . ." Her head tilted up-wards to indicate not only the heavens but her hus-band, who'd probably be given his say in the matter. "I'd like to do something foreign, I think. Portraits still, I do love portraits. But foreign faces this time. Not foreign-in-London faces, because obviously I could find hundreds of thousands of those but they've been Britished, haven't they, even if they don't think so themselves. So what I'd like is something quite dif-ferent. Africa? India? Turkey? Russia? I don't quite know."

"But portraits all the same?"

"People don't hide from the camera when the picture's not for their own use. That's what I like about it: the openness, the candour with which they gaze at the lens. It's rather addictive, looking at all those faces being real for once." She took another swallow of sherry and said, "But you can't have come to talk about my pictures."

He took the opportunity for escape even as he loathed himself for doing so. He said, "Is Simon in the lab?"

"Shall I fetch him for you?"

"I'll just go up if that's all right."

She said that it was, of course it was, he knew the way. And she crossed back to the desk where she'd been working, set down her glass, and came back to him. He finished his whisky, thinking she meant to have his own glass back, but she squeezed his arm and kissed him on the cheek. "Lovely to see you. D'you need help with that computer?"

"I can manage," he said. And he did just that, not feeling particularly proud of himself for accepting the escape route she offered, but telling himself that there was work to be done and work came first, which was certainly a fact that Deborah St. James understood.

Her husband was on the fourth floor of the house, where he had a work room that had long been called his laboratory, and Deborah had a darkroom adjacent to it. Lynley climbed to this floor, pausing at the top of the stairs to say, "Simon? Are you in the middle of something?" before he walked across the landing to the open door.

Simon St. James was at his own computer, where he appeared to be studying a complicated structure that resembled a three-dimensional graph. When he tapped a few keys, the graphic altered. When he tapped a few more, it revolved on its side. He murmured, "That's damn curious," and then turned to the door. "Tommy. I thought I heard someone come in a few minutes ago."

"Deb offered me a glass of your Lagavulin. She was seeking confirmation as to its quality."

"And?"

"Pretty damn good. May I . . . ?" He nodded down at the computer.

St. James said, "Sorry. Here. Let me move. . . . Well, something can be moved, I think."

He rolled his chair back from his computer table and hit the side of his leg brace at the knee with a metal ruler when it didn't adjust properly as he rose. He said, "I've been having the most blasted trouble with this thing. It's worse than arthritis. As soon as the rain starts, the knee hinge doesn't want to work properly. It's time for an overhaul. That or a visit to Oz." He spoke with an utter lack of concern that Lynley knew he felt but could not feel himself. Whenever St. James had taken a step in Lynley's line of vision in the last thirteen years, it had required every ounce of control he had not to avert his eyes in abject shame for having wreaked such physical devastation on his friend.

St. James cleared a space on the worktable nearest to the door by stacking up papers and manila folders and moving several scientific journals to one side. He said casually, "Is Helen all right? She was looking rather ill when she left this afternoon. All day, in fact, now that I think of it."

"She was fine this morning," Lynley said, and he told himself that the statement comprised the approximate if not the literal truth. She *was* fine. Morning sickness did not constitute illness in the usual sense. "Bit tired, I expect. We were out late at Web—" But that wasn't, he recalled, the story his wife had told Deborah and Simon earlier, was it? Blast Helen, he thought, for being so creative when it came to spinning tales. "No. Sorry. That was the other night, wasn't it. Christ. I can't keep anything straight. Anyway, she's fine. I expect it was a late night catching up with her."

"Right. Well. Yes," St. James said, but his examination of Lynley was rather too lengthy for Lynley's comfort. In the small silence that ensued, rain began to fall outside. It hit the window like timpani in miniature, and it was accompanied by a sudden gust of wind that rattled the casement like an unspoken accusation. St. James said, "What've you brought me?" with a nod at the computer.

"Some detective work."

"That's your bailiwick, isn't it?"

"This requires a more delicate touch."

St. James hadn't known Lynley for more than twenty years to find himself suddenly incapable of reading between the lines. He said, "Are we on thin ice, Tommy?"

Lynley said honestly, "A singular pronoun is all that's required. You're clean. If you'll help me, that is."

"That's remarkably reassuring," St. James said dryly. "Why do I picture myself in an unpleasant future scenario, sitting in the dock or standing in the witness box, but in either case sweating like a fat man in Miami?"

"That's your natural sense of fair play among men, a quality I deeply admire in you, by the way, if I've not mentioned the fact before. It's also, however, one of the first things that gets tossed out of the window after a few years dealing with the criminal element."

"This is from a case, then?" St. James said.

"You didn't hear that from me."

St. James fingered his upper lip thoughtfully as he gazed at the computer. He would know what Lynley ought to be doing with the piece of machinery. But as to why he wasn't doing it . . . That was something he'd be better off not asking. He finally drew a breath and let it out, giving a shake of his head that indicated it was against his better judgement to say, "What do you need?"

"All internet activity. Her use of e-mail particularly."

"Her?"

"Yes. Her. She may have received mail in the past from an internet Lothario who calls himself Tongue-Man—"

"Good God."

"—but there was nothing on the machine from him when we logged on to it in her office." Lynley went on to tell St. James Eugenie Davies' password, which the other man jotted down on a piece of yellow legal paper that he ripped from a pad on the worktable.

"Am I looking for anything besides TongueMan?"

"You're looking for all activity, Simon. E-mail in, e-mail out. Surfing the net. Whatever she's done once she's logged on, let's say, for the last two months. That's possible, isn't it?"

"Most of the time, yes. But I don't have to tell you how much more quickly an expert from the Yard could manage this for you, not to mention an order from some legal authority should you need to strong-arm the internet provider."

"Right. I know that."

"Which leads me to conclude that you suspect there's something here"—he placed his hand on the machine—"that puts someone in a difficult position, someone you'd rather not see get into a difficult position. Is that right?"

Lynley said steadily, "Yes. That's right."

"It's not you, I hope."

"Great Scot. No."

St. James nodded. "I'm glad of that, then." He looked momentarily uncomfortable and tried to hide the discomfort by lowering his head and rubbing the back of his neck. "So things are well with you and Helen, then," he settled on saying.

Lynley saw his line of reasoning. A mysterious *her,* a computer in Lynley's possession, an unnamed someone getting into difficulty should his e-mail address show up on Eugenie Davies' computer . . . It added up to an illicit something, and St. James's longstanding relationship with Lynley's wife—after all, he'd known Helen since she was eighteen—would make him more protective of her than one would expect of someone's employer.

Lynley hastened to say, "Simon, it's nothing to do with Helen. Nor with me. You have my word on that. So will you do this for me?"

"You're going to owe me, Tommy."

"In spades. But I'm so far in debt to you at this point that I might as well sign over the land in Cornwall and have done with it."

"That's a tempting offer." St. James smiled. "I've always fancied myself a country squire."

"You'll do it, then?"

"I expect I will. But without the land. God knows we don't want to set your ancestors spinning in their graves."

DC WINSTON NKATA knew the woman was Katja Wolff before she opened her mouth, but put to the rack he wouldn't have been able to tell anyone exactly how he knew. She had a key to the flat, true, so there was that to identify her since this flat in the Doddington Grove Estate had been listed as her address when he'd tracked down her parole officer at DI Lynley's request a short time earlier. But it was more than the key unlocking the door that told him whom he was looking at. There was the way she carried herself, like someone wary of every potential encounter, and there was also her expression, a perfect blank, the sort of expression a lag wore inside so as not to draw attention to herself.

She stopped right inside the door, and her glance went from Yasmin Edwards to Nkata and back to Yasmin, where it remained. She said, "Am I interrupting you, Yas?" in a husky voice that bore less of the German accent than Nkata had expected. But she'd been more than twenty years in the country at this point. And she hadn't been surrounded by her fellow Germans.

Yasmin said, "This is the Bill, this is. Detective Constable. He's called Nkata," and Katja Wolff's body went on the alert: a subtle, tensing awareness that someone not born into the land of gang activity like Winston Nkata might not have noticed.

Katja removed her coat—cherry red—and the close-fitting grey hat with its matching band of the coat's bright colour. Beneath, she had on a sky-blue pullover, looking like cashmere but worn to a paper-like thinness at the elbows, and pale grey trousers of a slick material threaded through with silver when she moved in the light.

She said to Yasmin, "Where's Dan?"

Yasmin indicated the bathroom with her head. "Doing wigs."

"And this bloke?" She tilted her chin at Nkata.

He took the reins while he had the chance, saying, "You're Katja Wolff?"

She didn't reply. Instead, she walked over to the bathroom and said hello to Yasmin Edwards' son, who appeared to be up to his elbows in bubbles. The boy looked over his shoulder at her, then into the sitting room, where he managed to lock eyes with Nkata for a moment. But he said nothing. Katja closed the bathroom door on him and strode to the old three-piece suite that constituted the sitting room furniture. She sat on the sofa, opened a packet of Dunhills that lay on the table next to it, and took out a cigarette, which she lit. She picked up the television remote and was about to punch the set on, when Yasmin said her name: not in supplication but in warning, it sounded to Nkata.

At that, Winston found that he wanted to study Yasmin Edwards because he wanted to understand: her, the situation here in Kennington, her son, the relationship between the two women. He'd got beyond the fact that she was beautiful. He was still sorting through her anger, though, as well as through the fears she was doing her best to hide. He wanted to say, "You're all *right* here, girl," but he recognised the foolishness of doing so.

He said to Katja Wolff, "Laundry up on Kennington High Street says you didn't show to work today."

She said, "I was ill this morning, all day in fact. I've just been to the chemist. There is no law broken in that, I believe," and she drew in on the cigarette and examined him.

Nkata saw Yasmin glance between them. She clasped her hands in front of her, just at the level of her sex, as if she wished to hide it. He said to Katja Wolff, "Go to the chemist by motor, then?"

"Yes. What about it?"

"Got your own motor, have you?"

Katja said, "Why? Have you come to request that I drive you somewhere?" Her English was perfect, remarkable really, as impressive as the woman herself.

"Got a car, Miss Wolff?" he repeated patiently.

"No. They don't generally provide parolees with transport when they release them. It's a pity, I think. Especially for those who serve time for armed robbery. How bleak their future must look to them, knowing they'll have to escape from the scenes of their future crimes on foot. While for someone like me . . . ?" She tapped her cigarette against a ceramic ashtray that was shaped, seasonally, like a pumpkin. "A car is quite inessential for working in a laundry. One only needs a high tolerance for both endless boredom and insufferable heat."

"So it's not your car, then?"

Yasmin crossed the room as Nkata completed the question. She joined Katja on the sofa and neatly rearranged a few magazines and tabloids on the iron-legged coffee table in front of it. Having done this, she placed a hand on Katja's knee. She looked at Nkata across the line she'd drawn as clearly as if she'd wielded chalk on the carpet squares.

She said, "What'd you want with us, man? Time to spit it out or time to leave."

"Got a car yourself?" Nkata asked her.

" 'F I do?"

"Like to see it, I would."

Katja said, "Why? Who is it you've come to speak to, Constable?"

"We'll get to that soon enough, I expect," Nkata said. "Where's the car?"

The two women were motionless for a moment, during which a resuming of water roaring into the bathtub told everyone that Daniel was taking his mother's wigs through a manual rinse cycle. Katja was the one to break the silence, and she did it with the confidence of a woman who'd spent two decades educating herself as to her rights with regard to the police. "Have you a warrant? For anything, by the way?"

"Didn't think I'd need one, conversation being what's on my mind."

"Conversation about Yasmin's car?"

"Missus Edwards' car. Ah. Right. Where is it?" Nkata tried not to look smug. The German woman flushed anyway, perhaps realising that her own dislike and distrust of Nkata had caused her to trip.

"What's this *about,* man?" Yasmin snapped, but her voice was higher now and anxiety was tightening her hold on Katja's knee. "You're wanting a warrant if you mean to go through my car, hear me?"

Nkata said, "I don't need to go through it, do I, Missus Edwards. But I'll have a look at it all the same."

The women exchanged a glance, after which Katja rose and went into the kitchen. There, cupboards opened and closed, a kettle clanged onto the cooker, and a burner hissed. For her part, Yasmin waited for a moment as if for a sign from the kitchen of some-

thing other than tea being made. When she didn't receive one, she got to her feet and snatched a key from
a hook to the right of the flat's front door. She said,
"Come on, then," to Nkata and, coatless despite the
weather, she led him outside. Katja Wolff remained
behind.

Yasmin took lengthy strides towards the lift, as if
she didn't care one way or another if the detective
was following her. When she moved, her plaits—so
long that they reached her shoulder blades—made a
music that was both hypnotic and soothing, and
Nkata realised that he couldn't account for the effect
that that music had on him. He felt the reaction in his
throat first, then behind his eyes, then in his chest.
He shook it away and looked down at the car park,
then over at what appeared to be allotments across
the street, then in the direction of Manor Place,
where he could glimpse the first of a row of derelict
buildings that expressed what years of government
indifference and urban decay had done to the neighbourhood.

In the lift, he said, " 'D you grow up round here?"

Yasmin stared him down in silence so he finally
moved his gaze to the words *eat me till I scream* that
someone had painted in nail varnish on the lift wall
in line with Yasmin's right shoulder. The graffito
brought his mother immediately to Nkata's mind: a
female vigilante who would no more allow graffiti to
foul her landscape than would she permit a profanity
uttered within her hearing. Alice Nkata would have
been so quickly inside that lift with the varnish re-

mover that the imperative wouldn't have had a chance even to dry before she had obliterated it. Thinking of this and his dignified mother and how she'd managed to maintain her dignity in a society that saw a black woman first and the woman herself only second and if she was lucky that day, Nkata smiled fondly.

Yasmin said, "Like to have women under your thumb, do you, man? That why you joined the Bill, was it?"

He wanted to tell her that she shouldn't sneer, not because the expression distorted her face and stretched the scar on her lip so that it seemed to bloom, but because when she sneered, she looked frightened. And fear was a woman's enemy on the streets.

He said, "Sorry. Thinking of my mum."

"Your mum." She rolled her eyes. "You telling me next I remind you 'f her, yeah?"

Nkata laughed outright at the thought of the comparison. He said, "Not at all, girl." And he chuckled more.

Her eyes narrowed. The lift door creaked open. She stalked outside.

Across a strip of dying lawn, the car park held a small array of cars that spoke of the general economic status of the people in the Doddington Grove Estate. Yasmin Edwards took Nkata to a Fiesta with a rear bumper that clung to the vehicle like an inebriate to a lamppost. The car had once been red but the colour had long ago oxidized so it was mostly rust. Nkata

walked round it carefully. The front right headlamp
had a jagged crack in it, but aside from the rear
bumper, that was the extent of the damage.

He squatted at the front of the Fiesta and peered
beneath it, using a pocket torch to shed some light on
its undercarriage. He did the same thing at the back
of the vehicle, taking his time. Yasmin Edwards stood
by in silence, her arms wrapped round her against the
chill, her summertime top meagre protection against
the wind that was blowing and the rain that had begun to fall.

Nkata straightened, his inspection finished. He
said, "When'd that headlamp get smashed?"

"What headlamp?" She went to the front of the car
and examined it herself. "I don't know," she said, and
for the first time since learning who and what Nkata
was, she did not sound combative as she ran her fingers across the uneven crack in the glass. "Lights still
work proper, so I didn't notice." She was shivering
now, but it seemed more likely with the cold than
with concern. Nkata removed his overcoat, saying,
"Here," and handing it over. She took it.

Nkata waited till she had slid her arms into his
coat, till she had snugly wrapped it round her, till he
saw what she looked like with the collar raised and
expressing a curve against her dark skin. Then he
said, "You both drive this car, Missus Edwards? Right
that, isn't it? You and Katja Wolff?"

And the coat was off and thrust back at him instantly, almost before he finished the question. If

there had been a moment of anything more than hostility between them, he'd just managed to shatter it. Yasmin looked up to the flat where Katja Wolff was making tea. She returned her glance to Nkata and said evenly, arms encircling her body once more, "That all you want with us, man?"

He said, "No. Where were you last night, Missus Edwards?"

She said, "Here. Where else would I be? I got a boy needs his mum, I expect you noticed."

"Miss Wolff here as well?"

She said, "Yeah. Tha's right. Katja was here." But there was an undercurrent in the way she made the statement that suggested the facts might prove otherwise.

Something always alters in a person when he lies. Nkata had been told that a hundred times. Listen to the timbre of the voice, he'd been lectured. Watch for changes in the pupils of the eyes. Look for the head's movement, the shoulders either relaxing or tensing, the muscles of the throat constricting. Look for something—anything—that wasn't there before, and that something will tell you exactly where the speaker stands in relation to the truth.

He said, "I'll need another word," and he nodded upwards.

"I've given you words."

"Yeah. I know." He headed back to the lift, and they went through the exercise they'd gone through before. But the silence between them felt charged to

Nkata, and charged with something more than a man-to-woman charge, more than copper to suspect, more than former lag to potential screw.

"She was here," Yasmin Edwards said. "But you don't believe me 'cause you can't believe me. 'Cause if you sussed where Katja was living, then you sussed the rest and you know I did time and lags and liars are one 'n the same when it comes to the filth. I'n't that right, man?"

He'd reached the door to her flat. She slid in front of it, blocking his way. She said, "You ask her what she did last night. You ask her where she was. She tell you she was here. An' just to make sure I can't mess with your process, I'll keep myself out here while you ask her."

Nkata said, "Suit yourself, but put this round you if you mean to stay outside," and he himself put the coat round her shoulders this time, drawing the collar up to protect her neck from the wind. She flinched. He wanted to say, "How'd you get this way, woman," but instead, he ducked back inside the flat to have his confrontation with Katja Wolff.

TEN

"THERE WERE letters, Helen." Lynley was standing at the cheval mirror in their bedroom, gloomily attempting to make a choice among three ties that dangled limply from his fingers. "Barbara found them in a chest of drawers, just like love letters, all of them together with envelopes included. Everything was in place except the traditional blue ribbon tying them up."

"Perhaps there's an innocent explanation."

"What the hell was the man even thinking?" Lynley went on as if his wife hadn't spoken. "The mother of a murdered child. The victim of a crime. You don't find anyone more vulnerable than that, and when you do, you put distance between yourself and her. You don't seduce her."

"If that's what happened in the first place, Tommy." Lynley's wife watched him from the bed.

"What else could it have been? 'Wait for me, Eugenie. I'm coming for you.' That doesn't sound to me like your average bread-and-butter letter straight out of Mrs. Beeton."

"I don't think Mrs. Beeton advised housewives on their letter writing, darling."

"You know what I mean."

Helen rolled onto her side, took his pillow, and cradled it to her stomach. She said, "Lord," in a hollow tone that he couldn't ignore.

"Bad this morning?" he asked.

"Awful. I've never felt like this in my life. When will it progress to the rosy glow of a woman fulfilled? And why are pregnant women in novels always described as *glowing* when in reality they'd have faces like paste and stomachs at war with the rest of their bodies?"

"Hmm." Lynley considered her question. "I don't actually know. Is it a conspiracy to keep the species propagating? I wish I could bear this for you, darling."

She laughed weakly. "You've always been such a terrible liar."

There was truth to that, and because of it, he held up the three ties for her inspection. "I was thinking about the dark blue with the ducks. What do you say?"

"Very appropriate for fostering in suspects the false belief that you'll be gentle with them."

"Just what I thought." He returned to the mirror, draping the other two ties round one of the bedposts on his way.

She said, "Did you tell DCI Leach about the letters?"

"No."

"What did you do with them?" Their glances met in the mirror, and she read his reply on his face. "You *took* them? Tommy . . ."

"I know. But consider the alternative: to hand them over as evidence or to leave them there for someone else who might track down Webberly at the worst possible time and return them. To his home, for instance. With Frances standing there, just waiting for someone to deal her a death blow. Or even to the Yard, where it wouldn't do much for his career to have it made public that he'd involved himself with the victim of a crime. Or how about to a tabloid or two? They've such a profound love for the Met, after all."

"Is that the only reason you took them? To protect Frances and Malcolm?"

"What other reason is there?"

"Perhaps the crime itself? They could be evidence."

"You aren't suggesting Webberly was involved in some way, are you? He was in our presence the evening long. As was Frances, who'd have far more reason to want to be rid of Eugenie Davies than would Webberly if it came down to it. Beyond that, the last of the letters was written over a decade ago. Eugenie Davies has been a closed book for Webberly for years. It was mad for him to have involved himself with her in the first place, but at least it ended before lives were shattered."

Helen read him, as usual. "But you're not sure of that, are you, Tommy?"

"I'm sure enough. So I don't see the letters' relevance to the present, to today."

"Unless there's been recent contact between them."

Which was, in part, why he'd taken Eugenie Davies' computer. Lynley was relying on gut instinct with regard to that, instinct which told him that his superior officer was a decent man who had a difficult life, a man who never sought to harm another human being but who had submitted to temptation in a moment of weakness that he no doubt regretted to this day.

"He's a good man," Lynley said into the mirror, more to himself than to his wife.

She responded all the same. "As are you. And that might explain why he asked DCI Leach to allow you in on the case. You believe in his decency, so you'll protect him, without his having to ask you to do so."

And that's the way it was playing out, Lynley thought morosely. Perhaps Barbara had been right. Hand the letters over as potential evidence; leave Malcolm Webberly to his fate.

Across the room, Helen suddenly threw back the covers and dashed to the bathroom. The retching began, just beyond the open door. Lynley looked at himself in the mirror and tried to close his ears to the sound.

Funny, how one could talk oneself into believing just about anything if one was desperate enough. In a twist of thinking, Helen's morning sickness could be-

come the result of a bad bit of chicken eaten yesterday on a lunchtime salad. Another twist, and she had
flu, which was going round now anyway. Or perhaps
it was a case of nerves. She was facing a challenge
later in the day, and this was the way her body reacted
to anxiety. Or pushed to an extreme of rationalisation, he could say that she was simply afraid. They
hadn't been together long, had they, and she wasn't as
easy being with him as he was being with her. There
were, after all, differences between them: of experience, of education, and of age. And all that counted
for something, didn't it, no matter how they tried to
talk themselves into believing otherwise?

The retching continued. He forced himself to deal
with it in some reasonable way. He turned from the
mirror and strode across to the bathroom. He flipped
on the light, which in her haste Helen had not
switched on. He found her draped round the toilet,
her back heaving mightily as she gulped in air.

He said, "Helen?" But he found he could not
move from the doorway.

Selfish *bastard,* he told himself as a prod to action.
This is the woman you love. Go to her. Touch her
hair. Wipe her face with a cool damp flannel. *Do
something.*

But he couldn't. He was frozen to one spot as if
he'd inadvertently looked upon Medusa, fixed on the
sight of his beautiful wife reduced to vomiting into
the toilet bowl, her now daily ritual that celebrated
the fact of their union.

He said, "Helen?" and he waited for her to tell him that she was all right, that she needed nothing. He waited hopefully for her to send him on his way.

She turned her face to him. He could see its damp sheen. And he knew that she was waiting for him to make some move in her direction that would underscore the love and concern that he felt for her.

He made do with a question. "Can I get you something, Helen?"

Her eyes held his. He saw the subtle change come over her as her dawning realisation that he would not go to her metamorphosed into hurt.

She shook her head and turned away. Her fingers gripped the edges of the toilet. "I'm fine," she murmured.

He was happy to accept the lie.

IN STAMFORD BROOK, the sound of a cup rattling in its saucer awakened Malcolm Webberly. He cracked open his eyes to see his wife setting a cup of morning tea on the scarred surface of the bedside table.

The room was claustrophobically hot, the result of a poorly designed central heating system and Frances's refusal to have any windows open at night. She couldn't bear the sensation of night air on her face. She also couldn't sleep for thinking that someone might break into their house should so much as an inch's gap exist between a window and its sill.

Webberly lifted his head from the pillow, then sank back down with a groan. It had been a rough night.

He ached in every joint in his body, which was secondary to the ache in his heart.

"I've brought you some nice Earl Grey," Frances said. "Milk and sugar. It's piping hot." She went to the window and opened the curtains. The limp light of late autumn filtered into the room. "All grey and nasty today, I'm afraid," she went on. "It looks like rain. There's to be a wind coming from the west later on. Well, November. What else can one expect?"

Webberly elbowed his way upwards through the covers, becoming aware of the fact that he'd sweated through another set of pyjamas during the night. He took up the cup and saucer and looked down at the steaming liquid, its colour telling him that Frances hadn't let it steep, that it would taste like milky water. He hadn't been a morning tea drinker for years. Coffee was his beverage of choice. But tea was what Frances herself drank and it was easier to plug in the kettle and pour the boiling water over the tea bags than it was to go through the scooping, measuring, and pouring that resulted in a decent cup of what he preferred.

It's all the same at the end of the day, he told himself. Getting caffeine into the body is the main point, boy. So drink up now and have at the morning.

"I've made out the shopping list," Frances said. "It's by the door."

He grunted an acknowledgment.

She seemed to take this sound as a protest, saying anxiously, "Really, there's not much to get. Just the odd thing. Tissues, kitchen rolls, that sort of thing.

We've still got all that food from the party. It shouldn't take long."

"Fine, Fran," he said. "No problem. I'll stop on my way home from work."

"If something comes up, you needn't—"

"I'll stop on my way home."

"Well, only if it's not too much trouble, dear."

Not too much trouble? Webberly thought, and he hated himself for the disloyalty he was showing even as he allowed himself to experience a momentary swelling of resentment towards his wife. Not too much trouble to see to everything and anything that involved an excursion into the world, Fran? Not too much trouble to shop for groceries, to drop by the chemist, to collect the dry cleaning, to have the car serviced, to see to the garden, to walk the dog, to— Webberly forced himself to stop. He reminded himself that his wife wouldn't have chosen this illness, that she wasn't attempting to make his life a misery, that she was doing her best to cope and so was he, and coping with what was dished onto your plate was what life was all about.

"It's no trouble, Fran," he told her as he sipped the tasteless drink she'd brought him. "Thanks for the tea."

"I hope it's all right. Something special this morning. Something a bit different."

"Good of you," he said.

He knew why she'd done it. She'd brought him tea for the same reason that she would go downstairs as soon as he was out of bed and begin to cook him a sumptuous breakfast. It was the only way she could apologise to him for not managing to do what she'd claimed she would do a brief twenty-four hours earlier. Her plan to work in the garden had come to nothing. Even protected behind the walls that marked the boundaries of their property, she hadn't felt safe, so she hadn't left the house. Perhaps she had tried: placing one hand on the doorknob—*I can manage this*—cracking the door open—*yes, I can do this as well*—feeling the fresh air wash against her cheeks—*there's nothing to fear*—and even curling the fingers of one hand round the door jamb before panic claimed her. But that's as far as she'd got and he knew it because—God forgive him for his own insanity—he'd inspected her wellingtons, the tines of the rake, the gardening gloves, and even the rubbish bags for evidence that she'd gone outside, done something, picked up a single leaf, made an inroad into her irrational fears.

He swung out of bed, swilling down the rest of the tea. He could smell the sweat on his pyjamas, and the feel of them was clammy against his skin. He felt weak, oddly off balance, as if he'd come through a long period of fever and was only now recovering from it.

Frances said, "I'm going to make you a proper breakfast, Malcolm Webberly. None of this cornflakes nonsense today."

"I need a shower," he said in reply.

"Brilliant. That'll give me just enough time." She headed to the door.

He said, "Fran," to stop her. And when she paused, "There's no need for all that."

"No need?" Her head tilted to one side. She'd combed her red hair—dyed with the colour that she sent him to Boots once a month to fetch so that it would match their daughter's hair, which it never did—and she wore her pink dressing gown precisely belted, with a perfect bow.

"It's all right," he said. "You don't need to . . ." To what? Saying the words would take them somewhere neither wanted to go. Webberly settled on, "You don't need to coddle me. I can manage with corn-flakes."

She smiled. "Of course you can *manage* with them, darling. But every once in a while, it's lovely to have a proper breakfast. You've the time, haven't you?"

"There's the dog to walk."

I'll walk him, Malcolm. But that was an announcement she could not make. Not after yesterday's proclamation about gardening. Two defeats in a row would be an injury that she wouldn't want to risk inflicting on herself. Webberly understood that. The hell of it was, he'd always understood it. So he was unsurprised when she said, "Let's see how the time goes, shall we? I expect there's enough. And if there's not, you can cut short Alfie's walk. Just down to the corner and back. He'll survive."

She crossed the room, kissed him fondly on the top of the head, and left. In less than a minute, he could hear her banging about in the kitchen. She started to sing.

He pushed himself off the edge of the bed and plodded along the corridor to the bathroom. It smelled of mildew from grout round the tub that needed cleaning and a shower curtain that needed replacing, and Webberly shoved open the window fully and stood in front of it, breathing in the sodden morning air. It was the heavy, tubercular air of an approaching winter that promised to be long, cold, wet, and grey. He thought of Spain, of Italy, of Greece, of the countless sun-drenched environments round the world that he would never see.

Roughly, he shook off the mental pictures of these places, turning from the window and shedding his pyjamas. He twisted the hot water tap in the tub till the steam rose like an optimist's hope, and when he'd added enough cold water to the mix to make it bearable, he stepped inside and began to work lather vigorously round his body.

He thought of his daughter's reasonable question about insisting that Frances return to the psychiatrist. He asked himself what harm it could do simply to make the suggestion to his wife. He hadn't mentioned her problem for the past two years. On the twenty-fifth anniversary of their marriage—with retirement looming—how unforgivable would it be to imply that the opportunity for a different life was fast approaching them, and in order to have that different life, Frances might want to consider how best to address her problem? We'll want to do some traveling, Frannie, he could tell her. Think of seeing Spain again. Think of Italy. Think of Crete. Why, we could even sell up and move to the country as we once talked of doing.

Her lips would form a smile as he spoke, but her eyes would show the incipient panic. "Why, Malcolm," she'd say, and her fingers would clutch: the edge of her apron, the belt of her dressing gown, the cuff of her shirt. "Why, Malcolm," she'd say.

Perhaps she'd make the attempt at that point, seeing that he was in earnest. But she'd make the attempt that she'd made two years ago, and it would doubtless end where that attempt had ended: with panic, tears, a phone call by strangers on the street to nine-nine-nine, paramedics and ambulance and police dispatched to Tesco's, where she'd taken herself by taxi to *prove* she could do it, darling . . . and afterwards a hospital, a period of sedation, and reinforcement for every terror she felt. She'd forced herself out of the house to please him. It hadn't worked then. It wouldn't work now.

"She has to want to get well," the psychiatrist had told him. "Without desire, there is no exigency. And the internal exigency that demands recovery cannot be manufactured."

So it had been, year after year. The world went on while her world shrank. His world was joined inextricably to her world; sometimes Webberly thought he would suffocate in its smallness.

He rinsed long in the water. He washed his thinning hair. When he was done, he stepped out of the tub into the bone chill of the bathroom where the

window still gaped, letting in a last few minutes of
the morning air.

Downstairs, he found that Frances had been as
good as her word. A full breakfast was laid out on the
kitchen table and the air was redolent with the scent
of bacon. Alfie was sitting at the corner of the cooker,
looking hopefully at the frying pan from which
Frances was removing the rashers. The table, however, was laid only for one.

"You aren't eating?" Webberly asked his wife.

"I live to serve you." She gestured with the frying
pan. "One word from you and the eggs go on. When
you're ready for them. Any way you want them. Any
way you want anything."

"D'you mean that, Fran?" He pulled out his chair.

"Scrambled, fried, or poached," she declared. "I'll
even do them deviled for you, if you've a mind for
that."

"If I've a mind for it," he said.

He didn't feel like eating, but he shoveled the food
into his mouth. He chewed and swallowed without
tasting much. Only the acidic tang of orange juice
made the journey from his tongue to his brain.

Frances chatted. What did he think about Randie's
weight? She hated to talk to their daughter about it,
but didn't he think she was getting just a bit too
chunky for a girl her age? And what of this recent plan
of hers to have a year in Turkey? *Turkey,* of all places.
She was always coming up with a new plan, so of
course one didn't want to get oneself in a dither over

something that she might not even do, but a girl her age . . . on her own . . . in Turkey . . . ? It wasn't wise, it wasn't safe, it wasn't sensible, Malcolm. Last month she was talking about a year in Australia, which was bad enough . . . all that distance without her family. But this? No. They had to talk her out of this. And wasn't Helen Lynley looking lovely the other night? She's one of those women who can wear *anything*. Naturally, it's the expense of the clothes that tells the tale. Buy French and you look like a . . . well, just like a countess, Malcolm. And she *can* buy French, can't she? No one's watching to see who she buys from. Not like the poor old dowdy Queen, who's always dressed by some English upholsterer by the look of her. Clothes do so make a woman, don't they?

Chat. Chat. Chat. It filled a silence that might otherwise be used for a conversation too painful to be endured. It simultaneously wore the guise of warmth and of closeness, offering a portrayal of the long-married couple breaking their fast *à deux*.

Webberly shoved his chair back abruptly. He scrubbed the paper napkin across his mouth. "Alfie," he commanded. "Come. Let's go." He grabbed the lead from the hook near the door, and the dog padded after him, through the sitting room and out of the front door.

Alfie came to life as soon as paws hit pavement. His tail began to wag, and his ears perked up. He was all at once on the alert for his sworn enemies—cats—and as he and his master headed down the street to Emlyn Road, the Alsatian kept an eye out for anything po-

tentially feline at which he could bark. He sat obediently, as he always did when they came to Stamford
Brook Road. Here, the traffic could be heavy depending upon the time of day, and even a zebra crossing didn't guarantee a driver's seeing a pedestrian.

They crossed and made their way to the garden.

The night's rain had made the garden thoroughly
sodden. The grass was heavily bent with moisture,
tree limbs dripped, and the benches along the
perimeter path were shining slickly with water. This
was no matter to Webberly. He didn't want to sit beneath the trees, and he had no interest in the lawn
across which Alfie gamboled as soon as Webberly had
him off the lead. Instead, he took to the perimeter
path. He walked determinedly, gravel crunching beneath his soles, but while his body was in the Stamford Brook neighbourhood in which he'd lived for
more than twenty years, his mind was centred on
Henley-on-Thames.

He'd come this far into his day without thinking
once of Eugenie. It seemed something of a miracle to
him. She hadn't left his thoughts for an instant during
the previous twenty-four hours. He hadn't heard
from Eric Leach yet, and he hadn't seen Tommy
Lynley at the Yard. He accepted the latter's request
for DC Winston Nkata as a sign that progress was being made, but he wanted to know what that progress
was, because knowing something—anything at this
point—was better than being left with nothing but
images best forgotten from the past.

Without that contact with his fellow officers,

though, the images came to him. Unprotected by the claustrophobic confines of his house, by Frances's chatter, by the duties that faced him once he got to work, he was assailed by mental pictures, pictures so distant now as to be fragments only, pieces of a puzzle he'd not been able to complete.

It was summer, sometime after the Regatta. He and Eugenie were rowing on the sluggish river.

Hers had not been the first marriage that had not survived the horror of a violent death in the family. It would not be the last that cracked irreparably under the combined weight of investigation-and-trial and the powerful load of guilt attendant to losing a child to someone in whom trust had been mistakenly placed. But Webberly had *felt* more at the dissolution of this particular marriage. It was many months before he admitted why.

After the trial, the tabloids had gone after her with the same rapacity that had driven their stories about Katja Wolff. Where the Wolff girl had been the reincarnation of every beast, from Mengele to Himmler, responsible in the eyes of the press for everything from the Holocaust to the Blitz, Eugenie had been the indifferent mother: she who worked outside the home, she who had employed an unskilled girl untutored in English and in the ways of the English to care for a badly disabled child. If Katja Wolff had been vilified in the press—and deservedly so, considering her crime—Eugenie had been pilloried.

She'd accepted this public scourging as her due. "I'm to blame," she'd said. "This is the least I deserve." She spoke with simple dignity, with neither hope nor desire of being contradicted. Indeed, she would not allow contradiction. "I just want it to end," she'd said.

He saw her again, two years after the trial, quite by chance at Paddington Station. He was on his way to a conference in Exeter. She was coming into town, she said, for an engagement with someone she did not name.

"Just coming in?" he'd said. "You've moved house, then? To the country? That's good for your boy, I expect."

But no, they hadn't moved to the country. She'd just moved herself, alone.

He'd said, "Oh. I'm sorry."

She'd said, "Thank you, Inspector Webberly."

He'd said, "Malcolm. Please, it's plain Malcolm."

She'd said, "Plain Malcolm, then," and her smile was infinitely sad.

He'd said impulsively and in a rush because it was mere minutes before his train left the station, "Would you give me your number, Eugenie? I'd like to check how you're doing now and then. As a friend. If that's all right with you."

She'd written it on the newspaper he'd been carrying. She'd said, "Thank you for your kindness, Inspector."

"Malcolm," he'd reminded her.

Summer on the river had been twelve months later and not the first time he'd found an excuse to drive to Henley-on-Thames to check on Eugenie. She was lovely that day, quiet as always but with a sense of peace that he'd not witnessed in her before. He rowed the boat and she leaned back and rested on her side, not trailing her hand in the water in the way some women might have done, hoping for a seductive pose, but merely watching the river's surface as if its depths hid something she was waiting to see. Her face reflected brightness and shadow as they glided along beneath the trees.

He was aware in a rush that he'd fallen in love with her. But they had those twelve months of chaste friendship between them: walks round town, drives in the country, lunches at pubs, the occasional dinner and the warmth of conversation, real conversation about who Eugenie Davies had been and how she'd come to be who she was.

"I believed in God when I was young," she told him. "But I lost God along the way to adulthood. I've been a long time without Him now, and I'd like to get Him back if I can."

"Even after what's happened?"

"Because of what's happened. But I'm afraid He won't have me, Malcolm. My sins are too great."

"You haven't sinned. You couldn't possibly sin."

"You of all people can't believe that."

But Webberly couldn't see sin in her no matter what she said about herself. He saw only perfection and—ultimately—what he himself wanted. But to speak of his feelings seemed a betrayal in every direction. He was married and the father of a child. She was fragile and vulnerable. And despite the time that had passed since her daughter's murder, he couldn't bring himself to take advantage of her grief.

So he settled on saying, "Eugenie, do you know that I'm married?"

She moved her gaze from the water to him. "I assumed that you were."

"Why?"

"Your kindness. No woman thinking straight would be foolish enough to let someone like you get away. Would you like to tell me about your wife and family?"

"No."

"Ah. What does that mean?"

"Marriages end sometimes."

"Sometimes they do."

"Yours did."

"Yes. My marriage ended." She moved her gaze back to the water. He continued to row, and he watched her face, feeling as if in a hundred years as a man long blind he would still be able to draw from memory every line and curve of it.

They'd brought a picnic with them, and when he saw the spot he wanted, Webberly bumped the boat into the bank. He said, "Wait. Stay there. Let me tie it up," and as he scrambled up the slippery little slope, he lost his footing and slid into the water, where he stood humiliated with the Thames lapping coolly round his thighs. The mooring rope draped over his hand, and the river ooze seeped into his shoes.

Eugenie sat up straight, saying, "Heavens, Malcolm! Are you all right?"

"I feel a perfect fool. It never happens this way in films."

"But this way is better," Eugenie said. And before he could speak again, she scrambled from the boat and joined him in the water.

"The mud—" he began in protest.

"Feels exquisite," she finished. And she began to laugh. "You've blushed to the roots of your hair. Why?"

"Because I want everything perfect," he admitted.

She said, "Malcolm, everything is."

He was flustered, wanting and not wanting, sure and unsure. He said nothing more. They clambered from the river onto the bank. He pulled the boat close and took from it the lunch they'd brought with them. They found a spot under a willow that they liked. It was when they sank to the ground that she spoke.

"I'm ready, Malcolm, if you are," she said.

Thus it began between them.

"SO THE KID was given up for adoption." Barbara Havers concluded her recitation by flipping closed her tatty notebook and digging round in her lump of a shoulder bag for a packet of Juicy Fruit which she brought forth and generously offered round Eric Leach's Hampstead office. The DCI took a stick. Lynley and DC Nkata demurred. Havers folded one into her mouth and began to chew vigorously. Her substitute for the weed, Lynley thought. He wondered idly when she'd give up smoking altogether.

Leach played with the foil interior wrapper of the gum. He folded it into a miniature fan and placed it at the base of a photograph of his daughter. He'd apparently been on the phone to her when the Scotland Yard detectives arrived, and they'd come upon him at the end of a conversation in which he was wearily saying, "For God's sake, Esmé, this is something you need to discuss with your mum. . . . Of *course* she'll listen. She loves you. . . . Now you're jumping the gun. No one's getting . . . Esmé, listen to me . . . Yes. Right. Someday she . . . So might I, but that will never mean we don't love—" At which point, the girl had apparently hung up on him because he stood behind his desk with his mouth open on what he'd intended to say. He'd replaced the phone in its cradle with undue care and sighed heavily.

Now he went on. "That could be what's driving our killer, then. Or our killers. The adopted kid. Wolff didn't put herself in the club without assistance. Let's keep that in mind."

The four of them continued their exchange of information. A hideous knot of traffic in Westminster had kept the Scotland Yard detectives from Leach's morning meeting with his team in the incident room, so the DCI took notes. At the conclusion of Havers' report on the Convent of the Immaculate Conception, Nkata said, "Could be the motive we're looking for, this. Wolff wants that kid and no one's giving her any help to find . . . is it him or her, Barb?" As was largely his habit, he hadn't taken a seat in the office. Rather, he stood not far from the doorway, lounging against the wall with one broad shoulder resting next to a framed commendation that Leach had received from the commissioner.

"It's him," Havers said. "But I don't think that's the case."

"Why?"

"According to Sister Cecelia, she gave him up for adoption straightaway. She could have kept him with her for nine months—longer than that if she did time somewhere other than Holloway—but she didn't want that. She didn't even request it and get denied. She just handed him over in the delivery room and never took a look at him."

Lynley said, "She wouldn't have wanted to get attached to the infant, Havers. What would be the point, facing a twenty-year sentence? It could be an indication of the strength of her maternal feelings for the baby. Had she not had him adopted, he would have spent his life in care."

"But if she was looking for the kid, why not start with the convent?" Havers asked. "Sister Cecelia handled the adoption."

"Could be she's not looking for him at all," Nkata pointed out. "Twenty years later? She might know the kid wouldn't likely want to meet his real mum and find out she's a yard bird. And that could be 'xactly why she did the job on Missus Davies in the first place. Maybe she's thinking she wouldn't've *been* a yard bird without Missus Davies. Live with that for twenty years, and when you get out, you want to do something about settling the score."

"I just don't buy that," Havers insisted. "Not with this bloke Wiley sitting out there in his bookshop, knowing every move Eugenie Davies made. Convenient, wouldn't you say, that he happened to come upon our victim and a mystery man having an argument on the very night she was killed? Who's to say it was an argument at all but just the opposite? And our Major Wiley took some nasty action as a result."

"We need to track this kid down one way or another," Leach said. "Katja Wolff's kid. She might be on his trail and he'll need to be advised. It's messy, but there's no way round it. You handle that, Constable."

Havers said, "Sir," in acquiescence, but she didn't look convinced about the value of the assignment.

Winston Nkata said, "I say Katja Wolff's the right direction. There's something off with that bird."

He went on to describe for the others the meeting he'd had with the German woman once he'd returned to Yasmin Edwards' flat on the previous evening. Asked for her whereabouts on the night in question, Katja Wolff had claimed to be at home with Yasmin and Daniel. Watching television, she'd said, although she couldn't name the programme, and when put to the rack about this gap in her recollection, she said they'd channel-surfed all evening and she hadn't kept track where they'd touched down. What was the point of having a satellite dish and a remote if you weren't going to use both to entertain yourself?

She'd lit a cigarette as they'd spoken, and from her demeanour it looked as if she hadn't a care in the world. She'd said, "What's this about, Constable?" in apparent innocence. But her glance flicked to the door before she answered the most important questions, and Nkata had known what that glance meant: She was hiding something from him and wondering if Yasmin Edwards had told a story similar to hers.

"What did the Edwards woman claim?" Lynley asked.

"That Wolff was there. Wouldn't say anything else about it, though."

"Old lags," Eric Leach pointed out. "They're sure as hell not going to finger each other for anything, not on a first go-round with the local rozzers. You need to go after them again, Constable. What else have you got?"

Nkata told them of the cracked headlamp on Yasmin Edwards' Fiesta. "Claimed she didn't know how it happened or when," he said. "But Wolff has access. She was driving it yesterday."

"Colour?" Lynley asked.

"Red gone bad."

"That's not helpful," Havers pointed out.

"Any of the neighbours have either one of them leaving the flat the night in question?" Leach asked this as a uniformed female constable came into his office with a sheaf of papers that she handed over. He glanced at them, grunted his thanks, and said, "Where are we with the Audis, then?"

"Still at it," she said. "Nearly two thousand in Brighton, sir."

"Who would've thought that?" Leach muttered as

the constable left them. "Whatever happened to *buy British*?" He hung on to the papers but didn't refer to them, going back to his previous topic and saying to Nkata, "The neighbours? What about it?"

"South of the river," Nkata said with a shrug. "No one willing to talk, even to me. Just one Bible basher who wanted to bang on 'bout women who live together in sin. Said the residents'd tried to get that baby killer—these're her words—off the premises with no luck."

"We've got some more digging to do out there, then," Leach noted. "See to it. Edwards might crack if you have a decent go. You said she has a boy, right? Bring him into the picture if you need to. Accessory to murder could get her arse in a sling, so point that out to her. In the meantime"—he rooted through some paperwork on his desk and brought out a photograph—"Holloway couriered this over last night. It needs to get taken round Henley-on-Thames." He handed it to Lynley, who saw by the line of typing beneath it that it was a photograph of Wolff. The picture wasn't flattering. She was ill-lit, looking haggard and unkempt. Looking, he thought, just like a convicted murderer. "If she did do the job on the Davies woman," Leach continued, "she would have had to begin by tracking her down to Henley. If she did that, someone was bound to see her. Check it out."

In the meantime, Leach concluded, they'd got a list of all phone calls made into and out of Eugenie Davies' cottage in the past three months. That list was being compared with the names in the dead woman's address book. The names and numbers in the address book were being matched to the calls on her answer machine. A few more hours and they should have some details as to who was last in contact with her.

"And we've got a name for the Cellnet number," Leach informed them. "One Ian Staines."

"That could be her brother," Lynley said. "Richard Davies mentioned that she had two brothers, one called Ian."

Leach jotted this down. He said, "D'we know our assignments, then, lads and lasses?" as a sign their meeting was at an end.

Havers and Lynley rose. Nkata disengaged from the wall. Leach stopped them before they left the office. He said, "Speak to Webberly, any of you?"

It was a casual enough question, Lynley thought. But its air of nonchalance didn't feel genuine. "He wasn't in this morning when we left the Yard," Lynley answered.

"Give him my best when you see him," Leach said. "Tell him I'll be in touch very soon."

"We will. When we see him."

Out on the street and once Nkata had gone on his way, Havers said to Lynley, "In touch about what? That's what I want to know."

"They're old friends."

"Hmmph. What've you done with those letters?"

"Nothing, as yet."

"Are you still planning to . . ." Havers peered at him. "You are, aren't you? Damn it, Inspector, if you'd listen for a minute—"

"I'm listening, Barbara."

"Good. Hear this: I know you, and I know how you think. 'Decent bloke, Webberly. He made a little mistake. But there's no sense letting one little mistake become a catastrophe.' Except it has done, Inspector. She's dead and those letters just might be why. We've got to face that. We've got to deal with it."

"Are you arguing that letters more than ten years old would provoke someone to murder?"

"Alone, no. I'm not saying that. But according to Wiley, she was going to tell him something important, something *he* thought would change their relationship. So, what if she already told him? Or what if he already knew because he came across those letters? We have only his word that he doesn't know what she had to say."

"Agreed. But you can't be thinking she wanted to speak to him about Webberly. That's ancient history."

"Not if they'd resumed their affair. Not if they'd never lost touch with each other. Not if they'd been meeting in . . . say . . . pubs and hotels? That would have to be dealt with. And maybe it was. Only it was dealt with badly and not in the way our principals— Mrs. Davies and Webberly—thought it would be."

"I don't see that happening. And it's far too coincidental for my liking that Eugenie Davies would be killed so soon after Katja Wolff was released from prison."

"You're jumping on *that* horse?" Havers scoffed. "It's a non-starter. Depend on it."

"I'm not jumping on any horse at all," Lynley

replied. "It's far too early to be doing that. And I suggest you employ the same hesitation with regard to Major Wiley. It gets us nowhere to fix our minds on one possibility and become blind to the others."

"You're *not* doing that? Inspector, you *haven't* decided those letters from Webberly are inconsequential?"

"What I've decided is to develop my opinions based on facts, Barbara. We haven't got a lot of them so far. Until we have, we can serve the cause of justice—not to mention pursue the course of wisdom—only by keeping our eyes open and our judgements suspended. Don't you agree?"

Havers fumed. "Listen to yourself. Bloody hell. I *hate* it when you go all toffs-in-town-for-the-season on me."

Lynley smiled. "Do you? Was I? I hope it doesn't provoke you to violence."

"Just to smoking," Havers informed him.

"Even worse," Lynley sighed.

GIDEON

8 OCTOBER

LAST NIGHT I dreamed of her, or of someone like her. But the time and the place were both out of joint because I was on the Eurostar and we were descending beneath the English Channel. It was like going down into a mine.

Everyone was there: Dad, Raphael, my grandparents, and someone shadowy and faceless whom I recognised as my mother. And she was there as well: the German girl, looking much the way she looked in the newspaper photo. And yes, Sarah-Jane Beckett was there, with a picnic basket from which she pulled not a meal but a baby. She offered the baby round like a plate of sandwiches and everyone refused. One can't eat a baby, Granddad instructed her.

Then it was dark outside the windows. Someone said, Oh yes, we're under the water now.

And that's when it happened.

The tunnel walls broke. The water came through. It wasn't black like the inside of the tunnel, though, but rather like the bottom of a riverbed where one might swim and look up through the water at the sun.

And suddenly in that way dreams have of changing, we were no longer in a train at all. The carriage disappeared, and we were out of the water and on the shore of a lake, all of us. A picnic basket lay on a blanket, and I wanted to open it because I was famished. But I couldn't unfasten the basket's leather straps, and although I asked for someone to open it for me, no one would because they didn't hear me.

They couldn't hear me because they were all on their feet, pointing and crying out about a boat that was floating some distance from the shore. And I became aware suddenly of what they were crying: It was my sister's name. Someone said, She's been left in the boat! We must fetch her! But no one moved.

Then the leather straps from the picnic basket were gone, as if they'd never been. Exultant, relieved, I flung the top open to get at the food, but there was no food inside. There was only the baby. And I somehow knew that the baby was my sister even though I couldn't see her face. She was covered head and shoulders by a veil, the sort you see on statues of the Virgin.

I said in the dream, Sosy's here. She's right *here*. But no one on the shore would listen. Instead, they began to swim towards the boat, and I couldn't stop them no matter how I shouted. I picked the baby up from the basket to show them I was telling the truth. I cried out, She's here! Look! Sosy's right here! Come back! There's no one in the boat! But they kept swimming, one by one entering the water in a single line, and one by one disappearing beneath the surface of the lake.

I was desperate to stop them. I thought that if they could see her face, if I could hold her high enough above my shoulders, they would believe me and come back. So I tore at the veil round my sister's face. But I found another veil beneath it, Dr. Rose. And under that another. And under that another. I tore at them till I was weeping and frantic and no one was left on the shore but me. Even Sonia was gone. Then I turned to the picnic basket again to find it filled not with food but with dozens of kites that I kept pulling out and tossing to one side. And as I pulled them out, I felt a desperation like nothing I've ever felt before. Desperation and tremendous fear because everyone was gone and I was alone.

So what did you do, you ask me gently.

I did nothing. Libby woke me. I found I was drenched in sweat, my heart was pounding, and I was actually weeping.

Weeping, Dr. Rose. My God, I was weeping over a dream.

I said to Libby, "There was nothing in the basket. I couldn't make them stop. I had her but they couldn't see I had her, so they went into the lake and didn't come out."

She said, "You were only dreaming. Here. Come here. Let me hold you, okay?"

And yes, Dr. Rose, she had spent the night the way she often spends the night. She cooks a meal or I cook a meal, we do the washing up, and we watch the television. That's what I have been reduced to: the television. If Libby notices that we no longer listen to Perlman, Rubinstein, and Menuhin—especially Yehudi, magnificent Yehudi, child of the instrument as I myself was—she does not mention it. Indeed, she's probably grateful for the television. She is, at heart, so much an American.

When we run out of programmes to watch, we drift into sleep. We sleep in the same bed and on the same bedclothes that haven't been changed for weeks. But they are not soiled with the mixture of our fluids. No. We have not managed that.

Libby held me while my heart hammered like a miner hewing coal. Her right hand fondled the back of my head while her left hand caressed the length of my spine. From my spine, she worked her way down to my bum till we were pelvis to pelvis with only the thin flannel of my pyjamas and the cotton of her knickers between us. She whispered, "It's nothing, it's all right, you're fine," and despite those words which might have been succour under other circumstances, I knew what was supposed to happen next. Blood would rush to my cock, and I would feel the pulse of it. The pulse of it would grow and the organ would ready. I would lift my head to find her mouth or lower my mouth to find her breasts, and I would grind against her, grind against her slowly. I would pin her to the bed beneath us and take her in a silence broken only by our cries of pleasure—like no other pleasure available to men and to women, as you know—when we come. Together, of course. We come together.

Anything less than simultaneous orgasm is completely unworthy of my prowess as a male.

Except, of course, that is not what happened. How could it, I being who and what I am?

Which is what? you ask me.

A carapace covering nothing, Dr. Rose. No, less even than that. With my music gone, I am nothing itself.

Libby doesn't understand this because she can't see that who I was until Wigmore Hall was the music I made. I myself was merely an extension of the instrument, and the instrument was merely the manner in which my being took form.

You say nothing at first when you hear this, Dr. Rose. You keep your eyes on me—sometimes I wonder at the discipline it must take to keep your eyes on someone so patently not even in the room with you—and you look thoughtful. But there is something more than consideration in your eyes. Is it pity? Confusion? Doubt? Frustration?

You sit unmoving, in your widow's black. You observe me over the top of your tea cup. What are you crying out in the dream? you say. When Libby wakes you, what are you crying out, Gideon?

Mummy.

But I expect you knew that before you asked.

10 OCTOBER

I can see my mother now because of the newspapers in the Press Association office. I glimpsed her—on the opposite page to Sonia's picture—before I thrust the tabloid out of my sight. I knew it was my mother because she was on my father's arm, because they were on the front step of the Old Bailey, because above them a headline declared Justice for Sonia! in four-inch type.

So now at last I see her where before she was a blur. I see her blonde hair, I see the angles of her face, I see the way her chin is sharp and her lower jaw points to form it like the bottom of a heart. She is wearing black trousers and a soft grey sweater, and she comes to fetch me in the corner of my bedroom where Sarah-Jane and I are having a geography lesson. The Amazon River is what we're studying. How it coils like a snake for four thousand miles, from the Andes, through Peru and Brazil, and into the vast Atlantic Ocean.

Mother tells Sarah-Jane that she must cut short the lesson, and I know that Sarah-Jane doesn't like this plan because her lips change from lips into an incision in her face although she says, "Of course, Mrs. Davies," and shuts our books.

I follow Mother. We go down the stairs. She takes me into the sitting room, where a man is waiting. He's a big man with lots of ginger hair.

Mother says that he's a policeman, and he wants to ask me some questions, but I'm not to be afraid because she won't leave the room while he talks to me. She sits on the sofa and pats the cushion, right next to her thigh. And when I sit, she puts her arm round my shoulders, and I can feel her trembling as she says, "Go ahead, Detective Inspector."

She's probably told me his name, but I can't remember it. What I do remember is that he pulls a chair over close to us and he leans forward with his elbows on his knees and his arms drawn up so that he can rest his chin on his thumbs. When he's close like this, I can smell cigars. The smoke must be in his clothes and his hair. It's not a bad smell, but I'm not used to it, and I shrink back against my mother.

He says, "Your mum's right, lad. You've no reason to be frightened. No one is going to hurt you." When he speaks, I twist to gaze up at my mother, and I see that she's looking only at her lap. In her lap lie our hands, hers and mine, because she's taken my hand so that we're connected there as well: by her arm round my shoulders, by our fingers linking. And she squeezes my fingers but makes no reply to what the ginger-haired policeman has said.

He asks me if I know what happened to my sister. I say I know something bad happened to Sosy. There were lots of people in the house, I tell him, and they took her to hospital.

"Your mum's told you that she's with God now, hasn't she?" he asks.

And I say yes. Sosy's with God.

He asks me if I know what that means, to be with God.

I tell him that it means Sosy died.

"Do you know how she died?" he asks me.

I lower my head. I feel my feet bounce against the front of the sofa. I say that I'm meant to practise my instrument for three hours, that Raphael has told me I must master something—an Allegro, is it?—if I want to meet Mr. Stern next month. Mother reaches down and stops my feet bouncing. She says that I'm to try to answer the policeman.

I know the answer. I've heard the tramp of foot-steps running up the stairs and into the bathroom. I've been a witness to the cries in the night. I've lis-tened to the whispered conversations. I've walked in on questions being asked and accusations being made. So I know what happened to my little sister.

In the bath, I tell him. Sosy died in the bath.

"Where were you when Sosy died?" he asks me.

Listening to the violin, I say.

Mother speaks then. She says that Raphael has given me some music to listen to twice each day be-cause I'm not playing it as well as I should.

"So you're learning to play the fiddle, are you?" the policeman asks me kindly.

"I'm a vio*lin*ist, not a fiddler," I reply.

"Ah," the policeman says, and he smiles. "A vio*lin*-ist. I stand corrected." He settles more comfortably into his chair, rests his hands on the tops of his thighs, and says, "Lad, your mum tells me that she and your dad haven't yet told you exactly how your little sister died."

In the bath, I repeat. She died in the bath.

"True. But, lad, it wasn't an accident. Someone

hurt the little girl. Someone meant to hurt her. Do you know what that means?"

I picture sticks and stones, and that's what I say. Hurt means throwing rocks, I tell him. Hurt means putting out a foot in front of someone, hurt means hitting or pinching or biting. I think of all those things happening to Sosy.

The policeman says, "That's one kind of hurting. But there's another sort, a sort done by an adult to a child. Do you know what I mean by that?"

Getting spanked, I say.

"More than that."

And this is when Dad comes into the room. Has he just got home from work? Has he been at work at all? How long after Sonia's death is this? I'm trying to place the recollection in a context, but the only context I have is that if the police are asking the family questions, it must be before Katja was charged with anything.

Dad sees what's going on and he puts a stop to it. I remember that. And he's angry: both at Mother and at the policeman. He says, "What's going on here, Eugenie?" as the policeman gets to his feet.

She says, "The inspector wanted to ask Gideon some questions."

He says, "Why?"

The policeman says, "Everyone must be questioned, Mr. Davies."

Dad says, "You aren't assuming that *Gideon*—"

And Mother says his name. She says it in the same

way Gran says *Jack* when she's hoping to forestall an episode.

Dad tells me to go to my room, and the policeman says that he's only prolonging the inevitable. I don't know what that means, but I do as I'm told—as I always do when Dad is the one giving the orders—and I leave the room. I hear the inspector say, "This only makes the situation more frightening for the lad," and I hear Dad say, "Now, you listen to me—" as Mother says, "Please, Richard," in a voice that breaks.

Mother weeping. I should be used to this by now. Wearing grey or black, grey of face as well, she has wept for more than two years, it seems. But weeping or otherwise, she isn't able to alter the circumstances of that day.

From the mezzanine, I see the policeman leave. I see Mother show him to the door. I see him speak to her bent head, watch her intently, reach out to her then withdraw his hand. Then Dad calls out Mother's name and she turns. She doesn't see me as she goes back to him. Dad shouts at her behind the closed door.

Then hands are on my shoulders and I'm pulled back from the railing. I look up to see Sarah-Jane Beckett standing over me. She crouches down. She puts her arm round my shoulders just as my mother did, but neither her arm nor her body is shaking. We stay just like that for several minutes—and all the while Dad's voice is loud and sharp and Mother's is tentative and afraid. ". . . No more of this, Eugenie," Dad says, "I won't have it. Do you hear me?"

I sense more than anger in those words. I sense violence, Granddad's kind of violence, violence that is forged on the wheel of a mind collapsing. I am afraid.

I look up at Sarah-Jane, seeking . . . what? Protection? Affirmation of what I'm hearing below? Distraction? Any of it, all of it. But she is rapt by the drawing room door, and her gaze is fixed to its dark panels. She watches that door, unblinking, and her fingers tighten on my shoulder, taking me to the threshold of pain. I whimper and glance down at her hand and see that her fingernails are bitten and torn, with angry hangnails that are chewed and bleeding. But her face is glowing and her breathing is deep and she doesn't move till the conversation below us ceases and footsteps fire against the parquet floor. Then she takes my hand and pulls me along in her wake, up the stairs to the second floor, past the door of the nursery—closed now—and back to my room where the school books have been re-opened to the Amazon River that crawls like a poisonous serpent across a continent.

What's happening between your parents? you ask me.

And the answer seems obvious to me now. Blame.

11 OCTOBER

Sonia's dead and there must be a reckoning. This reckoning must be made not only in a courtroom of the Old Bailey, not only in the courtroom of public opinion, but also in the courtroom of the family it-self. For someone must take the burden of responsi-bility for Sonia: first for her birth—imperfect as she was—then for the scores of medical problems that plagued her short life, and last for her violent and premature death. I know this now, although I could not have known it then: There is no surviving what occurred in that bathroom in Kensington Square if blame cannot be assigned somewhere.

Dad comes to me. Sarah-Jane and I have finished our lesson, and she's left with James the Lodger. I've watched them from my window as they cross the flag-stones at the front of the house and go out through the gate. Sarah-Jane has stepped back to let James the Lodger hold the gate open for her, and she's waited for him on the other side and taken his arm. She's leaned into him that way women do, so that he might feel her nearly non-existent breasts press against his arm. But if he's felt them, he's given no sign. Instead, he's started walking in the direction of the pub, and she's taken care to match her steps to his.

I've put on a piece of music assigned by Raphael. I'm listening to it when my father joins me. I'm try-ing to feel the notes as well as to hear them, because only if I feel the notes will I be able to find them on my instrument.

Dad searches me out where I sit on the floor in a corner of the room. He squats in front of me and the music swirls round us. We live in the music till the movement is over. Dad turns off the stereo. He says,

"Come here, son," and he sits on the bed. I go to him and stand before him.

He studies me, and I want to wriggle away, but I don't. He says, "You live for the music, don't you?" and he smooths his hand through my hair. "You concentrate on the music, Gideon. Just on the music and nothing else."

I can smell the scent of him: lemons and starch, so completely unlike the scent of cigars. I say, "He asked me how Sosy died."

Dad draws me to him. He says, "She's gone now. No one can harm you."

He's talking about Katja. I've heard her leave. I've seen her in the company of the nun, so perhaps she's returned to the convent. Her name isn't mentioned within our little world. Neither is Sonia's. Unless the policeman brings one of them up.

I say, "He said someone hurt Sosy."

Dad says, "Think of the music, Gideon. Listen to the music and master it, son. That's all you have to do just now."

But that turns out not to be the case, because the policeman instructs my father to bring me to the station on the Earl's Court Road, where we sit in a small, brightly lit room, in the company of a woman who wears a suit like a man and listens watchfully to the questions I'm asked, like a guardian who's there to protect me from something. Asking the questions is Ginger Hair himself.

What he wants to know is something simple, he

tells me. "You know who Katja Wolff is, don't you, lad?" I look from my father to the woman. She wears spectacles and when the light hits them, the lenses reflect it and hide her eyes.

Dad says, "Of course he knows who Katja Wolff is. He isn't an idiot. Get to the point."

The policeman won't be hurried. He talks to me as if Dad were not there. He takes me from Sosy's birth, through Katja's coming to live with us, to the care that Sosy received at her hands. Dad protests at this. "How is an eight-year-old boy supposed to answer these sorts of questions?"

The policeman says that children are observant, that I will be able to tell them more than Dad imagines possible.

I've been given a can of Coke and a biscuit studded with nuts and sultanas, and they sit before me on the table like a three-dimensional exclamation mark. I watch the moisture form its beadwork on the can, and I run my finger through it to shape a treble clef on the curving side. I'm missing my three-hour morning practice to be here in the police station. This makes me restless, anxious, and difficult. I am already quite afraid.

Of what? you ask me.

Of the questions themselves, of giving the wrong answers, of the tension that I sense in my father which, now that I consider it, seems so at odds with my mother's grief. Shouldn't he have been prostrate with sorrow, Dr. Rose? Or at least desperate to get to the bottom of what happened to Sonia? But he isn't sorrowful, and if he's desperate, it seems like a feeling born of an urgency that he hasn't explained to anyone.

Do you answer the questions despite your fear? you ask.

I answer them as well as I can. They lead me through the two years that Katja Wolff has lived in our home. For some reason, they seem to focus primarily on her relationship with James the Lodger and Sarah-Jane Beckett. But at long last they veer to her care of Sosy and to one particular point in that care.

"Did you ever hear Katja shout at your little sister?" the policeman asked.

No, I had not.

"Did you ever see her discipline Sonia if she misbehaved?"

No, I had not.

"Did you ever see her do anything a little bit rough with Sonia? Shake her a bit when she wouldn't stop crying? Smack her bottom when she didn't obey? Pull on her arm to get her attention? Grab her leg to move her about when she changed her nappies?"

Sosy cried a lot, I tell him. Katja got out of bed in the night to take care of Sosy. She talked German to her—

"In an angry voice?"

—and sometimes *she* cried as well. I could hear her from my room, and once I got up and looked into the corridor and saw her walking up and down, holding Sosy on her shoulder. Sosy wouldn't stop crying, so Katja put her back in her cot. She took a set of plastic baby keys and jangled them over Sosy's head and I heard her say, *"Bitte, bitte, bitte"* which is German for *please*. And when the keys didn't make Sosy stop crying, she grabbed the side of the cot and gave it a shake.

"You saw this?" The policeman leans towards me across the table. "You *saw* Katja do this? Are you certain, lad?"

And something in his voice tells me I've given an answer that's pleasing. I say I'm certain: Sosy cried and Katja shook the side of the cot.

"I think we're getting somewhere now," the policeman says.

12 OCTOBER

How much of what a child reports is the stuff of his memory, Dr. Rose? How much of what a child reports is the stuff of his dreams? How much of what I say to the detective in those hours in the police station comes from what I actually witnessed? How much grows from sources as diverse as the tension I feel between my father and the policeman and my desire to please them both?

It isn't much of a leap from shaking the side of a cot to shaking a child. And from there, it is the work of a moment to fancy having seen a small arm twisted, a small body jerked upright to put a coat on, a small round face squeezed and pinched when someone spits her food on the floor, a tangle of hair yanked through a comb, and legs wrenched into a pair of pink dungarees.

Ah, you say. Your voice is noncommittal and carefully, scrupulously without judgement, Dr. Rose. Your hands, however, rise, pressed together in an attitude that resembles prayer. You place them just beneath your chin. You don't avert your gaze but I avert mine.

I see what you're thinking, and I'm thinking it as well. My answers to that policeman's questions were what sent Katja Wolff to prison.

But I didn't give evidence at her trial, Dr. Rose. So if what I said was so important, why wasn't I called to give evidence? Anything less than the whole truth sworn to in a court of law was like an article appearing on the front page of a tabloid: something to be taken at face value only, something suggesting that further investigation into the matter by professionals might be required.

If I said that Katja Wolff harmed my sister, all that would have come from that is their looking into the allegation. Isn't that the case? And if corroboration existed for what I told them, they would have found it.

That has to be what happened, Dr. Rose.

15 OCTOBER

I might have truly seen it. I might have been a witness to those things which I declared as having occurred between my little sister and her nanny. If so many sections of my mind are blank when it comes to the past, how illogical is it to assume that somewhere on that vast canvas reside images too painful to be remembered accurately?

Pink dungarees are fairly accurate, you tell me. They come either from memory or from embellishment, Gideon.

How could I embellish with such a detail as the colour of her overalls if she didn't *wear* those overalls?

She was a little girl, you say with a shrug that's not dismissive so much as inconclusive. Little girls often wear pink.

So you're saying I was a liar, Dr. Rose? Simultaneously a child prodigy and a liar?

They're not mutually exclusive, you point out.

I reel from this and you see something—anguish, horror, guilt?—on my face.

You say, I'm not labeling you a liar now, Gideon. But you might have been then. Circumstances may have required you to lie.

What sort of circumstances, Dr. Rose?

You have no answer to give me other than this: Write what you remember.

17 OCTOBER

Libby found me at the top of Primrose Hill. I was standing before that metal engraving that allows one to identify the buildings and monuments that one can see from the summit, and I was forcing myself to look from the engraving to the view—working from east to west—in order to pick each one out. From the corner of my eye, I saw her coming up the path, dressed in her black leathers. She'd left her helmet elsewhere, and the wind whipped her curls round her face.

She said, "Saw your car in the square. I thought I'd find you here. No kite?"

"No kite." I touched the metal surface of the engraving, my fingers resting on St. Paul's Cathedral. I studied the skyline.

"What's up, then? You don't look so great. Aren't you cold? What're you doing out here without a sweater?"

Looking for answers, I thought.

She said, "Hey! Anyone home? I'm, like, *talking* to you here."

I said, "I needed a walk."

She said, "You saw the shrink today, didn't you?"

I wanted to say that I see you even when I don't see you, Dr. Rose. But I thought that she would misunderstand and take the comment for a patient's obsession with his doctor, which I do not have.

She came round the engraving to face me, blocking my view. She reached across the sheet of metal and touched her palm to my chest, saying, "What's wrong, Gid? How can I help?"

Her touch reminded me of all that isn't happening between us—of all that would have been happening between a woman and a normal man—and the weight of this idea was suddenly too much to bear in conjunction with what was already plaguing me. I said, "I may have sent a woman to prison."

"What?"

I told her the rest.

When I had finished, she said, "You were eight years old. A cop was asking questions. You did the best you could in a bad situation. *And* you might have seen that stuff, too. There've been studies on this, Gid, and they say that kids don't make things up when it comes to abuse. Where there's smoke, there's fire. And anyway, someone must have confirmed what you said if you didn't testify in court."

"That's just it. I'm not so sure that I didn't testify, Libby."

"But you said—"

"I said I'd managed to remember the policeman, the questions, the station: all of them aspects of a situation that I'd blocked from my mind. What's to say I haven't also blocked from my mind giving evidence at Katja Wolff's trial?"

"Oh. Yeah. I see." She looked out at the view and tried to tame her hair, sucking in on her lower lip as she thought about what I'd said. Finally, she declared, "Okay. Let's find out what really went on, then."

"How?"

"How tough can it be to dig up what happened at a trial that was probably covered by every newspaper in the country?"

19 OCTOBER

We started with Bertram Cresswell-White, the barrister who'd prosecuted Katja Wolff for the Crown.

Finding him, as Libby had promised, presented no problem. He had a room in chambers in the Temple, at Number Five Paper Buildings, and he agreed to see me once I managed to get him on the phone. He said, "I remember the case perfectly. Yes. I'm happy to speak with you about it, Mr. Davies."

Libby insisted on going with me. She said, "Two heads are better. What you won't think to ask him, I will."

So we drove to the river and entered the Temple from Victoria Embankment, where a cobblestone lane ducks beneath an ornate archway, which gives access to the best legal minds in the country. Paper Buildings sits on the east side of a leafy garden within the Temple, and the barristers who have chambers there possess the benefit of views of either the trees or the Thames.

Bertram Cresswell-White had views of both, and when Libby and I were ushered into his office by a young woman delivering him a set of pink-ribboned briefs, we found him in an alcove behind his desk, taking advantage of the sight of a barge sailing sluggishly in the direction of Waterloo Bridge. When he turned from the window, I felt confident that I'd never seen him before, that there was nothing I'd deliberately or unconsciously wiped from my mind involving him. For surely I would remember so imposing a figure had he questioned me inside a courtroom.

He must be six feet three inches tall, Dr. Rose, with the sort of shoulders one gets from rowing. He has the frightening eyebrows of a man over sixty, and when he looked at me, I felt the internal jolt one gets from being pierced by a stare that's used to intimidate witnesses.

He said, "I never expected to meet you. I heard you play some years ago at the Barbican." He said to the young woman as she placed the briefs on his desk where already a stack of manila folders lay in the centre, "Coffee please, Mandy." And to Libby and me, "Will you have some?"

I said yes. Libby said, "Sure. Thanks," and she looked round the room with her lips forming a small O through which she was blowing air. I know her well enough to see what she was thinking in her California fashion: "Some joint you got here." She wasn't wrong.

Cresswell-White's room in chambers was designed to impress: hung with brass chandeliers, lined with bookshelves holding well-bound legal volumes, and heated by a fireplace in which even now was burning a gas fire with a realistic arrangement of artificial coals. He gestured us to a sitting area of leather armchairs that were gathered round a coffee table on a Persian rug. A framed photograph stood on this table. In it, a youngish man dressed in a barrister's wig and gown posed at Cresswell-White's side, his arms crossed and a grin on his face.

"Is this your kid?" Libby said to Cresswell-White. "There's a big resemblance."

"That's my son Geoffrey, yes," the barrister replied, "at the conclusion of his first case."

"Looks like he won it," Libby noted.

"He did. He's just your age, by the way." This last was said to me with a nod as he set the folders on the coffee table. I saw that *Crown vs. Wolff* was written on each of their tabs. "You were born a week apart at the same hospital, I discovered. I didn't know that at the time of the trial. But later when I was reading about you somewhere—this would have been when you were a teenager, I suppose—the article included the facts of your birth and there it was: the date, place, and time. It's remarkable, really, how connected we all are."

Mandy returned with the coffee then and placed the tray on the table: three cups and three saucers, milk and sugar, but no pot: a subtle omission that seemed designed to determine the length of our stay. We doctored our drinks as she left us.

I said, "We've come with some specific questions about Katja Wolff's trial."

"You've not heard from her, have you?" Cresswell-White's tone was sharp.

"Heard from her? No. Once she left our house— when my sister died—I never saw her again. At least . . . I don't think I saw her."

"You don't think . . . ?" Cresswell-White picked up his cup of coffee and held it on his knee. He was wearing a good suit—grey wool and cut exactly to fit him—and the creases in his trousers looked as if they'd been placed there by royal decree.

"I have no recollection of the trial," I told him. "I have no actual *clear* recollection of that whole period of time. Large areas of my childhood are rather misty, and I've been trying to clarify them." I didn't tell him why I was making this attempt to recapture the past. I didn't use the word *repression,* and I couldn't bring myself to reveal anything more.

"I see." Cresswell-White gave a brief smile that disappeared as quickly as it flashed on his face. To me, the smile seemed both ironic and self-directed, and his next comment reinforced this assumption. "Gideon, would that we could all drink of the waters of Lethe like you. I, for one, would sleep better at night. May I call you Gideon, by the way? That's how I've always thought of you, although we've never met."

That was a decisive answer to the main question I'd come with, and the relief I felt at hearing it told me something of how great my fears had been. I said, "So I didn't give evidence, did I? At her trial? I didn't give evidence against her."

"Good God, no. I wouldn't put an eight-year-old child through that. Why do you ask?"

"Gideon talked to the cops when his sister died," Libby said frankly. "He couldn't remember much about the trial, but he thought his testimony might have been what put Katja Wolff away."

"Ah. I do see. And now that she's been released, you're wanting to prepare yourself in case—"

"She's been released?" I broke in.

"You didn't know? Neither of your parents informed you? They were both sent letters. She's been out for—" He glanced at some paperwork in one of the folders. "She's been out for just over a month."

"No. No. I didn't know." I felt a sudden pulsing within my skull, and I saw the familiar pattern of bright speckling that always suggests that the pulsing will turn into twenty-four hours of pounding. I thought, Oh no. Please. Not here and not now.

"Perhaps they didn't think it necessary," Cresswell-White said. "If she's going to approach anyone from that period of time, it's more likely to be one of them, isn't it? Or myself. Or someone who gave damning evidence against her." He went on to say something more, but I couldn't hear because the pulsing in my head was growing louder and the speckling was turning to an arc of light. My body was like an invading army, and I—who should have been its general—was instead its target.

I felt my feet begin a nervous tapping, as if they wanted to carry me from the room. I drew a breath and with the air came the image of that door once again: that blue blue door at the top of the stairs, those two locks upon it, that ring at its centre. I could see it as if I stood before it, and I wanted to open it but I could not raise my hand.

Libby said my name. I heard that much through the pulsing. I held up a hand, asking for a moment, just a moment please to recover.

From what? you want to know, and you lean towards me, ever ready for a loop in the yarn into which you can insert your needle. Recover from what? Go back, Gideon.

Go back to what?

To that moment in Bertram Cresswell-White's rooms, to the pulsing in your head, to what led to the pulsing.

All the talk about the trial led to the pulsing.

We've had the trial before now. It's more than that. What are you avoiding?

I'm avoiding *nothing*. . . . But you're not convinced, are you, Dr. Rose? I'm supposed to be writing what I remember, and you've begun to question how trolling through the trial of Katja Wolff is going to take me back to my music. You caution me. You point out that the human mind is strong, that it holds on to its neuroses with a fierce protection, that it possesses the ability to deny and distract, and that this expedition to Paper Buildings might well be a monumental effort on the part of my mind to engage in displacement.

Then that's how it will have to be, Dr. Rose. I do not know how else to go at this thing.

All right, you say. Did your time with Cresswell-White trigger anything else, then? Aside from the episode with your head?

Episode. You choose that word with deliberation, and I know it. But I will not bite at the bait you cast out. I will tell you about Sarah-Jane instead. For this is what I learn from Bertram Cresswell-White: the part that I did not have in Katja Wolff's trial, the part that Sarah-Jane Beckett had.

19 OCTOBER, 9:00 P.M.

"She lived in the house with your family and Wolff, after all," Bertram Cresswell-White said. He'd taken up the first of the folders with *Crown vs. Wolff* on them, and he'd begun to leaf through the documents inside, reading from time to time when his memory needed to be refreshed. "She was in a good position to observe what went on."

"So did she see something?" Libby asked. She'd moved her chair closer to mine, and she'd placed her hand on the back of my neck as if she knew without my telling her what state my head was in. She kneaded my neck gently, and I wanted to be grateful. But I could sense the displeasure that the barrister felt at this open display of her affection for me, and I tensed because of this displeasure as I always tense when an older man looks on me with a critical eye.

"She saw Wolff being sick in the mornings, every morning for a month before the child was killed," he said. "You know she was pregnant, don't you?"

"My father told me as much," I said.

"Yes. Well. Beckett saw the German girl's patience growing thin. The child—your sister—got her up three or four times each night, so she was short of sleep as well and that, in conjunction with the difficulties of morning sickness, wore her down. She began to leave Sonia too much alone, which was something that Miss Beckett came to realise since she gave you your lessons on the same floor of the house as your sister's nursery. Ultimately, she felt it her duty to report to your parents that Wolff was derelict in her duties. This precipitated a confrontation, which resulted in Wolff being sacked."

"On the spot?" Libby asked.

Cresswell-White consulted a file for the answer to this, saying, "No. She was given a month's notice. Your parents were quite generous considering the situation, Gideon."

"But she never said in court that she saw Katja Wolff abuse my sister?" I asked.

The barrister closed the folder, saying, "Beckett testified that they'd rowed—the German girl and your parents. She testified that Sonia, over a period of days, was left to cry for as long as an hour in her cot. She said that on the evening in question, she heard the German girl giving Sonia her bath. But she couldn't name the time or the place where she'd witnessed any direct physical abuse."

"Who did?" Libby asked.

"No one," the barrister replied.

"God," I murmured.

Cresswell-White seemed to know what I was thinking, because he set the folder back on the coffee table along with his cup and he spoke to me urgently. "A case in court is like a mosaic, Gideon. If there's no eyewitness to the crime itself—as there wasn't in this situation—then each piece of the case that the Crown presents must ultimately form a pattern from which an entire picture can be seen. The entire picture is what convinces the jury of the defendant's guilt. And that's what happened in Katja Wolff's case."

"Because there was other testimony against her?" Libby asked.

"Yes, indeed."

"Whose?" My voice was weak—I could *hear* the

weakness as well as I could hate it and as fully as I could not remove it from my tone.

"The police who took her first and only statement, the forensic pathologist who did the post-mortem, the friend with whom Wolff had initially claimed to be on the phone for one minute during which she left your sister alone, your mother, your father, your grandparents. It's less a case of encouraging anyone to say something directly against a defendant than of unfolding for the jury the situation as it existed and allowing them to draw their own conclusions about that situation. So everyone contributed to the overall mosaic. What we ended up with was a twenty-one-year-old German girl who had reveled in the publicity she got when she escaped from her country, who was able to emigrate to England because of the good will of a group of nuns, whose celebrity—which had fed her ego—quickly faded upon her arrival here, who was given a job that included room and board, who got herself pregnant, fell consequently ill, failed to cope, lost her job, and snapped."

"Sounds like manslaughter, not murder," Libby said.

"And would probably have gone down as such had she been willing to testify. But she wasn't. It was amazingly arrogant but quite in keeping with her background if it comes down to it, I suppose. She wouldn't testify. And she made matters worse for herself by refusing to speak to the police more than that single time, as well as by refusing to speak to her solicitor, or even her barrister."

"Why'd she clam up?" Libby asked.

"I couldn't say. But the post-mortem showed there were previously healed fractures on your sister's body that no doctor could account for and no one else was able to explain, Gideon, and the fact that the German girl would say *nothing* to anyone concerning Sonia didn't make it look as if she was in the dark about those older injuries. And while the jury was in-structed—as they were in those days—that Wolff's si-lence could not be held against her, juries are only human, aren't they? That silence is going to influence their thinking."

"So what I said to the police—"

Cresswell-White waved my words away, saying, "I read your statement. Naturally, it was part of the brief. I re-read it, in fact, when you phoned me. And while I would have taken it into account twenty years ago, believe me, I wouldn't have prosecuted Katja Wolff on the strength of it alone." He smiled. "After all, you were eight years old, Gideon. I had a son the very same age, so I was well aware of what boys are like. I had to consider the fact that Katja Wolff might have sorted you out about something in the days preceding your sister's death. And if that had been the case, you might have used your imagination for a bit of revenge on her, without knowing where your statement to the police could lead."

"There you go, Gideon," Libby said.

"So set your mind at rest if you're feeling guilty about Katja Wolff," Cresswell-White said, and his words were warm. "She did herself far more harm than you ever did her."

20 OCTOBER

So was it revenge or was it memory, Dr. Rose? And if it was revenge, what was it for? I can't think of a time that anyone save Raphael sought to discipline me, and the only times he did so were when he made me listen to a piece of music that I wasn't performing to his liking, and that was hardly punishment at all.

Was *The Archduke* something you listened to? you enquire.

I don't remember. But there were other pieces that I recall. The Lalo, compositions by Saint-Saëns and Bruch.

And did you master those other pieces? you ask. Once you listened to them, Gideon, were you able to play them?

Of course. Yes. I played them all.

But not *The Archduke*?

That piece has always been my *bête noire*.

Shall we talk about that?

There's nothing to say. *The Archduke* exists. I've never been able to play it well. And now I can't play the instrument itself. I'm not even close to being able to play it. So is my father right? Are we wasting our time? Is what I have just a case of nerves that has *un-*nerved me and caused me to look elsewhere for a so-lution? You know what I mean: Foist the problem onto someone else's shoulders so that I don't have to confront it myself. Hand it over to the shrink and see what she makes of it.

Do you believe that, Gideon?

I don't know what to believe.

We drove home from Bertram Cresswell-White's. I could tell that Libby thought we'd found a solution to my problems because the barrister had given me absolution. Her conversation was light—how she planned to "put it to Rock the next time he withholds my wages, the creep"—and when she wasn't changing gear, she kept her hand on my knee. She'd been the one to suggest that she drive my car, and I was only too happy to let her. Cresswell-White's absolution hadn't obliterated the growing pain in my head. I was definitely better off not behind the wheel.

Once back in Chalcot Square, Libby parked the car and turned my face to hers. "Hey," she said. "You've got the answers you were looking for, Gideon. Let's plan a celebration."

She leaned towards me and touched her mouth to mine. I felt her tongue against my lips, and I opened them and allowed her to kiss me.

Why? you ask.

Because I wanted to believe what she said: that I had the answers I'd been looking for.

Is that the only reason?

No. Of course not. I wanted to be normal.

And?

All right. I managed a response of sorts. My skull was cracking open, but I reached for her head, held her, and insinuated my fingers into her hair. We stayed like that, our tongues creating that dance of expectation between us. I tasted in her mouth the coffee she'd drunk in Cresswell-White's rooms and I drank of it deeply, with the hope that the sudden thirst I felt would lead to the hunger I'd not experienced in years. I wanted that hunger, Dr. Rose. Suddenly, I had to have it in order to know that I was alive.

One hand still in her hair, holding her to me, I kissed her face. I reached for her breast, and I felt her nipple hardening hardening erect and hardening through the material of her jersey and I squeezed that nipple to bring her both to pain and to pleasure and she moaned. She climbed from her seat onto mine, straddling me, kissing me. She called me baby and honey and Gid, and she unbuttoned my shirt as I squeezed and released and squeezed and released and her mouth was on my chest and her lips were tracing a trail from my neck and I wanted to feel, I wanted to feel, and so I groaned and put my face in her hair.

And there was the scent: fresh mint. From her shampoo, I suppose. But suddenly I was not in the car at all. I was in the back garden of our house in Kensington: in summer and at night. I've picked some mint leaves and I'm rolling them in my palms to release the smell and I hear the sounds before I see the people. They sound like diners smacking their lips over a meal, which is what I think the noise is at first until I pick them out of the darkness at the bottom of the garden, where a flash of colour that is her blonde hair attracts my attention.

They are standing against the brick shed where the gardening tools are kept. His back is to me. Her hands cover his head. One of her legs crosses behind him above his arse, holding him to her and they grind together, they grind and grind. Her head is thrown back and he kisses her neck and I can't *see* who he is but I can see her. It's Katja, my little sister's nanny. It's one of the men from the house.

Not someone else Katja knows? you ask. Not someone from the outside?

Who? Katja knows no one, Dr. Rose. She sees no one but the nun from the convent and a girl who comes to call now and then, a girl called Katie. And this isn't Katie out here in the darkness because I remember Katie, Good God I *remember* Katie now because she's fat and she's funny and she dresses with flair and she talks in the kitchen when Katja feeds Sonia and she says that Katja's escape from East Berlin was a metaphor for an organism only it wasn't *organism* that she said at all, it was *orgasm,* wasn't it, which is all she ever talks about.

Gideon, you say to me, who was the man? Look at the shape of him, look at his hair.

Her hands cover his head. He's bent to her anyway. I can't see his hair.

Can't or won't? Which is it, Gideon? Is it can't or won't?

I can't. I *can't.*

Have you seen the lodger? Your father? Your grandfather? Raphael Robson? Who is it, Gideon?

I DON'T KNOW.

And Libby reached for me then, reached her hands down, did what a normal woman does when she's aroused and wants to share her arousal. She laughed a breathless sort of laugh, said, "I can't even *believe* we're doing this in your car," and eased my belt out of its buckle, unfastened it, unbuttoned my trousers, put her fingers on the zipper, brought her mouth back to mine.

And there was nothing within me, Dr. Rose. No hunger, no thirst, no heat, no longing. No pulse of blood to awaken my lust, no throbbing in the veins to harden my cock.

I grabbed Libby's hands. I didn't need to make an excuse or say anything else to her. She may be American—a little loud at times, a little vulgar, a little too casual, too friendly, and too forthright—but she isn't a fool.

She pushed herself off me and got back in her seat. "It's me, isn't it?" she said. "I'm too fat for you."

"Don't be an idiot."

"Don't *call* me an idiot."

"Don't act like one."

She turned to the window. It was steaming up. Light from the square diffracted through the steam and cast a muted glow against her cheek. Round, the cheek looked, and I could see the colour in it, the flush of a peach as it grows and ripens. The despair I felt—for myself, for her, for the two of us together—was what made me continue. "You're fine, Libby. You're one hundred percent. You're perfect. It isn't you."

"Then what? Rock? It's Rock. It's that we're still married. It's that you know what he does to me, don't you? You've figured it out."

I didn't know what she was talking about, and I didn't want to know. I said, "Libby, if you haven't realised by now that there's something wrong with me—something seriously wrong—"

And at that, she got out of the car. She shoved the door open and slammed it shut, and she did what she never does. She shouted. "Nothing is wrong with you, Gideon! Do you hear me? Nothing is fucking *wrong* with you!"

I got out as well, and we faced each other over the bonnet of the car. I said, "You know that you're lying to yourself."

"I know what's before my eyes. And what's before my eyes is you."

"You've heard me try to play. You've sat in your flat and heard me. You know."

"The violin? Is *that* what this is all about, Gid? The God damn cock-sucking violin?" She smashed her fist against the car's bonnet so hard that I started. She cried, "You are *not* the violin. Playing music is what you do. It is not—and has never been—who you are."

"And if I can't play? What happens then?"

"Then you live, all right? You God damn start *living*. How about that for a profound idea?"

"You don't understand."

"I understand plenty. I understand that you've got yourself, like, all hooked into being Mr. Violin.

You've spent so many years scratching at the strings that you don't have any other identity. Why are you doing it? What's it s'posed to prove? Will your dad, maybe, *love* you enough if you play till your fingers bleed or something?" She swung away from the car and away from me. "Like, why am I even *bothering,* Gideon?"

She began striding towards the house and I followed her, which was when I saw that the front door was open and that someone was standing on the front steps and probably had been standing there since Libby had parked the car in the square. She saw him at that same moment that I did and for the first time I caught on her face an expression telling me she held an aversion to him that was as strong as—if not stronger than—the one my father held for her.

"Then perhaps it's time you stopped bothering," Dad said. His voice was quite pleasant, but his eyes were steel.

GIDEON

20 OCTOBER, 10:00 P.M.

DAD SAID, "Charming girl. Does she always shriek like a fishwife in the square, or was that something special this evening?"

"She was upset."

"That was obvious. As were her feelings about your work, by the way, which is something you might want to consider should you wish to carry on with her."

I didn't want to discuss Libby with him. He's made his attitude plain from the start. There's no point wasting energy trying to change it.

We were in the kitchen, where we'd repaired once Libby left us on the steps. She'd said to him, "Richard, stay out of my way," and had pushed open the gate to her steps with a clang. She'd pounded down and into her flat, from where the volume of her pop music was now illustrating the state of her mind.

"We went to see Bertram Cresswell-White," I told Dad. "Do you remember him?"

"I had a look at your garden earlier," Dad replied, canting his head towards the back of the house. "The weeds are starting to go rampant, Gideon. If you aren't careful, they're going to choke out the rest of the plants, what few there are. You know, you can hire a Filipino if you don't like gardening. Have you considered doing that?"

From below in Libby's flat, the pop music blared. She'd opened her windows. Distorted phrases pounded up from the lower ground floor: *How can your* man . . . loves *you . . . slow down,* bay-*bee . . .*

I said, "Dad, I asked you—"

"I've brought you two camellias, by the way." He walked to the window overlooking the garden.

. . . let him know . . . *he's* play*ing around!*

It was dark outside, so there was nothing to see except Dad's own reflection and mine on the glass. His was clear; mine wavered ghostlike as if affected by either the atmosphere or my inability to manifest strongly.

"I've planted them on either side of the steps," Dad said. "They're not quite what I want yet in the way of blooms, but I'm getting close."

"Dad, I'm asking you—"

"I've weeded both planters, but you're going to have to see to the rest of the garden yourself."

"Dad!"

. . . a chance to feel . . . free to . . . the feeling grab you, bay-*bee.*

"Or you can always ask your American friend if she wants to make herself useful in ways other than verbally assaulting you in the street or entertaining you with her quaint choice of music."

"God damn it, Dad. I'm asking you a question."

He turned from the window. "I heard the question. And—"

Love him. Love him, baby. Love him.

"—if I didn't have to compete with your little American's auditory entertainment, I might actually consider answering it."

I said loudly, "Ignore it, then. Ignore Libby as well. You're good at ignoring things you can't be bothered with, aren't you, Dad?"

The music suddenly stopped, as if I'd been heard. The silence following my question created nature's enemy, a vacuum, and I waited to see what would fill it. A moment later Libby's door banged shut. A moment after that the Suzuki fired up in the street. It roared as she angrily revved its motor. Then the sound faded as she spun out of Chalcot Square.

Dad leveled a look at me, his arms crossed. We'd arrived at dangerous territory, the two of us, and I could feel that danger, like a live wire snapping in the air between us. But he said evenly, "Yes. Yes, I suppose I do that, don't I? I ignore unpleasantness in order to get on with living."

I side-stepped the implication behind his words. I said slowly, as if speaking to someone who did not understand English, "Do you remember Cresswell-White?"

He sighed and moved away from the window. He walked into the music room. I followed him. He sat near my stereo and racks of CDs. I remained by the door.

"What do you want to know?" he asked me.

I accepted the question as acquiescence, saying, "I've remembered seeing Katja in the garden. It was night. She was with someone, a man. They were—" I shrugged, feeling heat in my face, aware of the juvenility of that heat, which only made it seem to grow stronger. "They were together. Intimately. I can't remember who he was. I don't think I saw him clearly."

"What's the point of this?"

"You know the point. We've been through it all. You know what she—what Dr. Rose—wants me to do."

"So tell me, is this particular memory supposed to relate to your music in some way?"

"I'm trying to remember whatever I can. In whatever order I can. When I can. One memory seems to trigger another, and if I hook enough of them together, there's a chance I can get to whatever it is that's causing the problem with my playing."

"There is no problem with your playing. There is no playing."

"Why won't you just answer? Why won't you help me? Just tell me who Katja—"

"Are you assuming that I know?" he demanded. "Or are you really asking if I was the man with Katja Wolff in the garden? My relationship with Jill certainly indicates a predilection for younger women, doesn't it? And if I have that predilection now, why not then?"

"Are you going to answer?"

"Let me assure you that my current predilection is recent and directed solely at Jill."

"So you weren't the man in the garden. The man with Katja Wolff."

"I was not."

I studied him. I wondered if he was telling the truth. I thought of that picture of Katja and my sister, of the way she smiled at whoever was taking it, of what that smile might mean.

He said with a tired gesture towards the racks near his chair, "I had the opportunity to look through your CDs while I was waiting for you, Gideon."

I waited, wary about this line of talk.

"You've quite a collection. How many are there? Three hundred? Four?"

I made no response.

"A number of different interpretations of some pieces by different artists as well."

"I'm sure there's a point in this," I said at last.

"But not a single copy of *The Archduke*. Why is that? I wonder."

"I've never been attracted to that particular piece."

"Then why were you going to play it at Wigmore Hall?"

"Beth suggested it. Sherrill went along. I had no real objection—"

"To playing a piece of music that doesn't attract you?" he demanded. "What the hell were you think- ing? You're the name, Gideon. Not Beth. Not

Sherrill. You call the shots when it comes to a concert. They do not."

"The concert's not what I want to talk about."

"I understand that. Believe me, I entirely understand. You haven't wanted to talk about the concert from the beginning. You're seeing this damned psychiatrist, in fact, because you don't want to talk about the concert."

"That's not true."

"Joanne heard from Philadelphia today. They wanted to know if you'll be able to make your appearance there. The rumours have traveled to America, Gideon. How much longer do you expect to be able to hold the world at bay?"

"I'm trying to get to the root of this in the only way I know."

" 'Trying to get to the root of this,' " he mocked. "You're doing nothing but opting for cowardice, and I wouldn't have thought that possible. I only thank God your grandfather didn't live to see this moment."

"Are you thankful for me or for yourself?"

He drew in a slow breath. One of his hands balled into a fist. The other hand reached to cradle it. "What exactly are you saying?"

I couldn't go further. We'd reached one of those moments when it seemed to me that irreparable harm could come from carrying on. And what good could have come from carrying on? What point would be served by forcing my father to turn the mirror from me onto his own childhood? onto his adulthood?

onto everything he'd done and been and attempted in order to be acceptable to the man who'd adopted him?

Freaks, freaks, freaks, Granddad had shouted at the son who'd created three of them. Because I, too, am a freak of nature, Dr. Rose. At heart I have always been one.

I said, "Cresswell-White said everyone gave evidence against Katja. Everyone from the house, he said."

Dad watched me through narrowed eyes before he made a comment, and I couldn't tell if his hesitation had to do with my words or with my refusal to answer his question. "That should hardly have come as a surprise to you in a murder trial," he finally responded.

"He told me I wasn't called to give evidence."

"That's what happened. Yes."

"I've remembered speaking to the police, though. I've remembered you and my mother arguing about my speaking to the police as well. I've remembered that there were a number of questions about the relationship between Sarah-Jane Beckett and James the Lodger."

"Pitchford." Dad's voice was heavier now, weary. "James Pitchford was his name."

"Pitchford. Right. Yes. James Pitchford." I'd been standing all the while, and now I picked up a chair and moved it to where Dad himself was sitting. I set it in front of him. "At the trial, someone said that you and my mother rowed with Katja in the days preceding . . . preceding what happened to Sonia."

"She was pregnant, Gideon. She'd become lax in her responsibilities. Your sister would have been a difficult charge for anyone and—"

"Why?"

"Why?" He rubbed his eyebrows as if trying to stimulate his own memory. When he dropped his hand, he looked up at the ceiling instead of at me, but when he lifted his head, I had time enough to see that his eyes had become red-rimmed. I felt a pang, but I did not stop him when he went on. "Gideon, I've already recited a litany of your sister's ailments for you. Down's Syndrome was only the tip of the iceberg. She was in and out of hospital for the two years that she was alive, and when she was *out* of hospital, she had to have someone to attend to her constantly. That someone was Katja."

"Why didn't you hire a professional nurse?"

He laughed without humour. "We hadn't the funds."

"The Government—"

"State support? Unthinkable."

And something within me jarred loose at that, my grandfather's words, spoken in a roar over the dinner table: "We do not lower ourselves to ask for charity, God damn it. A real man *supports* his family, and if he can't do so, he shouldn't produce one in the first place. Keep it in your bloody trousers, Dick, if you can't face the consequences of waving it about. You hear me, boy?"

And to this, Dad added, "And even if we'd tried for support, how far would we have got once the

Government sorted out how much we were already spending to employ Raphael and Sarah-Jane? There was belt-tightening that we could have done. We chose not to do it initially."

"What about the row with Katja?"

"What about it? We learned from Sarah-Jane that Katja had been lax. We talked to the girl, and during the conversation it came out that she was being sick in the morning. It was a short leap to the fact that she was pregnant. She didn't deny it."

"So you sacked her on the spot."

"What else were we supposed to do?"

"Who made her pregnant?"

"She wouldn't say. And we did not sack her because she wouldn't say, all right? That was hardly the issue. We sacked her because she couldn't look after your sister properly. And there were other problems, earlier problems that we'd overlooked because she'd seemed fond of Sonia, and we liked that."

"What sort of problems?"

"Her clothing, which was never appropriate. We'd asked her to wear either a uniform or a simple, plain skirt and blouse. She wouldn't, no matter how often we instructed her to do so. She felt she had to express herself, she said. Then there were her visitors, who came and went at all hours of the day and night despite our asking her to limit their calls."

"Who were they?"

"I don't recall them. Good God, this was more than twenty years ago."

"Katie?"

"What?"

"Someone called Katie. She was fat. She wore expensive clothes. I remember Katie."

"Perhaps there was a Katie. I don't know. They came from the convent. They sat in the kitchen and talked and drank coffee and smoked cigarettes. And several times when Katja went out with them on her evening off, she came back inebriated and overslept in the morning. What I'm trying to tell you is that there were problems *before* the pregnancy issue came up, Gideon. The pregnancy—as well as the illness that accompanied it—was just the final straw."

"But you and Mother argued with Katja when you gave her the sack."

He shoved himself to his feet, walked across the room, and stood looking down at my violin case, closed now as it had been for days, the Guarneri hidden away from my sight so that it might cease to taunt me. "She didn't want to be sacked, obviously. She was several months pregnant, and she wasn't likely to find anyone else to employ her. So she argued with us. She pleaded to be kept on."

"Then why not get rid of her baby? Even then, there were places . . . clinics . . ."

"That's not the decision she made, Gideon. I can't tell you why." He squatted and released the clips on the case. He lifted the top. Inside, the Guarneri lay burnished by the light, and the glow of the wood seemed to make an accusation to which I had no simple reply. "So we argued. The three of us argued. And the next time Sonia was difficult, which happened the following day, Katja . . . took care of the problem." He lifted the violin from the case and unclipped the bow. He said, and his voice was not unkind and the rims of his eyes were redder than before, "You know the truth now. Will you play for me, son?"

And I wanted to, Dr. Rose. But I knew that there was nothing within me, nothing of what had previously driven the music from my soul through my body to my arms and my fingers. That is my curse, even now.

I said, "I remember people in the house the night that . . . when Sonia . . . I remember voices, footsteps, my mother calling your name."

"We were panicked. Everyone was panicked. There were paramedics. Firemen. Your grandparents. Pitchford. Raphael."

"Raphael was there?"

"He was there."

"Doing what?"

"I don't recall. Perhaps he was on the phone to Juilliard. He'd been trying for months to come up with a way to convince us it was possible for you to attend. He was set on it, more set than you were."

"So all this happened round the time of Juilliard?"

Dad lowered his arms, which had been offering me the Guarneri. The violin hung from one hand and the bow from the other, orphans of my egregious impotence. He said, "Where is this taking us, Gideon? What the hell has this to do with your instrument?

God knows I'm trying to cooperate, but you're not giving me anything to measure with."

"Measure what?"

"How do I know if there's progress? How do *you* know if there's progress?"

And I could not answer him, Dr. Rose. Because the truth is what he fears and what I dread: I can not tell if this is any good, if the direction I'm heading is the direction that will take me back to the life I once knew and held so dear.

I said, "The night it happened . . . I was in my room. I've remembered that. I've remembered the shouting and the paramedics—the *sound* of them rather than the sight of them—and I've remembered Sarah-Jane listening at the door, inside my room with me, saying that she wouldn't be leaving after all. But I don't remember her *planning* to leave before Sonia . . . before what happened."

I could see Dad's right hand tighten on the neck of the Guarneri. Clearly, this wasn't the response he'd been looking for when he'd taken the instrument out of its case. He said, "A violin like this needs to be played. It also needs to be stored properly. Look at this bow, Gideon. Look at the condition of its hairs. And when was the last time you put a bow away without loosening it? Or don't you think about that sort of thing any longer, now that you're concentrating all your efforts on the past?"

I thought of the day that I'd tried to play, the day Libby had heard me, the day that I'd learned for certain what I'd only felt like a premonition before: that my music was gone, and irretrievably so.

Dad said, "You never used to do this sort of thing. This instrument wasn't just left lying on the floor. It was stored away from the heat and the cold. It wasn't near a radiator, nor was it within six yards of an open window."

"If Sarah-Jane was planning to leave before everything happened, why didn't she leave?" I asked.

"The strings haven't been cleaned since Wigmore Hall, have they? When was the last time you failed to clean the strings after a concert, Gideon?"

"There wasn't a concert. I didn't play."

"And haven't played since. Haven't thought to play. Haven't had the nerve to—"

"Tell me about Sarah-Jane Beckett!"

"God damn it! Sarah-Jane Beckett is *not* the issue."

"Then why won't you answer?"

"Because there's nothing to say. She was sacked. All right? Sarah-Jane Beckett was sacked as well."

This was the last answer I'd been expecting. I'd thought he would tell me she'd become engaged or found a better position or decided to make a change in career. But that she, too, had been sacked along with Katja Wolff . . . I'd not considered that possibility.

Dad said, "We'd had to cut back. We couldn't keep Sarah-Jane Beckett and Raphael Robson and have a nursemaid for Sonia as well. So we'd given Sarah-Jane two months' notice."

"When?"

"Shortly before we found that we'd have to sack Katja Wolff."

"So when Sonia died and Katja left . . ."

"There was no need for Sarah-Jane to go as well." He turned and replaced the Guarneri in its case. His movements were slow; his scoliosis made him seem like a man in his eighties.

I said, "Then Sarah-Jane herself might have—"

"She was with Pitchford when your sister was drowned, Gideon. She swore to that and Pitchford confirmed it." Dad straightened from the case and turned back to me. He looked done in. I felt anguish, guilt, and sorrow surge within me to know that I was forcing him to consider matters he'd buried along with my sister. But I had to continue. It seemed that we were making progress for the first time since I'd had the episode at Wigmore Hall—and yes, I use that word deliberately just as you have done, Dr. Rose, an *episode*—and feeling that progress was being made, I could not back away from it.

I said, "Why didn't she talk?"

"I just said she—"

"Katja Wolff, not Sarah-Jane Beckett. Cresswell-White said that she spoke to the police once and never spoke to anyone else. About the crime, that is. About Sonia."

"I can't answer that question. I don't know the answer. I don't care to know. And—" Here he took up the sheet music that I'd left on the stand when I'd thought to play, and he closed it slowly, seeming to put an end to something that neither one of us wanted to name. "I can't understand why you're dwelling on this at all. Hasn't Katja Wolff damaged our lives enough?"

"It's not Katja Wolff," I said. "It's what happened."

"You know what happened."

"I don't know everything."

"You know enough."

"I know that when I look over my life, when I write about it or talk about it, all I can remember with accuracy is the music: how I came to it, how I proceeded, the exercises that Raphael had me engage in, concerts I gave, orchestras I performed with, conductors, concertmasters, journalists who interviewed me, recordings I made."

"That's *been* your life. That's who you are."

But not according to Libby. I could hear her shouting at me once again. I could feel her frustration. I could drown in the wretchedness that flooded her heart.

And I am adrift, Dr. Rose. I am a man without a country any longer. I once existed in a world I recognised and was comfortable with, a world with definite borders, peopled by citizens all speaking a language I understood. All that is foreign territory to me now, but it is no less foreign than the land I wander in, without a guide or a map, at your instructions.

ELEVEN

YASMIN EDWARDS had a busy morning, for which she was grateful. She'd received half a dozen referrals from a women's shelter in Lambeth, and the six women in question all turned up at the shop at once. None of them were needing wigs—these usually went to women undergoing chemo or afflicted with alopecia—but all of them wanted make-overs, and Yasmin was happy to accommodate them. She knew what it felt like to be down and out because of a man, and she wasn't surprised when the women first hung back and spoke in hushed tones about their personal appearance and the changes they hoped Yasmin Edwards could make for them. So Yasmin started out gently, letting them decide for themselves over magazines, coffee, and biscuits.

"You make me look like this one?" was the question that broke the ice among them. One of the women—who wouldn't see sixty again and who must have tipped the scales at nearly twenty stone—had chosen a picture of a nubile black model with sumptuous breasts and pouting lips.

"You look like that when we done, girl, I'm taking up *residence* in this damn shop," one of the others said. Soft giggles among them turned to hearty laughter, and everything was easy after that.

Oddly, it was the scent of the cleaning fluid that Yasmin was using on the work tops after the women left that took her back abruptly to the morning. For a moment, she wondered why, until she recalled that she'd been cleaning the bathtub of the few wig hairs that Daniel hadn't managed to remove after his washing chore on the previous night when Katja came into the bathroom to clean her teeth.

"You going in to work today?" Yasmin asked her companion. Daniel had already left for school, so they were free to talk openly for the first time. Or at least they were free to make the attempt.

"Of course," Katja said. "Why would I not?"

She still made her W's into V's. Sometimes it seemed to Yasmin that twenty years away from her native language would have been enough to alter Katja's most deeply rooted habits, but that final one still remained. There had been a time when Yasmin had found her companion's way of speaking English appealing, but she did not find it so now. She couldn't determine when the charm had diminished for her. Recently, she thought. But she couldn't afford to put an exact date to the change in her feelings.

"He said that you'd missed. Four times in twelve weeks is what he said."

In the mirror above the basin, Katja's blue eyes fixed on Yasmin's. "You believe that, Yas? He's a cop-

per and you and I are . . . You know what we are to
him: fluff and dagger from inside, back in the street.
I saw how he looked at us if you didn't. So why
should a man like that tell us what really is when lies
will serve to put us apart from each other?"

Yasmin couldn't deny that there was truth in what
Katja was saying. In her experience, police couldn't be
trusted with anything. Indeed, no one in the whole
legal system could be trusted if it came down to it. In
the legal system, plods settled on a story and bent the
facts to fit it, presenting those facts to magistrates in
such a way that bail was deemed foolhardy and a trial
in the Old Bailey followed by a lengthy prison sentence was the only cure for what got called a social ill.
Like she had been a disease and Roger Edwards had
been what she'd infected instead of what each of them
had really been: she nineteen and the longtime play-
thing of step-fathers, step-brothers, and the friends of
both and he a yellow-haired Aussie who'd chased his
girlfriend to London where he'd been dumped, with
a book of poems tucked under his arm. That was the
same book of poems he'd left at the till at Sainsbury's
where she rang up his groceries once a week, a book
of poems that made her think he was something more
than what she was used to.

And he was, Roger Edwards. He was different and
more in so many ways. Just not in the ways that
counted.

It was never simple: what brought a man and a
woman together. Oh, it looked that way on the surface—hard cock and hot cunt—but it never was.

There was no way to explain it: her history and Roger's, her fears and his mighty desperation, their mutual needs and their unspoken beliefs about what each partner should be to the other. There was only what happened. And what happened was a tedious series of accusations that were the children born of his addictions and an even more tedious series of denials that were never enough, not without proof which was in itself a spur to more accusations. And these were flung with a building paranoia that was itself fueled by the drugs and the drink until she wanted him out of her life, out of their child's life, and out of her flat no matter that their son would go fatherless like so many boys within their community, fatherless despite the promise she'd made to herself that Daniel would not grow up trapped in a web of women.

Roger wouldn't go, though. He fought against going. He really fought. He fought the way a man fights another man, in silence and with strength and closed fists. But she was the one with the weapon, and she used it.

Five years she'd served. She'd been arrested and charged. Because she was six feet tall, she was more than five inches taller than her husband, so, gentlemen and ladies of the jury, why had this woman felt it was necessary to use a *knife* to stop him when he allegedly became abusive? He'd been what was called under the influence of a foreign substance so most of his punches had gone wide or been short or merely grazed her instead of connecting with her dusky flesh, instead of bruising or better yet breaking bones. Yet she used a *knife* on this unfortunate man, and she managed to connect that knife with his body no less than eight times.

More blood would have been useful in the subsequent investigation by the local police. Her blood, that is, instead of Roger's. As it was, all she had was the story itself in which an attractive bloke on the rebound catches the eye of a girl who's in hiding from the world. He coaxes her out from beneath her rock; she promises him a cool draught of forget. And if he used a little and he drank a lot, what worry was there in that? Those were, to her, familiar behaviours. It was the descent into squalor and the demand for money that she could earn at night in doorways, in parked cars, or leaning against a tree on the common with her legs spread wide that she hadn't been prepared to accept from Roger Edwards.

"Get out, get *out!*" she'd screamed at him. And it was her screaming and those words that she screamed that the neighbours later remembered.

"Just tell us the story, Mrs. Edwards," the coppers had said to her over her husband's bloodied and very dead body. "All you need to do is to tell us the story and we'll get all this sorted out straightaway."

Five years in prison had been the consequence of her telling her story to the police. Five years in prison had been their way of getting things sorted out straightaway. She'd lost those years with her son, she'd come out with nothing, and she'd spent the next five years working, planning, begging, and borrowing, making it up to them both. So Katja was right, and Yasmin knew it. Only a fool trusted anything a copper had to say.

But there was more than just the detective's words about Katja's absences—from work, from the flat, from anywhere at all—that she had to contend with. There was also the car. And no matter whether the black man could be trusted, the car itself could not lie to her.

Yasmin said, "Headlamp on the car got itself broke, Katja. He looked that over, the plod, last night. He asked how it broke."

"Are you asking me the same?"

"S'pose." Vigorously, Yasmin wiped the cleanser into the old bathtub, as if doing so and in such a manner could rub away the spots where the porcelain had worn through to the metal lining beneath it. "I didn't hit anything that I recall. You?"

"Why did he want to know? What business is it of his how a headlamp was broken?" Katja had finished with her teeth and she leaned forward into the mirror, inspecting her face as she always did, as Yasmin herself had done for months upon her final release from prison, checking to see that she was really there, in this particular room, guard-less, wall-less, lock-and-key-less, with what was left of her life in front of her and trying not to be completely terrified of that empty, unstructured stretch of years.

Katja washed her face and patted it dry. She turned from the basin and leaned against it, watching Yasmin finish with the tub. When the taps were turned off, Katja spoke again. "What is he after us for, Yas?"

"You," Yasmin said. "He's not after me. It's you. How'd that headlamp get busted?"

"I didn't know it was broken," Katja said. "I haven't looked . . . Yas, how often do you look at the front of the car? Did you know it was broken before he pointed it out to you? No? It could have been broken for weeks. How badly is it broken? Do the lights still work? Someone probably reversed into it in the car park. Or in the street."

True, Yasmin thought. But wasn't there something too quick, too anxious to be believed about Katja's words? And why didn't she ask which headlamp? Wouldn't it be logical for her to want to know which of the headlamps it was?

Katja added, "It could have happened when you were driving it, since neither one of us knew it was broken."

"Yeah," Yasmin admitted. "I see that."

"Then—"

"He wanted to know where you were. He went to where you work and he asked about you."

"So he says. But if he really talked to them, and if they really told him I'd missed four days, why did he give that information only to you and not to me as well? I was standing there, right in the room with the two of you. Why did he not ask me for my excuse? Think about that."

Yasmin did so. And she saw that what Katja was

pointing out did bear weight. The detective constable *hadn't* asked Katja about her absences from work when the three of them were in the sitting room together. Instead, he'd confided the information in Yasmin, just exactly like they were long-lost mates.

"You know what that means," Katja said. "He wants to tear us apart because it'll serve his purposes. And if he manages to do it—to tear us apart—he won't waste much effort putting us back together. Even if he gets what he wants . . . whatever it is."

"He's investigating something," Yasmin said. "Or someone. So . . ." She took a breath that was deep, that hurt. " 'S there something you're not telling me, Katja? Something you hiding from me?"

"This is just how it works," Katja said. "This is just exactly how he wants it to work."

"But you're not answering, are you?"

"Because I've nothing to say. Because I have nothing to hide from you or from anyone else."

Her eyes held Yasmin's. Her voice was firm. And they both made promises, those eyes and that voice. They also reminded Yasmin of the history between them, the solace that had been offered by one and grasped by the other, and what had finally grown from that solace to sustain them both. But nothing from the heart was indestructible. Experience had taught Yasmin Edwards that. She said, "Katja, you'd say if . . ."

"If what?"

"If . . ."

Katja knelt on the floor next to the bathtub, next to Yasmin. Gently, she ran her fingers round the curve of Yasmin's ear. "You waited five years for me to get out," she said. "There is no if, Yas."

They kissed long and tenderly, and Yasmin didn't think as she'd thought at first, How bloody mad, I'm kissing a woman . . . she's touching me . . . I'm *letting* her touch me . . . Her mouth is here, it's there, it's tasting me where I want to be tasted . . . this is a woman and what she's doing is . . . yes, yes, I want this, yes. All she thought was what it felt like to be with her and what it felt like to be safe and sure.

Now in the wig shop, she packed the make-up back into its case and threw into the rubbish the kitchen towels with which she'd wiped the work top at which the women had sat, one by one, and allowed her to make them beautiful. She smiled at the pictures she had of them in her mind, all of them laughing, giggling like schoolgirls, given for the morning a chance to be something more than what they'd chosen for themselves. Yasmin Edwards enjoyed her work. When she considered it, she had to shake her head in wonder that a stretch in prison had directed her not only to useful employment but also to a companion and to a life she loved. She knew this sort of conclusion to the kind of troubles she'd had was rare.

Behind her, the shop door opened. That would be Mrs. Newland's oldest daughter Ashaki, coming right on time to pick up Mum's freshly washed wig.

Yasmin turned to the door, offering a smile of welcome.

"Can I have a word?" the black constable said.

MAJOR TED WILEY was the last person in Henley-on-Thames to whom Lynley and Havers showed the photograph of Katja Wolff. They hadn't planned it that way. In the normal course of events, they would have shown him the picture first since, at least from his own account of it as Eugenie Davies' closest companion and neighbour across the street from Doll Cottage, he was the person most likely to have seen Katja Wolff in Henley had the woman come calling. But upon their arrival in Friday Street, they'd found Wiley's Books closed, with a be-right-back sign stating the time of the major's return. So they offered the photograph round every other establishment on Friday Street, having no luck anywhere.

Havers wasn't surprised. "This is the wrong tree, Inspector," she informed Lynley with martyred patience.

"It's an institutional picture," he replied, "as bad as a passport. It might not even resemble her. Let's try at the Sixty Plus Club before we count her out. If her other visitor waylaid her there, what's to say Katja Wolff didn't do likewise?"

The Sixty Plus Club was reasonably populated even at that hour of the day. Most of the members present were engaged in what looked like a bridge tournament, although an intense group of four women were also playing a serious game of Monop-

oly, with dozens of red hotels and green houses lit-
tering the board. Additionally, in a narrow room that
appeared to be a kitchen, three men and two women
sat round a table, manila folders open in front of
them. The fearsome red head of Georgia Ramsbottom bobbed among this latter group, and the sound
of her voice rose higher than even the singing of Fred
Astaire, who was dancing cheek to cheek—or at least
claiming to do so—with Ginger Rogers on a television screen in an alcove set up with comfortable armchairs.

"Recruiting internally is *much* more reasonable,"
Georgia Ramsbottom was saying. "We ought to at
least try it, Patrick. If someone amongst us wishes to
direct the club now that Eugenie's gone—"

One of the women interrupted her, but at a reduced volume.

She countered with, "I find that highly offensive,
Margery. *Someone* has to take the interests of the club
to heart. I suggest we set aside our grief and deal with
this now. If not today, then certainly before more
messages stack up to be answered"—here she gestured with a small fan of Post-its on which the afore-
mentioned messages were ostensibly written—"and
more bills go asking to be paid."

There was a rumble of what might have been either assent or disapproval, something that wasn't fully
clarified, because at that moment, Georgia Ramsbottom descried Lynley and Havers. She excused herself
from the table and came to them. The Sixty Plus
Club's Executive Committee were in a meeting, she

announced, every bit as if the agenda that the committee were following were of national significance. The Sixty Plus Club could not long remain rudderless and directorless, although explaining that a "suitable period of mourning" for Eugenie Davies did not necessarily obviate the process of replacing her was proving to be *quite* a challenge, Georgia revealed.

"I doubt this will take very long," Lynley told her. "We'll just need a few moments alone. With everyone. One at a time. If you'd be so good as to organise that . . ."

"Inspector," Georgia said, and she managed just the appropriate amount of effrontery in her words, "the members of Henley's Sixty Plus Club are very private, decent, upstanding people. If you've come here thinking that one of them was involved in Eugenie's death—"

"I come here thinking nothing in particular," Lynley broke in pleasantly, but he didn't miss the third person pronoun that Georgia had used to differentiate between herself and the rest of the club's members. "So perhaps we can start with you, Mrs. Ramsbottom. In Mrs. Davies' office . . . ?"

All members' eyes followed them as Georgia stiffly led the way to the office door. It was open today, and Lynley noted as they entered that all items remotely related to Eugenie Davies had already been packed away in a cardboard box that sat forlornly on her desk. He wondered idly what Mrs. Ramsbottom considered a suitable period of mourning for the club's director. She certainly wasn't letting any grass grow when it came to sweeping the club clean of her.

He wasted no time in small talk once Havers had shut the door and placed herself in front of it, notebook in hand. He took the seat behind the desk, gestured Georgia Ramsbottom into the chair in front of the desk, and brought out the photograph of Katja Wolff. Had Mrs. Ramsbottom seen this woman in the vicinity of the Sixty Plus Club or anywhere else in Henley, for that matter, in the weeks preceding Mrs. Davies' death?

The production of the photograph seemed to prompt Georgia to say, "The killer . . . ?" in the sort of reverential tone that would have done service in an Agatha Christie novel. She was suddenly all helpfulness, perhaps altered by the realisation that the police were not seeking the killer among the over-sixty crowd. She hastened to add, "I do know it was deliberate, Inspector, and not just an arbitrary hit-and-run. Dear Teddy told me when I rang him last evening."

Across the room, Havers mouthed *Dear Teddy*. Thwarted love among the ruins, her expression implied. She did some furious scribbling in her notebook. Georgia heard the sound of her pencil *scritching* across the paper. She glanced over her shoulder.

Lynley said, "If you'd have a look at the picture, Mrs. Ramsbottom . . ."

Georgia did so. She studied the photo. She held it close to her face. She held it at arm's length. She tilted her head. But no, she said at last, she'd never seen the woman in the picture. Not round Henley-on-Thames, at least.

"Somewhere else?" Lynley asked.

No, no. She didn't mean to imply *that*. Of course, she might have seen her in London—a stranger on the street, perhaps?—when she went up to visit her darling grandchildren. But if she had done, she couldn't remember.

"Thank you," Lynley said, and he prepared to dismiss her.

But he found that Georgia wasn't inclined to be so easily disposed of. She crossed her legs, ran a hand along one of the pleats in her skirt, reached down to smooth her tights, and said, "You'll want to talk to Teddy, of course, won't you, Inspector?" It sounded more like a suggestion than a question. "He lives near Eugenie, dear Teddy does—but I expect you already know that, don't you?—and if this woman was hanging about or perhaps paying calls on her, he might well know. Indeed, Eugenie might have told him herself because they were great friends, weren't they, the two of them, Teddy and Eugenie. So she might have confided in him should this woman have . . ." Then Georgia hesitated, a heavily ringed finger tapping against her cheek. "But no. Nooo. Perhaps not, after all."

Lynley sighed inwardly. He wasn't about to engage in the information game with the woman. If she wanted to enjoy the power of playing out what she knew like a fishing line, she was going to have to find someone else to swim in her river. He bluffed her with, "Thank you, Mrs. Ramsbottom," and he nodded at Havers to usher her from the room.

Georgia showed her hand. "All right. I spoke to dear Teddy," she confided. "As I said earlier, I phoned him last night. After all, one does want to offer condolences when someone loses a loved one, even in situations in which the scales of devotion aren't as evenly balanced as one would hope to see in a dear friend's love life."

"The dear friend being Major Wiley," Havers clarified with some impatience.

Georgia treated her to an imperious glance. She said to Lynley, "Inspector, I do feel you might benefit from knowing . . . not that I wish to speak ill of the dead . . . But I don't think we can call it speaking ill, can we, if what I say is simply a fact?"

"What are you getting at, Mrs. Ramsbottom?"

"It's just that I'm wondering if I should tell you something if it may not actually be germane to your case." She waited for some sort of reply or reassurance. When Lynley said nothing, she was forced to continue. "But then again, it *may* be germane. It probably is. And if I hold back . . . It's poor dear Teddy I'm thinking of, you see. The thought of something becoming public knowledge, something that might hurt him . . . That's difficult for me to bear."

Lynley thought that unlikely. He said, "Mrs. Ramsbottom, if you have information about Mrs. Davies that might lead to her killer, it's in your best interests to tell us directly."

It's in our interests as well, Havers' expression said. She looked as if she'd have liked to throttle the maddening woman.

"Otherwise," Lynley added, "we have work to do. Constable, if you'll assist Mrs. Ramsbottom in organising the others for interviews . . . ?"

"It's about Eugenie, then," Georgia said hastily. "I hate to say it. But I will. It's this: She didn't reciprocate, not completely."

"Reciprocate what?"

"Teddy's feelings. She didn't share the strength of his feelings for her, and he didn't realise that."

"But you did," Havers said from the door.

"I'm not blind," Georgia said over her shoulder to Havers. And then to Lynley, "I'm also not a fool. There was someone else, and Teddy didn't know. He still doesn't know, poor man."

"Someone else?"

"Some people might argue that there was something permanently on Eugenie's mind and that's what kept her from getting close to Teddy. But I say it was some*one* on her mind and she hadn't yet got round to dropping the bomb on the poor man."

"You saw her with someone?" Lynley asked.

"I didn't need to see her with someone," Georgia said. "I saw what she did when she was here: the phone calls that she took behind closed doors, the days when she left at half past eleven and never returned. And she drove her car to the club on those days, Inspector, though the rest of the time she walked here from Friday Street. And she wasn't doing her volunteer work at the nursing home on those days she drove, because she volunteered at Quiet Pines on Mondays and Wednesdays."

"And the days she left at half past eleven?"

"Thursday or Friday. Always. Once a month. Sometimes twice. What does that suggest to you, Inspector? It suggests an assignation to me."

It could well suggest anything, Lynley thought, from a doctor's appointment to a session with the hairdresser. But while what Georgia Ramsbottom was telling them was coloured by her obvious dislike of Eugenie Davies, Lynley could not ignore the fact that her information matched up with what they'd seen in the dead woman's diary.

After thanking her for her cooperation—no matter how much he'd had to wrest it from her—Lynley sent the woman back to her committee and had Havers assist her in organising the rest of the club members present for individual examinations of the photograph of Katja Wolff. He could tell that everyone wanted to be helpful, but no one was able to attest to having ever seen the pictured woman in the environs of the club.

They headed back to Friday Street, where Lynley had left his car in front of Eugenie Davies' tiny house. As they walked, Havers said, "Satisfied, Inspector?"

"About what?"

"The Wolff angle. Are you satisfied now?"

"Not entirely."

"But you can't still be considering her for the killer. Not after that." This, with a cock of her thumb back in the direction of the Sixty Plus Club. "If Katja Wolff ran over Eugenie Davies, she would have had to know where she was going that night in the first place, right? Or she would have had to follow her into London from here. Do you agree?"

"That seems obvious."

"So in either case, she would have had to establish some kind of contact with her once she got out of prison. Now, we may get some joy from those telephone records, and we may find out that Eugenie Davies and Katja Wolff were spending their evenings nattering like schoolgirls on the phone for the last twelve weeks for reasons that're completely obscure. But if we don't get something from those BT records, then what we're left with is someone following her up to town from here. And we both know which someone would have had an easy time of that, don't we?" She indicated the door of the bookshop where the be-right-back sign had been removed.

Lynley said, "Let's see what Major Wiley has to say about things," and he opened the door.

They found Ted Wiley unpacking a box of new books and arranging them on a table top that bore a hand-lettered sign reading *new releases*. He wasn't alone in the shop. At the far end a woman in a paisley headscarf sat in a comfortable armchair, happily sipping from a Thermos top with a book open upon her knees.

"Saw your motor when I got back," Wiley said in reference to the Bentley as he lifted three books from the box. He dusted each with a cloth before setting it on the table. "What've you come up with, then?"

The man appeared to have an interesting capacity to direct and demand, Lynley thought. He seemed to assume that the London detectives had come to Henley-on-Thames with the intention of reporting to him. He said, "It's too early in the investigation to reach a conclusion about anything, Major Wiley."

"What I know is this," Wiley said. "The longer things drag on, the less likely it is that you'll catch the bastard. You must have leads. Suspicions. Something."

Lynley offered the photograph of Katja Wolff. "Have you seen this woman? In the neighbourhood, perhaps. Or somewhere else round town."

Wiley fumbled in the breast pocket of his jacket and brought out a pair of heavy-looking horn-rimmed spectacles, which he flipped open with one hand and fixed on his large and florid nose. He squinted at Katja Wolff's likeness for a good fifteen seconds before saying, "Who is she?"

"She's called Katja Wolff. She's the woman who drowned Eugenie Davies' daughter. Do you recognise her?"

Wiley examined the picture again, and it was apparent from his expression that he very much *wanted* to recognise her, possibly to put an end to the anxiety of not knowing who had struck down and killed the woman he loved, possibly for another reason altogether. But ultimately, he shook his head and thrust the picture back at Lynley. "What about that bloke?"

he asked. "The Audi. He was raging, he was. Bent on hurting someone. I could feel it. And the way he drove off . . . He was just the sort of bastard who blows. Doesn't get what he wants, so he makes a statement and the statement is usually a body. Or bodies. You know what I mean. Hungerford. Dunblane."

"We haven't ruled him out," Lynley said. "Constables back in town are working through a list of Audis from Brighton. We should know something at that end soon."

Wiley grunted and removed his glasses. He shoved them into his jacket pocket.

Lynley said, "You mentioned that Mrs. Davies wanted to talk to you, that she said specifically that she had something to tell you. Have you any idea what that was, Major Wiley?"

"None." Wiley reached for more books. He checked the dust jackets of these, going so far as to open each one and to run his fingers along the inner flap as if he were looking for imperfections.

As he did so, Lynley reflected upon the fact that a man generally knows when the woman he loves does not reciprocate the emotion. A man also knows—he can't avoid knowing—when the passion within a woman he loves begins to wither. Sometimes he lies to himself about the fact, denying it till the moment comes when he can no longer avoid it or escape it altogether. But he always knows even subconsciously when things aren't right. Openly admitting this is a form of torture, though. And some men can't cope with such torture, so they choose another route to deal with the matter.

Lynley said, "Major Wiley, you heard the messages on Mrs. Davies' answer machine yesterday. You heard the men's voices, so it can't be a surprise to you when I ask if Mrs. Davies might have been involved elsewhere besides with you, if that's what she might have wanted to tell you."

"I've thought it," Wiley said quietly. "Nothing else has been in my mind since . . . Damn. God *damn.*" He shook his head and shoved his hand into his trouser pocket. He brought out a handkerchief and honked into it loudly enough to disturb the reading of the woman in the armchair. She looked round, saw Lynley and Havers, and said, "Major Wiley? Is everything all right?"

He nodded, raised a hand as if to underscore his assent, and turned his shoulder so she couldn't see his face. She seemed to feel this was answer enough, for she went back to her reading as Wiley said to Lynley, "I feel a perfect fool."

Lynley waited for more. Havers tapped her pencil against her notebook and frowned.

Wiley gathered himself together and told them the apparent worst there was for him to tell: about the nights he watched Eugenie Davies' cottage from his upstairs window and about one night in particular when his surveillance had finally been rewarded. "One A.M.," he said. "It was that bloke with the Audi. And the way she touched him . . . Yes. Yes. I loved her and she was involved somewhere else. So was that what she wanted to tell me, Inspector? I don't know. I didn't want to know then, and I don't want to know now. What's the point?"

"The point is finding her killer," Havers said.

"You think it's me?"

"What sort of car do you drive?"

"A Mercedes. It's right there, in front of the shop."

Havers looked to Lynley for direction, and he nodded. She went outside and the two men watched her giving the car's front end a thorough inspection. It was black, but the colour was inconsequential if there was no damage to report.

"I wouldn't have hurt her," Wiley said quietly. "I loved her. I trust you lot understand what that means."

And what it implies, Lynley thought. But he didn't speak, merely waiting till Havers had completed her inspection and returned to them. It's clean, her eyes told them. Lynley could see she was disappointed.

Wiley read the message. He allowed himself the pleasure of saying, "I hope that satisfies. Or do you want me on the rack as well?"

"I expect you want us to do our job," Havers pointed out.

Wiley said, "Then do it. There's a photo gone missing from Eugenie's house."

"What sort of photo?" Lynley said.

"The only one of the little girl alone."

"Why didn't you tell us this yesterday?"

"Didn't realise it. Not till this morning. She had them lined up on the kitchen table. Three rows of four. But she had thirteen pictures of those kids in the house—twelve of both of them and one of the girl—and unless she'd taken that one back upstairs, it's gone missing."

Lynley looked at Havers. She shook her head. There had been no picture in any of the three rooms she'd looked through on the first floor of Doll Cottage.

"When was the last time you saw that photo?" Lynley asked.

"Whenever I was there, I saw all of them. Not like they were yesterday—in the kitchen—but spread round. In the sitting room. And upstairs. On the landing. In her sewing room."

"P'rhaps she'd taken that one to have a new frame," Havers said. "Or thrown it away."

"She wouldn't have done," Wiley said, aghast.

"Or given it away or lent it somewhere."

"A picture of her daughter? Who'd she give it to, then?"

It was a question, Lynley knew, that had to be answered.

ONCE AGAIN ON the pavement in Friday Street, Havers offered another possibility. "She could have posted it somewhere. To the husband, d'you think? Did he have pictures of the girl in his flat when you spoke to him, Inspector?"

"None that I saw. There were only snapshots of Gideon."

"There you go, then. They'd been speaking, hadn't

they? About Gideon's stage fright? Why not about
the little girl as well? So he asked Eugenie for a picture of her, and she sent it along. That's easy enough
to find out, isn't it?"

"But it's odd that he had no pictures of the daughter already, Havers."

"Human nature's odd," Havers said. "This long on
the force, I'd think you'd know that."

Lynley couldn't argue. He said, "Let's have another
look at her house to make sure the photo's not
there."

It was a matter of only a few minutes to double-
check and to prove Major Wiley right. The twelve
photographs in the kitchen were all that were left in
the house.

Lynley and Havers were standing in the sitting
room, mulling this over, when Lynley's mobile began
to ring. It was Eric Leach phoning from the Hampstead incident room.

"We've got a match," he told Lynley without preamble, sounding pleased. "We've got the Brighton
Audi and the Cellnet customer rolled into one pretty
package."

"Ian Staines?" Lynley said, recalling the name connected to the Cellnet number. "Her brother?"

"The same." Leach recited the address and Lynley
wrote it down on the back of one of his business
cards. "Get on to him," Leach said. "What've you got
on Wolff?"

"Nothing." Lynley reported briefly on their conversations with the Sixty Plus Club's members as well

as with Major Wiley, and he went on to tell Leach of the missing photograph.

The DCI offered another interpretation. "She could have brought it with her to London."

"To show someone?"

"That takes us back to Pitchley."

"But why would she want to show him the picture? Or give it to him?"

"There's more to that story than we're hearing, I say," Leach pointed out. "Dig up a picture of the Davies woman. There's got to be a snapshot somewhere in her house. Or Wiley'll have one. Take it to the Valley of Kings and the Comfort Inn. There's a chance that someone remembers her there."

"With Pitchley?"

"He likes them older, doesn't he?"

WHEN THE POLICE departed, Ted Wiley left Mrs. Dilday watching over the shop. It had been a slow morning and was shaping up to be a slow afternoon, so he felt no compunction about putting his engrossed customer in charge of things. It was about time that she did something to earn the privilege of reading every best seller without ever making a purchase other than a greeting card, so he rousted her from her favourite armchair and gave her instructions on working the till. Then he went upstairs to his flat.

There, he found P.B. snoozing in a patch of weak sunlight. He stepped over the retriever and put himself at Connie's old davenport beneath whose sloping surface he'd stowed the brochures from the forthcoming opera seasons in Vienna, Santa Fe, and Sydney. It had been his hope that one of those seasons would serve as a backdrop to his broadened relationship with Eugenie. They would travel to Austria, America, or Australia and enjoy Rossini, Verdi, or Mozart as they enriched the joy they took in each other's company and deepened the nature of their love. They'd moved slowly towards this destination for three long and careful years together, building a structure comprising tenderness, devotion, affection, and support. They'd told each other that everything else that went with a man and a woman linking themselves together—most particularly sex—would find its way into the equation with time.

It had been a relief for Ted after Connie's death, not to mention after the esurient pursuing by other women to which he'd been exposed, to find himself in the company of a woman who wanted to build a structure first before taking up residence within it. But now, after the police had left him, Ted finally forced himself to acknowledge the reality that he'd not been able to bear even thinking about before this moment: that Eugenie's hesitation, her gentle and always kind "I'm not ready yet, Ted," were in actuality evidence that she was not ready for *him*. For what else could it mean that a man had phoned and left a message rife with desperation on her answer machine? that a man had left her house at one in the morning? that a man had accosted her in the car park of the Sixty Plus Club and pleaded with her the way a man pleads when everything—and most particularly his heart—is at stake? There was only one answer to these questions, and Ted knew what that answer was.

He'd been such a fool. Instead of being grateful for the blessed respite from performance that Eugenie's reserve had promised him, he should have suspected at once that she was involved elsewhere. But he hadn't because it had been such a relief after Georgia Ramsbottom's carnal demands.

She'd phoned last night. Her, "Teddy, I'm so sorry. I spoke to the police today and they said that Eugenie . . . Dearest Teddy, is there *anything* I can do?" had barely disguised the enthusiasm with which she'd made the call in the first place. "I'm coming over straightaway," she'd said. "No ifs or buts, dear. You're not to be left alone with this."

He'd not had a chance to protest and he'd not had the courage to decamp prior to her arrival. She'd swept in barely ten minutes later, bearing a baking dish in which she'd made him her speciality, which was shepherd's pie. She whipped off the aluminium foil that covered it, and he saw that the pie was depressingly perfect, with ornate little ridges like waves marking the mashed potatoes. She said, flashing a smile at him, "It's warmish, but if we pop it into the microwave, it'll be perfect. You must eat, Teddy, and I know that you haven't. Have you?" She hadn't waited for an answer. She'd marched to the microwave and shut its door smartly upon the shepherd's pie, whereupon she moved briskly round the kitchen, bringing forth plates and cutlery from cupboards and drawers with the unspoken authority of a woman showing that she was familiar with a man's domicile.

She said, "You're devastated. I can see it in your face. I am so sorry. I know what friends you two were. And to lose such a friend as Eugenie . . . You must let yourself feel the sorrow, Teddy."

Friend, he thought. Not lover. Not wife. Not companion. Not partner. Friend and everything that friend suggested.

He hated Georgia Ramsbottom in that moment. He hated her not only for barging into his solitude like a ship breaking ocean ice but also for the acuity of her perception. She said without saying what he had not allowed himself even to think: His imagination and his longing had created the bond he'd believed he'd had with Eugenie.

Women who were interested in a man showed their interest. They showed it soon, and they showed it unabashedly. They could do no less at an age and in a society in which they so vastly outnumbered available males. He had the proof of this in Georgia herself and in the women who had preceded Georgia in his widowed years. They had their knickers off before a man could reassuringly say to them, "I'm no Jack the lad." And if they kept their knickers on, it was only because their hands were busy in his crotch instead. But Eugenie had done none of that, had she? Demure Eugenie. Docile Eugenie. Damn Eugenie.

He'd felt such a swelling of anger that he couldn't reply at first to Georgia's comments. He wanted to pound his fist into something hard. He wanted to break it.

Georgia took his silence for stoicism, the stiff upper lip that was the proud achievement of every upstanding British male. She said, "I know, I know. And it's ghastly, isn't it? The older we get, the more we have to bear witness to our friends' passing. But what I've discovered is the importance of nurturing the precious friendships that are left to us. So you mustn't cut yourself off from those of us who care deeply about you, Teddy. We won't have that."

She'd reached across the table and placed on his arm her hand with its encrustation of rings. He'd thought fleetingly of Eugenie's hands and the contrast they made to this red-tipped snatcher. Ringless, they were, with the nails clipped short and slivers of moon showing at their bases.

"Don't turn away, Teddy," Georgia had said, and her hand had tightened upon him. "From any of us. We're here to help you through this. We care for you. Truly and deeply. You'll see."

Her own brief, unhappy past with Ted might not have existed for her. His failure and the contempt she'd felt being a witness to his failure were banished to a foreign land. The intervening manless years she'd lived through had obviously instructed her in what was important and what was not. She was a changed woman, as he would see once she wormed her way into his life again.

Ted read it all in the gesture of her placing her hand on his arm, and in the tender smile she directed at him. Bile rose in his throat, and his body burned. He needed air.

He rose abruptly. He said, "That old dog," and called out roughly, "P.B.? Where've you taken yourself off to? Come." And to Georgia, "Sorry. I was about to take the dog for her final nightly when you phoned."

He'd made his escape that way, without inviting Georgia to accompany him and giving her no chance to make the suggestion herself. He called out once again, "P.B.? Come, girl. Time for a walk," and he was gone before Georgia had the chance to regroup. He knew that she'd assume from his departure that she'd moved too quickly. He also knew that she wouldn't assume anything else. And that was important, Ted realised suddenly. That was crucial: to limit the woman's knowledge about him.

He'd walked rapidly, feeling it all again. Stupid, he told himself, stupid and blind. Hanging about like a schoolboy hoping for a go with the local tart, not seeing her as a tart at all because he was too young, too inexperienced, too eager, too . . . too limp. That's what it was, all right. Too limp.

He'd charged towards the river, dragging the poor dog behind him. He needed to put distance between himself and Georgia, and he wanted to be away from the flat long enough to ensure her departure in his absence. Even Georgia Ramsbottom would not throw all her chances away by playing her cards the first evening she was holding them. She would leave his flat; she would retire for a few days. Then, when she thought that he'd recovered from their initial skirmish, she would be back, offering a renewal of her sympathetic attention. Ted was certain he could depend upon that.

At the corner of Friday Street and the river, he'd turned left. He strode on the town side of the Thames. The lights along the street pooled buttermilk onto the pavement intermittently and the wind blew a heavy mist in sharp waves that felt as if they rose from the river itself. Ted turned up the collar of his waxed jacket and said, "Come on, girl," to the dog, who was looking longingly at a sapling planted nearby, possibly with the hope of snoozing awhile underneath it. "P.B. *Come.*" A jerk on the choke chain did it, as usual. They hurried on.

They were in the church yard before Ted really thought about it. They were in the church yard before he recalled the vision he'd had there on the night Eugenie died. P.B. made for the grass like a horse to its stall before Ted actually knew she was doing so. She squatted wearily and let forth her stream before he had the chance to urge her somewhere else.

Without intending, without thinking, without even considering what the action implied, Ted felt his eyes drift from the dog to the almshouses at the far end of the path. He'd just take a quick glance that way, he told himself, in order to see that the woman who lived in the third house from the right had her curtains closed. If she hadn't and if a light was burning, he'd do her a service and let her know that any stranger passing by could look right in and . . . well, assess her valuables for a burglary.

The light was on. Time to do his good deed for the day. Ted pulled P.B. away from the tipped gravestone round which she was sniffing and urged her as quickly as he could along the path. It was essential that he get to the almshouse before the woman within it did anything that could embarrass them both. Because if she began to undress, as she had the other night, he could hardly knock on her door, caution her about her indiscretion, and thereby admit to having watched her, could he?

"Hurry, P.B.," he said to the dog. "Come along."

He was just fifteen seconds too late. Five yards from the almshouse and she had begun. And she was quick about it, so very quick that before he had time to avert his eyes, she'd whisked her jersey off, shaken back her hair, and removed her brassiere. She bent to something—was it her shoes? her stockings? her trousers? what?—and her breasts hung heavily downward.

Ted swallowed. He thought two words—*Dear God*—and he felt the first throb of his body's answer to the sight before him. He'd watched her once, he'd stood here once, he'd traced with his eyes those sumptuous full curves. But he couldn't—*couldn't*—allow himself the guilty pleasure of doing so again. She had to be told. She had to be warned. She had to . . . had to know? he wondered. What woman didn't know? What woman had never learned about caution and nighttime windows? What woman threw her clothes off at night in a room fully lit without curtains or blinds without knowing that someone on the other side of those few millimeters of glass was probably watching, longing, fantasising, hardening . . . She knew, Ted realised. She *knew*.

So he'd watched the unknown woman in that almshouse bedroom a second night. He'd stayed longer this time, mesmerised by the sight of her smoothing lotion on her neck and her arms. He heard himself moan like a pre-adolescent having his first glimpse at *Playboy* when she used that same lotion on her succulent breasts.

There in the church yard, he'd wanked off surreptitiously. Beneath his waxed jacket as the rain began to fall, he worked his cock like a man pumping spray onto garden insects. He got about as much satisfaction from the resulting orgasm as one would get from using a garden sprayer, and in the aftermath of his release what he felt wasn't exultation and release. It was bitter shame.

He felt it again now in his sitting room, wave after wave of black humiliation, building and cresting as he sat at Connie's old davenport. He looked at the glossy photo of the Sydney Opera House, moved from it to a picture of the outdoor theatre in Santa Fe where *The Marriage of Figaro* was sung under the stars, set that to one side, and picked up a picture of a narrow antique street in Vienna. He stared at this last with a darkness of spirit enveloping him and hearing within him a voice that he recognised as the voice of his mother hovering over him so many years in the past, so eager to judge, even more eager to condemn, if not him then someone else: "What a waste of time, Teddy. Don't be such a little fool."

But he was, wasn't he? He'd spent so many good hours imagining himself and Eugenie in one location or another, like actors moving on a strip of celluloid that did not allow for a single blemish in either the moment or the individuals. In his mind's eye, there had been no harsh glare of sunlight upon skin that was ageing, no hair out of place on either of their heads, no breath wanting freshening, no sphincter tightening to prevent an embarrassing explosion of intestinal wind at an inopportune time, no thickened toenails, no sagging flesh, and most of all no failure on his part when the time was finally right. He'd pictured the two of them eternally young in each other's vision if not in the world's. And that was all that had mattered to Ted: the way they saw each other.

But for Eugenie, things had been different. He understood that now. Because it wasn't natural for a woman to hold a man at a distance for so many months that bled inexorably into so many years. It wasn't natural. It also wasn't fair.

She'd used him as a front, he concluded. There was no other explanation for the phone calls she'd received, the nocturnal visits to her house, and her inexplicable trip to London. She was using him as a front, because if their mutual friends and acquaintances in Henley—not to mention the board of directors at the Sixty Plus Club who employed her—believed that she was keeping chaste company with Major Ted Wiley, they'd be far less likely to speculate that she was keeping unchaste company with someone else.

Fool. Fool. Don't be such a little fool. Once burnt, twice shy. I'd've thought you'd know better.

But how did one ever know better? To hope for foresight meant never to venture forward at all into the company of another, and Ted didn't want that. His marriage to Connie—happy and fulfilling for so many years—had made him over-sanguine. His marriage to Connie had taught him to believe that such a union was possible again, not a rare thing at all but something to be worked for and if not easily achieved, then achieved through an effort that was based on love.

Lies, he thought. Every one of them lies. Lies he'd told to himself and lies that he'd willingly believed as Eugenie had said them. *I'm not ready yet, Ted.* But the reality was that Eugenie hadn't been ready for him.

The sense of betrayal he felt was like an illness coming upon him. It started in his head and began to work oozingly downward. It seemed to him that the only way to defeat it was to beat it from his body, and if he'd had a scourge, he would have used it upon himself and taken satisfaction from the pain. As it was, he had only the brochures on the davenport, those pathetic symbols of his puerile idiocy.

He felt them slick beneath his hand, and his fingers crumpled them first, then tore them. His chest bore a weight that might have been his arteries slowly closing but was, he knew, merely the dying of something other and far more necessary to his being than simply his old man's heart.

TWELVE

ENTERING THE shop on the heels of the black constable was Ashaki Newland, whose timely arrival gave Yasmin Edwards an opportunity that she would not otherwise have had of ignoring the man altogether. The girl politely hung back, apparently assuming that the man had come on business and was therefore to be given priority. All the Newland kids were like that, well brought up and thoughtful.

Yasmin said, "How's your mum today?" to the girl, avoiding eye contact with the constable.

Ashaki said, "Doin' fair so far. She had a round of chemo two days back, but she's not taking it 's bad as she did the last time. Don't know what that means, but we're hoping for the best. You know."

The best would be five more years of life, which was all the doctors had promised Mrs. Newland when they'd first found the tumour in her brain. She could go without treatment and she'd live eighteen months, they'd told her. With treatment she might have five years. But that would be the maximum, barring some miracle, and miracles were in short supply when it came to cancer. Yasmin wondered what it would be like to have seven children to raise with a death sentence hanging over one's head.

She fetched Mrs. Newland's wig from the back of the shop and brought it out on its Styrofoam stand. Ashaki said, "That doesn't look like—"

Yasmin interrupted. "It's a new one. I think she's going t' like the style. You ask if. She doesn't, you bring it back and we'll do the original for her. Right?"

Ashaki's face gleamed with pleasure. "That's real nice of you, Mrs. Edwards," she said as she scooped the wig stand under her arm. "Thanks. Mum'll have a surprise this way."

She was out in the street, with a bob of her head towards the constable, before Yasmin could do anything to prolong the conversation. When the door shut behind her, Yasmin looked at the man. She found that she couldn't remember his name, which was a delight to her.

She looked round for further employment in the shop, the better to continue ignoring him. Perhaps it was time to catalogue any supplies she now needed in her make-up case after having worked on those six women earlier. She brought the case out again, flipped the catches open, and began sorting through lotions, brushes, sponges, eye colour, lip colour, foundation, blushers, mascaras, and pencils. She laid each item on the counter.

The constable said, "Could I have a word, Missus Edwards?"

"You had a word last night. More 'an one, as I recall. And who are you, anyway?"

"Metropolitan police."

"I mean your name. I don't know your name."

He told her. She found that she was irritated by it. A surname that spoke of his roots was fine. But that Christian name—Winston—showed such a *groveling* wish to be English. It was worse than Colin or Nigel or Giles. What were his parents thinking of, naming him Winston like he was going to be a politician or something? Stupid, that was. Stupid, he was.

She said, "I'm working, as I expect you c'n see. I got another appointment coming in in"—she made a pretence of looking at her diary, which was, thankfully, out of his range of vision—"ten minutes. What d'you want, then? Make it quick."

He was big, she noticed. He'd looked big last night, both in the lift and in the flat. But somehow he looked even bigger today in the shop, perhaps because she was alone with him, with no Daniel there to offer a distraction. He seemed to fill the place, all broad shoulders and long-fingered hands and a face that looked friendly—pretended to be friendly because that's what they all did—even with that scar on his cheek.

"Like I said, a word, Missus Edwards." His voice was scrupulously polite. He kept his distance, the shop counter between them. But instead of going on with the word he wanted, he said, "Real nice that a new business opened up on a street like this. Always sad, you ask me, to see shop fronts boarded up. It's good to have a business go in, 'stead of some bloke buying up all the properties, bringing in a demolition crew, and putting up a Tesco's or something like."

She gave a mild snort. "Rent's cheap when you're willing to set up shop in a rubbish tip," she said, as if it meant nothing to her that she'd managed to actually achieve something she'd only dreamed of during her years in prison.

Nkata half-smiled. "I 'xpect that's the truth. But the neighbours must feel it a blessing. Gives them hope. What sort of work you do in here, then?"

It was more than obvious what sort of work she did. There were wigs on Styrofoam heads along one wall and a work room in the back where she styled them. He could see both the wigs and the work room from where he stood, so his question was maddening. It was such a blatant attempt to be friendly where friendliness between herself and someone like him was not only impossible but dangerous. Thus, she offered him her scorn, saying, "What you doing a plod?" with a contemptuous glance that took him in from head to toe.

He shrugged. "It's a living."

"At brothers' expense."

"Only if that's how it plays out."

He sounded as if he'd resolved the matter of possibly having to arrest one of his own a long time ago. That angered her so she jerked her head at his face, saying, "Where'd you get that, then?" as if the cicatrix that formed a curve on his cheek was his just reward for abandoning his people.

"Knife fight," he said. "Met some blokes on the 'llotments in Windmill Gardens when I was fifteen and full of myself. I was lucky."

"And I s'pose the other bloke wasn't?"

He fingered the scar as if trying to remember. He said, "Depends on how you think luck works."

She blew derision from her nostrils and went back to her make-up sorting. She arranged her eye shadows by colour, twisted tubes of lipstick open and did the same to them, flipped open the blushers and powders, and checked the levels on the liquid foundations. She made much of taking notes, writing on an order pad and being so extra scrupulous about her spelling that the lives of her customers might have depended upon the accuracy of her order form.

"I was in a gang, see," Nkata offered. "I got out after that fight. Mostly 'cause of my mum. She took a look at my face when they took me to Casualty and dropped to the floor like a stone. Gave herself a concussion and ended up in hospital. That was that."

"So you love your mum." What rubbish, she thought.

"Know better than not to," he replied.

She looked up quickly and saw he was smiling, but it seemed directed at himself, not at her. He said, "You got a real nice boy."

"You stay away from my Daniel!" Her panic surprised her.

"He miss his dad?"

"I said you stay away!"

Nkata came to the counter then. He laid down his

hands. He seemed to imply by the action that he was
weaponless, but Yasmin knew otherwise. Coppers always had weapons and they knew how to use them.
Nkata did so now. He said, "There's a woman died
two nights ago, Missus Edwards. Up in Hampstead.
She had a boy, too."

"What's that to me?"

"She was run down. Three times run over by the
same car."

"I don't know no one in Hampstead. I don't go to
Hampstead. I never been to Hampstead. I go there, I
stick out like a cactus in Siberia."

"You would, that."

She looked at him sharply to catch the sarcasm in
his face that she couldn't hear in his voice, but all she
saw was a gentleness in his eyes, and she knew exactly
what that gentleness meant. It was a gentleness manufactured for the moment that said he'd do her right
here in the shop if he could talk her into it, he'd do
her if he could get away with it, he'd do her even if
he had to scare her into doing it with him, because to
do it would prove he had the power, because she was
simply there, like a particularly challenging but
nonetheless potentially gratifying mountain he just
had to climb.

She said, "I hear coppers work different to this,
I do."

"What's that?" he asked, managing quite effectively
to look perplexed.

"You know what's that. You went to cop school,
didn't you? Plods look for lags who're falling back on

what they know best. They don't dig in new ground if they don't have to because they know that's a waste of time."

"I'm not wasting time, far's I see. And I got a feeling you know that, Missus Edwards."

"I knifed Roger Edwards. I cut him up good. I didn't run him down with a car. Didn't even have a car back then, Roger and me. Sold it, we did, when the money ran out and his little habit needed an urgent seeing to."

"I'm real sorry about that," the constable said. "Must've been a bad time for you."

"You try five years locked up if you want a bad time." She turned from him and went on taking her inventory of cosmetics.

He said, "Missus Edwards, you know it's not you I'm here about."

"I don't know nothing like that, Mr. Constable. But you can leave easy enough, I 'xpect, if it's not me you're wanting to talk to. I'm the only one here and the only one who's going to be here till my next client comes in. 'Course, you might want to have a word with her. She's got cancer in her ovaries but she's a real nice lady, and I expect she'll tell you last time she drove up to Hampstead. That's why you're in this part of town, right? Some black lady was driving in Hampstead and the neighbourhood's all in an uproar about it and you're here trying to suss her out?"

"You know that's not the fact 's well."

He sounded infinitely patient, and Yasmin wondered how far she could push him before he snapped.

She gave him her back. She had no intention of offering him anything, least of all what he apparently was after.

He said, "What happened to your boy when you were inside, Missus Edwards?"

She swung round so fast that the beads on the ends of her plaits struck her cheeks. "Don't you talk about him! Don't you try rattling me with Daniel. I didn't do nothing to anyone anywhere and you *bloody* well know it."

"I 'xpect that's the truth. But what's also the truth is that Katja Wolff knew this lady, Missus Edwards. This lady that got mashed over up in Hampstead. This was two nights back, Missus Edwards, and Katja Wolff used to work for her. Twenty years ago. Back in Kensington Square. She was nanny to her baby. You know the lady I'm talking about?"

Yasmin felt the panic like a swarm of bees attacking her face. She cried out, "You saw the car. Last night you saw it. You could tell it wasn't in no accident."

"What I could tell is it had a front headlamp that was broke, with no one able to say how it happened."

"Katja didn't run down no one! No one, you hear? You saying that Katja could run down a lady and only have a *headlamp* get broke?"

He didn't reply, merely letting her question and all that her question implied sing in the silence between them. She saw her mistake. He hadn't directly said that Katja was the person he was looking for. It was Yasmin herself who'd led them to that point.

She was furious with herself for letting panic get

the better of her. She went back to the make-up she'd been cataloguing, and she began to slam each article back into the large metal case.

Nkata said, "I don't think she was home, Missus Edwards. Not when this lady was run down. Happened sometime between ten and midnight. And I think Katja Wolff was gone from your flat just about that time. Maybe she was out for two hours, maybe three or four. Maybe she was gone for the night. But she wasn't there, was she? And neither was the car."

She wouldn't answer. She wouldn't meet his eyes. She wouldn't acknowledge he was in the shop. Just a counter separated them, so she could almost feel his breath. But she would not allow his presence— or his words—to gain access to her in any way. Still, her heart was slamming against her ribs, and her mind was filled with the image of Katja's face. It was a face that had observed her carefully during suicide watch when she first went inside, a face that studied her through their exercise period and through association later in the day, a face that locked on hers during tea, and ultimately—though she never would have thought it, expected it, or dreamed that she could have wanted it—a face that lingered above hers in the darkness. *Tell me your secrets. I'll tell you mine.*

She knew what had taken Katja inside. Everyone knew though Katja herself had never spoken of it to Yasmin. Whatever had happened in Kensington was not one of the secrets that Katja Wolff had been willing to reveal, and the single time that Yasmin had asked about the crime for which Katja was so much hated that she'd had to guard herself for years from retribution from the other women, Katja had said, "Do you think I would kill a child, Yasmin? Very well. So be it." And she had turned from Yasmin and had left her alone.

People didn't understand what it was like to be inside, to face the choice between solitude and companionship, between running the risks that went with solitude and embracing the protection that came with choosing—or allowing oneself to be chosen as—a lover, a partner, and a companion. To be alone was to be imprisoned within the prison, and the desolation that went with that secondary gaol term could break a woman and leave her fit for nothing when she was finally released.

So she'd put aside doubts and embraced the story that Katja's words had implied. Katja Wolff was no killer of babies. Katja Wolff was no killer at all.

"Missus Edwards," Constable Nkata said in that gentle, trustworthy voice that coppers always used till they saw it wasn't working like they wanted, "I see the situation you're in. You been together with her for a while. You got loyalty to her from when you were locked up, and loyalty's good. But when someone's dead and someone else is lyin'—"

"What do you know 'bout loyalty?" she cried out. "What do you know 'bout *anything,* man? You stand there like you think you're God 'cause you made a lucky choice that took you a different route to the rest of us. But you don't know nothing 'bout life, do you? 'Cause your choices always keep you safe but they got nothing in them that make you alive."

He observed her calmly, and it seemed that there was nothing she could do and nothing she could say to shatter that steady tranquility of his. And she hated him for the calm front he presented because she knew without having to be told that his serenity went right to the core of who he was.

"Katja was home," she snapped. "Just like we said. Now get out of here. I got work to do."

He said, "Where d'you 'xpect she went those days she phoned in to the laundry ill, Missus Edwards?"

"She didn't phone in to the laundry. She didn't phone in ill or anything else."

"She told you that?"

"She didn't need to tell me."

"You best ask her, then. You best watch her eyes when she answers, too. They fix on you, she's probably lying. They don't look at you at all, she's probably lying as well. 'Course, after twenty years inside, she'll be good at lying. So if she carries on with what she's doing when you ask your question, there's a good enough chance that she's lying."

"I asked you to get out," Yasmin said. "I don't 'tend to ask again."

"Missus Edwards, you're at risk in this situation, but you're not th' only one and you got to know that. You got a boy at risk. You got a fine boy. Clever and good. I c'n see he loves you 'bove everything on earth, and if anything takes you 'way from him again—"

"Get out!" she cried. "Get out 'f my shop. If you don't get out right now, I'll . . ." What? *What,* she thought raggedly. What in God's name would she do? Knife him like she'd knifed her husband? Assault him? And then what would they do to her? And to Daniel? What would happen to him? If they took her son from her—put him into care for even a day while they sorted things out the way they *always* did their sorting—she would not be able to bear the burden of responsibility for his pain and confusion.

She lowered her head. She would not give the detective her face. He could see her harsh breathing, he could take note of the beads of sweat that glistened on her neck. But more than that she would not give him. Not for the world, not for her freedom, not for anything else.

Into her line of vision, she suddenly saw his dark hand slide across the counter. She flinched till she realised he didn't mean to touch her. Instead, he passed her a business card, then slid his hand away. He said so quietly that it sounded like a prayer, "You phone me, Missus Edwards. There's my pager number on that card, so you phone me. Day or night. You phone. When you're ready—"

"I got nothing more to say." But she whispered the words because it hurt her throat too much to do more than that.

"When you're ready," he repeated. "Missus Edwards."

She didn't look up but she didn't need to. His heels sounded sharply against the yellow lino on the floor as he left the shop.

AFTER SHE AND Lynley went their separate ways, Barbara Havers visited the Valley of Kings first. It was filled with swarthy middle-eastern waiters. Once they appeared to come to terms with their collective disapproval of a woman wearing mufti instead of a black bed sheet, they studied in turn the snapshot of Eugenie Davies that Barbara and Lynley had managed to unearth from the woman's cottage in Friday Street. She had posed with Ted Wiley on the bridge that served as the gateway to Henley-on-Thames, and the picture had been taken during the Regatta, if the banners, boats, and colourfully dressed crowds in the background were anything to go by. Barbara had carefully folded the photograph to exclude Major Wiley. No need to muddy the waters of the waiters' memories by showing Eugenie Davies with someone whom the employees of the Valley of Kings might never have seen.

But they shook their heads anyway, one by one. The woman in the photo wasn't anyone they remembered.

She would have been with a man, Barbara told them helpfully. They would have come in separately but with the intention of meeting each other there, possibly in the bar. They would have seemed interested in each other, interested in a way that leads to sex.

Two of the waiters looked scandalised at this fascinating twist in the information. Another's expression of disgust said that mutual lust played out in public between a man and a woman was just what he'd come to expect from living in the UK's answer to Gomorrah. But the clarification that Barbara had sought to provide through her revelation gained her nothing. Soon enough she was back on the street, and plodding in the direction of the Comfort Inn.

It wasn't, she found, aptly named, but then, what affordable hotel on a busy street in their nation's capital ever was? She flashed Eugenie Davies' picture there—for the desk clerk, the maids, and everyone else having contact with the hotel's residents—but she received the same result. The night clerk, however, who would have been the person to see the pictured lady most closely had she ever checked into the hotel with a lover after dining at the Valley of Kings, was not yet on duty, Barbara was told by the hotel manager. So if the constable wanted to return . . . ?

She would have to do so, Barbara decided. There was no point to leaving any stone right side up.

She fetched her car from where she'd left it, illegally parked in front of a cobbled pedestrian path leading into a leafy neighbourhood. She sat inside, shook a fag from her packet of Players, and lit up, cracking open a window against the chill autumn air. She smoked thoughtfully and considered two topics: the lack of damage on Ted Wiley's car and everyone's failure to identify Eugenie Davies in this South Kensington neighbourhood.

On the subject of Wiley's car, the conclusion seemed obvious: Whatever Barbara's earlier thinking in the matter, Ted Wiley hadn't run down the woman he loved. On the subject of everyone's failure to identify Eugenie Davies, however, matters were less defined. One possible conclusion was that Eugenie had no connection with J. W. Pitchley, AKA James Pitchford, in the present day despite having had a connection with him in the past and despite the coincidence of her having his address in her possession and dying in the very street where he lived. Another possible conclusion was that a connection did exist between them—but that connection did not extend to a tryst at the Valley of Kings or a bout of mattress-bouncing afterwards at the Comfort Inn. A third conclusion was that they'd been longtime lovers who'd been meeting elsewhere prior to the night in question when they were to meet at Pitchley-Pitchford's place, which explained why Eugenie Davies had his address with her. And a fourth conclusion was that, sheer coincidence though it might be, Eugenie Davies had connected through the internet with TongueMan—Barbara shuddered at the name— and had met him like all his other lovers at the Valley of Kings for drinks and dinner, trailing him home afterwards and returning on another night to have some sort of encounter with him.

The fact of those other lovers seemed to be the point, though. If Pitchley-Pitchford was a regular at the restaurant and the hotel, then someone was going to remember his face, if not Eugenie's. So there was a chance that seeing his face next to Eugenie's would dislodge a memory helpful to the investigation. Thus, Barbara knew that she needed a picture of Pitchley-Pitchford. And there was only one way to get it.

She made the drive to Crediton Hill in forty-five minutes, wishing not for the first time that she had the talents of a taxi driver who'd passed the Knowledge with highest honours. There wasn't a single parking space on the street when she got there, but the houses had driveways, so Barbara made use of Pitchley's. It was a decent neighbourhood, she saw, lined with houses of a size that suggested no one in this part of the world was hurting for lolly. The area was not yet as trendy as Hampstead itself—with its coffee bars, narrow streets, and bohemian atmosphere—but it was pleasant, a good place for families with children and an unexpected place for a murder.

When she got out of her car, Barbara glanced up and saw a flicker of movement in Pitchley's front window. She rang the bell. There was no immediate answer, which she considered odd since the room in which she'd seen the movement was no great distance from the front door. She rang a second time and heard a man call out, "Coming, coming," and a moment later, the door swung open on a bloke who did not appear at all like the on-line Lothario Barbara had been imagining. She'd expected someone vaguely oleaginous, decidedly tight-trousered, blatantly open-shirted, and displaying a gold medallion like a prize to be disentangled from the snare of copious hairs on his chest. Instead, what she saw in front of her was a grey-eyed whippet of a man, well under six feet tall, possessing rounded cheeks splashed with the sort of natural colour that would have been the bane of his youth. He was wearing blue jeans and a striped cotton shirt with a button-down collar, and this latter garment was closed to the throat. A pair of glasses was tucked into his shirt pocket. He wore expensive looking slip-ons on his feet.

So much for preconceived notions, Barbara thought. It was obviously time to elevate her leisure reading because cheap romance novels were polluting her mind.

She drew out her warrant card and identified herself. "C'n I have a word?" she asked.

Pitchley's response was immediate as he half-shut the door. "Not without my solicitor present."

Barbara put out her hand and stopped the door's progress. "Look. I need a photo of you, Mr. Pitchley. If you have no connection with Eugenie Davies, it's no skin off your arse to hand one over."

"I've just said—"

"I heard. And what I say is this: I can go through the legal song and dance with everyone from your solicitor to the Lord Chancellor to get the picture I need, but it seems to me that that's not only going to prolong your problems but it's also going to make great entertainment for your neighbours when I show up in a panda with the police photographer.

With siren blaring and lights flashing on the roof to get the proper effect, of course."

"You wouldn't dare."

"Try me," she said.

He thought about it, his glance darting along the street. "I *said* I hadn't seen her in years. I didn't even recognise her when I saw her body. Why won't you lot believe me? I'm telling the truth."

"Fine. Brilliant. Then let me prove it to everyone interested. I don't know about the rest of the force, but I'm not keen to stick this murder onto someone with no direct claim on the territory."

He shifted from foot to foot like a schoolboy. He still held on to the door with one hand and his other hand now moved up to grasp the jamb.

It was an interesting reaction, Barbara thought. Despite what she'd said to reassure him, he was responding like a man barring the entry. He was acting like a man with something to hide. Barbara wanted to know what that something was. She said, "Mr. Pitchley . . . ? The photo . . . ?"

He said, "Very well. I'll fetch one. If you'll wait—"

Barbara shouldered her way inside the house, unwilling to give him the chance to add *here* or *on the step*, with or without a courteous *please* attached. She said heartily, "Thanks very much. Decent of you. I could do with a few minutes out of the cold."

His nostrils flared with his displeasure, but he said, "Fine. Wait here. I'll be just a moment," and he fairly threw himself up the stairs.

Barbara listened hard to his progress. She listened

hard to the sounds in the house. He'd admitted to trolling for older ladies on the net, but there was always the chance that he did some trolling where the younger fishies swam as well. If that was the case, and if he had the same degree of success with teenagers that he had with the others, he wouldn't risk taking one of them to the Comfort Inn. Any bloke who made I-want-my-solicitor his primary response to any interaction with the police was a bloke who knew his arse from his elbow when it came to doing the deed with an underage girl. If he was bent in that direction, he'd make sure he didn't take the risk in public. If he was bent in that direction, he'd make sure he took the risk at home.

The fact that she'd seen movement in the room just above the street upon her arrival suggested to Barbara that whatever Pitchley was up to, he was up to it on this floor of the house. So she sauntered to a closed door on her right as Pitchley thrashed about somewhere above her. She swung the door open and found herself in an orderly sitting room done up in antiques.

The only item that appeared out of place was a tattered waxed jacket that lay over a chair. It seemed an odd place for the neat-as-pins Pitchley to stow a garment of his own. He had that sort of everything-in-its-place look about him, suggesting that the very last spot he'd deposit such a jacket after his daily stroll-to-wherever would be in his sitting room among the nice furniture of ages past.

Barbara took a peek at the jacket, then more than a peek. She lifted it off the chair and held it out at arm's length. Bingo, she thought. Pitchley would have been dwarfed inside it. But so would have a teenaged girl. Or any woman, for that matter, who wasn't the size of a sumo wrestler.

She replaced the jacket as Pitchley pounded down the stairs and plunged into the sitting room. He said, "I asked you—" and stopped when he saw her smoothing down the garment's collar. At this, his eyes shifted to a second door in the room, which remained closed. Then they came back to Barbara, and he thrust his hand out. "This is what you want. The woman's a colleague, by the way."

Barbara said, "Thanks," and took the picture he offered. He'd chosen something flattering, she saw. In it, Pitchley wore black tie and he posed with a stunning brunette on his arm. She wore a sea-green form-fitting gown from which balloon-like bosoms threatened to spill. They were patently implants, rising abruptly from her chest like twin domes designed by Sir Christopher Wren. "Nice-looking lady," Barbara said. "American, I take it."

Pitchley looked surprised. "Yes. From Los Angeles. How did you guess?"

"Elementary deduction," Barbara said. She stowed the picture away. She went on pleasantly. "Nice digs. You live here alone?"

His eyes flicked to the jacket. But he said, "Yes."

"All this space. You're lucky. I've a place in Chalk

Farm. But it's nothing like this. Just a hedgehog hole." She indicated the second door. "What's through there?"

His tongue lapped against his lips. "The dining room. Constable, if there's nothing else . . ."

"Mind if I have a peek? It's always a treat to see how the other half lives."

"Yes. I do. I mean, see here. You've got what you came for, and I see no need—"

"I think you're hiding something, Mr. Pitchley."

He flushed to the roots of his hair. "I'm not."

"No? That's good, then. So I'll have a look at what's behind this door." She swung it open before he could protest further. He said, "I haven't given you permission," as she stepped into the next room.

It was empty, with stylish curtains at the far end drawn back against french windows. As in the sitting room, every article was in its place. Also as in the sitting room, however, one item struck a dissonant note. A chequebook sat on the walnut table. It was open, face down, and a pen lay next to it.

"Paying bills?" Barbara said idly. She took note that the air was tinctured heavily with the scent of male body odour as she advanced on the table.

"I'd like you to leave now, Constable." Pitchley made a move towards the table, but Barbara had the advantage of getting there first. She picked up the chequebook. Pitchley said hotly, "Hang on. How *dare* you? You have no right to invade my home."

"Hmm. Yes," Barbara said. She read the cheque

that had gone uncompleted, Pitchley's writing no doubt interrupted by her ringing on his front bell. The amount in question was three thousand pounds. The payee was Robert, and the missing surname marked the moment of Barbara's arrival.

"That's it," Pitchley said. "I've cooperated with you. Leave or I'll phone my solicitor."

"Who's Robert?" she asked. "Is that his jacket out there and his after shave in here?"

In reply, Pitchley headed for a swinging door. He said over his shoulder, "I'm finished with your questions."

But Barbara wasn't finished with him. She was hot on his heels into the kitchen.

He said, "Keep out of here."

"Why?"

A gust of cold air answered her as she entered. She saw that the window was open wide. From the garden beyond it, a clatter sounded. Barbara dashed to investigate while Pitchley dived for the phone. As he punched in numbers behind her, Barbara saw the source of the noise outside. A rake that had been leaning against the house near the kitchen window had been knocked over onto the flagstones. And the visitors to Pitchley's home who had done the knocking-over were at that moment slip-sliding down a narrow slope that separated the garden from a park behind it.

"Stop right there, you two!" Barbara shouted at the men. They were burly and badly dressed in crusty-looking blue jeans and muddy boots. One of

them had on a leather bomber jacket. The other wore
only a pullover against the cold.

Both flashed looks back over their shoulders when
they heard Barbara's shout. Pullover grinned and gave
her an insolent salute. Bomber Jacket shouted, "Have
at her, Jay," and both laughed as they slipped in the
mud, scrambled back to their feet, and took off at a
run across the park.

Barbara said, "Damn," and turned back to the
kitchen.

Pitchley had his solicitor on the line. He was babbling, "I want you over here now. I swear, Azoff, if
you're not at the house in the next ten minutes—"

Barbara snatched the phone from his hand. He
said, "You *bloody* little—"

"Take a stress pill, Pitchley," Barbara said. She said
into the phone, "Save yourself the trip, Mr. Azoff.
I'm leaving. I have what I need," and without waiting to hear the solicitor's reply, she handed the phone
back to Pitchley. She said, "I don't know what you're
up to, fast man, but I'm going to find out. And when
I do, I'll be back with a warrant and a team to tear
this house to shreds. If we find anything that connects
you to Eugenie Davies, you're meat on a skewer. *My*
skewer. Got it?"

"I have no connection with Eugenie Davies," he
said stiffly, although some of the colour was gone
from his cheeks and the rest of his face had gone
nearly white, "other than what I've already told Chief
Inspector Leach."

"Fine," she said. "So be it, Mr. Pitchley. You'd best hope that's what my spadework turns up."

She strode from the kitchen and made her way to the front door. Once outside, she went directly to her car. There was no point to trying to track down the two blokes, who'd leapt from Pitchley's kitchen window. By the time she worked her way round West Hampstead over to the other side of the park, they'd be either long gone or well in hiding.

Barbara fired up the Mini's engine and revved it a few times to let off steam. She'd been ready to go through the motions of taking Pitchley's photo and Eugenie Davies' photo back to the Valley of Kings and the Comfort Inn without the hope of gaining anything from the exercise. Indeed, she'd been nearly ready to dismiss J. W. Pitchley, AKA James Pitchford, AKA TongueMan from their list of suspects altogether. But now she wondered. He sure as hell wasn't acting like a man with nothing smelly on his conscience. He was acting like a man up to his neck in manure. And with a cheque for three thousand pounds half-written in his dining room and two gorilla-size yobbos climbing out of his kitchen window . . . Things no longer looked so cut-and-dried for Pitchley, Pitchford, TongueMan, or whoever the hell he was supposed to be.

Barbara reflected on this final idea as she reversed the Mini into the street. Pitchley, Pitchford, and TongueMan, she thought. There was something in that. She wondered idly if there was another name somewhere that the man from West Hampstead used for something.

She knew exactly how to suss that out.

LYNLEY FOUND THE home of Ian Staines on a quiet street not far from St. Ann's Well Gardens. Using the motorways, he'd made the drive down to Brighton from Henley-on-Thames in fairly good time, but the brief daylight of November was fast fading when he pulled up to the correct address.

The door was opened by a woman holding a cat like an infant against her shoulder. The cat was Persian, an insolent-looking pedigree who cast baleful blue eyes upon Lynley as he produced his identification. The woman was a striking Eurasian, no longer young and no longer beautiful as she once might have been, but difficult to look away from all the same because of a subtle hardness beneath her skin.

She took note of Lynley's identification and said, "Yes," and nothing more when he asked her if she was Mrs. Ian Staines. She waited for whatever was forthcoming from him, although a certain narrowing to her eyes suggested to Lynley that she had little doubt about who the subject of this visit was. He asked if he could have a word, and she stepped back from the doorway and led him to a partially furnished sitting room. Noting the deep impression of furniture feet left on the carpet, he asked if the Staineses were moving house. She said no, they were not moving house, and after the most minute of pauses, she added *yet* in such a way that Lynley felt the undercurrent of her contempt.

She didn't gesture him to one of the two remaining chairs in the sparsely furnished room, both of which were currently occupied with one cat apiece of the same breed as the feline she held. Neither of these was sleeping as one might expect of a cat perched on a comfortable chair. Rather, they were watchful, as if Lynley were a specimen of something in which they might become interested should a sudden burst of energy come upon them.

Mrs. Staines set the cat she held on to the floor. Bloomer-legged by fur that shone with careful grooming, he sauntered to one of the chairs, leapt effortlessly to its seat, and dispossessed his housemate of it. That cat joined the other and settled down on its haunches.

"They're beautiful animals," Lynley said. "Are you a breeder, Mrs. Staines?"

She didn't reply. She wasn't very different from the cats themselves: observing, withholding, and palpably hostile.

She walked to a table that stood by itself, next to the carpet impressions of what must have been a sofa. The table held nothing but a tortoiseshell box whose lid Mrs. Staines flipped open with one manicured finger. She took a cigarette out and from the pocket of her slender-legged trousers, she scooped up a lighter. She put flame to tobacco, inhaled, and said, "What's he done?" in the tone of a woman who very much wanted to add *this time* to the question.

There were no newspapers in the room. But their absence didn't mean that the Staineses were unaware

of Eugenie Davies' death. Lynley said, "There's a situation in London that I'd like to speak to your husband about, Mrs. Staines. Is he at home or still at
work?"

"At work?" She gave a short, breathy laugh before
saying, "London, is it? Ian doesn't like cities, Inspector. He can barely cope with the congestion in
Brighton."

"The traffic?"

"The people. Misanthropy is one of his less admirable qualities, although he manages to hide it most
of the time." She inhaled from her cigarette in the
studied manner of an old film star, her head tilted
back so that her hair—thick, stylishly cut, with the
occasional strand of grey highlighting it—hung free
from her shoulders. She walked to the window in
front of which were yet more carpet impressions of
furniture now removed. She said, "He wasn't here
when she died. He'd gone to see her. They'd had a
row, as you must have been told by someone, or why
else would you have come. But he didn't kill her."

"You've heard about what happened to Mrs.
Davies, then."

"*Daily Mail*," she said. "We didn't know about it
until this morning."

"Someone was seen having an argument with Mrs.
Davies in Henley-on-Thames, someone who took
off in an Audi with Brighton number plates. Was that
man your husband?"

"Yes," she said. "That would be Ian, in the midst
of yet another fine plan going awry."

"A plan?"

"Ian always has plans. And if he hasn't a plan, he has a promise. Plans and promises, promises and plans. All of which generally amount to nothing."

"That'll do, Lydia."

The statement, sharply spoken, came from the doorway. Lynley turned to see that they had been joined by a lanky man with the weathered and yellowing skin of a chronic smoker. He did as his wife had done, crossing the room to the tortoiseshell box and taking a cigarette. He jerked his head at his wife. This apparently communicated a desire to her, for in response she brought out her lighter a second time. She passed it to him and he used it, saying to Lynley, "What can I do for you?"

"He's come about your sister," Lydia Staines said. "I told you that you should expect him, Ian."

"Leave us." He lifted his chin in the direction of the two chairs to indicate the cats, adding, "And take them with you before they get turned into someone's new coat."

Lydia Staines threw her cigarette still smouldering into the fireplace. She scooped up a cat in each arm and said, "Come along, Caesar," to the one who remained. She went on with, "I'll leave you to your fun, then," and accompanied by the animals, she left the room.

Staines watched her go, something in his eyes of an animal's hunger as his glance traveled over her body, something round his mouth of a man's loathing for a woman with too much power over him. When he heard a radio click on somewhere in the back of the house, he gave his attention to Lynley. He said, "I saw Eugenie, yes. Twice. In Henley. We had a row. She'd given me her word, her promise that she'd speak to Gideon—that's her son, but I expect you know that already, don't you?—and I was depending on her to do it. But she said she'd changed her mind, said something had come up that made it impossible for her to ask him . . . And that was it. I took off out of there in a dead blind rage. But someone saw us, I take it. Saw me. Saw the car."

"Where is it?" Lynley asked.

"Being serviced."

"Where?"

"Local dealership. Why?"

"I'll need the address. I'll need to see it, to talk to the people at the dealership as well. They do body work there, I expect."

Staines' cigarette tip glowed, long and bright, as he took in enough smoke to see him through the moment. He said, "What's your name?"

"DI Lynley. New Scotland Yard."

"I didn't knock down my sister, DI Lynley. I was angry. I was damn well desperate. But running her over wouldn't take me an inch towards what I need, so I planned to wait a few days—a few weeks if it took that and if I could hold out—and try her again."

"Try her for what?"

Like his wife, he tossed his cigarette into the fireplace. He said, "Come with me," and headed out of the sitting room.

Lynley followed him. They went to the first floor of the house, up stairs so well-carpeted that their footfalls were soundless. They walked along a corridor where rectangles of darker paper on the walls indicated paintings or prints had been removed. They entered a darkened room that was set up as an office with a desk holding a computer monitor that glowed with text and numerical information. Lynley examined this and saw that Staines had logged on to the internet, having chosen an on-line stock broker as his reading or research material.

"You play the market," Lynley said.

"Abundance."

"What?"

"Abundance. It's all about thinking and living abundance. Thinking and living abundance *effects* abundance, and that abundance produces more of the same."

Lynley frowned, trying to piece this together with what he saw on the screen. Staines continued.

"It's all about thinking in the first place. Most people stay stuck in paucity because that's the only thing they know and that's what they've been taught. I was like that myself once. I was damn *bloody* like that." He came to join Lynley at the desk and laid his hand on a thick book that was open next to his computer's keyboard. This was heavily highlighted in a variety of colours, as if the reader had studied it for years and had taken something new from each perusal of its words. It looked like a text—Lynley thought vaguely of economics—but Staines' words sounded more like a new age philosophy. The man continued in a low, intense voice.

"We attract to our lives that which closely resembles our thoughts," he said insistently. "Think beauty, and we're beautiful. Think ugliness, and we're ugly. Think success, and we become successful."

"Think mastery of the international market, and we have it?" Lynley said.

"Yes. *Yes.* If you spend your life contemplating your limits, you can expect no freedom from limitation." Staines' eyes fixed on the glowing monitor. In its light, Lynley saw that his left eye was milky with a cataract, and the skin was puffy beneath it. He went on. "I used to live only within my limits. I was bound by drugs, by drink, by horses, by cards. If it wasn't one thing, it was another. I lost everything that way—my wife, my children, my home—but that'll not happen to me again. I swear it. Abundance will come. I *live* abundance."

Lynley was beginning to get the picture. He said, "It's a risky sort of business, playing the market, isn't it, Mr. Staines? A great deal of money can be made. Or lost."

"There is no risk, with faith, right action, and belief. Right thought produces the result that's intended by God, Who is Himself goodness and Who wants goodness for His children. If we are one with Him and part of Him, we are part of the good. We must tap into it." As he spoke, he stared intently at the screen. It was divided in such a way that the continually altering prices on a stock exchange somewhere flickered in a band along the bottom. Staines looked mesmerised by this band, as if its moving figures were coded directions to find the Holy Grail.

"But isn't the good open to interpretation?" Lynley asked. "And isn't it the case that man's time line and God's time line to reaching the good may be running on different calendars?"

"It's *abundance*," Staines said, and he spoke through his teeth. "We define it and it *comes*."

"And if it doesn't, we're in debt," Lynley said.

Abruptly, Staines reached forward and pressed a button on the monitor. The screen faded. He directed his words to it, and his tone underscored a rage that he held at bay. "I hadn't seen her for years. I hadn't bothered her for years. Last time was at our mother's funeral, and even then I held back because I knew if I talked to her, I'd have to talk to *him* as well, and I hated the bastard. I'd read the obituaries every day from the time I ran off, hoping to see his, waiting to read that the great man of God had finally left the hell he'd made for everyone round him and gone to his own. They stayed, though. Doug and Eugenie stayed. They sat like good little soldiers of Christ and listened to him preach on Sundays and felt the strap on their backs the rest of the week. But I ran off when I was fifteen and I never went back." He looked at Lynley. "I never *asked* my sister for a God damn thing. All those years with the drugs, the drink, the horses, I never asked. I thought, She was the youngest, she stayed, she took the brunt of the bastard's fury so she's owed the life she made for herself.

And it didn't matter to me that I lost it all—everything I ever owned or loved—because she was my sister and we were his victims and my time would come. So I went to Doug and he helped me when he could. But this last time he said, 'Can't do it, old man. Have a look at the chequebook if you don't believe me.' So what was I supposed to do?"

"You asked your sister for money to pay down your debt. What's it from, Mr. Staines? Selling short? Day trading? Buying futures? What?"

Staines swung away from the monitor, as if the sight of it now offended him. He said, "We've sold what we can. We have only a bed left in our room. We're eating from a card table in the kitchen. The silver's gone. Lydia's lost her jewellery. And all I need is a decent break, which she could have helped me to get, which she *promised* to help me to get. I told her I'd pay her back. I'd pay him back. He's got thousands, millions. He *has* to have."

"Gideon. Your nephew."

"I trusted her to speak to him. She changed her mind. Something's come up, she said. She couldn't ask him for money."

"Did she tell you this the other night when you saw her?"

"That's when she told me."

"Not earlier?"

"No."

"Did she tell you what the 'something' was?"

"We argued like hell. I begged. Begged my own sister, but . . . no. She didn't tell me."

Lynley wondered why the man was admitting so much. Addicts, he knew from personal experience, were themselves virtuosos when it came to playing the music that their intimates danced to. His own brother had played the tune for years. But he was no intimate of Eugenie Davies' brother, not a close relative whose overpowering sense of responsibility for something that was not in fact his responsibility was nevertheless going to compel him to hand over the cash that was needed "just this once." Yet he knew with the assurance of long experience that Staines was saying nothing without being fully aware of what it was.

"Where did you go when you left your sister, Mr. Staines?"

"Drove round till half past one in the morning, till I knew Lydia would be asleep when I got home."

"Is there anyone who can confirm that? Did you stop for petrol somewhere?"

"Didn't need to."

"I'll ask you to take me to the dealership where your car's being serviced, then."

"I didn't run Eugenie down. I didn't kill her. That would have gained me nothing."

"It's routine, Mr. Staines."

"She said she'd talk to him. I just needed a break."

What he needed, Lynley thought, was a cure for his delusions.

THIRTEEN

LIBBY NEALE took the corner into Chalcot Square so sharply that she had to put out a foot to prevent the Suzuki from going into a skid. She'd decided to take a break from her delivery route by scoring an English version of a BLT at a *Pret à Manger* on Victoria Street, and while she'd been munching at one of the stand-up counters, she'd spied a tabloid that a previous customer had left lying by an empty Evian bottle. She'd flipped it over to see that it was the *Sun,* the paper she loathed most due to the taunting presence of the Page Three Girl, who served as a daily reminder to Libby Neale of all she was not. She was about to shove it to one side, when the headline grabbed her attention. *Virtuoso's Mother Murdered* took up about four inches of space. Beneath it was a grainy picture that was dated by the hairstyle and the clothing of the woman in it: Gideon's mother.

Libby snatched up the paper and read it as she ate. She made the jump to page four, where the story continued, and what she saw on that page made her mouthful of sandwich begin to taste like wood shavings. The entire spread covered not the death of Gideon's mother—about which only a limited amount of information was currently available—but another death entirely.

Shit, Libby thought. The Fleet Street dickheads were digging *everything* up all over again. And tabloids being what they were, it was only a matter of time before they started hounding Gideon himself. In fact, they probably were *already* hounding him. A sidebar about Gideon blowing his concert at Wigmore Hall was a feature just begging for further exploration. And as if the poor dude didn't have enough messing up his mind, the paper looked like it was trying to make some sort of connection between Gideon's tough time at that concert and the hit-and-run in West Hampstead!

As *if*, Libby thought contemptuously. Like Gideon would even *recognise* his mother if he'd seen her on the street or something!

Uncharacteristically, she'd thrown half her sandwich away and stuffed the tabloid down the front of her leathers. She had another two deliveries to make, but to hell with that noise. She needed to see Gideon.

In Chalcot Square, she roared counterclockwise around the street and skidded to a stop right in front of the house. She pulled the motorcycle onto the sidewalk without bothering to chain it to the railing. Up the front steps in three strides, she banged on the door, then followed that with a long ring on the bell. He didn't answer, so she looked around the square to see if she could spy his Mitsubishi. She picked it out in front of a yellow house a few doors down on the right. He was at home. So come on, she thought, answer the door.

Within the house, she heard his telephone begin ringing. Four rings and it was abruptly cut off, which made her think he was at home and just not answering the door, but then a distant disembodied voice that she couldn't recognise told her that Gideon's answer machine was taking a message.

"Damn," she muttered. He must have gone off somewhere. He must have learned that the papers were digging up everything about his sister's death and decided to split for a while. She couldn't blame him. Most people had to live through shit only once. But it looked like he was going to have to live through everything connected with her murder a second time.

She went down to her flat. The day's mail lay on the mat, and she picked this up, unlocked her door, and looked through the letters as she stepped inside. Among the BT bill, a bank statement showing that her account was in dire need of an emergency transfusion, and a circular for a home alarm system, there was also a legal-sized envelope from her mother, which Libby dreaded opening because of the possibility of being confronted with yet another of her sister's success stories. But she tore the end off it anyway, and as she removed her helmet with one hand, with the other she shook out the single sheet of purple paper that her mother had sent.

Have What You Want . . . Be Everything You Dream

ran in heavy black script across the page. It seemed that Equality Neale—CEO of Neale Publicity and recently a *Money* magazine cover girl—was giving a seminar in Boston on the topic of Self-Assertion and Achievement in Business, which she would follow with another appearance in Amsterdam. Mrs. Neale had written in the precise hand that would have done proud the nuns who'd taught her, *Wouldn't it be nice if the two of you could get together? Ali could arrange for a stopover on her way back. How far is Amsterdam from London?*

Not far enough, Libby thought, and balled up the announcement. Still, the very idea of Ali and everything so righteously irritating about her that *made* her Ali caused Libby to bypass the refrigerator, where she'd normally have headed after being thwarted in her intentions to see Gideon. Instead, she poured herself a virtuous glass of Highland water in lieu of the six cheddar quesadillas she was feeling like scarfing down. As she drank it, she looked out the window. Against the wall that marked the side boundary of Gideon's backyard stood his kite-making shed, and its door was ajar, a light within throwing a wedge of illumination onto the ground in front of it.

She set her water glass on the counter and ducked outside, bounding up steps that were grey-green with lichen. She called out, "Hey, Gideon!" as she strode down the path in his direction. "You in there?"

There was no response, which gave Libby a qualm and slowed her steps for a moment. She hadn't seen Richard Davies' Granada out in the square, but she hadn't been looking for it. He might've come calling for another one of those pain-in-the-butt father/son talks of his that he appeared to be addicted to. And if he'd managed to piss off Gideon just enough, Gideon might've left on foot and Richard might even now be getting some vengeance on that leaving by wrecking Gideon's kites. That would be just like him, Libby thought. The one thing Gid did that wasn't connected to that stupid violin—besides gliding, which Richard *also* despised—and his father wouldn't hesitate a second to smash them to smithereens. He'd even come up with a good excuse afterwards. "It was taking you away from your music, son."

As *if*, Libby thought scornfully.

Richard continued, if only in her head, "I accepted it as a hobby before, Gideon, but I can't accept it now. We've got to get you well. We've got to get you playing. You've concerts scheduled, recordings to make, and a public waiting."

Fuck *off*, Libby told Richard Davies. He's got a life. He's got a good life. Why don't you think about getting one, too?

The thought of actually going *mano a mano* with Richard for once—of actually telling him off without Gideon there to stop her—renewed Libby's energetic surge along the path. She reached the shed and knocked the door the rest of the way open.

Gideon was there, no Richard with him. He was sitting at his makeshift design table. A piece of butcher paper was taped on the work surface before him, and he sat staring at it like it had something to say to him if he only listened to it long and hard enough.

Libby said, "Gid? Hi. I saw the light."

He didn't act like he'd heard her. He kept his gaze on the paper in front of him.

Libby said, "I knocked on the door upstairs. I rang the doorbell, too. I saw your car in the square, so I figured you were home. Then, when I saw the light out here . . ." She heard her own words die off, like a plant that's wilting without its necessary water.

He said, his eyes still fixed on the paper, "You're back from work early."

"I got my deliveries better organised today so I wouldn't be backtracking all over the place for once." Her aptitude for hasty lying surprised her. Something of Rock was rubbing off on her.

"I'm surprised your husband didn't want you to stay on anyway."

"He doesn't know, and I'm sure as hell not telling him." She shivered. A small electric heater stood on the floor near him, but Gideon didn't have it on. She said, "Aren't you cold without a sweater or something?"

"I hadn't actually noticed."

"Been out here long?"

"A few hours, I think."

"So what're you doing? Another kite?"

"Something to fly," he said. "Higher than the others."

"Sounds cool." She went to stand behind him, eager to see his latest design. She said, "You could do this professionally. No one makes kites like you do, Gid. They're incredible. They're—"

The sight of the design paper stopped her. What he'd produced was an elaborate mass of smudges where he'd drawn and then erased what he'd drawn. They covered the paper, with some of the erasures tearing through it.

Gideon turned to look at her when she didn't complete her remarks. He turned so quickly that she didn't have time to arrange her face.

He said, "I've lost this as well, it seems."

She said, "No, you haven't. Don't be dumb. You're just . . . blocked or stopped up or something. This is a creative thing, right? Making kites is creative. Anything creative gets stopped up now and then."

He read her face and apparently saw on it what she hadn't said. He shook his head. He looked the worst she'd seen him look in all the time since he'd been unable to play his music. He looked worse even than he'd looked just the previous night when he'd come to tell her that his mother was dead. His light hair lay flat and unwashed against his skull, his eyes seemed sunken, and his lips were so chapped that they looked like scales were growing on them. It all seemed so *extreme,* she thought. Hell, he hadn't even seen his mother in years, and he hadn't exactly been tied to her when she was alive, had he? Not like he was tied to his dad.

As if he knew her thoughts and wanted to respond to correct them, he said, "I saw her, Libby."

"Who?"

He said, "I saw her, and I forgot that I saw her."

"Your mom?" Libby asked. "You *saw* your mom?"

"I don't know how I'd forgotten that I saw her. I don't know how it works when you forget, but that's what happened."

He was looking at Libby, but she could tell he wasn't seeing her, and he seemed to be talking to himself. He sounded so filled with self-loathing that she hastened to reassure him. She said, "Maybe you didn't know who she was. It'd been . . . what . . . years and years . . . since you were a kid that you last saw her. And you don't have any pictures of her, do you? So how would you even remember what she looked like?"

"She was there," he said dully. "She said my name. 'Do you remember me, Gideon?' And she wanted money."

"Money?"

"I turned away from her. I am too important, you see, and I have important concerts to give. So I turned away. Because I didn't know who she was. But I'm at fault for that, no matter what I knew or when I knew it."

"Shit," Libby murmured as she began to realise what he was implying. "Gid, heck. You're not thinking you're, like, responsible for what's happened to your mom, are you?"

"I don't think," he said. "I know." And he moved his gaze away from her, fixing it on the open door-

way, where the daylight had faded and what remained of it were shadows that created great wells of
darkness.

She said, "That's bullshit. If you'd known who she
was when she came to you, you would've helped her
out. I know you, Gideon. You're good. You're decent. If your mother was on the ropes or something,
if she needed cash, you wouldn't've ever let her go
under. Yeah, she ran out on you. Yeah, she kept away
from you for years. But she was your mom and you
aren't the kind of guy who holds grudges against anyone, least of all your mom. You're not like Rock Peters." Libby gave a humourless laugh at the thought
of what her estranged husband might have done had
his mother shown up in *his* life asking for money after a twenty-year absence. He'd've given her a piece
of his mind, Libby thought. He'd've given her *more*
than a piece of his mind. Mother or not, he'd've
probably given her the sort of smacking around that
he reserved for women who righteously pissed him
off. And he would've been righteously pissed off at
that: having a deserting mom show up on his
doorstep asking for money without so much as a
how've-you-been-son first. In fact, he might've been
so pissed off that—

Libby put the brakes on her runaway thoughts. She
told herself that the whole idea that Gideon Davies of
all people would lift a hand to harm even a spider was
plain idiotic. He was an artist, after all, and an artist
wasn't the type of man who would run down someone in the street and expect to keep his creative flow

flowing afterwards. Except that here he was with the kites, unable to do what he'd earlier been able to do with ease.

She said, although her mouth was dry, "Did you hear from her, Gid? I mean after she asked you for money. Did you hear from her again?"

"I didn't know who she was," Gideon repeated. "I didn't know what she wanted, Libby, so I didn't understand what she was talking about."

Libby took that for negation because she didn't want to take it as anything else. She said, "Listen, why don't we go inside? I'll make you some tea. It's freezing in this place. You gotta be an ice cube if you've been out here awhile."

She took his arm and he allowed himself to be helped to his feet. She switched out the light and together they felt their way through the gloom to the door. He seemed like a heavy burden to Libby, leaning against her as if all his strength had been depleted in the hours he'd spent trying to design a simple kite.

"I don't know what I'm going to do," he said. "Mother would have helped me, and now she's gone."

"What you're going to do is have a cup of tea," Libby told him. "I'll throw in a tea cake on the side."

"I can't eat," he said. "I can't sleep."

"Then sleep with me tonight. You're always able to sleep with me." They didn't do anything else, she thought, that was for sure. For the first time, she wondered if he was a virgin, if he'd lost the ability to be close to a woman once his mother deserted him.

She knew next to nothing about psychology, but it seemed like a reasonable explanation for Gideon's apparent aversion to sex. How could he take the chance that a woman he grew to love might actually abandon him again?

Libby led him down the steps to her kitchen, where she discovered in short order that she didn't have any of the tea cakes she'd promised him. She didn't have anything to toast at all, but she bet that he did, so she hustled him up to his own part of the house and sat him at the kitchen table while she filled the kettle and rustled through his cupboards for tea and something edible that would go with it.

He sat looking like the living dead . . . although Libby winced when she came up with the analogy. She chatted about her day in an attempt to distract him and she found herself putting so much energy into the effort that she built up a sweat beneath her leathers. Without a thought, she unzipped the top and started to work her way out of it as she talked.

The tabloid she'd stuffed inside fell out. Just like a piece of buttered bread, it fell with the part she wouldn't wish to find face up exactly that: face up. The screaming headline managed what screaming headlines always seek to do: It got Gideon's attention and he bent from his chair and pulled the paper to him as Libby made a grab for it herself.

She said, "Don't. It'll just make things worse."

He looked up at her. "What things?"

"Why put yourself through more shit?" she asked him, her fingers closing over one side of the tabloid as his fingers closed over the other. "All it does is dig everything up all over again. You don't need that."

But Gideon's fingers were as insistent as hers and she knew that she could either let him have the paper or they would rip it in half between them like two women battling over a dress at a Nordstrom's sale. She released her half and mentally kicked her butt for having brought the tabloid with her in the first place and for having forgotten she had it in the second place.

Gideon read the article much as she had done. And just the same, he made the jump to the double spread of pages four and five. There, he saw the pictures that the paper had disinterred from its morgue: his sister, his mom and his dad, his own eight-year-old self, and the other parties involved. It must have been one hell of a slow news day, Libby thought bitterly.

She said, "Hey. Gideon. I forgot to say. Someone phoned when I was banging on your door. I heard a voice on the answer machine. You want to listen? You want me to play it back for you?"

"That can wait," he said.

"Could've been your dad. Might've been about Jill. How d' you feel about that anyway? You never said. It must be so weird to be going to have a little brother or sister when you're old enough to have a kid yourself. Do they know what it's going to be?"

"A girl," he said, although she could tell his mind was elsewhere. "Jill had the tests. It's going to be a girl."

"Cool. A little sister. What a trip for you. You'll be, like, so totally excellent a big brother."

He got to his feet abruptly. "I can't cope with any more nightmares. I don't sleep for hours when I go to bed. I lie there and I listen and I watch the ceiling. When I finally fall asleep, there're the dreams. The dreams and the dreams. I can't *cope* with the dreams."

The kettle clicked off behind her. Libby wanted to see to the tea, but there was something in his face, something so wild and despairing in his face. . . . She hadn't seen such an expression before, and she told herself that she was mesmerised by it, drawn into it in such a powerful way that any action other than looking at him was completely impossible. Better that, she thought, than go in any other direction . . . like wondering if his mother's death had pushed Gideon over the edge.

That couldn't be the case because what reason was there? Why would a man like him wig out if his mom died? If his mom whom he hadn't seen or heard from in years just died? Okay, so he saw her once, so she asked him for money, so he didn't know who she was and refused. . . . Was that something to totally lose it over? Libby didn't think so. But she knew that she was distinctly glad that Gideon was seeing a psychiatrist.

She said, "D' you tell your shrink about the dreams? They're supposed to know what they mean, aren't they? I mean, what else are you paying them for if not to tell you what your dreams mean so that you can stop having them. Right?"

"I've stopped seeing her."

Libby frowned. "The shrink? When?"

"I cancelled my appointment today. She can't help me get back to the violin. I've been wasting my time."

"But I thought you liked her."

"What does it mean that I *liked* her? If she can't help me, what the hell's the point? She wanted me to remember and I've remembered and what's been the result of that? Look at me. Look at this. Look. *Look.* Do you actually think I can play like *this*?"

He held out his hands, and she saw something she'd not noticed before, something she knew hadn't been there twenty-four hours ago when he'd first come to her and told her of his mother's death. His hands were shaking. They were shaking bad, like her grandpa's hands shook before his Parkinson's medication kicked in.

One part of her wanted to celebrate what it meant that Gideon had stopped seeing the psychiatrist: He was beginning to define himself as more than a violinist, which was definitely good. But another part of her felt a prickling of unease at what he was saying. Without the violin, he could discover who he was but he had to *want* to make the discovery, and he didn't much sound or look like a man willing to embark on a journey of self-actualisation.

Still, she said gently, "Not playing's not the end of the world, Gideon."

"It's the end of my world," he told her.

He went into the music room. She heard him stumble, hit against something, and curse. A light switched on, and as Libby saw to the tea—a recommendation on her part that she now recognised as the straw-grasping it most certainly was—Gideon listened to the message that had come in while he'd been trying to work in the shed.

"This is Detective Inspector Thomas Lynley," a plush costume-drama baritone informed them. "I'm on the way up to London from Brighton. Will you phone me on my mobile when you get this message? I need to speak to you regarding your uncle."

An *uncle* now? Libby wondered as the detective recited his cell phone number. What next? How much more was going to be heaped on Gideon and when would he finally shout, "Enough!"

She was about to say, "Wait till tomorrow, Gid. Sleep with me tonight. I'll make you not have nightmares. I promise," when she heard Gideon punching in numbers on his telephone. A moment later he began to speak. She tried to sound busy with the tea, but she listened all the same, in Gideon's best interests.

"Gideon Davies here," he said. "I got your message. . . . Thanks. . . . Yes, it was a shock." He listened long to something that the detective was telling him. He finally said, "I'd prefer it on the phone, if it's all the same to you."

Score one for our side, Libby thought. We'll have a quiet night and then we'll sleep. But as she took their tea cups to the table, Gideon went on, after another pause to listen to the cop.

"Very well, then. If there's no other way." He recited his address. "I'll be here, Inspector." And he hung up.

He came back to the kitchen. Libby tried to look as if she hadn't been eavesdropping. She went to a cupboard and opened it, searching for something to go with their tea. She settled on a bag of Japanese crackers. She ripped it open and dumped its contents into a bowl, searching out two peas and popping them into her mouth as she carried it back to the table.

"One of the detectives," Gideon said unnecessarily. "He wants to talk to me about my uncle."

"Something happen to your uncle, too?" Libby scooped a spoonful of sugar into her cup. She didn't really want the tea, but as she'd been the one to suggest it, she didn't see a way to get out of drinking it.

"I don't know," Gideon told her.

"Think you should call him before the cops get here, then? Check out what's going on?"

"I've no idea where he is."

"Brighton?" Libby felt her face get hot. "I overheard that guy say he was coming in from Brighton. On his message. When you played it."

"It could be Brighton. But I didn't think to ask his name."

"Whose?"

"My uncle's."

"You don't *know* . . . ? Oh. Well. Never mind, I guess." It was just another twist in his family history, Libby thought. Lots of people didn't know their relatives. As her father would have said, it was a sign of the times. "You couldn't put him off till tomorrow?"

"I didn't want to put him off. I want to know what's happening."

"Oh. Sure." She was disappointed, seeing herself ministering to him throughout the long evening, figuring inanely that ministering to him now that he was at his lowest might lead to something more between them, making a final breakthrough somehow. She said, "If you can trust him, I guess."

"Trust him how?"

"Trust him to tell you the truth. He's a cop, after all." She shrugged and scooped up a handful of the Japanese mix.

Gideon sat. He pulled his tea cup towards him, but he didn't drink. He said, "It doesn't matter one way or another."

"What doesn't?"

"Whether he tells me the truth or not."

"No? Why not?" Libby asked.

Gideon looked her square in the face when he delivered the blow. "Because I can't trust anyone with the truth. I didn't know that before. But I know that now."

THINGS WERE MOVING from bad to worse.

J. W. Pitchley, AKA TongueMan, AKA James Pitchford, logged off the internet, stared at the blank screen, and cursed it to hell. He'd finally managed to get CreamPants on the net for some cybertalk, but despite a good half hour of reasoning with her, she wasn't going to cooperate. All she had to do was walk into the Hampstead police station and have a five-minute conversation with DCI Leach and she wouldn't do it. She merely needed to confirm that she and a man she knew only as TongueMan had spent the evening together, first in a South Kensington restaurant and then in a claustrophobic little room above Cromwell Road where the ceaseless traffic noise disguised the frantic creaking of bedsprings and the cries of pleasure that he coaxed from her when he performed the services implied by his moniker. But no, she couldn't do that for him. No matter that he'd brought her off six times in under two hours, no matter that he'd held off taking his own satisfaction till she was weak, sodden, and limp with having taken hers, no matter that he'd fulfilled her every seamy fantasy about the rewards of anonymous sex. She wasn't going to step forward and "face the humiliation of having a complete stranger know the sort of woman I can be under certain unusual circumstances."

I'm a bloody stranger, you filthy bitch! Pitchley had roared, if only in his head. You didn't think twice about letting *me* know what you like to get up to when you're panting for it.

She'd seemed to know what he was thinking, though, despite the fact that he didn't communicate it on the screen. She'd written *They'd want my name, you see. I can't have that, Tongue. Not my name. Not with tabloids being what they are. I'm sorry, but you understand that, don't you?*

Which was how he'd come to realise that she wasn't divorced. She wasn't a woman in her declining years who was desperate for a man to prove she still had It. She was a woman in her declining years who was looking for a thrill to balance against the tedium of marriage.

That marriage had to be a longtime covenant, one made not with an Everyman or an Anyman but with a Somebody, an important Somebody, a politician, perhaps, or an entertainer, or a successful and well-known entrepreneur. And if she gave her name to DCI Leach, it would quickly leak through the porous substance that was the hierarchy of power at the police station. Having leaked through that, it would find its way to the ears of an informant from within, a snout who accepted cash from a journalist eager to make his name by outing someone on the front page of his filthy scream sheet.

Bitch, Pitchley thought. Bitch, bitch, bitch. She might have thought of that before she'd met him at the Valley of Kings, Mrs. Butter-Wouldn't-Melt-If-You-Put-It-On-Coals. She might have thought of all the potential consequences before she walked in, dressed to be seen as Mrs. Demure, Mrs. Out-Of-Style, Mrs. I've-Got-No-Experience-With-Men, Mrs. Please-Please-Show-Me-I'm-Still-Desirable-Because-I've-Been-So-Low-On-Myself-For-So-Long. She might have thought it could actually come to having to say Okay, I was there in the Valley of Kings, having drinks and then dinner with an utter stranger whom I met on-line in a chat room where people hide their identities while sharing their fantasies about wild, wet, and lubricious sex. She might have thought she could be asked to admit to hours lying splayed on a thin-mattressed bed above the South

Kensington traffic, naked on that bed with a man whose name she didn't know, didn't ask to know, and didn't want to know. She might have *thought,* the rotten little cow.

Pitchley pushed away from his computer and sank his elbows onto his knees. He took his forehead into his hands and dug into it with his fingertips. She could have helped. She wouldn't have been the complete solution to his problem—there was still that long period between the Comfort Inn and his arrival in Crediton Hill to be accounted for—but she would have been a bloody good start. As it was, he had only his story, his willingness to stick to his story, the unlikely possibility that the evening clerk at the Comfort Inn would confirm his presence two nights ago without confusing that night with the dozens of other nights he'd passed the requisite cash across the counter, and the hope that his face was guileless enough to convince the police to believe his story.

It didn't help matters that he knew the woman who'd died in his street in possession of his address. And it truly didn't help matters one iota that he'd once been involved—no matter how peripherally—with a heinous crime that had taken place when he'd lived under her roof.

He'd heard the shrieking that evening and he'd come running because he'd recognised who was crying out. When he'd got there, everyone else was there as well: the child's father and mother, the grandparents, the brother, Sarah-Jane Beckett, and Katja Wolff. "I do not leave her for more than a minute," she shrieked, frantically laying this information in front of everyone milling round the closed bathroom door. "I swear. I do not leave her for more than a minute!" And then looming behind her was Robson, the violin master, who grasped her by the shoulders and pulled her away. "You must believe me," she cried, and continued to cry as he pulled her with him down the stairs and out of sight.

He hadn't known at first what was going on. He hadn't wanted to know and couldn't afford to know. He'd heard the argument between her and the parents, she'd told him she'd been sacked, and the last thing he wanted to consider was whether the argument, the sacking, and the reason for the sacking— which he suspected but could not bear to contemplate—were in any way related to what lay behind that bathroom door.

"James, what's going *on*?" Sarah-Jane Beckett's hand had slipped into his, clutching at him as she breathed the whisper. "Oh God, something hasn't happened to Sonia, has it?"

He'd looked at her and saw that her eyes were glittering despite her sombre tone. But he hadn't wondered what that glitter meant. He'd only wondered how he could manage to get away from her and go to Katja.

"Take the boy," Richard Davies had instructed Sarah-Jane. "For God's sake, get Gideon out of here, Sarah."

She'd done as he commanded, taking the little white-faced boy into his bedroom, where music was playing, issuing blithely forth as if nothing terrible was going on in the house.

He himself went seeking Katja and he found her in the kitchen, where Robson was forcing a glass of brandy on her. She was trying to refuse, crying, "No. No. I cannot drink it," looking wild-haired, wild-eyed, and completely wrong for the part of loving, protective nanny to a child who was . . . what? He was afraid to ask, afraid because he already knew but didn't want to face because of what it might mean in his *own* life if what he thought and dreaded proved to be true.

"Drink this," Robson was saying. "Katja. For the love of God, pull yourself together. The paramedics will be here in a moment and you can't afford to be seen like this."

"I did not, I did not!" She swung round in her chair and grabbed onto his shirt, the collar of which she grasped and twisted. "You must *say*, Raphael! Say to them that I did not leave her."

"You're getting hysterical. It may be nothing."

But that did not prove to be the case.

He should have gone to her then, but he hadn't because he'd been afraid. The mere thought that something might have happened to that child, might have happened to *any* child within a house in which he was a resident, had paralysed him. And then later, when he could have talked to her and when he tried to talk to her, in order to declare himself the friend she needed and clearly did not have, she would not speak to him. It was as if the subtle flaying she was

taking in the press in the immediate aftermath of Sonia's death had driven her into a corner and the only
way she could survive was to become tiny and silent,
like a pebble on a path. Every story about the unfolding drama in Kensington Square began with the
reminder that Sonia Davies' nanny was the German
whose famed escape from East Germany—previously
considered laudable and miraculous—had cost a vital
young man his life, and that the luxurious environment in which she found herself in England was a
dire and bleak contrast to the situation to which her
ostentatious asylum-seeking had condemned the rest
of her family. Everything about her that was remotely
questionable or potentially interpretable was dug up
by the press. And anyone close to her was liable to the
same treatment. So he'd kept his distance, till it was
too late.

When she was finally charged and brought to trial,
the van that had taken her from Holloway to the Old
Bailey had been pelted with eggs and rotten fruit, and
shouts of "baby killer" greeted her when that same
van returned her to the prison at night and she had
to make the few yards' walk to the prison's door.
Public passion was aroused by the crime she had allegedly committed: because the victim was a child,
because the child was handicapped, and because—
although no one would say it directly—her putative
killer was German.

And now he was back in it all, Pitchley thought as
he rubbed his forehead. He was mixed up in it as effectively as if he'd never managed to put twenty years

between himself and what had happened in that miserable house. He'd changed his name, he'd switched jobs five times, but all his best efforts to remake himself were going to be brought to nothing if he couldn't get CreamPants to see that her statement was crucial to his survival.

Not that CreamPants' statement was the only thing he needed to put his house in order. He also needed to deal with Robbie and Brent, those two loose cannons who were about to fire.

He'd assumed they wanted money again when they'd shown up a second time in Crediton Hill. No matter that he'd already given them a cheque, he knew them well enough to realise there was a decent possibility that Robbie had been inspired by the sight of a Ladbrokes to deposit those funds not in a bank account but on the head of a horse whose name he rather fancied. This assumption on Pitchley's part was ratified when Robbie said, "Show 'im, Brent," not five minutes after the two of them had hulked through his front door, carrying with them the stench of their poor bathing habits. Accepting the instruction, Brent brought forth from his jacket a copy of *The Source,* which he opened like someone shaking out bed sheets.

"Look who it was got mashed on your doorstep, Jay," Brent said with a grin as he showed the scabrous paper's front page. And of course it would be *The Source,* Pitchley thought. God forbid that either Brent or Robbie would elevate their taste to something less sensational.

He couldn't avoid seeing what Brent dangled in front of him: the garish headline, the photograph of Eugenie Davies, the inset photograph of the street in which he himself lived, and the second inset photograph of the boy no longer a boy but a man now and a celebrity. It was all down to *him* that this death was taking up newsprint at all, Pitchley thought bitterly. If Gideon Davies hadn't achieved fame, fortune, and success in a world that increasingly valued those accomplishments, then the papers wouldn't even be covering this situation. It would simply be an unfortunate hit-and-run that the police were in the process of investigating. Full stop and end of story.

Robbie said, " 'Course, we di'n't know when we 'as here yesterday. Mind 'f I unload this, Jay?" And he'd shrugged his way out of his heavy waxed jacket and lobbed it onto the back of a chair. He made a circuit of the room and a point of examining everything in it. He said, "Nice gaff, this. You done good for yourself, Jay. I expect you got a big name in the City, least 'mong the people who count. That right, Jay? You massage their money and presto amazo, it makes more money and they trust you to do that, don't they?"

Pitchley said, "Just say what you want. I'm rather pressed for time."

"Don't see why," Robbie said. "Shoot. In New York . . ." He snapped his fingers in the direction of his companion. "Brent. Time in New York?"

Brent looked at his watch obediently. His lips moved as he did the maths. He frowned and employed the fingers of one hand. He finally said, "Early."

Robbie said, "Right. Early, Jay. Th' market's not closed yet in New York. You got plenty of time to make a few more quid before the day's over. Even with this little confab of ours."

Pitchley sighed. The only way to get rid of the two men would be to make it look as though he was playing Rob's game. He said, "You're right, of course," and nothing more. He merely walked to a bureau near the window that overlooked the street, and from inside he brought out his chequebook and a biro that he clicked open officially. He carried the chequebook into the dining room, where he pulled out a chair, sat, and began to write. He started with the amount: three thousand pounds. He couldn't imagine that Rob would ask for less.

Rob strode into the dining room. Brent, as always, followed his brother. Rob said, "That's what you think, is it, Jay? Us two show up and it's all about money?"

"What else?" Pitchley filled in the date and began to write the other man's name.

Robbie's hand smacked down on the dining room table. "Hey! You stop that and look at me." And for good measure, he knocked the biro from Pitchley's hand. "You think this is about *money*, Jay? Me and Brent trot round—all this way up to Hampstead, mind you—with business waiting to be tended to out there"—this with a jerk of his head back in the direction of the sitting room, by which Pitchley took that he meant the street—"with us losing dosh by the bucketful just to stand here and bunny with you for ten minutes and you think we come about money? Hell, man." And to the other, "What d'you think of that, Brent?"

Brent joined them at the table, *The Source* still dangling from his fingers. He wouldn't know what to do with the paper till Robbie gave him his next set of instructions. As for now, it gave him something to occupy his hands.

The poor oaf was pathetic, Pitchley thought. It was a wonder he'd ever learned to tie his shoes. He said, "All right. Fine," and sat back in his chair. "So why don't you tell me why you've come, Rob?"

"Can't just be a friendly visit, that it?"

"That's not exactly our history."

"Yeah? Well, you *think* about history. 'Cause it's ripe to come back and pay a call on you, Jay." Robbie flicked his thumb at *The Source*. Cooperatively, Brent held it higher, like a schoolboy displaying his primitive art work. "Slow going on the news front last few days. No Royals misbehaving, no MP getting caught with his dick in a schoolgirl's hole. The papers're going to start digging, Jay. And me and Brent come to see you to lay our plans."

"Plans." Pitchley repeated the word with a great deal of care.

"Sure. We took care of things once. We c'n do it again. Situation's bound to heat up fast once the coppers suss out who you really are and when they give the word to the press like they always do—"

"They know," Pitchley said, in the hope that he could head Robbie off, that he could bluff him with a partial truth that the man might take as a full admission. "I've already told them."

But Rob wasn't swallowing that tale. He said, "No way, Jay. 'Cause if you did, they'd feed you to the sharks soon 's they need something to make it look like they been working hard. You know that. So I 'xpect you told them something, true. But 'f I know you, you didn't tell them all." He eyed Pitchley shrewdly and seemed to like what he read on his face. He said, "Right. Good. So me and Brent here figger we got to lay some plans. You'll be wanting protection and we know how to give it."

And then I'll owe you forever, Pitchley thought. Double what I already owe you because it'll be twice in my life that you've played at keeping the hounds at bay.

"You need us, Jay," Robbie told him. "And me and Brent? We don't turn our backs when we know we're needed. Some people do, but that's not our way."

Pitchley could only imagine how it would play out: Robbie and Brent doing battle for him, strong-arming the press in the same ineffectual manner that they'd employed in the past.

He was about to tell them to go home to their wives, to their failing inadequate ill-managed business washing waxing buffing the cars of the rich among whom they would never be able to mix. He was about to tell them to piss off permanently because he was tired of being drained like a bathtub and played like a badly tuned piano. Indeed, he opened his mouth to say all of it, but that was when the doorbell rang, when he walked to the window and saw who it was, when he said, "Stay here," to Robbie and Brent and closed the dining room doors upon them.

And now, he thought miserably as he sat at his computer and tried and failed to come up with a way to bend the will of CreamPants to his own, he would owe them more. He would owe them more for Rob's quick thinking, the thinking that got him and Brent out of the house and into the park before the dumpy female detective constable was able to put her mitts on them when they'd hidden in the kitchen. No matter that what they might have told her would have added nothing harmful in his present situation. Robbie and Brent would not see it that way. They would see their actions as protecting him, and they would come calling when they thought it was time for him to pay.

LYNLEY MADE THE drive to London in fairly good time after paying a visit to the Audi dealership that was working on the car owned by Ian Staines. He'd taken Staines with him as a safeguard against the man making any phone calls in an attempt to direct the course of Lynley's enquiries, and once they'd pulled to a stop in front of the auto showroom, he'd told the man to wait in the Bentley while he went inside for a chat.

There, he corroborated much of what Eugenie

Davies' brother had told him. The car was indeed being serviced; it had been brought in at eight that morning. An appointment for the work had been scheduled on the previous Thursday, and nothing irregular—like a request for body work—had been noted in the computer when the service secretary had taken the call.

When Lynley asked to see the car, that presented no problem either. The service representative walked him out to it, chatting away about the great strides that Audi had made in craftsmanship, manoeuvrability, and design. If he was curious as to why a policeman had come round asking about a particular car, he gave no evidence of this. A potential customer was, after all, a potential customer.

The Audi in question stood in one of the service bays, raised some six feet on a hydraulic lift. Its position gave Lynley the opportunity to examine its undercarriage as well as the chance to scrutinise its front end and both of its wings for damage. The front end was fine, but there were scratches and a dent on the car's left wing that looked intriguing. They looked fresh as well.

"Any chance a smashed bumper was replaced before you got the car?" Lynley asked the mechanic who was working on it.

"Always a chance of that, mate," the man replied. "Bloke don't need to drop money at the dealership if he knows how to shop."

So despite the verification provided by the Audi's general condition and its presence just where Staines said it would be, there was still the chance that those scratches and that small dent meant something more than poor driving skills. Staines couldn't be crossed off the list despite his claim that the scratches and dent were a mystery to him, that "bloody Lydia uses the car as well, Inspector."

Lynley dropped the man at a bus stop and told him not to disappear from Brighton. "If you move house, phone me," he said to Staines, handing over his card. "I'll want to know."

Then he headed for London. Northeast of Regent's Park, Chalcot Square was yet another area of town that was undergoing gentrification. If the scaffolding on the front of several of the buildings hadn't told Lynley this much when he pulled into the square, the freshly painted façades of the rest of the residences would have filled him in on the information. The neighbourhood reminded him of Notting Hill. Here was the same bright paint in a variety of cheerful colours fronting the buildings along the streets.

Gideon Davies' house stood tucked into a corner of the square. It was bright blue in colour with a white front door. It possessed a narrow first-floor balcony along which ran a low white balustrade, and the french windows beyond that balcony were brightly lit.

His knock on the door was answered quickly, as if the house's owner had been waiting on the bottom step just beyond the entrance. Gideon Davies said quietly, "DI Lynley?" and when Lynley nodded, he added "Come upstairs," and led the way. He took him to the first floor, up a staircase whose walls displayed the framed hallmarks of his career, and he led him into the room that Lynley had seen from the street, where a CD system occupied one wall and comfortable furniture scattered across the floor was punctuated by tables and music stands. Sheet music stood on these stands and lay on the table tops, but none of it was open.

Davies said, "I've never met my uncle, Inspector Lynley. I don't know how much help I'll be to you."

Lynley had read the stories in the newspaper after the violinist had walked out on his concert at Wigmore Hall. He'd thought—probably like most of the public interested in the tale—that it was another instance of someone who had been feather-bedded for too many years getting his knickers in a twist about something. He'd seen the subsequent explanations put forth by the young man's publicity machine: exhaustion after a killing schedule of concerts in the spring. And he'd dismissed the entire subject as a three-day wonder that the papers needed to fill column space at a slow time of year.

But now he saw that the virtuoso looked ill. Lynley thought immediately of Parkinson's—Davies' walk was unsteady and his hands trembled—and of what that disease could do to finish his career. That would be something that the young man's publicity machine would indeed want to keep from the public for as long as possible, calling it everything from exhaustion to nerves until it was impossible for them to call it anything else.

Davies gestured to three overstuffed armchairs that formed a group near the fireplace. He himself sat nearest the fire itself: artificial coals between which blue and orange flames rhythmically lapped like a visual soporific. Despite his sickly appearance, Lynley could see the strong resemblance between the violinist and Richard Davies. They shared much the same body type, with an emphasis on bones and stringy muscles. The younger Davies had no spinal curvature, however, although the manner in which he kept his legs locked together and his clenched fists pressed into his stomach suggested that he had other physical problems.

Lynley said, "How old were you when your parents divorced, Mr. Davies?"

"When they divorced?" The violinist had to think about the question before he answered it. "I was about nine when my mother left, but they didn't divorce immediately. Well, they couldn't have done, not with the law being what it is. So it must have taken them what . . . four years? I don't actually know, now I think of it, Inspector. The subject never came up."

"The subject of their divorce or the subject of her leaving?"

"Either. She was just gone one day."

"You never asked why?"

"We never talked much about personal things in my family. There was a lot of . . . I suppose you could call it reticence amongst us. It wasn't just the three of us in the house, you see. There were my grandparents, my teacher, and a lodger as well. Something of a crowd. I suppose it was a way to have privacy: by letting everyone have a personal life that no one else ever mentioned. Everyone held their thinking and their feelings fairly close in. Well, that was the fashion anyway, wasn't it."

"And during the time of your sister's death?"

At that, Davies moved his gaze off Lynley and fixed it on the fire, but the rest of his body remained motionless. "What about my sister's death?"

"Did everyone hold their thinking and feelings close in when she was murdered? And during the trial that followed?"

Davies' legs tightened against each other as if they would defend him from the questions. "No one ever talked about it. 'Best to forget' was like a family motto, Inspector, and we lived by it." He raised his face towards the ceiling. He swallowed and said, "God. I expect that's why my mother finally left us. No one would ever talk about what desperately *needed* talking about in that house, and she just couldn't cope with it any longer."

"When was the last time you saw her, Mr. Davies?"

"Then," he said.

"When you were nine years old?"

"Dad and I left for a tour in Austria. When we returned, she was gone."

"You've not heard from her since?"

"I've not heard from her since."

"She never contacted you in the last several months?"

"No. Why?"

"Your uncle says she intended to see you. She in-tended to borrow money from you. He says that she told him something came up to prevent her from asking you for money. I'm wondering if you know what that something was."

Davies looked guarded at that, as if a barrier had come down like a thin shield of steel to cover his eyes. "I've had . . . I suppose you could call it some trouble with my playing." He let Lynley fill in the rest: A mother anxious about her son's well-being was unlikely to petition him for funds, either for her-self or for a ne'er-do-well brother.

That supposition didn't conflict with what Richard Davies had told Lynley about his former wife phon-ing him to learn more about their son's condition. But the timing was off if the musician's condition was supposed to be what had kept his mother from mak-ing her request for funds. Indeed, it was off by several months. For Gideon Davies had undergone his trauma at Wigmore Hall in July. It was now Novem-ber. And according to Ian Staines, his sister's change of heart concerning asking her son for money had occurred in the more immediate past than had Gideon's musical difficulties. It was a small point only, but it could not be overlooked.

"Your father tells me she'd been phoning him reg-ularly about you, so she did know that something was wrong," Lynley said in agreement. "But he made no mention of her wanting to see you or asking to see you. You're certain she didn't contact you directly?"

"I think I'd remember my own mother contacting me, Inspector. She didn't, and she couldn't have done. My number's ex-directory, so the only way she had to contact me would have been through my agent, through Dad, or by turning up at a concert and sending a note backstage."

"She did none of those things?"

"She did none of those things."

"And she passed no message to you through your father?"

"She passed no message," Davies said. "So perhaps my uncle's lying to you about my mother's intention of seeing me to ask for money. Or perhaps my mother lied to my uncle *about* her intention of seeing me to ask for money. Or perhaps my father's lying to you about her phone calls to him in the first place. But that last is unlikely."

"You sound sure of that. Why?"

"Because Dad himself wanted us to meet. He thought she could help me out."

"With what?"

"The trouble I've had with my playing. He thought she could . . ." Here, Davies went back to looking at the fire, his assurance of a moment before quite gone. His legs trembled. He said, more to the fire than to Lynley, "I don't really believe that she could have helped me, though. I don't believe anyone can help me at this point. But I was willing to try. Before she was killed. I was willing to try anything."

An artist, Lynley thought, who was being kept from his art due to fear. The violinist would be look-

ing for a talisman of some sort. He would want to believe his mother was the charm that could get him
back to his instrument. Lynley said to make certain,
"How, Mr. Davies?"

"What?"

"How could your mother have helped you?"

"By agreeing with Dad."

"Agreeing? About what?"

Davies considered the question, and when he answered, he told Lynley volumes about the difference
between what was going on in his professional life
and what the public was being told about it. "Agreeing that there's nothing wrong with me. Agreeing
that my head's playing me for a fool. That's what Dad
wanted her to do. He has to have her agree with him,
you see. Anything else is unthinkable. Now, unspeakable would be par for the course in my family. But
unthinkable . . . ? That would take too much effort."
He laughed weakly, a brief note that was as humourless as it was bitter. "I'd have seen her, though. And
I'd have tried to believe her."

So he would have reason to want his mother alive,
not dead. Especially if he held fast to the conviction
that she was the cure for what ailed his playing.
Nonetheless, Lynley said, "This is routine, Mr.
Davies, but I need to ask it: Where were you two
nights ago when your mother was killed? This would
have been between ten and midnight."

"Here," Davies said. "In bed. Alone."

"And since he left your home, have you had contact with a man called James Pitchford?"

Davies looked honestly surprised. "James the Lodger? No. Why?" The question seemed ingenuous enough.

"Your mother was on her way to see him when she was killed."

"On her way to see James? That doesn't make sense."

"No," Lynley said. "It doesn't."

Nor, he thought, did some of her other actions. Lynley wondered which of them had led to her death.

FOURTEEN

JILL FOSTER could see that Richard wasn't pleased at having to entertain another visit from the police. He was even less pleased to learn that the detective had just come from seeing Gideon. He took in this information politely enough as he motioned DI Lynley to a chair, but the manner in which his mouth tightened as the detective imparted his facts told Jill that he wasn't happy.

DI Lynley was watching Richard closely, as if gauging his most minute reaction. This gave Jill a sense of disquiet. She knew about the police from years of having read newspaper accounts of famously botched cases and even more famous miscarriages of justice, so she was fairly well-versed in the extremes they would go to in order to pin a crime on a suspect. When it came to murder, the police were more interested in building a strong case against some- one—against *anyone*—than they were in getting to the bottom of what happened because building a case against someone meant putting an investigation to rest, which meant getting home to their wives and their families at a reasonable hour for once. That desire underlay every move they made in a murder enquiry, and it behooved anyone being questioned by them to be wise to that fact.

The police are not our friends, Richard, she told her fiancé silently. Don't say a word that they can twist round and use against you later.

And surely that's what the detective was doing. He fastened his dark eyes—brown they were, not blue as one would have expected in a blond—on Richard and waited patiently for a reply to his statement, a neat notebook open in his large, handsome hand. "When we met yesterday, you didn't mention you'd been advocating a meeting between Gideon and his mother, Mr. Davies. I'm wondering why."

Richard sat on a straight-backed chair that he'd swung round from the table on which he and Jill took their meals. He'd made no offer of tea this time. That suggested welcome, which the detective definitely was not. Richard had said upon his arrival and prior to DI Lynley's mentioning the call he'd made on Gideon, "I do want to be helpful, Inspector, but I must ask you to be reasonable with your visits. Jill needs her rest and if we can reserve our interactions for daylight hours, I'd be very grateful."

The detective's lips had moved in what the naïve might have concluded was a smile. But his gaze took in Richard in such a way as to suggest he wasn't the sort of man used to being told what was expected of him, and he didn't apologise for his appearance in South Kensington or make routine noises about not taking up too much of their time.

"Mr. Davies?" Lynley repeated.

"I didn't mention that I was attempting to arrange a meeting between Gideon and his mother because you didn't ask me," Richard said. He looked to where Jill was sitting at one end of the table, her laptop open and her fifth attempt at Act III, Scene 1 of her television adaptation of *The Beautiful and Damned* taking up space on her screen. He said, "You'll probably want to continue working, Jill. There's the desk in the study . . . ?"

Jill wasn't about to be condemned to a sentence in that mausoleum-cum-memorial to his father that posed as Richard's study. She said, "I've gone about as far as I can with this just now," and she went through the exercise of saving and then backing up what she'd written. If Eugenie was going to be discussed, she intended to be present.

"Had she asked to see Gideon?" the detective asked Richard.

"No, she hadn't."

"Are you sure?"

"Of course I'm sure. She didn't want to see either of us. That's the choice she made years ago when she left without bothering to mention where she was going."

"What about why?" DI Lynley asked.

"Why what?"

"Why she was going, Mr. Davies. Did your wife mention that?"

Richard bristled. Jill held her breath, trying to ignore the stab she felt in her breast at those words: *your wife*. How she felt about hearing anyone other than herself referred to with that term could not be allowed to matter at the moment because the detective's question got right to the crux of the topic that was of interest to her. She longed to know not only why Richard's wife had left him but also how he'd felt about her leaving him, how he'd felt then and, much more importantly, how he felt now.

"Inspector," Richard said evenly, "have you ever lost a child? lost a child to violence? lost a child at the hands of someone who's living right inside your own home? No? You haven't? Well, then, I suggest you think about what a loss like that can do to a marriage. I didn't need Eugenie to give me chapter and verse on why she was leaving. Some marriages survive a trauma. Others do not."

"You didn't try to find her once she was gone?"

"I didn't see the point. I didn't want to keep Eugenie where she didn't want to be. There was Gideon to consider, and I'm not of the school who believe that two parents for a child are better than one no matter the condition of their marriage. If the marriage goes bad, it has to end. Children survive that better than living in a house that's little more than an armed encampment."

"Your break-up was hostile?"

"You're inferring."

"It's part of the job."

"It's taking you in the wrong direction. I'm sorry to disappoint you, but there was no bad blood between Eugenie and me."

Richard was irritated. Jill could hear it in his tone, and she was fairly sure that the detective could hear it also. This worried her, and she stirred on her seat and tried to get her lover's attention, to throw him a warning look that he would interpret and act upon, altering if not the substance of his replies then at least their timbre. She well understood the source of his irritation: Gideon, Gideon, always Gideon, what Gideon did and did not do, what Gideon said and did not say. Richard was upset because Gideon hadn't phoned and reported the detective's visit. But the detective wouldn't see it that way. He'd be far more likely to note it as Richard's reaction to being questioned too closely about Eugenie.

She said, "Richard, I'm sorry. If you could help me for a moment . . . ?" And to the detective, with an exasperated smile, "I'm running to the loo every fifteen minutes these days. Oh, thank you, darling. Heavens, I'm not quite right on my feet." She held on to Richard's arm for a moment, acting the part of a woman lightheaded, waiting for Richard to say that he'd help her along to the loo, which would thus buy him some time to regroup. But to her frustration, he just fastened his arm round her waist for a moment to steady her and said, "Do take care," but made no move to assist her from the room.

She tried to telegraph her intentions to him. *Come with me.* But he either ignored or didn't get the message, because once she was apparently solid in her stance, he let go of her and gave his attention back to the detective.

There was nothing for it but to go to the loo, which Jill did with as much dispatch as she could muster, considering her size. She needed to pee anyway—she always needed to pee now—and she squatted over the toilet while trying to hear what was going on in the room she'd just left.

Richard was speaking when she returned. Jill was gratified to see that he'd managed to wrest his quick temper under control. He was saying calmly, "My son is suffering from stage fright, Inspector, as I've already told you. He's completely lost his nerve. If you've seen him, you've no doubt also seen that something's badly wrong with the boy. Now, if Eugenie could have helped with that problem in any way, I was willing to try it. I was willing to try anything. I love my son. The last thing I want to see is his life's destruction brought about by an irrational fear."

"So you asked her to meet with him?"

"Yes."

"Why so long after the event?"

"The event?"

"The concert at Wigmore Hall."

Richard flushed. He hated, Jill knew, any mention of the venue. She had little doubt that, should Gideon ever regain his music, his father would never again allow him so much as to pass over its threshold. It was the scene of his public humiliation, after all. Better to burn it to the ground.

Richard said, "We'd tried everything else, Inspector. Aromatherapy, anti-anxiety treatments, pep talks, psychiatry, everything under the sun save having an astrologer do a reading of the stars. We'd been going those routes for several months, and Eugenie was simply the last resort." He watched Lynley writing in his notebook, and he added, "I'd very much appreciate it if this information is kept confidential, by the way."

Lynley looked up. "What?"

Richard said, "I'm no fool, Inspector. I know how you lot work. The pay's not good so you supplement it by passing along what you can without crossing the line. Fine. I understand. You've got mouths to feed. But the last thing Gideon needs right now is to see his problem displayed in the tabloids."

"I don't generally work with the newspapers," Lynley replied. And after a pause during which he made a note in his book, "Unless I'm forced to, of course, Mr. Davies."

Richard heard the implied threat because he said hotly, "You listen here. I'm cooperating with you and you can damn well—"

"Richard." Jill couldn't stop herself. There was too much at risk to let him continue when continuing only promised to alienate the detective in ways that were unproductive.

Richard clamped his jaws shut and cast a look at her. With her eyes, she appealed to his better judgement. *Tell him what he needs to know and he'll leave us.* This time, it seemed, he got the message.

He said, "All right." And then, "Sorry," to the detective. "This has put me on edge. First Gideon, then Eugenie. After all these years and when we needed her most . . . I tend to fly off the handle."

Lynley said, "Had you arranged a meeting between them?"

"No. I'd phoned and left a message on her machine. She'd not got back to me."

"When had you phoned?"

"Earlier in the week. I don't remember which day. Tuesday, perhaps."

"Was it like her not to return your call?"

"I didn't think anything of it. The message I left didn't say I was phoning her because of Gideon. I just asked her to ring me when she had the chance."

"And she never asked you to arrange a meeting with Gideon for reasons of her own?"

"No. Why would she? She phoned me when Gideon had his . . . that difficulty he had at the performance. In July. But I believe I told you that yesterday."

"And when she phoned you, it was only about your son's condition?"

"It isn't a condition," Richard said. "It's stage fright, Inspector. Nerves. It happens. Like writer's block. Like a sculptor making a mess of a few lumps of clay. Like a painter losing his vision for a week."

He sounded, Jill thought, very much like a man who was desperately attempting to convince himself, and she knew that the inspector had to hear this as well. She said to Lynley, attempting to sound unlike a woman making excuses for the man she loved, "Richard's given his life to Gideon's music. He's done it the way any parent of a prodigy must do it: with no thought of himself. And when one gives one's life to something, it's painful watching the project fall to pieces."

"If a person is a project," DI Lynley said.

She flushed and bit back a need to retort. All right, she thought. Let him have his moment. She wouldn't allow it to vex her.

Lynley said to Richard, "Did your ex-wife ever mention her brother to you in all these phone calls?"

"Who? Doug?"

"The other brother. Ian Staines."

"Ian?" Richard shook his head. "Never. As far as I know, Eugenie hadn't seen him in years."

"He tells me she was going to speak to Gideon about borrowing money. He's in a bad way—"

"When the hell is Ian not in a bad way?" Richard interrupted. "He ran off from home when he was a teenager, and spent the next thirty years trying to make Doug feel responsible for it. Obviously, Doug's dried up as a source of funds if Ian turned to Euge-nie. But she wouldn't help him in the past—this was when we were married and Doug was short of money—so I've little doubt she would have refused him now." He knotted his eyebrows as he realised where the detective was heading. He said, "Why're you asking about Ian?"

"He was seen with her the night she was killed."

"How awful," Jill murmured.

"He has a temper," Richard said. "He came by it honestly. Their dad was a rager. No one was safe from his temper. He excused it by saying he never lifted a hand against any of them, but his was a special form of torture. And the bastard was a *priest*, if you can credit that."

"That's not how Mr. Staines remembers it," Lynley said.

"What?"

"He mentioned beatings."

Richard snorted. "Beatings, is it? Ian probably said he took them personally so that the others wouldn't have to. That would be all the better to position Eugenie and Doug to feel guilty when he came calling on them for money."

"Perhaps he held something over them," Lynley said. "His brother and sister. What happened to their father?"

"What're you getting at?"

"Whatever it was that Eugenie wished to confess to Major Wiley."

Richard said nothing. Jill saw the pulse beat a rapid tattoo in the vein on his temple. He said, "I hadn't seen my wife in nearly twenty years, Inspector. She might have wanted to tell her lover anything."

My wife. Jill heard the words like a slim lance piercing her just beneath her heart. She reached blindly for the lid of her laptop. She lowered it and fastened it with more precision than was required.

The inspector was saying, "Did she mention this man—Major Wiley—in any of your conversations, Mr. Davies?"

"We spoke only of Gideon."

"So you know nothing that might have been on her mind?" the detective pressed on.

"For God's sake, I didn't even know she *had* a man in Henley, Inspector," Richard said testily. "So how the hell could I possibly have known what she intended to speak to him about?"

Jill tried to locate the feelings beneath his words. She laid his reaction—and whatever emotion underscored it—next to his earlier reference to Eugenie as his wife, and she excavated in the dust round both to see what fossilised emotions might remain there. She'd managed to put her hands on the *Daily Mail* that morning, and she'd flipped through it hungrily to find a picture of Eugenie. So she now knew that her rival had been attractive as Jill herself could never be attractive. And she wanted to ask the man she loved if that loveliness haunted him and, if so, what that haunting meant. She wouldn't share Richard with a ghost. Their marriage was going to be all or nothing and if it was meant to be nothing, then she wanted to know that so at least she could adjust her plans accordingly.

But how to ask? How to bring the subject up?

DI Lynley said, "She may not have identified it directly as something she wished to talk to Major Wiley about."

"Then I wouldn't have known what it was, Inspector. I'm not a mind read—" Richard stopped abruptly. He stood and for a moment Jill thought that, pushed to the extreme in having to talk about his former wife—*my wife,* he'd called her—he intended to ask the policeman to leave. But instead, he said, "What about the Wolff woman? Eugenie might have been worried about her. She must have got that letter telling her about the release. She might have been frightened. Eugenie gave evidence against her at the trial, and she might have fancied that she—Wolff—would come looking for her. D'you think that's possible?"

"She never told you that, though?"

"No. But him. This Wiley. He was there in Henley. If Eugenie wanted protection—or just a sense of security, of someone looking after her—he'd have been the one to give it to her. I wouldn't. And if that's what she wanted, she'd've had to explain why she wanted it in the first place."

Lynley nodded and looked thoughtful, saying, "That's possible. Major Wiley wasn't in England when your daughter was murdered. He did tell us that."

"So do you know where she is?" Richard asked. "Wolff?"

"Yes. We've tracked her down." Lynley flipped his notebook closed and stood. He thanked them for their time.

Richard said quickly, as if he suddenly didn't want the detective to leave them alone with what *alone* implied, "She might've been intent on settling the score, Inspector."

Lynley stowed his notebook in his pocket. He said, "Did you give evidence against her as well, Mr. Davies?"

"Yes. Most of us did."

"Then watch yourself till we get this cleared up."

Jill saw Richard swallow. He said, "Of course. I will."

With a nod to both of them, Lynley left.

Jill was suddenly frightened. She said, "Richard! You don't think . . . What if that woman killed her? If she tracked down Eugenie, there's every chance that she . . . You could be in danger as well."

"Jill. It's all right."

"How can you *say* that with Eugenie dead?"

Richard came to her. He said, "Please don't worry. It'll be all right. I'll be all right."

"But you've got to be careful. You must watch . . . Promise me."

"Yes. All right. I do promise that." He touched her cheek. "Good God. You've gone white as a ghost. You're not worried, are you?"

"Of course I'm worried. He as good as said—"

"Don't. We've had enough of this. I'm taking you home. No arguments, all right?" He helped her to her feet and lingered nearby as she made her preparations to leave. He said, "You told him an untruth, Jill. At least a partial untruth. I let it go when you said it, but I'd like to correct it now."

Jill slid her laptop into its carrying case and looked up as she closed its zip. She said, "Correct what?"

"What you said: that I've given my life to Gideon."

"Oh. That."

"Yes, that. It was true enough once; a year ago even, it was true. But not now. Oh, he'll always be important to me. How can he be otherwise? He's my son. But while he was the centre of my world for more than two decades, there's more to my life now, because of you."

He held out her coat. She slid her arms into it and turned to him. She said, "You are happy, aren't you? About us, the baby?"

"Happy?" He placed one hand on the mountain of her stomach. "If I could climb inside you and reside with our little Cara, I would. That's the only way the three of us could be any closer than we already are."

"Thank you," Jill said, and she kissed him, raising her mouth for the familiar joining to his, parting her lips, feeling his tongue, and experiencing the answering heat of desire.

Catherine, she thought. Her name is Catherine. But she kissed him with both longing and hunger, and she felt embarrassed: to be so hugely pregnant and still to want him sexually. But she suddenly possessed such a longing for him that the heat within her turned into an ache.

"Make love to me," she said against his mouth.

"Here?" he murmured. "In my lumpy bed?"

"No. At home. In Shepherd's Bush. Let's go. Make love to me, darling."

"Hmm." His fingers found her nipples. He

squeezed them gently. She sighed. He squeezed harder, and she felt her body shoot fire to her genitals in reply.

"Please," she murmured. "Richard. God."

He chuckled. "Are you certain that's what you want?"

"I'm dying for you."

"Well, we can't have that." He released her, held his hands on her shoulders, and examined her face. "But you do look completely done in."

Jill felt her spirits plummet. "Richard—"

He cut in. "So you must swear to me that you'll go to sleep and not open an eye for at least ten hours afterwards. Is that a deal?"

Love—or something she took for love—flooded her. She smiled. "Then take me home this instant, and have your way with me. If you don't do both, I won't answer for the consequences to your lumpy bed."

THERE WERE TIMES when you had to operate on instinct. DC Winston Nkata had seen that often enough while working an investigation in the company of one DI or another, and he recognised that inclination in himself.

He'd had that uneasy feeling for the entire afternoon once he'd visited Yasmin Edwards in her shop. It informed him that she wasn't telling him everything. So he stationed himself on Kennington Park Road and settled back with a lamb samosa in one hand and a carton of take-away dal as a dipping sauce in the other. His mum would keep his dinner warm, but it might be hours before he could put his lips round the jerk chicken she'd promised him for that night's meal. In the meantime he needed something to settle the growling in his stomach.

He munched and kept his attention on the steamed-up windows of Crushley's Laundry just across the street and down three doors from where he'd parked. He'd sauntered by and taken a glimpse inside when the door swung open, and he'd seen her big as life in the back, labouring over an ironing board with steam rising round her.

"She in today?" he'd asked her employer earlier over the phone not long after leaving Yasmin's shop. "Just a routine check, this is. No need to tell her I'm on the blower."

"Yeah," Betty Crushley had said, sounding like a woman talking round a cigar. "Got her mug where it ought to be for once."

"Good to hear, that."

"If good's enough."

So he was waiting for Katja Wolff to leave her place of employment for the evening. If she walked the short distance to the Doddington Grove Estate, his instinct would require adjustment. If she went somewhere else, he'd know his feeling about her was right.

Nkata was dipping the last bite of his samosa into the dal when the German woman finally came out of the laundry, carrying a jacket over her arm. He crammed the pastry into his mouth, ready for action, but Katja Wolff merely stood on the pavement for a minute, just outside the laundry's front door. It was cold, with a sharp wind blowing the smells of diesel fuel against the pedestrians' cheeks, but the temperature didn't appear to bother her.

She took a moment to don her jacket and pulled from its pocket a blue beret into which she tucked her short blonde hair. Then she turned up the collar of her coat and set off along Kennington Park Road in the direction of home.

Nkata was about to curse his instincts for wasting his time, when Katja did the unexpected. Instead of turning into Braganza Street, which led to the Doddington Grove Estate, she crossed and continued down Kennington Park Road without so much as a regretful glance in the direction in which she should have been heading. She passed a pub, the take-away where he'd bought his snack, a hairdresser, and a stationery shop, coming to rest at a bus stop where she lit a cigarette and waited among a small crowd of other potential passengers. She rejected the first two buses that stopped, finally climbing onto the third after she tossed her cigarette into the street. As the bus lumbered into the traffic, Nkata set off after it, glad that he wasn't in a panda car and grateful for the dark.

He didn't make himself popular with his fellow drivers as he tailed the bus, pulling to the kerb when it did, keeping an eye peeled at its every stop to make sure he didn't lose Katja Wolff in the growing gloom. More than one driver gave him two fingers as he wove in and out of the traffic, and he nearly hit a cyclist in a gas mask when a request stop loomed up faster than he was prepared for the bus to lurch over to it.

In this fashion, he halted across South London. Katja Wolff had taken a window seat on the street side of the bus, so Nkata could get a glimpse of her blue beret when the street curved ahead of him. He was fairly confident that he'd be able to pick her out when she disembarked, and that proved to be the case when, after suffering through the worst of the rush hour traffic, the bus pulled into Clapham station.

He thought she meant to get a train there, and he wondered how conspicuous he'd be if he had to get on the same carriage as she. Very, he decided. But there was no help for it and no time to consider any other option. He looked desperately for a place to park.

He kept one eye on her as she worked her way through the crowd outside the station. Instead of moving inside as he'd expected her to do, however, she went to a second bus stop, where, after a five-minute wait, she embarked on another ride through South London.

She had no window seat this time, so Nkata was forced to keep an eye peeled each time passengers disembarked. It was anxiety-producing—not to mention maddening to other drivers—but he ignored the rest of the traffic and kept his attention where it belonged.

At Putney Station, he was rewarded. Katja Wolff hopped off and, without a glance right or left, she set off along the Upper Richmond Road.

There was no way Nkata could tail her in a car and not stick out like an ostrich in Alaska or become the victim of a commuter's road rage, so he drove past her and, some fifty yards farther along, he found a section of double yellow just beyond a bus stop across the street. He veered over and parked there. Then he waited, his eyes on the rearview mirror, adjusting it to take in the pavement opposite.

In due course, Katja Wolff came into view. She had her head down and her collar up against the wind, so she didn't notice him. An illegally parked car in London was no anomaly. Even if she glimpsed him, in the fading light he would be just a bloke waiting to fetch someone from the bus stop.

When she'd gained some twenty yards past him, Nkata eased his car door open and took up after her. He shrugged his large frame into his overcoat as he trailed her, tucking a scarf round his neck and thanking his stars that his mum had insisted upon his wearing it that morning. He faded into the shadows created by the trunk of an aged sycamore as up ahead of him Katja Wolff paused, turned her back to the wind, and lit a cigarette. Then she strode to the kerb, waited for a break in the traffic, and dashed across to the opposite side.

At this point, the road opened into a commercial area comprising an assortment of businesses that were fashioned with residences off-set above them. Here were the sort of enterprises local residents would patronise: video shops, newsagents, restaurants, florists, and the like.

Katja Wolff chose to take her custom to Frère
Jacques Bar and Brasserie, where both the Union
Jack and the French national flag snapped in the
wind. It was a cheerful yellow building fronted by
multi-paned transom windows, brightly lit from the
interior. As she ducked inside, Nkata waited for a
chance to cross over. By the time he got there, she'd
removed her coat and handed it to a waiter, who was
gesturing her beyond the rows of small candlelit tables to a bar that ran along one wall. There were as
yet no other patrons in the brasserie, apart from a
well-dressed woman in a tailored black suit who sat
on a bar stool, nursing a drink.

She looked like money, Nkata thought. It spoke
from her haircut, which was fashioned so that her
short hair fell round her face like a polished helmet;
it spoke from her attire, which was tasteful and timeless as only significant money can buy. Nkata had
spent enough time leafing through *GQ* in the years
in which he'd reinvented himself to know how people looked when they did most of their clothes-
buying in places like Knightsbridge, where twenty
quid might get you a handkerchief but nothing else.

Katja Wolff approached this woman, who slid off
her bar stool with a smile and came to greet her.
They reached for each other's hands and pressed their
cheeks together, air-kissing in the batty way Euro-
peans had of greeting each other. The woman
gestured Katja Wolff to join her.

For his part, Nkata hunkered down into his overcoat and watched them from a place he made for

himself in the shadows just beyond the bank of the brasserie windows and at the side of an Oddbins. Should they turn his way, he could give his attention to the sale announcements painted in front of him on the window—Spanish wine was going for a real treat, he noted. And in the meantime he could watch them and attempt to suss out what they were to each other, although he already had developed a fair set of suspicions in that direction. He'd seen the familiarity in their greeting, after all. And the woman in black had money, which Katja Wolff would probably like just fine. So the pieces were starting to fall into place, aligning themselves with the German's lie about where she'd been on the night Eugenie Davies had died.

Nkata wished there were a way he could have overheard their conversation, however. The manner in which they hovered over their drinks shoulder to shoulder suggested a confidential chat that he would have given much to hear. And when Wolff raised a hand to her eyes and the other put her arm round her shoulders and said something into her ear, he even considered sauntering in and introducing himself, just to see how Katja Wolff reacted to being caught out.

Yes. There was something definitely going on here, he thought. This was probably what Yasmin Edwards knew but did not want to speak of. Because one could always tell when one's lover started stepping outside for more than a breath of air or a packet of fags in the evening. And the toughest bit about coping with that knowledge was coming to accept it in the first place. People walked miles to avoid having to look at, talk about, or actually confront something that might cause them pain. Short-sighted as it was to wear blinkers in relationships, it was still amazing to see how many people did exactly that.

Nkata stamped his feet in the cold and buried his hands in his coat pockets. He watched for another quarter of an hour and was considering his options, when the two women began to gather up their belongings.

He ducked into Oddbins as they came out of the brasserie door. Half-hidden behind a display of Chianti Classico, he picked up a bottle as if to study its label while the shop assistant eyed him the way all shop assistants eyed a black man who wasn't quick enough to buy what he was touching. Nkata ignored him, his head bent but his gaze fastened on the shop's front windows. When he saw Wolff and her companion pass by, he set the bottle back onto the display, stifled what he wanted to say to the young man behind the till—when would he outgrow the need to shout "I'm a copper, all right?" as he grabbed them by the necks of their shirts?—and slipped out of Oddbins in the women's wake.

Katja's companion had her by the arm, and she was continuing to talk to her as they strolled along. Over her right shoulder dangled a leather bag the size of a briefcase, and she held this firmly tucked under her arm like a woman who was wise to what life on the streets could offer the unaware. In this fashion, the two of them walked not to the station but along the Upper Richmond Road in the direction of Wandsworth.

Perhaps a quarter of a mile along, they turned left. This would take them into a heavily populated neighbourhood of terraced and semi-detached houses. If they went into a residence there, Nkata knew he would need more than luck to find them. He increased his pace and broke into a jog.

He was still in luck, he saw, as he turned the corner. Although several streets turned off this road and bored into the crowded neighbourhood, the two women hadn't taken any of them yet. Rather, they were continuing ahead of him, still in conversation but with the German woman talking this time, gesturing with her hands while the other listened.

They chose Galveston Road to turn into, a short thoroughfare of terraced houses, some converted into flats and some still standing as single homes. It was a middle-class neighbourhood of lace curtains, fresh paint, tended gardens, and window boxes where pansies were planted in anticipation of the coming winter. Wolff and her companion walked along to the midway point, where they turned in through a wrought iron gate and approached a red door. The brass number fifty-five was posted on it, between two narrow translucent windows.

The garden here was overgrown, unlike the other small gardens on the street. On either side of the front door, shrubbery had been allowed to flourish, and tentacles from a star jasmine bush at one side and a Spanish broom on the other hungered outward towards the front door as if for an anchoring spot. From across the street, Nkata watched as Katja sidled through the shrubbery and mounted the two steps onto the front porch. She didn't ring the bell. Rather, she opened the door and let herself in. Her companion followed.

The door shut behind them and a light went on right inside the entry. This was followed some five seconds later by a dimmer light, which began to glow behind the curtains at the front bay window. The curtains were such that only silhouettes were visible. But nothing more than silhouettes was necessary to understand what was going on when the two women melded into one figure and into each other's arms.

"Right," Nkata breathed. So at last he saw what he had come to see: a concrete illustration of Katja Wolff's infidelity.

Laying this information in front of the unsuspecting Yasmin Edwards should suffice to get her to start telling what was what with regard to her companion. And if he left this instant and jogged back to his car, he'd be able to make the drive to the Doddington Grove Estate far in advance of Katja herself, who thus wouldn't be able to prepare Yasmin to hear something which Katja could later label a lie.

But as the two figures in the Galveston Road sitting room moved apart to set about doing whatever it was that they intended to do for each other's pleasure, Nkata found himself hesitating. He found himself wondering how he could broach the subject of Katja's infidelity in such a way as to avoid making

Yasmin Edwards want to kill the messenger instead of absorbing the message.

Then he wondered why he was wondering that at all. The woman was a charlie. She was also a lag. She'd knifed her own husband and done five years and no doubt learned a few more tricks of the trade while she was inside. She was dangerous and he— Winston Nkata, who himself had escaped a life that could have sent him along a path similar to hers— would do well to remember that.

There was no need to rush over to the Doddington Grove Estate, he decided. From the looks of things here in Galveston Road, Katja Wolff wasn't going anywhere soon.

LYNLEY WAS SURPRISED to find his wife still at the St. James house when he arrived. It was nearly time for dinner, long past the hour at which she usually departed. But when Joseph Cotter—St. James's father-in-law and the man who had held the Cheyne Row household together for more than a decade— admitted Lynley into the house, the first thing he said was, "They're up in the lab, the whole flamin' lot of 'em. No surprise, that. His nibs's got them marching today. Deb's up there 's well, though I don't s'pose she's cooperating like Lady Helen's been doing. Even went without lunch. 'Can't stop now,' 'e said. 'We're almost done.' "

"Done with what?" Lynley asked, thanking Cotter when the other man set down a tray he'd been carrying and took his coat.

"God knows. Drink? Cuppa? I made fresh scones"—this with a nod at the tray—" 'f you c'n be bothered to take 'em up with you. I did 'em for tea, but no one came down."

"I'll investigate the situation." Lynley took the tray from where Cotter had balanced it precariously on an umbrella stand. He said, "Any message for them?"

Cotter said, "Tell 'em dinner's at half eight. Beef in port wine sauce. New potatoes. Courgettes and carrots."

"That should certainly tempt them."

Cotter snorted. "Should do, yes. But will do? Not likely. But mind you tell 'em there's no skipping this one 'f they want to keep me cooking. Peach is up there as well, by the way. Don't give her one of them scones, no matter what she does. She's on a diet."

"Right." Dutifully, Lynley mounted the stairs.

He found everyone where Cotter had promised they would be: Helen and Simon were poring over a set of graphs spread out on a worktable, while Deborah was examining a string of negatives just inside her darkroom. Peach was snuffling round the floor. She was the first to spy Lynley, and the sight of the tray he was carrying caused her to prance over to him happily, tail wagging and eyes alight.

"If I were naïve, I'd think you were welcoming me," Lynley said to the animal. "I've strict orders to refrain from feeding you, I'm afraid."

At this, St. James looked up and Helen said, "Tommy!" and glanced at the window with a frown, adding, "Good Lord. What time is it?"

"Our results aren't making sense," St. James said to Lynley without other explanation. "A gram as the minimum fatal dose? I'll be laughed out of the hearing."

"And when is the hearing?"

"Tomorrow."

"It looks like a late night, then."

"Or ritual suicide."

Deborah came to join them, saying, "Tommy, hello. What have you brought us?" Her face lit up. "Ah. *Brilliant.* Scones."

"Your father's sending a message about dinner."

"Eat or die?"

"Something along those lines." Lynley looked at his wife. "I thought you'd be long gone by now."

"No tea with the scones?" Deborah asked, relieving Lynley of the tray as Helen said, "We seem to have lost track of time."

"That's not like you," Deborah said to Helen as she set the tray next to a large book that lay open at a grisly illustration of a man apparently dead of something that had caused a glaucous-coloured vomit to discharge from his mouth and his nose. Either oblivious of this unappetising sight or completely used to it, Deborah scooped up a scone for herself. "If we can't depend on you to remind us of mealtimes, Helen, what *can* we depend upon?" She broke her scone in half and took a bite. She said, "Lovely. I hadn't realised I was famished. I can't eat one of these without something to drink, though. I'm fetching the sherry. Anyone else?"

"That sounds good." St. James took up a scone himself as his wife left the lab and headed for the stairs. He called out, "Glasses for all, my love."

"Will do," Deborah called back and added, "Peach, come. Time for your dinner." The dog obediently followed, her eyes glued to the scone in Deborah's hand.

Lynley said to Helen, "Tired?" She had very little colour in her face.

"A bit," she said, looping a lock of hair behind one ear. "He's been rather a slave driver today."

"When is he not?"

"I've a reputation for general beastliness to maintain," St. James said. "But I'm a decent sort underneath the foul exterior. I'll prove it to you. Have a look at this, Tommy."

He went to his computer table, where Lynley saw that he'd set up the terminal that he and Havers had taken from Eugenie Davies' office. A laser printer stood next to it, and from its tray, St. James took a sheaf of documents.

Lynley said, "You've tracked her internet use? Well done, Simon. I'm impressed and grateful."

"Save impressed. You could have done it yourself if you knew the first thing about technology."

"Be gentle with him, Simon." Helen smiled fondly at her husband. "He's only recently been strong-armed into accepting e-mail at work. Don't rush him too madly into the future."

"It might result in whiplash," Lynley agreed. He pulled his spectacles from his jacket pocket. "What've we got?"

"Her internet use first." St. James explained that
Eugenie Davies' computer—not to mention computers in general—always kept a record of the sites that
a user visited, and he handed over a list of what Lynley was pleased to see were recognisable even to him
as web addresses. "It's straightforward stuff," St. James
told him. "If you're looking for something untoward
in what she was doing on the net, I don't think you're
going to find it there."

Lynley glanced through what St. James identified
as the URLs he'd picked up by examining Eugenie
Davies' travel history: These were the addresses she
would have typed into the location bar, he said, in order to access individual web sites. If one merely chose
the dropdown arrow next to the location bar and
left-clicked on it, one had easy access to the trail an
internet user left when he or she logged on. Vaguely
listening to St. James's explanation about the source
of the information he'd handed over, Lynley made
noises of comprehension and ran his gaze over Eugenie Davies' chosen sites. He saw that the other man
had assessed the dead woman's usage of the internet
with his usual accuracy. Every site—at least by
name—appeared to relate to her job as director of the
Sixty Plus Club: She'd accessed everything from a site
dedicated to the NHS to a location for pensioners'
coach trips round the UK. She appeared to have
done some newspaper browsing as well, mostly in the
Daily Mail and the *Independent*. And those sites she'd
visited with regularity, particularly in the last four
months. This was possible support for Richard

Davies' contention that she'd been trying to assess Gideon's condition from the newspapers.

"Not much help here," Lynley agreed.

"No. But there's some hope with this." St. James handed over the rest of the papers he'd been holding. "Her e-mail."

"How much of it?"

"That's the lot. From the day she started corresponding on-line."

"She'd saved it?"

"Not intentionally."

"Meaning?"

"Meaning that people try to protect themselves on the net, but it doesn't always work. They choose passwords that turn out to be obvious to anyone who knows them—"

"As she did when she chose *Sonia*."

"Yes. Exactly. That's their first mistake. Their second is failing to note whether their computer is set up to save all the e-mail that comes into it. They think they've got privacy, but the reality is that their world is an open book to anyone who knows which icons turn which pages. In Mrs. Davies' case, her computer dumped all the messages it received into its trash bin whenever she deleted them, but till she emptied the trash bin itself—which she appears not to have done, ever—the messages were just stored inside it. It happens all the time. People hit the delete button and assume they've got rid of something when all the computer has actually done is to move it to another location."

"This is everything, then?" Lynley gestured with the stack of papers.

"Every message she received. Helen's to thank for printing them out. She's also gone through them and marked the ones that look like business messages to save you some time. The rest you'll want to have a more thorough look at."

Lynley said, "Thank you, darling," to his wife, who had taken a scone from the tray and was nibbling its edges. He went through the stack of papers, setting aside the ones that Helen had marked as business correspondence. He read the rest of them in chronological order. He was looking for anything even moderately suspicious, something from someone with the potential to do Eugenie Davies harm. And although he admitted this only to himself, he was also looking for anything from Webberly, anything recent, anything embarrassing to the superintendent.

Although some of the senders used not their own names but, rather, monikers apparently related to their line of work or their special interests, Lynley was relieved to see that there were none among them that he could easily associate with his superior at New Scotland Yard. There was also no Scotland Yard address listed, which was even better.

Lynley breathed easier and kept on reading to find that there was also nothing among the messages from anyone identifying himself as TongueMan, Pitchley, or Pitchford. And upon a second examination of the first document St. James had handed him, none of the URLs for the web sites Eugenie Davies had visited looked as if they might be a clever cover for a chat room where sexual encounters were set up. Which might or might not, he concluded, move TongueMan-Pitchley-Pitchford off their list.

He went back to the stack of e-mail as St. James and Helen returned to their perusal of the graphs they'd been working with upon his arrival, Helen saying, "The last e-mail she received was on the morning of the day she was killed, Tommy. It's at the bottom of the pile, but you might want to have a look at it now. It caught my eye."

Lynley saw why when he pulled it out. The message comprised three sentences, and he felt a corresponding chill when he read them: *I must see you again, Eugenie. I'm begging. Don't ignore me after all this time.*

"Damn," he whispered. *After all this time.*

"What do you think?" Helen asked although the tone of her voice indicated that she'd already reached her own conclusion in the matter.

"I don't know." There was no closing to the message, and the sender was among the group who used a handle rather than a Christian name. *Jete* was the word that preceded the provider's identification. The provider itself was Claranet, with no business name associated with it.

This indicated that a home computer had probably been used to communicate with Eugenie Davies, which brought Lynley at least some measure of reassurance. Because as far as he knew, Webberly had no personal computer at his home.

He said, "Simon, is there a way to trace the real name of an e-mail user if he's adopted a nickname?"

"Through the provider," St. James replied, "although I expect you'd have to strong-arm them into giving it to you. They're not obliged to."

"But in a murder investigation . . . ?" Helen said.

"That might be sufficient coercion," St. James admitted.

Deborah returned to them, carrying four glasses and a decanter. "Here we are," she announced. "Scones and sherry." She proceeded to pour.

Helen said quickly, "Nothing for me, Deborah. Thanks," and helped herself to a dab of butter that she dotted on a scrap of the scone she'd taken.

"You've got to have something," Deborah said. "We've been working like slaves. We deserve a reward. Would you rather a gin and tonic, Helen?" She wrinkled her nose. "What on earth am I thinking? Gin and tonic and scones? Now, *that* sounds appetising." She handed a glass to her husband and another to Lynley. "This is quite a red-letter day. I don't think I've ever heard you turn down a sherry, Helen, especially after being run ragged by Simon. Are you all right?"

"I'm perfectly fine," Helen said. And she glanced at Lynley.

Now was the moment, of course, Lynley thought. It was the perfect time for him to tell them. With the four of them congenially together in St. James's lab, what was to stop him from saying off-handedly, "We've an announcement, by the way, although you're probably moments away from guessing it. *Have* you guessed?" He could put his arm round Helen's shoulders as he spoke. He could carry on and kiss the side of her head. "Parenthood looms," he could say jokingly. "Goodbye to late nights and Sunday morning lie-ins. Hello to nappies and baby milk."

But he didn't say any of that. Instead, he held his glass up to St. James and declared, "Many thanks for the efforts with the computer, Simon. I'm in your debt once again," and he threw back a mouthful of the sherry.

Deborah looked from Lynley to Helen curiously. For her part, Helen quietly stacked up the graphs as St. James drank to Lynley's toast. A tight little silence fell among them, during which Peach scooted back up the stairs, her dinner consumed. She trotted into the lab expectantly, deposited herself beneath the worktable where the scones still sat, and gave one sharp bark as her plume of a tail dusted the floor.

"Yes. Well," Deborah said. And then brightly as the dog barked again, "No, Peach. You're not to have any scone. Simon, look at her. She's completely incorrigible."

Focusing on the little dog got them through the moment, at the end of which Helen began gathering her belongings. She said to St. James, "Simon, dearest, while I'd love to stay and help you labour through the night on this problem . . ."

His reply was, "You've been a brick to stay this long. I shall muddle onward heroically alone."

"He's worse than the dog," Deborah remarked.

"Shamelessly manipulative. You'd better be off before he traps you."

Helen took the advice. Lynley followed her. St. James and Deborah remained in the lab.

Lynley and his wife didn't speak until they were standing on the Cheyne Row pavement with the wind whipping up the street from the river. Then Helen said only, "Well." She spoke the word to herself, not to him. She looked a mixture of sad and tired. Lynley couldn't tell which was predominant, but he had a good idea.

Helen said, "Did it happen too soon?"

He didn't pretend to misunderstand. "No. *No.* Of course not."

"Then what?"

He searched for an explanation he could give her, one that both of them could live with, which would not come back to haunt him sometime in the future. He said, "I don't want to hurt them. I picture how they'll look, creating expressions of pleasure on their faces while inside they're screaming at the inequity of it all."

"Life's filled with inequities. You of all people know that. You can't make the playing field level for everyone, just as you can't know the future. What's in store for them. What's in store for us."

"I know that."

"Then . . ."

"It's just not as simple as knowing, Helen. Knowing doesn't take their feelings into account."

"What about my feelings?"

"They mean everything to me. You mean everything to me." He reached for her and fastened the top button of her coat, adjusting the scarf round her neck. "Let's get you out of the cold. Did you drive? Where's your car?"

"I want to talk about this. You've been acting as if . . ." She let her voice die. The only way to say it was to say it directly. No metaphor existed to describe what she feared, and he knew that.

He wanted to reassure her, but he couldn't. He'd expected joy, he'd expected excitement; he'd expected the bond of joint anticipation. What he hadn't expected was guilt and dread: the knowledge that he was obliged to bury his dead before he could wholeheartedly welcome his living.

He said, "Let's go home. It's been a long day, and you need your rest."

She said, "More than rest, Tommy," and she turned from him.

He watched as she walked to the end of the street where, next to the King's Head and Eight Bells, she'd left her car.

MALCOLM WEBBERLY REPLACED the telephone receiver in its cradle. Quarter to twelve and he shouldn't have rung them, but he couldn't stop himself. Even when his mind had said that it was late, that they would be asleep, that even if Tommy was still working at this hour, Helen would already be in bed and unlikely to be happy with a late-night phone call, he hadn't listened. Because throughout the day, he'd

waited for word, and when it hadn't come, he'd realised that he wouldn't sleep that night until he spoke
to Lynley.

He could have phoned Eric Leach. He could have
asked for an update on the investigation, and Eric
would have given him everything he had. But involving Eric would have brought everything back to
Webberly with more piercing clarity than he could
afford. For Eric had been too close to it all: there in
the house in Kensington Square where it had all begun, there at nearly every interview he'd conducted,
there to give evidence at the trial. He'd even been
there—standing right beside Webberly—when they'd
had their first look at the dead baby's body, an unmarried man then who had no idea what it was even
to have to consider the loss of a child.

He'd not been able to stop himself thinking of his
own Miranda when he'd seen the lifeless body of Sonia Davies lying on the post-mortem table. And as
the first cut into her flesh was made, that telltale
Y-incision that could never be disguised as anything
other than the brutal but necessary mutilation it was,
he'd flinched and held back a cry of protest that such
a cruelty had to be practised where such a cruelty had
gone before.

There was cruelty not only in the manner of Sonia
Davies' death, though. There was cruelty in her life
as well, even if it was only a natural cruelty, a minuscule blip on the genetic screen that had resulted in
her condition.

He'd seen the doctors' reports. He'd marveled at

the succession of operations and illnesses that such a tiny child had managed to endure in her first two years of life. He'd blessed his own luck in having produced with his wife a miracle of health and vitality in his daughter Miranda, and he wondered how individuals actually coped when what they were given demanded of them more than they'd ever thought they'd be asked to produce.

Eric Leach had wondered the same himself, saying, "Okay, I see why they had a nanny. It was too much to handle, with Granddad half a loon and the son another Mozart or whatever he is. But why'd they not get someone *qualified* to see to her? They needed a nurse, not a refugee."

"It was a bad decision," Webberly had agreed. "And they're going to take a beating for it. But no beating they take in court or in the press will match the beating they'll be giving themselves."

"Unless . . ." Leach hadn't completed his remark. He'd looked down at his feet and shuffled them, instead.

"Unless what, Sergeant?"

"Unless the choice was deliberate, sir. Unless they didn't really want proper care for the baby. For reasons of their own."

Webberly had allowed his face to reveal the disgust he felt. "You don't know what you're talking about. Wait till you have a kid and then see how it feels. No. Don't wait. I'll tell you myself. It feels like killing anyone who'd even *look* at her sideways."

And as more information came in over the next

few weeks, that's how he'd felt—like killing—because he'd not been able to get away from seeing his own Miranda in the death of this child, who was so unlike her. She was toddling round the house at that point, always with her tattered Eeyore clutched under her arm, and he started seeing danger to her everywhere. In every corner there was something that could claim her, ripping out his heart and gnawing at his entrails. So he'd begun to want to avenge the death of Sonia Davies as a way to ensure his own child's safety. If I bring her killer to an unquestioned justice, he told himself, I will buy God's protection for Randie with the studied coin of my righteousness.

Of course, he hadn't known there was a killer at all, at first. Like everyone else, he'd thought a moment of negligence had resulted in a tragedy that would haunt the lives of everyone concerned. But when the post-mortem uncovered the old fractures on her skeleton and when a closer examination of the body revealed the contusions along her shoulders and her neck that spoke of her being held down and deliberately drowned, he'd felt the blossoming of vengeance within him. It was vengeance for the death of this child, imperfect though she had been born. But it was also vengeance for the mother who had given birth to her.

There were no eyewitnesses and little enough evidence, which troubled Leach but did not worry Webberly. For the crime scene told a tale of its own, and he knew that he could use that tale to support a theory that was quick in coming. There was the bathtub itself with its tray so placidly undisturbed, disavowing the claim that a terrified nursemaid had come upon her charge slipped under the water and frantically called for help as she pulled her out of the tub and attempted to save her. There were the medicines—a cabinet of them—and afterwards the extensive medical records and the story both told about the burden of caring for a child in Sonia's condition. There were the arguments between the nanny and the parents, sworn to by more than one member of the household. And there were the statements given by the parents, the elder child, the grandparents, the teacher, the friend who was supposed to have phoned the nanny on the night in question, and the lodger, who was the only person who tried to avoid any discussion of the German girl at all. And then there was Katja Wolff herself, her preliminary statement, and after that her unbelievable and enduring silence.

Because she wouldn't speak, he had to rely on others who lived with her. *I didn't actually see anything that night, I'm afraid . . . Of course, there were moments of tension when she was dealing with the baby . . . She wasn't always as patient as she might have been but the circumstances were terribly difficult, weren't they . . . She seemed eager enough to please at first . . . It was an argument among the three of them because she'd overslept again . . . We'd decided to sack her . . . She didn't think it was fair . . . We weren't willing to give her a reference because we didn't think she was suited to childcare.* From the others if not from Wolff herself, a pattern of behaviour emerged. With the pattern had come the story, a stitched-together fabric of what had been seen, what had been heard, and what could be concluded from both.

"It's still a weak case," Leach had said respectfully during a pause in the proceedings at the magistrate's court.

"It's a case all the same," Webberly had replied. "As long as she keeps her lips locked up, she's doing half our job for us and hanging herself for good measure. I can't think her brief hasn't told her that."

"She's getting crucified in the press, sir. They're reporting the hearing verbatim, and every time you're talking about interviewing her, when you say 'she refused to answer the question,' it's making her look—"

"Eric, what's your bloody point?" Webberly had asked the other officer. "I can't help what the press are printing. That's not our problem. If she's worried how silence might look to potential jurors, then she might consider breaking it for us, mightn't she?"

Their concern, he told Leach, and their job, was to bring justice into an ugly equation, to lay out facts so the magistrate's court could decide to hold her over for trial. And that's what he had done. That was *all* he had done. He had made justice possible for Sonia Davies' family. He could not have brought them peace or an end to their nightmares. But he could have brought—and did bring—them that.

Now, in the kitchen of his home in Stamford Brook, Webberly sat at the table with a cup of Horlicks fast cooling in front of him, and he thought about what he'd learned in his late-night phone call to Tommy Lynley. Central to his thoughts was one item: that Eugenie Davies had found a man. He was glad of it. For the fact of Eugenie's finding a man might go some distance towards alleviating the remorse he'd never ceased to feel for the cowardly manner in which he'd ended the love between them.

He'd had the best of intentions towards her, right up until the day he knew their relationship could not continue. He'd begun as a dispassionate professional entering into her life to bring justice to her family, and when that rôle had begun to alter upon their chance encounter at Paddington Station, it had at first altered merely to the rôle of friend, and he'd convinced himself that he could maintain it, ignoring that part of him that soon wanted more. She's vulnerable, he'd told himself in a vain effort to hold his feelings in check. She's lost a child and she's lost a marriage, and you must never tread on ground that's so soft and insubstantial.

Had she not been the one to speak what should have remained unspoken, he wouldn't have ventured further. Or at least that was what he told himself during the long period of their affair. She wants this, he claimed, as much as I do, and there are instances when the shackles of social convention must be thrown off in order to embrace that which is obviously a higher good.

The only way for him to justify an affair such as theirs had been to see it in spiritual terms. She completes me, he told himself. What I share with her happens on the level of the *soul,* not just on the level of the body. And how is a man to live a full life if he has no nurture on the level of the soul?

He didn't have that with his wife. Their relationship, he decided, was the stuff of the temporal, ordinary world. It was a social contract founded on the largely outdated idea of sharing property, having traceable bloodlines for potential offspring, and possessing a mutual interest in cohabitation. Under the agreements of the contract, a man and a woman were to live together, to reproduce if possible, and to provide each other with a lifestyle mutually satisfactory to them both. But nowhere was it written or implied that they were to give succour to each other's imprisoned and earthbound spirit, and that, he told himself, was the problem with marriage. It effected in its participants a sense of complacency. That complacency effected a form of oblivion in which the man and the woman so joined together lost sight of themselves and each other as sentient individuals.

So it had happened in his own marriage. So, he determined, it would *not* happen within the amorphously described marriage of spirits that he had with Eugenie Davies.

He went further down the path of self-delusion as time passed and he continued to see her. He told himself that his chosen career was tailor-made to support the infidelity that he began to label his God-given right. His job had always called for late and unstructured hours, for entire weekends given to cases under investigation, for sudden absences resulting from phone calls in the night. Why had fate or God or coincidence brought him to such a line of work if he was not intended to use it to further his growth and development as a human being? Thus he persuaded himself to continue, acting the part of his own Mephistopheles, launching a thousand ships of faithlessness onto the sea of his life. The fact that he could maintain a virtual double existence by assigning responsibility for his absences to the Met began to convince him that such a double existence was his due.

But mankind's fatal failing is the desire for more of everything. And Webberly's desire had ultimately come to haunt what had begun as a celestial love, rendering it as temporal as everything else but simultaneously making it no less compelling. She'd ended her marriage, after all. He could end his. It would be a matter of a few uncomfortable conversations with his wife, and he would be free.

But he'd never managed to have those conversations with Frances. Her phobias had conversed with him instead, and he'd discovered that he, his love, and all the rightness he could muster to defend that love were no match for the affliction that possessed his wife and that ultimately came to possess them both.

He'd never told Eugenie. He'd written one final letter, asking her to wait, and he'd never written to her again. He'd never phoned her. He'd never seen her. Instead, he'd placed his life on hold, telling himself that he owed it to Frances to gauge each step of her recovery, anticipating the moment when she'd be well enough for him to tell her that he wanted to leave.

By the time he'd understood that his wife's condition would not be something that was easily vanquished, too many months had passed and he could not bear the thought of seeing Eugenie again, only to have to tear himself from her permanently. Cowardice stilled the hand that might have held the pen or dialed the phone number. Better to tell himself that they'd really had nothing—just a few years of passionate interludes that wore the guise of loving unity—than to face her, to have to release her, and to recognise that the rest of his life would be without the meaning he longed to give it. So he just let things go, let them drift away, and he allowed her to think of him what she would.

She hadn't phoned him or sought him out, and he'd used those facts to assure himself that she'd not been as deeply affected as he by either the relationship itself or by the ending that had been thrust upon it. And having thus assured himself, he'd set about obliterating the image of her in his mind, as well as the memory of their afternoons, evenings, and nights together. In doing so, he'd been as unfaithful to her as he'd been to his wife. And he'd paid the price.

But she'd found a man, a widower, he'd learned, someone free to love her and to be to her all that she deserved. "A chap called Wiley," Lynley had said over the phone. "He's told us she wanted to speak to him about something. Something, apparently, that had been keeping them from carrying on in a relationship together."

"You think she might have been murdered to prevent her from speaking to Wiley?" Webberly asked.

"That's only one of half a dozen possibilities," Lynley had answered.

He'd gone on to catalogue the rest of them, taking the care of the gentleman that he was—rather than employing the heartless determination of the investigator he should have been—not to mention whether he'd unearthed anything that pointed to Webberly's own ties to the murdered woman. Instead, he spoke at length of the brother, of Major Ted Wiley, of Gideon Davies, of J. W. Pitchley, who was also James Pitchford, and of Eugenie's former husband.

"Wolff is out of prison," Lynley said. "She's been on parole for just twelve weeks. Davies hasn't seen her, but that's not to say she hasn't seen him. And Eugenie gave evidence against her at the trial."

"As did nearly everyone else associated with that time. Eugenie's evidence was no more damning than anyone else's, Tommy."

"Yes. Well. I think everyone connected with that case would be wise to take care till we've got things sorted out."

"Are you considering this a stalking?"

"That can't be dismissed."

"But you can't think Wolff's stalking everyone."

"As I said, I'm thinking everyone should take a bit of care, sir. Winston phoned, by the way. He followed her earlier tonight to a house in Wandsworth. It looked like a rendezvous. She's more than she seems."

Webberly had waited for Lynley to segue from Katja Wolff's rendezvous—from the message of infidelity it implied—to his own infidelity. But the connection wasn't made. Instead, the DI said, "We're going through her e-mail and her internet usage. There's a message been left her—the morning of her death, and she read it because it was in the trash bin—from someone called *Jete* asking to see her. Begging her, incidentally. 'After all this time.' Those were the words."

"On e-mail you say?"

"Yes." Lynley paused on his end of the line before going on. "Technology's fast outpacing my ability to understand it, sir. Simon did the delving into her computer. He's given us all her e-mail and all her internet usage as well."

"Simon? What's her computer doing with St. James? Bugger it, Tommy. You should have taken it straight—"

"Yes. Yes, I know. But I wanted to see . . ." He hesitated again, then finally took the plunge. "There's no easy way to ask this, sir. Do you have a computer at home?"

"Randie's got a laptop."

"Do you have access?"

"When it's here. But she keeps it in Cambridge. Why?"

"I think you probably know why."

"You suspect that I'm *Jete*?"

" 'After all this time.' It's more a matter of crossing *Jete* off the list if it's you. You can't have killed her—"

"For God's *sake*."

"Sorry. I'm sorry. But it's got to be said. You can't have killed her because you were at home with two dozen witnesses celebrating your anniversary. So if you are *Jete,* sir, I'd like to know so that I don't waste time trying to track him down."

"Or her, Tommy. 'After all this time.' It could be Wolff."

"It could be Wolff. But it's not you?"

"No."

"Thanks. That's all I need to know, sir."

"You got to us quickly. To me and Eugenie."

"I didn't get to you. Havers did."

"Havers? How the hell . . . ?"

"Eugenie'd kept your letters. They were all together in a drawer in her bedroom. Barbara found them."

"Where are they now? Have you given them to Leach?"

"I didn't think they were germane to the case. Are they, sir? Because common sense tells me I shouldn't dismiss the possibility that Eugenie Davies wanted to talk to Ted Wiley about you."

"If she wanted to talk to Wiley about me, it would have been only to confess past transgressions before getting on with her life."

"Would that have been like her, Superintendent?"

"Oh yes," Webberly breathed. "Just exactly like."

She hadn't been brought up so, but she'd lived as a Catholic, with the Catholic's profound and powerful sense of guilt and remorse. That had coloured the way she'd lived in Henley, and that would have coloured the manner in which she faced the future. He was certain.

At his elbow, Webberly became aware of a gentle pressure. Alf, he saw, had lumbered up from his raggedy nighttime cushion by the stove and had come to join him, pressing the top of his head against his master's arm, perhaps sensing that canine solace was needed. The dog's presence reminded Webberly that he was late in taking the Alsatian for his regular nightly stroll.

He went upstairs first to check on Frances, compelled by the twinge of guilt he felt at having spent the last forty-eight hours dwelling in mind and in spirit, if not in body, with another woman. He found his wife in their double bed, snoring gently, and he stood, looking down at her. Sleep wiped the lines of anxiety from her face. While it did not render her youthful again, it served to provide her with an air of defencelessness that he'd never been able to ignore. How many times over the years had he done just this—stood looking down at his sleeping wife—and wondered how they'd come to this pass? how they'd gone so long just getting through days that turned into weeks that swiftly became months yet never once venturing each to understand what inner yearnings caused them to sing in their chains—faces held to the sky—when they were alone? But he had the answer to that question, at least on his own part, when he glanced at the window with its curtains shut tight, knowing that behind them the glass was locked and a wooden dowel lay on the floor for use as further security on the nights he wasn't at home.

They'd both been afraid from the start. It was just that Fran's fears had taken a form more readily apparent to the casual observer. Her fears had claimed him, making a plea for his constancy that was as eloquent as it was unspoken, and his own fears had bound him to her, terrified that he might have to become more than he'd lived his life as already.

A low whining from the foot of the stairs roused Webberly. He pulled the blankets over his wife's exposed right shoulder, whispered, "Sleep well, Frances," and left the room.

Below, Alfie had moved to the front door where he sat on his haunches expectantly. He got to his feet as Webberly went back to the kitchen for his jacket and the dog's lead. He was circling round in anticipation when Webberly returned to him and clipped the lead on his collar.

Webberly's intention was to take the Alsatian on a shorter walk this night: just a circuit of the rectangle described by walking to the end of Palgrave Road, up to Stamford Brook Road, and back to Palgrave via Hartswood Road. He was tired; he didn't much feel like trailing Alfie across the green that was Prebend Gardens. He realised that this wasn't giving the Alsatian his due. The dog was nothing if not patience, tolerance, and fidelity incarnate, and all he asked in return for his devotion was food, water, and the chance to run with happy abandon round, through, and across Prebend Gardens twice each day. It was small enough consideration for him, but tonight Webberly didn't feel up to it.

"I'll give you twice the time tomorrow, Alf," he said to the dog, and he vowed to do it.

At the corner of Stamford Brook Road, traffic trundled by, lighter now than at another hour but still coughing with the occasional noise of buses and cars. Alf sat obediently, as he'd been trained to do. But when Webberly would have turned to the left instead of crossing over to the garden, Alfie didn't move. He looked from his master to the gloomy expanse of trees, shrubs, and lawn across the street, wagging his tail urgently against the pavement.

"Tomorrow, Alf," Webberly told him. "Twice as much time. I promise. Tomorrow. Come, boy." He gave a tug on the lead.

The dog rose. But he looked over his shoulder at the garden in such a way that Webberly felt he could not commit yet another act of betrayal by pretending to ignore what the animal so patently wanted to do. He sighed. "All right. But just a few minutes. We've left Mum alone and she won't like it if she wakes up and finds neither one of us there."

They waited for the traffic lights to change, the dog's tail flapping and Webberly finding his own spirits lifting at the animal's pleasure. He thought what ease there was in doghood: So little in life equated with a dog's contentment.

They crossed over and entered the garden, its iron gate creaking with autumn rust. With the gate closed behind them, Webberly released Alfie from the lead and in the dim light provided from Stamford Brook Road on one side and South Side on the other, he watched the dog lope happily across the lawn.

He'd not thought to bring a ball, but the Alsatian didn't seem to mind. There were plenty of nighttime smells to entice him, and he partook of them in his romp.

They spent a quarter of an hour like this, Webberly slowly pacing the distance from the west to the east side of the garden. The wind had come up earlier in the day, and he drove his hands into his pockets, regretting the fact that he'd come out without either gloves or scarf.

He shivered and crunched along the cinder path that bordered the lawn. Beyond the iron fence and the shrubbery, traffic whizzed by on Stamford Brook Road. Aside from the wind creaking the bare limbs of the trees, that was the only sound in the night.

At the far end of the garden, Webberly took the lead from his pocket and called to the dog, who'd run once again to the opposite end of the green like a gamboling lamb. He whistled and waited as the Alsatian galloped the length of the lawn a final time, arriving in a happy heaving mass of damp fur hung with sodden leaves. Webberly chuckled at the sight of the animal. The night was far from over for them both. Alf would need brushing when they got home.

He clipped the lead back on. Outside the garden

gate, they headed up the avenue towards Stamford
Brook Road, where a zebra crossing marked a safe
passage to Hartswood. They had the right of way
here, although Alfie did again what he'd been trained
to do: He sat and waited for the command that indicated it was safe to cross.

Webberly waited for a break in the traffic which,
because of the hour, wasn't long in coming. After a
bus trundled past, he and the dog stepped off the
pavement. It was less than thirty yards across the
street.

Webberly was a careful pedestrian, but for a moment his attention drifted to the pillar box that stood
on the opposite side of the street. It had been there
since the reign of Queen Victoria, and it was there
that he'd dropped his letters to Eugenie over the years,
including the final one that had ended things without
ending things between them. His eyes fixed on it and
he saw himself there as he'd been on a hundred different mornings, hurriedly stuffing a letter through the
opening, casting a look over his shoulder in the unlikely event that Frances had come walking in his
wake. Seeing himself as he'd been long ago, engaged
by love and desire to act the apostate from vows that
were asking the impossible of him, he was unprepared. He was unprepared just for a second, but a
second was actually all it took.

To his right, Webberly heard the howl of an engine. At that same moment, Alfie began to bark.
Then Webberly felt the impact. As the dog's lead flew
up into the night, Webberly hurtled towards the pil-

lar box that had been the receptacle of his countless outpourings of unending love.

A blow crushed his chest.

A flash of light pierced his eyes like a beacon.

And then it was dark.

GIDEON

23 OCTOBER, 1:00 A.M.

I DREAMED again. I woke, remembering it. I sit up in bed now, notebook on my knees, in order to scribble a summary.

I'm in the house in Kensington Square. I'm in the drawing room. I'm watching children playing outside in the central garden, and they see me watching them. They wave and gesture for me to join them and I can see they're being entertained by a magician in a black cape and a top hat. He keeps drawing live doves from the ears of the children, tossing the birds high into the air. I want to be there, I want the magician to draw a bird from *my* ear, but when I go to the drawing room door, I find there is no handle, just a keyhole through which I can peer in order to see the reception hall and the staircase.

But when I peer through that keyhole, which turns out to be much more like a porthole than a keyhole, I see not what I expect to see but my sister's nursery on the other side. And although the light is bright in the drawing room, it's quite dim in the nursery, as if the curtains have been closed for naptime.

I hear crying on the other side of the door. I know the crying is Sonia's, but I can't see her. And then the door is suddenly not a door any longer but a heavy curtain through which I push, finding myself not in the house any longer but in the garden behind it.

The garden is much larger than it actually was in reality. There are enormous trees, huge ferns, and a waterfall that drops into a distant pool. In the middle of the pool is the garden shed, the same shed against which I saw Katja and the man on that night I've recalled.

Outside in the garden, I still hear Sonia crying, but she's wailing now, nearly screaming, and I know that I'm meant to find her. I'm surrounded by undergrowth that seems to grow by the moment, and I fight my way through it, beating down fronds and lilies to locate the crying. Just when I think I'm close to it, it seems to come from a different area entirely, and I'm forced to begin again.

I call for help: my mother, Dad, Gran, or Granddad. But no one comes. And then I reach the edge of the pool and I see that there are two people leaning against the shed, a man and woman. He's bent to her, he's sucking from her neck, and still Sonia is crying and crying.

I can tell by her hair that the woman is Libby, and I'm frozen there, watching, as the man I can't yet identify sucks upon her. I call to them; I ask them to help me find my little sister. The man raises his head when I call out, and I see he's my father.

I feel rage, betrayal. I am immobilised. Sonia still cries.

Then Mother is with me, or someone like Mother, someone of her height and her shape with hair the same colour. She takes my hand and I'm aware I must help her because Sonia needs us to calm her crying, which is angry now, high-pitched with rage like a tantrum being thrown.

"It's all right," the MotherPerson tells me. "She's just hungry, darling."

And we find her lying beneath a fern, covered completely by fronds. MotherPerson picks her up and holds her to her breast. She says, "Let her suck me. She'll calm, then."

But Sonia doesn't calm because she can't feed. MotherPerson doesn't free her breasts for Sonia, and even if she did, nothing would be accomplished. For when I look at my sister, I see she's wearing a mask that covers her face. I try to remove it, but I can't; my fingers keep slipping off. MotherPerson doesn't notice that there's anything wrong, and I can't make her look down at my sister. And I can't and I *can't* remove the mask that she's wearing. But I feel frantic to do so.

I ask the MotherPerson to help me, but that's no good because she doesn't even look down at Sonia. I hurry and fight my way back to the pool to find help there, and when I reach the edge, I slip and fall in, and I'm turning and turning beneath the water, unable to breathe.

That's when I awaken.

My heart was slamming. I could actually *feel* the way the adrenaline had shot into my blood stream. Writing all of it down has calmed my heartbeat, but I don't expect sleep to return to me tonight.

Libby isn't with you? you want to know.

No. She didn't return from wherever she jetted off to when we got back from Cresswell-White's office and found my father waiting at the house.

Are you worried about her?

Should I be worried?

There is no *should* to anything, Gideon.

But there is to me, Dr. Rose. I should be able to remember more. I should be able to play my instrument. I should be able to take a woman into my life and to share something with her without fearing that somehow I'll lose it all.

Lose what?

What's holding me together in the first place.

Do you need to be held together, Gideon?

That's how it feels.

23 OCTOBER

Raphael did his daily duty by me today, but instead of sitting in the music room and waiting for a miracle to happen, we walked down to Regent's Park and strolled through the zoo. One of the elephants was being hosed off by a keeper, and we paused by the enclosure and watched as sheets of water cascaded down the side of the enormous creature. Sprouts of hair along the elephant's backbone bristled like wires as the water hit them, and the animal shifted its weight as if trying to gain its footing.

"Odd, aren't they?" Raphael said. "One wonders about the design philosophy behind the elephant. When I see a biological oddity like this, I'm always sorry that I don't know more about evolution. How, for example, did something like an elephant develop out of the primordial muck?"

"He's probably thinking the same of us." I'd noticed upon Raphael's arrival that he was decidedly good-humoured. And he'd been the one to suggest we get out of the house and into the questionable air of the city and into the even more questionable fragrance of the zoo, where the atmosphere was redolent with the smells of urine and hay. This prompted me to wonder what was going on. I saw my father's hand in it. "Get him out of that house," he would have commanded.

And when Father commanded, Raphael obeyed.

That was the key to his longevity as my instructor: He held the reins to my musical training; Dad held the reins to the rest of my life. And Raphael had always accepted this division of their responsibilities towards me.

As an adult, of course, I could have chosen to replace Raphael with someone else to accompany me on my concert tours—apart from Dad, naturally— and to be a partner to my daily sessions of practice on the violin. But at this point with more than two decades of instruction, cooperation, and partnership between us, we knew each other's styles of living and working so well that to bring in someone else had never been a consideration. Besides, when I *could* play, I liked playing with Raphael Robson. He was—and is—a brilliant technician. There's a spark missing in him, an additional passion that would have long ago forced him to overcome his nerves and to play publicly, knowing that playing is forging a link with an audience, which makes the quadrinomial defined by composer-music-listener-performer complete. But aside from that spark, the artistry and the love are there, as is a remarkable ability to distil technique into a series of critiques, commands, adjustments, assignments, and instructions that are understandable to the neophyte artist and invaluable to the established violinist who seeks to improve himself on his instrument. So I never considered replacing Raphael, despite his obedience to—and loathing of—my father.

I must have always sensed the antipathy between them, even if I never saw it openly. They coped despite their dislike of each other, and it was only now, when they'd begun to seem at such pains to *hide* their mutual loathing, that I felt compelled to question why it had existed in the first place.

The natural answer was my mother: because of how Raphael may have felt about my mother. But that seemed to explain only why Raphael disliked my father so much, Dad being in possession of what Raphael might have wanted for himself. It didn't explain my father's aversion to Raphael. There had to be something more going on.

Perhaps it came from what Raphael could give you? you offer me as potential answer.

And it's true that my father played no instrument, but I think their dislike came from something more basic and atavistic than that.

I said to Raphael as we moved from the elephants to seek out the koalas, "You were told to get me out of the house today."

He didn't deny it. "He thinks you're dwelling too much on the past and avoiding the present."

"What do you think?"

"I trust Dr. Rose. At least I trust Dr. Rose the father. As to Dr. Rose the daughter, I assume she's discussing the case with him." He glanced at me anxiously as he said the word *case,* which reduced me to a phenomenon that would doubtless appear in a psychiatric journal at a later date, my name scrupulously withheld but everything else forming neon arrows that all pointed to me as the patient. "He's had decades of experience with the sort of thing you're going through, and that's going to count for something with her."

"What sort of thing do you think I'm going through?"

"I know what she's called it. The amnesia bit."

"Dad told you?"

"He would do, wouldn't he? I'm as much involved with your career as anyone."

"But you don't believe in the amnesia, do you?"

"Gideon, it's not my place to believe or disbelieve anything."

He led me into the koala enclosure, where simulated eucalyptus trees were formed by crisscrossing branches that rose out of the floor, and the forest in which the bears would have lived in the wild was expressed by a mural painted on a tall pink wall. A single diminutive bear slept in the V of two of the branches, nearby him hanging a bucket that contained the leaves upon which he was supposed to feed. The forest floor beneath the bear was concrete, and there were no bushes, no diversions, and no toys for him. He had no companions to break his solitude either, only the visitors to his enclosure, who whistled and called out to him, frustrated that a creature nocturnal by nature would not accommodate himself to their timetables.

I looked at all this and felt a heaviness settle onto my shoulders. "God. Why do people come to zoos?"

"To remind them of their freedom."

"To exult in their superiority."

"I suppose that's true as well. After all, as humans we hold the keys, don't we?"

"Ah," I said. "I did think there was a greater purpose behind this sojourn to Regent's Park than just getting some air. I've never seen you as interested either in exercise or in animals. So what did Dad say? 'Show him he ought to count his blessings. Show him how bad life really can be'?"

"There are worse places than a zoo if that was his intention, Gideon."

"Then what? And don't tell me you thought up the zoo on your own."

"You're brooding. It's not healthy. He knows it."

I laughed without humour. "As if what's happened already *is* healthy?"

"We don't know what's happened. We can only guess. And that's what this amnesia business is. It's a qualified guess."

"So he's brought you on board. I wouldn't have thought that possible, your past relationship with him considered."

Raphael kept his gaze on the pathetic koala, a ball of fur unmoving in the embrace of the wood that posed as branches from his native land. "My relationship with your father isn't your concern," he said steadily, but the pinpoints of perspiration—always his Nemesis—began to sprout on his forehead. Another two minutes and his face would be dripping and he'd be using his handkerchief to mop up the sweat.

"You were in the house the night Sonia drowned," I said. "Dad told me that. So you've always known everything, haven't you? Everything that happened, what led up to her death, and what followed it."

"Let's get some tea," Raphael said.

We went to the restaurant in Barclays Court, although a simple kiosk selling hot and cold drinks would have done as well. He wouldn't say anything until he'd meticulously looked over the mundane menu of grilled everything and ordered a pot of Darjeeling and a toasted tea cake from a middle-aged waitress wearing retro spectacles.

She said, "Got it, luv," and waited for my order, tapping her pencil against her pad. I ordered the same although I wasn't hungry. She took herself off to fetch it.

It wasn't a mealtime, so there were few people in the restaurant and no one at all near our table. We were next to a window, though, and Raphael directed his attention outside, where a man was struggling to unhook a blanket from the wheels of a push chair while a woman with a toddler in her arms gesticulated and gave him instructions.

I said, "It feels like night in my memory, when Sonia drowned. But if that's the case, what were you doing at the house? Dad told me you were there."

"It was late afternoon when she drowned, half past five, nearly six. I'd stayed to make some phone calls."

"Dad said you were probably contacting Juilliard that day."

"I wanted you to be able to attend once they'd made you the offer, so I was lining up support for the idea. It was inconceivable to me that anyone would think of turning down Juilliard—"

"How had they heard of me? I'd done those few concerts, but I don't remember actually applying to go there. I just remember being invited to attend."

"I'd written to them. I'd sent them tapes. Reviews. A piece that *Radio Times* did on you. They were interested and invited the application, which I filled out."

"Did Dad know about this?"

Again, the perspiration speckled his forehead, and this time he used one of the napkins on the table to mop it up. He said, "I wanted to present the invita-

accompli because I thought that if I had
___ in hand, your father would agree to
_ attending."

"But there wasn't the money, was there?" I concluded grimly. And just for a moment, oddly enough,
I felt it again, that searing disappointment bordering
on fury to know as an eight-year-old that Juilliard
was not and would never be available to me because
of money, because in our lives there *never* was nearly
enough money to live.

Raphael's next words surprised me, then. "Money
was never the issue. We would have come up with it
eventually. I was always certain of that. And they'd offered a scholarship for your tuition. But your father
wouldn't hear of your going. He didn't want to separate the family. I assumed his main concern was leaving his parents, and I offered to take you to New York
on my own, allowing everyone else to remain here in
London, but he wouldn't accept that solution either."

"So it wasn't financial? Because I'd thought—"

"No. Ultimately, it wasn't financial."

I must have looked either confused or betrayed by
this information, because Raphael continued, saying
quickly, "Your father believed you didn't need Juilliard, Gideon. It's a compliment to us both, I suppose.
He thought you could get the instruction you needed
right here in London, and he believed you'd succeed
without a move to New York. And time proved him
right. Look where you are today."

"Yes. Just look," I said ironically, as Raphael fell
into the same trap that I'd fallen into myself, Dr. Rose.

Look where I am today, huddled pathetically into the window seat in my music room where the last thing made in the room is the music that defines my life. I'm scribbling random thoughts in an effort that I don't quite believe in, trying to recall details that my subconscious has judged as better forgotten. And now I'm discovering that even some of the details that I *do* dredge up out of my memory—like the invitation to Juilliard and what prevented me from accepting it— are not accurate. If *that's* the case, what can I rely on, Dr. Rose?

You'll know, you answer quietly.

But I ask how you can be so sure. The facts of my past seem more and more like moving targets to me, and they're scurrying past a background of faces that I haven't seen in years. So *are* they actual facts, Dr. Rose, or are they merely what I wish the facts to be?

I said to Raphael, "Tell me what happened when Sonia drowned. That night. That afternoon. What happened? Getting Dad to talk about it . . ." I shook my head. The waitress returned with our tea and tea cakes spread across a plastic tray that, in keeping with the overall theme of the zoo, was painted to look like something else, in this case wood. She arranged cups, saucers, plates, and pots to her liking, and I waited till she was gone before I went on. "Dad won't say much. If I want to talk about music, the violin, that's fine. That looks like progress. If I want to go in an- other direction . . . He'll go, but it's hell for him. I can see that much."

"It was hell for everyone."

"Katja Wolff included?"

"Her hell came afterwards, I dare say. She couldn't have been anticipating the judge recommending she serve twenty years before parole."

"Is that why at the trial . . . I read that she jumped up and tried to make a statement once he'd passed sentence."

"Did she?" he asked. "I didn't know. I wasn't there on the day of the verdict. I'd had enough at that point."

"You went with her to the police station, though. In the beginning. There was that picture of the two of you coming out."

"I expect that was coincidence. The police had everyone down for questioning at one time or another. Most of us more than once."

"Sarah-Jane Beckett as well?"

"I expect so. Why?"

"I need to see her."

Raphael had buttered his tea cake and raised it to his mouth, but he didn't take a bite. Instead, he watched me over the top of it. "What's that going to accomplish, Gideon?"

"It's just the direction I think I should go. And that's what Dr. Rose suggested, following my instincts, looking for connections, trying to find anything that will jar loose memories."

"Your father's not going to be pleased."

"So take your telephone off the hook."

Raphael took a substantial bite of the tea cake, no doubt covering his chagrin at having been found out.

But what else would he expect me to assume other than that he and Dad are having daily conversations about my progress or lack thereof? They are, after all, the two people most involved with what has happened to me, and aside from Libby and you, Dr. Rose, they are the only two who know the extent of my troubles.

"What do you expect to gain from seeing Sarah-Jane Beckett, assuming you can even find her?"

"She's in Cheltenham," I told him. "She's been there for years. I get a card from her on my birthday and at Christmas. Don't you?"

"All right. She's in Cheltenham," he said, ignoring my question. "How can she help?"

"I don't know. Maybe she can tell me why Katja Wolff wouldn't talk about what happened."

"She had a right to silence, Gideon." He placed his tea cake on his plate and took up his cup, which he held in both hands as if warming them.

"In court, right. With the police, right. She didn't have to talk. But with her solicitor? With her barrister? Why not talk to them?"

"She wasn't fluent in English. Someone might have explained her right to silence and she could have misunderstood."

"And that brings up something else I don't understand," I told him. "If she was foreign, why did she serve her time in England? Why wasn't she sent back to Germany?"

"She fought repatriation through the courts, and she won."

"How do you know?"

"How could I help knowing? It was in all the newspapers at the time. She was like Myra Hindley: Every legal move she made from behind bars was scrutinised by the media. It was a nasty case, Gideon. It was a brutal case. It destroyed your parents, it killed both your grandparents within three years, and it damn well might have ruined you had not every effort in the world been made to keep you out of it. So to dig it all up now . . . all these years afterwards . . ." He set down his cup and added more tea to it. He said, "You aren't touching your food."

"I'm not hungry."

"When did you last have a meal? You look like hell. Eat the tea cake. Or at least drink the tea."

"Raphael, what if Katja Wolff didn't drown Sonia?"

He put the tea pot back on the table. He took the sugar and added a packet to his cup, following this with the milk. It came to me then that he did it all in reverse of the usual order.

He said once the pouring and sugaring was done, "It hardly makes sense that she'd keep quiet if she hadn't killed Sonia, Gideon."

"Perhaps she suspected that the police would twist her words. Or the Crown Prosecutors, should she have stood in the witness box."

"They might have done, all of them, yes. Indeed. But her solicitor and her barrister would have been unlikely to twist her words should she have seen fit to give them any."

"Did my father make her pregnant?"

He'd lifted his cup, but he set it back on its saucer. He looked out of the window, where the couple with the push chair had now unloaded it of a bag, two baby bottles, and a pack of disposable nappies. They'd turned the chair on its side and the man was attacking the wheel with the heel of his shoe. Raphael said quietly, "That has nothing to do with the problem," and I knew he was not speaking about the blanket that continued to make the push chair impossible to roll forward.

"How can you say that? How can you know? Did he make her pregnant? And is that what destroyed my parents' marriage?"

"Only the people within a marriage can say what destroyed it."

"All right. Accepted. And as to the rest? Did he make Katja pregnant?"

"What does he say? Have you asked him?"

"He says no. But he would do, wouldn't he?"

"So you've had your answer."

"Then who?"

"Perhaps the lodger. James Pitchford was in love with her. The day she walked into your parents' house, James fell hard and he never recovered."

"But I thought James and Sarah-Jane . . . I remember them together, James the Lodger and Sarah-Jane. From the window, I saw them heading out in the evening. And whispering together in the kitchen, like intimates."

"That would have been before Katja, I expect."

"Why?"

"Because after Katja arrived, James spent most of his free hours with her."

"So Katja displaced Sarah-Jane in more than one way."

"You could say that, yes, and I see where you're heading. But she was with James Pitchford when Sonia drowned. And James confirmed that. He had no reason to lie for her. If he was going to lie for anyone back then, he would have lied for the woman he loved. In fact, had Sarah-Jane *not* been with James when Sonia was murdered, I expect James would have gladly given Katja an alibi that would have made her seem merely derelict in her duties and consequently responsible for a tragic death but not a malevolent one."

"And as it was, it was murder," I said reflectively.

"When all the facts were presented, yes."

GIDEON

25 OCTOBER

WHEN ALL the facts were presented, Raphael Robson said. And that's what I'm looking for, isn't it, an accurate presentation of the facts.

You don't reply. Instead, you keep your face expressionless as you no doubt were instructed to do as a psychiatric intern or whatever it was that you were as a student, and you wait for me to offer an explanation for why I have veered so decidedly into this area. Seeing this, I flounder for words. In floundering, I begin to question myself. I examine my motivation for what might prompt me to engage in displacement—as you would call it—and I admit to every one of my fears.

What are they? you ask.

You already know what they are, Dr. Rose.

I suspect, you say, I consider, I speculate, and I wonder, but I do not know. You're the only one who knows, Gideon.

All right. I accept that. And to show you how

wholeheartedly I accept that, I'll name them for you: fear of crowds, fear of being trapped in the Underground, fear of excessive speed, complete terror of snakes.

All fairly common fears, you note.

As are fear of failure, fear of my father's disapproval, fear of enclosed spaces—

You raise an eyebrow at that, a momentary lapse in your lack of expression.

Yes, I'm afraid to be enclosed and I see how that relates to relationships, Dr. Rose. I'm afraid of being suffocated by someone, which fear in and of itself indicates a larger fear of being intimate with a woman. With anyone, for that matter. But this is hardly news to me. I've had years to consider how and why and at what point my affair with Beth fell completely apart, and believe me I've had plenty of opportunities to dwell on my lack of response to Libby. So if I know and admit my fears and take them out into the sunlight and shake them like dusters, how can you or Dad or anyone else accuse me of displacing them onto an unhealthy interest in my sister's death, in what led up to my sister's death, in the trial that followed it, and in what happened after that trial?

I'm not accusing you of anything, Gideon, you say, clasping your hands in your lap. Are you, however, accusing yourself?

Of what?

Perhaps you can tell me.

Oh, I see that game. And I know where you want me to head. It's where everyone wants me to head, everyone save Libby, that is. You want me to head to the music, Dr. Rose, to talk about the music, to delve into the music.

Only if that's where you want to go, you say.

And if I don't want to go there?

We might talk about why.

You see? You're trying to trick me. If you can get me to admit . . .

What? you ask when I hesitate, and your voice is as soft as goose down. Stay within the fear, you tell me. Fear is only a feeling; it is not a fact.

But the *fact* is that I cannot play. And the fear is of the music.

All music?

Oh, you know the answer to that, Dr. Rose. You know it's fear of one piece in particular. You know how *The Archduke* haunts my life. And you know that once Beth suggested it as our performance piece, I could not refuse. Because it was Beth who made the suggestion, not Sherrill. Had it been Sherrill, I could have tossed out a "Choose something else," without a thought, because even though Sherrill has no jinx himself and consequently might have questioned my rejection of *The Archduke,* the fact is that Sherrill's talent is such that for him to make the shift from one piece to another is so simple that even questioning that shift would have taken more energy than he'd have wished to expend on the matter. But Beth is not like Sherrill, Dr. Rose, either in talent or in *laissez-faire.* Beth had already prepared *The Archduke,* so Beth would have questioned. And questioning, she may have connected my failure to play *The Archduke* with that other more significant failure of mine with which she was once all too familiar. So I didn't ask for a different choice of music. I decided to confront the jinx head-on. And put to the test of that confrontation, I failed.

Before that? you ask.

Before what?

Before the performance at Wigmore Hall. You must have rehearsed.

We did. Of course.

And you played it then?

We would hardly have mounted a public concert of three instruments had one of them—

And you played it without difficulty then? During rehearsal?

I've *never* played it without difficulty, Dr. Rose. Either in private or in rehearsal, I've never played it without a bout of nerves, of burning in the gut, of pounding in the head, of sickness that makes me cling to the toilet for an hour first, and all *that* and I'm not even performing it publicly.

So what about the Wigmore night? you ask me. Did you have that same reaction to *The Archduke* before Wigmore Hall?

And I hesitate.

I see how your eyes spark with interest at my hesitation: evaluating, deciding, choosing whether to press forward now or to wait and let my realisations and admissions come when they will.

Because I did not suffer *before* that performance. And I haven't considered that fact before now.

26 OCTOBER

I've been to Cheltenham. Sarah-Jane Beckett is Sarah-Jane Hamilton now and has been Hamilton for the last twelve years. She's not much changed physically since she was my teacher: She's put on a bit of weight but she's still not developed breasts, and her hair is as red as it was when we lived in the same household. It's got a different style—she wears it held off her face with a hair band—but it's straight as a poker, as it always was.

The first thing I noticed that's different about her now was her manner of dress. She's apparently moved away from the sorts of dresses she wore as my teacher—which were heavily given to floppy collars and lace, as I recall—and she's advanced to skirts, twinsets, and pearls. The second thing I noticed that's different was her fingernails, which are no longer bitten to the quick with chewed-up cuticles but are instead long and bright with polish, the better to show off a sapphire and diamond ring that's the size of a small African nation. I noticed her fingernails because whilst we were together, she made a great job of waving her hands when she spoke, as if she wanted me to see how far she'd advanced in good fortune.

The means to her good fortune wasn't at home when I arrived in Cheltenham. Sarah-Jane was in the front garden of their house—which is in a very smart neighbourhood where Mercedes-Benzes and Range Rovers appear to be the vehicles of choice—and she was filling an enormous bird feeder with seed, standing on a three-step ladder and pouring from a weighty bag. I didn't want to startle her, so I said nothing till she was off the steps and rearranging her twinset as well as patting her chest to make sure the pearls were still in place. That was when I called her name, and after she greeted me with surprise and pleasure, she told me that Perry—husband and provider of largesse—was away on business in Manchester and would be disappointed to discover upon his return that he'd missed my visit.

"He's heard enough about you over the years," she said. "But I expect he's never believed that I actually *know* you." And here she trilled a little laugh that made me distinctly uncomfortable, although I could not tell you why except to say that laughs like that never sound genuine to me. She said, "Come in. Come *in*. Will you have coffee? Tea? A drink?"

She led the way into the house where everything was so tasteful that only an interior decorator could have managed it: just the right furniture, just the right colours, just the right *objets d'art,* subtle lighting designed to flatter, and a touch of homeliness in the careful selection of family photographs. She snatched up one on her way to make our coffee and she thrust it at me. "Perry," she said. "His girls and ours. They're with their mother most of the time. We have them every other weekend. Alternate holidays and

half terms. The modern British family, you know."
Again that laugh, and she disappeared behind a
swinging door through which, I assumed, the
kitchen lay.

Alone, I found myself looking at the family in a
studio portrait. The absent but seated Perry was surrounded by five women: his wife sitting next to him,
two older daughters behind him with one hand each
upon his shoulders, one smaller girl leaning into
Sarah-Jane, and the last—smaller still—upon Perry's
knee. He had that look of satisfaction that I can only
assume comes when a man successfully creates offspring. The older girls looked bored to tears, the
younger girls looked winsome, and Sarah-Jane
looked excessively pleased.

She popped back out of the kitchen as I was replacing the picture on the table from which she'd
fetched it. She said, "Step-mothering is rather like
teaching: It's a case of constantly encouraging without ever being actually *free* to say what one really
thinks. And always there are the parents to contend
with, in this case their mother. She drinks, I'm
afraid."

"Is that how it was with me?"

"Good heavens, your mother didn't drink."

"I meant the rest: not being able to say what you
think."

"One learns diplomacy," she replied. "This is my
Angelique." She indicated the child on Perry's knee.
"And this is Anastasia. She has something of a talent
for music herself."

I waited for her to identify the older girls. When she did not, I asked the obligatory question about Anastasia's choice of instrument. Harp, I was told. Suitable, I thought. Sarah-Jane had always possessed an air of the Regency about her, as if she'd somehow been a displaced person from a Jane Austen novel, more fitted for a life of writing letters, doing lace-work, and creating inoffensive water colours than for the scramble and dash of existence enjoyed by women today. I couldn't envisage Sarah-Jane Beckett Hamilton jogging through Regent's Park with a mobile phone pressed to her ear any more than I could see her fighting fires, mining coal, or crewing a yacht in the Fastnet Race. So steering her eldest natural daughter towards the harp rather than something like the electric guitar was a logical act of parental guidance on her part, and I had no doubt she'd employed it deftly once the girl had decided she wanted to play an instrument.

"Of course, she's no match for you," Sarah-Jane said, presenting me with another photograph, this one of Anastasia at her harp, arms raised gracefully so that her hands—stubby, unfortunately, like her mother's—could pluck the strings. "But she does well enough. I hope you'll hear her sometime. When you *have* the time, naturally." And she trilled her gay little laugh again. "I do so wish Perry were here to meet you, Gideon. Are you in town for a concert?"

I told her that I wasn't there for a concert but I didn't add the rest. She'd obviously not seen any accounts of the incident in Wigmore Hall, and the less

I had to delve into that with Sarah-Jane, the better I would feel about it. Instead, I told her that I was hoping to talk to her about my sister's death and the trial that followed her death.

She said, "Ah. Yes. I see." And she sat on a plump sofa the colour of newly cut grass and motioned me over to an armchair whose fabric featured a muted autumn hunting scene with dogs and deer.

I waited for the logical questions to come. *Why? Why now? Why dig up all that is past, Gideon?* But they did not come, which I found curious. Instead, Sarah-Jane composed herself, her legs crossed at the ankles, her hands lying one on top of the other—with the sapphired one on top—and her expression perfectly attentive and not the least guarded, as I'd come to expect.

"What is it you'd like to know?" she asked.

"Anything you can tell me. About Katja Wolff, mainly. About what she was like, what living in the same house with her was like."

"Yes. Of course." Sarah-Jane sat quietly, gathering her thoughts. Finally, she began by saying, "Well, it was obvious from the first that she didn't belong in the position as your sister's nanny. It was a mistake for your parents to employ her, but they didn't see that before it was too late."

"I've been told she was fond of Sonia."

"Oh, *fond* of her, yes. It was very easy to be fond of Sonia. She was a fragile little thing and she was fractious—well, what child wouldn't be, in that condition?—but she was terribly sweet and quite precious after all, and who finds it impossible to be fond of a baby? But she had other things on her mind, did Katja, and they got in the way of her devotion to Sonia. And devotion is what's required with children, Gideon. Fondness won't get you through the first bout of willfulness or tears."

"What sort of things?"

"She wasn't serious about childcare. It was a means to an end for her. She wanted to be a fashion designer—although God only knows why, considering the bizarre ensembles she put together for herself—and she intended to stay in your parents' employ only as long as it took her to save the money she needed for . . . for wherever it was that she intended to be trained. So there was that."

"What else?"

"Celebrity."

"She wanted fame?"

"She had fame already: The Girl Who Made It Over the Berlin Wall As Her Lover Died in Her Arms."

"In her arms?"

"Hmm. Yes. That's how she told the tale. She had a scrapbook, mind you, of all the interviews she'd done with newspapers and magazines from round the world after that escape, and to hear her tell the story was to be made to believe that she'd designed and inflated the balloon on her own, which I seriously doubt was the case. I always said it was a lucky turn of events that made her the only survivor of that escape. Had the boy lived—and what *was* his name?

Georg? Klaus?—I've little doubt he would have told an entirely different tale about whose idea it was and who did the work. So she came to England with her head enlarged, and it got larger during the year she spent at the Convent of the Immaculate Conception. More interviews, lunch with the Lord Mayor, a private audience at Buckingham Palace. She was ill-prepared psychologically to fade into the wood-work as your sister's nanny. And as for being physically and mentally prepared for what she was going to have to face—not to mention psychologically suited . . . She wasn't. Not in the least."

"So she was destined to fail," I remarked quietly, and I must have sounded contemplative because Sarah-Jane appeared to reach a conclusion about what I was thinking, and she hastened to make an adjustment.

"I don't mean to imply that your parents hired her *because* she was ill-prepared, Gideon. That wouldn't be an accurate assessment of the situation at all. And it might even go so far as to suggest that . . . Well, never mind. No."

"Yet it was obvious right off that she couldn't handle the responsibility?"

"Only if you were looking was it obvious," she replied. "And certainly, you and I were thrown together with Katja and the baby more than anyone else, so we could see and hear . . . And we were in the house—the four of us—far more than your parents, both of whom worked. So we saw more. Or at least I did."

"What about my grandparents? Where were they?"

"It's true that your granddad hung about a lot. He rather fancied Katja, so he kept her under his eye. But he wasn't actually altogether *there,* was he, if you understand my meaning? So he could hardly be prepared to report on anything irregular that he saw."

"Irregular?"

"Sonia's crying going unattended to. Katja's absences from the house when the baby was having a nap in the middle of the day. Telephone conversations during your sister's mealtimes. A general impatience with the baby when she was difficult. Those sorts of things that are questionable and disturbing while not being out-and-out grossly negligent."

"Did you tell anyone?"

"Indeed. I told your mother."

"What about Dad?"

Sarah-Jane gave a little bounce on the sofa. She said, "The coffee! I'd quite forgotten . . ." And she excused herself and hurried from the room.

What about Dad? The room was so quiet, and the neighbourhood outside was so quiet, that my question seemed to bounce off the walls like an echo in a canyon. *What about Dad?*

I got up from my chair and went to one of the two display cabinets that stood on either side of the fireplace. I examined its contents: four shelves filled with antique dolls of all shapes and sizes, representing everything from infants to adults, all of them dressed in period clothes, perhaps from the period during

which the dolls themselves had been manufactured. I
know nothing of dolls, so I had no idea what I was
looking at, but I could tell that the collection was impressive: by the numbers, the quality of the dress, and
the condition of the toys themselves, which was pris-
tine. Some of them looked as if they'd never actually
been handled by a child, and I wondered if Sarah-
Jane's own daughters or step-daughters had ever
stood before this case or the other, gazing inside wist-
fully at what they could never themselves possess.

I then noted that the walls of the room displayed a
collection of water colours that appeared to have
been painted by the same artist. These depicted
houses, bridges, castles, automobiles, and even buses,
and when I peered at the name penciled into the
right corner of two of them, I saw *SJBeckett* in a sloping script. I stood back and studied them. I hadn't recalled Sarah-Jane doing any painting when she'd been
my teacher, and I could see from her work that she
had a talent for detailed accuracy if not the confidence merely to let a stroke of paint read as an intended image.

"Ah. You've discovered my secret." She spoke
from the doorway, where she had paused, bearing a
large tray on which she'd assembled an ornate silver
coffee pot with a matching sugar bowl and cream jug.
She'd accompanied this with porcelain coffee cups,
spoons, and a plate of ginger biscuits that were, she
confided, "Homemade, just this morning." Unaccountably, I found myself wondering how Libby
would react to all this: to the dolls, to the water

colours, to the coffee presentation, to Sarah-Jane Beckett Hamilton herself, and most of all to what she had said so far and what she had avoided saying.

"I'm afraid I'm an utter failure with people," she said. "With animals as well. With anything living, when it comes to that, except trees. I can do trees. Flowers, on the other hand, defeat me entirely."

For a moment, I wondered what she was talking about. But then I saw that she meant her paintings and I made a suitable remark about the fine quality of her work.

"Flatterer," she laughed.

On a coffee table, she set down the tray and did the pouring. She said, "I was less than charitable about Katja's manner of dress just now. I do that sometimes. You must forgive me. I spend so much time alone—Perry travels, as I've said, and the girls are at school, of course—that I forget to monitor my tongue on the odd occasion when someone comes to call. What I *should* have said was that she had no experience with fashion or colour or design, having grown up in East Germany. And what would one actually expect from someone from an eastern bloc country, haute couture? So it was admirable, really, that she even had the *ambition* to go to college and learn fashion design. It was just unfortunate—it was tragic, really—that she brought both her dreams and her inexperience with children into your parents' home. That was a deadly combination. Sugar? Milk?"

I took the cup from her. I was not about to be sidetracked into a discussion of Katja Wolff's clothes.

I said, "Did Dad know that she was derelict in her duties towards Sonia?"

Sarah-Jane took up her own cup and stirred the coffee although she'd put nothing in it to require stirring. "Your mother would have told him, naturally."

"But you didn't."

"Having reported to one parent, I didn't think it would be necessary to report it to the other. And your mother was more often in the house, Gideon. Your father was rarely about, as he had more than one job, as you may recall. Have a biscuit. Do you still have a fondness for sweets? How funny. I've just recalled that Katja had a real passion for them. For chocolates, especially. Well, I suppose that comes of growing up in an eastern bloc country as well. Deprivation."

"Had she any other passions?"

"Any other . . . ?" Sarah-Jane looked perplexed.

"I know she was pregnant, and I've remembered seeing her in the garden with a man. I couldn't see him clearly, but I could tell what they were doing. Raphael says it was James Pitchford, the lodger."

"I *hardly* think that!" Sarah-Jane protested. "James and Katja? Heavens!" Then she laughed. "James Pitchford wasn't involved with *Katja*. What would make you think that? He helped her with her English, it's true, but apart from that . . . Well, James always had something of an air of indifference towards women, Gideon. One was forced to wonder about his . . . if I might say it . . . his sexual orientation at the end of the day. No, no. Katja wouldn't have been involved with James Pitchford." She took up another ginger biscuit. She said, "One naturally tends to *think* that when a group of adults live under one roof and when one of the *female* adults becomes pregnant, another of the co-inhabitants must be the father. I suppose it's logical, but in this case . . . ? It wasn't James. It couldn't have been your grandfather. And who else is there? Well, Raphael, of course. He could have been the pot calling the kettle when he named James Pitchford."

"What about my father?"

She looked disconcerted. "You can't possibly think your *father* and Katja—certainly you would have recognised your own father had he been the man you saw with her, Gideon. And even if you hadn't recognised him for some reason, he was utterly devoted to your mother."

"But the fact that they separated within two years after Sonia died . . ."

"That had to do with the death itself, with your mother's inability to cope afterwards. She went into a very black period after your sister was murdered— well, what mother wouldn't?—and she never pulled herself out of it. No. You mustn't think ill of your father on any account. I won't hear of that."

"But when she wouldn't name the father of her child . . . when she wouldn't talk at all about anything to do with my sister—"

"Gideon, listen to me." Sarah-Jane set down her coffee, placing the remainder of her biscuit on the saucer's edge. "Your father might have admired Katja

With Freud and sex. With sex and Freud. The significance of orgasm, the resolution of the Oedipal
drama, the gratification of childhood's unfulfilled and
forbidden wishes, the rôle of sex as a catalyst for
change, the sexual enslavement of women by men
and men by women . . ." Sarah-Jane leaned forward
and took up the coffee pot, smiling at me and saying,
"Another? Oh, but you haven't touched a drop yet,
have you? Here, then. Let me pour you a fresh one."

And before I could reply, she snatched up my coffee cup and disappeared into the kitchen, leaving me
with my thoughts: about celebrity and the abrupt loss
of it, about the destruction of immediate family,
about the possession of dreams and the crucial ability
to delay the immediate fulfilment of those dreams,
about physical beauty and the lack thereof, about lying out of malice and telling the truth for the very
same reason.

When Sarah-Jane came into the room, I had my
question ready. "What happened the night my sister
died? I remember this: I remember the emergency
people arriving, the paramedics or whoever they
were. I remember us—you and me—in my bedroom
while they were working on Sonia. I remember people crying. I think I remember Katja's voice. But
that's all. What actually happened?"

"Surely your father can give you a far better answer to that than I. You've asked him, I take it?"

"It's rough for him to talk about that time."

"Naturally, it would be . . . But as for me . . ." She
fingered her pearls. "Sugar? Milk? You must try my

coffee." And when I obliged her by raising the bitter brew to my mouth, she said, "I can't add much, I'm afraid. I was in my room when it happened. I'd been preparing your lessons for the following day and I'd just popped into James's room to ask him to help me devise a scheme that would get you interested in weights and measures. Since he was a man—well, is a man, assuming he's still alive, and there's certainly no reason to assume otherwise, is there?—I thought he'd be able to suggest some activity that would intrigue a little boy who was"—and here she winked at me—"not always cooperative when it came to learning something he thought was unrelated to his music. So James and I were going over some ideas, when we heard the commotion downstairs: shouting and pounding feet and doors slamming. We went running down and saw everyone in the corridor—"

"Everyone?"

"Yes. Everyone. Your mother, your father, Katja, Raphael Robson, your grandmother . . ."

"What about Granddad?"

"I don't . . . Well, he must have been there. Unless, of course, he was . . . well, out in the country for one of his rests? No, no, he must have been there, Gideon. Because there was such shouting going on, and I remember your grandfather as something of a shouter. At any rate, I was told to take you into your bedroom and stay with you there, so that's what I did. When the emergency services arrived, they told everyone else to get out of their way. Only your parents stayed. And we could still hear them from your room, you and I."

"I don't remember any of it," I said. "Just the part in my room."

"That's just as well, Gideon. You were a little boy. Seven? Eight?"

"Eight."

"Well, how many of us have explicit, full memories even of *good* times from when we were children? And this was a terrible, shocking time. I dare say, forgetting it was a blessing, dear."

"You said you wouldn't leave. I remember that."

"Of *course* I wouldn't have left you alone in the middle of what was going on!"

"No. I mean, you said that you wouldn't be leaving as my teacher. Dad told me he'd sacked you."

She coloured at that, a deep crimson that was the child of her red hair, hair that was dyed to its original hue now that she was approaching fifty. "There *was* a shortage of money, Gideon." Her voice was fainter than it had been.

"Right. Sorry. I know. I didn't mean to imply . . . Obviously, he wouldn't have kept you on till I was sixteen if you'd been anything less than extraordinary as my teacher."

"Thank you." Her reply was formal in the extreme. Either she had been wounded by my words or she wanted me to think so. And believe me, Dr. Rose, I could see how my believing I'd wounded her could serve to direct the course of the conversation.

But I chose to eschew that direction, saying, "What were you doing before you asked James for his advice on the weights-and-measures activity?"

"That evening? As I said, I was planning your lessons for the following day."

She didn't add the rest, but her face told me she knew I'd appended the information myself: She had been alone in her room before she asked James to help her.

FIFTEEN

THE RINGING forced Lynley to swim upwards, out of a deep sleep. He opened his eyes into the darkness of the bedroom and flailed out for the alarm clock, cursing when he knocked it to the floor without managing to silence it. Next to him, Helen didn't stir. Even when he switched on the light, she continued to sleep. That had long been her gift, and it remained so, even in pregnancy: She always slept like an effigy in a Gothic cathedral.

He blinked, became semi-conscious, and realised it was the phone sounding off and not the alarm. He saw the time—three-forty in the morning—and knew that the news wasn't good.

Assistant Commissioner Sir David Hillier was on the line. He snapped, "Charing Cross Hospital. Malcolm's been hit by a car."

Lynley said, "What? Malcolm? What?"

Hillier said, "Wake up, Inspector. Rub ice cubes over your face if necessary. Malcolm's in the operating theatre. Get down here. I want you on this. Now."

"When? What's happened?"

"God damn bastard didn't even stop," Hillier said, and his voice—uncharacteristically torn and sounding completely unlike the urbane and measured political tones that the AC usually employed at New Scotland Yard—illustrated the level of his concern.

Hit by a car. Bastard didn't stop. Lynley was instantly fully awake, as if a mixture of caffeine and adrenaline had been shot into his heart. He said, "Where? When?"

"Charing Cross Hospital. Get down here, Lynley." And Hillier rang off.

Lynley bolted from the bed and grabbed the first items of clothing that came to hand. He scrawled a note to his wife in lieu of waking her, giving her the bare details. He added the time and left the note on his pillow. Thrusting one arm into his overcoat, he went out into the night.

The earlier wind had died altogether, but the cold was unremitting and it had begun to rain. Lynley turned his coat collar up and jogged round the corner to the mews where he kept the Bentley in a locked garage.

He tried not to think about Hillier's terse message or the tone with which it had been given. He didn't want to make an interpretation of the facts till he had the facts, but he couldn't stop himself from making the leap anyway. One hit-and-run. And now another.

He assumed there would be little traffic on the King's Road at this time of night, so he headed directly for Sloane Square, coursed halfway round the leaf-clogged fountain in its centre, and shot past Peter Jones, where—in a bow to the growing commercialism of their society—Christmas decorations had long since been twinkling from its windows. He flew past the trendy shops of Chelsea, past the silent streets of dignified terraces. He saw a uniformed constable squatting to talk to a blanket-shrouded figure in the doorway of the town hall—the disenfranchised homeless yet another sign of their disparate times—but that was the only life he encountered beyond the few cars he passed on his flight towards Hammersmith.

Just short of King's College, he made a turn to the right, and he began to cut across and upwards to reach Lillie Road, which would take him closest to Charing Cross Hospital. When he zoomed into the car park and set off to Casualty at a sprint, he finally allowed himself a look at his watch. It had been less than twenty minutes since he'd taken Hillier's call.

The AC—as unshaven and disheveled as Lynley himself—was in the waiting area of the casualty ward, speaking tersely to a uniformed constable while three others clustered uneasily nearby. He caught sight of Lynley and flicked a finger at the uniform to dismiss him. As the constable rejoined his colleagues, Hillier strode to meet Lynley in the middle of the room.

Despite the hour, rain made the casualty ward a busy place. Someone called out, "Another ambulance coming from Earl's Court," which suggested what the next five minutes were going to be like in the immediate vicinity, and Hillier took Lynley by the arm, leading him beyond Casualty, down several corridors, and up several flights of stairs. He said nothing till they were in a private waiting area that served the families of those undergoing surgery in the operating theatre. No one else was there.

Lynley said, "Where's Frances? She's not—"

"Randie phoned us," Hillier cut in. "Round one-fifteen."

"Miranda? What happened?"

"Frances phoned her in Cambridge. Malcolm wasn't home. Frances'd gone to bed and she woke up with the dog barking outside in a frenzy. She found him in the front garden with the lead on his collar, but Malcolm not with him. She panicked, phoned Randie. Randie phoned us. By the time we got to Frances, the hospital had him in Casualty and had rung her. Frances thought he'd had a heart attack while walking the dog. She still doesn't know . . ." Hillier blew out a breath. "We couldn't get her out of the house. We got her to the door, even had it open, Laura on one arm and myself on the other. But the night air hit her and that was it. She got hysterical. The bloody dog went mad." Hillier took out a handkerchief and passed it over his face. Lynley realised that this moment constituted the first time he'd seen the assistant commissioner even slightly undone.

He said, "How bad is it?"

"They've gone into his brain to clear out a clot from beneath the skull fracture. There's swelling, so they're dealing with that as well. They're doing something with a monitor . . . I don't remember what. It's about the pressure. They do something with a monitor to keep note of the pressure. Do they put it in his brain? I don't know." He shoved his handkerchief away, clearing his throat roughly. "God," he said, and stared in front of him.

Lynley said, "Sir . . . can I get you a coffee?" and felt all the awkwardness of the offer as he spoke it. There were gallons of bad blood between himself and the assistant commissioner. Hillier had never made an effort to hide his antipathy for Lynley, and Lynley himself had never seen fit to disguise the disdain he felt for Hillier's rapacious pursuit of promotion. Seeing him like this, however, in an instance of vulnerability as Hillier confronted what had happened to his brother-in-law and friend of more than twenty-five years, painted Hillier in a different shade than previously. But Lynley wasn't sure what to do with the picture.

"They've said they're probably going to have to take out most of his spleen," Hillier said. "They think they can save the liver, perhaps half of it. But they don't know yet."

"Is he still—"

"Uncle David!" Miranda Webberly's arrival broke into Lynley's question. She flew through the door to the waiting area, wearing a baggy track suit with her curly hair pulled back and held in place with a knotted scarf. She was bare of foot and white in the face. She had a set of car keys clutched in her hand. She made a beeline for her uncle's arms.

"You got someone to drive you?" he asked her.

"I borrowed a car from one of the girls. I drove myself."

"Randie, I told you—"

"Uncle David." And to Lynley, "Have you seen him, Inspector?" And then back to her uncle without waiting for an answer, "How is he? Where's Mum? She's not . . . ? Oh, God. She wouldn't come, would she?" Miranda's eyes were bright liquid as she went on bitterly, saying, "Of course not, of *course* not," in a broken voice.

"Your aunt Laura's with her," Hillier said. "Come over here, Randie. Sit down. Where're your shoes?"

Miranda looked down at her feet blankly. "God, I've come without them, Uncle David. How *is* he?"

Hillier told her what he'd told Lynley, everything except the fact that the accident was a hit-and-run. He was just reaching the part about attempting to save the superintendent's liver, when a doctor in surgical garb pushed through the doorway, saying "Webberly?" He surveyed all three of them with the blood-shot eyes of a man who wasn't bearing good news.

Hillier identified himself, introduced Randie and Lynley, put his arm round his niece, and said, "What's happened?"

The surgeon said Webberly was in recovery and he'd go from there straight to intensive care where he would be kept in a chemically induced coma to rest the brain. Steroids would be used to ease the swelling there, barbiturates to render him unconscious. He'd be paralysed with muscle anaesthetics to keep him immobile until his brain recovered.

Randie seized upon the final word. "So he'll be all right? Dad'll be all right?"

They didn't know, the surgeon told her. His condition was critical. With cerebral oedema, it was always touch-and-go. One had to be vigilant with the swelling, to keep the brain from pushing down on its stem.

"What about the liver and the spleen?" Hillier asked.

"We've saved what we could. There're several fractures as well, but those are secondary in comparison to the rest."

"May I see him?" Randie asked.

"You're . . . ?"

"His daughter. He's my dad. May I see him?"

"No other next of kin?" This the doctor asked Hillier.

"She's ill," Hillier said.

"Rotten luck," was the reply. The surgeon nodded at Randie, saying, "We'll let you know when he's out of recovery. It won't be for several hours, though. You'd be wise to get some rest."

When he left, Randie turned to her uncle and Lynley, saying anxiously, "He won't die. That means he won't die. That's what it means."

"He's alive right now, and that's what counts," her uncle told her, but he didn't say what Lynley knew he was thinking: Webberly might not die, but he also might not recover, at least not to a degree that made him fit for something more than life as an invalid.

Without wanting it to happen, Lynley found himself thrust back in time to another head injury, and another bout of pressure on the brain. That had left his own friend Simon St. James much in the state he was in today, and the years that had passed since the man's long convalescence had not returned to him what Lynley's negligence had taken.

Hillier settled Randie on a PVC sofa, where a discarded hospital blanket marked another anxious relative's vigil. He said, "I'm going to fetch you some tea," and he indicated to Lynley that he was to follow. Out in the corridor, Hillier paused. He said, "You're acting superintendent till further notice. Put together a team to scour the town for the bastard that hit him."

"I've been working on a case that—"

"Is there something wrong with your hearing?" Hillier cut in. "Drop that case. I want you on this one. Use whatever resources you need. Report to me every morning. Clear? The uniforms below will put you in the picture of what we've got so far, which is sod bloody all in a basket. A driver going the opposite direction got a glimpse of the car, but it didn't register beyond something large like a limo or a taxicab. He thought the roof might be grey, but you can discount that. The reflection of street lights would have made it look grey, and when was the last time you saw a two-tone car?"

"Limo or taxi. Black vehicle, then," Lynley said.

"I'm glad to see you haven't lost your remarkable powers of deduction."

The gibe gave credence to how little Hillier actually wanted him involved in the case at hand. Hearing it, Lynley felt the old quick heat, felt his fingers draw inward to form a fist. But when he said, "Why me?" he did his best to make the question sound polite.

"Because Malcolm would choose you if he were able to speak," Hillier told him. "And I intend to honour his wishes."

"Then you think he won't make it."

"I don't think anything." But the tremor in Hillier's voice gave the lie to his words. "So just get onto it. Drop what you're doing and get onto it now. Find this son of a bitch. Drag him in. There're houses along the road where he was hit. Someone out there has got to have seen something."

"This may be related to what I'm working on already," Lynley said.

"How the hell—"

"Hear me out, if you will."

Hillier listened as Lynley sketched in the details of the hit-and-run two nights earlier. It was another black car, he explained, and there was a connection between Detective Superintendent Malcolm Webberly and the victim. Lynley didn't spell out the exact nature of their connection. He merely let it suffice that an investigation from two decades in the past might well be what lay beneath the two hit-and-runs.

Hillier hadn't reached his level of command without his fair share of brains, however. He said incredulously, "The mother of the child and the chief investigating officer? If this is connected, who the *hell* would wait two decades to go after them?"

"Someone who didn't know where they were till recently, I expect."

"And you've someone likely among the group you're interviewing?"

"Yes," Lynley said after a moment's reflection. "I believe we may have."

YASMIN EDWARDS SAT on the edge of her son's bed and curved her hand round his small, perfect shoulder. "C'me on, Danny. Time to get up." She gave him a shake. "Dan, di'n't you hear your alarm?"

Daniel scowled and burrowed further beneath the covers so that his bottom made an appealing hillock in the bed that caught at Yasmin's heart. He said, "Jus' a more minute, Mum. Please. C'me on. Jus' a more minute."

"No more minutes. They're adding up too fast. You'll be late for school. Or have to go without breakfast."

"Tha's okay."

"Not," she told him. She smacked his bum, then blew in his ear. "You don't get up, the kiss bugs're gonna go after you, Dan."

His lips curved in a smile, although his eyes stayed closed. "Won't," he said. "Got m' bug killer on."

"Bug killer? I think not. You can't kill a kiss bug. Just you watch and see."

She descended on him and planted kisses on his cheek, his ear, and his neck. She began to tickle him as she kissed him, until he finally came fully awake. He giggled, kicked, and fought her off half-heartedly, crying, "Yech! No! Get them bugs off me, Mum!"

"Can't," she said breathlessly. "Oh m'God, there's *more*, Dan. There's bugs crawling everywhere. I don't know what to *do*." She whipped back the covers and went for his stomach, crying, "Kiss, kiss, kiss," and reveling in what always seemed like the newness of her son's laughter despite the years that she'd been free. She'd had to teach him the kiss-bug game all over again when she'd come out, and they had a lot of kisses to recapture. For being the victim of kiss bugs wasn't the sort of hardship a child in care ever had to endure.

She lifted Daniel to a sitting position and rested him back against his *Star Trek* pillows. He caught his breath and ended his giggles, gazing at her with brown-eyed contentment. She felt her insides swelling and glowing when he looked at her like that. She said, "So what's for Christmas hols, Dan? 'D you think about it like I told you?"

"Disney World!" he crowed. "Orlando, Florida. We c'n go to the Magic Kingdom first and then the Epcot Centre and after that Universal Studios. *Then* we can go to Miami Beach, Mum, and you c'n lay on the strand and I c'n surf in the sea."

She smiled at him. "Disney World, is it? Where'd we get the dosh for that? You planning to rob a bank?"

"I got money saved."

"Do you? How much?"

"I got twenty-five pounds."

"Not a bad start, but not quite enough."

"Mum . . ." He gave that two-syllable expression of a child's disappointment.

Yasmin hated to deny him anything after what the early years of his life had been like. She felt tugged in the direction of her son's desires. But she knew there was no sense in getting his hopes up—or her own for that matter—because there was more to consider than his will or hers when it came to how they were going to spend Daniel's Christmas holiday.

"What about Katja? She wouldn't be able to go with us, Dan. She'd have to stay behind and work."

"So? Why can't you 'n me go, Mum? Just you 'n me? Like before."

"Because Katja's part of our family now. You know that."

He scowled and turned away.

"She's out there making your breakfast, she is," Yasmin said. "She's doing those little Dutch pancakes you fancy."

"She c'n do what she wants," Daniel muttered.

"Hey, luv." Yasmin bent over him. It was important to her that he understand. "Katja belongs here. She's my partner. You know what that means."

"Means we can't do *nothing* without her round, stupid cow."

"Hey!" She tapped his cheek lightly. "Don't talk nasty. Even if it was just you and me, Dan, we still couldn't go to Disney World. So don't you make Katja feel your disappointment, boy. I'm the one who's too short on money."

"Why'd you ask me, then?" he demanded with the manipulative shrewdness of the eleven-year-old. " 'F you knew we couldn't go in the first place, why'd you ask me where I want to go?"

"I asked you what you'd fancy *doing,* Dan. You changed it to where you'd fancy going."

He was caught at that, and he knew it, and the miracle of her son was that somehow he'd escaped learning and liking to argue the way so many children his age argued. But still he was just a boy, without a full arsenal of weapons to fight off disappointment. So his face grew cloudy, he crossed his arms, and he settled into the bed for a sulk.

She touched his chin to lift his head. He resisted. She sighed and said, "Someday we'll have more than we got right now. But you got to be patient. I love you. So does Katja." She rose from his bed and went to the door. "Up now, Dan. I want to hear you in that bathroom in twenty-two seconds."

"I wan' to go t' Disney World," he said stubbornly.

"Not half as much as I want to take you there."

She gave the door jamb a thoughtful pat and went back to the room she shared with Katja. There, she sat on the edge of the bed and listened to the sounds in the flat: Daniel rising and toddling to the bathroom, Katja making those tiny Dutch pancakes in the kitchen, the sizzle of the batter as she plopped a small portion into the shell-shaped crevasse where the hot butter waited, the *snick* of cupboard doors opening and closing as she fetched the plates and the powdered sugar, the click of the electric kettle switching off, and then her voice calling out, "Daniel? There are pancakes this morning. Your favourite breakfast I've made."

Why? Yasmin wondered. And she wanted to ask, but to ask meant to question much more than the simple actions of blending the flour and milk, adding the yeast, and stirring the batter.

She brushed her hand along the bed, still unmade, that bore the impressions of their two bodies. The pillows still held the indentations of their heads, and the tangle of blankets and sheets together reflected the manner in which they slept: Katja's arms round her, Katja's warm hands cupping her breasts.

She'd pretended sleep when her partner had slid into bed. The room was dark—no light from a prison corridor *ever* cutting again through the black of a nighttime room in which Yasmin Edwards lay—so she knew that Katja couldn't tell if her eyes were open or closed. She'd breathed, "Yas?" but Yasmin hadn't answered. And when the covers shifted as she lifted them, as she slipped into the bed like a sail boat docking so sleek and sure where it always docked, Yasmin made the sleep sounds of a woman only half roused from her dreams by the interruption, and she noted that Katja froze for an instant, as if waiting to see how far into consciousness Yasmin would be able to come.

That moment of immobility had said something to Yasmin, but its full meaning was not entirely clear. So Yasmin turned to Katja as she drew the covers up to her shoulders. She said, "Hey, baby," in a sleepy murmur, and eased her leg over Katja's hip. "Where you been?"

"In the morning," Katja whispered. "There's too much to tell."

"Too much? Why?"

"Shhh, now. Sleep."

"Been wanting you here," Yasmin murmured, and she tested Katja in spite of herself, knowing that she was testing her but not knowing what she'd do with the results. She lifted her mouth for her lover's kiss. She slid her fingers to graze the soft hair of her bush. Katja returned the kiss as always and after a moment gently pushed Yasmin onto her back. She whispered deep in her throat, "Crazy lipstick girl," to which Yasmin replied, "Crazy for you," and heard Katja's breathy laugh.

What was to tell from making love in the darkness? What was to tell from mouths and fingers and lingering contact with sweet soft flesh? What could anyone learn from riding the current till it flowed so fast that it no longer made a difference who was guiding the ship to the port just so long as it reached its destination? What the hell was there ever to be gained in the field of knowledge from that?

I should've switched on the light, Yasmin thought. I could tell for certain if I'd seen her face.

She told herself simultaneously that she had no doubts and that doubts were natural. She told herself that there was in life no single sure thing. But still she felt the hard knot of not knowing tighten inside her like a screw being turned by an unseen hand. Although she wanted to ignore it, she couldn't ignore it any more than she could have ignored a tumour that was threatening her life.

But she shook off these thoughts. The day ahead intruded. She rose from the edge of the bed and began to make it, telling herself that if the worst was true, there would be other opportunities to know it.

She joined Katja in the kitchen, where the air was sweet with the smell of the little Dutch pancakes that Daniel loved. Katja had made enough for all three of them, and they were mounded like snow-dashed cobblestones in a metal baking dish that stood keeping warm on the hob. She was adding to their breakfast something decidedly English: Several rashers of bacon were sizzling on the grill.

"Ah, here you are," Katja said with a smile. "Coffee's ready. Tea for Daniel. And where is our boy? Does he shower? This is new, yes? Is there a girl in his life?"

"Don't know," Yasmin said. "If there is, he hasn't said."

"That will happen soon, Daniel and girls. Sooner than you think. Children now grow up so very fast. Have you talked to him yet? Life talk. You know."

Yasmin poured herself a mug of coffee. "Facts of life?" she asked. "Daniel? You talking 'bout how babies get made?"

"It would be useful information if he yet knows nothing of the matter. Or would he have been told already? In the past, I mean."

Carefully, Katja didn't say "when he was in care," and Yasmin knew the German woman would avoid voicing those words and invoking the memories attached to them. Katja's way had always been to move forward, making no reference to the past. "How do you think I abide inside these walls?" she'd once said to Yasmin. "By making plans. I consider the future and not the past." And Yasmin, she'd gone on, would be wise if she followed that example. "Know what you're going to do when you're out of here," she'd insisted. "Know exactly who you will be. Then make it happen. You can do that. But start making that person now, in here, while you have the chance to concentrate on her."

And you? Yasmin thought in the kitchen as she watched her lover begin to scoop the pancakes onto their plates. What of you, Katja? What were your plans when you were inside and who was the person you wanted to be?

Katja had never said exactly, Yasmin realised now, just, "There will be time when I am free."

Time for who? Yasmin wondered. Time for what?

She'd never considered before what safety there was in imprisonment. The answers were simple when you were inside, and so were the questions. In freedom, there were too many of both.

Katja turned from the cooker, one plate in her hand. "Where *is* that boy? His pancakes will be like pucks for hockey if he doesn't hurry."

"He wants to go to Disney World for his Christmas hols," Yasmin told her.

"Does he?" Katja smiled. "Well, perhaps we can make that happen for him."

"How?"

"There are ways and there are ways," Katja said. "He is a good boy, our Daniel. He should have what he wants. So should you."

Here was the opening, so Yasmin took it at once, saying, "And if I want you? If that's all I want?"

Katja laughed, placed Daniel's plate on the table, and came back to Yasmin. "See how easy it is?" she said. "You speak your wish, and it is granted at once." She kissed her and went back to the cooker, calling out, "Daniel! Your pancakes are ready for you now! You must come. Come!"

The doorbell buzzed and Yasmin glanced at the small chipped clock that stood on the cooker. Half past seven. Who the hell . . . ? She frowned.

Katja said, "This is very early for a neighbour to call," as Yasmin loosed and retied the obi on the scarlet kimono she wore as a dressing gown. "I hope there is no trouble, Yas. Daniel has not played the truant, has he?"

"Better not have," Yasmin said. She strode to the door and looked through its spy hole. She drew in a sharp breath when she saw who stood there, waiting patiently for someone to answer, or perhaps not so patiently because he reached out and pushed the bell once again. Katja had come to the kitchen door, pan in one hand and pancake turner in the other. Yasmin said to her in a terse whisper, "It's that damn bloody *copper*."

"The black man from yesterday? Ah. Well. Let him in, Yas."

"I don't want—"

He rang the bell again, and as he did so, Daniel popped his head out of the bathroom, shouting, "Mum! There's the door! You gonna get it or wha'?" without noticing her standing in front of it like a disobedient child avoiding castigation. When he saw her, he looked from his mother to Katja.

Katja said, "Yas. Open the door." And to Daniel, "You've got pancakes waiting. Two dozen I've made you, just as you like them. Mum says you want Christmas at Disney World. Put your clothes on and tell me about it."

"We're not going," he said sullenly as the bell rang another time.

"Ah. You know the future that well? Get dressed. We need to talk about this."

"Why?"

"Because talking makes dreams more real. And when dreams are more real, they have a better chance of coming true. Yasmin, *mein Gott,* will you answer that door? He's heard us, that man. He plans to stay till you open."

Yasmin did so. She jerked on the door so hard, it nearly flew from her hand as behind her Daniel ducked into his bedroom and Katja returned to the kitchen. She said without preamble to the black constable, "How'd you get up here, then? I don't recollect buzzing you into the lift."

"Lift door was ajar," DC Nkata said. "I helped myself to it."

"Why? What more you want with us, man?"

"A few words. 'S your . . ." He hesitated and looked beyond her, into the flat where the kitchen light made an oblong of yellow on the carpet squares in the sitting room where no other lights were yet lit. "Katja Wolff here as well?"

"Half past seven in the morning, where'd you expect her to be?" Yasmin demanded, but she didn't like the expression on his face as she asked the question, so she hurried on. "We told you everything there is to tell when you 'as here before. Another time through everything i'n't going to make no difference to what we already said."

"This's something new," he told her evenly. "This's something else."

"Mum," Dan called out from his bedroom, "where's m' school jumper? Is it on the telly 'cause I can't find it with the rest—" His words trailed off as he left his bedroom in search of the piece of clothing. He was wearing his white shirt, his underpants, and socks, and his hair still glistened with the water from his shower.

" 'Morning, Daniel," the copper said to him with a nod and a smile. "Getting ready for school?"

"Never you mind what he's gettin' ready for," Yasmin snapped before Daniel could answer. And then to her son as she snatched his jumper from one of the hooks next to the door, "Dan, mind you see to that breakfast. Those pancakes're dead trouble to make. See you eat them all."

" 'Lo," Daniel said shyly to the cop, and he looked so pleased that Yasmin's insides quaked. "You 'membered my name."

"Did," Nkata said agreeably. "Mine's Winston, it is. You like school, Daniel?"

"Dan!" Yasmin spoke so sharply that her son started. She tossed him his sweater. "You heard me, right? Get dressed and get yourself into that breakfast."

Daniel nodded. But he didn't take his eyes from the cop. Instead, he *drank* him in with such unabashed interest and eagerness to know and be known that Yasmin wanted to step between them, to shove her son in one direction and the copper in another. Daniel backed into his bedroom, gaze still on Nkata, saying, "You like pancakes? They're little ones. They're special. I 'xpect we got enough to—"

"Daniel!"

"Right. Sorry, Mum." And he flashed that smile— thirty-thousand watts, it was—and disappeared into his room.

Yasmin turned to Nkata. She was suddenly aware of how cold the air was coming in the door, how it swept insidiously round her bare legs and bare feet, how it tickled her knees and caressed her thighs, how it hardened her nipples. The very *fact* of their hardness was an irritant to her, making her vulnerable to her own body. She shivered in the chill, undecided

about slamming the door upon the detective or allowing him in.

Katja made the decision for her. She said quietly,
"Let him in, Yas," from the kitchen doorway where
she stood with the pan of pancakes in her hand.

Yasmin stepped back as the constable gave a nod of
thanks to Katja. She shoved the door shut and
reached for her coat, taking it from its hook and
cinching it so tightly round her waist that it might
have been a corset and she a Victorian lady with an
hourglass figure on her mind. For his part, Nkata unbuttoned his own overcoat and loosened his scarf like
a guest come to dinner.

"We are having our breakfast," Katja said to him.
"And Daniel must not be late for school."

"What d'you want, then?" Yasmin demanded of
the detective.

"Want to see if you'd like to change anything you
told me 'bout the other night." He spoke to Katja.

"I have no change to make," Katja said.

"Tha's something you might want to think over,"
he told her.

Yasmin flared, her anger and fear triumphing over
her better judgement. She cried, "This is harassment,
this is. This is *harassment*. This is *bloody* harassment and
you *bloody* well know it."

"Yas," Katja said. She slid the pancake pan onto the
hob just inside the kitchen door. She remained where
she was, in its frame, and the light from the kitchen
behind her cast her face into shadow, which was
where she kept it. "Let him have his say."

"We heard his say once."

"I expect there's more, don't you?"

"No."

"Yas—"

"No! I bloody well don't intend to let some sodding nig-nog with a warrant card—"

"Mummy!" Daniel had come back into the room, dressed for school now, and on his face such an expression of horror that Yasmin wanted to pull the slur out of the air where it hung among them like a laughing bully, slapping her own face with far more power than it managed to slap the detective's.

She said abruptly, "Eat your breakfast," to her son. And to the copper, "Have your say and get out." For an awful moment, Daniel didn't move, as if waiting for direction from the detective, such as the black man's permission to do what his mother had just told him to do. Seeing this, Yasmin wanted to strike someone, but instead she breathed and tried to still her heart's vicious pounding. She said, "Dan," and her son moved to the kitchen, pushing past Katja, who told him, "There's juice in the fridge, Daniel," as she stepped to one side.

None of them said anything till muted sounds from the kitchen told them Daniel was at least making an attempt to eat his breakfast despite what was going on. All three of them maintained the positions they'd taken when the policeman had first come into the flat, forming a triangle described by the front door, the kitchen, and the television set. Yasmin wanted to leave her spot and join her lover, but just when she

made her first move to do so, the detective spoke, and
his words were what stopped her.

"Things don't look nice when a story gets changed
too far down the line, Miss Wolff. You sure you were
watching telly th' other night? That boy goin' t'say
the same 'f I ask him?"

"You leave Daniel alone!" Yasmin cried. "You
don't talk to my boy!"

"Yas," Katja said, her voice quiet but insistent.
"Have your breakfast, all right? It seems the detective
wishes to speak to me."

"I won't leave you talking to this bloke alone. You
know what cops do. You know how they are. You
can't trust them with anything but—"

"The facts," Nkata broke into her words. "And
you c'n trust us with the facts just fine. So 'bout the
other night . . . ?"

"I have nothing to add."

"Right. Then what about last night, Miss Wolff?"

Yasmin saw Katja's face alter at this question, just
round the eyes, which narrowed perceptibly. "What
about last night?"

"You watching telly like you did before?"

"Why d'you want to know?" Yasmin asked.
"Katja, you don't tell him *anything* till he says why
he's asking you. He's not going to trick us. He's going to tell us why he's asking what he's asking or he's
going to get his big black bum and his cut-up mug
right *out* of my flat. That clear to you, mister?"

"We got us another hit-and-run," Nkata said to

Katja. "You want to tell me where you were last night?"

Bells and alarms went off in Yasmin's head, so she very nearly didn't hear Katja say, "Here."

"Round half past eleven?"

"Here," she repeated.

"Got it," he said, and then he added what Yasmin realised he'd been meaning to say from the moment she opened the door to him, "So you didn't spend the whole night with her, then. You just met her, shagged her, and went on your way. That how it happened?"

There was a horrible silence, broken by nothing but the voice inside Yasmin's head shouting, "No!" She willed her partner to answer in some way, not to use silence and not to walk off.

Katja looked at Yasmin when she said to the copper, "I don't know what you're talking about."

"I'm talking 'bout a trip 'cross South London by bus last evening after work," the detective said. "I'm talking 'bout ending up in Putney at Frère Jacques Bar. 'Bout walking down to Wandsworth to Number Fifty-five Galveston Road. I'm talking 'bout what went on inside and who it went on with. This sounding familiar to you? Or were you still watching the telly last night? 'Cause if what I saw's any indication, if the telly was on, you two had your eyes glued elsewhere."

"You followed me." Katja said it carefully.

"You and the lady in black. That's right. White

lady in black," he added for good measure, and he cast a quick look at Yasmin as he said it. "Keep the lights off next time you do something interesting in front of the windows, Miss Wolff."

Yasmin felt wild birds fluttering in front of her face. She wanted to wave her arms to frighten them off, but her arms wouldn't move. *White lady in black* was all she heard. *Keep the lights off next time.*

Katja said, "I see. You've done your work well. You followed me—high marks for that. Then you followed us together—higher marks still. But had you lingered, which you obviously did not, you would have seen us leave within a quarter of an hour. And while this is no doubt the time you yourself would devote to doing something interesting—as you call it, Constable—Yasmin will confirm that I am a woman who takes rather longer when it comes to giving pleasure."

Nkata looked nonplussed, and Yasmin reveled in that look, as much as she reveled in Katja's seizing upon the advantage that she'd just gained by saying, "Had you done your homework more thoroughly, you would have discovered that the woman I met at Frère Jacques was my solicitor, Constable Nkata. She's called Harriet Lewis, and if you require her phone number to confirm my story, I shall give it to you."

"And Number Fifty-five Galveston Road?" he said.

"What about it?"

"Who lives there that you and"—his hesitation

and the emphasis he placed on the word told them he'd be checking her story—"your *solicitor* went calling on last night, Miss Wolff?"

"Her partner. And if you ask what I was consulting them about, I shall have to tell you it's a privileged matter, which is what Harriet Lewis will tell you herself when you phone her to confirm my story." Katja strode across the small sitting room to the sofa, where her shoulder bag lay against a faded tapestry pillow. She switched on a light and dispelled the morning gloom. She took out a packet of fags and lit one as she rooted in her bag for something else. This turned out to be a business card, which she brought over to Nkata and extended to him. She was the personification of calm, drawing in on the fag and sending a plume of smoke towards the ceiling as she said, "Phone her. And if there is nothing else you wish to learn from us this morning, we have our own breakfast to eat."

Nkata took the card and, his eyes on Katja as if they'd pin her to the spot she stood on, he put it in the breast pocket of his coat, saying, "You best hope she matches you A to Z. 'Cause if she doesn't—"

Yasmin cut in. "That all you want, then? 'Cause if it is, time for you to bunk off."

Nkata moved his glance to her. "You know where to find me," he said.

"Like I'd want to?" Yasmin laughed. She jerked the door open and didn't look at him as he left. She slammed the door behind him as Daniel called out, "Mummy?" from the kitchen.

She called back, "Be there in a moment, luv. You keep on with the pancakes."

"Don't forget that bacon as well," Katja said.

But as they spoke to Daniel, they looked at each other. They looked long and unwavering as each waited for the other to say what needed to be said.

"You didn't tell me you'd be meeting Harriet Lewis," Yasmin said.

Katja lifted her cigarette to her mouth and took her time about inhaling. She finally said, "There are matters to be dealt with. There are twenty years of matters to be dealt with. This will take time for us to work through."

"What d'you mean? What kind of matters? Katja, you in trouble or something?"

"There is trouble, yes. But it is not mine. Just something that needs to be resolved."

"What? What needs—"

"Yas. It is late." Katja rose and ground out her cigarette in an ashtray on the coffee table. "We must work. I cannot explain everything right now. The situation is far too complex."

Yasmin wanted to say, "And that's why it took so long to discuss it? Last night, Katja? Because the situation—whatever it is—is too complex?" but she didn't say it. She placed the question in the mental file that held all the other questions she'd not yet asked. Like the questions about Katja's absences from work, the questions about her absences from home, the questions about where she took the car when she borrowed it and why she needed to borrow it in the first place. If she and Katja were to establish something lasting—a connection to each other outside prison walls that was not defined by the need to maintain a bulwark against loneliness, despair, and depression—then they were going to have to start dispelling doubt. All her questions grew from doubt, and doubt was the virulent disease that could destroy them.

To drive it from her mind, she thought of her first days in Holloway on remand, of the medical unit where she was watched for signs that her despondency would lead to derangement, of the humiliation of the initial strip search—"Let's have a look up the grumble and grunt, Missy"—and of every strip search that followed it, of stuffing envelopes endlessly mindlessly in what went for rehabilitation in prison, of anger so deep and so profound that she thought it might eat its way into her bones. And she thought of Katja as Katja had been in those first few days and all through her trial, watching her from a distance but never speaking till Yasmin demanded what she wanted one day over tea in the dining room where Katja sat alone, as she always sat, a baby killer, the worst sort of monster: one who did not repent.

"Don't mess with Geraldine," she had been told. "That Kraut bitch's just *waiting* for a good sorting-out."

But she'd asked anyway. She'd sat at the German's table, slamming down her tea tray and saying, "What you *want* with me, bitch? You been watching me like I'm next week's dinner ever since I walked in here, and I'm dead sick of it. You got that straight?" She'd tried to sound tough. She knew without ever having been told that the key to survival behind walls and locked doors was never to show a sign of weakness.

"There are ways to cope," Katja had told her in answer. "But you will not manage if you do not submit."

"Sub*mit* to these fuckers?" Yasmin had shoved her own cup away so hard that tea sloshed out and soaked the paper napkin with milky-brown blood. "I don't *belong* in here. I 'as defending my life."

"And that is what you do when you submit. You defend your life. Not the life inside here but the life to come."

"What sort 'f life *that's* going to be? I get out of here, my baby won't know me. You know how that feels?"

And Katja had known, though she never spoke of the child she herself had given up on the day he was born. The miracle of Katja as Yasmin came to know her was that she knew how *everything* felt: from the loss of freedom to the loss of a child, from being tricked into trusting the wrong people to learning that only the self would stand steadfast. It was on the foundation of Katja's understanding that they'd put the first tentative stones of their association with each other. And during the time they spent together, Katja Wolff—who had been in prison ten years when Yasmin encountered her—and Yasmin developed a plan for their lives when they were finally released.

Revenge hadn't been part of the plan for either of

them. Indeed, the word *vengeance* hadn't crossed their lips. But now Yasmin wondered what Katja had meant all those years ago when she'd said, "I am owed," while imprisoned, without ever giving an explanation of what the debt was or who was to pay it.

She couldn't bring herself to ask where her lover had gone last night when she left that house on Galveston Road in the company of her solicitor, Harriet Lewis. The thought of the Katja who had counseled her, who had listened to and loved her throughout her sentence, was what kept Yasmin's every doubt in check.

But still, she couldn't shake off the memory of that moment when Katja had frozen in the act of getting into bed. She couldn't dismiss what that abrupt stillness in her lover meant. So she said, "I di'n't know Harriet Lewis had a partner."

Katja looked away from her at the window, where the curtains were closed upon the growing daylight. She said, "Funny enough, Yas. Neither did I."

"Think she'll be able to help you, then? Help with what you're trying to sort out?"

"Yes. Yes, I hope she will help me. That would be good, wouldn't it: to put an end to the struggle."

And then Katja stood there, waiting for more, waiting to hear the scores of questions that Yasmin Edwards could not bear to ask her.

When Yasmin said nothing, Katja finally nodded as if she herself had asked something and received a reply. "Things are being taken care of," she said. "I'll be home straight after work tonight."

SIXTEEN

BARBARA HAVERS got word of Webberly's condition at seven forty-five that morning when the superintendent's secretary phoned her as she was toweling herself dry from her wake-up shower. Upon instruction from DI Lynley, who'd been given the rank of acting superintendent, Barbara was told, Dorothea Harriman was ringing every detective under Webberly's command. She had little time to chat, so she was sparing with the details: Webberly was in Charing Cross Hospital, his condition was critical, he was in a coma, he'd been hit by a car late last night while walking his dog.

"Bloody hell, Dee," Barbara cried. "Hit by a *car*? How? Where? Will he . . . ? Is he going to . . . ?"

Harriman's voice grew tight, which told Barbara all she needed to know about the effort that Webberly's secretary was making to sound professional in the midst of her own concern for the man she'd worked for for nearly a decade. "That's all I know, Detective Constable. The Hammersmith police are investigating."

Barbara said, "Dee, what the hell happened?"

"A hit-and-run."

Barbara grew dizzy. At the same time, she felt the hand that held the telephone receiver turn numb, as if it were no longer part of her body. She rang off in a deadened state, and she dressed herself with even less regard than she normally gave to her appearance. Indeed, it wouldn't be until much later in the day that she'd glance in the mirror while making a visit to the ladies' toilet and discover that she'd donned pink socks, green stirrup trousers with sagging knees, and a faded purple T-shirt on which were printed the words "The truth ISN'T out there, it's under here" rendered in ornate Gothic script. She crammed a Pop-Tart into the toaster, and while it was heating, she dried her hair and smeared two blobs of fuchsia-tinted lipstick on her cheeks to give some colour to her face. Pop-Tart in hand, she gathered her belongings, grabbed her car keys, and dashed outside to set off into the morning . . . without coat, scarf, or the least idea of where she was supposed to be going.

The cold air brought her abruptly to her senses six steps from her own front door. She said, "Hang on, Barb," and scurried back to her bungalow, where she forced herself to sit at the table which she used for dining, ironing, working, and preparing most of what went for her daily dinners. She fired up a fag and told herself that she had to calm down if she was going to be any use to anyone. If Webberly's misfortune and the murder of Eugenie Davies were connected, she wasn't going to be able to assist in the enquiry if she continued to run round like an electri-fied mouse.

And there *was* a connection between the two events. She was willing to bet her career on that.

She had achieved very little joy from her second trip to the Valley of Kings and the Comfort Inn on the previous evening, learning only that J. W. Pitch-ley was a regular at both establishments, but so much a regular that neither the waiters at the restaurant nor the night clerk at the hotel had been able to say with certainty that he'd been there on the night Eugenie Davies had been murdered.

"Oh my yes, this gentleman has a way with the ladies," the night clerk had commented as he exam-ined Pitchley's photograph over the sound of Major James Bellamy and his wife having something of a class-driven set-to in an ancient episode of *Upstairs, Downstairs* that was playing nearby on a VCR. The night clerk had paused, had watched the unfolding drama for a moment, had shaken his head and sighed, "It will never last, that marriage," before turning to Barbara, handing back the picture she'd snagged in West Hampstead, and going on. "He brings them here often, these ladies of his. He always pays cash and the lady waits over there, out of sight in the lounge. This is so I will neither see her nor suspect that they intend to use the room for a few hours only, for sexual congress. He has been here many many times, this man."

And it was much the same at the Valley of Kings. J. W. Pitchley had eaten his way through the entire menu at the restaurant and the waiters could account for everything he'd ordered in the last five months. But as to his companions . . . ? They were blonde, brunette, red headed, and gray haired. And all of them were English, naturally. What else would one expect of such a decadent culture?

Flashing the picture of Eugenie Davies in the company of the picture of J. W. Pitchley had got Barbara exactly nowhere. Ah yes, she was another English-woman, wasn't she? both the waiters and the night clerk had asked. Yes, she might have been with him one night. But she might have not. It was the gentle-man, you see, who interested everyone: How did such an ordinary man have such an extraordinary way with ladies?

"Any port in a storm," Barbara had muttered in re-ply, "if you know what I mean."

They hadn't known and she hadn't explained. She'd just gone home, deciding to bide her time till St. Catherine's opened in the morning.

That was what she was supposed to be doing, Barbara realised as she sat at her little dining table, smoked, and hoped that the nicotine would rattle her brain into operation. There was something not right about J. W. Pitchley, and if his address in the posses-sion of the dead woman hadn't told her that much, then the thugs leaping out of his kitchen window and the cheque he'd been writing—to one of them, surely—did.

She could do nothing to improve the condition of Superintendent Webberly. But she could pursue her intended course, looking for whatever it was that J. W. Pitchley, AKA James Pitchford, was trying to hide. What that was might well be what tied him to murder and tied him to the attack on Webberly. And if that was the case, she wanted to be the person who brought the bugger down. She owed that much to the superintendent because she owed Malcolm Webberly more than she could ever repay.

With more calm this time, she rustled her pea jacket from the wardrobe, along with a tartan scarf that she wound round her neck. More appropriately garbed for the November chill, she set out again into the cold, damp morning.

She had a wait before St. Catherine's opened, and she used the time to tuck into a hot bacon and mushroom sandwich in the sort of fine, fried-bread-serving old caff that was fast disappearing from the metropolis. After that, she phoned Charing Cross Hospital, where she got word that Webberly's condition remained unchanged. She phoned Inspector Lynley next, getting him on his mobile on his way to the Yard. He'd been at the hospital till six, he told her, at which time it had become clear that hanging round in the intensive care waiting room was only going to rub his nerves raw while doing nothing to improve the superintendent's condition.

"Hillier's there," Lynley said abruptly, and those two words served as adequate explanation. AC Hillier wasn't a pleasant man to be around at the best of times. At the worst of times, he'd likely be impossible.

"What about the rest of the family?" Barbara asked.

"Miranda's come from Cambridge."

"And Frances?"

"Laura Hillier's with her. At home."

"At home?" Barbara frowned, going on to say, "That's a bit odd, isn't it, sir?" to which Lynley said, "Helen's taken some clothes over to the hospital. Some food as well. Randie came tearing up in such a hurry that she wasn't even wearing shoes, so Helen's taken her a pair of trainers and a track suit should she want to change her clothes. She'll phone me if there's any sudden change. Helen will, that is."

"Sir . . ." Barbara wondered at his reticence. There was ground to till here, and she meant to grab the hoe. She was a cop to her core, so—her suspicions about J. W. Pitchley aside for a moment—she couldn't help wondering whether Frances Webberly's absence from the scene might mean something that went beyond shock. Indeed, she couldn't help wondering if it meant something that indicated Frances's knowledge of her husband's past infidelity. She said, "Sir, as to Frances herself, have you thought—"

"What are you onto this morning, Havers?"

"Sir . . ."

"What did you come up with on Pitchley?"

Lynley was making it more than clear that Frances Webberly was a subject he wasn't about to discuss with her, so Barbara filed her irritation—if only at present—and instead recounted what she'd discovered about Pitchley on the previous day: his suspicious behaviour, the presence in his home of two yobbos who'd climbed out of a window rather than be confronted by her, the cheque he'd been writing, the confirmation of the night clerk and the waiters that Pitchley was indeed an habitué of the Comfort Inn and the Valley of Kings.

"So what I reckon is this: If he changed his name once because of a crime, what's to say he didn't change it before because of another?"

Lynley said that he thought it unlikely, but he gave Barbara the go-ahead. They would meet later at the Yard.

It didn't take too long for Barbara to troll through two decades of legal records in St. Catherine's, since she knew what she was looking for. And what she finally found sent her to New Scotland Yard posthaste, where she got on the blower to the station that served Tower Hamlets and spent an hour tracking down and talking to the only detective who'd spent his entire career there. His memory for detail and his possession of enough notes to write his memoirs several times over provided Barbara with the vein of gold she'd been seeking.

"Oh, right," he drawled. "That's not a name I'm likely to forget. The whole flaming lot of them've been giving us aggro 's long as they've been walking the earth."

"But as to the one . . ." Barbara said.

"I can spin a tale or two about *him*."

She took notes from the detective's recitation, and when she rang off, she went in search of Lynley.

She found him in his office, standing near the window, looking grave. He'd apparently been home between his early morning visit to the hospital and coming to the Yard, because he looked as he always looked: perfectly groomed, well-shaven, and suitably dressed. The only sign that things were not normal was in his posture. He'd always stood like a man with a fence pole for a spine, but now he seemed slumped, as if carrying sacks of grain on his shoulders.

"The only thing Dee told me was a coma," Barbara said by way of hello.

Lynley recounted for her the extent of the superintendent's injuries. He concluded with, "The only blessing is that the car didn't actually run over him. The force he was hit with threw him into a pillar box, which was bad enough. But it could have been worse."

"Were there any witnesses?"

"Just someone who saw a black vehicle tearing down Stamford Brook Road."

"Like the car that hit Eugenie?"

"It was large," Lynley said. "According to the witness, it could have been a taxi. He thought it was painted in two tones, black with a grey roof. Hillier claims the grey would be the street lights' reflection on black."

"Bugger Hillier for a lark," Barbara scoffed. "Taxis are painted all sorts of ways these days. Two tones, three tones, red and yellow, or covered tyres-to-top with advertisements. I say we should listen to what the witness says. And as we're talking about a black car once again, I expect we've got a connection, don't you?"

"With Eugenie Davies?" Lynley didn't wait for a reply. "Yes. I'd say we've got a connection." He gestured with a notebook he'd taken up from his desk and he put on his spectacles as he walked round to sit, nodding for Barbara to do likewise. "But we've still got virtually nothing to go on, Havers. I've been reading through my notes trying to find *something,* and I'm not getting far. All I can come up with is a conflict among what Richard Davies, his son, and Ian Staines are saying about Eugenie's seeing Gideon. Staines claims she intended to ask Gideon for money to get him out of debt before he loses his house and everything in it, but he also says that she told him— after having made the promise to see her son—that something had come up and because of it, she wouldn't ask Gideon for the money. In the meantime, Richard Davies claims she hadn't asked to see Gideon at all, but just the opposite. He says he wanted her to try to help Gideon with a problem he's having with stage fright and that's why they were going to meet: at *his* suggestion. Gideon supports this claim, more or less. He says his mother never asked to see him, at least not that he was told. All he knows is that his father wanted them to meet so she could help him out with his playing."

"She played the violin?" Barbara said. "There wasn't one at the cottage in Henley."

"Gideon didn't mean that she was going to tutor him. He said there was actually nothing she could do to help him with his problem other than to 'agree' with his father."

"What's that supposed to mean when it's dancing the polka?"

"I don't know. But I'll tell you this: He doesn't have stage fright. There's something seriously wrong with the man."

"Like a guilty conscience? Where was he three nights ago?"

"Home. Alone. So he says." Lynley tossed his notebook on his desk and removed his glasses. "And that doesn't even begin to address Eugenie Davies' e-mail, Barbara." He brought her into the picture on that front, saying in conclusion, "*Jete* was the name tagged onto the message. Does that mean anything to you?"

"An acronym?" She considered the possible words that the four letters could begin, with *just* and *eat* coming to mind at once. She followed that thought along the family tree to its cousin, saying, "Could be Pitchley branching out from his TongueMan handle?"

"What did you get from St. Catherine's on him?" Lynley asked her.

"Gold," she replied. "St. Catherine's confirms Pitchley's claim that he was James Pitchford twenty years ago."

"How is that gold?"

"Because of what follows," Barbara replied. "Before he was Pitchford, he was someone else: He was Jimmy Pytches, sir, little Jimmy Pytches from Tower Hamlets. He changed his name to Pitchford six years before the murder in Kensington Square."

"Unusual," Lynley agreed, "but hardly damning."

"By itself, right. But when you put two name changes in one lifetime into the same basket as having two blokes jumping out of his kitchen window when the rozzers come to call, you've got something that smells like cod in the sun. So I rang the station over there and asked if anyone remembered a Jimmy Pytches."

"And?" Lynley asked.

"And listen to this. The whole family're in and out of trouble all the time. Were back then. Still are now. And when Pitchley was Jimmy Pytches all those years ago, a baby died while he was minding her. He was a teenager at the time, and the investigation couldn't pin anything on him. The inquest finally called it cot death, but not before our Jimmy spent forty-eight hours being held and questioned as suspect number one. Here. Check my notes if you want to."

Lynley did so, putting his reading glasses back on.

Barbara said, "A second kid dying while he was in the same house," as Lynley looked over the information. "Doesn't feel very nice, does it, sir?"

"If he did indeed murder Sonia Davies and if Katja Wolff carried the can for him," Lynley began, and Barbara interrupted with, "Perhaps this is why she never said a word once she was arrested, sir. Say she and Pitchford had a thing—she was pregnant, right?—and when Sonia was drowned, they both knew that the cops would look hard at Pitchford because of the other death, once they found out who he really was. If they could play it out as an accident, as negligence—"

"Why would he have drowned the Davies girl?"

"Jealousy over what the family had and he hadn't got. Anger over how they were treating his beloved. He wants to rescue her from her situation, or he wants to get back at people he sees as having what he'll never put his mitts on, so he goes after the kid. Katja takes the fall for him, knowing about his past and thinking she'll get a year or two for negligence while he'd probably get life for premeditated murder. And she never once considers how a jury's going to react to her keeping silent about the death of a disabled toddler. And just think of what was probably going through their heads: shades of Mengele and all that, Inspector, and *she* won't even say what happened. So the judge throws the book at her, she gets twenty years, and Pitchford disappears from her life, leaving her to rot in prison while he becomes Pitchley and makes a killing in the City."

"And then what?" Lynley said. "She gets out of prison and then what, Havers?"

"She tells Eugenie what really happened, who really did it. Eugenie tracks down Pitchley the way I tracked down Pytches. She goes to confront him, but she never makes it."

"Because?"

"Because she gets it on the street."

"I realise that. But from whom, Barbara?"

"I think Leach might be onto it, sir."

"Pitchley? Why?"

"Katja Wolff wants justice. So does Eugenie. The only way to get it is to put Pitchley away, which I doubt he'd go for."

Lynley shook his head. "How do you explain Webberly, then?"

"I think you already know the answer to that."

"Those letters?"

"It's time to hand them over. You've got to see they're important, Inspector."

"Havers, they're more than ten years old. They're not an issue."

"Wrong, wrong, *wrong*." Barbara pulled on her sandy fringe in sheer frustration. "Look. Say Pitchley and Eugenie had something going. Say *that's* the reason she was in his street the other night. Say he's been to Henley to see her on the sly and during a tryst he's come across those letters. He's gone round the bend with jealousy, so he gives her the chop and then takes down the superintendent."

Lynley shook his head. "Barbara, you can't have it all ways. You're twisting the facts to fit a conclusion. But they don't fit it, and it doesn't fit the case."

"Why not?"

"Because it leaves too much unaccounted for." Lynley ticked off the items. "How could Pitchley have maintained an affair with Eugenie Davies without Ted Wiley's knowledge since Wiley appears to have kept close tabs on the comings and goings at Doll Cottage? What did Eugenie have to confess to Wiley, and why did she die the night before the scheduled confession? Who is *Jete*? Who was she meeting at those pubs and hotels? And what do we do about the coincidence of Katja Wolff's release from prison and two hit-and-runs in which the victims are significant people in the case that put her away?"

Barbara sighed, her shoulders slumping. "Okay. Where's Winston? What's he got to say about Katja Wolff?"

Lynley told her about Nkata's report on the German woman's movements from Kennington to Wandsworth on the previous night. He ended with, "He was confident that both Yasmin Edwards and Katja Wolff are hiding something. When he got the word about Webberly, he passed the message back that he wanted to have another chat with them."

"So he thinks there's a connection between the hit-and-runs as well."

"Right. And I agree. There *is* a connection, Havers. We just haven't seen it clearly." Lynley stood, handed Barbara her notes, and began gathering up material from his desk. He said, "Let's get on to Hampstead. Leach's team must have something we can work with by now."

WINSTON NKATA SAT in front of the Hampstead police station for a good five minutes before he clambered out of his car. Because of a four-car pileup on the huge roundabout just before the crossing to Vauxhall Bridge, it had taken him more than ninety minutes to make the drive from South London. He was glad of that. Sitting in the car while firemen, paramedics, and traffic police sorted out the tangle of metal and injured bodies had given him the time he needed to come to terms with the balls-up he'd made of his interview with Katja Wolff and Yasmin Edwards.

He'd cocked it up brilliantly. He'd shown his hand. He'd charged like a bull from the pen exactly sixty-seven minutes after opening his eyes that morning, galloping from his parents' flat to Kennington at the earliest hour he'd deemed reasonable. Snorting and pawing the ground, eager to lower his horns and attack, he'd ridden up in that creaking lift with a soaring sense of being about to break the case. And he'd gone to great lengths to assure himself that his mission to Kennington was indeed all about the case. Because if Katja Wolff had a little something on the side going on, and if Yasmin Edwards knew nothing about it, and if he could reveal the little something on the side in such a way as to create a fissure in their relationship, then what was to prevent Yasmin Edwards from admitting what he already knew in his bones to be true: that Katja Wolff had not been home on the night of the murder of Eugenie Davies.

He intended nothing more than that, he'd told himself. He was just a cop carrying out his duties. Her flesh meant nothing: smooth and taut, the colour of newly minted pennies. Her body was of no account either: lithe and firm, with a waist dipping in over welcoming hips. Her eyes were only windows: dark like the shadows and trying to hide what they couldn't hide, which was anger and fear. And that anger and fear were meant to be used, to be used by him to whom she was nothing, just a lezzie lag who'd chopped her husband one night and had taken up with a baby killer.

It wasn't his responsibility to sort out why Yasmin Edwards would bring that baby killer into her home, where her own child lived, and Nkata knew it. But he did tell himself that, aside from providing them the break they needed in the investigation, it would also be for the best if the fissure he was able to produce in the women's relationship led to a break-up that would take Daniel Edwards out of the reach of a convicted killer.

He shut his ears to the thought that the boy's own mother also was a convicted killer. After all, she'd struck out against an adult. There was nothing in her background to indicate she had it in for children.

So he was filled with the righteousness of his cause when he rang the buzzer at Yasmin Edwards' door. And when there was no answer at first, he merely used the lack of response as a spur. It dug into the sides of his reason for being there, and he rang again till he forced a reply.

Nkata was a man who'd encountered prejudice and hatred for most of his life. One couldn't be a member of a minority race in England and not be the recipient of hostility in a hundred subtle forms every day. Even at the Met, where he'd assumed performance counted for more than epidermal hue, he'd learned to watch himself, never allowing others in too close, never completely letting down his guard lest he pay the price of presuming that a familiarity of discourse meant an equality of mind. That was not the case, no matter how things looked to the uninitiated observer. And wise was the black man who remembered that.

Because of all this, Nkata had long thought himself incapable of the sort of judgement he'd learned to experience at the hands of others. But after his morning interview in the Doddington Grove Estate, he'd learned that his vision was just as narrow and just as fully capable of leading him to ill-founded conclusions as was the vision of the most illiterate, badly dressed, and ill-spoken member of the National Front.

He'd seen them together. He'd seen the way they greeted each other, the way they talked together, the way they walked like a couple to Galveston Road. He'd known the German was a woman whose life partner was another woman. So when they'd gone into that house and shut the door, he'd allowed an embrace silhouetted against the window to provoke his imagination into running from its pen like an untamed pony. A lesbian meeting another woman and trotting off with her for seclusion together meant only one thing. So he had believed. So he had let his belief colour his second interview in Yasmin Edwards' flat.

Had he not known how thoroughly he'd cocked things up right then, he would have been informed soon enough when he phoned the number on the business card that Katja had handed him. Harriet

Lewis herself confirmed the story: Yes, she was Katja Wolff's solicitor. Yes, she had been with her on the previous evening. Yes, they had gone to Galveston Road together.

"You leave after quarter of an hour?" Nkata asked her.

She said, "What's this about, Constable?"

"What sort of business 'd you engage in in Galveston Road?" he asked her.

"None that's any business of yours," the solicitor had said, just as Katja Wolff promised she would.

"How long's she been a client of yours?" he tried next.

"Our conversation is over," she'd said. "I work for Miss Wolff, not for you."

So he was left with nothing except the knowledge that he'd done everything wrong and that he'd have to explain himself to the one person he sought to emulate: DI Lynley. And when the traffic snarled up near Vauxhall Bridge, then stopped altogether as sirens blared and lights flashed up ahead, he was grateful not only for the diversion a smash-up provided but also for the time he would be handed to decide how to tell the tale of the last twelve hours.

Now he looked at the front of the Hampstead Police Station and forced himself out of his car. He walked inside, showed his ID, and trudged to do the penance his actions called for.

He found everyone in the incident room, where the morning meeting was just breaking up. The china board was filled with the day's list of actions and the men and women assigned to them, but the hush among the constables leaving told Nkata that they'd been informed about what had happened to Webberly.

DI Lynley and Barbara Havers remained behind, comparing two computer sheets. Nkata joined them, saying, "Sorry. Pileup at Vauxhall Bridge," to which Lynley replied, looking up over his spectacles, "Ah. Winston. How did it go?"

"Couldn't shake either one of them from what they already said."

"Damn," Barb muttered.

"Did you speak to the Edwards woman alone?" Lynley asked.

"Didn't need to. Wolff 'as meeting with her solicitor, 'Spector. That's who the bird was. Solicitor confirmed when I rang her." His face must have shown something of his chagrin, because Lynley examined him for a long moment, during which Nkata felt all the misery of a child who's displeased his parent.

"You sounded quite sure when we spoke," Lynley remarked, "and when you're feeling sure, you're usually right. Are you certain you spoke to the solicitor, Winnie? Wolff could have given you the number of a friend to play the role of solicitor when you rang her."

"She gave me her business card," Nkata said. "And what solicitor of your acquaintance's going to lie for a client when the answer the cops want is either yes or no? But I still think the women are hiding something. I just went at it wrong to suss out what it is." And then because his admiration for Lynley would always override his need to look good in the inspector's eyes, he added, "But I cocked it up with my whole approach. Whoever talks to them next, better not be me."

Barbara Havers said supportively, "Well, God knows I've done that more than once, Winnie," and Nkata shot her a grateful look. She *had* cocked up and it had cost her a suspension from duty, her previous rank, and probably the chance to rise in the Met. But she'd at least brought down a killer by the end of that case, while he'd done nothing more than complicate matters.

Lynley said, "Yes. Well. Haven't we all. No matter, Winston. We'll sort things out," although he did sound disappointed to Nkata's ears, which wasn't half of what his own mum was going to sound when he told *her* what had happened.

"Jewel," she'd say, "what were you *thinking,* son?"

And that was a question he preferred not to answer.

He brought himself round to listening to the update he'd missed from the morning's briefing. The BT records from Eugenie Davies' phone had been matched up with names and addresses. And the callers on her answer machine had likewise been identified. The woman who named herself Lynn had emerged as one Lynn Davies—

"A relation?" Nkata asked.

"Still to be discovered."

—with an address that put her close to East Dulwich.

"Havers will handle that interview," Lynley said. He went on to report that the unidentified male caller on the answer machine who'd angrily demanded that Mrs. Davies pick up the phone and talk to him was one Raphael Robson, whose address in Gospel Oak put him closer to the scene of the murder than anyone else, other than J. W. Pitchley, of course. "I'll take on Robson next," Lynley went on, and he added to Nkata, "I'd like you there as well," as if already knowing that he would need to bolster Nkata's faltering sense of competence.

Nkata said, "Right," as Lynley went on to explain that the BT records had also confirmed Richard Davies' story of phone calls taken from and made to his former wife. They'd begun in early August, round the time their son had had his problem at Wigmore Hall and they'd continued up to the morning before Eugenie's death, when Davies had made a brief call to her. There were plenty of calls from Staines as well, Lynley told him. So both men's stories were being corroborated by the evidence they had at hand.

"A word, you three?" came from the doorway upon the conclusion of Lynley's remarks. They swung round to see that DCI Leach had returned to the incident room, and he had a scrap of paper in his hand that he gestured with as he said, "In my office, if you will," after which he vanished, expecting them to follow.

"Where've you got to tracing the kid Wolff had while she was in prison?" Leach asked Barbara Havers when they joined him.

Barbara said, "I got side-tracked onto Pitchley once I stopped for his photo yesterday. I'm onto that today. But nothing's telling us that Katja Wolff even wants to know where the kid ended up, sir. If she wanted to find him, the first person she would've talked to is the nun. Which she hasn't done."

Leach made a dismissive noise in his throat. "Check it out, all the same."

"Right," Barbara said. "D'you want it before or after I track down Lynn Davies?"

"Before. After. Just do it, Constable," Leach said irritably. "We've had a report from across the river. Forensic have analysed the paint chips they found on the body."

"And?" Lynley asked.

"We're going to have to adjust our thinking. SO7 says the paint shows cellulose mixed with thinners to water it down. That doesn't match up with anything that's been used on cars for at least forty years. They're telling us the chips came from something old. Think nineteen-fifties at the latest, they're saying."

"Nineteen-*fifties*?" Barbara asked incredulously.

"That explains why last night's witness thought of a limousine," Lynley said. "Cars were big in the fifties. Jaguars. Rolls-Royces. Bentleys were enormous."

"So someone ran her down in his classic auto?" Barbara Havers asked. "Now, *that's* desperation."

"Could be a taxi," Nkata pointed out. "Taxi out of use, got sold to someone who fixed it up and uses it now for his regular motor."

"Taxi, classic car, or golden chariot," Barbara said, "everyone we've got under the microscope's out of the running."

"Unless one of them borrowed a car," Lynley noted.

"We can't discount that possibility," Leach concurred.

"Are we back to square one, then?" Barbara asked.

"I'll get someone to start checking it out. That and repair shops catering for old cars. Although we can't expect much body damage on something manufactured in the fifties. Cars were like tanks then."

"But they had chrome bumpers," Nkata said, "massive chrome bumpers that could've got mashed."

"So we'll need to check out old parts shops as well." Leach made a note. "It's easier to replace than to repair, especially if you know the cops are looking." He phoned into the incident room and allocated that assignment out, after which he rang off and said to Lynley, "It still could be a blind coincidence."

Lynley said, "Do you think that, sir?" in a measured tone that told Nkata the DI was looking for something beneath whatever reply the DCI might give.

"I'd like to. But I do see how it puts one in blinkers: thinking what we want to think in this situation." He gazed at his telephone as if willing it to ring. The others said nothing. Finally, he murmured, "He's a good man. He may have stepped wrong now and then, but which of us hasn't? Stepping wrong doesn't make him less of what he is." He looked at Lynley, and they seemed to communicate something that Nkata couldn't understand. Then he said, "Get on with it, you lot," and they left him.

Outside, Barbara Havers spoke to Lynley. "He knows, Inspector."

Nkata said, "Knows what? Who?"

Barbara said, "Leach. He knows Webberly's got a connection with the Davies woman."

" 'Course he knows it. They worked on that old case together. Nothing new there. And we already knew it as well."

"Right. But what we didn't know——"

"That'll do, Havers," Lynley said. The two of them exchanged a long look before Barbara said airily, "Oh. Right. Well, I'm off, then," and with a friendly nod at Nkata, she walked towards her car.

In the immediate aftermath of this brief exchange, Nkata felt the unspoken reprimand in Lynley's decision to keep from him what was obviously a new piece of information which he and Barbara had uncovered. Nkata realised he deserved to be left in the dark in this way—God knew he'd certainly not shown he possessed the requisite level of skill to do the *right* thing with a valuable new fact—but at the same time he thought he'd been circumspect enough with his recitation of his morning's cock-up so as not to be thought of as a complete incompetent. That obviously hadn't been the case.

Nkata felt all the misery of his position. He said, " 'Spector, you want me off this now?"

"Off what, Winston?"

"The case. You know. 'F I can't talk to two birds
without making a mess of things . . ."

In reply, Lynley looked completely confused, and
Nkata knew he'd have to go further, admitting what
he preferred to keep buried. He directed his gaze to
Barbara, who'd climbed into her soup-tin car and was
in the process of revving the Mini's sorely tried engine. He said, "I mean, 'f I don't know what to *do*
with a fact when I got a fact, I guess I c'n see how
you might not want me to *have* a fact in the first
place. But that doesn't give me a full hand, which c'n
make me less effective, right? Not that I showed how
'ffective I was this morning, of course. So what I'm
saying's . . . if you want me off the case . . . What I'm
saying's I understand. I should've known how to approach those two birds. 'Stead of thinking I knew
everything, I should've thought there might be
something I wasn't seeing. But I didn't, did I? So
when I talked to them, I ballsed it up. And—"

"Winston," Lynley cut in firmly. "A hair shirt
might be appropriate, given the circumstance—
whatever it is—but I assure you, the cat o' nine tails
can be dispensed with."

"What?"

Lynley smiled. "You've a brilliant career ahead of
you, Winnie. No blots on your copy book, unlike the
rest of us. I'd like to see you keep it that way. Do you
understand?"

"That I cocked things up? That another cock-up'd
mean a formal—"

"No. That I'd like to keep you in the clear

should . . ." Uncharacteristically, Lynley paused in what seemed like the search for a phrase that would explain something without revealing what he was explaining. He settled on, "Should our procedures come under scrutiny later on, I'd prefer them to be mine and not yours," and he made the statement with such delicacy, that Nkata followed it with a leap to comprehension once he put Lynley's words together with what Barbara Havers had inadvertently revealed just before leaving them.

He said in disbelief, "Holy God. You on to something you're keeping quiet about?"

Lynley said wryly, "Job well done. You didn't hear that from me."

"Barb knows 'bout it?"

"Only because she was there. I'm responsible, Winston. I'd like to keep it that way."

"Could it take us to the killer, what you're on to?"

"I don't think so. But yes, it may do."

"Is it evidence?"

"Let's not discuss that."

Nkata couldn't believe what he was hearing. "Then you got to turn it in! You got to 'stablish the chain. You can't not hand it over 'cause you think . . . What *do* you think?"

"That the hit-and-runs are probably connected but that I need to see exactly how they're connected before I make a move that could destroy someone's life. What's left of it. It's my decision, Winnie. And to protect yourself, I suggest you don't ask any more questions."

Nkata studied the DI, not believing that Lynley, of all people, should be operating in a grey area. He knew that he could insist and end up in there with him—with Barbara as well—but he was ambitious enough to heed the wisdom in the inspector's words. Still, he said, "Wish you wouldn't go at it like this, man."

"Objection noted," Lynley said.

SEVENTEEN

LIBBY NEALE decided to call in sick with the flu. She knew Rock Peters would have a conniption and threaten to withhold her week's pay—not that that actually *meant* anything, since he was currently three weeks behind paying her anyway—but she didn't care. When she'd parted from Gideon the previous night, she'd hoped he'd come down to her flat after the cop left him, and when he didn't, she slept so badly that she was as good as sick anyway. So calling it the flu wasn't *that* much of a lie.

She wandered around her flat in sweats for the first three hours after she got up, mostly pounding the heels of her palms together and straining her ears to hear any sound from above to indicate that Gideon was stirring. She didn't get very far in her efforts. Finally, she gave up the attempt at eavesdropping on him—not that it was *really* eavesdropping when all you were listening for was the sound of movement to indicate that someone was basically all right—and she decided to make sure in person that he was doing okay. He'd been a wreck yesterday *before* the cop got there. Who the hell knew what condition he'd been in once the cop left?

Should've gone to him then, she told herself. And while she made an earnest attempt not to ponder the reason that she *hadn't* gone to him once the cop departed, the thought of what she should have done in the first place led inexorably to the why of why she hadn't.

He'd spooked her. He'd been so not there. She'd talked to him in the kite shed and after that in the kitchen and he'd answered her—sort of—but still he'd been so somewhere else in his head that she'd wondered if he maybe needed to be committed or something. Just for a while. And then wondering *that* had made her feel so disloyal that she couldn't really face him, or at least that was what she told herself when she spent the evening watching old movies on Sky TV and eating two very large bags of cheddar-cheese popcorn which she could have done without thank you very much and finally going to bed alone, where she fought with the sheets and blankets all night when she wasn't having a soon-to-be-major-motion-picture nightmare.

So after spinning her wheels pacing the floor, browsing in the refrigerator for the bag of celery that was supposed to make her feel less guilty about the cheddar-cheese popcorn, and watching Kilroy yacking with women who'd married men young enough to be their sons and—in two cases—their frigging grandsons, she went upstairs to search out Gideon.

She found him on the floor in the music room, sitting beneath the window seat with his back against the wall. He had his legs drawn up to his chest, with his chin resting upon his knees like some kid who's been disciplined by a ticked-off parent. All around him were scattered papers, which turned out to be Xerox copies of newspaper articles, all of them covering the same subject. He'd been back to the Press Association's news library.

He didn't look at her when she came into the room. He was focused on the stories surrounding him, and she wondered if he even heard her. She said his name, but he didn't stir, other than to begin a gentle rocking.

Breakdown, she thought with alarm. Complete crack-up. He looked like someone who'd lost it. He was wearing exactly what he'd had on yesterday, so she figured he hadn't slept all night either.

"Hey," she said quietly, "what's up, Gideon? You been back down to Victoria? Why'n't you tell me? I'd've gone with you."

She scanned the papers that fanned around him, overlarge sheets on which newspaper clippings had been photocopied every which way. She saw that the British papers—in keeping with the country's general bent towards xenophobia—had gone after the nanny with a rusty hatchet. If she wasn't "the German" in every article, she was "the former Communist whose family lived particularly well"—not to mention *suspiciously* well, Libby thought sardonically—"under Russian domination." One paper had unearthed the news that her grandfather had been a member of the

Nazi party, while another had found a picture of her father, who'd evidently been a card-holding, uniform-wearing, *Siegheil!*-shouting member of the Hitler Youth.

The tireless ability of the press to milk a story for its every frigging ounce of liquid was totally amazing. It looked to Libby like the life of everyone even moderately involved with the death of Sonia Davies and the trial and conviction of her killer had been dissected by the tabloids at one time or another. So Gideon's home teacher had come under the microscope, as had the lodger, as well as Rafe Robson, both of Gideon's parents, and his grandparents, too. And long after the verdict, it seemed that anyone who'd wanted to make a buck had sold *his* version of the story to the papers.

Thus, people had crawled out from under rocks to comment on life as a nanny—NEWSREADER: I WAS A NANNY AND IT WAS HELL blared one headline—and those who had no experience as nannies had experience with Germans they wanted to reveal—A RACE APART, FORMER BERLIN GI SAYS, announced another. But what Libby noticed most of all was the number of stories that dealt with Gideon's family having had a nanny for his sister in the first place.

They went at the topic from several angles: There was the group who chose to dwell on what the German nanny was paid (a pittance, so no wonder she finally offed the poor kid, like in a greedy rage or something) compared to what something called "a well-trained Norland Nanny" was paid (a fortune that prompted Libby to seriously consider a change in career, pronto), crafting their nasty little articles in such a way as to suggest that the Davies family had gotten to the max what they'd paid for with their skinflint pennies. Then there was the group who chose to dwell on speculating what purposes were being served when a mother made the decision to "work outside the home." And then there was the group who chose to dwell on what it did to parental expectation, responsibility, and devotion when a family was burdened with a disabled child. Battle lines were drawn all over the place on the topic of how to deal with the birth of a Down's Syndrome baby, and all the options taken by parents of such children were given a good airing out: give them up for adoption, put them away at the Government's expense, devote your life to them, learn to cope by asking the aid of outside agencies, join a support group, soldier on with upper lips stiff, treat the child like any other, and on and on.

Libby found that she couldn't begin to imagine what it had been like for all of them when little Sonia Davies had died. Her birth would have been tough to deal with, but to love her—because they *must* have loved her, right?—and then to lose her and then to have every detail of what went into her existence and the existence of her family displayed for public entertainment and consumption . . . Whew, Libby thought. How did *anyone* deal with that?

Not well, if Gideon was anything to go by. He'd changed his position so his forehead was balanced on his knees. He continued to rock.

"Gideon," she asked him, "you all right?"

"I don't want to remember now that I remember," he replied numbly. "I don't want to think. And I can't stop either. Remembering. Thinking. I want to rip my brain from my head."

"I can buy that," Libby assured him. "So why don't we dump all this stuff in the trash? You been reading it all night?" She bent to the papers and began to gather them. "No wonder you can't get your mind off it, Gid."

He grabbed her wrist, crying out, "Don't!"

"But if you don't want to think—"

"No! I've been reading and reading and I want to know how anyone could continue to exist, could even *want* to exist . . . Look at it all, Libby. Look. Just look."

Libby looked again at the papers and she saw them the way Gideon must have seen them, coming upon them twenty years after the fact of being protected from the knowledge of what that time had been like for his family. Particularly, she saw the thinly veiled attacks on his parents in the light he would be seeing them. And she made the leap that he no doubt had already made from what the papers had printed: His mother had left them because of *this;* she had disappeared for nearly twenty years because she had no doubt begun to believe herself as ill-suited for parenthood as the newspapers had made her out to be. It seemed that Gideon was finally understanding his past. Little wonder that he was inches away from flipping out.

She was about to say all of this when he got to his feet. He took two steps, then swayed. She leapt up and grabbed him by the arm.

He said, "I've got to see Cresswell-White."

"Who? That attorney?"

He headed out of the room, fumbling in his pocket and bringing out his keys. The thought of him driving alone across London spurred Libby to follow. At the front door, she snatched his leather jacket from the coat rack, and she trailed him along the sidewalk to his GPS. As he attempted to insert the key in the lock with a hand that trembled like an octogenarian's, she threw the jacket over his shoulders and said, "You're *not* driving. You'd get in a wreck before you got to Regent's Park."

"I've got to get to Cresswell-White."

"Fine. Cool. Whatever. I'll drive."

During the drive, Gideon said not a word. He merely stared straight ahead, his knees knocking together spasmodically.

He got out the moment she turned off the ignition in the area of the Temple. He set off down the street. Libby locked the car and trotted to catch up, reaching him as he crossed over at the end and entered that holy of legal holies.

Gideon led her to the place she'd accompanied him previously: to a building that was part brick and part stone, sitting on the edge of a little park. He went in through the same narrow doorway, where black wooden slats on the wall were painted in white with the names of the lawyers who had offices inside.

They had to cool their heels in reception before Cresswell-White had a break in his schedule. They sat in silence on the black leather sofas, both of them staring alternately at the Persian carpet and the brass chandelier. Around them, telephones rang constantly and quietly as a group working in an office directly opposite the sofas fielded calls.

After forty minutes of pondering the crucial issue of whether the oak chest in reception had been built to store chamber pots, Libby heard someone say, "Gideon," and roused herself to see that Bertram Cresswell-White had himself come out to take them back to his corner office. Unlike their previous visit—which had been scheduled in advance—no coffee was on offer this time, although the fireplace was lit and it was doing at least something to cut the chill that pervaded the room.

The lawyer had been working hard at some task or another, for a computer's monitor was still glowing with a page of typescript and half a dozen books were open on his desk along with what looked like pretty ancient files. Among these, a black-and-white photograph of a woman lay. She was blonde with close-cropped hair, a bad complexion, and an expression saying "Don't mess with me."

Gideon saw the picture and said, "Are you trying to get her out?"

Cresswell-White closed the file, gestured them to the leather chairs near the fireplace, and said, "She would have been hanged if I'd had my way and the law were different. She's a monster. And I've made the study of monsters my avocation."

"What'd she do?" Libby asked.

"Killed children and buried their bodies on the moors. She liked to make audiotapes as she tortured them, she and her boyfriend." Libby swallowed. Cresswell-White glanced at his watch with some meaning but tempered this action with, "I heard about your mother, Gideon. On Radio Four News, I'm terribly sorry. I expect that's something to do with why you've come. How can I help you?"

"With her address." Gideon spoke as if he'd thought of nothing else since first getting into his car in Chalcot Square.

"Whose?"

"You have to know where she is. You were the one who put her away, so you would've been told when they let her out. That's why I've come. I need her address."

Libby thought, Hold *on* here, Gid.

Cresswell-White gave his version of that same re-action. He knotted his eyebrows, saying, "Are you asking me for Katja Wolff's address?"

"You have it, don't you? You have to have it. I don't expect they'd let her out without telling you where she went."

"Why do you want it? I'm not saying I do have it, by the way."

"She's owed."

Libby thought, This is *really* the limit. She said quietly but with what she hoped was gentle urgency, "Gideon. Gosh. The police're handling this, aren't they?"

"She's out now," Gideon said to Cresswell-White as if Libby hadn't spoken. "She's out and she's owed. Where is she?"

"I can't tell you that." Cresswell-White leaned forward, his body if not his hands reaching for Gideon. "I know you've had a very bad shock. Your life has probably been one long effort to recover from what she put you through. God knows the time that she spent in prison doesn't mitigate your suffering one iota."

"I've got to find her," Gideon said. "It's the only way."

"No. Listen to me. It's the wrong way. Oh, it feels right and I know that feeling: You'd climb back into the past if you could and you'd tear her limb from limb *before* the fact, just to prevent her from doing the harm she eventually did your family. But you'd gain as little as I gain, Gideon, when I hear the jury's verdict and I know that I've won but all the time I've lost because nothing can bring a dead child back to life. A woman who takes the life of a child is the worst kind of demon because she can *give* life if she chooses. And to take a life when you can give life is a crime that's compounded and one for which no sentence will ever be long enough and no punishment—even death—ever good enough."

"There's got to be reparation," Gideon said. He didn't sound so much stubborn as desperate. "My mother's dead, don't you see? There's got to be reparation, and this is the only way. I don't have a choice."

"You do," Cresswell-White said. "You can choose not to meet her at the level she operates on. You can choose to believe what I'm telling you because what I'm telling you comes from decades of experience. There is no vengeance for this sort of thing. Even death was no vengeance when death was both legal and possible, Gideon."

"You don't understand." Gideon closed his eyes, and for a moment, Libby thought he'd start crying. She wanted to do something to prevent him breaking down and humiliating himself further in the eyes of this man who did not really know him and could not therefore know what he'd been going through for more than three months. But she also wanted to do something to smooth things over, on the off-chance that something bad might accidentally happen to the German chick in the next few days, in which case Gideon would be the first person they'd be talking to after this little conversation in the Temple. Not that she really thought Gideon'd *do* anything to anyone. He was just talking; he was just looking for something to make him feel like his world wasn't falling apart.

Libby said to the lawyer in a low voice, "He's been up all night. And he's been having nightmares on the nights he *can* sleep. He saw her, see, and—"

Cresswell-White sat up and took notice of this, saying, "Katja Wolff? Has she contacted you, Gideon? The terms of her parole prevent her from contacting any member of the family, and if she violates those terms, we can see to it—"

"No, no. His mom," Libby interrupted. "He saw his mom. But he didn't know who she was because he hadn't seen her since he was a little kid. And that's been eating at him since he heard she was . . . you know, killed." She glanced cautiously at Gideon. His eyes were still closed, and his head was shaking as if he wanted to negate everything that had happened to bring him to this position of begging a lawyer he didn't even know to violate whatever it was he would have to violate in order to give out the information that Gideon wanted. That wasn't going to happen, and Libby knew it. Cresswell-White sure as hell wasn't going to hand the German nanny over to Gideon on a platter and risk his own reputation and career for having done so. Which was just as well and damn lucky to boot. All Gideon needed to really mess up his life at this point was access to the woman who'd killed his sister and maybe killed his mom as well.

But Libby knew how he felt, or at least she thought she knew. He felt like he'd blown his chance for some kind of redemption for some kind of sin, the punishment for which was not being able to play his violin. And that's what it all boiled down to after all: that frigging violin.

Cresswell-White said, "Gideon, Katja Wolff's not worth the time it would take to locate her. This is a woman who showed no remorse, who was so certain of her exoneration that she offered no defence of her actions. Her silence said, 'Let them prove they have a case,' and only when the facts piled up—those bruises, those fractures left to heal *untreated* on your sister's body—and she heard the verdict and the sentence did she decide a defence might be in order. Imagine that. Imagine what kind of person lies behind that simple refusal to cooperate—to answer the most *basic* of questions—when a child in her care has died. She didn't even weep once she made her initial statement. And she won't weep now. You can't expect that from her. She is not like us. Abusers of children are never like us."

Libby watched anxiously as Cresswell-White spoke, looking for a sign that what the lawyer was saying was somehow making an impression on Gideon. But she was left with a growing sense of despair when Gideon opened his eyes, got to his feet, and spoke.

He said, as if Cresswell-White's words meant nothing to him, "This is what it is: I didn't understand, but now I do. And I've got to find her." He walked towards the door of the office, raising his hands to his forehead as if he wanted to do what he'd said earlier: rip the brain from his head.

Cresswell-White said to Libby, "He's not well."

To which she responded, "Well, *duh*," as she went after Gideon.

RAPHAEL ROBSON'S HOME in Gospel Oak was set off one of the busier roads in the district. It turned out to be an enormous ramshackle Edwardian building in need of renovation, the front garden of which was hidden behind a yew hedge and graveled over to make it into a parking space. When Lynley and Nkata arrived, three vehicles were standing in front of the house: a dirty white van, a black Vauxhall, and a silver Renault. Lynley took quick note of the fact that the Vauxhall wasn't old enough to qualify as their hit-and-run vehicle.

A man came round the side of the house as they approached the front steps. He headed towards the Renault without noticing them. When Lynley called out, he stopped in his tracks, car keys extended to unlock his vehicle. Was he Raphael Robson? Lynley asked him, and produced his identification.

The man was an unappealing sort with a serious comb-over of dun-coloured hair that began just above his left ear and made his skull look as if someone were water-colouring a lattice across it. He was patchy-skinned from far too many holidays in the Mediterranean in August, and his shoulders bore a liberal sprinkling of dandruff. He gave a glance at Lynley's warrant card and said yes, he was Raphael Robson.

Lynley introduced Nkata and asked Robson if there was somewhere they could have a word with him, out of the noise of cars whooshing by just beyond the hedge. Robson said yes, yes, of course. If they'd follow him . . . ?

"The front door's warped," he said. "We haven't replaced it yet. We'll need to go in through the back."

Through the back took them along a brick path that led into a good-sized garden. This was overgrown with weeds and grass, edged by herbaceous borders long gone to ruin and dotted with trees that hadn't been pruned in years. Beneath them, wet fallen leaves were rotting to join their brothers from seasons past in the soil. In the midst of all the chaos and decay, however, a newish building stood. Robson saw both Lynley and Nkata giving this a look-over, and he said, "That was our first project. We do furniture in there."

"Building it?"

"Restoring it. We mean to do the house as well. Doing up furniture and selling it gives us something of a bank account to work from. Restoring a place like this"—with a nod at the imposing edifice—"takes a fortune. Whenever we get enough saved to do a room, we do it. It's taking forever, but no one's in a hurry. And there's a certain camaraderie that develops when everyone's behind a project, I think."

Lynley wondered at the word *camaraderie.* He'd been thinking Robson's *us* referred to his wife and family, but developing camaraderie suggested something else. He considered the vehicles he'd seen in front of the building and said, "This is a commune, then?"

Robson unlocked the door and swung it open onto a passageway with a wooden bench running along its wall and adult-sized wellingtons lined up beneath it and hooks holding jackets on the wall above it. He said, "That sounds like something from the summer-of-love era. But yes, I suppose you could call it a commune. Mostly it's a group with shared interests."

"Which are?"

"Making music and turning this house into something we can all enjoy."

"Not restoring furniture?" Nkata asked.

"That's merely a means to an end. Musicians don't make enough money to finance a restoration like this one without something else to fall back on."

He allowed them into the passage before him, shutting the door when they were inside and locking it scrupulously behind them. He said, "This way," and led them into what might once have been the dining room but now was a musty combination of draughting room, storeroom, and office, with water-stained wallpaper covering the upper half of the walls and battered wainscoting covering the lower half. A computer was part of the office function that the room was serving. From where he stood, Lynley could see the telephone line that was plugged into it.

He said, "We've tracked you through a message you left on the answer machine of a woman called Eugenie Davies, Mr. Robson. This was four days ago. At eight-fifteen in the evening."

Next to Lynley, Nkata got out his leather notebook and his propelling pencil, twisting it to produce a micro-millimeter of lead. Robson watched him do this, then walked to a worktable on which a set of blueprints were spread. He smoothed his hand over the top one as if to study it, but he answered the question with the single word. "Yes."

"Do you know Mrs. Davies was murdered three nights ago?"

"Yes. I know." His voice was low and his hand grasped a blueprint that lay still rolled up. His thumb played along the rubber band that held it formed into a tube. "Richard told me," he said, lifting his gaze to Lynley. "He'd been to tell Gideon when I arrived for one of our sessions."

"Sessions?"

"I teach the violin. Gideon's been my pupil since childhood. He isn't any longer, of course; he's no one's pupil. But we play together three hours a day when he's not recording, rehearsing, or touring. You've heard of him, doubtless."

"I was under the impression he hasn't played in several months."

Robson's hand had reached out to touch the opened blueprint again, but he hesitated and did nothing more with the gesture. He said on a heavy sigh, "Sit down, Inspector. You as well, Constable," and he turned back to them. "It's important not only to keep up appearances in a situation like Gideon's, but it's also important to go on as normally as possible. So I still turn up for our daily three hours together, and we keep hoping that when enough time passes, he'll be able to go back to the music."

" 'We'?" Nkata raised his head to look for the answer.

"Richard and I. Gideon's father."

Somewhere in the house, a scherzo began. Dozens of energetic notes ran riot on what sounded like a harpsichord at first but then abruptly changed to an oboe and then just as abruptly altered to a flute. This was accompanied by an increase in volume and the sudden rhythmic pounding of several percussion instruments. Robson went to the door and shut it, saying, "Sorry. Janet's gone a bit mad over the electric keyboard. She's enthralled with anything a computer chip can do."

"And you?" Lynley asked.

"I haven't the money for a keyboard."

"I meant computer chips, Mr. Robson. Do you use this computer? I see it has a telephone connection."

Robson's gaze flicked to it. He crossed the room and sat at a chair that he drew out from the sheet of plywood which served as a desk top. At this, Lynley and Nkata also sat, unfolding two metal chairs and swinging them into position so that, with Robson, they formed a triangle near the computer.

"We all use it," Robson said.

"For e-mail? Chat rooms? Surfing the net?"

"I mostly use it for e-mail. My sister's in Los Angeles. My brother's in Birmingham. My parents have a house on the Costa del Sol. It's an easy way for us to stay in contact."

"Your address is . . . ?"

"Why?"

"Curiosity," Lynley said.

Robson recited it, looking puzzled. Lynley heard what he'd suspected he'd hear when he saw the computer sitting in the room. *Jete* was Robson's on-line name and consequently part of his e-mail address.

"You've been fairly wrung out about Mrs. Davies, it seems," he said to the violinist. "Your message on her answer machine was agitated, Mr. Robson, and the last e-mail you sent her looked a bit frantic as well. 'I must see you. I'm begging.' Had you had some sort of falling-out?"

Robson's seat was a desk chair that swiveled, and he used it to rotate, to examine the computer's empty staring screen as if he could see his last message to Eugenie Davies there. He said, "You'd be checking everything. Of course. I see that," as if speaking to himself and not to them. Then he went on in a normal tone with, "We parted quite badly. I said some things that . . ." He removed a handkerchief from his pocket, pressing it to his forehead, where perspiration had begun to bead. "I expected I'd have a chance to apologise. Even as I drove away from the restaurant—and I was in a real fury, I admit it—I didn't drive off thinking, That's it, I'm done with this business forever, she's a blind silly cow and that's the end of it. What I thought was, Oh God, she looks rotten, she's thinner than ever, why can't she see what that *means,* for God's sake."

"Which was what?" Lynley asked.

"That she'd made a decision in her head, yes, and it probably sounded like a sensible one to her. But her body was rebelling against that decision, which was her . . . I don't know . . . I suppose it was her *spirit's* way of trying to tell her to stop, to carry things not one inch farther. And you could *see* the rebellion in her. Believe me, you could actually see it. It wasn't just that she'd let herself go. God knows she'd done that years ago. She'd been quite lovely, but to see her—especially as she was in these last few years—you'd never have realised how men would at one time slow down on the street as they passed her."

"What decision had she made, Mr. Robson?"

Robson said, "Come with me. I want to show you something," by way of answer. He took them from the house, out the same way they'd come in, out into the garden. He headed towards the building where he'd said the commune worked on their furniture.

The building comprised a single large room in which battered pieces stood in various stages of restoration. It smelled strongly of sawdust, turpentine, and wood stains, and a patina of the dust that comes from heavy sanding lay like a gauze veil on everything. Footprints tracked back and forth across the dirty floor, from a workbench above which a set of newly cleaned tools gleamed with oil to a three-legged wardrobe that listed tiredly, sanded down to bare walnut, disemboweled, and awaiting the next stage of rejuvenation.

"Here's my guess," Robson said. "Tell me how it matches to reality. I did a wardrobe for her. Cherry wood, it was. First rate. Beautiful. Not the sort of thing you see every day. I did her a commode as well, early eighteenth century. Oak. And a washstand. Vic-

torian. Ebony with a marble top. One of the drawer
pulls is missing, but you wouldn't want to replace it
because you couldn't match it and anyway leaving it
without the pull actually gives it more character. The
wardrobe took the longest, because you don't ever
want to refinish a piece unless there is no hope for it.
You just want to restore it. So it was six months before I had it the way I wanted it and no one"—he
nodded at the house to indicate his housemates—
"was pleased that I was working on that instead of
something we could get a profit from."

Lynley frowned at this, knowing that there were
lines upon lines being written by Robson and wondering how adept he himself could be to read between them in the time they had. He said, "You had
a falling-out with Mrs. Davies because of a decision
she'd made. But I can't think her decision was about
selling the pieces of furniture you'd done for her. Am
I right?"

Robson's shoulders dropped slightly, as if he'd been
hoping that Lynley wouldn't be able to confirm what
he himself suspected. He'd been clutching his handkerchief, and now he looked down at it as he said,
"So she didn't keep them, did she? She didn't keep
any of the pieces I gave to her. She sold them all and
gave the money to charity. Or she just gave the furniture itself away. But she didn't keep it. That's what
you're telling me."

"She had no antiques in her house in Henley, if
that's what you're wondering," Lynley said. "Her furniture was—" He looked for the right word to con-

vey the manner in which Eugenie Davies' house in
Friday Street had been furnished. "Spartan," he said.

"Just like a nun's cell, I expect." Robson's words
were bitter. "That's how she punished herself. But it
wasn't enough, that sort of deprivation, so she was
ready to take it to the next level."

"What would that be?" Nkata had given up writing during Robson's recitation of the antiques he'd
given to Eugenie Davies. *The next level,* however,
clearly promised more.

"Wiley," Robson said. "The bloke from the bookshop. She'd been seeing him for several years, but
she'd decided it was time to . . ." Robson shoved his
handkerchief into his pocket and gave his attention to
the listing wardrobe. To Lynley's eyes, the piece
didn't look even salvageable, with its missing leg and
its gaping interior that showed a large jagged hole in
its back, very much as if someone had taken an axe to
it. "She was going to marry him if he asked her. She
said that she believed—she *felt,* she said, with
women's bloody intuition, she said—that they were
heading towards it. I told her that if a man didn't
bother to make an attempt . . . In three years, if he
didn't try to make a move on her . . . God, I'm not
talking about rape. Not shoving her into a wall and
feeling her up. But just . . . He hadn't even tried to
get close to her. He hadn't even talked about *why* he
hadn't tried. They just went on their picnics, took
their walks, rode the bus on those stupid pensioners'
days out. . . . And I tried to tell her that it wasn't normal. It wasn't red-blooded. So if she made it perma-

nent with him, if she actually made herself his partner and took herself out of the *sodding* running . . ."
Robson ran out of steam. His eyes became red-
rimmed. "But I suppose that's what she wanted. To
take up life with someone who couldn't begin to give
her anything complete, who couldn't begin to give
her what a man can give to a woman when she means
everything to him."

Lynley examined Robson as he spoke, saw the
misery in the lines that etched their painful history on
his patchy-skinned face. "When was the last time you
saw Mrs. Davies?"

"A fortnight ago. Thursday."

"Where?"

"Marlow. The Swan and Three Roses. Just outside
of town."

"And you didn't see her again? Did you speak to
her?"

"On the phone twice. I was trying to . . . I'd reacted badly to what she'd told me about Wiley, and I
knew it. I wanted to make things right between us.
But it just got worse, because I still wanted to talk to
her about it, about him, about what it meant that he
never . . . never once in three years . . . But she
didn't want to hear. She didn't want to see. 'He's a
good man, Raphael,' she kept saying, 'and it's time
now.' "

"Time for what?"

Robson continued as if Nkata hasn't asked the
question, as if he himself were a silent Cyrano who'd
waited long for an opportunity to unburden himself.

He said, "I didn't disagree that it was time. She'd punished herself for years. She wasn't in prison, but she may as well have been because she made her life a prison anyway. She lived one step away from solitary confinement, in complete self-denial, surrounding herself with people with whom she had nothing in common, always volunteering for the worst jobs, and all of it so that she could pay and pay and pay."

"For what?" Nkata had been standing close to the door as he wrote, as if hoping a near contact with the outside environment might spare his fine wool charcoal suit from the worst of the dust that permeated the work room's air. But now he took a step closer to Robson, and he cast a glance towards Lynley, who indicated with his hand that they would wait for the violinist to continue. Silence on their part was as useful a tool as silence on his part was revealing.

Robson finally said, "When she was born, Eugenie didn't love her instantly the way she thought she was supposed to love her. At first she was just exhausted because the birth had been difficult and all she wanted was to recover from it. And that's not unnatural, when a woman's been in labour so long—thirty hours, it was—and she's got nothing left in her even to cuddle a newborn. That is not a sin."

"I wouldn't disagree," Lynley said.

"And they didn't know at first anyway, about the baby. Yes, of course, there were signs, but the birth had been rough. She didn't come out pink and perfect like a birth that's been orchestrated for a Hollywood production. So the doctors didn't know till she

was examined and then . . . Good God, *anyone* would
be slaughtered by the news. Anyone would have to
adjust and that takes time. But she thought she should
have been different, Eugenie. She thought she should
have loved her at once, felt like a fighter, had plans
how to care for her, known what to do, what to expect, how to *be*. When she couldn't do that, she hated
herself. And the rest of them didn't make it easier for
her to accept the baby, did they, especially Richard's
father—that mad bastard—who expected another
prodigy from them, and when he got the reverse—
there was just too much for Eugenie to cope with.
Sonia's physical problems, Gideon's needs—which
were mounting daily and what else could you expect
when it comes to dealing with a prodigy?—mad
Jack's raving, Richard's second failure—"

"Second failure?"

"Another damaged child, if you can believe it.
He'd had an earlier one. From another marriage. So
when a second one was born . . . It was terrible for all
of them, but Eugenie couldn't see that it was normal
to feel the anguish at first, to curse God, to do whatever one *has* to do to get through a bad time. Instead,
she heard her bloody father's voice, 'God speaks to us
directly. There is no mystery in His message. Examine your soul and your conscience to read God's
handwriting therein, Eugenie.' That's what he wrote
to her, if you can believe it. That was his blessing and
comfort upon the birth of that pathetic little baby. As
if an infant were a punishment from God. And there
was no one to talk her out of feeling like that, do you

see? Oh there was the nun, but she talked about God's will as if the entire situation were predetermined and Eugenie was meant to understand that, accept it, not to rage against it, grieve about it, feel whatever despair she needed to feel and then just get *on* with life. So then when the baby died . . . and the way she died . . . I expect there were moments when Eugenie had actually thought, 'better she be dead than have to live like this, with doctors and operations and lungs going bad and heart barely beating and stomach not working and ears not hearing and not even being able to shit properly for the love of God . . . Better she be dead.' And then, she actually was dead. It was as if someone had heard her and granted a wish that wasn't a real wish at all but just an expression of one moment's despair. So what was she to feel but guilt? And what was she to do to make reparation but deny herself everything that might mean comfort?"

"Until Major Wiley came along," Lynley noted.

"I suppose so." Robson's words were hollow. "Wiley was a new beginning for her. Or at least that's how she said she thought of it."

"But you disagreed."

"I think he was just another form of imprisonment. But worse than before because he'd be wearing the guise of something new."

"So you argued about it."

"And then I wanted to apologise," Robson added. "I was desperate to apologise—don't you see—because we'd shared years of friendship, the two of us,

Eugenie and I, and I couldn't see sending them down the drain because of Wiley. I wanted her to know that. That's all. For whatever it was worth."

Lynley set these words against what he'd learned from both Gideon and Richard Davies. "She ended contact with her family long ago, but not with you, then? Were you once lovers with Mrs. Davies, Mr. Robson?"

Colour flared into Robson's face, an unattractive smearing of crimson that battled with the various patches of his damaged skin. "We met twice a month," he said in answer.

"Where?"

"In London. In the country. Wherever she wanted. She asked for news of Gideon, and I provided it. That was the extent of what she and I had together."

The pubs and hotels in her diary, Lynley thought. Twice each month. But it didn't make sense. Her meetings with Robson didn't follow the pattern that Robson himself described as being the path of Eugenie Davies' life. If she had been intent upon punishing herself for the transgression of human despair, for the unspoken wish—so horribly granted—to be delivered from the struggle to care for a fragile daughter, why had she even allowed herself news of her son, news that might comfort her, might keep her in touch? Wouldn't she have denied herself that?

There was a piece missing somewhere, Lynley concluded. And his instincts told him that Raphael Robson knew exactly what that missing piece was.

He said, "I can understand part of her behaviour, but I can't understand all of it, Mr. Robson. Why cut out contact with her family but maintain contact with you?"

"As I said. It was how she punished herself."

"For something she'd thought but never acted on?"

It seemed that the answer to this simple question should have come easily to Raphael Robson. Yes or no. He'd spent years knowing the dead woman, after all. He'd engaged in regular meetings with her. But Robson didn't answer at first. He took a plane from among the tools instead, and he appeared to examine it with his long and thin musician's hands.

"Mr. Robson?" Lynley said.

Robson moved across the room to a window so covered in dust that it looked nearly opaque. He said, "She'd sacked her. It was Eugenie's decision. That began everything. So she blamed herself."

Nkata looked up. "Katja Wolff?"

Robson said, "Eugenie was the one who said the German girl had to go. If she hadn't made that decision . . . if they hadn't rowed . . ." He made an aimless gesture. "We can't relive a single moment, can we? We can't unsay things, and we can't undo things. We can only sweep up the pieces of the mess we make of our miserable lives."

True enough, Lynley thought, but the statements were also useful generalities that weren't going to take them one inch closer to the truth. He said, "Tell me about that time, before the baby was murdered. As you remember it, Mr. Robson."

"Why? What's that got to do with——"

"Humour me."

"There isn't much to tell. It's a grubby little story. The German girl got herself pregnant, and she was badly out of sorts. She was sick each morning and half the time sick at noon and at night. Sonia demanded someone's full-time attention, but Katja couldn't give it. She couldn't eat without sicking everything up. She was up with Sonia night after night, and she was trying to sleep when she got the chance. But she slept when she was meant to be doing something else once too often, and Eugenie sacked her. She snapped, then, the German. Sonia fussed too much one evening. And that was that."

"Did you give evidence at the Wolff woman's trial?" Nkata asked.

"Yes. I was there. Yes. I gave evidence."

"Against her?"

"I just testified to what I'd seen, where I'd been, what I knew."

"For the prosecution?"

"Ultimately. I suppose. Yes." Robson shifted on his feet and waited for another question, his gaze on Lynley as Nkata wrote. When Lynley said nothing and the silence among them lengthened, Robson finally spoke. "What I'd seen was practically nothing. I'd been giving Gideon some instruction, and the first I knew that something was wrong was when Katja began screaming from the bathroom. People came charging from all corners of the house, Eugenie phoned emergency, Richard tried the kiss of life."

"And the fault went down to Katja Wolff," Nkata noted.

"There was too much chaos to find fault anywhere at first," Robson said. "Katja was screaming that she hadn't left the baby alone, so it seemed as if she'd had some sort of seizure and died in an instant when Katja's back was turned, when she was reaching for a towel. Something like that. Then she said she'd been on the phone for a minute or two. But that fell through when Katie Waddington denied it. Then came the post-mortem. It became clear how Sonia died and that there had been earlier . . . earlier incidents that no one knew about and . . ." He opened his hands as if saying, The rest is as it was.

Lynley said, "Wolff is out of prison, Mr. Robson. Have you heard from her?"

Robson shook his head. "I can't think she'd want to talk to me."

"Talking might not be what she has in mind," Nkata said.

Robson looked from him to Lynley. "You're thinking Katja might have killed Eugenie."

Lynley said, "The investigating officer from that period of time was hit last night as well."

"Good God."

"We're thinking everyone needs to have a care till we get to the bottom of what happened to Mrs. Davies," Lynley said. "She had something to tell Major Wiley, by the way. He's told us that much. Would you have any idea what that was?"

"None at all," Robson said, shaking his head but all

the same saying the words far too quickly for Lynley's liking. As if realising that the speed of his reply was more revealing than the reply itself, Robson went on to say, "If there was something she wanted to reveal to Major Wiley, she didn't tell me. You see, Inspector."

Lynley didn't see. At least he didn't see what Robson hoped he would see. Instead, he saw a man holding something back. He said, "As Mrs. Davies' close friend, I'd think there might be something you've not yet considered, Mr. Robson. If you reflect on your most recent meetings with her and especially the last one when the two of you rowed, I expect a detail like a chance remark might give us an indication of what she wanted to tell Major Wiley."

"There's nothing. Really. I can't say . . ."

Lynley pressed on. "If what she had to tell Major Wiley is the reason she was killed—and we can't dismiss that possibility, Mr. Robson—anything you can remember is vital."

"She might have wanted him to know about Sonia's death and what led up to her death. Perhaps she believed she needed to tell him why she'd left Richard and Gideon. She might have felt she needed his forgiveness for having done that before they could proceed with each other."

"Would that have been like her?" Lynley asked. "The confessional bit before carrying on with a relationship, I mean."

"Yes," Robson said, and his affirmation seemed genuine. "Confession would have been exactly like Eugenie."

Lynley nodded and thought this over. Part of it made sense, but he couldn't escape a simple fact that had announced itself through Robson's helpful revelation: They hadn't mentioned to Robson that Major Wiley had been in Africa twenty years ago and hence hadn't known the circumstances of Sonia Davies' death.

But if Robson knew that, he probably knew more. And whatever that more was, Lynley was willing to wager it led to the death in West Hampstead.

GIDEON

1 NOVEMBER

I OBJECT, Dr. Rose. I am not avoiding anything. You might question my pursuit of the truth with regard to my sister's death, you might remark that it serves the powerful interests of distraction for me to spend half a day to-ing and fro-ing round Cheltenham, and you might scrutinise my reasons for lolling round the Press Association office for another three hours, copying and reading the cuttings about the arrest and the trial of Katja Wolff. But you cannot accuse me of avoiding the very activity you yourself assigned me in the first place.

Yes, you told me to write what I remember, which is what I've done. And it seems to me that until I get beyond this business of my sister's death, it's going to throw up a roadblock to any other memories that I might have. So I may as well get through all this. I may as well learn what happened back then. If this endeavour is an elaborate subconscious foil to what I am supposed to remember—whatever the hell that

is—then we'll know that eventually, won't we? And
in the meantime, you'll be all the richer for the
countless appointments that you and I shall have had
together. I may even become your patient for life.

And don't *tell* me you sense my frustration, please,
because I'm *obviously* frustrated, because just when I
think I'm on to something, you sit there asking me to
think about the process of rationalisation and to ponder what that could mean in my current pursuit.

I'll tell you what rationalisation means: It means
that I am consciously or unconsciously side-stepping
the reason for my loss of music. It means that I am
setting up an elaborate maze to thwart your attempts
to help me.

So you see? I am completely aware of what I *might*
be doing. And now I ask you to let me do it.

I've been to Dad's. He wasn't there when I arrived,
but Jill was. She's decided to paint his kitchen, and
she'd brought a selection of paint cards with her,
which she'd spread out on the kitchen table. I told her
I'd come by to go through some old paperwork that
Dad keeps in the Granddad Room. She gave me one
of those conspiratorial looks that suggest two people
are in agreement on a subject that's going undis-
cussed, and from that I concluded that Dad's museum
of devotion to his father is going to be packed away
when he and Jill have a home of their own. She
won't have told Dad this, naturally. Jill's way is not to
be so direct.

To me she said, "I hope you've got your gum

boots with you." I smiled but made no reply, instead taking myself to the Granddad Room and closing the door behind me.

I don't frequent this spot very often. It makes me uneasy to surround myself with such overwhelming evidence of my father's devotion to his father. I suppose I think that Dad's fervour for his father's memory is somewhat misguided. True, Granddad survived a prison camp, countless deprivations, forced labour, torture, and conditions suited more to an animal than a man, but he ruled my father's life with derision—if not with an iron fist—both before and after the war, and I have never been able to understand why Dad clings to his memory instead of burying him once and for all. It was because of Granddad, after all, that our lives were defined as they were in Kensington Square: Dad's superhuman employment history was because Granddad could not support himself, his own wife, and their standard of living; Mother's going out to work—despite having given birth to a handicapped child—was because the income Dad brought in to care for his own parents and the house and my music and my education was not sufficient; my own pursuit of music was encouraged and supported financially in the first place because Granddad decreed it would be so . . . And on top of all this always I can hear Granddad's accusation: *Freaks, Dick! You produce nothing but freaks.*

So within the room, I avoided the display of Granddad memorabilia. I went instead to the desk from which Dad had taken the picture of Katja Wolff and Sonia, and I opened the first of its drawers, which was filled to the top with papers and folders.

What were you looking for? you ask me.

Something to make me certain about what happened. Because I'm *not* certain, Dr. Rose, and with every piece of information I dig up, I find myself becoming that much less certain.

I've remembered something about my parents and Katja Wolff. It's been triggered by my conversation with Sarah-Jane Beckett and by what followed my conversation, which was those additional hours in the Press Association library. I found a diagram among those cuttings, Dr. Rose, a drawing of sorts that showed the previously healed injuries that Sonia had sustained over time. There was a fractured clavicle. A dislocated hip. An index finger had healed from a break, and a wrist showed evidence of a hairline fracture. I felt nausea overcome me when I read all this. In my mind one question rang out: How could Sonia have been injured by Katja—by *anyone*—without the rest of us knowing that something had happened to her?

The papers said that under cross-examination, the prosecution's expert witness—a physician specialising in child abuse cases—admitted that an infant's bones, more easily given to fractures, are also more easily given to healing from those fractures without the intervention of a doctor. He admitted that, as he was not a specialist in the skeletal anomalies of the Down's Syndrome child, he could not deny that the fractures and dislocations that Sonia had sustained might have been connected to her disability. But under re-examination by the prosecution, he drove home the point that was central to his testimony: A child whose body is undergoing trauma is going to react to that trauma. For that reaction to go unnoticed and for that trauma to go untreated, someone is being derelict in his duty.

And still Katja Wolff said nothing. Given an opportunity to rise to her own defence—even to talk about Sonia's condition, her operations, and all the attendant problems she had that made her difficult and fussy and a source of nearly constant and inconsolable crying—Katja Wolff remained silent in the dock as the prosecutor for the Crown savaged her "callous indifference to the suffering of a child," her "single-minded self-interest," and "the animosity that had sprung up between the German and her employer."

And that's when I remembered, Dr. Rose.

We're having breakfast, which we eat in the kitchen and not the dining room. Only the four of us are present: Dad, my mother, Sonia, and I. I'm playing with my Weetabix, lining up slices of banana like cargo on a barge despite having been told to eat it and not to play, and Sonia is sitting in her high chair while Mother spoons baby food into her mouth.

Mother says, "We can't keep putting up with this, Richard," and I look up from my Weetabix barge because I think she's cross that I'm still not eating and I think I'm about to be scolded. But Mother continues. "She was out till half past one again. We gave her a curfew, and if she can't adhere to it—"

"She has to have some evenings off," Dad says.

"But not the following morning as well. We did have an agreement, Richard."

And I understand from this that Katja is meant to be with us at breakfast, is meant to be feeding Sonia. She has failed to get up and go to my sister, so Mother is doing Katja's job.

"We're *paying* her to care for the baby," Mother says. "Not to go dancing, not to go to the cinema, not to watch television, and certainly not to advance her love life under our roof."

That's what I've remembered, Dr. Rose, that remark about Katja's love life. And I've also remembered what my parents said next.

"She's not interested in anyone in this house, Eugenie."

"Please don't expect me to believe that."

I look between them—first at Dad then at my mother—and I feel something in the air that I can't identify, perhaps a sense of unease. And into this unease comes Katja in a rush. She is filled with apologies for having slept through her morning alarm.

"I please to feed the little one," she says in her English which must become more broken whenever she's under stress.

My mother says, "Gideon, would you take your cereal to the dining room, please?" and because of the undercurrents in the kitchen, I obey. But I pause to listen just out of sight and I hear my mother say, "We've already had one talk about your morning duties, Katja," and Katja says, "Please to let me feed the baby, Frau Davies," in a clear, firm voice.

It is the voice of someone unafraid of her employer, I realise now, Dr. Rose. And that voice suggests there are very good reasons for Katja not to be afraid.

So I went to my father's flat. I said my hellos to Jill. I dodged certificates, display cases, and trunks containing my grandfather's belongings, and I homed in on my grandmother's desk, which Dad has used as his for years.

I was looking for something that could confirm the connection between Katja and the man who'd made her pregnant. Because I'd finally come to see that if Katja Wolff maintained silence, she could have done so for only one possible reason: to protect someone. And that someone had to be my father, who had kept her photo for more than twenty years.

1 NOVEMBER, 4:00 P.M.

I did not progress far in my search.

In the drawer that I'd opened, I discovered an accordion file of correspondence. Among the letters therein—most of which comprised subjects having to do with my career—there was one from a solicitor with a North London address. Her client Katja Veronika Wolff had authorised Harriet Lewis, Esq., to contact Richard Davies with regard to monies owed her. Since the terms of her parole forbade her

to contact any member of the Davies family personally, Miss Wolff was using this legal channel as a con-
duit through which the matter could be satisfactorily
settled. If Mr. Davies would be so kind as to phone
Ms. Lewis at the above-listed number at his earliest
convenience, this matter of money could be handled
expeditiously and to everyone's satisfaction. Ms.
Lewis remained yours truly, et cetera.

I studied this letter. It was less than two months
old. The language in it did not appear to contain the
sort of veiled threat one would expect from a solicitor with future litigation on her mind. It was all
straightforward, pleasant, and professional. As such, it
fairly screamed the question *Why?*

I was pondering the possible answers to this question when Dad arrived at the flat. I heard him come
in. I heard his voice and Jill's coming from the
kitchen. Shortly afterwards, his footsteps marked his
progress from the kitchen to the Granddad Room.

When he opened the door, I was still sitting there
with the accordion file open on the floor at my feet
and the letter from Harriet Lewis in my hand. I made
no attempt to hide the fact that I was going through
my father's belongings, and when he crossed the
room, saying sharply, "What are you doing,
Gideon?" my reply was to hand him the letter and
say, "What's behind this, Dad?"

He flicked his gaze over it. He returned it to the
accordion file and returned the file to the drawer before he replied.

"She wanted to be paid for the time she spent in

remand prior to the trial," he said. "The first month of the remand period constituted the notice we'd given her, and she wanted her money for that month as well as interest on it."

"All these years later?"

"Perhaps a more pertinent remark would be: 'After she murdered Sonia?'" He pushed the desk drawer shut.

"She was very sure of her place with our family, wasn't she? She never expected to be sacked."

"You've no idea what you're talking about."

"Have you answered that letter, then? Have you phoned that solicitor as requested?"

"I've no intention of doing anything to revisit that period, Gideon."

I nodded at the drawer where he'd returned the letter. "Someone apparently doesn't think so. Not only that, but despite what someone's supposed to have done to devastate your life, someone apparently has no compunction about re-entering it even via a solicitor. I don't understand why, unless there was something more between you than employer and employee. Because don't you think a letter like that indicates a sense of confidence that someone in Katja Wolff's position ought not to have with regard to you?"

"What the hell are you getting at?"

"I've remembered my mother talking to you about Katja. I've remembered her suspicions."

"You've remembered rubbish."

"Sarah-Jane Beckett says James Pitchford wasn't

interested in Katja. She says he wasn't actually interested in women at all. That leaves him out of the
equation, Dad, which brings it down to you or
Granddad, the only other men in the house. Or
Raphael, I suppose, although I think both you and I
know where Raphael's true affections lay."

"What are you implying?"

"Sarah-Jane says Granddad was fond of Katja. She
says he hung about when she was nearby. But somehow I can't see Granddad managing more than calf-
love. And that leaves you."

"Sarah-Jane Beckett was a jealous cow," Dad
replied. "She set her sights on Pitchford the day she
walked into the house. One pear-shaped syllable out
of his heavily tutored mouth and she thought she'd
encountered the Second Coming. She was a social
climber of the first order, Gideon, and before Katja
entered our lives, nothing stood between her and the
top of the mountain, which was that fool Pitchford.
The last thing she'd have wanted was to see a relationship developing where she herself wanted one.
And I assume you have enough basic human psychology under your belt to be able to think that one
through."

I was forced to do just that, sifting back through
my time in Cheltenham to weigh what Sarah-Jane
had said, placing it in the balance against what Dad
was claiming now. Had there been a vindictive satisfaction in Sarah-Jane's comments about Katja Wolff?
Or had she simply tried to accommodate a request
that I myself had made? Surely, had I called upon her

with no desire other than to re-establish a connection with her, she wouldn't have brought up Katja or that period of time on her own. And didn't the very cause of jealousy dictate that the object of the passion be derided at every opportunity? So if it *was* base jealousy that she felt, wouldn't she have sought to bring up the subject of Katja Wolff herself? And no matter what Sarah-Jane had felt for Katja Wolff twenty years ago, why would she still be wallowing in that feeling now? Tucked away in Cheltenham in her smartly decorated house, wife, mother, collector of dolls, painter of competent if not inspired water colours, she had little need to dwell on the past, hadn't she?

Into my thoughts, Dad said roughly, "This has gone on long enough, Gideon," in a tone that brought an abrupt end to my reflections.

"What?" I said.

"This mucking about. This contemplation of your navel. I'm at my limit with it all. Come with me. We're going to deal with this head-on."

I thought he meant to tell me something I'd not yet heard, so I followed him. I expected him to take me into the garden, the better to have a confidential talk far out of earshot of Jill, who remained in the kitchen contentedly setting up paint samples along the window sill. But instead he went to the door of the flat, and from there to the street. He strode to his car that was parked midway between Braemar Mansions and Gloucester Road. He said, "Get in," as he unlocked it. And when I hesitated, "God damn it, Gideon. You heard me. Get the hell *in*."

I said, "Where are we going?" as he started the engine.

He jerked the car into reverse, negotiated his way out of the space, and gunned the motor. We shot up Gloucester Road in the direction of those wrought iron gates that mark the entrance to Kensington Gardens. "We're going where we should have gone in the first place," he replied.

He headed east along Kensington Road, driving in a way that I'd never seen him do. He veered round taxis and buses and once leaned on the horn when two women dashed across the street near the Albert Hall. A sharp left at Exhibition Road took us into Hyde Park. He gained even more speed along South Carriage Drive. It wasn't until we'd got beyond Marble Arch that I realised where he was taking me. But I said nothing till he'd finally parked the car in the Portman Square underground car park, where he always went when I performed nearby.

"What's the point in this, Dad?" I asked him, trying for patience where I had fear.

"You're going to get past this nonsense," he told me. "Are you man enough to come with me, or have you lost your bollocks along with your nerve?"

He shoved open his door and stood waiting for me. I felt my insides go liquid at the thought of what the next few minutes might hold. But I got out of the car anyway. And we walked side by side along Wigmore Street, heading in the direction of Wigmore Hall.

How did that feel? you ask me. What were you experiencing, Gideon?

I was experiencing heading there that night. Only that night I'd been alone because I'd come directly from Chalcot Square.

I'm walking along the street, and I haven't a *clue* what's in store for me. I'm nervous, but not more than usual before a performance. I've mentioned that, haven't I? My nerves? Funny, I can't remember having nerves when I *ought* to have had them: performing in public the very first time as a six-year-old, performing several times thereafter as a seven-year-old, playing for Perlman, meeting Menuhin . . . What was it about me, then? How was I so capable of taking things in my stride? I lost that naïve confidence somewhere along the line. So this night on the way to Wigmore Hall is no different to all those other nights I've lived through, and my expectation is that the nervous anticipation that precedes this concert will pass as it usually does, the moment I lift the Guarneri and the bow.

I walk along, and I think about the music, revisiting it in my head as I usually do. I haven't had a flawless rehearsal of this piece—never have had one—but I'm telling myself that muscle memory will guide my playing past the sections that have given me difficulty.

Particular sections? you ask. The same sections each time?

No. That's what's always been so peculiar about *The Archduke.* I never know which part of the piece is going to trip me up. It's been a field not cleared of landmines, and no matter how slowly I've progressed over the rough terrain, I've always managed to encounter an explosive.

So I move along the street, dimly hear the after-work crowd at one of the pubs I pass, and think about my music. My fingers actually find the notes, although I carry the Guarneri in its case, and in doing this, they somewhat calm my anxiety, which I mistakenly take as a sign that all will be well.

I arrive ninety minutes early. Just before I round the corner to access the artists' entrance behind the concert hall, I can see up ahead extending over the pavement the covered-glass entry of the hall itself, peopled at this moment only by pedestrians hurrying home from work. I run through the first ten measures of the Allegro. I tell myself what a simple good thing it is, really, to play music with two friends like Beth and Sherrill. I have no idea of what will happen to me in those ninety minutes that are left of my career. I am, if you will, an innocent lamb on his way to be slaughtered, without a sense of peril and somehow lacking the ability to scent blood in the air.

On the way to the hall with Dad, I recalled all this. But there was no real immediacy to my trepidation because I knew already how the next few minutes would play out.

As I did that night, we rounded the corner into Welbeck Street. We hadn't spoken since emerging from the underground car park. I took Dad's silence to mean grim determination. He probably took mine as acquiescence to the plan instead of resignation to what I knew would be the outcome.

At Welbeck Way, we turned again, walking towards the red double doors above which the words *artistes entrance* are hewn into the stone pediment. I was thinking about the fact that Dad hadn't pondered his plan quite through. There would probably be people in the ticket booth at the front of the hall, but at this time of day the artists' entrance would be locked with no one near it to open it should we knock. So if Dad really wanted me to relive that night of *The Archduke,* he was going at it wrong, and he was about to be thwarted.

I was on the point of telling him this when my steps faltered, Dr. Rose. First they faltered, then they stopped altogether, and nothing on earth could have prompted me to continue walking.

Dad took my arm and said, "You won't get anywhere by running away, Gideon."

He thought I was afraid, of course, overcome by anxiety, and unwilling to place myself into the jeopardy that the music ostensibly represented. But it wasn't fear that paralysed me. It was what I saw right in front of me, what I couldn't believe I hadn't been able to dredge out of my mind before this moment, despite the number of times that I had played at Wigmore Hall in the past.

The blue door, Dr. Rose. The same blue door that has flashed periodically in my memory and in my dreams. It stands at the top of a flight of ten stairs, right next to the artists' entrance for Wigmore Hall.

1 NOVEMBER, 10:00 P.M.

It's identical to the door I've seen in my mind: bright blue, cerulean blue, the blue of a Highland summer sky. It has a silver ring in the centre, two security locks, and a fanlight above it. Beneath that window is a lighting fixture, mounted centrally above the door. There is a railing along the stairs, and this is painted like the door itself: that bright, clear, unforgettable blue that I had forgotten nonetheless.

I saw that the door appeared to lead to a residence: There were windows next to it, with curtains hanging in them, and from below in Welbeck Way I could see that there were pictures of some sort hanging high on the walls. I felt a surge of excitement the likes of which I haven't felt in months—perhaps in years—as I realised that behind that door might very well lie the explanation for what had happened to me, the cause of my troubles, and the cure.

I jerked myself out of Dad's grasp and bounded up those steps. Just as you have told me to do in my imagination, Dr. Rose, I tried that door, although I could see before I did so that it could be opened only from the exterior by means of a key. So I knocked upon it. I *pounded* upon it.

There my hopes for rescue ended. For the door was opened by a Chinese woman so small that at first I thought she was a child. I also thought she was wearing gloves till I saw that her hands were covered in flour. I had never seen her before.

She said, "Yes?" and looked at me politely. When I said nothing, her gaze shifted down to my father, who waited at the foot of the steps. "May I help you?" she asked, and she moved subtly as she spoke, placing her hip and the bulk of her weight—what little of it there was—behind the door.

I had no idea what to ask her. I had no idea why her front door had been haunting me. I had no idea why I'd gone bolting up the steps so *sure* of myself, so damnably certain that I was nearing an end to my troubles.

So I said, "Sorry. Sorry. There's been a mistake," although I added in what I already knew was a fruitless possibility, "Do you live here alone?"

Certainly, I knew this was the wrong question the moment after I asked it. What woman in her right mind is going to tell a strange man on her doorstep that she lives alone even if she *does*? But before she could offer a reply to the question, I heard a man's voice asking from somewhere behind her, "Who is that, Sylvia?" and I had my answer. I had more than that, because a moment after he asked the question, the man swung the door open wider and peered out. And I didn't know him any more than I knew Sylvia: a large, bald gentleman with hands the size of most people's skulls.

"Sorry. Wrong address," I told him.

"Who d'you want?" he asked.

"I don't know," I replied.

Like Sylvia, he looked from me to my father. He said, "Not the way it sounded from the thrashing you gave to the door just now."

"Yes. I'd thought . . ." What had I thought? That I was about to be given the gift of clarity? I suppose so.

But there was no clarity in Welbeck Way. And when I said to Dad later, once the blue door was closed upon us, "It's part of the answer. I swear that it's part," his reply was a thoroughly disgusted, "You don't even know the damn question."

EIGHTEEN

L YNN DAVIES?" Barbara Havers produced her
warrant card for the woman who'd answered the
door of the yellow stucco building. It stood at the end
of a line of terraced houses in Therapia Road, a split-
level Victorian conversion in an East Dulwich quad-
rant that Barbara had discovered was defined by two
cemeteries, a park, and a golf course.

"Yes," the woman replied, but she said the word as
a question, and she cocked her head to one side, puzzled, when she looked at Barbara's identification. She
was Barbara's own height—which made her short—
but her body looked fit under her simple clothing of
blue jeans, trainers, and a fisherman's sweater. She
would be the sister-in-law of Eugenie Davies, Barbara concluded, for Lynn looked about the same age
as the dead woman, although the wiry hair that
spilled round her shoulders and down her back was
only just beginning to grey.

"Could I have a word?" Barbara asked her.

"Yes, yes, of course." Lynn Davies opened the
door wider and admitted Barbara into an entrance

whose floor was covered by a small hooked rug. An umbrella stand stood in a corner there, next to it a rattan coat rack from which two identical rain slickers hung, both bright yellow and edged in black. She led Barbara to a sitting room, where a bay window overlooked the street. In the alcove that the window comprised, an easel held a heavy sheet of white paper that bore smears of colour in the unmistakable style of finger painting. More sheets of paper—these completed works of art—hung on the walls of the alcove, stuck higgledy piggledy with drawing pins. The sheet on the easel was not a finished work, but it was dry, and it looked as if the artist had been startled in the midst of its creation, for three fingers of paint lurched down towards one corner while the rest of the piece was done in happy, irregular swirls.

Lynn Davies said nothing as Barbara gave a look towards the alcove. She merely waited quietly.

Barbara said to her, "You're related to Eugenie Davies by marriage, I expect."

To which Lynn Davies said, "Not quite. What's this about, Constable?" and her brow furrowed in apparent concern. "Has something happened to Eugenie?"

"You're not Richard Davies' sister?"

"I was Richard's first wife. Please. Tell me. I'm getting rather frightened. Has something happened to Eugenie?" She clasped her hands in front of her, tightly, so that her arms made a perfect V along her torso. "Something must have done, because why else would you be here?"

Barbara readjusted her thinking, from Richard's sister to Richard's first wife to everything implied by *Richard's first wife*. She watched Lynn closely as she explained the whys and wherefores of New Scotland Yard's visit.

Lynn was olive-skinned, with darker crescents like coffee stains under her deep brown eyes. This skin paled slightly when she learned about the details of the hit-and-run in West Hampstead. She said, "Dear God," and walked to an ancient three-piece suite. She sat, staring in front of her but saying to Barbara, "Please . . ." then nodding to the armchair next to which stood a neat pile of children's books, *How the Grinch Stole Christmas* placed seasonably on the top.

"I'm sorry," Barbara said. "I can see it's a shock."

"I didn't know," Lynn said. "And it must have been in the papers, mustn't it? Because of Gideon. And because of . . . of how you say she died. But I didn't see them—the papers—because I've not been coping as well as I thought I would and . . . Oh God. Poor Eugenie. To have it all end like this."

This didn't seem at all to be the reaction of an embittered first wife thrown over for a second. Barbara said, "You knew her quite well, then."

"I've known Eugenie for years."

"When did you see her last?"

"Last week. She came to the service for my daughter. That's why I haven't seen . . . why I didn't know . . ." Lynn rubbed the palm of her right hand hard against her thigh, as if this action could quell something within her. "Virginia, my daughter, died quite suddenly last week, Constable. I knew it could happen at any time. I'd known that for years. But somehow one is never quite as prepared as one hopes to be."

"I'm sorry," Barbara said.

"She was painting as she did each afternoon. I was in the kitchen making our tea. I heard her fall. I came running out. And that was . . . What do they call it, Constable? *It*. The great, long-expected visitation arrived, and I wasn't with her. I wasn't even there to say goodbye."

Like Tony, Barbara thought, and it jolted her to have her brother shoot into her mind when she hadn't prepared herself to greet him. It was just like Tony, who had died alone without a single member of the family at his bedside. She didn't like to think about Tony, about his lingering death or the hell that his death had brought into her family. She said only, "Kids aren't meant to die before their parents, are they," and she felt an attendant tightness in her throat.

"The doctors said she was dead before she hit the floor," Lynn Davies told her. "And I know they mean to comfort me. But when you've spent most of your life caring for a child like Virginia—always and forever a little one no matter how large she grew—your world is still wrenched to pieces when she's taken, especially if you've simply stepped out of the room to see to her tea. So I haven't been able to read a paper—much less a novel or a magazine—and I haven't turned on the telly or the radio because although I'd like to distract myself, if I do that there's a chance I'll stop feeling and what I feel right now—at this moment, if you can understand what I'm saying—is how I stay connected to her. If you can understand." Lynn's eyes filled as she spoke.

Barbara gave her a moment as she herself adjusted to what she was learning. Among the information she was indexing in her mind was the unimaginable fact that Richard Davies had apparently fathered not one but two disabled children. For what else could Lynn Davies possibly mean when she described her daughter as "forever a little one"? "Virginia wasn't—" There *had* to be a euphemism somewhere, Barbara thought with frustration, and if she were from America—that great land of political correctness— she would probably have known it. "She wasn't well?" she settled on saying.

"My daughter was retarded from birth, Constable. She had the body of a woman and the mind of a two-year-old child."

"Oh. Hell. I'm sorry to hear that."

"Her heart wasn't right. We knew from the first it would fail her eventually. But her spirit was strong, so she surprised everyone and lived thirty-two years."

"Here at home with you?"

"It wasn't an easy life for either of us. But when I consider what might have been, I have no regrets. I gained more than I lost when my marriage ended. And ultimately, I couldn't blame Richard for asking for the divorce."

"And then he remarried and had another . . ." Again, there was no useful catch phrase. Lynn sup-

plied her own, saying, "A child imperfect as we measure perfection. Yes. Richard had another, and those
who believe in a vengeful God might argue that he
was being punished for having abandoned us, Virginia and me. But I don't think that's how God
works. Richard wouldn't have asked us to leave in
the first place if I'd only agreed to have more children."

"*Asked* you to leave?" What a prince among men,
Barbara thought. Here was something for a bloke to
be proud of: having asked his wife and his retarded
child to find themselves new digs.

Lynn hastened to explain. "We lived with his parents, in the house he himself had grown up in. So
when it came time to part, it didn't make sense that
Virginia and I should stay with Richard's parents
while Richard left. And, anyway, that was part of the
problem: Richard's parents. His father was completely unmoveable on the subject of Virginia. He
wanted her put away. He insisted on it. And Richard
was . . . It was so important to him to have his father's
approval. So he was won over to that way of thinking, about putting Virginia into a home. But I
wouldn't hear of it. After all, this was . . ." Her eyes
again showed her pain, and she stopped for a moment
before saying with simple dignity, "She was our child.
She hadn't asked to be born the way she was. Who
were we to think we could chuck her away? And
that's what Richard himself thought at first. Until his
father brought him round." She looked again to the
alcove, to the bright smeared paintings that decorated

it, saying, "He was a terrible man, Jack Davies was. I know he'd suffered horribly in the war. I know his mind was a ruin and he couldn't be blamed for the ugliness inside him. But to hate an innocent child so much that she wasn't allowed to be in the room with him . . . ? That was wrong, Constable. That was terribly wrong."

"It sounds like hell," Barbara acknowledged.

"A form of it. 'Thank God she doesn't spring from *my* blood,' he used to say. And Richard's mother would murmur, 'Jack, Jack, you don't actually mean that,' when all the time you could see that if there was a single way that he could wipe Virginia's existence from this planet, he would have gladly made the attempt without a second thought." Lynn's lips trembled. "And now she's gone. Wouldn't Jack be happy now." She shoved her hand into the pocket of her blue jeans and brought out a crumpled tissue, which she pressed beneath her eyes, saying, "I'm terribly sorry. Forgive me for running on in this way. I shouldn't be . . . God, how I miss her."

"It's okay," Barbara said. "You're trying to cope."

"And now Eugenie," Lynn Davies said. "How can I help with what's happened to Eugenie? I expect that's why you've come, isn't it? Not just to tell me but to ask for my help?"

"You and Mrs. Davies had a bond, I expect. Through your children."

"Not at first. It was when her little Sonia died that we met. Eugenie simply turned up on my doorstep one day. She wanted to talk. I was happy to listen."

"You saw her regularly, then?"

"Yes. She dropped round often. She needed to talk—what mother wouldn't in those circumstances?—and I was glad to be here for her. She felt she couldn't talk to Richard, you see, and while there was a Catholic nun she was close to, the nun wasn't a mother, was she? And that's what Eugenie needed: another mother to talk to, and especially the mother of a special child. She was grieving terribly, and there was no one in that household who could understand how she felt. But she knew about me and she knew about Virginia because Richard had told her shortly after they married."

"Not before they married? That's odd."

Lynn smiled resignedly. "That's Richard, Constable Havers. He paid maintenance till Virginia reached adulthood, but he never saw her once she and I left him. I did think he might come to the funeral. I let him know when she died. But he sent flowers and that was that."

"Brilliant," Barbara muttered.

"He is who he is. Not a bad man, but not a man equipped to cope with a handicapped child. And not everyone is. At least I'd had some practical training in nursing, while Richard . . . well, what did he have but his brief career in the Army? And anyway, he wanted to carry on the family name, which meant, naturally, that he would have to find a second wife. And that actually turned out to be the right thing to do, didn't it, because Eugenie gave him Gideon."

"The jackpot."

"In a way. But I expect the burden of giving birth to a prodigy is an enormous one. A different set of responsibilities but just as heavy."

"Eugenie didn't say?"

"She never spoke much of Gideon. And then, when she and Richard divorced, she never spoke of Gideon at all. Or of Richard. Or of any of them. Mostly, when she came, she helped me with Virginia. She loved the parks, Virginia did, the cemeteries as well. It was our special joy to take a ramble in Camberwell Old Cemetery. But I didn't like to do it without someone else with us, to help keep an eye on Virginia. If I was there with her alone, I had to fix my attention on her and I got no pleasure from the afternoon. But with Eugenie there, it was easier. She would watch her. I would watch her. We could talk, bask in the sun, read the gravestones. She was very good to us."

"Did you speak to her the day of Virginia's funeral?" Barbara asked.

"Of course. Yes. But we didn't speak of anything that could help your enquiry, I'm afraid. Just about Virginia. The loss. How I was coping. Eugenie was a great comfort to me. Indeed, she'd been a comfort for years. And Virginia . . . She actually came to *know* Eugenie. To recognise her. To—" Lynn stopped. She rose and went to the alcove where she stood in front of the easel on which her daughter's final painting marked her quick passage from life into death. She said in a contemplative voice, "Yesterday I did several of these myself. I wanted to *feel* what had given her

such joy. But I couldn't reach that place. I tried painting after painting till my hands were black from all
the colours I'd mixed together, and still I couldn't feel
it. So I finally saw how blessed she actually had been:
to be eternally a child who asked so little of life."

"There's a lesson in that," Barbara agreed.

"Yes. Isn't there." She studied the painting.

Barbara stirred in her seat, wanting to bring Lynn
Davies back. She said, "Eugenie'd been seeing a bloke
in Henley, Mrs. Davies. A retired Army bloke called
Ted Wiley. He owns the bookshop across the street
from her house. Did she ever speak of him?"

Lynn Davies turned from the painting. "Ted
Wiley? A bookshop? No. She never talked of Ted
Wiley."

"Of anyone else she might have been involved
with?"

Lynn thought about this. "She was careful with
what she revealed about herself. She'd always been
that way. But I think . . . I don't know if this is any
help, but the last time we spoke—this would be before I rang to tell her about Virginia's passing—she
mentioned . . . Well, I don't know if it actually meant
anything. At least I don't know if it meant she'd become involved."

"It might be of help," Barbara told her. "What did
she say?"

"It wasn't so much what she said but the way she
said it. There was a lightness to her voice that I'd
never heard before. She asked me if I believed that
one could fall in love where one wasn't expecting to

find love. She asked me if I thought that years could pass and one could suddenly look upon someone in a light entirely different from the way one had looked on him in the past. She asked me if I thought love could grow from that, from that new way of looking. Could she have been talking about the Army man with that? Someone she'd known for years but never thought of as a lover till now?"

Barbara wondered about this. It did seem likely. But there was something more to consider: Eugenie Davies' whereabouts at the time of her death and the address in her possession suggested something else.

She said, "Did she ever mention James Pitchford?"

Lynn shook her head.

"What about Pitchley? Or Pytches, perhaps?"

"She didn't mention anyone by name. But that's how she was: a very private person."

A very private person who'd ended up murdered, Barbara thought. And she wondered if the dead woman's need for privacy was at the core of her killing.

DCI ERIC LEACH listened to the sister in charge of the intensive care unit at Charing Cross Hospital as she essentially told him the worst. *No change* was what they said when the doctors were handing over the reins of someone's condition to God, fate, nature, or time. It was not what they said when someone made some sort of gain, side-stepped the grim reaper, or achieved a sudden and miraculous recovery. Leach hung up the phone and turned from his desk, brooding. He brooded not only over what had happened to Malcolm Webberly but also over his own inadequacies and what they were doing to his ability to anticipate the investigation's twists and turns.

He had to deal with the problem of Esmé. That much was clear. How to deal with it would come to him soon. But *that* he had to deal with it was obvious. Because had he not been distracted by Esmé's fears about her mum's new boyfriend—not to mention by his own feelings about Bridget having found a replacement for him—he surely would have remembered that J. W. Pitchley, AKA James Pitchford, had also once been Jimmy Pytches, whose ties to an infant's death in Tower Hamlets had long ago been the subject of the London tabloids' delight. Not when that infant died, of course, that situation having sorted itself out soon enough after the post-mortem. But years later, after another child died in Kensington.

Once that pug-like Yard woman had revealed this titbit, Leach had remembered it all. He'd tried to tell himself that he'd deleted the information from his memory banks because it hadn't amounted to anything but aggro for Pitchford during the investigation into the Davies baby's death. But the truth was, he should have remembered it, and it was down to Bridget and Bridget's boyfriend and especially Esmé's anxiety over Bridget's boyfriend that he hadn't. And he couldn't afford not to remember what he needed to remember about that long-ago case. Because it was seeming to him more and more probable that that case had a link to this one, which was unlikely to be easily severed.

A PC popped his head into his office doorway, saying, "We've got that bloke from West Hampstead you were asking for, sir. D'you want him in an interview room?"

"Got his brief with him?"

"What else? I don't expect he takes a dump in the morning without checking with his solicitor to see how many sheets of toilet paper he's got a right to use."

"Make it an interview room, then," Leach said. He didn't like allowing solicitors to think they'd somehow intimidated him, and showing Pitchley-Pitchford-Pytches into his office felt like something that would do just that.

He took a few minutes to make the call that would release Pitchley's motor to him. There was nothing more to be gained by holding the Boxter, and it seemed to Leach that their possession of past details about James Pitchford and Jimmy Pytches was more likely to chisel information from the man than was their continuing to hold on to his car.

After the call, he grabbed a cup of coffee and went to the interview room where Pitchley-Pitchford-Pytches—Leach was beginning to think of him as P-Man for simple ease of keeping track of all his names—and his solicitor were waiting, seated at the interview table. Azoff was smoking despite the posted sign expressly forbidding it, his way of sneering "bugger you for ten pence," while P-Man was working his hands through his hair like someone trying to rolf his brain.

"I've advised my client to say nothing," Azoff began, eschewing anything that might have done for a greeting. "He's cooperated thus far with no sign on your part of recompensing him in any way."

"Recompensing?" Leach said incredulously. "What d'you think this is, man? We're running a murder enquiry here, and if we need your boy to assist us, we're going to bloody well have him."

"I see no reason to carry on with these meetings if he's not going to be charged with something," Azoff countered.

At which P-Man looked up, mouth open, his face a veritable picture of "what the hell are you *saying,* you berk?" Leach liked this, because a man who was innocent of everything even remotely related to a case under investigation would hardly look at his solicitor like a back-alley thug with a garrote in his hand just because the lawyer said the words "charge him." A man who was innocent would wear an expression saying, "Yeah. Got *that,* Jack?" and he'd direct that expression at the cop. But P-Man wasn't doing that, which made Leach more certain than ever that he needed to be broken. He wasn't sure what breaking him would actually gain them, but he was more than willing to try it.

He said, "Well. Right. Mr. Pytches," quite affably.

To which Azoff said, "Pitchley," with an irritation that he underscored with a gust of tobacco smoke blown into the air, carrying on it the accompanying olfactory tincture of advanced halitosis.

Leach said, "Ah. Doesn't know it all, then, does he?" to P-Man with a nod at the solicitor. "Got some nooks and crannies in the skeleton cupboard you've not shone a torch into, yes?"

P-Man sank his head into his hands, body language for his sudden realisation that his bollixed-up life had just become a degree more bollixed up. "I've told you everything I can tell you," he said, side-stepping the Jimmy Pytches issue. "I've not seen that woman—I've not seen *any* of them—since six months after the trial. I moved on. Well, what else could I do? New house, new life—"

"New name," Leach said. "Just like before. But Mr. Azoff here doesn't seem to know that a bloke like you with a past like yours has a way of getting sucked into events, Mr. Pytches. Even when he thinks he's weighted that past in concrete boots and chucked it into the Thames."

"What the hell are you on about, Leach?" Azoff said.

"Get rid of that shit burner you've got in your mouth, and I'll do what I can to elucidate," Leach answered. "This is a non-smoking area, and I presume that reading is one of your talents, Mr. Azoff."

Azoff took his time about removing the cigarette from his mouth, and he took even more time to dislodge its ash against the sole of his shoe, carefully so as to preserve the remaining tobacco for his later pleasure. During this performance, P-Man, unbidden, unspooled most of his story for the solicitor. At the end of a recitation that was as brief and as positively slanted as possible, P-Man said, "I've not mentioned this cot-death business before because there was no need, Lou. And there's *still* no need. Or at least there wouldn't be if this"—a jerk of his head at Leach indicated that the demonstrative pronoun was as close as P-Man intended to come to dignifying Leach's presence by actually giving him a name—"hadn't made up his mind to something that bears no relationship whatsoever to the truth."

"Pytches," Azoff said, and while he sounded thoughtful as he said the name, his narrowing eyes suggested that his thoughts had less to do with absorbing a new piece of information than they had to do with what he planned as a disciplinary measure for a client who continued to withhold facts from him, making him look like a fool each time he was forced to face the police. "You say *another* kid who died, Jay?"

"Two kids and a woman," Leach reminded him. "And counting, by the way. Another victim got hit last night. Where were you, Pytches?"

"That's not fair!" P-Man cried. "I haven't seen a single one of those people . . . I haven't talked to . . . I don't know *why* she had my address with her . . . And I certainly don't believe—"

"Last night," Leach repeated.

"Nothing. *Nowhere.* At home. Where the hell else would I be when you've got my car?"

"Picked up by someone, perhaps," Leach said.

"Who? Someone I supposedly joined for a nice dash round London for a quick hit-and-run?"

"I don't think I mentioned it was hit-and-run."

"Don't make yourself out to be so bloody clever. You said another victim. You said another hit. You can't expect me to think you meant hitting someone with a cricket bat, can you? Else why would I be here?"

He was getting hot under the collar. Leach liked that. He also liked the fact that P-Man's brief was just cheesed off enough to let him twist in the wind for a minute or two. That could be distinctly useful.

He said, "Good question, Mr. Pytches."

"Pitchley," P-Man said.

"What have you seen of Katja Wolff lately?"

"Kat—" P-Man halted himself. "What about Katja Wolff?" he asked, quietly cautious.

"I had a look through ancient history this morning and I found you never gave evidence at her trial."

"I wasn't asked to give evidence. I was in the house, but I didn't see anything and there was no reason—"

"But the Beckett woman did. The boy's teacher. Sarah-Jane she was called. My notes—have I mentioned that I keep all my records from investigations?—show that you and she were together when the kid got the chop. You were together, which must mean you both saw everything or nothing at all, but in any event—"

"I didn't see *anything*."

"—in any event," Leach continued forcefully, "Beckett gave evidence while you stayed mum. Why was that?"

"She was the boy's teacher. Gideon. The brother. She saw more of the family. She saw more of the little girl. She saw what kind of care Katja gave her, so she must have thought she had something to contribute. And listen, I wasn't *asked* to give evidence. I spoke to the police, I gave my statement, I waited for more but I wasn't asked."

"Convenient, that."

"Why? Are you trying to suggest—"

"Plug it," Azoff said finally. And to Leach, "Get to the point or we're off."

"Not without my motor," P-Man said.

Leach fished in his jacket pocket and brought out the release form for the Boxter. He laid it on the table between himself and the two other men. He said, "You were the only one from that house who didn't give evidence against her, Mr. Pytches. I'd think she'd've dropped by to say thank you now that she's out of the coop."

"What're you *on* about?" P-Man cried.

"Beckett gave character evidence. Talked to us and to everyone else about which wires in Wolff's circuits were fraying. Bit of temper here. Dash of impatience there. Other things to do when the baby wanted a bit of looking after. Not always on her toes the way a properly trained nanny would be. And then getting herself in the club . . ."

"Yes? So? What about it?" P-Man said. "Sarah-

Jane saw more than I saw. She talked about that. Am I supposed to be her conscience or something? Twenty-odd years after the fact?"

Azoff intervened. "We're looking for a point to this confab, DCI Leach. If there isn't one, we'll have that paperwork and be off." He reached for it.

Leach pressed his fingers along its edge. "The point is Katja Wolff," he said. "And our boy's ties to her."

"I have no ties to her," P-Man protested.

"I'm not sure about that. Someone got her pregnant, and I'm not putting a fiver on the Holy Ghost."

"Don't put that down to me. We lived in the same house. That's all. We nodded on the staircase. I might have given her the odd lesson with her English and, yes, I might have *admired*— Look. She was attractive. She was sure of herself, confident, not the way you'd expect a foreigner who didn't even speak the language to feel or act. That's always nice to see in a woman. And for God's sake. I'm not blind."

"Had a bit of a thing with her, then. Tip-toeing round the house at night. Once or twice behind the garden shed, and oops, look what happened."

Azoff slapped his hand on the table between them. He said, "Once, twice, eighty-five times. If you're not intending to talk about the case in hand, we're off. You got that?"

"This *is* the case in hand, Mr. Azoff, especially if our boy spent the last twenty years brooding about a woman he diddled and then didn't do a thing to help once she'd—A—got herself up the spout thanks to him and—B—got herself charged with murder. He

might want to make amends for that. And what better way than to give a hand in a spot of revenge.
Which *she* might think she's owed, by the way. Time
passes a bit slow inside, you know. And you'd be dead
surprised to see the way that slow time makes a killer
decide *she's* the injured party."

"That's . . . that is *utterly* . . . that's preposterous,"
P-Man sputtered.

"Is it?"

"You know it is. What's supposed to have happened?"

"Jay—" Azoff counseled.

"She's supposed to have tracked me down, rung
my bell one night, and said, 'Hello, Jim. Know we
haven't seen each other for twenty, but how about
helping me rub out a few people? Just for a laugh, this
is. Not too busy, are you?' Is that how you picture it,
Inspector?"

"Shut up, Jay," Azoff said.

"No! I've spent half my life scouring down the
walls when *I'm* not the one who's pissed on them,
and I'm tired of it. I'm God damn bloody tired. If it's
not the police, then it's the papers. If it's not the papers, it's—" He stopped himself.

"Yes?" Leach leaned forward. "Who is it, then?
What's the nasty you've got back there, Mr. P? Something beyond that cot death, I reckon. You're a real
man of mystery, you are. And I'll tell you this much:
I'm not finished with you."

P-Man sank back in his chair, his throat working.
Azoff said, "Odd. I don't hear a caution, Inspector.

Forgive me if I lapsed into momentary unconscious-
ness sometime during this meeting, but I don't recall
having heard a caution yet. And if I *won't* be hearing
one in the next fifteen seconds, it's my suggestion that
we make our farewells to each other now, heartrend-
ing though those farewells may be."

Leach shoved the Boxter's paperwork at them. He
said, "Don't plan any holidays, Mr. P." And to Azoff,
"Keep that fag unlit till you're on the street or I'll
have you in for something."

"Cor. Blimey. I'm ackshully pissing me pants,
guv'nor," Azoff said.

Leach started to speak, then stopped himself. Then
he said, "Get out," and saw to it that they did just
that.

J. W. PITCHLEY, AKA TongueMan, AKA James
Pitchford, AKA Jimmy Pytches said his goodbye to
Lou Azoff in front of the Hampstead Police Station,
and he knew that this was a final one. Azoff was
cheesed off about the Jimmy Pytches revelation,
more cheesed off than he'd been by the James Pitchford revelation, and despite the fact that he'd been
declared blameless of the death of both children first
as Pytches and then as Pitchford, that wasn't "the issue," as Azoff put it. He wasn't about to put himself
in the position of getting sucker-punched again by
something that his client was withholding from him,
Azoff said. How'd he think it felt, sitting in there with
a sodding copper who'd probably not even passed his
bleeding O levels for Christ's sake, and having the rug

pulled out without even knowing there was a rug in the room? This effing situation wasn't *on*, Jay. Or is it James? Or Jimmy? Or someone else, for that matter?

It wasn't someone else. He wasn't someone else. And even if Azoff hadn't said, "You'll get my final bill by special courier tomorrow," he himself would have put the full stop to their legal dealings. No matter that he handled the labyrinth that was Azoff's tricky financial position. He could find someone else in the City equally talented at moving Azoff's money round faster than the Inland Revenue could track it.

So he said, "Right, Lou," and he didn't bother to try to talk the solicitor out of quitting on him. He couldn't blame the poor sod, really. Who could expect someone to want to play defence on a team that wouldn't give directions to the pitch?

He watched Azoff wind his scarf round his neck and fling its end over his shoulder, like the denouement of a play that had already gone on far too long. The solicitor made his exit, and Pitchley sighed. He could have told Azoff that sacking him had not only already crossed his mind but had also planted itself there half way through the interview with DCI Leach, but he decided to let the solicitor have his moment. The drama of quitting on the streets of Hampstead was meagre compensation for having endured the ignominy of ignorance to which Pitchley's omission of certain facts had recently exposed him. But it was all that Pitchley had to offer at the moment, so he offered it and stood, head bowed, while Azoff railed and till Azoff did his bit with the scarf. "I'll get on to a bloke I know who'll see you right with your money," he told the solicitor.

"You do just that," Azoff said. He made no similar offer on his part: recommending another solicitor willing to take on a client who asked him to work in the dark. But then, Pitchley didn't expect that of him. Indeed, he'd given up expecting anything.

That hadn't always been the case, although if it couldn't be said that he'd had expectations years ago, it *could* be said that he'd possessed dreams. She'd told him hers in that breathless, confiding, cheerful whisper, after hours when they had their English lessons and their chats at the top of the house, one ear to the speaker from the baby's room so that if she stirred, if she cried, if she needed her Katja, her Katja would be there, fast as could be. She said, "There are these fashion-for-clothes schools, yes? For design of what to wear. Yes? You see? And you see how I make these fashion drawings, yes? This is where I study when the money is saved. Where I come from, James, clothing . . . Oh, I cannot say, but your colours, your *colours* . . . And see at this scarf I have bought. This is Oxfam, James. Someone *gave* it away!" And she would bring it out and whirl it like an eastern dancer, a length of worn silk with fringe coming loose but to her a fabric to be turned into a sash, a belt, a drawstring bag, a hat. Two such scarves and she had a blouse. Five and a motley skirt emerged. "This I am meant to do," she would say, and her eyes were bright and her cheeks were flushed and the rest of her skin was velvet milk. All London wore black, but never Katja. Katja was a rainbow, a celebration of life.

And because of all that, he had dreams himself. Not plans as she had, not something spoken, but something held on to like a feather that will soil and be useless for flight if grasped too tightly or for too long.

He wouldn't move quickly, he'd told himself. They were both young. She had her schooling ahead of her and he wanted to establish himself in the City before taking on the sort of responsibilities that came with marriage. But when the time was right . . . Yes, she was the one. So completely different, so completely capable of *becoming,* so eager to learn, so willing—no, so *desperate*—to escape who she'd been in order to achieve who she believed she could become. She was, in effect, his female counterpart. She didn't know that yet and she never would if he had his way, but in the unlikely event that she discovered that fact, she was a woman who would understand. We all have our hot air balloons, he would tell her.

Had he loved her? he wondered. Or had he merely seen in her his best chance for a life where her foreign background would cast a useful shadow in which he could hide? He didn't know. He'd never got a chance to find out. And at a distance of two decades, he still didn't know how it might have worked out between the two of them. But what he did know without a single doubt was that at long last he'd had enough.

With the Boxter in his possession, he began the drive that he knew was a journey long in coming. It took him across London, first dropping down out of Hampstead and veering in the direction of Regent's Park, then wending his way eastward, ever eastward, to arrive in that Hades of postal codes: E3, where his nightmares had their roots.

Unlike many areas of London, Tower Hamlets had not become gentrified. Films made here did not feature actors who batted their eyelashes, fell in love, lived arty lives, and lent an air of genteel down-at-heel glamour to the place, thus resulting in its renaissance at the hands of yuppies in Range Rovers yearning to be trendy. For the word *renaissance* implied that a place had once seen better times to which an infusion of cash would return it. But to Pitchley's eyes, Tower Hamlets had been a dump from the moment its first building had its initial foundation stone set into place.

He'd spent more than half his life trying to scrub the grime of Tower Hamlets from beneath his fingernails. He'd worked jobs not fit for man or beast since his ninth birthday, squirreling away whatever he could towards a future he wanted but couldn't quite define. He'd endured bullying at a school where learning took a distant seventh place to tormenting teachers, demolishing ancient and nearly useless equipment, graffitiing every available inch, shagging birds on the stairwells, setting fires in the dustbins, and pinching everything from the third-formers' sweets money to the Christmas collection taken each year to give a decent meal to the area's homeless drunks. In that environment, he'd forced himself to learn, a sponge for *whatever* might get him out of the inferno he'd come to assume was his punishment for a transgression he'd committed in a previous lifetime.

His family didn't understand his passion to be free of the place. So his mother—unmarried as she always had been and would be to her grave—smoked her fags all day at the window of the council flat, collected the dole like it was owed to her for doing the nation the favour of breathing, raised the six offspring that were got by four fathers, and wondered aloud how she'd managed to produce such a git as Jimmy, all neat and tidy like he actually thought he was something other than a yobbo in disguise.

"Lookit '*im*, will you?" she'd ask his siblings. "Too good for us, our Jim. What's it to be today, laddie?"—as she looked him over—"Riding to the 'ounds, are we?"

He'd say, "Aw, Mum," and feel misery climbing from his navel up his chest and into his jaws.

"Tha's all right, lad," she'd reply. "Just pinch one of them nice doggies so we'll 'ave a watcher round these ol' digs, okay? Tha'd be nice, now, woul'n't it, kids? 'Ow'd you like our Jimmy to pinch us a dog?"

"Mum, I'm not going fox hunting," he'd say.

And they'd laugh. Laugh and laugh till he wanted to thrash the lot of them for being so useless.

His mother was the worst because she set the tone. She might have been clever. She might have been energetic. She might have been capable of doing something with her life. But she got herself a baby—Jimmy himself—when she was fifteen and that's when she learned that if she kept having them, she'd be paid. Child Benefit was what they called it. What Jimmy Pytches called it was Chains.

So he made his life's purpose the demolition of his past, taking every odd job he could get his mitts on as soon as he was able to do so. What the job was didn't matter to him: cleaning windows, scrubbing floors, vacuuming carpets, walking dogs, washing cars, minding children. He didn't care. If he was paid to do it, do it he would. Because although money couldn't buy him better blood, it could get him miles from the blood that threatened to drown him.

Then came that cot death, that god-awful moment when he went into her bedroom because it was long past the time she generally woke up from her nap. And there she was like a plastic doll, with one hand curled to her mouth like she'd been trying to help herself *breathe*—for God's sake—and her tiny fingernails were blue were blue were bluest of blue and he knew right then that she was a goner. Crikey, he'd been in the sitting room, hadn't he? He'd been right next door. He'd been watching Arsenal. He'd been thinking, Lucky day, this is, the brat's well away and I won't have to fuss with her during the game. He'd *thought* that—the brat—but he didn't mean it, never would have said it, actually smiled when he saw her in her push chair at the local grocery with her mum. He never thought "the brat" then. Just, Here's lit'le Sherry and her mum. Hello, Nubkins. Because that's

what he called her. He called her a nonsense name.
Nubkins.

Then she was dead and the police were there.
Questions and answers and tears all round. And what
kind of monster was *he* who watched Arsenal while a
baby was dying and who even to this *day* remembered the score?

There were whispers, of course. There were rumours. Both fueled his passion to be gone forever.
And forever was what he thought he'd achieved, a
kind of eternal paradise defined by a Dutch-fronted
house in Kensington, the kind of house so grand it
had a medallion carved 1879 on its gable. And this
house was peopled as grandly as it was situated, much
to his delight. A war hero, a child prodigy, a for-
God's-sake *governess* for that child, a foreign nanny . . .
Nothing could have been more different to where
he'd come from: Tower Hamlets via a bed-sit in
Hammersmith and a fortune spent on learning everything from how to say *haricots verts* and knowing what
it meant to how to use cutlery instead of one's fingers
for moving bits of food round one's plate. So when
he'd finally reached Kensington Square, no one knew.
Least of all Katja, who would never have known, having not had a lifetime of instruction on what it meant
to say *lounge* at an inopportune time.

And then she'd got pregnant, the worst sort of getting pregnant. Unlike his mum, who'd carried on
during her pregnancies as if growing a child inside
her body were nothing more than a minor inconvenience causing her to switch to a different set of

clothes for a few months, Katja'd had no easy time of
it, which made her condition impossible to hide. And
from that pregnancy had risen everything else, including his own past, threatening to seep from the
splitting pipes of their life in Kensington Square like
the sewage it was.

Even after all that, he'd thought he could escape it
again. James Pitchford, whose past had hung over
him like Damocles' sword, just waiting to be smeared
across the tabloids as Lodger Once Investigated in
Cot Death, just waiting to be revealed as Jimmy
Pytches: all aitches dropped and tee-aitches said as
effs, Jimmy Pytches the subject of laughter for trying
to be better than he was. So he changed again, mor-
phed himself into J. W. Pitchley, ace investor and financial wizard, but running, always running, and
always to run.

Which brought him to Tower Hamlets now: a
man who'd come to accept the fact that to escape
what he could not bear to face, he could kill himself,
he could change his identity yet another time, or he
could flee forever, not only the teeming city of London but everything that London—and England—
represented.

He parked the Boxter near the tower block that
had been his childhood home. He looked round and
saw that little had changed, including the presence of
local skinheads, three of them this time, who smoked
in the doorway of a nearby shop, watching him and
his car with studied attention. He called out to them,
"Want to make ten quid?"

One of them spat a gob of yellowish sputum into the street. "Each?" he said.

"All right. Each."

"What's to do, then?"

"Keep an eye on the motor for me. See that no one touches it. Okay?"

They shrugged. Pitchley took this for assent. He nodded at them, saying, "Ten now, twenty later."

"Give," said their leader, and he slouched over for the cash.

As he handed the ten-pound note over to the thug, Pitchley realised the bloke might well be his youngest half brother, Paul. It had been more than twenty years since he'd seen little Paulie. What an irony it would be if he were handing over what went for ex-torted dosh to his own brother without either of them knowing who the other was. But that was the case for most of his siblings now. For all he knew, there might even be more of them than the five there were when he did his runner.

He entered the tower block estate: a patch of dead lawn, chalk hopscotch squares drawn drunkenly on the uneven tarmac, a deflated football with a knife gouge in it, two shopping trolleys overturned and rendered wheel-less. Three little girls were attempt-ing to inline skate on one of the concrete paths, but its condition was as bad as the tarmac's, so they'd get about two and a half yards of even ground to glide on before they had to clomp over or around a spot where the concrete looked as if the bomb squad might want to come to have a look for a UXB.

Pitchley made his way to the tower block's lift and found that it was out of service. A block-lettered sign informed him of this, hanging on old chrome doors long ago decorated by the resident spray-paint artists.

He set off up the stairs, seven flights of them. She loved—as she said—" 'aving me a bit of a view." This was important since she never did anything but stand, sit, lounge, smoke, drink, eat, or watch telly in that sagging-seat chair that had stood forever next to the window.

He was out of breath by the second floor. He had to pause on the landing and breathe deeply of its urine-scented air before climbing upwards. When he got to the fifth floor, he stopped again. By the seventh, his armpits were dripping.

He rubbed down his neck as he walked to the door of her flat. He never suffered a moment's doubt that she would be there. Jen Pytches would move her arse only if the building were going up in flames. And even then she'd complain about it: "Wha' abou' me programme on the telly?"

He rapped on the door. From within he heard the sound of chatter, television voices that marked the time of day. Chat shows in the morning, afternoon and it was snooker—God only knew why—and evening brought the soaps.

No answer to his knock, so Pitchley rapped again, louder this time, and he called out, "Mum?" He tried the door and found it unlocked. He opened it a crack and said, "Mum?" another time.

She said, "Who's it, then? That you, Paulie? You

been to the job centre already, 'ave you? Don' think
so, lad. Don' be trying to pull the wool over, you go'
tha', son? I wasn' born this morning." She coughed
the deep, phlegm-cursed cough of the forty-year
smoker as Pitchley used the tips of his fingers to move
the door inward.

He slipped inside and faced his mother. It was the
first time he'd seen her in twenty-five years.

"Well," she said. She was by the window as he
thought she would be, but no longer the woman he
remembered from his childhood. Twenty-five years
of not stirring a muscle unless forced to do so had
made his mother into a great mound of a woman
wearing stretchy trousers and a jumper the size of a
parachute. He wouldn't have known her at all had he
passed her on the street. He wouldn't have known
her now had she not said, "Jim. Wha's a dolly to
make of this sor' 'f surprise?"

He said, "Hello, Mum," and he looked round the
flat. Nothing had changed. Here was the same
U-shaped blue sofa, there were the lamps with the
misshapen shades, up on the walls were the same set
of pictures: each little Pytches sitting on the knee of
his or her own dad on the only occasion Jen had
managed to make any of them act like fathers. God,
seeing them brought it back in a rush: the risible exercise of all the kids lined up and Jen pointing to the
pictures, saying, "Here's *your* dad, Jim. He was called
Trev. But I called him my little fancy boy." And,
"Yours was Derek, Bonnie. Look at the neck on that
bloke, will you, dear? Couldn't put me 'ands *any-*

where near round his neck. Oooh. Wha' a man your dad was, Bon." And on down the line, the same recitation, given once a week lest any of them forget.

"Wha' you want, then, Jim?" his mother asked him. She gave a grunt as she reached for the telly's remote. She squinted at the screen, made some sort of mental note about what it was she was watching, and pushed the button to mute the sound.

"I'm off," he said. "I wanted you to know."

She kept her gaze level on him and said, "You *been* off, lad. How many years? So wha's this off that's different from that?"

"Australia," he said. "New Zealand. Canada. I don't know yet. But I wanted to tell you I'm making it permanent. Cashing in everything. Starting over. I wanted you to know so you could tell the others."

"Don' think they been losing sleep wondering where you wanked off to," his mother said.

"I know. But all the same . . ." He wondered how much his mother knew. As far as he could recall, she didn't read a newspaper. The nation might go to hell in a wicker basket—politicians on the take, the Royals stepping down, the Lords taking up weapons to fight off the Commons' plans for their demise, sport figures dying, rock stars taking overdoses of designer drugs, trains crashing, bombs exploding in Piccadilly—and none of it mattered or had ever mattered, so she wouldn't know what had happened to one James Pitchford and what had been done to stop more from happening.

"Old times, I suppose," he settled on saying. "You're my mum. I thought you had a right."

She said, "Fetch me fags," and nodded to a table by the sofa, where a packet of Benson and Hedges spilled out onto the cover of *Woman's Weekly*. He took them to her and she lit up, watching the screen of the television where the camera was offering a bird's-eye view of a snooker table with a player bent over it studying a shot like a surgeon with a scalpel in his hand.

"Old times," she repeated. "Good of you, Jim. Cheers, then." And she pushed the sound button on the remote.

Pitchley shifted on his feet. He looked round for something that would do as employment. She wasn't really who he'd come to see, anyway, but he could tell that she wasn't about to part with any information on his siblings if he asked her directly. She owed him nothing, and both of them knew it. One didn't spend a quarter of a century pretending that one's past had never occurred only to come calling from the blue with the hope one's mum might decide to be helpful.

He said, "Look, Mum. I'm sorry. It was the only way."

She waved him off, cigarette smoke creating a filmy snake in the air. And seeing that cast him back through time, to this very room, to his mum on the floor, to the baby coming fast and her smoking one fag after another because *where* was the ambulance they'd rung for, God damn it, didn't they have rights to get their needs seen to? And he'd been there with her, alone when it happened. *Don't leave me, Jim. Don't leave me, lad.* And the thing was slimy like an un-cooked cod and bloody and still attached to the cord and she smoked, she *smoked* all the way through it and the smoke rose into the air like a snake.

Pitchley strode into the kitchen to rid himself of the memory of his ten-year-old self with a bloody newborn in his terrified hands. Three twenty-five in the morning, it had been. Brothers and sister asleep, neighbours asleep, the whole sodding world indiffer-ent, deep in their beds, dreaming their dreams.

He'd never much liked children after that. And the thought of producing one himself . . . The older he became, the more he'd realised he didn't need that drama twice in one life.

He went to the sink and turned on the water, thinking that a drink or a bathing of his face would drive the memory out of his head. As he reached for a glass, he heard the flat door open. He heard a man's voice say, "You made a right cock-up of *that* one, di'n't you? How many times I got to tell you to shut your gob when it comes to jollying the customers?"

Another man said, "I di'n't mean no harm. Birds always like a bit of oiling, don't they?"

To which the first said, "Bollocks. We lost them, you yob." And then, " 'Lo, Mum. How's going wha's going?"

"We got a visitor," Jen Pytches said.

Pitchley drank down his water and heard the foot-steps cross the sitting room and come into the kitchen. He placed his glass into the grimy sink and turned to face his two younger brothers. They filled the room, big men like their father with watermelon heads and hands the size of dustbin lids. Pitchley felt in their presence as he'd always felt—intimidated as the dickens. And he did what he'd always done at the first sight of those hulking creatures: He cursed the fate that had inspired his mother to couple with a veritable midget when she got him and to choose an all-in wrestler—or so it seemed—to father his brothers.

"Robbie," he said as a hello to the elder one. And "Brent," to the younger. They were dressed identically in boots and blue jeans topped with windcheaters on which the words *Rolling Suds* were printed front and back. They'd been working, Pitchley concluded, attempting to keep alive the mobile car-wash business that he himself had initiated when he was thirteen years old.

Robbie took the lead, as always. "Well, well, well. Lookit wha' we got here, Brent, our big bro. And don't he look a real pitcher in them fancy trousers?"

Brent snickered and chewed on his thumbnail and waited, as always, for direction from Rob.

Pitchley said, "You win, Rob. I'm shoving off."

"Shoving off like how?" Robbie went to the fridge and pulled out a can of beer, which he tossed to Brent, calling out, "Ma! You want somethin' in there? Eat? Drink?"

She said, "Cheers, Rob. Woul'n't say no to a bite o' that pork pie from yesterday. You see't there, luv? On the top shelf? Go' to eat it 'fore it goes off."

"Yeah. Go' it," Rob called back. He plopped the

crumbling remains of the pie onto a plate and shoved it at Brent, who disappeared for a moment as he delivered it to their mother. Rob ripped the ring-pull from his beer can and flicked it into the kitchen sink, pumping the beer directly into his mouth. He finished it in one long go and began on Brent's, which the younger man had foolishly left behind.

"So," Rob said. "Shoving off, are you? And where 'bouts you shoving off to, Jay?"

"I'm emigrating, Rob. I don't know where. It doesn't matter."

"Matters to me."

Of course, Pitchley thought. For where else would the money come from when he placed a bad bet, when he crashed another car, when he fancied a holiday by the sea? Without Pitchley there to write out the cheques when Robbie had a financial itch that wanted scratching, life as he'd known it was going to be different. He'd actually have to make a proper go of Rolling Suds, and if the business failed—as it had been threatening to do for years under Rob's quixotic management—then there would be no fallback position. Well, that was life, Rob, Pitchley thought. The milk cow's dried up, the golden egg's broken, the rainbow's vanishing permanently. You might've tracked me from East London to Hammersmith to Kensington to Hampstead and all points in between when you fancied, but you are going to be hard pressed to track me across the sea.

He said again, "I don't know where I'll end up. Not yet."

"So wha's the point in all this, then?" Robbie indicated Pitchley and his presence in their shabby
childhood flat by raising the empty can to him.
"Can't be ol' times now, can it, Jay? Ol' times's the
least of what you'd want to come round to have a
chat about, I 'xpect. You'd like to forget them, you
would, Jay. But here's the ringer. Some of us can't.
We don't got the *wherewithal*. So everything we been
through stays right up 'ere, circling round and
round." He used the can again, but this time to indicate the alleged movement in his head. Then he
shoved both cans into the plastic grocery bag that
hung from the pull of one of the kitchen drawers and
had long done service as the family dustbin.

"I know," Pitchley said.

"You know, you know," his brother mocked. "You
don't know nowt, Jay, and don't you forget it."

Pitchley said for the thousandth time to his
brother, "I didn't ask you to take them on. What you
did—"

"Oh *no*. You di'n't ask. You just said, 'You saw
what they wrote 'bout me, Rob!' Tha's what you
said. 'They're gonna end up pulling me limb to limb,'
you said. 'I'm gonna be nothing when this is over.' "

"I may have said that, but what I meant was—"

"Bugger what you meant!" Robbie kicked a cupboard door. Pitchley flinched.

"Wha's this, then?" Brent had returned to them,
having pinched their mother's packet of Benson &
Hedges. He was lighting up.

"This yob's doing another runner and claims he don't know where he's going. How'd you like that?"

Brent blinked. "Tha's shit, Jay."

"Bloody right tha's shit." Rob jabbed his finger into Pitchley's face. "I did time for you. I did six months. You know wha' it's like inside? Lemme tell you." And the catalogue began, the same dreary recitation that Pitchley had heard every time his brother wanted more money. It began with the reason for Robbie's run-in with the law: beating up the journalist who'd unearthed Jimmy Pytches from the carefully constructed past of James Pitchford, who'd not only printed the story pulled from a snout at the Tower Hamlets station but had the audacity to follow it up with another despite being warned off by Rob, who stood to gain nothing—"*sod all*, Jay, you hear me?"—for taking up arms to protect the reputation of a brother who'd *deserted* them years ago. "Us lot never came *near* to you till you needed us, Jay, and then you bled us dry," Robbie said.

His capacity for rewriting history was amazing, Pitchley thought. He said, "You came near me back then because you saw my picture in the paper, Rob. You saw a chance to put me in your debt. Bash a few heads. Break a few bones. All in the cause of keeping Jimmy's past hidden. He'll like that, he will. He's 'shamed of us. An' if we keep him thinkin' we're 'bout to pop out of his cupboard at any time, he'll pay, stupid git. He'll pay and he'll pay."

"I sat in a cell," Robbie roared. "I shat in a bucket.

You go' that, mate? I go' done over in the *shower*, Jay. And wha'd *you* get?"

"You!" Pitchley cried. "You and Brent. That's what I got. The two of you breathing down my neck ever since, hands out for the dosh, regular as rain in the winter."

"Can't wash cars in the rain, can we, Jay?" Brent offered.

"Shut up!" Rob threw the rubbish sack at Brent. "Blood and guts, you're so *fucking* stupid."

"He said—"

"Shut up! I heard wha' he said. Don' you know what he meant? He meant we're leeches. Tha's what he's saying. Like we owe him and not the reverse."

"I'm not saying that." Pitchley reached in his pocket. He brought out his chequebook, where inside was the incomplete cheque he'd been writing when the cop had shown up at his house. "But I am saying that it's ending now, because I'm leaving, Rob. I'll write this last cheque and after that you're on your own."

"Fuck that shit!" Rob advanced on him. Brent took a hasty step back towards the sitting room. Jen Pytches called, "Wha's goin' on, you lot?"

"Rob and Jay—"

"Shut up! Shut up! Christ on the cross! Why're you such a bleeding git, Brent?"

Pitchley took out a biro. He clicked out the ink. But before he could put pen to paper, Rob was on him. He ripped the chequebook from Pitchley's hand

and threw it against the wall, where it hit a rack of mugs which crashed to the floor.

"Hey!" Jen shouted.

Pitchley saw his life flash before him.

Brent dived into the sitting room.

"Bloody stupid wanker," Rob hissed. His hands went for the lapels of Pitchley's jacket. He jerked Pitchley forward. His head snapped back. "You don't understand fuck all, you git. You never did."

Pitchley closed his eyes and waited for the blow, but it didn't come. Instead, his brother released him as savagely as he'd taken hold of him, shoving him backwards against the kitchen sink.

"I di'n't do nowt wanting your stupid money," Rob said. "You handed it over, yeah, right. An' I was glad to take it, yeah, I was. But you're the one what go' out the chequebook every time you saw my mug. 'Give the bloody git a thousand or two and he'll disappear.' Tha's wha' you thought. And then you blamed *me* for takin' the handout when the handout was nothing but guilt money in the first place."

"I didn't do anything to feel guilty—"

Rob's hand chopped the air, silencing Pitchley. "You pr'tended we didn't exist, Jay. So don't blame me for wha' *you* did."

Pitchley swallowed. There was nothing more to say. There was too much truth in Robbie's claim and too much falsehood in his own past.

From the sitting room, the sound of the television rose, Jen raising the volume to drown out whatever her oldest two sons were doing in the kitchen. None of my business, her action said.

Right, Pitchley thought. All of their lives had been none of her business.

He said, "I'm sorry. It was the only way I knew to make a life, Rob."

Rob turned away. He went back to the fridge. He brought out another beer and opened it. He raised it to Pitchley in a mocking, farewell salute. He said, "I only ever wanted to be your brother, Jim."

GIDEON

2 NOVEMBER

IT SEEMS to me that the truth about James Pitchford and Katja Wolff lies between what Sarah-Jane
said about James's indifference to women and what
Dad said about James's besottedness with Katja. Both
of them had reason to twist the facts. If Sarah-Jane
had disliked Katja and wanted James for herself,
she'd not be likely to admit it if the lodger had
shown a preference elsewhere. And as for Dad . . . If
he was responsible for Katja's pregnancy, he'd hardly
be likely to confess that transgression to me, would
he? Fathers tend not to reveal that sort of thing to
their sons.

You listen to me with that expression of calm tranquility on your face, and *because* that expression is so
calm so tranquil so unjudging so open to receive
whatever it is that I choose to maunder on about, I
can see what you're thinking, Dr. Rose: He's *clinging*
to the fact of Katja Wolff's pregnancy as the only
means currently available to him to avoid . . .

What, Dr. Rose? And what if I'm not avoiding anything?

That could be the case precisely, Gideon. But consider that you've come up with no memory relating to your music in quite some time. You've offered very few memories of your mother. Your grandfather in your childhood has all but been deleted from your brain, as has your grandmother. And Raphael Robson—as he was in your childhood—has barely warranted a passing mention.

I can't *help* the way my brain is connecting the dots, can I?

Of course not. But in order to stimulate associative thoughts, one needs to be in a mental position in which the mind is free to roam. That's the point of becoming quiet, becoming restful, choosing a place to write and writing undisturbed. Actively pursuing the death of your sister and the subsequent trial—

How can I go on to something else when my mind is *filled* with this? I can't just clear my brain, forget about it, and pursue something else. She was *murdered,* Dr. Rose. I'd forgotten she was murdered. God forgive me, but I'd even forgotten she existed in the first place. I can't just set that to one side. I can't simply jot down details about playing *ansiosamente* as a nine-year-old when I was meant to play *animato,* and I can't dwell upon the psychological significance of misinterpreting a piece of music like that.

But what about the blue door, Gideon? you inquire, still reason incarnate. Considering the part that

that door has played in your mental processing, would it help if you reflected upon it and wrote about it rather than what you've been told by others?

No, Dr. Rose. That door—if you will pardon the pun—is closed.

Still, why not shut your eyes for a few moments and visualise that door again? you recommend. Why not see if you can put it into a context quite apart from Wigmore Hall? As you describe it, it appears to be an exterior door to a house or a flat. Could it be possible that it has nothing to do with Wigmore Hall? Perhaps it's the colour that you might think and write about for a time and not the door itself. Perhaps it's the presence of two locks instead of one. Perhaps it's the lighting fixture above it and the entire idea of what light is used for.

Freud, Jung, and whoever else occupy the consulting room with us . . . And yes, yes, yes, Dr. Rose. I am a field ready for the harvest.

3 NOVEMBER

Libby's come home. She was gone for three days after our altercation in the square. I heard nothing from her during that time, and the silence from her flat was an accusation, asserting that I'd driven her away through cowardice and monomania. The silence claimed that my monomania was merely a useful shield behind which I could hide so that I didn't have to face my failure with Libby herself, my failure to connect with a human being who had been dropped into my lap by the Almighty for the sole purpose of allowing me to form an attachment to her.

Here she is, Gideon, the Fates or God or Karma had said to me on that day when I agreed to let the lower ground floor flat to the curly-haired courier who needed a refuge from her husband. Here's your opportunity to resolve what has plagued you since Beth left your life.

But I had allowed that singular chance for redemption to slip through my fingers. More than that, I had done everything in my power to avoid having that chance in the first place. For what better way to circumvent intimate involvement with a woman than to subvert my career, thereby giving myself an exigent focal point for all my endeavours? No time to talk about our situation, Libby darling. No time to consider the oddity of it. No time to consider why I can hold your naked body, feel your soft breasts against my chest, feel the mound of your pubis pressing against me, and experience nothing save the raging humiliation of experiencing nothing. Indeed, there is no time for anything at all but resolving this plaguing persistent pernicious question regarding my music, Libby.

Or is the consideration of Libby right now a blind that helps cloud whatever it is that the blue door represents? And how the hell am I to know?

When Libby returned to Chalcot Square, she didn't bang on my door or phone me. Nor did she announce her presence through the means of either the Suzuki's engine gunning explosively outside or pop music blaring from her flat. The only way I knew that she was back at all was from the sudden sound of the old pipes clanging from within the walls of the building. She was having a bath.

I gave her forty minutes' leeway once the pipes were silent. Then I went downstairs, outside, and down the steps to her front door. I hesitated before knocking, almost giving up the idea of trying to mend my fences with her. But at the last moment when I thought, To hell with it, which I realise was my way of turning tail and running off, I found that I didn't want to be at odds with Libby. If nothing else, she'd been such a *friend*. I missed that friendship, and I wanted to make sure I still had it.

Several knocks were required to get a response from her. Even when she did answer, she asked, "Who is it?" from behind the closed door although she knew very well that I was the only person likely to be calling on her in Chalcot Square. I was patient with this. She's upset with me, I told myself. And, all things considered, that's her right.

When she opened the door, I said the conventional thing to her. "Hullo. I was worried about you. When you disappeared . . ."

"Don't lie," was her reply, although she didn't say it unkindly. She'd had time to dress, and she was wearing something other than her usual garb: a colourful skirt that dangled to her calves, a black sweater that reached her hips. Her feet were bare, although she had a gold chain round her ankle. She looked quite nice.

"It's not a lie. When you left, I thought you'd gone to work. When you didn't come back . . . I didn't know what to think."

"Another lie," she said.

I persisted, telling myself, The fault is mine. I'll take the punishment. "May I come in?"

She stepped back from the door in a movement that was not unlike a complete body shrug. I walked into the flat and saw that she'd been assembling a meal for herself. She had it laid out on the coffee table in front of the futon that serves as her sofa, and it was completely unlike her usual fare of take-away Chinese or curry: a grilled chicken breast, broccoli, and a salad of lettuce and tomatoes.

I said, "You're eating. Sorry. Shall I come back later?" and I hated the formality that I heard in my voice.

She said, "No problem as long as you don't mind if I eat in front of you."

"I don't mind. Do you mind being watched while you eat?"

"I don't mind."

It was a conversational check and counter-check. There were so many things that she and I could talk about and so many things that we were avoiding.

I said, "I'm sorry about the other day. About what happened. Between us, that is. I'm going through a bad patch just now. Well, obviously, you know that already. But until I see it through, I'm not going to be right for anyone."

"Were you before, Gideon?"

I was confused. "Was I what?"

"Right for anyone." She went back to the sofa, tucking her skirt beneath her as she sat, an oddly feminine movement that seemed completely out of character.

"I don't know how to answer that honestly and be honest with myself," I said. "I'm supposed to say Yes, I was right in the past and I'll be right again. But the truth of the matter is that I might not have been. Right, that is. I might not ever have been right for anyone, and I might never be. And that's all I know just now."

She was drinking water, I saw, not Coke, as had been her preference since I had known her. She had a glass with a slice of lemon floating amid the ice cubes, and she took this up as I was speaking and she watched me over the rim as she drank. "Fair enough," she said. "Is that what you've come to tell me?"

"As I said, I was worried about you. We didn't part on good terms. And when you left and didn't return . . . I suppose I thought you might have . . . Well, I'm glad you're back. And well. I'm glad you're well."

"Why?" she asked. "What did you think I might have done? Jumped into the river or something?"

"Of course not."

"Then?"

I didn't see at the moment that this was the wrong road to be traveling down. Idiotically, I turned into it, assuming it would take us to the destination that I had in mind. I said, "I know your position in London is tenuous, Libby. So I wouldn't blame you for . . . well, for doing whatever you felt you needed to do to shore it up . . . Especially since you and I parted badly. But I'm glad you're back. I'm awfully glad. I've missed having you here to talk to."

"Gotcha," she said with a wink, although she didn't smile. "I get it, Gid."

"What?"

She took up her knife and fork and cut into the chicken. Despite the fact that she'd been in England for several years at this point, I noted that she still ate like an American, with that inefficient shifting about of the knife and the fork from one hand to the other. I was dwelling on this fact when she answered me. "You think I've been with Rock, don't you?"

"I hadn't really . . . well, you do work for him. And after you and I had that row . . . I know that it would be only natural to . . ." I wasn't sure how to complete the thought. She was chewing her chicken slowly, and she was watching me flailing round verbally, perhaps determined not to do a single thing to help me.

She finally spoke. "What you thought was that I was back with Rock, doing what Rock wants me to do. Fucking him, basically, whenever he wants it. And totally putting up with him fucking everyone else he comes across. Right?"

"I know he holds the whip hand, Libby, but since you've been gone, I've been thinking that if you consult a solicitor who specialises in immigration law—"

"Bullshit what you've been thinking," she scoffed.

"Listen. If your husband is continuing to threaten you with going to the Home Office, we can—"

"It *is* what you think, isn't it?" She set down her fork. "I wasn't with Rock Peters, Gideon. Sure. It's hard for you to believe. I mean, why *wouldn't* I go running back to some complete asshole, since that's, like, my basic m.o. In fact, why wouldn't I move right in with him and put up with his shit all over again? I've been doing *such* a totally good job of putting up with yours."

"You're still angry, then." I sighed, frustrated with my inability to communicate with anyone, it seemed. I wanted very much to get us past this, but I didn't know where I wanted to get us *to*. I couldn't offer Libby what she had blatantly wanted from me for months, and I didn't actually know what else I could offer her that would satisfy, not only at that moment but in the future. But I wanted to offer her something. "Libby, I'm not right," I said. "You've seen that. You know it. We've not talked about the worst of what's wrong with me, but you know because you've experienced . . . You've seen . . . You've been with me . . . at night." God, it was excruciating trying to say it outright.

I hadn't taken a seat when she herself had, so I paced across the sitting room to the kitchen and back again. I was waiting for her to rescue me.

Have others done that before? you enquire.

Done . . . what?

Rescued you, Gideon. Because, you see, often we

wait for what we're used to from people. We develop the expectation that one person will give us what we've traditionally received from others.

God knows there have been few enough others, Dr. Rose. There was Beth, of course. But she reacted with wounded silence, which is certainly not what I wanted from Libby.

And from Libby, what was it that you wanted?

Understanding, I suppose. An acceptance that would make further conversation—and a fuller admission—unnecessary. But what I got was a statement that told me clearly she was going to give me none of that.

She said, "Life isn't all about you, Gideon."

I said, "I'm not implying that it is."

She said, "Sure you are. I'm gone for three days and you assume I've totally freaked because we can't get something going between us. You figure I've run back to Rock and he and I are bumping woolies all because of you."

"I wouldn't say that you were having relations with him because of me. But you have to admit that you wouldn't have gone to him in the first place if we hadn't . . . if things had gone differently for us. For you and me."

"Jeez. You are, like, deaf as a stone, aren't you? Have you even been listening to me? But then, why would you when we're not discussing *you*."

"That's not fair. And I have been listening."

"Yeah? Well, I said I wasn't with Rock. I saw him, sure. I went to work every day, so I saw him. And I could've gotten back with him if I wanted, but I *didn't* want. And if he wants to phone the Feds—or whoever it is that you guys phone—then he's going to do it and that'll be it: a one-way ticket to San Francisco. And there is, like, absolutely zilch that I can do about it. And that's the story."

"There's got to be a compromise. If he wants you as he seems to want you, perhaps you can get some counseling that would enable you to—"

"Are you out of your fucking mind? Or are you just freaked out that I might start wanting something from you?"

"I'm only trying to suggest a solution to the immigration problem. You don't want to be deported. I don't want you to be deported. Clearly, Rock doesn't want you to be deported, because if he did, he would have done something to alert the authorities—it's the Home Office, by the way—and they would have already come for you."

She had cut into her chicken again and she had lifted a forkful of meat to her mouth. But she hadn't taken it. Instead, she held the fork suspended while I spoke, and when I had finished, she laid the fork back onto her plate and stared at me for a good fifteen seconds before saying anything. And then what she said made no sense at all. "Tap dancing," were her words.

I said, "What?"

"Tap dancing, Gideon. That's where I went when I left here. That's what I do. I tap dance. I'm not very good, but it doesn't matter, because I don't, like, *do* it to be good. I do it because I get hot and sweaty and

I have fun and I like the way it makes me feel when I'm done."

I said, "Yes. I see," although I didn't, actually. We were talking about her marriage, we were talking about her status in the UK, we were talking about our own difficulties—at least we were trying to—and what tap dancing had to do with all this was unclear to me.

"There's this very nice chick at my tap-dancing class, an Indian girl who's taking the class on the sly. She invited me home to meet her family. And that's where I've been. With her. With them. I wasn't with Rock. Didn't even think of going to Rock. What I thought was what would be best for me. And that's what I did, Gid. Just like that."

"Yes. Well. I see." I was a broken record. I could sense her anger, but I didn't know what to do with it.

"No. You don't see. Everyone in your itty-bitty world lives and dies and breathes for you, and that's the way it's always been. So you figure that what's going on with me is the exact same deal. *You* can't get it up when we're together and I'm just so totally *bummed* about it that I rush off to the biggest dickhead in London and do the nasty with him because of *you*. You think I'm saying, Gid doesn't want me but good old Rock does, and if some total asshole *wants* me that makes me okay, that makes me real, that makes me really exist."

"Libby, I'm not saying any of that."

"You don't have to. It's the way you live, so it's the way you think everyone else lives, too. Only in your world, you live for that stupid violin instead of for another person, and if the violin *rejects* you or something, you don't know who you are any more. And that's what's going on, Gideon. But my life is, like, totally *not* about you. And yours isn't about your violin."

I stood there wondering how we'd reached this point. I couldn't think of a clear response. And in my head all I could hear was Dad saying, This is what comes of knowing Americans, and of all Americans, the worst are Californians. They don't converse. They psychologise.

I said, "I'm a musician, Libby."

"No. You're a person. Like I'm a person."

"People don't exist outside what they do."

" 'Course they do. Most people exist just fine. It's only people who don't have any real insides—people who've never taken the time to find out who they really *are*—that fall to pieces when stuff doesn't turn out the way they want it to."

"You can't know how this . . . this situation . . . between us is going to turn out. I've said that I'm in the middle of a bad patch, but I'm coming through it. I'm working at coming through it every day."

"You are *so* not listening to me." She threw down her fork. She'd not eaten half of her meal, but she carried her plate over to the kitchen, dumped the chicken and broccoli into a plastic bag, and flung that bag into the fridge. "You don't have anything to turn to if your music goes bad. And you think I don't have anything to turn to if you and me or Rock and me or me and *anything* goes bad either. But I'm not you. I have a life. You're the person who doesn't."

"Which is why I'm trying to get my life back. Because until I do, I won't be good for myself or for anyone."

"Wrong. No. You never had a life. All you had was the violin. Playing the violin wasn't ever who you are. But you *made* it who you are and that's why you're nothing right now."

Gibberish, I could hear Dad scoffing. Another month in this creature's company and what's left of your mind will turn to porridge. This is what comes of a steady diet of McDonald's, television chat shows, and self-help books.

With Dad in my head and Libby in front of me, I didn't stand a chance. The only course that seemed open to me was a dignified exit, which I attempted to make, saying, "I think we've said all we need to on the subject. It's safe to say that this is just going to be an area in which we disagree."

"Well, let's make sure we only say what's safe," was Libby's retort. " 'Cause if things get, like, too *scary* for us, we might actually be able to change."

I was at the door, but this parting shot of hers was going so far wide of the mark that I had to correct her. I said, "Some people don't need to change, Libby. They might need to understand what's happening to them, but they don't need to change."

Before she could answer, I left her. It seemed crucial that I have the last word. Still, as I closed the door behind me—and I did it carefully so as not to betray anything that she might take as an adverse reaction to our conversation—I heard her say, "Yeah. Right, Gideon," and something scraped viciously across the wooden floor, as if she'd kicked the coffee table.

4 NOVEMBER

I am the music. I am the instrument. She sees fault in this. I do not. What I see is the difference between us, that difference which Dad has been attempting to point out from the moment he and Libby met. Libby has never been a professional, and she's not an artist. It's easy for her to say that I am not the violin because she has never known what it is to have a life that is inextricably entwined with an artistic performance. Throughout her life, she's had a series of jobs, work that she's gone to and then left at the end of the day. Artists do not live that sort of life. Assuming that they do or can displays an ignorance which must give one pause to consider.

To consider what? you want to know.

To consider the possibilities for us. For Libby and me. Because there for a time, I had thought . . . Yes. There seemed to be a rightness in our knowing each other. There seemed to be a distinct advantage in the fact that Libby didn't know who I was, didn't recognise my name when she saw it that day on her courier parcel, didn't appreciate the facts of my career, didn't care whether I played the violin or made kites and sold them in Camden Market. I liked that about her. But now I see that being with someone who *understands* my life is crucial if I am going to *live* my life.

And that need for understanding was what prompted me to seek out Katie Waddington, the girl from the convent that I remembered sitting in the kitchen in Kensington Square, the most frequent visitor to Katja Wolff.

Katja Wolff was one half of the two KWs, Katie informed me when I tracked her down. Sometimes, she said, when one has a close friendship, one makes the mistake of assuming it will be there forever, unchanging and nurturing. But it rarely is.

It was no big problem to locate Katie Waddington. Nor was it any big surprise to discover that she'd followed a life course similar to what she'd suggested would be her mission two decades earlier. I located her through the telephone directory, and I found her in her clinic in Maida Vale. It's called Harmony of Bodies and Minds, this clinic, and it's a name which I suppose is useful to disguise its main function: sex therapy. They don't come right out and call it sex therapy, because who would have the nerve to engage in it if that were the case? Instead, they call it "relationship therapy," and an inability to take part in the sexual act itself is called "relationship dysfunction."

"You'd be astonished to know how many people have problems with sex," Katie informed me in a fashion that sounded personally friendly and professionally reassuring. "We get at least three referrals every day. Some are due to medical problems—diabetes, heart conditions, post-operative trauma. That sort of thing. But for every client with a medical problem, there are nine or ten with psychological troubles. I suppose that's not surprising, really, given our national obsession with sex and the pretence we maintain that sex *isn't* our national obsession. One only has to look at the tabloids and the glossies to know the level of interest everyone has in sex. I'm surprised not to find more people in therapy struggling with all this. God knows I've never encountered anyone without *some* sort of issue with sex. The healthy ones are those who deal with it."

She took me down a corridor painted in warm, earthy colours and we went to her office, which opened onto a terrace where a profusion of pot plants provided a verdant backdrop for a comfortable room of overstuffed furniture, cushions, and a collection of pottery ("South American," she informed me) and baskets ("North American . . . lovely, aren't they? They're my guilty pleasure. I can't afford them, but I buy them anyway. I suppose there are worse vices in life"). We sat and took stock of each other. Katie said in that same warm, personally friendly and professionally reassuring voice, "Now. How can I help you, Gideon?"

I realised that she thought I'd come to solicit her skills, and I hastened to disabuse her of the notion. Nothing in her area of speciality was required, I told her heartily. I'd really come for some information about Katja Wolff, if she didn't mind. I would recompense her for her time, since I'd be using up what would otherwise be someone's appointment. But as to having . . . shall we say, *difficulties* of the sort she was used to dealing with . . . ? Har, har. Chuckle. Well, at the moment there was no need for *that* sort of intervention.

Katie said, "Brilliant. So glad to hear it," and she settled more comfortably into her armchair. This was high-backed and upholstered in autumn colours similar to those which decorated the waiting room and the corridor. It was also extremely sturdy, a quality that would be necessary considering Katie's size. For if she'd been given to fat as a twenty-something university student sitting in the kitchen in Kensington Square, now she was downright obese, of a size that would no longer fit into a seat at the cinema or on a plane. But she was still dressed in hues that flattered her colouring, and the jewellery she wore was tasteful and looked expensive. Nonetheless, it was difficult for me to imagine how she managed to get round town. And, admittedly, I couldn't picture anyone telling their innermost libidinous secrets to her. It was obvious others hadn't shared my aversion, however. The clinic looked like a thriving enterprise, and I'd managed to get in to see Katie only because a regular client had canceled minutes before I phoned.

I told her that I was trying to refresh some memories of my childhood, and I'd remembered her. I'd recalled that she'd often been in the kitchen when Katja Wolff was feeding Sonia, and as I had no idea of Katja's whereabouts, it seemed to me that she—

Katie—might be able to fill in the gaps where my memories were dim.

Thankfully, she didn't ask why I'd developed this sudden interest in the past. Nor did she, from her place of professional wisdom, comment upon what it might mean that I had gaps in my recollections in the first place. Instead, she said, "People at Immaculate Conception used to call us the two KWs. 'Where are the KWs?' they'd ask. 'Someone fetch the KWs to have a look at this.' "

"So you were close friends."

"I wasn't the only one who sought her out when she first accepted a room at the convent. But our friendship . . . I suppose it *took*. So yes, we were close at the time."

There was a low table next to her chair, and on it stood an elaborate bird cage with two budgerigars inside, one a brilliant blue and the other green. As Katie spoke, she unfastened the door of the cage, and took the blue bird out, grasping him in her large fat fist. He squawked in protest and took a nip at her fingers. She said, "Naughty, *naughty*, Joey," and picked up a tongue depressor that lay on the table next to the cage. For a grim moment I thought she meant to use it to swat the little bird. But instead she used it to massage his head and neck in a way that calmed him. Indeed, it appeared to hypnotise him, and it did much the same for me, since I watched in fascination as the bird's eyes eased shut. Katie opened her palm, and he sank into it contentedly.

"Therapeutic," Katie told me as she went on with

the massage, using the tips of her fingers once the bird was gentled. "Lowers the blood pressure."

"I didn't know that birds had high blood pressure."

She laughed quietly. "Not Joey's. Mine. I've morbid obesity, to state the obvious. Doctor says I'll die before I'm fifty if I don't shed sixteen stone. 'You weren't born fat,' he tells me. 'No, but I've lived it,' I tell him. It's hell on one's heart, and what it does to one's blood pressure doesn't bear mentioning. But we all have to go some way. I'm just choosing mine." She ran her fingers along Joey's folded right wing. In response—eyes still closed—he stretched it out. "That's what attracted me to Katja. She was someone who made choices, and I loved that about her. Probably because in my own family, everyone just went into the restaurant business without thinking there might be something else out there to do with their lives. But Katja was someone who grabbed at life. She didn't just accept what was thrust upon her."

"East Germany," I acknowledged. "The balloon escape."

"Yes. That's an excellent example. The balloon escape and how she engineered it."

"Except she wasn't the one who built the balloon, was she? Not from what I've been told."

"No, she didn't build it. That's not what I meant by *engineered*. I meant how she convinced Hannes Hertel to take her with him. How she blackmailed him, actually, if what she told me was true, and I expect it was because why would someone lie about something so unflattering? But nasty as her plan might have been, she had real nerve to go to him and to make the threat. He was a big man—six foot three or four to hear her tell it—and he could have done her serious harm had he a mind to do so. He could have killed her, I expect, and gone on his way over the wall and disappeared from there. It was a calculated risk on her part, and she took it. That's how much she wanted life."

"What sort of risk?"

"The threat, you mean?" Katie had gone on to Joey's other wing, which he'd stretched out as cooperatively as he had done the first. Inside the cage, the second budgerigar had skittered along one of the perches and was watching the massage session with one bright eye. "She threatened to alert the authorities if Hannes didn't take her with him."

"That's not a story that's ever come out, is it?"

"I expect I'm the only person she ever told, and she probably never realised she told me. We'd both been drinking, and when Katja got pissed—which wasn't often, mind you—she'd say or do things that she couldn't even remember twenty-four hours later. I never mentioned the Hannes situation to her after she told me about it, but I admired her for it because it spoke of the lengths she was willing to go to in order to have what she wanted. And as I had to go to my own lengths to get what I wanted"—she indicated the office and the clinic itself, so many steps removed from her family's restaurant business—"it made us sisters, after a fashion."

"You lived at the convent as well?"

"God no. Katja did. She worked for the sisters—in their kitchen, I think—in exchange for her room while she was learning English. But I lived behind the convent. There were lodgings for students at the bottom of the grounds. Right on the District line, so the noise was ghastly. But the rent was cheap, and the location—near to so many colleges—made it convenient. Several hundred students lived there then, and most of us knew of Katja." Here she smiled. "Had we not known of her, we would have taken notice of her eventually. What she could do with a jumper, three scarves, and a pair of trousers was quite remarkable. She had an innovative mind when it came to fashion. That's what she wanted to do, by the way. And she would have done had things not turned out so badly for her."

This was exactly where I wanted the conversation to head: the way things had turned out for Katja Wolff and the why of those things.

"She wasn't really qualified to be my sister's nanny, was she?" I asked.

Katie was stroking the budgerigar's tail feathers now, and he spread them for her as cooperatively as he'd spread his wings, which still remained extended, as if he'd become paralysed by the sheer pleasure of the therapist's touch. "She was devoted to your sister," Katie said. "She loved her. She was brilliant with her. I never saw her be *anything* other than absolutely tender and gentle towards Sonia. She was a Godsend, Gideon."

That wasn't what I expected to hear, and I closed

my eyes, trying to find a picture in my mind of Katja and Sonia together. I wanted a picture that squared with what I'd said to the ginger-haired policeman, not one that squared with what Katie was claiming.

I said, "You would have seen them together mostly in the kitchen, though, when she was feeding Sonia," and I kept my eyes closed, trying to conjure that picture at least: the old red-and-black lino squares on the floor, the table scarred with the semi-circles of cups placed down on unprotected wood, the two windows set below the level of the street and the bars that fronted them. Odd that I could remember the sight of feet passing by on the pavement above those kitchen windows, but I could not at that moment envisage a scene in which something might have happened that would confirm what I'd later reported to the police.

Katie said, "I did see them in the kitchen. But I saw them at the convent as well. And in the square. And elsewhere. Part of Katja's job was to stimulate her senses and—" Here she cut herself off, stopped stroking the bird, and said, "But you already know all this, I suppose."

I murmured vaguely, "As I said, my memory . . ."

That seemed to be enough, because she went on. "Ah. Yes. Right. Well, all children, disabled or not, benefit from sensory stimulation, and Katja saw to it that Sonia had a variety of experiences. She worked with her in developing motor skills and she saw to it that she was exposed to the environment beyond the home. She was limited by your sister's health, but when Sonia was able to cope with it, Katja would take her out and about. And if I was free, I went as well. So I saw her with Sonia, not every day but several times a week, for the entire time your sister was . . . well, alive. And Katja was very good to Sonia. So when everything happened as it happened . . . Well, I still find it a bit difficult to understand."

So thoroughly different was this account to anything I'd heard or read in the papers that I felt compelled to attempt a frontal assault. I said, "This doesn't square at all with what I've been told."

"By whom?"

"By Sarah-Jane Beckett for one."

"That doesn't surprise me," Katie said. "You can take everything Sarah-Jane says with a pinch of salt. They were oil and water, Katja and she. And there was James to consider. He was wild about Katja, completely over the moon every time she so much as looked his way. Sarah-Jane didn't much like that. It was only too obvious that she'd earmarked James for herself."

This was down-the-rabbit-hole stuff, Dr. Rose, this bit about James the Lodger. No matter where, how, or to whom I turned, the story seemed to turn as well. And it turned in subtle ways, just a variation here and a little twist there but enough to throw me off my stride and make me wonder whose words I could believe.

Perhaps in no one's, you point out to me. Each person sees things in his own way, Gideon. Each person develops a version of past events that he can live with, and put to the rack, that's the version that he tells. Ultimately, it becomes his truth.

But what is Katie Waddington trying to live with, twenty years after the crime? I can understand what Dad is trying to live with, what Sarah-Jane Beckett is trying to live with. But Katie . . . ? She wasn't a member of the household. She had no interest in anything other than her friendship with Katja Wolff. Right?

Yet it had been Katie Waddington's evidence at the trial that, as much as anything, had sealed Katja Wolff's fate. I'd read that in the newspaper cutting where the words *Nanny Lied to Police* had formed a mammoth headline. In her only statement to the investigators, Katja had claimed that a phone call from Katie Waddington had taken her from the bathroom for no more than a minute on the night Sonia drowned. But Katie Waddington had, under oath, sworn that she was at an evening class at the same moment that that phone call had ostensibly been made. Her testimony had been supported by the records of the class instructor. And a serious blow had been dealt to Katja's nearly non-existent defence.

But wait. God. Had Katie *too* wanted James the Lodger? I wondered. Had she orchestrated events somehow in order to make James Pitchford available to *her*?

As if she perceived the subject festering in my mind, Katie continued with the theme she'd begun. "Katja wasn't interested in James. She saw him as someone who could help her with her English, and I suppose she used him if it comes down to it. She saw that he wanted her to spend her free time with him, and she was happy to do it so long as that free time was spent in language tutorials. James went along with that. I suppose he hoped she'd fall in love with him eventually if he was good enough to her."

"So he could have been the man who made her pregnant."

"As payment for the language lessons, d'you mean? I doubt it. Sex in exchange for anything wouldn't have been Katja's style. After all, she could have had sex with Hannes Hertel to get him to take her in the hot air balloon. But she chose a different route entirely, and one that could have got her badly hurt." Katie had ceased petting the blue budgerigar, and she watched the bird as he slowly regained his senses. His tail feathers returned to normal first, then his wings, and finally his eyes, which opened. He blinked as if wondering where he was.

I said, "Then she was in love with someone other than James. You must know who."

"I don't know that she was in love with anyone."

"But if she was pregnant—"

"Don't be naïve, Gideon. A woman doesn't need to be in love to become pregnant. She doesn't even need to be willing." She returned the blue bird to the cage.

"Are you suggesting . . ." I couldn't even say it, so horrified was I at the thought of what could have happened and at whose hands.

"No, no," Katie said hastily. "She wasn't raped. She

would have told me. I do believe that. What I meant was that . . ." A marked hesitation during which Katie took the green bird from the cage and began to give it the same massage as she'd given the other. "As I said, she drank a bit. Not a lot and not often. But when she did . . . well, I'm afraid she forgot things. So there was every chance that she herself didn't know . . . That's the only explanation I've ever been able to come up with."

"Explanation for what?"

"For the fact that I didn't know she was pregnant," Katie said. "We told each other everything. And the fact that she never told me she was pregnant suggests to me that she didn't know herself. Unless she wanted to keep the identity of the father a secret, I suppose."

I didn't want to head in that direction, and I didn't want her to do so. I said, "If she drank on her evenings off and one time ended up with someone she didn't even know, she might not have wanted that to come out. It would only have made her look worse, wouldn't it? Especially when she went to trial. Because they talked about her character at the trial, as I understand." Or at least, I thought, Sarah-Jane Beckett had done.

"As to that," Katie said, ceasing her stroking of the green bird's head for a moment, "I wanted to be a character witness. Despite her lie about the telephone call, I thought I could do that much for her. But I wasn't allowed. Her barrister wouldn't call me. And when the Crown Prosecutor discovered that I hadn't even known she was pregnant . . . You can imagine what he made of that when he was questioning me: How could I declare myself Katja Wolff's closest friend and an authority on what she was and wasn't capable of doing if she'd never trusted me enough to reveal she was pregnant?"

"I see how it went."

"Where it went was murder. I thought I could help her. I *wanted* to help her. But when she asked me to lie about that phone call—"

"She asked you to lie?"

"Yes. She asked me. But I just couldn't do it. Not in court. Not under oath. Not for anyone. That's where I had to draw the line, and it ended our friendship."

She lowered her gaze to the bird in her palm, its right wing extended now to receive the touch that the other bird had been given. Intelligent little creature, I thought. She'd not yet mesmerised it with her caress, but the bird was already cooperating.

"It's odd, isn't it?" she said to me. "One can earnestly believe one has a particular type of relationship with another person, only to discover it was never what one thought in the first place."

"Yes," I said. "It's very odd."

NINETEEN

YASMIN EDWARDS stood at the corner of Oakhill and Galveston Roads with the number fifty-five burning into her brain. She didn't want any part of what she was doing, but she was doing it anyway, compelled by a force that seemed at once outside herself and integral to her being.

Her heart was saying Go home, girl. Get away from this place. Go back to the shop and go back to pretending.

Her head was saying Nope, time to know the worst.

And the rest of her body was heaving between her head and her heart, leaving her feeling like a thick blonde heroine from a thriller film, the sort who tiptoes through the dark towards that creaking door while the audience shouts at her to stay away.

She'd stopped at the laundry before leaving Kennington. When she'd not been able to cope any longer with what her mind had been shouting for the past several days, she'd shut up the shop and picked up the Fiesta from the car park on the estate with the intention of heading to Wandsworth straight off. But at the top of Braganza Street, where she had to wait for the traffic to clear before she could turn into Kennington Park Road, she'd caught a glimpse of the laundry tucked between the grocery and the electrical shop, and she'd decided to pop round and ask Katja what she wanted for dinner.

No matter that she knew in her heart this was just an excuse to check up on her lover. She *hadn't* asked Katja about dinner before they'd parted that morning, had she? The unexpected visit from that bloody detective had rattled them away from their regular routine.

So she found a spot to park and she ducked into the shop, where she saw to her relief that Katja was at work: in the back, bending over a steaming iron that she was gliding along someone's lace-edged sheets. The combination of heat, humidity, and a smelly jungle of unwashed laundry made the shop feel like the tropics. Within ten seconds of entering the place, Yasmin was dizzy, with sweat beading on her forehead.

She'd never met Mrs. Crushley, but she recognised the laundry owner from the attitude she projected from her sewing machine when Yasmin approached the counter. She was of the England-fought-the-war-for-the-likes-of-you generation, a woman too young to have done service during any conflict in recent history but just old enough to remember a London that was largely Anglo-Saxon in origin. She said sharply, "Yes? What d' you want?" her glance darting all over

Yasmin's person, her face looking like she smelled something bad. Yasmin wasn't carrying laundry, which made her suspect to Mrs. Crushley. Yasmin was black, which went a good distance towards making her dangerous as well. She could have a knife in her kit, after all. She could have a poisoned dart taken from a fellow tribesman tucked away in her hair.

She said politely, "If I could have a word with Katja . . . ?"

"*Katja?*" Mrs. Crushley declared, sounding as if Yasmin had asked if Jesus Christ happened to be working that day. "What you want with her, then?"

"Just a word."

"Don't see as I need to allow that, do I? 'Nough that I'm employing her, i'n't it, without her taking social calls all day." Mrs. Crushley lifted the garment she was working on—a man's white shirt—and she used her crooked teeth to bite off a bit of thread from a button she'd been replacing.

At the back of the shop, Katja raised her head. But for some reason, rather than smile a greeting imme-diately, she looked beyond Yasmin to the door. And *then* she looked back at Yasmin and smiled.

It was the sort of thing anyone might have done, the sort of thing Yasmin once wouldn't have noticed. But now she found that she was acutely attuned to everything about Katja's behaviour. There were meanings everywhere; there were meanings within meanings. And *that* was down to that filthy detective.

She said to Katja, "Forgot to ask about your tea this morning," with a wary glance at Mrs. Crushley.

Mrs. Crushley snorted, saying, "Asking her about her *tea*, is it? In my day we ate wha' was put on our plates with no one out there taking requests."

Katja approached. Yasmin saw that she was soaked through with sweat. Her azure blouse clung to her torso like hunger. Her hair lay limply against her skull. But she'd never looked like this before—used up and bedraggled—at the end of a day since working at the laundry, and seeing her so now when the day was not even half over fired all of Yasmin's suspicions once again. If she *never* came home looking such a mess, Yasmin reasoned, she had to be going somewhere else before returning to the Doddington estate.

She'd come to the laundry just to check up on Katja, to make sure she hadn't bunked off and put herself in a bad place with her parole officer. But like most people who tell themselves they're merely sating their curiosity or doing something for someone else's benefit, Yasmin received more information than she wanted.

She said, "Wha' about it, then?" to Katja, her lips offering a smile that felt like a contortion. "Got any thoughts? I could do us lamb with couscous, if you like. That stew thing, remember?"

Katja nodded. She wiped her forehead on her sleeve and used her cuff against her upper lip. She said, "Yes. This is good. Lamb is good, Yas. Thank you."

And they stood there after that, perfectly mute. They exchanged a look as Mrs. Crushley watched

them both over her half-moon glasses. She said, "Go'
the information you 'as wanting, Missie Fancy
Hairdo, I believe. Then best take your leave."

Yasmin pressed her lips together to keep herself
from making a choice between saying, "Where?
Who?" to Katja or "Shit yourself, white cunt" to
Mrs. Crushley. Katja spoke instead. She said quietly,
"I must get back to work, Yas. See you tonight?"

"Yeah. All right," Yasmin replied, and she left
without asking Katja what time.

What time was the ultimate trap she could have
set, the trap that went beyond having a look at Katja's
appearance. With Mrs. Crushley sitting there, knowing what hour Katja got off work, it would have been
easy to ask exactly when Katja would return from the
laundry that evening and to watch for Mrs. Crushley's expression if the time didn't match up with
Katja's hours of employment. But Yasmin didn't want
to give the nasty sow the pleasure of drawing an inference of any kind about her relationship with Katja,
so she went on her way and drove to Wandsworth.

Now she stood on the street corner in the frigid
wind. She examined the neighbourhood, and she set
it down next to Doddington Grove Estate, which did
not gain from the comparison. The street was clean,
like it'd been swept. The pavement was clear of debris and fallen leaves. There were no stains from dog
urine on the lampposts and no piles of dog shit in the
gutters. The houses were free of graffiti and displayed
white curtains in the windows. No laundry hung
dispiritedly from balconies, because there were no

balconies: just a long row of terraced houses all well taken care of by their inhabitants.

Someone could be happy here, Yasmin thought. Someone could make a special life here. She began to walk cautiously down the pavement. No one was about, but she still felt watched. She adjusted the button at the top of her jacket and pulled out a scarf to cover her hair. She knew it was a stupid thing to do. She knew it marked her: scared, less than, and worried about. But she did it anyway because she wanted to feel safe, at ease, and confident here, and she was willing to try anything to get that way.

When she reached Number Fifty-five, she hesitated at the gate. She wondered at this final moment if she could really go through with it and she asked herself if she really wanted to know. She cursed the black man who'd brought her to this moment, loathing not only him but herself: him for passing her the information in the first place, herself for making something out of it.

But she had to know. She had too many questions that a simple knock on the door might answer. She couldn't leave until she'd confronted the fears that she'd too long been trying to ignore.

She opened the gate into an untidy front garden. The path to the door was flagstones and the door itself was shiny red with a polished brass knocker in the centre. Autumn-bare shrub branches arched over the porch, and a wire milk basket held three empty bottles, one of which had a note sticking out of it.

Yasmin bent to grasp this note, thinking at the last

moment that she wouldn't actually have to face . . . to see . . . Perhaps the note would tell her. She unrolled it against her palm and read the words: *We're switching to two skimmed, one silver top from now on, please.* That was all. The handwriting gave away nothing. Age, sex, race, creed. The message could have been penned by anyone.

She played her fingers into her palms, encouraging her hand to lift and do its work. She took a step back and looked at the bay window, in the hope that she might see something there that might save her from what she was about to do. But the curtains were like the others on the street: swathes of material that invited some little light into the room and against which a silhouette could be seen at night. But during the day they protected the room within from outside watchers. So Yasmin was left with the door again.

She thought, Bugger this. She had a *right* to know. She marched to the door and rapped the knocker forcefully against the wood.

She waited. Nothing. She rang the bell. She heard it sounding right near to the door, one of those fancy bells that played a tune. But the result was the same. Nothing.

Yasmin didn't want to think she'd come all the way from Kennington to learn nothing. She didn't want to think what it would be like, continuing with Katja as if she didn't have any doubts. It was better to know: the good or the bad. Because if she knew, then she'd have a clear sense of what she was meant to do next.

His card weighed in her pocket like a four-by-two-inch sheet of pure lead. She'd first looked at it, turning it over and over in her hands as the hours passed last night without Katja coming home. She'd phoned, of course. She'd said, "Yas, I'll be late," and she'd said, "It's a bit complicated for the phone. Tell you later, shall I?" when Yasmin had asked what was up. But *later* hadn't come when Yasmin expected and after several hours, she'd got out of bed, gone to the window, tried to use the darkness to understand something of what was happening, and finally gone to her jacket, where she'd found that card he'd given her in the shop.

She'd stared at the name: Winston Nkata. African, that was. But he sounded West Indies when he wasn't being dead careful to sound plod. A phone number was printed on the bottom, to the left of the name, a Met number that she'd sooner die than ring. A pager number was across from it, in the right corner. "You page me," he'd said. "Day or night."

Or had he said that? And in any case, what did it matter, because she wasn't about to grass to a cop. Not in this lifetime. She wasn't that stupid. So she'd shoved the card into her jacket pocket, where she felt it now, a little piece of lead growing hot, growing heavy, weighing her right shoulder down with the pull of it, drawing her like metal to a magnet and the magnet was an action she would not take.

She stepped away from the house. She backed down the flagstone path to the pavement. She felt behind her for the gate, and she backed through it as well. If someone intended to peer through those curtains as she departed, then she damn well intended to see who it was. But that didn't happen. The house was empty.

Yasmin made her decision when a DHL delivery van rumbled into Galveston Road. It puttered along as the driver looked for the correct address, and when he had the right house, he left the van running as he trotted up to the door to make his delivery three houses away from where Yasmin stood. She waited as he rang the bell. Ten seconds and that door was opened. An exchange of pleasantries, a signature on a clipboard, and the delivery man trotted back to his van and went on his way, glancing at Yasmin where she stood on the pavement, giving her a look that registered only *female, black, bad face, decent body, good for a shag.* Then he and his van were gone. But possibility was not.

Yasmin walked towards the house where he'd made the delivery. She rehearsed her lines. She paused out of sight of the window identical to the window on Number Fifty-five and took a moment to scribble that address—Number Fifty-five Galveston Road, Wandsworth—on the the back of the detective's card. Then she removed her headscarf and re-fashioned it into a turban. She took her earrings off and shoved the brass and beads of them into her pocket. And although her jacket was buttoned to her neck, she undid it and unclipped her necklace—just for good measure—depositing it into her shoulder bag, redoing her jacket, and flattening its collar to a humble and unfashionable angle.

Garbed as well as she could be for the part, she entered the garden of the DHL house and rapped hesitantly on its front door. There was a spy hole in it, so she lowered her head, took her bag from her shoulder, and held it awkwardly like a handbag in front of her. She arranged her features as best she could to portray humility, fear, worry, and a desperate eagerness to please. In a moment, she heard the voice.

"Yes? What can I do for you?" It came from behind the closed door, but the *fact* of it told Yasmin she'd cleared the first hurdle.

She looked up. "Please, can you help me?" she asked. "I have come to clean your neighbour's house, but she is not at home. Number Fifty-five?"

"She works during the day," the voice called back.

"But I do not understand . . ." Yasmin held up the detective's card. She said, "If you see . . . Her husband wrote it all down . . . ?"

"Husband?" The locks on the door were released and the door itself was opened. A middle-aged woman stood there, a pair of scissors in her hand. Seeing Yasmin's gaze go to the scissors and her expression alter, the woman said, "Oh. Sorry. I was opening a parcel. Here. Let me have a look at that."

Yasmin willingly handed over the card. The woman read the address.

"Yes. I see. It certainly does say . . . But you said her husband?" And when Yasmin nodded, the woman turned the card over and read the front of it, just exactly what Yasmin herself had read and read again on the previous night: *Winston Nkata, Detective Constable, Metropolitan Police.* A phone number and a pager number. Everything on the complete up and up.

"Well, of course, the fact that he's a policeman . . ." the woman said thoughtfully. But then, "No. There's a mistake, I'm sure. No one named Nkata lives there." She handed the card back.

"You are sure?" Yasmin asked, drawing her eyebrows together, attempting to look her most pathetic. "He said I should clean . . ."

"Yes, yes, my dear girl. I'm sure that he did. But he's given you the wrong address for some reason. No one named Nkata lives in that house or ever has done. It's been lived in for years by a family called McKay."

"McKay?" Yasmin asked. And her heart felt lighter. Because if there was a partner to Harriet Lewis the solicitor as Katja had claimed, then her fears were groundless if this was her home.

"Yes, yes, McKay," the woman said. "Noreen McKay. And her niece and nephew. Very nice woman, she is, very pleasant, but she isn't married. Never has been as far as I know. And certainly not to someone called Nkata, if you know what I mean, and no offence intended."

"I . . . yes. Yes. I see," Yasmin whispered, because that was all she could force from herself upon learning the full name of the occupant of Number Fifty-five. "I do thank you, madam. Thank you very much indeed." She backed away.

The woman came forward. "See here, are you all right, Miss?" she asked.

"Oh yes. Yes. Just . . . When one expects work and is disappointed . . ."

"I'm awfully sorry. If I hadn't had my own woman here yesterday, I'd not mind letting you have a go with my house. You seem decent enough. May I have your name and number on the chance my woman doesn't work out? She's one of those Filipinos, and they can't always be relied on, if you know what I mean."

Yasmin raised her head. What she wanted to say battled with what she needed to say, given the situation. Need won. There were other considerations beyond insult right now. She said, "You are very kind, madam," and she called herself Nora and recited eight digits at random, all of which the woman eagerly wrote onto a pad that she took from a table by the door.

"Well," she said as she wrote the last number with a flourish. "Our little encounter might turn out all for the best." She offered a smile. "You never know, do you?"

How true, Yasmin thought. She nodded, went back to the street, and returned to Number Fifty-five for a final look at it. She felt numb, and for a moment she encouraged herself to believe that the numbness was a sign of not caring about what she'd just learned. But she knew the reality was that she was in shock.

And between the time of the shock's wearing off and the rage's setting in, she hoped she'd have five minutes to decide what to do.

WINSTON NKATA'S PAGER went off while Lynley was reading the action reports that DCI Leach's team had been sending in to the incident room for compilation during the morning. In the absence of both eyewitnesses and evidence at the crime scene beyond the paint chips, the vehicle used in the first hit-and-run was what was left as the murder squad's focus. But according to the activities reports, the town's body shops were proving to be fallow ground so far, as were the parts shops, where something like a chrome bumper might possibly be purchased to replace one damaged in an accident.

Lynley looked up from one of the reports to see Nkata scrutinising his pager and contemplatively fingering his facial scar. He took off his reading glasses and said, "What is it, Winnie?" and the constable replied, "Don't know, man." But he said it slowly, as if he had his thoughts on the subject, after which he went to a phone on a nearby desk, where a WPC was entering data into the computer.

"I think our next step is Swansea, sir," Lynley had said to DCI Leach by mobile once they'd completed their interview with Raphael Robson. "It seems to me that we've got all the principals in hand at this point. Let's run their names through the DVLA and see if one of them has an older car registered, in addition to what they're driving round town. Start with Raphael Robson and see what he has. It could be in a lockup somewhere."

Leach had agreed. And this is what the WPC at the computer was doing at the moment: contacting the vehicle department, plugging in names, and looking for ownership of a classic—or simply an old car.

"We can't discount the possibility that one of our suspects just has access to cars—old or otherwise," Leach had pointed out. "Could be the friend of a collector, for instance. Friend of a car salesman. Friend of someone who works as a mechanic."

"And we also can't discount the possibility that the car was stolen, recently purchased from a private party but not registered, or brought over from Europe to do the job and already returned with no one the wiser," Lynley said. "In which case the DVLA will be a dead end. But in the absence of anything else . . ."

"Right," Leach said. "What've we got to lose?"

Both of them knew that what they had to lose was Webberly, whose condition had altered perilously in Charing Cross Hospital.

"Heart attack," Hillier had said tersely from intensive care. "Just three hours ago. Blood pressure went down, heart started acting dodgy, then . . . bam. It was massive."

"Jesus Christ," Lynley said.

"Used those things on him . . . what're they . . . electrical shocks . . ."

"Those paddles?"

"Ten times. Eleven. Randie was there. They got her out of the room but not before the alarms and the shouting and . . . It's a *bloody* mess, this."

"What are they telling you, sir?"

"He's monitored every which way to Sunday. IVs, tubes, machines, wires. Ventricular fibrillation, this was. It could happen again. Anything could."

"How's Randie?"

"Coping." Hillier didn't give Lynley a chance to enquire about anything else. Instead, he went on gruffly, as if wishing to dismiss a topic that was too frightening to entertain, "Who've you brought in for questioning?" He wasn't happy when he learned that Leach's best efforts had failed to gain anything substantial from Pitchley-Pitchford-Pytches upon his third interview. He was also not pleased to learn that the equally best efforts of the teams who were working the sites of the two hit-and-runs had uncovered nothing more useful than what they had already known about the car. He *was* moderately satisfied with the news from forensic about the paint chips and the age of the vehicle. But information was one thing; an arrest was another. And he God damn wanted a bloody arrest.

"Do you have that message, Acting Superintendent?"

Lynley took a deep breath and put the heightened level of Hillier's acerbity down to his understandable dread about Webberly. He did indeed have the message, he told the AC steadily. Was Miranda really all right, though? Was there anything he could . . . ?

Had Helen at least managed to get her to have a meal?

"She's gone to Frances," Hillier said.

"Randie?"

"Your wife. Laura's got exactly nowhere, can't even budge her from her bedroom, so Helen's decided to try her hand. Good woman, there." Hillier harrumphed. He would, Lynley knew, never venture any closer to a compliment.

"Thank you, sir."

"Get on with things. I'm staying here. I don't want Randie alone should anything . . . should she be asked to decide . . ."

"Right. Yes, sir. That's the best idea, isn't it?"

Now Lynley watched Nkata. Curiously, the constable was protecting his phone conversation from eavesdroppers with a broad shoulder lifted to shield the mouthpiece of the receiver. Lynley frowned at this, and when Nkata rang off, he said, "Get anything?"

Rubbing his hands together, the DC said, "Hope so, man. Bird who lives with Katja Wolff's asking for another word. That's who paged. Think I ought . . . ?" He nodded towards the doorway, but the motion seemed more a bow to obligation than an actual request for direction because the constable's fingers began tapping against the pocket of his trousers as if eager to dig out his car keys.

Lynley reflected upon what Nkata had already told him about his most recent interview with both women. "Did she say what she wanted?"

"Just a word. Said she didn't want to talk on the phone."

"Why not?"

Nkata shrugged and shifted his weight from one foot to the other. "Villains, man. You know how they are. Always like to be the ones pulling the strings."

That certainly rang an authentic note. If a convict was going to grass on a mate, that convict generally named the time, the place, and the circumstances under which the grassing would occur. It was a power play that acted as a salve to their conscience when they lived the part of no honour among thieves. But lags rarely bore love for cops, and caution suggested that a cop be wise to the fact that a villain liked nothing better than to throw spanners if he could, with the size of the spanners generally matching the proportions of his animosity for the police.

He said, "What's she called again, Winnie?"

"Who?"

"The woman who paged you. Wolff's flat mate." And when Nkata told him, Lynley asked what crime had sent Yasmin Edwards to prison.

"Knifed her husband," Nkata said. "Killed him. She was in five years. But I got the 'pression he beat her up a lot. She's got a bad face, 'Spector. Scarred up. She and the German live with her son. Daniel. Ten, eleven years old. Nice kid. Should I . . . ?" Again the anxious nod at the door.

Lynley pondered the wisdom of sending Nkata south of the river again on his own. His very zeal to take on the task gave Lynley pause. On the one hand,

Nkata would be eager to make up for his earlier gaffe. On the other hand, he was inexperienced, and the appetite he had for again confronting Yasmin Edwards suggested the potential for a loss of objectivity. As long as the potential was there, Nkata—not to mention the case itself—was in jeopardy. Just as Webberly had been, Lynley realised, all those years ago in another investigation.

They kept coming full circle to that other murder, he thought. There had to be a reason for that.

He said, "Has she got an axe to grind, this Yasmin Edwards?"

"With me, you mean?"

"With cops in general."

"Could have, yeah."

"Mind how you go, then."

Nkata said, "Will do," and he hastened out of the incident room, car keys already in his palm.

When the constable was gone, Lynley sat at a desk and put on his glasses. The situation they were in was maddening. He'd been involved in cases before in which they'd had mounds of evidence but no one to whom it could be attached. He'd been involved in cases in which they'd had motives leaping out from the wallpaper in the sitting room of every suspect they questioned but no evidence they could apply to the suspects. And he'd been involved in cases in which the means and the opportunity to kill could be applied left, right, and centre and all that was wanting was clarity on the motive. But this . . .

How was it possible that two people could be hit

and abandoned on populated streets without *someone* seeing something other than a black vehicle? Lynley wondered. And how was it possible that the first victim could actually be dragged from point A to point B in Crediton Hill once the hit took place without someone noticing what was going on?

The moving of the body was an important detail, and Lynley fetched the latest report from forensic to examine what they'd come up with from evidence taken from Eugenie Davies' body. The forensic pathologist would have combed it, probed it, studied it, and analysed it. And if there was a trace of evidence left on it—this despite the rain of the evening—the forensic pathologst would have found it.

Lynley flipped through the paperwork. Nothing under her fingernails, all blood on the body her own, remnants of earth fallen from tyres bearing no telling characteristics like minerals peculiar to one part of the country, granules caught up in her hair similar to those on the street itself, two hairs on her body—one grey and one brown—which, under analysis—

Lynley's interest sharpened. Two hairs, two different colours, an analysis. Surely this amounted to something. He read the report, frowning, wading through descriptions of cuticle, cortex, and medulla and celebrating the initial conclusion offered by SO7: The hairs were mammalian in origin.

But when he continued, fighting his way through the morass of technical terms from *the macrofibrillar ultrastructure of the medullary cells* to *the electrophoretic variants of the structural proteins,* he found that the results of the forensic examination of the hairs was inconclusive. How the hell could that possibly be?

He reached for a phone and punched in the number of the forensic lab across the river. After speaking to three technicians and a secretary, he was finally able to pin someone down who explained in layman's terms why a study of hair, made in this century of science so advanced that a microscopic particle of *skin*—for God's sake—could identify a killer, would offer inconclusive results.

"Actually," Dr. Claudia Knowles told him, "we have no way of telling if the hairs even came from the killer, Inspector. They could well be from the victim, you know."

"How can that be?"

"First, because we have no scalp attached to either of them. Second—and here's the trickier part—because there's a vast variation in features even within hairs that come from *one* individual. So we could take dozens of samples of your victim's hair and still not be able to match them to the two hairs found on her body. And all the time they could still be hers. Because of the possible variations. Do you see what I mean?"

"But what about DNA typing? What's the point of combing for hairs in the first place if we can't use them—"

"It's not that we can't use them," Dr. Knowles interrupted. "We can and we will. But even then, what we'll learn—and this isn't done overnight, which I'm sure you're already aware of—is whether the hairs did come from your victim. Which will help you, of course. But if the hairs *didn't* come from her, you'll be helped only as far as knowing that someone was close enough to her body either before or after her death to have left a hair or two on it."

"What about two people being close enough to her body to leave a hair? Since one hair was grey and one was brown?"

"That could have happened. But even then, you see, we can't discount the possibility that prior to her death she embraced someone who quite innocently left a hair behind in the process. And even if we *have* the DNA typing in front of us, to prove that she couldn't have embraced anyone who is currently in her life, what do we do with that typing, Inspector, without someone on the other end giving us a sample to match it to?"

God. Yes. That was the problem. That would always be the blasted problem. Lynley thanked Dr. Knowles and rang off, flinging the report to one side. They needed a break.

He read through the notes of his interviews again: what Wiley had said, what Staines had said, what Davies, Robson, and the younger Davies had said. There had to be something he was overlooking. But he couldn't dig it out of what he had written.

All right, he thought. Time to try another tack.

He left the station and made the quick drive to West Hampstead. He found Crediton Hill a short distance from Finchley Road, and he parked at the top end, got out, and began to pace. The street was lined with cars, and it possessed that uninhabited air of a place where all the occupants leave for work each morning, not to return till night.

Chalk marks on the tarmac indicated the spot where Eugenie Davies' body had lain, and Lynley stood upon these and gazed down the street in the direction the deadly vehicle would have come. She'd been hit and then driven over several times, which seemed to indicate that she'd either not been thrown as Webberly had or that she'd been thrown directly in front of the car, making the act of driving back and forth over her an easy piece of business. Then she'd been dragged to one side, her body half shoved beneath a Vauxhall.

But why? Why would her killer risk being seen? Why not just drive off and leave her lying in the middle of the road? Of course, putting her to one side might have served the purpose of keeping her from being noticed at once in the dark and the rain, thereby assuring she'd be dead when someone finally did find her. But it was such a risk to get out of the car at all. Unless the killer had a reason for doing so . . .

Such as living in the neighbourhood? Yes. It was possible.

But was anything else?

Lynley went onto the pavement, pacing along and thinking about every variation he could come up with on the theme of killer-victim-motive, killer-moving-the-broken-body, and killer-getting-out-of-the-car. All he could come up with was her handbag: something she'd carried inside it, something the killer had wanted, had known she'd have with her, had needed to obtain.

But the bag had been found beneath another car on the street, in a spot where it was unlikely that a killer—working in haste and in the darkness—would have seen it. And its contents were in order as far as anyone could tell. Unless, of course, the killer had removed a single item—like a letter, perhaps?—and then thrown the bag beneath the car, where it ultimately had been found.

Lynley paced and considered this and felt as if a Greek chorus had taken up residence in his head, reciting not only all the possibilities but also the consequences of his choosing one of them and investing an ounce of belief in it. He walked several yards past several houses, past the autumn-coloured hedges that edged their gardens. He was just about to turn back and walk to his car, when something glittering on the pavement caught his eye, quite near to a yew hedge that looked more recently planted than the others on the street.

He bent to this like Sherlock Holmes redeemed. But it proved to be just a shard of glass that, along with a few other shards, had been swept from the pavement into the flower bed where the hedge was planted. He took a pencil from his jacket pocket and turned the shards over, then dug round in the earth and found a few more. And because he'd never felt quite so much without resources as he was feeling in this investigation, he took out his handkerchief and collected them all.

Back in his car, he phoned home, seeking Helen. It was hours since she'd turned up at Charing Cross Hospital, hours since she'd trekked to Webberly's house to see what could be made of Frances. But she wasn't there. And she wasn't at work in Chelsea with St. James. This, he decided, was not a good sign.

He drove to Stamford Brook.

IN KENSINGTON SQUARE, Barbara Havers parked where she'd parked before: by the line of bollards that prevented traffic entering the square from the north on Derry Street. She walked to the Convent of the Immaculate Conception, but instead of going to the door straightaway and requesting to speak with Sister Cecilia Mahoney once again, she lit a cigarette and ventured farther along the pavement to the distinguished brick Dutch-gabled house where so much had happened two decades in the past.

It was the tallest building on its side of the street: five floors with a lower ground floor which was accessed by a narrow stairway that curved down from the flagstone-covered front garden. Two brick pillars topped with white stone finials sided the wrought iron entrance gate, and Barbara swung this gate open, entered, closed it behind her, and stood looking up at the house.

It was quite a contrast to Lynn Davies' small dwelling on the other side of the river. With its french windows and balconies, its creamy wood-

work, its solemn pediments and dog-toothed cor-
nices, its fanlights and its stained glass windows,
it—and the neighbourhood that surrounded it—
couldn't have been more different to the environment in which Virginia Davies had lived her life.

But there was another difference besides the
obvious physical one, and Barbara thought about it as
she surveyed the house. Inside had lived a terrible
man, in Lynn Davies' words, a man who couldn't
bear to be in the same room as a grandchild who was,
in his eyes, not what she should have been. The child
had been unwelcome in this house, she'd been an object of continual loathing, so her mother had taken
her away forever. And old Jack Davies—terrible Jack
Davies—had been appeased. More, he'd been gratified, as things turned out, because when his son got
round to marrying again, Jack's next grandchild
turned out to be a musical genius.

Delight all round at that one, Barbara thought. The
kid picked up a fiddle, made his mark, and gave the
name Davies the glory it deserved. But then came
the *next* grandchild's birth, and old Jack Davies—terrible Jack Davies—was made to look imperfection in
the face another time.

But on this second go with a defective child, things
were more dicey for Jack. Because if old Jack Davies
drove *this* mother off with his relentless demands to
"keep her out of my sight, put that creature *away*
somewhere," chances were that this mother would
take her other child with her. And that would mean
goodbye Gideon and goodbye to basking vicariously

in the glory of everything Gideon stood to accomplish.

When Sonia Davies was drowned in her bath, had the police even known about Virginia? Barbara wondered. And if they had, had the family managed to keep old Jack's attitude to her under wraps? Probably.

He'd gone through a horrific time in the war, he'd never recovered, he was a military hero. But he also sounded like a man who was five notes short of a full sonata, and how was anyone to know how far a man like that would go when he'd been thwarted?

Barbara went back to the pavement, closing the gate behind her. She flipped her cigarette into the street and retraced her steps to the Convent of the Immaculate Conception.

This time round, she found Sister Cecilia Mahoney in the enormous garden behind the main building. With another nun, she was raking up leaves from a mammoth sycamore tree that could have shaded an entire hamlet. They'd so far made five piles of leaves, which formed colourful mounds across the lawn. In the distance where a wall marked the end of the convent's property and protected it from the trains of the District line that rumbled above ground throughout the day, a man in a boiler suit and a knitted hat was tending a fire where some of the gathered leaves were burning.

"You need to have a care with that sort of thing," Barbara said to Sister Cecilia as she joined her. "One wrong move and all of Kensington'll go up in smoke. I don't expect you want that."

"With no Wren to build its replacement," Sister Cecilia noted. "Yes. We're being quite careful, Constable. George doesn't leave the fire unattended. And I'm thinking it's George who's got the better bargain. We do the gathering and he makes the offering that God receives with pleasure."

"Pardon?"

The nun drew her rake along the lawn, its tines snaring a cluster of leaves. "Biblical allusion, if you'll pardon me. Cain and Abel. Abel's fire produced smoke that went heavenward."

"Oh. Right."

"You don't know the Old Testament?"

"Just the lying, knowing, and begetting parts. And I've got most of those memorised."

Sister Cecilia laughed and took her rake to lean it against a bench that encircled the sycamore at the garden's centre. She returned to Barbara, saying, "Sure there was a great deal of lying and begetting going on in those days, wasn't there, Constable? But then, they had to set about it, didn't they, since they'd been told to populate the world."

Barbara smiled. "Could I have a word?"

"Of course. You'll be preferring to have it inside the convent, I expect." Sister Cecilia didn't wait for a reply. She merely said to her companion, "Sister Rose, if I can leave you to this for a quarter of an hour . . . ?" and when the other nun nodded, she led the way to a short flight of concrete stairs which took them to the back door of the dun brick building.

They walked down a lino-floored corridor to a

door marked *visitors' room*. Here, Sister Cecilia knocked, and when there was no reply, she swung the door open, saying, "Would you like a cup of tea, Constable? A coffee? I think we've a biscuit or two."

Barbara demurred. Just conversation, she told the nun.

"You don't mind if I . . . ?" Sister Cecilia indicated an electric kettle, which stood on a chipped plastic tray along with a tin of Earl Grey tea and several mismatched cups and saucers. She plugged the kettle in and fetched from the top of a small chest of drawers a box of sugar cubes, three of which she plopped into a cup, saying serenely to Barbara, "Sweet tooth. But God forgives small vices in us all. I would feel less guilty, though, if you'd be taking a biscuit at least. They're Weight Watchers. Oh but sure, I don't mean to imply that you're needing to—"

"No offence taken," Barbara interrupted. "I'll have one."

Sister Cecilia looked mischievous. "They do come in packets of two, Constable."

"Hand them over, then. I'll cope."

With her tea made and her biscuits in their little packet on a separate saucer, Sister Cecilia was prepared to join Barbara. They sat on two vinyl-covered chairs next to a window that overlooked the garden where Sister Rose was still raking leaves. A low veneer table separated them, its surface holding a variety of religious magazines and one copy of *Elle*, heavily thumbed.

Barbara told the nun that she'd met Lynn Davies

and asked if Sister Cecilia knew about this earlier marriage and this additional child of Richard Davies.

Sister Cecilia confirmed that she had long known, that she'd learned about Lynn and that "poor dear mite of hers" from Eugenie shortly after Gideon's birth. "It came as quite a shock to Eugenie, to be sure, Constable. She'd not known Richard was even divorced, and she spent some time reflecting on what it meant that he hadn't told her prior to their marriage."

"I expect she felt betrayed."

"Oh, it wasn't the personal side of the omission that concerned her. At least, if it was, she didn't discuss that part of it with me. It was the spiritual and religious implications that Eugenie wrestled with during those first years after Gideon's birth."

"What sort of implications?"

"Well, the holy Church recognises marriage as a permanent covenant between a man and a woman."

"Was Mrs. Davies concerned that if the Church saw her husband's first marriage as his legitimate one, her own marriage would be considered bigamous? And the kids from that marriage illegitimate?"

Sister Cecilia took a sip of tea. "Yes and no," she replied. "The situation was complicated by the fact that Richard himself wasn't Catholic. He wasn't actually anything, poor man. He hadn't been married in any church in the first place, so Eugenie's real question was whether he'd lived in sin with Lynn and if the child from that union—who would thus be conceived in sin—bore the mark of God's judgement upon her. And if that were the case, did Eugenie herself run the risk of calling down God's judgement upon herself as well?"

"For having married a man who'd 'lived in sin,' d'you mean?"

"Ah no. For not herself having married him in the Church."

"The Church wouldn't allow it?"

"It was never a question of what the Church would or would not allow. Richard didn't want a religious ceremony, so they never had one. Just the civil procedure at the register office."

"But as a Catholic, wouldn't Mrs. Davies have wanted a Church wedding as well? Wouldn't she have been obliged to have one? I mean, for everything to be on the up and up with God and the Pope."

"That's how it is, my dear. But Eugenie was Catholic only as far as it went."

"Meaning?"

"Meaning that she received some sacraments but not others. She accepted some beliefs but not others."

"When you join up, aren't you supposed to swear on the Bible or something that you'll abide by the rules? I mean, we know that she wasn't brought up Catholic, so does the Church take on members who abide by some rules and not by others?"

"You must remember that the Church has no secret police to make certain its members are walking the straight and narrow, Constable," the nun replied. She took a bite from her biscuit and munched. "God has given us each a conscience so that we can monitor our own behaviour. Isn't it true, of course, that there are many topics on which individual Catholics part ways with Holy Mother the Church, but whether that puts their eternal salvation into jeopardy is something that only God could tell us."

"Yet Mrs. Davies seemed to believe that God gets even with sinners during their lifetimes, if she thought that Virginia was God's way of dealing with Richard and Lynn."

"Sure it is that when a misfortune befalls someone, people often interpret it that way. But consider Job. What was his sin that he was so tried by God?"

"Knowing and begetting on the wrong side of the sheets?" Barbara asked. "I can't remember."

"You can't remember because there was no sin. Just the terrible trials of his faith in the Almighty." Sister Cecilia took up her tea, wiping the biscuit crumbs from her fingers onto the nubby material of her skirt.

"Is that what you told Mrs. Davies, then?"

"I pointed out that had God wished to punish her, He certainly wouldn't have started out by giving her Gideon—a perfectly healthy child—as the first fruit of her marriage to Richard."

"But as to Sonia?"

"Did she consider that child her punishment from God for her sins?" Sister Cecilia clarified. "She never said as much. But from the way she reacted when she was told about the wee one's condition . . . And then when she stopped attending church entirely once the baby died . . ." The nun sighed, brought her cup to her lips, and held it there as she considered how to reply. She finally said, "We can only surmise, Constable. We can only take the questions she asked with regard to Lynn and Virginia and infer from them how she herself might have felt and what she might have believed when she was faced with a similar trial."

"What about the rest of them?"

"The rest?"

"The rest of the family. Did she mention how they felt? About Sonia? Once they knew . . . ?"

"She never said."

"Lynn says she left in part because of Richard Davies' dad. She says he had a few cogs not working, but the ones that did work were nasty enough for her to be glad the rest were misfiring. If a cog misfires. But I expect you know what I mean."

"Eugenie didn't talk about the household."

"She didn't mention anyone wanting to get rid of Sonia? Like Richard? Or his dad? Or anyone?"

Sister Cecilia's blue eyes widened over the biscuit she'd raised to her lips. She said, "Mary and Joseph. No. *No.* This was not a house of evil people. Troubled people, perhaps, as we're all troubled from time to time. But to want to be rid of a baby so desperately that one of them might have . . . ? No. I can't think that of any of them."

"But someone did kill her, and you told me yesterday that you didn't believe it was Katja Wolff."

"Didn't and don't," the nun affirmed.

"But someone had to have done the deed, unless you believe that the hand of God swept down and held that baby under the water. So who? Eugenie herself? Richard? Granddad? The lodger? Gideon?"

"He was eight years old!"

"And jealous that a second child had come to take the spotlight off him?"

"She could hardly do that."

"But she could take everyone's attention from him. She could take up their time. She could take most of their money. She could tap the well till the well was dry. And if it went dry, where would that leave Gideon?"

"No eight-year-old child thinks that far into the future."

"But someone else might have, someone who had a vested interest in keeping him front and centre in the household."

"Yes. Well. I don't know who that someone might be."

Barbara watched the nun place half of the biscuit onto the saucer. She watched as Sister Cecilia went to the kettle and switched it on for a second cup of tea. She weighed her preconceived notions about nuns with what information she'd gathered from this one and the air with which Sister Cecilia had parted with it. She concluded that the nun was telling her everything she knew. In their earlier interview, Sister Cecilia had said that Eugenie stopped attending church when Sonia died. So she—Sister Cecilia—would no longer have had the opportunity she'd once had for heart-to-heart chats of the sort that passed along crucial information.

She said, "What happened to the other baby?"

"The other . . . ? Oh. Are you speaking of Katja's child?"

"My DCI wants me to track him down."

"He's in Australia, Constable. He's been there since he was twelve years old. And as I told you when we first spoke, if Katja wished to find him, she'd have come to me at once upon her release. You must believe me. The terms of the adoption asked the parents to provide annual updates about the child, so I've always known where he was and I'd have provided Katja with that information any time she asked for it."

"But she didn't?"

"She did not." Sister Cecilia headed for the door. "If you'll excuse me for a moment, I'll fetch something you might want to see."

The nun left the room just as the electric kettle brought the water to a boil and clicked off. Barbara rose and brewed a second cup of Earl Grey for Sister Cecilia, scoring another packet of the biscuits for herself. She'd crammed these down her throat and added the three cubes of sugar to Sister Cecilia's tea when the nun returned, a manila envelope in her hand.

She sat, knees and ankles together, and spread the contents of the envelope on her lap. Barbara saw they consisted of letters and photographs, both snapshots and studio portraits.

"He's called Jeremy, Katja's son," Sister Cecilia told

her. "He'll be twenty in February. He was adopted by a family called Watts, along with three other children. They're in Adelaide now, all of them. He favours his mother, I think."

Barbara took the photos that Sister Cecilia offered her. In them she saw that the nun had maintained a pictorial record of the child's life. Jeremy was fair and blue-eyed, although the blond hair of his childhood had darkened to pine in his adolescence. He'd gone through a gawky period round the time his family had taken him and his siblings to Australia, but once he'd passed through that, he was handsome enough. Straight nose, square jaw, ears flat against his skull, he would do for an Aryan, Barbara thought.

She said, "Katja Wolff doesn't know that you have these?"

Sister Cecilia said, "As I told you, she wouldn't ever see me. Even when it came time to arrange for Jeremy's adoption, she wouldn't speak with me. The prison acted as our go-between: The warden told me Katja wanted an adoption and the warden told me when the time had arrived. Sure, I don't know if Katja ever *saw* the baby. All I know is that she wanted him placed with a family at once, and she wanted me to see to it as soon as was possible after the birth."

Barbara handed the pictures back, saying, "She didn't want him to go to the father?"

"Adoption was what she wanted."

"Who was the dad?"

"We didn't speak—"

"Got that. I know. But you *knew* her. You knew all

of them. So you must have had an idea or two. There were three men in the house that we know of: the Granddad, Richard Davies, and the lodger, who was a bloke called James Pitchford. There were four if you count Raphael Robson, the violin teacher. Five if you want to count Gideon and think Katja might have liked to have at them young. He was precocious in one way. Why not in another?"

The nun looked affronted. "Katja was not a child molester."

"She might not have seen it as molestation. Women don't, do they, when they're initiating a male. Hell, there are tribes where it's *customary* for older women to take young boys in hand."

"Be that as it may, this was not a tribe. And Gideon was certainly *not* the father of that baby. I doubt"—and here the nun blushed hotly—"I doubt that he would have been capable of the act."

"Then whoever it was, he must have had reason to keep his part in it under wraps. Else why not come forward and lay claim to the kid once Katja got her twenty-year sentence? Unless, of course, he didn't want to be known as the man who put a killer in the club."

"Why does it have to be someone from the house at all?" Sister Cecilia asked. "And why is it important to know?"

"I'm not sure it is important," Barbara admitted. "But if the father of her baby is somehow involved with everything else that happened to Katja Wolff, then he might be in danger right now. If she's behind two hit-and-runs."

"*Two . . . ?*"

"The officer who headed the investigation into Sonia's death was hit last night. He's in a coma."

Sister Cecilia's fingers reached for the crucifix she wore round her neck. They curled round it and held on fast as the nun said, "I cannot believe Katja had anything to do with that."

"Right," Barbara said. "But sometimes we end up having to believe what we don't want to believe. That's the way of the world, Sister."

"It is not the way of my world," the nun declared.

GIDEON

6 NOVEMBER

I'VE DREAMED again, Dr. Rose. I'm standing on the stage at the Barbican, with the lights blindingly bright above me. The orchestra is behind me, and the maestro—whose face I cannot see—taps on his lectern. The music begins—four measures from the cellos—and I lift my instrument and prepare to join in. Then from somewhere in the vast hall, I hear it: A baby has begun crying.

It echoes through the hall, but I'm the only person who seems to notice. The cellos continue to play, the rest of the strings join them, and I know that my solo will be fast upon us.

I cannot think, I cannot play, I cannot do anything but wonder why the maestro won't stop the orchestra, won't turn to the audience, won't demand that someone have the simple courtesy to take the screaming child out of the auditorium so that we can concentrate on our playing. There is a full measure's rest before I'm to begin my solo, and as I wait for it to arrive, I keep glancing out to the audience. But I can see nothing because of the lights, and they are far more blinding than lights ever are in an actual auditorium. Indeed, they're the sort of lights one imagines to be shined upon a suspect who is under interrogation.

When the strings reach the full measure's rest, I count the time. I know somehow that I won't be able to play what I'm supposed to play while the distraction continues, but I feel that I must. I will thus have to do what I've never done before: As ludicrous as it sounds, I will have to fake it, to improvise if necessary, to maintain the same key but to play *anything* if I have to in order to get myself through the ordeal.

I begin. Of course, it isn't right. It isn't in the right key. To my left, the concertmaster stands abruptly and I see that he's Raphael Robson. I want to say, "Raphael, you're playing! With an audience, you're playing!" but the rest of the violins follow his lead and leap to their feet as well. They begin to protest to the maestro, as do the cellos and the basses. I hear all their voices. I try to drown them out with my playing and I try to drown the baby out, but I cannot. I want to tell them that it's not me, it's not my fault, and I say, "Can't you hear? Can't you hear it?" as I continue to play. And I watch the maestro as I do so, because he's continuing to direct the orchestra as if they'd never stopped playing in the first place.

Raphael then approaches the maestro, who turns to me. And he is my father. "Play!" he snarls. And I'm so surprised to see him there where he should not be that I back away and the darkness of the auditorium envelops me.

I begin to search for the screaming baby. I go up the aisle, feeling my way in the dark, until I hear that the crying is coming from behind a closed door.

I open this door. Suddenly, I am outside, in daylight, and in front of me is an enormous fountain. But this is not an ordinary fountain, because standing in the water are a minister of some sort dressed all in black and a woman in white who is holding the yowling infant to her bosom. As I watch, the minister submerges them both—the woman and the child that she holds—in the water, and I know that the woman is Katja Wolff and that she's holding my sister.

Somehow, I know I must get to that fountain, but my feet become too heavy to lift. So I watch, and when Katja Wolff emerges from the water, she emerges alone.

The water makes her white dress cling to her, and through the material her nipples show, as does her pubic hair, which is thick, dark as night, and coiling coiling coiling over her sex, which still glistens through the wet dress she's wearing as if she's not wearing a dress at all. And I feel that stirring within me, that rush of desire I haven't felt in years. The throb begins and I welcome it and I no longer think of the concert I've left or the ceremony I've witnessed in the water.

My feet are freed. I approach. Katja cups her breasts in her hands. But before I can reach the fountain and her, the minister blocks my way and I look at him and he is my father.

He goes to her. He does to her what I want to do, and I am forced to watch as her body draws him in and begins to work him as the water slaps languidly against their legs.

I cry out, and I awaken.

And there it was between my legs, Dr. Rose, what I hadn't been able to manage in . . . how many years? . . . since Beth. Throbbing, engorged, and ready for action, all because of a dream in which I was nothing but a voyeur of my father's pleasure.

I lay there in the darkness, despising myself, despising my body and my mind and what both of them were telling me through the means of a dream. And as I lay there, a memory came to me.

It is Katja, and she has come into the dining room where we're having dinner. She's carrying my sister, who is dressed for bed, and it's very clear that she's excited about something, because when Katja Wolff is excited, her English becomes more broken. She says, "See! See you must what she has done!"

Granddad says irritably, "What is it *now?*" and there's a moment that I recognise as tension while all the adults look at each other: Mother at Granddad, Dad at Gran, Sarah-Jane at James the Lodger. He—James—is looking at Katja. And Katja is looking at Sonia.

She says, "Show them, little one," and she sets my sister on the floor. She puts her on her bum but she doesn't prop her up as she's had to do in the past. Instead, she balances her carefully and removes her hands, and Sonia remains upright.

"She sits alone!" Katja announces proudly. "Is this not a dream?"

Mother gets to her feet, saying, "Wonderful, darling!" and goes to cuddle her. She says, "Thank you, Katja," and when she smiles, her face is radiant with delight.

Granddad makes no comment at all because he doesn't look to see what Sonia has managed to do. Gran murmurs, "Lovely, my dear," and watches Granddad.

Sarah-Jane Beckett makes a polite comment and attempts to draw James the Lodger into conversation. But it's an attempt that is all in vain: James is fixated on Katja the way a starving dog might fixate on a rare piece of beef.

And Katja herself is fixated on my father. "See how lovely is she!" Katja crows. "See what learns she and how quickly! What a good big girl is Sonia, yes. Every baby can thrive with Katja."

Every baby. How had I forgotten those words and that look? How had it escaped me till now: what those words and that look really meant? What they *had* to have meant, because everyone freezes the way people freeze when a motion picture is reduced to a single frame. And a moment later—in the breath of a second—Mother picks up Sonia and says, "We're all quite sure that's the case, my dear."

I saw it then, and I see it now. But I didn't understand because what was I, seven years old? What child that young can comprehend the full reality of the situation in which he's living? What child that young can infer from a single simple statement graciously said a woman's sudden understanding of a betrayal that has occurred and is continuing to occur within her own home?

9 NOVEMBER

He kept that picture, Dr. Rose. Everything I know goes back to the fact that my father kept that single picture, a photograph that he himself must have taken and hidden away because how else could it possibly have come to be in his possession?

So I see them, on a sunny afternoon in the summer, and he asks Katja to step into the garden so that he can take a photo of her with my sister. Sonia's presence, cradled in Katja's arms, legitimises the moment. Sonia serves as an excuse for the picture-taking despite the fact that she is cradled in such a way that her face isn't visible to the camera. And that's an important detail as well, because Sonia isn't perfect. Sonia is a freak, and a picture of Sonia whose face bears the manifestations of the congenital syndrome that afflicts her—oblique palpebral fissures, I have learned they are called, epicanthal folds, and a mouth that is disproportionately small—will serve as a constant reminder to Dad that he created for the second time in his life a child with physical and mental imperfections. So he doesn't want to capture her face on film, but he needs her there as an excuse.

Are he and Katja lovers at the time? Or do they both just think about it then, each of them waiting for some sign from the other that will express an interest that cannot yet be spoken? And when it happens between them for the first time, who makes the move and what is the move that signals the direction they will soon be taking?

She goes out for a breath of air on a stifling night, the kind of August night in London when a heat wave hits and there's no escaping the oppressive atmosphere created by bad air hanging too long over the city, which is daily heated by the scorching sun and further poisoned by the diesel lorries that belch exhaust fumes along the streets. Sonia is asleep at long last, and Katja has ten precious minutes to herself. The darkness outside makes a false promise of deliverance from the heat trapped inside the house, so she walks out into it, out into the garden behind the house, which is where he finds her.

"Terrible day," he says. "I'm burning up."

"I, too," she replies, and she watches him steadily. "I too burn, Richard."

And that is enough. That final statement and especially the use of his Christian name constitute implicit permission, and he needs no other invitation. He surges towards her, and it begins between them, and this is what I see from the garden.

TWENTY

LIBBY NEALE had never been to Richard Davies' flat, so she didn't know what to expect when she drove Gideon there from the Temple. Asked about it, she might have guessed that he'd be living high out of very deep pockets. He'd been making such a deal about Gideon's not playing the violin for the past four months, it seemed reasonable to conclude that he needed a hefty income that only cash from Gideon on a regular basis could provide.

So she said, "This is *it*?" when Gideon told her to pull to the kerb at a parking space on the north side of a street called Cornwall Gardens. She looked at the neighbourhood with a vague sense of disappointment, taking in buildings that were—okay—*genteel* enough but dilapidated to the max. True, there were some decent-looking places crammed in here and there, but the rest of them looked like they'd seen better days in another century.

It got worse. Gideon, without replying to her question, led the way to a building that looked like prayers were holding it up. He used a key on a front door so warped away from the jamb that using a key in the first place seemed like an unnecessary courtesy applied to spare the door's feelings. A credit card would have done as well. When they were inside, he led her upstairs to a second door. This one wasn't warped, but someone had decorated it with a trail of green spray paint in the shape of a Z, like an Irish Zorro had come to call.

Gideon said, "Dad?" as he swung the door open and they entered his father's flat. He said to Libby, "Wait here," which she was glad to do as he ducked into a kitchen that was just off the living room. The place gave her the major creeps. It was so not the kind of place she'd thought Richard Davies would've set himself up in.

First off, what was with the colour scheme? Libby wondered. She was no decorator—leave that to her mom and her sister, who were into Fêng Shui in a major way. But even she could tell that the colours in this place were guaranteed to make anyone want to take a leap from the nearest bridge. Puke-green walls. Diarrhoea-brown furniture. And weirdo art like that nude woman shown from neck to ankles with pubic hair looking like the inside of a toilet going through the flush cycle. What did *that* mean? Above the fire-place—which for some reason was filled with books—a circular display of tree branches had been pounded. These looked like they'd been made into walking sticks because they were sanded down and had holes punched through them and leather thongs threaded through the holes like wrist straps. But how weird to have them there in the first place.

The only thing in the room that Libby saw and had expected to see were pictures of Gideon. There were tons of those. And they were all unified by the same boring theme: the violin. Surprise, surprise, Libby thought. Richard couldn't *possibly* have a shot of Gideon doing something he might *like* to do. Why show him flying kites on Primrose Hill? Why catch him landing his glider? Why take a picture of him helping some kid from the East End learn how to hold a violin if he *himself* wasn't holding it, playing it, and making a bang-up salary for doing so? Richard, Libby thought, needed his butt kicked. He was so *not* helping Gideon get better.

She heard a window in the kitchen creak open, heard Gideon shout for his father in the direction of the garden that she'd seen to the left of the building itself. Richard obviously wasn't out there, though, because after thirty seconds and a few more shouts, the window closed. Gideon came back through the living room and headed down the hall.

He didn't say, "Wait here," this time, so Libby followed him. She'd had enough of the creepoid living room.

He worked through the place back to front, saying, "Dad?" as he opened a bedroom door and then a bathroom door. Libby followed. She was about to tell him it was sort of obvious that Richard wasn't at home, so why was Gideon yelling for him like he'd lost his hearing in the last twenty-four hours when he shoved on another door, swung it wide, and revealed the icing on the cake of the flat's overall weirdness.

Gideon ducked through the doorway, and she trailed him, saying, "Whoops! Oh, sorry," when she first caught a glimpse of the uniformed soldier standing just inside. It took her a moment to realise the soldier wasn't Richard playing dress-up with the hope of spooking the hell out of them. It was, instead, a mannequin. She approached it gingerly and said, "Jeez. What the hell . . . ?" and glanced at Gideon. But he was already at a desk at the far side of the room, and he had its fold-down front opened and was rooting through all its cubbyholes, looking so intense that she figured he wouldn't hear her even if she asked what she wanted to ask, which was what the hell Richard was *doing* with this weirdo piece of crap in his house and did Gid think Jill knew about it?

There were display cases as well, the kinds that you saw in museums. And these were filled with letters, medals, commendations, telegrams, and all sorts of junk that upon inspection appeared to have come from World War II. On the walls were pictures from the same era, all showing a dude in the Army. Here he was on his stomach, squinting down the barrel of a rifle like John Wayne in a war movie. There he was running alongside a tank. Next he was seated cross-legged on the ground, at the front of a pack of similar dudes with their weapons slung over their bodies all casual, like having an AK-47—or whatever it had been in those days—across your shoulder was pretty much par for the course. It wasn't what *any-one* with a grain of sense would show himself doing today. Not unless he was part of some neo-Nazi freedom fighter let's-get-rid-of-everyone-who's-not-a-WASP group.

Libby felt queasy. Getting out of this place in the next thirty seconds didn't seem like such a bad idea.

This thought was reinforced when she saw the last set of pictures, which showed the same guy as before but this time in completely different circumstances. He looked like someone from a Nazi death camp. He must have weighed about fifteen pounds, and his body was one big scab and approximately three million oozing sores. He was lying on a pallet in what looked like a jungle hut, and his eyes were so sunken into his head that it seemed they might burn right through his skull.

Behind Libby, drawers slammed shut and other drawers opened. Paperwork shuffled. Things flopped to the floor. She turned and watched what Gideon was doing, thinking, Richard's *really* going to blow a fuse over this one, but then, not much caring because Richard was reaping what Richard had spent a long time sowing.

She said, "Gideon. What are we looking for?"

"He's got her address. He has to have it."

"That doesn't make sense."

"He knows where she is. He's seen her."

"Did he tell you that?"

"She's written to him. He *knows*."

"Gid, did he *tell* you that?" Libby didn't think so. "Hey, why would she write to him? Why would she try to see him? Cresswell-White said she can't contact you guys. Her parole will be screwed up if she does. She's just spent twenty years in the joint, right? You think she wants to go back for three or four more?"

"He knows, Libby. And so do I."

"Then what are we doing here? I mean, if *you* know . . ." Gideon was making less and less sense by the hour. Libby thought fleetingly of his psychiatrist. She knew the shrink's name, Dr. Something Rose, but that was all. She wondered if she should phone every Dr. Rose in the book—how many could there be?—and say, Look, I'm a friend of Gideon Davies'. I'm getting freaked out. He's acting too weird. Can you help out?

Did psychiatrists make house calls? And more to the point, did they take it seriously if a friend of a patient called and said it looked like things were getting out of hand? Or did they then think the friend of the patient should be the next patient? Shit. Hell. *What* should she do? Not call Richard, that's for sure. He wasn't exactly playing the rôle of Mr. Sympathy By The Bucketful.

Gideon had dumped out each of the desk drawers on the floor and had done a thorough job of searching through their contents. The only thing left was a letter holder on top of the desk, which for some bizarre reason—but by then, who was counting them?—he went for last, opening envelopes and throwing them onto the floor after glancing at their contents. But the fifth one he came to, he read. Libby could see it was a card with flowers on the front and a printed greeting inside along with a note. His hand dropped hard as he read the message.

She thought, He's found it. She crossed the room to him. She said, "What? She, like, *wrote* to your dad?"

He said, "Virginia."

She said, "What? Who? Who's Virginia?"

His shoulders shook and his fist grabbed onto the card like he wanted to strangle it and he said again, "Virginia. *Virginia.* God damn him. He lied to me." And he began to cry. Not tears but sobs, heaves of his body like *everything* was trying to come up and out of him: the contents of his stomach, the thoughts in his mind, and the feelings of his heart.

Tentatively, Libby reached for the card. He let her take it from him and she ran her gaze over it, looking for what had caused Gideon's reaction. It said:

Dear Richard:

Thank you for the flowers. They were much appreciated. The ceremony was a brief one, but I tried to make it something Virginia herself would have liked. So I filled the chapel with her finger paintings and put her favourite toys round her coffin before the cremation.

Our daughter was a miracle child in many ways. Not only because she defied medical probability and lived thirty-two years but also because she managed to teach so much to anyone who came into contact with her. I

think you would have been proud to be her father,
Richard. Despite her problems, she had your tenacity
and your fighting spirit, no poor gifts to pass on to a
child.
　　Fondly,
　　Lynn

Libby re-read the message and understood. *She had*
your tenacity and your fighting spirit, no poor gifts to pass
on to a child. Virginia, she thought. Another kid.
Gideon had another sister and she was dead, too.

She looked at Gideon, at a loss for what to say.
He'd been taking so many body blows in the past few
days that she couldn't even begin to think where to
start with the psychic salve that might soothe him.

She said hesitantly, "You didn't know about her,
Gid?" And then, "Gideon?" again when he didn't reply. She reached out and touched his shoulder. He sat
unmoving except for the fact that his whole frame
was trembling. It was *vibrating,* almost, beneath his
clothes.

He said, "Dead."

She said, "Yeah. I read that in the note. Lynn
must've been . . . Well, obviously, she says 'our
daughter,' so she was her mom. Which means your
dad was married before and you had a half sister as
well. You didn't know?"

He took the card back from her. He heaved himself off the chair and clumsily shoved the card back
into its envelope, stuffing this into the back pocket of

his trousers. He said in a voice that was low, like someone talking while hypnotised, "He lies to me about everything. He always has. And he's lying now."

He walked through the litter he'd left on the floor, like a man without vision. Libby trailed him, saying, "Maybe he didn't lie at all," not so much because she wanted to defend Richard Davies—who probably would have lied about the second coming of Christ if that was the way to get what he wanted—but because she couldn't stand the thought of Gideon having to deal with anything else. "I mean, if he never told you about Virginia, it wouldn't have necessarily been a lie. It might've just been one of those things that never came up. Like, maybe he never had the opportunity to talk about her or something. Maybe your mom didn't want her discussed. Too painful? All's I'm saying is that it doesn't have to mean—"

"I knew," he said. "I've always known."

He went into the kitchen with Libby on his heels, chewing on this one. If Gideon knew about Virginia, then what was with him? Freaked out because she'd died, too? Distraught because no one had told him she'd died? Outraged because he'd been kept from the funeral? Except it looked like Richard himself didn't go, if the note was an indication of anything. So what was the lie?

She said, "Gid—" but stopped herself when he began punching numbers into the phone. Although he stood with one hand pressed to his stomach and one foot tapping against the floor, his expression was grim, the way a man looks when he's made up his mind about something.

He said into the phone, "Jill? Gideon. I want to speak with Dad . . . No? Then where . . . ? I'm at the flat. No, he's not here . . . I checked there. Did he give you any idea . . . ?" A rather long pause while Richard's lover either wracked her brains or recited a list of possibilities, at the end of which Gideon said, "Right. MotherCare. Fine . . . Thanks, Jill," and listened some more. He ended with, "No. No message. No message at all. If he rings you, in fact, don't tell him I phoned. I wouldn't want to . . . Right. Let's not worry him. He's got enough on his mind." Then he rang off. "She thinks he's gone off to Oxford Street. Supplies, she says. He wants an intercom for the baby's room. She hadn't yet got one because she intended the baby to sleep with them. Or with her. Or with him. Or with *someone*. But she didn't intend her to be alone. Because if a baby gets left alone, Libby, if a child goes untended for a while, if the parents aren't vigilant, if there's a distraction when they don't expect one, if there's a window open, if someone leaves a candle lit, if anything at all, then the worst can happen. The worst *will* happen. And who knows that better than Dad?"

"Let's go," Libby said. "Let's get out of here, Gideon. Come on. I'll buy you a latte, okay? There's got to be a Starbucks nearby."

He shook his head. "You go. Take the car. Go home."

"I'm not going to leave you here. Besides, how would you get—"

"I'll wait for Dad. He'll drive me back."

"That could be hours. If he goes back to Jill's and she starts labour and then she has the baby, it could be days. Come on. I don't want to leave you hanging around this place alone."

But she couldn't move him. He wouldn't have her there, and he wouldn't go with her. He would, however, speak with his father. "I don't care how long it takes," he told her. "This time I don't really care at all."

Reluctantly, then, she agreed to the plan, not liking it but also seeing that there wasn't much she could do about it. Besides, he seemed calmer after talking to Jill. Or at least he seemed moderately more himself. She said, "Will you call me, then, if you need anything?"

"I won't be needing a thing," he replied.

HELEN HERSELF ANSWERED the door when Lynley knocked at Webberly's house in Stamford Brook. He said, "Helen, why are you still here? When Hillier told me you'd come over from the hospital, I couldn't believe it. You shouldn't be doing this."

"Whyever not?" she asked in a perfectly reasonable voice.

He stepped inside as Webberly's dog came bounding from the direction of the kitchen, barking at full volume. Lynley backed towards the door while

Helen took the dog by the collar and said, "Alfie, no."
She gave him a shake. "He doesn't sound like a
friend, but he's quite all right. All bark and bluster."

"So I noticed," Lynley said.

She looked up from the animal. "Actually, I was
talking about you." She released the Alsatian once
he'd settled. The dog sniffed round Lynley's trouser
turn-ups, accepted the intrusion, and trotted back towards the kitchen. "Don't lecture me, darling,"
Helen said to her husband. "As you see, I have friends
in high places."

"With dangerous teeth."

"That's true." She gave a nod to the door and said,
"I didn't think it would be you. I was hoping for
Randie."

"She still won't leave him?"

"It's a stalemate. She won't leave her father;
Frances won't leave the house. I thought when we
got word about the heart attack . . . Surely, she'll
want to go to him, I thought. She'll force herself. Because he may die, and not to *be* there if he dies . . .
But no."

"It's not your problem, Helen. And considering
the kinds of days you've been having . . . You need to
get some rest. Where's Laura Hillier?"

"She and Frances had a row. Frances more than
Laura, actually. One of those don't-look-at-me-as-if-
I-were-a-monster sort of conversations that start out
with one party trying to convince the other party that
she's not thinking what the other party is determined
to believe she thinks she's thinking because at some

level—would that be subconsciously?—she actually *is* thinking it."

Lynley tried to wade through all this, saying, "Are these waters too deep for me, Helen?"

"They may require life belts."

"I thought I might be of help."

Helen had walked into the sitting room. There, an ironing board had been set up and an iron was sending steam ceilingward, which told Lynley—much to his astonishment—that his wife was actually in the process of seeing to the family laundry. A shirt lay across the board itself, one arm the subject of Helen's most recent ministrations. From the look of the wrinkles that appeared to have been permanently applied to the garment, it seemed that Lynley's wife hadn't exactly found a new calling in life.

She saw his glance and said, "Yes. Well. I'd hoped to be helpful."

"It's brilliant of you. Really," Lynley replied supportively.

"I'm not doing it properly. I can see that. I'm sure there's a logic to it—an order or something?—but I've not yet worked it out. Sleeves first? Front? Back? Collar? I do one part and the other part—which I've already done—wrinkles up again. Can you advise?"

"There must be a laundry nearby."

"That's terrifically helpful, Tommy." Helen smiled ruefully. "Perhaps I should stick to pillowcases. At least they're flat."

"Where's Frances?"

"Darling, no. We can't possibly ask her to—"

He chuckled. "That's not what I meant. I'd like to talk to her. Is she upstairs?"

"Oh. Yes. Once she and Laura had their argument, it was tears all round. Laura dashed out, absolutely sobbing. Frances tore up the stairs looking grim-faced. When I checked on her, she was sitting on the floor in a corner of her bedroom, clutching onto the curtains. She asked to be left alone."

"Randie needs to be with her. She needs to be with Randie."

"Believe me, Tommy, I've made that point. Carefully, subtly, straightforwardly, respectfully, cajolingly, and every other way I could think of, save belligerently."

"That could be what she needs. Bellicosity."

"Tone might work—although I doubt it—but volume I guarantee will get you nowhere. She asks to be left alone each time I go up to see her, and while I'd rather not leave her alone, I keep thinking I ought to respect her wishes."

"Let me have a go, then."

"I'll come as well. Have you any further news of Malcolm? We haven't had word from the hospital since Randie phoned, which is good, I suppose. Because surely Randie would have phoned at once if . . . Is there no change, Tommy?"

"No change," Lynley answered. "The heart complicates things. It's a waiting game."

"Do you think they might have to decide . . . ?" Helen paused on the stairway above him and looked back, reading in his expression the answer to her uncompleted question. "I'm so terribly sorry for all of them," she said. "For you as well. I do know what he means to you."

"Frances needs to be there. Randie can't be asked to do it alone, if it comes to that."

"Of course she can't," Helen said.

Lynley had never been above stairs in Webberly's home, so he allowed his wife to show him the way to the master bedroom. The first floor of the house was dominated by scents: potpourri from bowls on a three-tier stand that they passed at the top of the stairs, orange spice from a candle burning outside the bathroom door, lemon from polish used on the furniture. But the scents were not strong enough to cover the stronger odour of air overheated, overweighed with cigar smoke, and so long stale that it seemed only rainfall—violent and long—within the walls of the house would be enough to cleanse it.

"Every window is shut," Helen said quietly. "Well, of course, it's November, so one wouldn't expect . . . But still . . . It must be so difficult for them. Not just for Malcolm and Randie. They can get away. But for Frances, because she must so want to be . . . to be cured."

"One would think," Lynley agreed. "Through here, Helen?"

Only one of the doors was closed and Helen nodded when he indicated it. He tapped on its white panels and said, "Frances? It's Tommy. May I come in?"

No reply. He called out again, a little louder this

time, following that with another rap on the door.
When she didn't respond, he tried the knob. It
turned, so he eased the door open. Behind him,
Helen said, "Frances? Will you see Tommy?"

To which Webberly's wife finally said, "Yes," in a
voice that was neither fearful nor resentful at the intrusion, just quiet and tired.

They found her not in the corner where Helen last
had seen her but sitting on an undecorated straight-
backed chair that she'd drawn up to look at her reflection in a mirror that hung above a dressing table.
On the table she'd laid out hairbrushes, hair slides,
and ribbons. She was running two ribbons through
her fingers as they entered, as if studying the effect
that their colour had against her skin.

She was undoubtedly wearing, Lynley saw, what
she'd been wearing when she'd phoned her daughter
on the previous night. She had on a quilted pink
dressing gown belted at the waist, and an azure night-
dress beneath it. She hadn't combed her hair despite
the brushes laid out before her, so it was still asym-
metrically flattened by her head's pressure into her
pillow, as if an invisible hat were perched on it.

She looked so colourless that Lynley thought at
once of spirits despite the hour of the day: gin,
brandy, whisky, vodka, or anything else to bring some
blood to her face. He said to Helen, "Would you
bring up a drink, darling?" And to Webberly's wife,
"Frances, you could do with a brandy. I'd like you to
have one."

She said, "Yes. All right. A brandy."

Helen left them. Lynley saw that a linen chest extended across the foot of the bed, and he dragged this over to where Frances sat so that he could speak at her level rather than down at her like a lecturing uncle. He didn't know where to begin. He didn't know what would do any good. Considering the length of time that Frances Webberly had spent inside the walls of this house, paralysed by inexplicable terrors, it didn't seem likely that a simple declaration of her husband's peril and her daughter's need could convince her that her fears were groundless. He was wise enough to know that the human mind did not work that way. Common logic did not suffice to obliterate demons that lived within the tortuous caves of a woman's psyche.

He said, "Can I do anything, Frances? I know you want to go to him."

She'd raised one of the ribbons against her cheek, and she lowered this slowly to the top of the table. "Do you know that," she said, not a question but a statement. "If I had the heart of a woman who knows how to love her husband properly, I would have gone to him already. Directly they phoned from Casualty. Directly they said, 'Is this Mrs. Webberly? We're phoning you from Charing Cross Hospital. Casualty. Is this a relative of Malcolm Webberly that I'm speaking to?' I would have gone. I wouldn't have waited to hear a word more. No woman who loves her husband would have done that. No real woman—no adequate woman—would have said, 'What's happened? Oh God. *Why's* he not here? Please tell me. The dog came home but Malcolm wasn't *with* him and he's left me, hasn't he? He's left me, he's left me at last.' And they said, 'Mrs. Webberly, your husband's alive. But we would like to speak to you. Here, Mrs. Webberly. Can we send a taxi for you? Is there someone who can bring you down to the hospital?' And that was good of them, wasn't it, to pretend like that? To ignore what I'd said. But when they rang off, they said, 'We've got a real nutter here. Poor bloke, this Webberly. No wonder the old sod was out on the streets. Probably *threw* himself in front of the car.' " Her fingers curled round a navy ribbon, and her nails sank into it, making gullies in the satin.

Lynley said, "In the middle of the night when you have a shock, you don't weigh your words, Frances. Nurses, doctors, orderlies, and everyone else in hospitals know that."

" 'He's your *husband*,' she said. 'He's cared for you all these miserable years and you *owe* this to him. And to Miranda. Frances, you owe it to her. You must pull yourself together, because if you don't and if something should happen to Malcolm while you're not there . . . and if, God, if he should actually die . . . Get up, get up, get *up*, Frances Louise, because you and I know there is nothing God help me *nothing at all* that's wrong with you. The spotlight's *off* you. Accept that fact.' As if she knew what it's like. As if she's actually spent time in my world, in this world, right inside here"—savagely, she rapped her temple—"instead of in her own little space, where everything's perfect, always has been, always will be world without end amen. But it's not like that for me. That is not how it is."

"Of course," Lynley said. "We all look at the world through the prisms of our own experiences, don't we? But sometimes in a moment of crisis, people forget that. So they say things and do things . . . It's all for an end that everyone wants but no one knows how to reach. How can I help you?"

Helen came back into the room then, a wine glass in her hand. It was half-filled with brandy, and she placed it on the dressing table and looked towards Lynley with "What now?" on her face. He wished he knew. He had very little doubt that with every decent intention in the world Frances's sister had already run through the repertoire. Certainly, Laura Hillier had tried reasoning with Frances first, manipulating her second, inducing guilt in her third, and uttering threats fourth. What was probably needed—a slow process of getting the poor woman once again used to an external environment of which she'd been terrified for years—was something that none of them could manage and something for which they had no time.

What now? Lynley wondered along with his wife. *A miracle, Helen.*

He said, "Drink some of this, Frances," and lifted the glass for her. When she'd done so, he laid his hand on hers. He said, "What exactly have they told you about Malcolm?"

Frances murmured, " 'The doctors want to speak with you,' she said. 'You must go to the hospital. You

must be with him. You must be with Randie.' " For
the first time, Frances moved her gaze from her reflection. She looked at the joining of her hand with
Lynley's. She said, "If Randie's with him, that's nearly
all he would want. 'What a brave, new world that's
been given to us,' he said when she was born. That's
why he said she'd be called Miranda. And she was
perfect to him. Every way perfect. Perfect as I
couldn't hope to be. Ever. Not ever. Daddy's got a
princess." She reached for the wine glass where Lynley had placed it. She started to pick it up but stopped
herself and said, "No. No. That's not it. Not a
princess. Not at all. Daddy's found a queen." Her eyes
remained motionless, on the brandy in the glass, but
their rims slowly reddened as tears pooled against
them.

Lynley's glance met Helen's where she stood just
beyond Frances's right shoulder. He could read her
reaction to this and he knew it matched his own. Escape was called for. To be in the presence of a maternal jealousy so strong that it wouldn't loosen its grip
upon someone even in the midst of a life-and-death
crisis . . . It was more than disconcerting, Lynley
thought. It was obscene. He felt like a voyeur.

Helen said, "If Malcolm's anything at all like my father, Frances, I expect what he's felt is a special responsibility towards Randie, because she's a daughter
and not a son."

To which Lynley added, "I saw that in my own
family. The way my father was with my older sister
wasn't in the least the way he was with me. Or with

my younger brother, for that matter. We weren't as vulnerable, in his eyes. We needed toughening up. But I think what all that means is—"

Frances moved the hand that had been beneath his. She said, "No. They're right. What they're thinking at the hospital. The queen is dead and he can't cope now. He threw himself into the traffic last night." Then for the first time she looked directly at Lynley. She said it again, "The queen is finally dead. There's no one to replace her. Certainly not me."

And Lynley suddenly understood. He said, "You knew," as Helen began to say, "Frances, you must *never* believe—" but Frances stopped her by getting to her feet. She went to one of the two bedside tables, and she opened its drawer and set it on the bed. From the very back, tucked away as far as possible from the other contents, she took a small white square of linen. She unfolded it like a priest in a ritual, shaking it first, then smoothing it out against the counterpane on the bed.

Lynley joined her there. Helen did likewise. The three of them looked down on what was a handkerchief, ordinary save for two details: In one corner were twined the initials *E* and *D*, and directly in the centre of the material lay a rusty smear which described a little drama from the past. He cuts his finger his palm the back of his hand doing something for her . . . sawing a board pounding a nail drying a glass picking up the pieces of a jar accidentally smashed on the floor . . . and she quickly removes a handkerchief from her pocket her handbag the sleeve of her sweater the cup of her bra and she presses it upon him because he never remembers to carry one himself. This piece of linen finds its way into the pocket of his trousers his jacket the breast of his coat where he forgets about it till his wife preparing the laundry the dry cleaning the sorting of old things to go to Oxfam finds it sees it knows it for what it is and keeps it. For how many years? Lynley wondered. For how many blasted god-awful years in which she asked nothing about what it meant, giving her husband the opportunity to tell the truth, whatever that truth was, or to lie, fabricating a reason that might have been perfectly believable or at least something that she could cling to in order to lie to herself.

Helen said, "Frances, will you let me get rid of this?" and she placed her fingers not on the handkerchief itself but right next to it, as if it were a relic and she a novitiate in some obscure religion in which only the ordained could touch the blessed.

Frances said, "No!" and grabbed it. "He loved her," she said. "He loved her and I knew it. I saw it happening. I saw how it happened, as if it was a study of the whole *process* of love being played out in front of me. Like a television drama. And I kept waiting, you see, because right from the first I knew how he felt. He had to talk about it, he said. Because of Randie . . . because these poor people had lost a little girl not so much younger than our own Randie, and he could see how horrible it was for them, how much they suffered, especially the mother and 'No one seems to want to *talk* to her about it, Frances. She has no one. She's existing in a bubble of grief—no, an infected boil of grief—and not one of them is trying to lance it. It feels inhuman, Frances, *inhuman*. Someone must help her before she breaks.' So he decided to be the one. He would put that killer in gaol, by God, and he would not rest, Frances dear, till he had that killer signed, sealed, and delivered to justice. Because how would *we* feel if someone—God forbid—harmed our Randie? We would stay up nights, wouldn't we, we would search the streets, we would not sleep and we would not eat and we would not even darken our own doorstep for days on end if that's what it took to find the monster that hurt her."

Lynley released a slow breath, realising that he'd been holding it the entire time that Frances had been speaking. He felt so far out of his depth that drowning looked like the only option. He glanced at his wife for some sort of guidance and saw that she'd raised her fingers to her lips. And he knew it was sorrow that Helen felt, sorrow for the words that had gone too long unspoken between the Webberlys. He found himself wondering what was actually worse: years of enduring the iron maiden of imagining or seconds of experiencing the quick death of knowing.

Helen said, "Frances, if Malcolm hadn't loved you—"

"Duty." Frances began to refold the handkerchief carefully. She said nothing more.

Lynley said, "I think that's part of love, Frances. It's not the easy part. It's not that first rush of excitement:

wanting and believing something's been written in the stars and aren't we the lucky ones because we've just looked heavenwards and got the message. It's the part that's the choice to stay the course."

"I gave him no choice," Frances said.

"Frances," Helen murmured, and Lynley could tell from her voice just exactly how much her next words cost her, "believe me when I say that you don't have that power."

Frances looked at Helen then, but of course could not see beyond the structure that Helen had built to live in the world she'd long ago created for herself: the fashionable haircut, the carefully tended and un-blemished skin, the manicured hands, the perfect slim body weekly massaged, in the clothes designed for women who knew what elegance meant and how to use it. But as to seeing Helen herself, as to knowing her as the woman who'd once taken the quickest route out of the life of a man she'd dearly loved because she could not cope with staying a course that had altered too radically for her resources and her liking . . . Frances Webberly did not know that Helen and thus could not know that no one understood better than Helen that one person's condition—mental, spiritual, psychological, social, emotional, physical, or any combination thereof—could never really control the choices another person made.

Lynley said, "You need to know this, Frances. Malcolm didn't throw himself into traffic. Eric Leach phoned him to tell him about Eugenie Davies, yes, and I expect you read about her death in the paper."

"He was distraught. I thought he'd *forgotten* about her and then I knew he hadn't. All these years."

"Not forgotten her, true," Lynley said, "but not for the reasons you think. Frances, we don't forget. We can't forget. We don't walk away untouched when we hand our documents to the CPS. It doesn't work that way. But the fact of our remembering is just that: because that's what the mind does. It just remembers. And if we're lucky, the remembering doesn't turn into nightmares. But that's the best we can hope for. That's part of the job."

Lynley knew he was walking a fine line between truth and falsehood. He knew that whatever Webberly had experienced in his affair with Eugenie Davies and in the years that had followed that affair probably went far beyond mere memory. But that couldn't be allowed to matter at the moment. All that mattered was that the man's wife understand one part of the last forty-eight hours. So he repeated that part for her. "Frances, he didn't throw himself into the traffic. He was hit by a car. He was hit deliberately. Someone tried to kill him. And within the next few hours or days, we're going to know if that someone succeeded, because he may well die. He's had a serious heart attack as well. You've been told that, haven't you?"

A sound escaped her. It was something between the excruciating groan of a woman giving birth and the fearful moan of an abandoned child. "I don't want Malcolm to die," she said. "I'm so afraid."

"You're not alone in that," Lynley replied.

THE FACT THAT she had an appointment at a women's shelter was what kept Yasmin Edwards steady between the time she phoned the pager number on Constable Nkata's card and the time she was able to meet him at the shop. He'd said he'd have to drive down from Hampstead to see her, so he couldn't swear what time he'd get there but he would come as soon as possible, madam, and in the meantime if she began to worry that he wasn't coming at all or he'd forgotten or had got waylaid in some way, she could ring his pager again and he'd let her know where he was on the route, if that would suit her. She'd said she could come to him or meet him somewhere. She said, in fact, she'd prefer it that way. He'd said no, it was best that he come to her.

She'd nearly changed her mind then. But she thought about Number Fifty-five, about Katja's mouth closing over hers, about what it meant that Katja could still slide down and down and down to love her. And she said, "Right. I'll be at the shop, then."

In the meantime, she kept her appointment at the shelter in Camberwell. Three sisters in their thirties, an Asian lady, and an old bag married for forty-six years were the residents. Among them were shared countless bruises along with two black eyes, four split lips, a stitched-up cheek, a broken wrist, one dislocated shoulder, and a pierced eardrum. They were like beaten dogs recently let off the chain: cowering and undecided between flight and attack.

Do *not* let anyone do this to you, Yasmin wanted to shout at the women. The only thing that kept her from shouting was the scar on her own face and her badly set nose, both of which told the tale of what she herself had once allowed to be done to her.

So she flashed them a smile, said, "C'mon over here, you gorgeous tomatoes." She spent two hours at the women's shelter, with her make-up and her colour swatches, with her scarves, her scents, and her wigs. And when she finally left them, three of the residents had got used to smiling again, the fourth had actually managed a laugh, and the fifth had begun to raise her eyes from the floor. Yasmin considered it a good day's work.

She returned to the shop. When she arrived, the cop was striding up and down in front of it. She saw him check his watch and try to peer round the metal security door that she lowered over the shop front whenever she wasn't there. Then he looked at his watch again and took his beeper from his belt and tapped it.

Yasmin pulled up in the old Fiesta. When she opened her door, the detective was there before she put a foot on the pavement.

"This some kind of joke?" he demanded. "You think messing in a murder 'vestigation's something you can have fun with, Missus Edwards?"

"You said you didn't know how long—" Yasmin

stopped herself. What was *she* making excuses for? She said, "I had a 'pointment. You want to help me unload the car or you want to chew my bum?" She thrust out her chin as she spoke, hearing her final words for their double meaning only after she'd said them. Then she wouldn't give him the pleasure of her embarrassment. She faced him squarely—tall woman, tall man—and waited for *him* to go for the crude. *Hey, baby, I'll chew on more'n your bum, you give me the chance.*

But he didn't do that. Wordlessly, he went to the Fiesta's hatchback and waited for her to come round and unlock it.

She did so. She shoved her cardboard box of supplies into his arms and topped it with the case of lotions, make-up, and brushes. Then she smacked the hatch of the Fiesta closed and strode to the shop, where she unlocked the metal door and yanked it upwards, using her shoulder against it, as she usually did when it stuck midway.

He said, "Hang on," and put his burdens on the ground. Before she could stop it from happening, his hands—broad and flat and black with pale oval nails neatly trimmed to the tips of his fingers—planted themselves on either side of her. He heaved upwards as she pushed, and with a sound like *eeeerrreeek* of metal on metal, the door gave way. He stayed where he was, right behind her, too close by half, and said, "That needs seeing to. 'Fore much longer, you won't be able to slide it at all."

She said, "I c'n cope," and she grabbed up the

metal box of her make-up because she wanted to be doing something and because she wanted him to know she could manage the supplies, the door, and the shop itself just fine on her own.

But once inside, it was like before. He seemed to fill the place. He seemed to make it his. And that irritated her, especially since he did nothing at all to give the impression that he meant to intimidate or at least to dominate. He merely set the cardboard box onto the counter, saying gravely, "I wasted nearly an hour waiting for you, Missus Edwards. I hope you 'ntend to make it worth my while now you're finally here."

"You getting *nothing*—" She swung round. She'd been stowing her make-up case as he spoke, and her reaction was reflex, pure as the bell and those Russian dogs.

Now don't go playing Miss Ice Cubes, Yas. Girl got blessed with a body like yours, she need to use it to her bes' a'vantage.

So *You getting* nothing *off me* was what she'd intended to hurl at the cop. No kiss-and-don't-tell by the airing cupboard, no grope in the lap at the dinner table, no peeling back blouses and easing down trousers and no no no hands separating rigid legs. *Come on, Yas. Don't fight me on this.*

She felt her face freeze. He was watching her. She saw his gaze on her mouth, and she watched it travel to her nose. She was marked by what went for love from a man, and he read those marks and she would never be able to forget it.

He said, "Missus Edwards," and she hated the sound and she wondered why she'd kept Roger's name. She'd told herself she'd done it for Daniel, mother and son tied together by a name when they couldn't be tied by anything else. But now she wondered if she'd really done it to flay herself, not as a constant reminder of the fact that she'd killed her husband but as a way of doing penance for having hooked up with him in the first place.

She'd loved him, yes. But she'd soon learned that there was nothing whatsoever to be gained from loving. Still, the lesson hadn't stuck, had it? For she'd loved again and look where she was now: facing down a cop who would see this time the very same killer but an entirely different sort of corpse.

"You had something to tell me." DC Winston Nkata reached into the pocket of the jacket that fit him hand-to-a-leather-glove, and he brought out a notebook, the same one he'd been writing in before, with the same propelling pencil clipped to it.

Seeing this, Yasmin thought of the lies he'd already recorded and how bad it was going to go for her if she decided to clean house now. And the image of cleaning house opened her mind to the rest of it: how people could look on a person and because of her face, her speech, and the way she decided to carry herself, how people could reach a conclusion about her and cling to it in the face of all evidence to the contrary, and why? Because people were just so desperate to believe.

Yasmin said, "She wasn't at home. We weren't watching the telly. She wasn't there."

She saw the detective's chest slowly deflate, as if he'd been holding his breath since the moment he'd arrived, betting against his own respiration that Yasmin Edwards had paged him that morning with the express intention of betraying her lover.

"Where was she?" he asked. "She tell you, Missus Edwards? What time d'she get home?"

"Twelve forty-one."

He nodded. He wrote steadily and tried to look cool, but Yasmin could see it all happening in his head. He was doing the maths. He was matching the maths to Katja's lies. And underneath that, he was celebrating the fact that his gamble had won him the jackpot he'd bet for.

TWENTY-ONE

HER FINAL words to him were, "And let's not forget, Eric. *You* wanted the divorce. So if you can't cope with the fact that I've got Jerry now, don't let's pretend it's Esmé's problem." And she'd looked so flaming triumphant about it all, so filled with look-at-me-I've-found-someone-who-actually-wants-me-boyo that Leach actually found himself cursing his twelve-year-old daughter—God forgive him—for being capable of manipulating him into talking to her mother in the first place. "I've got a right to see other people," Bridget had asserted. "You were the one who gave it to me."

"Look, Bridg," he'd said. "It's not that I'm jealous. It's that Esmé's in a twist because she thinks you'll re-marry."

"I intend to remarry. I *want* to remarry."

"All right. Fine. But she thinks you've already chosen this bloke and—"

"What if I have? What if I've decided it feels good to be wanted? To be with a man who doesn't have a thing about breasts that droop a bit and lines of character on my face. That's what he calls them, by the way, lines of character, Eric."

"This is on the rebound," Leach tried to tell her.

"Do *not* inform me what this is. Or we'll get into what your behaviour is: midlife idiocy, extended immaturity, adolescent stupidity. Shall I go on? No? Right. I didn't think so." And she turned on her heel and left him. She returned to her classroom in the primary school, where ten minutes before Leach had motioned to her from the doorway, having dutifully stopped to speak to the head teacher first, asking if he could have a word, please, with Mrs. Leach. The head teacher had remarked how irregular it was that a parent should come calling on one of the teachers in the midst of the school day, but when Leach had introduced himself to her, she'd become simultaneously cooperative and compassionate, which told Leach that the word was out not only about the pending divorce but also about Bridget's new love interest. He felt like saying, "Hey. I don't give a flying one that she's got a new bloke," but he wasn't so sure that was the case. Nonetheless, the fact of the new bloke at least allowed him to feel less guilty about being the one who'd wanted to separate and, as his wife stalked off, he tried to keep his mind fixed on that.

He said, "Bridg, listen. I'm sorry," to her retreating back, but he didn't say it very loudly, he knew she couldn't hear him, and he wasn't sure what he was apologising about anyway.

Still, as he watched her retreat, he did feel the blow to his pride. So he tried to obliterate his regrets about how they'd parted, and he told himself he'd done the right thing. Considering how quickly she'd managed to replace him, there wasn't much doubt their marriage had been dead long before he'd first mentioned the fact.

Yet he couldn't help thinking that some couples managed to stay the course no matter what happened to their feelings for each other. Indeed, some couples swore that they were "absolutely desperate to grow together," when all the time the only real glue that kept them adhered to each other was a bank account, a piece of property, shared offspring, and an unwillingness to divide up the furniture and the Christmas decorations. Leach knew men on the force who were married to women they'd loathed forever. But the very thought of putting their children, their possessions—not to mention their pensions—at risk had kept them polishing their wedding rings for years.

Which thought led Leach ineluctably to Malcolm Webberly.

Leach had known that something was up from the phone calls, from the notes scribbled, shoved into envelopes, and posted, from the oft distracted manner in which Webberly engaged in a conversation. He'd had his suspicions. But he'd been able to discount them because he hadn't known for certain till he saw them together, seven years after the case itself, when quite by chance he and Bridget had taken the kids to the Regatta because Curtis'd had a project at school—The Culture and Traditions of Our Country . . . Jesus . . . Leach even remembered the bloody

name of it!—and there they were, the two of them,
standing on that bridge that crossed the Thames into
Henley, his arm round her waist and the sunlight on
them both. He didn't know who she was at first,
didn't remember her, saw only that she was good-
looking and that they comprised that unit which calls
itself In Love.

How odd, Leach thought now, to recall what he'd
felt at the sight of Webberly and his Lady Friend. He
realised that he'd never considered his superior officer a real breathing man before that moment. He realised that he'd seen Webberly in rather the same
manner as a child sees a much older adult. And the
sudden knowledge that Webberly had a secret life felt
like the blow an eight-year-old would take should
he walk in on his dad going at it with a lady from the
neighbourhood.

And she'd looked like that, the woman on the
bridge, familiar like a lady from the neighbourhood.
In fact, she looked so familiar to Leach that for a time
he expected to see her at work—perhaps a secretary
he'd not yet met?—or maybe emerging from an office on the Earl's Court Road. He'd reckoned that she
was just someone Webberly had happened to meet,
happened to strike up a conversation with, happened
to discover an attraction to, happened to say to himself "Oh, why not, Malc? No need to be such a
bloody Puritan," about.

Leach couldn't remember when or how he'd sussed
out that Webberly's lover was Eugenie Davies. But
when he had done, he hadn't been able to keep mum

any longer. He'd used his outrage as an excuse for speaking, no little boy fearful that Dad would leave home again but a full-grown adult who knew right from wrong. My God, he'd thought, that an officer from the murder squad—that his own partner—should cross the line like that, should take the opportunity to gratify himself with someone who'd been traumatised, victimised, and brutalised both by tragic events and the aftermath of those events. . . . It was inconceivable.

Webberly had been, if not deaf to the subject, at least willing to hear him out. He hadn't made a comment at all till Leach had recited every stanza of the ode to Webberly's unprofessional conduct that he'd been composing. Then he'd said, "What the hell do you think of me, Eric? It wasn't like that. This didn't start during the case. I hadn't seen her for years when we began to . . . Not till . . . It was at Paddington Station. Completely by chance. We spoke there for ten minutes or less, between trains. Then later . . . Hell. Why am I explaining this? If you think I'm out of order, put yourself up for transfer."

But he hadn't wanted that.

Why? he asked himself.

Because of what Malcolm Webberly had become to him.

How our pasts define our presents, Leach thought now. We're not even aware that it's happening, but every time we reach a conclusion, make a judgement, or take a decision, the years of our lives are stacked up behind us: all those dominoes of influence that we don't begin to acknowledge as part of defining who we are.

He drove to Hammersmith. He told himself he needed a few minutes to decompress from the scene with Bridget, and he did his decompressing in the car, wending his way south till he was in striking distance of Charing Cross Hospital. So he finished the journey and located intensive care.

He couldn't get in to see him, he was told by the sister in charge when he walked through the swinging doors. Only family were allowed in to see the patients in the Intensive Care. Was he a member of the Webberly family?

Oh yes, he thought. And of long standing, although he'd never truly admitted that to himself and Webberly hadn't ever twigged the idea. But what he said was, "No. Just another officer. The superintendent and I used to work together."

The nurse nodded. She remarked how good it was that so many members of the Met had stopped by, had phoned, had sent flowers, and had stood by with offers of blood for the patient. "Type B," she said to him. "Do you happen to be . . . ? Or O, which is universal, but I expect you know that."

"AB negative."

"That's very rare. We wouldn't be able to use it in this case, but you ought to be a regular donor, if you don't mind my saying."

"Is there anything . . . ?" He nodded in the direction of the rooms.

"His daughter's with him. His brother-in-law as

well. There's really nothing . . . But he's holding his own."

"Still hooked up to the machines?"

She looked regretful. "I'm awfully sorry. I can't exactly give out . . . I do hope you understand. But if I may ask . . . Do you pray . . . ?"

"Not regularly."

"Sometimes it helps."

But there was something more useful than prayer, Leach thought. Like cracking the whip over the murder team and at least making progress towards finding the bastard who did this to Malcolm. And he could do that.

He was about to nod a goodbye to the nurse, when a young woman wearing a track suit and untied trainers emerged from one of the rooms. The nurse called her over, saying, "This gentleman's asking after your dad."

Leach hadn't seen Miranda Webberly since her childhood, but he saw now that she'd grown up to look very much like her father: same stout body, same rust-coloured hair, same ruddy complexion, same smile that crinkled round her eyes and produced a single dimple on her left cheek. She looked like the sort of young woman who didn't bother with fashion magazines and he liked her for that.

She spoke quietly about her father's condition: that he hadn't regained consciousness, that there'd been "a rather serious crisis with his heart" earlier that day but now he had stabilised thank God, that his blood count—"I think it was the white cells? But maybe the other . . . ?"—indicated a point of internal bleeding that they were going to have to locate soon since right now they were transfusing him but that would be a waste of blood if he was losing it from somewhere inside.

"They say he can hear, even in a coma, so I've been reading to him," Miranda confided. "I hadn't thought to bring anything from Cambridge, so Uncle David went out and bought a book about narrow boating. I think it's the first thing that came to hand. But it's terribly dull and I'm afraid it'll send *me* into a coma before much longer. And I can't think it'll make Dad wake up because he's longing to hear how things turn out. Of course, he's in a coma mostly because they want him in a coma. At least, that's what they're telling me."

She seemed eager to make Leach feel comfortable, to let him know how much his pathetic effort to be of help was appreciated. She looked exhausted, but she was calm, with no apparent expectation that someone—other than herself—should rescue her from the situation in which she was involved. He liked her more.

He said, "Is there someone who could take over from you here? Give you a chance to get home for a bath? An hour's kip?"

"Oh, yes, of course," she said, and she fished in her track suit's jacket and brought out a rubber band that she used to discipline her steel-wool hair. "But I want to be here. He's my dad, and . . . He can hear me, you see. He knows I'm with him. And if that's a help . . . I mean, it's important that someone going through what he's going through know he's not alone, don't you think?"

Which implied that Webberly's wife wasn't with him. Which suggested a volume or two of what the years had been like since Webberly had made his decision not to leave Frances for Eugenie.

They'd talked about it the single time that Leach himself had brought up the subject. He couldn't remember now *why* he'd felt compelled to venture into such a private area of another man's life, but something had occurred—a veiled remark? a phone conversation with a subtext of hostility on Webberly's part? a departmental party to which Webberly had shown up alone for the dozenth time?—and that something had prompted Leach to say, "I don't see how you can act the lover of one and be the lover of the other. You could leave Frances, Malc. You know that. You've got someplace to go."

Webberly hadn't responded at first. Indeed, he hadn't responded for days. Leach thought he might never respond at all till two weeks later, when Webberly's car was in for repair and Leach had dropped him off at his home because it was not so far out of his way. Half past eight in the evening, and she was in her pyjamas when she came to the door and flung it open, crowing, "Daddy! Daddy! Daddy!" and dashing down the path to be caught up in her father's arms. Webberly had buried his face in her crinkly hair, had blown noisy kisses against her neck, had elicited more crows of joy from her.

"This is my Randie," he'd said to Leach. "This is why."

Leach said to Miranda now, "Your mum's not here, then? Gone home for a rest, has she?"

She said, "I'll tell her you were here, Inspector. She'll be so glad to know. Everyone's been so . . . so *decent*. Really." And she shook his hand and said that she would get back to her dad.

"If there's something I can do . . . ?"

"You've done it," she assured him.

But on the way back to the Hampstead station, Leach didn't feel that way. And once inside, he began pacing round the incident room as he reviewed one report after another, most of which he'd already read. He said to the WPC on the computer, "So what's Swansea given us?"

She shook her head. "Every car owned by every principal's a late model, sir. There's nothing earlier than ten years old."

"Who owns that one?"

She referred to a clipboard, ran her finger down the page. "Robson," she said. "Raphael. He's got a Renault. Colour is . . . let me see . . . silver."

"Blast. There's got to be something." Leach considered another way to approach the problem. He said, "Significant others. Go there."

She said, "Sir?"

"Go through the reports. Get all the names. Wives, husbands, boyfriends, girlfriends, teenagers who drive, anyone and everyone connected to this who has a driving licence. Run their names through the

DVLA and see if any of them have a car that fits our profile."

"All of them, sir?" the constable said.

"I believe we speak the same language, Vanessa."

She sighed, said, "Yes, sir," and returned to work as one of the newer constables came barreling into the room. He was called Solberg, a wet-behind-the-ears DC who'd been eager to prove himself from day one on the murder squad. He was trailing a sheaf of paperwork behind him, and his face was so red, he looked like a runner at the end of a marathon.

He cried out, "Guv! Check this out. Ten days ago, and it's hot. It's *hot*."

Leach said, "What're you on about, Solberg?"

"A bit of a complication," the constable replied.

NKATA DECIDED TO turn to Katja Wolff's solicitor after his conversation with Yasmin Edwards. She'd said, "You got what you want, now get out, Constable," once she'd watched him write *12:41* in his notebook, and she'd refused to speculate on where her lover had been on the night Eugenie Davies had died. He'd thought about pushing her— *You lied once, madam, so what's to say you aren't lying again and do you know what happens to lags who get ticks by their names as accessories to murder?*—but he hadn't done so. He hadn't had the heart because he'd seen the emotions running across her face while he was questioning her, and he had an idea of how much it had cost her to tell him the little she'd already told. Still, he'd not been able to stop himself from considering what would happen if he asked her why: Why was she betraying her lover and, more important, what did it mean that she was betraying her? But that wasn't his business, was it? It couldn't be his business because he was a copper and she was a lag. And that's the way it was.

So he'd closed his notebook. He'd intended to turn on his heel and get out of her shop with a simple yet pointed "Cheers, Missus Edwards. You did the right thing." But he didn't say that. Instead, what he'd said was, "You all right, Missus Edwards?" and found himself taken aback at the gentleness he felt. It was wrong as hell to feel gentle towards such a woman in such a situation, and when she said, "Just get out," he took the course of wisdom and did just that.

In his car, he'd slipped from his wallet the card that Katja Wolff had handed him early that morning. He'd removed the *A to Z* from his glove box and looked up the street on which Harriet Lewis had her office. As luck would have it, the solicitor's office was in Kentish Town, which meant the other side of the river and yet another drive through London. But wending his way there gave him time to plan an approach likely to dislodge information from the lawyer. And he knew he needed a decent approach, because the proximity of her office to HM Prison Holloway suggested that Harriet Lewis had more than one villain as a client, which suggested in turn that she wasn't likely to be easily finessed into revealing anything.

When at last he pulled to the kerb, Nkata discovered that Harriet Lewis had set herself up in humble offices between a newsagent and a grocery displaying limp broccoli and bruised cauliflower out on the pavement. A door was set at an oblique angle to the street, abutting the door to the newsagent's, and on its upper half of translucent glass was printed *Solicitors* and nothing more.

Directly inside, a staircase covered in thinning red carpet led up to two doors which faced each other on a landing. One of the doors was open, revealing an empty room with another adjoining it and a wide-planked wooden floor frosted with dust. The other door was closed, and a business card was tacked to the panels with a drawing pin. Nkata scrutinised this card and found it identical to the one Katja Wolff had given to him. He lifted it with the edge of his finger-nail and looked beneath it. There was no other card. Nkata smiled. He had the opening he wanted.

He entered without knocking and found himself in a reception room as unlike the neighbourhood, the immediate environment, and the suite across the landing as he could have imagined. A Persian rug covered most of the polished floor, and on it sat a reception desk, sofa, chairs, and tables of a severely modern design. They were all sharp edges, wood, and leather, and they should have argued with not only the rug but also the wainscoting and the wallpaper, but instead, they suggested just the right degree of daring one would hope for when one hired a solicitor.

"May I help you?" The question came from a

middle-aged woman who sat at the desk in front of a keyboard and monitor, wearing tiny earphones from which she appeared to have been taking dictation. She was done up in professional navy-and-cream, her hair short and neat and just beginning to grey in a streak that wove back from above her left temple. She had the darkest eyebrows Nkata had ever seen, and in a world in which he was used to being looked at with suspicion by white women, he'd never encountered a more hostile stare.

He produced his identification and asked to speak to the solicitor. He didn't have an appointment, he told Mrs. Eyebrows before she could ask, but he expected Miss Lewis—

"*Ms.* Lewis," the receptionist said, removing her earphones and setting them aside.

—would see him once she was told he was calling about Katja Wolff. He laid his card on the desk and added, "Pass that to her if you like. Tell her we talked on the phone this morning. I 'xpect she'll remember."

Mrs. Eyebrows made a point of not touching the card till Nkata's fingers had left it. Then she picked it up, saying, "Wait here, please," and went through to the inner office. She came out perhaps two minutes later and repositioned the earphones on her head. She resumed her typing without a glance in his direction, which might have caused his blood to start heating had he not learned early in life to take white women's behaviour for what it usually was: obvious and ignorant as hell.

So he studied the pictures on the walls—old black-and-white head shots of women that put him in mind of days when the British Empire stretched round the globe—and when he was done inspecting these, he picked up a copy of *Ms.* from America and engrossed himself in an article about alternatives to hysterectomies that seemed to be written by a woman who was balancing on her shoulder a chip the size of the Blidworth Boulder.

He did not sit, and when Mrs. Eyebrows said to him meaningfully, "It will be a while, Constable, as you've come without an appointment," he said, "Murder's like that, i'n't it? Never does let you know when it's coming." And he leaned his shoulder against the pale striped wallpaper and gave it a smack with the palm of his hand, saying, "Very nice, this is. What d'you call the design?"

He could see the receptionist eyeing the spot he'd touched, looking for grease marks. She made no reply. He nodded at her pleasantly, snapped his magazine more fully open, and rested his head against the wall.

"We've a sofa, Constable," Mrs. Eyebrows said.

"Been sitting all day," he told her, and added, "Piles," with a grimace for good measure.

That appeared to do it. She got to her feet, disappeared into the inner office once again, and returned in a minute. She was bearing a tray with the remains of afternoon tea on it, and she said that the solicitor was ready to see him now.

Nkata smiled to himself. He bet she was.

Harriet Lewis, dressed in black as she had been on the previous evening, was standing behind her desk when he entered. She said, "We've had our conversation already, Constable Nkata. Am I going to have to ring for counsel?"

"You feeling the need?" Nkata asked her. "Woman like you, 'fraid to go it alone?"

" 'Woman like me,' " she mimicked, "no bloody fool. I spend my life telling clients to keep their mouths shut in the presence of the police. I'd be fairly stupid not to heed my own advice, now wouldn't I?"

"You'd be stupider—"

"More stupid," she said.

"—stupider," he repeated, "to find yourself dis'tangling your way out of a charge of obstruction in a police enquiry."

"You've charged no one with anything. You haven't a leg to stand on."

"Day's not over."

"Don't threaten me."

"Make your phone call, then," Nkata told her. He looked round and saw that a seating area of three chairs and a coffee table had been fashioned at one end of the room. He sauntered over, sat down, and said, "Ah. Whew. Nice to take a load off at the end of the day," and nodded at her telephone. "Go ahead. I got the time to wait. My mum's a fine cook and she'll keep dinner warm."

"What's this about, Constable? We've already spoken. I have nothing to add to what I've already told you."

"Don't have a partner, I notice," he said, " 'less she's hiding under your desk."

"I don't believe I said there was a partner. You made that assumption."

"Based on Katja Wolff's lie. Number Fifty-five Galveston Road, Miss Lewis. Care to speculate with me on that topic? Tha's where your partner's s'posed to live, by the way."

"My relationship with my client is privileged."

"Right. You got a client there, then?"

"I didn't say that."

Nkata leaned forward, elbows on knees. He said, "Listen to what I say, then." He looked at his watch. "Seventy-seven minutes ago Katja Wolff lost her alibi for the time of a hit-and-run in West Hampstead. You got that straight? And losing that alibi sends her straight to the top of the class. My experience, people don't lie 'bout where they were the night someone goes down 'less they got a good reason. This case, the reason looks like she was involved. Woman who was killed—"

"I know who was killed," the solicitor snapped.

"Do you? Good. Then you also proba'ly know that your client might've had an axe she wanted to grind with that individual."

"That idea's laughable. If anything, the complete opposite is the truth."

"Katja Wolff wanting Eugenie Davies to stay alive? Why's that, Miss Lewis?"

"That's privileged information."

"Cheers. So add to your privileged information

this bit: Last night a second hit happened in Hammersmith. Round midnight this one was. The officer who first put Katja away. He's not dead, but he's hanging on the edge. And you got to know how cops feel 'bout a suspect when one of their own goes down."

This piece of news seemed to make the first dent in Harriet Lewis's armour of calm. She adjusted her spine microscopically and said, "Katja Wolff is not involved in any of this."

"So you get paid to say. And paid to believe. So your partner would proba'ly say and proba'ly believe if you had a partner."

"Stop harping on that. You and I both know that I'm not responsible for a piece of misinformation passed to you by a client when I'm not present."

"Right. But you are present now. And now that it's clear you got no partner, p'rhaps we need to dwell on why I 'as told that you had."

"I have no idea."

"Don't you." Nkata took out his notebook and his pencil, and he tapped the pencil against the notebook's leather cover for emphasis. "Here's what it's looking like to me: You're Katja Wolff's brief, but you're something else 's well, something tastier and something that's lying just the other side of what's on the up and up in your business. Now—"

"You're incredible."

"—word of that gets out, you start looking bad, Miss Lewis. You got some code of ethics or other, and solicitor playing love monkeys with her client isn't part of that code. 'Fact, it starts looking like that's *why* you take on lags in the first place: Get 'em when they're at their lowest, you do, and it's plain sailing when you want to pop 'em in bed."

"That's outrageous." Harriet Lewis finally came round from behind her desk. She strode across the room, took position behind one of the chairs in the grouping by the coffee table, and gripped onto its back. "Leave this office, Constable."

"Let's play at this," he said reasonably, settling back into his chair. "Let's think out loud."

"Your sort's not even capable of doing that silently."

Nkata smiled. He gave himself a point. He said, "Stick with me, then, all the same."

"I've no intention of speaking with you further. Now leave, or I'll see to it you're brought to the attention of the PCA."

"What're you going to complain 'bout? And how's it likely to look when the story gets out that you couldn't cope with one lone copper come to talk to you about a killer? And not jus' any killer, Miss Lewis. A baby killer, twenty years put away."

The solicitor made no reply to this.

Nkata pressed on, nodding in the direction of Harriet Lewis's desk. "So you phone up Police Complaints right now, and you shout harassment and you file whatever you want to file. And when the story finds its way to the papers, you watch and see who gets the smear."

"You're blackmailing me."

"I'm telling you the facts. You c'n do with them what you want. What *I* want is the truth about Galveston Road. Give me that and I'm gone."

"Go there yourself."

"Been there once. Not going again without ammunition."

"Galveston Road has *nothing* to do with—"

"Miss Lewis? Don't play me like a fool." Nkata nodded at her telephone. "You making that call to the PCA? You ready to file your complaint 'gainst me?"

Harriet Lewis appeared to consider her options as she let out a breath. She came round the chair. She sat. She said, "Katja Wolff's alibi lives in that house, Constable Nkata. She's a woman called Noreen McKay, and she's unwilling to step forward and clear Katja from suspicion. We went there last night to talk to her about it. We weren't successful. And I very much doubt you'll be."

"Why's that?" Nkata asked.

Harriet Lewis smoothed down her skirt. She fingered a minute length of thread that she found at the edge of a button on her jacket. "I suppose you'd call it a code of ethics," she finally said.

"She's a solicitor?"

Harriet Lewis stood. "I'm going to have to phone Katja and request her permission to answer that question," she said.

LIBBY NEALE WENT straight to the refrigerator when she got home from South Kensington. She was having a major white jones, and she considered herself deserving of having the attack taken care of. She kept a pint of vanilla Häagen-Dazs in the freezer for just such emergencies. She dug this out, ferreted a spoon from the utensil drawer, and prised open the lid. She'd gobbled up approximately one dozen spoonfuls before she was even able to think.

When she finally did think, what she thought was *more white,* so she rustled through the trash under the kitchen sink and found part of the bag of cheddar popcorn that she'd thrown away in a moment of disgust on the previous day. She sat on the floor and proceeded to cram into her mouth the two handfuls of popcorn that were left in the bag. From there, she went to a package of flour tortillas, which she'd long kept as a challenge to herself to stay away from anything white. These, she found, weren't exactly white any longer, as spots of mould were growing on them like ink stains on linen. But mould was easy enough to remove, and if she ingested some by mistake, it couldn't hurt, could it? Consider penicillin.

She rustled a cube of Wensleydale from its wrapper and sliced enough for a quesadilla. She plopped the cheese slices onto the tortilla, topped that with another, and slapped the whole mess into a frying pan. When the Wensleydale was melted and the tortilla was browned, she took the treat from the fire, rolled it into a tube, and settled herself on the kitchen floor. She proceeded to shove the food into her mouth, eating like a victim of famine.

When she'd polished off the quesadilla, she remained on the floor, her head against one of the cupboard doors. She'd needed that, she told herself. Things were getting too weird, and when things got too weird, you had to keep your blood sugar high. There was no telling when you'd need to take action.

Gideon hadn't walked her from his father's flat to his car. He'd just shown her to the door and shut it behind her. She'd said, "You going to be okay, Gid?" as they'd made their way from the study. "I mean, this can't be the nicest place for you to wait. Look. Why'n't you come home with me? We can leave a note for your dad, and when he gets back, he can call you and we can drive back over."

"I'll wait here," he'd said. And he'd opened the door and shut it without ever once looking at her.

What did it *mean* that he wanted to wait for his dad? she wondered. Was this going to be the Big Showdown between them? She certainly hoped so. The Big Showdown had been a long time coming between Davies father and son.

She tried to picture it, a confrontation provoked, for some reason, by Gideon's discovery of a second sister he hadn't even known he'd had. He'd take that card written to Richard by Virginia's mother and he'd wave it in front of his father's nose. He'd say, "*Tell* me about her, you bastard. Tell me why I wasn't allowed to know *her* either."

Because that seemed to be the crux of what had set Gideon off when he'd read the card: His dad had denied him another sibling when Virginia had been there all along.

And why? Libby thought. Why had Richard made this move to isolate Gid from his surviving sister? It had to be the same reason that Richard did everything else: to keep Gid focused on the violin.

No, no, no. Can't have friends, Gideon. Can't go to parties. Can't play at sports. Can't go to a *real* school. Must practise, play, perform, and provide. And you can't do that if you've got any interests away from your instrument. Like a sister, for example.

God, Libby thought. He was such a shit. He was *so* totally screwing up Gideon's life.

What, she wondered, would that life have been like had he not spent it playing his music? He would have gone to school like a regular kid. He would have played sports, like soccer or something. He would have ridden a bike, fallen out of trees, and maybe broken a bone or two. He would have met his buddies for beer in the evening and gone out on dates and screwed around in girls' pants and been normal. He would be so *not* who he was right now.

Gideon deserved what other people had and took for granted, Libby told herself. He deserved friends. He deserved love. He deserved a family. He deserved a life. But he wasn't going to get any of that as long as Richard kept him under his thumb and as long as no one was willing to take positive action to alter the relationship Gideon had with his frigging father.

Libby stirred at that and realised her scalp was tingling. She rolled her head against the cupboard door so that she could look at the kitchen table. She'd left Gideon's car keys there when she'd dashed into the kitchen to admit defeat to her attack of the whites, and it seemed to her now that her possession of those keys was meant to be, like a sign from God that she'd been sent into Gideon's life to be the one who took a stand.

Libby got to her feet. She approached the keys in a state of pure resolution. She snatched them up from the table before she could talk herself out of it. She left the flat.

TWENTY-TWO

YASMIN EDWARDS sent Daniel across the street to the Army Centre, a chocolate cake in his hands. He was surprised, considering how she'd reacted in the past to his lingering round the uniformed men, but he said, "Wicked, Mum!" and grinned at her and was gone in an instant to make what she'd called a thank-you visit to them. "Good of those blokes to offer you tea time to time," she told her son, and if Daniel recognised the contradiction in this statement from her earlier fury at the idea of someone pitying her son, he didn't mention it.

Alone, Yasmin sat in front of the television set. She had the lamb stew simmering because—bloody fool that she was—she was *still* incapable of not doing what she'd said earlier she was going to do. She was also as unable to change her mind or to draw the line as she had been as Roger Edwards' girlfriend, his lover, his wife, and then as an inmate in Holloway Prison.

She wondered why now, but the answer lay before her in the hollowness she felt and the budding of a fear that she'd long ago buried. It seemed to her that her entire life had been described and dominated by that fear, a gripping terror of one thing that she'd been entirely unwilling to name, let alone to face. But all the running she'd done from the Bogey Man had only brought her to his embrace yet again.

She tried not to think. She wanted not to ponder the fact that she'd been reduced once more to discovering that there was no sanctuary no matter how determinedly she believed there would be.

She hated herself. She hated herself as much as she'd ever hated Roger Edwards and more—far more—than she hated Katja, who'd brought her to this mirror of a moment and asked her to gaze long and gaze hard. It made no difference that every kiss, embrace, act of love, and conversation had been built on a lie she could not have discerned. What mattered was that she, Yasmin Edwards, had even allowed herself to be a party to it. So she was filled with self-loathing. She was consumed by a thousand "I should've known's."

When Katja came in, Yasmin glanced at the clock. She was right on time, but she would be, wouldn't she, because the one thing Katja Wolff wasn't blind to was what was going on within others. It was a survival technique she'd learned inside. So she'd have read a whole book from Yasmin's visit to the laundry that morning. Thus, she'd be home on the stroke of dinner time, and she'd be prepared.

What she'd be prepared for, Katja wouldn't know. That was the only advantage Yasmin had. The rest of the advantages were all her lover's, and the single most important one was exactly like a beacon that had long been shining although Yasmin had always refused to acknowledge it.

Single-mindedness. That Katja Wolff had always had a goal was what had kept her sane in prison. She was a woman with plans, and she'd always been that. "You must know what you want and who you will become when you are out of here," she'd told Yasmin time and again. "Do not let what they have done to you become their triumph. That will happen if you fail." Yasmin had learned to admire Katja Wolff for that stubborn determination to become who she'd always intended to become despite her situation. And then she'd learned to love Katja Wolff for the solid foundation of the future she represented for them both, even while held within prison walls.

She'd said to her, "You got twenty *years* in here. You think you're going to step outside and start designing clothes when you're forty-five years old?"

"I will have a life," Katja had asserted. "I will prevail, Yas. I will have a life."

That life needed to start somewhere once Katja did her time, made her way through open conditions, proved herself there, and was released into society. She needed a place where she would be safe from notice so that she could begin to build her world again. She wouldn't have wanted any spotlight on her. She wouldn't be able to achieve her dream if she failed to fit easily back into the world. Even then it would prove to be tough: establishing herself in the competitive arena of fashion, when all she was, at best, was a notorious graduate of the criminal justice system.

When she'd first fixed herself up in Kennington with Yasmin, Yasmin had understood that Katja would have to undergo a period of adjustment before she began to fulfil the dreams she'd spoken of. So she'd given her time to reacquaint herself with freedom, and she had not questioned the fact that Katja's talk of goals within prison did not immediately translate to action once she was outside. People were different, she told herself. It meant nothing that she—Yasmin—had begun to work at her new life furiously and single-mindedly the moment she was finally released. She, after all, had a son to provide for and a lover whose arrival she spent years anticipating. She had more incentive to put her world in order so that Daniel first and then Katja afterwards would have the home they both deserved.

But now she saw that Katja's talk had been that: merely talk. Katja had no inclination to make her way in the world because she did not need to. Her spot in the world had long been reserved.

Yasmin didn't move from the sofa as Katja shrugged out of her coat, saying, "*Mein Gott.* I'm exhausted," and then, seeing her, "What're you doing in the dark there, Yas?" She crossed the room and switched on the table lamp, homing in as she usually did on the cigarettes that Mrs. Crushley wouldn't allow her to smoke anywhere near the laundry. She lit up from a book of matches that she took from her pocket and tossed down on the coffee table next to the packet of Dunhills from which she'd scored the cigarette. Yasmin leaned forward and picked up the matches. *Frère Jacques Bar and Brasserie* were the words printed on it.

"Where's Daniel?" Katja said, looking round the flat. She stepped into the kitchen and took note of the fact that the table was set only for two, because the next thing she said was, "Has he gone to a mate's for dinner, Yas?"

"No," Yasmin said. "He'll be home soon." She'd set it up that way to make sure she didn't cave in to her cowardice at the final moment.

"Then why's the table—" Katja stopped. She was a woman who had the discipline not to betray herself, and Yasmin saw her use that discipline now, silencing her own question.

Yasmin smiled bitterly. Right, she told her lover in silence. Didn't think little Pinky would open her eyes, did you, Kat? And if she opened them or had them opened, didn't expect *her* to make a move, make the *first* move, put herself *out* there alone and afraid, did you, Kat? 'Cause you had five years to suss out how to get inside her skin and make her feel like she had a future with you. 'Cause even then you knew that if anyone ever made this little bitch start seeing possibilities where there wasn't a hope in hell of planting one, she'd give herself over to that worthless cow and do anything it took to make her happy. And that's what you needed, isn't it, Kat? That's what you were counting on.

She said, "I been to Number Fifty-five."

Katja said guardedly, "You've been where?" And those V's were present in her voice again, those once-charming hallmarks of her dissimilarity.

"Number Fifty-five Galveston Road. Wandsworth. South London," Yasmin said.

Katja didn't reply, but Yasmin could see her thinking despite the fact that her face was the perfect blank she'd learned to produce for anyone looking her way in prison. Her expression said, Nothing going on inside here. Her eyes, however, locked too tightly on Yasmin's.

Yasmin noticed for the first time that Katja was grimy: Her face was oily and her blonde hair clung in spears to her skull. "Didn't go there tonight," she noted evenly. "Decided to shower at home, I s'pose."

Katja came nearer. She drew in deeply on her cigarette, and Yasmin could see that still she was thinking. She was thinking it could all be a trick to force her into admitting something that Yasmin was only guessing at in the first place. She said, "Yas," and put out her hand and grazed it along the line of plaits that Yasmin had drawn back from her face and tied at the nape of her neck with a scarf. Yasmin jerked away.

"Didn't need to shower there, I s'pose," Yasmin said. "No cunt juice on your face tonight. Right?"

"Yasmin, what are you talking about?"

"I'm *talking* about Number Fifty-five, Katja. Galveston Road. I'm talking about what you *do* when you go there."

"I go there to meet my solicitor," Katja said. "Yas,

you heard me tell that detective so this morning. Do you think I'm lying? Why would I lie? If you wish to phone Harriet and ask her if she and I went there to-gether—"

"*I* went there," Yasmin announced flatly. "I *went* there, Katja. Are you listenin' to me?"

"And?" Katja asked. Still so calm, Yasmin thought, still so sure of herself or at least still so capable of looking that way. And why? Because she knew that no one was at home during the day. She believed that anyone ringing the bell would have no luck learning who lived within. Or perhaps she was just buying time to think how to explain it all away.

Yasmin said, "No one was home."

"I see."

"So I went to a neighbour and asked who lives there." She felt the betrayal swelling inside her, like a balloon too inflated that climbed to her throat. She forced herself to say, "Noreen McKay," and she waited to hear her lover's response. What's it going to be? she thought. An excuse? A declaration of misun-derstanding? An attempt at a reasonable explanation?

Katja   said,   "Yas . . ." Then   she   murmured, "Bloody hell," and the Englishism sounded so strange coming from her that Yasmin felt, if only for an in-stant, as if she were talking to a different person en-tirely to the Katja Wolff she'd loved for the last three of her years in prison and all of the five years that had followed them. "I do not know what to say," she sighed. She came round the coffee table and joined

Yasmin on the sofa. Yasmin flinched at her nearness. Katja moved away.

"I packed your things," Yasmin said. "They're in the bedroom. I didn't want Dan to see . . . I'll tell him tomorrow. He's used to you not being here some nights anyway."

"Yas, it wasn't always—"

Yasmin could hear her voice go higher as she said, "There's dirty clothes to be washed. I put them separate in a Sainsbury's bag. You can do them tomorrow or borrow a washing machine tonight or stop at a launderette or—"

"Yasmin, you must hear me. We were not always . . . Noreen and I . . . We were not always together as you're thinking we were. This is something . . ." Katja moved closer again. She put her hand on Yasmin's thigh, and Yasmin felt her body go rigid at the touch and that tensing of muscles, that hardening of joints, brought too much back, brought everything back, shot her into her past, where the faces overhung her. . . .

She leapt to her feet. She covered her ears. "Stop it! You burn in hell!" she cried.

Katja held out her hand but didn't rise from the sofa. She said, "Yasmin, listen to me. This is something I cannot explain. It's here inside and it's been here forever. I cannot get it out of my system. I try. It fades. Then it comes back again. With you, Yasmin, you must listen to me. With you, I thought . . . I hoped . . ."

"You used," Yasmin said. "No thinking, no hoping. *Using,* Katja. Because what you thought was if things looked like you moved on from her, she'd finally have to step forward and say who she really was. But she didn't do that when you were inside. And she didn't do that when you came out. But you keep thinking she's going to do that, so you set up with me to force her hand. Only that's not how it works 'less she knows what you're up to and with who, right? And it sure's *hell* don't work 'less you give her a taste now and then of what she's missing."

"That is not how it is."

"You telling me you haven't done it, the two of you? You haven't been with her since you got out? You haven't been slithering over there after work, after dinner, even after you been with me and say you can't sleep and need a walk and know I won't wake up till morning and I can see it *all* now, Katja. And I want you gone."

"Yas, I have no place to go."

Yasmin breathed out a laugh. "I expect one phone call'll sort that out."

"Please, Yasmin. Come. Sit. Let me tell you how it has been."

"How it's *been* is you waiting. Oh, I d'n't see't at first. I thought you 're trying to adjust to outside. I thought you 're getting ready to make a life for yourself—for you and me and Dan, Katja—but all the time you were waiting for her. You were *always* waiting. You were waiting to make yourself part of *her* life and once you got there, everything in yours'd be taken care of just fine."

"That's not how it is."

"No? Really? You make one move to get yourself together since you been out? You phone up design schools? You talk to anyone? You walk into one of those Knightsbridge shops and offer yourself as a 'prentice?"

"No. I have not done that."

"And we both know why. You don't need to make a life for yourself if she does it for you."

"That is not the case." Katja rose from the sofa, crushing out her cigarette in the ashtray, spilling ash onto the table top, where it lay like the remnants of disappointed dreams. "I make my own life as always," she said. "It's different from the life I thought I'd have, yes. It's different from the life I spoke of inside, yes. But Noreen doesn't make that life for me any more than you do, Yasmin. I make it myself. And that is what I have been doing since I was released. That is what Harriet is helping me to do. That is why I spent twenty years in prison and did not go mad. Because I knew—I *knew*—what waited for me when I got out."

"Her," Yasmin said. "She waited, right? So go to her. Leave."

"No. You must understand. I will make you—"

Make you, make you, make you. Too many people had *made her* already. Yasmin clutched her hands to her head.

"Yasmin, I did three evil things in my life. I made Hannes take me over the wall by threatening to tell the authorities."

"That's ancient history."

"It's more than that. Listen. That was my first evil, what I did to Hannes. But I also did not speak up when I once should have spoken. That's the second thing. And then, once—only once, Yas, but once was enough—I listened when I should have covered my ears. And I paid for all of it. Twenty years I paid. Because *I* was lied to. And now others must pay. That's what I have been setting about."

"No! I won't hear!" In panic, Yasmin dashed to the bedroom, where she'd packed up Katja's small wardrobe of bright secondhand clothes—all those clothes that defined who Katja was, a woman who would never wear black in a city where black was everywhere—into a duffel bag that she'd bought for that purpose, laying out her own money as a way of paying for every mistake she'd made in trust. She didn't want to hear, but more than that, she knew she couldn't afford to hear. Hearing what Katja had to say put her at risk, put her future with Daniel at risk, and she wouldn't do that.

She grabbed the duffel bag and slung it out into the sitting room. She followed it with the Sainsbury bag of dirty laundry and then the single cardboard box that contained the toiletries and other supplies Katja had brought with her when she'd first moved into the flat. She cried out, "I told him, Katja. He knows. You got that? I told him. I *told*."

She said, "Who?"

"You know who. *Him.*" Yasmin drew her fingers down her cheek to indicate the scar that marked the black detective's face. "You weren't here watching the telly, and he knows."

"But he is . . . they are . . . all of them . . . Yas, you know they are your enemy. What they did to you when you defended yourself against Roger . . . What they put you through? How could you trust—"

"That's what you were depending on, wasn't it? Old Yas won't ever trust a copper, no matter what he says, no matter what I do. So I'll just set myself up with good old Yas, and she'll protect me when they come calling. She'll follow my lead, just like she did inside. But that's over, Katja. Whatever it was, and I don't much care. It's over."

Katja looked down at the bags. She said quietly, "We are so close to ending things after all these—"

Yasmin slammed the bedroom door to cut off her words and to cut herself off from further danger. And then, finally, she began to weep. Over her tears, she could hear the sound of Katja gathering up her belongings. When the flat door opened and closed a moment later, Yasmin Edwards knew her lover was gone.

"SO IT'S NOT about the kid," Havers said to Lynley, concluding the update of her second visit to the Convent of the Immaculate Conception. "He's called Jeremy Watts, by the way. The nun's always known where he was; Katja Wolff's always known that she's known. She's gone twenty years without asking about him. She's gone twenty years without talking to Sister Cecilia at all. So it's not about the kid."

"There's something not natural in that," Lynley said reflectively.

"There's plenty not natural in all of her," Havers replied. "In all of *them*. I mean, what's going on with Richard Davies, Inspector? Okay, all right. Virginia was retarded. He was cut up about that. Who wouldn't be? But never even to see her again . . . and to let his *dad* dictate . . . And why the hell were he and Lynn living with his dad anyway? Sure, those were impressive digs in Kensington and maybe Richard's a bloke who likes to make an impression. And p'rhaps Mum and Dad might've lost the ancestral pile or something if Richard didn't contribute by living there and paying through the nose or whatever, but still . . ."

"The relationship between fathers and sons is always complicated," Lynley said.

"More than mothers and daughters?"

"Indeed. Because so much more goes unspoken."

They were in a café on Hampstead High Street, not far from the station on Downshire Hill. They'd rendezvoused there by prior arrangement, Havers phoning Lynley on his mobile as he was setting out from Stamford Brook. He'd told her about Webberly's heart attack, and she'd cursed fervently and asked what she could do. His answer had been what Randie's had been when she'd phoned the house from the hospital to share an update with her mother not long before Lynley left: They could do nothing but pray; the doctors were watching him.

She'd said, "What the hell does 'watching him' mean?"

Lynley hadn't replied because it seemed to him that "watching the patient's progress" was a medical euphemism for waiting for an appropriate moment to pull the plug. Now, across the table from Havers with an undoctored espresso (his) and a coffee loaded with milk and sugar not to mention a *pain au chocolat* (both hers) between them, Lynley dug out his handkerchief from his pocket and spread it out on the table, disclosing its contents.

He said, "We may be down to this," and indicated the shards of glass he'd taken from the edge of the pavement in Crediton Hill.

Havers scrutinised them. "Headlamp?" she asked.

"Not considering where I found them. Swept under a hedge."

"Could be nothing, sir."

"I know," Lynley said gloomily.

"Where's Winnie? What's he come up with, Inspector?"

"He's on Katja Wolff's trail." Lynley filled her in on what Nkata had reported to him earlier.

She said, "So are you leaning towards Wolff? Because like I said—"

"I know. If she's our killer, it's not about her son. So what's her motive?"

"Revenge? Could they have framed her, Inspector?"

"With Webberly part of the *they*? Christ. I don't want to think so."

"But with him involved with Eugenie Davies . . ." Havers had brought her coffee to her lips, but she didn't drink, instead, looking at him over the top of it. "I'm not saying he would've done it deliberately, sir. But if he was involved, he could've been blinded, could've been . . . well, *led* to believe . . . You know."

"That presupposes the CPS, a jury, and a judge were all led to believe as well," Lynley said.

"It's happened," Havers pointed out. "And more than once. You know that."

"All right. Accepted. But why didn't she speak? If evidence was altered, if testimony was false, why didn't she *speak*?"

"There's that," Havers sighed. "We always come back to it."

"We do." Lynley took a pencil from his breast pocket. With it, he moved about the pieces of glass at the centre of his handkerchief. "Too thin for a head-lamp," he told Havers. "The first pebble that hit it—on the motorway, for instance—would have smashed to bits a headlamp made of this sort of glass."

"Broken glass in a hedgerow? It's probably from a bottle. Someone coming out of a party with a bottle of plonk under his arm. He's had a few and he stag-gers. It drops, breaks, and he kicks the shards to one side."

"But there's no curve, Havers. Look at the larger pieces. They're straight."

"Okay. They're straight. But if you expect to tie

these to one of our principals, I think you're going to be wandering in the outback without a guide."

Lynley knew she was right. He gathered the handkerchief together again, slipped it into his pocket, and brooded. His fingers played with the top of his espresso cup as his eyes examined the ring of sludge left in it. For her part, Havers polished off her *pain au chocolat,* emerging from the exercise with flakes of pastry on her lips.

He said, "You're hardening your arteries, Constable."

"And now I'm going after my lungs." She wiped her mouth with a paper napkin and dug out her packet of Players. She said in advance of his protest, "I'm owed this. It's been a long day. I'll blow it over my shoulder, okay?"

Lynley was too dispirited to argue. Webberly's condition was heavy in his mind, weighing only slightly less than Frances's knowledge of her husband's affair. He forced himself away from these thoughts, saying, "All right. Let's look at everyone again. Notes?"

Havers blew out a lungful of smoke impatiently. "We've *done* this, Inspector. We don't have a thing."

"We've got to have something," Lynley said, putting on his reading glasses. "Notes, Havers."

She groused but brought them out of her shoulder bag. Lynley took his from his jacket pocket. They started with those individuals without alibis that could be corroborated.

Ian Staines was Lynley's first offering. He was desperate for money, which his sister had promised to request from her son. But she'd reneged on that promise, leaving Staines in dangerous straits. "He looks about to lose his home," Lynley said. "The night of the death, they rowed. He could have followed her up to London. He didn't get home till after one."

"But the car's not right," Havers said. "Unless he had a second vehicle with him in Henley."

"Which he may have done," Lynley noted. "Parked there previously just in case. Someone has access to a second vehicle, Havers."

They went on to the multi-named J. W. Pitchley, Havers' prime candidate at this point. "What the hell," she wanted to know, "was his address doing in Eugenie's possession? Why was she heading to see him? Staines says she told him something came up. Was that something Pitchley?"

"Possibly, save for the fact that we can establish no tie between them. No phone tie, internet tie—"

"Snail mail?"

"How did she track him down?"

"Same way I did, Inspector. She figured he'd changed identities once, why not again?"

"All right. But why would she arrange to see him?"

Havers took a different tack from all the possibilities she'd offered earlier in the case. She said, "Maybe *he* arranged to see her once she'd located him. And she contacted him because . . ." Havers considered the potential reasons, settling on, "because Katja Wolff just got out of the slammer. If the whole boiling lot of them framed her and she was finally out of prison, they'd have plans to lay, right? About how to deal with her if she came calling?"

"But we're back to that, Havers. An entire household of people framing an individual who then doesn't utter a word in her own defence? *Why?*"

"Fear of what they could do to her? The granddad sounds like a real terror. P'rhaps he got to her in some way. He said, 'Play our game or we'll let the world know . . .'" Havers considered this and rejected her own idea, saying, "Know what? That she was in the club? Big deal. Like anyone cared at that point? It came out that she was pregnant anyway."

Lynley held up a hand to stop her from dismissing the thought. He said, "But you could be on to something, Barbara. It could have been 'Play our game or we'll let it out who the father of your baby is.'"

"Big deal again."

"Yes, big deal," Lynley argued, "if it's not a case of letting the world know who the father is but letting Eugenie Davies know."

"Richard?"

"It wouldn't be the first time the man of the house got entangled with the nanny."

"What about him, then?" Havers said. "What about Davies knocking off Eugenie?"

"Motive and alibi," Lynley pointed out. "He doesn't have one. He has the other. Although the reverse could be said of Robson."

"But where does Webberly fit in? In fact, where does he fit in no matter who we go with?"

"He fits in only with Wolff. And that takes us back to the original crime: the murder of Sonia Davies. And that takes us back to the initial group who were involved in the subsequent investigation."

"P'rhaps someone's just making it look like everything's connected to that period of time, sir. Because isn't it the truth that a more profound connection exists: the romantic one between Webberly and Eugenie Davies? And that takes us to Richard, doesn't it? To Richard or to Frances Webberly."

Lynley didn't want to think of Frances. He said, "Or to Gideon, blaming Webberly for the end of his parents' marriage."

"That's weak."

"But something's going on with him, Havers. If you met him, you'd agree. And he has no alibi other than being home alone."

"Where was his dad?"

Lynley referred to his notes once again. "With the fiancée. She confirms."

"But he's got a much better motive than Gideon if the Webberly-Eugenie connection's behind this."

"Hmm. Yes. I do see that. But to assign him the motive of rubbing out his wife *and* Webberly begs the question of why he would wait all these years to see to the job."

"He had to wait till now. This is when Katja Wolff was released. He'd know we'd establish a trail to her."

"That's nursing a grievance for a hell of a long time."

"So maybe it's a more recent grievance."

"More recent . . . ? Are you arguing he's fallen in love with her a second time in his life?" Lynley considered his question. "All right. I think it's unlikely, but for the sake of argument, I'll go with it. Let's consider the possibility that he's had his love for his former wife reawakened. We begin with him divorced from her."

"Destroyed by the fact that she walked out on him," Havers added.

"Right. Now, Gideon has trouble with the violin. His mother reads about that trouble in the papers or hears it from Robson. She gets back in touch with Davies."

"They talk often. They begin to reminisce. *He* thinks they're going to make a go of it again, and he's hot to trot—"

"This is, of course, ignoring the entire question of Jill Foster," Lynley pointed out.

"Hang on, Inspector. Richard and Eugenie talk about Gideon. They talk about old times, their marriage, whatever. Everything he's felt gets fired up again. He becomes a potato all hot for the oven, only to find out that Eugenie's got someone lined up in her knickers already: Wiley."

"Not Wiley," Lynley said. "He's too old. Davies wouldn't see him as competition. Besides, Wiley told us she had something she wanted to reveal to him. She'd said as much. But she didn't want to reveal it three nights ago—"

"Because she was headed to London," Havers said. "To Crediton Hill."

"To Pitchley-Pitchford-Pytches," Lynley said. "The end is always the beginning, isn't it?" He found the reference in his notes that supplied a single piece of information that had been there all along, just waiting for the correct interpretation. He said, "Wait. When I brought up the idea of another man, Havers, Davies went straight to him. By name, in fact. Without a doubt in his mind. I've got him naming Pytches right here in my notes."

"Pytches?" Havers asked. "No. It's not Pytches, Inspector. That can't—"

Lynley's mobile rang. He grabbed it from the table top and held up a finger to stop Havers from continuing. She was itching to do so, however. She'd stubbed out her cigarette impatiently, saying, "What day did you talk to Davies, Inspector?"

Lynley waved her off, clicked on his mobile, said, "Lynley," and turned away from Havers' smoke.

His caller was DCI Leach. "We've got another victim," he announced.

WINSTON NKATA READ the sign—*HM Prison Holloway*—and reflected on the fact that had his life taken a slightly different turn, had his mum not fainted dead away at the sight of her son in a casualty ward with thirty-four stitches closing an ugly slash on his face, he might have ended up in such a place. Not in this place, naturally, which imprisoned only women, but in a place just like it. The Scrubs, perhaps, or Dartmoor or the Ville. Doing time inside because what he'd not been able to manage was doing life outside.

But his mum had fainted. She had murmured, "Oh, Jewel," and had slid to the floor like her legs'd turned to jelly. And the sight of her there with her turban askew—so that he could see what he'd never noticed before, that her hair was actually going grey—made him finally accept her not as the indomitable force he thought she was but instead as a real woman for once, a woman who loved and relied on him to make her proud that she'd given birth. And that had been that.

But had the moment not occurred, had his dad come to fetch him instead, flinging him into the back seat of the car with a demonstration of the full measure of the disgust he deserved, the outcome might have been quite different. He might have felt the need to prove he didn't care that he'd become the recipient of his father's displeasure, and he might have felt the need to prove it by upping the stakes in the Brixton Warriors' longtime battle with the smaller upstart Longborough Bloods to secure a patch of ground called Windmill Gardens and make it part of their turf. But the moment had happened, and his life course had altered, bringing him to where he was now: staring at the windowless brick bulk of Holloway Prison inside which Katja Wolff had met both Yasmin Edwards and Noreen McKay.

He'd parked across the street from the prison, in front of a pub with boarded-up windows that looked

like something straight out of Belfast. He'd eaten an
orange, studied the prison entrance, and meditated on
what everything meant. Particularly, he meditated on
what it meant that the German woman was living
with Yasmin Edwards but messing around with
someone else, just as he'd suspected when he'd seen
those shadows merging on the curtains in the window of Number Fifty-five Galveston Road.

His orange consumed, he ducked across the street
when the heavy traffic on Parkhurst Road was halted
at the traffic lights. He approached reception and dug
out his warrant card, presenting it to the officer behind the desk. She said, "Is Miss McKay expecting
you?"

He said, "Official business. She won't be surprised
to know I'm here."

The receptionist said she would phone, if Constable Nkata wanted to have a seat. It was late in the day,
and whether Miss McKay would be able to see
him . . .

"Oh, I 'xpect she'll be able to see me," Nkata said.

He didn't sit but rather walked to the window,
where he looked out on more of the vast brick walls.
As he watched the traffic passing by on the street, a
guard gate raised to accommodate a prison van, no
doubt returning an inmate at the end of a day's trial
at the Old Bailey. This would have been how Katja
Wolff had come and gone during those long-ago days
of her own trial. She'd have been accompanied daily
by a prison officer, who would remain in court with
her, right inside the dock. That officer would have

ferried her to and from her cell beneath the court-room, made her tea, escorted her to lunch, and seen her back to Holloway for the night. An officer and an inmate alone, during the most difficult period of that inmate's life.

"Constable Nkata?"

Nkata swung round to see the receptionist holding a telephone receiver out to him. He took it from her, said his name, and heard a woman say in response, "There's a pub across the street. On the corner of Hillmarton Road. I can't see you in here, but if you wait in the pub, I'll join you in quarter of an hour."

He said, "Make it five minutes and I'm on my way without hanging about chatting to anyone."

She exhaled loudly, said, "Five minutes, then," and slammed down the phone at her end.

Nkata went back to the pub, which turned out to be a nearly empty room as cold as a barn where the air was redolent mostly of dust. He ordered himself a cider, and he took his drink to a table that faced the door.

She didn't make it in five, but she arrived under ten, coming through the door with a gust of wind. She looked round the pub, and when her eyes fell upon Nkata, she nodded once and came over to him, taking the long sure strides of a woman with power and confidence. She was quite tall, not as tall as Yasmin Edwards but taller than Katja Wolff, perhaps five foot ten.

She said, "Constable Nkata?"

He said, "Miss McKay?"

She pulled out a chair, unbuttoned her coat, shrugged out of it, and sat, elbows on the table and hands fingering back her hair. This was blonde and cut short, leaving her ears bare. She wore small pearl studs in their lobes. For a moment, she kept her head bent, but when she drew in a breath and looked up, her blue eyes fixed on Nkata with plain dislike.

"What do you want from me? I don't like interruptions while I'm at work."

"Could've caught up with you at home," Nkata said. "But here was closer than Galveston Road from Harriet Lewis's office."

At the mention of the solicitor, her face became guarded. "You know where I live," she said cautiously.

"Followed a bird called Katja Wolff there last night. From Kennington to Wandsworth by bus, this was. It was in'ersting to note that she went the whole route and didn't stop once to ask directions. Seems like she knew where she was going good enough."

Noreen McKay sighed. She was middle-aged— probably near fifty, Nkata thought—but the fact that she wore little make-up served her well. She heightened what she had without looking painted, so her colour seemed authentic. She was neatly dressed in the uniform of the prison. Her white blouse was crisp, the navy epaulets bore their brass ornamentation brightly, and her trousers had creases that would have done a military man proud. She had keys on her belt, a radio as well, and some sort of pouch. She looked impressive.

She said, "I don't know what this is about, but I've nothing to say to you, Constable."

"Not even 'bout Katja Wolff?" he asked her. " 'Bout what she was doing calling on you with her solicitor in tow? They filing a law suit 'gainst you, or something?"

"As I just said, I've nothing to say, and there's no room for compromise in my position. I've a future and two adolescents to consider."

"Not a husband, though?"

She brushed one hand through her hair again. It seemed to be a characteristic gesture. "I've never been married, Constable. I've had my sister's children since they were four and six years old. Their father didn't want them when Susie died—too busy playing the footloose bachelor—but he's started coming round now he's realising he won't be twenty years old forever. Frankly, I don't want to give him a reason to take them."

"There's a reason, then? What would that be?"

Noreen McKay shoved away from the table and went to the bar instead of replying. There, she placed an order and waited while her gin was poured over two ice cubes and a bottle of tonic set next to it.

Nkata watched her, trying to fill in the blanks with a simple scrutiny of her person. He wondered which part of prison work had first attracted Noreen McKay: the power it provided over other people, the sense of superiority it offered, or the chance it represented to cast a fishing line in waters where the trout had no psychological protection.

She returned to the table, her drink in hand. She said, "You saw Katja Wolff and her solicitor come to my home. That's the extent of what you saw."

"Saw her let herself in 's well. She didn't knock."

"Constable, she's a German."

Nkata cocked his head. "I got no recollection of Germans not knowing they're s'posed to knock on strangers' doors before walking in on them, Miss McKay. Mostly, I think they know the rules. Especially the ones telling them they don't have to knock where they already've got themselves well established."

Noreen McKay lifted her gin and tonic. She drank but made no reply.

Nkata said, "What I'm wondering 'bout the whole situation is this: Is Katja the first lag you had some rabbit with or was she just one in a line of nellies?"

The woman flushed. "You don't know what you're talking about."

"What I'm talking about's your position at Holloway and how you might've used and abused it over the years, and what action the guv'nors might think of taking if word got out you've been doing the nasty where you ought to be just locking the doors. You got how many years in the job? You got a pension? In line for promotion to warden? What?"

She smiled without humour, saying, "You know, I wanted to be a policeman, Constable, but I've dyslexia and I couldn't pass the exams. So I turned to prison work because I like the idea of citizens upholding the law, and I believe in punishing those who cross the line."

"Which you yourself did. With Katja. She 'as doing twenty years—"

"She didn't do all her time at Holloway. Virtually no one does. But I've been here for twenty-four years. So I expect your assumption—whatever it is—has a number of holes in it."

"She was here on remand, she was here for the trial, she did some time here. And when she went off—to Durham, was it?—she'd be able to list her visitors, wouldn't she? And whose name d'you think I'd find in her records as the one to admit—proba'ly the *only* one to admit aside from her brief—for her visits? And she'd be back in Holloway to do some of her time, I expect. Yeah. I expect that could've been fixed up easy enough from within. What's your job, Miss McKay?"

"Deputy warden," she said. "I imagine you know that."

"Deputy warden with a taste for the ladies. You always been bent?"

"That's none of your business."

Nkata slapped his hand on the table and leaned towards the woman. "It's all my business," he told her. "Now, you want me to troll through Katja's records, find all the prisons she 'as locked up in, get all the visitors lists she filled out, see your name topping them, and put the thumbscrews to you? I c'n do that, Miss McKay, but I don't like to. It wastes my time."

She lowered her gaze to her drink, turning the glass slowly on the mat beneath it. The pub door opened, letting in another gust of chill evening air and the smell of exhaust fumes from Parkhurst Road, and two men in the uniform of prison workers walked inside. They fixed on Noreen, then on Nkata, then back to Noreen. One smiled and made a low comment. Noreen looked up and saw them.

She breathed an oath and said, "I've got to get out of here," beginning to rise.

Nkata closed his hand over her wrist. "Not without giving me something," he told her. "Else I'm going to have to look through her records, Miss McKay. And 'f your name's there, I 'xpect you'll have some real 'xplaining to do to your guv."

"Do you threaten people often?"

"Not a threat. Just a simple fact. Now, sit back down and 'tend to your drink." He nodded towards her colleagues. "I 'xpect I'm doing your reputation some good."

Her face flared with red. "You completely *despicable*—"

"Chill," he said. "Let's talk about Katja. She gave me the go-ahead to talk to you, by the way."

"I don't believe—"

"Phone her."

"She—"

"She's a suspect in a hit-and-run murder. And a suspect in a second hit-and-run as well. 'F you can clear her name, you better set to it. She's 'bout two breaths away from getting arrested. And you think we'll be able to keep *that* from the press? Notorious baby killer 'helping the police with their enquiries' again? Not likely, Miss McKay. Her whole life's about to go under the microscope. And I 'xpect you know what that means."

"I can't clear her name," Noreen McKay said, her fingers tightening on her gin and tonic. "That's just it, don't you see? I can't clear her name."

TWENTY-THREE

"WADDINGTON," DCI Leach informed them when Lynley and Havers joined him in the incident room. He was all exultation: his face brighter than it had been in days and his step lighter as he dashed across the room to scrawl *Kathleen Waddington* at the top of one of the china boards.

"Where was she hit?" Lynley asked.

"Maida Vale. And it's the same m.o. Quiet neighbourhood. Pedestrian alone. Night. Black car. *Smash.*"

"Last night?" Barbara Havers asked. "But that would mean—"

"No, no. This was ten days ago."

"Could be a coincidence," Lynley said.

"Not bloody likely. She's a player from before." Leach went on to explain precisely who Kathleen Waddington was: a sex therapist who'd left her clinic on the night in question after ten o'clock. She'd been hit on the street and left with a broken hip and a dislocated shoulder. When she was interviewed by the police, she'd said the car that hit her was big, "like a gangster car," that it moved fast, that it was dark, possibly black. Leach said, "I went through my notes from the other case, the baby drowning. Waddington was the woman who broke Katja Wolff's story about being out of the bathroom for a minute or less on the night that Sonia Davies drowned. The woman Wolff claimed phoned her. Without Waddington, it still might have gone down to negligence and a few years in prison. With her showing Wolff up to be a liar . . . It was another nail in the coffin. We need to bring Wolff in. Pass that word to Nkata. Let him have the glory. He's been working her hard."

"What about the car?" Lynley asked.

"That'll come in due course. You can't tell me she spent two decades inside without having formed more than one association she could depend on when she got out."

"Someone with an old motor?" Barbara Havers asked.

"Bet on it. I've got a PC going through the significant others right now," with a jerk of his head towards a female constable sitting at one of the terminals in the room. "She's picking up every name mentioned in every action report and running each through the system. We'll get our mitts on the prison records as well and run through everyone Wolff had contact with while she was inside. We can do that while we've got her in for questioning. D'you want to page your man and give him the message? Or shall I?" Leach rubbed his hands together briskly.

The constable at the computer terminal rose from her seat at that moment with a paper in her hand. She said, "I think I've got it, sir," and Leach bounded to her with a happy, "Brilliant. Good work, Vanessa. What've we got?"

"A Humber," she said.

The vehicle in question was a post-war saloon manufactured in the days when the relationship between petrol consumed and kilometers covered was not the first thing on a driver's mind. It was smaller than a Rolls-Royce, a Bentley, or a Daimler—not to mention less costly—but it was larger than the average car on the street today. And whereas the modern car was manufactured from aluminium and alloy to keep its weight low and its mileage high, the Humber was fashioned from steel and chrome with a front end comprising a toothy sneer of heavy grillwork suitable for scooping from the air everything from winged insects to small birds.

"Excellent," Leach said.

"Whose is it?" Lynley asked.

"Belongs to a woman," Vanessa told them. "She's called Jill Foster."

"Richard Davies' fiancée?" Havers looked at Lynley. Her face broke into a smile. She said, "That's it. That's bloody *it*, Inspector. When you—"

But Lynley interrupted her. "Jill Foster? I can't see that, Havers. I've met the woman. She's enormously pregnant. She's not capable of this. And even if she were, why would she go after Waddington?"

Havers said, "Sir—"

Leach cut in, "There's got to be another car, then. Another old one."

"How likely is that?" the PC said doubtfully.

"Page Nkata," Leach told Lynley. And to Vanessa, "Get Wolff's prison records. We need to go through them. There's got to be a car—"

"Hang *on*!" Havers said explosively. "There's another way to look at this, you lot. Listen. He said Pytches. Richard Davies said Pytches. Not Pitchley or Pitchford, but *Pytches*." She grasped Lynley's arm for emphasis. "You said he said Pytches when we were having coffee. You said you had Pytches in your notes. When you interviewed Richard Davies? Yes?"

Lynley said, "Pytches? What's Jimmy Pytches have to do with this, Havers?"

"It was a slip of the tongue, don't you see?"

"Constable," Leach said irritably, "what the hell are you on about?"

Havers went on, directing her comments to Lynley. "Richard Davies wouldn't have made that kind of verbal mistake when he'd just been told his former wife was murdered. He couldn't have *known* J. W. Pitchley was Jimmy Pytches right at that moment. He might have known James Pitchford was Jimmy Pytches, yes, all right, but he didn't think of him as Pytches, he'd never known him as Pytches, so why the hell would he call him that in front of you, since you yourself didn't know who Pytches even was at that point? Why would he *ever* call him that, in fact? He wouldn't unless it was on his mind because he'd had to go through what I'd gone through: the records in St. Catherine's. And why? In order to locate James Pitchford himself."

"What is this?" Leach demanded.

Lynley held up a hand, saying, "Hang on a moment, sir. She's got something. Havers, go on."

"Too right I've got something," Havers asserted. "He'd been speaking to Eugenie for months. You've got that in your notes. He said it and the BT records corroborate."

"They do," Lynley said.

"And Gideon told you they were supposed to meet, he and his mother. Right?"

"Yes."

"Eugenie was supposed to be able to help him get over his stage fright. That's what he said. That's also in your notes. Only they didn't meet, did they? They weren't able to meet because she was killed first. So what if she was killed to *prevent* them from meeting? She didn't know where Gideon lived, did she? The only way she could have found out was from Richard."

Lynley said thoughtfully, "Davies wants to kill her, and he sees a way. Give her what she thinks is Gideon's address, arrange a time when they're supposed to meet, lie in wait for her—"

"—and when she goes wandering down the street with the address in her hand or wherever it was, *blam*. He runs her down," Havers concluded. "Then he drives over her to finish her off. But he makes it look like it's related to the older crime by taking Waddington out first and Webberly afterwards."

"Why?" Leach asked.

"That's the question," Lynley acknowledged. He said to Havers, "It works, Barbara. I do see that it works. But if Eugenie Davies could help her son regain his music, why would Richard Davies want to stop her? From talking to the man—not to mention from seeing his flat, which is a virtual shrine to Gideon's accomplishments—the only reasonable conclusion is that Richard Davies was determined to get his son playing again."

"So what if we've been looking at it wrong?" Havers asked.

"In what way?"

"I accept that Richard Davies wants Gideon to play again. If he had an issue with his playing—like jealousy or something, like his kid being more of a success than he is and how can he handle that—then he probably would have done something a long time ago to stop him. But from what we know, the kid's been playing since he was just out of nappies. So what if Eugenie Davies was going to meet Gideon in order to *stop* him ever playing again?"

"Why would she do that?"

"What about *quid pro quo* to Richard? If their marriage ended because of something he'd done—"

"Like putting the nanny in the club?" Leach suggested.

"Or devoting his every waking moment to Gideon and forgetting he had a wife at all, a woman in mourning, a woman with needs . . . Eugenie loses a child and instead of having someone to lean on, she has Richard, and all he cares about is getting *Gideon* through the trauma so he doesn't freak out and stop playing his music and stop being the son who's admired so much and on the edge of being famous and gratifying his daddy's every dream and what about *her* through all this? What about his mum? She's been forgotten, left to cope on her own, and she never forgets what it was like, so when she has the chance to put the screws on Richard, she knows just how to do it: when *he* needs her just like she needed him." Havers drew a deep breath at the end of all this, looking from the DCI to Lynley for their reaction.

Leach was the one to give it. "How?"

"How what?"

"How's she supposed to be able to stop her son playing? What's she going to do, Constable: break his fingers? Run *him* down?"

Havers drew a second breath, but she let it out on a sigh. "I don't know," she said, her shoulders sagging.

"Right," Leach snorted. "Well, when you do—"

"No," Lynley cut in. "There's some sense to this, sir."

"You're joking," Leach said.

"There's something in it. Following Havers' line of thinking, we've got an explanation of why Eugenie Davies was carrying Pitchley's address that night, and nothing else we've come up with so far gets anywhere near explaining that."

"Bollocks," Leach said.

"What other explanation can we come up with?

Nothing ties her to Pitchley. No letter, no phone call, no e-mail."

"She had e-mail?" Leach demanded.

Havers said, "Right. And her computer—" But she stopped herself abruptly, swallowing the rest of her sentence with a wince.

"*Computer?*" Leach echoed. "Where the hell's her computer? There's no computer mentioned in your reports."

Lynley felt Havers look at him, then drop her glance to her shoulder bag, where she rooted industriously for something that she probably didn't need. He wondered what would serve them better, truth or lie at this point. He opted for "I checked the computer. There was nothing on it. She had e-mail, yes. But there was nothing from Pitchley. So I saw no need—"

"To put it in your report?" Leach demanded. "What the *hell* kind of police work is that?"

"It seemed unnecessary."

"*What?* Good Christ. I want that computer in here, Lynley. I want our people on it like ants over ice cream. You're no computer expert. You might have missed . . . God damn it. Have you gone out of your mind? What the *hell* were you thinking?"

What could he say? That he was thinking of saving time? saving trouble? saving a reputation? saving a marriage? He said carefully, "Getting into her e-mail wasn't a problem, sir. Once we managed that, we could see there was virtually nothing—"

"*Virtually?*"

"Just a message from Robson, and we've spoken to him. He's holding something back, I think. But it's not the fact that he had anything to do with Mrs. Davies' death."

"You know that, do you?"

"It's a gut feeling, yes."

"The same one that prompted you to hold back— or is it *remove?*—a piece of evidence?"

"It was a judgement call, sir."

"You've no place making judgement calls. I want that computer. In here. *Now.*"

"As to the Humber?" Havers ventured delicately.

"Bugger the Humber. And bugger Davies. Vanessa, get those sodding prison records of Wolff's. For all we know, she's got ten people on a string, all with vehicles as old as Methuselah, *all* of them some-how related to this case."

"That's not what we have," Lynley said. "What you've come up with here, the Humber, can lead us—"

"I said *bugger* the Humber, Lynley. We're back to square one as far as you're concerned. Bring in that computer. And when you're done, get on your knees and thank God I don't report you to your superiors."

"IT'S TIME YOU came home with me, Jill." Dora Foster finished drying the last of the dishes and folded the tea towel neatly over its rack by the sink. She straightened its edges with her usual attention to mi-croscopic detail, and she turned back to Jill, who was resting at the kitchen table, her feet up and her fingers kneading the aching muscles of her lower back. Jill felt as if she were carrying a fifty-pound bag of flour in her stomach, and she wondered how on God's holy earth she was going to be able to get herself back into shape for her wedding just two months after the birth. "Our little Catherine's dropped into position," her mother said. "It's a matter of days. Any day now, in fact."

"Richard's not quite resigned to the plan," Jill told her.

"You're in better hands with me than you'd be alone in a delivery room with a nurse popping by occasionally to see that you're still among the living."

"Mum, I know that. But Richard's concerned."

"I've delivered—"

"He knows."

"Then—"

"It's not that he thinks you aren't competent. But it's different, he says, when it's your own flesh and blood involved. He says a doctor wouldn't operate on his own child. A doctor couldn't remain objective if something were to happen. Like an emergency. A crisis. You know."

"In an emergency, we go to hospital. Ten minutes in the car."

"I've told him that. He says anything could happen in ten minutes."

"Nothing will happen. This entire pregnancy has gone like a dream."

"Yes. But Richard—"

"Richard isn't your husband." Dora Foster said it

firmly. "He could have been, but he chose not to be. And that gives him no rights in this decision. Have you pointed that out to him?"

Jill sighed. "Mum . . ."

"Don't *Mum* me."

"What difference does it make that we're not married just now? We're *getting* married: the church, the priest, down the aisle on Dad's arm, the hotel reception, everything properly seen to. What more do you need?"

"It's not what I need," Dora said. "It's what you deserve. And don't tell me again this was your idea, because I know that's nonsense. You've had your wedding planned since you were ten years old, from the flowers down to the cake decoration, and as I recall, nowhere in your plans did it ever state there'd be a baby in attendance."

Jill didn't want to go into that. She said, "Times change, Mum."

"But you do not. Oh, I know it's the fashion for women to find themselves a partner rather than a husband. A *partner*, like someone they've gone into the baby-making business with. And when they have their babies, they parade them round in public without the slightest degree of embarrassment. I know this happens all the time. I'm not blind. But you aren't an actress or rock singer, Jill. You've always known your own mind, and you've never been one to do something just because it's in vogue."

Jill stirred on her chair. Her mother knew her better than anyone, and what she was saying was true.

But what was also true was the fact that compromise was necessary to have a successful relationship, and beyond wanting a child, she wanted to have a marriage that was happy, which she certainly wasn't guaranteed if she forced Richard's hand. "Well, it's done," she said. "And it's too late to change things. I'm not about to waddle down the aisle like this."

"Which makes you a woman without ties," her mother said. "So you can state how and where you want your baby delivered. And if Richard doesn't like it, you can point out to him that, as his preference was *not* to become your husband in the traditional fashion prior to the baby's birth, he can step out of the picture and stay out of the picture until after you're married. Now"—her mother joined her at the table, where a box of wedding invitations sat waiting to be addressed—"let's get your bag and take you home to Wiltshire. You can leave him a note. Or you can phone him. Shall I fetch the phone for you?"

"I'm not going to Wiltshire tonight," Jill said. "I'll speak to Richard. I'll ask him again—"

"*Ask* him?" Her mother put her hand on Jill's hugely swollen ankle. "Ask him what? Ask him if you can please have your baby—"

"Catherine's his baby as well."

"That has nothing to do with this. You're having her. Jill, this isn't at all like you. You've always known your own mind, but you're acting as if you're worried now, as if you might do something to drive him away. That's absurd, you know. He's lucky to have you. Considering his age, he's lucky to have any—"

"Mum." This was one area that they'd long ago agreed not to discuss: Richard's age and the fact that he was two years older than Jill's own father and five years older than her mother. "You're right. I know my own mind. It's made up: I'll speak to Richard when he comes home. But I won't go to Wiltshire without speaking to him and I certainly won't go and just leave him a note." She gave her voice The Edge, a tone she'd long used at the BBC, just the inflection that had been needed to bring every production in on time and on budget. No one argued with her when her voice had The Edge.

And Dora Foster didn't argue with her now. Instead, she sighed. She gazed on the ivory wedding dress that hung beneath its transparent shroud on the door. She said, "I never thought it would be like this."

"It'll be fine, Mum." Jill told herself that she meant it.

But when her mother had departed, she was left with her thoughts, those mischievous companions of one's solitude. They insisted she consider her mother's words carefully, which took her over the ground of her association with Richard.

It didn't *mean* anything that he'd been the one who wished to wait. There had been logic involved in the decision. And they'd taken it mutually, hadn't they? What difference did it make that he'd been the one to suggest it? He'd used sound reasoning. She'd told him she was pregnant, and he'd been joyful at the news, as joyful as she herself had been. He'd said,

"We'll get married. *Tell* me we'll get married," and she had laughed at the sight of his face looking so much like a little boy's, afraid of being disappointed. She'd said, "Of course we'll get married," and he'd pulled her into his arms and led her off into the bedroom.

After their coupling they lay entwined and he talked about their wedding. She'd been filled with bliss, with that gratified and grateful aftermath of orgasm during which everything seems possible and anything seems reasonable, so when he declared that he wanted her to have a *proper* wedding and no rushed affair, she sleepily had said, "Yes. Yes. A proper wedding, darling." To which he'd added, "With a proper gown for you. Flowers and attendants. A church. A photographer. A reception. I want to celebrate, Jill."

Which, of course, he could not do if they had to shoe-horn the planning into the seven months before the baby's birth. And even if they were able to manage that, no amount of shoe-horning would fit her into an elegant wedding gown once she had a bump. It was so practical to wait. In fact, Jill realised as she thought about it, Richard had led her right up to the idea so that when he said at the conclusion of her recitation of everything that had to be done in order to produce the kind of wedding he wanted her to have, "I'd no idea how *many* months . . . Will you be comfortable, Jill, with a wedding that far along into your pregnancy?" she'd been more than ready for his next line of thinking. "No one ought to enjoy the

day more than you. And as you're so small . . ." He
put his hand on her stomach as if for emphasis. It was
flat and taut, but it wouldn't be soon. "D'you think
we ought to wait?" he'd suggested.

Why not, she'd thought. She'd waited thirty-seven
years for her wedding day. There was no problem
waiting a few months more.

But that had been before Gideon's troubles had
taken up primary residence in Richard's mind. And
Gideon's troubles had brought on Eugenie.

Jill could see now that Richard's preoccupation after Wigmore Hall may have had a secondary source
beyond his son's failure to perform that night. And
when she set that secondary source next to his apparent reluctance to marry, she felt an uneasiness creep
over her, like a fog bank gliding noiselessly onto an
unsuspecting shore.

She blamed her mother for this. Dora Foster was
happy enough to be on the road to having her first
grandchild, but she wasn't pleased with Jill's choice of
father, although she knew better than to say so directly. Still, she *would* feel the need to voice her ob-
jections subtly, and what better way than to create an
inroad in Jill's implicit faith in Richard's honour. Not
that she actually *thought* in terms of a man doing "the
honourable thing." She didn't, after all, live in a
Hardy novel. When she thought of honour, she
merely thought of a man telling the truth about his
actions and intentions. Richard said they would
marry; ergo, they would.

They could have married at once, of course, once she'd become pregnant. She wouldn't have minded. It was, after all, marriage and children that she'd placed on her list as having to accomplish by her thirty-fifth birthday. She'd never written the word *wedding*, and she had seen a wedding only as one of the means she could use to achieve her end. Indeed, had she not been so blissful there in bed after their lovemaking, she probably would have said, "Bother the wedding, Richard. Let's marry now," and he would have agreed.

Wouldn't he? she wondered. Just as he'd agreed to the name she'd chosen for the baby? Just as he'd agreed to her mother's delivering the baby? Just as he'd agreed to selling her flat first instead of his? To buying that house she'd found in Harrow? To simply *going* with the estate agent to at least take a look at that house?

What did it mean that Richard was thwarting her at every turn, thwarting her in the most reasonable of fashions, making it seem as if every decision they reached was reached mutually and not a case of her giving in because she was . . . what? Afraid? And if so, of what?

And the answer was there even though the woman was dead, even though she could not come back to harm them, to stand in the way, to prevent what was meant to be . . .

The phone rang. Jill started. She looked round, dazed at first. So deep into her thoughts had she been that she wasn't aware for a moment that she was still in the kitchen and the cordless phone was somewhere in the sitting room. She lumbered to get it.

"Is this Miss Foster?" a woman's voice said. It was a professional voice, a competent voice, a voice such as Jill's voice once had been.

Jill said, "Yes."

"Miss Jill Foster?"

"Yes. Yes. Who is this please?"

And the answer fractured Jill's world into pieces.

THERE WAS SOMETHING about the way Noreen McKay made the statement—"I can't clear her name"—that gave Nkata pause before lighting the fireworks of celebration. There was a desperation behind the deputy warden's eyes and an incipient panic in the manner in which she downed the rest of her drink in a gulp. He said, "Can't or won't clear her name, Miss McKay?"

She said, "I have two teenage children to consider. They're all I have left as family. I don't want a custody battle with their father."

"Courts're more liberal these days."

"I also have a career. It's not the one I wanted, but it's the one I've got. The one I've made for myself. Don't you see? If it comes to light that I ever—" She stopped herself.

Nkata sighed. He couldn't take *ever* to the bank and deposit it, one way or the other. He said, "She was with you, then. Three nights back? Last night as well? Late last night?"

Noreen McKay blinked. She was sitting so straight and tall in her chair that she looked like a cardboard cutout of herself.

"Miss McKay, I got to know whether I c'n cross her name off."

"And I've got to know whether I can trust you. The fact that you've come here, right to the prison itself . . . Don't you see what that suggests?"

"Suggests I'm busy. Suggests it doesn't make sense for me to go driving back and forth 'cross London when you're . . . what . . . a mile? two miles? from Harriet Lewis's office."

"It suggests more than that," Noreen McKay said. "It tells me that you're self-interested, Constable, and if you're self-interested, what's to prevent you from passing on my name to a snout for a nice fifty quid? Or from being the snout yourself, for fifty more? It's a good story to sell to the *Mail*. You've threatened worse already in this conversation."

"I could do that now, comes down to it. You given me enough already, you have."

"I've given you what? The fact that a solicitor and her client came to my house one evening? What do you expect the *Mail* to do with that?"

Nkata had to acknowledge that Noreen McKay was making a good point. There was hardly seed for anyone's planting in what little information he had. There was, however, what he knew already and what he could assume from what he knew and what he ultimately could do with *that*. But the truth of the matter, however reluctantly he admitted it to himself, was that he actually needed from her only confirmation and a period of time to go with that confirmation. As for the rest of it, all the whys and the wherefores . . . If the truth were told, he *wanted* them, but he did not need them, not professionally.

He said, "The hit-and-run in Hampstead happened round half ten or eleven th' other night. Harriet Lewis says you c'n give Katja Wolff an alibi for the time. She also says you won't, which's what makes me think you and Katja got something between yourselves that's going to make one of you look bad if it gets out."

"I've said: I'm not going to talk about that."

"I get that, Miss McKay. Loud and clear. So what about you talking about what you're willing to talk about. What about bare facts with no window-dressing on them?"

"What do you mean?"

"Yeses and nos."

Noreen McKay glanced over at the bar, where her colleagues were downing pints of Guinness. The pub door opened, and three more employees of the prison walked in, all of them women in uniforms similar to the deputy warden's. Two of them called out to her and looked as if they were considering a saunter over for an introduction to McKay's companion. Noreen turned from them abruptly and said in a low voice, "This is impossible. I shouldn't have . . . We've got to get out of here."

"You running out wouldn't look so good," Nkata murmured. "Especially when I jump up and start shouting your name. But yeses and nos, and I'm gone, Miss McKay. Quiet as a mouse and you c'n tell them I'm anyone. Truant officer come to talk about your kids. Scout for Manchester United interested in the boy. I don't care. Just yeses and nos, and you got your life back, whatever it is."

"You don't *know* what it is."

" 'Course. Like I said. Whatever it is."

She stared at him for a moment before saying, "All right. Ask."

"Was she with you three nights ago?"

"Yes."

"Between ten and midnight?"

"Yes."

"What time d'she leave?"

"We said yeses or nos."

"Right. Yeah. She leave before midnight?"

"No."

"She arrive before ten?"

"Yes."

"She come alone?"

"Yes."

"Missus Edwards know where she was?"

Noreen McKay moved her gaze at this question, but it didn't appear to be because she was about to lie. "No," she said.

"And last night?"

"What about last night?"

"Katja Wolff with you last night? Say, after her solicitor left?"

Noreen McKay looked back at him. "Yes."

"She stay? Was she there round half eleven, midnight?"

"Yes. She left. . . . It was probably half past one when she left."

"You know Missus Edwards?"

Her gaze moved again. He saw a muscle tighten in her jaw. She said, "Yes. Yes, I know Yasmin Edwards. She served most of her time in Holloway."

"You know she and Katja—"

"Yes."

"Then what're you doing mixed up with them?" he asked abruptly, abjuring the previous yeses and nos in a sudden need for weapons, a personal need that he could barely acknowledge let alone begin to understand. "You got some sort of plan, you and Katja? You two using her and her boy for some reason?"

She looked at him but did not reply.

He said, "These're *people,* Miss McKay. They got lives and they got feelings. If you and Katja're planning to put something down to Yasmin, like laying a trail to her door, making her look bad, putting her at risk—"

Noreen snapped forward, saying in a hiss, "Isn't it obvious that just the *opposite* has happened? *I* look bad. *I'm* at risk. And why? Because I love her, Constable. That's my sin. You think this is about quirky sex, don't you? The abuse of power. Coercion leading to perversion, and nauseating scenes of desperate women with dildos strapped to their hips mounting desperate women behind bars. But what you don't think is that this is complicated, that it has to do with loving someone but not being able to love her openly so loving her the only way I can and having to know that on the nights we're apart—which are far more than we're together, believe me—she's with someone else, loving someone else, or at least playing at it because that's what *I* want. And every argument we *ever* have has *no* solution because both of us are right in the choices we've made. I can't give her what she wants from me, and I can't accept what she wants to give. So she gives it elsewhere and I take scraps from her and she takes scraps from me, and *that's* how it is, no matter what she says about how and when and for whom things will change." She leaned back in her chair after the speech, her breath coming jerkily as she fumbled her way into her navy coat once more. She got to her feet and headed for the door.

Nkata followed her. Outside, the wind was blowing ferociously, and Noreen McKay was standing in it. She was breathing like a runner in the light from a streetlamp, one hand curled round the pole. She was looking at Holloway Prison across the street.

She appeared to feel rather than to see Nkata come up next to her. She didn't look at him when she spoke. "At first, I was just curious about her. They put her in the medical unit after her trial, which is where I was assigned back then. She was on suicide watch. But I could tell that she had no intention of harming herself. There was this *resolve* about her, this knowing completely who she was. And I found that attractive, compelling really, because while I knew who I was as well, I'd never been able to admit it to myself. Then she went to the pregnancy unit and she could have gone to the mother-and-baby unit after the child was born, but she didn't want that, she didn't want him, and I found that I needed to know what she wanted and what she was made of that she could exist so sure and so alone."

Nkata said nothing. He blocked some of the wind with his back as he positioned himself before the deputy warden.

"So I just watched her. She was in jeopardy, of course, once she was off the medical unit. There's a form of honour among them, and the worst in their eyes is the killer of babies, so she wasn't safe unless she was with other Schedule One offenders. But she didn't care that she wasn't safe, and that fascinated me. I thought at first it was because she saw her life as over, and I wanted to talk to her about that. I called it my duty, and since I was in charge of the Samaritans at that point—"

"Samaritans?" Nkata asked.

"We have a programme of visits for them here at the prison. If a prisoner wishes to participate, she tells the staff member in charge."

"Katja wanted to participate?"

"No. Never. But I used that as an excuse to talk to her." She examined Nkata's face and seemed to read something into his expression, because she went on with, "I am *good* at my job. We've got twelve-step programmes now. We've got an increase in visits. We've got better rehabilitation and easier means for families to see mothers who're doing time. I *am* good at my job." She looked away from him, into the street, where the evening traffic was pouring out towards the northern suburbs. She said, "She didn't want any of it, and I couldn't understand why. She'd fought deportation to Germany, and I couldn't understand why. She talked to no one unless spoken to first. But all the time she watched. And so she eventually saw me watching her. When I was assigned to her wing—this is later—we started talking. She went first, which surprised me. She said, 'Why do you watch me?' I remember that. And what followed. I remember that also."

"She's holding all the cards, Miss McKay," Nkata noted.

"This isn't about blackmail, Constable. Katja could destroy me, but I know she won't."

"Why?"

"There are things you just know."

"We're talking 'bout a lag."

"We're talking about Katja." The deputy warden pushed away from the streetlamp and approached the traffic lights that would allow her to cross the road and return to the prison. Nkata walked beside her. She said, "I knew what I was from an early age. I expect my parents knew as well when I played dressing up and dressed like a soldier, a pirate, a fireman. But never like a princess or a nurse or a mum. And that's not normal, is it, and when at last you're fifteen, all you want is what's normal. So I tried it: short skirts, high heels, low necklines, the whole bit. I went after men and I shagged every boy I could get my hands on. Then one day in the paper I saw an ad for women looking for women and I phoned a number. For a joke, I told myself. Just for a lark. We met at a health club and had a swim and went out for coffee and then went to her place. She was twenty-four. I was nineteen. We were together five years, till I went into the prison service. And then . . . I couldn't live that life. It felt like too much of a risk. And then my sister got Hodgkin's and I got her children and for a long time that was enough."

"Till Katja."

"I've had scores of bed mates in the form of men, but only two lovers, both of them women. Katja's one of them."

"For how long?"

"Seventeen years. Off and on."

"You mean to go at it like this forever?"

"With Yasmin in the middle, d'you mean?" She glanced at Nkata, seeming to try to read an answer in his silence. "If it can be said that we choose where we love, then I chose Katja for two reasons. She never spoke about what put her in prison, so I knew she could hold her tongue about me. And she had an enormous secret she was keeping, which I thought at the time was a lover outside prison. I'll be safe getting involved, I thought. When she leaves, she'll go to her or to him, and I'll have had the chance to get this out of my system so I can live the rest of my life celibate but still knowing I once had *something*. . . ." The traffic lights on Parkhurst Road changed, and the walking figure altered along with it from red to green.

Noreen stepped off the pavement, but looked back over her shoulder as she made a final comment. "It's been seventeen years, Constable. She's the only prisoner I ever touched . . . that way. She's the only woman I've ever loved . . . this way."

"Why?" he asked as she began to cross the street.

"Because she's safe," Noreen McKay said in parting. "And because she's strong. No one can break Katja Wolff."

"BLOODY HELL. THIS is just brilliant," Barbara Havers muttered. She was beginning to feel the peril of her own situation: Two months demoted for insubordination and assault on a superior officer, she couldn't afford yet another pot hole on the ill-paved road of her career. "If Leach tells Hillier about that computer, we're done for, Inspector. You know that, don't you?"

"We're only done for if there's something useful to the investigation on the computer," Lynley pointed out as he nosed the Bentley into the heavy evening traffic of Rosslyn Hill. "And there isn't, Havers."

His utter calm rubbed against the sore of Barbara's apprehension. Their progress to his car had been so rapid after leaving Leach's office that she hadn't had a chance for a cigarette, and she was itching for a hit of tobacco to steady her nerves, which made her irritable along with afraid. "You know that, do you?" she asked him. "And what about those letters? From the superintendent to her? If we need those letters to build a case against Richard Davies . . . for why he

went after Webberly . . . for why he made it look like
Wolff was after people . . ." She ran her hand through
her hair and felt it bristle. She needed to cut it. She'd
do that tonight, take the nail scissors to it and do a
proper job. Maybe she'd hack it all off and punk it up
with hair goo. *That* should serve to distract AC
Hillier from the rôle she'd played in evidence tampering.

"You can't have it all ways," Lynley said.

"What's that s'posed to mean when it's home with
its mother?"

"He can't have killed Eugenie because she threatened Gideon's career, Havers, and then gone after
Webberly because he'd been harbouring jealousy over
his affair with Eugenie. If you go that direction,
where does that put Kathleen Waddington?"

"So maybe I'm wrong about Gideon's career," she
said. "Maybe he ran down Eugenie because she'd
taken up with Webberly."

"No. You're right. His objective was Eugenie, the
only person he killed. But he went after Webberly
and Waddington as well to focus our attention onto
Katja Wolff." Lynley sounded so certain, so completely unfazed by the danger they were in, that Barbara wanted to smack him. He could afford to be
unruffled, she decided. Out from New Scotland Yard
on *his* ear, he'd just motor down to the family pile in
Cornwall and live out his days like the landed gentry.
She, on the other hand, didn't have that option.

"You sound dead bloody sure of yourself," she
groused.

"Davies had the letter, Havers."

"What letter?" she demanded.

"The letter telling him Katja Wolff was out of prison. He knew I'd suspect her once he showed me that letter."

"So he knocks down the superintendent and this Waddington bird to make it look like Eugenie's death was for revenge? Katja going after the crowd who sent her away?"

"That's my guess."

"But maybe it *is* revenge, Inspector. Not Katja's but his. P'rhaps he knew about Eugenie and Webberly. P'rhaps he's always known but just bided his time and eaten himself up with jealousy and vowed that someday—"

"It doesn't work, Havers. Webberly's letters to Eugenie Davies are addressed to Henley. They all postdate her separation from her husband. Davies had no reason to be jealous. He probably never even knew about them."

"So *why* choose Webberly? Why not someone else from the trial? The Crown Prosecutor, the judge, another witness."

"I expect Webberly was easier to locate. He's lived in the same house for twenty-five years."

"But Davies has to know where the others lived if he found Waddington."

"What others do you mean?"

"The people who testified against her. Robson, for instance. What about Robson?"

"Robson served Gideon. He told me that himself.

I don't see Davies doing anything that might hurt his son, do you? Your entire scenario—the one you came up with in Leach's office—depends on the contention that Davies acted to save his son."

"Okay. All right. Maybe I'm wrong. Maybe it's all to do with Eugenie and Webberly and their affair. Maybe the letters and the computer are pieces of evidence we could've used to prove it. And maybe we're buggered."

He glanced over at her. "Barbara, we're not." Lynley looked at her hands, and she realised she was actually wringing them, like the unfortunate, impotent heroine in a melodrama featuring Simon Legree. He said, "Have one."

She said, "What?"

"A cigarette. Have one. You're owed. I can cope." He even punched in the Bentley's cigarette lighter, and when it popped out, he handed it over, saying, "Light up. This is a situation you're not likely to find yourself in again."

"I bloody well hope not," Havers muttered.

He shot her a look. "I was talking about smoking in the Bentley, Barbara."

"Yeah. Well, I wasn't." She dug out her Players and used the hot coil of the lighter against one. She inhaled deeply and grudgingly thanked her superior for humouring her vice for once. They inched their way south along the high street, and Lynley glanced at his pocket watch. He handed his mobile over to Barbara and said, "Phone St. James and ask him to have the computer ready."

Barbara was about to do as he asked, when the mobile rang in her hand. She flipped it on and Lynley nodded at her to take the call, so she said, "Havers here."

"Constable?" It was DCI Leach, speaking not so much in a tone as in a snarl. "Where the hell are you?"

"Heading to fetch the computer, sir." *Leach*, she mouthed to Lynley, *in another twist.*

"Bugger the computer," Leach said. "Get over to Portman Street. Between Oxford Street and Portman Square. You'll see the action when you get there."

"Portman Street?" Barbara said. "But, sir, don't you want—"

"Is your hearing as bad as your judgement?"

"I—"

"We've got another hit-and-run," Leach snapped.

"*What?*" Barbara said. "Another? Who is it?"

"Richard Davies. But there're witnesses this time. And I want you and Lynley over there shaking the lot of them through a sieve before they disappear."

GIDEON

10 NOVEMBER

CONFRONTATION IS the only answer. He has lied to me. For nearly three quarters of my life, my father has lied. He's lied not with what he said but with what he's allowed me to believe by saying nothing for twenty years: that we—he and I—were the injured parties when my mother left us. But all the time the truth was that she left us because she'd realised why Katja had murdered my sister and why she kept silent about having done so.

11 NOVEMBER

So this is how it happened, Dr. Rose. No memories now, if you will forgive me, no traveling back through time. Just this:

I phoned him. I said, "I know why Sonia died. I know why Katja refused to talk. You bastard, Dad."

He said nothing.

I said, "I know why my mother left us. I know

what happened. Do you understand me? Say something, Dad. It's time for the truth. I *know* what happened."

I could hear Jill's voice in the background. I could hear her question, and both the tone and the manner of her question—"Richard? Darling, who on earth *is* it?"—told me something of Dad's reaction to what I was saying. So I was not surprised when he said harshly, "I'm coming over there. Don't leave the house."

How he got to me so quickly, I don't know. All I can say is that when he entered the house and came up the stairs at a decisive pace, it seemed that mere minutes had passed since I had rung off from our conversation.

But I'd seen the two of them in those minutes: Katja Wolff, who grabbed at life, who used a deadly threat to get out of East Germany, and who would have used death itself if necessary to achieve the end that she had in mind; and my father, who had impregnated her, perhaps in the hope of producing a perfect specimen to carry on a family line that began with himself. He, after all, discarded women when they failed to produce something healthy. He'd done that to his first wife, and he'd been more than likely setting up to do the same to my mother. But he hadn't been moving fast enough for Katja. Katja Katja, who *grabbed* at life and who did not wait for what life provided her.

They argued about it.

When will you tell her about us, Richard?

When the time is right.

But we have no time! You know *we have no time.*

Katja, don't act like an hysterical fool.

And then, when the moment came when he could have taken a stand, he wouldn't speak up to defend her, excuse her, or commit himself as my mother confronted the German girl with the fact of her pregnancy and with the fact of her failure to perform her duties towards my sister *because* of her pregnancy. So Katja had finally taken matters into her own hands. Exhausted with arguing and with attempting to defend herself, ill from her pregnancy, and feeling deeply betrayed on all sides, she had snapped. She had drowned Sonia.

What did she hope to gain?

Perhaps she hoped to free my father from a burden she believed was keeping them apart. Perhaps she saw drowning Sonia as her way of making a statement that needed to be made. Perhaps she wished to punish my mother for having a hold on my father that seemed unbreakable. But kill Sonia she did, and then she refused, by means of a stoic silence, to acknowledge her crime, my sister's brief life, or what sins of her own had led to the taking of that life.

Why, though? Because she was protecting the man she loved? Or because she was punishing him?

All this I saw, and all this I thought of as I waited for my father's arrival.

"What is this cock, Gideon?"

Those were his first words to me as he strode into the music room, where I was sitting in the window seat, fighting off the first tentative stabs in my gut that proclaimed me frightened, childish, and cowardly as the time for our final engagement approached. I gestured to the notebook I'd been writing in all these weeks, and I hated the fact that my voice was strained. I hated what that strain revealed: about myself, about him, about what I feared.

"I know what happened," I said. "I've remembered what happened."

"Have you picked up your instrument?"

"You thought I wouldn't work it out, didn't you?"

"Have you picked up the Guarnerius, Gideon?"

"You thought you could pretend for the rest of your life."

"Damn it. Have you played? Have you tried to play? Have you even *looked* at your violin?"

"You thought I'd do what I've always done."

"I've had enough of this." He began to move, but not to the violin case. Instead, he walked to the stereo system, and as he did so he removed a new CD from his pocket.

"You thought I'd go along with anything you told me because that's what I've always done, right? Throw out something that resembles an acceptable tale and he'll swallow it: hook, line, and sinker."

He swung round. "You don't know what you're talking about. *Look* at yourself. Look what she's done to you with all this psycho-mumbo-jumbo of hers. You've been reduced to a puling mouse afraid of his shadow."

"Isn't that what you've done, Dad? Isn't that what

you did back then? You lied, you cheated, you betrayed—"

"Enough!" He was battling to free the CD from its
wrapping, and he tore at it with his teeth like a dog,
spitting the shreds of cellophane onto the floor. "I'm
telling you now that there's *one* way to deal with this,
and it's the way you should have dealt with it from
the first. A real man faces his fear head-on. He doesn't
turn tail and run from it."

"You're running. Right now."

"Like bloody God damn *hell* I am." He punched
the button to open the CD player. He jammed the
compact disk inside. He hit play and twisted the volume knob. "You listen," he hissed. "You bloody well
listen. And act like a man."

He'd turned up the sound so high that when the
music started, I didn't know what it was at first. But
my confusion lasted only for a second, because he'd
chosen *it,* Dr. Rose. Beethoven. *The Archduke.* He'd
chosen it.

The Allegro Moderato began. And it swelled
round the room. And over it I could hear Dad's
shout.

"Listen. *Listen.* Listen to what's unmade you,
Gideon. Listen to what you're terrified to play."

I covered my ears. "I can't." But still I heard. It. I
heard it. And I heard him above it.

"*Listen* to what you're letting control you. Listen
to what you've let a simple bloody piece of music do
to your entire career."

"I don't—"

"Black smudges on a damn piece of *paper*. That's all it is. That's what you've given your power to."

"Don't make me—"

"Stop it. *Listen*. Is it impossible for a musician like you to play this piece? No, it's not. Is it too difficult? It is not. Is it even challenging? No, no, no. Is it mildly, remotely, or vaguely—"

"Dad!" I pressed my hands to my ears. The room was going black. It was shrinking to a pinpoint of light and the light was blue, it was blue, it was *blue*.

"What it is is weakness made flesh in you, Gideon. You had a bout of nerves and you've transformed yourself into flaming Mr. Robson. That's what you've done."

The piano introduction was nearly complete. The violin was due to begin. I knew the notes. The music was in me. But in front of my eyes I saw only that door. And Dad—my father—continued to rail.

"I'm surprised you haven't started sweating like him. That's where you'll be next. Sweating and shaking like a freak who—"

"Stop it!"

And the music. The music. The *music*. Swelling, exploding, demanding. All round me, the music that I dreaded and feared.

And in front of me the door, with *her* standing there on the steps that lead up to it, with the light shining down on her, a woman I wouldn't have known on the street, a woman whose accent has faded in time, in the twenty years she has spent in prison.

She says, "Do you remember me, Gideon? It is Katja Wolff. I must speak with you."

I say politely because I do not know who she is but I have been taught through the years to be polite to the public no matter the demands they make upon me because it is the public who attend my concerts who buy my recordings who support the East London Conservatory and what it is trying to do to better the lives of impoverished children children like me in so many ways save for the circumstances of birth . . . I say, "I'm afraid I have a concert, Madam."

"This will not take long."

She descends the steps. She crosses the bit of Welbeck Way that separates us. I've moved to the red double doors of the artists' entrance to Wigmore Hall and I'm about to knock to gain admittance, when she says she says oh God she says, "I've come for payment, Gideon," and I do not know what she means.

But somehow I understand that danger is about to engulf me. I clutch the case in which the Guarneri is protected by leather and velvet, and I say, "As I said, I do have a concert."

"Not for more than an hour," she says. "This I have been told in the front."

She nods towards Wigmore Street, where the box office is, where she apparently has gone at first to seek me out. They would have told her that the performers for the evening had not yet arrived, Madam, and that when they do arrive, they use the back entrance and not the front. So if she cared to wait there, she might have the opportunity to speak to Mr.

Davies, although the box office couldn't guarantee that Mr. Davies would have the time to speak to her.

She says, "Four hundred thousand pounds, Gideon. Your father claims he does not have it. So I come to you because I know that you must."

And the world as I know it is shrinking shrinking disappearing entirely into a single bead of light. From that bead grows sound, and I hear the Beethoven, the Allegro Moderato, *The Archduke's* first movement, and then Dad's voice.

He said, "Act like a man, for the love of God. Sit up. Stand up. Stop cowering there like a beaten dog! Jesus! Stop *sniveling*. You're acting like this is—"

I heard no more because I knew suddenly what all of *this* was, and I knew what *this* had always been. I remembered it all in a piece—like the music itself— and the music was the background and the act that went with that music as background was what I had forced myself to forget.

I am in my room. Raphael is displeased, more displeased than he has ever been, and he has been displeased, on edge, anxious, nervous, and irritable for days. I have been petulant and uncooperative. Juilliard has been denied me. Juilliard has been listed amongst the impossibilities that I am growing used to hearing about. This isn't possible, that isn't possible, trim here, cut there, make allowances for. So I'll show them, I decide. I won't play this stupid violin again. I won't practise. I won't have lessons. I won't perform in public. I won't perform in private, for myself or for anyone. *I* will show them.

Raphael marches me to my room. He puts on the recording of *The Archduke* and says, "I'm losing patience with you, Gideon. This is not a difficult piece. I want you to listen to the first movement till you can hum it in your sleep."

He leaves me, shuts the door. And the Allegro Moderato begins.

I say, "I won't, I won't, I *won't!*" And I upset a table and kick over a chair and slam my body into the door. "You can't make me!" I shout. "You can't make me do anything!"

And the music swells. The piano introduces the melody. All is hushed and ready for the violin and cello. Mine is not a difficult part to learn, not for someone with natural gifts like myself. But what will be the point of learning it when I cannot go to Juilliard? Although Perlman did. As a boy, he went there. But I will not. And this is unfair. This is *bloody* unfair. Everything about my world is unfair. I will not do this. I will not accept this.

And the music swells.

I fling open my door. I shout "No!" and "I won't!" into the corridor. I think someone will come, will march me somewhere and administer discipline, but no one comes because they are all busy with their own concerns and not with mine. And I'm angry at this because it is *my* world that is being affected. It is *my* life that is being moulded. It is *my* will that is being thwarted, and I want to punch my fist into the wall.

And the music swells. And the violin soars. And I will not play this piece of music at Juilliard or anywhere else because I must remain here. In this house, where we're all prisoners. Because of her.

The knob is under my hand before I realise it, the panels of the door inches from my face. I will burst in and frighten her. I will make her cry. I will make her pay. I will make them pay.

She isn't frightened. But she is alone. Alone in the tub with the yellow ducklings bobbing nearby and a bright red boat that she's slapping at happily with her fist. And she deserves to be frightened, to be thrashed, to be made to understand what she's done to me, so I grab her and shove her beneath the water and see her eyes widen and widen and widen and feel her struggle to sit up again.

And the music—*that* music—swells and swells. On and on it goes. For minutes. For days.

And then Katja is there. She screams my name. And Raphael is right behind her yes, because yes, I understand it all now: They have been talking the two of them talking, which is why Sonia has been left alone, and he has been demanding to know if what Sarah-Jane Beckett has whispered is true. Because he has a right to know, he says. He says this as he enters the bathroom on Katja's heels. It is what he's saying as he enters and she screams. He says, ". . . Because if you are, it's mine and you know it. I do have the right—"

And the music swells.

And Katja screams, screams for my father and Raphael shouts, "Oh my God! Oh my God" but I do not release her. I do not release her even then because I know that the end of my world began with her.

TWENTY-FOUR

JILL STAGGERED to her bedroom. Her movements were clumsy. She was hampered by her size. She flung open the cupboard that held her clothes, thinking only, Richard, oh my God, *Richard*, and coming round to wonder wildly what she was doing standing incoherently in front of a rack of garments. All she could think was her lover's name. All she could feel was a mixture of terror and a profound self-hatred at the doubts she'd had, doubts that she'd been harbouring and nursing at the very moment that . . . that what? What had *happened* to him?

"Is he *alive?*" she'd cried into the telephone when the voice asked if she was Miss Foster, Miss Jill Foster, the woman whose name Richard carried in his wallet in the event that something . . .

"My God, what's happened?" Jill had continued.

"Miss Foster, if you'll come to the hospital," the Voice had said. "Do you need a taxi? Shall I phone one for you? If you'll give me an address, I can ring a minicab."

The idea of waiting five minutes—or ten or

fifteen—for a cab was inconceivable. Jill dropped the telephone and stumbled for her coat.

Her coat. That was it. She'd come into her bedroom in search of her coat. She shoved through the hanging garments in the cupboard till her hands came into contact with cashmere. She jerked this from its hanger and struggled into it. She fumbled with the horn buttons, miscalculated where they went, and didn't bother to refasten them more precisely when the hem of the coat hung like a lopsided curtain upon her. From her chest of drawers she took a scarf—the first one that came to hand, it didn't matter—and she wrapped this round her throat. She slammed a black wool cap on her head and snatched up her shoulder bag. She went for the door.

In the lift, she punched for the underground car park, and she willed the little cubicle downwards without stopping at any other floors. She told herself that it was a *good* sign the hospital had rung her and asked her to come. If the news was bad, if the situation was—could she risk the word?—fatal, they wouldn't have rung her at all, would they? Wouldn't they instead have sent a constable round to fetch her or to speak with her? So what it meant that they had phoned was that he was alive. He *was* alive.

She found herself making bargains with God as she pushed through the doors to the car park. If Richard would live, if his heart or whatever it was would mend, then she would compromise on the baby's name. They would christen her Cara Catherine. Richard could call her Cara at home behind closed doors, among the family, and Jill herself would call her the same. Then outside, in the world at large, both of them could refer to her as Catherine. They'd register her at school as Catherine. Her friends would call her Catherine. And Cara would be even more special because it would be what only her parents called her. That was fair, wasn't it, God? If only Richard would live.

The car was parked seven bays along. She unlocked it, praying that it would start, and for the first time seeing the wisdom in having something modern and reliable. But the Humber loomed large in her past— her granddad had been its single owner—and when he'd left the vehicle to her in his will, she'd kept it out of love for him and in memory of the countryside drives they'd taken together. Her friends had laughed at it in earlier years, and Richard had lectured her about its dangers—no airbags, no headrests, inadequate restraints—but Jill had stubbornly continued to drive it and had no intention of giving it up.

"It's safer than what's on the streets these days," she'd declared loyally whenever Richard had attempted to wrestle from her a promise not to drive it. "It's like a tank."

"Just stay out of it till you've had the baby, and promise me you won't let Cara anywhere near it," he had replied.

Catherine, she had thought. Her name is Catherine. But that was before. That was when she thought nothing could happen in an instant the way things happened: things like this that changed everything, making what had seemed so important yesterday less than a bagatelle today.

Still, she'd made the promise not to drive the Humber, and she'd kept that promise for the last two months. So she had added reason to wonder if it would start.

It did. Like a dream. But the increase in Jill's size required her to make an adjustment to the heavy front seat. She reached forward and beneath it for the metal lever. She flipped it up and shifted her weight. The seat wouldn't budge.

She said, "Damn it. Come on," and tried again. But either the device itself had corroded over the years or something was blocking the track on which the enormous seat ran.

Her anxiety rising, she scrabbled her fingers on the floor beneath her. She felt the lever, then the edge of the lever. She felt the seat springs. She felt the track. And then she found it. Something hard and thin and rectangular was blocking the old metal track, wedged in in such a way as to make it virtually immovable.

She frowned. She pulled on the object. She jockeyed it back and forth when it got stuck. She cursed. Her hands became damp with sweat. And finally, finally, she managed to dislodge it. She slid it out, lifted it, and laid it on the broad seat next to her.

It was a photograph, she saw, a picture in a stark monastic wooden frame.

GIDEON

11 NOVEMBER

I RAN, Dr. Rose. I bolted for the music room door and crashed down the stairs. I threw open the door. It slammed back against the wall. I flung myself into Chalcot Square. I didn't know where I was going or what I intended to do. But I had to be away: away from my father and away from what he'd inadvertently forced me to face.

I ran blindly, but I saw her face. Not as she might have looked in joy or innocence or even in suffering, but in losing consciousness as I drowned her. I saw her head turn side to side, her baby's hair fan out, her mouth gulp fishlike, her eyes roll back and disappear. She fought to stay alive, but she couldn't match the strength of my rage. I held her down and held her down, and when Katja and Raphael burst into the room, she was no longer moving or struggling against me. But still my rage was not satisfied.

My feet pounded the pavement as I tore along the square. I did not head for Primrose Hill, for Primrose

Hill is exposed, and exposure to anything, anyone, any longer, was an unbearable thought to me. So I thundered in another direction, veering round the first corner I came to, charging through the silent neighbourhood till I burst into the upper reaches of Regent's Park Road.

Moments later, I heard him shouting my name. As I stood panting at the junction where Regent's Park and Gloucester Roads meet, he came round the corner, holding his side against a stitch. He raised his arm. He shouted, "Wait!" I ran again.

What I thought as I ran was a simple phrase: *He's always known.* For I remembered more, and I saw what I remembered as a series of images.

Katja screams and shrieks. Raphael pushes past her to get to me. Shouts and footsteps rise up the stairs and along the corridor. A voice cries out, "God *damn* it!"

Dad is in the bathroom. He tries to pull me away from the tub, where my fingers have dug and dug and dug into my sister's fragile shoulders. He shouts my name and slaps my face. He yanks me by the hair, and I finally release her.

"Get him out of here!" he roars, and for the first time he sounds just like Granddad and I am frightened.

As Raphael jerks me across the corridor, I hear others on their way. My mother is calling, "Richard? Richard?" as she runs up the stairs. Sarah-Jane Beckett and James the Lodger are talking to each other as they hurry down from above. Somewhere Granddad is bellowing, "Dick! Where's my whisky? Dick!" And

Gran is calling out fearfully from below, "Has something happened to Jack?"

Then Sarah-Jane Beckett is with me, saying, "What's happened? What's going on?" She takes me from Raphael's fierce grip saying, "Raphael, what are you *doing* to him?" and "What on earth is *she* going on about?" in reference to Katja Wolff, who is weeping and saying, "I do not leave her. For a minute only," to which comment Raphael Robson is adding nothing at all.

After that I am in my room. I hear Dad cry, "Don't come in here, Eugenie. Dial nine-nine-nine."

She says, "What's *happened*? Sosy! What's happened?"

A door shuts. Katja weeps. Raphael says, "Let me take her below."

Sarah-Jane Beckett goes to stand at the door to my room, where she listens, her head bent, and there she remains. I sit against the headboard of the bed, arms wet to the elbows, shaking now, finally aware of the terrible enormity of what I have done. And all along the music has played, that same music, the cursed *Archduke* that has haunted and pursued me like a relentless demon for the last twenty years.

That is what I remembered as I ran, and when I crossed the junction, I did not attempt to avoid the traffic. It seemed to me that the only mercy would be if a car or lorry struck me.

None did. I made it to the other side. But Dad was hard on my heels, still shouting my name.

I set off again running, running away from him,

running into the past. And I saw that past like a kalei-
doscope of pictures: that genial ginger-haired policeman who smelled of cigars and spoke in a kindly
paternal voice . . . that night in bed with my mother
holding me holding me holding me and my face
pressed firmly into her breasts as if she would do to
me what I had done to my sister . . . my father sitting
on the edge of my bed, his hands on my shoulders as
my hands were on hers . . . his voice saying, "You're
quite safe, Gideon, no one will harm you" . . .
Raphael with flowers, flowers for my mother, flowers of sympathy to assuage her grief . . . and always
hushed voices, in every room, for days on end . . .

Finally Sarah-Jane leaves the door where she has
stood motionless, waiting and listening. She walks to
the tape player, where the violin in the Beethoven
trio is executing a passage of doublestops. She
punches a button and the music blessedly ceases, leaving behind a silence so hollow that I wish only for the
music again.

Into this silence comes the sound of sirens. They
grow louder and louder as the vehicles approach. Although it's probably taken them minutes, it seems like
an hour since Dad yanked on my hair and forced me
to release the grip I had on my sister.

"Up here, in here," Dad shouts down the stairs as
someone lets the paramedics into the house.

And then begins the effort to save what cannot be
saved, what I know cannot be saved, because I was
the one who destroyed her.

I can't bear the images, the thoughts, the sounds.

I ran blindly, wildly, without caring where I was
going. I crossed the street and came to my senses directly in front of the Pembroke Castle pub. And beyond it I saw the terrace where the drinkers sit in
summer, the terrace that was empty now, but bordered by a wall, a low brick wall onto which I leapt,
along which I ran, and from which I sprang, sprang
without thinking onto the iron archway of the pedestrian footbridge that spans the railway line thirty feet
beneath it. I sprang thinking, This is how it will be.

I heard the train before I saw it. In the hearing, I
took my answer. The train wasn't traveling fast, so the
engineer would well be able to stop it and I would
not die . . . unless I timed my jump with precision.

I moved to the edge of the arch. I saw the train. I
watched its approach.

"Gideon!"

Dad was at the end of the footbridge. "Stay where
you are!" he shouted.

"It's too late."

And like a baby, I began to cry, and I waited for the
moment, the perfect moment, when I could drop
onto the tracks in front of the train and enter
oblivion.

"What are you saying?" he shouted. "Too late for
what?"

"I know what I did," I cried. "To Sonia. I remember."

"You remember what?" He looked from me to the
train, both of us watching its steady approach. He
took a single step closer to me.

"You know. What I did. That night. To Sonia. How she died. You know what I did to Sonia."

"No! Wait!" This as I moved my feet so that the soles of my shoes overhung the drop. "Don't do this, Gideon. Tell me what you think happened."

"I drowned her, Dad! I drowned my sister!"

He took another step towards me, his hand extended.

The train drew closer. Twenty seconds and it would be over. Twenty seconds and a debt would be paid.

"Stay where you are! For the love of God, Gideon!"

"I drowned her!" I cried, and my breath caught on a sob. "I drowned her and I didn't even *remember*. Do you know what that means? Do you know how it feels?"

His glance went to the train, then back to me. He took another step forward. "Don't!" he shouted. "Listen to me. You didn't kill your sister."

"You pulled me off her. I *remember* now. And that's why Mother left. She left us without a word because she knew what I'd done. Isn't that right? Isn't that the truth?"

"No! No, it's not!"

"It is. I remember."

"Listen to me. Wait." His words were rapid. "You hurt her, yes. And yes, yes, she was unconscious. But, Gideon, son, hear what I'm saying. You didn't drown Sonia."

"Then who—"

"I did."

"I don't believe you." I looked beneath me to the waiting rail tracks. A single step was all I needed to take, and I would be on the tracks and a moment later it would all be over. A burst of pain then a wiping of the slate.

"*Look* at me, Gideon. For God's sake, hear me out. Don't do this before you understand what happened."

"You're trying to stall."

"If I am, there'll be another train, won't there? So listen to me. You owe it to yourself."

No one had been present, he told me. Raphael had taken Katja to the kitchen. My mother had gone to ring the emergency number. Gran had gone to Granddad to settle him down. Sarah-Jane had taken me to my room. And James the Lodger had disappeared back upstairs.

"I could have taken her from the bath just then," he said. "I could have given her the kiss of life. I could have used CPR on her. But I held her there, Gideon. I held her down beneath the water until I heard your mother finish her call to emergency."

"That wouldn't have done it. There wouldn't have been enough time."

"There was. Your mother stayed on the phone with emergency till we heard the paramedics pounding on the front door. She relayed emergency's instructions to me. I pretended to do what they directed. But she couldn't *see* me, Gideon, so she didn't know that I hadn't taken Sonia out of the bath."

"I don't believe you. You've lied to me my whole life. You said nothing. You told me *nothing*."

"I'm telling you now."

Below me, the train passed. I saw the engineer look up at the last moment. Our eyes met, his widened, and he reached for his radio transmitter. The warning was sent to trains that would follow. My opportunity for oblivion was past.

Dad said, "You must believe me. I'm telling you the truth."

"What about Katja, then?"

"What about Katja?"

"She went to prison. And we sent her there, didn't we? We lied to the police and she went to prison. For twenty years, Dad. We're to blame for that."

"No. Gideon, she agreed to go."

"*What?*"

"Come back to me. Here. I'll explain."

So I gave him that much: the belief that he'd talked me away from the tracks when in fact I knew that we were moments away from being joined by the transport police. I climbed back onto the footbridge proper, and I approached my father. When I was close enough to him, he grabbed me as if dragging me from the brink of a chasm. He held me to him, and I could feel the hammering of his heart. I didn't believe anything that he'd told me so far, but I was willing to listen, to hear him out, and to try to see past the façade he wore and to ascertain what facts lay beneath it.

He spoke in a rush, never once releasing me as he

told me the story. Believing that I—and not my father—had drowned my sister, Katja Wolff had known instantly that she bore a large part of the responsibility because she had left Sonia alone. If she agreed to take the blame—claiming to have left the child for a minute only while she took a phone call—then Dad would see that she was rewarded. He would pay her twenty thousand pounds for this service to his family. And in the event that she should come to trial for negligence, he would add to that amount another twenty thousand for every year she was inconvenienced thereafter.

"We didn't know the police would build a case against her," he said into my ear. "We didn't know about the healed fractures on your sister's body. We didn't know the tabloids would seize the case with such ferocity. And we didn't know that Bertram Cresswell-White would prosecute her like a man with a chance to convict Myra Hindley all over again. In the normal course of events, she might have been given a suspended sentence for negligence. Or at the most five years. But everything went wrong. And when the judge recommended twenty years because of the abuse . . . It was too late."

I pulled away from him. Truth or lie? I wondered as I studied his face. "Who abused Sonia?"

"No one," he said.

"But the fractures—"

"She was frail, Gideon. Her skeleton was delicate. It was part of her condition. Katja's defence counsel put this to the jury, but Cresswell-White tore their experts to pieces. Everything went badly. Everything went wrong."

"Then why didn't she give evidence in her own defence? Why didn't she talk to the police? Her own lawyers?"

"That was part of the deal."

"The deal."

"Twenty thousand pounds if she remained silent."

"But you must have *known*—" What? I thought. What must he have known? That her friend Katie Waddington wouldn't lie under oath, wouldn't testify to having made a phone call that she hadn't made? That Sarah-Jane Beckett would paint her in the worst possible light? That the Crown Prosecutor would try her as a child abuser and limn her as the devil incarnate? That the judge would recommend a draconian sentence? What exactly was my father to have known?

I released myself from the hold he had on me. I began to retrace my route from Chalcot Square. He followed closely on my heels, not speaking. But I could feel his eyes on me. I could feel the burn of their penetration. He's made all of this up, I concluded. He has too many answers, and they're coming too quickly.

I told him on the front steps to my house. I said, "I don't believe you, Dad."

He countered with, "Why else would she have remained silent? It was hardly in her interests to do so."

"Oh, I believe that part," I told him. "I believe the part about the twenty thousand pounds. You would have paid her that much to keep me from harm. And to keep it from Granddad that your freak of a son had deliberately drowned your freak of a daughter."

"That's not what happened!"

"We both know it is." I turned to go inside.

He grabbed my arm. "Will you believe your mother?" he asked me.

I turned. He must have seen the question, the disbelief, and the wariness on my face because he went on without my speaking.

"She's been phoning me. Since Wigmore Hall, she's been phoning at least twice a week. She read about what happened, she phoned to ask about you, and she's been phoning ever since. I'll arrange a meeting between you if you like."

"What good would that do? You said she didn't see—"

"Gideon, for God's sake. Why do you think she left me? Why do you suppose she took every picture of your sister with her?"

I stared at him. I tried to read him. And more than that, I tried to find the answer to a single question that I didn't give voice to: Even if I saw her, would she tell me the truth?

But Dad appeared to see this question in my eyes, because quickly he said, "Your mother has no reason to lie to you, son. And surely the manner of her disappearance from our lives tells you she couldn't bear the guilt of living the pretence that I'd forced her into living."

"It also might mean that she couldn't bear to live in the same house with a son who'd murdered his sister."

"Then let her tell you that."

We were eye to eye, and I waited for a sign that he was the least apprehensive. But no sign came.

"You can trust me," he told me.

And I wanted more than anything to believe that promise.

TWENTY-FIVE

HAVERS SAID, "I wish the situation would stop changing direction every twenty-five minutes. If it would, we *might* actually be able to get a handle on this case."

Lynley made a turn into Belsize Avenue and did a quick recce of the *A to Z* in his brain to plot out a decent route to Portman Street. Next to him, Havers was continuing to grouse.

"So if Davies is down, who're we on to? Leach must be right. It's got to be back to Wolff with another antique car in possession of someone she knows that we haven't sussed out yet. That someone loans the car to her—probably not knowing what she wants it for—and she goes gunning for the principals who put her into the nick. Or maybe the two of them go gunning together. We haven't considered that possibility yet."

"That scenario argues an innocent woman going to prison for twenty years," Lynley pointed out.

"It's been known to happen," Havers said.

"But not with the innocent person saying nothing about *being* innocent in the first place."

"She's from East Germany, former totalitarian state. She'd been in England . . . what? Two years? Three? When Sonia Davies drowned? She finds herself questioned by the local rozzers and she gets paranoid and won't talk to them. That makes sense to me. I don't expect she had the warm fuzzies for the police where she came from, do you?"

Lynley said, "I agree that she might have been rattled by police. But she would have told *someone* she was innocent, Havers. She would have spoken to her lawyers, surely. But she didn't. What does that suggest to you?"

"Someone got to her."

"How?"

"Hell, I don't know." Havers pulled at her hair in frustration, as if this action would dislodge another possibility in her brain, which it did not.

Lynley thought about what Havers had suggested, however. He said, "Page Winston. He may have something for us."

Havers used Lynley's mobile to do so. They worked their way down to Finchley Road. The wind, which had been brisk all day, had picked up in force during the late afternoon, and now it was hurtling autumn leaves and rubbish along the street. It was also carrying a storm in from the northeast, and as they made the turn into Baker Street, drops began to splatter the Bentley's windscreen. November's early darkness had fallen on London, and the lights from passing vehicles coned forward, creating a playing area for the first sheet of rain.

Lynley cursed. "This'll make a fine mess of the crime scene."

Havers agreed. Lynley's mobile rang. Havers handed it over.

Winston Nkata reported that unless Katja Wolff's longtime lover was lying, the German woman was in the clear. Both for the murder of Eugenie Davies and for the hit-and-run of Malcolm Webberly. They were together both nights, he said.

Lynley said, "That's nothing new, Winston. You've told us that Yasmin Edwards confirms that she and Katja—"

This lover wasn't Yasmin Edwards, Nkata informed him. This lover was the deputy warden at Holloway, one Noreen McKay, who'd been involved with Katja Wolff for years. McKay hadn't wanted to come forward for obvious reasons, but put on the rack, she'd admitted to being with the German woman on both nights in question.

"Phone her name into the incident room anyway," Lynley told Nkata. "Have them run her through the DVLA. Where's Wolff now?"

" 'Xpect she's home in Kennington," Nkata said. "I'm heading over there now."

"Why?"

There was a pause on Nkata's end before the constable said, "Thought it best to let her know she's in the clear. I was rough on her."

Lynley wondered exactly whom the constable meant when he said *her*. "First phone Leach with the McKay woman's name. Her address as well."

"After that?"

"See to the Kennington situation. But, Winnie, go easy."

"Why's that, 'Spector?"

"We've another hit-and-run." Lynley brought him into the picture, telling him that he and Havers were heading to Portman Street. "With Davies down, we've got a new match. New rules, new players, and for all we know, an entirely new objective."

"But with the Wolff woman having an alibi—"

"Just go easy," Lynley cautioned. "There's more to know."

When Lynley rang off, he brought Havers into the picture. She said at his conclusion, "The pickings are getting slim, Inspector."

"Aren't they just," Lynley replied.

Another ten minutes and they had made the circuit to come into Portman Street, where, had they not known an accident had happened, they would have concluded as much from the flashing lights a short distance from the square and the car-park quality of the stationary traffic. They pulled to the kerb, half in a bus lane and half on the pavement.

They trudged through the rain in the direction of the flashing lights, shouldering their way through a crowd of onlookers. The lights came from two panda cars that were blocking the bus lane and a third that was impeding the flow of traffic. The constables from one of the cars were in conversation with a traffic warden in the middle of the street, while those from the other two cars were divided between talking to people on the pavement and wedging themselves into the upper and lower parts of a bus that was itself parked at an angle with one tyre on the kerb. There was no ambulance anywhere in sight. Nor was there any sign of a scene-of-crime team. And the actual point of impact—which certainly had to be where the panda was parked in the traffic lane—had yet to be cordoned off. Which meant that what valuable evidence might be there wasn't being safeguarded and would soon be lost. Lynley muttered a curse.

With Havers on his heels, he squeezed through the crowd and showed his identification to the nearest policeman, a bobby in an anorak. Water dripped from his helmet onto his neck. Periodically, he slapped it away.

"What's happened?" Lynley asked the constable. "Where's the victim?"

"Off to hospital," the constable said.

"He's alive, then?" Lynley glanced at Havers. She gave him a thumbs-up. "What's his condition?"

"Damn lucky, I'd say. Last time we had something like this, we were scraping the corpse off the pavement for a week, and the driver wasn't fit to go another hundred yards."

"You've witnesses? We'll need to speak with them."

"Oh, aye? How's that?"

"We've a similar hit-and-run in West Hampstead,"

Lynley told him. "Another in Hammersmith. And a third in Maida Vale. This one today involves a man who's related to one of our earlier victims."

"Your facts are off."

"What?" Havers was the one to ask.

"This isn't a hit-and-run." The constable nodded at the bus, where inside, one of his colleagues was taking a statement from a woman in the seat directly behind the driver's. The driver himself was out on the pavement, gesticulating to his left front headlamp and speaking earnestly to another policeman. "Bus hit someone," the constable clarified. "Pedestrian was shoved out from the pavement directly into its path. Lucky he wasn't killed. Mr. Nai"—here he gave a nod to the driver of the bus—"has good reflexes and the bus had its brakes serviced last week. We've got some bumps and bruises from the sudden stop—this is on the passengers inside—and the victim's got a bone or two broken, but that's the extent of it."

"Did anyone see who pushed him?" Lynley asked.

"That's what we're trying to find out, mate."

JILL LEFT THE Humber in a spot marked clearly for ambulances only, but she didn't care. Let them tow, clamp, or fine her. She squirmed out from beneath the steering wheel and walked rapidly to the entrance for accidents and emergencies. There was no receptionist to greet her, just a guard behind a plain wooden desk.

He took a look at Jill and said, "Shall I ring your doctor, Madam, or is he meeting you here?"

Jill said, "What?" before she understood the inference that the guard was drawing from her condition,
her personal appearance, and her frantic state. She
said, "No. No doctor," to which the man said, "You
have no doctor?" in a disapproving tone.

Ignoring him, Jill made a lumbering dash in the direction of someone who looked like a doctor. He was
consulting a clipboard and wore a stethoscope round
his neck, which gave him an air of authority that the
guard did not possess. Jill cried, "Richard Davies?"
and the doctor looked up. "Where is Richard
Davies? I was phoned. I was told to come. He's been
brought in and don't tell me . . . you mustn't tell me
he's . . . Please. Where *is* he?"

"Jill . . ."

She swung round. He was leaning against a jamb
whose door opened into what appeared to be some
sort of treatment room just behind the guard's desk.
Beyond him, she could see trolleys with people lying
upon them, covered to their chins in thin pastel blankets, and beyond the trolleys she could see cubicles
formed by curtains at the bottom of which the feet of
those ministering to the injured, the critically ill, or
the dying were only just visible.

Richard was from among the merely injured. Jill
felt her knees grow weak at the sight of him. She
cried, "Oh God, I thought you were . . . They said
. . . When they *phoned* . . ." and she began to weep,
which was utterly unlike her and told her just how
terrified she'd been.

He stumbled to her and they held each other. He said, "I asked them not to phone you. I told them I'd ring you myself so that you'd know, but they insisted . . . It's their procedure . . . If I'd known how upset . . . Here, Jill, don't cry . . ."

He tried to fish out a handkerchief for her, which was how she first noticed that his right arm was in plaster. And then she noticed the rest of it: the walking cast on his right foot which she could now see beyond the ripped-open seam of his navy trousers, the ugly bruising on one side of his face, and the row of stitches beneath his right eye.

"What *happened*?" she cried.

He said, "Get me home, darling. They want me to spend the night—but I don't need . . . I can't think . . ." He gazed at her earnestly. "Jill, will you take me home?"

She said of course. Had he ever doubted that she'd be there, do what he asked of her, tend to him, nurse him?

He thanked her with a gratitude that she found touching. And when they gathered his things together, she was even more touched to see that he'd managed the shopping he'd gone out to do. He brought five mangled and soiled shopping bags out of the treatment room with him. "At least I found the intercom," he said wryly.

They made their way to the car, ignoring the protest of the young doctor and even younger nurse who tried to stop them. Their progress was slow,

Richard needing to stop to rest every four paces or so. As they went out of the ambulance entrance, he told her briefly what had happened.

He'd gone into more than one shop, he said, looking for what he had in mind. He ended up making more purchases than he'd expected, and the shopping bags were unwieldy in the crowds out on the pavement.

"I wasn't paying attention, and I should have been," he told her. "There were so many people."

He was making his way along Portman Street to where he'd left his Granada in the underground car park in Portman Square. The pavement was packed: shoppers running for one last purchase in Oxford Street before the shops closed, business people heading for home, streams of students jostling one another, the homeless eager to find doorways for the night and a handout of coins to keep them from hunger. "You know how it can be in that part of town," he said. "It was madness to go there, but I just didn't want to put it off any longer."

The shove, he said, came out of nowhere just as a Number 74 bus was pulling out from its stop. Before he knew what was happening, he was hurtling straight into the vehicle's path. One tyre drove over—

"Your arm," Jill said. "Your *arm*. Oh Richard—"

"The police said how lucky I was," Richard finished. "It could have been . . . You know what might have happened." He'd paused again in their walk to the car.

Jill said angrily, "People don't take care any longer. They're in such a *hurry* all the time. They walk down the street with their mobiles fixed to their skulls and they don't even *see* anyone else." She touched his bruised cheek. "Let me get you home, darling. Let me baby you a bit." She smiled at him fondly. "I'll make you some soup and soldiers, and I'll pop you into bed."

"I'll need to be at my own place tonight," he said. "Forgive me, Jill, but I couldn't face sleeping on your sofa."

"Of *course* you couldn't," she said. "Let's get you home." She repositioned the five shopping bags that she had taken from him in Casualty. They *were* heavy and awkward, she thought. It was no wonder he'd been distracted by them.

She said, "What did the police do with the person who pushed you?"

"They don't know who it was."

"Don't *know* . . . ? How is that possible, Richard?"

He shrugged. She knew him well enough to understand at once that he wasn't telling her everything.

She said, "Richard?"

"Whoever it was, he didn't come forward once I was hit. For all I know, he—or she—didn't even know I fell into the traffic. It happened so fast, and just as the bus was pulling away from the kerb. If they were in a rush . . ." He adjusted his jacket over his shoulder, where it hung cape-like because he could not fit it over the cast on his arm. "I just want to forget it happened."

Jill said, "Surely someone would have seen something."

"They were interviewing people when the ambulance fetched me." He spied the Humber where Jill had left it and lurched towards it in silence. Jill followed him, saying, "Richard, are you telling me everything?"

He didn't reply until they were at the car. Then he said, "They think it was deliberate, Jill," and then, "Where's Gideon? He needs to be warned."

Jill hardly knew what she was doing as she opened the car door, flipped the seat forward, and deposited Richard's packages in the back. Jill saw her lover safely into his seat and then joined him behind the wheel of the car. She said, "What do you mean, deliberate?" and she looked straight ahead at the worm tracks that the rain was making on her windscreen and she tried to hide her fear.

He made no reply. She turned to him. She said, "Richard, what do you mean by deliberate? Is this connected to—" and then she saw that he was holding in his lap the frame she'd found beneath her seat.

He said, "Where did you get this?"

She told him and added, "But I can't understand . . . Where did it come from? Who is she? I don't know her. I don't recognise . . . And surely she can't be . . ." Jill hesitated, not wanting to say it.

Richard did so for her. "This is Sonia. My daughter."

And Jill felt a ring of ice take a sudden position round her heart. In the half light coming from the hospital entrance, she reached for the picture and tilted it towards her. In it, a child—blonde as her brother had been in childhood—held a stuffed panda up to her cheek. She laughed at the camera as if she hadn't a care in the world. Which she probably hadn't known that she did have, Jill thought as she looked at the picture again.

She said, "Richard, you never mentioned that Sonia . . . Why has no one ever *told* me . . . ? Richard. Why didn't you tell me your daughter was Down's Syndrome?"

He looked at her then. "I don't talk about Sonia," he said evenly. "I never talk about Sonia. You know that."

"But I needed to know. I ought to have known. I *deserved* to know."

"You sound like Gideon."

"What's Gideon to do with . . . ? Richard, why haven't you spoken to me about her before? And what's this picture doing in my car?" The stresses of the evening—the conversation with her mother, the phone call from the hospital, the frantic drive—all of it descended upon Jill at once. "Are you trying to frighten me?" she cried. "Are you hoping that if I see what happened to Sonia, I'll agree to have Catherine in hospital and not at my mother's? Is that what you're doing? Is that what this is all about?"

Richard tossed the picture into the back seat, where it landed on one of the packages. He said, "Don't be absurd. Gideon wants a picture of her— God only knows why—and I dug that one out to have it reframed. It needs to be, as you probably saw. The frame's banged up and the glass . . . You've seen for yourself. That's it, Jill. Nothing more than that."

"But why didn't you tell me? Don't you see the risk we were running? If she was Down's Syndrome because of something genetic . . . We could have gone to a doctor. We could have had blood tests or something. *Something.* Whatever they do. But instead you let me become pregnant and I never knew that there was a chance . . ."

"*I* knew," he said. "There was no chance. I knew you'd have the amnio test. And once we were told Cara's fine, what would've been the point of upsetting you?"

"But when we decided to try for a baby, I had the right . . . Because if the tests had shown that something was wrong, I would have had to decide . . . Don't you see that I needed to know from the start? I needed to know the risk so that I'd have the time to think it through, in case I *had* to decide . . . Richard, I can't believe you kept this from me."

He said, "Start the car, Jill. I want to go home."

"You can't think I can dismiss this so easily."

He sighed, raised his head towards the roof, and took a deep breath. He said, "Jill, I've been hit by a bus. The police think someone pushed me deliberately. That means someone intended me dead. Now, I understand that you're upset. You argue that you've a right to be and I'll accept that for now. But if you'd look beyond your own concerns for one moment, you'll see that I need to get home. My face hurts, my ankle's throbbing, and my arm is swelling. We can thrash this out in the car and I can end up back in Casualty, asking to see a doctor, or we can go home and revisit this situation in the morning. Have it either way."

Jill stared at him till he turned his head and met her gaze. She said, "Not telling me about her is tantamount to lying."

She started the car before he could reply, putting it into gear with a jerk. He winced. "Had I known you'd react this way, I would have told you. Do you think I actually *want* anything to estrange us? Now? With the baby due any moment? Do you think I want that? For the love of God, we nearly lost each other tonight."

Jill moved the car out into Grafton Way. She knew intuitively that something wasn't right, but what she couldn't intuit was whether that something was wrong within her or wrong within the man she loved.

Richard didn't speak till they'd crisscrossed over into Portland Place and headed through the rain in the direction of Cavendish Square. And then he said, "I must speak with Gideon as soon as possible. He could be in danger as well. If something happens to him . . . after everything else . . ."

The *as well* told Jill volumes. She said, "This *is* connected to what happened to Eugenie, isn't it?"

His silence comprised an eloquent response. Fear began to eat away at her again.

Too late Jill saw that the route she'd chosen was

going to take them directly past Wigmore Hall. And the worst of it was that there was apparently a concert on this night, because a glut of taxis were crowding the street there, all of them jockeying to disgorge their passengers directly under the glass marquee. She saw Richard turn from the sight of it.

He said, "She's out of prison. And twelve weeks to the day that she got out of prison, Eugenie was murdered."

"You think that German woman . . . ? The woman who killed . . . ?" And then it was all back before her again, rendering any other discussion impossible: the image of that pitiable baby and the fact that her condition had been hidden, hidden from Jill Foster, who'd had a serious and vested interest in knowing all there was to know about Richard Davies and his fathering of children. She said, "Were you afraid to tell me? Is that it?"

"You knew Katja Wolff was out of prison. We even spoke of that with the detective the other day."

"I'm not talking about Katja Wolff. I'm talking about . . . You know what I'm talking about." She swung the car into Portman Square and from there dropped down and over to Park Lane, saying, "You were afraid that I wouldn't want to try for a baby if I knew. I'd have too many fears. You were afraid of that, so you didn't tell me because you didn't trust me."

"How did you expect me to give you the information?" Richard asked. "Was I supposed to say,

'Oh, by the way, my ex-wife gave birth to a handicapped child'? It wasn't relevant."

"How can you say that?"

"Because we weren't trying for a baby, you and I.
We were having sex. Good sex. The best. And we
were in love. But we weren't—"

"I wasn't taking precautions. You knew that."

"But what I didn't know was that you weren't
aware that Sonia had been . . . My God, it was in all
the papers when she died: the fact that she was
drowned, that she was Down's Syndrome and that
she was drowned. I never thought I *had* to mention it."

"I *didn't* know it. She died over twenty years ago,
Richard. I was sixteen years old. What sixteen-year-
old do you know who reads the newspaper and remembers what she's read two decades later?"

"I'm not responsible for what you can and can't
remember."

"But you *are* responsible for making me aware of
something that could affect my future and our baby's
future."

"You were going at it without precautions. I assumed you had your future planned out."

"Are you telling me you think I *entrapped* you?"
They'd reached the traffic lights at the end of Park
Lane, and Jill pivoted awkwardly in her seat to face
him. "Is that what you're saying? Are you telling me
that I was so desperate to have you as a husband that
I got myself pregnant to ensure you'd be willing to

trot up to the altar? Well, it hasn't exactly worked out that way, has it? I've compromised right, left, and centre for you." A taxi blared its horn behind her. Jill glanced in the rearview mirror first, then took note that the lights were now green. They edged their way round the Wellington Arch, and Jill was grateful for the size of the Humber that made her more than visible to the buses and more intimidating to the smaller cars.

"What I'm telling you," Richard said steadily, "is that I don't want to argue about this. It happened. I didn't tell you something I thought you knew. I may not have mentioned it, but I never tried to hide it."

"How can you say that when you've not a single picture of her anywhere?"

"That's been for Gideon's sake. Do you think I wanted my son to spend his life looking at his murdered sister? How do you expect that would affect his music? When Sonia was killed, we all went through hell. *All* of us, Jill, including Gideon. We needed to forget, and removing all the pictures of her seemed one way to do it. Now, if you can't understand that or forgive it, if you wish to end our relationship because of it—" His voice quavered. He put his hand to his face, pulling on the skin along his jaw, savagely pulling it, saying nothing.

And neither did Jill for the remainder of the journey to Cornwall Gardens. She took the route along Kensington Gore. Seven minutes more and they were parking at a spot midway along the leaf-blown square.

In silence, Jill helped her lover from the car and reached into the back seat to collect the parcels. On the one hand, since they were for Catherine, it made more sense to leave them where they were. On the other hand, since everything was suddenly so unsettled about the future of Catherine's parents, it seemed to send a subtle but unmistakable message to take them inside to Richard's flat. Jill scooped them up. She also scooped up the picture that had been the cause of their argument.

Richard said, "Here. Let me take something," and offered his good hand.

She said, "I can manage."

"Jill . . ."

"I can manage." She walked to Braemar Mansions, the decrepit building yet another reminder of how she was compromising with her fiancé. Who would want to live in such a place? she wondered. Who would be willing to purchase a flat in a building that was falling apart at the seams? If she and Richard waited to sell his flat before they tried to sell her own, they'd be forever denied their house, their garden, and their place to be a family with Catherine. Which was, perhaps, what he had wanted all along.

He never remarried, she told herself. Twenty years since his divorce—sixteen? eighteen? oh, it didn't even *matter*—and he'd never taken another woman into his life. And now, on this day, on this night during which he himself could have died, he thought of her. Of what had happened to her and why and what he must now do to safeguard . . .

whom? Not Jill Foster, not his pregnant companion, not their unborn child, but his son. Gideon. His son. His *bloody* son.

Richard came up behind her as she mounted the steps to the building. He reached round her and unlocked the door, pushing it open so that she could enter the unlit hall with its cracking tiles on the floor and its wallpaper sagging from its mildewed walls. It seemed a further affront that there was no lift and only a partial curve in the staircase to serve as a landing should someone wish to rest while ascending. But Jill didn't want to rest. She climbed to the first floor and let her lover struggle up behind her.

He was breathing heavily when he reached the top. She would have felt repentant to have left him fumbling upwards with only the rickety railing to assist in a climb made awkward by the plaster on his leg—but she thought the lesson was a good one for him.

"My building has a lift," she said. "People want lifts, you know, when they're looking for flats. And how much do you actually expect to get for this place, compared with what we could get for mine? We could move house, then. We could *have* a house. And then you'd have the time to paint, redecorate, whatever it might take to make this place sellable."

"I'm exhausted," he said. "I can't continue like this." He shouldered past her and limped to the door of his flat.

She said, "That's convenient, isn't it?" as they went inside and Richard closed the door behind them. The lights were on. Richard frowned at this. He walked to the window and peered out. "You never continue what you want to avoid."

"That's not true. You're becoming unreasonable. You've had a fright, we've both had a fright, and you're reacting to that. When you've had a chance to rest—"

"Don't tell me what to do!" Her voice rose shrilly. She knew at heart that Richard was right, that she was being unreasonable, but she couldn't stop. Somehow all the unspoken doubts she'd been harbouring for months were mingling with her unacknowledged fears. Everything was bubbling up inside her, like noxious gases looking for a fissure through which they could seep. "You've had your way. I've given it and given it. And now you're going to give me mine."

He didn't move from the window. "Has all of this come from seeing that ancient picture?" he asked, and extended his hand to her. "Give it to me, then. I want to destroy it."

"I thought you meant it for Gideon," she cried.

"I did, but if it's going to cause this kind of trouble between us . . . Give it to me, Jill."

"No. I'll give it to Gideon. Gideon's what's important, after all. How Gideon feels, what Gideon does, when Gideon plays his music. He's stood between us from the very first—my God, we even *met* because of Gideon—and I don't intend to displace him now. You want Gideon to have this picture, and he shall have it. Let's phone him at once and tell him we've got it."

"Jill. Don't be a fool. I haven't told him you know he's afraid to play, and if you phone him about the picture, he's going to feel betrayed."

"You can't have it all ways, my darling. He wants the picture and he shall have it tonight. I'll take it over to him myself." She picked up the phone and began to punch the number.

"Jill!" Richard said, and started to approach her.

"What're you going to take over to me, Jill?" Gideon asked.

Both whirled round at the sound of his voice. He was standing in the doorway to the sitting room, in the dim passage that led to the bedroom and to Richard's study. He held a square envelope in one hand and a floral card in the other. His face was the colour of sand, and his eyes were ringed by the circles of insomnia.

"What were you going to take over to me?" he repeated.

GIDEON

12 NOVEMBER

YOU SIT in your father's leather armchair, Dr. Rose, watching me as I stumble through the recitation of the dreadful facts. Your face remains as it always is— interested in what I'm saying but without judgement—and your eyes shine with a compassion that makes me feel like a child in desperate need of comfort.

And that is what I have become: phoning you and weeping, begging that you see me at once, claiming that there is no one else whom I can trust.

You say, Meet me at the office in ninety minutes.

Precise, like that. Ninety minutes. I want to know what you are doing that you cannot meet me there in this instant.

You say, Calm yourself, Gideon. Go within. Breathe deeply.

I need to see you *now*, I cry.

You tell me that you're with your father, but you will be there as soon as you can. You say, Wait on the steps if you get there ahead of me. Ninety minutes, Gideon. Can you remember that?

So now we are here and now I tell you everything that I have remembered on this terrible day. I end it all by saying, How is it possible that I forgot all this? What sort of monster am I that I wasn't able to remember *anything* of what happened all those years ago?

It's clear to you that I have finished my recitation, and that is when you explain things to me. You say in your calm and dispassionate voice that the memory of harming my sister and believing myself to have killed her was something that was not only horrific but associatively connected to the music playing when I committed the act. The act was the memory I repressed, but because music was connected to it, I ultimately repressed the music as well. Remember, you say, that a repressed memory is like a magnet, Gideon. It attracts to it other things that are associated with the memory and pulls them in, repressing them also. *The Archduke* was intimately related to your actions that night. You repressed those actions—and it appears that everyone either overtly or subtly *encouraged* you to repress them—and the music got drawn into the repression.

But I've always been able to play everything else. Only *The Archduke* defeated me.

Indeed, you say. But when Katja Wolff appeared unexpectedly at Wigmore Hall and introduced herself to you, the complete repression was finally triggered.

Why? *Why?*

Because Katja Wolff, your violin, *The Archduke,* and your sister's death were all associatively connected in your mind. That's how it works, Gideon. The main repressed memory was your belief that you had drowned your sister. That repression drew to it the memory of Katja, the person most associated with your sister. What followed Katja into the black hole was *The Archduke,* the piece that was playing that night. Finally, the rest of the music—symbolised by the violin itself—followed that single piece you'd always had trouble playing. That's how it works.

I am silent at this. I am afraid to ask the next question—Will I be able to play again?—because I despise what it reveals about me. We are all the centres of our individual worlds, but most of us are capable of seeing others who exist within our singular boundaries. But I have never been capable of that. I have seen only myself from the very first time I became conscious that I had a self to see. To ask about my music now seems monstrous to me. That question would act as a repudiation of my innocent sister's entire existence. And I've done enough repudiating of Sonia to last me the rest of my life.

Do you believe your father? you ask me. What he said about Sonia's death and the part he himself played in her death . . . Do you believe him, Gideon?

I'll believe nothing till I talk to my mother.

13 NOVEMBER

I begin to see my life in a perspective that makes much clear to me, Dr. Rose. I begin to see how the relationships I've attempted to form or have formed successfully were actually ruled by that which I didn't want to face: my sister's death. The people who didn't know how I was involved in the circumstances of her death were the people I was able to be with, and those were the people most concerned with my own prime concern, which was my professional life: Sherrill and my other fellow musicians, recording artists, conductors, producers, concert organisers round the globe. But the people who might have wanted more from me than a performance on my instrument . . . those were the people with whom I failed.

Beth is the best example of this. Of course I couldn't be the partner in life that she wanted me to be. Partnership of that sort suggested to me a level of intimacy, trust, and revelation in which I could not afford to participate. My only hope for survival was to effect an escape from her.

And so it is with Libby now. That prime symbol of intimacy between us—the Act—is beyond my power. We lie in each other's arms, and feeling desire is so far removed from what I'm experiencing that Libby may as well be a sack of potatoes.

At least I know why. And until I speak to my mother and learn the full truth of what happened that night, I can have nothing with any woman, no matter who she is, no matter how little she expects of me.

16 NOVEMBER

I was returning from Primrose Hill when I saw Libby again. I'd taken one of the kites out, a new one that

I'd worked on for several weeks and was eager to try. I'd employed what I thought was an intriguingly aerodynamic design, crafted to ensure that the height reached would be a record-breaking one.

On the top of Primrose Hill, there is nothing to impede the flight of a kite. The trees are distant, and the only structures that could get in the way of anything airborne are the buildings that stand far beyond the hill's crest, on the other side of the roads that border the park. As it was a day of good wind, I assumed that I'd have the kite aloft within moments of releasing it.

That wasn't the case. Every time I released it, began to jog forward, and played out the twine, the kite shuddered, tossed and turned on the wind, and plummeted to the ground like a missile. Time and again, I made the attempt, after adjusting the leading edge, the standoffs, even the bridle. Nothing helped. Eventually, one of the bottom spreaders fractured, and I had to give up the whole enterprise.

I was trudging along Chalcot Crescent when I encountered Libby. She was heading in the direction I had just come from, a Boots bag dangling from one hand and a can of diet Coke in the other. Picnic lunch, I assumed. I could see the top of a baguette rising out of the bag like a crusty appendage.

"The wind'll give you aggravation if you're planning to eat your lunch out there," I said with a nod in the direction I'd just walked.

"Hi to you, too," was her reply.

She said it politely, but her smile was brief. We

hadn't seen each other since our unhappy encounter in her flat, and although I'd heard her come in and go out and had admittedly anticipated her ringing my bell, she hadn't done so. I'd missed her, but once I'd remembered what I needed to remember about Sonia, about Katja, and about my part in the death of one and the imprisonment of the other, I realised it was just as well. I wasn't fit to be any woman's companion, be that her friend, her lover, or her husband. So whether she realised it or not, Libby was wise to steer clear.

"I've been trying to get this one up," I said, lifting the broken kite by way of explaining my statement about the wind. "If you stay off the hill and eat down below, you might be all right."

"Ducks," she said.

For a moment I thought the word was another strange California term I'd never heard before. She went on.

"I'm going to feed them. In Regent's Park."

"Ah. I see. I thought . . . Well, seeing the bread—"

"And associating me with food. Yeah. It makes good sense."

"I don't associate you with food, Libby."

"Okay," she said. "You don't."

I shifted the kite from my left hand to my right. I didn't like the feeling of being at odds with her, but I had no clear idea how to bridge the chasm between us. We are, at heart, such different people, I thought. Perhaps, just as Dad had seen it from the first, it was always a ridiculous affiliation: Libby Neale and Gideon Davies. What had they in common, after all?

"I haven't seen Rafe in a couple of days," Libby said, indicating the direction of Chalcot Square with a toss of her head. "I was wondering if something happened to him."

The fact that she'd given me an opening prompted me to realise that she always had been the person to provide the openings in our conversations. And that realisation was what prompted me to say, "Something *has* happened. But not to him."

She looked at me earnestly. "Your dad's okay, right?"

"He's fine."

"His girlfriend?"

"Jill's fine. Everyone's fine."

"Oh. Good."

I took a deep breath. "Libby, I'm going to see my mother. After all this time, I'm actually going to see her. Dad told me she's been phoning him about me, so we're going to meet. Just the two of us. And when we do, there's a chance that I'll get to the bottom of the violin problem."

She put her can of diet Coke into the Boots bag and rubbed her hand down her hip. "I guess that's cool, Gid. If you want it to be. It's, like, what you want in life, right?"

"It *is* my life."

"Sure. It's your life. That's what you've made it."

I could tell by her tone that we were back to the

uneven ground we'd walked over before, and I felt a surge of frustration run through me. "Libby, I'm a musician. If nothing else, it's how I support myself. It's where the money to live comes from. You can understand that."

"I understand," she said.

"Then——"

"Look, Gid. Like I said, I'm heading out to feed the ducks."

"Why don't you come up afterwards? We could have a meal."

"I've got plans for tapping."

"Tapping?"

She looked away. For a moment, her face expressed a reaction I couldn't quite grasp. When she turned her head back to me, her eyes appeared sorrowful. But when she spoke, her voice was resigned. "Tap dancing," she said. "It's what I like to do."

"Sorry. I'd forgotten."

"Yeah," she said. "I know."

"What about later, then? I should be home. I'm just hanging about, waiting to hear from Dad. Come up after your dancing. If you've a mind to, that is."

"Sure," she said. "I'll see you around."

At that, I knew she wouldn't come up. The fact that I'd forgotten her dancing was, apparently, the final blow to her. I said, "Libby, I've had a lot on my mind. You know that. You must see——"

"Jesus," she interrupted me. "You don't get anything."

"I 'get' that you're angry."

"I'm not angry. I'm not anything. I'm going to the park to feed the ducks. Because I've got the time and I like ducks. I've always liked ducks. And after that, I'm going to a tap-dancing lesson. Because I like tap dancing."

"You're avoiding me, aren't you?"

"This isn't about you. *I'm* not about you. The rest of the world isn't about you. If you, like, stop playing the violin tomorrow, the rest of the world will just go on being the rest of the world. But how can you go on being you if there's no you in the first place, Gid?"

"That's what I'm trying to recapture."

"You can't recapture what's never been there. You can create it if you want to. But you can't just go out with a net and bag it."

"Why won't you see—"

"I want to feed the ducks," she cut in. And with that, she swung past me and headed down to Regent's Park Road.

I watched her go. I wanted to run after her and argue my point. How easy it was for her to talk about one's simply being oneself when she didn't have a past that was littered with accomplishments, all of which served as guideposts to a future that had long been determined. It was easy for her simply to exist in a given moment of a given day because moments were all she had ever had. But my life had never been like that, and I wanted her to acknowledge that fact.

She must have read my mind. She turned when she came to the corner and shouted something back at me.

"What?" I called to her as her words were taken by the wind.

She cupped her hands round her mouth and tried again. "Good luck with your mother," she shouted.

17 NOVEMBER

I'd been able to put my mother from my mind for years because of my work. Preparing for this concert or that recording session, practising my instrument with Raphael, filming a documentary, rehearsing with this or that orchestra, touring Europe or the US, meeting my agent, negotiating contracts, working with the East London Conservatory . . . My days and my hours had been filled with music for two decades. There had been no place in them for speculation about the parent who'd deserted me.

But now there was time, and she dominated my thoughts. And I knew even as I thought about it, even as I wondered, imagined, and pondered, that keeping my mind fixed on my mother was a way to keep it at a distance from Sonia.

I wasn't altogether successful. For my sister still came to me in unguarded moments.

"She doesn't look right, Mummy," I remembered saying, hovering over the bed on which my sister lay, swaddled in blankets, wearing a cap, in possession of a face that didn't look as it should.

"Don't say that, Gideon," Mother replied. "Don't ever say that about your sister."

"But her eyes are squishy. She's got a funny mouth."

"I said don't talk like that about your sister!"

We began in that way, making the subject of Sonia's disabilities *verboten* among us. When they began to dominate our lives, we made no mention of them. Sonia was fretful, Sonia cried through the night, Sonia went into hospital for two or three weeks. But still we pretended that life was normal, that this was the way things always happened in families when a baby was born. We went about life in that way till Granddad fractured the glass wall of our denial.

"What good are either of them?" he raged. "What good is any one of you, Dick?"

Is that when it began in my head? Is that when I first saw the necessity to prove myself different from my sister? Granddad had lumped me together with Sonia, but I would show him the truth.

Yet how could I do that when everything revolved round *her*? Her health, her growth, her disabilities, her development. A cry in the night and the household was rallied to see to her needs. A change in her temperature and life was halted till a doctor could explain what had brought it about. An alteration in the manner of her feeding and specialists were consulted for an explanation. She was the topic of every conversation but at the same time the cause of her ailments could never be directly mentioned.

And I remembered this, Dr. Rose. I remembered because when I thought of my mother, my sister was clinging to the shirttails of any memory I was able to evoke. She was there in my mind as persistently as she'd been there in my life. And as I waited for the time when I would see my mother, I sought to shake her from me with as much determination as I'd sought to shake her from me when she was alive.

Yes, I do see what that means. She is in my way now. She was in my way then. Because of her, life had altered. Because of her, it was going to alter still more.

"You'll be going to school, Gideon."

That must be when the seed was planted: the seed of disappointment, anger, and thwarted dreams that grew into a forest of blame. Dad was the one who broke the news to me.

He comes into my bedroom. I'm sitting at the table by the window, where Sarah-Jane Beckett and I do our lessons. I'm working on school prep. Dad pulls out the chair in which Sarah-Jane generally sits, and he watches me with his arms crossed.

He says, "We've had a good run of it, Gideon. You've thrived, haven't you, son?"

I don't know what he's talking about, and what I hear in his words makes me wary immediately. I know now that what I heard must have been resignation, but at the moment I cannot put a name to what he's apparently feeling.

That is when he tells me that I will be going out to school, to a C of E school that he's managed to locate, a day school not too far away. I say what first comes to my mind.

"What about my playing? When will I practise?"

"We'll have to work that out."

"But what will happen to Sarah-Jane? She won't like it if she can't teach me."

"She'll have to cope. We're letting her go, son."

Letting her go. At first I think he means that Sarah-Jane *wants* to leave us, that she's made a request and he's acceded to it with as much good grace as he can muster. But when I say, "I shall talk to her, then. I shall stop her from going," he says, "We can't afford her any longer, Gideon." He doesn't add the rest, but I do, in my head. *We can't afford her because of Sonia.* "We have to cut back somewhere," Dad informs me. "We don't want to let Raphael go, and we can't let Katja go. So it's come down to Sarah-Jane."

"But when will I play if I'm at school? They won't let me come to school only when I want to, will they, Dad? And there'll be rules. So how will I have my lessons?"

"We've spoken to them, Gideon. They're willing to make allowances. They know the situation."

"But I don't want to go! I want Sarah-Jane to keep teaching me."

"So do I," Dad said. "So do we all. But it's not possible, Gideon. We haven't the funds."

We haven't the funds, the money, the funds. Hasn't this been the leitmotiv for all of our lives? So should I be the least surprised when the Juilliard offer comes and must be rejected? Isn't it logical that I would attach my inability to attend Juilliard to money?

But I *am* surprised. I am outraged. I am maddened.

And the seed that was planted sends shoots upwards, sends roots downwards, and begins to multiply in the soil.

I learn to hate. I acquire a need for revenge. A target for my vengeance becomes essential. I hear it at first, in her ceaseless crying and the inhuman demands she places upon everyone. And then I see it, in her, in my sister.

Thinking of my mother, I dwelled upon these other thoughts as well. In considering them, I had to conclude that even if Dad had not acted to save Sonia as he might have done, what did it matter? I had begun the process of killing her. He had only allowed that process to run its course.

You say to me: Gideon, you were just a little boy. This was a sibling situation. You weren't the first person who has attempted to harm a younger sibling, and you won't be the last.

But she *died,* Dr. Rose.

Yes. She died. But not at your hands.

I don't *know* that for certain.

You don't know—and can't know—what's true right now. But you will. Soon.

You're right, Dr. Rose, as you usually are. Mother will tell me what actually happened. If there's salvation for me anywhere in the world, it will come to me from her.

TWENTY-SIX

"HE WOULDN'T even take a wheelchair," the nurse in charge of Casualty told them. Her name badge said she was Sister Darla Magnana and she was in high dudgeon over the manner in which Richard Davies had departed the hospital. Patients were to leave in *wheelchairs,* accompanied by an appropriate staff member who would see them to their vehicles. They were *not* meant to decline this service, and if they *did* decline it, they were not to be discharged. *This* gentleman had actually walked off on his own without being discharged at all. So the hospital could *not* be held responsible if his injuries intensified or caused him further problems. Sister Darla Magnana hoped that was clear. "When we wish to keep someone overnight for observation, we have a very good reason for doing so," she declared.

Lynley asked to speak to the doctor who'd seen Richard Davies, and from that gentleman—a harassed-looking resident physician with several days' growth of whiskers—he and Havers learned the extent of Davies' injuries: a compound fracture of the right ulna, a single break of the right lateral malleolus. "Right arm and right ankle," the doctor translated for Havers when she said, "Fractures of the whats?" He went on to say, "Cuts and abrasions on the hands. A possible concussion. He needed some stitches on the face. Overall, he was very lucky, however. It could have been fatal."

Lynley thought about this as he and Havers left the hospital, having been told that Richard had departed in the company of a heavily pregnant woman. They went to the Bentley, phoned in to Leach, and learned from him that Winston Nkata had given the incident room Noreen McKay's name to be put through the DVLA. Leach had the results: Noreen McKay owned a late-model Toyota RAV4. That was her only vehicle.

"If we get no joy from those prison records, we're back to the Humber," Leach said. "Bring that car in for a once-over."

Lynley said, "Right. And as to Eugenie Davies' computer, sir?"

"Deal with that later. After we get our hands on that car. And talk to Foster. I want to know where *she* was this afternoon."

"Surely not pushing her fiancé under a bus," Lynley said despite his better judgement, which told him not to do or say anything that might remind Leach of Lynley's own transgressions. "In her condition, she'd be rather conspicuous to witnesses."

"Just deal with her, Inspector. And get that car." Leach recited Jill Foster's address. It was a flat in

Shepherd's Bush. Directory enquiries gave Lynley a phone number to go along with the address, and within a minute he knew what he'd already assumed when Leach gave him the assignment: Jill wasn't at home. She'd have taken Davies to his own flat in South Kensington.

As they were spinning down Park Lane in preparation for the last leg of the trip from Gower Street to South Kensington, Havers said, "You know, Inspector, we're down to Gideon or Robson shoving Davies into the street this evening. But if either one of them did the job, the basic question remains, doesn't it? *Why?*"

"*If*'s the operative word," Lynley said.

She obviously heard his doubts, because she said, "You don't think either of them pushed him, do you?"

"Killers nearly always choose the same means," Lynley pointed out.

"But a bus *is* a vehicle," Havers said.

"But it's not a car and driver. And it's not *that* car, the Humber. Or any antique car for that matter. Nor was the hit as serious as the others, considering what it could have been."

"And no one saw the shove," Havers said thoughtfully. "At least so far."

"I'm betting no one saw it at all, Havers."

"Okay. So we're back to Davies again. Davies tracking down Kathleen Waddington before going after Eugenie. Davies setting his sights on Webberly to guide our suspicion onto Katja Wolff when we don't get there fast enough. Davies then throwing himself into the traffic because he's got the sense we're not taking Wolff seriously as a suspect. All right. I see. But *why*'s the question."

"Because of Gideon. It has to be. Because she was threatening Gideon in some way and Davies lives for Gideon. If, as you suggested, Barbara, she actually meant to stop him playing—"

"I like the idea, but what was it to her? I mean, if anything, it seems that she'd want to keep him playing, not stop him, right? She had a history of his whole career up in her attic. She obviously cared that he played. Why cock it up?"

"Perhaps cocking it up wasn't her intention," Lynley said. "But perhaps cocking it up was what would have happened—without her knowing it—if she met Gideon again."

"So Davies killed her? Why not just tell her the truth? Why not just say, 'Hang on, old girl. 'F you see Gideon, he's done for, professionally speaking.' "

"Perhaps he did say that," Lynley pointed out. "And perhaps she said, 'I've not got a choice, Richard. It's been years and it's time . . .' "

"For what?" Havers asked. "A family reunion? An explanation of why she ran off in the first place? An announcement that she was going to hook up with Major Wiley? What?"

"Something," Lynley said. "Something that we may never find out."

"Which toasts our muffins good and proper," Havers noted. "And doesn't go very far towards putting Richard Davies in the nick. *If* he's our man. And we've got sod all for evidence of that. He has an alibi, Inspector. Hasn't he?"

"Asleep. With Jill Foster. Who was, herself, most likely asleep. So he could have gone and returned without her knowledge, Havers, using her car and then bringing it back."

"We're at the car again."

"It's the only thing we have."

"Right. Well. The CPS aren't likely to do backflips over that, Inspector. Access to the car's not exactly hard evidence."

"Access isn't," Lynley agreed. "But it's not access alone that I'm depending on."

GIDEON

20 NOVEMBER

I SAW Dad before he looked up and saw me. He was coming along the pavement in Chalcot Square, and I could tell from his posture that he was brooding. I felt some concern but no alarm.

Then something odd happened. Raphael appeared at the far end of the garden in the centre of the square. He must have called out to Dad, because Dad hesitated on the pavement, turned, and then waited for him a few doors away from my own house. As I watched from the music room window, they exchanged a few words, Dad doing the talking. As he spoke, Raphael staggered back two steps, his face crumpling the way a man's face crumples when he's received a punch to the gut. Dad continued to talk. Raphael turned back towards the garden. Dad watched as Raphael walked back through the gates to where two wooden benches face each other. He sat. No, he *dropped,* all of his weight falling in a mass that was merely bones and flesh, reaction incarnate.

I should have known then. But I did not.

Dad walked on, at which point he looked up and saw me watching from the window. He raised a hand but didn't wait for me to respond. In a moment, he disappeared beneath me and I heard the sound of his key in the lock of my front door. When he came into the music room, he removed his coat and laid it deliberately along the back of a chair.

"What's Raphael doing?" I asked him. "Has something happened?"

He looked at me, and I could see that his face was awash with sorrow. "I've some news," he told me, "some very bad news."

"What?" I felt fear lap against my skin.

"There's no easy way to tell you," he said.

"Then tell me."

"Your mother's dead, son."

"But you said she's been phoning you. About what happened at Wigmore Hall. She can't be—"

"She was killed last night, Gideon. She was hit by a car in West Hampstead. The police rang me this morning." He cleared his throat and squeezed his temples as if to contain an emotion there. "They asked if I would try to identify her body. I looked. I couldn't tell for certain. . . . It's been years since I saw her. . . ." He made an aimless gesture. "I'm so sorry, son."

"But she can't be . . . If you didn't recognise her, perhaps it's not—"

"The woman was carrying your mother's identification. Driving licence, credit cards, chequebook.

What are the possibilities that someone else would have had all of Eugenie's identification?"

"So you said it was her? You said it was my mother?"

"I said I didn't know, that I couldn't be sure. I gave them the name of her dentist . . . the man she used to see when we were still together. They'll be able to check that way. And there are fingerprints, I suppose."

"Did you ring her?" I asked. "Did she know I wanted to . . . Was she *willing* . . . ?" But what was the point of asking, the point of knowing? What did it matter if she was dead?

"I left a message for her, son. She hadn't got back to me yet."

"That's it, then."

Dad's head had been dropped forward, but he raised it then. "That's what?" he asked.

"There's no one to tell me."

"I've told you."

"No."

"Gideon, for God's sake . . ."

"You've told me what you think will make me believe that I'm not at fault. But you'd say anything to get me back on the violin."

"Gideon, please."

"No." Everything was becoming so much clearer. It was as if the shock of learning of her death suddenly blew the fog from my mind. I said, "It doesn't make sense that Katja Wolff would have agreed to your plan. That she would give up so many years of her life . . . for what, Dad? For me? For you? I wasn't anything to her and neither were you. Isn't that true? You weren't her lover. You weren't the father of her child. Raphael was, wasn't he? So it makes no sense that she agreed. You must have tricked her. You must have . . . what? Planted evidence? Twisted the facts?"

"How the hell can you accuse me of that?"

"Because I see it. Because I understand. Because how would Granddad have reacted, Dad, to the news that his freak of a granddaughter had just been drowned by her freak of a brother? And that's what it must have come down to in the end: Keep the truth from Granddad no matter what."

"She was a willing participant because of the money. Twenty thousand pounds for admitting to a negligent act that led to Sonia's death. I explained all that. I told you that we didn't expect the press's reaction to the case or the Crown Prosecutor's passion to put her in prison. We had no idea—"

"You did it to protect me. And all your talk about leaving Sonia in the bath to die—of holding her down yourself—is just that: talk. It serves the same purpose as letting Katja Wolff take the blame twenty years ago. It keeps me playing the violin. Or at least it's supposed to."

"What are you saying?"

"You know what I'm saying. It's over. Or it will be once I collect the money to pay Katja Wolff her four hundred thousand pounds."

"No! You don't owe her . . . For God's sake, think. She may well have been the person who ran over your mother!"

I stared at him. My mouth said the word, "What?" but my voice did not. And my brain could not take in what he was saying.

He continued to talk, saying words that I heard but did not assimilate. Hit-and-run, I heard. No accident, Gideon. A car ploughing over her twice. Three times. A deliberate death. Indeed, a murder.

"I didn't have the money to pay her," he said. "You didn't know who she was. So she would have tracked down your mother next. And when Eugenie hadn't the money to pay her . . . You see what happened, don't you? You *do* see what happened?"

They were words falling against my ears, but they meant nothing to me. I heard them, but I didn't comprehend. All I knew was that my hope for deliverance from my crime was gone. For if I had been unable to believe anything else, I did believe in her. I did believe in my mother.

Why? you ask.

Because she left us, Dr. Rose. And while she might indeed have left us because she couldn't come to terms with her grief over my sister's death, I believe that she left us because she couldn't come to terms with the lie she'd have had to live should she have stayed.

20 NOVEMBER, 2:00 P.M.

Dad departed when it became apparent that I had finished talking. But I was alone ten minutes only—perhaps even less—when Raphael took his place.

He looked like hell. Blood red traced a curve along his lower eyelashes. That and flesh in a shade like ashes were the only colours in his face.

He came to me and put his hand on my shoulder. We faced each other and I watched his features begin to dissolve, as if he had no skull beneath his skin to hold him together but, rather, a substance that had always been soluble, vulnerable to the right element that could melt it.

He said, "She wouldn't stop punishing herself." His hand tightened and tightened on my shoulder. I wanted to cry out or jerk back from the pain, but I couldn't move because I couldn't risk even a gesture that might make him stop talking. "She couldn't forgive herself, Gideon, but she never—she *never,* I swear it—stopped thinking of you."

"Thinking of me?" I repeated numbly as I tried to absorb what he was saying. "How do you know? How do you know she never stopped thinking . . . ?"

His face gave me the answer before he spoke it: He'd not lost contact with my mother in all the years that she'd been gone from our lives. He'd never stopped talking to her on the phone. He'd never stopped seeing her: in pubs, restaurants, hotel lounges, parks, and museums. She would say, "Tell me how Gideon is getting on, Raphael," and he would supply her with the information that newspapers, critical reviews of my playing, magazine articles, and gossip within the community of classical musicians couldn't give her.

"You've seen her," I said. "You've *seen* her. Why?"

"Because she loved you."

"No. I mean, why did you do it?"

"She wouldn't let me tell you," he said brokenly. "Gideon, she swore she would stop our meetings if she ever learned that I'd told you I'd seen her."

"And you couldn't bear that, could you," I said bitterly, because finally I understood it all. I'd seen the answers in those long-ago flowers he'd brought to her and I read them in his reaction now, when she was gone and he could no longer entertain the fantasy that there might be something of significance that would bloom one day between them. "Because if she stopped seeing you, then what would happen to your little dream?"

He said nothing.

"You were in love with her. Isn't that right, Raphael? You've always been in love with her. And seeing her once a month, once a week, once a day, or once a year had nothing to do with anything but what you wanted and hoped to get. So you wouldn't tell me. You just let me believe she walked out on us and never looked back, and never *cared* to look back. When all the time you *knew*—" I couldn't go on.

"It's the way she wanted it," he said. "I had to honour her choice."

"You had to *nothing*."

"I'm sorry," he said. "Gideon, if I'd known . . . How was I to know?"

"Tell me what happened that night."

"What night?"

"You know what night. Don't let's play the happy

idiot now. What happened the night my sister drowned? And don't try to tell me that Katja Wolff did it, all right? You were with her. You were arguing with her. I got into the bathroom. I held Sonia down. And then what happened?"

"I don't know."

"I don't believe you."

"It's the truth. We came upon you in the bathroom. Katja began screaming. Your father came running. I took Katja downstairs. That's all I know. I didn't go back up when the paramedics arrived. I didn't leave the kitchen till the police turned up."

"Was Sonia moving in the bathtub?"

"I don't know. I don't think so. But that doesn't mean you harmed her. It *never* meant that."

"For Christ's sake, Raphael, I held her down!"

"You can't remember that. It's impossible. You were far too young. Gideon, Katja had left her alone for five or six minutes. I'd gone to talk to her and we began to argue. We stepped out of the room and into the nursery because I wanted to know what she intended to do about . . ." He faltered. He couldn't say it, even now.

I said it for him. "Why the hell did you make her pregnant when you were in love with my mother?"

"Blonde," was his miserable, pathetic reply. It came after a long fifteen seconds in which he did nothing but breathe erratically. "They both were blonde."

"God," I whispered. "And did she let you call her Eugenie?"

"Don't," he said. "It happened only once."

"And you couldn't afford to let anyone know, could you? Neither of you could afford that. She couldn't afford to let anyone know she'd left Sonia alone as long as five minutes and you couldn't afford to let anyone know you'd got her pregnant while pretending you were fucking my mother."

"She could have got rid of it. It would have been easy."

"Nothing," I said, "is that easy, Raphael. Except lying. And that was easy for all of us, wasn't it?"

"Not for your mother," Raphael said. "That's why she left."

He reached for me again, then. He put his hand on my shoulder, tightly, as he had done before. He said, "She would have told you the truth, Gideon. You must believe your father in this. Your mother would have told you the truth."

21 NOVEMBER, 1:30 A.M.

So that is what I'm left with, Dr. Rose: an assurance only. Had she lived, had we had the opportunity to meet, she would have told me everything.

She would have taken me back through my own history and corrected where my impressions were false and my memory incomplete.

She would have explained the details I recall. She would have filled in the gaps.

But she is dead, so she can do nothing.

And what I'm left with is only what I can remember.

TWENTY-SEVEN

RICHARD SAID to his son, "Gideon. What are you doing here?"

Gideon said, "What's happened to you?"

"Someone tried to kill him," Jill said. "He thinks it's Katja Wolff. He's afraid she'll come after you next."

Gideon looked at her, then he looked at his father. He seemed, if anything, inordinately puzzled. Not shocked, Jill concluded, not horrified that Richard had nearly died that day, but merely puzzled. He said, "Why would Katja want to do that? It would hardly get her what she's after."

"Gideon . . ." Richard said heavily.

"Richard thinks she's after you as well," Jill said. "He thinks she's the one who pushed him into the traffic. He might have been killed."

"Is that what he's telling you?"

"My God. That's what happened," Richard countered. "What are you doing here? How long have you been here?"

Gideon didn't answer at first. Instead, he appeared

to make a mental catalogue of his father's injuries, his gaze going first to Richard's leg, then to his arm, then coming back to rest on his face.

"Gideon," Richard said. "I asked you how long—"

"Long enough to find this." Gideon gestured with the card he held.

Jill looked at Richard. She saw his eyes narrow.

"You lied to me about this as well," Gideon said.

Richard's attention was fixed on the card. "Lied about what?"

"About my sister. She didn't die. Not as a baby and not as a child." His hand crumpled the envelope. It dropped to the floor.

Jill looked down at the photograph she was holding. She said, "But, Gideon, you know that your sister—"

"You've been going through my belongings," Richard cut in.

"I wanted to find her address, which I expect you have squirreled away somewhere, haven't you? But what I found instead—"

"Gideon!" Jill held out the picture Richard intended for his son. "You're not making sense. Your sister was—"

"What I found," Gideon went doggedly on, shaking the card at his father, "was this, and now I know exactly who you are: a liar who couldn't stop if he had to, Dad, if his life depended on telling the truth, if everyone's life depended upon it."

"Gideon!" Jill was aghast not at the words but at the glacial tone in which Gideon spoke them. Her horror momentarily drove from her thoughts her own affront at Richard's behaviour. She pushed from her mind that Gideon was speaking the truth at least as it applied to her own life if not to his: In never mentioning Sonia's condition, Richard had indeed lied to her, if only by omission. Instead, she dwelt on the intemperance of what the son was saying to the father. "Richard was nearly killed less than three hours ago."

"Are you sure of that?" Gideon asked her. "If he lied to me about Virginia, who's to know what else he's willing to lie about?"

"Virginia?" Jill asked. "Who—"

Richard said to his son, "We'll talk about this later."

"No," Gideon said. "We're going to talk about Virginia now."

Jill said, "Who is Virginia?"

"Then you don't know either."

Jill said, "Richard?" and turned to her fiancé. "Richard, what's this all about?"

"Here's what it's all about," Gideon said, and he read the inside of the card aloud. His voice carried the strength of indignation although it trembled twice: once when he read out the words *our daughter* and a second time when he came to *lived thirty-two years.*

For her part, Jill heard the echo of a different two phrases reverberating round the room: *She defied medical probability* was one, and the other comprised the first three words of the final sentence: *Despite her prob-*

lems. She felt a wave of sickness rise up in her, and a terrible cold worked its way into her bones. "Who is she?" she cried. "Richard, who is she?"

"A freak," Gideon said. "Isn't that right, Dad? Virginia Davies was another freak."

"What does he mean?" Jill asked, although she knew, already knew and couldn't bear the knowing. She willed Richard to answer her question, but he stood like granite, bent-shouldered, crooked-backed, with his eyes fixed steadily on his son. "Say something!" Jill implored.

"He's thinking how to shape an answer for you," Gideon told her. "He's wondering what excuse he can make for letting me think my older sister died as a baby. There was something badly wrong with her, you see. And I expect it was easier to pretend she was dead than to have to accept that she wasn't perfect."

Richard finally spoke. "You don't know what you're talking about," he said as Jill's thoughts began to spin wildly out of control: another Down's Syndrome, the voices shouted inside her skull, a second Down's Syndrome, a second Down's Syndrome or something else something worse something he couldn't bring himself even to mention and all the while her precious Catherine was at risk for something God only knew what that the antenatal tests had not identified and he stood there just stood there and stood there and stood there and looked at his son and refused to discuss . . . She was aware that the picture she was holding was becoming slick in her hands, was becoming heavy, was becoming a burden she could hardly manage. It slipped from her fingers as she cried out, "Talk to me, Richard!"

Richard and his son moved simultaneously as the picture clattered on the bare wood floor and Jill stepped past it, stepped around it, feeling she couldn't bear her own impossible weight a moment longer. So she stumbled to the sofa, where she became a mute onlooker to what then followed.

Hastily, Richard bent for the picture, but his actions were hampered by the plaster on his leg. Gideon got there first. He snatched it up, crying, "Something else, Dad?" and then he stared down at it with his fingers whitening to the colour of bone upon the wooden frame. He said hoarsely, "Where did this come from?" He raised his eyes to his father.

Richard said, "You must calm down, Gideon," and he sounded desperate and Jill watched both of them and saw their tension, Richard's held like a whip in his hand, Gideon's coiled and ready to spring.

Gideon said, "You told me she'd taken every picture of Sonia with her. Mother left us and she took all the pictures, you said. She took all of the pictures except that one you kept in your desk."

"I had a very good reason—"

"Have you had this all along?"

"I have." Richard's eyes bored into his son's.

"I don't believe you," Gideon said. "You said she took them and she took them. You wanted her to take them. Or you sent them to her. But you didn't have this, because if you'd had it, on that day when I wanted it, when I needed to see her, when I asked you, begged you—"

"Rubbish. This is bollocks. I didn't give it to you then because I thought you might—"

"What? Throw myself onto the railway tracks? I didn't know then. I didn't even suspect. I was panicked about my music and so were you. So if you'd had this then, on that day, Dad, you'd have handed it over straightaway. If you thought for a moment it would get me back to the violin, you would have done anything."

"Listen to me." Richard spoke rapidly. "I had that picture. I'd forgotten about it. I'd merely misplaced it among your grandfather's papers. When I saw it yesterday, I intended at once to give it to you. I remembered you wanted a picture of Sonia . . . that you'd asked about one. . . ."

"It wouldn't be in a frame," Gideon said. "Not if it was yours. Not if you'd misplaced it among his papers."

"You're twisting my words."

"It would have been like the other. It would have been in an envelope or stuffed into a book or placed in a bag or lying somewhere loose, but it wouldn't— it wouldn't—have been in a frame."

"You're getting hysterical. This is what comes of psychoanalysis. I hope you see that."

"What I see," Gideon cried, "is a self-involved hypocrite who'd say anything at all, who'd do anything at all if that's what it took—" Gideon stopped himself.

On the sofa, Jill felt the atmosphere between the two men suddenly become electric and hot. Her own thoughts were charging round madly in her head, so at first when Gideon spoke again, she didn't comprehend his meaning.

"It was you," he said. "Oh my God. You killed her. You had spoken to her. You had asked her to support your lies about Sonia, but she wouldn't do that, would she? So she had to die."

"For the love of God, Gideon. You don't know what you're saying."

"I do. For the first time in my life, I do. She was going to tell me the truth, wasn't she? You didn't think she would, you were so certain she'd go along with anything you planned, because she did at first, all those years ago. But that's not who she was and why the hell did you think it might be? She'd left us, Dad. She couldn't live a lie and live with us, so she walked out. It was too much for her, knowing that we'd sent Katja to prison."

"She agreed to go. She was party to it all."

"But not to twenty years," Gideon said. "Katja Wolff wouldn't have been party to that. To five years, perhaps. Five years and one hundred thousand pounds, all right. But twenty years? No one expected it. And Mother couldn't live with it, could she? So she left us and she would have stayed away forever had I not lost my music at Wigmore Hall."

"You've got to stop thinking that Wigmore Hall is connected to anything but Wigmore Hall. I've told you that from the first."

"Because you wanted to believe it," Gideon said. "But the truth is that Mother was going to tell me that my memory wasn't lying to me, wasn't she, Dad? She knew I killed Sonia. She knew I did it alone."

"You didn't. I've told you. I explained what happened."

"Tell me again, then. In front of Jill."

Richard said nothing, although he cast a look at Jill. She wanted to see it as a look that begged for her help and her understanding. But she saw instead the calculation behind it. Richard said, "Gideon. Let's put this aside. Let's talk about it later."

"We'll talk about it now. One of us will. Shall I be the one? I killed my sister, Jill. I drowned her in her bath. She was a millstone round everyone's neck—"

"Gideon. Stop it."

"—but especially round mine. She stood in the way of my music. I saw the world revolving round her, and I couldn't cope with that, so I killed her."

"No!" Richard said.

"Dad wants me to think—"

"No!" Richard shouted.

"—that he was the one, that when he came into the bathroom that evening and saw her underwater in the tub, he held her there and finished the job. But he's lying about that because he knows that if I continue to believe I killed her, there's a very good chance I'll never pick up the violin again."

"That's not what happened," Richard said.

"Which part of it?"

Richard said nothing for a moment, then,

"Please," and Jill saw that he was caught between the two choices that Gideon's accusations had brought him to facing. And no matter which way he chose to go, both choices amounted to a single one in the end. Either he killed his child. Or he killed his child.

Gideon apparently saw the answer he wanted within his father's silence. He said, "Yes. Right, then," and dropped the picture of his sister onto the floor.

He strode to the door. He drew it open.

"For God's sake, I did it," Richard cried out. "Gideon! Stop! Listen to me. Believe what I say. She was still alive when you left her. I held her down in the bath. I was the one who drowned Sonia."

Jill caught herself in a wail of horror. It was all too logical. She knew. She saw. He was talking to his son but he was doing more: He was finally explaining to Jill what was keeping him from marriage.

Gideon said, "Those are lies," and he began to leave.

Richard started to go after him, hampered by his injuries. Jill struggled to her feet. She said, "They're all daughters. That's it, isn't it? Virginia. Sonia. And now Catherine."

Richard stumbled to the door, leaned against the jamb. He roared, "Gideon! God damn it! Listen!" He shoved himself out into the corridor.

Jill staggered after him. She cried, "You didn't want to marry because it's a daughter." She grabbed on to his arm. He was hobbling towards the staircase, and heavy as she was, he dragged her with him. She could hear Gideon clattering downwards. His footsteps pounded across the tiled entry.

"Gideon!" Richard shouted. "Wait!"

"You're afraid she'll be like the other two, aren't you?" Jill cried, clinging to Richard's arm. "You created Virginia. You created Sonia and you think our baby's going to be damaged as well. That's why you haven't wanted to marry me, isn't it?"

The front door opened. Richard and Jill reached the top of the stairs. Richard shouted, "Gideon! Listen to me."

"I've listened long enough," came the reply. Then the front door banged closed. Richard bellowed as if struck in the chest. He started to descend.

Jill dragged down on his arm. "That's why. Isn't it? You've been waiting to see if the baby's normal before you're willing to—"

He shook her off. She grabbed at him again. "Get away!" he cried. "Get off me. Go! Don't you see I've got to stop him?"

"Answer me. Tell me. You've thought there was something wrong because she's a daughter and if we married, then you'd be stuck. With me. With her. Just like before."

"You don't know what you're saying."

"Then tell me I'm wrong."

"Gideon!" he shouted. "God damn it, Jill. I'm his father. He needs me. You don't know . . . Let me go."

"I won't! Not until you—"

"I. Said. Let. Me . . ." His teeth were clenched. His

face was rigid. Jill felt his hand—his good hand—climb up her chest and push at her savagely.

She clung to him harder, crying, "No! What are you doing? Talk to me!"

She pulled him towards her, but he swung away. He jerked free and as he did so, their positions shifted precariously. He was now above her. She was below. And so she blocked him, blocked his passage to Gideon and his re-entry into a life she could not afford to understand.

Both of them were panting. The smell of their sweat was rank in the air. "That's why, isn't it?" Jill demanded. "I want to hear it from you, Richard."

But instead of replying, he gave an inarticulate cry. Before she could move to safety, he was trying to get past her. He used his good arm against her breasts. She backed away in reflex. She lost her footing. In an instant she was tumbling down the stairs.

TWENTY-EIGHT

RICHARD HEARD only the breath in his ears. She fell and he watched her and he heard banisters cracking when she hit them. And the sheer weight of her body increased her velocity, so even at the meagre excuse for a landing—that single inadequate slightly wider step that Jill so hated—she continued to hurtle towards the ground floor.

It didn't happen in a second. It happened in an arc of time so wide and so long that forever seemed inadequate for it. And every second that passed was a second in which Gideon, a Gideon able-bodied and unhampered by a plaster cast enclosing his leg from foot to knee, gained more distance from his father. But even more than distance, he gained certainty as well. And that could not be allowed.

Richard descended the stairs as quickly as he could. At the bottom, Jill lay sprawled and motionless. When he reached her, her eyelids—looking blue in the faint light from the entry windows—fluttered, and her lips parted in a moan.

"Mummy?" she whispered.

Her clothing rucked up, her great huge stomach was obscenely exposed. Her coat spread above her head like a monstrous fan.

"Mummy?" she whispered again. Then she groaned. And then cried out and arched her back.

Richard moved to her head. Furiously, he searched through the pockets of the coat. He'd seen her put her keys in the coat, hadn't he? God damn it, he'd *seen* her. He had to find those keys. If he didn't, Gideon would be gone and he had to find him, had to speak to him, had to make him know. . . .

There were no keys. Richard cursed. He shoved himself to his feet. He went back to the stairs and began to haul himself furiously upwards. Below him, Jill cried out, "Catherine," and Richard pulled on the stair rail and breathed like a runner and thought about how he could stop his son.

Inside the flat, he looked for Jill's bag. It was by the sofa, lying on the floor. He scooped it up. He wrestled with its maddening clasp. His hands were shaking. His fingers were clumsy. He couldn't manage to—

A buzzer went off. He raised his head, looked round the room. But there was nothing. He went back to the bag. He managed to unfasten the clasp, and he jerked the bag open. He dumped its contents onto the sofa.

A buzzer went off. He ignored it. He pawed through lipsticks, powders, chequebook, purse, crumpled tissues, pens, a small notebook, and there they were. Hooked together by the familiar chrome ring: five keys, two brass, three silver. One for her flat, one for his, one for the family home in Wiltshire, and two for the Humber, ignition and boot. He grabbed them.

A buzzer went off. Long, loud, insistent this time. Demanding immediate acknowledgment.

He cursed, located the buzzing at its source. The front bell on the street. Gideon? God, Gideon? But he had his own key. He wouldn't ring.

The buzzing continued. Richard ignored it. He made for the door.

The buzzing faded. The buzzing stopped. In his ears, Richard heard only his breathing. It sounded like the shriek of lost souls, and pain began to accompany it, searing up his right leg and, simultaneously, burning and throbbing from right hand to shoulder. His side began to ache with the exertion. He didn't seem able to catch his breath.

At the top of the stairs, he paused, looked down. His heart was pounding. His chest was heaving. He drew in air, stale and damp.

He began to descend. He clutched on to the rail. Jill hadn't moved. Could she? Would she? It hardly mattered. Not with Gideon on the run.

"Mummy? Will you help?" Her voice was faint. But Mummy was not here. Mummy could not help.

But Daddy was. Daddy could. He would always be there. Not as in the past, that figure cloaked by an artful madness that came and went and stood between Daddy and yes my son you are my son. But Daddy in the present who could not did not would not fail because yes my son you are my son. You, what you do, what you're capable of doing. All of it you. You are my son.

Richard reached the landing.

Below him, he heard the entry door open.

He called out, "Gideon?"

"Bloody sodding hell!" came a woman's reply.

A squat creature in a navy pea jacket seemed to fling herself at Jill. Behind her came a raincoated figure whom Richard Davies recognised only too well. He held a credit card in his hand, the means by which he'd gained access through the warped old door to Braemar Mansions.

"Good God," Lynley said, dashing over to kneel by Jill as well. "Phone an ambulance, Havers." Then he raised his head.

At once his eyes came to rest on Richard, midway down the stairs, Jill's car keys in his hand.

HAVERS RODE WITH Jill Foster to hospital. Lynley took Richard Davies to the nearest police station. This turned out to be on the Earl's Court Road, the same station from which Malcolm Webberly had departed more than twenty years ago on the evening he was assigned to investigate the suspicious drowning of Sonia Davies.

If Richard Davies was aware of the irony involved therein, he didn't mention it. Indeed, he said nothing, as was his right, when Lynley gave him the official caution. The duty solicitor was brought in to advise him, but the only advice Davies asked for was how he could get a message to his son.

"I must speak to Gideon," he said to the solicitor. "Gideon Davies. You've heard of him. The violinist . . . ?"

Other than that, he had nothing to say. He would stand by his original story, given to Lynley during earlier interviews. He knew his rights, and the police had nothing on which to build a case against the father of Gideon Davies.

What they had, however, was the Humber, and Lynley went back to Cornwall Gardens with the official team to oversee the acquisition of that vehicle. As Winston Nkata had predicted, what damage the car had sustained in striking two—and probably three—individuals was centred round its front chrome bumper, which was fairly mangled. But this was something that any adroit defence lawyer would be able to argue away, and consequently Lynley was not depending upon it to build a case against Richard Davies. What he was depending upon and what that same adroit barrister would find difficult to discount was trace evidence both beneath the bumper and upon the undercarriage of the Humber. For it was hardly possible that Davies could strike Kathleen Waddington and Malcolm Webberly and run over his former wife three times and leave not a deposit of blood, a fragment of skin, or the kind of hair they desperately needed—hair with human scalp attached to it—on the underside of the car. To get rid of that sort of evidence, Davies would have had to think of that possibility. And Lynley was betting that he hadn't done so. No killer, he knew from long experience, ever thought of everything.

He phoned the news to DCI Leach and asked him to pass the message along to AC Hillier. He would wait in Cornwall Gardens to see the Humber safely off the street, he said, after which he'd fetch Eugenie Davies' computer, as had been his original destination. Did DCI Leach still wish him to fetch that computer?

He did, Leach told him. Despite the arrest, Lynley was still out of order for having taken it and it needed to be logged among the belongings of the victim. "Anything else you lifted, while we're at it?" Leach asked shrewdly.

Lynley replied there was nothing else belonging to Eugenie Davies that he had taken, nothing at all. And he was content with the truth of this answer. For he had come to understand for better or worse that the words born of passion which a man puts on paper and sends to a woman—indeed, even those words that he speaks—are on loan to her only, for whatever length of time serves their purpose. The words themselves always belong to the man.

"HE DIDN'T PUSH me," was what Jill Foster said to Barbara Havers in the ambulance. "You mustn't think that he pushed me." Her voice was faint, a weak murmur only, and her lower body was soiled from the pool of urine, water, and blood that had been spreading out beneath her when Barbara knelt by her side at the foot of the stairs. But that was all she was able to say, because pain was taking her, or at least that was how it seemed to Barbara as she heard Jill cry out and she watched the paramedic monitor the woman's vital signs and listened to him say to the driver, "Hit the sirens, Cliff," which was explanation enough of Jill Foster's condition.

"The baby?" Barbara asked the medic in a low voice.

He cast her a look, said nothing, and moved his gaze to the IV bag he'd fixed to a pole above his patient.

Even with the siren, the ride to the nearest hospital with a casualty ward seemed endless to Barbara. But once they arrived, the response was immediate and gratifying. The paramedics trundled their charge inside the building at a run. There, she was met by a swarm of personnel, who whisked her away, calling out for equipment, for phone calls to be made to Obstetrics, for obscure drugs and arcane procedures with names that camouflaged their purposes.

"Is she going to make it?" Barbara asked anyone who would listen. "She's in labour, right? She's okay? The baby?"

"This is not how babies are intended to get born," was the only reply she was able to obtain.

She remained in Casualty, pacing the waiting area, till Jill Foster was taken in a rush to an operating theatre. "She's been through enough trauma," was the explanation she was given and "Are you family?" was the reason that nothing else was revealed. Barbara couldn't have said why she felt it was important for her to know that the woman was going to be all right. She put it down to an unusual sisterhood she found herself feeling for Jill Foster. It had not, after all, been so many months since Barbara herself had been whisked away by an ambulance after her own encounter with a killer.

She didn't believe that Richard Davies had not pushed Jill Foster down the stairs. But that was something to be sorted out later, once a recovery period gave the other woman time to learn what else her fiancé had been up to. And she *would* recover, Barbara learned within the hour. She'd been delivered of a daughter: healthy despite her precipitate entry into the world.

Barbara felt she could leave at that point, and she was doing so—indeed, she was out in front of the hospital and sussing out what buses, if any, served Fulham Palace Road—when she saw that she was standing in front of Charing Cross Hospital, where Superintendent Webberly was a patient. She ducked back inside.

On the eleventh floor, she waylaid a nurse just outside the intensive care ward. *Critical* and *unchanged* were the words the nurse used to describe the superintendent's condition, from which Barbara inferred that he was still in a coma, still on life support, and still in so much danger of so many further complications that praying for his recovery seemed as risky a business as thinking about the possibility of his death. When people were struck by cars, when they sustained injuries to the brain, more often than not they emerged from the crisis radically altered. Barbara didn't know if she wished such a change upon her superior officer. She didn't want him to die. She dreaded the thought of it. But she couldn't imagine him caught up in months or years of torturous convalescence.

She said to the nurse, "Is his family with him? I'm one of the officers investigating what happened. I've news for them. If they'd like to hear it, that is."

The nurse eyed Barbara doubtfully. Barbara sighed and fished out her warrant card. The nurse squinted at it and said, "Wait here, then," leaving Barbara waiting to see what would happen next.

Barbara expected AC Hillier to emerge from the ward, but instead it was Webberly's daughter who came to greet her. Miranda looked just about done in, but she smiled and said, "Barbara! Hello! How very good of you to come. You can't still be on duty at this hour."

Barbara said, "We've made an arrest. Will you tell your dad? I mean, I know he can't hear you or anything . . . Still, you know . . ."

"Oh, but he can hear," Miranda said.

Barbara's hopes rose. "He's come out of it?"

"No. Not that. But the doctors say that people in comas can hear what's being said round them. And he'll certainly want to know that you've caught who hit him, won't he?"

"How is he?" Barbara asked. "I talked to a nurse,

but I couldn't get much. Just that there wasn't any change yet."

Miranda smiled, but it seemed a response that was generated to soothe Barbara's worries more than a reflection of what the girl herself was feeling. "There isn't, really. But he hasn't had another heart attack, which everyone considers a very good sign. So far he's been stable, and we're . . . well, we're very hopeful. Yes. We're quite hopeful."

Her eyes were too bright, too frightened. Barbara wanted to tell Miranda that she had no need to play the part for her sake, but she understood that the girl's attempt at optimism was more for herself than anyone else. She said, "Then I'll be hopeful as well. We all will. D'you need anything?"

"Oh gosh, no. At least, I don't think so. I did come from Cambridge in a terrible rush and I've left a paper behind that I have due for a supervision. But that's not till next week and perhaps by then . . . Well, perhaps."

"Yeah. Perhaps."

Footsteps coming along the corridor diverted their attention. They turned to see AC Hillier and his wife approaching. Between them, they were supporting Frances Webberly.

Miranda cried out, "Mum!"

"Randie," Frances said. "Randie, darling . . ."

Miranda said again, "Mum! I'm so glad. Oh, *Mum.*" She went to her and hugged her long and hard. And then, perhaps feeling a weight lifting off her that she should never have had to bear in the first place, she began to cry. She said, "The doctors said if he has another heart attack, he might . . . He really might—"

"Hush. Yes," Frances Webberly said, her cheek pressed against her daughter's hair. "Take me in to see Daddy, won't you, dear? We'll sit with him together."

When Miranda and her mother had gone through the door, AC Hillier said to his wife, "Stay with them, Laura. Please. Make sure . . ." and nodded meaningfully. Laura Hillier followed them.

The AC eyed Barbara with a degree less than his usual level of disapproval. She became acutely aware of her clothing. She'd been doing her best to stay out of his way for months now, and when she'd known she'd be running into him, she'd always managed to dress with that expectation in mind. But now . . . She felt her high-top red trainers take on neon proportions, and the green stirrup trousers she'd donned that morning seemed only marginally less inappropriate.

She said, "We've made the arrest, sir. I thought I'd come to tell—"

"Leach phoned me." Hillier walked to a door across the corridor and inclined his head at it. She was meant to follow. When they were inside what turned out to be a waiting room, he went to a sofa and sank into it. For the first time, Barbara noted how tired he looked, and she realised he'd been on family duty since the middle of the previous night. Her guard slipped a notch at this thought. Hillier had always seemed superhuman.

He said, "Good work, Barbara. Both of you."

She said cautiously, "Thank you, sir," and waited for what would happen next.

He said, "Sit."

She said, "Sir," and although she'd have preferred to be off on her way home, she went to a chair of limited comfort and perched on its edge. In a better world, she thought, AC Hillier would at this moment of emotional *in extremis* see the error of his ways. He'd look at her, recognise her finer qualities—one of which was decidedly not her fashion sense—and he'd summarily acknowledge them. He'd elevate her on the spot to her previous professional position and that would be the end of the punishment he'd inflicted upon her at the end of the summer.

But this was not a better world, and AC Hillier did none of that. He merely said, "He might not make it. We're pretending otherwise—especially round Frances, for what little good it's doing—but it's got to be faced."

Barbara didn't know what to say, so she murmured, "Bloody hell," because that's what she felt: bloody, bowed, and consigned to helplessness. And sentenced, with the rest of mankind, to interminable waiting.

"I've known him ages," Hillier said. "There've been times when I haven't much liked him and God knows I've never understood him, but he's been there for years, a presence that I could somehow depend upon, just to . . . to *be* there. And I find I don't like the thought of his going."

"Perhaps he won't go," Barbara said. "Perhaps he'll recover."

Hillier shot her a look. "You don't recover from something like this. He may live. But recover? No. He'll not be the same. He'll not recover." He crossed one leg over the other, which was the first time Barbara noticed *his* clothes, which were what he'd thrown on the night before and had never got round to changing during the day. And she saw him for once not as superior but as human being: in hound's-tooth and Tattersall, with a pullover that had a hole in the cuff. He said, "Leach tells me it was all done to divert suspicion."

"Yes. That's what DI Lynley and I think."

"What a waste." And then he peered at her. "There's nothing else?"

"What do you mean?"

"No other reason behind Malcolm's being hit?"

She met his gaze steadily and read the question behind it, the one that asked if what AC Hillier assumed, believed, or wanted to believe about the Webberly marriage and its partners therein was really true. And Barbara didn't intend to give the assistant commissioner any part of that piece of information. She said, "No other reason. Turns out the superintendent was just easy for Davies to track down."

"That's what you *think*," Hillier said. "Leach told me Davies himself isn't talking."

"I expect he'll talk eventually," Barbara replied. "He knows better than most where keeping mum can get you."

"I've made Lynley acting superintendent till this is sorted out," Hillier said. "You know that, don't you?"

"Dee Harriman passed along the word." Barbara drew in a breath and held it, hoping, wishing, and dreaming for what did not then come.

Instead, he said, "Winston Nkata does good work, doesn't he, all things considered."

What things? she wondered. But she said, "Yes, sir. He does good work."

"He'll be looking at a promotion soon."

"He'll be glad of that, sir."

"Yes. I expect he will." Hillier looked at her long, then he looked away. His eyes closed. His head rested back against the sofa.

Barbara sat there in silence, wondering what she was meant to do. She finally settled on saying, "You ought to go home and get some sleep, sir."

"I intend to," Hillier replied. "We all should, Constable Havers."

IT WAS HALF past ten when Lynley parked on Lawrence Street and walked back round the corner to the St. James house. He hadn't phoned ahead to let them know he was coming, and on the way down from the Earl's Court Road, he'd determined that if the ground floor lights in the house were off, he wouldn't disturb its occupants. This was, he knew, in large part cowardice. The time was fast approaching when he was going to have to deal with harvesting the crop he'd long-ago sown, and he didn't particularly want to do that. But he'd seen how his past was seeping insidiously into his present, and he knew that he owed the future he wanted an exorcism that could only be managed if he spoke. Still, he would have liked to put it off and as he rounded the corner, he hoped for darkness in the house's windows as a sign that further procrastination was acceptable.

He had no such luck. Not only was the light above the front door blazing, but the windows of St. James's study cast yellow shafts onto the wrought iron fence that edged the property.

He mounted the steps and rang the bell. Inside the house, the dog barked in response. She was still barking when Deborah St. James opened the door.

She said, "Tommy! Good Lord, you're *soaked*. What a night. Have you forgotten your umbrella? Peach, here. Stop it at once." She scooped the barking little dachshund from the floor and tucked her under her arm. "Simon's not in," she confided, "and Dad's watching a documentary about dormice, don't ask me why. So she's taking guard duty more seriously than usual. Peach, none of your growling, now."

Lynley stepped inside and removed his wet coat. He hung it on the rack to the right of the door. He extended his hand to the dog for purposes of olfactory identification, and Peach ceased both barking and growling and indicated her willingness to accept his obeisance in the form of a few scratches behind her ears.

"She's impossibly spoiled," Deborah said.

"She's doing her job. You shouldn't just open the

door like that at night anyway, Deb. It's not very wise."

"I always assume that if a burglar's calling, Peach will go for his ankles before he can get into the first room. Not that we have much worth taking, although I wouldn't mind seeing the last of that hideous thing with peacock feathers that sits on the sideboard in the dining room." She smiled. "How *are* you, Tommy? I'm in here. Working."

She led him into the study where, he saw, she was in the process of wrapping the pictures she'd selected for her December show. The floor was spread with framed photographs yet to be protected by plastic, along with a bottle of window cleaner that she'd been using to see to the glass that covered them, a roll of kitchen towels, myriad sheets of bubble-wrap, tape, and scissors. She'd lit the gas fire in the room, and Peach repaired to her ramshackle basket that stood before it.

"It's an obstacle course," Deborah said, "but if you can find your way to the trolley, have some more of Simon's whisky."

"Where is he?" Lynley asked. He worked his way round her photographs and went to the drinks trolley.

"He went to a lecture at the Royal Geographic Society: somebody's journey somewhere and a book signing to follow. I think there are polar bears involved. In the lecture, that is."

Lynley smiled. He tossed down a hefty gulp of the whisky. It would do for courage. To give himself time for the spirits to work in his bloodstream, he said, "We've made an arrest in the case I've been working on."

"It didn't take you long. You know, you're completely suited to police work, Tommy. Who would ever have thought it, the way you grew up?"

She rarely mentioned his upbringing. A child of privilege born to another child of privilege, he'd long chafed beneath the burdens of blood, family history, and his duties to both. The thought of it now— family, useless titles that were every year rendered more meaningless, velvet capes trimmed in ermine, and more than two hundred and fifty years of lineage always determining what his next move should be— served as a stark reminder of what he had come to tell her and why. Still, he stalled, saying, "Yes. Well. One always has to move quickly in a homicide. If the trail begins to cool, you stand less chance of making an arrest. I've come for that computer, by the way. The one I left with Simon. Is it still up in the lab? May I fetch it, Deb?"

"Of course," she said, although she gave him a curious glance, either at his choice of subject— considering her husband's line of work, she was more than aware of the need for speed in a murder investigation—or the tone with which he spoke about it, which was too hearty to be at all believable. She said, "Go on up. You don't mind my carrying on down here, do you?"

He said, "Not at all," and made his escape, taking his time to trudge up the stairs to the top floor of the house. There, he flipped on the lights in the lab and found the computer exactly where St. James had left it. He unplugged it, cradled it in his arms, and went back down the stairs. He placed it by the front door and considered calling out a cheerful goodnight and going on his way. It was late, after all, and the conversation that he needed to have with Deborah St. James could wait.

Just as he was thinking of another postponement, though, Deborah came to the study door and observed him. She said, "All's not right with your world. There's nothing wrong with Helen, is there?"

And Lynley found at last that he couldn't avoid it no matter how much he wanted to. He said, "No. There's nothing wrong with Helen."

"I'm glad," she said. "The first months of pregnancy can be awful."

He opened his mouth to reply but lost the words. Then he found them again. He said, "So you know."

She smiled. "I couldn't help knowing. After . . . what is it, now? seven pregnancies? . . . I've become pretty well-attuned to the signs. I never got far in them—the pregnancies, I mean . . . well, you know that—but far enough to feel that I'd *never* get over being sick."

Lynley swallowed. Deborah went back into the study. He followed her, found the glass of whisky where he'd left it, and took a momentary refuge in its depths. He said when he could, "We know how you want . . . And how you've tried . . . You and Simon . . ."

"Tommy," she said firmly, "I'm pleased for you. You mustn't ever think that my situation—Simon's and mine . . . well, no . . . mine, really—would ever keep me from feeling happiness for yours. I know what this means to you both, and the fact that I'm not able to carry a baby . . . Well, it's painful, yes. Of *course* it's painful. But I don't want the rest of the world to wallow round in my grief. And I surely don't want to put anyone else in my situation just for the company."

She knelt among her photographs. She seemed to have dismissed the subject, but Lynley could not because, as far as he was concerned, they had not yet come to the real topic. He went to sit opposite her, in the leather chair St. James used when he was in the room. He said, "Deb," and when she looked up, "There's something else."

Her green eyes darkened. "What else?"

"Santa Barbara."

"Santa Barbara?"

"That summer when you were eighteen, when you were at school at the institute. That year when I made those four trips to see you: October, January, May, and July. July, especially, when we drove the coastal road into Oregon."

She said nothing, but her face blanched, so he knew that she understood where he was heading. Even as he headed there, he wished that something would happen to stop him so he wouldn't have to admit to her what he could hardly bear to face himself.

"You said it was the car on that trip," he told her.

"You weren't used to so much driving. Or perhaps it was the food, you said. Or the change in climate. Or the heat when it was hot outside or the cool when it was cold indoors. You weren't used to being in and out of air-conditioning so much, and aren't Americans addicted to their air conditioners? I listened to every excuse you made, and I chose to believe you. But all the time . . ." He didn't wish to say it, would have given anything to avoid it. But at the last moment he forced himself to admit what he'd long pushed from his mind. "I knew."

She lowered her gaze. He saw her reach out for the scissors and bubble-wrap, pulling one of her pictures towards her. She did nothing with it.

"After that trip, I waited for you to tell me," he said. "What I thought was that when you told me, we'd decide together what we wanted to do. We're in love, so we'll marry, I told myself. As soon as Deb admits that she's pregnant."

"Tommy . . ."

"Let me go on. This has been years in the making, and now we're here, I have to see it through."

"Tommy, you can't—"

"I always knew. I think I knew the night that it happened. That night in Montecito."

She said nothing.

He said, "Deborah. Please tell me."

"It's no longer important."

"It *is* important to me."

"Not after all this time."

"Yes. After all this time. Because I did nothing.

Don't you see? I knew, but I did nothing. I just left you to face it alone, whatever 'it' was going to be. You were the woman I loved, the woman I wanted, and I ignored what was happening because . . ." He became aware that still she wasn't looking at him, her face fully hidden by the angle of her head and the way her hair fell round her shoulders. But he didn't stop speaking because he finally understood what had motivated him then, what was indeed the source of his shame. "Because I couldn't sort out how to work it," he said. "Because I hadn't planned it to happen like that and God help anything that stood in the way of how I planned my life to work out. And as long as you said nothing about it, I could let the entire situation slide, let everything slide, let my whole damned life slide right on by without the least inconvenience to me. Ultimately, I could even pretend that there was no baby. I could tell myself that surely if there was, you'd have said something. And when you didn't, I allowed myself to believe I'd been mistaken. When all the time I knew at heart that I hadn't. So I said nothing throughout July. In August. September. And whatever you faced when you finally made your decision to act, you faced alone."

"It was my responsibility."

"It was ours. Our child. Our responsibility. But I left you there. And I'm sorry."

"There's no need to be."

"There is. Because when you and Simon married, when you lost all those babies, what I had to think was that if you'd had that first child, ours—"

"Tommy, no!" She raised her head.

"—then none of this would have happened to you."

"That's not how it was," she said. "Believe me. That's *not* how it is. You've no need to punish yourself over this. You've no obligation to me."

"Now, perhaps not. But then I did."

"No. And it wouldn't have mattered, anyway. You could have spoken about it, yes. You could have phoned. You could have returned on the very next plane, and confronted me with what you believed was going on. But nothing would have changed with all that. Oh, we might have married in a rush or something. You might even have stayed with me in Santa Barbara so that I could finish at the institute. But at the end of it all, there still wouldn't have been a baby. Not mine and yours. Not mine and Simon's. Not mine and anyone's as it turns out."

"What do you mean?"

She leaned back on her heels, setting the scissors and the tape to one side. She said, "Just what I say. There wouldn't have been a baby no matter what I did. I just didn't wait long enough to find that out." She blinked rapidly and turned her head to look hard at the bookshelves. After a moment, she returned her gaze to him. "I would have lost our baby as well, Tommy. It's something called balanced translocation."

"What is?"

"My . . . what do I call it? My problem? Condition? Situation?" She offered him a shaky smile.

"Deborah, what are you telling me?"

"That I can't have a baby. I'll never be able to have one. It's incredible to think that a single chromosome could hold such power, but there you have it." She pressed her fingers to her chest, saying, "Phenotype: normal in every way. Genotype . . . Well, when one has 'excessive foetal wastage'—that's what they call it . . . all the miscarriages . . . isn't that obscene?—there's got to be a medical reason. In my case, it's genetics: One arm of the twenty-first chromosome is upside down."

"My God," he said. "Deb, I'm—"

"Simon doesn't know yet," she said quickly, as if to stop him from going on. "And I'd rather he not just now. I did promise him that I'd let a full year go by before having any more tests and I'd like him to think I've kept that promise. I intended to. But last June . . . that case you were working on when the little girl died . . . ? I just had to know after that, Tommy. I don't know why except that I was . . . well, I was so struck by her death. Its uselessness. The terrible shame and waste of it, this sweet little life gone . . . So I went back to the doctor then. But Simon doesn't know."

"Deborah." Lynley said her name quietly. "I am so terribly sorry."

Her eyes filled at that. She blinked the tears back furiously, then shook her head just as furiously when he reached out to her. "No. It's fine. I'm fine. I mean, I'm all *right*. Most of the time I don't think about it. And we're going through the process of adoption. We've filled out so many applications . . . all this paperwork . . . that we're *bound* to . . . at some time. And we're trying in other countries as well. I just wish it could be different for Simon's sake. It's selfish and I know it, it's all sorts of ego, but I wanted us to create a child together. I think he wanted . . . would have liked that as well, but he's too good to say so directly." And then she smiled despite one large tear that she couldn't contain. "You're not to think I'm not all right, Tommy. I *am*. I've learned that things work out the way they're meant to work out no matter what we want, so it's best to keep our wants to a minimum and to thank our stars, our luck, or our gods that we've been given as much as we have."

"But this doesn't absolve me from my part in what happened," he told her. "Back then. In Santa Barbara. My going off and never saying a word. This doesn't absolve me of that, Deb."

"No, this doesn't," she agreed. "It doesn't at all. But, Tommy, you must believe me. I do."

HELEN WAS WAITING for him when he got home. She was already in bed with a book lying open in her lap. But she'd dozed off while she was reading, and her head rested back against the pillows she'd piled behind her, her hair a dark blur against white cotton.

Quietly, Lynley crossed to his wife and stood gazing down at her. She was light and shadow, perfectly omnipotent and achingly vulnerable. He sat on the edge of the bed.

She didn't start as some might have done, roused

suddenly from sleep by someone's presence. Instead, her eyes opened and were immediately focused on him with preternatural comprehension. "Frances finally went to him," she said as if they'd been talking all along. "Laura Hillier phoned with the news."

"I'm glad," he said. "It's what she needed to do. How is he?"

"There's no change. But he's holding on."

Lynley sighed and nodded. "Anyway, it's over. We've made an arrest."

"I know. Barbara phoned me as well. She said I should tell you all's right with the world at her end of things. She would have rung you on the mobile, but she wanted to check in with me."

"That was good of her."

"She's a very good person. She says Hillier's planning to give Winston a promotion, by the way. Did you know that, Tommy?"

"Is he really?"

"She says Hillier wanted to make sure she knew. Although, she says, he complimented her first. On the case. He complimented both of you."

"Yes. Well, that sounds like Hillier. Never say 'well done' without pulling the rug out just in case you're feeling cocky."

"She'd like her rank back. But, of course, you know that."

"And I'd like the power to give it to her." He picked up the book she'd been reading. He turned it over and examined its title. *A Lesson Before Dying.* How apt, he thought.

She said, "I found it among your novels in the library. I've not got far, I'm afraid. I dropped off to sleep. Lord. Why have I become so exhausted? If this goes on all nine months, by the end of the pregnancy I'll be sleeping twenty hours a day. And the rest of the time I'll spend being sick. It's supposed to be more romantic than this. At least, that's what I was always led to believe."

"I've told Deborah." He explained why he'd gone to Chelsea in the first place, adding, "She already knew, as things turned out."

"Did she really?"

"Yes. Well, obviously, she knows the signs. She's very pleased, Helen. You were right to want to share the news with her. She was only waiting for you to tell her."

Helen searched his face then, perhaps hearing something in his tone that seemed misplaced, given the situation. And something *was* there. He could hear it himself. But what it was had nothing to do with Helen and even less to do with the future Lynley intended to share with her.

She said, "And you, Tommy? Are *you* pleased? Oh, you've said that you are, but what else *can* you say? Husband, gentleman, and a party to the process, you can hardly go tearing from the room with your head in your hands. But I've had the feeling that something's gone badly wrong between us lately. I didn't have that feeling before we made the baby, so it's seemed to me that perhaps you aren't as ready as you thought you were."

"No," he said. "Everything's right, Helen. And I *am* pleased. More than I can say."

"I suppose we could have done with a longer period of adjustment together all the same," she said.

Lynley thought of what Deborah had said to him, about the source of happiness coming from what's given. "We have the rest of our lives to adjust," he told his wife. "If we don't seize the moment, the moment's gone."

He set the novel on her bedside table then. He bent and kissed her forehead. He said, "I love you, darling," and she pulled him down to her mouth and parted her lips against his. She murmured, "Talking of seizing the moment . . ." and she returned his kiss in a way, he realised, that connected them as they hadn't been connected since she'd first told him she was pregnant.

He felt a stirring for her then, that mixture of lust and love that always left him at once both weak and resolute, determined to be her master and at the same time completely within her power. He laid a trail of kisses down her neck to her shoulders, and he felt her shiver as he eased the straps of her nightgown gently down her arms. As he cupped her bare breasts and bent to them, her fingers went to his tie and unknotted it and began to work on the buttons of his shirt.

He looked up at her then, passion suddenly tempered by concern. "What about the baby?" he asked. "Is it safe?"

She smiled and drew him into her arms. "The baby, darling Tommy, will be fine."

TWENTY-NINE

WINSTON NKATA came out of the bathroom and found his mother seated beneath a standard lamp whose shade had been removed to give her better light in which to work. What she was working on was her tatting. She'd taken a class in this form of lace-making with a group of ladies from her church, and she was determined to perfect the art. Nkata didn't know why. When he'd asked her the reason she'd begun messing about with cotton reels, shuttles, and knots, she said, "Keeps my hands busy, Jewel. And just 'cause something's not done much any longer doesn't make it worth chucking out."

Nkata thought it actually had to do with his father. Benjamin Nkata snored so ferociously that it was impossible for anyone to sleep in the same room with him unless they managed to drop off first and lie like the dead once they got there. If Alice Nkata was up past her usual retiring time of ten forty-five, it stood to reason that she was practising her lacework in lieu of suffocating her snorting and bellowing husband in sheer insomniac frustration.

Nkata could tell that was the case this night. The moment he stepped from the bathroom, he was greeted not only with the sight of his mother at her lace but also with the sound of his father at his dreams. It sounded as if bears were being baited inside his parents' bedroom.

Alice Nkata looked up from her work, over the top of her half-moon glasses. She was wearing her ancient yellow chenille dressing gown, and her son frowned with displeasure when he saw this.

He said, "Where's that one I got you for Mothering Sunday?"

"Where's what one?" his mother asked.

"You know what one. That new dressing gown."

"Too nice to sit round in, Jewel," she said. And before he could protest that dressing gowns weren't intended to be saved just in case one was invited to tea with the Queen so why wasn't she *using* the one he'd paid two weeks' wages to buy her at Liberty's, she said, "Where you going this hour?"

"Thought I'd go round to see what's up with the super," he told her. "Case got resolved—th' inspector nabbed the bloke who made the hits—but the super's still out and . . ." He shrugged. "I don't know. Seemed like it's the right thing to do."

"At this hour?" Alice Nkata asked, casting a look at the tiny Wedgwood clock on the table beside her, a gift presented by her son at Christmas. "Don't know of any hospital round here that likes having visitors in the middle of the night."

"Not the middle of the night, Mum."

"You know what I mean."

"Can't sleep anyway. Too wired up. If I c'n give a hand to the family . . . Like I said, it seems the right thing to do."

She eyed him. "Dressed nice enough to be going to his wedding," she noted acerbically.

Or his funeral, for that matter, Nkata thought. But he didn't like even getting *close* to that idea with regard to Webberly, so he made himself think of something else: like the reasons he'd set his sights on Katja Wolff as the killer of Eugenie Davies as well as the driver who'd injured the superintendent so grievously, like what it actually *meant* that Katja Wolff was not guilty of either offence.

He said, "Nice to show respect where respect's due, Mum. You brought up a boy knows what's called for."

His mother said, "Hmph," but he could tell she was pleased. She said, "Mind how you go, then. You see any no-hair white boys in army boots hanging 'bout on the corner, you give them a wide berth. You walk th' other way. I mean what I say."

"Right, Mum."

"No 'Right, Mum' like I don't know what I'm talking about."

"Don't worry," he said. "I know that you do."

He kissed her on the top of the head and left the flat. He felt a twinge of guilt at having fibbed—he hadn't done that since adolescence—but he told himself it was all in a good cause. It was late; there would have been too much explaining to do; he needed to be on his way.

Outside, the rain was making its usual mess of the estate where the Nkatas lived. Pools of water had collected along the outdoor passages between the flats, deposited on the unprotected uppermost level by the wind and seeping down to the other levels through cracks between the floor of the passages and the building itself that had long existed and not been repaired. The staircase was consequently slick and dangerous, also as usual, because the rubber treads on the individual steps had been worn away—or sometimes had been cut away by kids with too much time on their hands and too little to do to fill it—leaving bare the concrete that comprised them. And down below at what went for the garden, the grass and flower beds of ancient times were now an expanse of mud across which lager cans, take-away food wrappers, disposable nappies, and other assorted human detritus made an eloquent statement about the level of frustration and despair that people sank to when they believed— or their experience taught them—that their options were limited by the colour of their skin.

Nkata had suggested to his parents more than once that they move house, indeed that he would *help* them move house. But they had refused his every offer. If people set about digging up their roots first chance they had, Alice Nkata explained to her son, the whole plant could die. Besides, by staying right where they were and by having one son who'd managed to escape what could indeed have ruined him forever, they were setting an example for everyone else. No need to think their own lives had limits when among them lived someone who showed them that it wasn't so.

"Besides," Alice Nkata said, "we got Brixton Station close. And Loughborough Junction as well. That suits me fine, Jewel. Suits your dad as well."

So they stayed, his parents. And he stayed with them. Living on his own was as yet too expensive, and even if it weren't, he wanted to remain in his parents' flat. He afforded them a source of pride that they needed, and he himself needed to give that to them.

His car was gleaming under a streetlamp, washed clean by the rain. He climbed inside and belted himself in.

The drive was a short one. A few twists and turns put him on the Brixton Road, where he headed north, cruising in the direction of Kennington. He parked in front of the agricultural centre, where he sat for a moment, looking across the street through the sheets of rain that the wind was waving between his car and Yasmin Edwards' flat.

He'd been propelled to Kennington in part by the knowledge that he'd done wrong. He'd told himself earlier that he'd done this wrong for all the right reasons, and he believed there was a lot of truth to the assurance. He was fairly certain that Inspector Lynley might have used the same ploys with Yasmin Edwards and her lover, and he was absolutely positive that Barbara Havers would have done the same or more. But of course, they'd have had intentions a good sight nobler than his own had been, and beneath their behaviour would not have run the strong current of an aggression that was inconsistent with their invasion into the women's lives.

Nkata wasn't sure where the aggression came from or what it indicated about him as an officer of the police. He only knew that he felt it and that he needed to lose it before he could move with absolute comfort again.

He shoved open the car door, carefully locked it behind him, and dashed across the street to the block of flats. The lift door was closed. He began to ring the buzzer for Yasmin Edwards' flat, but he stopped with his finger suspended above the appropriate button. Instead, he rang the flat beneath it and when a man's voice asked who it was, he gave his name, said he'd been phoned about some vandalism in the car park, and would Mr.—he looked at the list of names quickly—Mr. Houghton be willing to look at some pictures to see if he recognised any faces among a group of youths arrested in the vicinity? Mr. Houghton agreed to do so and buzzed the lift open. Nkata rode to Yasmin Edwards' floor with a pang of guilt for the manner in which he'd gained access, but he told himself he'd stop below afterwards and apologise to Mr. Houghton for the ruse.

The curtains were shut upon Yasmin Edwards' windows, but a thread of light licked at the bottom of them and behind the door, the sound of television voices spoke. When he knocked, she wisely asked who it was and when he gave his name, he was forced to wait thirty eternal seconds while she made up her mind whether to admit him.

When she had done, she merely opened the door six inches, enough for him to see her in her leggings and her oversized sweater. Red this was, the colour of poppies. She said nothing. She looked at him squarely, her face without the slightest expression, which reminded him inadvertently again of who she was and what she always would be.

He said, "C'n I come in?"

"Why?"

"Talk."

"About?"

"Is she here?"

"What d'you think?"

He heard the door open on the floor beneath them, knew it was Mr. Houghton wondering what had happened to the cop who'd come to show him pictures. He said, "Raining. Cold and damp're getting inside. You let me in and I stay a minute. Five at the most. I swear."

She said, "Dan's asleep. I don't want him waked. He's got school—"

"Yeah. I'll keep my voice low."

She took another moment to make up her mind, but at last she stepped back. She turned from the door and walked to where she'd been before he'd knocked, leaving him to open the door wider and then to close it quietly behind him.

He saw that she was watching a film. In it, Peter Sellers began to walk across water. It was an illusion, of course, the stuff of make-believe but suggestive of possibility nonetheless.

She took up the remote control but did not turn the television off. She merely muted the sound and continued to watch the picture.

He got the message and did not blame her for it. He would be even less welcome when he'd said what he'd come to say.

"We got the hit-and-run driver," he told her. "It wasn't . . . Not Katja Wolff. She had a square alibi, 's things turned out."

"I know her alibi," Yasmin said. "Number Fifty-five."

"Ah." He looked at the television, then at her. She sat straight-backed. She looked like a model. She had a model's fine body, and she would have been perfect wearing trendy clothes for pictures except for her face, the scar on her mouth that made her look fierce and used and angry. He said, "Following leads 's part of the job, Missus Edwards. She had a connection with who got hit, and I couldn't ignore that."

"I 'xpect you did what you had to do."

"You did 's well," he said to her. "That's what I came to say."

"Sure I did," she said. "Grassing's always the thing to do, isn't it?"

"She didn't give you a choice once she lied to me 'bout where she was when that woman was hit. You either went along for the ride and put yourself in danger—'long with your boy—or you told the truth. If she wasn't here, then she was somewhere and f'r all anyone knew about it, that somewhere could've been up in West Hampstead. You couldn't stand by that, keep your mug shut, and take another fall."

"Yeah. Well, Katja wasn't up in West Hampstead, was she? And now we know where she was and why, we c'n both rest easy. I won't be getting into trouble with the cops, I won't be losing Dan into care, and you won't be tossing round in your bed nights, wond'ring how the hell you're goin' t' stick something onto Katja Wolff when she never thought once of doing it."

Nkata found it hard to digest that Yasmin would still defend Katja despite Katja's betrayal of her. But he made himself think before he replied, and he saw that there was sense in what the woman was doing. He was still the enemy in Yasmin Edwards' eyes. Not only was he a copper, which would always put them at odds with each other, he was also the person who'd forced her to see that she was living within a charade, one party to a relationship that existed only in lieu of another, one that was of longer standing to Katja, more desired, and just out of reach.

He said, "No. I wouldn't be tossing in bed 'cause of that."

"Like I say," was her contemptuous reply.

"What I mean," he said, "is I'd still be tossing. But not over that."

"Whatever," she said. She held the remote at the television again. "That all you come to say? That I did the right thing and be happy, Madam, 'cause you're safe from being called an accessory to something someone never did?"

"No," he said. "That's not all I come to say."

"Yeah? Then what else?"

He didn't really know. He wanted to tell her that he'd had to come because his motives in forcing her hand had been mixed from the first. But in saying that, he'd be saying the obvious and telling her what she already knew. And he was more than acutely aware that she'd long ago realised that the motives of every man who looked at her, spoke to her, asked something of her—lithe and warm and decidedly alive—would always be mixed. And he was also more than acutely aware that he didn't want to be counted among those other men.

So he said, "Your boy's on my mind, Missus Edwards."

"Then take him off of your mind."

"Can't," he said, and when she would have made a retort, he went on with, "It's like this. He's got the look of a winner, you know, if he follows a course. But lots out there c'n get in his way."

"You think I don't know it?"

"Didn't say that," he said. "But whether you like me or hate me, I c'n be his friend. I'd like to do that."

"Do what?"

"Be somebody to your boy. He likes me. You c'n see that yourself. I take him out and about now and then, he gets a chance to mix it up with someone who's playing it straight. With a man who's playing it straight, Missus Edwards," he hastened to add. "A boy his age? He needs that pretty bad."

"Why? You had it yourself, you saying?"

"I had it, yeah. Like to pass it along."

She snorted. "Save it for your own kids, man."

"When I have them, sure. I'll pass it to them. In the meanwhile . . ." He sighed. "It's this: I like him, Missus Edwards. When I got the free time, I'd like to spend it with him."

"Doing what?"

"Don't know."

"He doesn't need you."

"Not saying he needs me," Nkata told her. "But he needs someone. A man. You c'n see it. And the way I'm thinking—"

"I don't care what you're thinking." She pressed the button and the sound came on. She raised it a notch lest he miss the message.

He looked in the direction of the bedrooms, wondering if the boy would wake up, would walk into the sitting room, would show by his smile of welcome that everything Winston Nkata was saying was true. But the increase in volume didn't penetrate the closed door, or if it did, to Daniel Edwards it was just another sound in the night.

Nkata said, "You got my card still?"

Yasmin didn't reply, her eyes fastened on the television screen.

Nkata took out another and set it on the coffee

table in front of her. "You ring me if you change your mind," he said. "Or you c'n page me. Anytime. It's okay."

She made no reply, so he left the flat. He closed the door quietly, gently, behind him.

He was below in the car park, crossing its puddle-strewn expanse to reach the street, before he realised that he'd forgotten his promise to himself to stop at Mr. Houghton's flat, show his warrant card, and apologise for the ruse that had gained him admittance. He turned back to do so and looked up at the building.

Yasmin Edwards, he saw, was standing at her window. She was watching him. And she was holding in her hands something he very much wanted to believe was the card he'd given her.

THIRTY

GIDEON WALKED. At first he'd run: up the leafy confines of Cornwall Gardens and across the wet, narrow strip of traffic that was Gloucester Road. He hurtled into Queen's Gate Gardens, then up past the old hotels in the direction of the park. And then mindlessly he ducked to the right and dashed past the Royal College of Music. He hadn't actually known where he was till he'd veered up a little incline and burst out into the well-lit surroundings of the Royal Albert Hall, where an audience was just pouring out of the auditorium's circumference of doors.

There, the irony of the location had hit him, and he'd stopped running. Indeed, he'd stumbled to a complete halt, chest heaving, with the rain pelting him, and not even noticing that his jacket was hanging heavy with the damp upon his shoulders and his trousers were slapping wetly against his shins. Here was the greatest venue for public performance in the land: the most sought-after showplace for anyone's talent. Here, Gideon Davies had first performed as a nine-year-old prodigy with his father and Raphael Robson in attendance, all three of them eager for the opportunity to establish the name Davies in the classical firmament. How appropriate was it, then, that his final flight from Braemar Mansions—from his father, from his father's words and what they did and did not mean—should bring him to the very *raison d'être* of everything that had happened: to Sonia, to Katja Wolff, to his mother, to all of them. And how even more appropriate was it that the very *raison d'être* behind the other *raison d'être*—the audience—did not even know that he was there.

Across the street from the Albert Hall, Gideon watched the crowd raise their umbrellas to the weeping sky. Although he could see their lips moving, he did not hear their excited chatter, that all-too-familiar sound of ravenous culture vultures who were sated for the moment, the happy noise of just the sort of people whose approbation he'd sought. Instead, what he heard were his father's words, like an incantation within his brain: *For God's sake I did it I did it I did it* Believe *what I say I say I say She was* alive *when you left her you left her I held her* down *in the bath the bath I was the one who* drowned *her who drowned her. It wasn't you Gideon my son my* son.

Over and over the words repeated, but they called forth a vision that made a different claim. What he saw was his hands on his sister's small shoulders. What he felt was the water closing over his arms. And above the repetition of his father's declaration, what he heard was the cries of the woman and the man, then the sound of running, the *blam* of doors closing, and the other hoarse cries, then the wail of sirens and the guttural orders of rescue workers going about their business where rescue was futile. And everyone knew that save the workers themselves because they were trained to one job only: maintaining and resuscitating life in the face of anything that stood in life's way.

But *For God's sake I did it I did it I did it Believe what I say I say I say.*

Gideon struggled for the memory that would allow this belief, but what he came up with was the same image as before: his hands on her shoulders and added to that now the sight of her face, her mouth opening and closing and opening and closing and her head turning slowly back and forth.

His father argued that this was a dream because *She was alive when you left her when you left her.* And even more importantly because *I held her down in the bath in the bath.*

Yet the only person who might have confirmed that story—was dead herself, Gideon thought. And what did that mean? What did that tell him?

That she didn't know the truth herself, his father told him insistently, as if he walked at Gideon's side in the wind and the rain. She didn't know because I *never* admitted it, not then when it counted, not then when I saw another far easier way to resolve the situation. And when I finally told her—

She didn't believe you. She knew that I'd done it. And you killed her to keep her from telling me that. She's dead, Dad. She's dead, she's dead.

Yes. All right. Your mother is dead. But she's dead because of me, not because of you. She's dead because of what I'd led her to believe and what I'd forced her into accepting.

Which was what, Dad? *What?* Gideon demanded.

You *know* the answer, his father replied. I let her believe you'd killed your sister. I said *Gideon was in here in here in the bathroom he was holding her down I pulled him off her but my God my God Eugenie she was gone.* And she believed me. And that's why she agreed to the arrangement with Katja: because she thought she was saving you. From an investigation. From a juvenile trial. From a hideous burden that would weigh upon you for the rest of your life. You were Gideon Davies, for the love of God. She wanted to keep you safe from scandal, and I *used* that, Gideon, to keep everyone safe.

Except Katja Wolff.

She *agreed*. For the money.

So she thought that I—

Yes, she thought. She thought, she *thought*. But she did not know. Any more than you know right now. You were not in the room. You were dragged away, and she was taken downstairs. Your mother went to phone for help. And that left me alone with your sister. Don't you see what that means?

But I remember—

You remember what you remember because that's

what happened: You held her down. But holding her down and keeping her down are not the same. And you know that, Gideon. By God, you *know* it.

But I remember—

You remember what you did as far as you did it. I did the rest. I stand guilty of *all* the crimes that were committed. I am the man, after all, who could not bear to have my own daughter Virginia in my life.

No. It was Granddad.

Granddad was simply the excuse I used. I dismissed her, Gideon. I pretended she was dead because I wanted her dead. Don't forget that. Never forget that. You know what it means. You *know* it, Gideon.

But Mother . . . Mother was going to tell me—

Eugenie was going to perpetuate the lie. She was going to tell you what I'd let her *believe* was the truth for years. She was going to explain why she'd left us without a word of goodbye, why she'd taken every picture of your sister with her, why she'd stayed away for nearly twenty years. . . . Yes. She was going to tell you what she thought was the truth—that you drowned your sister—and I refused to let that happen. So I killed her, Gideon. I murdered your mother. I did it for you.

So now there's no one left who can tell me—

I am telling you. You can believe me and you must believe me. Am I not a man who killed the mother of his own children? Am I not a man who hit her on the street, who drove a car over her, who removed the picture she'd brought to town with her to sustain your guilt? Am I not a man who drove off quietly and felt *nothing* afterwards? Am I not a man who went happily home to his young lover and got on with his life? So am I not thus also a man who is fully capable of killing a sickly worthless cretin of a child, a burden to us all, a living illustration of my own failure? Am I not that man, Gideon? Am I not that man? The question echoed through the years. It forced upon Gideon a hundred memories, He saw them flicker, unspooling before him, each asking the same question: Am I not that man?

And he was. He was. Of course. He was. Richard Davies had *always* been that man. Gideon saw it and read it in every word, nuance, and gesture of his father over the last two decades. Richard Davies was indeed that man.

But an admission of the fact—a final embracing of it—did not produce one gram of absolution.

So Gideon walked. His face was streaked with rain, and his hair was painted onto his skull. Rivulets ran like veins down his neck, but he felt nothing of the cold or the damp. The path he followed felt aimless to him, but it was not so despite the fact that he barely recognised when Park Lane gave way to Oxford Street and when Orchard Street turned into Baker.

From the morass of what he remembered, what he had been told, and what he had learned emerged a single point that he clung to at the last: Acceptance was the only option available because only acceptance allowed reparation finally to be made. And he was the one who had to make that reparation because he was the only one left who could do so.

He could not bring his sister back to life, he could not save his mother from destruction, he could not give Katja Wolff back the twenty years she'd sacrificed in the service of his father's plans. But he could pay the debt of those twenty years and at least in that one way he could make amends for the unholy deal his father had struck with her.

And there was indeed a way to pay her back that would also close the circle of everything else that had happened: from his mother's death to the loss of his music, from Sonia's death to the public exposure of everyone associated with Kensington Square. It was embodied in the long and elegant inner bouts, the perfect scrolls, and the lovely perpendicular F holes crafted two hundred and fifty years ago by Bartolomeo Giuseppe Guarneri.

He would sell the violin. Whatever price it fetched at auction, no matter how high, and it *would* be astronomical, he would give that money to Katja Wolff. And in taking those two specific actions, he would in effect be making a statement of apology and sorrow that no other effort on his part would permit him to make.

He would allow those two actions to serve to close the circle of crime, lies, guilt, and punishment. His life would not be the same thereafter, but it would be his own life at last. He wanted that.

Gideon had no idea what the time was when he finally arrived in Chalcot Square. He was soaked to the skin and drained of energy from the long walk. But at last, secure in the knowledge of the plan he would follow, he felt possessed by a modicum of peace. Still, the last yards to his house seemed endless. When he finally arrived, he had to pull himself up the front steps by the handrail, and he sagged against the door and fumbled in his trouser pockets for his keys.

He didn't have them. He frowned at this. He re-lived the day. He'd started out with the keys. He'd started out with the car. He'd driven to see Bertram Cresswell-White and after that he'd gone to his father's flat, where—

Libby, he recalled. She'd done the driving. She'd been with him. He'd asked her to leave him all those hours ago and she had obliged. She'd taken his car on his own instructions. She would have the keys.

He was turning to go down the stairs to her flat, when the front door swung open, however.

Libby cried out, "Gideon! What the *hell*? Jeez, you're totally drenched! Couldn't you get a taxi? Why didn't you call me? I would've come . . . Hey, that cop rang, the one who was here the other day to talk to you, remember? I didn't pick up, but he left a message for you to call him. Is everything . . . ? Jeez, why didn't you *call* me?"

She held the door wide as she was speaking, and she drew him inside and slammed it behind him. Gideon said nothing. She continued as if he'd made a reply.

"Here, Gid. Put your arm around me. There.

Where've you been? Did you talk to your dad? Is everything okay?"

They climbed to the first floor. Gideon headed towards the music room. Libby guided him towards the kitchen instead.

"You need tea," she insisted. "Or soup. Or something. Sit. Let me get it . . ."

He obliged.

She chatted on. Her voice was quick. Her colour was high. She said, "I figured I should wait up here since I had the keys. I could've waited in my own place, I guess. I did go down a while ago. But Rock called, and I made the mistake of answering because I thought it was you. God, he is *so* not who I thought he was when I hooked up with him. He actually wanted to come over. Let's talk things out, was how he put it. Unbelievable."

Gideon heard her and did not hear her. At the kitchen table, he was restless and wet.

Libby said, even more rapidly now as he stirred on his seat, "Rock wants us to get back together. 'Course, it's all totally dog-in-the-haystack stuff, or whatever you call it, but he actually said 'I'm good for you, Lib,' if you can believe that. Like he never spent our whole frigging marriage screwing everything with the right body parts that he ran into. He said, 'You know we're good for each other,' and I said back, 'Gid's good for me, Rocco. You are, like, so totally bad.' And that's what I believe, you know. You're good for me, Gideon. And I'm good for you."

She was moving about the kitchen. She'd settled

on soup, evidently, because she rooted through the fridge, found a carton of tomato and basil, and produced it triumphantly, saying, "Not even past its sell-by date. I'll heat it in a flash." She rustled out a pan and dumped the soup inside it. She set it on the cooker and took a bowl from the cupboard. She continued to talk. "How I figured it is this. We could blow London off for a while. You need a rest. And I need a vacation. So we could travel. We could go over to Spain for some decent weather. Or we could go to Italy. We could go to California, even, and you could meet my family. I told them about you. They know I know you. I mean, I told them we live together and everything. I mean, well, sort of. Not I sort of told them but we sort of live . . . you know."

She put the bowl on the table along with a spoon. She folded a paper napkin into a triangle. She said, "There," and reached for one of the straps of her dungarees, which was held together by a safety pin. She clutched at this as he looked at her. She used her thumb against it, opening and closing the pin spasmodically.

This display of nerves wasn't like her. It gave Gideon pause. He studied her, puzzled.

She said, "What?"

He rose. "I need to change my clothes."

She said, "I'll get them," and headed towards the music room and his bedroom which lay beyond it. "What d'you want? Levi's? A sweater? You're right. You need to get out of those clothes." And as he moved, "I'll get them. I mean, wait. Gideon. We need to talk first. I mean, I need to explain . . ." She stopped. She swallowed, and he heard the sound of it from five feet away. It was the noise a fish makes when it flops on the deck of a boat, breathing its last.

Gideon looked beyond her then and saw that the lights in the music room were off, which served to warn him although he could not have said what the warning was. He took in the fact that Libby was blocking his way to the room, though. He took a step towards it.

Libby said quickly, "Here's what you've got to understand, Gideon. You are number one with me. And here's what I thought: I thought, How can I help him—how can I help us to really be a real us? Because it's not normal that we'd be together but not really *be* together, is it. And it would be totally good for both of us if we . . . you know . . . look, it's what you need. It's what I need. Each other, being who we really are. And who we are is who we *are*. It's not what we do. And the only way I knew to make you, like, see that and understand it—because talking myself blue in the face sure as hell wasn't doing it and you know that—was to—"

"Oh God. No." Gideon pushed past her, shoving her to one side with an inarticulate cry.

He fumbled to the nearest lamp in the music room. He grabbed it. He switched it on.

He saw.

The Guarneri—what was left of it—lay next to the radiator. Its neck was fractured, its top was shattered, its sides were broken into pieces. Its bridge was snapped in half and its strings were wrapped round what remained of its tailpiece. The only part of the violin that wasn't destroyed was its perfect scroll, elegantly curving as if it still could bend forward to reach towards the player's fingers.

Libby was speaking behind him. High and rapid. Gideon heard the words but not their meaning. "You'll thank me," she said. "Maybe not now. But you will. I swear it. I did it for you And now that it's finally gone from your life, you can—"

"Never," he said to himself. "Never."

"Never what?" she said, and as he approached the violin, as he knelt before it, as he touched the chin rest and felt the cool of it mix with the heat that was coming into his hands, "Gideon?" Her voice was insistent, ringing. "Listen to me. It's going to be okay. I know you're upset, but you've got to see it was the only way. You're free of it now. Free to be who you are, which is more than just a guy who plays the fiddle. You were always more than that guy, Gideon. And now you can know it, just like I do."

The words beat against him, but he registered only the sound of her voice. And past that sound was the roar of the future as it rushed upon him, rising like a tidal wave, black and profound. He was rendered powerless as it overcame him. He was caught within it and all he knew was reduced in that instant to a single thought: what he wanted and what he planned to do had been denied him. Again. *Again.*

He cried out, "No!" And "No!" And "No!" He surged to his feet.

He did not hear Libby cry out in turn as he leapt towards her. His weight fell against her, fell hard upon her. Both of them toppled to the floor.

She screamed, "Gideon! Gideon! No! Stop!"

But the words were nothing, less than sound and fury. His hands went for her shoulders as they'd done in the past.

And he held her down.

ACKNOWLEDGMENTS

I couldn't have completed a project of this size in the time I allowed myself without the contributions and assistance of various individuals both in the United States and in England.

In England, I would like to express my appreciation to Louise Davis, Principal of Norland College, for allowing me to watch nannies in training and for giving me background information on the professional lives of child care givers; to Godfrey Carey, Q.C., Joanna Korner, Q.C., and Charlotte Bircher of the Inner Temple, all of whom were instrumental in assisting me in my understanding of British jurisprudence; to Sister Mary O'Gorman of the Convent of the Assumption in Kensington Square for giving me access to the convent and the chapel and for providing me with two decades of information about the square itself; to Chief Superintendent Paul Scotney of the Metropolitan Police (Belgravia Police Station) for assisting me with police procedures and for proving once again that the most forgiving audience among my readers exists within the ranks of the British police; to Chief Inspector Pip Lane, who always and generously acts as liaison between the local police and me; to John Oliver and Maggie Newton of HM Prison Holloway for information about the penal system in England; to Swati Gamble for everything from bus schedules to the locations of hospitals with casualty wards; to Jo-Ann Goodwin of the *Daily Mail* for assistance with the laws that deal with press coverage of murder investigations and trials; to Sue Fletcher for generously lending me the services of the resourceful Swati Gamble; and to my agent, Stephanie Cabot of William Morris Agency, to whom no obstacle is too much of a challenge.

In the United States, I'm deeply grateful to Amy Sims of the Orange County Philharmonic, who took the time to make certain I was able to write about the violin with a fair degree of accuracy; to Cynthia Faisst, who allowed me to sit in on some violin instruction; to Dr. Gordon Globus, who added to my understanding of psychogenic amnesia and therapeutic protocols; to Dr. Tom Ruben and Dr. Robert Greenburg, who weighed in with medical information whenever I needed it; and to my writing students, who listened to early sections of the novel and gave helpful feedback.

I am particularly indebted to my wonderful assistant, Dannielle Azoulay, without whom I could not possibly have written the rough draft of this rather lengthy novel in ten months. Dannielle's assistance in every area—from doing necessary research to running errands—was absolutely crucial to my well-being and my sanity, and I extend to her my deepest thanks.

Finally, I'm grateful, as always, to my longtime editor at Bantam—Kate Miciak—who always asked the best questions about the most convoluted turns of plot; to my literary agent in the U.S.—Robert Gottlieb of Trident Media—who represents me with energy and creativity; to my fellow writer Don McQuinn, who gallantly stood on the receiving end of my doubts and fears; and to Tom McCabe, who graciously stepped out of the way of the creative locomotive whenever it was necessary.

ABOUT THE AUTHOR

ELIZABETH GEORGE's first novel, *A Great Deliverance,* was honored with the Anthony and Agatha Best First Novel Awards and received the *Grand Prix de Littérature Policière.* Her third novel, *Well-Schooled in Murder,* was awarded the prestigious German prize for suspense fiction, the MIMI. *A Suitable Vengeance, For the Sake of Elena, Missing Joseph, Playing for the Ashes, In the Presence of the Enemy, Deception on His Mind,* and *In Pursuit of the Proper Sinner* were international bestsellers. Elizabeth George divides her time between Huntington Beach, California, and London. Her novels are currently being dramatized by the BBC. Visit her website at www.ElizabethGeorgeOnline.com.